# Classic
# Westerns

*Introduction by Michael A. Cramer, PhD*

**Canterbury Classics**

San Diego

Canterbury Classics
An imprint of Printers Row Publishing Group
10350 Barnes Canyon Road, Suite 100, San Diego, CA 92121
www.thunderbaybooks.com

Printers Row Publishing Group is a division of Readerlink Distribution Services, LLC.
Canterbury Classics is a registered trademark of Readerlink Distribution Services, LLC.

All correspondence concerning the content of this book should be addressed to
Canterbury Classics, Editorial Department, at the above address.

Publisher: Peter Norton
Publishing Team: Ana Parker, Vicki Jaeger, Kathryn Chipinka, Aaron Guzman
Editorial Team: JoAnn Padgett, Melinda Allman, Dan Mansfield, Traci Douglas
Production Team: Jonathan Lopes, Rusty von Dyl

Library of Congress Cataloging-in-Publication Data available on request.

ISBN: 978-1-68412-097-0

Printed in China
21 20 19 18 17  1 2 3 4 5

# CONTENTS

# INTRODUCTION

The Western is the most potent myth in American culture. It is how we view ourselves. It is our ideal. It is the dream of easterners, the birthright of westerners. Its traces can be found to this day in Texas and California and Montana and Wyoming, where gold miners still toil, where hunters still pursue deer, and where ranchers still ride the range. Of course, it can also be found on cable TV, in video games, at rodeos, and at cowboy action shooting competitions around the world. From the books in this volume, to the movies of John Wayne and John Ford, to the plays of Sam Shepard, to HBO's *Westworld*, the West permeates how we view our history and how we view ourselves as Americans—more than the colonial era, the Industrial Revolution, the Civil War, Prohibition, World War II, or the 1960s.

The Western myth was popularized immediately—it arose as westward expansion was occurring, turning the political idea of Manifest Destiny into mass entertainment. It comes from dime novels and from Buffalo Bill's Wild West shows, from the chronicles of Teddy Roosevelt and the artwork of Frederic Remington. It's usually associated with the 1870s, but it was going on as late as the 1910s and, in a way, it was brought here by the first European colonists in the sixteenth century, always moving west into the setting sun, toward a new frontier. By the time Horace Greeley advised "Go west, young man," the myth was already established.

The Western myth is a standard melodrama, a triangle consisting of a persecutor/villain, a rescuer/hero, and a victim. Sometimes the villain is a gunfighter, sometimes it's Native Americans, sometimes it's greedy ranchers. The victims may be townspeople, homesteaders, or virtuous maidens. But the hero is always the same: some variation of a man on a horse with a gun. The Western hero is a man out of place. He is never truly at home. He moves between the savage and the civilized because he belongs to both but doesn't fully belong to either. He moves among Native Americans, among outlaws, and represents a buffer between them and the coming civilization of towns and farms and railroads, protecting the settlers, if reluctantly, in the end. He is a product of civilization but is always trying to stay ahead of it. He is part of the wilderness but can't stay there forever. He must always keep moving on, praying never to be fenced in, yet occasionally returning—at least for a time—to town and its comforts. He is most at home when he's alone, save for his horse, on the range. The Western myth is not confined to cowboys. James Fenimore

Cooper's *The Last of the Mohicans* is a classic Western, as is the 1981 science-fiction film *Outland*, starring Sean Connery.

Many of the ideas that modern-day readers have of the Old West and the frontier era come from the four authors in this volume.

Of course, that familiar gunslinger romance of Zane Grey and Louis L'Amour, of Hopalong Cassidy and Roy Rogers, is not the true West, nor is it the only West. The bucolic West of hardy settlers and beautiful rolling prairies peopled not by outlaws and lawmen but by farmers and townsfolk, of people who *do* want to settle down and stay put—that is part of the Western tradition as well. This is the West of *Little House on the Prairie* and *Oklahoma!* It's this West that Willa Cather and, to a lesser extent, Owen Wister write about—and it can be found in Zane Grey and Max Brand, but only in an ancillary way. It is this world that the Western hero is trying to escape, the one he must occasionally go back to and sometimes protect. As with all such myths, it is the normal—the West of toiling farmers and common landowners and townsmen—that made up most of that real West (and Cather's gift, in particular, is to give that world weight).

## *The Virginian*, Owen Wister

O wen Wister was an unlikely candidate to be the most important writer of Western fiction. He was a lawyer, a classical composer, and an aristocrat. He was not a son of the West. Wister was born into a wealthy Philadelphia family in 1860. He studied music at Harvard and graduated summa cum laude in 1882. He went to Paris to study composition, and was known to both Franz Liszt and Richard Wagner. In 1885 a dispute between his parents over his future (his father wanted him to go into business) forced a deep melancholy on Wister. As a cure, he was advised to travel west by his friend Theodore Roosevelt, who had famously sought out the West after his mother and his wife both died on the same day just a year prior. Wister traveled to Wyoming, the first of fifteen trips he took to the West, often accompanying Roosevelt on his hunting and ranching expeditions. Like Roosevelt, Wister found there not just a cure for melancholy but a cure for the soft Victorian lifestyle and values of the East. In several books, Roosevelt documents the severity of Western life and the hardiness of those who lived it. Roosevelt wrote of cowboys and horse thieves. He was among the first to write about another of those larger-than-life Western heroes, his friend Seth Bullock. But while Roosevelt was an important historian and chronicler of the West, it would be Wister's gift to fictionalize it and bring the Western myth from the dime novel into the mainstream. In 1890, as the story goes,

Wister decided to fashion himself into the Rudyard Kipling of the West, writing about the things he had witnessed with his own eyes. Over the next twelve years, he published several short stories about life on the plains.

*The Virginian* (1902) was dedicated to Roosevelt, who by then was president of the United States. To say, as some do, that Wister invented the Western myth is too broad a claim. The dime novels existed already, and many Western themes go back as far as James Fennimore Cooper in the 1820s, but the importance of *The Virginian* is hard to overstate. In it, Wister introduces most of the well-known Western tropes. There's the green tenderfoot, the strong silent hero, and the virtuous schoolmarm; there's the sidekick, the dastardly villain, and the benevolent ranch owner. There's also the shootout in the street and the lynching of cattle rustlers. The latter incident, justified in the story as a necessary piece of frontier justice, presents the hero with a moment of Shakespearean tragedy straight out of *Henry V*. This moment of torment is one of the many elements that elevates *The Virginian* above the dime novels that had come before it.

Unlike a lot of Victorian novels, *The Virginian* is very readable for a modern audience. Wister was a minimalist and something of a naturalist. His prose was terse and his stories often violent and uncompromising. He had a strong influence on Ernest Hemingway, who knew Wister later in life. His best device is how he uses the narrative voice. *The Virginian* is told in first person by the tenderfoot, who, like Wister himself, takes the train to Medicine Bow, Wyoming, in 1885 and steps off into a strange new land. Both narrator and hero, the tenderfoot and the Virginian, are unnamed throughout the book. Both are émigrés from the eastern United States; they are the yin and yang of the Western experience.

While the dime novels, Buffalo Bill's Wild West shows, Remington's paintings, and Roosevelt's chronicles all helped to popularize the American West, Wister created its most enduring images. *The Virginian* was adapted for the stage in 1904 by Wister and the Broadway impresario Kirke La Shelle, in a production starring Dustin Farnum. The play was adapted to the screen (or, as it says in the credits, "picturized") by Cecil B. DeMille in 1914, with Farnum reprising the lead role. It was remade as a movie five times, and inspired the popular TV show that ran from 1962 to 1971. Wister created a heroic type that Hollywood turned into a global phenomenon, especially in the films of John Ford. John Wayne played heroes closely modeled on Wister's Virginian—from *Stagecoach* at the height of the Western story, to *The Man Who Shot Liberty Valance* and *The Shootist* at its sad end, when the encroachment of civilization that both Wister and Roosevelt predicted and mourned had fenced in the West.

## *O Pioneers!*, Willa Cather

Of the four authors in this volume, none stands as tall in literary history as Willa Cather. A Pulitzer Prize winner and author of twelve critically acclaimed novels, Cather is an important figure in both modernist literature and American feminism. She is the subject of countless scholarly articles, books, and dissertations. Critical assessment of her work is the stuff of graduate seminars and PhD dissertations. The University of Nebraska, Lincoln, in conjunction with the Willa Cather Foundation, publishes a biennial journal, *Cather Studies*, devoted to criticism of her work. In literary and scholarly circles, she is considered to be as important as William Faulkner and Edith Wharton.

Willa Cather was born in 1873 in Back Creek Valley, near Winchester, Virginia. When she was nine years old, her family moved to an area near Red Cloud, Nebraska, to join her grandparents and some other relatives in what is now known as Catherton. The change was a shock. She described moving from hills and streams and woods that were a part of her to a land as barren as a sheet of iron. In *O Pioneers!* she wrote of Nebraska: "Of all the bewildering things about a new country, the absence of human landmarks is one of the most depressing and disheartening."

After failing as a farmer, her father Charles became a businessman in Red Cloud and Willa began attending school. She also wrote for the local newspaper. She attended the University of Nebraska, intending to become a doctor. She edited the school newspaper, and began to be published regularly in the *Nebraska State Journal.* She changed her major to English and graduated in 1894.

Cather moved back East, first to Pittsburgh and then, eventually, to Greenwich Village in New York City. She taught English and Latin, edited women's magazines, and wrote: first essays and short stories, then books. *O Pioneers!* (1913) was her second novel. It was both popular and highly acclaimed. It was followed by *The Song of the Lark* (1915) and *My Ántoina* (1918), which together form the Prairie Trilogy for which she is best known.

Cather's West is not the West of cattle drives and gunslingers. It is the lonely West of immigrants pushing into a land emptied of its inhabitants by disease and war, scratching a living out of dirt. It is a land of sod shacks and diseased hogs. Violence here is not the casual byproduct of conquest, as it is in so many Westerns. It is terrible and pathetic, a twisted, unnecessary thing brought on by drunkenness and jealousy. Most of Cather's characters are immigrants not just to Nebraska but to the United States. Instead of displaced Virginians and New Yorkers, Cather's settlers are Swedes and Bohemians and Russians, a population doubly out of place—the population she came to know in Red Cloud.

As in *The Virginian*, the land itself is a character in *O Pioneers!*, but here, instead of a land big and beautiful, sublime and rejuvenating, the land is bleak and hard, a place where men don't really belong. This sense of bleakness is an oppressive force in *O Pioneers!* "But the great fact was the land itself, which seemed to overwhelm the little beginnings of human society that struggled in its sombre wastes. It was from facing this vast hardness that the boy's mouth had become so bitter; because he felt that men were too weak to make any mark here, that the land wanted to be let alone, to preserve its own fierce strength, its peculiar, savage kind of beauty, its uninterrupted mournfulness." Of the settlers' houses she writes, "Most of them were built of the sod itself, and were only the unescapable ground in another form."

The writing in *O Pioneers!* evokes loneliness, hope, and forgiveness with a descriptive delicacy not found in most Westerns. Many Western writers write about bleakness; Cather makes the bleakness palpable. But the thing that stands out in her writing is a strong female viewpoint. Cather is a type of prairie feminist, one of the strong independent women who helped settle the West and often had to fend for themselves. To the rest of the Edwardian world, prairie women like Annie Oakley and Calamity Jane seemed transgressive, but on the plains, where it was a struggle just to survive to the next day, self-sufficient women were not exotic or threatening, they were the norm.

Cather was one of these independent women, and so is Alexandra Bergson, the protagonist of *O Pioneers!* Molly, the love interest in *The Virginian*, is innocent and a bit helpless, with a heart too feeling for the harsh life of the frontier. She needs men—the Virginian and Judge Henry—to help her navigate Western life. Not so Alexandra. While she eventually marries, she has no need for a man. When her father dies he puts her—not her brothers—in charge of the farm, because she's the most competent. While the other farms fail, hers prospers. When her brothers object to her choices, she ignores them. She does not try to conquer the West, as men do; she learns to work with it, to coax it, to nurture it. Even when she has reason to hate and seek revenge, she forgives, not out of religious fervor but out of practicality. Revenge and hate are wastes of her time. At times Alexandra is feminine, but at others she is quite masculine. Gender roles are somewhat fluid in Cather's world.

## The Lone Star Ranger and The Mysterious Rider, Zane Grey

The writer most closely associated with cowboys and gunfighters, Pearl Zane Grey was born on January 31, 1872, in Zanesville, Ohio, a city founded by his great-grandfather Ebenezer Zane. His father was a dentist. He grew up with a love of fishing, baseball, reading, and writing, the last of which his father disapproved. When Grey wrote his first story, his father tore it up and beat him. When his father's practice collapsed, the Greys moved to Columbus, where Zane performed dentistry (without a license), and he and his brother Romer played minor league baseball. Grey was scouted by several universities, and eventually took a baseball scholarship at the University of Pennsylvania, where he studied dentistry. He was a star baseball player but a mediocre student. He was also involved in a scandal that resulted in a paternity suit. After graduating, he played minor league baseball in New Jersey and set up a dental practice in New York City. In 1900 he met Dolly Roth, whom he married in 1905. She became his editor and business manager. Though Grey had several affairs, which were known to Dolly, they stayed married and their partnership flourished.

Grey was strongly influenced by James Fenimore Cooper's *The Leatherstocking Tales*, as well as the art of Frederic Remington, but his biggest influence was *The Virginian*. He meticulously copied Wister's style. His first few novels, based on the adventures of his ancestors in the American Revolution, were rejected, but after a hunting trip to Arizona, he started to write about the Old West, and his novels began to be accepted. They quickly became best-sellers. In 1912 he had his greatest success with *Riders of the Purple Sage*. He grew rich, moved to California, and split his time between writing and fishing. Grey spent an average of 300 days each year fishing. Like Ernest Hemingway, he pursued everything, from brook trout to marlin; and, also like Hemingway, he wrote about it, as a regular contributor to *Outdoor Life* magazine. Living in California put him close to Hollywood, where his stories were grist for the Western movie mill—well over a hundred films have been based on his works.

*The Lone Star Ranger* represents an early phase of Grey's development as a writer. It doesn't have the flow of Cather's or Wister's novels. It's less imaginative and less evocative. His characters are wooden, like cutouts of people, with little depth and predictable emotions. Exposition comes in the form of tedious speeches being made from one character to another. Grey hasn't yet mastered the descriptive style for which he will become famous. What's best in *The Lone Star Ranger* is action. It's exciting, thrilling even, and wonderfully plotted.

*The Lone Star Ranger* is a story told in two parts. In the first half, the hero, Buck Duane, kills a man in self-defense. Duane is the son of an outlaw and feels the rage of blood pump whenever he finds himself threatened. In Buck Duane, the Western hero has moved past the literary realism of Wister and Cather. Where the Virginian and Alexandra Bergson were the most competent people around them, Buck Duane is superhuman. He is the biggest, the toughest, the fastest draw, the best shot. He can split a playing card on edge at twenty paces. He rides the biggest and the ugliest horse. With Buck Duane, we have entered the realm of the tall tale.

The killing forces Duane to go on the run. He has a series of adventures among the outlaw gangs of the Big Bend country—and a series of gunfights, by which his reputation grows. He hates the outlaw life, and wants desperately to clear his name. He feels remorse, not so much for the men he killed but for the act of killing itself. He also finds friendship where he didn't expect it. To his surprise, Duane discovers a few outlaws who are decent men. There's something of a familiarity of blood among them: good people can spot the good qualities in Duane. His curse is not simply to be an outlaw, it's to be the best. He is warned early on that winning a gunfight enhances his reputation, but that, in turn, makes him a target for men seeking theirs. "An' every town you ride into will scare up some cowpuncher full of booze or a long-haired four-flush gunman or a sheriff—an' these men will be playin' to the crowd an' yellin' for your blood. Thet's the Texas of it."

In the second half, Duane joins the Rangers and works to clear west Texas of outlaws. He's been guaranteed a pardon if he helps the Rangers settle Texas. He becomes the first literary version of the lone ranger, working along the border, alone, undercover as an outlaw, bringing violence to violent men. The gunfights become more violent and the dangers greater. But now he has the law on his side. As with all his books, Grey insisted that *The Lone Star Ranger* was based on real events and people. Grey was an obsessive note taker and strived for realism. This is even true of Buck Duane. Grey had spent time meeting members of the Texas Rangers in order to get to know them and to collect story ideas. *The Lone Star Ranger* is based on a story one of the Rangers told him. In a dedication written as a letter to Captain John Hughes of the Texas Rangers, Grey described how the story, learned from a Ranger named Coffee, had haunted him (there was later speculation that the hero of *The Lone Star Ranger* was modeled on Hughes himself; Hughes is also believed to be the inspiration for the masked Lone Ranger of radio and television).

*The Mysterious Rider* is a very different book from *The Lone Star Ranger*. It was written six years later, and by then Grey had developed the descriptive style for which he is now known. As in the stories of Cather and Wister, the land is now a fully fleshed-out character in Grey's novels. The main character, Columbine, is much more interested in the beauty of the Colorado hillsides than Buck Duane was of the landscape of southwest Texas. The story is a love triangle. Columbine is in love—though she won't admit it to herself— with the gallant cowboy Wils Moore. Belllounds, the rancher who raised her after she was found by some miners, wants her to marry his drunkard son Jack. All of the conflict revolves around their tension.

This story is problematic from a modern viewpoint. The main concern of the rancher Belllounds is to rid the mountains of the predators attacking his cattle. He keeps a huge pack of dogs for this purpose, and won't rest until every predator is exterminated: "'Yes, an' the range'll be thankin' me when I rid it of all these varmints,' declared Belllounds. 'Lass, I swore I'd buy every dog fetched to me, until I had enough to kill off the coyotes an' lofers an' lions. I'll do it, too. But I need a hunter.'" This paradigm is still a source of tension between rural westerners who want to conquer and mold the West, and environmentalists—usually from the cities—who want to preserve it. The reintroduction of wolves into areas around Yellowstone National Park continues to spark conflicts between ranchers and environmentalists today.

The presence of predators—coyotes and wolves in particular—hangs like a shadow over *The Mysterious Rider*. There are sinister forces lurking just beyond sight. To Belllounds they are a threat, but Columbine finds their calls soothing. There is a suppressed wildness inside her, and these predators have a freedom she comes to envy. She loves the coyotes in particular, and doesn't want them to be wiped out. Columbine's reaction to the wolves and to the cowboy Wils Moore demonstrates the place that instinct plays in Zane Grey's world. Not only are his characters true to their essence, but that essence drives them to action without thought. Columbine feels her love for Wils without knowing that she loves him. Buck Duane feels the instinct to kill that he inherited from his father without knowing, at first, what it means. Both these protagonists struggle against their instincts in vain. They can't control what they are.

The Mysterious Rider of the title is neither Wils nor Jack, but an older gunfighter named Hell-Bent Wade, who appears, like some sort of guardian angel, to unravel the tangle of loyalties and secrets that make up the plot. He's an early example of the Western antihero, a prototype of Clint Eastwood's Man with No Name. But he's even more than this—not just a lone man with a horse and a gun, not a tortured soul never at home in civilization or the wild, but a divine and vengeful presence. He is, as Belllounds describes him, a pale rider, and hell travels with him. The link to the Bible's book of Revelations and the fourth horseman of the apocalypse—the Pale Rider who is so often referenced in Westerns—should not be ignored. Hell-Bent Wade is divine retribution.

## *Gunman's Reckoning* and *The Untamed*, Max Brand

Max Brand is one of the many pen names of Frederick Schiller Faust. He was a prolific writer of short stories, novels, and screenplays in many genres. Of the four authors in this volume, Faust is the only one who actually worked as a cowboy. He is also, by far, the most prolific. Born in Seattle and orphaned at an early age, he grew up in central California and worked as a ranch hand there. He attended the University of California, Berkeley, where he began his writing career, but he never graduated. He joined the Canadian Army, deserted, and wound up in New York City, writing pulp fiction. He was so prolific, writing fourteen pages a day, every day, for thirty years, that he often had two or three pieces, under different pen names, in one magazine issue. Faust wrote under fifteen pen names, and was said to have produced 1.5 million words a year throughout his entire career. In the 1930s, he was among the highest-paid authors in the world. His most famous creation— not a Western character—was Dr. Kildare, which made him a fortune when the stories were turned into a series of MGM films. The series was revived on radio and (twice) on television. He also wrote the Western classic *Destry Rides Again*. For all his success, Faust never signed his real name to anything but his poetry, which was the work he most cared about. He became a war correspondent during World War II and died in action, in Italy, in 1944.

The two Max Brand novels in this collection are the type of pulp fiction that he was famous for. He is a meticulous storyteller, and his narrative is deeply layered. He spends entire chapters on action that takes just a moment. He also moves easily between points of view and, writing in the third person, switches from one character to another from chapter to chapter, each time with a clear difference in psychology and perspective.

*Gunman's Reckoning* begins with a murder attempt. Several pages are devoted to the murderer contemplating his act and stalking his prey. Then what should have been the knifing of a sleeping man turns into a fight to the death, painstakingly detailed. Only at the end of the fight do we realize that the character whose point of view we've been following is not the protagonist—it's his victim. All of the action is like that—complex, intricate, and extremely entertaining. *Gunman's Reckoning* is a mining town mystery. The hero, Donnegan, links up with an evil robber baron and his beautiful daughter to try and coax her wayward fiancée—who's struck it rich—back into the fold. Donnegan, a confirmed railroad tramp who loathes the very idea of work, is happy to hire himself out as a gunfighter. He is on a mysterious quest that will come to a head in a boom town, oddly named The Corner. Like Hell Bent Wade, Donnegan is an early version of the dark Western antihero, who is the good guy only in this instance, and only out of circumstance. He's a criminal and a murderer—he never even tries to hide the fact. He's lazy and selfish. He's at home fighting on the railroad, running with outlaws, or matching wits with a clever femme fatale. This is a pretty dark tale for an early Western. It's a dense, complicated book that defies convention. The plot never plays out like you expect it to: People get shot, but not quite the ones you expect. People fall in love, but confusedly. The double-twist ending leaves much unresolved.

In *The Untamed*, we again meet a rancher with a beautiful daughter who is just becoming a woman—we've found another Western trope. Once again, she must find a way to love a wild cowboy, but in this case he's what the title calls him—untamed. He loves deeply, wanders endlessly, his vengeance is terrible, he's always true, but he'll never stick around. *The Untamed* is just as convoluted, formulaic, and entertaining as *Gunman's Reckoning*. It begins with a short, eleven-paragraph side story. It's not marked as such. It's marked as a chapter called "Pan of the Desert." But really, it's a self-contained story, a brief encounter between a man, a horse, a wolf, and a rattlesnake. It tells us all we need to know about the hero and his animal sidekicks. He is noble, the horse is beautiful, the wolf dog is cunning, and all three are wild. He's also fast. He cuts the head off the rattler in midstrike. He's called "Pan of the desert" because of his melodic whistling, akin to "the exultant improvisations of a master violinist," but also because he's not quite human. Faust had a long fascination with mythology. A common complaint about his writing is that his characters are often more mythic than human. Referring to his hero as a god right off the bat reinforces this. Whistling Dan, as he's called, is indeed mythic. He is more of a caricature than a character. He is too heroic, too wild, and, like Buck Duane, superhuman. Cumberland, the old rancher, describes him as not like regular folks, as though he's part of a fairy tale. He's slight, but he's stronger than the biggest of men. He can calm savage beasts. No one but Dan could ride the wild Arabian horse Satan. No one but Dan could tame the wolf Black Bart. Dan is, as Cumberland puts it, "queer—powerful queer," just like Pan. To top it off, Dan goes up against a band of outlaws led by Jim Silent. Just as Pan breaks the silence of the morning, Whistling Dan will break the Silent Gang. Along the way Dan will get framed, get jailed, break out, and kill—all in the single-minded pursuit of justice. Like Pan, he will be terrible in his vengeance; and, like Pan, he will drift away, incapable of settling down.

## Conclusion

These six novels helped to create the Western myth that lives on to this day. They provided the blueprints for movies, television, plays, and even opera. But, more than that, they are the expression of a deeply held American ideal, one that seeks out the wild places where one can be alone, one where right and wrong are simple and obvious, and where a lone man on a horse with a gun, half civilized and half wild, can save the world.

Michael A. Cramer, PhD
Brooklyn, New York
April 14, 2017

# THE VIRGINIAN

## Owen Wister

### TO THEODORE ROOSEVELT

Some of these pages you have seen, some you have praised, one stands new-written because you blamed it; and all, my dear critic, beg leave to remind you of their author's changeless admiration.

### TO THE READER

Certain of the newspapers, when this book was first announced, made a mistake most natural upon seeing the subtitle as it then stood, *A Tale of Sundry Adventures.* "This sounds like a historical novel," said one of them, meaning (I take it) a colonial romance. As it now stands, the title will scarce lead to such interpretation; yet nonetheless is this book historical—quite as much so as any colonial romance. Indeed, when you look at the root of the matter, it is a colonial romance. For Wyoming between 1874 and 1890 was a colony as wild as was Virginia one hundred years earlier. As wild, with a scantier population, and the same primitive joys and dangers. There were, to be sure, not so many Chippendale settees.

We know quite well the common understanding of the term "historical novel." *Hugh Wynne* exactly fits it. But *Silas Lapham* is a novel as perfectly historical as is *Hugh Wynne,* for it pictures an era and personifies a type. It matters not that in the one we find George Washington and in the other none save imaginary figures; else *The Scarlet Letter* were not historical. Nor does it matter that Dr. Mitchell did not live in the time of which he wrote, while Mr. Howells saw many Silas Laphams with his own eyes; else *Uncle Tom's Cabin* were not historical. Any narrative which presents faithfully a day and a generation is of necessity historical; and this one presents Wyoming between 1874 and 1890.

Had you left New York or San Francisco at ten o'clock this morning, by noon the day after tomorrow you could step out at Cheyenne. There you would stand at the heart of the world that is the subject of my picture, yet you would look around you in vain for the reality. It is a vanished world. No journeys, save those which memory can take, will bring you to it now. The mountains are there, far and shining, and the sunlight, and the infinite earth, and the air that seems forever the true fountain of youth, but where is the buffalo, and the wild antelope, and where the horseman with his pasturing thousands? So like its old self does the sagebrush seem when revisited, that you wait for the horseman to appear.

But he will never come again. He rides in his historic yesterday. You will no more see him gallop out of the unchanging silence than you will see Columbus on the unchanging sea come sailing from Palos with his caravels.

And yet the horseman is still so near our day that in some chapters of this book, which were published separate at the close of the nineteenth century, the present tense was used. It is true no longer. In those chapters it has been changed, and verbs like "is" and "have" now read "was" and "had." Time has flowed faster than my ink.

What is become of the horseman, the cowpuncher, the last romantic figure upon our soil? For he was romantic. Whatever he did, he did with his might. The bread that he earned was earned hard, the wages that he squandered were squandered hard—half a year's pay sometimes gone in a night—"blown in," as he expressed it, or "blowed in," to be perfectly accurate. Well, he will be here among us always, invisible, waiting his chance to live and play as he would like. His wild kind has been among us always, since the beginning: a young man with his temptations, a hero without wings.

The cowpuncher's ungoverned hours did not unman him. If he gave his word, he kept it; Wall Street would have found him behind the times. Nor did he talk lewdly to women; Newport would have thought him old-fashioned. He and his brief epoch make a complete picture, for in themselves they were as complete as the pioneers of the land or the explorers of the sea. A transition has followed the horseman of the plains; a shapeless state, a condition of men and manners as unlovely as is that moment in the year when winter is gone and spring not come, and the face of Nature is ugly. I shall not dwell upon it here. Those who have seen it know well what I mean. Such transition was inevitable. Let us give thanks that it is but a transition, and not a finality.

Sometimes readers inquire, Did I know the Virginian? As well, I hope, as a father should know his son. And sometimes it is asked, Was such and such a thing true? Now to this I have the best answer in the world. Once a cowpuncher listened patiently while I read him a manuscript. It concerned an event upon an Indian reservation. "Was that the Crow reservation?" he inquired at the finish. I told him that it was no real reservation and no real event; and his face expressed displeasure. "Why," he demanded, "do you waste your time writing what never happened, when you know so many things that did happen?"

And I could no more help telling him that this was the highest compliment ever paid me than I have been able to help telling you about it here!

CHARLESTON, S.C., MARCH 31ST, 1902

# CHAPTER I

## ENTER THE MAN

S ome notable sight was drawing the passengers, both men and women, to the window; and therefore I rose and crossed the car to see what it was. I saw near the track an enclosure, and round it some laughing men, and inside it some whirling dust, and amid the dust some horses, plunging, huddling, and dodging. They were cow ponies in a corral, and one of them would not be caught, no matter who threw the rope. We had plenty of time to watch this sport, for our train had stopped that the engine might take water at the tank before it pulled us up beside the station platform of Medicine Bow. We were also six hours late, and starving for entertainment. The pony in the corral was wise, and rapid of limb. Have you seen a skilful boxer watch his antagonist with a quiet, incessant eye? Such an eye as this did the pony keep upon whatever man took the rope. The man might pretend to look at the weather, which was fine; or he might affect earnest conversation with a bystander: it was bootless. The pony saw through it. No feint hoodwinked him. This animal was thoroughly a man of the world. His undistracted eye stayed fixed upon the dissembling foe, and the gravity of his horse-expression made the matter one of high comedy. Then the rope would sail out at him, but he was already elsewhere; and if horses laugh, gayety must have abounded in that corral. Sometimes the pony took a turn alone; next he had slid in a flash among his brothers, and the whole of them like a school of playful fish whipped round the corral, kicking up the fine dust, and (I take it) roaring with laughter. Through the window-glass of our Pullman the thud of their mischievous hoofs reached us, and the strong, humorous curses of the cowboys. Then for the first time I noticed a man who sat on the high gate of the corral, looking on. For he now climbed down with the undulations of a tiger, smooth and easy, as if his muscles flowed beneath his skin. The others had all visibly whirled the rope, some of them even shoulder high. I did not see his arm lift or move. He appeared to hold the rope down low, by his leg. But like a sudden snake I saw the noose go out its length and fall true; and the thing was done. As the captured pony walked in with a sweet, church-door expression, our train moved slowly on to the station, and a passenger remarked, "That man knows his business."

But the passenger's dissertation upon roping I was obliged to lose, for Medicine Bow was my station. I bade my fellow-travelers good-by, and descended, a stranger, into the great cattle land. And here in less than ten minutes I learned news which made me feel a stranger indeed.

My baggage was lost; it had not come on my train; it was adrift somewhere back in the two thousand miles that lay behind me. And by way of comfort, the baggage-man remarked that passengers often got astray from their trunks, but the trunks mostly found them after a while. Having offered me this encouragement, he turned whistling to his affairs and left me planted in the baggage-room at Medicine Bow. I stood deserted among crates and boxes, blankly holding my check, hungry and forlorn. I stared out through the door at the sky and the plains; but I did not see the antelope shining among the sagebrush, nor the great sunset light of Wyoming. Annoyance blinded my eyes to all things save my grievance: I saw only a lost trunk. And I was muttering half-aloud, "What a forsaken hole this is!" when suddenly from outside on the platform came a slow voice: "Off to get married *again*? Oh, don't!"

The voice was Southern and gentle and drawling; and a second voice came in immediate answer, cracked and querulous. "It ain't again. Who says it's again? Who told you, anyway?"

And the first voice responded caressingly: "Why, your Sunday clothes told me, Uncle Hughey. They are speakin' mighty loud o' nuptials."

"You don't worry me!" snapped Uncle Hughey, with shrill heat.

And the other gently continued, "Ain't them gloves the same yu' wore to your last weddin'?"

"You don't worry me! You don't worry me!" now screamed Uncle Hughey.

Already I had forgotten my trunk; care had left me; I was aware of the sunset, and had no desire but for more of this conversation. For it resembled none that I had heard in my life so far. I stepped to the door and looked out upon the station platform.

Lounging there at ease against the wall was a slim young giant, more beautiful than pictures. His broad, soft hat was pushed back; a loose-knotted, dull-scarlet handkerchief sagged from his throat; and one casual thumb was hooked in the cartridge-belt that slanted across his hips. He had plainly come many miles from somewhere across the vast horizon, as the dust upon him showed. His boots were white with it. His overalls were gray with it. The weather-beaten bloom of his face shone through it duskily, as the ripe peaches look upon their trees in a dry season. But no dinginess of travel or shabbiness of attire could tarnish the splendor that radiated from his youth and strength. The old man upon whose temper his remarks were doing such deadly work was combed and curried to a finish, a bridegroom swept and garnished; but alas for age! Had I been the bride, I should have taken the giant, dust and all. He had by no means done with the old man.

"Why, yu've hung weddin' gyarments on every limb!" he now drawled, with admiration. "Who is the lucky lady this trip?"

The old man seemed to vibrate. "Tell you there ain't been no other! Call me a Mormon, would you?"

"Why, that—"

"Call me a Mormon? Then name some of my wives. Name two. Name one. Dare you!"

"—that Laramie wido' promised you—"

"Shucks!"

"—only her doctor suddenly ordered Southern climate and—"

"Shucks! You're a false alarm."

"—so nothing but her lungs came between you. And next you'd most got united with Cattle Kate, only—"

"Tell you you're a false alarm!"

"—only she got hung."

"Where's the wives in all this? Show the wives! Come now!"

"That corn-fed biscuit-shooter at Rawlins yu' gave the canary—"

"Never married her. Never did marry—"

"But yu' come so near, uncle! She was the one left yu' that letter explaining how she'd got married to a young cyard-player the very day before her ceremony with you was due, and—"

"Oh, you're nothing; you're a kid; you don't amount to—"

"—and how she'd never, never forgot to feed the canary."

"This country's getting full of kids," stated the old man, witheringly. "It's doomed." This crushing assertion plainly satisfied him. And he blinked his eyes with renewed anticipation. His tall tormentor continued with a face of unchanging gravity, and a voice of gentle solicitude: "How is the health of that unfortunate—"

"That's right! Pour your insults! Pour 'em on a sick, afflicted woman!"

The eyes blinked with combative relish.

"Insults? Oh, no, Uncle Hughey!"

"That's all right! Insults goes!"

"Why, I was mighty relieved when she began to recover her mem'ry. Las' time I heard, they told me she'd got it pretty near all back. Remembered her father, and her mother, and her sisters and brothers, and her friends, and her happy childhood, and all her doin's except only your face. The boys was bettin' she'd get that far too, give her time. But I reckon afteh such a turrable sickness as she had, that would be expectin' most too much."

At this Uncle Hughey jerked out a small parcel. "Shows how much you know!" he cackled. "There! See that! That's my ring she sent me back, being too unstrung for marriage. So she don't remember me, don't she? Ha-ha! Always said you were a false alarm."

The Southerner put more anxiety into his tone. "And so you're a-takin' the ring right on to the next one!" he exclaimed. "Oh, don't go to get married again, Uncle Hughey! What's the use o' being married?"

"What's the use?" echoed the bridegroom, with scorn. "Hm! When you grow up you'll think different."

"Course I expect to think different when my age is different. I'm havin' the thoughts proper to twenty-four, and you're havin' the thoughts proper to sixty."

"Fifty!" shrieked Uncle Hughey, jumping in the air.

The Southerner took a tone of self-reproach. "Now, how could I forget you was fifty," he murmured, "when you have been telling it to the boys so careful for the last ten years!"

Have you ever seen a cockatoo—the white kind with the top-knot—enraged by insult? The bird erects every available feather upon its person. So did Uncle Hughey seem to swell, clothes, mustache, and woolly white beard; and without further speech he took himself on board the East-bound train, which now arrived from its siding in time to deliver him.

Yet this was not why he had not gone away before. At any time he could have escaped into the baggage-room or withdrawn to a dignified distance until his train should come up. But the old man had evidently got a sort of joy from this teasing. He had reached that inevitable age when we are tickled to be linked with affairs of gallantry, no matter how.

With him now the East-bound departed slowly into that distance whence I had come. I stared after it as it went its way to the far shores of civilization. It grew small in the unending gulf of space, until all sign of its presence was gone save a faint skein of smoke against the evening sky. And now my lost trunk came back into my thoughts, and Medicine Bow seemed a lonely spot. A sort of ship had left me marooned in a foreign ocean; the Pullman was comfortably steaming home to port, while I—how was I to find Judge Henry's ranch? Where in this unfeatured wilderness was Sunk Creek? No creek or any water at all flowed here that I could perceive. My host had written he should meet me at the station and drive me to his ranch. This was all that I knew. He was not here. The baggage-man had not seen him lately. The ranch was almost certain to be too far to walk to, tonight. My trunk—I discovered myself still staring dolefully after the vanished East-bound; and at the same instant I became aware that the tall man was looking gravely at me—as gravely as he had looked at Uncle Hughey throughout their remarkable conversation.

To see his eye thus fixing me and his thumb still hooked in his cartridge-belt, certain tales of travelers from these parts forced themselves disquietingly into my recollection. Now that Uncle Hughey was gone, was I to take his place and be, for instance, invited to dance on the platform to the music of shots nicely aimed?

"I reckon I am looking for you, seh," the tall man now observed.

## CHAPTER II

## "WHEN YOU CALL ME THAT, SMILE!"

We cannot see ourselves as others see us, or I should know what appearance I cut at hearing this from the tall man. I said nothing, feeling uncertain.

"I reckon I am looking for you, seh," he repeated politely.

"I am looking for Judge Henry," I now replied.

He walked toward me, and I saw that in inches he was not a giant. He was not more than six feet. It was Uncle Hughey that had made him seem to tower. But in his eye, in his face, in his step, in the whole man, there dominated a something potent to be felt, I should think, by man or woman.

"The Judge sent me afteh you, seh," he now explained, in his civil Southern voice; and he handed me a letter from my host. Had I not witnessed his facetious performances with Uncle Hughey, I should have judged him wholly ungifted with such powers. There was nothing external about him but what seemed the signs of a nature as grave as you could meet. But I had witnessed; and therefore supposing that I knew him in spite of his appearance, that I was, so to speak, in his secret and could give him a sort of wink, I adopted at once a method of easiness. It was so pleasant to be easy with a large stranger, who instead of shooting at your heels had very civilly handed you a letter.

"You're from old Virginia, I take it?" I began.

He answered slowly, "Then you have taken it correct, seh."

A slight chill passed over my easiness, but I went cheerily on with a further inquiry. "Find many oddities out here like Uncle Hughey?"

"Yes, seh, there is a right smart of oddities around. They come in on every train."

At this point I dropped my method of easiness.

"I wish that trunks came on the train," said I. And I told him my predicament.

It was not to be expected that he would be greatly moved at my loss; but he took it with no comment whatever. "We'll wait in town for it," said he, always perfectly civil.

Now, what I had seen of "town" was, to my newly arrived eyes, altogether horrible. If I could possibly sleep at the Judge's ranch, I preferred to do so.

"Is it too far to drive there tonight?" I inquired.

He looked at me in a puzzled manner.

"For this valise," I explained, "contains all that I immediately need; in fact, I could do without my trunk for a day or two, if it is not convenient to send. So if we could arrive there not too late by starting at once—" I paused.

"It's two hundred and sixty-three miles," said the Virginian.

To my loud ejaculation he made no answer, but surveyed me a moment longer, and then said, "Supper will be about ready now." He took my valise, and I followed his steps toward the eating-house in silence. I was dazed.

As we went, I read my host's letter—a brief hospitable message. He was very sorry not to meet me himself. He had been getting ready to drive over, when the surveyor appeared and detained him. Therefore in his stead he was sending a trustworthy man to town, who would look after me and drive me over. They were looking forward to my visit with much pleasure. This was all.

Yes, I was dazed. How did they count distance in this country? You spoke in a neighborly fashion about driving over to town, and it meant—I did not know yet how many days. And what would be meant by the term "dropping in," I wondered. And how many miles would be considered really far? I abstained from further questioning the "trustworthy man." My questions had not fared excessively well. He did not propose making me dance, to be sure: that would scarcely be trustworthy. But neither did he propose to have me familiar with him. Why was this? What had I done to elicit that veiled and skilful sarcasm about oddities coming in on every train? Having been sent to look after me, he would do so, would even carry my valise; but I could not be jocular with him. This handsome, ungrammatical son of the soil had set between us the bar of his cold and perfect civility. No polished person could have done it better. What was the matter? I looked at him, and suddenly it came to me. If he had tried familiarity with me the first two minutes of our acquaintance, I should have resented it; by what right, then, had I tried it with him? It smacked of patronizing: on this occasion he had come off the better gentleman of the two. Here in flesh and blood was a truth which I had long believed in words, but never met before. The creature we call a *gentleman* lies deep in the hearts of thousands that are born without chance to master the outward graces of the type.

Between the station and the eating-house I did a deal of straight thinking. But my thoughts were destined presently to be drowned in amazement at the rare personage into whose society fate had thrown me.

Town, as they called it, pleased me the less, the longer I saw it. But until our language stretches itself and takes in a new word of closer fit, town will have to do for the name of such a place as was Medicine Bow. I have seen and slept in many like it since. Scattered wide, they littered the frontier from the Columbia to the Rio Grande, from the Missouri to the Sierras. They lay stark, dotted over a planet of treeless dust, like soiled packs of cards. Each was similar to the next, as one old five-spot of clubs resembles another. Houses, empty bottles, and garbage, they were forever of the same shapeless pattern. More forlorn they were than stale bones. They seemed to have been strewn there by the wind and to be waiting till the wind should come again and blow them away. Yet serene above their foulness swam a pure and quiet light, such as the East never sees; they might be bathing in the air of creation's first morning. Beneath sun and stars their days and nights were immaculate and wonderful.

Medicine Bow was my first, and I took its dimensions, twenty-nine buildings in all—one coal shute, one water tank, the station, one store, two eating-houses, one billiard hall, two tool-houses, one feed stable, and twelve others that for one reason and another I shall not name. Yet this wretched husk of squalor spent thought upon appearances; many houses in it wore a false front to seem as if they were two stories high. There they stood, rearing their pitiful masquerade amid a fringe of old tin cans, while at their very doors began a world of crystal light, a land without end, a space across which Noah and Adam might come straight from Genesis. Into that space went wandering a road, over a hill and down out of sight, and up again smaller in the distance, down once more, and up once more, straining the eyes, and so away.

Then I heard a fellow greet my Virginian. He came rollicking out of a door, and made a pass with his hand at the Virginian's hat. The Southerner dodged it, and I saw once more the tiger undulation of body, and knew my escort was he of the rope and the corral.

"How are yu' Steve?" he said to the rollicking man. And in his tone I heard instantly old friendship speaking. With Steve he would take and give familiarity.

Steve looked at me, and looked away—and that was all. But it was enough. In no company had I ever felt so much an outsider. Yet I liked the company, and wished that it would like me.

"Just come to town?" inquired Steve of the Virginian.

"Been here since noon. Been waiting for the train."

"Going out tonight?"

"I reckon I'll pull out to-morro'."

"Beds are all took," said Steve. This was for my benefit.

"Dear me," said I.

"But I guess one of them drummers will let yu' double up with him."

Steve was enjoying himself, I think. He had his saddle and blankets, and beds were nothing to him.

"Drummers, are they?" asked the Virginian.

"Two Jews handling cigars, one American with consumption killer, and a Dutchman with jew'lry."

The Virginian set down my valise, and seemed to meditate. "I did want a bed tonight," he murmured gently.

"Well," Steve suggested, "the American looks like he washed the oftenest."

"That's of no consequence to me," observed the Southerner.

"Guess it'll be when yu' see 'em."

"Oh, I'm meaning something different. I wanted a bed to myself."

"Then you'll have to build one."

"Bet yu' I have the Dutchman's."

"Take a man that won't scare. Bet yu' drinks yu' can't have the American's."

"Go yu'" said the Virginian. "I'll have his bed without any fuss. Drinks for the crowd."

"I suppose you have me beat," said Steve, grinning at him affectionately. "You're such a son-of-a—— when you get down to work. Well, so long! I got to fix my horse's hoofs."

I had expected that the man would be struck down. He had used to the Virginian a term of heaviest insult, I thought. I had marvelled to hear it come so unheralded from Steve's friendly lips. And now I marvelled still more. Evidently he had meant no harm by it, and evidently no offence had been taken. Used thus, this language was plainly complimentary. I had stepped into a world new to me indeed, and novelties were occurring with scarce any time to get breath between them. As to where I should sleep, I had forgotten that problem altogether in my curiosity. What was the Virginian going to do now? I began to know that the quiet of this man was volcanic.

"Will you wash first, sir?"

We were at the door of the eating-house, and he set my valise inside. In my tenderfoot innocence I was looking indoors for the washing arrangements.

"It's out hyeh, seh," he informed me gravely, but with strong Southern accent. Internal mirth seemed often to heighten the local flavor of his speech. There were other times when it had scarce any special accent or fault in grammar.

A trough was to my right, slippery with soapy water; and hanging from a roller above one end of it was a rag of discouraging appearance. The Virginian caught it, and it performed one whirling revolution on its roller. Not a dry or clean inch could be found on it. He took off his hat, and put his head in the door.

"Your towel, ma'am," said he, "has been too popular."

She came out, a pretty woman. Her eyes rested upon him for a moment, then upon me with disfavor; then they returned to his black hair.

"The allowance is one a day," said she, very quietly. "But when folks are particular—" She completed her sentence by removing the old towel and giving a clean one to us.

"Thank you, ma'am," said the cowpuncher.

She looked once more at his black hair, and without any word returned to her guests at supper.

A pail stood in the trough, almost empty; and this he filled for me from a well. There was some soap sliding at large in the trough, but I got my own. And then in a tin basin I removed as many of the stains of travel as I was able. It was not much of a toilet that I made in this first wash-trough of my experience, but it had to suffice, and I took my seat at supper.

Canned stuff it was—corned beef. And one of my table companions said the truth about it. "When I slung my teeth over that," he remarked, "I thought I was chewing a hammock." We had strange coffee, and condensed milk; and I have never seen more flies. I made no attempt to talk, for no one in this country seemed favorable to me. By reason of something—my clothes, my hat, my pronunciation, whatever it might be, I possessed the secret of estranging people at sight. Yet I was doing better than I knew; my strict silence and attention to the corned beef made me in the eyes of the cowboys at table compare well with the over-talkative commercial travelers.

The Virginian's entrance produced a slight silence. He had done wonders with the wash-trough, and he had somehow brushed his clothes. With all the roughness of his dress, he was now the neatest of us. He nodded to some of the other cowboys, and began his meal in quiet.

But silence is not the native element of the drummer. An average fish can go a longer time out of water than this breed can live without talking. One of them now looked across the table at the grave, flannel-shirted Virginian; he inspected, and came to the imprudent conclusion that he understood his man.

"Good evening," he said briskly.

"Good evening," said the Virginian.

"Just come to town?" pursued the drummer.

"Just come to town," the Virginian suavely assented.

"Cattle business jumping along?" inquired the drummer.

"Oh, fair." And the Virginian took some more corned beef.

"Gets a move on your appetite, anyway," suggested the drummer.

The Virginian drank some coffee. Presently the pretty woman refilled his cup without his asking her.

"Guess I've met you before," the drummer stated next.

The Virginian glanced at him for a brief moment.

"Haven't I, now? Ain't I seen you somewhere? Look at me. You been in Chicago, ain't you? You look at me well. Remember Ikey's, don't you?"

"I don't reckon I do."

"See, now! I knowed you'd been in Chicago. Four or five years ago. Or maybe it's two years. Time's nothing to me. But I never forget a face. Yes, sir. Him and me's met at Ikey's, all right." This important point the drummer stated to all of us. We were called to witness how well he had proved old acquaintanceship. "Ain't the world small, though!" he exclaimed complacently. "Meet a man once and you're sure to run on to him again. That's straight.

That's no barroom josh." And the drummer's eye included us all in his confidence. I wondered if he had attained that high perfection when a man believes his own lies.

The Virginian did not seem interested. He placidly attended to his food, while our landlady moved between dining room and kitchen, and the drummer expanded.

"Yes, sir! Ikey's over by the stockyards, patronized by all cattlemen that know what's what. That's where. Maybe it's three years. Time never was nothing to me. But faces! Why, I can't quit 'em. Adults or children, male and female; onced I seen 'em I couldn't lose one off my memory, not if you were to pay me bounty, five dollars a face. White men, that is. Can't do nothing with niggers or Chinese. But you're white, all right." The drummer suddenly returned to the Virginian with this high compliment. The cowpuncher had taken out a pipe, and was slowly rubbing it. The compliment seemed to escape his attention, and the drummer went on.

"I can tell a man when he's white, put him at Ikey's or out loose here in the sagebrush." And he rolled a cigar across to the Virginian's plate.

"Selling them?" inquired the Virginian.

"Solid goods, my friend. Havana wrappers, the biggest tobacco proposition for five cents got out yet. Take it, try it, light it, watch it burn. Here." And he held out a bunch of matches.

The Virginian tossed a five-cent piece over to him.

"Oh, no, my friend! Not from you! Not after Ikey's. I don't forget you. See? I knowed your face right away. See? That's straight. I seen you at Chicago all right."

"Maybe you did," said the Virginian. "Sometimes I'm mighty careless what I look at."

"Well, py damn!" now exclaimed the Dutch drummer, hilariously. "I am ploom disappointed. I vas hoping to sell him somedings myself."

"Not the same here," stated the American. "He's too healthy for me. I gave him up on sight."

Now it was the American drummer whose bed the Virginian had in his eye. This was a sensible man, and had talked less than his brothers in the trade. I had little doubt who would end by sleeping in his bed; but how the thing would be done interested me more deeply than ever.

The Virginian looked amiably at his intended victim, and made one or two remarks regarding patent medicines. There must be a good deal of money in them, he supposed, with a live man to manage them. The victim was flattered. No other person at the table had been favored with so much of the tall cowpuncher's notice. He responded, and they had a pleasant talk. I did not divine that the Virginian's genius was even then at work, and that all this was part of his satanic strategy. But Steve must have divined it. For while a few of us still sat finishing our supper, that facetious horseman returned from doctoring his horse's hoofs, put his head into the dining room, took in the way in which the Virginian was engaging his victim in conversation, remarked aloud, "I've lost!" and closed the door again.

"What's he lost?" inquired the American drummer.

"Oh, you mustn't mind him," drawled the Virginian. "He's one of those box-head jokers goes around openin' and shuttin' doors that-a-way. We call him harmless. Well," he broke off, "I reckon I'll go smoke. Not allowed in hyeh?" This last he addressed to the landlady, with especial gentleness. She shook her head, and her eyes followed him as he went out.

Left to myself I meditated for some time upon my lodging for the night, and smoked a cigar for consolation as I walked about. It was not a hotel that we had supped in. Hotel at Medicine Bow there appeared to be none. But connected with the eating-house was that place where, according to Steve, the beds were all taken, and there I went to see for myself. Steve had spoken the truth. It was a single apartment containing four or five beds, and nothing else whatever. And when I looked at these beds, my sorrow that I could sleep in none of them grew less. To be alone in one offered no temptation, and as for this courtesy of the country, this doubling up—!

"Well, they have got ahead of us." This was the Virginian standing at my elbow.

I assented.

"They have staked out their claims," he added.

In this public sleeping room they had done what one does to secure a seat in a railroad train. Upon each bed, as notice of occupancy, lay some article of travel or of dress. As we stood there, the two Jews came in and opened and arranged their valises, and folded and refolded their linen dusters. Then a railroad employee entered and began to go to bed at this hour, before dusk had wholly darkened into night. For him, going to bed meant removing his boots and placing his overalls and waistcoat beneath his pillow. He had no coat. His work began at three in the morning; and even as we still talked he began to snore.

"The man that keeps the store is a friend of mine," said the Virginian; "and you can be pretty near comfortable on his counter. Got any blankets?"

I had no blankets.

"Looking for a bed?" inquired the American drummer, now arriving.

"Yes, he's looking for a bed," answered the voice of Steve behind him.

"Seems a waste of time," observed the Virginian. He looked thoughtfully from one bed to another. "I didn't know I'd have to lay over here. Well, I have sat up before."

"This one's mine," said the drummer, sitting down on it. "Half's plenty enough room for me."

"You're cert'nly mighty kind," said the cowpuncher. "But I'd not think o' disconveniencing yu'."

"That's nothing. The other half is yours. Turn in right now if you feel like it."

"No. I don't reckon I'll turn in right now. Better keep your bed to yourself."

"See here," urged the drummer, "if I take you I'm safe from drawing some party I might not care so much about. This here sleeping proposition is a lottery."

"Well," said the Virginian (and his hesitation was truly masterly), "if you put it that way—"

"I do put it that way. Why, you're clean! You've had a shave right now. You turn in when you feel inclined, old man! I ain't retiring just yet."

The drummer had struck a slightly false note in these last remarks. He should not have said "old man." Until this I had thought him merely an amiable person who wished to do a favor. But "old man" came in wrong. It had a hateful taint of his profession; the being too soon with everybody, the celluloid good-fellowship that passes for ivory with nine in ten of the city crowd. But not so with the sons of the sagebrush. They live nearer nature, and they know better.

But the Virginian blandly accepted "old man" from his victim: he had a game to play. "Well, I cert'nly thank yu'," he said. "After a while I'll take advantage of your kind offer."

I was surprised. Possession being nine points of the law, it seemed his very chance to intrench himself in the bed. But the cowpuncher had planned a campaign needing no intrenchments. Moreover, going to bed before nine o'clock upon the first evening in many weeks that a town's resources were open to you, would be a dull proceeding. Our entire company, drummer and all, now walked over to the store, and here my sleeping arrangements were made easily. This store was the cleanest place and the best in Medicine Bow, and would have been a good store anywhere, offering a multitude of things for sale, and kept by a very civil proprietor. He bade me make myself at home, and placed both of his counters at my disposal. Upon the grocery side there stood a cheese too large and strong to sleep near comfortably, and I therefore chose the dry-goods side. Here thick quilts were unrolled for me, to make it soft; and no condition was placed upon me, further than that I should remove my boots, because the quilts were new, and clean, and for sale. So now my rest was assured. Not an anxiety remained in my thoughts. These therefore turned themselves wholly to the other man's bed, and how he was going to lose it.

I think that Steve was more curious even than myself. Time was on the wing. His bet must be decided, and the drinks enjoyed. He stood against the grocery counter, contemplating the Virginian. But it was to me that he spoke. The Virginian, however, listened to every word.

"Your first visit to this country?"

I told him yes.

"How do you like it?"

I expected to like it very much.

"How does the climate strike you?"

I thought the climate was fine.

"Makes a man thirsty though."

This was the subcurrent which the Virginian plainly looked for. But he, like Steve, addressed himself to me.

"Yes," he put in, "thirsty while a man's soft yet. You'll harden."

"I guess you'll find it a drier country than you were given to expect," said Steve.

"If your habits have been frequent that way," said the Virginian.

"There's parts of Wyoming," pursued Steve, "where you'll go hours and hours before you'll see a drop of wetness."

"And if yu' keep a-thinkin' about it," said the Virginian, "it'll seem like days and days."

Steve, at this stroke, gave up, and clapped him on the shoulder with a joyous chuckle. "You old son-of-a!" he cried affectionately.

"Drinks are due now," said the Virginian. "My treat, Steve. But I reckon your suspense will have to linger a while yet."

Thus they dropped into direct talk from that speech of the fourth dimension where they had been using me for their telephone.

"Any cyards going tonight?" inquired the Virginian.

"Stud and draw," Steve told him. "Strangers playing."

"I think I'd like to get into a game for a while," said the Southerner. "Strangers, yu' say?"

And then, before quitting the store, he made his toilet for this little hand at poker. It was a simple preparation. He took his pistol from its holster, examined it, then shoved it between his overalls and his shirt in front, and pulled his waistcoat over it. He might have been combing his hair for all the attention anyone paid to this, except myself. Then the two friends went out, and I bethought me of that epithet which Steve again had used to the Virginian as he clapped him on the shoulder. Clearly this wild country spoke a language other than mine—the word here was a term of endearment. Such was my conclusion.

The drummers had finished their dealings with the proprietor, and they were gossiping together in a knot by the door as the Virginian passed out.

"See you later, old man!" This was the American drummer accosting his prospective bedfellow.

"Oh, yes," returned the bedfellow, and was gone.

The American drummer winked triumphantly at his brethren. "He's all right," he observed, jerking a thumb after the Virginian. "He's easy. You got to know him to work him. That's all."

"Und vat is your point?" inquired the German drummer.

"Point is—he'll not take any goods off you or me; but he's going to talk up the killer to any consumptive he runs across. I ain't done with him yet. Say," (he now addressed the proprietor), "what's her name?"

"Whose name?"

"Woman runs the eating-house."

"Glen. Mrs. Glen."

"Ain't she new?"

"Been settled here about a month. Husband's a freight conductor."

"Thought I'd not seen her before. She's a good-looker."

"Hm! Yes. The kind of good looks I'd sooner see in another man's wife than mine."

"So that's the gait, is it?"

"Hm! Well, it don't seem to be. She come here with that reputation. But there's been general disappointment."

"Then she ain't lacked suitors any?"

"Lacked! Are you acquainted with cowboys?"

"And she disappointed 'em? Maybe she likes her husband?"

"Hm! Well, how are you to tell about them silent kind?"

"Talking of conductors," began the drummer. And we listened to his anecdote. It was successful with his audience; but when he launched fluently upon a second I strolled out. There was not enough wit in this narrator to relieve his indecency, and I felt shame at having been surprised into laughing with him.

I left that company growing confidential over their leering stories, and I sought the saloon. It was very quiet and orderly. Beer in quart bottles at a dollar I had never met before; but saving its price, I found no complaint to make of it. Through folding doors I passed from the bar proper with its bottles and elk head back to the hall with its various tables. I saw a man sliding cards from a case, and across the table from him another man laying counters down. Near by was a second dealer pulling cards from the bottom of a pack, and opposite him a solemn old rustic piling and changing coins upon the cards which lay already exposed.

But now I heard a voice that drew my eyes to the far corner of the room.

"Why didn't you stay in Arizona?"

Harmless looking words as I write them down here. Yet at the sound of them I noticed the eyes of the others directed to that corner. What answer was given to them I did not hear, nor did I see who spoke. Then came another remark.

"Well, Arizona's no place for amateurs."

This time the two card dealers that I stood near began to give a part of their attention to the group that sat in the corner. There was in me a desire to leave this room. So far my hours at Medicine Bow had seemed to glide beneath a sunshine of merriment, of easy-going jocularity. This was suddenly gone, like the wind changing to north in the middle of a warm day. But I stayed, being ashamed to go.

Five or six players sat over in the corner at a round table where counters were piled. Their eyes were close upon their cards, and one seemed to be dealing a card at a time to each, with pauses and betting between. Steve was there and the Virginian; the others were new faces.

"No place for amateurs," repeated the voice; and now I saw that it was the dealer's. There was in his countenance the same ugliness that his words conveyed.

"Who's that talkin'?" said one of the men near me, in a low voice.

"Trampas."

"What's he?"

"Cowpuncher, bronco-buster, tin-horn, most anything."

"Who's he talkin' at?"

"Think it's the black-headed guy he's talking at."

"That ain't supposed to be safe, is it?"

"Guess we're all goin' to find out in a few minutes."

"Been trouble between 'em?"

"They've not met before. Trampas don't enjoy losin' to a stranger."

"Fello's from Arizona, yu' say?"

"No. Virginia. He's recently back from havin' a look at Arizona. Went down there last year for a change. Works for the Sunk Creek outfit." And then the dealer lowered his voice still further and said something in the other man's ear, causing him to grin. After which both of them looked at me.

There had been silence over in the corner; but now the man Trampas spoke again.

"And ten," said he, sliding out some chips from before him. Very strange it was to hear him, how he contrived to make those words a personal taunt. The Virginian was looking at his cards. He might have been deaf.

"And twenty," said the next player, easily.

The next threw his cards down.

It was now the Virginian's turn to bet, or leave the game, and he did not speak at once.

Therefore Trampas spoke. "Your bet, you son-of-a——."

The Virginian's pistol came out, and his hand lay on the table, holding it unaimed. And with a voice as gentle as ever, the voice that sounded almost like a caress, but drawling a very little more than usual, so that there was almost a space between each word, he issued his orders to the man Trampas: "When you call me that, *smile.*" And he looked at Trampas across the table.

Yes, the voice was gentle. But in my ears it seemed as if somewhere the bell of death was ringing; and silence, like a stroke, fell on the large room. All men present, as if by some magnetic current, had become aware of this crisis. In my ignorance, and the total stoppage of my thoughts, I stood stock-still, and noticed various people crouching, or shifting their positions.

"Sit quiet," said the dealer, scornfully to the man near me. "Can't you see he don't want to push trouble? He has handed Trampas the choice to back down or draw his steel."

Then, with equal suddenness and ease, the room came out of its strangeness. Voices and cards, the click of chips, the puff of tobacco, glasses lifted to drink—this level of smooth relaxation hinted no more plainly of what lay beneath than does the surface tell the depth of the sea.

For Trampas had made his choice. And that choice was not to "draw his steel." If it was knowledge that he sought, he had found it, and no mistake! We heard no further reference to what he had been pleased to style "amateurs." In no company would the black-headed man who had visited Arizona be rated a novice at the cool art of self-preservation.

One doubt remained: what kind of a man was Trampas? A public back-down is an unfinished thing—for some natures at least. I looked at his face, and thought it sullen, but tricky rather than courageous.

Something had been added to my knowledge also. Once again I had heard applied to the Virginian that epithet which Steve so freely used. The same words, identical to the letter. But this time they had produced a pistol. "When you call me that, *smile!*" So I perceived a new example of the old truth, that the letter means nothing until the spirit gives it life.

## CHAPTER III

## STEVE TREATS

It was for several minutes, I suppose, that I stood drawing these silent morals. No man occupied himself with me. Quiet voices, and games of chance, and glasses lifted to drink, continued to be the peaceful order of the night. And into my thoughts broke the voice of that card-dealer who had already spoken so sagely. He also took his turn at moralizing.

"What did I tell you?" he remarked to the man for whom he continued to deal, and who continued to lose money to him.

"Tell me when?"

"Didn't I tell you he'd not shoot?" the dealer pursued with complacence. "You got ready to dodge. You had no call to be concerned. He's not the kind a man need feel anxious about."

The player looked over at the Virginian, doubtfully. "Well," he said, "I don't know what you folks call a dangerous man."

"Not him!" exclaimed the dealer with admiration. "He's a brave man. That's different."

The player seemed to follow this reasoning no better than I did.

"It's not a brave man that's dangerous," continued the dealer. "It's the cowards that scare me." He paused that this might sink home.

"Fello' came in here las' Toosday," he went on. "He got into some misunderstanding about the drinks. Well, sir, before we could put him out of business, he'd hurt two perfectly innocent onlookers. They'd no more to do with it than you have," the dealer explained to me.

"Were they badly hurt?" I asked.

"One of 'em was. He's died since."

"What became of the man?"

"Why, we put him out of business, I told you. He died that night. But there was no occasion for any of it; and that's why I never like to be around where there's a coward. You can't tell. He'll always go to shooting before it's necessary, and there's no security who he'll hit. But a man like that black-headed guy is (the dealer indicated the Virginian) need never worry you. And there's another point why there's no need to worry about him: *it'd be too late.*"

These good words ended the moralizing of the dealer. He had given us a piece of his mind. He now gave the whole of it to dealing cards. I loitered here and there, neither welcome nor unwelcome at present, watching the cowboys at their play. Saving Trampas, there was scarce a face among them that had not in it something very likable. Here were lusty horsemen ridden from the heat of the sun, and the wet of the storm, to divert themselves awhile. Youth untamed sat here for an idle moment, spending easily its hard-earned wages. City saloons rose into my vision, and I instantly preferred this Rocky Mountain place. More of death it undoubtedly saw, but less of vice, than did its New York equivalents.

And death is a thing much cleaner than vice. Moreover, it was by no means vice that was written upon these wild and manly faces. Even where baseness was visible, baseness was not uppermost. Daring, laughter, endurance—these were what I saw upon the countenances of the cowboys. And this very first day of my knowledge of them marks a date with me. For something about them, and the idea of them, smote my American heart, and I have never forgotten it, nor ever shall, as long as I live. In their flesh our natural passions ran tumultuous; but often in their spirit sat hidden a true nobility, and often beneath its unexpected shining their figures took on heroic stature.

The dealer had styled the Virginian "a black-headed guy." This did well enough as an unflattered portrait. Judge Henry's trustworthy man, with whom I was to drive two hundred and sixty-three miles, certainly had a very black head of hair. It was the first thing to notice now, if one glanced generally at the table where he sat at cards. But the eye came back to him—drawn by that inexpressible something which had led the dealer to speak so much at length about him.

Still, "black-headed guy" justly fits him and his next performance. He had made his plan for this like a true and (I must say) inspired devil. And now the highly appreciative town of Medicine Bow was to be treated to a manifestation of genius.

He sat playing his stud-poker. After a decent period of losing and winning, which gave Trampas all proper time for a change of luck and a repairing of his fortunes, he looked at Steve and said amiably: "How does bed strike you?"

I was beside their table, learning gradually that stud-poker has in it more of what I will call red pepper than has our Eastern game. The Virginian followed his own question: "Bed strikes me," he stated.

Steve feigned indifference. He was far more deeply absorbed in his bet and the American drummer than he was in this game; but he chose to take out a fat, florid gold watch, consult it elaborately, and remark, "It's only eleven."

"Yu' forget I'm from the country," said the black-headed guy. "The chickens have been roostin' a right smart while."

His sunny Southern accent was again strong. In that brief passage with Trampas it had been almost wholly absent. But different moods of the spirit bring different qualities of utterance—where a man comes by these naturally. The Virginian cashed in his checks.

"Awhile ago," said Steve, "you had won three months' salary."

"I'm still twenty dollars to the good," said the Virginian. "That's better than breaking a laig."

Again, in some voiceless, masonic way, most people in that saloon had become aware that something was in process of happening. Several left their games and came to the front by the bar.

"If he ain't in bed yet—" mused the Virginian.

"I'll find out," said I. And I hurried across to the dim sleeping room, happy to have a part in this.

They were all in bed; and in some beds two were sleeping. How they could do it—but in those days I was fastidious. The American had come in recently and was still awake.

"Thought you were to sleep at the store?" said he.

So then I invented a little lie, and explained that I was in search of the Virginian.

"Better search the dives," said he. "These cowboys don't get to town often."

At this point I stumbled sharply over something.

"It's my box of Consumption Killer," explained the drummer. "Well, I hope that man will stay out all night."

"Bed narrow?" I inquired.

"For two it is. And the pillows are mean. Takes both before you feel anything's under your head."

He yawned, and I wished him pleasant dreams.

At my news the Virginian left the bar at once; and crossed to the sleeping room. Steve and I followed softly, and behind us several more strung out in an expectant line. "What is this going to be?" they inquired curiously of each other. And upon learning the great novelty of the event, they clustered with silence intense outside the door where the Virginian had gone in.

We heard the voice of the drummer, cautioning his bedfellow. "Don't trip over the Killer," he was saying. "The Prince of Wales barked his shin just now." It seemed my English clothes had earned me this title.

The boots of the Virginian were next heard to drop.

"Can yu' make out what he's at?" whispered Steve.

He was plainly undressing. The rip of swift unbuttoning told us that the black-headed guy must now be removing his overalls.

"Why, thank yu', no," he was replying to a question of the drummer. "Outside or in's all one to me."

"Then, if you'd just as soon take the wall—"

"Why, cert'nly." There was a sound of bedclothes, and creaking. "This hyeh pillo' needs a Southern climate," was the Virginian's next observation.

Many listeners had now gathered at the door. The dealer and the player were both here. The storekeeper was present, and I recognized the agent of the Union Pacific Railroad among the crowd. We made a large company, and I felt that trembling sensation which is common when the cap of a camera is about to be removed upon a group.

"I should think," said the drummer's voice, "that you'd feel your knife and gun clean through that pillow."

"I do," responded the Virginian.

"I should think you'd put them on a chair and be comfortable."

"I'd be uncomfortable, then."

"Used to the feel of them, I suppose?"

"That's it. Used to the feel of them. I would miss them, and that would make me wakeful."

"Well, good night."

"Good night. If I get to talkin' and tossin', or what not, you'll understand you're to—"

"Yes, I'll wake you."

"No, don't yu', for God's sake!"

"Not?"

"Don't yu' touch me."

"What'll I do?"

"Roll away quick to your side. It don't last but a minute." The Virginian spoke with a reassuring drawl.

Upon this there fell a brief silence, and I heard the drummer clear his throat once or twice.

"It's merely the nightmare, I suppose?" he said after a throat clearing.

"Lord, yes. That's all. And don't happen twice a year. Was you thinkin' it was fits?"

"Oh, no! I just wanted to know. I've been told before that it was not safe for a person to be waked suddenly that way out of a nightmare."

"Yes, I have heard that too. But it never harms me any. I didn't want you to run risks."

"Me?"

"Oh, it'll be all right now that yu' know how it is." The Virginian's drawl was full of assurance.

There was a second pause, after which the drummer said:

"Tell me again how it is."

The Virginian answered very drowsily: "Oh, just don't let your arm or your laig touch me if I go to jumpin' around. I'm dreamin' of Indians when I do that. And if anything touches me then, I'm liable to grab my knife right in my sleep."

"Oh, I understand," said the drummer, clearing his throat. "Yes."

Steve was whispering delighted oaths to himself, and in his joy applying to the Virginian one unprintable name after another.

We listened again, but now no further words came. Listening very hard, I could half make out the progress of a heavy breathing, and a restless turning I could clearly detect. This was the wretched drummer. He was waiting. But he did not wait long. Again there was a light creak, and after it a light step. He was not even going to put his boots on in the fatal neighborhood of the dreamer. By a happy thought Medicine Bow formed into two lines, making an avenue from the door. And then the commercial traveler forgot his Consumption Killer. He fell heavily over it.

Immediately from the bed the Virginian gave forth a dreadful howl.

And then everything happened at once; and how shall mere words narrate it? The door burst open, and out flew the commercial traveler in his stockings. One hand held a lump of coat and trousers with suspenders dangling, his boots were clutched in the other. The sight of us stopped his flight short. He gazed, the boots fell from his hand; and at his profane explosion, Medicine Bow set up a united, unearthly noise and began to play Virginia reel with him. The other occupants of the beds had already sprung out of them, clothed chiefly with their pistols, and ready for war. "What is it?" they demanded. "What is it?"

"Why, I reckon it's drinks on Steve," said the Virginian from his bed. And he gave the first broad grin that I had seen from him.

"I'll set 'em up all night!" Steve shouted, as the reel went on regardless. The drummer was bawling to be allowed to put at least his boots on. "This way, Pard," was the answer; and another man whirled him round. "This way, Beau!" they called to him; "This way, Budd!" and he was passed like a shuttlecock down the line. Suddenly the leaders bounded into the sleeping-room. "Feed the machine!" they said. "Feed her!" And seizing the German drummer who sold jewelry, they flung him into the trough of the reel. I saw him go bouncing like an ear of corn to be shelled, and the dance engulfed him. I saw a Jew sent rattling after him; and next they threw in the railroad employee, and the other Jew; and while I stood mesmerized, my own feet left the earth. I shot from the room and sped like a bobbing cork into this mill race, whirling my turn in the wake of the others amid cries of, "Here comes the Prince of Wales!" There was soon not much English left about my raiment.

They were now shouting for music. Medicine Bow swept in like a cloud of dust to where a fiddler sat playing in a hall; and gathering up fiddler and dancers, swept out again, a larger Medicine Bow, growing all the while. Steve offered us the freedom of the house, everywhere. He implored us to call for whatever pleased us, and as many times as we should please. He ordered the town to be searched for more citizens to come and help him pay his bet. But changing his mind, kegs and bottles were now carried along with us. We had found three fiddlers, and these played busily for us; and thus we set out to visit all cabins and houses where people might still by some miracle be asleep. The first man put out his head to decline. But such a possibility had been foreseen by the proprietor of the store. This seemingly respectable man now came dragging some sort of apparatus from his place, helped by the Virginian. The cowboys cheered, for they knew what this was. The man in his window likewise recognized it, and uttering a groan, came immediately out and joined us. What it was, I also learned in a few minutes. For we found a house where the people made no sign at either our fiddlers or our knocking.

And then the infernal machine was set to work. Its parts seemed to be no more than an empty keg and a plank. Some citizen informed me that I should soon have a new idea of noise; and I nerved myself for something severe in the way of gunpowder. But the Virginian and the proprietor now sat on the ground holding the keg braced, and two others got down apparently to play see-saw over the top of it with the plank. But the keg and plank had been rubbed with rosin, and they drew the plank back and forth over the keg. Do you know the sound made in a narrow street by a dray loaded with strips of iron? That noise is a lullaby compared with the staggering, blinding bellow which rose from the keg. If you were to try it in your native town, you would not merely be arrested, you would be hanged, and everybody would be glad, and the clergyman would not bury you. My head, my teeth, the whole system of my bones leaped and chattered at the din, and out of the house like drops squirted from a lemon came a man and his wife. No time was given them. They were swept along with the rest; and having been routed from their own bed, they now became most furious in assailing the remaining homes of Medicine Bow. Everybody was to come out. Many were now riding horses at top speed out into the plains and back, while the procession of the plank and keg continued its work, and the fiddlers played incessantly.

Suddenly there was a quiet. I did not see who brought the message; but the word ran among us that there was a woman—the engineer's woman down by the water-tank—very sick. The doctor had been to see her from Laramie. Everybody liked the engineer. Plank and keg were heard no more. The horsemen found it out and restrained their gambols. Medicine Bow went gradually home. I saw doors shutting, and lights go out; I saw a late few reassemble at the card tables, and the drummers gathered themselves together for sleep; the proprietor of the store (you could not see a more respectable-looking person) hoped that I would be comfortable on the quilts; and I heard Steve urging the Virginian to take one more glass.

"We've not met for so long," he said.

But the Virginian, the black-headed guy who had set all this nonsense going, said No to Steve. "I have got to stay responsible," was his excuse to his friend. And the friend looked at me. Therefore I surmised that the Judge's trustworthy man found me an embarrassment to his holiday. But if he did, he never showed it to me. He had been sent to meet a stranger and drive him to Sunk Creek in safety, and this charge he would allow no temptation to imperil. He nodded good night to me. "If there's anything I can do for yu', you'll tell me."

I thanked him. "What a pleasant evening!" I added.

"I'm glad yu' found it so."

Again his manner put a bar to my approaches. Even though I had seen him wildly disporting himself, those were matters which he chose not to discuss with me.

Medicine Bow was quiet as I went my way to my quilts. So still, that through the air the deep whistles of the freight trains came from below the horizon across great miles of silence. I passed cowboys, whom half an hour before I had seen prancing and roaring, now rolled in their blankets beneath the open and shining night.

"What world am I in?" I said aloud. "Does this same planet hold Fifth Avenue?"

And I went to sleep, pondering over my native land.

## CHAPTER IV

## DEEP INTO CATTLE LAND

Morning had been for some while astir in Medicine Bow before I left my quilts. The new day and its doings began around me in the store, chiefly at the grocery counter. Dry-goods were not in great request. The early rising cowboys were off again to their work; and those to whom their night's holiday had left any dollars were spending these for tobacco, or cartridges, or canned provisions for the journey to their distant camps. Sardines were called for, and potted chicken, and devilled ham: a sophisticated nourishment, at first sight, for these sons of the sagebrush. But portable ready-made food plays of necessity a great part in the opening of a new country. These picnic pots and cans were the first of her trophies that Civilization dropped upon Wyoming's virgin soil. The cowboy is now gone to worlds invisible; the wind has blown away the white ashes of his campfires; but the empty sardine box lies rusting over the face of the Western earth.

So through my eyes half closed I watched the sale of these tins, and grew familiar with the ham's inevitable trademark—that label with the devil and his horns and hoofs and tail very pronounced, all colored a sultry prodigious scarlet. And when each horseman had made his purchase, he would trail his spurs over the floor, and presently the sound of his horse's hoofs would be the last of him. Through my dozing attention came various fragments of talk, and sometimes useful bits of knowledge. For instance, I learned the true value of tomatoes in this country. One fellow was buying two cans of them.

"Meadow Creek dry already?" commented the proprietor.

"Been dry ten days," the young cowboy informed him. And it appeared that along the road he was going, water would not be reached much before sundown, because this Meadow Creek had ceased to run. His tomatoes were for drink. And thus they have refreshed me many times since.

"No beer?" suggested the proprietor.

The boy made a shuddering face. "Don't say its name to me!" he exclaimed. "I couldn't hold my breakfast down." He rang his silver money upon the counter. "I've swore off for three months," he stated. "I'm going to be as pure as the snow!" And away he went jingling out of the door, to ride seventy-five miles. Three more months of hard, unsheltered work, and he would ride into town again, with his adolescent blood crying aloud for its own.

"I'm obliged," said a new voice, rousing me from a new doze. "She's easier this morning, since the medicine." This was the engineer, whose sick wife had brought a hush over Medicine Bow's rioting. "I'll give her them flowers soon as she wakes," he added.

"Flowers?" repeated the proprietor.

"You didn't leave that bunch at our door?"

"Wish I'd thought to do it."

"She likes to see flowers," said the engineer. And he walked out slowly, with his thanks unachieved. He returned at once with the Virginian; for in the band of the Virginian's hat were two or three blossoms.

"It don't need mentioning," the Southerner was saying, embarrassed by any expression of thanks. "If we had knowed last night—"

"You didn't disturb her any," broke in the engineer. "She's easier this morning. I'll tell her about them flowers."

"Why, it don't need mentioning," the Virginian again protested, almost crossly. "The little things looked kind o' fresh, and I just picked them." His eye now fell upon me, where I lay upon the counter. "I reckon breakfast will be getting through," he remarked.

I was soon at the wash trough. It was only half-past six, but many had been before me—one glance at the roller-towel told me that. I was afraid to ask the landlady for a clean one, and so I found a fresh handkerchief, and accomplished a sparing toilet. In the midst of this the drummers joined me, one by one, and they used the degraded towel without hesitation. In a way they had the best of me; filth was nothing to them.

The latest risers in Medicine Bow, we sat at breakfast together; and they essayed some light familiarities with the landlady. But these experiments were failures. Her eyes did not see, nor did her ears hear them. She brought the coffee and the bacon with a sedateness that propriety itself could scarce have surpassed. Yet impropriety lurked noiselessly all over her. You could not have specified how; it was interblended with her sum total. Silence was her apparent habit and her weapon; but the American drummer found that she could speak to the point when need came for this. During the meal he had praised her golden hair. It was golden indeed, and worth a high compliment; but his kind displeased her. She had let it pass, however, with no more than a cool stare. But on taking his leave, when he came to pay for the meal, he pushed it too far.

"Pity this must be our last," he said; and as it brought no answer, "Ever travel?" he inquired. "Where I go, there's room for a pair of us."

"Then you'd better find another jackass," she replied quietly.

I was glad that I had not asked for a clean towel.

From the commercial travelers I now separated myself, and wandered alone in pleasurable aimlessness. It was seven o'clock. Medicine Bow stood voiceless and unpeopled. The cowboys had melted away. The inhabitants were indoors, pursuing the business or the idleness of the forenoon. Visible motion there was none. No shell upon the dry sands could lie more lifeless than Medicine Bow. Looking in at the store, I saw the proprietor sitting with his pipe extinct. Looking in at the saloon, I saw the dealer dealing dumbly to himself. Up in the sky there was not a cloud nor a bird, and on the earth the lightest straw lay becalmed. Once I saw the Virginian at an open door, where the golden-haired landlady stood talking with him. Sometimes I strolled in the town, and sometimes out on the plain I lay down with my daydreams in the sagebrush. Pale herds of antelope were in the distance, and near by the demure prairie-dogs sat up and scrutinized me. Steve, Trampas, the riot of horsemen, my lost trunk, Uncle Hughey, with his abortive brides—all things merged in my thoughts in a huge, delicious indifference. It was like swimming slowly at random in an ocean that was smooth, and neither too cool nor too warm. And before I knew it, five lazy imperceptible hours had gone thus. There was the Union Pacific train, coming as if from shores forgotten.

Its approach was silent and long drawn out. I easily reached town and the platform before it had finished watering at the tank. It moved up, made a short halt, I saw my trunk come out of it, and then it moved away silently as it had come, smoking and dwindling into distance unknown.

Beside my trunk was one other, tied extravagantly with white ribbon. The fluttering bows caught my attention, and now I suddenly saw a perfectly new sight. The Virginian was further down the platform, doubled up with laughing. It was good to know that with sufficient cause he could laugh like this; a smile had thus far been his limit of external mirth. Rice now flew against my hat, and hissing gusts of rice spouted on the platform. All the men left in Medicine Bow appeared like magic, and more rice choked the atmosphere. Through the general clamor a cracked voice said, "Don't hit her in the eye, boys!" and Uncle Hughey rushed proudly by me with an actual wife on his arm. She could easily have been his granddaughter. They got at once into a vehicle. The trunk was lifted in behind. And amid cheers, rice, shoes, and broad felicitations, the pair drove out of town, Uncle Hughey shrieking to the horses and the bride waving unabashed adieus.

The word had come over the wires from Laramie: "Uncle Hughey has made it this time. Expect him on today's number two." And Medicine Bow had expected him.

Many words arose on the departure of the new-married couple.

"Who's she?"

"What's he got for her?"

"Got a gold mine up Bear Creek."

And after comment and prophecy, Medicine Bow returned to its dinner.

This meal was my last here for a long while. The Virginian's responsibility now returned; duty drove the Judge's trustworthy man to take care of me again. He had not once sought my society of his own accord; his distaste for what he supposed me to be (I don't exactly know what this was) remained unshaken. I have thought that matters of dress and speech should not carry with them so much mistrust in our democracy; thieves are presumed innocent until proved guilty, but a starched collar is condemned at once. Perfect civility and obligingness I certainly did receive from the Virginian, only not a word of fellowship. He harnessed the horses, got my trunk, and gave me some advice about taking provisions for our journey, something more palatable than what food we should find along the road. It was well thought of, and I bought quite a parcel of dainties, feeling that he would despise both them and me. And thus I took my seat beside him, wondering what we should manage to talk about for two hundred and sixty-three miles.

Farewell in those days was not said in Cattle Land. Acquaintances watched our departure with a nod or with nothing, and the nearest approach to "Good-by" was the proprietor's "So-long." But I caught sight of one farewell given without words.

As we drove by the eating-house, the shade of a side window was raised, and the landlady looked her last upon the Virginian. Her lips were faintly parted, and no woman's eyes ever said more plainly, "I am one of your possessions." She had forgotten that it might be seen. Her glance caught mine, and she backed into the dimness of the room. What look she may have received from him, if he gave her any at this too public moment, I could not tell. His eyes seemed to be upon the horses, and he drove with the same mastering ease that had roped the wild pony yesterday. We passed the ramparts of Medicine Bow—thick heaps and fringes of tin cans, and shelving mounds of bottles cast out of the saloons. The sun struck these at a hundred glittering points. And in a moment we were in the clean plains, with the prairie-dogs and the pale herds of antelope. The great, still air bathed us, pure as water and strong as wine; the sunlight flooded the world; and shining upon the breast of the Virginian's flannel shirt lay a long gold thread of hair! The noisy American drummer had met defeat, but this silent free lance had been easily victorious.

It must have been five miles that we traveled in silence, losing and seeing the horizon among the ceaseless waves of the earth. Then I looked back, and there was Medicine Bow, seemingly a stone's throw behind us. It was a full half-hour before I looked back again, and there sure enough was always Medicine Bow. A size or two smaller, I will admit, but visible in every feature, like something seen through the wrong end of a field glass. The East-bound express was approaching the town, and I noticed the white steam from its whistle; but when the sound reached us, the train had almost stopped. And in reply to my comment upon this, the Virginian deigned to remark that it was more so in Arizona.

"A man come to Arizona," he said, "with one of them telescopes to study the heavenly bodies. He was a Yankee, seh, and a right smart one, too. And one night we was watchin' for some little old fallin' stars that he said was due, and I saw some lights movin' along across the mesa pretty lively, an' I sang out. But he told me it was just the train. And I told him I didn't know yu' could see the cyars that plain from his place, 'Yu' can see them,' he said to me, 'but it is las' night's cyars you're lookin' at.'" At this point the Virginian spoke severely to one of the horses. "Of course," he then resumed to me, "that Yankee man did not mean quite all he said.—You, Buck!" he again broke off suddenly to the horse. "But Arizona, seh," he continued, "it cert'nly has a mos' deceivin' atmospheah. Another man told me he had seen a lady close one eye at him when he was two minutes hard run from her." This time the Virginian gave Buck the whip.

"What effect," I inquired with a gravity equal to his own, "does this extraordinary foreshortening have upon a quart of whiskey?"

"When it's outside yu', seh, no distance looks too far to go to it."

He glanced at me with an eye that held more confidence than hitherto he had been able to feel in me. I had made one step in his approval. But I had many yet to go. This day he preferred his own thoughts to my conversation, and so he did all the days of this first journey; while I should have greatly preferred his conversation to my thoughts. He dismissed some attempts that I made upon the subject of Uncle Hughey so that I had not the courage to touch upon Trampas, and that chill brief collision which might have struck the spark of death. Trampas! I had forgotten him till this silent drive I was beginning. I wondered if I should ever see him, or Steve, or any of those people again. And this wonder I expressed aloud.

"There's no tellin' in this country," said the Virginian. "Folks come easy, and they go easy. In settled places, like back in the States, even a poor man mostly has a home. Don't care if it's only a barrel on a lot, the fello' will keep frequentin' that lot, and if yu' want him yu' can find him. But out hyeh in the sagebrush, a man's home is apt to be his saddle blanket. First thing yu' know, he has moved it to Texas."

"You have done some moving yourself," I suggested.

But this word closed his mouth. "I have had a look at the country," he said, and we were silent again. Let me, however, tell you here that he had set out for a "look at the country" at the age of fourteen; and that by his present age of twenty-four he had seen Arkansas, Texas, New Mexico, Arizona, California, Oregon, Idaho, Montana, and Wyoming. Everywhere he had taken care of himself, and survived; nor had his strong heart yet waked up to any hunger for a home. Let me also tell you that he was one of thousands drifting and living thus, but (as you shall learn) one in a thousand.

Medicine Bow did not forever remain in sight. When next I thought of it and looked behind, nothing was there but the road we had come; it lay like a ship's wake across the huge ground swell of the earth. We were swallowed in a vast solitude. A little while before sunset, a cabin came in view; and here we passed our first night. Two young men lived here, tending their cattle. They were fond of animals. By the stable a chained coyote rushed nervously in a circle, or sat on its haunches and snapped at gifts of food ungraciously. A tame young elk walked in and out of the cabin door, and during supper it tried to push me off my chair. A half-tame mountain sheep practiced jumping from the ground to the roof. The cabin was papered with posters of a circus, and skins of bear and silver fox lay upon the floor. Until nine o'clock one man talked to the Virginian, and one played gayly upon a concertina; and then we all went to bed. The air was like December, but in my blankets and a buffalo robe I kept warm, and luxuriated in the Rocky Mountain silence. Going to wash before breakfast at sunrise, I found needles of ice in a pail. Yet it was hard to remember that this quiet, open, splendid wilderness (with not a peak in sight just here) was six thousand feet high. And when breakfast was over there was no December left; and by the time the Virginian and I were ten miles upon our way, it was June. But always every breath that I breathed was pure as water and strong as wine.

We never passed a human being this day. Some wild cattle rushed up to us and away from us; antelope stared at us from a hundred yards; coyotes ran skulking through the sagebrush to watch us from a hill; at our noon meal we killed a rattlesnake and shot some young sage chickens, which were good at supper, roasted at our campfire.

By half-past eight we were asleep beneath the stars, and by half-past four I was drinking coffee and shivering. The horse, Buck, was hard to catch this second morning. Whether some hills that we were now in had excited him, or whether the better water up here had caused an effervescence in his spirits, I cannot say. But I was as hot as July by the time we had him safe in harness, or, rather, unsafe in harness. For Buck, in the mysterious language of horses, now taught wickedness to his side partner, and about eleven o'clock they laid their evil heads together and decided to break our necks.

We were passing, I have said, through a range of demi-mountains. It was a little country where trees grew, water ran, and the plains were shut out for a while. The road had steep places in it, and places here and there where you could fall off and go bounding to the bottom among stones. But Buck, for some reason, did not think these opportunities good enough for him. He selected a more theatrical moment. We emerged from a narrow canyon suddenly upon five hundred cattle and some cowboys branding calves by a fire in a corral. It was a sight that Buck knew by heart. He instantly treated it like an appalling phenomenon. I saw him kick seven ways; I saw Muggins kick five ways; our furious motion snapped my spine like a whip. I grasped the seat. Something gave a forlorn jingle. It was the brake.

"Don't jump!" commanded the trustworthy man.

"No," I said, as my hat flew off.

Help was too far away to do anything for us. We passed scatheless through a part of the cattle, I saw their horns and backs go by. Some earth crumbled, and we plunged downward into water rocking among stones, and upward again through some more crumbling earth. I heard a crash, and saw my trunk landing in the stream.

"She's safer there," said the trustworthy man.

"True," I said.

"We'll go back for her," said he, with his eye on the horses and his foot on the crippled brake. A dry gully was coming, and no room to turn. The farther side of it was terraced with rock. We should simply fall backward, if we did not fall forward first. He steered the horses straight over, and just at the bottom swung them, with astonishing skill, to the right along the hard-baked mud. They took us along the bed up to the head of the gully, and through a thicket of quaking asps. The light trees bent beneath our charge and bastinadoed the wagon as it went over them. But their branches enmeshed the horses' legs, and we came to a harmless standstill among a bower of leaves.

I looked at the trustworthy man, and smiled vaguely. He considered me for a moment.

"I reckon," said he, "you're feelin' about halfway between 'Oh, Lord!' and 'Thank God!'"

"That's quite it," said I, as he got down on the ground.

"Nothing's broke," said he, after a searching examination. And he indulged in a true Virginian expletive. "Gentlemen, hush!" he murmured gently, looking at me with his grave eyes; "one time I got pretty near scared. You, Buck," he continued, "some folks would beat you now till yu'd be uncertain whether yu' was a hawss or a railroad accident. I'd do it myself, only it wouldn't cure yu'."

I now told him that I supposed he had saved both our lives. But he detested words of direct praise. He made some grumbling rejoinder, and led the horses out of the thicket. Buck, he explained to me, was a good horse, and so was Muggins. Both of them generally meant well, and that was the Judge's reason for sending them to meet me. But these broncos had their off days. Off days might not come very often; but when the humor seized a bronco, he had to have his spree. Buck would now behave himself as a horse should for probably two months. "They are just like humans," the Virginian concluded.

Several cowboys arrived on a gallop to find how many pieces of us were left. We returned down the hill; and when we reached my trunk, it was surprising to see the distance that our runaway had covered. My hat was also found, and we continued on our way.

Buck and Muggins were patterns of discretion through the rest of the mountains. I thought when we camped this night that it was strange Buck should be again allowed to graze at large, instead of being tied to a rope while we slept. But this was my ignorance. With the hard work that he was gallantly doing, the horse needed more pasture than a rope's length would permit him to find. Therefore he went free, and in the morning gave us but little trouble in catching him.

We crossed a river in the forenoon, and far to the north of us we saw the Bow Leg Mountains, pale in the bright sun. Sunk Creek flowed from their western side, and our two hundred and sixty-three miles began to grow a small thing in my eyes. Buck and Muggins, I think, knew perfectly that tomorrow would see them home. They recognized this region; and once they turned off at a fork in the road. The Virginian pulled them back rather sharply.

"Want to go back to Balaam's?" he inquired of them. "I thought you had more sense."

I asked, "Who was Balaam?"

"A maltreater of hawsses," replied the cowpuncher. "His ranch is on Butte Creek oveh yondeh." And he pointed to where the diverging road melted into space. "The Judge bought Buck and Muggins from him in the spring."

"So he maltreats horses?" I repeated.

"That's the word all through this country. A man that will do what they claim Balaam does to a hawss when he's mad, ain't fit to be called human." The Virginian told me some particulars.

"Oh!" I almost screamed at the horror of it, and again, "Oh!"

"He'd have prob'ly done that to Buck as soon as he stopped runnin' away. If I caught a man doin' that—"

We were interrupted by a sedate-looking traveler riding upon an equally sober horse.

"Mawnin', Taylor," said the Virginian, pulling up for gossip. "Ain't you strayed off your range pretty far?"

"You're a nice one!" replied Mr. Taylor, stopping his horse and smiling amiably.

"Tell me something I don't know," retorted the Virginian.

"Hold up a man at cards and rob him," pursued Mr. Taylor. "Oh, the news has got ahead of you!"

"Trampas has been hyeh explainin', has he?" said the Virginian with a grin.

"Was that your victim's name?" said Mr. Taylor, facetiously. "No, it wasn't him that brought the news. Say, what did you do, anyway?"

"So that thing has got around," murmured the Virginian. "Well, it wasn't worth such wide repawtin'." And he gave the simple facts to Taylor, while I sat wondering at the contagious powers of Rumor. Here, through this voiceless land, this desert, this vacuum, it had spread like a change of weather. "Any news up your way?" the Virginian concluded.

Importance came into Mr. Taylor's countenance. "Bear Creek is going to build a schoolhouse," said he.

"Goodness gracious!" drawled the Virginian. "What's that for?"

Now Mr. Taylor had been married for some years. "To educate the offspring of Bear Creek," he answered with pride.

"Offspring of Bear Creek," the Virginian meditatively repeated. "I don't remember noticin' much offspring. There was some white tail deer, and a right smart o' jack rabbits."

"The Swintons have moved up from Drybone," said Mr. Taylor, always seriously. "They found it no place for young children. And there's Uncle Carmody with six, and Ben Dow. And Westfall has become a family man, and—"

"Jim Westfall!" exclaimed the Virginian. "Him a fam'ly man! Well, if this hyeh Territory is goin' to get full o' fam'ly men and empty o' game, I believe I'll—"

"Get married yourself," suggested Mr. Taylor.

"Me! I ain't near reached the marriageable age. No, seh! But Uncle Hughey has got there at last, yu' know."

"Uncle Hughey!" shouted Mr. Taylor. He had not heard this. Rumor is very capricious. Therefore the Virginian told him, and the family man rocked in his saddle.

"Build your schoolhouse," said the Virginian. "Uncle Hughey has qualified himself to subscribe to all such propositions. Got your eye on a schoolmarm?"

## CHAPTER V

## ENTER THE WOMAN

"We are taking steps," said Mr. Taylor. "Bear Creek ain't going to be hasty about a schoolmarm."

"Sure," assented the Virginian. "The children wouldn't want yu' to hurry."

But Mr. Taylor was, as I have indicated, a serious family man. The problem of educating his children could appear to him in no light except a sober one. "Bear Creek," he said, "don't want the experience they had over at Calef. We must not hire an ignoramus."

"Sure!" assented the Virginian again.

"Nor we don't want no gad-a-way flirt," said Mr. Taylor.

"She must keep her eyes on the blackboa'd," said the Virginian, gently.

"Well, we can wait till we get a guaranteed article," said Mr. Taylor. "And that's what we're going to do. It can't be this year, and it needn't to be. None of the kids is very old, and the schoolhouse has got to be built." He now drew a letter from his pocket, and looked at me. "Are you acquainted with Miss Mary Stark Wood of Bennington, Vermont?" he inquired.

I was not acquainted with her at this time.

"She's one we are thinking of. She's a correspondent with Mrs. Balaam."

Taylor handed me the letter. "She wrote that to Mrs. Balaam, and Mrs. Balaam said the best thing was for to let me see it and judge for myself. I'm taking it back to Mrs. Balaam. Maybe you can give me your opinion how it sizes up with the letters they write back East?"

The communication was mainly of a business kind, but also personal, and freely written. I do not think that its writer expected it to be exhibited as a document. The writer wished very much that she could see the West. But she could not gratify this desire merely for pleasure, or she would long ago have accepted the kind invitation to visit Mrs. Balaam's ranch. Teaching school was something she would like to do, if she were fitted for it. "Since the mills failed" (the writer said) "we have all gone to work and done a lot of things so that mother might keep on living in the old house. Yes, the salary would be a temptation. But, my dear, isn't Wyoming bad for the complexion? And could I sue them if mine got damaged? It is still admired. I could bring one male witness *at least* to prove that!" Then the writer became businesslike again. Even if she came to feel that she could leave home, she did not at all know that she could teach school. Nor did she think it right to accept a position in which one had had no experience. "I do love children, boys especially," she went on. "My small nephew and I get on famously. But imagine if a whole benchful of boys began asking me questions that I couldn't answer! What should I do? For one could not spank them all, you know! And mother says that I ought not to teach anybody spelling, because I leave the U out of *honor.*"

Altogether it was a letter which I could assure Mr. Taylor "sized up" very well with the letters written in my part of the United States. And it was signed, "Your very sincere spinster, Molly Stark Wood."

"I never seen *honor* spelled with a U," said Mr. Taylor, over whose not highly civilized head certain portions of the letter had lightly passed.

I told him that some old-fashioned people still wrote the word so.

"Either way would satisfy Bear Creek," said Mr. Taylor, "if she's otherwise up to requirements."

The Virginian was now looking over the letter musingly, and with awakened attention.

"'Your very sincere spinster,'" he read aloud slowly.

"I guess that means she's forty," said Taylor.

"I reckon she is about twenty," said the Virginian. And again he fell to musing over the paper that he held.

"Her handwriting ain't like any I've saw," pursued Mr. Taylor. "But Bear Creek would not object to that, provided she knows 'rithmetic and George Washington, and them kind of things."

"I expect she is not an awful sincere spinster," surmised the Virginian, still looking at the letter, still holding it as if it were some token.

Has any botanist set down what the seed of love is? Has it anywhere been set down in how many ways this seed may be sown? In what various vessels of gossamer it can float across wide spaces? Or upon what different soils it can fall, and live unknown, and bide its time for blooming?

The Virginian handed back to Taylor the sheet of notepaper where a girl had talked as the women he had known did not talk. If his eyes had ever seen such maidens, there had been no meeting of eyes; and if such maidens had ever spoken to him, the speech was from an established distance. But here was a free language, altogether new to him. It proved, however, not alien to his understanding, as it was alien to Mr. Taylor's.

We drove onward, a mile perhaps, and then two. He had lately been full of words, but now he barely answered me, so that a silence fell upon both of us. It must have been all of ten miles that we had driven when he spoke of his own accord.

"Your real spinster don't speak of her lot that easy," he remarked. And presently he quoted a phrase about the complexion, "'Could I sue them if mine got damaged?'" and he smiled over this to himself, shaking his head. "What would she be doing on Bear Creek?" he next said. And finally: "I reckon that witness will detain her in Vermont. And her mother'll keep livin' at the old house."

Thus did the cowpuncher deliver himself, not knowing at all that the seed had floated across wide spaces, and was biding its time in his heart.

On the morrow we reached Sunk Creek. Judge Henry's welcome and his wife's would have obliterated any hardships that I had endured, and I had endured none at all.

For a while I saw little of the Virginian. He lapsed into his native way of addressing me occasionally as "seh"—a habit entirely repudiated by this land of equality. I was sorry. Our common peril during the runaway of Buck and Muggins had brought us to a familiarity that I hoped was destined to last. But I think that it would not have gone farther, save for a certain personage—I must call her a personage. And as I am indebted to her for gaining me a friend whose prejudice against me might never have been otherwise overcome, I shall tell you her little story, and how her misadventures and her fate came to bring the Virginian and me to an appreciation of one another. Without her, it is likely I should also not have heard so much of the story of the schoolmarm, and how that lady at last came to Bear Creek.

## CHAPTER VI

### EM'LY

My personage was a hen, and she lived at the Sunk Creek Ranch.

Judge Henry's ranch was notable for several luxuries. He had milk, for example. In those days his brother ranchmen had thousands of cattle very often, but not a drop of milk, save the condensed variety. Therefore they had no butter. The Judge had plenty. Next rarest to butter and milk in the cattle country were eggs. But my host had chickens. Whether this was because he had followed cockfighting in his early days, or whether it was due to Mrs. Henry, I cannot say. I only know that when I took a meal elsewhere, I was likely to find nothing but the eternal "sowbelly," beans, and coffee; while at Sunk Creek the omelet and the custard were frequent. The passing traveler was glad to tie his horse to the fence here, and sit down to the Judge's table. For its fame was as wide as Wyoming. It was an oasis in the Territory's desolate bill-of-fare.

The long fences of Judge Henry's home ranch began upon Sunk Creek soon after that stream emerged from its canyon through the Bow Leg. It was a place always well cared for by the owner, even in the days of his bachelorhood. The placid regiments of cattle lay in the cool of the cottonwoods by the water, or slowly moved among the sagebrush, feeding upon the grass that in those forever departed years was plentiful and tall. The steers came fat off his unenclosed range and fattened still more in his large pasture; while his small pasture, a field some eight miles square, was for several seasons given to the Judge's horses, and over this ample space there played and prospered the good colts which he raised from Paladin, his imported stallion. After he married, I have been assured that his wife's influence became visible in and about the house at once. Shade trees were planted, flowers attempted, and to the chickens was added the much more troublesome turkey. I, the visitor, was pressed into service when I arrived, green from the East. I took hold of the farmyard and began building a better chicken house, while the Judge was off creating meadowland in his gray and yellow wilderness. When any cowboy was unoccupied, he would lounge over to my neighborhood, and silently regard my carpentering.

Those cowpunchers bore names of various denominations. There was Honey Wiggin; there was Nebrasky, and Dollar Bill, and Chalkeye. And they came from farms and cities, from Maine and from California. But the romance of American adventure had drawn them all alike to this great playground of young men, and in their courage, their generosity, and their amusement at me they bore a close resemblance to each other. Each one would silently observe my achievements with the hammer and the chisel. Then he would retire to the bunk-house, and presently I would overhear laughter. But this was only in the morning. In the afternoon on many days of the summer which I spent at the Sunk Creek Ranch I would go shooting, or ride up toward the entrance of the canyon and watch the men working on the irrigation ditches. Pleasant systems of water running in channels were being led through the soil, and there was a sound of rippling here and there among the yellow grain; the green thick alfalfa grass waved almost, it seemed, of its own accord, for the wind never blew; and when at evening the sun lay against the plain, the rift of the canyon was filled with a violet light, and the Bow Leg Mountains became transfigured with hues of floating and unimaginable color. The sun shone in a sky where never a cloud came, and noon was not too warm nor the dark too cool. And so for two months I went through these pleasant uneventful days, improving the chickens, an object of mirth, living in the open air, and basking in the perfection of content.

I was justly styled a tenderfoot. Mrs. Henry had in the beginning endeavored to shield me from this humiliation; but when she found that I was inveterate in laying my inexperience of Western matters bare to all the world, begging to be enlightened upon rattlesnakes, prairie-dogs, owls, blue and willow grouse, sage-hens, how to rope a horse or tighten the front cinch of my saddle, and that my spirit soared into enthusiasm at the mere sight of so ordinary an animal as a white-tailed deer, she let me rush about with my firearms and made no further effort to stave off the ridicule that my blunders perpetually earned from the ranch hands, her own humorous husband, and any chance visitor who stopped for a meal or stayed the night.

I was not called by my name after the first feeble etiquette due to a stranger in his first few hours had died away. I was known simply as "the tenderfoot." I was introduced to the neighborhood (a circle of eighty miles) as "the tenderfoot." It was thus that Balaam, the maltreater of horses, learned to address me when he came a two days' journey to pay a visit. And it was this name and my notorious helplessness that bid fair to end what relations I had with the Virginian. For when Judge Henry ascertained that nothing could prevent me from losing myself, that it was not uncommon for me to saunter out after breakfast with a gun and in thirty minutes cease to know north from south, he arranged for my protection. He detailed an escort for me; and the escort was once more the trustworthy man! The poor Virginian was taken from his work and his comrades and set to playing nurse for me. And for a while this humiliation ate into his untamed soul. It was his lugubrious lot to accompany me in my rambles, preside over my blunders, and save me from calamitously passing into the next world. He bore it in courteous silence, except when speaking was necessary. He would show me the lower ford, which I could never find for myself, generally mistaking a quicksand for it. He would tie my horse properly. He would recommend me not to shoot my rifle at a white-tailed deer in the particular moment that the outfit wagon was passing behind the animal on the further side of the brush. There was seldom a day that he was not obliged to hasten and save me from sudden death or from ridicule, which is worse. Yet never once did he lose his patience and his gentle, slow voice, and apparently lazy manner remained the same, whether we were sitting at lunch together, or up in the mountain during a hunt, or whether he was bringing me back my horse, which had run away because I had again forgotten to throw the reins over his head and let them trail.

"He'll always stand if yu' do that," the Virginian would say. "See how my hawss stays right quiet yondeh."

After such admonition he would say no more to me. But this tame nursery business was assuredly gall to him. For though utterly a man in countenance and in his self-possession and incapacity to be put at a loss, he was still boyishly proud of his wild calling, and wore his leather straps and jingled his spurs with obvious pleasure. His tiger limberness and his beauty were rich with unabated youth; and that force which lurked beneath his surface must often have curbed his intolerance of me. In spite of what I knew must be his opinion of me, the tenderfoot, my liking for him grew, and I found his silent company more and more agreeable. That he had spells of talking, I had already learned at Medicine Bow. But his present taciturnity might almost have effaced this impression, had I not happened to pass by the bunkhouse one evening after dark, when Honey Wiggin and the rest of the cowboys were gathered inside it.

That afternoon the Virginian and I had gone duck shooting. We had found several in a beaver dam, and I had killed two as they sat close together; but they floated against the breastwork of sticks out in the water some four feet deep, where the escaping current might carry them down the stream. The Judge's red setter had not accompanied us, because she was expecting a family.

"We don't want her along anyways," the cowpuncher had explained to me. "She runs around mighty irresponsible, and she'll stand a prairie-dog 'bout as often as she'll stand a bird. She's a triflin' animal."

My anxiety to own the ducks caused me to pitch into the water with all my clothes on, and subsequently crawl out a slippery, triumphant, weltering heap. The Virginian's serious eyes had rested upon this spectacle of mud; but he expressed nothing, as usual.

"They ain't overly good eatin'," he observed, tying the birds to his saddle. "They're divers."

"Divers!" I exclaimed. "Why didn't they dive?"

"I reckon they was young ones and hadn't experience."

"Well," I said, crestfallen, but attempting to be humorous, "I did the diving myself."

But the Virginian made no comment. He handed me my double-barreled English gun, which I was about to leave deserted on the ground behind me, and we rode home in our usual silence, the mean little white-breasted, sharp-billed divers dangling from his saddle.

It was in the bunkhouse that he took his revenge. As I passed I heard his gentle voice silently achieving some narrative to an attentive audience, and just as I came by the open window where he sat on his bed in shirt and drawers, his back to me, I heard his concluding words, "And the hat on his haid was the one mark showed yu' he weren't a snappin'-turtle."

The anecdote met with instantaneous success, and I hurried away into the dark. The next morning I was occupied with the chickens. Two hens were fighting to sit on some eggs that a third was daily laying, and which I did not want hatched, and for the third time I had kicked Em'ly off seven potatoes she had rolled together and was determined to raise I know not what sort of family from. She was shrieking about the henhouse as the Virginian came in to observe (I suspect) what I might be doing now that could be useful for him to mention in the bunk-house.

He stood awhile, and at length said, "We lost our best rooster when Mrs. Henry came to live hyeh."

I paid no attention.

"He was a right elegant Dominicker," he continued.

I felt a little riled about the snapping-turtle, and showed no interest in what he was saying, but continued my functions among the hens. This unusual silence of mine seemed to elicit unusual speech from him.

"Yu' see, that rooster he'd always lived round hyeh when the Judge was a bachelor, and he never seen no ladies or any persons wearing female gyarments. You ain't got rheumatism, seh?"

"Me? No."

"I reckoned maybe them little odd divers yu' got damp goin' afteh—" He paused.

"Oh, no, not in the least, thank you."

"Yu' seemed sort o' grave this mawnin', and I'm cert'nly glad it ain't them divers."

"Well, the rooster?" I inquired finally.

"Oh, him! He weren't raised where he could see petticoats. Mrs. Henry she come hyeh from the railroad with the Judge afteh dark. Next mawnin' early she walked out to view her new home, and the rooster was a-feedin' by the door, and he seen her. Well, seh, he screeched that awful I run out of the bunk-house; and he jus' went over the fence and took down Sunk Creek shoutin' fire, right along. He has never come back."

"There's a hen over there now that has no judgment," I said, indicating Em'ly. She had got herself outside the house, and was on the bars of a corral, her vociferations reduced to an occasional squawk. I told him about the potatoes.

"I never knowed her name before," said he. "That runaway rooster, he hated her. And she hated him same as she hates 'em all."

"I named her myself," said I, "after I came to notice her particularly. There's an old maid at home who's charitable, and belongs to the Cruelty to Animals, and she never knows whether she had better cross in front of a streetcar or wait. I named the hen after her. Does she ever lay eggs?"

The Virginian had not "troubled his haid" over the poultry.

"Well, I don't believe she knows how. I think she came near being a rooster."

"She's sure manly-lookin'," said the Virginian. We had walked toward the corral, and he was now scrutinizing Em'ly with interest.

She was an egregious fowl. She was huge and gaunt, with great yellow beak, and she stood straight and alert in the manner of responsible people. There was something wrong with her tail. It slanted far to one side, one feather in it twice as long as the rest. Feathers on her breast there were none. These had been worn entirely off by her habit of sitting upon potatoes and other rough abnormal objects. And this lent to her appearance an air of being decollete, singularly at variance with her otherwise prudish ensemble. Her eye was remarkably bright, but somehow it had an outraged expression.

It was as if she went about the world perpetually scandalized over the doings that fell beneath her notice. Her legs were blue, long, and remarkably stout.

"She'd ought to wear knickerbockers," murmured the Virginian. "She'd look a heap better 'n some o' them college students. And she'll set on potatoes, yu' say?"

"She thinks she can hatch out anything. I've found her with onions, and last Tuesday I caught her on two balls of soap."

In the afternoon the tall cowpuncher and I rode out to get an antelope.

After an hour, during which he was completely taciturn, he said: "I reckon maybe this hyeh lonesome country ain't been healthy for Em'ly to live in. It ain't for some humans. Them old trappers in the mountains gets skewed in the haid mighty often, an' talks out loud when nobody's nigher 'n a hundred miles."

"Em'ly has not been solitary," I replied. "There are forty chickens here."

"That's so," said he. "It don't explain her."

He fell silent again, riding beside me, easy and indolent in the saddle. His long figure looked so loose and inert that the swift, light spring he made to the ground seemed an impossible feat. He had seen an antelope where I saw none.

"Take a shot yourself," I urged him, as he motioned me to be quick. "You never shoot when I'm with you."

"I ain't hyeh for that," he answered. "Now you've let him get away on yu'!"

The antelope had in truth departed.

"Why," he said to my protest, "I can hit them things any day. What's your notion as to Em'ly?"

"I can't account for her," I replied.

"Well," he said musingly, and then his mind took one of those particular turns that made me love him, "Taylor ought to see her. She'd be just the schoolmarm for Bear Creek!"

"She's not much like the eating-house lady at Medicine Bow," I said.

He gave a hilarious chuckle. "No, Em'ly knows nothing o' them joys. So yu' have no notion about her? Well, I've got one. I reckon maybe she was hatched after a big thunderstorm."

"In a big thunderstorm!" I exclaimed.

"Yes. Don't yu' know about them, and what they'll do to aiggs? A big case o' lightnin' and thunder will addle aiggs and keep 'em from hatchin'. And I expect one came along, and all the other aiggs of Em'ly's set didn't hatch out, but got plumb addled, and she happened not to get addled that far, and so she just managed to make it through. But she cert'nly ain't got a strong haid."

"I fear she has not," said I.

"Mighty hon'ble intentions," he observed. "If she can't make out to lay anything, she wants to hatch somethin', and be a mother anyways."

"I wonder what relation the law considers that a hen is to the chicken she hatched but did not lay?" I inquired.

The Virginian made no reply to this frivolous suggestion. He was gazing over the wide landscape gravely and with apparent inattention. He invariably saw game before I did, and was off his horse and crouched among the sage while I was still getting my left foot clear of the stirrup. I succeeded in killing an antelope, and we rode home with the head and hindquarters.

"No," said he. "It's sure the thunder, and not the lonesomeness. How do yu' like the lonesomeness yourself?"

I told him that I liked it.

"I could not live without it now," he said. "This has got into my system." He swept his hand out at the vast space of world. "I went back home to see my folks onced. Mother was dyin' slow, and she wanted me. I stayed a year. But them Virginia mountains could please me no more. Afteh she was gone, I told my brothers and sisters good-by. We like each other well enough, but I reckon I'll not go back."

We found Em'ly seated upon a collection of green California peaches, which the Judge had brought from the railroad.

"I don't mind her anymore," I said; "I'm sorry for her."

"I've been sorry for her right along," said the Virginian. "She does hate the roosters so." And he said that he was making a collection of every class of object which he found her treating as eggs.

But Em'ly's egg-industry was terminated abruptly one morning, and her unquestioned energies diverted to a new channel. A turkey which had been sitting in the root-house appeared with twelve children, and a family of bantams occurred almost simultaneously. Em'ly was importantly scratching the soil inside Paladin's corral when the bantam tribe of newly born came by down the lane, and she caught sight of them through the bars. She crossed the corral at a run, and intercepted two of the chicks that were trailing somewhat behind their real mamma. These she undertook to appropriate, and assumed a high tone with the bantam, who was the smaller, and hence obliged to retreat with her still numerous family. I interfered, and put matters straight; but the adjustment was only temporary. In an hour I saw Em'ly immensely busy with two more bantams, leading them about and taking a care of them which I must admit seemed perfectly efficient.

And now came the first incident that made me suspect her to be demented.

She had proceeded with her changelings behind the kitchen, where one of the irrigation ditches ran under the fence from the hay-field to supply the house with water. Some distance along this ditch inside the field were the twelve turkeys in the short, recently cut stubble. Again Em'ly set off instantly like a deer. She left the dismayed bantams behind her. She crossed the ditch with one jump of her stout blue legs, flew over the grass, and was at once among the turkeys, where, with an instinct of maternity as undiscriminating as it was reckless, she attempted to huddle some of them away. But this other mamma was not a bantam, and in a few moments Em'ly was entirely routed in her attempt to acquire a new variety of family.

This spectacle was witnessed by the Virginian and myself, and it overcame him. He went speechless across to the bunk-house, by himself, and sat on his bed, while I took the abandoned bantams back to their own circle.

I have often wondered what the other fowls thought of all this. Some impression it certainly did make upon them. The notion may seem out of reason to those who have never closely attended to other animals than man; but I am convinced that any community which shares some of our instincts will share some of the resulting feelings, and that birds and beasts have conventions, the breach of which startles them. If there be anything in evolution, this would seem inevitable. At all events, the chicken-house was upset during the following several days. Em'ly disturbed now the bantams and now the turkeys, and several of these latter had died, though I will not go so far as to say that this was the result of her misplaced attentions. Nevertheless, I was seriously thinking of locking her up till the broods should be a little older, when another event happened, and all was suddenly at peace.

The Judge's setter came in one morning, wagging her tail. She had had her puppies, and she now took us to where they were housed, in between the floor of a building and the hollow ground. Em'ly was seated on the whole litter.

"No," I said to the Judge, "I am not surprised. She is capable of anything."

In her new choice of offspring, this hen had at length encountered an unworthy parent. The setter was bored by her own puppies. She found the hole under the house an obscure and monotonous residence compared with the dining room, and our company more stimulating and sympathetic than that of her children. A much-petted contact with our superior race had developed her dog intelligence above its natural level, and turned her into an unnatural, neglectful mother, who was constantly forgetting her nursery for worldly pleasures.

At certain periods of the day she repaired to the puppies and fed them, but came away when this perfunctory ceremony was accomplished; and she was glad enough to have a governess bring them up. She made no quarrel with Em'ly, and the two understood each other perfectly. I have never seen among animals any arrangement so civilized and so perverted. It made Em'ly perfectly happy. To see her sitting all day jealously spreading her wings over some blind puppies was sufficiently curious; but when they became large enough to come out from under the house and toddle about in the proud hen's wake, I longed for some distinguished naturalist. I felt that our ignorance made us inappropriate spectators of such a phenomenon. Em'ly scratched and clucked, and the puppies ran to her, pawed her with their fat limp little legs, and retreated beneath her feathers in their games of hide and seek. Conceive, if you can, what confusion must have reigned in their infant minds as to who the setter was!

"I reckon they think she's the wet-nurse," said the Virginian.

When the puppies grew to be boisterous, I perceived that Em'ly's mission was approaching its end. They were too heavy for her, and their increasing scope of playfulness was not in her line. Once or twice they knocked her over, upon which she arose and pecked them severely, and they retired to a safe distance, and sitting in a circle, yapped at her. I think they began to suspect that she was only a hen after all. So Em'ly resigned with an indifference which surprised me, until I remembered that if it had been chickens, she would have ceased to look after them by this time.

But here she was again "out of a job," as the Virginian said.

"She's raised them puppies for that triflin' setter, and now she'll be huntin' around for something else useful to do that ain't in her business."

Now there were other broods of chickens to arrive in the henhouse, and I did not desire any more bantam and turkey performances. So, to avoid confusion, I played a trick upon Em'ly. I went down to Sunk Creek and fetched some smooth, oval stones. She was quite satisfied with these, and passed a quiet day with them in a box. This was not fair, the Virginian asserted.

"You ain't going to jus' leave her fooled that a-way?"

I did not see why not.

"Why, she raised them puppies all right. Ain't she showed she knows how to be a mother anyways? Em'ly ain't going to get her time took up for nothing while I'm round hyeh," said the cowpuncher.

He laid a gentle hold of Em'ly and tossed her to the ground. She, of course, rushed out among the corrals in a great state of nerves.

"I don't see what good you do meddling," I protested.

To this he deigned no reply, but removed the unresponsive stones from the straw.

"Why, if they ain't right warm!" he exclaimed plaintively. "The poor, deluded son-of-a-gun!" And with this unusual description of a lady, he sent the stones sailing like a line of birds. "I'm regular getting stuck on Em'ly," continued the Virginian. "Yu' needn't to laugh. Don't yu' see she's got sort o' human feelin's and desires? I always knowed hawsses was like people, and my collie, of course. It is kind of foolish, I expect, but that hen's goin' to have a real aigg di-rectly, right now, to set on." With this he removed one from beneath another hen. "We'll have Em'ly raise this hyeh," said he, "so she can put in her time profitable."

It was not accomplished at once; for Em'ly, singularly enough, would not consent to stay in the box whence she had been routed. At length we found another retreat for her, and in these new surroundings, with a new piece of work for her to do, Em'ly sat on the one egg which the Virginian had so carefully provided for her.

Thus, as in all genuine tragedies, was the stroke of Fate wrought by chance and the best intentions.

Em'ly began sitting on Friday afternoon near sundown. Early next morning my sleep was gradually dispersed by a sound unearthly and continuous. Now it dwindled, receding to a distance; again it came near, took a turn, drifted to the other side of the house; then, evidently, whatever it was, passed my door close, and I jumped upright in my bed. The high, tense strain of vibration, nearly, but not quite, a musical note, was like the threatening scream of machinery, though weaker, and I bounded out of the house in my pajamas.

There was Em'ly, dishevelled, walking wildly about, her one egg miraculously hatched within ten hours. The little lonely yellow ball of down went cheeping along behind, following its mother as best it could. What, then, had happened to the established period of incubation? For an instant the thing was like a portent, and I was near joining Em'ly in her horrid surprise, when I saw how it all was. The Virginian had taken an egg from a hen which had already been sitting for three weeks.

I dressed in haste, hearing Em'ly's distracted outcry. It steadily sounded, without perceptible pause for breath, and marked her erratic journey back and forth through stables, lanes, and corrals. The shrill disturbance brought all of us out to see her, and in the henhouse I discovered the new brood making its appearance punctually.

But this natural explanation could not be made to the crazed hen. She continued to scour the premises, her slant tail and its one preposterous feather waving as she aimlessly went, her stout legs stepping high with an unnatural motion, her head lifted nearly off her neck, and in her brilliant yellow eye an expression of more than outrage at this overturning of a natural law. Behind her, entirely ignored and neglected, trailed the little progeny. She never looked at it. We went about our various affairs, and all through the clear, sunny day that unending metallic scream pervaded the premises. The Virginian put out food and water for her, but she tasted nothing. I am glad to say that the little chicken did. I do not think that the hen's eyes could see, except in the way that sleep-walkers' do.

The heat went out of the air, and in the canyon the violet light began to show. Many hours had gone, but Em'ly never ceased. Now she suddenly flew up in a tree and sat there with her noise still going; but it had risen lately several notes into a slim, acute level of terror, and was not like machinery anymore, nor like any sound I ever heard before or since. Below the tree stood the bewildered little chicken, cheeping, and making tiny jumps to reach its mother.

"Yes," said the Virginian, "it's comical. Even her aigg acted different from anybody else's." He paused, and looked across the wide, mellowing plain with the expression of easy-going gravity so common with him. Then he looked at Em'ly in the tree and the yellow chicken.

"It ain't so damned funny," said he.

We went in to supper, and I came out to find the hen lying on the ground, dead. I took the chicken to the family in the henhouse.

No, it was not altogether funny anymore. And I did not think less of the Virginian when I came upon him surreptitiously digging a little hole in the field for her.

"I have buried some citizens here and there," said he, "that I have respected less."

And when the time came for me to leave Sunk Creek, my last word to the Virginian was, "Don't forget Em'ly."

"I ain't likely to," responded the cowpuncher. "She is just one o' them parables."

Save when he fell into his native idioms (which, they told me, his wanderings had well-nigh obliterated until that year's visit to his home again revived them in his speech), he had now for a long while dropped the "seh," and all other barriers between us. We were thorough friends, and had exchanged many confidences both of the flesh and of the spirit. He even went the length of saying that he would write me the Sunk Creek news if I would send him a line now and then. I have many letters from him now. Their spelling came to be faultless, and in the beginning was little worse than George Washington's.

The Judge himself drove me to the railroad by another way—across the Bow Leg Mountains, and south through Balaam's Ranch and Drybone to Rock Creek.

"I'll be very homesick," I told him.

"Come and pull the latch-string whenever you please," he bade me. I wished that I might! No lotus land ever cast its spell upon man's heart more than Wyoming had enchanted mine.

## CHAPTER VII

### THROUGH TWO SNOWS

"Dear Friend [thus in the spring the Virginian wrote me], Yours received. It must be a poor thing to be sick. That time I was shot at Canada de Oro would have made me sick if it had been a littel lower or if I was much of a drinking man. You will be well if you give over city life and take a hunt with me about August or say September for then the elk will be out of the velvett.

"Things do not please me here just now and I am going to settel it by vamosing. But I would be glad to see you. It would be pleasure not business for me to show you plenty elk and get you strong. I am not crybabying to the Judge or making any kick about things. He will want me back after he has swallowed a litter tincture of time. It is the best dose I know.

"Now to answer your questions. Yes the Emmily hen might have ate loco weed if hens do. I never saw anything but stock and horses get poisoned with loco weed. No the school is not built yet. They are always big talkers on Bear Creek. No I have not seen Steve. He is around but I am sorry for him. Yes I have been to Medicine Bow. I had the welcom I wanted. Do you remember a man I played poker and he did not like it? He is working on the upper ranch near Ten Sleep. He does not amount to a thing except with weaklings. Uncle Hewie has twins. The boys got him vexed some about it, but I think they are his. Now that is all I know today and I would like to see you poco presently as they say at Los Cruces. There's no sense in you being sick."

The rest of this letter discussed the best meeting point for us should I decide to join him for a hunt.

That hunt was made, and during the weeks of its duration something was said to explain a little more fully the Virginian's difficulty at the Sunk Creek Ranch, and his reason for leaving his excellent employer the Judge. Not much was said, to be sure; the Virginian seldom spent many words upon his own troubles. But it appeared that owing to some jealousy of him on the part of the foreman, or the assistant foreman, he found himself continually doing another man's work, but under circumstances so skilfully arranged that he got neither credit nor pay for it. He would not stoop to telling tales out of school. Therefore his ready and prophetic mind devised the simple expedient of going away altogether. He calculated that Judge Henry would gradually perceive there was a connection between his departure and the cessation of the satisfactory work. After a judicious interval it was his plan to appear again in the neighborhood of Sunk Creek and await results.

Concerning Steve he would say no more than he had written. But it was plain that for some cause this friendship had ceased.

Money for his services during the hunt he positively declined to accept, asserting that he had not worked enough to earn his board. And the expedition ended in an untraveled corner of the Yellowstone Park, near Pitchstone Canyon, where he and young Lin McLean and others were witnesses of a sad and terrible drama that has been elsewhere chronicled.

His prophetic mind had foreseen correctly the shape of events at Sunk

Creek. The only thing that it had not foreseen was the impression to be made upon the Judge's mind by his conduct.

Toward the close of that winter, Judge and Mrs. Henry visited the East. Through them a number of things became revealed. The Virginian was back at Sunk Creek.

"And," said Mrs. Henry, "he would never have left you if I had had my way, Judge H.!"

"No, Madam Judge," retorted her husband; "I am aware of that. For you have always appreciated a fine appearance in a man."

"I certainly have," confessed the lady, mirthfully. "And the way he used to come bringing my horse, with the ridges of his black hair so carefully brushed and that blue spotted handkerchief tied so effectively round his throat, was something that I missed a great deal after he went away."

"Thank you, my dear, for this warning. I have plans that will keep him absent quite constantly for the future."

And then they spoke less flightily. "I always knew," said the lady, "that you had found a treasure when that man came."

The Judge laughed. "When it dawned on me," he said, "how cleverly he caused me to learn the value of his services by depriving me of them, I doubted whether it was safe to take him back."

"Safe!" cried Mrs. Henry.

"Safe, my dear. Because I'm afraid he is pretty nearly as shrewd as I am. And that's rather dangerous in a subordinate." The Judge laughed again. "But his action regarding the man they call Steve has made me feel easy."

And then it came out that the Virginian was supposed to have discovered in some way that Steve had fallen from the grace of that particular honesty which respects another man's cattle. It was not known for certain. But calves had begun to disappear in Cattle Land, and cows had been found killed. And calves with one brand upon them had been found with mothers that bore the brand of another owner. This industry was taking root in Cattle Land, and of those who practised it, some were beginning to be suspected. Steve was not quite fully suspected yet. But that the Virginian had parted company with him was definitely known. And neither man would talk about it.

There was the further news that the Bear Creek schoolhouse at length stood complete, floor, walls, and roof; and that a lady from Bennington, Vermont, a friend of Mrs. Balaam's, had quite suddenly decided that she would try her hand at instructing the new generation.

The Judge and Mrs. Henry knew this because Mrs. Balaam had told them of her disappointment that she would be absent from the ranch on Butte Creek when her friend arrived, and therefore unable to entertain her. The friend's decision had been quite suddenly made, and must form the subject of the next chapter.

## CHAPTER VIII

## THE SINCERE SPINSTER

I do not know with which of the two estimates—Mr. Taylor's or the Virginian's—you agreed. Did you think that Miss Mary Stark Wood of Bennington, Vermont, was forty years of age? That would have been an error. At the time she wrote the letter to Mrs. Balaam, of which letter certain portions have been quoted in these pages, she was in her twenty-first year; or, to be more precise, she had been twenty some eight months previous.

Now, it is not usual for young ladies of twenty to contemplate a journey of nearly two thousand miles to a country where Indians and wild animals live unchained, unless they are to make such journey in company with a protector, or are going to a protector's arms at the other end. Nor is school teaching on Bear Creek a usual ambition for such young ladies.

But Miss Mary Stark Wood was not a usual young lady for two reasons.

First, there was her descent. Had she so wished, she could have belonged to any number of those patriotic societies of which our American ears have grown accustomed to hear so much. She could have been enrolled in the Boston Tea Party, the Ethan Allen Ticonderogas, the Green Mountain Daughters, the Saratoga Sacred Circle, and the Confederated Colonial Chatelaines. She traced direct descent from the historic lady whose name she bore, that Molly Stark who was not a widow after the battle where her lord, her Captain John, battled so bravely as to send his name thrilling down through the blood of generations of schoolboys. This ancestress was her chief claim to be a member of those shining societies which I have enumerated. But she had been willing to join none of them, although invitations to do so were by no means lacking. I cannot tell you her reason. Still, I can tell you this. When these societies were much spoken of in her presence, her very sprightly countenance became more sprightly, and she added her words of praise or respect to the general chorus. But when she received an invitation to join one of these bodies, her countenance, as she read the missive, would assume an expression which was known to her friends as "sticking her nose in the air." I do not think that Molly's reason for refusing to join could have been a truly good one. I should add that her most precious possession—a treasure which accompanied her even if she went away for only one night's absence—was an heirloom, a little miniature portrait of the old Molly Stark, painted when that far-off dame must have been scarce more than twenty. And when each summer the young Molly went to Dunbarton, New Hampshire, to pay her established family visit to the last survivors of her connection who bore the name of Stark, no word that she heard in the Dunbarton houses pleased her so much as when a certain great-aunt would take her by the hand, and, after looking with fond intentness at her, pronounce: "My dear, you're getting more like the General's wife every year you live."

"I suppose you mean my nose," Molly would then reply.

"Nonsense, child. You have the family length of nose, and I've never heard that it has disgraced us."

"But I don't think I'm tall enough for it."

"There now, run to your room, and dress for tea. The Starks have always been punctual."

And after this annual conversation, Molly would run to her room, and there in its privacy, even at the risk of falling below the punctuality of the Starks, she would consult two objects for quite a minute before she began to dress. These objects, as you have already correctly guessed, were the miniature of the General's wife and the looking glass.

So much for Miss Molly Stark Wood's descent.

The second reason why she was not a usual girl was her character. This character was the result of pride and family pluck battling with family hardship.

Just one year before she was to be presented to the world—not the great metropolitan world, but a world that would have made her welcome and done her homage at its little dances and little dinners in Troy and Rutland and Burlington—fortune had turned her back upon the Woods. Their possessions had never been great ones; but they had sufficed. From generation to generation the family had gone to school like gentlefolk, dressed like gentlefolk, used the speech and ways of gentlefolk, and as gentlefolk lived and died. And now the mills failed.

Instead of thinking about her first evening dress, Molly found pupils to whom she could give music lessons. She found handkerchiefs that she could embroider with initials. And she found fruit that she could make into preserves. That machine called the typewriter was then in existence, but the day of women typewriters had as yet scarcely begun to dawn, else I think Molly would have preferred this occupation to the handkerchiefs and the preserves.

There were people in Bennington who "wondered how Miss Wood could go about from house to house teaching the piano, and she a lady." There always have been such people, I suppose, because the world must always have a rubbish heap. But we need not dwell upon them further than to mention one other remark of theirs regarding Molly. They all with one voice declared that Sam Bannett was good enough for anybody who did fancy embroidery at five cents a letter.

"I dare say he had a great-grandmother quite as good as hers," remarked Mrs. Flynt, the wife of the Baptist minister.

"That's entirely possible," returned the Episcopal rector of Hoosic, "only we don't happen to know who she was." The rector was a friend of Molly's. After this little observation, Mrs. Flynt said no more, but continued her purchases in the store where she and the rector had happened to find themselves together. Later she stated to a friend that she had always thought the Episcopal Church a snobbish one, and now she knew it.

So public opinion went on being indignant over Molly's conduct. She could stoop to work for money, and yet she pretended to hold herself above the most rising young man in Hoosic Falls, and all just because there was a difference in their grandmothers!

Was this the reason at the bottom of it? The very bottom? I cannot be certain, because I have never been a girl myself. Perhaps she thought that work is not a stooping, and that marriage may be. Perhaps—but all I really know is that Molly Wood continued cheerfully to embroider the handkerchiefs, make the preserves, teach the pupils—and firmly to reject Sam Bannett.

Thus it went on until she was twenty. There certain members of her family began to tell her how rich Sam was going to be—was, indeed, already. It was at this time that she wrote Mrs. Balaam her doubts and her desires as to migrating to Bear Creek. It was at this time also that her face grew a little paler, and her friends thought that she was overworked, and Mrs. Flynt feared she was losing her looks. It was at this time, too, that she grew very intimate with that great-aunt over at Dunbarton, and from her received much comfort and strengthening.

"Never!" said the old lady, "especially if you can't love him."

"I do like him," said Molly; "and he is very kind."

"Never!" said the old lady again. "When I die, you'll have something—and that will not be long now."

Molly flung her arms around her aunt, and stopped her words with a kiss. And then one winter afternoon, two years later, came the last straw.

The front door of the old house had shut. Out of it had stepped the persistent suitor. Mrs. Flynt watched him drive away in his smart sleigh.

"That girl is a fool!" she said furiously; and she came away from her bedroom window where she had posted herself for observation.

Inside the old house a door had also shut. This was the door of Molly's own room. And there she sat, in floods of tears. For she could not bear to hurt a man who loved her with all the power of love that was in him.

It was about twilight when her door opened, and an elderly lady came softly in.

"My dear," she ventured, "and you were not able—"

"Oh, mother!" cried the girl, "have you come to say that too?"

The next day Miss Wood had become very hard. In three weeks she had accepted the position on Bear Creek. In two months she started, heart-heavy, but with a spirit craving the unknown.

# CHAPTER IX

## THE SPINSTER MEETS THE UNKNOWN

On a Monday noon a small company of horsemen strung out along the trail from Sunk Creek to gather cattle over their allotted sweep of range. Spring was backward, and they, as they rode galloping and gathering upon the cold week's work, cursed cheerily and occasionally sang. The Virginian was grave in bearing and of infrequent speech; but he kept a song going—a matter of some seventy-nine verses. Seventy-eight were quite unprintable, and rejoiced his brother cowpunchers monstrously. They, knowing him to be a singular man, forebore ever to press him, and awaited his own humor, lest he should weary of the lyric; and when after a day of silence apparently saturnine, he would lift his gentle voice and begin:

> "If you go to monkey with my Looloo girl,
> I'll tell you what I'll do:
> I'll cyarve your heart with my razor, *and*
> I'll shoot you with my pistol, too—"

then they would stridently take up each last line, and keep it going three, four, ten times, and kick holes in the ground to the swing of it.

By the levels of Bear Creek that reach like inlets among the promontories of the lonely hills, they came upon the schoolhouse, roofed and ready for the first native Wyoming crop. It symbolized the dawn of a neighborhood, and it brought a change into the wilderness air. The feel of it struck cold upon the free spirits of the cowpunchers, and they told each other that, what with women and children and wire fences, this country would not long be a country for men. They stopped for a meal at an old comrade's. They looked over his gate, and there he was pattering among garden furrows.

"Pickin' nosegays?" inquired the Virginian and the old comrade asked if they could not recognize potatoes except in the dish. But he grinned sheepishly at them, too, because they knew that he had not always lived in a garden. Then he took them into his house, where they saw an object crawling on the floor with a handful of sulphur matches. He began to remove the matches, but stopped in alarm at the vociferous result; and his wife looked in from the kitchen to caution him about humoring little Christopher.

When she beheld the matches she was aghast but when she saw her baby grow quiet in the arms of the Virginian, she smiled at that cowpuncher and returned to her kitchen.

Then the Virginian slowly spoke again: "How many little strangers have yu' got, James?"

"Only two."

"My! Ain't it most three years since yu' maried? Yu' mustn't let time creep ahaid o' yu', James."

The father once more grinned at his guests, who themselves turned sheepish and polite; for Mrs. Westfall came in, brisk and hearty, and set the meat upon the table. After that, it was she who talked. The guests ate scrupulously, muttering, "Yes, ma'am," and "No, ma'am," in their plates, while their hostess told them of increasing families upon Bear Creek, and the expected school-teacher, and little Alfred's early teething, and how it was time for all of them to become husbands like James. The bachelors of the saddle listened, always diffident, but eating heartily to the end; and soon after they rode away in a thoughtful clump. The wives of Bear Creek were few as yet, and the homes scattered; the schoolhouse was only a sprig on the vast face of a world of elk and bear and uncertain Indians; but that night, when the earth near the fire was littered with the cowpunchers' beds, the Virginian was heard drawling to himself: "Alfred and Christopher. Oh, sugar!"

They found pleasure in the delicately chosen shade of this oath. He also recited to them a new verse about how he took his Looloo girl to the schoolhouse for to learn her A B C; and as it was quite original and unprintable, the camp laughed and swore joyfully, and rolled in its blankets to sleep under the stars.

Upon a Monday noon likewise (for things will happen so) some tearful people in petticoats waved handkerchiefs at a train that was just leaving Bennington, Vermont. A girl's face smiled back at them once, and withdrew quickly, for they must not see the smile die away.

She had with her a little money, a few clothes, and in her mind a rigid determination neither to be a burden to her mother nor to give in to that mother's desires. Absence alone would enable her to carry out this determination. Beyond these things, she possessed not much except spelling-books, a colonial miniature, and that craving for the unknown which has been mentioned. If the ancestors that we carry shut up inside us take turns in dictating to us our actions and our state of mind, undoubtedly Grandmother Stark was empress of Molly's spirit upon this Monday.

At Hoosic Junction, which came soon, she passed the up-train bound back to her home, and seeing the engineer and the conductor—faces that she knew well—her courage nearly failed her, and she shut her eyes against this glimpse of the familiar things that she was leaving. To keep herself steady she gripped tightly a little bunch of flowers in her hand.

But something caused her eyes to open; and there before her stood Sam Bannett, asking if he might accompany her so far as Rotterdam Junction.

"No!" she told him with a severity born from the struggle she was making with her grief. "Not a mile with me. Not to Eagle Bridge. Good-by."

And Sam—what did he do? He obeyed her, I should like to be sorry for him. But obedience was not a lover's part here. He hesitated, the golden moment hung hovering, the conductor cried "All aboard!" the train went, and there on the platform stood obedient Sam, with his golden moment gone like a butterfly.

After Rotterdam Junction, which was some forty minutes farther, Molly Wood sat bravely up in the through car, dwelling upon the unknown. She thought that she had attained it in Ohio, on Tuesday morning, and wrote a letter about it to Bennington. On Wednesday afternoon she felt sure, and wrote a letter much more picturesque. But on the following day, after breakfast at North Platte, Nebraska, she wrote a very long letter indeed, and told them that she had seen a black pig on a white pile of buffalo bones, catching drops of water in the air as they fell from the railroad tank. She also wrote that trees were extraordinarily scarce. Each hour westward from the pig confirmed this opinion, and when she left the train at Rock Creek, late upon that fourth night—in those days the trains were slower—she knew that she had really attained the unknown, and sent an expensive telegram to say that she was quite well.

At six in the morning the stage drove away into the sagebrush, with her as its only passenger; and by sundown she had passed through some of the primitive perils of the world. The second team, virgin to harness, and displeased with this novelty, tried to take it off, and went down to the bottom of a gully on its eight hind legs, while Miss Wood sat mute and unflinching beside the driver. Therefore he, when it was over, and they on the proper road again, invited her earnestly to be his wife during many of the next fifteen miles, and told her of his snug cabin and his horses and his mine. Then she got down and rode inside, Independence and Grandmother Stark shining in her eye. At Point of Rocks, where they had supper and his drive ended, her face distracted his heart, and he told her once more about his cabin, and lamentably hoped she would remember him. She answered sweetly that she would try, and gave him her hand. After all, he was a frank-looking boy, who had paid her the highest compliment that a boy (or a man for that matter) knows; and it is said that Molly Stark, in her day, was not a New Woman.

The new driver banished the first one from the maiden's mind. He was not a frank-looking boy, and he had been taking whiskey. All night long he took it, while his passenger, helpless and sleepless inside the lurching stage, sat as upright as she possibly could; nor did the voices that she heard at Drybone reassure her. Sunrise found the white stage lurching eternally on across the alkali, with a driver and a bottle on the box, and a pale girl staring out at the plain, and knotting in her handkerchief some utterly dead flowers. They came to a river where the man bungled over the ford. Two wheels sank down over an edge, and the canvas toppled like a descending kite. The ripple came sucking through the upper spokes, and as she felt the seat careen, she put out her head and tremulously asked if anything was wrong. But the driver was addressing his team with much language, and also with the lash.

Then a tall rider appeared close against the buried axles, and took her out of the stage on his horse so suddenly that she screamed. She felt splashes, saw a swimming flood, and found herself lifted down upon the shore. The rider said something to her about cheering up, and its being all right, but her wits were stock-still, so she did not speak and thank him. After four days of train and thirty hours of stage, she was having a little too much of the unknown at once. Then the tall man gently withdrew leaving her to become herself again. She limply regarded the river pouring round the slanted stage, and a number of horsemen with ropes, who righted the vehicle, and got it quickly to dry land, and disappeared at once with a herd of cattle, uttering lusty yells.

She saw the tall one delaying beside the driver, and speaking. He spoke so quietly that not a word reached her, until of a sudden the driver protested loudly. The man had thrown something, which turned out to be a bottle. This twisted loftily and dived into the stream. He said something more to the driver, then put his hand on the saddle-horn, looked half-lingeringly at the passenger on the bank, dropped his grave eyes from hers, and swinging upon his horse, was gone just as the passenger opened her mouth and with inefficient voice murmured, "Oh, thank you!" at his departing back.

The driver drove up now, a chastened creature. He helped Miss Wood in, and inquired after her welfare with a hanging head; then meek as his own drenched horses, he climbed back to his reins, and nursed the stage on toward the Bow Leg Mountains much as if it had been a perambulator.

As for Miss Wood, she sat recovering, and she wondered what the man on the horse must think of her. She knew that she was not ungrateful, and that if he had given her an opportunity she would have explained to him. If he supposed that she did not appreciate his act—here into the midst of these meditations came an abrupt memory that she had screamed—she could not be sure when. She rehearsed the adventure from the beginning, and found one or two further uncertainties—how it had all been while she was on the horse, for instance. It was confusing to determine precisely what she had done with her arms. She knew where one of his arms had been. And the handkerchief with the flowers was gone. She made a few rapid dives in search of it. Had she, or had she not, seen him putting something in his pocket? And why had she behaved so unlike herself? In a few miles Miss Wood entertained sentiments of maidenly resentment toward her rescuer, and of maidenly hope to see him again.

To that river crossing he came again, alone, when the days were growing short. The ford was dry sand, and the stream a winding lane of shingle. He found a pool—pools always survive the year round in this stream—and having watered his pony, he lunched near the spot to which he had borne the frightened passenger that day. Where the flowing current had been he sat, regarding the now extremely safe channel.

"She cert'nly wouldn't need to grip me so close this mawnin'," he said, as he pondered over his meal. "I reckon it will mightily astonish her when I tell her how harmless the torrent is lookin'." He held out to his pony a slice of bread matted with sardines, which the pony expertly accepted. "You're a plumb pie-biter you Monte," he continued. Monte rubbed his nose on his master's shoulder. "I wouldn't trust you with berries and cream. No, seh; not though yu' did rescue a drownin' lady."

Presently he tightened the forward cinch, got in the saddle, and the pony fell into his wise mechanical jog; for he had come a long way, and was going a long way, and he knew this as well as the man did.

To use the language of Cattle Land, steers had "jumped to seventy-five."

This was a great and prosperous leap in their value. To have flourished in that golden time you need not be dead now, nor even middle-aged; but it is Wyoming mythology already—quite as fabulous as the high-jumping cow. Indeed, people gathered together and behaved themselves much in the same pleasant and improbable way. Johnson County, and Natrona, and Converse, and others, to say nothing of the Cheyenne Club, had been jumping over the moon for some weeks, all on account of steers; and on the strength of this vigorous price of seventy-five, the Stanton Brothers were giving a barbecue at the Goose Egg outfit, their ranch on Bear Creek. Of course the whole neighborhood was bidden, and would come forty miles to a man; some would come further—the Virginian was coming a hundred and eighteen. It had struck him—rather suddenly, as shall be made plain—that he should like to see how they were getting along up there on Bear Creek. "They," was how he put it to his acquaintances. His acquaintances did not know that he had bought himself a pair of trousers and a scarf, unnecessarily excellent for such a general visit. They did not know that in the spring, two days after the adventure with the stage, he had learned accidentally who the lady in the stage was. This he had kept to himself; nor did the camp ever notice that he had ceased to sing that eightieth stanza he had made about the A B C—the stanza which was not printable. He effaced it imperceptibly, giving the boys the other seventy-nine at judicious intervals. They dreamed of no guile, but merely saw in him, whether frequenting camp or town, the same not over-angelic comrade whom they valued and could not wholly understand.

All spring he had ridden trail, worked at ditches during summer, and now he had just finished with the beef round-up. Yesterday, while he was spending a little comfortable money at the Drybone hog-ranch, a casual traveler from the north gossiped of Bear Creek, and the fences up there, and the farm crops, the Westfalls, and the young schoolmarm from Vermont, for whom the Taylors had built a cabin next door to theirs. The traveler had not seen her, but Mrs. Taylor and all the ladies thought the world of her, and Lin McLean had told him she was "away up in G."

She would have plenty of partners at this Swinton barbecue. Great boon for the country, wasn't it, steers jumping that way?

The Virginian heard, asking no questions; and left town in an hour, with the scarf and trousers tied in his slicker behind his saddle. After looking upon the ford again, even though it was dry and not at all the same place, he journeyed in attentively. When you have been hard at work for months with no time to think, of course you think a great deal during your first empty days. "Step along, you Monte hawss!" he said, rousing after some while. He disciplined Monte, who flattened his ears affectedly and snorted. "Why, you surely ain' thinkin' of you'-self as a hero? She wasn't really a-drownin', you pie-biter." He rested his serious glance upon the alkali. "She's not likely to have forgot that mix-up, though. I guess I'll not remind her about grippin' me, and all that. She wasn't the kind a man ought to josh about such things. She had a right clear eye." Thus, tall and loose in the saddle, did he jog along the sixty miles which still lay between him and the dance.

# CHAPTER X

## WHERE FANCY WAS BRED

Two camps in the open, and the Virginian's Monte horse, untired, brought him to the Swintons' in good time for the barbecue. The horse received good food at length, while his rider was welcomed with good whiskey. *Good* whiskey—for had not steers jumped to seventy-five?

Inside the Goose Egg kitchen many small delicacies were preparing, and a steer was roasting whole outside. The bed of flame under it showed steadily brighter against the dusk that was beginning to veil the lowlands. The busy hosts went and came, while men stood and men lay near the fire-glow. Chalkeye was there, and Nebrasky, and Trampas, and Honey Wiggin, with others, enjoying the occasion; but Honey Wiggin was enjoying himself: he had an audience; he was sitting up discoursing to it.

"Hello!" he said, perceiving the Virginian. "So you've dropped in for your turn! Number—six, ain't he, boys?"

"Depends who's a-runnin' the countin'," said the Virginian, and stretched himself down among the audience.

"I've saw him number one when nobody else was around," said Trampas.

"How far away was you standin' when you beheld that?" inquired the lounging Southerner.

"Well, boys," said Wiggin, "I expect it will be Miss Schoolmarm says who's number one tonight."

"So she's arrived in this hyeh country?" observed the Virginian, very casually.

"Arrived!" said Trampas again. "Where have you been grazing lately?"

"A right smart way from the mules."

"Nebrasky and the boys was tellin' me they'd missed yu' off the range," again interposed Wiggin. "Say, Nebrasky, who have yu' offered your canary to the schoolmarm said you mustn't give her?"

Nebrasky grinned wretchedly.

"Well, she's a lady, and she's square, not takin' a man's gift when she don't take the man. But you'd ought to get back all them letters yu' wrote her. Yu' sure ought to ask her for them tell-tales."

"Ah, pshaw, Honey!" protested the youth. It was well known that he could not write his name.

"Why, if here ain't Bokay Baldy!" cried the agile Wiggin, stooping to fresh prey. "Found them slippers yet, Baldy? Tell yu' boys, that was turruble sad luck Baldy had. Did yu' hear about that? Baldy, yu' know, he can stay on a tame horse most as well as the schoolmarm. But just you give him a pair of young knittin'-needles and see him make 'em sweat! He worked an elegant pair of slippers with pink cabbages on 'em for Miss Wood."

"I bought 'em at Medicine Bow," blundered Baldy.

"So yu' did!" assented the skilful comedian. "Baldy he bought 'em. And on the road to her cabin there at the Taylors' he got thinkin' they might be too big, and he got studyin' what to do. And he fixed up to tell her about his not bein' sure of the size, and how she was to let him know if they dropped off her, and he'd exchange 'em, and when he got right near her door, why, he couldn't find his courage. And so he slips the parcel under the fence and starts serenadin' her. But she ain't inside her cabin at all. She's at supper next door with the Taylors, and Baldy singin' 'Love has conqwered pride and angwer' to a lone house. Lin McLean was comin' up by Taylor's corral, where Taylor's Texas bull was. Well, it was turrible sad. Baldy's pants got tore, but he fell inside the fence, and Lin druv the bull back and somebody stole them Medicine Bow galoshes. Are you goin' to knit her some more, Bokay?"

"About half that ain't straight," Baldy commented, with mildness.

"The half that was tore off yer pants? Well, never mind, Baldy; Lin will get left too, same as all of yu'."

"Is there many?" inquired the Virginian. He was still stretched on his back, looking up at the sky.

"I don't know how many she's been used to where she was raised," Wiggin answered. "A kid stage-driver come from Point of Rocks one day and went back the next. Then the foreman of the 76 outfit, and the horse-wrangler from the Bar-Circle-L, and two deputy marshals, with punchers, stringin' right along—all got their tumble. Old Judge Burrage from Cheyenne come up in August for a hunt and stayed round here and never hunted at all. There was that horse thief—awful good-lookin'. Taylor wanted to warn her about him, but Mrs. Taylor said she'd look after her if it was needed. Mr. Horse-thief gave it up quicker than most; but the schoolmarm couldn't have knowed he had a Mrs. Horse-thief camped on Poison Spider till afterwards. She wouldn't go ridin' with him. She'll go with some, takin' a kid along."

"Bah!" said Trampas.

The Virginian stopped looking at the sky, and watched Trampas from where he lay.

"I think she encourages a man some," said poor Nebrasky.

"Encourages? Because she lets yu' teach her how to shoot," said Wiggin. "Well—I don't guess I'm a judge. I've always kind o' kep' away from them good women. Don't seem to think of anything to chat about to 'em. The only folks I'd say she encourages is the school kids. She kisses them."

"Riding and shooting and kissing the kids," sneered Trampas. "That's a heap too pussy-kitten for me."

They laughed. The sagebrush audience is readily cynical.

"Look for the man, I say," Trampas pursued. "And ain't he there? She leaves Baldy sit on the fence while she and Lin McLean—"

They laughed loudly at the blackguard picture which he drew; and the laugh stopped short, for the Virginian stood over Trampas.

"You can rise up now, and tell them you lie," he said.

The man was still for a moment in the dead silence. "I thought you claimed you and her wasn't acquainted," said he then.

"Stand on your laigs, you polecat, and say you're a liar!"

Trampas's hand moved behind him.

"Quit that," said the Southerner, "or I'll break your neck!"

The eye of a man is the prince of deadly weapons. Trampas looked in the Virginian's, and slowly rose. "I didn't mean—" he began, and paused, his face poisonously bloated.

"Well, I'll call that sufficient. Keep a-standin' still. I ain' going to trouble yu' long. In admittin' yourself to be a liar you have spoke God's truth for onced. Honey Wiggin, you and me and the boys have hit town too frequent for any of us to play Sunday on the balance of the gang." He stopped and surveyed Public Opinion, seated around in carefully inexpressive attention. "We ain't a Christian outfit a little bit, and maybe we have most forgotten what decency feels like. But I reckon we haven't forgot what it means. You can sit down now, if you want."

The liar stood and sneered experimentally, looking at Public Opinion. But this changeful deity was no longer with him, and he heard it variously assenting, "That's so," and "She's a lady," and otherwise excellently moralizing. So he held his peace. When, however, the Virginian had departed to the roasting steer, and Public Opinion relaxed into that comfort which we all experience when the sermon ends, Trampas sat down amid the reviving cheerfulness, and ventured again to be facetious.

"Shut your rank mouth," said Wiggin to him, amiably. "I don't care whether he knows her or if he done it on principle. I'll accept the roundin' up he gave us—and say! You'll swallo' your dose, too! Us boys'll stand in with him in this."

So Trampas swallowed. And what of the Virginian?

He had championed the feeble, and spoken honorably in meeting, and according to all the constitutions and by-laws of morality, he should have been walking in virtue's especial calm. But there it was! he had spoken; he had given them a peep through the key-hole at his inner man; and as he prowled away from the assemblage before whom he stood convicted of decency, it was vicious rather than virtuous that he felt. Other matters also disquieted him—so Lin McLean was hanging round that schoolmarm! Yet he joined Ben Swinton in a seemingly Christian spirit. He took some whiskey and praised the size of the barrel, speaking with his host like this: "There cert'nly ain' goin' to be trouble about a second helpin'."

"Hope not. We'd ought to have more trimmings, though. We're shy on ducks."

"Yu' have the barrel. Has Lin McLean seen that?"

"No. We tried for ducks away down as far as the Laparel outfit. A real barbecue—"

"There's large thirsts on Bear Creek. Lin McLean will pass on ducks."

"Lin's not thirsty this month."

"Signed for one month, has he?"

"Signed! He's spooning our schoolmarm!"

"They claim she's a right sweet-faced girl."

"Yes; yes; awful agreeable. And next thing you're fooled clean through."

"Yu' don't say!"

"She keeps a-teaching the darned kids, and it seems like a good growed-up man can't interest her."

*"Yu' don't say!"*

"There used to be all the ducks you wanted at the Laparel, but their fool cook's dead stuck on raising turkeys this year."

"That must have been mighty close to a drowndin' the schoolmarm got at South Fork."

"Why, I guess not. When? She's never spoken of any such thing—that I've heard."

"Mos' likely the stage-driver got it wrong, then."

"Yes. Must have drownded somebody else. Here they come! That's her ridin' the horse. There's the Westfalls. Where are you running to?"

"To fix up. Got any soap around hyeh?"

"Yes," shouted Swinton, for the Virginian was now some distance away; "towels and everything in the dugout." And he went to welcome his first formal guests.

The Virginian reached his saddle under a shed. "So she's never mentioned it," said he, untying his slicker for the trousers and scarf. "I didn't notice Lin anywheres around her." He was over in the dugout now, whipping off his overalls; and soon he was excellently clean and ready, except for the tie in his scarf and the part in his hair. "I'd have knowed her in Greenland," he remarked. He held the candle up and down at the looking-glass, and the looking-glass up and down at his head. "It's mighty strange why she ain't mentioned that." He worried the scarf a fold or two further, and at length, a trifle more than satisfied with his appearance, he proceeded most serenely toward the sound of the tuning fiddles. He passed through the storeroom behind the kitchen, stepping lightly lest he should rouse the ten or twelve babies that lay on the table or beneath it. On Bear Creek babies and children always went with their parents to a dance, because nurses were unknown. So little Alfred and Christopher lay there among the wraps, parallel and crosswise with little Taylors, and little Carmodys, and Lees, and all the Bear Creek offspring that was not yet able to skip at large and hamper its indulgent elders in the ballroom.

"Why, Lin ain't hyeh yet!" said the Virginian, looking in upon the people.

There was Miss Wood, standing up for the quadrille. "I didn't remember her hair was that pretty," said he. "But ain't she a little, little girl!"

Now she was in truth five feet three; but then he could look away down on the top of her head.

"Salute your honey!" called the first fiddler. All partners bowed to each other, and as she turned, Miss Wood saw the man in the doorway. Again, as it had been at South Fork that day, his eyes dropped from hers, and she divining instantly why he had come after half a year, thought of the handkerchief and of that scream of hers in the river, and became filled with tyranny and anticipation; for indeed he was fine to look upon. So she danced away, carefully unaware of his existence.

"First lady, center!" said her partner, reminding her of her turn. "Have you forgotten how it goes since last time?"

Molly Wood did not forget again, but quadrilled with the most sprightly devotion.

"I see some new faces tonight," said she, presently.

"Yu' always do forget our poor faces," said her partner.

"Oh, no! There's a stranger now. Who is that black man?"

"Well—he's from Virginia, and he ain't allowin' he's black."

"He's a tenderfoot, I suppose?"

"Ha, ha, ha! That's rich, too!" and so the simple partner explained a great deal about the Virginian to Molly Wood. At the end of the set she saw the man by the door take a step in her direction.

"Oh," said she, quickly, to the partner, "how warm it is! I must see how those babies are doing." And she passed the Virginian in a breeze of unconcern.

His eyes gravely lingered where she had gone. "She knowed me right away," said he. He looked for a moment, then leaned against the door. "'How warm it is!' said she. Well, it ain't so screechin' hot hyeh; and as for rushin' after Alfred and Christopher, when their natural motheh is bumpin' around handy—she cert'nly can't be offended?" he broke off, and looked again where she had gone. And then Miss Wood passed him brightly again, and was dancing the schottische almost immediately. "Oh, yes, she knows me," the swarthy cowpuncher mused. "She has to take trouble not to see me. And what she's a-fussin' at is mighty interestin'. Hello!"

"Hello!" returned Lin McLean, sourly. He had just looked into the kitchen.

"Not dancin'?" the Southerner inquired.

"Don't know how."

"Had scyarlet fever and forgot your past life?"

Lin grinned.

"Better persuade the schoolmarm to learn it. She's goin' to give me instruction."

"Huh!" went Mr. McLean, and skulked out to the barrel.

"Why, they claimed you weren't drinkin' this month!" said his friend, following.

"Well, I am. Here's luck!" The two pledged in tin cups. "But I'm not waltzin' with her," blurted Mr. McLean grievously. "She called me an exception."

"Waltzin'," repeated the Virginian quickly, and hearing the fiddles he hastened away.

Few in the Bear Creek Country could waltz, and with these few it was mostly an unsteered and ponderous exhibition; therefore was the Southerner bent upon profiting by his skill. He entered the room, and his lady saw him come where she sat alone for the moment, and her thoughts grew a little hurried.

"Will you try a turn, ma'am?"

"I beg your pardon?" It was a remote, well-schooled eye that she lifted now upon him.

"If you like a waltz, ma'am, will you waltz with me?"

"You're from Virginia, I understand?" said Molly Wood, regarding him politely, but not rising. One gains authority immensely by keeping one's seat. All good teachers know this.

"Yes, ma'am, from Virginia."

"I've heard that Southerners have such good manners."

"That's correct." The cowpuncher flushed, but he spoke in his unvaryingly gentle voice.

"For in New England, you know," pursued Miss Molly, noting his scarf and clean-shaven chin, and then again steadily meeting his eye, "gentlemen ask to be presented to ladies before they ask them to waltz."

He stood a moment before her, deeper and deeper scarlet; and the more she saw his handsome face, the keener rose her excitement. She waited for him to speak of the river; for then she was going to be surprised, and gradually to remember, and finally to be very nice to him. But he did not wait. "I ask your pardon, lady," said he, and bowing, walked off, leaving her at once afraid that he might not come back. But she had altogether mistaken her man. Back he came serenely with Mr. Taylor, and was duly presented to her. Thus were the conventions vindicated.

It can never be known what the cowpuncher was going to say next; for Uncle Hughey stepped up with a glass of water which he had left Wood to bring, and asking for a turn, most graciously received it. She danced away from a situation where she began to feel herself getting the worst of it. One moment the Virginian stared at his lady as she lightly circulated, and then he went out to the barrel.

Leave him for Uncle Hughey! Jealousy is a deep and delicate thing, and works its spite in many ways. The Virginian had been ready to look at Lin McLean with a hostile eye; but finding him now beside the barrel, he felt a brotherhood between himself and Lin, and his hostility had taken a new and whimsical direction.

"Here's how!" said he to McLean. And they pledged each other in the tin cups.

"Been gettin' them instructions?" said Mr. McLean, grinning. "I thought I saw yu' learning your steps through the window."

"Here's your good health," said the Southerner. Once more they pledged each other handsomely.

"Did she call you an exception, or anything?" said Lin.

"Well, it would cipher out right close in that neighborhood."

"Here's how, then!" cried the delighted Lin, over his cup.

"Jest because yu' happen to come from Vermont," continued Mr. McLean, "is no cause for extra pride. Shoo! I was raised in Massachusetts myself, and big men have been raised there, too—Daniel Webster and Israel Putnam: and a lot of them politicians."

"Virginia is a good little old state," observed the Southerner.

"Both of 'em's a sight ahead of Vermont. She told me I was the first exception she'd struck."

"What rule were you provin' at the time, Lin?"

"Well yu' see, I started to kiss her."

"Yu' didn't!"

"Shucks! I didn't mean nothin'."

"I reckon yu' stopped mighty sudden?"

"Why, I'd been ridin' out with her—ridin' to school, ridin' from school, and a-comin' and a-goin', and she chattin' cheerful and askin' me a heap o' questions all about myself every day, and I not lyin' much neither. And so I figured she wouldn't mind. Lots of 'em like it. But she didn't, you bet!"

"No," said the Virginian, deeply proud of his lady who had slighted him. He had pulled her out of the water once, and he had been her unrewarded knight even today, and he felt his grievance; but he spoke not of it to Lin; for he felt also, in memory, her arms clinging round him as he carried her ashore upon his horse. But he muttered, "Plumb ridiculous!" as her injustice struck him afresh, while the outraged McLean told his tale.

"Trample is what she has done on me tonight, and without notice. We was startin' to come here; Taylor and Mrs. were ahead in the buggy, and I was holdin' her horse, and helpin' her up in the saddle, like I done for days and days. Who was there to see us? And I figured she'd not mind, and she calls me an exception! Yu'd ought to've just heard her about Western men respectin' women. So that's the last word we've spoke. We come twenty-five miles then, she scootin' in front, and her horse kickin' the sand in my face. Mrs. Taylor, she guessed something was up, but she didn't tell."

"Miss Wood did not tell?"

"Not she! She'll never open her head. She can take care of herself, you bet!"

The fiddles sounded hilariously in the house, and the feet also. They had warmed up altogether, and their dancing figures crossed the windows back and forth. The two cowpunchers drew near to a window and looked in gloomily.

"There she goes," said Lin.

"With Uncle Hughey again," said the Virginian, sourly. "Yu' might suppose he didn't have a wife and twins, to see the way he goes gambollin' around."

"Westfall is takin' a turn with her now," said McLean.

"James!" exclaimed the Virginian. "He's another with a wife and fam'ly, and he gets the dancin', too."

"There she goes with Taylor," said Lin, presently.

"Another married man!" the Southerner commented. They prowled round to the storeroom, and passed through the kitchen to where the dancers were robustly tramping. Miss Wood was still the partner of Mr. Taylor. "Let's have some whiskey," said the Virginian. They had it, and returned, and the Virginian's disgust and sense of injury grew deeper. "Old Carmody has got her now," he drawled. "He polkas like a landslide. She learns his monkey-faced kid to spell dog and cow all the mawnin'. He'd ought to be tucked up cosey in his bed right now, old Carmody ought."

They were standing in that place set apart for the sleeping children; and just at this moment one of two babies that were stowed beneath a chair uttered a drowsy note. A much louder cry, indeed a chorus of lament, would have been needed to reach the ears of the parents in the room beyond, such was the noisy volume of the dance. But in this quiet place the light sound caught Mr. McLean's attention, and he turned to see if anything were wrong. But both babies were sleeping peacefully.

"Them's Uncle Hughey's twins," he said.

"How do you happen to know that?" inquired the Virginian, suddenly interested.

"Saw his wife put 'em under the chair so she could find 'em right off when she come to go home."

"Oh," said the Virginian, thoughtfully. "Oh, find 'em right off. Yes. Uncle Hughey's twins." He walked to a spot from which he could view the dance. "Well," he continued, returning, "the schoolmarm must have taken quite a notion to Uncle Hughey. He has got her for this quadrille." The Virginian was now speaking without rancor; but his words came with a slightly augmented drawl, and this with him was often a bad omen. He now turned his eyes upon the collected babies wrapped in various colored shawls and knitted work. "Nine, ten, eleven, beautiful sleepin' strangers," he counted, in a sweet voice. "Any of 'em your'n, Lin?"

"Not that I know of," grinned Mr. McLean.

"Eleven, twelve. This hyeh is little Christopher in the blue-stripe quilt—or maybe that other yello'-head is him. The angels have commenced to drop in on us right smart along Bear Creek, Lin."

"What trash are yu' talkin' anyway?"

"If they look so awful alike in the heavenly gyarden," the gentle Southerner continued, "I'd just hate to be the folks that has the cuttin' of 'em out o' the general herd. And that's a right quaint notion too," he added softly. "Them under the chair are Uncle Hughey's, didn't you tell me?" And stooping, he lifted the torpid babies and placed them beneath a table. "No, that ain't thorough," he murmured. With wonderful dexterity and solicitude for their welfare, he removed the loose wrap which was around them, and this soon led to an intricate process of exchange. For a moment Mr. McLean had been staring at the Virginian, puzzled. Then, with a joyful yelp of enlightenment, he sprang to abet him.

And while both busied themselves with the shawls and quilts, the unconscious parents went dancing vigorously on, and the small, occasional cries of their progeny did not reach them.

## CHAPTER XI

### "YOU'RE GOING TO LOVE ME BEFORE WE GET THROUGH"

The Swinton barbecue was over. The fiddles were silent, the steer was eaten, the barrel emptied, or largely so, and the tapers extinguished; round the house and sunken fire all movement of guests was quiet; the families were long departed homeward, and after their hospitable turbulence, the Swintons slept.

Mr. and Mrs. Westfall drove through the night, and as they neared their cabin there came from among the bundled wraps a still, small voice.

"Jim," said his wife, "I said Alfred would catch cold."

"Bosh! Lizzie, don't you fret. He's a little more than a yearlin', and of course he'll snuffle." And young James took a kiss from his love.

"Well, how you can speak of Alfred that way, calling him a yearling, as if he was a calf, and he just as much your child as mine, I don't see, James Westfall!"

"Why, what under the sun do you mean?"

"There he goes again! Do hurry up home, Jim. He's got a real strange cough."

So they hurried home. Soon the nine miles were finished, and good James was unhitching by his stable lantern, while his wife in the house hastened to commit their offspring to bed. The traces had dropped, and each horse marched forward for further unbuckling, when James heard himself called. Indeed, there was that in his wife's voice which made him jerk out his pistol as he ran. But it was no bear or Indian—only two strange children on the bed. His wife was glaring at them.

He sighed with relief and laid down the pistol.

"Put that on again, James Westfall. You'll need it. Look here!"

"Well, they won't bite. Whose are they? Where have you stowed ourn?"

"Where have I—" Utterance forsook this mother for a moment. "And you ask me!" she continued. "Ask Lin McLean. Ask him that sets bulls on folks and steals slippers, what he's done with our innocent lambs, mixing them up with other people's coughing, unhealthy brats. That's Charlie Taylor in Alfred's clothes, and I know Alfred didn't cough like that, and I said to you it was strange; and the other one that's been put in Christopher's new quilts is not even a bub—bub—boy!"

As this crime against society loomed clear to James Westfall's understanding, he sat down on the nearest piece of furniture, and heedless of his wife's tears and his exchanged children, broke into unregenerate laughter. Doubtless after his sharp alarm about the bear, he was unstrung. His lady, however, promptly restrung him; and by the time they had repacked the now clamorous changelings, and were rattling on their way to the Taylors', he began to share her outraged feelings properly, as a husband and a father should; but when he reached the Taylors' and learned from Miss Wood that at this house a child had been unwrapped whom nobody could at all identify, and that Mr. and Mrs. Taylor were already far on the road to the Swintons', James Westfall whipped up his horses and grew almost as thirsty for revenge as was his wife.

Where the steer had been roasted, the powdered ashes were now cold white, and Mr. McLean, feeling through his dreams the change of dawn come over the air, sat up cautiously among the outdoor slumberers and waked his neighbor.

"Day will be soon," he whispered, "and we must light out of this. I never suspicioned yu' had that much of the devil in you before."

"I reckon some of the fellows will act haidstrong," the Virginian murmured luxuriously, among the warmth of his blankets.

"I tell yu' we must skip," said Lin, for the second time; and he rubbed the Virginian's black head, which alone was visible.

"Skip, then, you," came muffled from within, "and keep you'self mighty sca'ce till they can appreciate our frolic."

The Southerner withdrew deeper into his bed, and Mr. McLean, informing him that he was a fool, arose and saddled his horse. From the saddlebag, he brought a parcel, and lightly laying this beside Bokay Baldy, he mounted and was gone. When Baldy awoke later, he found the parcel to be a pair of flowery slippers.

In selecting the inert Virginian as the fool, Mr. McLean was scarcely wise; it is the absent who are always guilty.

Before ever Lin could have been a mile in retreat, the rattle of the wheels roused all of them, and here came the Taylors. Before the Taylors' knocking had brought the Swintons to their door, other wheels sounded, and here were Mr. and Mrs. Carmody, and Uncle Hughey with his wife, and close after them Mr. Dow, alone, who told how his wife had gone into one of her fits—she upon whom Dr. Barker at Drybone had enjoined total abstinence from all excitement. Voices of women and children began to be uplifted; the Westfalls arrived in a lather, and the Thomases; and by sunrise, what with fathers and mothers and spectators and loud offspring, there was gathered such a meeting as has seldom been before among the generations of speaking men. Today you can hear legends of it from Texas to Montana; but I am giving you the full particulars.

Of course they pitched upon poor Lin. Here was the Virginian doing his best, holding horses and helping ladies descend, while the name of McLean began to be muttered with threats. Soon a party led by Mr. Dow set forth in search of him, and the Southerner debated a moment if he had better not put them on a wrong track. But he concluded that they might safely go on searching.

Mrs. Westfall found Christopher at once in the green shawl of Anna Maria Dow, but all was not achieved thus in the twinkling of an eye. Mr. McLean had, it appeared, as James Westfall lugubriously pointed out, not merely "swapped the duds; he had shuffled the whole doggone deck"; and they cursed this Satanic invention. The fathers were but of moderate assistance; it was the mothers who did the heavy work; and by ten o'clock some unsolved problems grew so delicate that a ladies' caucus was organized in a private room—no admittance for men—and what was done there I can only surmise.

During its progress the search party returned. It had not found Mr. McLean. It had found a tree with a notice pegged upon it, reading, "God bless our home!" This was captured.

But success attended the caucus; each mother emerged, satisfied that she had received her own, and each sire, now that his family was itself again, began to look at his neighbor sideways. After a man has been angry enough to kill another man, after the fire of righteous slaughter has raged in his heart as it had certainly raged for several hours in the hearts of these fathers, the flame will usually burn itself out. This will be so in a generous nature, unless the cause of the anger is still unchanged. But the children had been identified; none had taken hurt. All had been humanely given their nourishment. The thing was over. The day was beautiful. A tempting feast remained from the barbecue. These Bear Creek fathers could not keep their ire at red heat. Most of them, being as yet more their wives' lovers than their children's parents, began to see the mirthful side of the adventure; and they ceased to feel very severely toward Lin McLean.

Not so the women. They cried for vengeance; but they cried in vain, and were met with smiles.

Mrs. Westfall argued long that punishment should be dealt the offender. "Anyway," she persisted, "it was real defiant of him putting that up on the tree. I might forgive him but for that."

"Yes," spoke the Virginian in their midst, "that wasn't sort o' right. Especially as I am the man you're huntin'."

They sat dumb at his assurance.

"Come and kill me," he continued, round upon the party. "I'll not resist."

But they could not resist the way in which he had looked round upon them. He had chosen the right moment for his confession, as a captain of a horse awaits the proper time for a charge. Some rebukes he did receive; the worst came from the mothers. And all that he could say for himself was, "I am getting off too easy."

"But what was your point?" said Westfall.

"Blamed if I know anymore. I expect it must have been the whiskey."

"I would mind it less," said Mrs. Westfall, "if you looked a bit sorry or ashamed."

The Virginian shook his head at her penitently. "I'm tryin' to," he said.

And thus he sat disarming his accusers until they began to lunch upon the copious remnants of the barbecue. He did not join them at this meal. In telling you that Mrs. Dow was the only lady absent upon this historic morning, I was guilty of an inadvertence. There was one other.

The Virginian rode away sedately through the autumn sunshine; and as he went he asked his Monte horse a question. "Do yu' reckon she'll have forgotten you too, you pie-biter?" said he. Instead of the new trousers, the cowpuncher's leathern chaps were on his legs. But he had the new scarf knotted at his neck. Most men would gladly have equaled him in appearance. "You Monte," said he, "will she be at home?"

It was Sunday, and no school day, and he found her in her cabin that stood next the Taylors' house. Her eyes were very bright.

"I'd thought I'd just call," said he.

"Why, that's such a pity! Mr. and Mrs. Taylor are away."

"Yes; they've been right busy. That's why I thought I'd call. Will yu' come for a ride, ma'am?"

"Dear me! I—"

"You can ride my hawss. He's gentle."

"What! And you walk?"

"No, ma'am. Nor the two of us ride him *this* time, either." At this she turned entirely pink, and he, noticing, went on quietly: "I'll catch up one of Taylor's hawsses. Taylor knows me."

"No. I don't really think I could do that. But thank you. Thank you very much. I must go now and see how Mrs. Taylor's fire is."

"I'll look after that, ma'am. I'd like for yu' to go ridin' mighty well. Yu' have no babies this mawnin' to be anxious after."

At this shaft, Grandmother Stark flashed awake deep within the spirit of her descendant, and she made a haughty declaration of war. "I don't know what you mean, sir," she said.

Now was his danger; for it was easy to fall into mere crude impertinence and ask her why, then, did she speak thus abruptly? There were various easy things of this kind for him to say. And any rudeness would have lost him the battle. But the Virginian was not the man to lose such a battle in such a way. His shaft had hit. She thought he referred to those babies about whom last night she had shown such superfluous solicitude. Her conscience was guilty. This was all that he had wished to make sure of before he began operations.

"Why, I mean," said he, easily, sitting down near the door, "that it's Sunday. School don't hinder yu' from enjoyin' a ride today. You'll teach the kids all the better for it to-morro', ma'am. Maybe it's your duty." And he smiled at her.

"My duty! It's quite novel to have strangers—"

"Am I a stranger?" he cut in, firing his first broadside. "I was introduced, ma'am," he continued, noting how she had flushed again. "And I would not be oversteppin' for the world. I'll go away if yu' want."

And hereupon he quietly rose, and stood, hat in hand.

Molly was flustered. She did not at all want him to go. No one of her admirers had ever been like this creature. The fringed leathern chaparreros, the cartridge belt, the flannel shirt, the knotted scarf at the neck, these things were now an old story to her. Since her arrival she had seen young men and old in plenty dressed thus. But worn by this man now standing by her door, they seemed to radiate romance. She did not want him to go—and she wished to win her battle. And now in her agitation she became suddenly severe, as she had done at Hoosic Junction. He should have a punishment to remember!

"You call yourself a man, I suppose," she said.

But he did not tremble in the least. Her fierceness filled him with delight, and the tender desire of ownership flooded through him.

"A grown-up, responsible man," she repeated.

"Yes, ma'am. I think so." He now sat down again.

"And you let them think that—that Mr. McLean—you dare not look me in the face and say that Mr. McLean did that last night!"

"I reckon I dassent."

"There! I knew it! I said so from the first!"

"And me a stranger to you!" he murmured.

It was his second broadside. It left her badly crippled. She was silent.

"Who did yu' mention it to, ma'am?"

She hoped she had him. "Why, are you afraid?" And she laughed lightly.

"I told 'em myself. And their astonishment seemed so genu-wine I'd just hate to think they had fooled me that thorough when they knowed it all along from you seeing me."

"I did not see you. I knew it must—of course I did not tell anyone. When I said I said so from the first, I meant—you can understand perfectly what I meant."

"Yes, ma'am."

Poor Molly was near stamping her foot. "And what sort of a trick," she rushed on, "was that to play? Do you call it a manly thing to frighten and distress women because you—for no reason at all? I should never have imagined it could be the act of a person who wears a big pistol and rides a big horse. I should be afraid to go riding with such an immature protector."

"Yes; that was awful childish. Your words do cut a little; for maybe there's been times when I have acted pretty near like a man. But I cert'nly forgot to be introduced before I spoke to yu' last night. Because why? You've found me out dead in one thing. Won't you take a guess at this too?"

"I cannot sit guessing why people do not behave themselves—who seem to know better."

"Well, ma'am, I've played square and owned up to yu'. And that's not what you're doin' by me. I ask your pardon if I say what I have a right to say in language not as good as I'd like to talk to yu' with. But at South Fork Crossin' who did any introducin'? Did yu' complain I was a stranger then?"

"I—no!" she flashed out; then, quite sweetly, "The driver told me it wasn't *really* so dangerous there, you know."

"That's not the point I'm makin'. You are a grown-up woman, a responsible woman. You've come ever so far, and all alone, to a rough country to instruct young children that play games—tag, and hide-and-seek, and fooleries they'll have to quit when they get old. Don't you think pretendin' yu' don't know a man—his name's nothin', but *him*—a man whom you were glad enough to let assist yu' when somebody was needed—don't you think that's mighty close to hide-and-seek them children plays? I ain't so sure but what there's a pair of us children in this hyeh room."

Molly Wood was regarding him saucily. "I don't think I like you," said she.

"That's all square enough. You're goin' to love me before we get through. I wish yu'd come a-ridin, ma'am."

"Dear, dear, dear! So I'm going to love you? How will you do it? I know men think that they only need to sit and look strong and make chests at a girl—"

"Goodness gracious! I ain't makin' any chests at yu'!" Laughter overcame him for a moment, and Miss Wood liked his laugh very much. "Please come a-ridin'," he urged. "It's the prettiest kind of a day."

She looked at him frankly, and there was a pause. "I will take back two things that I said to you," she then answered him. "I believe that I do like you. And I know that if I went riding with you, I should not have an immature protector." And then, with a final gesture of acknowledgment, she held out her hand to him. "And I have always wanted," she said, "to thank you for what you did at the river."

He took her hand, and his heart bounded. "You're a gentleman!" he exclaimed.

It was now her turn to be overcome with merriment. "I've always wanted to be a man," she said.

"I am mighty glad you ain't," said he, looking at her.

But Molly had already received enough broadsides for one day. She could allow no more of them, and she took herself capably in hand. "Where did you learn to make such pretty speeches?" she asked. "Well, never mind that. One sees that you have had plenty of practice for one so young."

"I am twenty-seven," blurted the Virginian, and knew instantly that he had spoken like a fool.

"Who would have dreamed it!" said Molly, with well-measured mockery. She knew that she had scored at last, and that this day was hers. "Don't be too sure you are glad I'm not a man," she now told him. There was something like a challenge in her voice.

"I risk it," he remarked.

"For I am almost twenty-three myself," she concluded. And she gave him a look on her own account.

"And you'll not come a-ridin'?" he persisted.

"No," she answered him; "no." And he knew that he could not make her.

"Then I will tell yu' good-by," said he. "But I am comin' again. And next time I'll have along a gentle hawss for yu'."

"Next time! Next time! Well, perhaps I will go with you. Do you live far?"

"I live on Judge Henry's ranch, over yondeh." He pointed across the mountains. "It's on Sunk Creek. A pretty rough trail; but I can come hyeh to see you in a day, I reckon. Well, I hope you'll cert'nly enjoy good health, ma'am."

"Oh, there's one thing!" said Molly Wood, calling after him rather quickly. "I—I'm not at all afraid of horses. You needn't bring such a gentle one. I—was very tired that day, and—and I don't scream as a rule."

He turned and looked at her so that she could not meet his glance. "Bless your heart!" said he. "Will yu' give me one o' those flowers?"

"Oh, certainly! I'm always so glad when people like them."

"They're pretty near the color of your eyes."

"Never mind my eyes."

"Can't help it, ma'am. Not since South Fork."

He put the flower in the leather band of his hat, and rode away on his Monte horse. Miss Wood lingered a moment, then made some steps toward her gate, from which he could still be seen; and then, with something like a toss of the head, she went in and shut her door.

Later in the day the Virginian met Mr. McLean, who looked at his hat and innocently quoted, "'My Looloo picked a daisy.'"

"Don't yu', Lin," said the Southerner.

"Then I won't," said Lin.

Thus, for this occasion, did the Virginian part from his lady—and nothing said one way or another about the handkerchief that had disappeared during the South Fork incident.

As we fall asleep at night, our thoughts will often ramble back and forth between the two worlds.

"What color were his eyes?" wondered Molly on her pillow. "His mustache is not bristly like so many of them. Sam never gave me such a look at Hoosic Junction. No . . . You can't come with me . . . Get off your horse . . . The passengers are all staring . . ."

And while Molly was thus dreaming that the Virginian had ridden his horse into the railroad car, and sat down beside her, the fire in the great stone chimney of her cabin flickered quietly, its gleams now and again touching the miniature of Grandmother Stark upon the wall.

Camped on the Sunk Creek trail, the Virginian was telling himself in his blankets: "I ain't too old for education. Maybe she will lend me books. And I'll watch her ways and learn . . . stand still, Monte. I can learn a lot more than the kids on that. There's Monte . . . you pie-biter, stop . . . He has ate up your book, ma'am, but I'll get yu' . . ."

And then the Virginian was fast asleep.

# CHAPTER XII

# QUALITY AND EQUALITY

To the circle at Bennington, a letter from Bear Creek was always a welcome summons to gather and hear of doings very strange to Vermont. And when the tale of the changed babies arrived duly by the post, it created a more than usual sensation, and was read to a large number of pleased and scandalized neighbors. "I hate her to be where such things can happen," said Mrs. Wood.

"I wish I could have been there," said her son-in-law, Andrew Bell.

"She does not mention who played the trick," said Mrs. Andrew Bell.

"We shouldn't be any wiser if she did," said Mrs. Wood.

"I'd like to meet the perpetrator," said Andrew.

"Oh, no!" said Mrs. Wood. "They're all horrible."

And she wrote at once, begging her daughter to take good care of herself, and to see as much of Mrs. Balaam as possible. "And of any other ladies that are near you. For you seem to me to be in a community of roughs. I wish you would give it all up. Did you expect me to laugh about the babies?"

Mrs. Flynt, when this story was repeated to her (she had not been invited in to hear the letter), remarked that she had always felt that Molly Wood must be a little vulgar, ever since she began to go about giving music lessons like any ordinary German.

But Mrs. Wood was considerably relieved when the next letter arrived. It contained nothing horrible about barbecues or babies. It mentioned the great beauty of the weather, and how well and strong the fine air was making the writer feel. And it asked that books might be sent, many books of all sorts, novels, poetry, all the good old books and any good new ones that could be spared. Cheap editions, of course.

"Indeed she shall have them!" said Mrs. Wood. "How her mind must be starving in that dreadful place!" The letter was not a long one, and, besides the books, spoke of little else except the fine weather and the chances for outdoor exercise that this gave. "You have no idea," it said, "how delightful it is to ride, especially on a spirited horse, which I can do now quite well."

"How nice that is!" said Mrs. Wood, putting down the letter. "I hope the horse is not too spirited."

"Who does she go riding with?" asked Mrs. Bell.

"She doesn't say, Sarah. Why?"

"Nothing. She has a queer way of not mentioning things, now and then."

"Sarah!" exclaimed Mrs. Wood, reproachfully. "Oh, well, mother, you know just as well as I do that she can be very independent and unconventional."

"Yes; but not in that way. She wouldn't ride with poor Sam Bannett, and after all he is a suitable person."

Nevertheless, in her next letter, Mrs. Wood cautioned her daughter about trusting herself with anyone of whom Mrs. Balaam did not thoroughly approve. The good lady could never grasp that Mrs. Balaam lived a long day's journey from Bear Creek, and that Molly saw her about once every three months. "We have sent your books," the mother wrote; "everybody has contributed from their store—Shakespeare, Tennyson, Browning, Longfellow; and a number of novels by Scott, Thackeray, George Eliot, Hawthorne, and lesser writers; some volumes of Emerson; and Jane Austen complete, because you admire her so particularly."

This consignment of literature reached Bear Creek about a week before Christmastime.

By New Year's Day, the Virginian had begun his education.

"Well, I have managed to get through 'em," he said, as he entered Molly's cabin in February. And he laid two volumes upon her table.

"And what do you think of them?" she inquired.

"I think that I've cert'nly earned a good long ride today."

"Georgie Taylor has sprained his ankle."

"No, I don't mean that kind of a ride. I've earned a ride with just us two alone. I've read every word of both of 'em, yu' know."

"I'll think about it. Did you like them?"

"No. Not much. If I'd knowed that one was a detective story, I'd have got yu' to try something else on me. Can you guess the murderer, or is the author too smart for yu'? That's all they amount to. Well, he was too smart for me this time, but that didn't distress me any. That other book talks too much."

Molly was scandalized, and she told him it was a great work.

"Oh, yes, yes. A fine book. But it will keep up its talkin'. Don't let you alone."

"Didn't you feel sorry for poor Maggie Tulliver?"

"Hmp. Yes. Sorry for her, and for Tawmmy, too. But the man did right to drownd 'em both."

"It wasn't a man. A woman wrote that."

"A woman did! Well, then, o' course she talks too much."

"I'll not go riding with you!" shrieked Molly.

But she did. And he returned to Sunk Creek, not with a detective story, but this time with a Russian novel.

It was almost April when he brought it back to her—and a heavy sleet storm lost them their ride. So he spent his time indoors with her, not speaking a syllable of love. When he came to take his departure, he asked her for some other book by this same Russian. But she had no more.

"I wish you had," he said. "I've never saw a book could tell the truth like that one does."

"Why, what do you like about it?" she exclaimed. To her it had been distasteful.

"Everything," he answered. "That young come-outer, and his fam'ly that can't understand him—for he is broad gauge, yu' see, and they are narro' gauge." The Virginian looked at Molly a moment almost shyly. "Do you know," he said, and a blush spread over his face, "I pretty near cried when that young come-outer was dyin', and said about himself, 'I was a giant.' Life made him broad gauge, yu' see, and then took his chance away."

Molly liked the Virginian for his blush. It made him very handsome. But she thought that it came from his confession about "pretty near crying."

The deeper cause she failed to divine—that he, like the dying hero in the novel, felt himself to be a giant whom life had made "broad gauge," and denied opportunity. Fecund nature begets and squanders thousands of these rich seeds in the wilderness of life.

He took away with him a volume of Shakespeare. "I've saw good plays of his," he remarked.

Kind Mrs. Taylor in her cabin next door watched him ride off in the sleet, bound for the lonely mountain trail.

"If that girl don't get ready to take him pretty soon," she observed to her husband, "I'll give her a piece of my mind."

Taylor was astonished. "Is he thinking of *her?*" he inquired.

"Lord, Mr. Taylor, and why shouldn't he?"

Mr. Taylor scratched his head and returned to his newspaper.

It was warm—warm and beautiful upon Bear Creek. Snow shone upon the peaks of the Bow Leg range; lower on their slopes the pines were stirring with a gentle song; and flowers bloomed across the wide plains at their feet.

Molly and her Virginian sat at a certain spring where he had often ridden with her. On this day he was bidding her farewell before undertaking the most important trust which Judge Henry had as yet given him. For this journey she had provided him with Sir Walter Scott's Kenilworth. Shakespeare he had returned to her. He had bought Shakespeare for himself. "As soon as I got used to readin' it," he had told her, "I knowed for certain that I liked readin' for enjoyment."

But it was not of books that he had spoken much today. He had not spoken at all. He had bade her listen to the meadow-lark, when its song fell upon the silence like beaded drops of music. He had showed her where a covey of young willow-grouse were hiding as their horses passed. And then, without warning, as they sat by the spring, he had spoken potently of his love.

She did not interrupt him. She waited until he was wholly finished.

"I am not the sort of wife you want," she said, with an attempt of airiness.

He answered roughly, "I am the judge of that." And his roughness was a pleasure to her, yet it made her afraid of herself. When he was absent from her, and she could sit in her cabin and look at Grandmother Stark, and read home letters, then in imagination she found it easy to play the part which she had arranged to play regarding him—the part of the guide, and superior, and indulgent companion. But when he was by her side, that part became a difficult one. Her woman's fortress was shaken by a force unknown to her before. Sam Bannett did not have it in him to look as this man could look, when the cold lustre of his eyes grew hot with internal fire. What color they were baffled her still. "Can it possibly change?" she wondered. It seemed to her that sometimes when she had been looking from a rock straight down into clear sea water, this same color had lurked in its depths. "Is it green, or is it gray?" she asked herself, but did not turn just now to see. She kept her face toward the landscape.

"All men are born equal," he now remarked slowly.

"Yes," she quickly answered, with a combative flash. "Well?"

"Maybe that don't include women?" he suggested.

"I think it does."

"Do yu' tell the kids so?"

"Of course I teach them what I believe!"

He pondered. "I used to have to learn about the Declaration of Independence. I hated books and truck when I was a kid."

"But you don't anymore."

"No. I cert'nly don't. But I used to get kep' in at recess for bein' so dumb. I was most always at the tail end of the class. My brother, he'd be head sometimes."

"Little George Taylor is my prize scholar," said Molly.

"Knows his tasks, does he?"

"Always. And Henry Dow comes next."

"Who's last?"

"Poor Bob Carmody. I spend more time on him than on all the rest put together."

"My!" said the Virginian. "Ain't that strange!"

She looked at him, puzzled by his tone. "It's not strange when you know Bob," she said.

"It's very strange," drawled the Virginian. "Knowin' Bob don't help it any."

"I don't think that I understand you," said Molly, sticky.

"Well, it is mighty confusin'. George Taylor, he's your best scholar, and poor Bob, he's your worst, and there's a lot in the middle—and you tell me we're all born equal!"

Molly could only sit giggling in this trap he had so ingeniously laid for her.

"I'll tell you what," pursued the cowpuncher, with slow and growing intensity, "equality is a great big bluff. It's easy called."

"I didn't mean——" began Molly.

"Wait, and let me say what I mean." He had made an imperious gesture with his hand. "I know a man that mostly wins at cyards. I know a man that mostly loses. He says it is his luck. All right. Call it his luck. I know a man that works hard and he's gettin' rich, and I know another that works hard and is gettin' poor. He says it is his luck. All right. Call it his luck. I look around and I see folks movin' up or movin' down, winners or losers everywhere. All luck, of course. But since folks can be born that different in their luck, where's your equality? No, seh! call your failure luck, or call it laziness, wander around the words, prospect all yu' mind to, and yu'll come out the same old trail of inequality." He paused a moment and looked at her. "Some holds four aces," he went on, "and some holds nothin', and some poor fello' gets the aces and no show to play 'em; but a man has got to prove himself my equal before I'll believe him."

Molly sat gazing at him, silent.

"I know what yu' meant," he told her now, "by sayin' you're not the wife I'd want. But I am the kind that moves up. I am goin' to be your best scholar." He turned toward her, and that fortress within her began to shake.

"Don't," she murmured. "Don't, please."

"Don't what?"

"Why—spoil this."

"Spoil it?"

"These rides—I don't love you—I can't—but these rides are——"

"What are they?"

"My greatest pleasure. There! And, please, I want them to go on so."

"Go on so! I don't reckon yu' know what you're sayin'. Yu' might as well ask fruit to stay green. If the way we are now can keep bein' enough for you, it can't for me. A pleasure to you, is it? Well, to me it is—I don't know what to call it. I come to yu' and I hate it, and I come again and I hate it, and I ache and grieve all over when I go. No! You will have to think of some other way than just invitin' me to keep green."

"If I am to see you——" began the girl.

"You're not to see me. Not like this. I can stay away easier than what I am doin'."

"Will you do me a favor, a great one?" said she, now.

"Make it as impossible as you please!" he cried. He thought it was to be some action.

"Go on coming. But don't talk to me about—don't talk in that way—if you can help it."

He laughed out, not permitting himself to swear.

"But," she continued, "if you can't help talking that way—sometimes—I promise I will listen. That is the only promise I make."

"That is a bargain," he said.

Then he helped her mount her horse, restraining himself like a Spartan, and they rode home to her cabin.

"You have made it pretty near impossible," he said, as he took his leave. "But you've been square today, and I'll show you I can be square when I come back. I'll not do more than ask you if your mind's the same. And now I'll not see you for quite a while. I am going a long way. But I'll be very busy. And bein' busy always keeps me from grievin' too much about you."

Strange is woman! She would rather have heard some other last remark than this.

"Oh, very well!" she said. "I'll not miss you either."

He smiled at her. "I doubt if yu' can help missin' me," he remarked. And he was gone at once, galloping on his Monte horse.

Which of the two won a victory this day?

# CHAPTER XIII

## THE GAME AND THE NATION—ACT FIRST

There can be no doubt of this: All America is divided into two classes—the quality and the equality.

The latter will always recognize the former when mistaken for it. Both will be with us until our women bear nothing but kings.

It was through the Declaration of Independence that we Americans acknowledged the *eternal inequality* of man. For by it we abolished a cut-and-dried aristocracy. We had seen little men artificially held up in high places, and great men artificially held down in low places, and our own justice-loving hearts abhorred this violence to human nature. Therefore, we decreed that every man should thenceforth have equal liberty to find his own level. By this very decree we acknowledged and gave freedom to true aristocracy, saying, "Let the best man win, whoever he is." Let the best man win! That is America's word. That is true democracy. And true democracy and true aristocracy are one and the same thing. If anybody cannot see this, so much the worse for his eyesight.

The above reflections occurred to me before reaching Billings, Montana, some three weeks after I had unexpectedly met the Virginian at Omaha, Nebraska. I had not known of that trust given to him by Judge Henry, which was taking him East. I was looking to ride with him before long among the clean hills of Sunk Creek. I supposed he was there. But I came upon him one morning in Colonel Cyrus Jones's eating palace.

Did you know the palace? It stood in Omaha, near the trains, and it was ten years old (which is middle-aged in Omaha) when I first saw it. It was a shell of wood, painted with golden emblems—the steamboat, the eagle, the Yosemite—and a live bear ate gratuities at its entrance. Weather permitting, it opened upon the world as a stage upon the audience. You sat in Omaha's whole sight and dined, while Omaha's dust came and settled upon the refreshments. It is gone the way of the Indian and the buffalo, for the West is growing old. You should have seen the palace and sat there. In front of you passed rainbows of men—Chinese, Indian chiefs, Africans, General Miles, younger sons, Austrian nobility, wide females in pink. Our continent drained prismatically through Omaha once.

So I was passing that way also, walking for the sake of ventilation from a sleeping-car toward a bath, when the language of Colonel Cyrus Jones came out to me. The actual colonel I had never seen before. He stood at the rear of his palace in gray flowery mustaches and a Confederate uniform, telling the wishes of his guests to the cook through a hole. You always bought meal tickets at once, else you became unwelcome. Guests here had foibles at times, and a rapid exit was too easy. Therefore I bought a ticket. It was spring and summer since I had heard anything like the colonel. The Missouri had not yet flowed into New York dialect freely, and his vocabulary met me like the breeze of the plains. So I went in to be fanned by it, and there sat the Virginian at a table, alone.

His greeting was up to the code of indifference proper on the plains; but he presently remarked, "I'm right glad to see somebody," which was a good deal to say. "Them that comes hyeh," he observed next, "don't eat. They feed." And he considered the guests with a sombre attention. "D' yu' reckon they find joyful digestion in this swallo'-an'-get-out trough?"

"What are you doing here, then?" said I.

"Oh, pshaw! When yu' can't have what you choose, yu' just choose what you have." And he took the bill-of-fare. I began to know that he had something on his mind, so I did not trouble him further.

Meanwhile he sat studying the bill-of-fare.

"Ever heard o' them?" he inquired, shoving me the spotted document.

Most improbable dishes were there—salmis, canapes, supremes—all perfectly spelt and absolutely transparent. It was the old trick of copying some metropolitan menu to catch travelers of the third and last dimension of innocence; and whenever this is done the food is of the third and last dimension of awfulness, which the cowpuncher knew as well as anybody.

"So they keep that up here still," I said.

"But what about them?" he repeated. His finger was at a special item, *Frogs' Legs à la Delmonico*. "Are they true anywheres?" he asked. And I told him, certainly. I also explained to him about Delmonico of New York and about Augustin of Philadelphia.

"There's not a little bit o' use in lyin' to me this mawnin'," he said, with his engaging smile. "I ain't goin' to awdeh anything's laigs."

"Well, I'll see how he gets out of it," I said, remembering the odd Texas legend. (The traveler read the bill-of-fare, you know, and called for a vol-au-vent. And the proprietor looked at the traveler, and running a pistol into his ear, observed, "You'll take hash.") I was thinking of this and wondering what would happen to me. So I took the step.

"Wants frogs' legs, does he?" shouted Colonel Cyrus Jones. He fixed his eye upon me, and it narrowed to a slit. "Too many brain workers breakfasting before yu' came in, professor," said he. "Missionary ate the last leg off me just now. Brown the wheat!" he commanded, through the hole to the cook, for someone had ordered hot cakes.

"I'll have fried aiggs," said the Virginian. "Cooked both sides."

"White wings!" sang the colonel through the hole. "Let 'em fly up and down."

"Coffee an' no milk," said the Virginian.

"Draw one in the dark!" the colonel roared.

"And beefsteak, rare."

"One slaughter in the pan, and let the blood drip!"

"I should like a glass of water, please," said I. The colonel threw me a look of pity.

"One Missouri and ice for the professor!" he said.

"That fello's a right live man," commented the Virginian. But he seemed thoughtful. Presently he inquired, "Yu' say he was a foreigner, an' learned fancy cookin' to New Yawk?"

That was this cowpuncher's way. Scarcely ever would he let drop a thing new to him until he had got from you your whole information about it. So I told him the history of Lorenzo Delmonico and his pioneer work, as much as I knew, and the Southerner listened intently.

"Mighty inter-estin'," he said—"mighty. He could just take little old o'rn'ry frawgs, and dandy 'em up to suit the bloods. Mighty inter-estin'. I expaict, though, his cookin' would give an outraiged stomach to a plain-raised man."

"If you want to follow it up," said I, by way of a sudden experiment, "Miss Molly Wood might have some book about French dishes."

But the Virginian did not turn a hair. "I reckon she wouldn't," he answered. "She was raised in Vermont. They don't bother overly about their eatin' up in Vermont. Hyeh's what Miss Wood recommended the las' time I was seein' her," the cowpuncher added, bringing Kenilworth from his pocket. "Right fine story. That Queen Elizabeth must have cert'nly been a competent woman."

"She was," said I. But talk came to an end here. A dusty crew, most evidently from the plains, now entered and drifted to a table; and each man of them gave the Virginian about a quarter of a slouchy nod. His greeting to them was very serene. Only, Kenilworth went back into his pocket, and he breakfasted in silence. Among those who had greeted him I now recognized a face.

"Why, that's the man you played cards with at Medicine Bow!" I said.

"Yes. Trampas. He's got a job at the ranch now." The Virginian said no more, but went on with his breakfast.

His appearance was changed. Aged I would scarcely say, for this would seem as if he did not look young. But I think that the boy was altogether gone from his face—the boy whose freak with Steve had turned Medicine Bow upside down, whose other freak with the babies had outraged Bear Creek, the boy who had loved to jingle his spurs. But manhood had only trained, not broken, his youth. It was all there, only obedient to the rein and curb.

Presently we went together to the railway yard.

"The Judge is doing a right smart o' business this year," he began, very casually indeed, so that I knew this was important. Besides bells and coal smoke, the smell and crowded sounds of cattle rose in the air around us. "Hyeh's our first gather o' beeves on the ranch," continued the Virginian. "The whole lot's shipped through to Chicago in two sections over the Burlington. The Judge is fighting the Elkhorn road."

We passed slowly along the two trains—twenty cars, each car packed with huddled, round-eyed, gazing steers. He examined to see if any animals were down. "They ain't ate or drank anything to speak of," he said, while the terrified brutes stared at us through their slats. "Not since they struck the railroad they've not drank. Yu' might suppose they know somehow what they're travelin' to Chicago for." And casually, always casually, he told me the rest. Judge Henry could not spare his foreman away from the second gather of beeves. Therefore these two ten-car trains with their double crew of cowboys had been given to the Virginian's charge. After Chicago, he was to return by St. Paul over the Northern Pacific; for the Judge had wished him to see certain of the road's directors and explain to them persuasively how good a thing it would be for them to allow especially cheap rates to the Sunk Creek outfit henceforth. This was all the Virginian told me; and it contained the whole matter, to be sure.

"So you're acting foreman," said I.

"Why, somebody has to have the say, I reckon."

"And of course you hated the promotion?"

"I don't know about promotion," he replied. "The boys have been used to seein' me one of themselves. Why don't you come along with us far as

Plattsmouth?" Thus he shifted the subject from himself, and called to my notice the locomotives backing up to his cars, and reminded me that from Plattsmouth I had the choice of two trains returning. But he could not hide or belittle this confidence of his employer in him. It was the care of several thousand perishable dollars and the control of men. It was a compliment. There were more steers than men to be responsible for; but none of the steers had been suddenly picked from the herd and set above his fellows. Moreover, Chicago finished up the steers; but the new-made deputy foreman had then to lead his six highly unoccupied brethren away from towns, and back in peace to the ranch, or disappoint the Judge, who needed their services. These things sometimes go wrong in a land where they say you are all born equal; and that quarter of a nod in Colonel Cyrus Jones's eating palace held more equality than any whole nod you could see. But the Virginian did not see it, there being a time for all things.

We trundled down the flopping, heavy-eddied Missouri to Plattsmouth, and there they backed us on to a siding, the Christian Endeavor being expected to pass that way. And while the equality absorbed themselves in a deep but harmless game of poker by the side of the railway line, the Virginian and I sat on the top of a car, contemplating the sandy shallows of the Platte.

"I should think you'd take a hand," said I.

"Poker? With them kittens?" One flash of the inner man lightened in his eyes and died away, and he finished with his gentle drawl, "When I play, I want it to be interestin'." He took out Sir Walter's Kenilworth once more, and turned the volume over and over slowly, without opening it. You cannot tell if in spirit he wandered on Bear Creek with the girl whose book it was. The spirit will go one road, and the thought another, and the body its own way sometimes. "Queen Elizabeth would have played a mighty pow'ful game," was his next remark.

"Poker?" said I.

"Yes, seh. Do you expaict Europe has got any queen equal to her at present?"

I doubted it.

"Victoria'd get pretty nigh slain sliding chips out agaynst Elizabeth. Only mos' prob'ly Victoria she'd insist on a half-cent limit. You have read this hyeh *Kenilworth?* Well, deal Elizabeth ace high, an' she could scare Robert Dudley with a full house plumb out o' the bettin'."

I said that I believed she unquestionably could.

"And," said the Virginian, "if Essex's play got next her too near, I reckon she'd have stacked the cyards. Say, d' yu' remember Shakespeare's fat man?"

"Falstaff? Oh, yes, indeed."

"Ain't that grand? Why, he makes men talk the way they do in life. I reckon he couldn't get printed today. It's a right down shame Shakespeare couldn't know about poker. He'd have had Falstaff playing all day at that Tearsheet outfit. And the Prince would have beat him."

"The Prince had the brains," said I.

"Brains?"

"Well, didn't he?"

"I neveh thought to notice. Like as not he did."

"And Falstaff didn't, I suppose?"

"Oh, yes, seh! Falstaff could have played whist."

"I suppose you know what you're talking about; I don't," said I, for he was drawling again.

The cowpuncher's eye rested a moment amiably upon me. "You can play whist with your brains," he mused—"brains and cyards. Now cyards are only one o' the manifestations of poker in this hyeh world. One o' the shapes yu fool with it in when the day's work is oveh. If a man is built like that Prince boy was built (and it's away down deep beyond brains), he'll play winnin' poker with whatever hand he's holdin' when the trouble begins. Maybe it will be a mean, triflin' army, or an empty six-shooter, or a lame hawss, or maybe just nothin' but his natural countenance. 'Most any old thing will do for a fello' like that Prince boy to play poker with."

"Then I'd be grateful for your definition of poker," said I.

Again the Virginian looked me over amiably. "You put up a mighty pretty game o' whist yourself," he remarked. "Don't that give you the contented spirit?" And before I had any reply to this, the Christian Endeavor began to come over the bridge. Three instalments crossed the Missouri from Pacific Junction, bound for Pike's Peak, every car swathed in bright bunting, and at each window a Christian with a handkerchief, joyously shrieking. Then the cattle trains got the open signal, and I jumped off. "Tell the Judge the steers was all right this far," said the Virginian.

That was the last of the deputy foreman for a while.

## CHAPTER XIV

## BETWEEN THE ACTS

My road to Sunk Creek lay in no straight line. By rail I diverged northwest to Fort Meade, and thence, after some stay with the kind military people, I made my way on a horse. Up here in the Black Hills it sluiced rain most intolerably. The horse and I enjoyed the country and ourselves but little; and when finally I changed from the saddle into a stagecoach, I caught a thankful expression upon the animal's face, and returned the same.

"Six legs inside this jerky tonight?" said somebody, as I climbed the wheel. "Well, we'll give thanks for not havin' eight," he added cheerfully. "Clamp your mind on to that, Shorty." And he slapped the shoulder of his neighbor. Naturally I took these two for old companions. But we were all total strangers. They told me of the new gold excitement at Rawhide, and supposed it would bring up the Northern Pacific; and when I explained the millions owed to this road's German bondholders, they were of opinion that a German would strike it richer at Rawhide. We spoke of all sorts of things, and in our silence I gloated on the autumn holiday promised me by Judge Henry. His last letter had said that an outfit would be starting for his ranch from Billings on the seventh, and he would have a horse for me. This was the fifth. So we six legs in the jerky traveled harmoniously on over the rain-gutted road, getting no deeper knowledge of each other than what our outsides might imply.

Not that we concealed anything. The man who had slapped Shorty introduced himself early. "Scipio le Moyne, from Gallipolice, Ohio," he said. "The eldest of us always gets called Scipio. It's French. But us folks have been white for a hundred years." He was limber and light-muscled, and fell skilfully about, evading bruises when the jerky reeled or rose on end. He had a strange, long, jocular nose, very wary-looking, and a bleached blue eye. Cattle was his business, as a rule, but of late he had been "looking around some," and Rawhide seemed much on his brain. Shorty struck me as "looking around" also. He was quite short, indeed, and the jerky hurt him almost every time. He was light-haired and mild. Think of a yellow dog that is lost, and fancies each newcomer in sight is going to turn out his master, and you will have Shorty.

It was the Northern Pacific that surprised us into intimacy. We were nearing Medora. We had made a last arrangement of our legs. I lay stretched in silence, placid in the knowledge it was soon to end. So I drowsed. I felt something sudden, and, waking, saw Scipio passing through the air. As Shorty next shot from the jerky, I beheld smoke and the locomotive. The Northern Pacific had changed its schedule. A valise is a poor companion for catching a train with. There was rutted sand and lumpy, knee-high grease wood in our short cut. A piece of stray wire sprang from some hole and hung caracoling about my ankle. Tin cans spun from my stride. But we made a conspicuous race. Two of us waved hats, and there was no moment that someone of us was not screeching. It meant twenty-four hours to us.

Perhaps we failed to catch the train's attention, though the theory seems monstrous. As it moved off in our faces, smooth and easy and insulting, Scipio dropped instantly to a walk, and we two others outstripped him and came desperately to the empty track. There went the train. Even still its puffs were the separated puffs of starting, that bitten-off, snorty kind, and sweat and our true natures broke freely forth.

I kicked my valise, and then sat on it, dumb.

Shorty yielded himself up aloud. All his humble secrets came out of him. He walked aimlessly round, lamenting. He had lost his job, and he mentioned the ranch. He had played cards, and he mentioned the man. He had sold his horse and saddle to catch a friend on this train, and he mentioned what the friend had been going to do for him. He told a string of griefs and names to the air, as if the air knew.

Meanwhile Scipio arrived with extreme leisure at the rails. He stuck his hands into his pockets and his head out at the very small train. His bleached blue eyes shut to slits as he watched the rear car in its smoke-blur ooze away westward among the mounded bluffs. "Lucky it's out of range," I thought. But now Scipio spoke to it.

"Why, you seem to think you've left me behind," he began easily, in fawning tones. "You're too much of a kid to have such thoughts. Age some." His next remark grew less wheedling. "I wouldn't be a bit proud to meet yu'. Why, if I was seen travelin' with yu', I'd have to explain it to my friends! Think you've got me left, do yu'? Just because yu' ride through this country on a rail, do yu' claim yu' can find your way around? I could take yu' out ten yards in the brush and lose yu' in ten seconds, you spangle-roofed hobo! Leave *me* behind? You recent blanket-mortgage yearlin'! You plush-lined, nickel-plated, whistlin' wash room, d' yu' figure I can't go east just as soon as west? Or I'll stay right here if it suits me, yu' dude-inhabited hot-box! Why, yu' coon-bossed face-towel—" But from here he rose in flights of novelty that appalled and held me spellbound, and which are not for me to say to you. Then he came down easily again, and finished with expressions of sympathy for it because it could never have known a mother.

"Do you expaict it could show a male parent offhand?" inquired a slow voice behind us. I jumped round, and there was the Virginian.

"Male parent!" scoffed the prompt Scipio. "Ain't you heard about *them* yet?"

"Them? Was there two?"

"Two? The blamed thing was sired by a whole doggone Dutch syndicate."

"Why, the piebald son of a gun!" responded the Virginian, sweetly. "I got them steers through all right," he added to me. "Sorry to see yu' get so out o' breath afteh the train. Is your valise sufferin' any?"

"Who's he?" inquired Scipio, curiously, turning to me.

The Southerner sat with a newspaper on the rear platform of a caboose. The caboose stood hitched behind a mile or so of freight train, and the train was headed west. So here was the deputy foreman, his steers delivered in Chicago, his men (I could hear them) safe in the caboose, his paper in his lap, and his legs dangling at ease over the railing. He wore the look of a man for whom things are going smooth. And for me the way to Billings was smooth now, also.

"Who's he?" Scipio repeated.

But from inside the caboose loud laughter and noise broke on us. Someone was reciting "And it's my night to howl."

"We'll all howl when we get to Rawhide," said some other one; and they howled now.

"These hyeh steam cyars," said the Virginian to Scipio, "make a man's language mighty nigh as speedy as his travel." Of Shorty he took no notice whatever—no more than of the manifestations in the caboose.

"So yu' heard me speakin' to the express," said Scipio. "Well, I guess, sometimes I—see here," he exclaimed, for the Virginian was gravely considering him, "I may have talked some, but I walked a whole lot. You didn't catch *me* squandering no speed. Soon as—"

"I noticed," said the Virginian, "thinkin' came quicker to yu' than runnin'."

I was glad I was not Shorty, to have my measure taken merely by my way of missing a train. And of course I was sorry that I had kicked my valise.

"Oh, I could tell yu'd been enjoyin' us!" said Scipio. "Observin' somebody else's scrape always kind o' rests me too. Maybe you're a philosopher, but maybe there's a pair of us drawd in this deal."

Approval now grew plain upon the face of the Virginian. "By your laigs," said he, "you are used to the saddle."

"I'd be called used to it, I expect."

"By your hands," said the Southerner, again, "you ain't roped many steers lately. Been cookin' or something?"

"Say," retorted Scipio, "tell my future some now. Draw a conclusion from my mouth."

"I'm right distressed," answered the gentle Southerner, "we've not a drop in the outfit."

"Oh, drink with me uptown!" cried Scipio. "I'm pleased to death with yu'."

The Virginian glanced where the saloons stood just behind the station, and shook his head.

"Why, it ain't a bit far to whiskey from here!" urged the other, plaintively. "Step down, now. Scipio le Moyne's my name. Yes, you're lookin' for my brass ear-rings. But there ain't no ear-rings on me. I've been white for a hundred years. Step down. I've a forty-dollar thirst."

"You're certainly white," began the Virginian. "But—"

Here the caboose resumed:

> "I'm wild, and woolly, and full of peas;
> I'm hard to curry above the knees;
> I'm a she-wolf from Bitter Creek, and
> It's my night to ho-o-wl—"

And as they howled and stamped, the wheels of the caboose began to turn gently and to murmur.

The Virginian rose suddenly. "Will yu' save that thirst and take a forty-dollar job?"

"Missin' trains, profanity, or what?" said Scipio.

"I'll tell yu' soon as I'm sure."

At this Scipio looked hard at the Virginian. "Why, you're talkin' business!" said he, and leaped on the caboose, where I was already. "I *was* thinkin' of Rawhide," he added, "but I ain't anymore."

"Well, good luck!" said Shorty, on the track behind us.

"Oh, say!" said Scipio, "he wanted to go on that train, just like me."

"Get on," called the Virginian. "But as to getting a job, he ain't just like you." So Shorty came, like a lost dog when you whistle to him.

Our wheels clucked over the main-line switch. A train-hand threw it shut after us, jumped aboard, and returned forward over the roofs. Inside the caboose they had reached the third howling of the she-wolf.

"Friends of yourn?" said Scipio.

"My outfit," drawled the Virginian.

"Do yu' always travel outside?" inquired Scipio.

"It's lonesome in there," returned the deputy foreman. And here one of them came out, slamming the door.

"Hell!" he said, at sight of the distant town. Then, truculently, to the Virginian, "I told you I was going to get a bottle here."

"Have your bottle, then," said the deputy foreman, and kicked him off into Dakota. (It was not North Dakota yet; they had not divided it.) The Virginian had aimed his pistol at about the same time with his boot. Therefore the man sat in Dakota quietly, watching us go away into Montana, and offering no objections. Just before he became too small to make out, we saw him rise and remove himself back toward the saloons.

## CHAPTER XV

## THE GAME AND THE NATION—ACT SECOND

"That is the only step I have had to take this whole trip," said the Virginian. He holstered his pistol with a jerk. "I have been fearing he would force it on me." And he looked at empty, receding Dakota with disgust. "So nyeh back home!" he muttered.

"Known your friend long?" whispered Scipio to me.

"Fairly," I answered.

Scipio's bleached eyes brightened with admiration as he considered the Southerner's back. "Well," he stated judicially, "start awful early when yu' go to fool with him, or he'll make you feel unpunctual."

"I expaict I've had them almost all of three thousand miles," said the Virginian, tilting his head toward the noise in the caboose. "And I've strove to deliver them back as I received them. The whole lot. And I would have. But he has spoiled my hopes." The deputy foreman looked again at Dakota. "It's a disappointment," he added. "You may know what I mean."

I had known a little, but not to the very deep, of the man's pride and purpose in this trust. Scipio gave him sympathy. "There must be quite a balance of 'em left with yu' yet," said Scipio, cheeringly.

"I had the boys plumb contented," pursued the deputy foreman, hurt into open talk of himself. "Away along as far as Saynt Paul I had them reconciled to my authority. Then this news about gold had to strike us."

"And they're a-dreamin' nuggets and Parisian bowleyvards," suggested Scipio.

The Virginian smiled gratefully at him.

"Fortune is shinin' bright and blindin' to their delicate young eyes," he said, regaining his usual self.

We all listened a moment to the rejoicings within.

"Energetic, ain't they?" said the Southerner. "But none of 'em was whelped savage enough to sing himself bloodthirsty. And though they're strainin' mighty earnest not to be tame, they're goin' back to Sunk Creek with me accordin' to the Judge's awders. Never a calf of them will desert to Rawhide, for all their dangerousness; nor I ain't goin' to have any fuss over it. Only one is left now that don't sing. Maybe I will have to make some arrangements about him. The man I have parted with," he said, with another glance at Dakota, "was our cook, and I will ask yu' to replace him, Colonel."

Scipio gaped wide. "Colonel! Say!" He stared at the Virginian. "Did I meet yu' at the palace?"

"Not exackly meet," replied the Southerner. "I was present one mawnin' las' month when this gentleman awdehed frawgs' laigs."

"Sakes and saints, but that was a mean position!" burst out Scipio. "I had to tell all comers anything all day. Stand up and jump language hot off my brain at 'em. And the pay don't near compensate for the drain on the system. I don't care how good a man is, you let him keep a-tappin' his presence of mind right along, without takin' a lay-off, and you'll have him sick. Yes, sir. You'll hit his nerves. So I told them they could hire some fresh man, for I was goin' back to punch cattle or fight Indians, or take a rest somehow, for I didn't propose to get jaded, and me only twenty-five years old. There ain't no regular Colonel Cyrus Jones anymore, yu' know. He met a Cheyenne telegraph pole in seventy-four, and was buried. But his palace was doin' big business, and he had been a kind of attraction, and so they always keep a live bear outside, and some poor fello', fixed up like the Colonel used to be, inside. And it's a turruble mean position. Course I'll cook for yu'. Yu've a dandy memory for faces!"

"I wasn't right convinced till I kicked him off and you gave that shut to your eyes again," said the Virginian.

Once more the door opened. A man with slim black eyebrows, slim black mustache, and a black shirt tied with a white handkerchief was looking steadily from one to the other of us.

"Good day!" he remarked generally and without enthusiasm; and to the Virginian, "Where's Schoffner?"

"I expaict he'll have got his bottle by now, Trampas."

Trampas looked from one to the other of us again. "Didn't he say he was coming back?"

"He reminded me he was going for a bottle, and afteh that he didn't wait to say a thing."

Trampas looked at the platform and the railing and the steps. "He told me he was coming back," he insisted.

"I don't reckon he has come, not without he clumb up ahaid somewhere. An' I mus' say, when he got off he didn't look like a man does when he has the intention o' returnin'."

At this Scipio coughed, and pared his nails attentively. We had already been avoiding each other's eye. Shorty did not count. Since he got aboard, his meek seat had been the bottom step.

The thoughts of Trampas seemed to be in difficulty. "How long's this train been started?" he demanded.

"This hyeh train?" The Virginian consulted his watch. "Why, it's been fanning it a right smart little while," said he, laying no stress upon his indolent syllables.

"Huh!" went Trampas. He gave the rest of us a final unlovely scrutiny. "It seems to have become a passenger train," he said. And he returned abruptly inside the caboose.

"Is he the member who don't sing?" asked Scipio.

"That's the specimen," replied the Southerner.

"He don't seem musical in the face," said Scipio.

"Pshaw!" returned the Virginian. "Why, you surely ain't the man to mind ugly mugs when they're hollow!"

The noise inside had dropped quickly to stillness. You could scarcely catch the sound of talk. Our caboose was clicking comfortably westward, rail after rail, mile upon mile, while night was beginning to rise from earth into the clouded sky.

"I wonder if they have sent a search party forward to hunt Schoffner?" said the Virginian. "I think I'll maybe join their meeting." He opened the door upon them. "Kind o' dark hyeh, ain't it?" said he. And lighting the lantern, he shut us out.

"What do yu' think?" said Scipio to me. "Will he take them to Sunk Creek?"

"He evidently thinks he will," said I. "He says he will, and he has the courage of his convictions."

"That ain't near enough courage to have!" Scipio exclaimed. "There's times in life when a man has got to have courage *without* convictions—*without* them—or he is no good. Now your friend is that deep constitooted that you don't know and I don't know what he's thinkin' about all this."

"If there's to be any gunplay," put in the excellent Shorty, "I'll stand in with him."

"Ah, go to bed with your gunplay!" retorted Scipio, entirely good-humored. "Is the Judge paying for a carload of dead punchers to gather his beef for him? And this ain't a proposition worth a man's gettin' hurt for himself, anyway."

"That's so," Shorty assented.

"No," speculated Scipio, as the night drew deeper round us and the caboose click-clucked and click-clucked over the rail joints; "he's waitin' for somebody else to open this pot. I'll bet he don't know but one thing now, and that's that nobody else shall know he don't know anything."

Scipio had delivered himself. He lighted a cigarette, and no more wisdom came from him. The night was established. The rolling badlands sank away in it. A train-hand had arrived over the roof, and hanging the red lights out behind, left us again without remark or symptom of curiosity. The train-hands seemed interested in their own society and lived in their own caboose. A chill wind with wet in it came blowing from the invisible draws, and brought the feel of the distant mountains.

"That's Montana!" said Scipio, snuffing. "I am glad to have it inside my lungs again."

"Ain't yu' getting cool out there?" said the Virginian's voice. "Plenty room inside."

Perhaps he had expected us to follow him; or perhaps he had meant us to delay long enough not to seem like a reenforcement. "These gentlemen missed the express at Medora," he observed to his men, simply.

What they took us for upon our entrance I cannot say, or what they believed. The atmosphere of the caboose was charged with voiceless currents of thought. By way of a friendly beginning to the three hundred miles of caboose we were now to share so intimately, I recalled myself to them. I trusted no more of the Christian Endeavor had delayed them. "I am so lucky to have caught you again," I finished. "I was afraid my last chance of reaching the Judge's had gone."

Thus I said a number of things designed to be agreeable, but they met my small talk with the smallest talk you can have. "Yes," for instance, and "Pretty well, I guess," and grave strikings of matches and thoughtful looks at the floor. I suppose we had made twenty miles to the imperturbable clicking of the caboose when one at length asked his neighbor had he ever seen New York.

"No," said the other. "Flooded with dudes, ain't it?"

"Swimmin'," said the first.

"Leakin', too," said a third.

"Well, my gracious!" said a fourth, and beat his knee in private delight. None of them ever looked at me. For some reason I felt exceedingly ill at ease.

"Good clothes in New York," said the third.

"Rich food," said the first.

"Fresh eggs, too," said the third.

"Well, my gracious!" said the fourth, beating his knee.

"Why, yes," observed the Virginian, unexpectedly; "they tell me that aiggs there ain't liable to be so rotten as yu'll strike 'em in this country."

None of them had a reply for this, and New York was abandoned. For some reason I felt much better.

It was a new line they adopted next, led off by Trampas.

"Going to the excitement?" he inquired, selecting Shorty.

"Excitement?" said Shorty, looking up.

"Going to Rawhide?" Trampas repeated. And all watched Shorty.

"Why, I'm all adrift missin' that express," said Shorty.

"Maybe I can give you employment," suggested the Virginian. "I am taking an outfit across the basin."

"You'll find most folks going to Rawhide, if you're looking for company," pursued Trampas, fishing for a recruit.

"How about Rawhide, anyway?" said Scipio, skillfully deflecting this missionary work. "Are they taking much mineral out? Have yu' seen any of the rock?"

"Rock?" broke in the enthusiast who had beaten his knee. "There!" And he brought some from his pocket.

"You're always showing your rock," said Trampas, sulkily; for Scipio now held the conversation, and Shorty returned safely to his dozing.

"H'm!" went Scipio at the rock. He turned it back and forth in his hand, looking it over; he chucked and caught it slightingly in the air, and handed it back. "Porphyry, I see." That was his only word about it. He said it cheerily.

He left no room for discussion. You could not damn a thing worse. "Ever been in Santa Rita?" pursued Scipio, while the enthusiast slowly pushed his rock back into his pocket. "That's down in New Mexico. Ever been to Globe, Arizona?" And Scipio talked away about the mines he had known. There was no getting at Shorty anymore that evening. Trampas was foiled of his fish, or of learning how the fish's heart lay. And by morning Shorty had been carefully instructed to change his mind about once an hour. This is apt to discourage all but very superior missionaries. And I too escaped for the rest of this night. At Glendive we had a dim supper, and I bought some blankets; and after that it was late, and sleep occupied the attention of us all.

We lay along the shelves of the caboose, a peaceful sight I should think, in that smoothly trundling cradle. I slept almost immediately, so tired that not even our stops or anything else waked me, save once, when the air I was breathing grew suddenly pure, and I roused. Sitting in the door was the lonely figure of the Virginian. He leaned in silent contemplation of the occasional moon, and beneath it the Yellowstone's swift ripples. On the caboose shelves the others slept sound and still, each stretched or coiled as he had first put himself. They were not untrustworthy to look at, it seemed to me—except Trampas. You would have said the rest of that young humanity was average rough male blood, merely needing to be told the proper things at the right time; and one big bunchy stocking of the enthusiast stuck out of his blanket, solemn and innocent, and I laughed at it. There was a light sound by the door, and I found the Virginian's eye on me. Finding who it was, he nodded and motioned with his hand to go to sleep. And this I did with him in my sight, still leaning in the open door, through which came the interrupted moon and the swimming reaches of the Yellowstone.

# CHAPTER XVI

## THE GAME AND THE NATION—LAST ACT

It has happened to you, has it not, to wake in the morning and wonder for a while where on earth you are? Thus I came half to life in the caboose, hearing voices, but not the actual words at first.

But presently, "Hathaway!" said someone more clearly. "Portland 1291!"

This made no special stir in my intelligence, and I drowsed off again to the pleasant rhythm of the wheels. The little shock of stopping next brought me to, somewhat, with the voices still round me; and when we were again in motion, I heard: "Rosebud! Portland 1279!" These figures jarred me awake, and I said, "It was 1291 before," and sat up in my blankets.

The greeting they vouchsafed and the sight of them clustering expressionless in the caboose brought last evening's uncomfortable memory back to me. Our next stop revealed how things were going today.

"Forsythe," one of them read on the station. "Portland 1266."

They were counting the lessening distance westward. This was the undercurrent of war. It broke on me as I procured fresh water at Forsythe and made some toilet in their stolid presence. We were drawing nearer the Rawhide station—the point, I mean, where you left the railway for the new mines. Now Rawhide station lay this side of Billings. The broad path of desertion would open ready for their feet when the narrow path to duty and Sunk Creek was still some fifty miles more to wait. Here was Trampas's great strength; he need make no move meanwhile, but lie low for the immediate temptation to front and waylay them and win his battle over the deputy foreman. But the Virginian seemed to find nothing save enjoyment in this sunny September morning, and ate his breakfast at Forsythe serenely.

That meal done and that station gone, our caboose took up again its easy trundle by the banks of the Yellowstone. The mutineers sat for a while digesting in idleness.

"What's your scar?" inquired one at length inspecting casually the neck of his neighbor.

"Foolishness," the other answered.

"Yourn?"

"Mine."

"Well, I don't know but I prefer to have myself to thank for a thing," said the first.

"I was displaying myself," continued the second. "One day last summer it was. We come on a big snake by Torrey Creek corral. The boys got betting pretty lively that I dassent make my word good as to dealing with him, so I loped my cayuse full tilt by Mr. Snake, and swung down and catched him up by the tail from the ground, and cracked him same as a whip, and snapped his head off. You've saw it done?" he said to the audience.

The audience nodded wearily.

"But the loose head flew agin me, and the fangs caught. I was pretty sick for a while."

"It don't pay to be clumsy," said the first man. "If you'd snapped the snake away from yu' instead of toward yu', its head would have whirled off into the brush, same as they do with me."

"How like a knife-cut your scar looks!" said I.

"Don't it?" said the snake-snapper. "There's many that gets fooled by it."

"An antelope knows a snake is his enemy," said another to me. "Ever seen a buck circling round and round a rattler?"

"I have always wanted to see that," said I, heartily. For this I knew to be a respectable piece of truth.

"It's worth seeing," the man went on. "After the buck gets close in, he gives an almighty jump up in the air, and down comes his four hoofs in a bunch right on top of Mr. Snake. Cuts him all to hash. Now you tell me how the buck knows that."

Of course I could not tell him. And again we sat in silence for a while—friendlier silence, I thought.

"A skunk'll kill yu' worse than a snake bite," said another, presently. "No, I don't mean that way," he added. For I had smiled. "There is a brown skunk down in Arkansaw. Kind of prairie-dog brown. Littler than our variety, he is. And he is mad the whole year round, same as a dog gets. Only the dog has a spell and dies but this here Arkansaw skunk is mad right along, and it don't seem to interfere with his business in other respects. Well, suppose you're camping out, and suppose it's a hot night, or you're in a hurry, and you've made camp late, or anyway you haven't got inside any tent, but you have just bedded down in the open. Skunk comes traveling along and walks on your blankets. You're warm. He likes that, same as a cat does. And he tramps with pleasure and comfort, same as a cat. And you move. You get bit, that's all. And you die of hydrophobia. Ask anybody."

"Most extraordinary!" said I. "But did you ever see a person die from this?"

"No, sir. Never happened to. My cousin at Bald Knob did."

"Died?"

"No, sir. Saw a man."

"But how do you know they're not sick skunks?"

"No, sir! They're well skunks. Well as anything. You'll not meet skunks in any state of the Union more robust than them in Arkansaw. And thick."

"That's awful true," sighed another. "I have buried hundreds of dollars' worth of clothes in Arkansaw."

"Why didn't yu' travel in a sponge bag?" inquired Scipio. And this brought a slight silence.

"Speakin' of bites," spoke up a new man, "how's that?" He held up his thumb.

"My!" breathed Scipio. "Must have been a lion."

The man wore a wounded look. "I was huntin' owl eggs for a botanist from Boston," he explained to me.

"Chiropodist, weren't he?" said Scipio. "Or maybe a sonnabulator?"

"No, honest," protested the man with the thumb; so that I was sorry for him, and begged him to go on.

"I'll listen to you," I assured him. And I wondered why this politeness of mine should throw one or two of them into stifled mirth. Scipio, on the other hand, gave me a disgusted look and sat back sullenly for a moment, and then took himself out on the platform, where the Virginian was lounging.

"The young feller wore knee-pants and ever so thick spectacles with a half-moon cut in 'em," resumed the narrator, "and he carried a tin box strung to a strap I took for his lunch till it flew open on him and a horn toad hustled out. Then I was sure he was a botanist—or whatever yu' say they're called. Well, he would have owl eggs—them little prairie-owl that some claim can turn their head clean around and keep a-watchin' yu', only that's nonsense. We was ridin' through that prairie-dog town, used to be on the flat just after yu' crossed the south fork of Powder River on the Buffalo trail, and I said I'd dig an owl nest out for him if he was willing to camp till I'd dug it. I wanted to know about them owls some myself—if they did live with the dogs and snakes, yu' know," he broke off, appealing to me.

"Oh, yes," I told him eagerly.

"So while the botanist went glarin' around the town with his glasses to see if he could spot a prairie-dog and an owl usin' the same hole, I was diggin' in a hole I'd seen an owl run down. And that's what I got." He held up his thumb again.

"The snake!" I exclaimed.

"Yes, sir. Mr. Rattler was keepin' house that day. Took me right there. I hauled him out of the hole hangin' to me. Eight rattles."

"Eight!" said I. "A big one."

"Yes, sir. Thought I was dead. But the woman—"

"The woman?" said I.

"Yes, woman. Didn't I tell yu' the botanist had his wife along? Well, he did. And she acted better than the man, for he was losin' his head, and shoutin' he had no whiskey, and he didn't guess his knife was sharp enough to amputate my thumb, and none of us chewed, and the doctor was twenty miles away, and if he had only remembered to bring his ammonia—well, he was screeching out 'most everything he knew in the world, and without arranging it any, neither. But she just clawed his pocket and burrowed and kep' yelling, 'Give him the stone, Augustus!' And she whipped out one of them Injun medicine-stones—first one I ever seen—and she clapped it on to my thumb, and it started in right away."

"What did it do?" said I.

"Sucked. Like blotting-paper does. Soft and funny it was, and gray. They get 'em from elks' stomachs, yu' know. And when it had sucked the poison out of the wound, off it falls of my thumb by itself! And I thanked the woman for saving my life that capable and keeping her head that cool. I never knowed how excited she had been till afterward. She was awful shocked."

"I suppose she started to talk when the danger was over," said I, with deep silence around me.

"No; she didn't say nothing to me. But when her next child was born, it had eight rattles."

Din now rose wild in the caboose. They rocked together. The enthusiast beat his knee tumultuously. And I joined them. Who could help it? It had been so well conducted from the imperceptible beginning. Fact and falsehood blended with such perfect art. And this last, an effect so new made with such world-old material! I cared nothing that I was the victim, and I joined them; but ceased, feeling suddenly somehow estranged or chilled. It was in their laughter. The loudness was too loud. And I caught the eyes of Trampas fixed upon the Virginian with exultant malevolence. Scipio's disgusted glance was upon me from the door.

Dazed by these signs, I went out on the platform to get away from the noise. There the Virginian said to me: "Cheer up! You'll not be so easy for 'em that-a-way next season."

He said no more; and with his legs dangled over the railing, appeared to resume his newspaper.

"What's the matter?" said I to Scipio.

"Oh, I don't mind if he don't," Scipio answered. "Couldn't yu' see? I tried to head 'em off from yu' all I knew, but yu' just ran in among 'em yourself. Couldn't yu' see? Kep' hinderin' and spoilin' me with askin' those urgent questions of yourn—why, I had to let yu' go your way! Why, that wasn't the ordinary play with the ordinary tenderfoot they treated you to! You ain't a common tenderfoot this trip. You're the foreman's friend. They've hit him through you. That's the way they count it. It's made them encouraged. Can't yu' see?"

Scipio stated it plainly. And as we ran by the next station, "Howard!" they harshly yelled. "Portland 1256!"

We had been passing gangs of workmen on the track. And at that last yell the Virginian rose. "I reckon I'll join the meeting again," he said. "This filling and repairing looks like the washout might have been true."

"Washout?" said Scipio.

"Big Horn bridge, they say—four days ago."

"Then I wish it came this side Rawhide station."

"Do yu'?" drawled the Virginian. And smiling at Scipio, he lounged in through the open door.

"He beats me," said Scipio, shaking his head. "His trail is turrible hard to anticipate."

We listened.

"Work bein' done on the road, I see," the Virginian was saying, very friendly and conversational.

"We see it too," said the voice of Trampas.

"Seem to be easin' their grades some."

"Roads do."

"Cheaper to build 'em the way they want 'em at the start, a man would think," suggested the Virginian, most friendly. "There go some more I-talians."

"They're Chinese," said Trampas.

"That's so," acknowledged the Virginian, with a laugh.

"What's he monkeyin' at now?" muttered Scipio.

"Without cheap foreigners they couldn't afford all this hyeh new gradin'," the Southerner continued.

"Grading! Can't you tell when a flood's been eating the banks?"

"Why, yes," said the Virginian, sweet as honey. "But 'ain't yu' heard of the improvements west of Big Timber, all the way to Missoula, this season? I'm talkin' about them."

"Oh! Talking about them. Yes, I've heard."

"Good money-savin' scheme, ain't it?" said the Virginian. "Lettin' a freight run down one hill an' up the next as far as she'll go without steam, an' shavin' the hill down to that point." Now this was an honest engineering fact. "Better'n settin' dudes squintin' through telescopes and cypherin' over one percent reductions," the Southerner commented.

"It's common sense," assented Trampas. "Have you heard the new scheme about the water-tanks?"

"I ain't right certain," said the Southerner.

"I must watch this," said Scipio, "or I shall bust." He went in, and so did I.

They were all sitting over this discussion of the Northern Pacific's recent policy as to betterments, as though they were the board of directors. Pins could have dropped. Only nobody would have cared to hear a pin.

"They used to put all their tanks at the bottom of their grades," said Trampas.

"Why, yu' get the water easier at the bottom."

"You can pump it to the top, though," said Trampas, growing superior. "And it's cheaper."

"That gets me," said the Virginian, interested.

"Trains after watering can start down hill now and get the benefit of the gravity. It'll cut down operating expenses a heap."

"That's cert'nly common sense!" exclaimed the Virginian, absorbed. "But ain't it kind o' tardy?"

"Live and learn. So they gained speed, too. High speed on half the coal this season, until the accident."

"Accident!" said the Virginian, instantly.

"Yellowstone Limited. Man fired at engine driver. Train was flying past that quick the bullet broke every window and killed a passenger on the back platform. You've been running too much with aristocrats," finished Trampas, and turned on his heel.

"Haw, hew!" began the enthusiast, but his neighbor gripped him to silence. This was a triumph too serious for noise. Not a mutineer moved; and I felt cold.

"Trampas," said the Virginian, "I thought yu'd be afeared to try it on me."

Trampas whirled round. His hand was at his belt. "Afraid!" he sneered.

"Shorty!" said Scipio, sternly, and leaping upon that youth, took his half-drawn pistol from him.

"I'm obliged to yu'," said the Virginian to Scipio. Trampas's hand left his belt. He threw a slight, easy look at his men, and keeping his back to the Virginian, walked out on the platform and sat on the chair where the Virginian had sat so much.

"Don't you comprehend," said the Virginian to Shorty, amiably, "that this hyeh question has been discussed peaceable by civilized citizens? Now you sit down and be good, and Mr. Le Moyne will return your gun when we're across that broken bridge, if they have got it fixed for heavy trains yet."

"This train will be lighter when it gets to that bridge," spoke Trampas, out on his chair.

"Why, that's true, too!" said the Virginian. "Maybe none of us are crossin' that Big Horn bridge now, except me. Funny if yu' should end by persuadin' me to quit and go to Rawhide myself! But I reckon I'll not. I reckon I'll worry along to Sunk Creek, somehow."

"Don't forget I'm cookin' for yu'," said Scipio, gruffy.

"I'm obliged to yu'," said the Southerner.

"You were speaking of a job for me," said Shorty.

"I'm right obliged. But yu' see—I ain't exackly foreman the way this comes out, and my promises might not bind Judge Henry to pay salaries."

A push came through the train from forward. We were slowing for the Rawhide station, and all began to be busy and to talk. "Going up to the mines today?" "Oh, let's grub first." "Guess it's too late, anyway."

And so forth; while they rolled and roped their bedding, and put on their coats with a good deal of elbow motion, and otherwise showed off. It was wasted. The Virginian did not know what was going on in the caboose. He was leaning and looking out ahead, and Scipio's puzzled eye never left him. And as we halted for the water-tank, the Southerner exclaimed, "They 'ain't got away yet!" as if it were good news to him.

He meant the delayed trains. Four stalled expresses were in front of us, besides several freights. And two hours more at least before the bridge would be ready.

Travelers stood and sat about forlorn, near the cars, out in the sagebrush, anywhere. People in hats and spurs watched them, and Indian chiefs offered them painted bows and arrows and shiny horns.

"I reckon them passengers would prefer a laig o' mutton," said the Virginian to a man loafing near the caboose.

"Bet your life!" said the man. "First lot has been stuck here four days."

"Plumb starved, ain't they?" inquired the Virginian.

"Bet your life! They've eat up their dining cars and they've eat up this town."

"Well," said the Virginian, looking at the town, "I expaict the dining-cyars contained more nourishment."

"Say, you're about right there!" said the man. He walked beside the caboose as we puffed slowly forward from the water-tank to our siding. "Fine business here if we'd only been ready," he continued. "And the Crow agent has let his Indians come over from the reservation. There has been a little beef brought in, and game, and fish. And big money in it, bet your life! Them Eastern passengers has just been robbed. I wisht I had somethin' to sell!"

"Anything starting for Rawhide this afternoon?" said Trampas, out of the caboose door.

"Not until morning," said the man. "You going to the mines?" he resumed to the Virginian.

"Why," answered the Southerner, slowly and casually, and addressing himself strictly to the man, while Trampas, on his side, paid obvious inattention, "this hyeh delay, yu' see, may unsettle our plans some. But it'll be one of two ways—we're all goin' to Rawhide, or we're all goin' to Billings. We're all one party, yu' see."

Trampas laughed audibly inside the door as he rejoined his men. "Let him keep up appearances," I heard him tell them. "It don't hurt us what he says to strangers."

"But I'm goin' to eat hearty either way," continued the Virginian. "And I ain' goin' to be robbed. I've been kind o' promisin' myself a treat if we stopped hyeh."

"Town's eat clean out," said the man.

"So yu' tell me. But all you folks has forgot one source of revenue that yu' have right close by, mighty handy. If you have got a gunny sack, I'll show you how to make some money."

"Bet your life!" said the man.

"Mr. Le Moyne," said the Virginian, "the outfit's cookin' stuff is aboard, and if you'll get the fire ready, we'll try how frawgs' laigs go fried." He walked off at once, the man following like a dog. Inside the caboose rose a gust of laughter.

"Frogs!" muttered Scipio. And then turning a blank face to me, "Frogs?"

"Colonel Cyrus Jones had them on his bill of fare," I said. "'*Frogs' Legs à la Delmonico.*'"

"Shoo! I didn't get up that thing. They had it when I came. Never looked at it. Frogs?" He went down the steps very slowly, with a long frown. Reaching the ground, he shook his head. "That man's trail is surely hard to anticipate," he said. "But I must hurry up that fire. For his appearance has given me encouragement," Scipio concluded, and became brisk. Shorty helped him, and I brought wood. Trampas and the other people strolled off to the station, a compact band.

Our little fire was built beside the caboose, so the cooking things might be easily reached and put back. You would scarcely think such operations held any interest, even for the hungry, when there seemed to be nothing to cook. A few sticks blazing tamely in the dust, a frying-pan, half a tin bucket of lard, some water, and barren plates and knives and forks, and three silent men attending to them—that was all. But the travelers came to see. These waifs drew near us, and stood, a sad, lone, shifting fringe of audience; four to begin with; and then two wandered away; and presently one of these came back, finding it worse elsewhere. "Supper, boys?" said he. "Breakfast," said Scipio, crossly. And no more of them addressed us. I heard them joylessly mention Wall Street to each other, and Saratoga; I even heard the name Bryn Mawr, which is near Philadelphia. But these fragments of home dropped in the wilderness here in Montana beside a freight caboose were of no interest to me now.

"Looks like frogs down there, too," said Scipio. "See them marshy sloos full of weeds?" We took a little turn and had a sight of the Virginian quite active among the ponds. "Hush! I'm getting some thoughts," continued Scipio. "He wasn't sorry enough. Don't interrupt me."

"I'm not," said I.

"No. But I'd 'most caught a-hold." And Scipio muttered to himself again, "He wasn't sorry enough." Presently he swore loud and brilliantly. "Tell yu'!" he cried. "What did he say to Trampas after that play they exchanged over railroad improvements and Trampas put the josh on him? Didn't he say, 'Trampas, I thought you'd be afraid to do it?' Well, sir, Trampas had better have been afraid. And that's what he meant. There's where he was bringin' it to. Trampas made an awful bad play then. You wait. Glory, but he's a knowin' man! Course he wasn't sorry. I guess he had the hardest kind of work to look as sorry as he did. You wait."

"Wait? What for? Go on, man! What for?"

"I don't know! I don't know! Whatever hand he's been holdin' up, this is the showdown. He's played for a showdown here before the caboose gets off the bridge. Come back to the fire, or Shorty'll be leavin' it go out. Grow happy some, Shorty!" he cried on arriving, and his hand cracked on Shorty's shoulder. "Supper's in sight, Shorty. Food for reflection."

"None for the stomach?" asked the passenger who had spoken once before.

"We're figuring on that too," said Scipio. His crossness had melted entirely away.

"Why, they're cowboys!" exclaimed another passenger; and he moved nearer.

From the station Trampas now came back, his herd following him less compactly. They had found famine, and no hope of supplies until the next train from the East. This was no fault of Trampas's; but they were following him less compactly. They carried one piece of cheese, the size of a fist, the weight of a brick, the hue of a corpse. And the passengers, seeing it, exclaimed, "There's Old Faithful again!" and took off their hats.

"You gentlemen met that cheese before, then?" said Scipio, delighted.

"It's been offered me three times a day for four days," said the passenger. "Did he want a dollar or a dollar and a half?"

"Two dollars!" blurted out the enthusiast. And all of us save Trampas fell into fits of imbecile laughter.

"Here comes our grub, anyway," said Scipio, looking off toward the marshes. And his hilarity sobered away in a moment.

"Well, the train will be in soon," stated Trampas. "I guess we'll get a decent supper without frogs."

All interest settled now upon the Virginian. He was coming with his man and his gunny sack, and the gunny sack hung from his shoulder heavily, as a full sack should. He took no notice of the gathering, but sat down and partly emptied the sack. "There," said he, very businesslike, to his assistant, "that's all we'll want. I think you'll find a ready market for the balance."

"Well, my gracious!" said the enthusiast. "What fool eats a frog?"

"Oh, I'm fool enough for a tadpole!" cried the passenger. And they began to take out their pocketbooks.

"You can cook yours right hyeh, gentlemen," said the Virginian, with his slow Southern courtesy. "The dining-cyars don't look like they were fired up."

"How much will you sell a couple for?" inquired the enthusiast.

The Virginian looked at him with friendly surprise. "Why, help yourself! We're all together yet awhile. Help yourselves," he repeated, to Trampas and his followers. These hung back a moment, then, with a slinking motion, set the cheese upon the earth and came forward nearer the fire to receive some supper.

"It won't scarcely be Delmonico style," said the Virginian to the passengers, "nor yet Saynt Augustine." He meant the great Augustin, the traditional chef of Philadelphia, whose history I had sketched for him at Colonel Cyrus Jones's eating palace.

Scipio now officiated. His frying-pan was busy, and prosperous odors rose from it.

"Run for a bucket of fresh water, Shorty," the Virginian continued, beginning his meal. "Colonel, yu' cook pretty near good. If yu' had sold 'em as advertised, yu'd have cert'nly made a name."

Several were now eating with satisfaction, but not Scipio. It was all that he could do to cook straight. The whole man seemed to glisten. His eye was shut to a slit once more, while the innocent passengers thankfully swallowed.

"Now, you see, you have made some money," began the Virginian to the native who had helped him get the frogs.

"Bet your life!" exclaimed the man. "Divvy, won't you?" And he held out half his gains.

"Keep 'em," returned the Southerner. "I reckon we're square. But I expaict they'll not equal Delmonico's, seh?" he said to a passenger.

"Don't trust the judgment of a man as hungry as I am!" exclaimed the traveler, with a laugh. And he turned to his fellow-travelers. "Did you ever enjoy supper at Delmonico's more than this?"

"Never!" they sighed.

"Why, look here," said the traveler, "what fools the people of this town are! Here we've been all these starving days, and you come and get ahead of them!"

"That's right easy explained," said the Virginian. "I've been where there was big money in frawgs, and they 'ain't been. They're all cattle hyeh. Talk cattle, think cattle, and they're bankrupt in consequence. Fallen through. Ain't that so?" he inquired of the native.

"That's about the way," said the man.

"It's mighty hard to do what your neighbors ain't doin'," pursued the Virginian. "Montana is all cattle, an' these folks must be cattle, an' never notice the country right hyeh is too small for a range, an' swampy, anyway, an' just waitin' to be a frawg ranch."

At this, all wore a face of careful reserve.

"I'm not claimin' to be smarter than you folks hyeh," said the Virginian, deprecatingly, to his assistant. "But travelin' learns a man many customs. You wouldn't do the business they done at Tulare, California, north side o' the lake. They cert'nly utilized them hopeless swamps splendid. Of course they put up big capital and went into it scientific, gettin' advice from the government Fish Commission, an' such like knowledge. Yu' see, they had big markets for their frawgs—San Francisco, Los Angeles, and clear to New York afteh the Southern Pacific was through. But up hyeh yu' could sell to passengers every day like yu' done this one day. They would get to know yu' along the line. Competing swamps are scarce. The dining-cyars would take your frawgs, and yu' would have the Yellowstone Park for four months in the year. Them hotels are anxious to please, an' they would buy off yu' what their Eastern patrons esteem as fine-eatin'. And you folks would be sellin' something instead o' nothin'."

"That's a practical idea," said a traveler. "And little cost."

"And little cost," said the Virginian.

"Would Eastern people eat frogs?" inquired the man.

"Look at us!" said the traveler.

"Delmonico doesn't give yu' such a treat!" said the Virginian.

"Not exactly!" the traveler exclaimed.

"How much would be paid for frogs?" said Trampas to him. And I saw Scipio bend closer to his cooking.

"Oh, I don't know," said the traveler. "We've paid pretty well, you see."

"You're late for Tulare, Trampas," said the Virginian.

"I was not thinking of Tulare," Trampas retorted. Scipio's nose was in the frying-pan.

"Mos' comical spot you ever struck!" said the Virginian, looking round upon the whole company. He allowed himself a broad smile of retrospect. "To hear 'em talk frawgs at Tulare! Same as other folks talks hawsses or steers or whatever they're raising to sell. Yu'd fall into it yourselves if yu' started the business. Anything a man's bread and butter depends on, he's going to be earnest about. Don't care if it is a frawg."

"That's so," said the native. "And it paid good?"

"The only money in the county was right there," answered the Virginian. "It was a dead county, and only frawgs was movin'. But that business was a-fannin' to beat four of a kind. It made yu' feel strange at first, as I said. For all the men had been cattlemen at one time or another. Till yu' got accustomed, it would give 'most anybody a shock to hear 'em speak about herdin' the bulls in a pasture by themselves." The Virginian allowed himself another smile, but became serious again. "That was their policy," he explained. "Except at certain times o' year they kept the bulls separate. The Fish Commission told 'em they'd better, and it cert'nly worked mighty well. It or something did— for, gentlemen, hush! But there was millions. You'd have said all the frawgs in the world had taken charge at Tulare. And the money rolled in! Gentlemen, hush! 'Twas a gold mine for the owners. Forty percent they netted some years. And they paid generous wages. For they could sell to all them French restaurants in San Francisco, yu' see. And there was the Cliff House. And the Palace Hotel made it a specialty. And the officers took frawgs at the Presidio, an' Angel Island, an' Alcatraz, an' Benicia. Los Angeles was beginnin' its boom. The corner-lot sharps wanted something by way of varnish. An' so they dazzled Eastern investors with advertisin' Tulare frawgs clear to New Orleans an' New York. 'Twas only in Sacramento frawgs was dull. I expaict the California legislature was too or'n'ry for them fine-raised luxuries. They tell of one of them senators that he raked a million out of Los Angeles real estate, and started in for a bang-up meal with champagne. Wanted to scatter his new gold thick an' quick. But he got astray among all the fancy dishes, an' just yelled right out before the ladies, 'Damn it! bring me forty dollars' worth of ham and aiggs.' He was a funny senator, now."

The Virginian paused, and finished eating a leg. And then with diabolic art he made a feint at wandering to new fields of anecdote. "Talkin' of senators," he resumed, "Senator Wise—"

"How much did you say wages were at Tulare?" inquired one of the Trampas faction.

"How much? Why, I never knew what the foreman got. The regular hands got a hundred. Senator Wise—"

"A hundred a *month?*"

"Why, it was wet an' muddy work, yu' see. A man risked rheumatism some. He risked it a good deal. Well, I was going to tell about Senator Wise. When Senator Wise was speaking of his visit to Alaska—"

"Forty percent, was it?" said Trampas.

"Oh, I must call my wife," said the traveler behind me. "This is what I came West for." And he hurried away.

"Not forty percent the bad years," replied the Virginian. "The frawgs had enemies, same as cattle. I remember when a pelican got in the spring pasture, and the herd broke through the fence—"

"Fence?" said a passenger.

"Ditch, seh, and wire net. Every pasture was a square swamp with a ditch around, and a wire net. Yu've heard the mournful, mixed-up sound a big bunch of cattle will make? Well, seh, as yu' druv from the railroad to the Tulare frawg ranch yu' could hear 'em a mile. Springtime they'd sing like girls in the organ loft, and by August they were about ready to hire out for bass. And all was fit to be soloists, if I'm a judge. But in a bad year it might only be twenty percent. The pelican rushed 'em from the pasture right into the San Joaquin River, which was close by the property. The big balance of the herd stampeded, and though of course they came out on the banks again, the news had went around, and folks below at Hemlen eat most of 'em just to spite the company. Yu' see, a frawg in a river is more hopeless than any maverick loose on the range. And they never struck any plan to brand their stock and prove ownership."

"Well, twenty percent is good enough for me," said Trampas, "if Rawhide don't suit me."

"A hundred a month!" said the enthusiast. And busy calculations began to arise among them.

"It went to fifty percent," pursued the Virginian, "when New York and

Philadelphia got to biddin' agaynst each other. Both cities had signs all over
'em claiming to furnish the Tulare frawg. And both had 'em all right. And
same as cattle trains, yu'd see frawg trains tearing acrosst Arizona—big glass
tanks with wire over 'em—through to New York, an' the frawgs starin' out."

"Why, George," whispered a woman's voice behind me, "he's merely
deceiving them! He's merely making that stuff up out of his head."

"Yes, my dear, that's merely what he's doing."

"Well, I don't see why you imagined I should care for this. I think I'll go
back."

"Better see it out, Daisy. This beats the geysers or anything we're likely to
find in the Yellowstone."

"Then I wish we had gone to Bar Harbor as usual," said the lady, and she
returned to her Pullman.

But her husband stayed. Indeed, the male crowd now was a goodly sight to
see, how the men edged close, drawn by a common tie. Their different kinds
of feet told the strength of the bond—yellow sleeping-car slippers planted
miscellaneous and motionless near a pair of Mexican spurs. All eyes watched
the Virginian and gave him their entire sympathy. Though they could not
know his motive for it, what he was doing had fallen as light upon them—all
except the excited calculators. These were loudly making their fortunes at
both Rawhide and Tulare, drugged by their satanically aroused hopes of gold,
heedless of the slippers and the spurs. Had a man given any sign to warn
them, I think he would have been lynched. Even the Indian chiefs had come
to see in their show war bonnets and blankets. They naturally understood
nothing of it, yet magnetically knew that the Virginian was the great man.
And they watched him with approval. He sat by the fire with the frying-
pan, looking his daily self—engaging and saturnine. And now as Trampas
declared tickets to California would be dear and Rawhide had better come
first, the Southerner let loose his heaven-born imagination.

"There's a better reason for Rawhide than tickets, Trampas," said he. "I
said it was too late for Tulare."

"I heard you," said Trampas. "Opinions may differ. You and I don't think
alike on several points."

"Gawd, Trampas!" said the Virginian, "D' yu' reckon I'd be rotting hyeh on
forty dollars if Tulare was like it used to be? Tulare is broke."

"What broke it? Your leaving?"

"Revenge broke it, and disease," said the Virginian, striking the frying-pan
on his knee, for the frogs were all gone. At those lurid words their untamed
child minds took fire, and they drew round him again to hear a tale of blood.
The crowd seemed to lean nearer.

But for a short moment it threatened to be spoiled. A passenger came along, demanding in an important voice, "Where are these frogs?" He was a prominent New York after-dinner speaker, they whispered me, and out for a holiday in his private car. Reaching us and walking to the Virginian, he said cheerily, "How much do you want for your frogs, my friend?"

"You got a friend hyeh?" said the Virginian. "That's good, for yu' need care taken of yu'." And the prominent after-dinner speaker did not further discommode us.

"That's worth my trip," whispered a New York passenger to me.

"Yes, it was a case of revenge," resumed the Virginian, "and disease. There was a man named Saynt Augustine got run out of Domingo, which is a Dago island. He come to Philadelphia, an' he was dead broke. But Saynt Augustine was a live man, an' he saw Philadelphia was full o' Quakers that dressed plain an' eat humdrum. So he started cookin' Domingo way for 'em, an' they caught right ahold. Terrapin, he gave 'em, an' croakeets, an' he'd use forty chickens to make a broth he called consommay. An' he got rich, and Philadelphia got well known, an' Delmonico in New York he got jealous. He was the cook that had the say-so in New York."

"Was Delmonico one of them I-talians?" inquired a fascinated mutineer.

"I don't know. But he acted like one. Lorenzo was his front name. He aimed to cut—"

"Domingo's throat?" breathed the enthusiast.

"Aimed to cut away the trade from Saynt Augustine an' put Philadelphia back where he thought she belonged. Frawgs was the fashionable rage then. These foreign cooks set the fashion in eatin', same as foreign dressmakers do women's clothes. Both cities was catchin' and swallowin' all the frawgs Tulare could throw at 'em. So he—"

"Lorenzo?" said the enthusiast.

"Yes, Lorenzo Delmonico. He bid a dollar a tank higher. An' Saynt Augustine raised him fifty cents. An' Lorenzo raised him a dollar. An' Saynt Augustine shoved her up three. Lorenzo he didn't expect Philadelphia would go that high, and he got hot in the collar, an' flew round his kitchen in New York, an' claimed he'd twist Saynt Augustine's Domingo tail for him and crack his ossified system. Lorenzo raised his language to a high temperature, they say. An' then quite sudden off he starts for Tulare. He buys tickets over the Santa Fe, and he goes a-fannin' and a-foggin'. But, gentlemen, hush! The very same day Saynt Augustine he tears out of Philadelphia. He traveled by the way o' Washington, an' out he comes a-fannin' an' a-foggin' over the Southern Pacific. Of course Tulare didn't know nothin' of this. All it knowed was how the frawg market was on soarin' wings, and it was feelin' like a flight o' rawckets. If only there'd been some preparation—a telegram or something—the disaster would never have occurred. But Lorenzo and Saynt Augustine was that absorbed watchin' each other—for, yu' see, the Santa Fe and the Southern Pacific come together at Mojave, an' the two cooks traveled a matter of two hundred an' ten miles in the same cyar—they never thought about a telegram. And when they arruv, breathless, an' started in to screechin' what they'd give for the monopoly, why, them unsuspectin' Tulare boys got amused at 'em. I never heard just all they done, but they had Lorenzo singin' and dancin', while Saynt Augustine played the fiddle for him. And one of Lorenzo's heels did get a trifle grazed. Well, them two cooks quit that ranch without disclosin' their identity, and soon as they got to a safe distance they swore eternal friendship, in their excitable foreign way. And they went home over the Union Pacific, sharing the same stateroom. Their revenge killed frawgs. The disease—"

"How killed frogs?" demanded Trampas.

"Just killed 'em. Delmonico and Saynt Augustine wiped frawgs off the slate of fashion. Not a banker in Fifth Avenue'll touch one now if another banker's around watchin' him. And if ever yu' see a man that hides his feet an' won't take off his socks in company, he has worked in them Tulare swamps an' got the disease. Catch him wadin', and yu'll find he's web-footed. Frawgs are dead, Trampas, and so are you."

"Rise up, liars, and salute your king!" yelled Scipio. "Oh, I'm in love with you!" And he threw his arms round the Virginian.

"Let me shake hands with you," said the traveler, who had failed to interest his wife in these things. "I wish I was going to have more of your company."

"Thank ye', seh," said the Virginian.

Other passengers greeted him, and the Indian chiefs came, saying, "How!" because they followed their feelings without understanding.

"Don't show so humbled, boys," said the deputy foreman to his most sheepish crew. "These gentlemen from the East have been enjoying yu' some, I know. But think what a weary wait they have had hyeh. And you insisted on playing the game with me this way, yu' see. What outlet did yu' give me? Didn't I have it to do? And I'll tell yu' one thing for your consolation: when I got to the middle of the frawgs I 'most believed it myself." And he laughed out the first laugh I had heard him give.

The enthusiast came up and shook hands. That led off, and the rest followed, with Trampas at the end. The tide was too strong for him. He was not a graceful loser; but he got through this, and the Virginian eased him down by treating him precisely like the others—apparently. Possibly the supreme—the most American—moment of all was when word came that the bridge was open, and the Pullman trains, with noise and triumph, began to move westward at last. Everyone waved farewell to everyone, craning from steps and windows, so that the cars twinkled with hilarity; and in twenty minutes the whole procession in front had moved, and our turn came.

"Last chance for Rawhide," said the Virginian.

"Last chance for Sunk Creek," said a reconstructed mutineer, and all sprang aboard. There was no question who had won his spurs now.

Our caboose trundled on to Billings along the shingly cotton-wooded Yellowstone; and as the plains and bluffs and the distant snow began to grow well known, even to me, we turned to our baggage that was to come off, since camp would begin in the morning. Thus I saw the Virginian carefully rewrapping Kenilworth, that he might bring it to its owner unharmed; and I said, "Don't you think you could have played poker with Queen Elizabeth?"

"No; I expaict she'd have beat me," he replied. "She was a lady."

It was at Billings, on this day, that I made those reflections about equality. For the Virginian had been equal to the occasion: that is the only kind of equality which I recognize.

# CHAPTER XVII

## SCIPIO MORALIZES

Into what mood was it that the Virginian now fell? Being less busy, did he begin to "grieve" about the girl on Bear Creek? I only know that after talking so lengthily he fell into a nine days' silence. The talking part of him deeply and unbrokenly slept.

Official words of course came from him as we rode southward from the railroad, gathering the Judge's stray cattle. During the many weeks since the spring round-up, some of these animals had as usual got very far off their range, and getting them on again became the present business of our party.

Directions and commands—whatever communications to his subordinates were needful to the forwarding of this—he duly gave. But routine has never at any time of the world passed for conversation. His utterances, such as, "We'll work Willo' Creek tomorro' mawnin'," or, "I want the wagon to be at the fawks o' Stinkin' Water by Thursday," though on some occasions numerous enough to sound like discourse, never once broke the man's true silence. Seeming to keep easy company with the camp, he yet kept altogether to himself. That talking part of him—the mood which brings out for you your friend's spirit and mind as a free gift or as an exchange—was down in some dark cave of his nature, hidden away. Perhaps it had been dreaming; perhaps completely reposing. The Virginian was one of those rare ones who are able to refresh themselves in sections. To have a thing on his mind did not keep his body from resting. During our recent journey—it felt years ago now!—while our caboose on the freight train had trundled endlessly westward, and the men were on the ragged edge, the very jumping-off place, of mutiny and possible murder, I had seen him sleep like a child. He snatched the moments not necessary for vigil. I had also seen him sit all night watching his responsibility, ready to spring on it and fasten his teeth in it. And now that he had confounded them with their own attempted weapon of ridicule, his powers seemed to be profoundly dormant. That final pitched battle of wits had made the men his captives and admirers—all save Trampas. And of him the Virginian did not seem to be aware.

But Scipio le Moyne would say to me now and then, "If I was Trampas, I'd pull my freight." And once he added, "Pull it kind of casual, yu' know, like I wasn't noticing myself do it."

"Yes," our friend Shorty murmured pregnantly, with his eye upon the quiet Virginian, "he's sure studying his revenge."

"Studying your pussy-cat," said Scipio. "He knows what he'll do. The time ain't arrived." This was the way they felt about it; and not unnaturally this was the way they made me, the inexperienced Easterner, feel about it. That Trampas also felt something about it was easy to know. Like the leaven which leavens the whole lump, one spot of sulkiness in camp will spread its dull flavor through any company that sits near it; and we had to sit near Trampas at meals for nine days.

His sullenness was not wonderful. To feel himself forsaken by his recent adherents, to see them gone over to his enemy, could not have made his reflections pleasant. Why he did not take himself off to other climes—"pull his freight casual," as Scipio said—I can explain only thus: pay was due him— "time," as it was called in cow-land; if he would have this money, he must stay under the Virginian's command until the Judge's ranch on Sunk Creek should be reached; meanwhile, each day's work added to the wages in store for him; and finally, once at Sunk Creek, it would be no more the Virginian who commanded him; it would be the real ranch foreman. At the ranch he would be the Virginian's equal again, both of them taking orders from their officially recognized superior, this foreman. Shorty's word about "revenge" seemed to me like putting the thing backwards. Revenge, as I told Scipio, was what I should be thinking about if I were Trampas.

"He dassent," was Scipio's immediate view. "Not till he's got strong again. He got laughed plumb sick by the bystanders, and whatever spirit he had was broke in the presence of us all. He'll have to recuperate."

Scipio then spoke of the Virginian's attitude. "Maybe revenge ain't just the right word for where this affair has got to now with him. When yu' beat another man at his own game like he done to Trampas, why, yu've had all the revenge yu' can want, unless you're a hog. And he's no hog. But he has got it in for Trampas. They've not reckoned to a finish. Would you let a man try such spite-work on you and quit thinkin' about him just because yu'd headed him off?" To this I offered his own notion about hogs and being satisfied. "Hogs!" went on Scipio, in a way that dashed my suggestion to pieces; "hogs ain't in the case. He's got to deal with Trampas somehow—man to man. Trampas and him can't stay this way when they get back and go workin' same as they worked before. No, sir; I've seen his eye twice, and I know he's goin' to reckon to a finish."

I still must, in Scipio's opinion, have been slow to understand, when on the afternoon following this talk I invited him to tell me what sort of "finish" he wanted, after such a finishing as had been dealt Trampas already. Getting "laughed plumb sick by the bystanders" (I borrowed his own not overstated expression) seemed to me a highly final finishing. While I was running my notions off to him, Scipio rose, and, with the frying-pan he had been washing, walked slowly at me.

"I do believe you'd oughtn't to be let travel alone the way you do."

He put his face close to mine. His long nose grew eloquent in its shrewdness, while the fire in his bleached blue eye burned with amiable satire. "What has come and gone between them two has only settled the one point he was aimin' to make. He was appointed boss of this outfit in the absence of the regular foreman. Since then all he has been playin' for is to hand back his men to the ranch in as good shape as they'd been handed to him, and without losing any on the road through desertion or shooting or what not. He had to kick his cook off the train that day, and the loss made him sorrowful, I could see. But I'd happened to come along, and he jumped me into the vacancy, and I expect he is pretty near consoled. And as boss of the outfit he beat Trampas, who was settin' up for opposition boss. And the outfit is better than satisfied it come out that way, and they're stayin' with him; and he'll hand them all back in good condition, barrin' that lost cook. So for the present his point is made, yu' see. But look ahead a little. It may not be so very far ahead yu'll have to look. We get back to the ranch. He's not boss there anymore. His responsibility is over. He is just one of us again, taking orders from a foreman they tell me has showed partiality to Trampas more'n a few times. Partiality! That's what Trampas is plainly trusting to. Trusting it will fix him all right and fix his enemy all wrong. He'd not otherwise dare to keep sour like he's doing. Partiality! D' yu' think it'll scare off the enemy?" Scipio looked across a little creek to where the Virginian was helping throw the gathered cattle on the bedground. "What odds"—he pointed the frying-pan at the Southerner—"d' yu' figure Trampas's being under any foreman's wing will make to a man like him? He's going to remember Mr. Trampas and his spite-work if he's got to tear him out from under the wing, and maybe tear off the wing in the operation. And I am goin' to advise your folks," ended the complete Scipio, "not to leave you travel so much alone—not till you've learned more life."

He had made me feel my inexperience, convinced me of innocence, undoubtedly; and during the final days of our journey I no longer invoked his aid to my reflections upon this especial topic: What would the Virginian do to Trampas? Would it be another intellectual crushing of him, like the frog story, or would there be something this time more material—say muscle, or possibly gunpowder—in it? And was Scipio, after all, infallible? I didn't pretend to understand the Virginian; after several years' knowledge of him he remained utterly beyond me. Scipio's experience was not yet three weeks long. So I let him alone as to all this, discussing with him most other things good and evil in the world, and being convinced of much further innocence; for Scipio's twenty odd years were indeed a library of life. I have never met a better heart, a shrewder wit, and looser morals, with yet a native sense of decency and duty somewhere hard and fast enshrined.

But all the while I was wondering about the Virginian: eating with him, sleeping with him (only not so sound as he did), and riding beside him often for many hours.

Experiments in conversation I did make—and failed. One day particularly while, after a sudden storm of hail had chilled the earth numb and white like winter in fifteen minutes, we sat drying and warming ourselves by a fire that we built, I touched upon that theme of equality on which I knew him to hold opinions as strong as mine. "Oh," he would reply, and "Cert'nly"; and when I asked him what it was in a man that made him a leader of men, he shook his head and puffed his pipe. So then, noticing how the sun had brought the earth in half an hour back from winter to summer again, I spoke of our American climate.

It was a potent drug, I said, for millions to be swallowing every day.

"Yes," said he, wiping the damp from his Winchester rifle.

Our American climate, I said, had worked remarkable changes, at least.

"Yes," he said; and did not ask what they were.

So I had to tell him. "It has made successful politicians of the Irish. That's one. And it has given our whole race the habit of poker."

Bang went his Winchester. The bullet struck close to my left. I sat up angrily.

"That's the first foolish thing I ever saw you do!" I said.

"Yes," he drawled slowly, "I'd ought to have done it sooner. He was pretty near lively again." And then he picked up a rattlesnake six feet behind me. It had been numbed by the hail, part revived by the sun, and he had shot its head off.

# CHAPTER XVIII

## "WOULD YOU BE A PARSON?"

After this I gave up my experiments in conversation. So that by the final afternoon of our journey, with Sunk Creek actually in sight, and the great grasshoppers slatting their dry song over the sagebrush, and the time at hand when the Virginian and Trampas would be "man to man," my thoughts rose to a considerable pitch of speculation.

And now that talking part of the Virginian, which had been nine days asleep, gave its first yawn and stretch of waking. Without preface, he suddenly asked me, "Would you be a parson?"

I was mentally so far away that I couldn't get back in time to comprehend or answer before he had repeated: "What would yu' take to be a parson?"

He drawled it out in his gentle way, precisely as if no nine days stood between it and our last real intercourse.

"Take?" I was still vaguely moving in my distance. "How?"

His next question brought me home.

"I expect the Pope's is the biggest of them parson jobs?"

It was with an "Oh!" that I now entirely took his idea. "Well, yes; decidedly the biggest."

"Beats the English one? Archbishop—ain't it?—of Canterbury? The Pope comes ahead of him?"

"His Holiness would say so if his Grace did not."

The Virginian turned half in his saddle to see my face—I was, at the moment, riding not quite abreast of him—and I saw the gleam of his teeth beneath his mustache. It was seldom I could make him smile, even to this slight extent. But his eyes grew, with his next words, remote again in their speculation.

"His Holiness and his Grace. Now if I was to hear 'em namin' me that-a-way every mawnin', I'd sca'cely get down to business."

"Oh, you'd get used to the pride of it."

"'Tisn't the pride. The laugh is what would ruin me. 'Twould take 'most all my attention keeping a straight face. The Archbishop"—here he took one of his wide mental turns—"is apt to be a big man in them Shakespeare plays. Kings take talk from him they'd not stand from anybody else; and he talks fine, frequently. About the bees, for instance, when Henry is going to fight France. He tells him a beehive is similar to a kingdom. I learned that piece." The Virginian could not have expected to blush at uttering these last words. He knew that his sudden color must tell me in whose book it was he had learned the piece. Was not her copy of Kenilworth even now in his cherishing pocket? So he now, to cover his blush, very deliberately recited to me the Archbishop's discourse upon bees and their kingdom:

> "'Where some, like magistrates, correct at home . . .
> Others, like soldiers, armed in their stings,
> Made loot upon the summer's velvet buds;
> Which pillage they with merry march bring home
> To the tent-royal of their emperor:
> He, busied in his majesty, surveys
> The singing masons building roofs of gold.'

"Ain't that a fine description of bees a-workin'? 'The singing masons building roofs of gold!' Puts 'em right before yu', and is poetry without bein' foolish. His Holiness and his Grace. Well, they could not hire me for either o' those positions. How many religions are there?"

"All over the earth?"

"Yu' can begin with ourselves. Right hyeh at home I know there's Romanists, and Episcopals—"

"Two kinds!" I put in. "At least two of Episcopals."

"That's three. Then Methodists and Baptists, and—"

"Three Methodists!"

"Well, you do the countin'."

I accordingly did it, feeling my revolving memory slip cogs all the way round. "Anyhow, there are safely fifteen."

"Fifteen." He held this fact a moment. "And they don't worship a whole heap o' different gods like the ancients did?"

"Oh, no!"

"It's just the same one?"

"The same one."

The Virginian folded his hands over the horn of his saddle, and leaned forward upon them in contemplation of the wide, beautiful landscape.

"One God and fifteen religions," was his reflection. "That's a right smart of religions for just one God."

This way of reducing it was, if obvious to him, so novel to me that my laugh evidently struck him as a louder and livelier comment than was required. He turned on me as if I had somehow perverted the spirit of his words.

"I ain't religious. I know that. But I ain't unreligious. And I know that too."

"So do I know it, my friend."

"Do you think there ought to be fifteen varieties of good people?" His voice, while it now had an edge that could cut anything it came against, was still not raised. "There ain't fifteen. There ain't two. There's one kind. And when I meet it, I respect it. It is not praying nor preaching that has ever caught me and made me ashamed of myself, but one or two people I have knowed that never said a superior word to me. They thought more o' me than I deserved, and that made me behave better than I naturally wanted to. Made me quit a girl onced in time for her not to lose her good name. And so that's one thing I have never done. And if ever I was to have a son or somebody I set store by, I would wish their lot to be to know one or two good folks mighty well—men or women—women preferred."

He had looked away again to the hills behind Sunk Creek ranch, to which our walking horses had now almost brought us.

"As for parsons"—the gesture of his arm was a disclaiming one—"I reckon some parsons have a right to tell yu' to be good. The bishop of this hyeh Territory has a right. But I'll tell yu' this: a middlin' doctor is a pore thing, and a middlin' lawyer is a pore thing; but keep me from a middlin' man of God."

Once again he had reduced it, but I did not laugh this time. I thought there should in truth be heavy damages for malpractice on human souls. But the hot glow of his words, and the vision of his deepest inner man it revealed, faded away abruptly.

"What do yu' make of the proposition yondeh?" As he pointed to the cause of this question he had become again his daily, engaging, saturnine self.

Then I saw over in a fenced meadow, to which we were now close, what he was pleased to call "the proposition." Proposition in the West does, in fact, mean whatever you at the moment please—an offer to sell you a mine, a cloud-burst, a glass of whiskey, a steamboat. This time it meant a stranger clad in black, and of a clerical deportment which would in that atmosphere and to a watchful eye be visible for a mile or two.

"I reckoned yu' hadn't noticed him," was the Virginian's reply to my ejaculation. "Yes. He set me goin' on the subject a while back. I expect he is another missionary to us pore cowboys."

I seemed from a hundred yards to feel the stranger's forceful personality. It was in his walk—I should better say stalk—as he promenaded along the creek. His hands were behind his back, and there was an air of waiting, of displeased waiting, in his movement.

"Yes, he'll be a missionary," said the Virginian, conclusively; and he took to singing, or rather to whining, with his head tilted at an absurd angle upward at the sky:

> " 'Dar is a big Car'lina nigger,
> About de size of dis chile or p'raps a little bigger,
> By de name of Jim Crow.
> Dat what de white folks call him.

If ever I sees him I 'tends for to maul him,
Just to let de white folks see
Such an animos as he
Can't walk around the streets and scandalize me.'"

The lane which was conducting us to the group of ranch buildings now turned a corner of the meadow, and the Virginian went on with his second verse:

"'Great big fool, he hasn't any knowledge.
Gosh! how could he, when he's never been to scollege?
Neither has I.
But I'se come mighty nigh;
I peaked through de door as I went by.'"

He was beginning a third stanza, but stopped short; a horse had neighed close behind us.

"Trampas," said he, without turning his head, "we are home."

"It looks that way." Some ten yards were between ourselves and Trampas, where he followed.

"And I'll trouble yu' for my rope yu' took this mawnin' instead o' your own."

"I don't know as it's your rope I've got." Trampas skilfully spoke this so that a precisely opposite meaning flowed from his words.

If it was discussion he tried for, he failed. The Virginian's hand moved, and for one thick, flashing moment my thoughts were evidently also the thoughts of Trampas. But the Virginian only held out to Trampas the rope which he had detached from his saddle.

"Take your hand off your gun, Trampas. If I had wanted to kill yu' you'd be lying nine days back on the road now. Here's your rope. Did yu' expect I'd not know it? It's the only one in camp the stiffness ain't all drug out of yet. Or maybe yu' expected me to notice and—not take notice?"

"I don't spend my time in expectations about you. If—"

The Virginian wheeled his horse across the road. "Yu're talkin' too soon after reachin' safety, Trampas. I didn't tell yu' to hand me that rope this mawnin', because I was busy. I ain't foreman now; and I want that rope."

Trampas produced a smile as skilful as his voice. "Well, I guess your having mine proves this one is yours." He rode up and received the coil which the Virginian held out, unloosing the disputed one on his saddle. If he had meant to devise a slippery, evasive insult, no small trick in cow-land could be more offensive than this taking another man's rope. And it is the small tricks which lead to the big bullets. Trampas put a smooth coating of plausibility over the whole transaction. "After the rope corral we had to make this morning"—his tone was mock explanatory—"the ropes was all strewed round camp, and in the hustle I—"

"Pardon me," said a sonorous voice behind us, "do you happen to have seen Judge Henry?" It was the reverend gentleman in his meadow, come to the fence. As we turned round to him he spoke on, with much rotund authority in his eye. "From his answer to my letter, Judge Henry undoubtedly expects me here. I have arrived from Fetterman according to my plan which I announced to him, to find that he has been absent all day—absent the whole day."

The Virginian sat sidewise to talk, one long, straight leg supporting him on one stirrup, the other bent at ease, the boot half lifted from its dangling stirrup. He made himself the perfection of courtesy. "The Judge is frequently absent all night, seh."

"Scarcely tonight, I think. I thought you might know something about him."

"I have been absent myself, seh."

"Ah! On a vacation, perhaps?" The divine had a ruddy facet. His strong glance was straight and frank and fearless; but his smile too much reminded me of days bygone, when we used to return to school from the Christmas holidays, and the masters would shake our hands and welcome us with: "Robert, John, Edward, glad to see you all looking so well! Rested, and ready for hard work, I'm sure!"

That smile does not really please even good, tame little boys; and the Virginian was nearing thirty.

"It has not been vacation this trip, seh," said he, settling straight in his saddle. "There's the Judge driving in now, in time for all questions yu' have to ask him."

His horse took a step, but was stopped short. There lay the Virginian's rope on the ground. I had been aware of Trampas's quite proper departure during the talk; and as he was leaving, I seemed also to be aware of his placing the coil across the cantle of its owner's saddle. Had he intended it to fall and have to be picked up? It was another evasive little business, and quite successful, if designed to nag the owner of the rope. A few hundred yards ahead of us Trampas was now shouting loud cowboy shouts. Were they to announce his return to those at home, or did they mean derision? The Virginian leaned, keeping his seat, and, swinging down his arm, caught up the rope, and hung it on his saddle somewhat carefully. But the hue of rage spread over his face.

From his fence the divine now spoke, in approbation, but with another strong, cheerless smile. "You pick up that rope as if you were well trained to it."

"It's part of our business, seh, and we try to mind it like the rest."

But this, stated in a gentle drawl, did not pierce the missionary's armor; his superiority was very thick.

We now rode on, and I was impressed by the reverend gentleman's robust, dictatorial back as he proceeded by a short cut through the meadow to the ranch. You could take him for nothing but a vigorous, sincere, dominating man, full of the highest purpose. But whatever his creed, I already doubted if he were the right one to sow it and make it grow in these new, wild fields. He seemed more the sort of gardener to keep old walks and vines pruned in their antique rigidity. I admired him for coming all this way with his clean, short, gray whiskers and his black, well-brushed suit. And he made me think of a powerful locomotive stuck puffing on a grade.

Meanwhile, the Virginian rode beside me, so silent in his volcanic wrath that I did not perceive it. The missionary coming on top of Trampas had been more than he could stand. But I did not know, and I spoke with innocent cheeriness.

"Is the parson going to save us?" I asked; and I fairly jumped at his voice: "Don't talk so much!" he burst out. I had got the whole accumulation!

"Who's been talking?" I in equal anger screeched back. "I'm not trying to save you. I didn't take your rope." And having poured this out, I whipped up my pony.

But he spurred his own alongside of me; and glancing at him, I saw that he was now convulsed with internal mirth. I therefore drew down to a walk, and he straightened into gravity.

"I'm right obliged to yu'," he laid his hand in its buckskin gauntlet upon my horse's mane as he spoke, "for bringing me back out o' my nonsense. I'll be as serene as a bird now—whatever they do. A man," he stated reflectively, "any full-sized man, ought to own a big lot of temper. And like all his valuable possessions, he'd ought to keep it and not lose any." This was his full apology. "As for salvation, I have got this far: somebody," he swept an arm at the sunset and the mountains, "must have made all that, I know. But I know one more thing I would tell Him to His face: if I can't do nothing long enough and good enough to earn eternal happiness, I can't do nothing long enough and bad enough to be damned. I reckon He plays a square game with us if He plays at all, and I ain't bothering my haid about other worlds."

As we reached the stables, he had become the serene bird he promised, and was sentimentally continuing:

> " 'De sun is made of mud from de bottom of de river;
> De moon is made o' fox-fire, as you might disciver;
> De stars like de ladies' eyes,
> All round de world dey flies,
> To give a little light when de moon don't rise.' "

If words were meant to conceal our thoughts, melody is perhaps a still thicker veil for them. Whatever temper he had lost, he had certainly found again; but this all the more fitted him to deal with Trampas, when the dealing should begin. I had half a mind to speak to the Judge, only it seemed beyond a mere visitor's business. Our missionary was at this moment himself speaking to Judge Henry at the door of the home ranch.

"I reckon he's explaining he has been a-waiting." The Virginian was throwing his saddle off as I loosened the cinches of mine. "And the Judge don't look like he was hopelessly distressed."

I now surveyed the distant parley, and the Judge, from the wagonful of guests whom he had evidently been driving upon a day's excursion, waved me a welcome, which I waved back. "He's got Miss Molly Wood there!" I exclaimed.

"Yes." The Virginian was brief about this fact. "I'll look afteh your saddle. You go and get acquainted with the company."

This favor I accepted; it was the means he chose for saying he hoped, after our recent boiling over, that all was now more than right between us. So for the while I left him to his horses, and his corrals, and his Trampas, and his foreman, and his imminent problem.

## CHAPTER XIX

## DR. MACBRIDE BEGS PARDON

Judge and Mrs. Henry, Molly Wood, and two strangers, a lady and a gentleman, were the party which had been driving in the large three-seated wagon. They had seemed a merry party. But as I came within hearing of their talk, it was a fragment of the minister's sonority which reached me first: "—more opportunity for them to have the benefit of hearing frequent sermons," was the sentence I heard him bring to completion.

"Yes, to be sure, sir." Judge Henry gave me (it almost seemed) additional warmth of welcome for arriving to break up the present discourse. "Let me introduce you to the Rev. Dr. Alexander MacBride. Doctor, another guest we have been hoping for about this time," was my host's cordial explanation to him of me. There remained the gentleman with his wife from New York, and to these I made my final bows. But I had not broken up the discourse.

"We may be said to have met already." Dr. MacBride had fixed upon me his full, mastering eye; and it occurred to me that if they had policemen in heaven, he would be at least a centurion in the force. But he did not mean to be unpleasant; it was only that in a mind full of matters less worldly, pleasure was left out. "I observed your friend was a skilful horseman," he continued. "I was saying to Judge Henry that I could wish such skilful horsemen might ride to a church upon the Sabbath. A church, that is, of right doctrine, where they would have opportunity to hear frequent sermons."

"Yes," said Judge Henry, "yes. It would be a good thing."

Mrs. Henry, with some murmur about the kitchen, here went into the house.

"I was informed," Dr. MacBride held the rest of us, "before undertaking my journey that I should find a desolate and mainly godless country. But nobody gave me to understand that from Medicine Bow I was to drive three hundred miles and pass no church of any faith."

The Judge explained that there had been a few a long way to the right and left of him. "Still," he conceded, "you are quite right. But don't forget that this is the newest part of a new world."

"Judge," said his wife, coming to the door, "how can you keep them standing in the dust with your talking?"

This most efficiently did break up the discourse. As our little party, with the smiles and the polite holdings back of new acquaintanceship, moved into the house, the Judge detained me behind all of them long enough to whisper dolorously, "He's going to stay a whole week."

I had hopes that he would not stay a whole week when I presently learned of the crowded arrangements which our hosts, with many hospitable apologies, disclosed to us. They were delighted to have us, but they hadn't foreseen that we should all be simultaneous. The foreman's house had been prepared for two of us, and did we mind? The two of us were Dr. MacBride and myself; and I expected him to mind. But I wronged him grossly. It would be much better, he assured Mrs. Henry, than straw in a stable, which he had tried several times, and was quite ready for. So I saw that though he kept his vigorous body clean when he could, he cared nothing for it in the face of his mission. How the foreman and his wife relished being turned out during a week for a missionary and myself was not my concern, although while he and I made ready for supper over there, it struck me as hard on them. The room with its two cots and furniture was as nice as possible; and we closed the door upon the adjoining room, which, however, seemed also untenanted.

Mrs. Henry gave us a meal so good that I have remembered it, and her husband the Judge strove his best that we should eat it in merriment. He poured out his anecdotes like wine, and we should have quickly warmed to them; but Dr. MacBride sat among us, giving occasional heavy ha-ha's, which produced, as Miss Molly Wood whispered to me, a "dreadfully cavernous effect." Was it his sermon, we wondered, that he was thinking over? I told her of the copious sheaf of them I had seen him pull from his wallet over at the foreman's. "Goodness!" said she. "Then are we to hear one every evening?" This I doubted; he had probably been picking one out suitable for the occasion. "Putting his best foot foremost," was her comment; "I suppose they have best feet, like the rest of us." Then she grew delightfully sharp. "Do you know, when I first heard him I thought his voice was hearty. But if you listen, you'll find it's merely militant. He never really meets you with it. He's off on his hill watching the battle-field the whole time."

"He will find a hardened pagan here."

"Judge Henry?"

"Oh, no! The wild man you're taming brought you Kenilworth safe back."

She was smooth. "Oh, as for taming him! But don't you find him intelligent?"

Suddenly I somehow knew that she didn't want to tame him. But what did she want to do? The thought of her had made him blush this afternoon. No thought of him made her blush this evening.

A great laugh from the rest of the company made me aware that the Judge had consummated his tale of the "Sole Survivor."

"And so," he finished, "they all went off as mad as hops because it hadn't been a massacre." Mr. and Mrs. Ogden—they were the New Yorkers—gave this story much applause, and Dr. MacBride half a minute later laid his "ha-ha," like a heavy stone, upon the gayety.

"I'll never be able to stand seven sermons," said Miss Wood to me.

"Talking of massacres"—I now hastened to address the already saddened table—"I have recently escaped one myself."

The Judge had come to an end of his powers. "Oh, tell us!" he implored.

"Seriously, sir, I think we grazed pretty wet tragedy but your extraordinary man brought us out into comedy safe and dry."

This gave me their attention; and, from that afternoon in Dakota when I had first stepped aboard the caboose, I told them the whole tale of my experience: how I grew immediately aware that all was not right, by the Virginian's kicking the cook off the train; how, as we journeyed, the dark bubble of mutiny swelled hourly beneath my eyes; and how, when it was threatening I know not what explosion, the Virginian had pricked it with humor, so that it burst in nothing but harmless laughter.

Their eyes followed my narrative: the New Yorkers, because such events do not happen upon the shores of the Hudson; Mrs. Henry, because she was my hostess; Miss Wood followed for whatever her reasons were—I couldn't see her eyes; rather, I *felt* her listening intently to the deeds and dangers of the man she didn't care to tame. But it was the eyes of the Judge and the missionary which I saw riveted upon me indeed until the end; and they forthwith made plain their quite dissimilar opinions.

Judge Henry struck the table lightly with his fist. "I knew it!" And he leaned back in his chair with a face of contentment. He had trusted his man, and his man had proved worthy.

"Pardon me." Dr. MacBride had a manner of saying "pardon me," which rendered forgiveness well-nigh impossible.

The Judge waited for him.

"Am I to understand that these—a—cowboys attempted to mutiny, and were discouraged in this attempt upon finding themselves less skilful at lying than the man they had plotted to depose?"

I began an answer. "It was other qualities, sir, that happened to be revealed and asserted by what you call his lying that—"

"And what am I to call it, if it is not lying? A competition in deceit in which, I admit, he outdid them."

"It's their way to—"

"Pardon me. Their way to lie? They bow down to the greatest in this?"

"Oh," said Miss Wood in my ear, "give him up."

The Judge took a turn. "We-ell, Doctor—" He seemed to stick here.

Mr. Ogden handsomely assisted him. "You've said the word yourself, Doctor. It's the competition, don't you see? The trial of strength by no matter what test."

"Yes," said Miss Wood, unexpectedly. "And it wasn't that George Washington couldn't tell a lie. He just wouldn't. I'm sure if he'd undertaken to he'd have told a much better one than Cornwall's."

"Ha-ha, madam! You draw an ingenious subtlety from your books."

"It's all plain to me," Ogden pursued. "The men were morose. This foreman was in the minority. He cajoled them into a bout of tall stories, and told the tallest himself. And when they found they had swallowed it whole—well, it would certainly take the starch out of me," he concluded. "I couldn't be a serious mutineer after that."

Dr. MacBride now sounded his strongest bass. "Pardon me. I cannot accept such a view, sir. There is a levity abroad in our land which I must deplore. No matter how leniently you may try to put it, in the end we have the spectacle of a struggle between men where lying decides the survival of the fittest. Better, far better, if it was to come, that they had shot honest bullets. There are worse evils than war."

The Doctor's eye glared righteously about him. None of us, I think, trembled; or, if we did, it was with emotions other than fear. Mrs. Henry at once introduced the subject of trout-fishing, and thus happily removed us from the edge of whatever sort of precipice we seemed to have approached; for Dr. MacBride had brought his rod. He dilated upon this sport with fervor, and we assured him that the streams upon the west slope of the Bow Leg Mountains would afford him plenty of it. Thus we ended our meal in carefully preserved amity.

## CHAPTER XX

## THE JUDGE IGNORES PARTICULARS

"Do you often have these visitations?" Ogden inquired of Judge Henry. Our host was giving us whiskey in his office, and Dr. MacBride, while we smoked apart from the ladies, had repaired to his quarters in the foreman's house previous to the service which he was shortly to hold.

The Judge laughed. "They come now and then through the year. I like the bishop to come. And the men always like it. But I fear our friend will scarcely please them so well."

"You don't mean they'll—"

"Oh, no. They'll keep quiet. The fact is, they have a good deal better manners than he has, if he only knew it. They'll be able to bear him. But as for any good he'll do—"

"I doubt if he knows a word of science," said I, musing about the Doctor.

"Science! He doesn't know what Christianity is yet. I've entertained many guests, but none— The whole secret," broke off Judge Henry, "lies in the way you treat people. As soon as you treat men as your brothers, they are ready to acknowledge you—if you deserve it—as their superior. That's the whole bottom of Christianity, and that's what our missionary will never know."

There was a somewhat heavy knock at the office door, and I think we all feared it was Dr. MacBride. But when the Judge opened, the Virginian was standing there in the darkness.

"So!" The Judge opened the door wide. He was very hearty to the man he had trusted. "You're back at last."

"I came to repawt."

While they shook hands, Ogden nudged me. "That the fellow?" I nodded. "Fellow who kicked the cook off the train?" I again nodded, and he looked at the Virginian, his eye and his stature.

Judge Henry, properly democratic, now introduced him to Ogden.

The New Yorker also meant to be properly democratic. "You're the man I've been hearing such a lot about."

But familiarity is not equality. "Then I expect yu' have the advantage of me, seh," said the Virginian, very politely. "Shall I repawt tomorro'?" His grave eyes were on the Judge again. Of me he had taken no notice; he had come as an employee to see his employer.

"Yes, yes; I'll want to hear about the cattle tomorrow. But step inside a moment now. There's a matter—" The Virginian stepped inside, and took off his hat. "Sit down. You had trouble—I've heard something about it," the Judge went on.

The Virginian sat down, grave and graceful. But he held the brim of his hat all the while. He looked at Ogden and me, and then back at his employer. There was reluctance in his eye. I wondered if his employer could be going to make him tell his own exploits in the presence of us outsiders; and there came into my memory the Bengal tiger at a trained-animal show I had once seen.

"You had some trouble," repeated the Judge.

"Well, there was a time when they maybe wanted to have notions. They're good boys." And he smiled a very little.

Contentment increased in the Judge's face. "Trampas a good boy too?"

But this time the Bengal tiger did not smile. He sat with his eye fastened on his employer.

The Judge passed rather quickly on to his next point. "You've brought them all back, though, I understand, safe and sound, without a scratch?"

The Virginian looked down at his hat, then up again at the Judge, mildly. "I had to part with my cook."

There was no use; Ogden and myself exploded. Even upon the embarrassed Virginian a large grin slowly forced itself. "I guess yu' know about it," he murmured. And he looked at me with a sort of reproach. He knew it was I who had told tales out of school.

"I only want to say," said Ogden, conciliatingly, "that I know I couldn't have handled those men."

The Virginian relented. "Yu' never tried, seh."

The Judge had remained serious; but he showed himself plainly more and more contented. "Quite right," he said. "You had to part with your cook. When I put a man in charge, I put him in charge. I don't make particulars my business. They're to be always his. Do you understand?"

"Thank yu'." The Virginian understood that his employer was praising his management of the expedition. But I don't think he at all discerned—as I did presently—that his employer had just been putting him to a further test, had laid before him the temptation of complaining of a fellow-workman and blowing his own trumpet, and was delighted with his reticence. He made a movement to rise.

"I haven't finished," said the Judge. "I was coming to the matter. There's one particular—since I do happen to have been told. I fancy Trampas has learned something he didn't expect."

This time the Virginian evidently did not understand, anymore than I did. One hand played with his hat, mechanically turning it round.

The Judge explained. "I mean about Roberts."

A pulse of triumph shot over the Southerner's face, turning it savage for that fleeting instant. He understood now, and was unable to suppress this much answer. But he was silent.

"You see," the Judge explained to me, "I was obliged to let Roberts, my old foreman, go last week. His wife could not have stood another winter here, and a good position was offered to him near Los Angeles."

I did see. I saw a number of things. I saw why the foreman's house had been empty to receive Dr. MacBride and me. And I saw that the Judge had been very clever indeed. For I had abstained from telling any tales about the present feeling between Trampas and the Virginian; but he had divined it. Well enough for him to say that "particulars" were something he let alone; he evidently kept a deep eye on the undercurrents at his ranch. He knew that in Roberts, Trampas had lost a powerful friend. And this was what I most saw, this final fact, that Trampas had no longer any intervening shield. He and the Virginian stood indeed man to man.

"And so," the Judge continued speaking to me, "here I am at a very inconvenient time without a foreman. Unless," I caught the twinkle in his eyes before he turned to the Virginian, "unless you're willing to take the position yourself. Will you?"

I saw the Southerner's hand grip his hat as he was turning it round. He held it still now, and his other hand found it and gradually crumpled the soft crown in. It meant everything to him: recognition, higher station, better fortune, a separate house of his own, and—perhaps—one step nearer to the woman he wanted. I don't know what words he might have said to the Judge had they been alone, but the Judge had chosen to do it in our presence, the whole thing from beginning to end. The Virginian sat with the damp coming out on his forehead, and his eyes dropped from his employer's.

"Thank yu'," was what he managed at last to say.

"Well, now, I'm greatly relieved!" exclaimed the Judge, rising at once. He spoke with haste, and lightly. "That's excellent. I was in some thing of a hole," he said to Ogden and me; "and this gives me one thing less to think of. Saves me a lot of particulars," he jocosely added to the Virginian, who was now also standing up. "Begin right off. Leave the bunkhouse. The gentlemen won't mind your sleeping in your own house."

Thus he dismissed his new foreman gayly. But the new foreman, when he got outside, turned back for one gruff word—"I'll try to please yu'."

That was all. He was gone in the darkness. But there was light enough for me, looking after him, to see him lay his hand on a shoulder-high gate and vault it as if he had been the wind. Sounds of cheering came to us a few moments later from the bunkhouse. Evidently he had "begun right away," as the Judge had directed. He had told his fortune to his brother cowpunchers, and this was their answer.

"I wonder if Trampas is shouting too?" inquired Ogden.

"Hm!" said the Judge. "That is one of the particulars I wash my hands of."

I knew that he entirely meant it. I knew, once his decision taken of appointing the Virginian his lieutenant for good and all, that, like a wise commander-in-chief, he would trust his lieutenant to take care of his own business.

"Well," Ogden pursued with interest, "haven't you landed Trampas plump at his mercy?"

The phrase tickled the Judge. "That is where I've landed him!" he declared. "And here is Dr. MacBride."


## CHAPTER XXI

## IN A STATE OF SIN

Thunder sat imminent upon the missionary's brow. Many were to be at his mercy soon. But for us he had sunshine still. "I am truly sorry to be turning you upside down," he said importantly. "But it seems the best place for my service." He spoke of the tables pushed back and the chairs gathered in the hall, where the storm would presently break upon the congregation. "Eight-thirty?" he inquired.

This was the hour appointed, and it was only twenty minutes off. We threw the unsmoked fractions of our cigars away, and returned to offer our services to the ladies. This amused the ladies. They had done without us. All was ready in the hall.

"We got the cook to help us," Mrs. Ogden told me, "so as not to disturb your cigars. In spite of the cowboys, I still recognize my own country."

"In the cook?" I rather densely asked.

"Oh, no! I don't have a Chinaman. It's in the length of after-dinner cigars."

"Had you been smoking," I returned, "you would have found them short this evening."

"You make it worse," said the lady; "we have had nothing but Dr. MacBride."

"We'll share him with you now," I exclaimed.

"Has he announced his text? I've got one for him," said Molly Wood, joining us. She stood on tiptoe and spoke it comically in our ears. "'I said in my haste, All men are liars.'" This made us merry as we stood among the chairs in the congested hall.

I left the ladies, and sought the bunkhouse. I had heard the cheers, but I was curious also to see the men, and how they were taking it. There was but little for the eye. There was much noise in the room. They were getting ready to come to church—brushing their hair, shaving, and making themselves clean, amid talk occasionally profane and continuously diverting.

"Well, I'm a Christian, anyway," one declared.

"I'm a Mormon, I guess," said another.

"I belong to the Knights of Pythias," said a third.

"I'm a Mohammedist," said a fourth; "I hope I ain't goin' to hear nothin' to shock me."

And they went on with their joking. But Trampas was out of the joking. He lay on his bed reading a newspaper, and took no pains to look pleasant. My eyes were considering him when the blithe Scipio came in.

"Don't look so bashful," said he. "There's only us girls here."

He had been helping the Virginian move his belongings from the bunkhouse over to the foreman's cabin. He himself was to occupy the Virginian's old bed here. "And I hope sleepin' in it will bring me some of his luck," said Scipio. "Yu'd ought to've seen us when he told us in his quiet way. Well," Scipio sighed a little, "it must feel good to have your friends glad about you."

"Especially Trampas," said I. "The Judge knows about that," I added.

"Knows, does he? What's he say?" Scipio drew me quickly out of the bunkhouse.

"Says it's no business of his."

"Said nothing but that?" Scipio's curiosity seemed strangely intense. "Made no suggestion? Not a thing?"

"Not a thing. Said he didn't want to know and didn't care."

"How did he happen to hear about it?" snapped Scipio. "You told him!" he immediately guessed. "He never would." And Scipio jerked his thumb at the Virginian, who appeared for a moment in the lighted window of the new quarters he was arranging. "He never would tell," Scipio repeated. "And so the Judge never made a suggestion to him," he muttered, nodding in the darkness. "So it's just his own notion. Just like him, too, come to think of it. Only I didn't expect—well, I guess he could surprise me any day he tried."

"You're surprising me now," I said. "What's it all about?"

"Oh, him and Trampas."

"What? Nothing surely happened yet?" I was as curious as Scipio had been.

"No, not yet. But there will."

"Great Heavens, man! When?"

"Just as soon as Trampas makes the first move," Scipio replied easily.

I became dignified. Scipio had evidently been told things by the Virginian.

"Yes, I up and asked him plumb out," Scipio answered. "I was liftin' his trunk in at the door, and I couldn't stand it no longer, and I asked him plumb out. 'Yu've sure got Trampas where yu' want him.' That's what I said. And he up and answered and told me. So I know." At this point Scipio stopped; I was not to know.

"I had no idea," I said, "that your system held so much meanness."

"Oh, it ain't meanness!" And he laughed ecstatically.

"What do you call it, then?"

"He'd call it discretion," said Scipio. Then he became serious. "It's too blamed grand to tell yu'. I'll leave yu' to see it happen. Keep around, that's all. Keep around. I pretty near wish I didn't know it myself."

What with my feelings at Scipio's discretion, and my human curiosity, I was not in that mood which best profits from a sermon. Yet even though my expectations had been cruelly left quivering in mid air, I was not sure how much I really wanted to "keep around." You will therefore understand how Dr. MacBride was able to make a prayer and to read Scripture without my being conscious of a word that he had uttered. It was when I saw him opening the manuscript of his sermon that I suddenly remembered I was sitting, so to speak, in church, and began once more to think of the preacher and his congregation. Our chairs were in the front line, of course; but, being next the wall, I could easily see the cowboys behind me. They were perfectly decorous. If Mrs. Ogden had looked for pistols, daredevil attitudes, and so forth, she must have been greatly disappointed. Except for their weather-beaten cheeks and eyes, they were simply American young men with mustaches and without, and might have been sitting, say, in Danbury, Connecticut. Even Trampas merged quietly with the general placidity. The Virginian did not, to be sure, look like Danbury, and his frame and his features showed out of the mass; but his eyes were upon Dr. MacBride with a creamlike propriety.

Our missionary did not choose Miss Wood's text. He made his selection from another of the Psalms; and when it came, I did not dare to look at anybody; I was much nearer unseemly conduct than the cowboys. Dr. MacBride gave us his text sonorously, " 'They are altogether become filthy; There is none of them that doeth good, no, not one.' " His eye showed us plainly that present company was not excepted from this. He repeated the text once more, then, launching upon his discourse, gave none of us a ray of hope.

I had heard it all often before; but preached to cowboys it took on a new glare of untimeliness, of grotesque obsoleteness—as if someone should say, "Let me persuade you to admire woman," and forthwith hold out her bleached bones to you. The cowboys were told that not only they could do no good, but that if they did contrive to, it would not help them. Nay, more: not only honest deeds availed them nothing, but even if they accepted this especial creed which was being explained to them as necessary for salvation, still it might not save them. Their sin was indeed the cause of their damnation, yet, keeping from sin, they might nevertheless be lost. It had all been settled for them not only before they were born, but before Adam was shaped. Having told them this, he invited them to glorify the Creator of the scheme. Even if damned, they must praise the person who had made them expressly for damnation. That is what I heard him prove by logic to these cowboys. Stone upon stone he built the black cellar of his theology, leaving out its beautiful park and the sunshine of its garden. He did not tell them the splendor of its past, the noble fortress for good that it had been, how its tonic had strengthened generations of their fathers. No; wrath he spoke of, and never once of love. It was the bishop's way, I knew well, to hold cowboys by homely talk of their special hardships and temptations. And when they fell he spoke to them of forgiveness and brought them encouragement. But Dr. MacBride never thought once of the lives of these waifs. Like himself, like all mankind, they were invisible dots in creation; like him, they were to feel as nothing, to be swept up in the potent heat of his faith. So he thrust out to them none of the sweet but all the bitter of his creed, naked and stern as iron. Dogma was his all in all, and poor humanity was nothing but flesh for its canons.

Thus to kill what chance he had for being of use seemed to me more deplorable than it did evidently to them. Their attention merely wandered. Three hundred years ago they would have been frightened; but not in this electric day. I saw Scipio stifling a smile when it came to the doctrine of original sin. "We know of its truth," said Dr. MacBride, "from the severe troubles and distresses to which infants are liable, and from death passing upon them before they are capable of sinning."

Yet I knew he was a good man; and I also knew that if a missionary is to be tactless, he might almost as well be bad.

I said their attention wandered, but I forgot the Virginian. At first his attitude might have been mere propriety. One can look respectfully at a preacher and be internally breaking all the commandments. But even with the text I saw real attention light in the Virginian's eye. And keeping track of the concentration that grew on him with each minute made the sermon short for me. He missed nothing. Before the end his gaze at the preacher had become swerveless. Was he convert or critic? Convert was incredible. Thus was an hour passed before I had thought of time.

When it was over we took it variously. The preacher was genial and spoke of having now broken ground for the lessons that he hoped to instil. He discoursed for a while about trout-fishing and about the rumored uneasiness of the Indians northward where he was going. It was plain that his personal safety never gave him a thought. He soon bade us good night. The Ogdens shrugged their shoulders and were amused. That was their way of taking it. Dr. MacBride sat too heavily on the Judge's shoulders for him to shrug them. As a leading citizen in the Territory he kept open house for all comers. Policy and good nature made him bid welcome a wide variety of travelers. The cowboy out of employment found bed and a meal for himself and his horse, and missionaries had before now been well received at Sunk Creek Ranch.

"I suppose I'll have to take him fishing," said the Judge, ruefully.

"Yes, my dear," said his wife, "you will. And I shall have to make his tea for six days."

"Otherwise," Ogden suggested, "it might be reported that you were enemies of religion."

"That's about it," said the Judge. "I can get on with most people. But elephants depress me."

So we named the Doctor "Jumbo," and I departed to my quarters.

At the bunkhouse, the comments were similar but more highly salted. The men were going to bed. In spite of their outward decorum at the service, they had not liked to be told that they were "altogether become filthy."

It was easy to call names; they could do that themselves. And they appealed to me, several speaking at once, like a concerted piece at the opera: "Say, do you believe babies go to hell?"—"Ah, of course he don't."—"There ain't no hereafter, anyway."—"Ain't there?"—"Who told yu'?"—"Same man as told the preacher we were all a sifted set of sons-of-guns."—"Well, I'm going to stay a Mormon."—"Well, I'm going to quit fleeing from temptation."—"That's so! Better get it in the neck after a good time than a poor one." And so forth. Their wit was not extreme, yet I should like Dr. MacBride to have heard it. One fellow put his natural soul pretty well into words, "If I happened to learn what they had predestinated me to do, I'd do the other thing, just to show 'em!"

And Trampas? And the Virginian? They were out of it. The Virginian had gone straight to his new abode. Trampas lay in his bed, not asleep, and sullen as ever.

"He ain't got religion this trip," said Scipio to me.

"Did his new foreman get it?" I asked.

"Huh! It would spoil him. You keep around that's all. Keep around."

Scipio was not to be probed; and I went, still baffled, to my repose.

No light burned in the cabin as I approached its door.

The Virginian's room was quiet and dark; and that Dr. MacBride slumbered was plainly audible to me, even before I entered. Go fishing with him! I thought, as I undressed. And I selfishly decided that the Judge might have this privilege entirely to himself. Sleep came to me fairly soon, in spite of the Doctor. I was wakened from it by my bed's being jolted—not a pleasant thing that night. I must have started. And it was the quiet voice of the Virginian that told me he was sorry to have accidentally disturbed me. This disturbed me a good deal more. But his steps did not go to the bunkhouse, as my sensational mind had suggested. He was not wearing much, and in the dimness he seemed taller than common. I next made out that he was bending over Dr. MacBride. The divine at last sprang upright.

"I am armed," he said. "Take care. Who are you?"

"You can lay down your gun, seh. I feel like my spirit was going to bear witness. I feel like I might get an enlightening."

He was using some of the missionary's own language. The baffling I had been treated to by Scipio melted to nothing in this. Did living men petrify, I should have changed to mineral between the sheets. The Doctor got out of bed, lighted his lamp, and found a book; and the two retired into the Virginian's room, where I could hear the exhortations as I lay amazed. In time the Doctor returned, blew out his lamp, and settled himself. I had been very much awake, but was nearly gone to sleep again, when the door creaked and the Virginian stood by the Doctor's side.

"Are you awake, seh?"

"What? What's that? What is it?"

"Excuse me, seh. The enemy is winning on me. I'm feeling less inward opposition to sin."

The lamp was lighted, and I listened to some further exhortations. They must have taken half an hour. When the Doctor was in bed again, I thought that I heard him sigh. This upset my composure in the dark; but I lay face downward in the pillow, and the Doctor was soon again snoring. I envied him for a while his faculty of easy sleep. But I must have dropped off myself; for it was the lamp in my eyes that now waked me as he came back for the third time from the Virginian's room. Before blowing the light out he looked at his watch, and thereupon I inquired the hour of him.

"Three," said he.

I could not sleep anymore now, and I lay watching the darkness.

"I'm afeared to be alone!" said the Virginian's voice presently in the next room. "I'm afeared." There was a short pause, and then he shouted very loud, "I'm losin' my desire afteh the sincere milk of the Word!"

"What? What's that? What?" The Doctor's cot gave a great crack as he started up listening, and I put my face deep in the pillow.

"I'm afeared! I'm afeared! Sin has quit being bitter in my belly."

"Courage, my good man." The Doctor was out of bed with his lamp again, and the door shut behind him. Between them they made it long this time. I saw the window become gray; then the corners of the furniture grow visible; and outside, the dry chorus of the blackbirds began to fill the dawn. To these the sounds of chickens and impatient hoofs in the stable were added, and some cow wandered by loudly calling for her calf. Next, someone whistling passed near and grew distant. But although the cold hue that I lay staring at through the window warmed and changed, the Doctor continued working hard over his patient in the next room. Only a word here and there was distinct; but it was plain from the Virginian's fewer remarks that the sin in his belly was alarming him less. Yes, they made this time long. But it proved, indeed, the last one. And though some sort of catastrophe was bound to fall upon us, it was myself who precipitated the thing that did happen.

Day was wholly come. I looked at my own watch, and it was six. I had been about seven hours in my bed, and the Doctor had been about seven hours out of his. The door opened, and he came in with his book and lamp. He seemed to be shivering a little, and I saw him cast a longing eye at his couch. But the Virginian followed him even as he blew out the now quite superfluous light. They made a noticeable couple in their underclothes: the Virginian with his lean racehorse shanks running to a point at his ankle, and the Doctor with his stomach and his fat sedentary calves.

"You'll be going to breakfast and the ladies, seh, pretty soon," said the Virginian, with a chastened voice. "But I'll worry through the day somehow without yu'. And tonight you can turn your wolf loose on me again."

Once more it was no use. My face was deep in the pillow, but I made sounds as of a hen who has laid an egg. It broke on the Doctor with a total instantaneous smash, quite like an egg.

He tried to speak calmly. "This is a disgrace. An infamous disgrace. Never in my life have I—" Words forsook him, and his face grew redder. "Never in my life—" He stopped again, because, at the sight of him being dignified in his red drawers, I was making the noise of a dozen hens. It was suddenly too much for the Virginian. He hastened into his room, and there sank on the floor with his head in his hands. The Doctor immediately slammed the door upon him, and this rendered me easily fit for a lunatic asylum. I cried into my pillow, and wondered if the Doctor would come and kill me. But he took no notice of me whatever. I could hear the Virginian's convulsions through the door, and also the Doctor furiously making his toilet within three feet of my head; and I lay quite still with my face the other way, for I was really afraid to look at him. When I heard him walk to the door in his boots, I ventured to peep; and there he was, going out with his bag in his hand. As I still continued to lie, weak and sore, and with a mind that had ceased all operation, the Virginian's door opened. He was clean and dressed and decent, but the devil still sported in his eye. I have never seen a creature more irresistibly handsome.

Then my mind worked again. "You've gone and done it," said I. "He's packed his valise. He'll not sleep here."

The Virginian looked quickly out of the door. "Why, he's leavin' us!" he exclaimed. "Drivin' away right now in his little old buggy!" He turned to me, and our eyes met solemnly over this large fact. I thought that I perceived the faintest tincture of dismay in the features of Judge Henry's new, responsible, trusty foreman. This was the first act of his administration. Once again he looked out at the departing missionary. "Well," he vindictively stated, "I cert'nly ain't goin' to run afteh him." And he looked at me again.

"Do you suppose the Judge knows?" I inquired.

He shook his head. "The windo' shades is all down still oveh yondeh."

He paused. "I don't care," he stated, quite as if he had been ten years old. Then he grinned guiltily. "I was mighty respectful to him all night."

"Oh, yes, respectful! Especially when you invited him to turn his wolf loose."

The Virginian gave a joyous gulp. He now came and sat down on the edge of my bed. "I spoke awful good English to him most of the time," said he. "I can, yu' know, when I cinch my attention tight on to it. Yes, I cert'nly spoke a lot o' good English. I didn't understand some of it myself!"

He was now growing frankly pleased with his exploit. He had builded so much better than he knew. He got up and looked out across the crystal world of light. "The Doctor is at one-mile crossing," he said. "He'll get breakfast at the N-lazy-Y." Then he returned and sat again on my bed, and began to give me his real heart. "I never set up for being better than others. Not even to myself. My thoughts ain't apt to travel around making comparisons. And I shouldn't wonder if my memory took as much notice of the meannesses I have done as of—as of the other actions. But to have to sit like a dumb lamb and let a stranger tell yu' for an hour that yu're a hawg and a swine, just after you have acted in a way which them that know the facts would call pretty near white—"

"Trampas!" I could not help exclaiming.

For there are moments of insight when a guess amounts to knowledge.

"Has Scipio told—"

"No. Not a word. He wouldn't tell me."

"Well, yu' see, I arrived home hyeh this evenin' with several thoughts workin' and stirrin' inside me. And not one o' them thoughts was what yu'd call Christian. I ain't the least little bit ashamed of 'em. I'm a human. But after the Judge—well, yu' heard him. And so when I went away from that talk and saw how positions was changed—"

A step outside stopped him short. Nothing more could be read in his face, for there was Trampas himself in the open door.

"Good morning," said Trampas, not looking at us. He spoke with the same cool sullenness of yesterday.

We returned his greeting.

"I believe I'm late in congratulating you on your promotion," said he.

The Virginian consulted his watch. "It's only half afteh six," he returned.

Trampas's sullenness deepened. "Any man is to be congratulated on getting a rise, I expect."

This time the Virginian let him have it. "Cert'nly. And I ain't forgetting how much I owe mine to you."

Trampas would have liked to let himself go. "I've not come here for any forgiveness," he sneered.

"When did yu' feel yu' needed any?" The Virginian was impregnable.

Trampas seemed to feel how little he was gaining this way. He came out straight now. "Oh, I haven't any Judge behind me, I know. I heard you'd be paying the boys this morning, and I've come for my time."

"You're thinking of leaving us?" asked the new foreman. "What's your dissatisfaction?"

"Oh, I'm not needing anybody back of me. I'll get along by myself." It was thus he revealed his expectation of being dismissed by his enemy.

This would have knocked any meditated generosity out of my heart. But I was not the Virginian. He shifted his legs, leaned back a little, and laughed. "Go back to your job, Trampas, if that's all your complaint. You're right about me being in luck. But maybe there's two of us in luck."

It was this that Scipio had preferred me to see with my own eyes. The fight was between man and man no longer. The case could not be one of forgiveness; but the Virginian would not use his official position to crush his subordinate.

Trampas departed with something muttered that I did not hear, and the Virginian closed intimate conversation by saying, "You'll be late for breakfast." With that he also took himself away.

The ladies were inclined to be scandalized, but not the Judge. When my whole story was done, he brought his fist down on the table, and not lightly this time. "I'd make him lieutenant general if the ranch offered that position!" he declared.

Miss Molly Wood said nothing at the time. But in the afternoon, by her wish, she went fishing, with the Virginian deputed to escort her. I rode with them, for a while. I was not going to continue a third in that party; the Virginian was too becomingly dressed, and I saw *Kenilworth* peeping out of his pocket. I meant to be fishing by myself when that volume was returned.

But Miss Wood talked with skilful openness as we rode. "I've heard all about you and Dr. MacBride," she said. "How could you do it, when the Judge places such confidence in you?"

He looked pleased. "I reckon," he said, "I couldn't be so good if I wasn't bad onced in a while."

"Why, there's a skunk," said I, noticing the pretty little animal trotting in front of us at the edge of the thickets.

"Oh, where is it? Don't let me see it!" screamed Molly. And at this deeply feminine remark, the Virginian looked at her with such a smile that, had I been a woman, it would have made me his to do what he pleased with on the spot.

Upon the lady, however, it seemed to make less impression. Or rather, I had better say, whatever were her feelings, she very naturally made no display of them, and contrived not to be aware of that expression which had passed over the Virginian's face.

It was later that these few words reached me while I was fishing alone: "Have you anything different to tell me yet?" I heard him say.

"Yes; I have." She spoke in accents light and well intrenched. "I wish to say that I have never liked any man better than you. But I expect to!"

He must have drawn small comfort from such an answer as that. But he laughed out indomitably: "Don't yu' go betting on any such expectation!"

And then their words ceased to be distinct, and it was only their two voices that I heard wandering among the windings of the stream.

## CHAPTER XXII

### "WHAT IS A RUSTLER?"

We all know what birds of a feather do. And it may be safely surmised that if a bird of any particular feather has been for a long while unable to see other birds of its kind, it will flock with them all the more assiduously when they happen to alight in its vicinity.

Now the Ogdens were birds of Molly's feather. They wore Eastern, and not Western, plumage, and their song was a different song from that which the Bear Creek birds sang. To be sure, the piping of little George Taylor was full of hopeful interest; and many other strains, both striking and melodious, were lifted in Cattle Land, and had given pleasure to Molly's ear. But although Indians, and bears, and mavericks, make worthy themes for song, these are not the only songs in the world. Therefore the Eastern warblings of the Ogdens sounded doubly sweet to Molly Wood. Such words as Newport, Bar Harbor, and Tiffany's thrilled her exceedingly. It made no difference that she herself had never been to Newport or Bar Harbor, and had visited Tiffany's more often to admire than to purchase. On the contrary, this rather added a dazzle to the music of the Ogdens. And Molly, whose Eastern song had been silent in this strange land, began to chirp it again during the visit that she made at the Sunk Creek Ranch.

Thus the Virginian's cause by no means prospered at this time. His forces were scattered, while Molly's were concentrated. The girl was not at that point where absence makes the heart grow fonder. While the Virginian was trundling his long, responsible miles in the caboose, delivering the cattle at Chicago, vanquishing Trampas along the Yellowstone, she had regained herself.

Thus it was that she could tell him so easily during those first hours that they were alone after his return, "I expect to like another man better than you."

Absence had recruited her. And then the Ogdens had reenforced her. They brought the East back powerfully to her memory, and her thoughts filled with it. They did not dream that they were assisting in any battle. No one ever had more unconscious allies than did Molly at that time. But she used them consciously, or almost consciously. She frequented them; she spoke of Eastern matters; she found that she had acquaintances whom the Ogdens also knew, and she often brought them into the conversation. For it may be said, I think, that she was fighting a battle—nay, a campaign. And perhaps this was a hopeful sign for the Virginian (had he but known it), that the girl resorted to allies. She surrounded herself, she steeped herself, with the East, to have, as it were, a sort of counteractant against the spell of the black-haired horseman.

And his forces were, as I have said, scattered. For his promotion gave him no more time for lovemaking. He was foreman now. He had said to Judge Henry, "I'll try to please yu'." And after the throb of emotion which these words had both concealed and conveyed, there came to him that sort of intention to win which amounts to a certainty. Yes, he would please Judge Henry!

He did not know how much he had already pleased him. He did not know that the Judge was humorously undecided which of his new foreman's first acts had the more delighted him: his performance with the missionary, or his magnanimity to Trampas.

"Good feeling is a great thing in anyone," the Judge would say; "but I like to know that my foreman has so much sense."

"I am personally very grateful to him," said Mrs. Henry.

And indeed so was the whole company. To be afflicted with Dr. MacBride for one night instead of six was a great liberation.

But the Virginian never saw his sweetheart alone again; while she was at the Sunk Creek Ranch, his duties called him away so much that there was no chance for him. Worse still, that habit of birds of a feather brought about a separation more considerable. She arranged to go East with the Ogdens. It was so good an opportunity to travel with friends, instead of making the journey alone!

Molly's term of ministration at the schoolhouse had so pleased Bear Creek that she was warmly urged to take a holiday. School could afford to begin a little late. Accordingly, she departed.

The Virginian hid his sore heart from her during the moment of farewell that they had.

"No, I'll not want any more books," he said, "till yu' come back." And then he made cheerfulness. "It's just the other way round!" said he.

"What is the other way round?"

"Why, last time it was me that went traveling, and you that stayed behind."

"So it was!" And here she gave him a last scratch. "But you'll be busier than ever," she said; "no spare time to grieve about me!"

She could wound him, and she knew it. Nobody else could. That is why she did it.

But he gave her something to remember, too.

"Next time," he said, "neither of us will stay behind. We'll both go together."

And with these words he gave her no laughing glance. It was a look that mingled with the words; so that now and again in the train, both came back to her, and she sat pensive, drawing near to Bennington and hearing his voice and seeing his eyes.

How is it that this girl could cry at having to tell Sam Bannett she could not think of him, and then treat another lover as she treated the Virginian? I cannot tell you, having never (as I said before) been a woman myself.

Bennington opened its arms to its venturesome daughter. Much was made of Molly Wood. Old faces and old places welcomed her. Fatted calves of varying dimensions made their appearance. And although the fatted calf is an animal that can assume more divergent shapes than any other known creature—being sometimes champagne and partridges, and again cake and currant wine—through each disguise you can always identify the same calf. The girl from Bear Creek met it at every turn.

The Bannetts at Hoosic Falls offered a large specimen to Molly—a dinner (perhaps I should say a banquet) of twenty-four. And Sam Bannett of course took her to drive more than once.

"I want to see the Hoosic Bridge," she would say. And when they reached that well-remembered point, "How lovely it is!" she exclaimed. And as she gazed at the view up and down the valley, she would grow pensive. "How natural the church looks," she continued. And then, having crossed both bridges, "Oh, there's the dear old lodge gate!" Or again, while they drove up the valley of the little Hoosic: "I had forgotten it was so nice and lonely. But after all, no woods are so interesting as those where you might possibly see a bear or an elk." And upon another occasion, after a cry of enthusiasm at the view from the top of Mount Anthony, "It's lovely, lovely, lovely," she said, with diminishing cadence, ending in pensiveness once more. "Do you see that little bit just there? No, not where the trees are—that bare spot that looks brown and warm in the sun. With a little sagebrush, that spot would look something like a place I know on Bear Creek. Only of course you don't get the clear air here."

"I don't forget you," said Sam. "Do you remember me? Or is it out of sight out of mind?"

And with this beginning he renewed his suit. She told him that she forgot no one; that she should return always, lest they might forget her.

"Return always!" he exclaimed. "You talk as if your anchor was dragging."

Was it? At all events, Sam failed in his suit.

Over in the house at Dunbarton, the old lady held Molly's hand and looked a long while at her. "You have changed very much," she said finally.

"I am a year older," said the girl.

"Pshaw, my dear!" said the great-aunt. "Who is he?"

"Nobody!" cried Molly, with indignation.

"Then you shouldn't answer so loud," said the great-aunt.

The girl suddenly hid her face. "I don't believe I can love anyone," she said, "except myself."

And then that old lady, who in her day had made her courtesy to Lafayette, began to stroke her niece's buried head, because she more than half understood. And understanding thus much, she asked no prying questions, but thought of the days of her own youth, and only spoke a little quiet love and confidence to Molly.

"I am an old, old woman," she said. "But I haven't forgotten about it. They objected to him because he had no fortune. But he was brave and handsome, and I loved him, my dear. Only I ought to have loved him more. I gave him my promise to think about it. And he and his ship were lost."

The great-aunt's voice had become very soft and low, and she spoke with many pauses. "So then I knew. If I had—if—perhaps I should have lost him; but it would have been after—ah, well! So long as you can help it, never marry! But when you cannot help it a moment longer, then listen to nothing but that; for, my dear, I know your choice would be worthy of the Starks. And now—let me see his picture."

"Why, aunty!" said Molly.

"Well, I won't pretend to be supernatural," said the aunt, "but I thought you kept one back when you were showing us those Western views last night."

Now this was the precise truth. Molly had brought a number of photographs from Wyoming to show to her friends at home. These, however, with one exception, were not portraits. They were views of scenery and of cattle round-ups, and other scenes characteristic of ranch life. Of young men she had in her possession several photographs, and all but one of these she had left behind her. Her aunt's penetration had in a way mesmerized the girl; she rose obediently and sought that picture of the Virginian. It was full length, displaying him in all his cowboy trappings—the leathern chaps, the belt and pistol, and in his hand a coil of rope.

Not one of her family had seen it, or suspected its existence. She now brought it downstairs and placed it in her aunt's hand.

"Mercy!" cried the old lady.

Molly was silent, but her eye grew warlike.

"Is that the way—" began the aunt. "Mercy!" she murmured; and she sat staring at the picture.

Molly remained silent.

Her aunt looked slowly up at her. "Has a man like that presumed—"

"He's not a bit like that. Yes, he's exactly like that," said Molly. And she would have snatched the photograph away, but her aunt retained it.

"Well," she said, "I suppose there are days when he does not kill people."

"He never killed anybody!" And Molly laughed.

"Are you seriously—" said the old lady.

"I almost might—at times. He is perfectly splendid."

"My dear, you have fallen in love with his clothes."

"It's not his clothes. And I'm not in love. He often wears others. He wears a white collar like anybody."

"Then that would be a more suitable way to be photographed, I think. He couldn't go round like that here. I could not receive him myself."

"He'd never think of such a thing. Why, you talk as if he were a savage."

The old lady studied the picture closely for a minute. "I think it is a good face," she finally remarked. "Is the fellow as handsome as that, my dear?"

More so, Molly thought. And who was he, and what were his prospects? were the aunt's next inquiries. She shook her head at the answers which she received; and she also shook her head over her niece's emphatic denial that her heart was lost to this man. But when their parting came, the old lady said: "God bless you and keep you, my dear. I'll not try to manage you. They managed me—" A sigh spoke the rest of this sentence. "But I'm not worried about you—at least, not very much. You have never done anything that was not worthy of the Starks. And if you're going to take him, do it before I die so that I can bid him welcome for your sake. God bless you, my dear."

And after the girl had gone back to Bennington, the great-aunt had this thought: "She is like us all. She wants a man that is a man." Nor did the old lady breathe her knowledge to any member of the family. For she was a loyal spirit, and her girl's confidence was sacred to her.

"Besides," she reflected, "if even I can do nothing with her, what a mess they'd make of it! We should hear of her elopement next."

So Molly's immediate family never saw that photograph, and never heard a word from her upon this subject. But on the day that she left for Bear Creek, as they sat missing her and discussing her visit in the evening, Mrs. Bell observed: "Mother, how did you think she was?"—"I never saw her better, Sarah. That horrible place seems to agree with her."—"Oh, yes, agree. It seemed to me—"—"Well?"—"Oh, just somehow that she was thinking."—"Thinking?"—"Well, I believe she has something on her mind."—"You mean a man," said Andrew Bell.—"A man, Andrew?"—"Yes, Mrs. Wood, that's what Sarah always means."

It may be mentioned that Sarah's surmises did not greatly contribute to her mother's happiness. And rumor is so strange a thing that presently from the malicious outside air came a vague and dreadful word—one of those words that cannot be traced to its source. Somebody said to Andrew Bell that they heard Miss Molly Wood was engaged to marry a *rustler*.

"Heavens, Andrew!" said his wife; "what is a rustler?"

It was not in any dictionary, and current translations of it were inconsistent. A man at Hoosic Falls said that he had passed through Cheyenne, and heard the term applied in a complimentary way to people who were alive and pushing. Another man had always supposed it meant some kind of horse. But the most alarming version of all was that a rustler was a cattle thief.

Now the truth is that all these meanings were right. The word ran a sort of progress in the cattle country, gathering many meanings as it went. It gathered more, however, in Bennington. In a very few days, gossip had it that Molly was engaged to a gambler, a gold miner, an escaped stage robber, and a Mexican bandit; while Mrs. Flynt feared she had married a Mormon.

Along Bear Creek, however, Molly and her "rustler" took a ride soon after her return. They were neither married nor engaged, and she was telling him about Vermont.

"I never was there," said he. "Never happened to strike in that direction."

"What decided your direction?"

"Oh, looking for chances. I reckon I must have been more ambitious than my brothers—or more restless. They stayed around on farms. But I got out. When I went back again six years afterward, I was twenty. They was talking about the same old things. Men of twenty-five and thirty—yet just sittin' and talkin' about the same old things. I told my mother about what I'd seen here and there, and she liked it, right to her death. But the others—well, when I found this whole world was hawgs and turkeys to them, with a little gunnin' afteh small game throwed in, I put on my hat one mawnin' and told 'em maybe when I was fifty I'd look in on 'em again to see if they'd got any new subjects. But they'll never. My brothers don't seem to want chances."

"You have lost a good many yourself," said Molly.

"That's correct."

"And yet," said she, "sometimes I think you know a great deal more than I ever shall."

"Why, of course I do," said he, quite simply. "I have earned my living since I was fourteen. And that's from old Mexico to British Columbia. I have never stolen or begged a cent. I'd not want yu' to know what I know."

She was looking at him, half listening and half thinking of her great-aunt.

"I am not losing chances anymore," he continued. "And you are the best I've got."

She was not sorry to have Georgie Taylor come galloping along at this moment and join them. But the Virginian swore profanely under his breath. And on this ride nothing more happened.

# CHAPTER XXIII

## VARIOUS POINTS

Love had been snowbound for many weeks. Before this imprisonment its course had run neither smooth nor rough, so far as eye could see; it had run either not at all, or, as an undercurrent, deep out of sight. In their rides, in their talks, love had been dumb, as to spoken words at least; for the Virginian had set himself a heavy task of silence and of patience. Then, where winter barred his visits to Bear Creek, and there was for the while no ranch work or responsibility to fill his thoughts and blood with action, he set himself a task much lighter. Often, instead of Shakespeare and fiction, schoolbooks lay open on his cabin table; and penmanship and spelling helped the hours to pass. Many sheets of paper did he fill with various exercises, and Mrs. Henry gave him her assistance in advice and corrections.

"I shall presently be in love with him myself," she told the Judge. "And it's time for you to become anxious."

"I am perfectly safe," he retorted. "There's only one woman for him anymore."

"She is not good enough for him," declared Mrs. Henry. "But he'll never see that."

So the snow fell, the world froze, and the spelling-books and exercises went on. But this was not the only case of education which was progressing at the Sunk Creek Ranch while love was snowbound.

One morning Scipio le Moyne entered the Virginian's sitting room—that apartment where Dr. MacBride had wrestled with sin so courageously all night.

The Virginian sat at his desk. Open books lay around him; a half-finished piece of writing was beneath his fist; his fingers were coated with ink. Education enveloped him, it may be said. But there was none in his eye. That was upon the window, looking far across the cold plain.

The foreman did not move when Scipio came in, and this humorous spirit smiled to himself. "It's Bear Creek he's havin' a vision of," he concluded. But he knew instantly that this was not so. The Virginian was looking at something real, and Scipio went to the window to see for himself.

"Well," he said, having seen, "when is he going to leave us?"

The foreman continued looking at two horsemen riding together. Their shapes, small in the distance, showed black against the universal whiteness.

"When d' yu' figure he'll leave us?" repeated Scipio.

"He," murmured the Virginian, always watching the distant horsemen; and again, "he."

Scipio sprawled down, familiarly, across a chair. He and the Virginian had come to know each other very well since that first meeting at Medora. They were birds many of whose feathers were the same, and the Virginian often talked to Scipio without reserve. Consequently, Scipio now understood those two syllables that the Virginian had pronounced precisely as though the sentences which lay between them had been fully expressed.

"Hm," he remarked. "Well, one will be a gain, and the other won't be no loss."

"Poor Shorty!" said the Virginian. "Poor fool!"

Scipio was less compassionate. "No," he persisted, "I ain't sorry for him. Any man old enough to have hair on his face ought to see through Trampas."

The Virginian looked out of the window again, and watched Shorty and Trampas as they rode in the distance. "Shorty is kind to animals," he said. "He has gentled that hawss Pedro he bought with his first money. Gentled him wonderful. When a man is kind to dumb animals, I always say he had got some good in him."

"Yes," Scipio reluctantly admitted. "Yes. But I always did hate a fool."

"This hyeh is a mighty cruel country," pursued the Virginian. "To animals that is. Think of it! Think what we do to hundreds an' thousands of little calves! Throw 'em down, brand 'em, cut 'em, ear mark 'em, turn 'em loose, and on to the next. It has got to be, of course. But I say this. If a man can go jammin' hot irons on to little calves and slicin' pieces off 'em with his knife, and live along, keepin' a kindness for animals in his heart, he has got some good in him. And that's what Shorty has got. But he is lettin' Trampas get a hold of him, and both of them will leave us." And the Virginian looked out across the huge winter whiteness again. But the riders had now vanished behind some foothills.

Scipio sat silent. He had never put these thoughts about men and animals to himself, and when they were put to him, he saw that they were true.

"Queer," he observed finally.

"What?"

"Everything."

"Nothing's queer," stated the Virginian, "except marriage and lightning. Them two occurrences can still give me a sensation of surprise."

"All the same it is queer," Scipio insisted.

"Well, let her go at me."

"Why, Trampas. He done you dirt. You pass that over. You could have fired him, but you let him stay and keep his job. That's goodness. And badness is resultin' from it, straight. Badness right from goodness."

"You're off the trail a whole lot," said the Virginian.

"Which side am I off, then?"

"North, south, east, and west. First point. I didn't expect to do Trampas any good by not killin' him, which I came pretty near doin' three times. Nor I didn't expect to do Trampas any good by lettin' him keep his job. But I am foreman of this ranch. And I can sit and tell all men to their face: 'I was above that meanness.' Point two: it ain't any *goodness,* it is *Trampas* that badness has resulted from. Put him anywhere and it will be the same. Put him under my eye, and I can follow his moves a little, anyway. You have noticed, maybe, that since you and I run on to that dead Polled Angus cow, that was still warm when we got to her, we have found no more cows dead of sudden death. We came mighty close to catchin' whoever it was that killed that cow and ran her calf off to his own bunch. He wasn't ten minutes ahead of us. We can prove nothin'; and he knows that just as well as we do. But our cows have all quit dyin' of sudden death. And Trampas he's gettin' ready for a change of residence. As soon as all the outfits begin hirin' new hands in the spring, Trampas will leave us and take a job with some of them. And maybe our cows'll commence gettin' killed again, and we'll have to take steps that will be more emphatic—maybe."

Scipio meditated. "I wonder what killin' a man feels like?" he said.

"Why, nothing to bother yu'—when he'd ought to have been killed. Next point: Trampas he'll take Shorty with him, which is certainly bad for Shorty. But it's me that has kept Shorty out of harm's way this long. If I had fired Trampas, he'd have worked Shorty into dissatisfaction that much sooner."

Scipio meditated again. "I knowed Trampas would pull his freight," he said. "But I didn't think of Shorty. What makes you think it?"

"He asked me for a raise."

"He ain't worth the pay he's getting now."

"Trampas has told him different."

"When a man ain't got no ideas of his own," said Scipio, "he'd ought to be kind o' careful who he borrows 'em from."

"That's mighty correct," said the Virginian. "Poor Shorty! He has told me about his life. It is sorrowful. And he will never get wise. It was too late for him to get wise when he was born. D' yu' know why he's after higher wages? He sends most all his money East."

"I don't see what Trampas wants him for," said Scipio.

"Oh, a handy tool some day."

"Not very handy," said Scipio.

"Well, Trampas is aimin' to train him. Yu' see, supposin' yu' were figuring to turn professional thief—yu'd be lookin' around for a nice young trustful accomplice to take all the punishment and let you take the rest."

"No such thing!" cried Scipio, angrily. "I'm no shirker." And then, perceiving the Virginian's expression, he broke out laughing. "Well," he exclaimed, "yu' fooled me that time."

"Looks that way. But I do mean it about Trampas."

Presently Scipio rose, and noticed the half-finished exercise upon the Virginian's desk. "Trampas is a rolling stone," he said.

"A rolling piece of mud," corrected the Virginian.

"Mud! That's right. I'm a rolling stone. Sometimes I'd most like to quit being."

"That's easy done," said the Virginian.

"No doubt, when yu've found the moss yu' want to gather." As Scipio glanced at the schoolbooks again, a sparkle lurked in his bleached blue eye. "I can cipher some," he said. "But I expect I've got my own notions about spelling."

"I retain a few private ideas that way myself," remarked the Virginian, innocently; and Scipio's sparkle gathered light.

"As to my geography," he pursued, "that's away out loose in the brush. Is Bennington the capital of Vermont? And how d' yu' spell bridegroom?"

"Last point!" shouted the Virginian, letting a book fly after him: "don't let badness and goodness worry yu', for yu'll never be a judge of them."

But Scipio had dodged the book, and was gone. As he went his way, he said to himself, "All the same, it must pay to fall regular in love."

At the bunkhouse that afternoon it was observed that he was unusually silent. His exit from the foreman's cabin had let in a breath of winter so chill that the Virginian went to see his thermometer, a Christmas present from Mrs. Henry. It registered twenty below zero. After reviving the fire to a white blaze, the foreman sat thinking over the story of Shorty: what its useless, feeble past had been; what would be its useless, feeble future. He shook his head over the sombre question, Was there any way out for Shorty?

"It may be," he reflected, "that them whose pleasure brings yu' into this world owes yu' a living. But that don't make the world responsible. The world did not beget you. I reckon man helps them that help themselves. As for the universe, it looks like it did too wholesale a business to turn out an article up to standard every clip. Yes, it is sorrowful. For Shorty is kind to his hawss."

In the evening the Virginian brought Shorty into his room. He usually knew what he had to say, usually found it easy to arrange his thoughts; and after such arranging the words came of themselves. But as he looked at Shorty, this did not happen to him. There was not a line of badness in the face; yet also there was not a line of strength; no promise in eye, or nose, or chin; the whole thing melted to a stubby, featureless mediocrity. It was a countenance like thousands; and hopelessness filled the Virginian as he looked at this lost dog, and his dull, wistful eyes.

But some beginning must be made.

"I wonder what the thermometer has got to be," he said. "Yu' can see it, if yu'll hold the lamp to that right side of the window."

Shorty held the lamp. "I never used any," he said, looking out at the instrument, nevertheless.

The Virginian had forgotten that Shorty could not read. So he looked out of the window himself, and found that it was twenty-two below zero. "This is pretty good tobacco," he remarked; and Shorty helped himself, and filled his pipe.

"I had to rub my left ear with snow today," said he. "I was just in time."

"I thought it looked pretty freezy out where yu' was riding," said the foreman.

The lost dog's eyes showed plain astonishment. "We didn't see you out there," said he.

"Well," said the foreman, "it'll soon not be freezing anymore; and then we'll all be warm enough with work. Everybody will be working all over the range. And I wish I knew somebody that had a lot of stable work to be attended to. I cert'nly do for your sake."

"Why?" said Shorty.

"Because it's the right kind of a job for you."

"I can make more—" began Shorty, and stopped.

"There is a time coming," said the Virginian, "when I'll want somebody that knows how to get the friendship of hawsses. I'll want him to handle some special hawsses the Judge has plans about. Judge Henry would pay fifty a month for that."

"I can make more," said Shorty, this time with stubbornness.

"Well, yes. Sometimes a man can—when he's not worth it, I mean. But it don't generally last."

Shorty was silent. "I used to make more myself," said the Virginian.

"You're making a lot more now," said Shorty.

"Oh, yes. But I mean when I was fooling around the earth, jumping from job to job, and helling all over town between whiles. I was not worth fifty a month then, nor twenty-five. But there was nights I made a heap more at cyards."

Shorty's eyes grew large.

"And then, bang! It was gone with treatin' the men and the girls."

"I don't always—" said Shorty, and stopped again.

The Virginian knew that he was thinking about the money he sent East. "After a while," he continued, "I noticed a right strange fact. The money I made easy that I *wasn't* worth, it went like it came. I strained myself none gettin' or spendin' it. But the money I made hard that I *was* worth, why I began to feel right careful about that. And now I have got savings stowed away. If once yu' could know how good that feels—"

"So I would know," said Shorty, "with your luck."

"What's my luck?" said the Virginian, sternly.

"Well, if I had took up land along a creek that never goes dry and proved upon it like you have, and if I had saw that land raise its value on me with me lifting no finger—"

"Why did you lift no finger?" cut in the Virginian. "Who stopped yu' taking up land? Did it not stretch in front of yu', behind yu', all around yu', the biggest, baldest opportunity in sight? That was the time I lifted my finger; but yu' didn't."

Shorty stood stubborn.

"But never mind that," said the Virginian. "Take my land away tomorrow, and I'd still have my savings in bank. Because, you see, I had to work right hard gathering them in. I found out what I could do, and I settled down and did it. Now you can do that too. The only tough part is the finding out what you're good for. And for you, that is found. If you'll just decide to work at this thing you can do, and gentle those hawsses for the Judge, you'll be having savings in a bank yourself."

"I can make more," said the lost dog.

The Virginian was on the point of saying, "Then get out!" But instead, he spoke kindness to the end. "The weather is freezing yet," he said, "and it will be for a good long while. Take your time, and tell me if yu' change your mind."

After that Shorty returned to the bunkhouse, and the Virginian knew that the boy had learned his lesson of discontent from Trampas with a thoroughness past all unteaching. This petty triumph of evil seemed scarce of the size to count as any victory over the Virginian. But all men grasp at straws. Since that first moment, when in the Medicine Bow saloon the

Virginian had shut the mouth of Trampas by a word, the man had been trying to get even without risk; and at each successive clash of his weapon with the Virginian's, he had merely met another public humiliation. Therefore, now at the Sunk Creek Ranch in these cold white days, a certain lurking insolence in his gait showed plainly his opinion that by disaffecting Shorty he had made some sort of reprisal.

Yes, he had poisoned the lost dog. In the springtime, when the neighboring ranches needed additional hands, it happened as the Virginian had foreseen—Trampas departed to a "better job," as he took pains to say, and with him the docile Shorty rode away upon his horse Pedro.

Love now was not any longer snowbound. The mountain trails were open enough for the sure feet of love's steed—that horse called Monte. But duty blocked the path of love. Instead of turning his face to Bear Creek, the foreman had other journeys to make, full of heavy work, and watchfulness, and councils with the Judge. The cattle thieves were growing bold, and winter had scattered the cattle widely over the range. Therefore the Virginian, instead of going to see her, wrote a letter to his sweetheart. It was his first.

## CHAPTER XXIV

## A LETTER WITH A MORAL

The letter which the Virginian wrote to Molly Wood was, as has been stated, the first that he had ever addressed to her. I think, perhaps, he may have been a little shy as to his skill in the epistolary art, a little anxious lest any sustained production from his pen might contain blunders that would too staringly remind her of his scant learning. He could turn off a business communication about steers or stock cars, or any other of the subjects involved in his profession, with a brevity and a clearness that led the Judge to confide three-quarters of such correspondence to his foreman. "Write to the 76 outfit," the Judge would say, "and tell them that my wagon cannot start for the round-up until," etc.; or "Write to Cheyenne and say that if they will hold a meeting next Monday week, I will," etc. And then the Virginian would write such communications with ease.

But his first message to his lady was scarcely written with ease. It must be classed, I think, among those productions which are styled literary *efforts*. It was completed in pencil before it was copied in ink; and that first draft of it in pencil was well-nigh illegible with erasures and amendments. The state of mind of the writer during its composition may be gathered without further description on my part from a slight interruption which occurred in the middle.

The door opened, and Scipio put his head in. "You coming to dinner?" he inquired.

"You go to hell," replied the Virginian.

"My jinks!" said Scipio, quietly, and he shut the door without further observation.

To tell the truth, I doubt if this letter would ever have been undertaken, far less completed and despatched, had not the lover's heart been wrung with disappointment. All winter long he had looked to that day when he should knock at the girl's door, and hear her voice bid him come in. All winter long he had been choosing the ride he would take her. He had imagined a sunny afternoon, a hidden grove, a sheltering cleft of rock, a running spring, and some words of his that should conquer her at last and leave his lips upon hers. And with this controlled fire pent up within him, he had counted the days, scratching them off his calendar with a dig each night that once or twice snapped the pen. Then, when the trail stood open, this meeting was deferred, put off for indefinite days, or weeks; he could not tell how long. So, gripping his pencil and tracing heavy words, he gave himself what consolation he could by writing her.

The letter, duly stamped and addressed to Bear Creek, set forth upon its travels; and these were devious and long. When it reached its destination, it was some twenty days old. It had gone by private hand at the outset, taken the stagecoach at a way point, become late in that stagecoach, reached a point of transfer, and waited there for the postmaster to begin, continue, end, and recover from a game of poker, mingled with whiskey. Then it once more proceeded, was dropped at the right way point, and carried by private hand to Bear Creek. The experience of this letter, however, was not at all a remarkable one at that time in Wyoming.

Molly Wood looked at the envelope. She had never before seen the Virginian's handwriting. She knew it instantly. She closed her door and sat down to read it with a beating heart.

SUNK CREEK RANCH, *May 5, 188–*
MY DEAR MISS WOOD: I am sorry about this. My plan was different. It was to get over for a ride with you about now or sooner. This year Spring is early. The snow is off the flats this side the range and where the sun gets a chance to hit the earth strong all day it is green and has flowers too, a good many. You can see them bob and mix together in the wind. The quaking-asps down low on the South side are in small leaf and will soon be twinkling like the flowers do now. I had planned to take a look at this with you and that was a better plan than what I have got to do. The water is high but I could have got over and as for the snow on top of the mountain a man told

me nobody could cross it for a week yet, because he had just done it himself. Was not he a funny man? You ought to see how the birds have streamed across the sky while Spring was coming. But you have seen them on your side of the mountain. But I can't come now Miss Wood. There is a lot for me to do that has to be done and Judge Henry needs more than two eyes just now. I could not think much of myself if I left him for my own wishes.

But the days will be warmer when I come. We will not have to quit by five, and we can get off and sit too. We could not sit now unless for a very short while. If I know when I can come I will try to let you know, but I think it will be this way. I think you will just see me coming for I have things to do of an unsure nature and a good number of such. Do not believe reports about Indians. They are started by editors to keep the soldiers in the country. The friends of the editors get the hay and beef contracts. Indians do not come to settled parts like Bear Creek is. It is all editors and politicianists.

Nothing has happened worth telling you. I have read that play Othello. No man should write down such a thing. Do you know if it is true? I have seen one worse affair down in Arizona. He killed his little child as well as his wife but such things should not be put down in fine language for the public. I have read Romeo and Juliet. That is beautiful language but Romco is no man. I like his friend Mercutio that gets killed. He is a man. If he had got Juliet there would have been no foolishness and trouble.

Well Miss Wood I would like to see you today. Do you know what I think Monte would do if I rode him out and let the rein slack? He would come straight to your gate for he is a horse of great judgement. ("That's the first word he has misspelled," said Molly.) I suppose you are sitting with George Taylor and those children right now. Then George will get old enough to help his father but Uncle Hewie's twins will be ready for you about then and the supply will keep coming from all quarters all sizes for you to say big A little a to them. There is no news here. Only calves and cows and the hens are laying now which does always seem news to a hen every time she does it. Did I ever tell you about a hen Emily we had here? She was venturesome to an extent I have not seen in other hens only she had poor judgement and would make no family ties. She would keep trying to get interest in the ties of others taking charge of little chicks and bantams and turkeys and puppies one time, and she thought most anything was an egg. I will tell you about her sometime. She died without family ties one day while I was building a house for her to teach school in. ("The outrageous wretch!" cried Molly! And her cheeks turned deep pink as she sat alone with her lover's letter.)

I am coming the first day I am free. I will be a hundred miles from you most of the time when I am not more but I will ride a hundred miles for one hour and Monte is up to that. After never seeing you for so long I will make one hour do if I have to. Here is a flower I have just been out and picked. I have kissed it now. That is the best I can do yet.

Molly laid the letter in her lap and looked at the flower. Then suddenly she jumped up and pressed it to her lips, and after a long moment held it away from her.

"No," she said. "No, no, no." She sat down.

It was some time before she finished the letter. Then once more she got up and put on her hat.

Mrs. Taylor wondered where the girl could be walking so fast. But she was not walking anywhere, and in half an hour she returned, rosy with her swift exercise, but with a spirit as perturbed as when she had set out.

Next morning at six, when she looked out of her window, there was Monte tied to the Taylor's gate. Ah, could he have come the day before, could she have found him when she returned from that swift walk of hers!

## CHAPTER XXV

## PROGRESS OF THE LOST DOG

It was not even an hour's visit that the Virginian was able to pay his lady love. But neither had he come a hundred miles to see her. The necessities of his wandering work had chanced to bring him close enough for a glimpse of her, and this glimpse he took, almost on the wing. For he had to rejoin a company of men at once.

"Yu' got my letter?" he said.

"Yesterday."

"Yesterday! I wrote it three weeks ago. Well, yu' got it. This cannot be the hour with you that I mentioned. That is coming, and maybe very soon."

She could say nothing. Relief she felt, and yet with it something like a pang.

"Today does not count," he told her, "except that every time I see you counts with me. But this is not the hour that I mentioned."

What little else was said between them upon this early morning shall be told duly. For this visit in its own good time did count momentously, though both of them took it lightly while its fleeting minutes passed. He returned to her two volumes that she had lent him long ago and with Taylor he left a horse which he had brought for her to ride. As a good-by, he put a bunch of flowers in her hand. Then he was gone, and she watched him going by the thick bushes along the stream. They were pink with wild roses; and the meadowlarks, invisible in the grass, like hiding choristers, sent up across the empty miles of air their unexpected song. Earth and sky had been propitious, could he have stayed; and perhaps one portion of her heart had been propitious too. So, as he rode away on Monte, she watched him, half chilled by reason, half melted by passion, self-thwarted, self-accusing, unresolved. Therefore the days that came for her now were all of them unhappy ones, while for him they were filled with work well done and with changeless longing.

One day it seemed as if a lull was coming, a pause in which he could at last attain that hour with her. He left the camp and turned his face toward Bear Creek. The way led him along Butte Creek. Across the stream lay Balaam's large ranch; and presently on the other bank he saw Balaam himself, and reined in Monte for a moment to watch what Balaam was doing.

"That's what I've heard," he muttered to himself. For Balaam had led some horses to the water, and was lashing them heavily because they would not drink. He looked at this spectacle so intently that he did not see Shorty approaching along the trail.

"Morning," said Shorty to him, with some constraint.

But the Virginian gave him a pleasant greeting, "I was afraid I'd not catch you so quick," said Shorty. "This is for you." He handed his recent foreman a letter of much battered appearance. It was from the Judge. It had not come straight, but very gradually, in the pockets of three successive cowpunchers. As the Virginian glanced over it and saw that the enclosure it contained was for Balaam, his heart fell. Here were new orders for him, and he could not go to see his sweetheart.

"Hello, Shorty!" said Balaam, from over the creek. To the Virginian he gave a slight nod. He did not know him, although he knew well enough who he was.

"Hyeh's a letter from Judge Henry for yu'," said the Virginian, and he crossed the creek.

Many weeks before, in the early spring, Balaam had borrowed two horses from the Judge, promising to return them at once. But the Judge, of course, wrote very civilly. He hoped that "this dunning reminder" might be excused. As Balaam read the reminder, he wished that he had sent the horses before. The Judge was a greater man than he in the Territory. Balaam could not but excuse the "dunning reminder"—but he was ready to be disagreeable to somebody at once.

"Well," he said, musing aloud in his annoyance, "Judge Henry wants them by the 30th. Well, this is the 24th, and time enough yet."

"This is the 27th," said the Virginian, briefly.

That made a difference! Not so easy to reach Sunk Creek in good order by the 30th! Balaam had drifted three sunrises behind the progress of the month. Days look alike, and often lose their very names in the quiet depths of Cattle Land. The horses were not even here at the ranch. Balaam was ready to be very disagreeable now. Suddenly he perceived the date of the Judge's letter. He held it out to the Virginian, and struck the paper.

"What's your idea in bringing this here two weeks late?" he said.

Now, when he had struck that paper, Shorty looked at the Virginian. But nothing happened beyond a certain change of light in the Southerner's eyes. And when the Southerner spoke, it was with his usual gentleness and civility. He explained that the letter had been put in his hands just now by Shorty.

"Oh," said Balaam. He looked at Shorty. How had he come to be a messenger? "You working for the Sunk Creek outfit again?" said he.

"No," said Shorty.

Balaam turned to the Virginian again. "How do you expect me to get those horses to Sunk Creek by the 30th?"

The Virginian levelled a lazy eye on Balaam. "I ain' doin' any expecting," said he. His native dialect was on top today. "The Judge has friends goin' to arrive from New Yawk for a trip across the Basin," he added. "The hawsses are for them."

Balaam grunted with displeasure, and thought of the sixty or seventy days since he had told the Judge he would return the horses at once. He looked across at Shorty seated in the shade, and through his uneasy thoughts his instinct irrelevantly noted what a good pony the youth rode. It was the same animal he had seen once or twice before. But something must be done. The Judge's horses were far out on the big range, and must be found and driven in, which would take certainly the rest of this day, possibly part of the next.

Balaam called to one of his men and gave some sharp orders, emphasizing details, and enjoining haste, while the Virginian leaned slightly against his horse, with one arm over the saddle, hearing and understanding, but not smiling outwardly. The man departed to saddle up for his search on the big range, and Balaam resumed the unhitching of his team.

"So you're not working for the Sunk Creek outfit now?" he inquired of Shorty. He ignored the Virginian. "Working for the Goose Egg?"

"No," said Shorty.

"Sand Hill outfit, then?"

"No," said Shorty.

Balaam grinned. He noticed how Shorty's yellow hair stuck through a hole in his hat, and how old and battered were Shorty's overalls. Shorty had been glad to take a little accidental pay for becoming the bearer of the letter which he had delivered to the Virginian. But even that sum was no longer in his possession. He had passed through Drybone on his way, and at Drybone there had been a game of poker. Shorty's money was now in the pocket of Trampas. But he had one valuable possession in the world left to him, and that was his horse Pedro.

"Good pony of yours," said Balaam to him now, from across Butte Creek. Then he struck his own horse in the jaw because he held back from coming to the water as the other had done.

"Your trace ain't unhitched," commented the Virginian, pointing.

Balaam loosed the strap he had forgotten, and cut the horse again for consistency's sake. The animal, bewildered, now came down to the water, with its head in the air, and snuffing as it took short, nervous steps.

The Virginian looked on at this, silent and sombre. He could scarcely interfere between another man and his own beast. Neither he nor Balaam was among those who say their prayers. Yet in this omission they were not equal. A half-great poet once had a wholly great day, and in that great day he was able to write a poem that has lived and become, with many, a household word. He called it *The Rime of the Ancient Mariner.* And it is rich with many lines that possess the memory; but these are the golden ones:

> "He prayeth well who loveth well
> Both man and bird and beast.
> He prayeth best who loveth best
> All things both great and small;
> For the dear God who loveth us,
> He made and loveth all."

These lines are the pure gold. They are good to teach children; because after the children come to be men, they may believe at least some part of them still. The Virginian did not know them—but his heart had taught him many things. I doubt if Balaam knew them either. But on him they would have been as pearls to swine.

"So you've quit the round-up?" he resumed to Shorty.

Shorty nodded and looked sidewise at the Virginian.

For the Virginian knew that he had been turned off for going to sleep while night-herding.

Then Balaam threw another glance on Pedro the horse.

"Hello, Shorty!" he called out, for the boy was departing. "Don't you like dinner anymore? It's ready about now."

Shorty forded the creek and slung his saddle off, and on invitation turned Pedro, his buckskin pony, into Balaam's pasture. This was green, the rest of the wide world being yellow, except only where Butte Creek, with its bordering cottonwoods, coiled away into the desert distance like a green snake without end. The Virginian also turned his horse into the pasture. He must stay at the ranch till the Judge's horses should be found.

"Mrs. Balaam's East yet," said her lord, leading the way to his dining room.

He wanted Shorty to dine with him, and could not exclude the Virginian, much as he should have enjoyed this.

"See any Indians?" he enquired.

"Na-a!" said Shorty, in disdain of recent rumors.

"They're headin' the other way," observed the Virginian. "Bow Laig Range is where they was repawted."

"What business have they got off the reservation, I'd like to know," said the ranchman, "Bow Leg, or anywhere?"

"Oh, it's just a hunt, and a kind of visitin' their friends on the South Reservation," Shorty explained. "Squaws along and all."

"Well, if the folks at Washington don't keep squaws and all where they belong," said Balaam, in a rage, "the folks in Wyoming Territory 'ill do a little job that way themselves."

"There's a petition out," said Shorty. "Paper's goin' East with a lot of names to it. But they ain't no harm, them Indians ain't."

"No harm?" rasped out Balaam. "Was it white men druv off the O. C. yearlings?"

Balaam's Eastern grammar was sometimes at the mercy of his Western feelings. The thought of the perennial stultification of Indian affairs at Washington, whether by politician or philanthropist, was always sure to arouse him. He walked impatiently about while he spoke, and halted impatiently at the window. Out in the world the unclouded day was shining, and Balaam's eye traveled across the plains to where a blue line, faint and pale, lay along the end of the vast yellow distance. That was the beginning of the Bow Leg Mountains. Somewhere over there were the red men, ranging in unfrequented depths of rock and pine—their forbidden ground.

Dinner was ready, and they sat down.

"And I suppose," Balaam continued, still hot on the subject, "you'd claim Indians object to killing a white man when they run on to him good and far from human help? These peaceable Indians are just the worst in the business."

"That's so," assented the easy-opinioned Shorty, exactly as if he had always maintained this view. "Chap started for Sunk Creek three weeks ago. Trapper he was; old like, with a red shirt. One of his horses come into the round-up Toosday. Man ain't been heard from." He ate in silence for a while, evidently brooding in his childlike mind. Then he said, querulously, "I'd sooner trust one of them Indians than I would Trampas."

Balaam slanted his fat bullet head far to one side, and laying his spoon down (he had opened some canned grapes) laughed steadily at his guest with a harsh relish of irony.

The guest ate a grape, and perceiving he was seen through, smiled back rather miserably.

"Say, Shorty," said Balaam, his head still slanted over, "what's the figures of your bank balance just now?"

"I ain't usin' banks," murmured the youth.

Balaam put some more grapes on Shorty's plate, and drawing a cigar from his waistcoat, sent it rolling to his guest.

"Matches are behind you," he added. He gave a cigar to the Virginian as an afterthought, but to his disgust, the Southerner put it in his pocket and lighted a pipe.

Balaam accompanied his guest, Shorty, when he went to the pasture to saddle up and depart. "Got a rope?" he asked the guest, as they lifted down the bars.

"Don't need to rope him. I can walk right up to Pedro. You stay back."

Hiding his bridle behind him, Shorty walked to the river-bank, where the pony was switching his long tail in the shade; and speaking persuasively to him, he came nearer, till he laid his hand on Pedro's dusky mane, which was many shades darker than his hide. He turned expectantly, and his master came up to his expectations with a piece of bread.

"Eats that, does he?" said Balaam, over the bars.

"Likes the salt," said Shorty. "Now, n-n-ow, here! Yu' don't guess yu'll be bridled, don't you? Open your teeth! Yu'd like to play yu' was nobody's horse and live private? Or maybe yu'd prefer ownin' a saloon?"

Pedro evidently enjoyed this talk, and the dodging he made about the bit. Once fairly in his mouth, he accepted the inevitable, and followed Shorty to the bars. Then Shorty turned and extended his hand.

"Shake!" he said to his pony, who lifted his forefoot quietly and put it in his master's hand. Then the master tickled his nose, and he wrinkled it and flattened his ears, pretending to bite. His face wore an expression of knowing relish over this performance. "Now the other hoof," said Shorty; and the horse and master shook hands with their left. "I learned him that," said the cowboy, with pride and affection. "Say, Pede," he continued, in Pedro's ear, "ain't yu' the best little horse in the country? What? Here, now! Keep out of that, you deadbeat! There ain't no more bread." He pinched the pony's nose, one quarter of which was wedged into his pocket.

"Quite a lady's little pet!" said Balaam, with the rasp in his voice. "Pity this isn't New York, now, where there's a big market for harmless horses. Gee-gees, the children call them."

"He ain't no gee-gee," said Shorty, offended. "He'll beat any cow-pony workin' you've got. Yu' can turn him on a half-dollar. Don't need to touch the reins. Hang 'em on one finger and swing your body, and he'll turn."

Balaam knew this, and he knew that the pony was only a four-year-old. "Well," he said, "Drybone's had no circus this season. Maybe they'd buy tickets to see Pedro. He's good for that, anyway."

Shorty became gloomy. The Virginian was grimly smoking. Here was something else going on not to his taste, but none of his business.

"Try a circus," persisted Balaam. "Alter your plans for spending cash in town, and make a little money instead."

Shorty having no plans to alter and no cash to spend, grew still more gloomy.

"What'll you take for that pony?" said Balaam.

Shorty spoke up instantly. "A hundred dollars couldn't buy that piece of stale mud off his back," he asserted, looking off into the sky grandiosely.

But Balaam looked at Shorty, "You keep the mud," he said, "and I'll give you thirty dollars for the horse."

Shorty did a little professional laughing, and began to walk toward his saddle.

"Give you thirty dollars," repeated Balaam, picking a stone up and slinging it into the river.

"How far do yu' call it to Drybone?" Shorty remarked, stooping to investigate the bucking-strap on his saddle—a superfluous performance, for Pedro never bucked.

"You won't have to walk," said Balaam. "Stay all night, and I'll send you over comfortably in the morning, when the wagon goes for the mail."

"Walk?" Shorty retorted. "Drybone's twenty-five miles. Pedro'll put me there in three hours and not know he done it." He lifted the saddle on the horse's back. "Come, Pedro," said he.

"Come, Pedro!" mocked Balaam.

There followed a little silence.

"No, sir," mumbled Shorty, with his head under Pedro's belly, busily cinching. "A hundred dollars is bottom figures."

Balaam, in his turn, now duly performed some professional laughing, which was noted by Shorty under the horse's belly. He stood up and squared round on Balaam. "Well, then," he said, "what'll yu give for him?"

"Thirty dollars," said Balaam, looking far off into the sky, as Shorty had looked.

"Oh, come, now," expostulated Shorty.

It was he who now did the feeling for an offer and this was what Balaam liked to see. "Why yes," he said, "thirty," and looked surprised that he should have to mention the sum so often.

"I thought yu'd quit them first figures," said the cowpuncher, "for yu' can see I ain't goin' to look at em."

Balaam climbed on the fence and sat there "I'm not crying for your Pedro," he observed dispassionately. "Only it struck me you were dead broke, and wanted to raise cash and keep yourself going till you hunted up a job and could buy him back." He hooked his right thumb inside his waistcoat pocket. "But I'm not cryin' for him," he repeated. "He'd stay right here, of course. I wouldn't part with him. Why does he stand that way? Hello!" Balaam suddenly straightened himself, like a man who has made a discovery.

"Hello, what?" said Shorty, on the defensive.

Balaam was staring at Pedro with a judicial frown. Then he stuck out a finger at the horse, keeping the thumb hooked in his pocket. So meagre a gesture was felt by the ruffled Shorty to be no just way to point at Pedro. "What's the matter with that foreleg there?" said Balaam.

"Which? Nothin's the matter with it!" snapped Shorty.

Balaam climbed down from his fence and came over with elaborate deliberation. He passed his hand up and down the off foreleg. Then he spit slenderly. "Mm!" he said thoughtfully; and added, with a shade of sadness, "that's always to be expected when they're worked too young."

Shorty slid his hand slowly over the disputed leg. "What's to be expected?" he inquired—"that they'll eat hearty? Well, he does."

At this retort the Virginian permitted himself to laugh in audible sympathy.

"Sprung," continued Balaam, with a sigh. "Whirling round short when his bones were soft did that. Yes."

"Sprung!" Shorty said, with a bark of indignation. "Come on, Pede; you and me'll spring for town."

He caught the horn of the saddle, and as he swung into place the horse rushed away with him. "O-ee! Yoi-yup, yup, yup!" sang Shorty, in the shrill cow dialect. He made Pedro play an exhibition game of speed, bringing him round close to Balaam in a wide circle, and then he vanished in dust down the left-bank trail.

Balaam looked after him and laughed harshly. He had seen trout dash about like that when the hook in their jaw first surprised them. He knew Shorty would show the pony off, and he knew Shorty's love for Pedro was not equal to his need of money. He called to one of his men, asked something about the dam at the mouth of the canyon, where the main irrigation ditch began, made a remark about the prolonged drought, and then walked to his dining-room door, where, as he expected, Shorty met him.

"Say," said the youth, "do you consider that's any way to talk about a good horse?"

"Any dude could see the leg's sprung," said Balaam. But he looked at

Pedro's shoulder, which was well laid back; and he admired his points, dark in contrast with the buckskin, and also the width between the eyes.

"Now you know," whined Shorty, "that it ain't sprung any more than your leg's cork. If you mean the right leg ain't plumb straight, I can tell you he was born so. That don't make no difference, for it ain't weak. Try him onced. Just as sound and strong as iron. Never stumbles. And he don't never go to jumpin' with yu'. He's kind and he's smart." And the master petted his pony, who lifted a hoof for another handshake.

Of course Balaam had never thought the leg was sprung, and he now took on an unprejudiced air of wanting to believe Shorty's statements if he only could.

"Maybe there's two years' work left in that leg," he now observed.

"Better give your hawss away, Shorty," said the Virginian.

"Is this your deal, my friend?" inquired Balaam. And he slanted his bullet head at the Virginian.

"Give him away, Shorty," drawled the Southerner. "His laig is busted. Mr. Balaam says so."

Balaam's face grew evil with baffled fury. But the Virginian was gravely considering Pedro. He, too, was not pleased. But he could not interfere. Already he had overstepped the code in these matters. He would have dearly liked—for reasons good and bad, spite and mercy mingled—to have spoiled Balaam's market, to have offered a reasonable or even an unreasonable price for Pedro, and taken possession of the horse himself. But this might not be. In bets, in card games, in all horse transactions and other matters of similar business, a man must take care of himself, and wiser onlookers must suppress their wisdom and hold their peace.

That evening Shorty again had a cigar. He had parted with Pedro for forty dollars, a striped Mexican blanket, and a pair of spurs. Undressing over in the bunkhouse, he said to the Virginian, "I'll sure buy Pedro back off him just as soon as ever I rustle some cash." The Virginian grunted. He was thinking he should have to travel hard to get the horses to the Judge by the 30th; and below that thought lay his aching disappointment and his longing for Bear Creek.

In the early dawn Shorty sat up among his blankets on the floor of the bunkhouse and saw the various sleepers coiled or sprawled in their beds; their breathing had not yet grown restless at the nearing of day. He stepped to the door carefully, and saw the crowding blackbirds begin their walk and chatter in the mud of the littered and trodden corrals. From beyond among the cottonwoods, came continually the smooth unemphatic sound of the doves answering each other invisibly; and against the empty ridge of the river-bluff lay the moon, no longer shining, for there was established a new light through the sky. Pedro stood in the pasture close to the bars. The cowboy slowly closed the door behind him, and sitting down on the step, drew his money out and idly handled it, taking no comfort just then from its possession. Then he put it back, and after dragging on his boots, crossed to the pasture, and held a last talk with his pony, brushing the cakes of mud from his hide where he had rolled, and passing a lingering hand over his mane. As the sounds of the morning came increasingly from tree and plain, Shorty glanced back to see that no one was yet out of the cabin, and then put his arms round the horse's neck, laying his head against him. For a moment the cowboy's insignificant face was exalted by the emotion he would never have let others see. He hugged tight this animal, who was dearer to his heart than anybody in the world.

"Good-by, Pedro," he said—"good-by." Pedro looked for bread.

"No," said his master, sorrowfully, "not anymore. Yu' know well I'd give it yu' if I had it. You and me didn't figure on this, did we, Pedro? Good-by!"

He hugged his pony again, and got as far as the bars of the pasture, but returned once more. "Good-by, my little horse, my dear horse, my little, little Pedro," he said, as his tears wet the pony's neck. Then he wiped them with his hand, and got himself back to the bunkhouse. After breakfast he and his belongings departed to Drybone, and Pedro from his field calmly watched this departure; for horses must recognize even less than men the black corners that their destinies turn. The pony stopped feeding to look at the mail-wagon pass by; but the master sitting in the wagon forebore to turn his head.

# CHAPTER XXVI

## BALAAM AND PEDRO

Resigned to wait for the Judge's horses, Balaam went into his office this dry, bright morning and read nine accumulated newspapers; for he was behindhand. Then he rode out on the ditches, and met his man returning with the troublesome animals at last. He hastened home and sent for the Virginian. He had made a decision.

"See here," he said; "those horses are coming. What trail would you take over to the Judge's?"

"Shortest trail's right through the Bow Laig Mountains," said the foreman, in his gentle voice.

"Guess you're right. It's dinnertime. We'll start right afterward. We'll make Little Muddy Crossing by sundown, and Sunk Creek tomorrow, and the next day'll see us through. Can a wagon get through Sunk Creek Canyon?"

The Virginian smiled. "I reckon it can't, seh, and stay resembling a wagon."

Balaam told them to saddle Pedro and one packhorse, and drive the bunch of horses into a corral, roping the Judge's two, who proved extremely wild. He had decided to take this journey himself on remembering certain politics soon to be rife in Cheyenne. For Judge Henry was indeed a greater man than Balaam. This personally conducted return of the horses would temper its tardiness, and, moreover, the sight of some New York visitors would be a good thing after seven months of no warmer touch with that metropolis than the Sunday *Herald*, always eight days old when it reached the Butte Creek Ranch.

They forded Butte Creek, and, crossing the well-traveled trail which follows down to Drybone, turned their faces toward the uninhabited country that began immediately, as the ocean begins off a sandy shore. And as a single mast on which no sail is shining stands at the horizon and seems to add a loneliness to the surrounding sea, so the long gray line of fence, almost a mile away, that ended Balaam's land on this side the creek, stretched along the waste ground and added desolation to the plain. No solitary watercourse with margin of cottonwoods or willow thickets flowed here to stripe the dingy, yellow world with interrupting green, nor were cattle to be seen dotting the distance, nor moving objects at all, nor any bird in the soundless air. The last gate was shut by the Virginian, who looked back at the pleasant trees of the ranch, and then followed on in single file across the alkali of No Man's Land.

No cloud was in the sky. The desert's grim noon shone sombrely on flat and hill. The sagebrush was dull like zinc. Thick heat rose near at hand from the caked alkali, and pale heat shrouded the distant peaks.

There were five horses. Balaam led on Pedro, his squat figure stiff in the saddle, but solid as a rock, and tilted a little forward, as his habit was. One of the Judge's horses came next, a sorrel, dragging back continually on the rope by which he was led. After him ambled Balaam's wise pack-animal, carrying the light burden of two days' food and lodging. She was an old mare who could still go when she chose, but had been schooled by the years, and kept the trail, giving no trouble to the Virginian who came behind her. He also sat solid as a rock, yet subtly bending to the struggles of the wild horse he led, as a steel spring bends and balances and resumes its poise.

Thus they made but slow time, and when they topped the last dull rise of ground and looked down on the long slant of ragged, caked earth to the crossing of Little Muddy, with its single tree and few mean bushes, the final distance where eyesight ends had deepened to violet from the thin, steady blue they had stared at for so many hours, and all heat was gone from the universal dryness. The horses drank a long time from the sluggish yellow water, and its alkaline taste and warmth were equally welcome to the men.

They built a little fire, and when supper was ended, smoked but a short while and in silence, before they got in the blankets that were spread in a smooth place beside the water.

They had picketed the two horses of the Judge in the best grass they could find, letting the rest go free to find pasture where they could. When the first light came, the Virginian attended to breakfast, while Balaam rode away on the sorrel to bring in the loose horses. They had gone far out of sight, and when he returned with them, after some two hours, he was on Pedro. Pedro was soaking with sweat, and red froth creamed from his mouth. The Virginian saw the horses must have been hard to drive in, especially after Balaam brought them the wild sorrel as a leader.

"If you'd kep' ridin' him, 'stead of changin' off on your hawss, they'd have behaved quieter," said the foreman.

"That's good seasonable advice," said Balaam, sarcastically. "I could have told you that now."

"I could have told you when you started," said the Virginian, heating the coffee for Balaam.

Balaam was eloquent on the outrageous conduct of the horses. He had come up with them evidently striking back for Butte Creek, with the old mare in the lead.

"But I soon showed her the road she was to go," he said, as he drove them now to the water.

The Virginian noticed the slight limp of the mare, and how her pastern was cut as it with a stone or the sharp heel of a boot.

"I guess she'll not be in a hurry to travel except when she's wanted to," continued Balaam. He sat down, and sullenly poured himself some coffee. "We'll be in luck if we make any Sunk Creek this night."

He went on with his breakfast, thinking aloud for the benefit of his companion, who made no comments, preferring silence to the discomfort of talking with a man whose vindictive humor was so thoroughly uppermost. He did not even listen very attentively, but continued his preparations for departure, washing the dishes, rolling the blankets, and moving about in his usual way of easy and visible good nature.

"Six o'clock, already," said Balaam, saddling the horses. "And we'll not get started for ten minutes more." Then he came to Pedro. "So you haven't quit fooling yet, haven't you?" he exclaimed, for the pony shrank as he lifted the bridle. "Take that for your sore mouth!" and he rammed the bit in, at which Pedro flung back and reared.

"Well, I never saw Pedro act that way yet," said the Virginian.

"Ah, rubbish!" said Balaam. "They're all the same. Not a bastard one but's laying for his chance to do for you. Some'll buck you off, and some'll roll with you, and some'll fight you with their fore feet. They may play good for a year, but the Western pony's man's enemy, and when he judges he's got his chance, he's going to do his best. And if you come out alive it won't be his fault." Balaam paused for a while, packing. "You've got to keep them afraid of you," he said next; "that's what you've got to do if you don't want trouble. That Pedro horse there has been fed, hand-fed, and fooled with like a damn pet, and what's that policy done? Why, he goes ugly when he thinks it's time, and decides he'll not drive any horses into camp this morning. He knows better now."

"Mr. Balaam," said the Virginian, "I'll buy that hawss off yu' right now."

Balaam shook his head. "You'll not do that right now or any other time," said he. "I happen to want him."

The Virginian could do no more. He had heard cowpunchers say to refractory ponies, "You keep still, or I'll Balaam you!" and he now understood the aptness of the expression.

Meanwhile Balaam began to lead Pedro to the creek for a last drink before starting across the torrid drought. The horse held back on the rein a little, and Balaam turned and cut the whip across his forehead. A delay of forcing and backing followed, while the Virginian, already in the saddle, waited. The minutes passed, and no immediate prospect, apparently, of getting nearer Sunk Creek.

"He ain' goin' to follow you while you're beatin' his haid," the Southerner at length remarked.

"Do you think you can teach me anything about horses?" retorted Balaam.

"Well, it don't look like I could," said the Virginian, lazily.

"Then don't try it, so long as it's not your horse, my friend."

Again the Southerner levelled his eye on Balaam. "All right," he said, in the same gentle voice. "And don't you call me your friend. You've made that mistake twiced."

The road was shadeless, as it had been from the start, and they could not travel fast. During the first few hours all coolness was driven out of the glassy morning, and another day of illimitable sun invested the world with its blaze. The pale Bow Leg Range was coming nearer, but its hard hot slants and rifts suggested no sort of freshness, and even the pines that spread for wide miles along near the summit counted for nothing in the distance and the glare, but seemed mere patches of dull dry discoloration. No talk was exchanged between the two travelers, for the cowpuncher had nothing to say and Balaam was sulky, so they moved along in silent endurance of each other's company and the tedium of the journey.

But the slow succession of rise and fall in the plain changed and shortened. The earth's surface became lumpy, rising into mounds and knotted systems of steep small hills cut apart by staring gashes of sand, where water poured in the spring from the melting snow. After a time they ascended through the foothills till the plain below was for a while concealed, but came again into view in its entirety, distant and a thing of the past, while some magpies sailed down to meet them from the new country they were entering. They passed up through a small transparent forest of dead trees standing stark and white, and a little higher came on a line of narrow moisture that crossed the way and formed a stale pool among some willow thickets. They turned aside to water their horses, and found near the pool a circular spot of ashes and some poles lying, and beside these a cage-like edifice of willow wands built in the ground.

"Indian camp," observed the Virginian.

There were the tracks of five or six horses on the farther side of the pool, and they did not come into the trail, but led off among the rocks on some system of their own.

"They're about a week old," said Balaam. "It's part of that outfit that's been hunting."

"They've gone on to visit their friends," added the cowpuncher.

"Yes, on the Southern Reservation. How far do you call Sunk Creek now?"

"Well," said the Virginian, calculating, "it's mighty nigh fo'ty miles from Muddy Crossin', an' I reckon we've come eighteen."

"Just about. It's noon." Balaam snapped his watch shut. "We'll rest here till 12:30."

When it was time to go, the Virginian looked musingly at the mountains. "We'll need to travel right smart to get through the canyon tonight," he said.

"Tell you what," said Balaam; "we'll rope the Judge's horses together and drive 'em in front of us. That'll make speed."

"Mightn't they get away on us?" objected the Virginian. "They're pow'ful wild."

"They can't get away from me, I guess," said Balaam, and the arrangement was adopted. "We're the first this season over this piece of the trail," he observed presently.

His companion had noticed the ground already, and assented. There were no tracks anywhere to be seen over which winter had not come and gone since they had been made. Presently the trail wound into a sultry gulch that hemmed in the heat and seemed to draw down the sun's rays more vertically. The sorrel horse chose this place to make a try for liberty. He suddenly whirled from the trail, dragging with him his less inventive fellow. Leaving the Virginian with the old mare, Balaam headed them off, for Pedro was quick, and they came jumping down the bank together, but swiftly crossed up on the other side, getting much higher before they could be reached. It was no place for this sort of game, as the sides of the ravine were ploughed with steep channels, broken with jutting knobs of rock, and impeded by short twisted pines that swung out from their roots horizontally over the pitch of the hill. The Virginian helped, but used his horse with more judgment, keeping as much on the level as possible, and endeavoring to anticipate the next turn of the runaways before they made it, while Balaam attempted to follow them close, wheeling short when they doubled, heavily beating up the face of the slope, veering again to come down to the point he had left, and whenever he felt Pedro begin to flag, driving his spurs into the horse and forcing him to keep up the pace. He had set out to overtake and capture on the side of the mountain these two animals who had been running wild for many weeks, and now carried no weight but themselves, and the futility of such work could not penetrate his obstinate and rising temper. He had made up his mind not to give in. The Virginian soon decided to move slowly along for the present, preventing the wild horses from passing down the gulch again, but otherwise saving his own animal from useless fatigue. He saw that Pedro was reeking wet, with mouth open, and constantly stumbling, though he galloped on. The cowpuncher kept the group in sight, driving the packhorse in front of him, and watching the tactics of the sorrel, who had now undoubtedly become the leader of the expedition, and was at the top of the gulch, in vain trying to find an outlet through its rocky rim to the levels above. He soon judged this to be no thoroughfare, and changing his plan, trotted down to the bottom and up the other side, gaining more and more; for in this new descent Pedro had fallen twice. Then the sorrel showed the cleverness of a genuinely vicious horse. The Virginian saw him stop and fall to kicking his companion with all the energy that a short rope would permit. The rope slipped, and both, unencumbered, reached the top and disappeared. Leaving the packhorse for Balaam, the Virginian started after them and came into a high tableland, beyond which the mountains began in earnest. The runaways were moving across toward these at an easy rate. He followed for a moment, then looking back, and seeing no sign of Balaam, waited, for the horses were sure not to go fast when they reached good pasture or water.

He got out of the saddle and sat on the ground, watching, till the mare came up slowly into sight, and Balaam behind her. When they were near, Balaam dismounted and struck Pedro fearfully, until the stick broke, and he raised the splintered half to continue.

Seeing the pony's condition, the Virginian spoke, and said, "I'd let that hawss alone."

Balaam turned to him, but wholly possessed by passion did not seem to hear, and the Southerner noticed how white and like that of a maniac his face was. The stick slid to the ground.

"He played he was tired," said Balaam, looking at the Virginian with glazed eyes. The violence of his rage affected him physically, like some stroke of illness. "He played out on me on purpose." The man's voice was dry and light. "He's perfectly fresh now," he continued, and turned again to the coughing, swaying horse, whose eyes were closed. Not having the stick, he seized the animal's unresisting head and shook it. The Virginian watched him a moment, and rose to stop such a spectacle. Then, as if conscious he was doing no real hurt, Balaam ceased, and turning again in slow fashion looked across the level, where the runaways were still visible.

"I'll have to take your horse," he said, "mine's played out on me."

"You ain' goin' to touch my hawss."

Again the words seemed not entirely to reach Balaam's understanding, so dulled by rage were his senses. He made no answer, but mounted Pedro; and the failing pony walked mechanically forward, while the Virginian, puzzled, stood looking after him. Balaam seemed without purpose of going anywhere, and stopped in a moment. Suddenly he was at work at something. This sight was odd and new to look at. For a few seconds it had no meaning to the Virginian as he watched. Then his mind grasped the horror, too late. Even with his cry of execration and the tiger spring that he gave to stop Balaam, the monstrosity was wrought. Pedro sank motionless, his head rolling flat on the earth. Balaam was jammed beneath him. The man had struggled to his feet before the Virginian reached the spot, and the horse then lifted his head and turned it piteously round.

Then vengeance like a blast struck Balaam. The Virginian hurled him to the ground, lifted and hurled him again, lifted him and beat his face and struck his jaw. The man's strong ox-like fighting availed nothing. He fended his eyes as best he could against these sledgehammer blows of justice. He felt blindly for his pistol. That arm was caught and wrenched backward, and crushed and doubled. He seemed to hear his own bones, and set up a hideous screaming of hate and pain. Then the pistol at last came out, and together with the hand that grasped it was instantly stamped into the dust. Once again the creature was lifted and slung so that he lay across Pedro's saddle a blurred, dingy, wet pulp.

Vengeance had come and gone. The man and the horse were motionless. Around them, silence seemed to gather like a witness.

"If you are dead," said the Virginian, "I am glad of it." He stood looking down at Balaam and Pedro, prone in the middle of the open tableland. Then he saw Balaam looking at him. It was the quiet stare of sight without thought or feeling, the mere visual sense alone, almost frightful in its separation from any self. But as he watched those eyes, the self came back into them. "I have not killed you," said the Virginian. "Well, I ain't goin' to do anymore to yu'— if that's a satisfaction to know."

Then he began to attend to Balaam with impersonal skill, like someone hired for the purpose. "He ain't hurt bad," he asserted aloud, as if the man were some nameless patient; and then to Balaam he remarked, "I reckon it might have put a less tough man than you out of business for quite a while. I'm goin' to get some water now." When he returned with the water, Balaam was sitting up, looking about him. He had not yet spoken, nor did he now speak. The sunlight flashed on the six-shooter where it lay, and the Virginian secured it. "She ain't so pretty as she was," he remarked, as he examined the weapon. "But she'll go right handy yet."

Strength was in a measure returning to Pedro. He was a young horse, and the exhaustion neither of anguish nor of overriding was enough to affect him long or seriously. He got himself on his feet and walked waveringly over to the old mare, and stood by her for comfort. The cowpuncher came up to him, and Pedro, after starting back slightly, seemed to comprehend that he was in friendly hands. It was plain that he would soon be able to travel slowly if no weight was on him, and that he would be a very good horse again. Whether they abandoned the runaways or not, there was no staying here for night to overtake them without food or water. The day was still high, and what its next few hours had in store the Virginian could not say, and he left them to take care of themselves, determining meanwhile that he would take command of the minutes and maintain the position he had assumed both as to Balaam and Pedro. He took Pedro's saddle off, threw the mare's pack to the ground, put Balaam's saddle on her, and on that stowed or tied her original pack, which he could do, since it was so light. Then he went to Balaam, who was sitting up.

"I reckon you can travel," said the Virginian. "And your hawss can. If you're comin' with me, you'll ride your mare. I'm goin' to trail them hawsses. If you're not comin' with me, your hawss comes with me, and you'll take fifty dollars for him."

Balaam was indifferent to this good bargain. He did not look at the other or speak, but rose and searched about him on the ground. The Virginian was also indifferent as to whether Balaam chose to answer or not. Seeing Balaam searching the ground, he finished what he had to say.

"I have your six-shooter, and you'll have it when I'm ready for you to. Now, I'm goin'," he concluded.

Balaam's intellect was clear enough now, and he saw that though the rest of this journey would be nearly intolerable, it must go on. He looked at the impassive cowpuncher getting ready to go and tying a rope on Pedro's neck to lead him, then he looked at the mountains where the runaways had vanished, and it did not seem credible to him that he had come into such straits. He was helped stiffly on the mare, and the three horses in single file took up their journey once more, and came slowly among the mountains. The perpetual desert was ended, and they crossed a small brook, where they missed the trail. The Virginian dismounted to find where the horses had turned off, and discovered that they had gone straight up the ridge by the watercourse.

"There's been a man camped in hyeh inside a month," he said, kicking up a rag of red flannel. "White man and two hawsses. Ours have went up his old tracks."

It was not easy for Balaam to speak yet, and he kept his silence. But he remembered that Shorty had spoken of a trapper who had started for Sunk Creek.

For three hours they followed the runaways' course over softer ground, and steadily ascending, passed one or two springs, at length, where the mud was not yet settled in the hoofprints. Then they came through a corner of pine forest and down a sudden bank among quaking-asps to a green park. Here the runaways beside a stream were grazing at ease, but saw them coming, and started on again, following down the stream. For the present all to be done was to keep them in sight. This creek received tributaries and widened, making a valley for itself. Above the bottom, lining the first terrace of the ridge, began the pines, and stretched back, unbroken over intervening summit and basin, to cease at last where the higher peaks presided.

"This hyeh's the middle fork of Sunk Creek," said the Virginian. "We'll get on to our right road again where they join."

Soon a game trail marked itself along the stream. If this would only continue, the runaways would be nearly sure to follow it down into the canyon. Then there would be no way for them but to go on and come out into their own country, where they would make for the Judge's ranch of their own accord. The great point was to reach the canyon before dark. They passed into permanent shadow; for though the other side of the creek shone in full day, the sun had departed behind the ridges immediately above them. Coolness filled the air, and the silence, which in this deep valley of invading shadow seemed too silent, was relieved by the birds. Not birds of song, but a freakish band of gray talkative observers, who came calling and croaking along through the pines, and inspected the cavalcade, keeping it company for a while, and then flying up into the woods again. The travelers came round a corner on a little spread of marsh, and from somewhere in the middle of it rose a buzzard and sailed on its black pinions into the air above them, wheeling and wheeling, but did not grow distant. As it swept over the trail, something fell from its claw, a rag of red flannel; and each man in turn looked at it as his horse went by.

"I wonder if there's plenty elk and deer hyeh?" said the Virginian.

"I guess there is," Balaam replied, speaking at last. The travelers had become strangely reconciled.

"There's game 'most all over these mountains," the Virginian continued;

"country not been settled long enough to scare them out." So they fell into casual conversation, and for the first time were glad of each other's company.

The sound of a new bird came from the pines above—the hoot of an owl—and was answered from some other part of the wood. This they did not particularly notice at first, but soon they heard the same note, unexpectedly distant, like an echo. The game trail, now quite a defined path beside the river, showed no sign of changing its course or fading out into blank ground, as these uncertain guides do so often. It led consistently in the desired direction, and the two men were relieved to see it continue. Not only were the runaways easier to keep track of, but better speed was made along this valley. The pervading imminence of night more and more dispelled the lingering afternoon, though there was yet no twilight in the open, and the high peaks opposite shone yellow in the invisible sun. But now the owls hooted again. Their music had something in it that caused both the Virginian and Balaam to look up at the pines and wish that this valley would end. Perhaps it was early for night-birds to begin; or perhaps it was that the sound never seemed to fall behind, but moved abreast of them among the trees above, as they rode on without pause down below; some influence made the faces of the travelers grave. The spell of evil which the sight of the wheeling buzzard had begun, deepened as evening grew, while ever and again along the creek the singular call and answer of the owls wandered among the darkness of the trees not far away.

The sun was gone from the peaks when at length the other side of the stream opened into a long wide meadow. The trail they followed, after crossing a flat willow thicket by the water, ran into dense pines, that here for the first time reached all the way down to the water's edge. The two men came out of the willows, and saw ahead the capricious runaways leave the bottom and go up the hill and enter the wood.

"We must hinder that," said the Virginian; and he dropped Pedro's rope. "There's your six-shooter. You keep the trail, and camp down there"—he pointed to where the trees came to the water—"till I head them hawsses off. I may not get back right away." He galloped up the open hill and went into the pine, choosing a place above where the vagrants had disappeared.

Balaam dismounted, and picking up his six-shooter, took the rope off Pedro's neck and drove him slowly down toward where the wood began. Its interior was already dim, and Balaam saw that here must be their stopping-place tonight, since there was no telling how wide this pine strip might extend along the trail before they could come out of it and reach another suitable camping-ground. Pedro had recovered his strength, and he now showed signs of restlessness. He shied where there was not even a stone in the trail, and finally turned sharply round. Balaam expected he was going to rush back on the way they had come; but the horse stood still, breathing excitedly. He was urged forward again, though he turned more than once. But when they were a few paces from the wood, and Balaam had got off preparatory to camping, the horse snorted and dashed into the water, and stood still there. The astonished Balaam followed to turn him; but Pedro seemed to lose control of himself, and plunged to the middle of the river, and was evidently intending to cross. Fearing that he would escape to the opposite meadow and add to their difficulties, Balaam, with the idea of turning him round, drew his six-shooter and fired in front of the horse, divining, even as the flash cut the dusk, the secret of all this—the Indians; but too late. His bruised hand had stiffened, marring his aim, and he saw Pedro fall over in the water then rise and struggle up the bank on the farther shore, where he now hurried also, to find that he had broken the pony's leg.

He needed no interpreter for the voices of the seeming owls that had haunted the latter hour of their journey, and he knew that his beast's keener instinct had perceived the destruction that lurked in the interior of the wood. The history of the trapper whose horse had returned without him might have been—might still be—his own; and he thought of the rag that had fallen from the buzzard's talons when he had been disturbed at his meal in the marsh. "Peaceable" Indians were still in these mountains, and some few of them had for the past hour been skirting his journey unseen, and now waited for him in the wood which they expected him to enter. They had been too wary to use their rifles or show themselves, lest these travelers should be only part of a larger company following, who would hear the noise of a shot, and catch them in the act of murder. So, safe under the cover of the pines, they had planned to sling their silent noose, and drag the white man from his horse as he passed through the trees.

Balaam looked over the river at the ominous wood, and then he looked at Pedro, the horse that he had first maimed and now ruined, to whom he probably owed his life. He was lying on the ground, quietly looking over the green meadow, where dusk was gathering. Perhaps he was not suffering from his wound yet, as he rested on the ground; and into his animal intelligence there probably came no knowledge of this final stroke of his fate. At any rate, no sound of pain came from Pedro, whose friendly and gentle face remained turned toward the meadow. Once more Balaam fired his pistol, and this time the aim was true, and the horse rolled over, with a ball through his brain. It was the best reward that remained for him.

Then Balaam rejoined the old mare, and turned from the middle fork of Sunk Creek. He dashed across the wide field, and went over a ridge, and found his way along in the night till he came to the old trail—the road which they would never have left but for him and his obstinacy. He unsaddled the weary mare by Sunk Creek, where the canyon begins, letting her drag a rope and find pasture and water, while he, lighting no fire to betray him, crouched close under a tree till the light came. He thought of the Virginian in the wood. But what could either have done for the other had he stayed to look for him among the pines? If the cowpuncher came back to the corner, he would follow Balaam's tracks or not. They would meet, at any rate, where the creeks joined.

But they did not meet. And then to Balaam the prospect of going onward to the Sunk Creek Ranch became more than he could bear. To come without the horses, to meet Judge Henry, to meet the guests of the Judge's, looking as he did now after his punishment by the Virginian, to give the news about the Judge's favorite man—no, how could he tell such a story as this? Balaam went no farther than a certain cabin, where he slept, and wrote a letter to the Judge. This the owner of the cabin delivered. And so, having spread news which would at once cause a search for the Virginian, and having constructed such sentences to the Judge as would most smoothly explain how, being overtaken by illness, he had not wished to be a burden at Sunk Creek, Balaam turned homeward by himself. By the time he was once more at Butte Creek, his general appearance was a thing less to be noticed. And there was Shorty, waiting!

One way and another, the lost dog had been able to gather some ready money. He was cheerful because of this momentary purseful of prosperity.

"And so I come back, yu' see," he said. "For I figured on getting Pedro back as soon as I could when I sold him to yu'."

"You're behind the times, Shorty," said Balaam.

Shorty looked blank. "You've sure not sold Pedro?" he exclaimed.

"Them Indians," said Balaam, "got after me on the Bow Leg trail. Got after me and that Virginia man. But they didn't get me."

Balaam wagged his bullet head to imply that this escape was due to his own superior intelligence. The Virginian had been stupid, and so the Indians had got him. "And they shot your horse," Balaam finished. "Stop and get some dinner with the boys."

Having eaten, Shorty rode away in mournful spirits. For he had made so sure of once more riding and talking with Pedro, his friend whom he had taught to shake hands.

## CHAPTER XXVII

## GRANDMOTHER STARK

Except for its chair and bed, the cabin was stripped almost bare. Amid its emptiness of dismantled shelves and walls and floor, only the tiny ancestress still hung in her place, last token of the home that had been. This miniature, tacked against the despoiled boards, and its descendant, the angry girl with her hand on an open box-lid, made a sort of couple in the loneliness: she on the wall sweet and serene, she by the box sweet and stormy. The picture was her final treasure waiting to be packed for the journey. In whatever room she had called her own since childhood, there it had also lived and looked at her, not quite familiar, not quite smiling, but in its prim colonial hues delicate as some pressed flower. Its pale oval, of color blue and rose and flaxen, in a battered, pretty gold frame, unconquerably pervaded any surroundings with a something like last year's lavender. Till yesterday a Crow Indian war-bonnet had hung next it, a sumptuous cascade of feathers; on the other side a bow with arrows had dangled; opposite had been the skin of a silver fox; over the door had spread the antlers of a black-tail deer; a bearskin stretched beneath it. Thus had the whole cosey log cabin been upholstered, lavish with trophies of the frontier; and yet it was in front of the miniature that the visitors used to stop.

Shining quietly now in the cabin's blackness this summer day, the heirloom was presiding until the end. And as Molly Wood's eyes fell upon her ancestress of Bennington, 1777, there flashed a spark of steel in them, alone here in the room that she was leaving forever. She was not going to teach school anymore on Bear Creek, Wyoming; she was going home to Bennington, Vermont. When time came for school to open again, there should be a new schoolmarm.

This was the momentous result of that visit which the Virginian had paid her. He had told her that he was coming for his hour soon. From that hour she had decided to escape. She was running away from her own heart. She did not dare to trust herself face to face again with her potent, indomitable lover. She longed for him, and therefore she would never see him again. No great-aunt at Dunbarton, or anybody else that knew her and her family, should ever say that she had married below her station, had been an unworthy Stark! Accordingly, she had written to the Virginian, bidding him good-by, and wishing him everything in the world. As she happened to be aware that she was taking everything in the world away from him, this letter was not the most easy of letters to write. But she had made the language very kind. Yes; it was a thoroughly kind communication. And all because of that momentary visit, when he had brought back to her two novels, *Emma* and *Pride and Prejudice*.

"How do you like them?" she had then inquired; and he had smiled slowly at her. "You haven't read them!" she exclaimed.

"No."

"Are you going to tell me there has been no time?"

"No."

Then Molly had scolded her cowpuncher, and to this he had listened with pleasure undisguised, as indeed he listened to every word that she said.

"Why, it has come too late," he had told her when the scolding was over. "If I was one of your little scholars hyeh in Bear Creek schoolhouse, yu' could learn me to like such frillery I reckon. But I'm a mighty ignorant, growed-up man."

"So much the worse for you!" said Molly.

"No. I am pretty glad I am a man. Else I could not have learned the thing you have taught me."

But she shut her lips and looked away. On the desk was a letter written from Vermont. "If you don't tell me at once when you decide," had said the arch writer, "never hope to speak to me again. Mary Wood, seriously, I am suspicious. Why do you never mention him nowadays? How exciting to have you bring a live cowboy to Bennington! We should all come to dinner. Though of course I understand now that many of them have excellent manners. But would he wear his pistol at table?" So the letter ran on. It recounted the latest home gossip and jokes. In answering it Molly Wood had taken no notice of its childish tone here and there.

"Hyeh's some of them cactus blossoms yu' wanted," said the Virginian. His voice recalled the girl with almost a start. "I've brought a good hawss I've gentled for yu', and Taylor'll keep him till I need him."

"Thank you so much! But I wish—"

"I reckon yu' can't stop me lendin' Taylor a hawss. And you cert'nly'll get sick schoolteachin' if yu' don't keep outdoors some. Good-by—till that next time."

"Yes; there's always a next time," she answered, as lightly as she could.

"There always will be. Don't yu' know that?"

She did not reply.

"I have discouraged spells," he pursued, "but I down them. For I've told yu' you were going to love me. You are goin' to learn back the thing you have taught me. I'm not askin' anything now; I don't want you to speak a word to me. But I'm never goin' to quit till 'next time' is no more, and it's 'all the time' for you and me."

With that he had ridden away, not even touching her hand. Long after he had gone she was still in her chair, her eyes lingering upon his flowers, those yellow cups of the prickly pear. At length she had risen impatiently, caught up the flowers, gone with them to the open window—and then, after all, set them with pains in water.

But today Bear Creek was over. She was going home now. By the week's end she would be started. By the time the mail brought him her good-by letter she would be gone. She had acted.

To Bear Creek, the neighborly, the friendly, the not comprehending, this move had come unlooked for, and had brought regret. Only one hard word had been spoken to Molly, and that by her next-door neighbor and kindest friend. In Mrs. Taylor's house the girl had daily come and gone as a daughter, and that lady reached the subject thus: "When I took Taylor," said she, sitting by as Robert Browning and Jane Austen were going into their box, "I married for love."

"Do you wish it had been money?" said Molly, stooping to her industries.

"You know both of us better than that, child."

"I know I've seen people at home who couldn't possibly have had any other reason. They seemed satisfied, too."

"Maybe the poor ignorant things were!"

"And so I have never been sure how I might choose."

"Yes, you are sure, deary. Don't you think I know you? And when it comes over Taylor once in a while, and he tells me I'm the best thing in his life, and I tell him he ain't merely the best thing but the only thing in mine—him and the children—why, we just agree we'd do it all over the same way if we had the chance."

Molly continued to be industrious.

"And that's why," said Mrs. Taylor, "I want every girl that's anything to me to know her luck when it comes. For I was that near telling Taylor I wouldn't!"

"If ever my luck comes," said Molly, with her back to her friend, "I shall say 'I will' at once."

"Then you'll say it at Bennington next week."

Molly wheeled round.

"Why, you surely will. Do you expect he's going to stay here, and you in Bennington?" And the campaigner sat back in her chair.

"He? Goodness! Who is he?"

"Child, child, you're talking cross today because you're at outs with yourself. You've been at outs ever since you took this idea of leaving the school and us and everything this needless way. You have not treated him right. And why, I can't make out to save me. What have you found out all of a sudden? If he was not good enough for you, I—but, oh, it's a prime one you're losing, Molly. When a man like that stays faithful to a girl 'spite all the chances he gets, her luck is come."

"Oh, my luck! People have different notions of luck."

"Notions!"

"He has been very kind."

"Kind!" And now without further simmering, Mrs. Taylor's wrath boiled up and poured copiously over Molly Wood. "Kind! There's a word you shouldn't use, my dear. No doubt you can spell it. But more than its spelling I guess you don't know. The children can learn what it means from some of the rest of us folks that don't spell so correct, maybe."

"Mrs. Taylor, Mrs. Taylor—"

"I can't wait, deary. Since the roughness looks bigger to you than the diamond, you had better go back to Vermont. I expect you'll find better grammar there, deary."

The good dame stalked out, and across to her own cabin, and left the angry girl among her boxes. It was in vain she fell to work upon them. Presently something had to be done over again, and when it was the box held several chattels less than before the readjustment. She played a sort of desperate dominos to fit these objects in the space, but here were a paperweight, a portfolio, with two wretched volumes that no chink would harbor; and letting them fall all at once, she straightened herself, still stormy with revolt, eyes and cheeks still hot from the sting of long-parried truth. There, on her wall still, was the miniature, the little silent ancestress; and upon this face the girl's glance rested. It was as if she appealed to Grandmother Stark for support and comfort across the hundred years which lay between them. So the flaxen girl on the wall and she among the boxes stood a moment face to face in seeming communion, and then the descendant turned again to her work. But after a desultory touch here and there she drew a long breath and walked to the open door. What use was in finishing today, when she had nearly a week? This first spurt of toil had swept the cabin bare of all indwelling charm, and its look was chill. Across the lane his horse, the one he had "gentled" for her, was grazing idly. She walked there and caught him, and led him to her gate. Mrs. Taylor saw her go in, and soon come out in riding-dress; and she watched the girl throw the saddle on with quick ease—the ease he had taught her. Mrs. Taylor also saw the sharp cut she gave the horse, and laughed grimly to herself in her window as horse and rider galloped into the beautiful sunny loneliness.

To the punished animal this switching was new! and at its third repetition he turned his head in surprise, but was no more heeded than were the bluffs and flowers where he was taking his own undirected choice of way. He carried her over ground she knew by heart—Corncliff Mesa, Crowheart Butte, Westfall's Crossing, Upper Canyon; open land and woodland, pines and sagebrush, all silent and grave and lustrous in the sunshine. Once and again a ranchman greeted her, and wondered if she had forgotten who he was; once she passed some cowpunchers with a small herd of steers, and they stared after her too. Bear Creek narrowed, its mountainsides drew near, its little falls began to rush white in midday shadow, and the horse suddenly pricked his ears. Unguided, he was taking this advantage to go home. Though he had made but little way—a mere beginning yet—on this trail over to Sunk Creek, here was already a Sunk Creek friend whinnying good day to him, so he whinnied back and quickened his pace, and Molly started to life. What was Monte doing here? She saw the black horse she knew also, saddled, with reins dragging on the trail as the rider had dropped them to dismount. A cold spring bubbled out beyond the next rock, and she knew her lover's horse was waiting for him while he drank. She pulled at the reins, but loosed them, for to turn and escape now was ridiculous; and riding boldly round the rock, she came upon him by the spring. One of his arms hung up to its elbow in the pool, the other was crooked beside his head, but the face was sunk downward against the shelving rock, so that she saw only his black, tangled hair. As her horse snorted and tossed his head she looked swiftly at Monte, as if to question him. Seeing now the sweat matted on his coat, and noting the white rim of his eye, she sprang and ran to the motionless figure. A patch of blood at his shoulder behind stained the soft flannel shirt, spreading down beneath his belt, and the man's whole strong body lay slack and pitifully helpless.

She touched the hand beside his head, but it seemed neither warm nor cold to her; she felt for the pulse, as nearly as she could remember the doctors did, but could not tell whether she imagined or not that it was still; twice with painful care her fingers sought and waited for the beat, and her face seemed like one of listening. She leaned down and lifted his other arm and hand from the water, and as their ice-coldness reached her senses, clearly she saw the patch near the shoulder she had moved grow wet with new blood, and at that sight she grasped at the stones upon which she herself now sank. She held tight by two rocks, sitting straight beside him, staring, and murmuring aloud, "I must not faint; I will not faint"; and the standing horses looked at her, pricking their ears.

In this cup-like spread of the ravine the sun shone warmly down, the tall red cliff was warm, the pines were a warm film and filter of green; outside the shade across Bear Creek rose the steep, soft, open yellow hill, warm and high to the blue, and Bear Creek tumbled upon its sunsparkling stones. The two horses on the margin trail still looked at the spring and trees, where sat the neat flaxen girl so rigid by the slack prone body in its flannel shirt and leathern chaps. Suddenly her face livened. "But the blood ran!" she exclaimed, as if to the horses, her companions in this. She moved to him, and put her hand in through his shirt against his heart.

Next moment she had sprung up and was at his saddle, searching, then swiftly went on to her own and got her small flask and was back beside him. Here was the cold water he had sought, and she put it against his forehead and drenched the wounded shoulder with it. Three times she tried to move him, so he might lie more easy, but his dead weight was too much, and desisting, she sat close and raised his head to let it rest against her. Thus she saw the blood that was running from in front of the shoulder also; but she said no more about fainting. She tore strips from her dress and soaked them, keeping them cold and wet upon both openings of his wound, and she drew her pocketknife out and cut his shirt away from the place. As she continually rinsed and cleaned it, she watched his eyelashes, long and soft and thick, but they did not stir. Again she tried the flask, but failed from being still too gentle, and her searching eyes fell upon ashes near the pool. Still undispersed by the weather lay the small charred ends of a fire he and she had made once here together, to boil coffee and fry trout. She built another fire now, and when the flames were going well, filled her flask-cup from the spring and set it to heat. Meanwhile, she returned to nurse his head and wound. Her cold water had stopped the bleeding. Then she poured her brandy in the steaming cup, and, made rough by her desperate helplessness, forced some between his lips and teeth.

Instantly, almost, she felt the tremble of life creeping back, and as his deep eyes opened upon her she sat still and mute. But the gaze seemed luminous with an unnoting calm, and she wondered if perhaps he could not recognize her; she watched this internal clearness of his vision, scarcely daring to breathe, until presently he began to speak, with the same profound and clear impersonality sounding in his slowly uttered words.

"I thought they had found me. I expected they were going to kill me."

He stopped, and she gave him more of the hot drink, which he took, still lying and looking at her as if the present did not reach his senses. "I knew hands were touching me. I reckon I was not dead. I knew about them soon as they began, only I could not interfere." He waited again. "It is mighty strange where I have been. No. Mighty natural." Then he went back into his revery, and lay with his eyes still full open upon her where she sat motionless.

She began to feel a greater awe in this living presence than when it had been his body with an ice-cold hand; and she quietly spoke his name, venturing scarcely more than a whisper.

At this, some nearer thing wakened in his look. "But it was you all along," he resumed. "It is you now. You must not stay—" Weakness overcame him, and his eyes closed. She sat ministering to him, and when he roused again, he began anxiously at once: "You must not stay. They would get you, too."

She glanced at him with a sort of fierceness, then reached for his pistol, in which was nothing but blackened empty cartridges. She threw these out and drew six from his belt, loaded the weapon, and snapped shut its hinge.

"Please take it," he said, more anxious and more himself. "I ain't worth tryin' to keep. Look at me!"

"Are you giving up?" she inquired, trying to put scorn in her tone. Then she seated herself.

"Where is the sense in both of us—"

"You had better save your strength," she interrupted.

He tried to sit up.

"Lie down!" she ordered.

He sank obediently, and began to smile.

When she saw that, she smiled too, and unexpectedly took his hand. "Listen, friend," said she. "Nobody shall get you, and nobody shall get me. Now take some more brandy."

"It must be noon," said the cowpuncher, when she had drawn her hand away from him. "I remember it was dark when—when—when I can remember. I reckon they were scared to follow me in so close to settlers. Else they would have been here."

"You must rest," she observed.

She broke the soft ends of some evergreen, and putting them beneath his head, went to the horses, loosened the cinches, took off the bridles, led them to drink, and picketed them to feed. Further still, to leave nothing undone which she could herself manage, she took the horses' saddles off to refold the blankets when the time should come, and meanwhile brought them for him. But he put them away from him. He was sitting up against a rock, stronger evidently, and asking for cold water. His head was fire-hot, and the paleness beneath his swarthy skin had changed to a deepening flush.

"Only five miles!" she said to him, bathing his head.

"Yes. I must hold it steady," he answered, waving his hand at the cliff.

She told him to try and keep it steady until they got home.

"Yes," he repeated. "Only five miles. But it's fightin' to turn around."

Half aware that he was becoming light-headed, he looked from the rock to her and from her to the rock with dilating eyes.

"We can hold it together," she said. "You must get on your horse." She took his handkerchief from round his neck, knotting it with her own, and to make more bandage she ran to the roll of clothes behind his saddle and tore in halves a clean shirt. A handkerchief fell from it, which she seized also, and opening, saw her own initials by the hem. Then she remembered: she saw again their first meeting, the swollen river, the overset stage, the unknown horseman who carried her to the bank on his saddle and went away unthanked—her whole first adventure on that first day of her coming to this new country—and now she knew how her long-forgotten handkerchief had gone that day. She refolded it gently and put it back in his bundle, for there was enough bandage without it. She said not a word to him, and he placed a wrong meaning upon the look which she gave him as she returned to bind his shoulder.

"It don't hurt so much," he assured her (though extreme pain was clearing his head for the moment, and he had been able to hold the cliff from turning). "Yu' must not squander your pity."

"Do not squander your strength," said she.

"Oh, I could put up a pretty good fight now!" But he tottered in showing her how strong he was, and she told him that, after all, he was a child still.

"Yes," he slowly said, looking after her as she went to bring his horse, "the same child that wanted to touch the moon, I guess." And during the slow climb down into the saddle from a rock to which she helped him he said, "You have got to be the man all through this mess."

She saw his teeth clinched and his drooping muscles compelled by will; and as he rode and she walked to lend him support, leading her horse by a backward-stretched left hand, she counted off the distance to him continually—the increasing gain, the lessening road, the landmarks nearing and dropping behind; here was the tree with the wasp-nest gone; now the burned cabin was passed; now the cottonwoods at the ford were in sight. He was silent, and held to the saddle-horn, leaning more and more against his two hands clasped over it; and just after they had made the crossing he fell, without a sound slipping to the grass, and his descent broken by her. But it started the blood a little, and she dared not leave him to seek help. She gave him the last of the flask and all the water he craved.

Revived, he managed to smile. "Yu' see, I ain't worth keeping."

"It's only a mile," said she. So she found a log, a fallen trunk, and he crawled to that, and from there crawled to his saddle, and she marched on with him, talking, bidding him note the steps accomplished. For the next half-mile they went thus, the silent man clinched on the horse, and by his side the girl walking and cheering him forward, when suddenly he began to speak: "I will say good-by to you now, ma'am."

She did not understand, at first, the significance of this.

"He is getting away," pursued the Virginian. "I must ask you to excuse me, ma'am."

It was a long while since her lord had addressed her as "ma'am." As she looked at him in growing apprehension, he turned Monte and would have ridden away, but she caught the bridle.

"You must take me home," said she, with ready inspiration. "I am afraid of the Indians."

"Why, you—why, they've all gone. There he goes. Ma'am—that hawss—"

"No," said she, holding firmly his rein and quickening her step. "A gentleman does not invite a lady to go out riding and leave her."

His eyes lost their purpose. "I'll cert'nly take you home. That sorrel has gone in there by the wallow, and Judge Henry will understand." With his eyes watching imaginary objects, he rode and rambled and it was now the girl who was silent, except to keep his mind from its half-fixed idea of the sorrel. As he grew more fluent she hastened still more, listening to head off that notion of return, skilfully inventing questions to engage him, so that when she brought him to her gate she held him in a manner subjected, answering faithfully the shrewd unrealities which she devised, whatever makeshifts she could summon to her mind; and next she had got him inside her dwelling and set him down docile, but now completely wandering; and then—no help was at hand, even here. She had made sure of aid from next door, and there she hastened, to find the Taylors' cabin locked and silent; and this meant that parents and children were gone to drive; nor might she be luckier at her next nearest neighbors', should she travel the intervening mile to fetch them. With a mind jostled once more into uncertainty, she returned to her room, and saw a change in him already. Illness had stridden upon him; his face was not as she had left it, and the whole body, the splendid supple horseman, showed sickness in every line and limb, its spurs and pistol and bold leather chaps a mockery of trappings. She looked at him, and decision came back to her, clear and steady. She supported him over to her bed and laid him on it. His head sank flat, and his loose, nerveless arms stayed as she left them. Then among her packing-boxes and beneath the little miniature, blue and flaxen and gold upon its lonely wall, she undressed him. He was cold, and she covered him to the face, and arranged the pillow, and got from its box her scarlet and black Navajo blanket and spread it over him. There was no more that she could do, and she sat down by him to wait. Among the many and many things that came into her mind was a word he said to her lightly a long while ago. "Cowpunchers do not live long enough to get old," he had told her. And now she looked at the head upon the pillow, grave and strong, but still the head of splendid, unworn youth.

At the distant jingle of the wagon in the lane she was out, and had met her returning neighbors midway. They heard her with amazement, and came in haste to the bedside; then Taylor departed to spread news of the Indians and bring the doctor, twenty-five miles away. The two women friends stood alone again, as they had stood in the morning when anger had been between them.

"Kiss me, deary," said Mrs. Taylor. "Now I will look after him—and you'll need some looking after yourself."

But on returning from her cabin with what store she possessed of lint and stimulants, she encountered a rebel, independent as ever. Molly would hear no talk about saving her strength, would not be in any room but this one until the doctor should arrive; then perhaps it would be time to think about resting. So together the dame and the girl rinsed the man's wound and wrapped him in clean things, and did all the little that they knew—which was, in truth, the very thing needed. Then they sat watching him toss and mutter. It was no longer upon Indians or the sorrel horse that his talk seemed to run, or anything recent, apparently, always excepting his work. This flowingly merged with whatever scene he was inventing or living again, and he wandered unendingly in that incompatible world we dream in. Through the medley of events and names, often thickly spoken, but rising at times to grotesque coherence, the listeners now and then could piece out the reference from their own knowledge. "Monte," for example, continually addressed, and Molly heard her own name, but invariably as "Miss Wood"; nothing less respectful came out, and frequently he answered someone as "ma'am."

At these fragments of revelation Mrs. Taylor abstained from speech, but eyed Molly Wood with caustic reproach. As the night wore on, short lulls of silence intervened, and the watchers were deceived into hope that the fever was abating. And when the Virginian sat quietly up in bed, essayed to move his bandage, and looked steadily at Mrs. Taylor, she rose quickly and went to him with a question as to how he was doing.

"Rise on your laigs, you polecat," said he, "and tell them you're a liar."

The good dame gasped, then bade him lie down, and he obeyed her with that strange double understanding of the delirious; for even while submitting, he muttered "liar," "polecat," and then "Trampas."

At that name light flashed on Mrs. Taylor, and she turned to Molly; and there was the girl struggling with a fit of mirth at his speech; but the laughter was fast becoming a painful seizure. Mrs. Taylor walked Molly up and down, speaking immediately to arrest her attention.

"You might as well know it," she said. "He would blame me for speaking of it, but where's the harm all this while after? And you would never hear it from his mouth. Molly, child, they say Trampas would kill him if he dared, and that's on account of you."

"I never saw Trampas," said Molly, fixing her eyes upon the speaker.

"No, deary. But before a lot of men—Taylor has told me about it—Trampas spoke disrespectfully of you, and before them all he made Trampas say he was a liar. That is what he did when you were almost a stranger among us, and he had not started seeing so much of you. I expect Trampas is the only enemy he ever had in this country. But he would never let you know about that."

"No," whispered Molly; "I did not know."

"Steve!" the sick man now cried out, in poignant appeal. "Steve!" To the women it was a name unknown—unknown as was also this deep inward tide of feeling which he could no longer conceal, being himself no longer. "No, Steve," he said next, and muttering followed. "It ain't so!" he shouted; and then cunningly in a lowered voice, "Steve, I have lied for you."

In time Mrs. Taylor spoke some advice.

"You had better go to bed, child. You look about ready for the doctor yourself."

"Then I will wait for him," said Molly.

So the two nurses continued to sit until darkness at the windows weakened into gray, and the lamp was no more needed. Their patient was rambling again. Yet, into whatever scenes he went, there in some guise did the throb of his pain evidently follow him, and he lay hitching his great shoulder as if to rid it of the cumbrance. They waited for the doctor, not daring much more than to turn pillows and give what other ease they could; and then, instead of the doctor, came a messenger, about noon, to say he was gone on a visit some thirty miles beyond, where Taylor had followed to bring him here as soon as might be. At this Molly consented to rest and to watch, turn about; and once she was over in her friend's house lying down, they tried to keep her there. But the revolutionist could not be put down, and when, as a last pretext, Mrs. Taylor urged the proprieties and conventions, the pale girl from Vermont laughed sweetly in her face and returned to sit by the sick man. With the approach of the second night his fever seemed to rise and master him more completely than they had yet seen it, and presently it so raged that the women called in stronger arms to hold him down. There were times when he broke out in the language of the round-up, and Mrs. Taylor renewed her protests. "Why," said Molly, "don't you suppose I knew they could swear?" So the dame, in deepening astonishment and affection, gave up these shifts at decorum. Nor did the delirium run into the intimate, coarse matters that she dreaded. The cowpuncher had lived like his kind, but his natural daily thoughts were clean, and came from the untamed but unstained mind of a man. And toward morning, as Mrs. Taylor sat taking her turn, suddenly he asked had he been sick long, and looked at her with a quieted eye. The wandering seemed to drop from him at a stroke, leaving him altogether himself. He lay very feeble, and inquired once or twice of his state and how he came here; nor was anything left in his memory of even coming to the spring where he had been found.

When the doctor arrived, he pronounced that it would be long—or very short. He praised their clean water treatment; the wound was fortunately well up on the shoulder, and gave so far no bad signs; there were not any bad signs; and the blood and strength of the patient had been as few men's were; each hour was now an hour nearer certainty, and meanwhile—meanwhile the doctor would remain as long as he could. He had many inquiries to satisfy. Dusty fellows would ride up, listen to him, and reply, as they rode away, "Don't yu' let him die, Doc." And Judge Henry sent over from Sunk Creek to answer for any attendance or medicine that might help his foreman. The country was moved with concern and interest; and in Molly's ears its words of good feeling seemed to unite and sum up a burden, "Don't yu' let him die, Doc." The Indians who had done this were now in military custody. They had come unpermitted from a southern reservation, hunting, next thieving, and as the slumbering spirit roused in one or two of the young and ambitious, they had ventured this in the secret mountains, and perhaps had killed a trapper found there. Editors immediately reared a tall war out of it; but from five Indians in a guardhouse waiting punishment not even an editor can supply spar for more than two editions, and if the recent alarm was still a matter of talk anywhere, it was not here in the sick-room. Whichever way the case should turn, it was through Molly alone (the doctor told her) that the wounded man had got this chance—this good chance, he related.

And he told her she had not done a woman's part, but a man's part, and now had no more to do; no more till the patient got well, and could thank her in his own way, said the doctor, smiling, and supposing things that were not so—misled perhaps by Mrs. Taylor.

"I'm afraid I'll be gone by the time he is well," said Molly, coldly; and the discreet physician said ah, and that she would find Bennington quite a change from Bear Creek.

But Mrs. Taylor spoke otherwise, and at that the girl said: "I shall stay as long as I am needed. I will nurse him. I want to nurse him. I will do everything for him that I can!" she exclaimed, with force.

"And that won't be anything, deary," said Mrs. Taylor, harshly. "A year of nursing don't equal a day of sweetheart."

The girl took a walk—she was of no more service in the room at present—but she turned without going far, and Mrs. Taylor spied her come to lean over the pasture fence and watch the two horses—that one the Virginian had "gentled" for her, and his own Monte. During this suspense came a new call for the doctor, neighbors profiting by his visit to Bear Creek; and in his going away to them, even under promise of quick return, Mrs. Taylor suspected a favorable sign. He kept his word as punctually as had been possible, arriving after some six hours with a confident face, and spending now upon the patient a care not needed, save to reassure the bystanders. He spoke his opinion that all was even better than he could have hoped it would be, so soon. Here was now the beginning of the fifth day; the wound's look was wholesome, no further delirium had come, and the fever had abated a degree while he was absent. He believed the serious danger-line lay behind, and (short of the unforeseen) the man's deep untainted strength would reassert its control. He had much blood to make, and must be cared for during weeks—three, four, five—there was no saying how long yet. These next few days it must be utter quiet for him; he must not talk nor hear anything likely to disturb him; and then the time for cheerfulness and gradual company would come—sooner than later, the doctor hoped. So he departed, and sent next day some bottles, with further cautions regarding the wound and dirt, and to say he should be calling the day after tomorrow.

Upon that occasion he found two patients. Molly Wood lay in bed at Mrs. Taylor's, filled with apology and indignation. With little to do, and deprived of the strong stimulant of anxiety and action, her strength had quite suddenly left her, so that she had spoken only in a sort of whisper. But upon waking from a long sleep, after Mrs. Taylor had taken her firmly, almost severely, in hand, her natural voice had returned, and now the chief treatment the doctor gave her was a sort of scolding, which it pleased Mrs. Taylor to hear. The doctor even dropped a phrase concerning the arrogance of strong nerves in slender bodies, and of undertaking several people's work when several people were at hand to do it for themselves, and this pleased Mrs. Taylor remarkably. As for the wounded man, he was behaving himself properly. Perhaps in another week he could be moved to a more cheerful room. Just now, with cleanliness and pure air, any barn would do.

"We are real lucky to have such a sensible doctor in the country," Mrs. Taylor observed, after the physician had gone.

"No doubt," said Molly. "He said my room was a barn."

"That's what you've made it, deary. But sick men don't notice much."

Nevertheless, one may believe, without going widely astray, that illness, so far from veiling, more often quickens the perceptions—at any rate those of the naturally keen. On a later day—and the interval was brief—while Molly was on her second drive to take the air with Mrs. Taylor, that lady informed her that the sick man had noticed. "And I could not tell him things liable to disturb him," said she, "and so I—well, I expect I just didn't exactly tell him the facts. I said yes, you were packing up for a little visit to your folks. They had not seen you for quite a while, I said. And he looked at those boxes kind of silent like."

"There's no need to move him," said Molly. "It is simpler to move them—the boxes. I could take out some of my things, you know, just while he has to be kept there. I mean—you see, if the doctor says the room should be cheerful—"

"Yes, deary."

"I will ask the doctor next time," said Molly, "if he believes I am—competent to spread a rug upon a floor." Molly's references to the doctor were usually acid these days. And this he totally failed to observe, telling her when he came, why, to be sure! The very thing! And if she could play cards or read aloud, or afford any other light distractions, provided they did not lead the patient to talk and tire himself, that she would be most useful. Accordingly she took over the cribbage board, and came with unexpected hesitation face to face again with the swarthy man she had saved and tended. He was not so swarthy now, but neat, with chin clean, and hair and mustache trimmed and smooth, and he sat propped among pillows watching for her.

"You are better," she said, speaking first, and with uncertain voice.

"Yes. They have given me awdehs not to talk," said the Southerner, smiling.

"Oh, yes. Please do not talk—not today."

"No. Only this"—he looked at her, and saw her seem to shrink—"thank you for what you have done," he said simply.

She took tenderly the hand he stretched to her; and upon these terms they set to work at cribbage. She won, and won again, and the third time laid down her cards and reproached him with playing in order to lose.

"No," he said, and his eye wandered to the boxes. "But my thoughts get away from me. I'll be strong enough to hold them on the cyards next time, I reckon."

Many tones in his voice she had heard, but never the tone of sadness until today.

Then they played a little more, and she put away the board for this first time.

"You are going now?" he asked.

"When I have made this room look a little less forlorn. They haven't wanted to meddle with my things, I suppose." And Molly stooped once again among the chattels destined for Vermont. Out they came; again the bearskin was spread on the floor, various possessions and ornaments went back into their ancient niches, the shelves grew comfortable with books, and, last, some flowers were stood on the table.

"More like old times," said the Virginian, but sadly.

"It's too bad," said Molly, "you had to be brought into such a looking place."

"And your folks waiting for you," said he.

"Oh, I'll pay my visit later," said Molly, putting the rug a trifle straighter.

"May I ask one thing?" pleaded the Virginian, and at the gentleness of his voice her face grew rosy, and she fixed her eyes on him with a sort of dread.

"Anything that I can answer," said she.

"Oh, yes. Did I tell yu' to quit me, and did yu' load up my gun and stay? Was that a real business? I have been mixed up in my haid."

"That was real," said Molly. "What else was there to do?"

"Just nothing—for such as you!" he exclaimed. "My haid has been mighty crazy; and that little grandmother of yours yondeh, she—but I can't just quite catch a-hold of these things"—he passed a hand over his forehead—"so many—or else one right along—well, it's all foolishness!" he concluded, with something almost savage in his tone. And after she had gone from the cabin he lay very still, looking at the miniature on the wall.

He was in another sort of mood the next time, cribbage not interesting him in the least. "Your folks will be wondering about you," said he.

"I don't think they will mind which month I go to them," said Molly. "Especially when they know the reason."

"Don't let me keep you, ma'am," said he. Molly stared at him; but he pursued, with the same edge lurking in his slow words: "Though I'll never forget. How could I forget any of all you have done—and been? If there had been none of this, why, I had enough to remember! But please don't stay, ma'am. We'll say I had a claim when yu' found me pretty well dead, but I'm gettin' well, yu' see—right smart, too!"

"I can't understand, indeed I can't," said Molly, "why you're talking so!"

He seemed to have certain moods when he would address her as "ma'am," and this she did not like, but could not prevent.

"Oh, a sick man is funny. And yu' know I'm grateful to you."

"Please say no more about that, or I shall go this afternoon. I don't want to go. I am not ready. I think I had better read something now."

"Why, yes. That's cert'nly a good notion. Why, this is the best show you'll ever get to give me education. Won't yu' please try that *Emma* book now, ma'am? Listening to you will be different." This was said with softness and humility.

Uncertain—as his gravity often left her—precisely what he meant by what he said, Molly proceeded with *Emma*, slackly at first, but soon with the enthusiasm that Miss Austen invariably gave her. She held the volume and read away at it, commenting briefly, and then, finishing a chapter of the sprightly classic, found her pupil slumbering peacefully. There was no uncertainty about that.

"You couldn't be doing a healthier thing for him, deary," said Mrs. Taylor. "If it gets to make him wakeful, try something harder." This was the lady's scarcely sympathetic view.

But it turned out to be not obscurity in which Miss Austen sinned.

When Molly next appeared at the Virginian's threshold, he said plaintively, "I reckon I am a dunce." And he sued for pardon. "When I waked up," he said, "I was ashamed of myself for a plumb half-hour." Nor could she doubt this day that he meant what he said. His mood was again serene and gentle, and without referring to his singular words that had distressed her, he made her feel his contrition, even in his silence.

"I am right glad you have come," he said. And as he saw her going to the bookshelf, he continued, with diffidence: "As regyards that *Emma* book, yu' see—yu' see, the doin's and sayin's of folks like them are above me. But I think" (he spoke most diffidently), "if yu' could read me something that was about something, I—I'd be liable to keep awake." And he smiled with a certain shyness.

"Something *about* something?" queried Molly, at a loss.

"Why, yes. Shakespeare. *Henry the Fourth*. The British king is fighting, and there is his son the prince. He cert'nly must have been a jim-dandy boy if that is all true. Only he would go around town with a mighty triflin' gang. They sported and they held up citizens. And his father hated his traveling with trash like them. It was right natural—the boy and the old man! But the boy showed himself a man too. He killed a big fighter on the other side who was another jim-dandy—and he was sorry for having it to do." The Virginian warmed to his recital. "I understand most all of that. There was a fat man kept everybody laughing. He was awful natural too; except yu' don't commonly meet 'em so fat. But the prince—that play is bedrock, ma'am! Have you got something like that?"

"Yes, I think so," she replied. "I believe I see what you would appreciate."

She took her Browning, her idol, her imagined affinity. For the pale decadence of New England had somewhat watered her good old Revolutionary blood too, and she was inclined to think under glass and to live underdone—when there were no Indians to shoot! She would have joyed to venture "Paracelsus" on him, and some lengthy rhymed discourses; and she fondly turned leaves and leaves of her pet doggerel analytics. "Pippa Passes" and others she had to skip, from discreet motives—pages which he would have doubtless stayed awake at; but she chose a poem at length. This was better than *Emma*, he pronounced. And short. The horse was a good horse. He thought a man whose horse must not play out on him would watch the ground he was galloping over for holes, and not be likely to see what color the rims of his animal's eye-sockets were. You could not see them if you sat as you ought to for such a hard ride. Of the next piece that she read him he thought still better. "And it is short," said he. "But the last part drops."

Molly instantly exacted particulars.

"The soldier should not have told the general he was killed," stated the cowpuncher.

"What should he have told him, I'd like to know?" said Molly.

"Why, just nothing. If the soldier could ride out of the battle all shot up, and tell his general about their takin' the town—that was being gritty, yu' see. But that truck at the finish—will yu' please say it again?"

So Molly read:—

> " 'You're wounded!' 'Nay,' the soldier's pride
> Touched to the quick, he said,
> 'I'm killed, sire!' And, his chief beside,
> Smiling the boy fell dead."

" 'Nay, I'm killed, sire,' " drawled the Virginian, amiably; for (symptom of convalescence) his freakish irony was revived in him. "Now a man who was man enough to act like he did, yu' see, would fall dead without mentioning it."

None of Molly's sweet girl friends had ever thus challenged Mr. Browning. They had been wont to cluster over him with a joyous awe that deepened proportionally with their misunderstanding. Molly paused to consider this novelty of view about the soldier. "He was a Frenchman, you know," she said, under inspiration.

"A Frenchman," murmured the grave cowpuncher. "I never knowed a Frenchman, but I reckon they might perform that class of foolishness."

"But why was it foolish?" she cried.

"His soldier's pride—don't you see?"

"No."

Molly now burst into a luxury of discussion. She leaned toward her cowpuncher with bright eyes searching his; with elbow on knee and hand propping chin, her lap became a slant, and from it Browning the poet slid and toppled, and lay unrescued. For the slow cowpuncher unfolded his notions of masculine courage and modesty (though he did not deal in such high-sounding names), and Molly forgot everything to listen to him, as he forgot himself and his inveterate shyness and grew talkative to her. "I would never have supposed that!" she would exclaim as she heard him; or, presently again, "I never had such an idea!" And her mind opened with delight to these new things which came from the man's mind so simple and direct. To Browning they did come back, but the Virginian, though interested, conceived a dislike for him. "He is a smarty," said he, once or twice.

"Now here is something," said Molly. "I have never known what to think."

"Oh, Heavens!" murmured the sick man, smiling. "Is it short?"

"Very short. Now please attend." And she read him twelve lines about a lover who rowed to a beach in the dusk, crossed a field, tapped at a pane, and was admitted.

"That is the best yet," said the Virginian. "There's only one thing yu' can think about that."

"But wait," said the girl, swiftly. "Here is how they parted:

'Round the cape of a sudden came the sea,
    And the sun looked over the mountain's rim—
    And straight was a path of gold for him,
    And the need of a world of men for me.'"

"That is very, very true," murmured the Virginian, dropping his eyes from the girl's intent ones.

"Had they quarreled?" she inquired.

"Oh, no!"

"But—"

"I reckon he loved her very much."

"Then you're sure they hadn't quarreled?"

"Dead sure, ma'am. He would come back afteh he had played some more of the game."

"The game?"

"Life, ma'am. Whatever he was a-doin' in the world of men. That's a bedrock piece, ma'am!"

"Well, I don't see why you think it's so much better than some of the others."

"I could sca'cely explain," answered the man. "But that writer does know something."

"I am glad they hadn't quarreled," said Molly, thoughtfully. And she began to like having her opinions refuted.

His bandages, becoming a little irksome, had to be shifted, and this turned their discourse from literature to Wyoming; and Molly inquired, had he ever been shot before? Only once, he told her. "I have been lucky in having few fusses," said he. "I hate them. If a man has to be killed—"

"You never—" broke in Molly. She had started back a little. "Well," she added hastily, "don't tell me if—"

"I shouldn't wonder if I got one of those Indians," he said quietly. "But I wasn't waitin' to see! But I came mighty near doing for a white man that day. He had been hurtin' a hawss."

"Hurting?" said Molly.

"Injurin.' I will not tell yu' about that. It would hurt yu' to hear such things. But hawsses—don't they depend on us? Ain't they somethin' like children? I did not lay up the man very bad. He was able to travel 'most right away. Why, you'd have wanted to kill him yourself!"

So the Virginian talked, nor knew what he was doing to the girl. Nor was she aware of what she was receiving from him as he unwittingly spoke himself out to her in these Browning meetings they had each day. But Mrs. Taylor grew pleased. The kindly dame would sometimes cross the road to see if she were needed, and steal away again after a peep at the window. There, inside, among the restored home treasures, sat the two: the rosy alert girl, sweet as she talked or read to him; and he, the grave, half-weak giant among his wraps, watching her.

Of her delayed home visit he never again spoke, either to her or to Mrs. Taylor; and Molly veered aside from any trend of talk she foresaw was leading toward that subject. But in those hours when no visitors came, and he was by himself in the quiet, he would lie often sombrely contemplating the girl's room, her little dainty knickknacks, her home photographs, all the delicate manifestations of what she came from and what she was. Strength was flowing back into him each day, and Judge Henry's latest messenger had brought him clothes and mail from Sunk Creek and many inquiries of kindness, and returned taking the news of the cowpuncher's improvement, and how soon he would be permitted the fresh air. Hence Molly found him waiting in a flannel shirt of highly becoming shade, and with a silk handkerchief knotted round his throat; and he told her it was good to feel respectable again.

She had come to read to him for the allotted time; and she threw around his shoulders the scarlet and black Navajo blanket, striped with its splendid zigzags of barbarity. Thus he half sat, half leaned, languid but at ease. In his lap lay one of the letters brought over by the messenger: and though she was midway in a book that engaged his full attention—*David Copperfield*—his silence and absent look this morning stopped her, and she accused him of not attending.

"No," he admitted; "I am thinking of something else."

She looked at him with that apprehension which he knew.

"It had to come," said he. "And today I see my thoughts straighter than I've been up to managing since—since my haid got clear. And now I must say these thoughts—if I can, if I can!" He stopped. His eyes were intent upon her; one hand was gripping the arm of his chair.

"You promised—" trembled Molly.

"I promised you should love me," he sternly interrupted. "Promised that to myself. I have broken that word."

She shut *David Copperfield* mechanically, and grew white.

"Your letter has come to me hyeh," he continued, gentle again.

"My—" She had forgotten it.

"The letter you wrote to tell me good-by. You wrote it a little while ago— not a month yet, but it's away and away long gone for me."

"I have never let you know—" began Molly.

"The doctor," he interrupted once more, but very gently now, "he gave awdehs I must be kept quiet. I reckon yu' thought tellin' me might—"

"Forgive me!" cried the girl. "Indeed I ought to have told you sooner! Indeed I had no excuse!"

"Why, should yu' tell me if yu' preferred not? You had written. And you speak" (he lifted the letter) "of never being able to repay kindness; but you have turned the tables. I can never repay you by anything! by anything! So I had figured I would just jog back to Sunk Creek and let you get away, if you did not want to say that kind of good-by. For I saw the boxes. Mrs. Taylor is too nice a woman to know the trick of lyin', and she could not deceive me. I have knowed yu' were going away for good ever since I saw those boxes. But now hyeh comes your letter, and it seems no way but I must speak. I have thought a deal, lyin' in this room. And—today—I can say what I have thought. I could not make you happy." He stopped, but she did not answer. His voice had grown softer than whispering, but yet was not a whisper. From its quiet syllables she turned away, blinded with sudden tears.

"Once, I thought love must surely be enough," he continued. "And I thought if I could make you love me, you could learn me to be less—less—more your kind. And I think I could give you a pretty good sort of love. But that don't help the little mean pesky things of day by day that make roughness or smoothness for folks tied together so awful close. Mrs. Taylor hyeh—she don't know anything better than Taylor does. She don't want anything he can't give her. Her friends will do for him and his for her. And when I dreamed of you in my home—" he closed his eyes and drew a long breath. At last he looked at her again. "This is no country for a lady. Will yu' forget and forgive the bothering I have done?"

"Oh!" cried Molly. "Oh!" And she put her hands to her eyes. She had risen and stood with her face covered.

"I surely had to tell you this all out, didn't I?" said the cowpuncher, faintly, in his chair.

"Oh!" said Molly again.

"I have put it clear how it is," he pursued. "I ought to have seen from the start I was not the sort to keep you happy."

"But," said Molly—"but I—you ought—please try to keep me happy!" And sinking by his chair, she hid her face on his knees.

Speechless, he bent down and folded her round, putting his hands on the hair that had been always his delight. Presently he whispered: "You have beat me; how can I fight this?"

She answered nothing. The Navajo's scarlet and black folds fell over both. Not with words, not even with meeting eyes, did the two plight their troth in this first new hour. So they remained long, the fair head nesting in the great arms, and the black head laid against it, while over the silent room presided the little Grandmother Stark in her frame, rosy, blue, and flaxen, not quite familiar, not quite smiling.

## CHAPTER XXVIII

### NO DREAM TO WAKE FROM

For a long while after she had left him, he lay still, stretched in his chair. His eyes were fixed steadily upon the open window and the sunshine outside. There he watched the movement of the leaves upon the green cottonwoods. What had she said to him when she went? She had said, "Now I know how unhappy I have been." These sweet words he repeated to himself over and over, fearing in some way that he might lose them. They almost slipped from him at times; but with a jump of his mind he caught them again and held them—and then—"I'm not all strong yet," he murmured. "I must have been very sick." And, weak from his bullet wound and fever, he closed his eyes without knowing it. There were the cottonwoods again, waving, waving; and he felt the cool, pleasant air from the window. He saw the light draught stir the ashes in the great stone fireplace. "I have been asleep," he said. "But she was cert'nly here herself. Oh, yes. Surely. She always has to go away every day because the doctor says—why, she was readin'!" he broke off, aloud. "*David Copperfield.*" There it was on the floor. "Aha! Nailed you anyway!" he said. "But how scared I am of myself! You're a fool. Of course it's so. No fever business could make yu' feel like this."

His eye dwelt awhile on the fireplace, next on the deer horns, and next it traveled toward the shelf where her books were; but it stopped before reaching them.

"Better say off the names before I look," said he. "I've had a heap o' misreading visions. And—and supposin'—if this was just my sickness fooling me some more—I'd want to die. I would die! Now we'll see. If *Copperfield* is on the floor" (he looked stealthily to be sure that it was), "then she was readin' to me when everything happened, and then there should be a hole in the book row, top, left. Top, left," he repeated, and warily brought his glance to the place. "Proved!" he cried. "It's all so!"

He now noticed the miniature of Grandmother Stark. "You are awful like her," he whispered. "You're cert'nly awful like her. May I kiss you too, ma'am?"

Then, tottering, he rose from his sick-chair. The Navajo blanket fell from his shoulders, and gradually, experimentally, he stood upright.

Helping himself with his hand slowly along the wall of the room, and round to the opposite wall with many a pause, he reached the picture, and very gently touched the forehead of the ancestral dame with his lips. "I promise to make your little girl happy," he whispered.

He almost fell in stooping to the portrait, but caught himself and stood carefully quiet, trembling, and speaking to himself. "Where is your strength?" he demanded. "I reckon it is joy that has unsteadied your laigs."

The door opened. It was she, come back with his dinner.

"My Heavens!" she said; and setting the tray down, she rushed to him. She helped him back to his chair, and covered him again. He had suffered no hurt, but she clung to him; and presently he moved and let himself kiss her with fuller passion.

"I will be good," he whispered.

"You must," she said. "You looked so pale!"

"You are speakin' low like me," he answered. "But we have no dream we can wake from."

Had she surrendered on this day to her cowpuncher, her wild man? Was she forever wholly his? Had the Virginian's fire so melted her heart that no rift in it remained? So she would have thought if any thought had come to her. But in his arms today, thought was lost in something more divine.

# CHAPTER XXIX

## WORD TO BENNINGTON

They kept their secret for a while, or at least they had that special joy of believing that no one in all the world but themselves knew this that had happened to them. But I think that there was one person who knew how to keep a secret even better than these two lovers. Mrs. Taylor made no remarks to anyone whatever. Nobody on Bear Creek, however, was so extraordinarily cheerful and serene. That peculiar severity which she had manifested in the days when Molly was packing her possessions, had now altogether changed. In these days she was endlessly kind and indulgent to her "deary." Although, as a housekeeper, Mrs. Taylor believed in punctuality at meals, and visited her offspring with discipline when they were late without good and sufficient excuse, Molly was now exempt from the faintest hint of reprimand.

"And it's not because you're not her mother," said George Taylor, bitterly. "She used to get it, too. And we're the only ones that get it. There she comes, just as we're about ready to quit! Aren't you going to say *nothing* to her?"

"George," said his mother, "when you've saved a man's life it'll be time for you to talk."

So Molly would come in to her meals with much irregularity; and her remarks about the imperfections of her clock met with no rejoinder. And yet one can scarcely be so severe as had been Mrs. Taylor, and become wholly as mild as milk. There was one recurrent event that could invariably awaken hostile symptoms in the dame. Whenever she saw a letter arrive with the Bennington postmark upon it, she shook her fist at that letter. "What's family pride?" she would say to herself. "Taylor could be a Son of the Revolution if he'd a mind to. I wonder if she has told her folks yet."

And when letters directed to Bennington would go out, Mrs. Taylor would inspect every one as if its envelope ought to grow transparent beneath her eyes, and yield up to her its great secret, if it had one. But in truth these letters had no great secret to yield up, until one day—yes; one day Mrs. Taylor would have burst, were bursting a thing that people often did. Three letters were the cause of this emotion on Mrs. Taylor's part; one addressed to Bennington, one to Dunbarton, and the third—here was the great excitement—to Bennington, but not in the little schoolmarm's delicate writing. A man's hand had traced those plain, steady vowels and consonants.

"It's come!" exclaimed Mrs. Taylor, at this sight. "He has written to her mother himself."

That is what the Virginian had done, and here is how it had come about.

The sick man's convalescence was achieved. The weeks had brought back to him, not his whole strength yet—that could come only by many miles of open air on the back of Monte; but he was strong enough now to *get* strength. When a patient reaches this stage, he is out of the woods.

He had gone for a little walk with his nurse. They had taken (under the doctor's recommendation) several such little walks, beginning with a five-minute one, and at last today accomplishing three miles.

"No, it has not been too far," said he. "I am afraid I could walk twice as far."

"Afraid?"

"Yes. Because it means I can go to work again. This thing we have had together is over."

For reply, she leaned against him.

"Look at you!" he said. "Only a little while ago you had to help me stand on my laigs. And now—" For a while there was silence between them. "I have never had a right down sickness before," he presently went on. "Not to remember, that is. If any person had told me I could *enjoy* such a thing—" He said no more, for she reached up, and no more speech was possible.

"How long has it been?" he next asked her.

She told him.

"Well, if it could be forever—no. Not forever with no more than this. I reckon I'd be sick again! But if it could be forever with just you and me, and no one else to bother with. But any longer would not be doing right by your mother. She would have a right to think ill of me."

"Oh!" said the girl. "Let us keep it."

"Not after I am gone. Your mother must be told."

"It seems so—can't we—oh, why need anybody know?"

"Your mother ain't 'anybody.' She is your mother. I feel mighty responsible to her for what I have done."

"But I did it!"

"Do you think so? Your mother will not think so. I am going to write to her today."

"You! Write to my mother! Oh, then everything will be so different! They will all—" Molly stopped before the rising visions of Bennington. Upon the fairy-tale that she had been living with her cowboy lover broke the voices of the world. She could hear them from afar. She could see the eyes of Bennington watching this man at her side. She could imagine the ears of Bennington listening for slips in his English. There loomed upon her the round of visits which they would have to make. The ringing of the door-bells, the waiting in drawing-rooms for the mistress to descend and utter her prepared congratulations, while her secret eye devoured the Virginian's appearance, and his manner of standing and sitting. He would be wearing gloves, instead of fringed gauntlets of buckskin. In a smooth black coat and waistcoat, how could they perceive the man he was? During those short formal interviews, what would they ever find out of the things that she knew about him? The things for which she was proud of him? He would speak shortly and simply; they would say, "Oh, yes!" and "How different you must find this from Wyoming!"—and then, after the door was shut behind his departing back they would say—He would be totally underrated, not in the least understood. Why should he be subjected to this? He should never be!

Now in all these half-formed, hurried, distressing thoughts which streamed through the girl's mind, she altogether forgot one truth. True it was that the voice of the world would speak as she imagined. True it was that in the eyes of her family and acquaintance this lover of her choice would be examined even more like a *specimen* than are other lovers upon these occasions: and all accepted lovers have to face this ordeal of being treated like specimens by the other family. But dear me! most of us manage to stand it, don't we? It isn't, perhaps, the most delicious experience that we can recall in connection with our engagement. But it didn't prove fatal. We got through it somehow. We dined with Aunt Jane, and wined with Uncle Joseph, and perhaps had two fingers given to us by old Cousin Horatio, whose enormous fortune was of the greatest importance to everybody. And perhaps fragments of the other family's estimate of us subsequently reached our own ears. But if a chosen lover cannot stand being treated as a specimen by the other family, he's a very weak vessel, and not worth any good girl's love. That's all I can say for him.

Now the Virginian was scarcely what even his enemy would term a weak vessel; and Molly's jealousy of the impression which he might make upon Bennington was vastly superfluous. She should have known that he would indeed care to make a good impression; but that such anxiety on his part would be wholly for her sake, that in the eyes of her friends she might stand justified in taking him for her wedded husband. So far as he was concerned apart from her, Aunt Jane and Uncle Joseph might say anything they pleased, or think anything they pleased. His character was open for investigation. Judge Henry would vouch for him.

This is what he would have said to his sweetheart had she but revealed to him her perturbations. But she did not reveal them; and they were not of the order that he with his nature was likely to divine. I do not know what good would have come from her speaking out to him, unless that perfect understanding between lovers which indeed is a good thing. But I do not believe that he could have reassured her; and I am certain that she could not have prevented his writing to her mother.

"Well, then," she sighed at last, "if you think so, I will tell her."

That sigh of hers, be it well understood, was not only because of those far-off voices which the world would in consequence of her news be lifting presently. It came also from bidding farewell to the fairy-tale which she must leave now; that land in which she and he had been living close together alone, unhindered, unmindful of all things.

"Yes, you will tell her," said her lover. "And I must tell her too."

"Both of us?" questioned the girl.

What would he say to her mother? How would her mother like such a letter as he would write to her? Suppose he should misspell a word? Would not sentences from him at this time—written sentences—be a further bar to his welcome acceptance at Bennington?

"Why don't you send messages by me?" she asked him.

He shook his head. "She is not going to like it, anyway," he answered. "I must speak to her direct. It would be like shirking."

Molly saw how true his instinct was here; and a little flame shot upward from the glow of her love and pride in him. Oh, if they could all only know that he was like this when you understood him! She did not dare say out to him what her fear was about this letter of his to her mother. She did not dare because—well, because she lacked a little faith. That is it, I am afraid. And for that sin she was her own punishment. For in this day, and in many days to come, the pure joy of her love was vexed and clouded, all through a little lack of faith; while for him, perfect in his faith, his joy was like crystal.

"Tell me what you're going to write," she said.

He smiled at her. "No."

"Aren't you going to let me see it when it's done?"

"No." Then a freakish look came into his eyes. "I'll let yu' see anything I write to other women." And he gave her one of his long kisses. "Let's get through with it together," he suggested, when they were once more in his sick-room, that room which she had given to him. "You'll sit one side o' the table, and I'll sit the other, and we'll go ahaid; and pretty soon it will be done."

"O dear!" she said. "Yes, I suppose that is the best way."

And so, accordingly, they took their places. The inkstand stood between them. Beside each of them she distributed paper enough, almost, for a presidential message. And pens and pencils were in plenty. Was this not the headquarters of the Bear Creek schoolmarm?

"Why, aren't you going to do it in pencil first?" she exclaimed, looking up from her vacant sheet. His pen was moving slowly, but steadily.

"No, I don't reckon I need to," he answered, with his nose close to the paper. "Oh, damnation, there's a blot!" He tore his spoiled beginning in small bits, and threw them into the fireplace. "You've got it too full," he commented; and taking the inkstand, he tipped a little from it out of the window. She sat lost among her false starts. Had she heard him swear, she would not have minded. She rather liked it when he swore. He possessed that quality in his profanity of not offending by it. It is quite wonderful how much worse the same word will sound in one man's lips than in another's. But she did not hear him. Her mind was among a litter of broken sentences. Each thought which she began ran out into the empty air, or came against some stone wall. So there she sat, her eyes now upon that inexorable blank sheet that lay before her, waiting, and now turned with vacant hopelessness upon the sundry objects in the room. And while she thus sat accomplishing nothing, opposite to her the black head bent down, and the steady pen moved from phrase to phrase.

She became aware of his gazing at her, flushed and solemn. That strange color of the seawater, which she could never name, was lustrous in his eyes. He was folding his letter.

"You have finished?" she said.

"Yes." His voice was very quiet. "I feel like an honester man."

"Perhaps I can do something tonight at Mrs. Taylor's," she said, looking at her paper.

On it were a few words crossed out. This was all she had to show. At this set task in letter-writing, the cowpuncher had greatly excelled the schoolmarm!

But that night, while he lay quite fast asleep in his bed, she was keeping vigil in her room at Mrs. Taylor's.

Accordingly, the next day, those three letters departed for the mail, and Mrs. Taylor consequently made her exclamation, "It's come!"

On the day before the Virginian returned to take up his work at Judge Henry's ranch, he and Molly announced their news. What Molly said to Mrs. Taylor and what Mrs. Taylor said to her, is of no interest to us, though it was of much to them.

But Mr. McLean happened to make a call quite early in the morning to inquire for his friend's health.

"Lin," began the Virginian, "there is no harm in your knowing an hour or so before the rest, I am—"

"Lord!" said Mr. McLean, indulgently. "Everybody has knowed that since the day she found yu' at the spring."

"It was not so, then," said the Virginian, crossly.

"Lord! Everybody has knowed it right along."

"Hmp!" said the Virginian. "I didn't know this country was that rank with gossips."

Mr. McLean laughed mirthfully at the lover. "Well," he said, "Mrs. McLean will be glad. She told me to give yu' her congratulations quite a while ago. I was to have 'em ready just as soon as ever yu' asked for 'em yourself." Lin had been made a happy man some twelve months previous to this. And now, by way of an exchange of news, he added: "We're expectin' a little McLean down on Box Elder. That's what you'll be expectin' some of these days, I hope."

"Yes," murmured the Virginian, "I hope so too."

"And I don't guess," said Lin, "that you and I will do much shufflin' of other folks' children anymore."

Whereupon he and the Virginian shook hands silently, and understood each other very well.

On the day that the Virginian parted with Molly, beside the weight of farewell which lay heavy on his heart, his thoughts were also grave with news. The cattle thieves had grown more audacious. Horses and cattle both were being missed, and each man began almost to doubt his neighbor.

"Steps will have to be taken soon by somebody, I reckon," said the lover.

"By you?" she asked quickly.

"Most likely I'll get mixed up with it."

"What will you have to do?"

"Can't say. I'll tell yu' when I come back."

So did he part from her, leaving her more kisses than words to remember.

And what was doing at Bennington, meanwhile, and at Dunbarton? Those three letters which by their mere outside had so moved Mrs. Taylor, produced by their contents much painful disturbance.

It will be remembered that Molly wrote to her mother, and to her great-aunt. That announcement to her mother was undertaken first. Its composition occupied three hours and a half, and it filled eleven pages, not counting a postscript upon the twelfth. The letter to the great-aunt took only ten minutes. I cannot pretend to explain why this one was so greatly superior to the other; but such is the remarkable fact. Its beginning, to be sure, did give the old lady a start; she had dismissed the cowboy from her probabilities.

"Tut, tut, tut!" she exclaimed out loud in her bedroom. "She has thrown herself away on that fellow!"

But some sentences at the end made her pause and sit still for a long while. The severity upon her face changed to tenderness, gradually. "Ah, me," she sighed. "If marriage were as simple as love!" Then she went slowly downstairs, and out into her garden, where she walked long between the box borders. "But if she has found a great love," said the old lady at length. And she returned to her bedroom, and opened an old desk, and read some old letters.

There came to her the next morning a communication from Bennington. This had been penned frantically by poor Mrs. Wood. As soon as she had been able to gather her senses after the shock of her daughter's eleven pages and the postscript, the mother had poured out eight pages herself to the eldest member of the family. There had been, indeed, much excuse for the poor lady. To begin with, Molly had constructed her whole opening page with the express and merciful intention of preparing her mother. Consequently, it made no sense whatever. Its effect was the usual effect of remarks designed to break a thing gently. It merely made Mrs. Wood's head swim, and filled her with a sickening dread. "Oh, mercy, Sarah," she had cried, "come here. What does this mean?" And then, fortified by her elder daughter, she had turned over that first page and found what it meant on the top of the second. "A savage with knives and pistols!" she wailed.

"Well, mother, I always told you so," said her daughter Sarah.

"What is a foreman?" exclaimed the mother. "And who is Judge Henry?"

"She has taken a sort of upper servant," said Sarah. "If it is allowed to go as far as a wedding, I doubt if I can bring myself to be present."

(This threat she proceeded to make to Molly, with results that shall be set forth in their proper place.)

"The man appears to have written to me himself," said Mrs. Wood.

"He knows no better," said Sarah.

"Bosh!" said Sarah's husband later. "It was a very manly thing to do."

Thus did consternation rage in the house at Bennington. Molly might have spared herself the many assurances that she gave concerning the universal esteem in which her cowpuncher was held, and the fair prospects which were his. So, in the first throes of her despair, Mrs. Wood wrote those eight not maturely considered pages to the great-aunt.

"Tut, tut, tut!" said the great-aunt as she read them. Her face was much more severe today. "You'd suppose," she said, "that the girl had been kidnapped! Why, she has kept him waiting three years!" And then she read more, but soon put the letter down with laughter. For Mrs. Wood had repeated in writing that early outburst of hers about a savage with knives and pistols. "Law!" said the great-aunt. "Law, what a fool Lizzie is!"

So she sat down and wrote to Mrs. Wood a wholesome reply about putting a little more trust in her own flesh and blood, and reminding her among other things that General Stark had himself been wont to carry knives and pistols owing to the necessities of his career, but that he had occasionally taken them off, as did probably this young man in Wyoming. "You had better send me the letter he has written you," she concluded. "I shall know much better what to think after I have seen that."

It is not probable that Mrs. Wood got much comfort from this communication; and her daughter Sarah was actually enraged by it. "She grows more perverse as she nears her dotage," said Sarah. But the Virginian's letter was sent to Dunbarton, where the old lady sat herself down to read it with much attention.

Here is what the Virginian had said to the unknown mother of his sweetheart.

> *Mrs. John Stark Wood,* BENNINGTON, VERMONT.
> MADAM: If your daughter Miss Wood has ever told you about her saving a man's life here when some Indians had shot him that is the man who writes to you now. I don't think she can have told you right about that affair for she is the only one in this country who thinks it was a little thing. So I must tell you it, the main points. Such an action would have been thought highly of in a Western girl, but with Miss Wood's raising nobody had a right to expect it.

"Indeed!" snorted the great-aunt. "Well, he would be right, if I had not had a good deal more to do with her 'raising' than ever Lizzie had." And she went on with the letter.

> I was starting in to die when she found me. I did not know anything then, and she pulled me back from where I was half in the next world. She did not know but what Indians would get her too but I could not make her leave me. I am a heavy man one hundred and seventy-three stripped when in full health. She lifted me herself from the ground me helping scarce any for there was not much help in me that day. She washed my wound and brought me to with her own whiskey. Before she could get me home I was out of my head but she kept me on my horse somehow and talked wisely to me so I minded her and did not go clean crazy till she had got me safe to bed. The doctor says I would have died all the same if she had not nursed me the way she did. It made me love her more which I did not know I could. But there is no end, for this writing it down makes me love her more as I write it.
>
> And now Mrs. Wood I am sorry this will be bad news for you to hear. I know you would never choose such a man as I am for her for I have got no education and must write humble against my birth. I wish I could make the news easier but truth is the best.

I am of old stock in Virginia. English and one Scotch Irish grandmother my father's father brought from Kentucky. We have always stayed at the same place farmers and hunters not bettering our lot and very plain. We have fought when we got the chance, under Old Hickory and in Mexico and my father and two brothers were killed in the Valley sixty-four. Always with us one son has been apt to run away and I was the one this time. I had too much older brothering to suit me. But now I am doing well being in full sight of prosperity and not too old and very strong my health having stood the sundries it has been put through. She shall teach school no more when she is mine. I wish I could make this news easier for you Mrs. Wood. I do not like promises I have heard so many. I will tell any man of your family anything he likes to ask one, and Judge Henry would tell you about my reputation. I have seen plenty rough things but can say I have never killed for pleasure or profit and am not one of that kind, always preferring peace. I have had to live in places where they had courts and lawyers so called but an honest man was all the law you could find in five hundred miles. I have not told her about those things not because I am ashamed of them but there are so many things too dark for a girl like her to hear about.

I had better tell you the way I know I love Miss Wood. I am not a boy now, and women are no new thing to me. A man like me who has traveled meets many of them as he goes and passes on but I stopped when I came to Miss Wood. That is three years but I have not gone on. What right has such as he? you will say. So did I say it after she had saved my life. It was hard to get to that point and keep there with her around me all day. But I said to myself you have bothered her for three years with your love and if you let your love bother her you don't love her like you should and you must quit for her sake who has saved your life. I did not know what I was going to do with my life after that but I supposed I could go somewhere and work hard and so Mrs. Wood I told her I would give her up. But she said no. It is going to be hard for her to get used to a man like me—

But at this point in the Virginian's letter, the old great-aunt could read no more. She rose, and went over to that desk where lay those faded letters of her own. She laid her head down upon the package, and as her tears flowed quietly upon it, "O dear," she whispered, "O dear! And this is what I lost!"

To her girl upon Bear Creek she wrote the next day. And this word from Dunbarton was like balm among the harsh stings Molly was receiving. The voices of the world reached her in gathering numbers, and not one of them save that great-aunt's was sweet. Her days were full of hurts; and there was no one by to kiss the hurts away. Nor did she even hear from her lover anymore now. She only knew he had gone into lonely regions upon his errand.

That errand took him far: Across the Basin, among the secret places of Owl Creek, past the Washakie Needles, over the Divide to Gros Ventre, and so through a final barrier of peaks into the borders of East Idaho. There, by reason of his bidding me, I met him, and came to share in a part of his errand.

It was with no guide that I traveled to him. He had named a little station on the railroad, and from thence he had charted my route by means of landmarks. Did I believe in omens, the black storm that I set out in upon my horse would seem like one today. But I had been living in cities and smoke; and Idaho, even with rain, was delightful to me.

# CHAPTER XXX

## A STABLE ON THE FLAT

When the first landmark, the lone clump of cottonwoods, came at length in sight, dark and blurred in the gentle rain, standing out perhaps a mile beyond the distant buildings, my whole weary body hailed the approach of repose. Saving the noon hour, I had been in the saddle since six, and now six was come round again. The ranch, my resting-place for this night, was a ruin—cabin, stable, and corral. Yet after the twelve hours of pushing on and on through silence, still to have silence, still to eat and go to sleep in it, perfectly fitted the mood of both my flesh and spirit. At noon, when for a while I had thrown off my long oilskin coat, merely the sight of the newspaper half crowded into my pocket had been a displeasing reminder of the railway, and cities, and affairs. But for its possible help to build fires, it would have come no farther with me. The great levels around me lay cooled and freed of dust by the wet weather, and full of sweet airs. Far in front the foothills rose through the rain, indefinite and mystic. I wanted no speech with anyone, nor to be near human beings at all. I was steeped in a revery as of the primal earth; even thoughts themselves had almost ceased motion. To lie down with wild animals, with elk and deer, would have made my waking dream complete; and since such dream could not be, the cattle around the deserted buildings, mere dots as yet across separating space, were my proper companions for this evening.

Tomorrow night I should probably be camping with the Virginian in the foothills. At his letter's bidding I had come eastward across Idaho, abandoning my hunting in the Saw Tooth Range to make this journey with him back through the Tetons. It was a trail known to him, and not to many other honest men. Horse Thief Pass was the name his letter gave it. Business (he was always brief) would call him over there at this time. Returning, he must attend to certain matters in the Wind River country. There I could leave by stage for the railroad, or go on with him the whole way back to Sunk Creek. He designated for our meeting the forks of a certain little stream in the foothills which today's ride had brought in sight. There would be no chance for him to receive an answer from me in the intervening time. If by a certain day—which was four days off still—I had not reached the forks, he would understand I had other plans. To me it was like living back in ages gone, this way of meeting my friend, this choice of a stream so far and lonely that its very course upon the maps was wrongly traced. And to leave behind all noise and mechanisms, and set out at ease, slowly, with one packhorse, into the wilderness, made me feel that the ancient earth was indeed my mother and that I had found her again after being lost among houses, customs, and restraints. I should arrive three days early at the forks—three days of margin seeming to me a wise precaution against delays unforeseen. If the Virginian were not there, good; I could fish and be happy. If he were there but not ready to start, good; I could still fish and be happy. And remembering my Eastern helplessness in the year when we had met first, I enjoyed thinking how I had come to be trusted. In those days I had not been allowed to go from the ranch for so much as an afternoon's ride unless tied to him by a string, so to speak; now I was crossing unmapped spaces with no guidance. The man who could do this was scarce any longer a "tenderfoot."

My vision, as I rode, took in serenely the dim foothills—tomorrow's goal—and nearer in the vast wet plain the clump of cottonwoods, and still nearer my lodging for tonight with the dotted cattle round it. And now my horse neighed. I felt his gait freshen for the journey's end, and leaning to pat his neck I noticed his ears no longer slack and inattentive, but pointing forward to where food and rest awaited both of us. Twice he neighed, impatiently and long; and as he quickened his gait still more, the packhorse did the same, and I realized that there was about me still a spice of the tenderfoot: those dots were not cattle; they were horses.

My horse had put me in the wrong. He had known his kind from afar, and was hastening to them. The plainsman's eye was not yet mine; and I smiled a little as I rode. When was I going to know, as by instinct, the different look of horses and cattle across some two or three miles of plain?

These miles we finished soon. The buildings changed in their aspect as they grew to my approach, showing their desolation more clearly, and in some way bringing apprehension into my mood. And around them the horses, too, all standing with ears erect, watching me as I came—there was something about them; or was it the silence? For the silence which I had liked until now seemed suddenly to be made too great by the presence of the deserted buildings. And then the door of the stable opened, and men came out and stood, also watching me arrive. By the time I was dismounting more were there. It was senseless to feel as unpleasant as I did, and I strove to give to them a greeting that should sound easy. I told them that I hoped there was room for one more here tonight. Some of them had answered my greeting, but none of them answered this; and as I began to be sure that I recognized several of their strangely imperturbable faces, the Virginian came from the stable; and at that welcome sight my relief spoke out instantly.

"I am here, you see!"

"Yes, I do see." I looked hard at him, for in his voice was the same strangeness that I felt in everything around me. But he was looking at his companions. "This gentleman is all right," he told them.

"That may be," said one whom I now knew that I had seen before at Sunk Creek; "but he was not due tonight."

"Nor tomorrow," said another.

"Nor yet the day after," a third added.

The Virginian fell into his drawl. "None of you was ever early for anything, I presume."

One retorted, laughing, "Oh, we're not suspicioning you of complicity."

And another, "Not even when we remember how thick you and Steve used to be."

Whatever jokes they meant by this he did not receive as jokes. I saw something like a wince pass over his face, and a flush follow it. But he now spoke to me. "We expected to be through before this," he began. "I'm right sorry you have come tonight. I know you'd have preferred to keep away."

"We want him to explain himself," put in one of the others. "If he satisfies us, he's free to go away."

"Free to go away!" I now exclaimed. But at the indulgence in their frontier smile I cooled down. "Gentlemen," I said, "I don't know why my movements interest you so much. It's quite a compliment! May I get under shelter while I explain?"

No request could have been more natural, for the rain had now begun to fall in straight floods. Yet there was a pause before one of them said, "He might as well."

The Virginian chose to say nothing more; but he walked beside me into the stable. Two men sat there together, and a third guarded them. At that sight I knew suddenly what I had stumbled upon; and on the impulse I murmured to the Virginian, "You're hanging them tomorrow."

He kept his silence.

"You may have three guesses," said a man behind me.

But I did not need them. And in the recoil of my insight the clump of cottonwoods came into my mind, black and grim. No other trees high enough grew within ten miles. This, then, was the business that the Virginian's letter had so curtly mentioned. My eyes went into all corners of the stable, but no other prisoners were here. I half expected to see Trampas, and I half feared to see Shorty; for poor stupid Shorty's honesty had not been proof against frontier temptations, and he had fallen away from the company of his old friends. Often of late I had heard talk at Sunk Creek of breaking up a certain gang of horse and cattle thieves that stole in one Territory and sold in the next, and knew where to hide in the mountains between. And now it had come to the point; forces had been gathered, a long expedition made, and here they were, successful under the Virginian's lead, but a little later than their calculations. And here was I, a little too early, and a witness in consequence. My presence seemed a simple thing to account for; but when I had thus accounted for it, one of them said with good nature: "So you find us here, and we find you here. Which is the most surprised, I wonder?"

"There's no telling," said I, keeping as amiable as I could; "nor any telling which objects the most."

"Oh, there's no objection here. You're welcome to stay. But not welcome to go, I expect. He ain't welcome to go, is he?"

By the answers that their faces gave him it was plain that I was not. "Not till we are through," said one.

"He needn't to see anything," another added.

"Better sleep late tomorrow morning," a third suggested to me.

I did not wish to stay here. I could have made some sort of camp apart from them before dark; but in the face of their needless caution I was helpless. I made no attempt to inquire what kind of spy they imagined I could be, what sort of rescue I could bring in this lonely country; my too early appearance seemed to be all that they looked at. And again my eyes sought the prisoners. Certainly there were only two. One was chewing tobacco, and talking now and then to his guard as if nothing were the matter. The other sat dull in silence, not moving his eyes; but his face worked, and I noticed how he continually moistened his dry lips. As I looked at these doomed prisoners, whose fate I was invited to sleep through tomorrow morning, the one who was chewing quietly nodded to me.

"You don't remember me?" he said.

It was Steve! Steve of Medicine Bow! The pleasant Steve of my first evening in the West. Some change of beard had delayed my instant recognition of his face. Here he sat sentenced to die. A shock, chill and painful, deprived me of speech.

He had no such weak feelings. "Have yu' been to Medicine Bow lately?" he inquired. "That's getting to be quite a while ago."

I assented. I should have liked to say something natural and kind, but words stuck against my will, and I stood awkward and ill at ease, noticing idly that the silent one wore a gray flannel shirt like mine. Steve looked me over, and saw in my pocket the newspaper which I had brought from the railroad and on which I had pencilled a few expenses. He asked me, Would I mind letting him have it for a while? And I gave it to him eagerly, begging him to keep it as long as he wanted. I was overeager in my embarrassment. "You need not return it at all," I said; "those notes are nothing. Do keep it."

He gave me a short glance and a smile. "Thank you," he said; "I'll not need it beyond tomorrow morning." And he began to search through it. "Jake's election is considered sure," he said to his companion, who made no response. "Well, Fremont County owes it to Jake." And I left him interested in the local news.

Dead men I have seen not a few times, even some lying pale and terrible after violent ends, and the edge of this wears off; but I hope I shall never again have to be in the company with men waiting to be killed. By this time tomorrow the gray flannel shirt would be buttoned round a corpse. Until what moment would Steve chew? Against such fancies as these I managed presently to barricade my mind, but I made a plea to be allowed to pass the night elsewhere, and I suggested the adjacent cabin. By their faces I saw that my words merely helped their distrust of me. The cabin leaked too much, they said; I would sleep drier here. One man gave it to me more directly: "If you figured on camping in this stable, what has changed your mind?" How could I tell them that I shrunk from any contact with what they were doing, although I knew that only so could justice be dealt in this country? Their wholesome frontier nerves knew nothing of such refinements.

But the Virginian understood part of it. "I am right sorry for your annoyance," he said. And now I noticed he was under a constraint very different from the ease of the others.

After the twelve hours' ride my bones were hungry for rest. I spread my blankets on some straw in a stall by myself and rolled up in them; yet I lay growing broader awake, every inch of weariness stricken from my excited senses. For a while they sat over their councils, whispering cautiously, so that I was made curious to hear them by not being able; was it the names of Trampas and Shorty that were once or twice spoken—I could not be sure. I heard the whisperers cease and separate. I heard their boots as they cast them off upon the ground. And I heard the breathing of slumber begin and grow in the interior silence. To one after one sleep came, but not to me. Outside, the dull fall of the rain beat evenly, and in some angle dripped the spouting pulses of a leak. Sometimes a cold air blew in, bearing with it the keen wet odor of the sagebrush. On hundreds of other nights this perfume had been my last waking remembrance; it had seemed to help drowsiness; and now I lay staring, thinking of this. Twice through the hours the thieves shifted their positions with clumsy sounds, exchanging muted words with their guard. So, often, had I heard other companions move and mutter in the darkness and lie down again. It was the very naturalness and usualness of every fact of the night—the stable straw, the rain outside, my familiar blankets, the cool visits of the wind—and with all this the thought of Steve chewing and the man in the gray flannel shirt, that made the hours unearthly and strung me tight with suspense. And at last I heard someone get up and begin to dress. In a little while I saw light suddenly through my closed eyelids, and then darkness shut again abruptly upon them. They had swung in a lantern and found me by mistake. I was the only one they did not wish to rouse. Moving and quiet talking set up around me, and they began to go out of the stable. At the gleams of new daylight which they let in my thoughts went to the clump of cottonwoods, and I lay still with hands and feet growing steadily cold. Now it was going to happen. I wondered how they would do it; one instance had been described to me by a witness, but that was done from a bridge, and there had been but a single victim. This morning, would one have to wait and see the other go through with it first?

The smell of smoke reached me, and next the rattle of tin dishes. Breakfast was something I had forgotten, and one of them was cooking it now in the dry shelter of the stable. He was alone, because the talking and the steps were outside the stable, and I could hear the sounds of horses being driven into the corral and saddled. Then I perceived that the coffee was ready, and almost immediately the cook called them. One came in, shutting the door behind him as he reentered, which the rest as they followed imitated; for at each opening of the door I saw the light of day leap into the stable and heard the louder sounds of the rain. Then the sound and the light would again be shut out, until someone at length spoke out bluntly, bidding the door be left open on account of the smoke. What were they hiding from? he asked. The runaways that had escaped? A laugh followed this sally, and the door was left open. Thus I learned that there had been more thieves than the two that were captured. It gave a little more ground for their suspicion about me and my anxiety to pass the night elsewhere. It cost nothing to detain me, and they were taking no chances, however remote.

The fresh air and the light now filled the stable, and I lay listening while their breakfast brought more talk from them. They were more at ease now than was I, who had nothing to do but carry out my role of slumber in the stall; they spoke in a friendly, ordinary way, as if this were like every other morning of the week to them. They addressed the prisoners with a sort of fraternal kindness, not bringing them pointedly into the conversation, nor yet pointedly leaving them out. I made out that they must all be sitting round the breakfast together, those who had to die and those who had to kill them. The Virginian I never heard speak. But I heard the voice of Steve; he discussed with his captors the sundry points of his capture.

"Do you remember a haystack?" he asked. "Away up the south fork of Gros Ventre?"

"That was Thursday afternoon," said one of the captors. "There was a shower."

"Yes. It rained. We had you fooled that time. I was laying on the ledge above to report your movements."

Several of them laughed. "We thought you were over on Spread Creek then."

"I figured you thought so by the trail you left after the stack. Saturday we watched you turn your back on us up Spread Creek. We were snug among the trees the other side of Snake River. That was another time we had you fooled."

They laughed again at their own expense. I have heard men pick to pieces a hand of whist with more antagonism.

Steve continued: "Would we head for Idaho? Would we swing back over the Divide? You didn't know which! And when we generalled you on to that band of horses you thought was the band you were hunting—ah, we were a strong combination!" He broke off with the first touch of bitterness I had felt in his words.

"Nothing is any stronger than its weakest point." It was the Virginian who said this, and it was the first word he had spoken.

"Naturally," said Steve. His tone in addressing the Virginian was so different, so curt, that I supposed he took the weakest point to mean himself. But the others now showed me that I was wrong in this explanation.

"That's so," one said. "Its weakest point is where a rope or a gang of men is going to break when the strain comes. And you was linked with a poor partner, Steve."

"You're right I was," said the prisoner, back in his easy, casual voice.

"You ought to have got yourself separated from him, Steve."

There was a pause. "Yes," said the prisoner, moodily. "I'm sitting here because one of us blundered." He cursed the blunderer. "Lighting his fool fire queered the whole deal," he added. As he again heavily cursed the blunderer, the others murmured to each other various I told you so's.

"You'd never have built that fire, Steve," said one.

"I said that when we spied the smoke," said another. "I said, 'That's none of Steve's work, lighting fires and revealing to us their whereabouts.'"

It struck me that they were plying Steve with compliments.

"Pretty hard to have the fool get away and you get caught," a third suggested. At this they seemed to wait. I felt something curious in all this last talk.

"Oh, did he get away?" said the prisoner, then.

Again they waited; and a new voice spoke huskily: "I built that fire, boys." It was the prisoner in the gray flannel shirt.

"Too late, Ed," they told him kindly. "You ain't a good liar."

"What makes you laugh, Steve?" said someone.

"Oh, the things I notice."

"Meaning Ed was pretty slow in backing up your play? The joke is really on you, Steve. You'd ought never to have cursed the fire-builder if you wanted us to believe he was present. But we'd not have done much to Shorty, even if we had caught him. All he wants is to be scared good and hard, and he'll go back into virtuousness, which is his nature when not traveling with Trampas."

Steve's voice sounded hard now. "You have caught Ed and me. That should satisfy you for one gather."

"Well, we think different, Steve. Trampas escaping leaves this thing unfinished."

"So Trampas escaped too, did he?" said the prisoner.

"Yes, Steve, Trampas escaped—this time; and Shorty with him—this time. We know it most as well as if we'd seen them go. And we're glad Shorty is loose, for he'll build another fire or do some other foolishness next time, and that's the time we'll get Trampas."

Their talk drifted to other points, and I lay thinking of the skirmish that had played beneath the surface of their banter. Yes, the joke, as they put it, was on Steve. He had lost one point in the game to them. They were playing for names. He, being a chivalrous thief, was playing to hide names. They could only, among several likely confederates, guess Trampas and Shorty. So it had been a slip for him to curse the man who built the fire. At least, they so held it. For, they with subtlety reasoned, one curses the absent. And I agreed with them that Ed did not know how to lie well; he should have at once claimed the disgrace of having spoiled the expedition. If Shorty was the blunderer, then certainly Trampas was the other man; for the two were as inseparable as don and master. Trampas had enticed Shorty away from good, and trained him in evil. It now struck me that after his single remark the Virginian had been silent throughout their shrewd discussion.

It was the other prisoner that I heard them next address. "You don't eat any breakfast, Ed."

"Brace up, Ed. Look at Steve, how hardy he eats!"

But Ed, it seemed, wanted no breakfast. And the tin dishes rattled as they were gathered and taken to be packed.

"Drink this coffee, anyway," another urged; "you'll feel warmer."

These words almost made it seem like my own execution. My whole body turned cold in company with the prisoner's, and as if with a clank the situation tightened throughout my senses.

"I reckon if everyone's ready we'll start." It was the Virginian's voice once more, and different from the rest. I heard them rise at his bidding, and I put the blanket over my head. I felt their tread as they walked out, passing my stall. The straw that was half under me and half out in the stable was stirred as by something heavy dragged or half lifted along over it. "Look out, you're hurting Ed's arm," one said to another, as the steps with tangled sounds passed slowly out. I heard another among those who followed say, "Poor Ed couldn't swallow his coffee." Outside they began getting on their horses; and next their hoofs grew distant, until all was silence round the stable except the dull, even falling of the rain.

## CHAPTER XXXI

## THE COTTONWOODS

I do not know how long I stayed there alone. It was the Virginian who came back, and as he stood at the foot of my blankets his eye, after meeting mine full for a moment, turned aside. I had never seen him look as he did now, not even in Pitchstone Canyon when we came upon the bodies of Hank and his wife. Until this moment we had found no chance of speaking together, except in the presence of others.

"Seems to be raining still," I began after a little.

"Yes. It's a wet spell."

He stared out of the door, smoothing his mustache.

It was again I that spoke. "What time is it?"

He brooded over his watch. "Twelve minutes to seven."

I rose and stood drawing on my clothes.

"The fire's out," said he; and he assembled some new sticks over the ashes. Presently he looked round with a cup.

"Never mind that for me," I said.

"We've a long ride," he suggested.

"I know. I've crackers in my pocket."

My boots being pulled on, I walked to the door and watched the clouds. "They seem as if they might lift," I said. And I took out my watch.

"What time is it?" he asked.

"A quarter of—it's run down."

While I wound it he seemed to be consulting his own.

"Well?" I inquired.

"Ten minutes past seven."

As I was setting my watch he slowly said:

"Steve wound his all regular. I had to night-guard him till two." His speech was like that of one in a trance: so, at least, it sounds in my memory today.

Again I looked at the weather and the rainy immensity of the plain. The foothills eastward where we were going were a soft yellow. Over the gray-green sagebrush moved shapeless places of light—not yet the uncovered sunlight, but spots where the storm was wearing thin; and wandering streams of warmth passed by slowly in the surrounding air. As I watched the clouds and the earth, my eyes chanced to fall on the distant clump of cottonwoods. Vapors from the enfeebled storm floated round them, and they were indeed far away; but I came inside and began rolling up my blankets.

"You will not change your mind?" said the Virginian by the fire. "It is thirty-five miles."

I shook my head, feeling a certain shame that he should see how unnerved I was.

He swallowed a hot cupful, and after it sat thinking; and presently he passed his hand across his brow, shutting his eyes. Again he poured out a cup, and emptying this, rose abruptly to his feet as if shaking himself free from something.

"Let's pack and quit here," he said.

Our horses were in the corral and our belongings in the shelter of what had been once the cabin at this forlorn place. He collected them in silence while I saddled my own animal, and in silence we packed the two packhorses, and threw the diamond hitch, and hauled tight the slack, damp ropes. Soon we had mounted, and as we turned into the trail I gave a look back at my last night's lodging.

The Virginian noticed me. "Good-by forever!" he interpreted.

"By God, I hope so!"

"Same here," he confessed. And these were our first natural words this morning.

"This will go well," said I, holding my flask out to him; and both of us took some, and felt easier for it and the natural words.

For an hour we had been shirking real talk, holding fast to the weather, or anything, and all the while that silent thing we were keeping off spoke plainly in the air around us and in every syllable that we uttered. But now we were going to get away from it; leave it behind in the stable, and set ourselves free from it by talking it out. Already relief had begun to stir in my spirits.

"You never did this before," I said.

"No. I never had it to do." He was riding beside me, looking down at his saddle-horn.

"I do not think I should ever be able," I pursued.

Defiance sounded in his answer. "I would do it again this morning."

"Oh, I don't mean that. It's all right here. There's no other way."

"I would do it all over again the same this morning. Just the same."

"Why, so should I—if I could do it at all." I still thought he was justifying their justice to me.

He made no answer as he rode along, looking all the while at his saddle. But again he passed his hand over his forehead with that frown and shutting of the eyes.

"I should like to be sure I should behave myself if I were condemned," I said next. For it now came to me—which should I resemble? Could I read the newspaper, and be interested in county elections, and discuss coming death as if I had lost a game of cards? Or would they have to drag me out? That poor wretch in the gray flannel shirt—"It was bad in the stable," I said aloud. For an after-shiver of it went through me.

A third time his hand brushed his forehead, and I ventured some sympathy. "I'm afraid your head aches."

"I don't want to keep seeing Steve," he muttered.

"Steve!" I was astounded. "Why he—why all I saw of him was splendid. Since it had to be. It was—"

"Oh, yes; Ed. You're thinking about him. I'd forgot him. So you didn't enjoy Ed?"

At this I looked at him blankly. "It isn't possible that—"

Again he cut me short with a laugh almost savage. "You needn't to worry about Steve. He stayed game."

What then had been the matter that he should keep seeing Steve—that his vision should so obliterate from him what I still shivered at, and so shake him now? For he seemed to be growing more stirred as I grew less. I asked him no further questions, however, and we went on for several minutes, he brooding always in the same fashion, until he resumed with the hard indifference that had before surprised me: "So Ed gave you feelings! Dumb ague and so forth."

"No doubt we're not made the same way," I retorted.

He took no notice of this. "And you'd have been more comfortable if he'd acted same as Steve did. It cert'nly was bad seeing Ed take it that way, I reckon. And you didn't see him when the time came for business. Well, here's what it is: a man may be such a confirmed miscreant that killing's the only cure for him; but still he's your own species, and you don't want to have him fall around and grab your laigs and show you his fear naked. It makes you feel ashamed. So Ed gave you feelings, and Steve made everything right easy for you!" There was irony in his voice as he surveyed me, but it fell away at once into sadness. "Both was miscreants. But if Steve had played the coward, too, it would have been a whole heap easier for me." He paused before adding, "And Steve was not a miscreant once."

His voice had trembled, and I felt the deep emotion that seemed to gain upon him now that action was over and he had nothing to do but think. And his view was simple enough: you must die brave. Failure is a sort of treason to the brotherhood, and forfeits pity. It was Steve's perfect bearing that had caught his heart so that he forgot even his scorn of the other man.

But this was by no means all that was to come. He harked back to that notion of a prisoner helping to make it easy for his executioner. "Easy plumb to the end," he pursued, his mind reviewing the acts of the morning. "Why, he tried to give me your newspaper. I didn't—"

"Oh, no," I said hastily. "I had finished with it."

"Well, he took dying as naturally as he took living. Like a man should. Like I hope to." Again he looked at the pictures in his mind. "No play-acting nor last words. He just told good-by to the boys as we led his horse under the limb—you needn't to look so dainty," he broke off. "You ain't going to get any more shocking particulars."

"I know I'm white-livered," I said with a species of laugh. "I never crowd and stare when somebody is hurt in the street. I get away."

He thought this over. "You don't mean all of that. You'd not have spoke just that way about crowding and staring if you thought well of them that stare. Staring ain't courage; it's trashy curiosity. Now you did not have this thing—"

He had stretched out his hand to point, but it fell, and his utterance stopped, and he jerked his horse to a stand. My nerves sprang like a wire at his suddenness, and I looked where he was looking. There were the cottonwoods, close in front of us. As we had traveled and talked we had forgotten them. Now they were looming within a hundred yards; and our trail lay straight through them.

"Let's go around them," said the Virginian.

When we had come back from our circuit into the trail he continued: "You did not have that thing to do. But a man goes through with his responsibilities—and I reckon you could."

"I hope so," I answered. "How about Ed?"

"He was not a man, though we thought he was till this. Steve and I started punching cattle together at the Bordeaux outfit, north of Cheyenne. We did everything together in those days—work and play. Six years ago. Steve had many good points onced."

We must have gone two miles before he spoke again. "You prob'ly didn't notice Steve? I mean the way he acted to me?" It was a question, but he did not wait for my answer. "Steve never said a word to me all through. He shunned it. And you saw how neighborly he talked to the other boys."

"Where have they all gone?" I asked.

He smiled at me. "It cert'nly is lonesome now, for a fact."

"I didn't know you felt it," said I.

"Feel it! They've went to the railroad. Three of them are witnesses in a case at Evanston, and the Judge wants our outfit at Medicine Bow. Steve shunned me. Did he think I was going back on him?"

"What if he did? You were not. And so nobody's going to Wind River but you?"

"No. Did you notice Steve would not give us any information about Shorty? That was right. I would have acted that way, too." Thus, each time, he brought me back to the subject.

The sun was now shining warm during two or three minutes together, and gulfs of blue opened in the great white clouds. These moved and met among each other, and parted, like hands spread out, slowly weaving a spell of sleep over the day after the wakeful night storm. The huge contours of the earth lay basking and drying, and not one living creature, bird or beast, was in sight. Quiet was returning to my revived spirits, but there was none for the Virginian. And as he reasoned matters out aloud, his mood grew more overcast.

"You have a friend, and his ways are your ways. You travel together, you spree together confidentially, and you suit each other down to the ground. Then one day you find him putting his iron on another man's calf. You tell him fair and square those ways have never been your ways and ain't going to be your ways. Well, that does not change him any, for it seems he's disturbed over getting rich quick and being a big man in the Territory. And the years go on, until you are foreman of Judge Henry's ranch and he—is dangling back in the cottonwoods. What can he claim? Who made the choice? He cannot say, 'Here is my old friend that I would have stood by.' Can he say that?"

"But he didn't say it," I protested.

"No. He shunned me."

"Listen," I said. "Suppose while you were on guard he had whispered, 'Get me off'—would you have done it?"

"No, sir!" said the Virginian, hotly.

"Then what do you want?" I asked. "What did you want?"

He could not answer me—but I had not answered him, I saw; so I pushed it farther. "Did you want indorsement from the man you were hanging? That's asking a little too much."

But he had now another confusion. "Steve stood by Shorty," he said musingly. "It was Shorty's mistake cost him his life, but all the same he didn't want us to catch—"

"You are mixing things," I interrupted. "I never heard you mix things before. And it was not Shorty's mistake."

He showed momentary interest. "Whose then?"

"The mistake of whoever took a fool into their enterprise."

"That's correct. Well, Trampas took Shorty in, and Steve would not tell on him either."

I still tried it, saying, "They were all in the same boat." But logic was useless; he had lost his bearings in a fog of sentiment. He knew, knew passionately, that he had done right; but the silence of his old friend to him through those last hours left a sting that no reasoning could assuage. "He told good-by to the rest of the boys; but not to me."

And nothing that I could point out in common sense turned him from the thread of his own argument. He worked round the circle again to self-justification. "Was it him I was deserting? Was not the deserting done by him the day I spoke my mind about stealing calves? I have kept my ways the same. He is the one that took to new ones. The man I used to travel with is not the man back there. Same name, to be sure. And same body. But different in— and yet he had the memory! You can't never change your memory!"

He gave a sob. It was the first I had ever heard from him, and before I knew what I was doing I had reined my horse up to his and put my arm around his shoulders. I had no sooner touched him than he was utterly overcome. "I knew Steve awful well," he said.

Thus we had actually come to change places; for early in the morning he had been firm while I was unnerved, while now it was I who attempted to steady and comfort him.

I had the sense to keep silent, and presently he shook my hand, not looking at me as he did so. He was always very shy of demonstration. And he took to patting the neck of his pony. "You Monte hawss," said he, "you think you are wise, but there's a lot of things you don't savvy."

Then he made a new beginning of talk between us.

"It is kind of pitiful about Shorty."

"Very pitiful," I said.

"Do you know about him?" the Virginian asked.

"I know there's no real harm in him, and some real good, and that he has not got the brains necessary to be a horse thief."

"That's so. That's very true. Trampas has led him in deeper than his stature can stand. Now back East you can be middling and get along. But if you go to try a thing on in this Western country, you've got to do it *well*. You've got to deal cyards *well*; you've got to steal *well*; and if you claim to be quick with your gun, you must be quick, for you're a public temptation, and some man will not resist trying to prove he is the quicker. You must break all the Commandments *well* in this Western country, and Shorty should have stayed in Brooklyn, for he will be a novice his livelong days. You don't know about him? He has told me his circumstances. He don't remember his father, and it was like he could have claimed three or four. And I expect his mother was not much interested in him before or after he was born. He ran around, and when he was eighteen he got to be help to a grocery man. But a girl he ran with kept taking all his pay and teasing him for more, and so one day the grocery man caught Shorty robbing his till, and fired him. There wasn't no one to tell good-by to, for the girl had to go to the country to see her aunt, she said. So Shorty hung around the store and kissed the grocery cat good-by. He'd been used to feeding the cat, and she'd sit in his lap and purr, he told me. He sends money back to that girl now. This hyeh country is no country for Shorty, for he will be a conspicuous novice all his days."

"Perhaps he'll prefer honesty after his narrow shave," I said.

But the Virginian shook his head. "Trampas has got hold of him."

The day was now all blue above, and all warm and dry beneath. We had begun to wind in and rise among the first slopes of the foothills, and we had talked ourselves into silence. At the first running water we made a long nooning, and I slept on the bare ground. My body was lodged so fast and deep in slumber that when the Virginian shook me awake I could not come back to life at once; it was the clump of cottonwoods, small and far out in the plain below us, that recalled me.

"It'll not be watching us much longer," said the Virginian. He made it a sort of joke; but I knew that both of us were glad when presently we rode into a steeper country, and among its folds and carvings lost all sight of the plain. He had not slept, I found. His explanation was that the packs needed better balancing, and after that he had gone up and down the stream on the chance of trout. But his haunted eyes gave me the real reason—they spoke of Steve, no matter what he spoke of; it was to be no short thing with him.

## CHAPTER XXXII

## SUPERSTITION TRAIL

We did not make thirty-five miles that day, nor yet twenty-five, for he had let me sleep. We made an early camp and tried some unsuccessful fishing, over which he was cheerful, promising trout tomorrow when we should be higher among the mountains. He never again touched or came near the subject that was on his mind, but while I sat writing my diary, he went off to his horse Monte, and I could hear that he occasionally talked to that friend.

Next day we swung southward from what is known to many as the Conant trail, and headed for that short cut through the Tetons which is known to but a few. Bitch Creek was the name of the stream we now followed, and here there was such good fishing that we idled; and the horses and I at least enjoyed ourselves. For they found fresh pastures and shade in the now plentiful woods; and the mountain odors and the mountain heights were enough for me when the fish refused to rise. This road of ours now became the road which the pursuit had taken before the capture. Going along, I noticed the footprints of many hoofs, rain-blurred but recent, and these were the tracks of the people I had met in the stable.

"You can notice Monte's," said the Virginian. "He is the only one that has his hind feet shod. There's several trails from this point down to where we have come from."

We mounted now over a long slant of rock, smooth and of wide extent. Above us it went up easily into a little side canyon, but ahead, where our way was, it grew so steep that we got off and led our horses. This brought us to the next higher level of the mountain, a space of sagebrush more open, where the rain-washed tracks appeared again in the softer ground.

"Someone has been here since the rain," I called to the Virginian, who was still on the rock, walking up behind the packhorses.

"Since the rain!" he exclaimed. "That's not two days yet." He came and examined the footprints. "A man and a hawss," he said, frowning. "Going the same way we are. How did he come to pass us, and us not see him?"

"One of the other trails," I reminded him.

"Yes, but there's not many that knows them. They are pretty rough trails."

"Worse than this one we're taking?"

"Not much; only how does he come to know any of them? And why don't he take the Conant trail that's open and easy and not much longer? One man and a hawss. I don't see who he is or what he wants here."

"Probably a prospector," I suggested.

"Only one outfit of prospectors has ever been here, and they claimed there was no mineral-bearing rock in these parts."

We got back into our saddles with the mystery unsolved. To the Virginian it was a greater one, apparently, than to me; why should one have to account for every stray traveler in the mountains?

"That's queer, too," said the Virginian. He was now riding in front of me, and he stopped, looking down at the trail. "Don't you notice?"

It did not strike me.

"Why, he keeps walking beside his hawss; he don't get on him."

Now we, of course, had mounted at the beginning of the better trail after the steep rock, and that was quite half a mile back. Still, I had a natural explanation. "He's leading a packhorse. He's a poor trapper, and walks."

"Packhorses ain't usually shod before and behind," said the Virginian; and sliding to the ground he touched the footprints. "They are not four hours old," said he. "This bank's in shadow by one o'clock, and the sun has not cooked them dusty."

We continued on our way; and although it seemed no very particular thing to me that a man should choose to walk and lead his horse for a while—I often did so to limber my muscles—nevertheless I began to catch the Virginian's uncertain feeling about this traveler whose steps had appeared on our path in mid-journey, as if he had alighted from the mid-air, and to remind myself that he had come over the great face of rock from another trail and thus joined us, and that indigent trappers are to be found owning but a single horse and leading him with their belongings through the deepest solitudes of the mountains—none of this quite brought back to me the comfort which had been mine since we left the cottonwoods out of sight down in the plain. Hence I called out sharply, "What's the matter now?" when the Virginian suddenly stopped his horse again.

He looked down at the trail, and then he very slowly turned round in his saddle and stared back steadily at me. "There's two of them," he said.

"Two what?"

"I don't know."

"You must know whether it's two horses or two men," I said, almost angrily.

But to this he made no answer, sitting quite still on his horse and contemplating the ground. The silence was fastening on me like a spell, and I spurred my horse impatiently forward to see for myself. The footprints of two men were there in the trail.

"What do you say to that?" said the Virginian. "Kind of ridiculous, ain't it?"

"Very quaint," I answered, groping for the explanation. There was no rock here to walk over and step from into the softer trail. These second steps came more out of the air than the first. And my brain played me the evil trick of showing me a dead man in a gray flannel shirt.

"It's two, you see, traveling with one hawss, and they take turns riding him."

"Why, of course!" I exclaimed; and we went along for a few paces.

"There you are," said the Virginian, as the trail proved him right. "Number one has got on. My God, what's that?"

At a crashing in the woods very close to us we both flung round and caught sight of a vanishing elk.

It left us confronted, smiling a little, and sounding each other with our eyes. "Well, we didn't need him for meat," said the Virginian.

"A spike-horn, wasn't it?" said I.

"Yes, just a spike-horn."

For a while now as we rode we kept up a cheerful conversation about elk. We wondered if we should meet many more close to the trail like this; but it was not long before our words died away. We had come into a veritable gulf of mountain peaks, sharp at their bare summits like teeth, holding fields of snow lower down, and glittering still in full day up there, while down among our pines and parks the afternoon was growing sombre. All the while the fresh hoofprints of the horse and the fresh footprints of the man preceded us. In the trees, and in the opens, across the levels, and up the steeps, they were there. And so they were not four hours old! Were they so much? Might we not, round some turn, come upon the makers of them? I began to watch for this. And again my brain played me an evil trick, against which I found myself actually reasoning thus: if they took turns riding, then walking must tire them as it did me or any man. And besides, there was a horse. With such thoughts I combated the fancy that those footprints were being made immediately in front of us all the while, and that they were the only sign of any presence which our eyes could see. But my fancy overcame my thoughts. It was shame only which held me from asking this question of the Virginian: Had one horse served in both cases of Justice down at the cottonwoods? I wondered about this. One horse—or had the strangling nooses dragged two saddles empty at the same signal? Most likely; and therefore these people up here—Was I going back to the nursery? I brought myself up short. And I told myself to be steady; there lurked in this brain-process which was going on beneath my reason a threat worse than the childish apprehensions it created. I reminded myself that I was a man grown, twenty-five years old, and that I must not merely seem like one, but feel like one. "You're not afraid of the dark, I suppose?" This I uttered aloud, unwittingly.

"What's that?"

I started; but it was only the Virginian behind me. "Oh, nothing. The air is getting colder up here."

I had presently a great relief. We came to a place where again this trail mounted so abruptly that we once more got off to lead our horses. So likewise had our predecessors done; and as I watched the two different sets of footprints, I observed something and hastened to speak of it.

"One man is much heavier than the other."

"I was hoping I'd not have to tell you that," said the Virginian.

"You're always ahead of me! Well, still my education is progressing."

"Why, yes. You'll equal an Injun if you keep on."

It was good to be facetious; and I smiled to myself as I trudged upward. We came off the steep place, leaving the canyon beneath us, and took to horseback. And as we proceeded over the final gentle slant up to the rim of the great basin that was set among the peaks, the Virginian was jocular once more.

"Pounds has got on," said he, "and Ounces is walking."

I glanced over my shoulder at him, and he nodded as he fixed the weather-beaten crimson handkerchief round his neck. Then he threw a stone at a pack animal that was delaying on the trail. "Damn your buckskin hide," he drawled. "You can view the scenery from the top."

He was so natural, sitting loose in the saddle, and cursing in his gentle voice, that I laughed to think what visions I had been harboring. The two dead men riding one horse through the mountains vanished, and I came back to every day.

"Do you think we'll catch up with those people?" I asked.

"Not likely. They're traveling about the same gait we are."

"Ounces ought to be the best walker."

"Up hill, yes. But Pounds will go down a-foggin'."

We gained the rim of the basin. It lay below us, a great cup of country—rocks, woods, opens, and streams. The tall peaks rose like spires around it, magnificent and bare in the last of the sun; and we surveyed this upper world, letting our animals get breath. Our bleak, crumbled rim ran like a rampart between the towering tops, a half circle of five miles or six, very wide in some parts, and in some shrinking to a scanty foothold, as here. Here our trail crossed over it between two eroded and fantastic shapes of stone, like mushrooms, or misshapen heads on pikes. Banks of snow spread up here against the black rocks, but half an hour would see us descended to the green and the woods. I looked down, both of us looked down, but our forerunners were not there.

"They'll be camping somewhere in this basin, though," said the Virginian, staring at the dark pines. "They have not come this trail by accident."

A cold little wind blew down between our stone shapes, and upward again, eddying. And round a corner upward with it came fluttering a leaf of newspaper, and caught against an edge close to me.

"What's the latest?" inquired the Virginian from his horse. For I had dismounted, and had picked up the leaf.

"Seems to be interesting," I next heard him say. "Can't you tell a man what's making your eyes bug out so?"

"Yes," my voice replied to him, and it sounded like some stranger speaking lightly near by; "oh, yes! Decidedly interesting." My voice mimicked his pronunciation. "It's quite the latest, I imagine. You had better read it yourself." And I handed it to him with a smile, watching his countenance, while my brain felt as if clouds were rushing through it.

I saw his eyes quietly run the headings over. "Well?" he inquired, after scanning it on both sides. "I don't seem to catch the excitement. Fremont County is going to hold elections. I see they claim Jake——"

"It's mine," I cut him off. "My own paper. Those are my pencil marks."

I do not think that a microscope could have discerned a change in his face. "Oh," he commented, holding the paper, and fixing it with a critical eye. "You mean this is the one you lent Steve, and he wanted to give me to give back to you. And so them are your own marks." For a moment more he held it judicially, as I have seen men hold a contract upon whose terms they were finally passing. "Well, you have got it back now, anyway." And he handed it to me.

"Only a piece of it!" I exclaimed, always lightly. And as I took it from him his hand chanced to touch mine. It was cold as ice.

"They ain't through readin' the rest," he explained easily. "Don't you throw it away! After they've taken such trouble."

"That's true," I answered. "I wonder if it's Pounds or Ounces I'm indebted to."

Thus we made further merriment as we rode down into the great basin. Before us, the horse and boot tracks showed plain in the soft slough where melted snow ran half the day.

"If it's a paper chase," said the Virginian, "they'll drop no more along here."

"Unless it gets dark," said I.

"We'll camp before that. Maybe we'll see their fire."

We did not see their fire. We descended in the chill silence, while the mushroom rocks grew far and the sombre woods approached. By a stream we got off where two banks sheltered us; for a bleak wind cut down over the crags now and then, making the pines send out a great note through the basin, like breakers in a heavy sea. But we made cosey in the tent. We pitched the tent this night, and I was glad to have it shut out the mountain peaks. They showed above the banks where we camped; and in the starlight their black shapes rose stark against the sky. They, with the pines and the wind, were a bedroom too unearthly this night. And as soon as our supper dishes were washed we went inside to our lantern and our game of cribbage.

"This is snug," said the Virginian, as we played. "That wind don't get down here."

"Smoking is snug, too," said I. And we marked our points for an hour, with no words save about the cards.

"I'll be pretty near glad when we get out of these mountains," said the Virginian. "They're most too big."

The pines had altogether ceased; but their silence was as tremendous as their roar had been.

"I don't know, though," he resumed. "There's times when the plains can be awful big, too."

Presently we finished a hand, and he said, "Let me see that paper."

He sat reading it apparently through, while I arranged my blankets to make a warm bed. Then, since the paper continued to absorb him, I got myself ready, and slid between my blankets for the night. "You'll need another candle soon in that lantern," said I.

He put the paper down. "I would do it all over again," he began. "The whole thing just the same. He knowed the customs of the country, and he played the game. No call to blame me for the customs of the country. You leave other folks' cattle alone, or you take the consequences, and it was all known to Steve from the start. Would he have me take the Judge's wages and give him the wink? He must have changed a heap from the Steve I knew if he expected that. I don't believe he expected that. He knew well enough the only thing that would have let him off would have been a regular jury. For the thieves have got hold of the juries in Johnson County. I would do it all over, just the same."

The expiring flame leaped in the lantern, and fell blue. He broke off in his words as if to arrange the light, but did not, sitting silent instead, just visible, and seeming to watch the death struggle of the flame. I could find nothing to say to him, and I believed he was now winning his way back to serenity by himself. He kept his outward man so nearly natural that I forgot about that cold touch of his hand, and never guessed how far out from reason the tide of emotion was even now whirling him. "I remember at Cheyenne onced," he resumed. And he told me of a Thanksgiving visit to town that he had made with Steve. "We was just colts then," he said. He dwelt on their coltish doings, their adventures sought and wrought in the perfect fellowship of youth. "For Steve and me most always hunted in couples back in them gamesome years," he explained. And he fell into the elemental talk of sex, such talk as would be an elk's or tiger's; and spoken so by him, simply and naturally, as we speak of the seasons, or of death, or of any actuality, it was without offense. It would be offense should I repeat it. Then, abruptly ending these memories of himself and Steve, he went out of the tent, and I heard him dragging a log to the fire. When it had blazed up, there on the tent wall was his shadow and that of the log where he sat with his half-broken heart. And all the while I supposed he was master of himself, and self-justified against Steve's omission to bid him good-by.

I must have fallen asleep before he returned, for I remember nothing except waking and finding him in his blankets beside me. The fire shadow was gone, and gray, cold light was dimly on the tent. He slept restlessly, and his forehead was ploughed by lines of pain. While I looked at him he began to mutter, and suddenly started up with violence. "No!" he cried out; "no! Just the same!" and thus wakened himself, staring. "What's the matter?" he demanded. He was slow in getting back to where we were; and full consciousness found him sitting up with his eyes fixed on mine. They were more haunted than they had been at all, and his next speech came straight from his dream. "Maybe you'd better quit me. This ain't your trouble."

I laughed. "Why, what is the trouble?"

His eyes still intently fixed on mine. "Do you think if we changed our trail we could lose them from us?"

I was framing a jocose reply about Ounces being a good walker, when the sound of hoofs rushing in the distance stopped me, and he ran out of the tent with his rifle. When I followed with mine he was up the bank, and all his powers alert. But nothing came out of the dimness save our three stampeded horses. They crashed over fallen timber and across the open to where their picketed comrade grazed at the end of his rope. By him they came to a stand, and told him, I suppose, what they had seen; for all four now faced in the same direction, looking away into the mysterious dawn. We likewise stood peering, and my rifle barrel felt cold in my hand. The dawn was all we saw, the inscrutable dawn, coming and coming through the black pines and the gray open of the basin. There above lifted the peaks, no sun yet on them, and behind us our stream made a little tinkling.

"A bear, I suppose," said I, at length.

His strange look fixed me again, and then his eyes went to the horses. "They smell things we can't smell," said he, very slowly. "Will you prove to me they don't see things we can't see?"

A chill shot through me, and I could not help a frightened glance where we had been watching. But one of the horses began to graze and I had a wholesome thought. "He's tired of whatever he sees, then," said I, pointing.

A smile came for a moment in the Virginian's face. "Must be a poor show," he observed. All the horses were grazing now, and he added, "It ain't hurt their appetites any."

We made our own breakfast then. And what uncanny dread I may have been touched with up to this time henceforth left me in the face of a real alarm. The shock of Steve was working upon the Virginian. He was aware of it himself; he was fighting it with all his might; and he was being overcome. He was indeed like a gallant swimmer against whom both wind and tide have conspired. And in this now foreboding solitude there was only myself to throw him ropes. His strokes for safety were as bold as was the undertow that ceaselessly annulled them.

"I reckon I made a fuss in the tent?" said he, feeling his way with me.

I threw him a rope. "Yes. Nightmare—indigestion—too much newspaper before retiring."

He caught the rope. "That's correct! I had a hell of a foolish dream for a growed-up man. You'd not think it of me."

"Oh, yes, I should. I've had them after prolonged lobster and champagne."

"Ah," he murmured, "prolonged! Prolonged is what does it." He glanced behind him. "Steve came back—"

"In your lobster dream," I put in.

But he missed this rope. "Yes," he answered, with his eyes searching me. "And he handed me the paper—"

"By the way, where is that?" I asked.

"I built the fire with it. But when I took it from him it was a six-shooter I had hold of, and pointing at my breast. And then Steve spoke. 'Do you think you're fit to live?' Steve said; and I got hot at him, and I reckon I must have told him what I thought of him. You heard me, I expect?"

"Glad I didn't. Your language sometimes is—"

He laughed out. "Oh, I account for all this that's happening just like you do. If we gave our explanations, they'd be pretty near twins."

"The horses saw a bear, then?"

"Maybe a bear. Maybe"—but here the tide caught him again—"What's your idea about dreams?"

My ropes were all out. "Liver—nerves," was the best I could do.

But now he swam strongly by himself.

"You may think I'm discreditable," he said, "but I know I am. It ought to take more than—well, men have lost their friendships before. Feuds and wars have cloven a right smart of bonds in twain. And if my haid is going to get shook by a little old piece of newspaper—I'm ashamed I burned that. I'm ashamed to have been that weak."

"Any man gets unstrung," I told him. My ropes had become straws; and I strove to frame some policy for the next hours.

We now finished breakfast and set forth to catch the horses. As we drove them in I found that the Virginian was telling me a ghost story. "At half-past three in the morning she saw her runaway daughter standing with a babe in her arms; but when she moved it was all gone. Later they found it was the very same hour the young mother died in Nogales. And she sent for the child and raised it herself. I knowed them both back home. Do you believe that?"

I said nothing.

"No more do I believe it," he asserted. "And see here! Nogales time is three hours different from Richmond. I didn't know about that point then."

Once out of these mountains, I knew he could right himself; but even I, who had no Steve to dream about, felt this silence of the peaks was preying on me.

"Her daughter and her might have been thinkin' mighty hard about each other just then," he pursued. "But Steve is dead. Finished. You cert'nly don't believe there's anything more?"

"I wish I could," I told him.

"No, I'm satisfied. Heaven didn't never interest me much. But if there was a world of dreams after you went—" He stopped himself and turned his searching eyes away from mine. "There's a heap o' darkness wherever you try to step," he said, "and I thought I'd left off wasting thoughts on the subject. You see"—he dexterously roped a horse, and once more his splendid sanity was turned to gold by his imagination—"I expect in many growed-up men you'd call sensible there's a little boy sleepin'—the little kid they onced was—that still keeps his fear of the dark. You mentioned the dark yourself yesterday. Well, this experience has woke up that kid in me, and blamed if I can coax the little cuss to go to sleep again! I keep a-telling him daylight will sure come, but he keeps a-crying and holding on to me."

Somewhere far in the basin there was a faint sound, and we stood still.

"Hush!" he said.

But it was like our watching the dawn; nothing more followed.

"They have shot that bear," I remarked.

He did not answer, and we put the saddles on without talk. We made no haste, but we were not over half an hour, I suppose, in getting off with the packs. It was not a new thing to hear a shot where wild game was in plenty; yet as we rode that shot sounded already in my mind different from others. Perhaps I should not believe this today but for what I look back to. To make camp last night we had turned off the trail, and now followed the stream down for a while, taking next a cut through the wood. In this way we came upon the tracks of our horses where they had been galloping back to the camp after their fright. They had kicked up the damp and matted pine needles very plainly all along.

"Nothing has been here but themselves, though," said I.

"And they ain't showing signs of remembering any scare," said the Virginian.

In a little while we emerged upon an open.

"Here's where they was grazing," said the Virginian; and the signs were clear enough. "Here's where they must have got their scare," he pursued. "You stay with them while I circle a little." So I stayed; and certainly our animals were very calm at visiting this scene. When you bring a horse back to where he has recently encountered a wild animal his ears and his nostrils are apt to be wide awake.

The Virginian had stopped and was beckoning to me.

"Here's your bear," said he, as I arrived. "Two-legged, you see. And he had a hawss of his own." There was a stake driven down where an animal had been picketed for the night.

"Looks like Ounces," I said, considering the footprints.

"It's Ounces. And Ounces wanted another hawss very bad, so him and Pounds could travel like gentlemen should."

"But Pounds doesn't seem to have been with him."

"Oh, Pounds, he was making coffee, somewhere in yonder, when this happened. Neither of them guessed there'd be other hawsses wandering here in the night, or they both would have come." He turned back to our pack animals.

"Then you'll not hunt for this camp to make sure?"

"I prefer making sure first. We might be expected at that camp."

He took out his rifle from beneath his leg and set it across his saddle at half-cock. I did the same; and thus cautiously we resumed our journey in a slightly different direction. "This ain't all we're going to find out," said the Virginian. "Ounces had a good idea; but I reckon he made a bad mistake later."

We had found out a good deal without any more, I thought. Ounces had gone to bring in their single horse, and coming upon three more in the pasture had undertaken to catch one and failed, merely driving them where he feared to follow.

"Shorty never could rope a horse alone," I remarked.

The Virginian grinned. "Shorty? Well, Shorty sounds as well as Ounces. But that ain't the mistake I'm thinking he made."

I knew that he would not tell me, but that was just like him. For the last twenty minutes, having something to do, he had become himself again, had come to earth from that unsafe country of the brain where beckoned a spectral Steve. Nothing was left but in his eyes that question which pain had set there; and I wondered if his friend of old, who seemed so brave and amiable, would have dealt him that hurt at the solemn end had he known what a poisoned wound it would be.

We came out on a ridge from which we could look down. "You always want to ride on high places when there's folks around whose intentions ain't been declared," said the Virginian. And we went along our ridge for some distance. Then, suddenly he turned down and guided us almost at once to the trail. "That's it," he said. "See."

The track of a horse was very fresh on the trail. But it was a galloping horse now, and no bootprints were keeping up with it anymore. No boots could have kept up with it. The rider was making time today. Yesterday that horse had been ridden up into the mountains at leisure. Who was on him? There was never to be any certain answer to that. But who was not on him? We turned back in our journey, back into the heart of that basin with the tall peaks all rising like teeth in the cloudless sun, and the snow-fields shining white.

"He was afraid of us," said the Virginian. "He did not know how many of us had come up here. Three hawsses might mean a dozen more around."

We followed the backward trail in among the pines, and came after a time upon their camp. And then I understood the mistake that Shorty had made.

He had returned after his failure, and had told that other man of the presence of new horses. He should have kept this a secret; for haste had to be made at once, and two cannot get away quickly upon one horse. But it was poor Shorty's last blunder. He lay there by their extinct fire, with his wistful, lost-dog face upward, and his thick yellow hair unparted as it had always been. The murder had been done from behind. We closed the eyes.

"There was no natural harm in him," said the Virginian. "But you must do a thing well in this country."

There was not a trace, not a clew, of the other man; and we found a place where we could soon cover Shorty with earth. As we lifted him we saw the newspaper that he had been reading. He had brought it from the clump of cottonwoods where he and the other man had made a later visit than ours to be sure of the fate of their friends—or possibly in hopes of another horse. Evidently, when the party were surprised, they had been able to escape with only one. All of the newspaper was there save the leaf I had picked up—all and more, for this had pencil writing on it that was not mine, nor did I at first take it in. I thought it might be a clew, and I read it aloud. "Good-by, Jeff," it said. "I could not have spoke to you without playing the baby."

"Who's Jeff?" I asked. But it came over me when I looked at the Virginian. He was standing beside me quite motionless; and then he put out his hand and took the paper, and stood still, looking at the words. "Steve used to call me Jeff," he said, "because I was Southern. I reckon nobody else ever did."

He slowly folded the message from the dead, brought by the dead, and rolled it in the coat behind his saddle. For a half-minute he stood leaning his forehead down against the saddle. After this he came back and contemplated Shorty's face awhile. "I wish I could thank him," he said. "I wish I could."

We carried Shorty over and covered him with earth, and on that laid a few pine branches; then we took up our journey, and by the end of the forenoon we had gone some distance upon our trail through the Teton Mountains. But in front of us the hoofprints ever held their stride of haste, drawing farther from us through the hours, until by the next afternoon somewhere we noticed they were no longer to be seen; and after that they never came upon the trail again.

# CHAPTER XXXIII

## THE SPINSTER LOSES SOME SLEEP

Somewhere at the eastern base of the Tetons did those hoofprints disappear into a mountain sanctuary where many crooked paths have led. He that took another man's possessions, or he that took another man's life, could always run here if the law or popular justice were too hot at his heels. Steep ranges and forests walled him in from the world on all four sides, almost without a break; and every entrance lay through intricate solitudes. Snake River came into the place through canyons and mournful pines and marshes, to the north, and went out at the south between formidable chasms. Every tributary to this stream rose among high peaks and ridges, and descended into the valley by well-nigh impenetrable courses: Pacific Creek from Two Ocean Pass, Buffalo Fork from no pass at all, Black Rock from the To-wo-ge-tee Pass—all these, and many more, were the waters of loneliness, among whose thousand hiding-places it was easy to be lost. Down in the bottom was a spread of level land, broad and beautiful, with the blue and silver Tetons rising from its chain of lakes to the west, and other heights presiding over its other sides. And up and down and in and out of this hollow square of mountains, where waters plentifully flowed, and game and natural pasture abounded, there skulked a nomadic and distrustful population. This in due time built cabins, took wives, begot children, and came to speak of itself as "The honest settlers of Jackson's Hole." It is a commodious title, and doubtless today more accurate than it was once.

Into this place the hoofprints disappeared. Not many cabins were yet built there; but the unknown rider of the horse knew well that he would find shelter and welcome among the felons of his stripe. Law and order might guess his name correctly, but there was no next step, for lack of evidence; and he would wait, whoever he was, until the rage of popular justice, which had been pursuing him and his brother thieves, should subside. Then, feeling his way gradually with prudence, he would let himself be seen again.

And now, as mysteriously as he had melted away, rumor passed over the country. No tongue seemed to be heard telling the first news; the news was there, one day, a matter of whispered knowledge. On Sunk Creek and on Bear Creek, and elsewhere far and wide, before men talked men seemed secretly to know that Steve, and Ed, and Shorty, would never again be seen. Riders met each other in the road and drew rein to discuss the event, and its bearing upon the cattle interests. In town saloons men took each other aside, and muttered over it in corners.

Thus it reached the ears of Molly Wood, beginning in a veiled and harmless shape.

A neighbor joined her when she was out riding by herself.

"Good morning," said he. "Don't you find it lonesome?" And when she answered lightly, he continued, meaning well: "You'll be having company again soon now. He has finished his job. Wish he'd finished it *more!* Well, good day."

Molly thought these words over. She could not tell why they gave her a strange feeling. To her Vermont mind no suspicion of the truth would come naturally. But suspicion began to come when she returned from her ride. For, entering the cabin of the Taylors', she came upon several people who all dropped their talk short, and were not skilful at resuming it. She sat there awhile, uneasily aware that all of them knew something which she did not know, and was not intended to know. A thought pierced her—had anything happened to her lover? No; that was not it. The man she had met on horseback spoke of her having company soon again. How soon? she wondered. He had been unable to say when he should return, and now she suddenly felt that a great silence had enveloped him lately: not the mere silence of absence, of receiving no messages or letters, but another sort of silence which now, at this moment, was weighing strangely upon her.

And then the next day it came out at the schoolhouse. During that interval known as recess, she became aware through the open window that they were playing a new game outside. Lusty screeches of delight reached her ears.

"Jump!" a voice ordered. "Jump!"

"I don't want to," returned another voice, uneasily.

"You said you would," said several. "Didn't he say he would? Ah, he said he would. Jump now, quick!"

"But I don't want to," quavered the voice in a tone so dismal that Molly went out to see.

They had got Bob Carmody on the top of the gate by a tree, with a rope round his neck, the other end of which four little boys were joyously holding. The rest looked on eagerly, three little girls clasping their hands, and springing up and down with excitement.

"Why, children!" exclaimed Molly.

"He's said his prayers and everything," they all screamed out. "He's a rustler, and we're lynchin' him. Jump, Bob!"

"I don't want—"

"Ah, coward, won't take his medicine!"

"Let him go, boys," said Molly. "You might really hurt him." And so she broke up this game, but not without general protest from Wyoming's young voice.

"He said he would," Henry Dow assured her.

And George Taylor further explained: "He said he'd be Steve. But Steve didn't scare." Then George proceeded to tell the schoolmarm, eagerly, all about Steve and Ed, while the schoolmarm looked at him with a rigid face.

"You promised your mother you'd not tell," said Henry Dow, after all had been told. "You've gone and done it," and Henry wagged his head in a superior manner.

Thus did the New England girl learn what her cowboy lover had done.

She spoke of it to nobody; she kept her misery to herself. He was not there to defend his act. Perhaps in a way that was better. But these were hours of darkness indeed to Molly Wood.

On that visit to Dunbarton, when at the first sight of her lover's photograph in frontier dress her aunt had exclaimed, "I suppose there are days when he does not kill people," she had cried in all good faith and mirth, "He never killed anybody!" Later, when he was lying in her cabin weak from his bullet wound, but each day stronger beneath her nursing, at a certain word of his there had gone through her a shudder of doubt. Perhaps in his many wanderings he had done such a thing in self-defence, or in the cause of popular justice. But she had pushed the idea away from her hastily, back into the days before she had ever seen him. If this had ever happened, let her not know of it. Then, as a cruel reward for his candor and his laying himself bare to her mother, the letters from Bennington had used that very letter of his as a weapon against him. Her sister Sarah had quoted from it. "He says with apparent pride," wrote Sarah, "that he has 'never killed for pleasure or profit.' Those are his exact words, and you may guess their dreadful effect upon mother. I congratulate you, my dear, on having chosen a protector so scrupulous."

Thus her elder sister had seen fit to write; and letters from less near relatives made hints at the same subject. So she was compelled to accept this piece of knowledge thrust upon her. Yet still, still, those events had been before she knew him. They were remote, without detail or context. He had been little more than a boy. No doubt it was to save his own life. And so she bore the hurt of her discovery all the more easily because her sister's tone roused her to defend her cowboy.

But now!

In her cabin, alone, after midnight, she arose from her sleepless bed, and lighting the candle, stood before his photograph.

"It is a good face," her great-aunt had said, after some study of it. And these words were in her mind now. There his likeness stood at full length, confronting her: the spurs on the boots, the fringed leathern chaparreros, the coiled rope in hand, the pistol at hip, the rough flannel shirt, and the scarf knotted at the throat—and then the grave eyes, looking at her. It thrilled her to meet them, even so. She could read life into them. She seemed to feel passion come from them, and then something like reproach. She stood for a long while looking at him, and then, beating her hands together suddenly, she blew out her light and went back into bed, but not to sleep.

"You're looking pale, deary," said Mrs. Taylor to her, a few days later.

"Am I?"

"And you don't eat anything."

"Oh, yes, I do." And Molly retired to her cabin.

"George," said Mrs. Taylor, "you come here."

It may seem severe—I think that it was severe. That evening when Mr. Taylor came home to his family, George received a thrashing for disobedience.

"And I suppose," said Mrs. Taylor to her husband, "that she came out just in time to stop 'em breaking Bob Carmody's neck for him."

Upon the day following Mrs. Taylor essayed the impossible. She took herself over to Molly Wood's cabin. The girl gave her a listless greeting, and the dame sat slowly down, and surveyed the comfortable room.

"A very nice home, deary," said she, "if it was a home. But you'll fix something like this in your real home, I have no doubt."

Molly made no answer.

"What we're going to do without you I can't see," said Mrs. Taylor. "But I'd not have it different for worlds. He'll be coming back soon, I expect."

"Mrs. Taylor," said Molly, all at once, "please don't say anything now. I can't stand it." And she broke into wretched tears.

"Why, deary, he—"

"No; not a word. Please, please—I'll go out if you do."

The older woman went to the younger one, and then put her arms round her. But when the tears were over, they had not done any good; it was not the storm that clears the sky—all storms do not clear the sky. And Mrs. Taylor looked at the pale girl and saw that she could do nothing to help her toward peace of mind.

"Of course," she said to her husband, after returning from her profitless errand, "you might know she'd feel dreadful."

"What about?" said Taylor.

"Why, you know just as well as I do. And I'll say for myself, I hope you'll never have to help hang folks."

"Well," said Taylor, mildly, "if I had to, I'd have to, I guess."

"Well, I don't want it to come. But that poor girl is eating her heart right out over it."

"What does she say?"

"It's what she don't say. She'll not talk, and she'll not let me talk, and she sits and sits."

"I'll go talk some to her," said the man.

"Well, Taylor, I thought you had more sense. You'd not get a word in. She'll be sick soon if her worry ain't stopped someway, though."

"What does she want this country to do?" inquired Taylor. "Does she expect it to be like Vermont when it—"

"We can't help what she expects," his wife interrupted. "But I wish we could help *her*."

They could not, however; and help came from another source. Judge Henry rode by the next day. To him good Mrs. Taylor at once confided her anxiety. The Judge looked grave.

"Must I meddle?" he said.

"Yes, Judge, you must," said Mrs. Taylor.

"But why can't I send him over here when he gets back? Then they'll just settle it between themselves."

Mrs. Taylor shook her head. "That would unsettle it worse than it is," she assured him. "They mustn't meet just now."

The Judge sighed. "Well," he said, "very well. I'll sacrifice my character, since you insist."

Judge Henry sat thinking, waiting until school should be out. He did not at all relish what lay before him. He would like to have got out of it. He had been a federal judge; he had been an upright judge; he had met the responsibilities of his difficult office not only with learning, which is desirable, but also with courage and common sense besides, and these are essential. He had been a stanch servant of the law. And now he was invited to defend that which, at first sight, nay, even at second and third sight, must always seem a defiance of the law more injurious than crime itself. Every good man in this world has convictions about right and wrong. They are his soul's riches, his spiritual gold. When his conduct is at variance with these, he knows that it is a departure, a falling; and this is a simple and clear matter. If falling were all that ever happened to a good man, all his days would be a simple matter of striving and repentance. But it is not all. There come to him certain junctures, crises, when life, like a highwayman, springs upon him, demanding that he stand and deliver his convictions in the name of some righteous cause, bidding him do evil that good may come. I cannot say that I believe in doing evil that good may come. I do not. I think that any man who honestly justifies such course deceives himself. But this I can say: to call any act evil, instantly begs the question. Many an act that man does is right or wrong according to the time and place which form, so to speak, its context; strip it of its surrounding circumstances, and you tear away its meaning. Gentlemen reformers, beware of this common practice of yours! Beware of calling an act evil on Tuesday because that same act was evil on Monday!

Do you fail to follow my meaning? Then here is an illustration. On Monday I walk over my neighbor's field; there is no wrong in such walking. By Tuesday he has put up a sign that trespassers will be prosecuted according to law. I walk again on Tuesday, and am a law-breaker. Do you begin to see my point? or are you inclined to object to the illustration because the walking on Tuesday was not *wrong*, but merely *illegal*? Then here is another illustration which you will find it a trifle more embarrassing to answer. Consider carefully, let me beg you, the case of a young man and a young woman who walk out of a door on Tuesday, pronounced man and wife by a third party inside the door. It matters not that on Monday they were, in their own hearts, sacredly vowed to each other. If they had omitted stepping inside that door, if they had dispensed with that third party, and gone away on Monday sacredly vowed to each other in their own hearts, you would have scarcely found their conduct moral. Consider these things carefully—the sign-post and the third party—and the difference they make. And now, for a finish, we will return to the sign-post.

Suppose that I went over my neighbor's field on Tuesday, after the sign-post was put up, because I saw a murder about to be committed in the field, and therefore ran in and stopped it. Was I doing evil that good might come? Do you not think that to stay out and let the murder be done would have been the evil act in this case? To disobey the sign-post was *right;* and I trust that you now perceive the same act may wear as many different hues of right or wrong as the rainbow, according to the atmosphere in which it is done. It is not safe to say of any man, "He did evil that good might come." Was the thing that he did, in the first place, evil? That is the question.

Forgive my asking you to use your mind. It is a thing which no novelist should expect of his reader, and we will go back at once to Judge Henry and his meditations about lynching.

He was well aware that if he was to touch at all upon this subject with the New England girl, he could not put her off with mere platitudes and humdrum formulas; not, at least, if he expected to do any good. She was far too intelligent, and he was really anxious to do good. For her sake he wanted the course of the girl's true love to run more smoothly, and still more did he desire this for the sake of his Virginian.

"I sent him myself on that business," the Judge reflected uncomfortably. "I am partly responsible for the lynching. It has brought him one great unhappiness already through the death of Steve. If it gets running in this girl's mind, she may—dear me!" the Judge broke off, "what a nuisance!" And he sighed. For as all men know, he also knew that many things should be done in this world in silence, and that talking about them is a mistake.

But when school was out, and the girl gone to her cabin, his mind had set the subject in order thoroughly, and he knocked at her door, ready, as he had put it, to sacrifice his character in the cause of true love.

"Well," he said, coming straight to the point, "some dark things have happened." And when she made no answer to this, he continued: "But you must not misunderstand us. We're too fond of you for that."

"Judge Henry," said Molly Wood, also coming straight to the point, "have you come to tell me that you think well of lynching?"

He met her. "Of burning Southern negroes in public, no. Of hanging Wyoming cattle thieves in private, yes. You perceive there's a difference, don't you?"

"Not in principle," said the girl, dry and short.

"Oh—dear—me!" slowly exclaimed the Judge. "I am sorry that you cannot see that, because I think that I can. And I think that you have just as much sense as I have." The Judge made himself very grave and very good-humored at the same time. The poor girl was strung to a high pitch, and spoke harshly in spite of herself.

"What is the difference in principle?" she demanded.

"Well," said the Judge, easy and thoughtful, "what do you mean by principle?"

"I didn't think you'd quibble," flashed Molly. "I'm not a lawyer myself."

A man less wise than Judge Henry would have smiled at this, and then war would have exploded hopelessly between them, and harm been added to what was going wrong already. But the Judge knew that he must give to every word that the girl said now his perfect consideration.

"I don't mean to quibble," he assured her. "I know the trick of escaping from one question by asking another. But I don't want to escape from anything you hold me to answer. If you can show me that I am wrong, I want you to do so. But," and here the Judge smiled, "I want you to play fair, too."

"And how am I not?"

"I want you to be just as willing to be put right by me as I am to be put right by you. And so when you use such a word as principle, you must help me to answer by saying what principle you mean. For in all sincerity I see no likeness in principle whatever between burning Southern negroes in public and hanging Wyoming horse-thieves in private. I consider the burning a proof that the South is semi-barbarous, and the hanging a proof that Wyoming is determined to become civilized. We do not torture our criminals when we lynch them. We do not invite spectators to enjoy their death agony. We put no such hideous disgrace upon the United States. We execute our criminals by the swiftest means, and in the quietest way. Do you think the principle is the same?"

Molly had listened to him with attention. "The way is different," she admitted.

"Only the way?"

"So it seems to me. Both defy law and order."

"Ah, but do they both? Now we're getting near the principle."

"Why, yes. Ordinary citizens take the law in their own hands."

"The principle at last!" exclaimed the Judge.

"Now tell me some more things. Out of whose hands do they take the law?"

"The court's."

"What made the courts?"

"I don't understand."

"How did there come to be any courts?"

"The Constitution."

"How did there come to be any Constitution? Who made it?"

"The delegates, I suppose."

"Who made the delegates?"

"I suppose they were elected, or appointed, or something."

"And who elected them?"

"Of course the people elected them."

"Call them the ordinary citizens," said the Judge. "I like your term. They are where the law comes from, you see. For they chose the delegates who made the Constitution that provided for the courts. There's your machinery. These are the hands into which ordinary citizens have put the law. So you see, at best, when they lynch they only take back what they once gave. Now we'll take your two cases that you say are the same in principle. I think that they are not. For in the South they take a negro from jail where he was waiting to be duly hung. The South has never claimed that the law would let him go. But in Wyoming the law has been letting our cattle-thieves go for two years. We are in a very bad way, and we are trying to make that way a little better until civilization can reach us. At present we lie beyond its pale. The courts, or rather the juries, into whose hands we have put the law, are not dealing the law. They are withered hands, or rather they are imitation hands made for show, with no life in them, no grip. They cannot hold a cattle-thief. And so when your ordinary citizen sees this, and sees that he has placed justice in a dead hand, he must take justice back into his own hands where it was once at the beginning of all things. Call this primitive, if you will. But so far from being a *defiance* of the law, it is an *assertion* of it—the fundamental assertion of self governing men, upon whom our whole social fabric is based. There is your principle, Miss Wood, as I see it. Now can you help me to see anything different?"

She could not.

"But perhaps you are of the same opinion still?" the Judge inquired.

"It is all terrible to me," she said.

"Yes; and so is capital punishment terrible. And so is war. And perhaps some day we shall do without them. But they are none of them so terrible as unchecked theft and murder would be."

After the Judge had departed on his way to Sunk Creek, no one spoke to Molly upon this subject. But her face did not grow cheerful at once. It was plain from her fits of silence that her thoughts were not at rest. And sometimes at night she would stand in front of her lover's likeness, gazing upon it with both love and shrinking.

# CHAPTER XXXIV

## TO FIT HER FINGER

It was two rings that the Virginian wrote for when next I heard from him.

After my dark sight of what the Cattle Land could be, I soon had journeyed home by way of Washakie and Rawlins. Steve and Shorty did not leave my memory, nor will they ever, I suppose.

The Virginian had touched the whole thing the day I left him. He had noticed me looking a sort of farewell at the plains and mountains.

"You will come back to it," he said. "If there was a headstone for every man that once pleasured in his freedom here, yu'd see one most every time yu' turned your head. It's a heap sadder than a graveyard—but yu' love it all the same."

Sadness had passed from him—from his uppermost mood, at least, when he wrote about the rings. Deep in him was sadness of course, as well as joy. For he had known Steve, and he had covered Shorty with earth. He had looked upon life with a marksman's eyes, very close; and no one, if he have a heart, can pass through this and not carry sadness in his spirit with him forever. But he seldom shows it openly; it bides within him, enriching his cheerfulness and rendering him of better service to his fellow-men.

It was a commission of cheerfulness that he now gave, being distant from where rings are to be bought. He could not go so far as the East to procure what he had planned. Rings were to be had in Cheyenne, and a still greater choice in Denver; and so far as either of these towns his affairs would have permitted him to travel. But he was set upon having rings from the East. They must come from the best place in the country; nothing short of that was good enough "to fit her finger," as he said. The wedding ring was a simple matter. Let it be right, that was all: the purest gold that could be used, with her initials and his together graven round the inside, with the day of the month and the year.

The date was now set. It had come so far as this. July third was to be the day. Then for sixty days and nights he was to be a bridegroom, free from his duties at Sunk Creek, free to take his bride wheresoever she might choose to go. And she had chosen.

Those voices of the world had more than angered her; for after the anger a set purpose was left. Her sister should have the chance neither to come nor to stay away. Had her mother even answered the Virginian's letter, there could have been some relenting. But the poor lady had been inadequate in this, as in all other searching moments of her life: she had sent messages—kind ones, to be sure—but only messages. If this had hurt the Virginian, no one knew it in the world, least of all the girl in whose heart it had left a cold, frozen spot. Not a good spirit in which to be married, you will say. No; frozen spots are not good at any time. But Molly's own nature gave her due punishment. Through all these days of her warm happiness a chill current ran, like those which interrupt the swimmer's perfect joy. The girl was only half as happy as her lover; but she hid this deep from him—hid it until that final, fierce hour of reckoning that her nature had with her—nay, was bound to have with her, before the punishment was lifted, and the frozen spot melted at length from her heart.

So, meanwhile, she made her decree against Bennington. Not Vermont, but Wyoming, should be her wedding place. No world's voices should be whispering, no world's eyes should be looking on, when she made her vow to him and received his vow. Those voices should be spoken and that ring put on in this wild Cattle Land, where first she had seen him ride into the flooded river, and lift her ashore upon his horse. It was this open sky which should shine down on them, and this frontier soil upon which their feet should tread. The world should take its turn second.

After a month with him by stream and canyon, a month far deeper into the mountain wilds than ever yet he had been free to take her, a month with sometimes a tent and sometimes the stars above them, and only their horses besides themselves—after such a month as this, she would take him to her mother and to Bennington; and the old aunt over at Dunbarton would look at him, and be once more able to declare that the Starks had always preferred a man who was a man.

And so July third was to be engraved inside the wedding ring. Upon the other ring the Virginian had spent much delicious meditation, all in his secret mind. He had even got the right measure of her finger without her suspecting the reason. But this step was the final one in his plan.

During the time that his thoughts had begun to be busy over the other ring, by a chance he had learned from Mrs. Henry a number of old fancies regarding precious stones. Mrs. Henry often accompanied the Judge in venturesome mountain climbs, and sometimes the steepness of the rocks required her to use her hands for safety. One day when the Virginian went with them to help mark out certain boundary corners, she removed her rings lest they should get scratched; and he, being just behind her, took them during the climb.

"I see you're looking at my topaz," she had said, as he returned them. "If I could have chosen, it would have been a ruby. But I was born in November."

He did not understand her in the least, but her words awakened exceeding interest in him; and they had descended some five miles of mountain before he spoke again. Then he became ingenious, for he had half worked out what Mrs. Henry's meaning must be; but he must make quite sure. Therefore, according to his wild, shy nature, he became ingenious.

"Men wear rings," he began. "Some of the men on the ranch do. I don't see any harm in a man's wearin' a ring. But I never have."

"Well," said the lady, not yet suspecting that he was undertaking to circumvent her, "probably those men have sweethearts."

"No, ma'am. Not sweethearts worth wearin' rings for—in two cases, anyway. They won 'em at cyards. And they like to see 'em shine. I never saw a man wear a topaz."

Mrs. Henry did not have any further remark to make.

"I was born in January myself," pursued the Virginian, very thoughtfully.

Then the lady gave him one look, and without further process of mind perceived exactly what he was driving at.

"That's very extravagant for rings," said she. "January is diamonds."

"Diamonds," murmured the Virginian, more and more thoughtfully. "Well, it don't matter, for I'd not wear a ring. And November is—what did yu' say, ma'am?"

"Topaz."

"Yes. Well, jewels are cert'nly pretty things. In the Spanish Missions yu'll see large ones now and again. And they're not glass, I think. And so they have got some jewel that kind of belongs to each month right around the twelve?"

"Yes," said Mrs. Henry, smiling. "One for each month. But the opal is what you want."

He looked at her, and began to blush.

"October is the opal," she added, and she laughed outright, for Miss Wood's birthday was on the fifteenth of that month.

The Virginian smiled guiltily at her through his crimson.

"I've no doubt you can beat around the bush very well with men," said Mrs. Henry. "But it's perfectly transparent with us—in matters of sentiment, at least."

"Well, I am sorry," he presently said. "I don't want to give her an opal. I have no superstition, but I don't want to give her an opal. If her mother did, or anybody like that, why, all right. But not from me. D' yu' understand, ma'am?"

Mrs. Henry did understand this subtle trait in the wild man, and she rejoiced to be able to give him immediate reassurance concerning opals.

"Don't worry about that," she said. "The opal is said to bring ill luck, but not when it is your own month stone. Then it is supposed to be not only deprived of evil influence, but to possess peculiarly fortunate power. Let it be an opal ring."

Then he asked her boldly various questions, and she showed him her rings, and gave him advice about the setting. There was no special custom, she told him, ruling such rings as this he desired to bestow. The gem might be the lady's favorite or the lover's favorite; and to choose the lady's month stone was very well indeed.

Very well indeed, the Virginian thought. But not quite well enough for him. His mind now busied itself with this lore concerning jewels, and soon his sentiment had suggested something which he forthwith carried out.

When the ring was achieved, it was an opal, but set with four small embracing diamonds. Thus was her month stone joined with his, that their luck and their love might be inseparably clasped.

He found the size of her finger one day when winter had departed, and the early grass was green. He made a ring of twisted grass for her, while she held her hand for him to bind it. He made another for himself. Then, after each had worn their grass ring for a while, he begged her to exchange. He did not send his token away from him, but most carefully measured it. Thus the ring fitted her well, and the lustrous flame within the opal thrilled his heart each time he saw it. For now June was near its end; and that other plain gold ring, which, for safe keeping, he cherished suspended round his neck day and night, seemed to burn with an inward glow that was deeper than the opal's.

So in due course arrived the second of July. Molly's punishment had got as far as this: she longed for her mother to be near her at this time; but it was too late.

## CHAPTER XXXV

## WITH MALICE AFORETHOUGHT

Town lay twelve straight miles before the lover and his sweetheart, when they came to the brow of the last long hill. All beneath them was like a map: neither man nor beast distinguishable, but the veined and tinted image of a country, knobs and flats set out in order clearly, shining extensive and motionless in the sun. It opened on the sight of the lovers as they reached the sudden edge of the tableland, where since morning they had ridden with the head of neither horse ever in advance of the other.

At the view of their journey's end, the Virginian looked down at his girl beside him, his eyes filled with a bridegroom's light, and, hanging safe upon his breast, he could feel the gold ring that he would slowly press upon her finger tomorrow. He drew off the glove from her left hand, and stooping, kissed the jewel in that other ring which he had given her. The crimson fire in the opal seemed to mingle with that in his heart, and his arm lifted her during a moment from the saddle as he held her to him. But in her heart the love of him was troubled by that cold pang of loneliness which had crept upon her like a tide as the day drew near. None of her own people were waiting in that distant town to see her become his bride. Friendly faces she might pass on the way; but all of them new friends, made in this wild country: not a face of her childhood would smile upon her; and deep within her, a voice cried for the mother who was far away in Vermont. That she would see Mrs. Taylor's kind face at her wedding was no comfort now.

There lay the town in the splendor of Wyoming space. Around it spread the watered fields, westward for a little way, eastward to a great distance, making squares of green and yellow crops; and the town was but a poor rag in the midst of this quilted harvest. After the fields to the east, the tawny plain began; and with one faint furrow of river lining its undulations, it stretched beyond sight. But west of the town rose the Bow Leg Mountains, cool with their still unmelted snows and their dull blue gulfs of pine. From three canyons flowed three clear forks which began the river. Their confluence was above the town a good two miles; it looked but a few paces from up here, while each side the river straggled the margin cottonwoods, like thin borders along a garden walk. Over all this map hung silence like a harmony, tremendous yet serene.

"How beautiful! How I love it!" whispered the girl. "But, oh, how big it is!" And she leaned against her lover for an instant. It was her spirit seeking shelter. Today, this vast beauty, this primal calm, had in it for her something almost of dread. The small, comfortable, green hills of home rose before her. She closed her eyes and saw Vermont: a village street, and the post-office, and ivy covering an old front door, and her mother picking some yellow roses from a bush.

At a sound, her eyes quickly opened; and here was her lover turned in his saddle, watching another horseman approach. She saw the Virginian's hand in a certain position, and knew that his pistol was ready. But the other merely overtook and passed them, as they stood at the brow of the hill.

The man had given one nod to the Virginian, and the Virginian one to him; and now he was already below them on the descending road. To Molly Wood he was a stranger; but she had seen his eyes when he nodded to her lover, and she knew, even without the pistol, that this was not enmity at first sight. It was not indeed. Five years of gathered hate had looked out of the man's eyes. And she asked her lover who this was.

"Oh," said he, easily, "just a man I see now and then."

"Is his name Trampas?" said Molly Wood.

The Virginian looked at her in surprise. "Why, where have you seen him?" he asked.

"Never till now. But I knew."

"My gracious! Yu' never told me yu' had mind-reading powers." And he smiled serenely at her.

"I knew it was Trampas as soon as I saw his eyes."

"My gracious!" her lover repeated with indulgent irony. "I must be mighty careful of my eyes when you're lookin' at 'em."

"I believe he did that murder," said the girl.

"Whose mind are yu' readin' now?" he drawled affectionately.

But he could not joke her off the subject. She took his strong hand in hers, tremulously, so much of it as her little hand could hold. "I know something about that—that—last autumn," she said, shrinking from words more definite. "And I know that you only did—"

"What I had to," he finished, very sadly, but sternly, too.

"Yes," she asserted, keeping hold of his hand. "I suppose that—lynching—" (she almost whispered the word) "is the only way. But when they had to die just for stealing horses, it seems so wicked that this murderer—"

"Who can prove it?" asked the Virginian.

"But don't you know it?"

"I know a heap o' things inside my heart. But that's not proving. There was only the body, and the hoofprints—and what folks guessed."

"He was never even arrested!" the girl said.

"No. He helped elect the sheriff in that county."

Then Molly ventured a step inside the border of her lover's reticence. "I saw—" she hesitated, "just now, I saw what you did."

He returned to his caressing irony. "You'll have me plumb scared if you keep on seein' things."

"You had your pistol ready for him."

"Why, I believe I did. It was mighty unnecessary." And the Virginian took out the pistol again, and shook his head over it, like one who has been caught in a blunder.

She looked at him, and knew that she must step outside his reticence again. By love and her surrender to him their positions had been exchanged.

He was not now, as through his long courting he had been, her half-obeying, half-refractory worshipper. She was no longer his half-indulgent, half-scornful superior. Her better birth and schooling that had once been weapons to keep him at his distance, or bring her off victorious in their encounters, had given way before the onset of the natural man himself. She knew her cowboy lover, with all that he lacked, to be more than ever she could be, with all that she had. He was her worshipper still, but her master, too. Therefore now, against the baffling smile he gave her, she felt powerless. And once again a pang of yearning for her mother to be near her today shot through the girl. She looked from her untamed man to the untamed desert of Wyoming, and the town where she was to take him as her wedded husband. But for his sake she would not let him guess her loneliness.

He sat on his horse Monte, considering the pistol. Then he showed her a rattlesnake coiled by the roots of some sagebrush. "Can I hit it?" he inquired.

"You don't often miss them," said she, striving to be cheerful.

"Well, I'm told getting married unstrings some men." He aimed, and the snake was shattered. "Maybe it's too early yet for the unstringing to begin!" And with some deliberation he sent three more bullets into the snake. "I reckon that's enough," said he.

"Was not the first one?"

"Oh, yes, for the snake." And then, with one leg crooked cowboy fashion across in front of his saddle-horn, he cleaned his pistol, and replaced the empty cartridges.

Once more she ventured near the line of his reticence. "Has—has Trampas seen you much lately?"

"Why, no; not for a right smart while. But I reckon he has not missed me."

The Virginian spoke this in his gentlest voice. But his rebuffed sweetheart turned her face away, and from her eyes she brushed a tear.

He reined his horse Monte beside her, and upon her cheek she felt his kiss. "You are not the only mind-reader," said he, very tenderly. And at this she clung to him, and laid her head upon his breast. "I had been thinking," he went on, "that the way our marriage is to be was the most beautiful way."

"It is the most beautiful," she murmured.

He slowly spoke out his thought, as if she had not said this. "No folks to stare, no fuss, no jokes and ribbons and best bonnets, no public eye nor talkin' of tongues when most yu' want to hear nothing and say nothing."

She answered by holding him closer.

"Just the bishop of Wyoming to join us, and not even him after we're once joined. I did think that would be ahead of all ways to get married I have seen."

He paused again, and she made no rejoinder.

"But we have left out your mother."

She looked in his face with quick astonishment. It was as if his spirit had heard the cry of her spirit.

"That is nowhere near right," he said. "That is wrong."

"She could never have come here," said the girl.

"We should have gone there. I don't know how I can ask her to forgive me."

"But it was not you!" cried Molly.

"Yes. Because I did not object. I did not tell you we must go to her. I missed the point, thinking so much about my own feelings. For you see—and I've never said this to you until now—your mother did hurt me. When you said you would have me after my years of waiting, and I wrote her that letter telling her all about myself, and how my family was not like yours, and—and—all the rest I told her, why you see it hurt me never to get a word back from her except just messages through you. For I had talked to her about my hopes and my failings. I had said more than ever I've said to you, because she was your mother. I wanted her to forgive me, if she could, and feel that maybe I could take good care of you after all. For it was bad enough to have her daughter quit her home to teach school out hyeh on Bear Creek. Bad enough without havin' me to come along and make it worse. I have missed the point in thinking of my own feelings."

"But it's not your doing!" repeated Molly.

With his deep delicacy he had put the whole matter as a hardship to her mother alone. He had saved her any pain of confession or denial. "Yes, it is my doing," he now said. "Shall we give it up?"

"Give what—?" She did not understand.

"Why, the order we've got it fixed in. Plans are—well, they're no more than plans. I hate the notion of changing, but I hate hurting your mother more. Or, anyway, I *ought* to hate it more. So we can shift, if yu' say so. It's not too late."

"Shift?" she faltered.

"I mean, we can go to your home now. We can start by the stage tonight. Your mother can see us married. We can come back and finish in the mountains instead of beginning in them. It'll be just merely shifting, yu' see."

He could scarcely bring himself to say this at all; yet he said it almost as if he were urging it. It implied a renunciation that he could hardly bear to think of. To put off his wedding day, the bliss upon whose threshold he stood after his three years of faithful battle for it, and that wedding journey he had arranged: for there were the mountains in sight, the woods and canyons where he had planned to go with her after the bishop had joined them; the solitudes where only the wild animals would be, besides themselves. His horses, his tent, his rifle, his rod, all were waiting ready in the town for their start tomorrow. He had provided many dainty things to make her comfortable. Well, he could wait a little more, having waited three years. It would not be what his heart most desired: there would be the "public eye and the talking of tongues"—but he could wait. The hour would come when he could be alone with his bride at last. And so he spoke as if he urged it.

"Never!" she cried. "Never, never!"

She pushed it from her. She would not brook such sacrifice on his part. Were they not going to her mother in four weeks? If her family had warmly accepted him—but they had not; and in any case, it had gone too far, it was too late. She told her lover that she would not hear him, that if he said any more she would gallop into town separately from him. And for his sake she would hide deep from him this loneliness of hers, and the hurt that he had given her in refusing to share with her his trouble with Trampas, when others must know of it.

Accordingly, they descended the hill slowly together, lingering to spin out these last miles long. Many rides had taught their horses to go side by side, and so they went now: the girl sweet and thoughtful in her sedate gray habit; and the man in his leathern chaps and cartridge belt and flannel shirt, looking gravely into the distance with the level gaze of the frontier.

Having read his sweetheart's mind very plainly, the lover now broke his dearest custom. It was his code never to speak ill of any man to any woman. Men's quarrels were not for women's ears. In his scheme, good women were to know only a fragment of men's lives. He had lived many outlaw years, and his wide knowledge of evil made innocence doubly precious to him. But today he must depart from his code, having read her mind well. He would speak evil of one man to one woman, because his reticence had hurt her—and was she not far from her mother, and very lonely, do what he could? She should know the story of his quarrel in language as light and casual as he could veil it with.

He made an oblique start. He did not say to her: "I'll tell you about this. You saw me get ready for Trampas because I have been ready for him any time these five years." He began far off from the point with that rooted caution of his—that caution which is shared by the primal savage and the perfected diplomat.

"There's cert'nly a right smart o' difference between men and women," he observed.

"You're quite sure?" she retorted.

"Ain't it fortunate?—that there's both, I mean."

"I don't know about fortunate. Machinery could probably do all the heavy work for us without your help."

"And who'd invent the machinery?"

She laughed. "We shouldn't need the huge, noisy things you do. Our world would be a gentle one."

"Oh, my gracious!"

"What do you mean by that?"

"Oh, my gracious! Get along, Monte! A gentle world all full of ladies!"

"Do you call men gentle?" inquired Molly.

"Now it's a funny thing about that. Have yu' ever noticed a joke about fathers-in-law? There's just as many fathers—as mothers-in-law; but which side are your jokes?"

Molly was not vanquished. "That's because the men write the comic papers," said she.

"Hear that, Monte? The men write 'em. Well, if the ladies wrote a comic paper, I expect that might be gentle."

She gave up this battle in mirth; and he resumed: "But don't you really reckon it's uncommon to meet a father-in-law flouncin' around the house? As for gentle—once I had to sleep in a room next a ladies' temperance meetin'. Oh, heavens! Well, I couldn't change my room, and the hotel man, he apologized to me next mawnin'. Said it didn't surprise him the husbands drank some."

Here the Virginian broke down over his own fantastic inventions, and gave a joyous chuckle in company with his sweetheart. "Yes, there's a big heap o' difference between men and women," he said. "Take that fello' and myself, now."

"Trampas?" said Molly, quickly serious. She looked along the road ahead, and discerned the figure of Trampas still visible on its way to town.

The Virginian did not wish her to be serious—more than could be helped. "Why, yes," he replied, with a waving gesture at Trampas. "Take him and me. He don't think much o' me! How could he? And I expect he'll never. But yu' saw just now how it was between us. We were not a bit like a temperance meetin'."

She could not help laughing at the twist he gave to his voice. And she felt happiness warming her; for in the Virginian's tone about Trampas was something now that no longer excluded her. Thus he began his gradual recital, in a cadence always easy, and more and more musical with the native accent of the South. With the light turn he gave it, its pure ugliness melted into charm.

"No, he don't think anything of me. Once a man in the John Day Valley didn't think much, and by Canada de Oro I met another. It will always be so here and there, but Trampas beats 'em all. For the others have always expressed themselves—got shut of their poor opinion in the open air."

"Yu' see, I had to explain myself to Trampas a right smart while ago, long before ever I laid my eyes on yu'. It was just nothing at all. A little matter of cyards in the days when I was apt to spend my money and my holidays pretty headlong. My gracious, what nonsensical times I have had! But I was apt to win at cyards, 'specially poker. And Trampas, he met me one night, and I expect he must have thought I looked kind o' young. So he hated losin' his money to such a young-lookin' man, and he took his way of sayin' as much. I had to explain myself to him plainly, so that he learned right away my age had got its growth.

"Well, I expect he hated that worse, having to receive my explanation with folks lookin' on at us publicly that-a-way, and him without further ideas occurrin' to him at the moment. That's what started his poor opinion of me, not havin' ideas at the moment. And so the boys resumed their cyards.

"I'd most forgot about it. But Trampas's mem'ry is one of his strong points. Next thing—oh, it's a good while later—he gets to losin' flesh because Judge Henry gave me charge of him and some other punchers taking cattle—"

"That's not next," interrupted the girl.

"Not? Why—"

"Don't you remember?" she said, timid, yet eager. "Don't you?"

"Blamed if I do!"

"The first time we met?"

"Yes; my mem'ry keeps that—like I keep this." And he brought from his pocket her own handkerchief, the token he had picked up at a river's brink when he had carried her from an overturned stage.

"We did not exactly meet, then," she said. "It was at that dance. I hadn't seen you yet; but Trampas was saying something horrid about me, and you said—you said, 'Rise on your legs, you pole cat, and tell them you're a liar.' When I heard that, I think—I think it finished me." And crimson suffused Molly's countenance.

"I'd forgot," the Virginian murmured. Then sharply, "How did you hear it?"

"Mrs. Taylor—"

"Oh! Well, a man would never have told a woman that."

Molly laughed triumphantly. "Then who told Mrs. Taylor?"

Being caught, he grinned at her. "I reckon husbands are a special kind of man," was all that he found to say. "Well, since you do know about that, it was the next move in the game. Trampas thought I had no call to stop him sayin' what he pleased about a woman who was nothin' to me—then. But all women ought to be somethin' to a man. So I had to give Trampas another explanation in the presence of folks lookin' on, and it was just like the cyards. No ideas occurred to him again. And down goes his opinion of me some more!

"Well, I have not been able to raise it. There has been this and that and the other—yu' know most of the later doings yourself—and today is the first time I've happened to see the man since the doings last autumn. Yu' seem to know about them, too. He knows I can't prove he was with that gang of horse thieves. And I can't prove he killed poor Shorty. But he knows I missed him awful close, and spoiled his thieving for a while. So d' yu' wonder he don't think much of me? But if I had lived to be twenty-nine years old like I am, and with all my chances made no enemy, I'd feel myself a failure."

His story was finished. He had made her his confidant in matters he had never spoken of before, and she was happy to be thus much nearer to him. It diminished a certain fear that was mingled with her love of him.

During the next several miles he was silent, and his silence was enough for her. Vermont sank away from her thoughts, and Wyoming held less of loneliness. They descended altogether into the map which had stretched below them, so that it was a map no longer, but earth with growing things, and prairie-dogs sitting upon it, and now and then a bird flying over it. And after a while she said to him, "What are you thinking about?"

"I have been doing sums. Figured in hours it sounds right short. Figured in minutes it boils up into quite a mess. Twenty by sixty is twelve hundred. Put that into seconds, and yu' get seventy-two thousand seconds. Seventy-two thousand. Seventy-two thousand seconds yet before we get married."

"Seconds! To think of its having come to seconds!"

"I am thinkin' about it. I'm choppin' sixty of 'em off every minute."

With such chopping time wears away. More miles of the road lay behind them, and in the virgin wilderness the scars of new-scraped water ditches began to appear, and the first wire fences. Next, they were passing cabins and occasional fields, the outposts of habitation. The free road became wholly imprisoned, running between unbroken stretches of barbed wire. Far off to the eastward a flowing column of dust marked the approaching stage, bringing the bishop, probably, for whose visit here they had timed their wedding. The day still brimmed with heat and sunshine; but the great daily shadow was beginning to move from the feet of the Bow Leg Mountains outward toward the town. Presently they began to meet citizens. Some of these knew them and nodded, while some did not, and stared. Turning a corner into the town's chief street, where stood the hotel, the bank, the drug store, the general store, and the seven saloons, they were hailed heartily. Here were three friends—Honey Wiggin, Scipio Le Moyne, and Lin McLean—all desirous of drinking the Virginian's health, if his lady—would she mind? The three stood grinning, with their hats off; but behind their gayety the Virginian read some other purpose.

"We'll all be very good," said Honey Wiggin.

"Pretty good," said Lin.

"Good," said Scipio.

"Which is the honest man?" inquired Molly, glad to see them.

"Not one!" said the Virginian. "My old friends scare me when I think of their ways."

"It's bein' engaged scares yu'," retorted Mr. McLean. "Marriage restores your courage, I find."

"Well, I'll trust all of you," said Molly. "He's going to take me to the hotel, and then you can drink his health as much as you please."

With a smile to them she turned to proceed, and he let his horse move with hers; but he looked at his friends. Then Scipio's bleached blue eyes narrowed to a slit, and he said what they had all come out on the street to say: *"Don't change your clothes."*

"Oh!" protested Molly, "isn't he rather dusty and countrified?"

But the Virginian had taken Scipio's meaning. "Don't change your clothes." Innocent Molly appreciated these words no more than the average reader who reads a masterpiece, complacently unaware that its style differs from that of the morning paper. Such was Scipio's intention, wishing to spare her from alarm.

So at the hotel she let her lover go with a kiss, and without a thought of Trampas. She in her room unlocked the possessions which were there waiting for her, and changed her dress.

Wedding garments, and other civilized apparel proper for a genuine frontiersman when he comes to town, were also in the hotel, ready for the Virginian to wear. It is only the somewhat green and unseasoned cowpuncher who struts before the public in spurs and deadly weapons. For many a year the Virginian had put away these childish things. He made a sober toilet for the streets. Nothing but his face and bearing remained out of the common when he was in a town. But Scipio had told him not to change his clothes; therefore he went out with his pistol at his hip. Soon he had joined his three friends.

"I'm obliged to yu'," he said. "He passed me this mawnin'."

"We don't know his intentions," said Wiggin.

"Except that he's hangin' around," said McLean.

"And fillin' up," said Scipio, "which reminds me—"

They strolled into the saloon of a friend, where, unfortunately, sat some foolish people. But one cannot always tell how much of a fool a man is, at sight.

It was a temperate health-drinking that they made. "Here's how," they muttered softly to the Virginian; and "How," he returned softly, looking away from them. But they had a brief meeting of eyes, standing and lounging near each other, shyly; and Scipio shook hands with the bridegroom. "Someday," he stated, tapping himself; for in his vagrant heart he began to envy the man who could bring himself to marry. And he nodded again, repeating, "Here's how."

They stood at the bar, full of sentiment, empty of words, memory and affection busy in their hearts. All of them had seen rough days together, and they felt guilty with emotion.

"It's hot weather," said Wiggin.

"Hotter on Box Elder," said McLean. "My kid has started teething."

Words ran dry again. They shifted their positions, looked in their glasses, read the labels on the bottles. They dropped a word now and then to the proprietor about his trade, and his ornaments.

"Good head," commented McLean.

"Big old ram," assented the proprietor. "Shot him myself on Gray Bull last fall."

"Sheep was thick in the Tetons last fall," said the Virginian.

On the bar stood a machine into which the idle customer might drop his nickel. The coin then bounced among an arrangement of pegs, descending at length into one or another of various holes. You might win as much as ten times your stake, but this was not the most usual result; and with nickels the three friends and the bridegroom now mildly sported for a while, buying them with silver when their store ran out.

"Was it sheep you went after in the Tetons?" inquired the proprietor, knowing it was horse thieves.

"Yes," said the Virginian. "I'll have ten more nickels."

"Did you get all the sheep you wanted?" the proprietor continued.

"Poor luck," said the Virginian.

"Think there's a friend of yours in town this afternoon," said the proprietor.

"Did he mention he was my friend?"

The proprietor laughed. The Virginian watched another nickel click down among the pegs.

Honey Wiggin now made the bridegroom a straight offer. "We'll take this thing off your hands," said he.

"Any or all of us," said Lin.

But Scipio held his peace. His loyalty went every inch as far as theirs, but his understanding of his friend went deeper. "Don't change your clothes," was the first and the last help he would be likely to give in this matter. The rest must be as such matters must always be, between man and man. To the other two friends, however, this seemed a very special case, falling outside established precedent. Therefore they ventured offers of interference.

"A man don't get married every day," apologized McLean. "We'll just run him out of town for yu'."

"Save yu' the trouble," urged Wiggin. "Say the word."

The proprietor now added his voice. "It'll sober him up to spend his night out in the brush. He'll quit his talk then."

But the Virginian did not say the word, or any word. He stood playing with the nickels.

"Think of her," muttered McLean.

"Who else would I be thinking of?" returned the Southerner. His face had become very sombre. "She has been raised so different!" he murmured. He pondered a little, while the others waited, solicitous.

A new idea came to the proprietor. "I am acting mayor of this town," said he. "I'll put him in the calaboose and keep him till you get married and away."

"Say the word," repeated Honey Wiggin.

Scipio's eye met the proprietor's, and he shook his head about a quarter of an inch. The proprietor shook his to the same amount. They understood each other. It had come to that point where there was no way out, save only the ancient, eternal way between man and man. It is only the great mediocrity that goes to law in these personal matters.

"So he has talked about me some?" said the Virginian.

"It's the whiskey," Scipio explained.

"I expect," said McLean, "he'd run a mile if he was in a state to appreciate his insinuations."

"Which we are careful not to mention to yu'," said Wiggin, "unless yu' inquire for 'em."

Some of the fools present had drawn closer to hear this interesting conversation. In gatherings of more than six there will generally be at least one fool; and this company must have numbered twenty men.

"This country knows well enough," said one fool, who hungered to be important, "that you don't brand no calves that ain't your own."

The saturnine Virginian looked at him. "Thank yu'," said he, gravely, "for your indorsement of my character." The fool felt flattered. The Virginian turned to his friends. His hand slowly pushed his hat back, and he rubbed his black head in thought.

"Glad to see yu've got your gun with you," continued the happy fool. "You know what Trampas claims about that affair of yours in the Tetons? He claims that if everything was known about the killing of Shorty—"

"Take one on the house," suggested the proprietor to him, amiably. "Your news will be fresher." And he pushed him the bottle. The fool felt less important.

"This talk had went the rounds before it got to us," said Scipio, "or we'd have headed it off. He has got friends in town."

Perplexity knotted the Virginian's brows. This community knew that a man had implied he was a thief and a murderer; it also knew that he knew it. But the case was one of peculiar circumstances, assuredly. Could he avoid meeting the man? Soon the stage would be starting south for the railroad. He had already today proposed to his sweetheart that they should take it. Could he for her sake leave unanswered a talking enemy upon the field? His own ears had not heard the enemy.

Into these reflections the fool stepped once more. "Of course this country don't believe Trampas," said he. "This country—"

But he contributed no further thoughts. From somewhere in the rear of the building, where it opened upon the tin cans and the hinder purlieus of the town, came a movement, and Trampas was among them, courageous with whiskey.

All the fools now made themselves conspicuous. One lay on the floor, knocked there by the Virginian, whose arm he had attempted to hold. Others struggled with Trampas, and his bullet smashed the ceiling before they could drag the pistol from him. "There now! there now!" they interposed; "you don't want to talk like that," for he was pouring out a tide of hate and vilification. Yet the Virginian stood quiet by the bar, and many an eye of astonishment was turned upon him. "I'd not stand half that language," some muttered to each other. Still the Virginian waited quietly, while the fools reasoned with Trampas. But no earthly foot can step between a man and his destiny. Trampas broke suddenly free.

"Your friends have saved your life," he rang out, with obscene epithets. "I'll give you till sundown to leave town."

There was total silence instantly.

"Trampas," spoke the Virginian, "I don't want trouble with you."

"He never has wanted it," Trampas sneered to the bystanders. "He has been dodging it five years. But I've got him corralled."

Some of the Trampas faction smiled.

"Trampas," said the Virginian again, "are yu' sure yu' really mean that?"

The whiskey bottle flew through the air, hurled by Trampas, and crashed through the saloon window behind the Virginian.

"That was surplusage, Trampas," said he, "if yu' mean the other."

"Get out by sundown, that's all," said Trampas. And wheeling, he went out of the saloon by the rear, as he had entered.

"Gentlemen," said the Virginian, "I know you will all oblige me."

"Sure!" exclaimed the proprietor, heartily, "We'll see that everybody lets this thing alone."

The Virginian gave a general nod to the company, and walked out into the street.

"It's a turruble shame," sighed Scipio, "that he couldn't have postponed it."

The Virginian walked in the open air with thoughts disturbed. "I am of two minds about one thing," he said to himself uneasily.

Gossip ran in advance of him; but as he came by, the talk fell away until he had passed. Then they looked after him, and their words again rose audibly. Thus everywhere a little eddy of silence accompanied his steps.

"It don't trouble him much," one said, having read nothing in the Virginian's face.

"It may trouble his girl some," said another.

"She'll not know," said a third, "until it's over."

"He'll not tell her?"

"I wouldn't. It's no woman's business."

"Maybe that's so. Well, it would have suited me to have Trampas die sooner."

"How would it suit you to have him live longer?" inquired a member of the opposite faction, suspected of being himself a cattle thief.

"I could answer your question, if I had other folks' calves I wanted to brand." This raised both a laugh and a silence.

Thus the town talked, filling in the time before sunset.

The Virginian, still walking aloof in the open air, paused at the edge of the town. "I'd sooner have a sickness than be undecided this way," he said, and he looked up and down. Then a grim smile came at his own expense. "I reckon it would make me sick—but there's not time."

Over there in the hotel sat his sweetheart alone, away from her mother, her friends, her home, waiting his return, knowing nothing. He looked into the west. Between the sun and the bright ridges of the mountains was still a space of sky; but the shadow from the mountains' feet had drawn halfway toward the town. "About forty minutes more," he said aloud. "She has been raised so different." And he sighed as he turned back. As he went slowly, he did not know how great was his own unhappiness. "She has been raised so different," he said again.

Opposite the post-office the bishop of Wyoming met him and greeted him. His lonely heart throbbed at the warm, firm grasp of this friend's hand. The bishop saw his eyes glow suddenly, as if tears were close. But none came, and no word more open than, "I'm glad to see you."

But gossip had reached the bishop, and he was sorely troubled also. "What is all this?" said he, coming straight to it.

The Virginian looked at the clergyman frankly. "Yu' know just as much about it as I do," he said. "And I'll tell yu' anything yu' ask."

"Have you told Miss Wood?" inquired the bishop.

The eyes of the bridegroom fell, and the bishop's face grew at once more keen and more troubled. Then the bridegroom raised his eyes again, and the bishop almost loved him. He touched his arm, like a brother. "This is hard luck," he said.

The bridegroom could scarce keep his voice steady. "I want to do right today more than any day I have ever lived," said he.

"Then go and tell her at once."

"It will just do nothing but scare her."

"Go and tell her at once."

"I expected you was going to tell me to run away from Trampas. I can't do that, yu' know."

The bishop did know. Never before in all his wilderness work had he faced such a thing. He knew that Trampas was an evil in the country, and that the Virginian was a good. He knew that the cattle thieves—the rustlers—were gaining, in numbers and audacity; that they led many weak young fellows to ruin; that they elected their men to office, and controlled juries; that they were a staring menace to Wyoming. His heart was with the Virginian. But there was his Gospel, that he preached, and believed, and tried to live. He stood looking at the ground and drawing a finger along his eyebrow. He wished that he might have heard nothing about all this. But he was not one to blink his responsibility as a Christian server of the church militant.

"Am I right," he now slowly asked, "in believing that you think I am a sincere man?"

"I don't believe anything about it. I know it."

"I should run away from Trampas," said the bishop.

"That ain't quite fair, seh. We all understand you have got to do the things you tell other folks to do. And you do them, seh. You never talk like anything but a man, and you never set yourself above others. You can saddle your own horses. And I saw yu' walk unarmed into that White River excitement when those two other parsons was a-foggin' and a-fannin' for their own safety. Damn scoundrels!"

The bishop instantly rebuked such language about brothers of his cloth, even though he disapproved both of them and their doctrines. "Everyone may be an instrument of Providence," he concluded.

"Well," said the Virginian, "if that is so, then Providence makes use of instruments I'd not touch with a ten-foot pole. Now if you was me, seh, and not a bishop, would you run away from Trampas?"

"That's not quite fair, either!" exclaimed the bishop, with a smile. "Because you are asking me to take another man's convictions, and yet remain myself."

"Yes, seh. I am. That's so. That don't get at it. I reckon you and I can't get at it."

"If the Bible," said the bishop, "which I believe to be God's word, was anything to you—"

"It is something to me, seh. I have found fine truths in it."

"'Thou shalt not kill,'" quoted the bishop. "That is plain."

The Virginian took his turn at smiling. "Mighty plain to me, seh. Make it plain to Trampas, and there'll be no killin'. We can't get at it that way."

Once more the bishop quoted earnestly. "'Vengeance is mine, I will repay, saith the Lord.'"

"How about instruments of Providence, seh? Why, we can't get at it that way. If you start usin' the Bible that way, it will mix you up mighty quick, seh."

"My friend," the bishop urged, and all his good, warm heart was in it, "my dear fellow—go away for the one night. He'll change his mind."

The Virginian shook his head. "He cannot change his word, seh. Or at least I must stay around till he does. Why, I have given him the say-so. He's got the choice. Most men would not have took what I took from him in the saloon. Why don't you ask him to leave town?"

The good bishop was at a standstill. Of all kicking against the pricks none is so hard as this kick of a professing Christian against the whole instinct of human man.

"But you have helped me some," said the Virginian. "I will go and tell her. At least, if I think it will be good for her, I will tell her."

The bishop thought that he saw one last chance to move him.

"You're twenty-nine," he began.

"And a little over," said the Virginian.

"And you were fourteen when you ran away from your family."

"Well, I was weary, yu' know, of havin' elder brothers lay down my law night and mawnin'."

"Yes, I know. So that your life has been your own for fifteen years. But it is not your own now. You have given it to a woman."

"Yes; I have given it to her. But my life's not the whole of me. I'd give her twice my life—fifty—a thousand of 'em. But I can't give her—her nor anybody in heaven or earth—I can't give my—my—we'll never get at it, seh! There's no good in words. Good-by." The Virginian wrung the bishop's hand and left him.

"God bless him!" said the bishop. "God bless him!"

The Virginian unlocked the room in the hotel where he kept stored his tent, his blankets, his pack-saddles, and his many accoutrements for the bridal journey in the mountains. Out of the window he saw the mountains blue in shadow, but some cottonwoods distant in the flat between were still bright green in the sun. From among his possessions he took quickly a pistol, wiping and loading it. Then from its holster he removed the pistol which he had tried and made sure of in the morning. This, according to his wont when going into a risk, he shoved between his trousers and his shirt in front. The untried weapon he placed in the holster, letting it hang visibly at his hip. He glanced out of the window again, and saw the mountains of the same deep blue. But the cottonwoods were no longer in the sunlight. The shadow had come past them, nearer the town; for fifteen of the forty minutes were gone. "The bishop is wrong," he said. "There is no sense in telling her." And he turned to the door, just as she came to it herself.

"Oh!" she cried out at once, and rushed to him.

He swore as he held her close. "The fools!" he said. "The fools!"

"It has been so frightful waiting for you," said she, leaning her head against him.

"Who had to tell you this?" he demanded.

"I don't know. Somebody just came and said it."

"This is mean luck," he murmured, patting her. "This is mean luck."

She went on: "I wanted to run out and find you; but I didn't! I didn't! I stayed quiet in my room till they said you had come back."

"It is mean luck. Mighty mean," he repeated.

"How could you be so long?" she asked. "Never mind, I've got you now. It is over."

Anger and sorrow filled him. "I might have known some fool would tell you," he said.

"It's all over. Never mind." Her arms tightened their hold of him. Then she let him go. "What shall we do?" she said. "What now?"

"Now?" he answered. "Nothing now."

She looked at him without understanding.

"I know it is a heap worse for you," he pursued, speaking slowly. "I knew it would be."

"But it is over!" she exclaimed again.

He did not understand her now. He kissed her. "Did you think it was over?" he said simply. "There is some waiting still before us. I wish you did not have to wait alone. But it will not be long." He was looking down, and did not see the happiness grow chilled upon her face, and then fade into bewildered fear. "I did my best," he went on. "I think I did. I know I tried. I let him say to me before them all what no man has ever said, or ever will again. I kept thinking hard of you—with all my might, or I reckon I'd have killed him right there. And I gave him a show to change his mind. I gave it to him twice. I spoke as quiet as I am speaking to you now. But he stood to it. And I expect he knows he went too far in the hearing of others to go back on his threat. He will have to go on to the finish now."

"The finish?" she echoed, almost voiceless.

"Yes," he answered very gently.

Her dilated eyes were fixed upon him. "But—" she could scarce form utterance, "but you?"

"I have got myself ready," he said. "Did you think—why, what did you think?"

She recoiled a step. "What are you going—" She put her two hands to her head. "Oh, God!" she almost shrieked, "you are going—" He made a step, and would have put his arm round her, but she backed against the wall, staring speechless at him.

"I am not going to let him shoot me," he said quietly.

"You mean—you mean—but you can come away!" she cried. "It's not too late yet. You can take yourself out of his reach. Everybody knows that you are brave. What is he to you? You can leave him in this place. I'll go with you anywhere. To any house, to the mountains, to anywhere away. We'll leave this horrible place together and—and—oh, won't you listen to me?" She stretched her hands to him. "Won't you listen?"

He took her hands. "I must stay here."

Her hands clung to his. "No, no, no. There's something else. There's something better than shedding blood in cold blood. Only think what it means! Only think of having to remember such a thing! Why, it's what they hang people for! It's murder!"

He dropped her hands. "Don't call it that name," he said sternly.

"When there was the choice!" she exclaimed, half to herself, like a person stunned and speaking to the air. "To get ready for it when you have the choice!"

"He did the choosing," answered the Virginian. "Listen to me. Are you listening?" he asked, for her gaze was dull.

She nodded.

"I work hyeh. I belong hyeh. It's my life. If folks came to think I was a coward—"

"Who would think you were a coward?"

"Everybody. My friends would be sorry and ashamed, and my enemies would walk around saying they had always said so. I could not hold up my head again among enemies or friends."

"When it was explained—"

"There'd be nothing to explain. There'd just be the fact." He was nearly angry.

"There is a higher courage than fear of outside opinion," said the New England girl.

Her Southern lover looked at her. "Cert'nly there is. That's what I'm showing in going against yours."

"But if you know that you are brave, and if I know that you are brave, oh, my dear, my dear! what difference does the world make? How much higher courage to go your own course—"

"I am goin' my own course," he broke in. "Can't yu' see how it must be about a man? It's not for their benefit, friends or enemies, that I have got this thing to do. If any man happened to say I was a thief and I heard about it, would I let him go on spreadin' such a thing of me? Don't I owe my own honesty something better than that? Would I sit down in a corner rubbin' my honesty and whisperin' to it, 'There! There! I know you ain't a thief?' No, seh; not a little bit! What men say about my nature is not just merely an outside thing. For the fact that I let 'em keep on sayin' it is a proof I don't value my nature enough to shield it from their slander and give them their punishment. And that's being a poor sort of a jay."

She had grown very white.

"Can't yu' see how it must be about a man?" he repeated.

"I cannot," she answered, in a voice that scarcely seemed her own. "If I ought to, I cannot. To shed blood in cold blood. When I heard about that last fall—about the killing of those cattle thieves—I kept saying to myself: 'He had to do it. It was a public duty.' And lying sleepless I got used to Wyoming being different from Vermont. But this"—she gave a shudder—"when I think of tomorrow, of you and me, and of—if you do this, there can be no tomorrow for you and me."

At these words he also turned white.

"Do you mean—" he asked, and could go no farther.

Nor could she answer him, but turned her head away.

"This would be the end?" he asked.

Her head faintly moved to signify yes.

He stood still, his hand shaking a little. "Will you look at me and say that?" he murmured at length. She did not move. "Can you do it?" he said.

His sweetness made her turn, but could not pierce her frozen resolve. She gazed at him across the great distance of her despair.

"Then it is really so?" he said.

Her lips tried to form words, but failed.

He looked out of the window, and saw nothing but shadow. The blue of the mountains was now become a deep purple. Suddenly his hand closed hard.

"Good-by, then," he said.

At that word she was at his feet, clutching him. "For my sake," she begged him. "For my sake."

A tremble passed through his frame. She felt his legs shake as she held them, and, looking up, she saw that his eyes were closed with misery. Then he opened them, and in their steady look she read her answer. He unclasped her hands from holding him, and raised her to her feet.

"I have no right to kiss you anymore," he said. And then, before his desire could break him down from this, he was gone, and she was alone.

She did not fall, or totter, but stood motionless. And next—it seemed a moment and it seemed eternity—she heard in the distance a shot, and then two shots. Out of the window she saw people beginning to run. At that she turned and fled to her room, and flung herself face downward upon the floor.

Trampas had departed into solitude from the saloon, leaving behind him his *ultimatum*. His loud and public threat was town knowledge already, would very likely be county knowledge tonight. Riders would take it with them to entertain distant cabins up the river and down the river; and by dark the stage would go south with the news of it—and the news of its outcome.

For everything would be over by dark. After five years, here was the end coming—coming before dark. Trampas had got up this morning with no such thought. It seemed very strange to look back upon the morning; it lay so distant, so irrevocable. And he thought of how he had eaten his breakfast. How would he eat his supper? For supper would come afterward. Some people were eating theirs now, with nothing like this before them. His heart ached and grew cold to think of them, easy and comfortable with plates and cups of coffee.

He looked at the mountains, and saw the sun above their ridges, and the shadow coming from their feet. And there close behind him was the morning he could never go back to. He could see it clearly; his thoughts reached out like arms to touch it once more, and be in it again. The night that was coming he could not see, and his eyes and his thoughts shrank from it. He had given his enemy until sundown. He could not trace the path which had led him to this. He remembered their first meeting—five years back, in Medicine Bow, and the words which at once began his hate. No, it was before any words; it was the encounter of their eyes. For out of the eyes of every stranger looks either a friend or an enemy, waiting to be known. But how had five years of hate come to play him such a trick, suddenly, today? Since last autumn he had meant sometime to get even with this man who seemed to stand at every turn of his crookedness, and rob him of his spoils. But how had he come to choose such a way of getting even as this, face to face? He knew many better ways; and now his own rash proclamation had trapped him. His words were like doors shutting him in to perform his threat to the letter, with witnesses at hand to see that he did so.

Trampas looked at the sun and the shadow again. He had till sundown. The heart inside him was turning it round in this opposite way: it was to *himself* that in his rage he had given this lessening margin of grace. But he dared not leave town in all the world's sight after all the world had heard him. Even his friends would fall from him after such an act. Could he—the thought actually came to him—could he strike before the time set? But the thought was useless. Even if his friends could harbor him after such a deed, his enemies would find him, and his life would be forfeit to a certainty. His own trap was closing upon him.

He came upon the main street, and saw some distance off the Virginian standing in talk with the bishop. He slunk between two houses, and cursed both of them. The sight had been good for him, bringing some warmth of rage back to his desperate heart. And he went into a place and drank some whiskey.

"In your shoes," said the barkeeper, "I'd be afraid to take so much."

But the nerves of Trampas were almost beyond the reach of intoxication, and he swallowed some more, and went out again. Presently he fell in with some of his brothers in cattle stealing, and walked along with them for a little.

"Well, it will not be long now," they said to him. And he had never heard words so desolate.

"No," he made out to say; "soon now." Their cheerfulness seemed unearthly to him, and his heart almost broke beneath it.

"We'll have one to your success," they suggested.

So with them he repaired to another place; and the sight of a man leaning against the bar made him start so that they noticed him. Then he saw that the man was a stranger whom he had never laid eyes on till now.

"It looked like Shorty," he said, and could have bitten his tongue off.

"Shorty is quiet up in the Tetons," said a friend. "You don't want to be thinking about him. Here's how!"

Then they clapped him on the back and he left them. He thought of his enemy and his hate, beating his rage like a failing horse, and treading the courage of his drink. Across a space he saw Wiggin, walking with McLean and Scipio. They were watching the town to see that his friends made no foul play.

"We're giving you a clear field," said Wiggin.

"This race will not be pulled," said McLean.

"Be with you at the finish," said Scipio.

And they passed on. They did not seem like real people to him.

Trampas looked at the walls and windows of the houses. Were they real? Was he here, walking in this street? Something had changed. He looked everywhere, and feeling it everywhere, wondered what this could be. Then he knew: it was the sun that had gone entirely behind the mountains, and he drew out his pistol.

The Virginian, for precaution, did not walk out of the front door of the hotel. He went through back ways, and paused once. Against his breast he felt the wedding ring where he had it suspended by a chain from his neck. His hand went up to it, and he drew it out and looked at it. He took it off the chain, and his arm went back to hurl it from him as far as he could. But he stopped and kissed it with one sob, and thrust it in his pocket. Then he walked out into the open, watching. He saw men here and there, and they let him pass as before, without speaking. He saw his three friends, and they said no word to him. But they turned and followed in his rear at a little distance, because it was known that Shorty had been found shot from behind. The Virginian gained a position soon where no one could come at him except from in front; and the sight of the mountains was almost more than he could endure, because it was there that he had been going tomorrow.

"It is quite a while after sunset," he heard himself say.

A wind seemed to blow his sleeve off his arm, and he replied to it, and saw Trampas pitch forward. He saw Trampas raise his arm from the ground and fall again, and lie there this time, still. A little smoke was rising from the pistol on the ground, and he looked at his own, and saw the smoke flowing upward out of it.

"I expect that's all," he said aloud.

But as he came nearer Trampas, he covered him with his weapon. He stopped a moment, seeing the hand on the ground move. Two fingers twitched, and then ceased; for it was all. The Virginian stood looking down at Trampas.

"Both of mine hit," he said, once more aloud. "His must have gone mighty close to my arm. I told her it would not be me."

He had scarcely noticed that he was being surrounded and congratulated. His hand was being shaken, and he saw it was Scipio in tears. Scipio's joy made his heart like lead within him. He was near telling his friend everything, but he did not.

"If anybody wants me about this," he said, "I will be at the hotel."

"Who'll want you?" said Scipio. "Three of us saw his gun out." And he vented his admiration. "You were that cool! That quick!"

"I'll see you boys again," said the Virginian, heavily; and he walked away.

Scipio looked after him, astonished. "Yu' might suppose he was in poor luck," he said to McLean.

The Virginian walked to the hotel, and stood on the threshold of his sweetheart's room. She had heard his step, and was upon her feet. Her lips were parted, and her eyes fixed on him, nor did she move, or speak.

"Yu' have to know it," said he. "I have killed Trampas."

"Oh, thank God!" she said; and he found her in his arms. Long they embraced without speaking, and what they whispered then with their kisses, matters not.

Thus did her New England conscience battle to the end, and, in the end, capitulate to love. And the next day, with the bishop's blessing, and Mrs. Taylor's broadest smile, and the ring on her finger, the Virginian departed with his bride into the mountains.

# CHAPTER XXXVI

## AT DUNBARTON

For their first bridal camp he chose an island. Long weeks beforehand he had thought of this place, and set his heart upon it. Once established in his mind, the thought became a picture that he saw waking and sleeping. He had stopped at the island many times alone, and in all seasons; but at this special moment of the year he liked it best. Often he had added several needless miles to his journey that he might finish the day at this point, might catch the trout for his supper beside a certain rock upon its edge, and fall asleep hearing the stream on either side of him.

Always for him the first signs that he had gained the true world of the mountains began at the island. The first pine trees stood upon it; the first white columbine grew in their shade; and it seemed to him that he always met here first of the true mountain air—the coolness and the new fragrance. Below, there were only the cottonwoods, and the knolls and steep foothills with their sagebrush, and the great warm air of the plains; here at this altitude came the definite change. Out of the lower country and its air he would urge his horse upward, talking to him aloud, and promising fine pasture in a little while.

Then, when at length he had ridden abreast of the island pines, he would ford to the sheltered circle of his camp-ground, throw off the saddle and blanket from the horse's hot, wet back, throw his own clothes off, and, shouting, spring upon the horse bare, and with a rope for bridle, cross with him to the promised pasture. Here there was a pause in the mountain steepness, a level space of open, green with thick grass. Riding his horse to this, he would leap off him, and with the flat of his hand give him a blow that cracked sharp in the stillness and sent the horse galloping and gambolling to his night's freedom. And while the animal rolled in the grass, often his master would roll also, and stretch, and take the grass in his two hands, and so draw his body along, limbering his muscles after a long ride. Then he would slide into the stream below his fishing place, where it was deep enough for swimming, and cross back to his island, and dressing again, fit his rod together and begin his casting. After the darkness had set in, there would follow the lying drowsily with his head upon his saddle, the campfire sinking as he watched it, and sleep approaching to the murmur of the water on either side of him.

So many visits to this island had he made, and counted so many hours of revery spent in its haunting sweetness, that the spot had come to seem his own. It belonged to no man, for it was deep in the unsurveyed and virgin wilderness; neither had he ever made his camp here with any man, nor shared with any the intimate delight which the place gave him. Therefore for many weeks he had planned to bring her here after their wedding, upon the day itself, and show her and share with her his pines and his fishing rock. He would bid her smell the first true breath of the mountains, would watch with her the sinking campfire, and with her listen to the water as it flowed round the island.

Until this wedding plan, it had by no means come home to him how deep a hold upon him the island had taken. He knew that he liked to go there, and go alone; but so little was it his way to scan himself, his mind, or his feelings (unless some action called for it), that he first learned his love of the place through his love of her. But he told her nothing of it. After the thought of taking her there came to him, he kept his island as something to let break upon her own eyes, lest by looking forward she should look for more than the reality.

Hence, as they rode along, when the houses of the town were shrunk to dots behind them, and they were nearing the gates of the foothills, she asked him questions. She hoped they would find a camp a long way from the town. She could ride as many miles as necessary. She was not tired. Should they not go on until they found a good place far enough within the solitude? Had he fixed upon any? And at the nod and the silence that he gave her for reply, she knew that he had thoughts and intentions which she must wait to learn.

They passed through the gates of the foothills, following the stream up among them. The outstretching fences and the widely trodden dust were no more. Now and then they rose again into view of the fields and houses down in the plain below. But as the sum of the miles and hours grew, they were glad to see the road less worn with travel, and the traces of men passing from sight. The ploughed and planted country, that quilt of many-colored harvests which they had watched yesterday, lay in another world from this where they rode now. No hand but nature's had sown these crops of yellow flowers, these willow thickets and tall cottonwoods. Somewhere in a passage of red rocks the last sign of wagon wheels was lost, and after this the trail became a wild mountain trail. But it was still the warm air of the plains, bearing the sagebrush odor and not the pine, that they breathed; nor did any forest yet cloak the shapes of the tawny hills among which they were ascending. Twice the steepness loosened the pack ropes, and he jumped down to tighten them, lest the horses should get sore backs. And twice the stream that they followed went into deep canyons, so that for a while they parted from it. When they came back to its margin for the second time, he bade her notice how its water had become at last wholly clear. To her it had seemed clear enough all along, even in the plain above the town. But now she saw that it flowed lustrously with flashes; and she knew the soil had changed to mountain soil. Lower down, the water had carried the slightest cloud of alkali, and this had dulled the keen edge of its transparence. Full solitude was around them now, so that their words grew scarce, and when they spoke it was with low voices. They began to pass nooks and points favorable for camping, with wood and water at hand, and pasture for the horses. More than once as they reached such places, she thought he must surely stop; but still he rode on in advance of her (for the trail was narrow) until, when she was not thinking of it, he drew rein and pointed.

"What?" she asked timidly.

"The pines," he answered.

She looked, and saw the island, and the water folding it with ripples and with smooth spaces. The sun was throwing upon the pine boughs a light of deepening red gold, and the shadow of the fishing rock lay over a little bay of quiet water and sandy shore. In this forerunning glow of the sunset, the pasture spread like emerald; for the dry touch of summer had not yet come near it. He pointed upward to the high mountains which they had approached, and showed her where the stream led into their first unfoldings.

"Tomorrow we shall be among them," said he.

"Then," she murmured to him, "tonight is here?"

He nodded for answer, and she gazed at the island and understood why he had not stopped before; nothing they had passed had been so lovely as this place.

There was room in the trail for them to go side by side; and side by side they rode to the ford and crossed, driving the packhorses in front of them, until they came to the sheltered circle, and he helped her down where the soft pine needles lay. They felt each other tremble, and for a moment she stood hiding her head upon his breast. Then she looked round at the trees, and the shores, and the flowing stream, and he heard her whispering how beautiful it was.

"I am glad," he said, still holding her. "This is how I have dreamed it would happen. Only it is better than my dreams." And when she pressed him in silence, he finished, "I have meant we should see our first sundown here, and our first sunrise."

She wished to help him take the packs from their horses, to make the camp together with him, to have for her share the building of the fire, and the cooking. She bade him remember his promise to her that he would teach her how to loop and draw the pack-ropes, and the swing-ropes on the pack-saddles, and how to pitch a tent. Why might not the first lesson be now? But he told her that this should be fulfilled later. This night he was to do all himself. And he sent her away until he should have camp ready for them. He bade her explore the island, or take her horse and ride over to the pasture, where she could see the surrounding hills and the circle of seclusion that they made.

"The whole world is far from here," he said. And so she obeyed him, and went away to wander about in their hiding-place; nor was she to return, he told her, until he called her.

Then at once, as soon as she was gone, he fell to. The packs and saddles came off the horses, which he turned loose upon the pasture on the main land. The tent was unfolded first. He had long seen in his mind where it should go, and how its white shape would look beneath the green of the encircling pines. The ground was level in the spot he had chosen, without stones or roots, and matted with the fallen needles of the pines. If there should come any wind, or storm of rain, the branches were thick overhead, and around them on three sides tall rocks and undergrowth made a barrier. He cut the pegs for the tent, and the front pole, stretching and tightening the rope, one end of it pegged down and one round a pine tree. When the tightening rope had lifted the canvas to the proper height from the ground, he spread and pegged down the sides and back, leaving the opening so that they could look out upon the fire and a piece of the stream beyond. He cut tufts of young pine and strewed them thickly for a soft floor in the tent, and over them spread the buffalo hide and the blankets. At the head he placed the neat sack of her belongings. For his own he made a shelter with crossed poles and a sheet of canvas beyond the first pines. He built the fire where its smoke would float outward from the trees and the tent, and near it he stood the cooking things and his provisions, and made this first supper ready in the twilight. He had brought much with him; but for ten minutes he fished, catching trout enough. When at length she came riding over the stream at his call, there was nothing for her to do but sit and eat at the table he had laid. They sat together, watching the last of the twilight and the gentle oncoming of the dusk. The final after-glow of day left the sky, and through the purple which followed it came slowly the first stars, bright and wide apart. They watched the spaces between them fill with more stars, while near them the flames and embers of their fire grew brighter. Then he sent her to the tent while he cleaned the dishes and visited the horses to see that they did not stray from the pasture. Some while after the darkness was fully come, he rejoined her. All had been as he had seen it in his thoughts beforehand: the pines with the setting sun upon them, the sinking campfire, and now the sound of the water as it flowed murmuring by the shores of the island.

The tent opened to the east, and from it they watched together their first sunrise. In his thoughts he had seen this morning beforehand also: the waking, the gentle sound of the water murmuring ceaselessly, the growing day, the vision of the stream, the sense that the world was shut away far from them. So did it all happen, except that he whispered to her again: "Better than my dreams."

They saw the sunlight begin upon a hilltop; and presently came the sun itself, and lakes of warmth flowed into the air, slowly filling the green solitude. Along the island shores the ripples caught flashes from the sun.

"I am going into the stream," he said to her; and rising, he left her in the tent. This was his side of the island, he had told her last night; the other was hers, where he had made a place for her to bathe. When he was gone, she found it, walking through the trees and rocks to the water's edge. And so, with the island between them, the two bathed in the cold stream. When he came back, he found her already busy at their camp. The blue smoke of the fire was floating out from the trees, loitering undispersed in the quiet air, and she was getting their breakfast. She had been able to forestall him because he had delayed long at his dressing, not willing to return to her unshaven. She looked at his eyes that were clear as the water he had leaped into, and at his soft silk neckerchief, knotted with care.

"Do not let us ever go away from here!" she cried, and ran to him as he came. They sat long together at breakfast, breathing the morning breath of the earth that was fragrant with woodland moisture and with the pines. After the meal he could not prevent her helping him make everything clean. Then, by all customs of mountain journeys, it was time they should break camp and be moving before the heat of the day. But first, they delayed for no reason, save that in these hours they so loved to do nothing. And next, when with some energy he got upon his feet and declared he must go and drive the horses in, she asked, Why? Would it not be well for him to fish here, that they might be sure of trout at their nooning? And though he knew that where they should stop for noon, trout would be as sure as here, he took this chance for more delay.

She went with him to his fishing rock, and sat watching him. The rock was tall, higher than his head when he stood. It jutted out halfway across the stream, and the water flowed round it in quick foam, and fell into a pool. He caught several fish; but the sun was getting high, and after a time it was plain the fish had ceased to rise.

Yet still he stood casting in silence, while she sat by and watched him. Across the stream, the horses wandered or lay down in their pasture. At length he said with half a sigh that perhaps they ought to go.

"Ought?" she repeated softly.

"If we are to get anywhere today," he answered.

"Need we get anywhere?" she asked.

Her question sent delight through him like a flood. "Then you do not want to move camp today?" said he.

She shook her head.

At this he laid down his rod and came and sat by her. "I am very glad we shall not go till tomorrow," he murmured.

"Not tomorrow," she said. "Nor next day. Nor any day until we must."

And she stretched her hands out to the island and the stream exclaiming, "Nothing can surpass this!"

He took her in his arms. "You feel about it the way I do," he almost whispered. "I could not have hoped there'd be two of us to care so much."

Presently, while they remained without speaking by the pool, came a little wild animal swimming round the rock from above. It had not seen them, nor suspected their presence. They held themselves still, watching its alert head cross through the waves quickly and come down through the pool, and so swim to the other side. There it came out on a small stretch of sand, turned its gray head and its pointed black nose this way and that, never seeing them, and then rolled upon its back in the warm dry sand. After a minute of rolling, it got on its feet again, shook its fur, and trotted away.

Then the bridegroom husband opened his shy heart deep down.

"I am like that fellow," he said dreamily. "I have often done the same."

And stretching slowly his arms and legs, he lay full length upon his back, letting his head rest upon her. "If I could talk his animal language, I could talk to him," he pursued. "And he would say to me: 'Come and roll on the sands. Where's the use of fretting? What's the gain in being a man? Come roll on the sands with me.' That's what he would say." The Virginian paused. "But," he continued, "the trouble is, I am responsible. If that could only be forgot forever by you and me!"

Again he paused and went on, always dreamily. "Often when I have camped here, it has made me want to become the ground, become the water, become the trees, mix with the whole thing. Not know myself from it. Never unmix again. Why is that?" he demanded, looking at her. "What is it? You don't know, nor I don't. I wonder would everybody feel that way here?"

"I think not everybody," she answered.

"No; none except the ones who understand things they can't put words to. But you did!" He put up a hand and touched her softly. "You understood about this place. And that's what makes it—makes you and me as we are now—better than my dreams. And my dreams were pretty good."

He sighed with supreme quiet and happiness, and seemed to stretch his length closer to the earth. And so he lay, and talked to her as he had never talked to anyone, not even to himself. Thus she learned secrets of his heart new to her: his visits here, what they were to him, and why he had chosen it for their bridal camp. "What I did not know at all," he said, "was the way a man can be pining for—for this—and never guess what is the matter with him."

When he had finished talking, still he lay extended and serene; and she looked down at him and the wonderful change that had come over him, like a sunrise. Was this dreamy boy the man of two days ago? It seemed a distance immeasurable; yet it was two days only since that wedding eve when she had shrunk from him as he stood fierce and implacable. She could look back at that dark hour now, although she could not speak of it. She had seen destruction like sharp steel glittering in his eyes. Were these the same eyes? Was this youth with his black head of hair in her lap the creature with whom men did not trifle, whose hand knew how to deal death? Where had the man melted away to in this boy? For as she looked at him, he might have been no older than nineteen today. Not even at their first meeting—that night when his freakish spirit was uppermost—had he looked so young. This change their hours upon the island had wrought, filling his face with innocence.

By and by they made their nooning. In the afternoon she would have explored the nearer woods with him, or walked up the stream. But since this was to be their camp during several days, he made it more complete. He fashioned a rough bench and a table; around their tent he built a tall wind-break for better shelter in case of storm; and for the fire he gathered and cut much wood, and piled it up. So they were provided for, and so for six days and nights they stayed, finding no day or night long enough.

Once his hedge of boughs did them good service, for they had an afternoon of furious storm. The wind rocked the pines and ransacked the island, the sun went out, the black clouds rattled, and white bolts of lightning fell close by. The shower broke through the pine branches and poured upon the tent. But he had removed everything inside from where it could touch the canvas and so lead the water through, and the rain ran off into the ditch he had dug round the tent. While they sat within, looking out upon the bounding floods and the white lightning, she saw him glance at her apprehensively, and at once she answered his glance.

"I am not afraid," she said. "If a flame should consume us together now, what would it matter?"

And so they sat watching the storm till it was over, he with his face changed by her to a boy's, and she leavened with him.

When at last they were compelled to leave the island, or see no more of the mountains, it was not a final parting. They would come back for the last night before their journey ended. Furthermore, they promised each other like two children to come here every year upon their wedding day, and like two children they believed that this would be possible. But in after years they did come, more than once, to keep their wedding day upon the island, and upon each new visit were able to say to each other, "Better than our dreams."

For thirty days by the light of the sun and the campfire light they saw no faces except their own; and when they were silent it was all stillness, unless the wind passed among the pines, or some flowing water was near them. Sometimes at evening they came upon elk, or black-tailed deer, feeding out in the high parks of the mountains; and once from the edge of some concealing timber he showed her a bear, sitting with an old log lifted in its paws. She forbade him to kill the bear, or any creature that they did not require. He took her upward by trail and canyon, through the unfooted woods and along dwindling streams to their headwaters, lakes lying near the summit of the range, full of trout, with meadows of long grass and a thousand flowers, and above these the pinnacles of rock and snow.

They made their camps in many places, delaying several days here, and one night there, exploring the high solitudes together, and sinking deep in their romance. Sometimes when he was at work with their horses, or intent on casting his brown hackle for a fish, she would watch him with eyes that were fuller of love than of understanding. Perhaps she never came wholly to understand him; but in her complete love for him she found enough. He loved her with his whole man's power. She had listened to him tell her in words of transport, "I could enjoy dying"; yet she loved him more than that. He had come to her from a smoking pistol, able to bid her farewell—and she could not let him go. At the last white-hot edge of ordeal, it was she who renounced, and he who had his way. Nevertheless she found much more than enough, in spite of the sigh that now and again breathed through her happiness when she would watch him with eyes fuller of love than of understanding.

They could not speak of that grim wedding eve for a long while after; but the mountains brought them together upon all else in the world and their own lives. At the end they loved each other doubly more than at the beginning, because of these added confidences which they exchanged and shared. It was a new bliss to her to know a man's talk and thoughts, to be given so much of him; and to him it was a bliss still greater to melt from that reserve his lonely life had bred in him. He never would have guessed so much had been stored away in him, unexpressed till now. They did not want to go to Vermont and leave these mountains, but the day came when they had to turn their backs upon their dream. So they came out into the plains once more, well established in their familiarity, with only the journey still lying between themselves and Bennington.

"If you could," she said, laughing. "If only you could ride home like this."

"With Monte and my six-shooter?" he asked. "To your mother?"

"I don't think mother could resist the way you look on a horse."

But he said, "It's this way she's fearing I will come."

"I have made one discovery," she said. "You are fonder of good clothes than I am."

He grinned. "I cert'nly like 'em. But don't tell my friends. They would say it was marriage. When you see what I have got for Bennington's special benefit, you—why, you'll just trust your husband more than ever."

She undoubtedly did. After he had put on one particular suit, she arose and kissed him where he stood in it.

"Bennington will be sorrowful," he said. "No wild-west show, after all. And no ready-made guy, either." And he looked at himself in the glass with unbidden pleasure.

"How did you choose that?" she asked. "How did you know that homespun was exactly the thing for you?"

"Why, I have been noticing. I used to despise an Eastern man because his clothes were not Western. I was very young then, or maybe not so very young, as very—as what you saw I was when you first came to Bear Creek. A Western man is a good thing. And he generally knows that. But he has a heap to learn. And he generally don't know that. So I took to watching the Judge's Eastern visitors. There was that Mr. Ogden especially, from New Yawk—the gentleman that was there the time when I had to sit up all night with the missionary, yu' know. His clothes pleased me best of all. Fit him so well, and nothing flash. I got my ideas, and when I knew I was going to marry you, I sent my measure East—and I and the tailor are old enemies now."

Bennington probably was disappointed. To see get out of the train merely a tall man with a usual straw hat, and Scotch homespun suit of a rather better cut than most in Bennington—this was dull. And his conversation—when he indulged in any—seemed fit to come inside the house.

Mrs. Flynt took her revenge by sowing broadcast her thankfulness that poor Sam Bannett had been Molly's rejected suitor. He had done so much better for himself. Sam had married a rich Miss Van Scootzer, of the second families of Troy; and with their combined riches this happy couple still inhabit the most expensive residence in Hoosic Falls.

But most of Bennington soon began to say that Molly's cowboy could be invited anywhere and hold his own. The time came when they ceased to speak of him as a cowboy, and declared that she had shown remarkable sense. But this was not quite yet.

Did this bride and groom enjoy their visit to her family? Well—well, they did their best. Everybody did their best, even Sarah Bell. She said that she found nothing to object to in the Virginian; she told Molly so. Her husband Sam did better than that. He told Molly he considered that she was in luck. And poor Mrs. Wood, sitting on the sofa, conversed scrupulously and timidly with her novel son-in-law, and said to Molly that she was astonished to find him so gentle. And he was undoubtedly fine-looking; yes, very handsome. She believed that she would grow to like the Southern accent. Oh, yes! Everybody did their best; and, dear reader, if ever it has been your earthly portion to live with a number of people who were all doing their best, you do not need me to tell you what a heavenly atmosphere this creates.

And then the bride and groom went to see the old great-aunt over at Dunbarton.

Their first arrival, the one at Bennington, had been thus: Sam Bell had met them at the train, and Mrs. Wood, waiting in her parlor, had embraced her daughter and received her son-in-law. Among them they had managed to make the occasion as completely mournful as any family party can be, with the window blinds up. "And with you present, my dear," said Sam Bell to Sarah, "the absence of a coffin was not felt."

But at Dunbarton the affair went off differently. The heart of the ancient lady had taught her better things. From Bennington to Dunbarton is the good part of a day's journey, and they drove up to the gate in the afternoon. The great-aunt was in her garden, picking some August flowers, and she called as the carriage stopped, "Bring my nephew here, my dear, before you go into the house."

At this, Molly, stepping out of the carriage, squeezed her husband's hand. "I knew that she would be lovely," she whispered to him. And then she ran to her aunt's arms, and let him follow. He came slowly, hat in hand.

The old lady advanced to meet him, trembling a little, and holding out her hand to him. "Welcome, nephew," she said. "What a tall fellow you are, to be sure. Stand off, sir, and let me look at you."

The Virginian obeyed, blushing from his black hair to his collar.

Then his new relative turned to her niece, and gave her a flower. "Put this in his coat, my dear," she said. "And I think I understand why you wanted to marry him."

After this the maid came and showed them to their rooms. Left alone in her garden, the great-aunt sank on a bench and sat there for some time; for emotion had made her very weak.

Upstairs, Molly, sitting on the Virginian's knee, put the flower in his coat, and then laid her head upon his shoulder.

"I didn't know old ladies could be that way," he said. "D' yu' reckon there are many?"

"Oh, I don't know," said the girl. "I'm so happy!"

Now at tea, and during the evening, the great-aunt carried out her plans still further. At first she did the chief part of the talking herself. Nor did she ask questions about Wyoming too soon. She reached that in her own way, and found out the one thing that she desired to know. It was through General Stark that she led up to it.

"There he is," she said, showing the family portrait. "And a rough time he must have had of it now and then. New Hampshire was full of fine young men in those days. But nowadays most of them have gone away to seek their fortunes in the West. Do they find them, I wonder?"

"Yes, ma'am. All the good ones do."

"But you cannot all be—what is the name? Cattle Kings."

"That's having its day, ma'am, right now. And we are getting ready for the change—some of us are."

"And what may be the change, and when is it to come?"

"When the natural pasture is eaten off," he explained. "I have seen that coming a long while. And if the thieves are going to make us drive our stock away, we'll drive it. If they don't, we'll have big pastures fenced, and hay and shelter ready for winter. What we'll spend in improvements, we'll more than save in wages. I am well fixed for the new conditions. And then, when I took up my land, I chose a place where there is coal. It will not be long before the new railroad needs that."

Thus the old lady learned more of her niece's husband in one evening than the Bennington family had ascertained during his whole sojourn with them. For by touching upon Wyoming and its future, she roused him to talk. He found her mind alive to Western questions: irrigation, the Indians, the forests; and so he expanded, revealing to her his wide observation and his shrewd intelligence. He forgot entirely to be shy. She sent Molly to bed, and kept him talking for an hour. Then she showed him old things that she was proud of, "because," she said, "we, too, had something to do with making our country. And now go to Molly, or you'll both think me a tiresome old lady."

"I think—" he began, but was not quite equal to expressing what he thought, and suddenly his shyness flooded him again.

"In that case, nephew," said she, "I'm afraid you'll have to kiss me good night."

And so she dismissed him to his wife, and to happiness greater than either of them had known since they had left the mountains and come to the East. "He'll do," she said to herself, nodding.

Their visit to Dunbarton was all happiness and reparation for the doleful days at Bennington. The old lady gave much comfort and advice to her niece in private, and when they came to leave, she stood at the front door holding both their hands a moment.

"God bless you, my dears," she told them. "And when you come next time, I'll have the nursery ready."

And so it happened that before she left this world, the great-aunt was able to hold in her arms the first of their many children.

Judge Henry at Sunk Creek had his wedding present ready. His growing affairs in Wyoming needed his presence in many places distant from his ranch, and he made the Virginian his partner. When the thieves prevailed at length, as they did, forcing cattle owners to leave the country or be ruined, the Virginian had forestalled this crash. The herds were driven away to Montana. Then, in 1889, came the cattle war, when, after putting their men in office, and coming to own some of the newspapers, the thieves brought ruin on themselves as well. For in a broken country there is nothing left to steal.

But the railroad came, and built a branch to that land of the Virginian's where the coal was. By that time he was an important man, with a strong grip on many various enterprises, and able to give his wife all and more than she asked or desired.

Sometimes she missed the Bear Creek days, when she and he had ridden together, and sometimes she declared that his work would kill him. But it does not seem to have done so. Their eldest boy rides the horse Monte; and, strictly between ourselves, I think his father is going to live a long while.

# O Pioneers!

## Willa Cather

### PART I. THE WILD LAND

### CHAPTER I

One January day, thirty years ago, the little town of Hanover, anchored on a windy Nebraska tableland, was trying not to be blown away. A mist of fine snowflakes was curling and eddying about the cluster of low drab buildings huddled on the gray prairie, under a gray sky. The dwelling-houses were set about haphazard on the tough prairie sod; some of them looked as if they had been moved in overnight, and others as if they were straying off by themselves, headed straight for the open plain. None of them had any appearance of permanence, and the howling wind blew under them as well as over them. The main street was a deeply rutted road, now frozen hard, which ran from the squat red railway station and the grain "elevator" at the north end of the town to the lumber yard and the horse pond at the south end. On either side of this road straggled two uneven rows of wooden buildings; the general merchandise stores, the two banks, the drug store, the feed store, the saloon, the post-office. The board sidewalks were gray with trampled snow, but at two o'clock in the afternoon the shopkeepers, having come back from dinner, were keeping well behind their frosty windows. The children were all in school, and there was nobody abroad in the streets but a few rough-looking countrymen in coarse overcoats, with their long caps pulled down to their noses. Some of them had brought their wives to town, and now and then a red or a plaid shawl flashed out of one store into the shelter of another. At the hitch-bars along the street a few heavy work-horses, harnessed to farm wagons, shivered under their blankets. About the station everything was quiet, for there would not be another train in until night.

On the sidewalk in front of one of the stores sat a little Swede boy, crying bitterly. He was about five years old. His black cloth coat was much too big for him and made him look like a little old man. His shrunken brown flannel dress had been washed many times and left a long stretch of stocking between the hem of his skirt and the tops of his clumsy, copper-toed shoes.

His cap was pulled down over his ears; his nose and his chubby cheeks were chapped and red with cold. He cried quietly, and the few people who hurried by did not notice him. He was afraid to stop anyone, afraid to go into the store and ask for help, so he sat wringing his long sleeves and looking up a telegraph pole beside him, whimpering, "My kitten, oh, my kitten! Her will fweeze!" At the top of the pole crouched a shivering gray kitten, mewing faintly and clinging desperately to the wood with her claws. The boy had been left at the store while his sister went to the doctor's office, and in her absence a dog had chased his kitten up the pole. The little creature had never been so high before, and she was too frightened to move. Her master was sunk in despair. He was a little country boy, and this village was to him a very strange and perplexing place, where people wore fine clothes and had hard hearts. He always felt shy and awkward here, and wanted to hide behind things for fear someone might laugh at him. Just now, he was too unhappy to care who laughed. At last he seemed to see a ray of hope: his sister was coming, and he got up and ran toward her in his heavy shoes.

His sister was a tall, strong girl, and she walked rapidly and resolutely, as if she knew exactly where she was going and what she was going to do next. She wore a man's long ulster (not as if it were an affliction, but as if it were very comfortable and belonged to her; carried it like a young soldier), and a round plush cap, tied down with a thick veil. She had a serious, thoughtful face, and her clear, deep blue eyes were fixed intently on the distance, without seeming to see anything, as if she were in trouble. She did not notice the little boy until he pulled her by the coat. Then she stopped short and stooped down to wipe his wet face.

"Why, Emil! I told you to stay in the store and not to come out. What is the matter with you?"

"My kitten, sister, my kitten! A man put her out, and a dog chased her up there." His forefinger, projecting from the sleeve of his coat, pointed up to the wretched little creature on the pole.

"Oh, Emil! Didn't I tell you she'd get us into trouble of some kind, if you brought her? What made you tease me so? But there, I ought to have known better myself." She went to the foot of the pole and held out her arms, crying, "Kitty, kitty, kitty," but the kitten only mewed and faintly waved its tail. Alexandra turned away decidedly. "No, she won't come down. Somebody will have to go up after her. I saw the Linstrums' wagon in town. I'll go and see if I can find Carl. Maybe he can do something. Only you must stop crying, or I won't go a step. Where's your comforter? Did you leave it in the store? Never mind. Hold still, till I put this on you."

She unwound the brown veil from her head and tied it about his throat. A shabby little traveling man, who was just then coming out of the store on his way to the saloon, stopped and gazed stupidly at the shining mass of hair she bared when she took off her veil; two thick braids, pinned about her head in the German way, with a fringe of reddish-yellow curls blowing out from under her cap. He took his cigar out of his mouth and held the wet end between the fingers of his woolen glove. "My God, girl, what a head of hair!" he exclaimed, quite innocently and foolishly. She stabbed him with a glance of Amazonian fierceness and drew in her lower lip—most unnecessary severity. It gave the little clothing drummer such a start that he actually let his cigar fall to the sidewalk and went off weakly in the teeth of the wind to the saloon. His hand was still unsteady when he took his glass from the bartender. His feeble flirtatious instincts had been crushed before, but never so mercilessly. He felt cheap and ill-used, as if someone had taken advantage of him. When a drummer had been knocking about in little drab towns and crawling across the wintry country in dirty smoking-cars, was he to be blamed if, when he chanced upon a fine human creature, he suddenly wished himself more of a man?

While the little drummer was drinking to recover his nerve, Alexandra hurried to the drug store as the most likely place to find Carl Linstrum. There he was, turning over a portfolio of chromo "studies" which the druggist sold to the Hanover women who did china-painting. Alexandra explained her predicament, and the boy followed her to the corner, where Emil still sat by the pole.

"I'll have to go up after her, Alexandra. I think at the depot they have some spikes I can strap on my feet. Wait a minute." Carl thrust his hands into his pockets, lowered his head, and darted up the street against the north wind. He was a tall boy of fifteen, slight and narrow-chested. When he came back with the spikes, Alexandra asked him what he had done with his overcoat.

"I left it in the drug store. I couldn't climb in it, anyhow. Catch me if I fall, Emil," he called back as he began his ascent. Alexandra watched him anxiously; the cold was bitter enough on the ground. The kitten would not budge an inch. Carl had to go to the very top of the pole, and then had some difficulty in tearing her from her hold. When he reached the ground, he handed the cat to her tearful little master. "Now go into the store with her, Emil, and get warm." He opened the door for the child. "Wait a minute, Alexandra. Why can't I drive for you as far as our place? It's getting colder every minute. Have you seen the doctor?"

"Yes. He is coming over tomorrow. But he says father can't get better; can't get well." The girl's lip trembled. She looked fixedly up the bleak street as if she were gathering her strength to face something, as if she were trying with all her might to grasp a situation which, no matter how painful, must be met and dealt with somehow. The wind flapped the skirts of her heavy coat about her.

Carl did not say anything, but she felt his sympathy. He, too, was lonely. He was a thin, frail boy, with brooding dark eyes, very quiet in all his movements. There was a delicate pallor in his thin face, and his mouth was too sensitive for a boy's. The lips had already a little curl of bitterness and skepticism. The two friends stood for a few moments on the windy street corner, not speaking a word, as two travelers, who have lost their way, sometimes stand and admit their perplexity in silence. When Carl turned away he said, "I'll see to your team." Alexandra went into the store to have her purchases packed in the egg-boxes, and to get warm before she set out on her long cold drive.

When she looked for Emil, she found him sitting on a step of the staircase that led up to the clothing and carpet department. He was playing with a little Bohemian girl, Marie Tovesky, who was tying her handkerchief over the kitten's head for a bonnet. Marie was a stranger in the country, having come from Omaha with her mother to visit her uncle, Joe Tovesky. She was a dark child, with brown curly hair, like a brunette doll's, a coaxing little red mouth, and round, yellow-brown eyes. Everyone noticed her eyes; the brown iris had golden glints that made them look like gold-stone, or, in softer lights, like that Colorado mineral called tiger-eye.

The country children thereabouts wore their dresses to their shoe-tops, but this city child was dressed in what was then called the "Kate Greenaway" manner, and her red cashmere frock, gathered full from the yoke, came almost to the floor. This, with her poke bonnet, gave her the look of a quaint little woman. She had a white fur tippet about her neck and made no fussy objections when Emil fingered it admiringly. Alexandra had not the heart to take him away from so pretty a playfellow, and she let them tease the kitten together until Joe Tovesky came in noisily and picked up his little niece, setting her on his shoulder for everyone to see. His children were all boys, and he adored this little creature. His cronies formed a circle about him, admiring and teasing the little girl, who took their jokes with great good nature. They were all delighted with her, for they seldom saw so pretty and carefully nurtured a child. They told her that she must choose one of them for a sweetheart, and each began pressing his suit and offering her bribes; candy, and little pigs, and spotted calves. She looked archly into the big, brown, mustached faces, smelling of spirits and tobacco, then she ran her tiny forefinger delicately over Joe's bristly chin and said, "Here is my sweetheart."

The Bohemians roared with laughter, and Marie's uncle hugged her until she cried, "Please don't, Uncle Joe! You hurt me." Each of Joe's friends gave her a bag of candy, and she kissed them all around, though she did not like country candy very well. Perhaps that was why she bethought herself of Emil. "Let me down, Uncle Joe," she said, "I want to give some of my candy to that nice little boy I found." She walked graciously over to Emil, followed by her lusty admirers, who formed a new circle and teased the little boy until he hid his face in his sister's skirts, and she had to scold him for being such a baby.

The farm people were making preparations to start for home. The women were checking over their groceries and pinning their big red shawls about their heads. The men were buying tobacco and candy with what money they had left, were showing each other new boots and gloves and blue flannel shirts. Three big Bohemians were drinking raw alcohol, tinctured with oil of cinnamon. This was said to fortify one effectually against the cold, and they smacked their lips after each pull at the flask. Their volubility drowned every other noise in the place, and the overheated store sounded of their spirited language as it reeked of pipe smoke, damp woolens, and kerosene.

Carl came in, wearing his overcoat and carrying a wooden box with a brass handle. "Come," he said, "I've fed and watered your team, and the wagon is ready." He carried Emil out and tucked him down in the straw in the wagonbox. The heat had made the little boy sleepy, but he still clung to his kitten.

"You were awful good to climb so high and get my kitten, Carl. When I get big I'll climb and get little boys' kittens for them," he murmured drowsily. Before the horses were over the first hill, Emil and his cat were both fast asleep.

Although it was only four o'clock, the winter day was fading. The road led southwest, toward the streak of pale, watery light that glimmered in the leaden sky. The light fell upon the two sad young faces that were turned mutely toward it: upon the eyes of the girl, who seemed to be looking with such anguished perplexity into the future; upon the sombre eyes of the boy, who seemed already to be looking into the past. The little town behind them had vanished as if it had never been, had fallen behind the swell of the prairie, and the stern frozen country received them into its bosom. The homesteads were few and far apart; here and there a windmill gaunt against the sky, a sod house crouching in a hollow. But the great fact was the land itself, which seemed to overwhelm the little beginnings of human society that struggled in its sombre wastes. It was from facing this vast hardness that the boy's mouth had become so bitter; because he felt that men were too weak to make any mark here, that the land wanted to be let alone, to preserve its own fierce strength, its peculiar, savage kind of beauty, its uninterrupted mournfulness.

The wagon jolted along over the frozen road. The two friends had less to say to each other than usual, as if the cold had somehow penetrated to their hearts.

"Did Lou and Oscar go to the Blue to cut wood today?" Carl asked.

"Yes. I'm almost sorry I let them go, it's turned so cold. But mother frets if the wood gets low." She stopped and put her hand to her forehead, brushing back her hair. "I don't know what is to become of us, Carl, if father has to die. I don't dare to think about it. I wish we could all go with him and let the grass grow back over everything."

Carl made no reply. Just ahead of them was the Norwegian graveyard, where the grass had, indeed, grown back over everything, shaggy and red, hiding even the wire fence. Carl realized that he was not a very helpful companion, but there was nothing he could say.

"Of course," Alexandra went on, steadying her voice a little, "the boys are strong and work hard, but we've always depended so on father that I don't see how we can go ahead. I almost feel as if there were nothing to go ahead for."

"Does your father know?"

"Yes, I think he does. He lies and counts on his fingers all day. I think he is trying to count up what he is leaving for us. It's a comfort to him that my chickens are laying right on through the cold weather and bringing in a little money. I wish we could keep his mind off such things, but I don't have much time to be with him now."

"I wonder if he'd like to have me bring my magic lantern over some evening?"

Alexandra turned her face toward him. "Oh, Carl! Have you got it?"

"Yes. It's back there in the straw. Didn't you notice the box I was carrying? I tried it all morning in the drugstore cellar, and it worked ever so well, makes fine big pictures."

"What are they about?"

"Oh, hunting pictures in Germany, and Robinson Crusoe and funny pictures about cannibals. I'm going to paint some slides for it on glass, out of the Hans Andersen book."

Alexandra seemed actually cheered. There is often a good deal of the child left in people who have had to grow up too soon. "Do bring it over, Carl. I can hardly wait to see it, and I'm sure it will please father. Are the pictures colored? Then I know he'll like them. He likes the calendars I get him in town. I wish I could get more. You must leave me here, mustn't you? It's been nice to have company."

Carl stopped the horses and looked dubiously up at the black sky. "It's pretty dark. Of course the horses will take you home, but I think I'd better light your lantern, in case you should need it."

He gave her the reins and climbed back into the wagon-box, where he crouched down and made a tent of his overcoat. After a dozen trials he succeeded in lighting the lantern, which he placed in front of Alexandra, half covering it with a blanket so that the light would not shine in her eyes. "Now, wait until I find my box. Yes, here it is. Good-night, Alexandra. Try not to worry." Carl sprang to the ground and ran off across the fields toward the Linstrum homestead. "Hoo, hoo-o-o-o!" he called back as he disappeared over a ridge and dropped into a sand gully. The wind answered him like an echo, "Hoo, hoo-o-o-o-o-o!" Alexandra drove off alone. The rattle of her wagon was lost in the howling of the wind, but her lantern, held firmly between her feet, made a moving point of light along the highway, going deeper and deeper into the dark country.

## CHAPTER II

On one of the ridges of that wintry waste stood the low log house in which John Bergson was dying. The Bergson homestead was easier to find than many another, because it overlooked Norway Creek, a shallow, muddy stream that sometimes flowed, and sometimes stood still, at the bottom of a winding ravine with steep, shelving sides overgrown with brush and cottonwoods and dwarf ash. This creek gave a sort of identity to the farms that bordered upon it. Of all the bewildering things about a new country, the absence of human landmarks is one of the most depressing and disheartening. The houses on the Divide were small and were usually tucked away in low places; you did not see them until you came directly upon them. Most of them were built of the sod itself, and were only the unescapable ground in another form. The roads were but faint tracks in the grass, and the fields were scarcely noticeable. The record of the plow was insignificant, like the feeble scratches on stone left by prehistoric races, so indeterminate that they may, after all, be only the markings of glaciers, and not a record of human strivings.

In eleven long years John Bergson had made but little impression upon the wild land he had come to tame. It was still a wild thing that had its ugly moods; and no one knew when they were likely to come, or why. Mischance hung over it. Its Genius was unfriendly to man. The sick man was feeling this as he lay looking out of the window, after the doctor had left him, on the day following Alexandra's trip to town. There it lay outside his door, the same land, the same lead-colored miles. He knew every ridge and draw and gully between him and the horizon. To the south, his plowed fields; to the east, the sod stables, the cattle corral, the pond—and then the grass.

Bergson went over in his mind the things that had held him back. One winter his cattle had perished in a blizzard. The next summer one of his plow horses broke its leg in a prairie dog hole and had to be shot. Another summer he lost his hogs from cholera, and a valuable stallion died from a rattlesnake bite. Time and again his crops had failed. He had lost two children, boys, that came between Lou and Emil, and there had been the cost of sickness and death. Now, when he had at last struggled out of debt, he was going to die himself. He was only forty-six, and had, of course, counted upon more time.

Bergson had spent his first five years on the Divide getting into debt, and the last six getting out. He had paid off his mortgages and had ended pretty much where he began, with the land. He owned exactly six hundred and forty acres of what stretched outside his door; his own original homestead and timber claim, making three hundred and twenty acres, and the half-section adjoining, the homestead of a younger brother who had given up the fight, gone back to Chicago to work in a fancy bakery and distinguish himself in a Swedish athletic club. So far John had not attempted to cultivate the second half-section, but used it for pasture land, and one of his sons rode herd there in open weather.

John Bergson had the Old-World belief that land, in itself, is desirable. But this land was an enigma. It was like a horse that no one knows how to break to harness, that runs wild and kicks things to pieces. He had an idea that no one understood how to farm it properly, and this he often discussed with Alexandra. Their neighbors, certainly, knew even less about farming than he did. Many of them had never worked on a farm until they took up their homesteads. They had been *handwerkers* at home; tailors, locksmiths, joiners, cigar-makers, etc. Bergson himself had worked in a shipyard.

For weeks, John Bergson had been thinking about these things. His bed stood in the sitting room, next to the kitchen. Through the day, while the baking and washing and ironing were going on, the father lay and looked up at the roof beams that he himself had hewn, or out at the cattle in the corral. He counted the cattle over and over. It diverted him to speculate as to how much weight each of the steers would probably put on by spring. He often called his daughter in to talk to her about this. Before Alexandra was twelve years old she had begun to be a help to him, and as she grew older he had come to depend more and more upon her resourcefulness and good judgment. His boys were willing enough to work, but when he talked with them they usually irritated him. It was Alexandra who read the papers and followed the markets, and who learned by the mistakes of their neighbors. It was Alexandra who could always tell about what it had cost to fatten each steer, and who could guess the weight of a hog before it went on the scales closer than John Bergson himself. Lou and Oscar were industrious, but he could never teach them to use their heads about their work.

Alexandra, her father often said to himself, was like her grandfather; which was his way of saying that she was intelligent. John Bergson's father had been a shipbuilder, a man of considerable force and of some fortune. Late in life he married a second time, a Stockholm woman of questionable character, much younger than he, who goaded him into every sort of extravagance. On the shipbuilder's part, this marriage was an infatuation, the despairing folly of a powerful man who cannot bear to grow old. In a few years his unprincipled wife warped the probity of a lifetime. He speculated, lost his own fortune and funds entrusted to him by poor seafaring men, and died disgraced, leaving his children nothing. But when all was said, he had come up from the sea himself, had built up a proud little business with no capital but his own skill and foresight, and had proved himself a man. In his daughter, John Bergson recognized the strength of will, and the simple direct way of thinking things out, that had characterized his father in his better days. He would much rather, of course, have seen this likeness in one of his sons, but it was not a question of choice. As he lay there day after day he had to accept the situation as it was, and to be thankful that there was one among his children to whom he could entrust the future of his family and the possibilities of his hard-won land.

The winter twilight was fading. The sick man heard his wife strike a match in the kitchen, and the light of a lamp glimmered through the cracks of the door. It seemed like a light shining far away. He turned painfully in his bed and looked at his white hands, with all the work gone out of them. He was ready to give up, he felt. He did not know how it had come about, but he was quite willing to go deep under his fields and rest, where the plow could not find him. He was tired of making mistakes. He was content to leave the tangle to other hands; he thought of his Alexandra's strong ones.

*"Dotter,"* he called feebly, *"Dotter!"* He heard her quick step and saw her tall figure appear in the doorway, with the light of the lamp behind her. He felt her youth and strength, how easily she moved and stooped and lifted. But he would not have had it again if he could, not he! He knew the end too well to wish to begin again. He knew where it all went to, what it all became.

His daughter came and lifted him up on his pillows. She called him by an old Swedish name that she used to call him when she was little and took his dinner to him in the shipyard.

"Tell the boys to come here, daughter. I want to speak to them."

"They are feeding the horses, father. They have just come back from the Blue. Shall I call them?"

He sighed. "No, no. Wait until they come in. Alexandra, you will have to do the best you can for your brothers. Everything will come on you."

"I will do all I can, father."

"Don't let them get discouraged and go off like Uncle Otto. I want them to keep the land."

"We will, father. We will never lose the land."

There was a sound of heavy feet in the kitchen. Alexandra went to the door and beckoned to her brothers, two strapping boys of seventeen and nineteen. They came in and stood at the foot of the bed. Their father looked at them searchingly, though it was too dark to see their faces; they were just the same boys, he told himself, he had not been mistaken in them. The square head and heavy shoulders belonged to Oscar, the elder. The younger boy was quicker, but vacillating.

"Boys," said the father wearily, "I want you to keep the land together and to be guided by your sister. I have talked to her since I have been sick, and she knows all my wishes. I want no quarrels among my children, and so long as there is one house there must be one head. Alexandra is the oldest, and she knows my wishes. She will do the best she can. If she makes mistakes, she will not make so many as I have made. When you marry, and want a house of your own, the land will be divided fairly, according to the courts. But for the next few years you will have it hard, and you must all keep together. Alexandra will manage the best she can."

Oscar, who was usually the last to speak, replied because he was the older, "Yes, father. It would be so anyway, without your speaking. We will all work the place together."

"And you will be guided by your sister, boys, and be good brothers to her, and good sons to your mother? That is good. And Alexandra must not work in the fields anymore. There is no necessity now. Hire a man when you need help. She can make much more with her eggs and butter than the wages of a man. It was one of my mistakes that I did not find that out sooner. Try to break a little more land every year; sod corn is good for fodder. Keep turning the land, and always put up more hay than you need. Don't grudge your mother a little time for plowing her garden and setting out fruit trees, even if it comes in a busy season. She has been a good mother to you, and she has always missed the old country."

When they went back to the kitchen the boys sat down silently at the table. Throughout the meal they looked down at their plates and did not lift their red eyes. They did not eat much, although they had been working in the cold all day, and there was a rabbit stewed in gravy for supper, and prune pies.

John Bergson had married beneath him, but he had married a good housewife. Mrs. Bergson was a fair-skinned, corpulent woman, heavy and placid like her son, Oscar, but there was something comfortable about her; perhaps it was her own love of comfort. For eleven years she had worthily striven to maintain some semblance of household order amid conditions that made order very difficult. Habit was very strong with Mrs. Bergson, and her unremitting efforts to repeat the routine of her old life among new surroundings had done a great deal to keep the family from disintegrating morally and getting careless in their ways. The Bergsons had a log house, for instance, only because Mrs. Bergson would not live in a sod house. She missed the fish diet of her own country, and twice every summer she sent the boys to the river, twenty miles to the southward, to fish for channel cat. When the children were little she used to load them all into the wagon, the baby in its crib, and go fishing herself.

Alexandra often said that if her mother were cast upon a desert island, she would thank God for her deliverance, make a garden, and find something to preserve. Preserving was almost a mania with Mrs. Bergson. Stout as she was, she roamed the scrubby banks of Norway Creek looking for fox grapes and goose plums, like a wild creature in search of prey. She made a yellow jam of the insipid ground-cherries that grew on the prairie, flavoring it with lemon peel; and she made a sticky dark conserve of garden tomatoes. She had experimented even with the rank buffalo-pea, and she could not see a fine bronze cluster of them without shaking her head and murmuring, "What a pity!" When there was nothing more to preserve, she began to pickle. The amount of sugar she used in these processes was sometimes a serious drain upon the family resources. She was a good mother, but she was glad when her children were old enough not to be in her way in the kitchen. She had never quite forgiven John Bergson for bringing her to the end of the earth; but, now that she was there, she wanted to be let alone to reconstruct her old life in so far as that was possible. She could still take some comfort in the world if she had bacon in the cave, glass jars on the shelves, and sheets in the press. She disapproved of all her neighbors because of their slovenly housekeeping, and the women thought her very proud. Once when Mrs. Bergson, on her way to Norway Creek, stopped to see old Mrs. Lee, the old woman hid in the haymow "for fear Mis' Bergson would catch her barefoot."

## CHAPTER III

One Sunday afternoon in July, six months after John Bergson's death, Carl was sitting in the doorway of the Linstrum kitchen, dreaming over an illustrated paper, when he heard the rattle of a wagon along the hill road. Looking up he recognized the Bergsons' team, with two seats in the wagon, which meant they were off for a pleasure excursion. Oscar and Lou, on the front seat, wore their cloth hats and coats, never worn except on Sundays, and Emil, on the second seat with Alexandra, sat proudly in his new trousers, made from a pair of his father's, and a pink-striped shirt, with a wide ruffled collar. Oscar stopped the horses and waved to Carl, who caught up his hat and ran through the melon patch to join them.

"Want to go with us?" Lou called. "We're going to Crazy Ivar's to buy a hammock."

"Sure." Carl ran up panting, and clambering over the wheel sat down beside Emil. "I've always wanted to see Ivar's pond. They say it's the biggest in all the country. Aren't you afraid to go to Ivar's in that new shirt, Emil? He might want it and take it right off your back."

Emil grinned. "I'd be awful scared to go," he admitted, "if you big boys weren't along to take care of me. Did you ever hear him howl, Carl? People say sometimes he runs about the country howling at night because he is afraid the Lord will destroy him. Mother thinks he must have done something awful wicked."

Lou looked back and winked at Carl. "What would you do, Emil, if you was out on the prairie by yourself and seen him coming?"

Emil stared. "Maybe I could hide in a badger-hole," he suggested doubtfully.

"But suppose there wasn't any badger-hole," Lou persisted. "Would you run?"

"No, I'd be too scared to run," Emil admitted mournfully, twisting his fingers. "I guess I'd sit right down on the ground and say my prayers."

The big boys laughed, and Oscar brandished his whip over the broad backs of the horses.

"He wouldn't hurt you, Emil," said Carl persuasively. "He came to doctor our mare when she ate green corn and swelled up most as big as the water-tank. He petted her just like you do your cats. I couldn't understand much he said, for he don't talk any English, but he kept patting her and groaning as if he had the pain himself, and saying, 'There now, sister, that's easier, that's better!'"

Lou and Oscar laughed, and Emil giggled delightedly and looked up at his sister.

"I don't think he knows anything at all about doctoring," said Oscar scornfully. "They say when horses have distemper he takes the medicine himself, and then prays over the horses."

Alexandra spoke up. "That's what the Crows said, but he cured their horses, all the same. Some days his mind is cloudy, like. But if you can get him on a clear day, you can learn a great deal from him. He understands animals. Didn't I see him take the horn off the Berquist's cow when she had torn it loose and went crazy? She was tearing all over the place, knocking herself against things. And at last she ran out on the roof of the old dugout and her legs went through and there she stuck, bellowing. Ivar came running with his white bag, and the moment he got to her she was quiet and let him saw her horn off and daub the place with tar."

Emil had been watching his sister, his face reflecting the sufferings of the cow. "And then didn't it hurt her anymore?" he asked.

Alexandra patted him. "No, not anymore. And in two days they could use her milk again."

The road to Ivar's homestead was a very poor one. He had settled in the rough country across the county line, where no one lived but some Russians— half a dozen families who dwelt together in one long house, divided off like barracks. Ivar had explained his choice by saying that the fewer neighbors he had, the fewer temptations. Nevertheless, when one considered that his chief business was horse-doctoring, it seemed rather short-sighted of him to live in the most inaccessible place he could find. The Bergson wagon lurched along over the rough hummocks and grass banks, followed the bottom of winding draws, or skirted the margin of wide lagoons, where the golden coreopsis grew up out of the clear water and the wild ducks rose with a whirr of wings.

Lou looked after them helplessly. "I wish I'd brought my gun, anyway, Alexandra," he said fretfully. "I could have hidden it under the straw in the bottom of the wagon."

"Then we'd have had to lie to Ivar. Besides, they say he can smell dead birds. And if he knew, we wouldn't get anything out of him, not even a hammock. I want to talk to him, and he won't talk sense if he's angry. It makes him foolish."

Lou sniffed. "Whoever heard of him talking sense, anyhow! I'd rather have ducks for supper than Crazy Ivar's tongue."

Emil was alarmed. "Oh, but, Lou, you don't want to make him mad! He might howl!"

They all laughed again, and Oscar urged the horses up the crumbling side of a clay bank. They had left the lagoons and the red grass behind them. In Crazy Ivar's country the grass was short and gray, the draws deeper than they were in the Bergsons' neighborhood, and the land was all broken up into hillocks and clay ridges. The wild flowers disappeared, and only in the bottom of the draws and gullies grew a few of the very toughest and hardiest: shoestring, and ironweed, and snow-on-the-mountain.

"Look, look, Emil, there's Ivar's big pond!" Alexandra pointed to a shining sheet of water that lay at the bottom of a shallow draw. At one end of the pond was an earthen dam, planted with green willow bushes, and above it a door and a single window were set into the hillside. You would not have seen them at all but for the reflection of the sunlight upon the four panes of window-glass. And that was all you saw. Not a shed, not a corral, not a well, not even a path broken in the curly grass. But for the piece of rusty stovepipe sticking up through the sod, you could have walked over the roof of Ivar's dwelling without dreaming that you were near a human habitation. Ivar had lived for three years in the clay bank, without defiling the face of nature any more than the coyote that had lived there before him had done.

When the Bergsons drove over the hill, Ivar was sitting in the doorway of his house, reading the Norwegian Bible. He was a queerly shaped old man, with a thick, powerful body set on short bow-legs. His shaggy white hair, falling in a thick mane about his ruddy cheeks, made him look older than he was. He was barefoot, but he wore a clean shirt of unbleached cotton, open at the neck. He always put on a clean shirt when Sunday morning came round, though he never went to church. He had a peculiar religion of his own and could not get on with any of the denominations. Often he did not see anybody from one week's end to another. He kept a calendar, and every morning he checked off a day, so that he was never in any doubt as to which day of the week it was. Ivar hired himself out in threshing and corn-husking time, and he doctored sick animals when he was sent for. When he was at home, he made hammocks out of twine and committed chapters of the Bible to memory.

Ivar found contentment in the solitude he had sought out for himself. He disliked the litter of human dwellings: the broken food, the bits of broken china, the old wash-boilers and tea-kettles thrown into the sunflower patch. He preferred the cleanness and tidiness of the wild sod. He always said that the badgers had cleaner houses than people, and that when he took a housekeeper her name would be Mrs. Badger. He best expressed his preference for his wild homestead by saying that his Bible seemed truer to him there. If one stood in the doorway of his cave, and looked off at the rough land, the smiling sky, the curly grass white in the hot sunlight; if one listened to the rapturous song of the lark, the drumming of the quail, the burr of the locust against that vast silence, one understood what Ivar meant.

On this Sunday afternoon his face shone with happiness. He closed the book on his knee, keeping the place with his horny finger, and repeated softly:

> He sendeth the springs into the valleys, which run among the hills;
> They give drink to every beast of the field; the wild asses quench their thirst.
> The trees of the Lord are full of sap; the cedars of Lebanon which he hath planted;
> Where the birds make their nests: as for the stork, the fir trees are her house.
> The high hills are a refuge for the wild goats; and the rocks for the conies.

Before he opened his Bible again, Ivar heard the Bergsons' wagon approaching, and he sprang up and ran toward it.

"No guns, no guns!" he shouted, waving his arms distractedly.

"No, Ivar, no guns," Alexandra called reassuringly.

He dropped his arms and went up to the wagon, smiling amiably and looking at them out of his pale blue eyes.

"We want to buy a hammock, if you have one," Alexandra explained, "and my little brother, here, wants to see your big pond, where so many birds come."

Ivar smiled foolishly, and began rubbing the horses' noses and feeling about their mouths behind the bits. "Not many birds just now. A few ducks this morning; and some snipe come to drink. But there was a crane last week. She spent one night and came back the next evening. I don't know why. It is not her season, of course. Many of them go over in the fall. Then the pond is full of strange voices every night."

Alexandra translated for Carl, who looked thoughtful. "Ask him, Alexandra, if it is true that a sea gull came here once. I have heard so."

She had some difficulty in making the old man understand.

He looked puzzled at first, then smote his hands together as he remembered. "Oh, yes, yes! A big white bird with long wings and pink feet. My! what a voice she had! She came in the afternoon and kept flying about the pond and screaming until dark. She was in trouble of some sort, but I could not understand her. She was going over to the other ocean, maybe, and did not know how far it was. She was afraid of never getting there. She was more mournful than our birds here; she cried in the night. She saw the light from my window and darted up to it. Maybe she thought my house was a boat, she was such a wild thing. Next morning, when the sun rose, I went out to take her food, but she flew up into the sky and went on her way." Ivar ran his fingers through his thick hair. "I have many strange birds stop with me here. They come from very far away and are great company. I hope you boys never shoot wild birds?"

Lou and Oscar grinned, and Ivar shook his bushy head. "Yes, I know boys are thoughtless. But these wild things are God's birds. He watches over them and counts them, as we do our cattle; Christ says so in the New Testament."

"Now, Ivar," Lou asked, "may we water our horses at your pond and give them some feed? It's a bad road to your place."

"Yes, yes, it is." The old man scrambled about and began to loose the tugs. "A bad road, eh, girls? And the bay with a colt at home!"

Oscar brushed the old man aside. "We'll take care of the horses, Ivar. You'll be finding some disease on them. Alexandra wants to see your hammocks."

Ivar led Alexandra and Emil to his little cave house. He had but one room, neatly plastered and whitewashed, and there was a wooden floor. There was a kitchen stove, a table covered with oilcloth, two chairs, a clock, a calendar, a few books on the window-shelf; nothing more. But the place was as clean as a cupboard.

"But where do you sleep, Ivar?" Emil asked, looking about.

Ivar unslung a hammock from a hook on the wall; in it was rolled a buffalo robe. "There, my son. A hammock is a good bed, and in winter I wrap up in this skin. Where I go to work, the beds are not half so easy as this."

By this time Emil had lost all his timidity. He thought a cave a very superior kind of house. There was something pleasantly unusual about it and about

Ivar. "Do the birds know you will be kind to them, Ivar? Is that why so many come?" he asked.

Ivar sat down on the floor and tucked his feet under him. "See, little brother, they have come from a long way, and they are very tired. From up there where they are flying, our country looks dark and flat. They must have water to drink and to bathe in before they can go on with their journey. They look this way and that, and far below them they see something shining, like a piece of glass set in the dark earth. That is my pond. They come to it and are not disturbed. Maybe I sprinkle a little corn. They tell the other birds, and next year more come this way. They have their roads up there, as we have down here."

Emil rubbed his knees thoughtfully. "And is that true, Ivar, about the head ducks falling back when they are tired, and the hind ones taking their place?"

"Yes. The point of the wedge gets the worst of it; they cut the wind. They can only stand it there a little while—half an hour, maybe. Then they fall back and the wedge splits a little, while the rear ones come up the middle to the front. Then it closes up and they fly on, with a new edge. They are always changing like that, up in the air. Never any confusion; just like soldiers who have been drilled."

Alexandra had selected her hammock by the time the boys came up from the pond. They would not come in, but sat in the shade of the bank outside while Alexandra and Ivar talked about the birds and about his housekeeping, and why he never ate meat, fresh or salt.

Alexandra was sitting on one of the wooden chairs, her arms resting on the table. Ivar was sitting on the floor at her feet. "Ivar," she said suddenly, beginning to trace the pattern on the oilcloth with her forefinger, "I came today more because I wanted to talk to you than because I wanted to buy a hammock."

"Yes?" The old man scraped his bare feet on the plank floor.

"We have a big bunch of hogs, Ivar. I wouldn't sell in the spring, when everybody advised me to, and now so many people are losing their hogs that I am frightened. What can be done?"

Ivar's little eyes began to shine. They lost their vagueness.

"You feed them swill and such stuff? Of course! And sour milk? Oh, yes! And keep them in a stinking pen? I tell you, sister, the hogs of this country are put upon! They become unclean, like the hogs in the Bible. If you kept your chickens like that, what would happen? You have a little sorghum patch, maybe? Put a fence around it, and turn the hogs in. Build a shed to give them shade, a thatch on poles. Let the boys haul water to them in barrels, clean water, and plenty. Get them off the old stinking ground, and do not let them go back there until winter. Give them only grain and clean feed, such as you would give horses or cattle. Hogs do not like to be filthy."

The boys outside the door had been listening. Lou nudged his brother. "Come, the horses are done eating. Let's hitch up and get out of here. He'll fill her full of notions. She'll be for having the pigs sleep with us, next."

Oscar grunted and got up. Carl, who could not understand what Ivar said, saw that the two boys were displeased. They did not mind hard work, but they hated experiments and could never see the use of taking pains. Even Lou, who was more elastic than his older brother, disliked to do anything different from their neighbors. He felt that it made them conspicuous and gave people a chance to talk about them.

Once they were on the homeward road, the boys forgot their ill-humor and joked about Ivar and his birds. Alexandra did not propose any reforms in the care of the pigs, and they hoped she had forgotten Ivar's talk. They agreed that he was crazier than ever, and would never be able to prove up on his land because he worked it so little. Alexandra privately resolved that she would have a talk with Ivar about this and stir him up. The boys persuaded Carl to stay for supper and go swimming in the pasture pond after dark.

That evening, after she had washed the supper dishes, Alexandra sat down on the kitchen doorstep, while her mother was mixing the bread. It was a still, deep-breathing summer night, full of the smell of the hay fields. Sounds of laughter and splashing came up from the pasture, and when the moon rose rapidly above the bare rim of the prairie, the pond glittered like polished metal, and she could see the flash of white bodies as the boys ran about the edge, or jumped into the water. Alexandra watched the shimmering pool dreamily, but eventually her eyes went back to the sorghum patch south of the barn, where she was planning to make her new pig corral.

## CHAPTER IV

For the first three years after John Bergson's death, the affairs of his family prospered. Then came the hard times that brought everyone on the Divide to the brink of despair; three years of drouth and failure, the last struggle of a wild soil against the encroaching plowshare. The first of these fruitless summers the Bergson boys bore courageously. The failure of the corn crop made labor cheap. Lou and Oscar hired two men and put in bigger crops than ever before. They lost everything they spent. The whole country was discouraged. Farmers who were already in debt had to give up their land. A few foreclosures demoralized the county. The settlers sat about on the wooden sidewalks in the little town and told each other that the country was never meant for men to live in; the thing to do was to get back to Iowa, to Illinois, to any place that had been proved habitable. The Bergson boys, certainly, would have been happier with their uncle Otto, in the bakery shop in Chicago. Like most of their neighbors, they were meant to follow in paths already marked out for them, not to break trails in a new country. A steady job, a few holidays, nothing to think about, and they would have been very happy. It was no fault of theirs that they had been dragged into the wilderness when they were little boys. A pioneer should have imagination, should be able to enjoy the idea of things more than the things themselves.

The second of these barren summers was passing. One September afternoon Alexandra had gone over to the garden across the draw to dig sweet potatoes—they had been thriving upon the weather that was fatal to everything else. But when Carl Linstrum came up the garden rows to find her, she was not working. She was standing lost in thought, leaning upon her pitchfork, her sunbonnet lying beside her on the ground. The dry garden patch smelled of drying vines and was strewn with yellow seed-cucumbers and pumpkins and citrons. At one end, next the rhubarb, grew feathery asparagus, with red berries. Down the middle of the garden was a row of gooseberry and currant bushes. A few tough zenias and marigolds and a row of scarlet sage bore witness to the buckets of water that Mrs. Bergson had carried there after sundown, against the prohibition of her sons. Carl came quietly and slowly up the garden path, looking intently at Alexandra. She did not hear him. She was standing perfectly still, with that serious ease so characteristic of her. Her thick, reddish braids, twisted about her head, fairly burned in the sunlight. The air was cool enough to make the warm sun pleasant on one's back and shoulders, and so clear that the eye could follow a hawk up and up, into the blazing blue depths of the sky. Even Carl, never a very cheerful boy, and considerably darkened by these last two bitter years, loved the country on days like this, felt something strong and young and wild come out of it, that laughed at care.

"Alexandra," he said as he approached her, "I want to talk to you. Let's sit down by the gooseberry bushes." He picked up her sack of potatoes and they crossed the garden. "Boys gone to town?" he asked as he sank down on the warm, sun-baked earth. "Well, we have made up our minds at last, Alexandra. We are really going away."

She looked at him as if she were a little frightened. "Really, Carl? Is it settled?"

"Yes, father has heard from St. Louis, and they will give him back his old job in the cigar factory. He must be there by the first of November. They are taking on new men then. We will sell the place for whatever we can get, and auction the stock. We haven't enough to ship. I am going to learn engraving with a German engraver there, and then try to get work in Chicago."

Alexandra's hands dropped in her lap. Her eyes became dreamy and filled with tears.

Carl's sensitive lower lip trembled. He scratched in the soft earth beside him with a stick. "That's all I hate about it, Alexandra," he said slowly. "You've stood by us through so much and helped father out so many times, and now it seems as if we were running off and leaving you to face the worst of it. But it isn't as if we could really ever be of any help to you. We are only one more drag, one more thing you look out for and feel responsible for. Father was never meant for a farmer, you know that. And I hate it. We'd only get in deeper and deeper."

"Yes, yes, Carl, I know. You are wasting your life here. You are able to do much better things. You are nearly nineteen now, and I wouldn't have you stay. I've always hoped you would get away. But I can't help feeling scared when I think how I will miss you—more than you will ever know." She brushed the tears from her cheeks, not trying to hide them.

"But, Alexandra," he said sadly and wistfully, "I've never been any real help to you, beyond sometimes trying to keep the boys in a good humor."

Alexandra smiled and shook her head. "Oh, it's not that. Nothing like that. It's by understanding me, and the boys, and mother, that you've helped me. I expect that is the only way one person ever really can help another. I think you are about the only one that ever helped me. Somehow it will take more courage to bear your going than everything that has happened before."

Carl looked at the ground. "You see, we've all depended so on you," he said, "even father. He makes me laugh. When anything comes up he always says, 'I wonder what the Bergsons are going to do about that? I guess I'll go and ask her.' I'll never forget that time, when we first came here, and our horse had the colic, and I ran over to your place—your father was away, and you came home with me and showed father how to let the wind out of the horse. You were only a little girl then, but you knew ever so much more about farm work than poor father. You remember how homesick I used to get, and what long talks we used to have coming from school? We've someway always felt alike about things."

"Yes, that's it; we've liked the same things and we've liked them together, without anybody else knowing. And we've had good times, hunting for Christmas trees and going for ducks and making our plum wine together every year. We've never either of us had any other close friend. And now—" Alexandra wiped her eyes with the corner of her apron, "and now I must remember that you are going where you will have many friends, and will find the work you were meant to do. But you'll write to me, Carl? That will mean a great deal to me here."

"I'll write as long as I live," cried the boy impetuously. "And I'll be working for you as much as for myself, Alexandra. I want to do something you'll like and be proud of. I'm a fool here, but I know I can do something!" He sat up and frowned at the red grass.

Alexandra sighed. "How discouraged the boys will be when they hear. They always come home from town discouraged, anyway. So many people are trying to leave the country, and they talk to our boys and make them low-spirited. I'm afraid they are beginning to feel hard toward me because I won't listen to any talk about going. Sometimes I feel like I'm getting tired of standing up for this country."

"I won't tell the boys yet, if you'd rather not."

"Oh, I'll tell them myself, tonight, when they come home. They'll be talking wild, anyway, and no good comes of keeping bad news. It's all harder on them than it is on me. Lou wants to get married, poor boy, and he can't until times are better. See, there goes the sun, Carl. I must be getting back. Mother will want her potatoes. It's chilly already, the moment the light goes."

Alexandra rose and looked about. A golden afterglow throbbed in the west, but the country already looked empty and mournful. A dark moving mass came over the western hill, the Lee boy was bringing in the herd from the other half-section. Emil ran from the windmill to open the corral gate. From the log house, on the little rise across the draw, the smoke was curling. The cattle lowed and bellowed. In the sky the pale half-moon was slowly silvering. Alexandra and Carl walked together down the potato rows. "I have to keep telling myself what is going to happen," she said softly. "Since you have been here, ten years now, I have never really been lonely. But I can remember what it was like before. Now I shall have nobody but Emil. But he is my boy, and he is tender-hearted."

That night, when the boys were called to supper, they sat down moodily. They had worn their coats to town, but they ate in their striped shirts and suspenders. They were grown men now, and, as Alexandra said, for the last few years they had been growing more and more like themselves. Lou was still the slighter of the two, the quicker and more intelligent, but apt to go off at half-cock. He had a lively blue eye, a thin, fair skin (always burned red to the neckband of his shirt in summer), stiff, yellow hair that would not lie down on his head, and a bristly little yellow mustache, of which he was very proud. Oscar could not grow a mustache; his pale face was as bare as an egg, and his white eyebrows gave it an empty look. He was a man of powerful body and unusual endurance; the sort of man you could attach to a corn-sheller as you would an engine. He would turn it all day, without hurrying, without slowing down. But he was as indolent of mind as he was unsparing of his body. His love of routine amounted to a vice. He worked like an insect, always doing the same thing over in the same way, regardless of whether it was best or no. He felt that there was a sovereign virtue in mere bodily toil, and he rather liked to do things in the hardest way. If a field had once been in corn, he couldn't bear to put it into wheat. He liked to begin his corn-planting at the same time every year, whether the season were backward or forward. He seemed to feel that by his own irreproachable regularity he would clear himself of blame and reprove the weather. When the wheat crop failed, he threshed the straw at a dead loss to demonstrate how little grain there was, and thus prove his case against Providence.

Lou, on the other hand, was fussy and flighty; always planned to get through two days' work in one, and often got only the least important things done. He liked to keep the place up, but he never got round to doing odd jobs until he had to neglect more pressing work to attend to them. In the middle of the wheat harvest, when the grain was over-ripe and every hand was needed, he would stop to mend fences or to patch the harness; then dash down to the field and overwork and be laid up in bed for a week. The two boys balanced each other, and they pulled well together. They had been good friends since they were children. One seldom went anywhere, even to town, without the other.

Tonight, after they sat down to supper, Oscar kept looking at Lou as if he expected him to say something, and Lou blinked his eyes and frowned at his plate. It was Alexandra herself who at last opened the discussion.

"The Linstrums," she said calmly, as she put another plate of hot biscuit on the table, "are going back to St. Louis. The old man is going to work in the cigar factory again."

At this Lou plunged in. "You see, Alexandra, everybody who can crawl out is going away. There's no use of us trying to stick it out, just to be stubborn. There's something in knowing when to quit."

"Where do you want to go, Lou?"

"Any place where things will grow," said Oscar grimly.

Lou reached for a potato. "Chris Arnson has traded his half-section for a place down on the river."

"Who did he trade with?"

"Charley Fuller, in town."

"Fuller the real estate man? You see, Lou, that Fuller has a head on him. He's buying and trading for every bit of land he can get up here. It'll make him a rich man, someday."

"He's rich now, that's why he can take a chance."

"Why can't we? We'll live longer than he will. Someday the land itself will be worth more than all we can ever raise on it."

Lou laughed. "It could be worth that, and still not be worth much. Why, Alexandra, you don't know what you're talking about. Our place wouldn't bring now what it would six years ago. The fellows that settled up here just made a mistake. Now they're beginning to see this high land wasn't never meant to grow nothing on, and everybody who ain't fixed to graze cattle is trying to crawl out. It's too high to farm up here. All the Americans are skinning out. That man Percy Adams, north of town, told me that he was going to let Fuller take his land and stuff for four hundred dollars and a ticket to Chicago."

"There's Fuller again!" Alexandra exclaimed. "I wish that man would take me for a partner. He's feathering his nest! If only poor people could learn a little from rich people! But all these fellows who are running off are bad farmers, like poor Mr. Linstrum. They couldn't get ahead even in good years, and they all got into debt while father was getting out. I think we ought to hold on as long as we can on father's account. He was so set on keeping this land. He must have seen harder times than this, here. How was it in the early days, mother?"

Mrs. Bergson was weeping quietly. These family discussions always depressed her, and made her remember all that she had been torn away from. "I don't see why the boys are always taking on about going away," she said, wiping her eyes. "I don't want to move again; out to some raw place, maybe, where we'd be worse off than we are here, and all to do over again. I won't move! If the rest of you go, I will ask some of the neighbors to take me in, and stay and be buried by father. I'm not going to leave him by himself on the prairie, for cattle to run over." She began to cry more bitterly.

The boys looked angry. Alexandra put a soothing hand on her mother's shoulder. "There's no question of that, mother. You don't have to go if you don't want to. A third of the place belongs to you by American law, and we can't sell without your consent. We only want you to advise us. How did it use to be when you and father first came? Was it really as bad as this, or not?"

"Oh, worse! Much worse," moaned Mrs. Bergson. "Drouth, chince-bugs, hail, everything! My garden all cut to pieces like sauerkraut. No grapes on the creek, no nothing. The people all lived just like coyotes."

Oscar got up and tramped out of the kitchen. Lou followed him. They felt that Alexandra had taken an unfair advantage in turning their mother loose on them. The next morning they were silent and reserved. They did not offer to take the women to church, but went down to the barn immediately after breakfast and stayed there all day. When Carl Linstrum came over in the afternoon, Alexandra winked to him and pointed toward the barn. He understood her and went down to play cards with the boys. They believed that a very wicked thing to do on Sunday, and it relieved their feelings.

Alexandra stayed in the house. On Sunday afternoon Mrs. Bergson always took a nap, and Alexandra read. During the week she read only the newspaper, but on Sunday, and in the long evenings of winter, she read a good deal; read a few things over a great many times. She knew long portions of the "Frithjof Saga" by heart, and, like most Swedes who read at all, she was fond of Longfellow's verse—the ballads and the "Golden Legend" and "The Spanish Student."

Today she sat in the wooden rocking-chair with the Swedish Bible open on her knees, but she was not reading. She was looking thoughtfully away at the point where the upland road disappeared over the rim of the prairie. Her body was in an attitude of perfect repose, such as it was apt to take when she was thinking earnestly. Her mind was slow, truthful, steadfast. She had not the least spark of cleverness.

All afternoon the sitting room was full of quiet and sunlight. Emil was making rabbit traps in the kitchen shed. The hens were clucking and scratching brown holes in the flower beds, and the wind was teasing the prince's feather by the door.

That evening Carl came in with the boys to supper.

"Emil," said Alexandra, when they were all seated at the table, "how would you like to go traveling? Because I am going to take a trip, and you can go with me if you want to."

The boys looked up in amazement; they were always afraid of Alexandra's schemes. Carl was interested.

"I've been thinking, boys," she went on, "that maybe I am too set against making a change. I'm going to take Brigham and the buckboard tomorrow and drive down to the river country and spend a few days looking over what they've got down there. If I find anything good, you boys can go down and make a trade."

"Nobody down there will trade for anything up here," said Oscar gloomily.

"That's just what I want to find out. Maybe they are just as discontented down there as we are up here. Things away from home often look better than they are. You know what your Hans Andersen book says, Carl, about the Swedes liking to buy Danish bread and the Danes liking to buy Swedish bread, because people always think the bread of another country is better than their own. Anyway, I've heard so much about the river farms, I won't be satisfied till I've seen for myself."

Lou fidgeted. "Look out! Don't agree to anything. Don't let them fool you."

Lou was apt to be fooled himself. He had not yet learned to keep away from the shell-game wagons that followed the circus.

After supper Lou put on a necktie and went across the fields to court Annie Lee, and Carl and Oscar sat down to a game of checkers, while Alexandra read "The Swiss Family Robinson" aloud to her mother and Emil. It was not long before the two boys at the table neglected their game to listen. They were all big children together, and they found the adventures of the family in the tree house so absorbing that they gave them their undivided attention.

# CHAPTER V

Alexandra and Emil spent five days down among the river farms, driving up and down the valley. Alexandra talked to the men about their crops and to the women about their poultry. She spent a whole day with one young farmer who had been away at school, and who was experimenting with a new kind of clover hay. She learned a great deal. As they drove along, she and Emil talked and planned. At last, on the sixth day, Alexandra turned Brigham's head northward and left the river behind.

"There's nothing in it for us down there, Emil. There are a few fine farms, but they are owned by the rich men in town, and couldn't be bought. Most of the land is rough and hilly. They can always scrape along down there, but they can never do anything big. Down there they have a little certainty, but up with us there is a big chance. We must have faith in the high land, Emil. I want to hold on harder than ever, and when you're a man you'll thank me." She urged Brigham forward.

When the road began to climb the first long swells of the Divide, Alexandra hummed an old Swedish hymn, and Emil wondered why his sister looked so happy. Her face was so radiant that he felt shy about asking her. For the first time, perhaps, since that land emerged from the waters of geologic ages, a human face was set toward it with love and yearning. It seemed beautiful to her, rich and strong and glorious. Her eyes drank in the breadth of it, until her tears blinded her. Then the Genius of the Divide, the great, free spirit which breathes across it, must have bent lower than it ever bent to a human will before. The history of every country begins in the heart of a man or a woman.

Alexandra reached home in the afternoon. That evening she held a family council and told her brothers all that she had seen and heard.

"I want you boys to go down yourselves and look it over. Nothing will convince you like seeing with your own eyes. The river land was settled before this, and so they are a few years ahead of us, and have learned more about farming. The land sells for three times as much as this, but in five years we will double it. The rich men down there own all the best land, and they are buying all they can get. The thing to do is to sell our cattle and what little old corn we have, and buy the Linstrum place. Then the next thing to do is to take out two loans on our half-sections, and buy Peter Crow's place; raise every dollar we can, and buy every acre we can."

"Mortgage the homestead again?" Lou cried. He sprang up and began to wind the clock furiously. "I won't slave to pay off another mortgage. I'll never do it. You'd just as soon kill us all, Alexandra, to carry out some scheme!"

Oscar rubbed his high, pale forehead. "How do you propose to pay off your mortgages?"

Alexandra looked from one to the other and bit her lip. They had never seen her so nervous. "See here," she brought out at last. "We borrow the money for six years. Well, with the money we buy a half-section from Linstrum and a half from Crow, and a quarter from Struble, maybe. That will give us upwards of fourteen hundred acres, won't it? You won't have to pay off your mortgages for six years. By that time, any of this land will be worth thirty dollars an acre—it will be worth fifty, but we'll say thirty; then you can sell a garden patch anywhere, and pay off a debt of sixteen hundred dollars. It's not the principal I'm worried about, it's the interest and taxes. We'll have to strain to meet the payments. But as sure as we are sitting here tonight, we can sit down here ten years from now independent landowners, not struggling farmers any longer. The chance that father was always looking for has come."

Lou was pacing the floor. "But how do you *know* that land is going to go up enough to pay the mortgages and—"

"And make us rich besides?" Alexandra put in firmly. "I can't explain that, Lou. You'll have to take my word for it. I *know*, that's all. When you drive about over the country you can feel it coming."

Oscar had been sitting with his head lowered, his hands hanging between his knees. "But we can't work so much land," he said dully, as if he were talking to himself. "We can't even try. It would just lie there and we'd work ourselves to death." He sighed, and laid his calloused fist on the table.

Alexandra's eyes filled with tears. She put her hand on his shoulder. "You poor boy, you won't have to work it. The men in town who are buying up other people's land don't try to farm it. They are the men to watch, in a new country. Let's try to do like the shrewd ones, and not like these stupid fellows. I don't want you boys always to have to work like this. I want you to be independent, and Emil to go to school."

Lou held his head as if it were splitting. "Everybody will say we are crazy. It must be crazy, or everybody would be doing it."

"If they were, we wouldn't have much chance. No, Lou, I was talking about that with the smart young man who is raising the new kind of clover. He says the right thing is usually just what everybody don't do. Why are we better fixed than any of our neighbors? Because father had more brains. Our people were better people than these in the old country. We *ought* to do more than they do, and see further ahead. Yes, mother, I'm going to clear the table now."

Alexandra rose. The boys went to the stable to see to the stock, and they were gone a long while. When they came back Lou played on his *dragharmonika* and Oscar sat figuring at his father's secretary all evening. They said nothing more about Alexandra's project, but she felt sure now that they would consent to it. Just before bedtime Oscar went out for a pail of water. When he did not come back, Alexandra threw a shawl over her head and ran down the path to the windmill. She found him sitting there with his head in his hands, and she sat down beside him.

"Don't do anything you don't want to do, Oscar," she whispered. She waited a moment, but he did not stir. "I won't say any more about it, if you'd rather not. What makes you so discouraged?"

"I dread signing my name to them pieces of paper," he said slowly. "All the time I was a boy we had a mortgage hanging over us."

"Then don't sign one. I don't want you to, if you feel that way."

Oscar shook his head. "No, I can see there's a chance that way. I've thought a good while there might be. We're in so deep now, we might as well go deeper. But it's hard work pulling out of debt. Like pulling a threshing-machine out of the mud; breaks your back. Me and Lou's worked hard, and I can't see it's got us ahead much."

"Nobody knows about that as well as I do, Oscar. That's why I want to try an easier way. I don't want you to have to grub for every dollar."

"Yes, I know what you mean. Maybe it'll come out right. But signing papers is signing papers. There ain't no maybe about that." He took his pail and trudged up the path to the house.

Alexandra drew her shawl closer about her and stood leaning against the frame of the mill, looking at the stars which glittered so keenly through the frosty autumn air. She always loved to watch them, to think of their vastness and distance, and of their ordered march. It fortified her to reflect upon the great operations of nature, and when she thought of the law that lay behind them, she felt a sense of personal security. That night she had a new consciousness of the country, felt almost a new relation to it. Even her talk with the boys had not taken away the feeling that had overwhelmed her when she drove back to the Divide that afternoon. She had never known before how much the country meant to her. The chirping of the insects down in the long grass had been like the sweetest music. She had felt as if her heart were hiding down there, somewhere, with the quail and the plover and all the little wild things that crooned or buzzed in the sun. Under the long shaggy ridges, she felt the future stirring.

# PART II. NEIGHBORING FIELDS

## CHAPTER I

It is sixteen years since John Bergson died. His wife now lies beside him, and the white shaft that marks their graves gleams across the wheat fields. Could he rise from beneath it, he would not know the country under which he has been asleep. The shaggy coat of the prairie, which they lifted to make him a bed, has vanished forever. From the Norwegian graveyard one looks out over a vast checkerboard, marked off in squares of wheat and corn; light and dark, dark and light. Telephone wires hum along the white roads, which always run at right angles. From the graveyard gate one can count a dozen gayly painted farmhouses; the gilded weather-vanes on the big red barns wink at each other across the green and brown and yellow fields. The light steel windmills tremble throughout their frames and tug at their moorings, as they vibrate in the wind that often blows from one week's end to another across that high, active, resolute stretch of country.

The Divide is now thickly populated. The rich soil yields heavy harvests; the dry, bracing climate and the smoothness of the land make labor easy for men and beasts. There are few scenes more gratifying than a spring plowing in that country, where the furrows of a single field often lie a mile in length, and the brown earth, with such a strong, clean smell, and such a power of growth and fertility in it, yields itself eagerly to the plow; rolls away from the shear, not even dimming the brightness of the metal, with a soft, deep sigh of happiness. The wheat-cutting sometimes goes on all night as well as all day, and in good seasons there are scarcely men and horses enough to do the harvesting. The grain is so heavy that it bends toward the blade and cuts like velvet.

There is something frank and joyous and young in the open face of the country. It gives itself ungrudgingly to the moods of the season, holding nothing back. Like the plains of Lombardy, it seems to rise a little to meet the sun. The air and the earth are curiously mated and intermingled, as if the one were the breath of the other. You feel in the atmosphere the same tonic, puissant quality that is in the tilth, the same strength and resoluteness.

One June morning a young man stood at the gate of the Norwegian graveyard, sharpening his scythe in strokes unconsciously timed to the tune he was whistling. He wore a flannel cap and duck trousers, and the sleeves of his white flannel shirt were rolled back to the elbow. When he was satisfied with the edge of his blade, he slipped the whetstone into his hip pocket and began to swing his scythe, still whistling, but softly, out of respect to the quiet folk about him. Unconscious respect, probably, for he seemed intent upon his own thoughts, and, like the Gladiator's, they were far away. He was a splendid figure of a boy, tall and straight as a young pine tree, with a handsome head, and stormy gray eyes, deeply set under a serious brow. The space between his two front teeth, which were unusually far apart, gave him the proficiency in whistling for which he was distinguished at college. (He also played the cornet in the University band.)

When the grass required his close attention, or when he had to stoop to

cut about a headstone, he paused in his lively air—the "Jewel" song—taking
it up where he had left it when his scythe swung free again. He was not
thinking about the tired pioneers over whom his blade glittered. The old wild
country, the struggle in which his sister was destined to succeed while so
many men broke their hearts and died, he can scarcely remember. That is all
among the dim things of childhood and has been forgotten in the brighter
pattern life weaves today, in the bright facts of being captain of the track
team, and holding the interstate record for the high jump, in the all-suffusing
brightness of being twenty-one. Yet sometimes, in the pauses of his work,
the young man frowned and looked at the ground with an intentness which
suggested that even twenty-one might have its problems.

When he had been mowing the better part of an hour, he heard the rattle
of a light cart on the road behind him. Supposing that it was his sister coming
back from one of her farms, he kept on with his work. The cart stopped at
the gate and a merry contralto voice called, "Almost through, Emil?" He
dropped his scythe and went toward the fence, wiping his face and neck with
his handkerchief. In the cart sat a young woman who wore driving gauntlets
and a wide shade hat, trimmed with red poppies. Her face, too, was rather
like a poppy, round and brown, with rich color in her cheeks and lips, and her
dancing yellow-brown eyes bubbled with gayety. The wind was flapping her
big hat and teasing a curl of her chestnut-colored hair. She shook her head
at the tall youth.

"What time did you get over here? That's not much of a job for an athlete.
Here I've been to town and back. Alexandra lets you sleep late. Oh, I know!
Lou's wife was telling me about the way she spoils you. I was going to give
you a lift, if you were done."

She gathered up her reins.

"But I will be, in a minute. Please wait for me, Marie," Emil coaxed.
"Alexandra sent me to mow our lot, but I've done half a dozen others, you
see. Just wait till I finish off the Kourdnas'. By the way, they were Bohemians.
Why aren't they up in the Catholic graveyard?"

"Free-thinkers," replied the young woman laconically.

"Lots of the Bohemian boys at the University are," said Emil, taking up his
scythe again. "What did you ever burn John Huss for, anyway? It's made an
awful row. They still jaw about it in history classes."

"We'd do it right over again, most of us," said the young woman hotly.
"Don't they ever teach you in your history classes that you'd all be heathen
Turks if it hadn't been for the Bohemians?"

Emil had fallen to mowing. "Oh, there's no denying you're a spunky little
bunch, you Czechs," he called back over his shoulder.

Marie Shabata settled herself in her seat and watched the rhythmical movement of the young man's long arms, swinging her foot as if in time to some air that was going through her mind. The minutes passed. Emil mowed vigorously and Marie sat sunning herself and watching the long grass fall. She sat with the ease that belongs to persons of an essentially happy nature, who can find a comfortable spot almost anywhere; who are supple, and quick in adapting themselves to circumstances. After a final swish, Emil snapped the gate and sprang into the cart, holding his scythe well out over the wheel. "There," he sighed. "I gave old man Lee a cut or so, too. Lou's wife needn't talk. I never see Lou's scythe over here."

Marie clucked to her horse. "Oh, you know Annie!" She looked at the young man's bare arms. "How brown you've got since you came home. I wish I had an athlete to mow my orchard. I get wet to my knees when I go down to pick cherries."

"You can have one, any time you want him. Better wait until after it rains." Emil squinted off at the horizon as if he were looking for clouds.

"Will you? Oh, there's a good boy!" She turned her head to him with a quick, bright smile. He felt it rather than saw it. Indeed, he had looked away with the purpose of not seeing it. "I've been up looking at Angelique's wedding clothes," Marie went on, "and I'm so excited I can hardly wait until Sunday. Amedee will be a handsome bridegroom. Is anybody but you going to stand up with him? Well, then it will be a handsome wedding party." She made a droll face at Emil, who flushed. "Frank," Marie continued, flicking her horse, "is cranky at me because I loaned his saddle to Jan Smirka, and I'm terribly afraid he won't take me to the dance in the evening. Maybe the supper will tempt him. All Angelique's folks are baking for it, and all Amedee's twenty cousins. There will be barrels of beer. If once I get Frank to the supper, I'll see that I stay for the dance. And by the way, Emil, you mustn't dance with me but once or twice. You must dance with all the French girls. It hurts their feelings if you don't. They think you're proud because you've been away to school or something."

Emil sniffed. "How do you know they think that?"

"Well, you didn't dance with them much at Raoul Marcel's party, and I could tell how they took it by the way they looked at you—and at me."

"All right," said Emil shortly, studying the glittering blade of his scythe.

They drove westward toward Norway Creek, and toward a big white house that stood on a hill, several miles across the fields. There were so many sheds and outbuildings grouped about it that the place looked not unlike a tiny village. A stranger, approaching it, could not help noticing the beauty and fruitfulness of the outlying fields. There was something individual about the great farm, a most unusual trimness and care for detail. On either side of the road, for a mile before you reached the foot of the hill, stood tall osage orange hedges, their glossy green marking off the yellow fields. South of the hill, in a low, sheltered swale, surrounded by a mulberry hedge, was the orchard, its fruit trees knee-deep in timothy grass. Anyone thereabouts would have told you that this was one of the richest farms on the Divide, and that the farmer was a woman, Alexandra Bergson.

If you go up the hill and enter Alexandra's big house, you will find that it is curiously unfinished and uneven in comfort. One room is papered, carpeted, over-furnished; the next is almost bare. The pleasantest rooms in the house are the kitchen—where Alexandra's three young Swedish girls chatter and cook and pickle and preserve all summer long—and the sitting room, in which Alexandra has brought together the old homely furniture that the Bergsons used in their first log house, the family portraits, and the few things her mother brought from Sweden.

When you go out of the house into the flower garden, there you feel again the order and fine arrangement manifest all over the great farm; in the fencing and hedging, in the windbreaks and sheds, in the symmetrical pasture ponds, planted with scrub willows to give shade to the cattle in fly-time. There is even a white row of beehives in the orchard, under the walnut trees. You feel that, properly, Alexandra's house is the big out-of-doors, and that it is in the soil that she expresses herself best.

## CHAPTER II

Emil reached home a little past noon, and when he went into the kitchen Alexandra was already seated at the head of the long table, having dinner with her men, as she always did unless there were visitors. He slipped into his empty place at his sister's right. The three pretty young Swedish girls who did Alexandra's housework were cutting pies, refilling coffee cups, placing platters of bread and meat and potatoes upon the red tablecloth, and continually getting in each other's way between the table and the stove. To be sure they always wasted a good deal of time getting in each other's way and giggling at each other's mistakes. But, as Alexandra had pointedly told her sisters-in-law, it was to hear them giggle that she kept three young things in her kitchen; the work she could do herself, if it were necessary. These girls, with their long letters from home, their finery, and their love-affairs, afforded her a great deal of entertainment, and they were company for her when Emil was away at school.

Of the youngest girl, Signa, who has a pretty figure, mottled pink cheeks, and yellow hair, Alexandra is very fond, though she keeps a sharp eye upon her. Signa is apt to be skittish at mealtime, when the men are about, and to spill the coffee or upset the cream. It is supposed that Nelse Jensen, one of the six men at the dinner-table, is courting Signa, though he has been so careful not to commit himself that no one in the house, least of all Signa, can tell just how far the matter has progressed. Nelse watches her glumly as she waits upon the table, and in the evening he sits on a bench behind the stove with his *dragharmonika*, playing mournful airs and watching her as she goes about her work. When Alexandra asked Signa whether she thought Nelse was in earnest, the poor child hid her hands under her apron and murmured, "I don't know, ma'm. But he scolds me about everything, like as if he wanted to have me!"

At Alexandra's left sat a very old man, barefoot and wearing a long blue blouse, open at the neck. His shaggy head is scarcely whiter than it was sixteen years ago, but his little blue eyes have become pale and watery, and his ruddy face is withered, like an apple that has clung all winter to the tree. When Ivar lost his land through mismanagement a dozen years ago, Alexandra took him in, and he has been a member of her household ever since. He is too old to work in the fields, but he hitches and unhitches the work-teams and looks after the health of the stock. Sometimes of a winter evening Alexandra calls him into the sitting room to read the Bible aloud to her, for he still reads very well. He dislikes human habitations, so Alexandra has fitted him up a room in the barn, where he is very comfortable, being near the horses and, as he says, further from temptations. No one has ever found out what his temptations are. In cold weather he sits by the kitchen fire and makes hammocks or mends harness until it is time to go to bed. Then he says his prayers at great length behind the stove, puts on his buffalo-skin coat and goes out to his room in the barn.

Alexandra herself has changed very little. Her figure is fuller, and she has more color. She seems sunnier and more vigorous than she did as a young girl. But she still has the same calmness and deliberation of manner, the same clear eyes, and she still wears her hair in two braids wound round her head. It is so curly that fiery ends escape from the braids and make her head look like one of the big double sunflowers that fringe her vegetable garden. Her face is always tanned in summer, for her sunbonnet is oftener on her arm than on her head. But where her collar falls away from her neck, or where her sleeves are pushed back from her wrist, the skin is of such smoothness and whiteness as none but Swedish women ever possess; skin with the freshness of the snow itself.

Alexandra did not talk much at the table, but she encouraged her men to talk, and she always listened attentively, even when they seemed to be talking foolishly.

Today Barney Flinn, the big red-headed Irishman who had been with

Alexandra for five years and who was actually her foreman, though he had no such title, was grumbling about the new silo she had put up that spring. It happened to be the first silo on the Divide, and Alexandra's neighbors and her men were skeptical about it. "To be sure, if the thing don't work, we'll have plenty of feed without it, indeed," Barney conceded.

Nelse Jensen, Signa's gloomy suitor, had his word. "Lou, he says he wouldn't have no silo on his place if you'd give it to him. He says the feed outen it gives the stock the bloat. He heard of somebody lost four head of horses, feedin' 'em that stuff."

Alexandra looked down the table from one to another. "Well, the only way we can find out is to try. Lou and I have different notions about feeding stock, and that's a good thing. It's bad if all the members of a family think alike. They never get anywhere. Lou can learn by my mistakes and I can learn by his. Isn't that fair, Barney?"

The Irishman laughed. He had no love for Lou, who was always uppish with him and who said that Alexandra paid her hands too much. "I've no thought but to give the thing an honest try, mum. 'T would be only right, after puttin' so much expense into it. Maybe Emil will come out an' have a look at it wid me." He pushed back his chair, took his hat from the nail, and marched out with Emil, who, with his university ideas, was supposed to have instigated the silo. The other hands followed them, all except old Ivar. He had been depressed throughout the meal and had paid no heed to the talk of the men, even when they mentioned cornstalk bloat, upon which he was sure to have opinions.

"Did you want to speak to me, Ivar?" Alexandra asked as she rose from the table. "Come into the sitting room."

The old man followed Alexandra, but when she motioned him to a chair he shook his head. She took up her workbasket and waited for him to speak. He stood looking at the carpet, his bushy head bowed, his hands clasped in front of him. Ivar's bandy legs seemed to have grown shorter with years, and they were completely misfitted to his broad, thick body and heavy shoulders.

"Well, Ivar, what is it?" Alexandra asked after she had waited longer than usual.

Ivar had never learned to speak English and his Norwegian was quaint and grave, like the speech of the more old-fashioned people. He always addressed Alexandra in terms of the deepest respect, hoping to set a good example to the kitchen girls, whom he thought too familiar in their manners.

"Mistress," he began faintly, without raising his eyes, "the folk have been looking coldly at me of late. You know there has been talk."

"Talk about what, Ivar?"

"About sending me away; to the asylum."

Alexandra put down her sewing-basket. "Nobody has come to me with such talk," she said decidedly. "Why need you listen? You know I would never consent to such a thing."

Ivar lifted his shaggy head and looked at her out of his little eyes. "They say that you cannot prevent it if the folk complain of me, if your brothers complain to the authorities. They say that your brothers are afraid—God forbid!—that I may do you some injury when my spells are on me. Mistress, how can anyone think that? That I could bite the hand that fed me!" The tears trickled down on the old man's beard.

Alexandra frowned. "Ivar, I wonder at you, that you should come bothering me with such nonsense. I am still running my own house, and other people have nothing to do with either you or me. So long as I am suited with you, there is nothing to be said."

Ivar pulled a red handkerchief out of the breast of his blouse and wiped his eyes and beard. "But I should not wish you to keep me if, as they say, it is against your interests, and if it is hard for you to get hands because I am here."

Alexandra made an impatient gesture, but the old man put out his hand and went on earnestly:

"Listen, mistress, it is right that you should take these things into account. You know that my spells come from God, and that I would not harm any living creature. You believe that everyone should worship God in the way revealed to him. But that is not the way of this country. The way here is for all to do alike. I am despised because I do not wear shoes, because I do not cut my hair, and because I have visions. At home, in the old country, there were many like me, who had been touched by God, or who had seen things in the graveyard at night and were different afterward. We thought nothing of it, and let them alone. But here, if a man is different in his feet or in his head, they put him in the asylum. Look at Peter Kralik; when he was a boy, drinking out of a creek, he swallowed a snake, and always after that he could eat only such food as the creature liked, for when he ate anything else, it became enraged and gnawed him. When he felt it whipping about in him, he drank alcohol to stupefy it and get some ease for himself. He could work as good as any man, and his head was clear, but they locked him up for being different in his stomach. That is the way; they have built the asylum for people who are different, and they will not even let us live in the holes with the badgers. Only your great prosperity has protected me so far. If you had had ill-fortune, they would have taken me to Hastings long ago."

As Ivar talked, his gloom lifted. Alexandra had found that she could often break his fasts and long penances by talking to him and letting him pour out the thoughts that troubled him. Sympathy always cleared his mind, and ridicule was poison to him.

"There is a great deal in what you say, Ivar. Like as not they will be wanting to take me to Hastings because I have built a silo; and then I may take you with me. But at present I need you here. Only don't come to me again telling me what people say. Let people go on talking as they like, and we will go on living as we think best. You have been with me now for twelve years, and I have gone to you for advice oftener than I have ever gone to anyone. That ought to satisfy you."

Ivar bowed humbly. "Yes, mistress, I shall not trouble you with their talk again. And as for my feet, I have observed your wishes all these years, though you have never questioned me; washing them every night, even in winter."

Alexandra laughed. "Oh, never mind about your feet, Ivar. We can remember when half our neighbors went barefoot in summer. I expect old Mrs. Lee would love to slip her shoes off now sometimes, if she dared. I'm glad I'm not Lou's mother-in-law."

Ivar looked about mysteriously and lowered his voice almost to a whisper. "You know what they have over at Lou's house? A great white tub, like the stone water-troughs in the old country, to wash themselves in. When you sent me over with the strawberries, they were all in town but the old woman Lee and the baby. She took me in and showed me the thing, and she told me it was impossible to wash yourself clean in it, because, in so much water, you could not make a strong suds. So when they fill it up and send her in there, she pretends, and makes a splashing noise. Then, when they are all asleep, she washes herself in a little wooden tub she keeps under her bed."

Alexandra shook with laughter. "Poor old Mrs. Lee! They won't let her wear nightcaps, either. Never mind; when she comes to visit me, she can do all the old things in the old way, and have as much beer as she wants. We'll start an asylum for old-time people, Ivar."

Ivar folded his big handkerchief carefully and thrust it back into his blouse. "This is always the way, mistress. I come to you sorrowing, and you send me away with a light heart. And will you be so good as to tell the Irishman that he is not to work the brown gelding until the sore on its shoulder is healed?"

"That I will. Now go and put Emil's mare to the cart. I am going to drive up to the north quarter to meet the man from town who is to buy my alfalfa hay."

## CHAPTER III

Alexandra was to hear more of Ivar's case, however. On Sunday her married brothers came to dinner. She had asked them for that day because Emil, who hated family parties, would be absent, dancing at Amedee Chevalier's wedding, up in the French country. The table was set for company in the dining room, where highly varnished wood and colored glass and useless pieces of china were conspicuous enough to satisfy the standards of the new prosperity. Alexandra had put herself into the hands of the Hanover furniture dealer, and he had conscientiously done his best to make her dining room look like his display window. She said frankly that she knew nothing about such things, and she was willing to be governed by the general conviction that the more useless and utterly unusable objects were, the greater their virtue as ornament. That seemed reasonable enough. Since she liked plain things herself, it was all the more necessary to have jars and punchbowls and candlesticks in the company rooms for people who did appreciate them. Her guests liked to see about them these reassuring emblems of prosperity.

The family party was complete except for Emil, and Oscar's wife who, in the country phrase, "was not going anywhere just now."

Oscar sat at the foot of the table and his four tow-headed little boys, aged from twelve to five, were ranged at one side. Neither Oscar nor Lou has changed much; they have simply, as Alexandra said of them long ago, grown to be more and more like themselves. Lou now looks the older of the two; his face is thin and shrewd and wrinkled about the eyes, while Oscar's is thick and dull. For all his dullness, however, Oscar makes more money than his brother, which adds to Lou's sharpness and uneasiness and tempts him to make a show. The trouble with Lou is that he is tricky, and his neighbors have found out that, as Ivar says, he has not a fox's face for nothing. Politics being the natural field for such talents, he neglects his farm to attend conventions and to run for county offices.

Lou's wife, formerly Annie Lee, has grown to look curiously like her husband. Her face has become longer, sharper, more aggressive. She wears her yellow hair in a high pompadour, and is bedecked with rings and chains and "beauty pins." Her tight, high-heeled shoes give her an awkward walk, and she is always more or less preoccupied with her clothes. As she sat at the table, she kept telling her youngest daughter to "be careful now, and not drop anything on mother."

The conversation at the table was all in English. Oscar's wife, from the malaria district of Missouri, was ashamed of marrying a foreigner, and his boys do not understand a word of Swedish. Annie and Lou sometimes speak Swedish at home, but Annie is almost as much afraid of being "caught" at it as ever her mother was of being caught barefoot. Oscar still has a thick accent, but Lou speaks like anybody from Iowa.

"When I was in Hastings to attend the convention," he was saying, "I saw the superintendent of the asylum, and I was telling him about Ivar's symptoms. He says Ivar's case is one of the most dangerous kind, and it's a wonder he hasn't done something violent before this."

Alexandra laughed good-humoredly. "Oh, nonsense, Lou! The doctors would have us all crazy if they could. Ivar's queer, certainly, but he has more sense than half the hands I hire."

Lou flew at his fried chicken. "Oh, I guess the doctor knows his business, Alexandra. He was very much surprised when I told him how you'd put up with Ivar. He says he's likely to set fire to the barn any night, or to take after you and the girls with an axe."

Little Signa, who was waiting on the table, giggled and fled to the kitchen. Alexandra's eyes twinkled. "That was too much for Signa, Lou. We all know that Ivar's perfectly harmless. The girls would as soon expect me to chase them with an axe."

Lou flushed and signaled to his wife. "All the same, the neighbors will be having a say about it before long. He may burn anybody's barn. It's only necessary for one property-owner in the township to make complaint, and he'll be taken up by force. You'd better send him yourself and not have any hard feelings."

Alexandra helped one of her little nephews to gravy. "Well, Lou, if any of the neighbors try that, I'll have myself appointed Ivar's guardian and take the case to court, that's all. I am perfectly satisfied with him."

"Pass the preserves, Lou," said Annie in a warning tone. She had reasons for not wishing her husband to cross Alexandra too openly. "But don't you sort of hate to have people see him around here, Alexandra?" she went on with persuasive smoothness. "He *is* a disgraceful object, and you're fixed up so nice now. It sort of makes people distant with you, when they never know when they'll hear him scratching about. My girls are afraid as death of him, aren't you, Milly, dear?"

Milly was fifteen, fat and jolly and pompadoured, with a creamy complexion, square white teeth, and a short upper lip. She looked like her grandmother Bergson, and had her comfortable and comfort-loving nature. She grinned at her aunt, with whom she was a great deal more at ease than she was with her mother. Alexandra winked a reply.

"Milly needn't be afraid of Ivar. She's an especial favorite of his. In my opinion Ivar has just as much right to his own way of dressing and thinking as we have. But I'll see that he doesn't bother other people. I'll keep him at home, so don't trouble any more about him, Lou. I've been wanting to ask you about your new bathtub. How does it work?"

Annie came to the fore to give Lou time to recover himself. "Oh, it works something grand! I can't keep him out of it. He washes himself all over three times a week now, and uses all the hot water. I think it's weakening to stay in as long as he does. You ought to have one, Alexandra."

"I'm thinking of it. I might have one put in the barn for Ivar, if it will ease people's minds. But before I get a bathtub, I'm going to get a piano for Milly."

Oscar, at the end of the table, looked up from his plate. "What does Milly want of a pianny? What's the matter with her organ? She can make some use of that, and play in church."

Annie looked flustered. She had begged Alexandra not to say anything about this plan before Oscar, who was apt to be jealous of what his sister did for Lou's children. Alexandra did not get on with Oscar's wife at all. "Milly can play in church just the same, and she'll still play on the organ. But practicing on it so much spoils her touch. Her teacher says so," Annie brought out with spirit.

Oscar rolled his eyes. "Well, Milly must have got on pretty good if she's got past the organ. I know plenty of grown folks that ain't," he said bluntly.

Annie threw up her chin. "She has got on good, and she's going to play for her commencement when she graduates in town next year."

"Yes," said Alexandra firmly, "I think Milly deserves a piano. All the girls around here have been taking lessons for years, but Milly is the only one of them who can ever play anything when you ask her. I'll tell you when I first thought I would like to give you a piano, Milly, and that was when you learned that book of old Swedish songs that your grandfather used to sing. He had a sweet tenor voice, and when he was a young man he loved to sing. I can remember hearing him singing with the sailors down in the shipyard, when I was no bigger than Stella here," pointing to Annie's younger daughter.

Milly and Stella both looked through the door into the sitting room, where a crayon portrait of John Bergson hung on the wall. Alexandra had had it made from a little photograph, taken for his friends just before he left Sweden; a slender man of thirty-five, with soft hair curling about his high forehead, a drooping mustache, and wondering, sad eyes that looked forward into the distance, as if they already beheld the New World.

After dinner Lou and Oscar went to the orchard to pick cherries—they had neither of them had the patience to grow an orchard of their own—and Annie went down to gossip with Alexandra's kitchen girls while they washed the dishes. She could always find out more about Alexandra's domestic economy from the prattling maids than from Alexandra herself, and what she discovered she used to her own advantage with Lou. On the Divide, farmers' daughters no longer went out into service, so Alexandra got her girls from Sweden, by paying their fare over. They stayed with her until they married, and were replaced by sisters or cousins from the old country.

Alexandra took her three nieces into the flower garden. She was fond of the little girls, especially of Milly, who came to spend a week with her aunt now and then, and read aloud to her from the old books about the house, or listened to stories about the early days on the Divide. While they were walking among the flower beds, a buggy drove up the hill and stopped in front of the gate. A man got out and stood talking to the driver. The little girls were delighted at the advent of a stranger, someone from very far away, they knew by his clothes, his gloves, and the sharp, pointed cut of his dark beard. The girls fell behind their aunt and peeped out at him from among the castor beans. The stranger came up to the gate and stood holding his hat in his hand, smiling, while Alexandra advanced slowly to meet him. As she approached he spoke in a low, pleasant voice.

"Don't you know me, Alexandra? I would have known you, anywhere."

Alexandra shaded her eyes with her hand. Suddenly she took a quick step forward. "Can it be!" she exclaimed with feeling; "can it be that it is Carl Linstrum? Why, Carl, it is!" She threw out both her hands and caught his across the gate. "Sadie, Milly, run tell your father and Uncle Oscar that our old friend Carl Linstrum is here. Be quick! Why, Carl, how did it happen? I can't believe this!" Alexandra shook the tears from her eyes and laughed.

The stranger nodded to his driver, dropped his suitcase inside the fence, and opened the gate. "Then you are glad to see me, and you can put me up overnight? I couldn't go through this country without stopping off to have a look at you. How little you have changed! Do you know, I was sure it would be like that. You simply couldn't be different. How fine you are!" He stepped back and looked at her admiringly.

Alexandra blushed and laughed again. "But you yourself, Carl—with that beard—how could I have known you? You went away a little boy." She reached for his suitcase and when he intercepted her she threw up her hands. "You see, I give myself away. I have only women come to visit me, and I do not know how to behave. Where is your trunk?"

"It's in Hanover. I can stay only a few days. I am on my way to the coast."

They started up the path. "A few days? After all these years!"

Alexandra shook her finger at him. "See this, you have walked into a trap. You do not get away so easy." She put her hand affectionately on his shoulder. "You owe me a visit for the sake of old times. Why must you go to the coast at all?"

"Oh, I must! I am a fortune hunter. From Seattle I go on to Alaska."

"Alaska?" She looked at him in astonishment. "Are you going to paint the Indians?"

"Paint?" the young man frowned. "Oh! I'm not a painter, Alexandra. I'm an engraver. I have nothing to do with painting."

"But on my parlor wall I have the paintings—"

He interrupted nervously. "Oh, watercolor sketches—done for amusement. I sent them to remind you of me, not because they were good. What a wonderful place you have made of this, Alexandra."

He turned and looked back at the wide, map-like prospect of field and hedge and pasture. "I would never have believed it could be done. I'm disappointed in my own eye, in my imagination."

At this moment Lou and Oscar came up the hill from the orchard. They did not quicken their pace when they saw Carl; indeed, they did not openly look in his direction. They advanced distrustfully, and as if they wished the distance were longer.

Alexandra beckoned to them. "They think I am trying to fool them. Come, boys, it's Carl Linstrum, our old Carl!"

Lou gave the visitor a quick, sidelong glance and thrust out his hand. "Glad to see you."

Oscar followed with "How d' do." Carl could not tell whether their offishness came from unfriendliness or from embarrassment. He and Alexandra led the way to the porch.

"Carl," Alexandra explained, "is on his way to Seattle. He is going to Alaska."

Oscar studied the visitor's yellow shoes. "Got business there?" he asked.

Carl laughed. "Yes, very pressing business. I'm going there to get rich. Engraving's a very interesting profession, but a man never makes any money at it. So I'm going to try the goldfields."

Alexandra felt that this was a tactful speech, and Lou looked up with some interest. "Ever done anything in that line before?"

"No, but I'm going to join a friend of mine who went out from New York and has done well. He has offered to break me in."

"Turrible cold winters, there, I hear," remarked Oscar. "I thought people went up there in the spring."

"They do. But my friend is going to spend the winter in Seattle and I am to stay with him there and learn something about prospecting before we start north next year."

Lou looked skeptical. "Let's see, how long have you been away from here?"

"Sixteen years. You ought to remember that, Lou, for you were married just after we went away."

"Going to stay with us some time?" Oscar asked.

"A few days, if Alexandra can keep me."

"I expect you'll be wanting to see your old place," Lou observed more cordially. "You won't hardly know it. But there's a few chunks of your old sod house left. Alexandra wouldn't never let Frank Shabata plough over it."

Annie Lee, who, ever since the visitor was announced, had been touching up her hair and settling her lace and wishing she had worn another dress, now emerged with her three daughters and introduced them. She was greatly impressed by Carl's urban appearance, and in her excitement talked very loud and threw her head about. "And you ain't married yet? At your age, now!

Think of that! You'll have to wait for Milly. Yes, we've got a boy, too. The youngest. He's at home with his grandma. You must come over to see mother and hear Milly play. She's the musician of the family. She does pyrography, too. That's burnt wood, you know. You wouldn't believe what she can do with her poker. Yes, she goes to school in town, and she is the youngest in her class by two years."

Milly looked uncomfortable and Carl took her hand again. He liked her creamy skin and happy, innocent eyes, and he could see that her mother's way of talking distressed her. "I'm sure she's a clever little girl," he murmured, looking at her thoughtfully. "Let me see—Ah, it's your mother that she looks like, Alexandra. Mrs. Bergson must have looked just like this when she was a little girl. Does Milly run about over the country as you and Alexandra used to, Annie?"

Milly's mother protested. "Oh, my, no! Things has changed since we was girls. Milly has it very different. We are going to rent the place and move into town as soon as the girls are old enough to go out into company. A good many are doing that here now. Lou is going into business."

Lou grinned. "That's what she says. You better go get your things on. Ivar's hitching up," he added, turning to Annie.

Young farmers seldom address their wives by name. It is always "you," or "she."

Having got his wife out of the way, Lou sat down on the step and began to whittle. "Well, what do folks in New York think of William Jennings Bryan?" Lou began to bluster, as he always did when he talked politics. "We gave Wall Street a scare in ninety-six, all right, and we're fixing another to hand them. Silver wasn't the only issue," he nodded mysteriously. "There's a good many things got to be changed. The West is going to make itself heard."

Carl laughed. "But, surely, it did do that, if nothing else."

Lou's thin face reddened up to the roots of his bristly hair. "Oh, we've only begun. We're waking up to a sense of our responsibilities, out here, and we ain't afraid, neither. You fellows back there must be a tame lot. If you had any nerve you'd get together and march down to Wall Street and blow it up. Dynamite it, I mean," with a threatening nod.

He was so much in earnest that Carl scarcely knew how to answer him. "That would be a waste of powder. The same business would go on in another street. The street doesn't matter. But what have you fellows out here got to kick about? You have the only safe place there is. Morgan himself couldn't touch you. One only has to drive through this country to see that you're all as rich as barons."

"We have a good deal more to say than we had when we were poor," said Lou threateningly. "We're getting on to a whole lot of things."

As Ivar drove a double carriage up to the gate, Annie came out in a hat that looked like the model of a battleship. Carl rose and took her down to the carriage, while Lou lingered for a word with his sister.

"What do you suppose he's come for?" he asked, jerking his head toward the gate.

"Why, to pay us a visit. I've been begging him to for years."

Oscar looked at Alexandra. "He didn't let you know he was coming?"

"No. Why should he? I told him to come at any time."

Lou shrugged his shoulders. "He doesn't seem to have done much for himself. Wandering around this way!"

Oscar spoke solemnly, as from the depths of a cavern. "He never was much account."

Alexandra left them and hurried down to the gate where Annie was rattling on to Carl about her new dining room furniture. "You must bring Mr. Linstrum over real soon, only be sure to telephone me first," she called back, as Carl helped her into the carriage. Old Ivar, his white head bare, stood holding the horses. Lou came down the path and climbed into the front seat, took up the reins, and drove off without saying anything further to anyone. Oscar picked up his youngest boy and trudged off down the road, the other three trotting after him. Carl, holding the gate open for Alexandra, began to laugh. "Up and coming on the Divide, eh, Alexandra?" he cried gayly.

## CHAPTER IV

Carl had changed, Alexandra felt, much less than one might have expected. He had not become a trim, self-satisfied city man. There was still something homely and wayward and definitely personal about him. Even his clothes, his Norfolk coat and his very high collars, were a little unconventional. He seemed to shrink into himself as he used to do; to hold himself away from things, as if he were afraid of being hurt. In short, he was more self-conscious than a man of thirty-five is expected to be. He looked older than his years and not very strong. His black hair, which still hung in a triangle over his pale forehead, was thin at the crown, and there were fine, relentless lines about his eyes. His back, with its high, sharp shoulders, looked like the back of an over-worked German professor off on his holiday. His face was intelligent, sensitive, unhappy.

That evening after supper, Carl and Alexandra were sitting by the clump of castor beans in the middle of the flower garden. The gravel paths glittered in the moonlight, and below them the fields lay white and still.

"Do you know, Alexandra," he was saying, "I've been thinking how strangely things work out. I've been away engraving other men's pictures, and you've stayed at home and made your own." He pointed with his cigar toward the sleeping landscape. "How in the world have you done it? How have your neighbors done it?"

"We hadn't any of us much to do with it, Carl. The land did it. It had its little joke. It pretended to be poor because nobody knew how to work it right; and then, all at once, it worked itself. It woke up out of its sleep and stretched itself, and it was so big, so rich, that we suddenly found we were rich, just from sitting still. As for me, you remember when I began to buy land. For years after that I was always squeezing and borrowing until I was ashamed to show my face in the banks. And then, all at once, men began to come to me offering to lend me money—and I didn't need it! Then I went ahead and built this house. I really built it for Emil. I want you to see Emil, Carl. He is so different from the rest of us!"

"How different?"

"Oh, you'll see! I'm sure it was to have sons like Emil, and to give them a chance, that father left the old country. It's curious, too; on the outside Emil is just like an American boy—he graduated from the State University in June, you know—but underneath he is more Swedish than any of us. Sometimes he is so like father that he frightens me; he is so violent in his feelings like that."

"Is he going to farm here with you?"

"He shall do whatever he wants to," Alexandra declared warmly. "He is going to have a chance, a whole chance; that's what I've worked for. Sometimes he talks about studying law, and sometimes, just lately, he's been talking about going out into the sand hills and taking up more land. He has his sad times, like father. But I hope he won't do that. We have land enough, at last!" Alexandra laughed.

"How about Lou and Oscar? They've done well, haven't they?"

"Yes, very well; but they are different, and now that they have farms of their own I do not see so much of them. We divided the land equally when Lou married. They have their own way of doing things, and they do not altogether like my way, I am afraid. Perhaps they think me too independent. But I have had to think for myself a good many years and am not likely to change. On the whole, though, we take as much comfort in each other as most brothers and sisters do. And I am very fond of Lou's oldest daughter."

"I think I liked the old Lou and Oscar better, and they probably feel the same about me. I even, if you can keep a secret"—Carl leaned forward and touched her arm, smiling—"I even think I liked the old country better. This is all very splendid in its way, but there was something about this country when it was a wild old beast that has haunted me all these years. Now, when I come back to all this milk and honey, I feel like the old German song, 'Wo bist du, wo bist du, mein geliebtest Land?'—Do you ever feel like that, I wonder?"

"Yes, sometimes, when I think about father and mother and those who are gone; so many of our old neighbors." Alexandra paused and looked up thoughtfully at the stars. "We can remember the graveyard when it was wild prairie, Carl, and now—"

"And now the old story has begun to write itself over there," said Carl softly. "Isn't it queer: there are only two or three human stories, and they go on repeating themselves as fiercely as if they had never happened before; like the larks in this country, that have been singing the same five notes over for thousands of years."

"Oh, yes! The young people, they live so hard. And yet I sometimes envy them. There is my little neighbor, now; the people who bought your old place. I wouldn't have sold it to anyone else, but I was always fond of that girl. You must remember her, little Marie Tovesky, from Omaha, who used to visit here? When she was eighteen she ran away from the convent school and got married, crazy child! She came out here a bride, with her father and husband. He had nothing, and the old man was willing to buy them a place and set them up. Your farm took her fancy, and I was glad to have her so near me. I've never been sorry, either. I even try to get along with Frank on her account."

"Is Frank her husband?"

"Yes. He's one of these wild fellows. Most Bohemians are good-natured, but Frank thinks we don't appreciate him here, I guess. He's jealous about everything, his farm and his horses and his pretty wife. Everybody likes her, just the same as when she was little. Sometimes I go up to the Catholic church with Emil, and it's funny to see Marie standing there laughing and shaking hands with people, looking so excited and gay, with Frank sulking behind her as if he could eat everybody alive. Frank's not a bad neighbor, but to get on with him you've got to make a fuss over him and act as if you thought he was a very important person all the time, and different from other people. I find it hard to keep that up from one year's end to another."

"I shouldn't think you'd be very successful at that kind of thing, Alexandra." Carl seemed to find the idea amusing.

"Well," said Alexandra firmly, "I do the best I can, on Marie's account. She has it hard enough, anyway. She's too young and pretty for this sort of life. We're all ever so much older and slower. But she's the kind that won't be downed easily. She'll work all day and go to a Bohemian wedding and dance all night, and drive the hay wagon for a cross man next morning. I could stay by a job, but I never had the go in me that she has, when I was going my best. I'll have to take you over to see her tomorrow."

Carl dropped the end of his cigar softly among the castor beans and sighed. "Yes, I suppose I must see the old place. I'm cowardly about things that remind me of myself. It took courage to come at all, Alexandra. I wouldn't have, if I hadn't wanted to see you very, very much."

Alexandra looked at him with her calm, deliberate eyes. "Why do you dread things like that, Carl?" she asked earnestly. "Why are you dissatisfied with yourself?"

Her visitor winced. "How direct you are, Alexandra! Just like you used to be. Do I give myself away so quickly? Well, you see, for one thing, there's nothing to look forward to in my profession. Wood-engraving is the only thing I care about, and that had gone out before I began. Everything's cheap metal work nowadays, touching up miserable photographs, forcing up poor drawings, and spoiling good ones. I'm absolutely sick of it all." Carl frowned. "Alexandra, all the way out from New York I've been planning how I could deceive you and make you think me a very enviable fellow, and here I am telling you the truth the first night. I waste a lot of time pretending to people, and the joke of it is, I don't think I ever deceive anyone. There are too many of my kind; people know us on sight."

Carl paused. Alexandra pushed her hair back from her brow with a puzzled, thoughtful gesture. "You see," he went on calmly, "measured by your standards here, I'm a failure. I couldn't buy even one of your cornfields. I've enjoyed a great many things, but I've got nothing to show for it all."

"But you show for it yourself, Carl. I'd rather have had your freedom than my land."

Carl shook his head mournfully. "Freedom so often means that one isn't needed anywhere. Here you are an individual, you have a background of your own, you would be missed. But off there in the cities there are thousands of rolling stones like me. We are all alike; we have no ties, we know nobody, we own nothing. When one of us dies, they scarcely know where to bury him. Our landlady and the delicatessen man are our mourners, and we leave nothing behind us but a frock-coat and a fiddle, or an easel, or a typewriter, or whatever tool we got our living by. All we have ever managed to do is to pay our rent, the exorbitant rent that one has to pay for a few square feet of space near the heart of things. We have no house, no place, no people of our own. We live in the streets, in the parks, in the theatres. We sit in restaurants and concert halls and look about at the hundreds of our own kind and shudder."

Alexandra was silent. She sat looking at the silver spot the moon made on the surface of the pond down in the pasture. He knew that she understood what he meant. At last she said slowly, "And yet I would rather have Emil grow up like that than like his two brothers. We pay a high rent, too, though we pay differently. We grow hard and heavy here. We don't move lightly and easily as you do, and our minds get stiff. If the world were no wider than my cornfields, if there were not something beside this, I wouldn't feel that it was much worth while to work. No, I would rather have Emil like you than like them. I felt that as soon as you came."

"I wonder why you feel like that?" Carl mused.

"I don't know. Perhaps I am like Carrie Jensen, the sister of one of my hired men. She had never been out of the cornfields, and a few years ago she got despondent and said life was just the same thing over and over, and she didn't see the use of it. After she had tried to kill herself once or twice, her folks got worried and sent her over to Iowa to visit some relations. Ever since she's come back she's been perfectly cheerful, and she says she's contented to live and work in a world that's so big and interesting. She said that anything as big as the bridges over the Platte and the Missouri reconciled her. And it's what goes on in the world that reconciles me."

## CHAPTER V

Alexandra did not find time to go to her neighbor's the next day, nor the next. It was a busy season on the farm, with the corn-plowing going on, and even Emil was in the field with a team and cultivator. Carl went about over the farms with Alexandra in the morning, and in the afternoon and evening they found a great deal to talk about. Emil, for all his track practice, did not stand up under farmwork very well, and by night he was too tired to talk or even to practise on his cornet.

On Wednesday morning Carl got up before it was light, and stole downstairs and out of the kitchen door just as old Ivar was making his morning ablutions at the pump. Carl nodded to him and hurried up the draw, past the garden, and into the pasture where the milking cows used to be kept.

The dawn in the east looked like the light from some great fire that was burning under the edge of the world. The color was reflected in the globules of dew that sheathed the short gray pasture grass. Carl walked rapidly until he came to the crest of the second hill, where the Bergson pasture joined the one that had belonged to his father. There he sat down and waited for the sun to rise. It was just there that he and Alexandra used to do their milking together, he on his side of the fence, she on hers. He could remember exactly how she looked when she came over the close-cropped grass, her skirts pinned up, her head bare, a bright tin pail in either hand, and the milky light of the early morning all about her. Even as a boy he used to feel, when he saw her coming with her free step, her upright head and calm shoulders, that she looked as if she had walked straight out of the morning itself. Since then, when he had happened to see the sun come up in the country or on the water, he had often remembered the young Swedish girl and her milking pails.

Carl sat musing until the sun leaped above the prairie, and in the grass about him all the small creatures of day began to tune their tiny instruments. Birds and insects without number began to chirp, to twitter, to snap and whistle, to make all manner of fresh shrill noises. The pasture was flooded with light; every clump of ironweed and snow-on-the-mountain threw a long shadow, and the golden light seemed to be rippling through the curly grass like the tide racing in.

He crossed the fence into the pasture that was now the Shabatas' and continued his walk toward the pond. He had not gone far, however, when he discovered that he was not the only person abroad. In the draw below, his gun in his hands, was Emil, advancing cautiously, with a young woman beside him. They were moving softly, keeping close together, and Carl knew that they expected to find ducks on the pond. At the moment when they came in sight of the bright spot of water, he heard a whirr of wings and the ducks shot up into the air. There was a sharp crack from the gun, and five of the birds fell to the ground. Emil and his companion laughed delightedly, and Emil ran to pick them up. When he came back, dangling the ducks by their feet, Marie held her apron and he dropped them into it. As she stood looking down at them, her face changed. She took up one of the birds, a rumpled ball of feathers with the blood dripping slowly from its mouth, and looked at the live color that still burned on its plumage.

As she let it fall, she cried in distress, "Oh, Emil, why did you?"

"I like that!" the boy exclaimed indignantly. "Why, Marie, you asked me to come yourself."

"Yes, yes, I know," she said tearfully, "but I didn't think. I hate to see them when they are first shot. They were having such a good time, and we've spoiled it all for them."

Emil gave a rather sore laugh. "I should say we had! I'm not going hunting with you anymore. You're as bad as Ivar. Here, let me take them." He snatched the ducks out of her apron.

"Don't be cross, Emil. Only—Ivar's right about wild things. They're too happy to kill. You can tell just how they felt when they flew up. They were scared, but they didn't really think anything could hurt them. No, we won't do that anymore."

"All right," Emil assented. "I'm sorry I made you feel bad." As he looked down into her tearful eyes, there was a curious, sharp young bitterness in his own.

Carl watched them as they moved slowly down the draw. They had not seen him at all. He had not overheard much of their dialogue, but he felt the import of it. It made him, somehow, unreasonably mournful to find two young things abroad in the pasture in the early morning. He decided that he needed his breakfast.

## CHAPTER VI

At dinner that day Alexandra said she thought they must really manage to go over to the Shabatas' that afternoon. "It's not often I let three days go by without seeing Marie. She will think I have forsaken her, now that my old friend has come back."

After the men had gone back to work, Alexandra put on a white dress and her sun-hat, and she and Carl set forth across the fields. "You see we have kept up the old path, Carl. It has been so nice for me to feel that there was a friend at the other end of it again."

Carl smiled a little ruefully. "All the same, I hope it hasn't been *quite* the same."

Alexandra looked at him with surprise. "Why, no, of course not. Not the same. She could not very well take your place, if that's what you mean. I'm friendly with all my neighbors, I hope. But Marie is really a companion, someone I can talk to quite frankly. You wouldn't want me to be more lonely than I have been, would you?"

Carl laughed and pushed back the triangular lock of hair with the edge of his hat. "Of course I don't. I ought to be thankful that this path hasn't been worn by—well, by friends with more pressing errands than your little Bohemian is likely to have." He paused to give Alexandra his hand as she stepped over the stile. "Are you the least bit disappointed in our coming together again?" he asked abruptly. "Is it the way you hoped it would be?"

Alexandra smiled at this. "Only better. When I've thought about your coming, I've sometimes been a little afraid of it. You have lived where things move so fast, and everything is slow here; the people slowest of all. Our lives are like the years, all made up of weather and crops and cows. How you hated cows!" She shook her head and laughed to herself.

"I didn't when we milked together. I walked up to the pasture corners this morning. I wonder whether I shall ever be able to tell you all that I was thinking about up there. It's a strange thing, Alexandra; I find it easy to be frank with you about everything under the sun except—yourself!"

"You are afraid of hurting my feelings, perhaps." Alexandra looked at him thoughtfully.

"No, I'm afraid of giving you a shock. You've seen yourself for so long in the dull minds of the people about you, that if I were to tell you how you seem to me, it would startle you. But you must see that you astonish me. You must feel when people admire you."

Alexandra blushed and laughed with some confusion. "I felt that you were pleased with me, if you mean that."

"And you've felt when other people were pleased with you?" he insisted.

"Well, sometimes. The men in town, at the banks and the county offices, seem glad to see me. I think, myself, it is more pleasant to do business with people who are clean and healthy-looking," she admitted blandly.

Carl gave a little chuckle as he opened the Shabatas' gate for her. "Oh, do you?" he asked dryly.

There was no sign of life about the Shabatas' house except a big yellow cat, sunning itself on the kitchen doorstep.

Alexandra took the path that led to the orchard. "She often sits there and sews. I didn't telephone her we were coming, because I didn't want her to go to work and bake cake and freeze ice-cream. She'll always make a party if you give her the least excuse. Do you recognize the apple trees, Carl?"

Linstrum looked about him. "I wish I had a dollar for every bucket of water I've carried for those trees. Poor father, he was an easy man, but he was perfectly merciless when it came to watering the orchard."

"That's one thing I like about Germans; they make an orchard grow if they can't make anything else. I'm so glad these trees belong to someone who takes comfort in them. When I rented this place, the tenants never kept the orchard up, and Emil and I used to come over and take care of it ourselves. It needs mowing now. There she is, down in the corner. Maria-a-a!" she called.

A recumbent figure started up from the grass and came running toward them through the flickering screen of light and shade.

"Look at her! Isn't she like a little brown rabbit?" Alexandra laughed.

Maria ran up panting and threw her arms about Alexandra. "Oh, I had begun to think you were not coming at all, maybe. I knew you were so busy. Yes, Emil told me about Mr. Linstrum being here. Won't you come up to the house?"

"Why not sit down there in your corner? Carl wants to see the orchard. He kept all these trees alive for years, watering them with his own back."

Marie turned to Carl. "Then I'm thankful to you, Mr. Linstrum. We'd never have bought the place if it hadn't been for this orchard, and then I wouldn't have had Alexandra, either." She gave Alexandra's arm a little squeeze as she walked beside her. "How nice your dress smells, Alexandra; you put rosemary leaves in your chest, like I told you."

She led them to the northwest corner of the orchard, sheltered on one side by a thick mulberry hedge and bordered on the other by a wheat field, just beginning to yellow. In this corner the ground dipped a little, and the bluegrass, which the weeds had driven out in the upper part of the orchard, grew thick and luxuriant. Wild roses were flaming in the tufts of bunchgrass along the fence. Under a white mulberry tree there was an old wagon-seat. Beside it lay a book and a workbasket.

"You must have the seat, Alexandra. The grass would stain your dress," the hostess insisted. She dropped down on the ground at Alexandra's side and tucked her feet under her. Carl sat at a little distance from the two women, his back to the wheat field, and watched them. Alexandra took off her shade-hat and threw it on the ground. Marie picked it up and played with the white ribbons, twisting them about her brown fingers as she talked. They made a pretty picture in the strong sunlight, the leafy pattern surrounding them like a net; the Swedish woman so white and gold, kindly and amused, but armored in calm, and the alert brown one, her full lips parted, points of yellow light dancing in her eyes as she laughed and chattered. Carl had never forgotten little Marie Tovesky's eyes, and he was glad to have an opportunity to study them. The brown iris, he found, was curiously slashed with yellow, the color of sunflower honey, or of old amber. In each eye one of these streaks must have been larger than the others, for the effect was that of two dancing points of light, two little yellow bubbles, such as rise in a glass of champagne. Sometimes they seemed like the sparks from a forge. She seemed so easily excited, to kindle with a fierce little flame if one but breathed upon her. "What a waste," Carl reflected. "She ought to be doing all that for a sweetheart. How awkwardly things come about!"

It was not very long before Marie sprang up out of the grass again. "Wait a moment. I want to show you something." She ran away and disappeared behind the low-growing apple trees.

"What a charming creature," Carl murmured. "I don't wonder that her husband is jealous. But can't she walk? does she always run?"

Alexandra nodded. "Always. I don't see many people, but I don't believe there are many like her, anywhere."

Marie came back with a branch she had broken from an apricot tree, laden with pale yellow, pink-cheeked fruit. She dropped it beside Carl. "Did you plant those, too? They are such beautiful little trees."

Carl fingered the blue-green leaves, porous like blotting-paper and shaped like birch leaves, hung on waxen red stems. "Yes, I think I did. Are these the circus trees, Alexandra?"

"Shall I tell her about them?" Alexandra asked. "Sit down like a good girl, Marie, and don't ruin my poor hat, and I'll tell you a story. A long time ago, when Carl and I were, say, sixteen and twelve, a circus came to Hanover and we went to town in our wagon, with Lou and Oscar, to see the parade. We hadn't money enough to go to the circus. We followed the parade out to the circus grounds and hung around until the show began and the crowd went inside the tent. Then Lou was afraid we looked foolish standing outside in the pasture, so we went back to Hanover feeling very sad. There was a man in the streets selling apricots, and we had never seen any before. He had driven down from somewhere up in the French country, and he was selling them twenty-five cents a peck. We had a little money our fathers had given us for candy, and I bought two pecks and Carl bought one. They cheered us a good deal, and we saved all the seeds and planted them. Up to the time Carl went away, they hadn't borne at all."

"And now he's come back to eat them," cried Marie, nodding at Carl. "That *is* a good story. I can remember you a little, Mr. Linstrum. I used to see you in Hanover sometimes, when Uncle Joe took me to town. I remember you because you were always buying pencils and tubes of paint at the drug store. Once, when my uncle left me at the store, you drew a lot of little birds and flowers for me on a piece of wrapping-paper. I kept them for a long while. I thought you were very romantic because you could draw and had such black eyes."

Carl smiled. "Yes, I remember that time. Your uncle bought you some kind of a mechanical toy, a Turkish lady sitting on an ottoman and smoking a hookah, wasn't it? And she turned her head backwards and forwards."

"Oh, yes! Wasn't she splendid! I knew well enough I ought not to tell Uncle Joe I wanted it, for he had just come back from the saloon and was feeling good. You remember how he laughed? She tickled him, too. But when we got home, my aunt scolded him for buying toys when she needed so many things. We wound our lady up every night, and when she began to move her head my aunt used to laugh as hard as any of us. It was a music-box, you know, and the Turkish lady played a tune while she smoked. That was how she made you feel so jolly. As I remember her, she was lovely, and had a gold crescent on her turban."

Half an hour later, as they were leaving the house, Carl and Alexandra were met in the path by a strapping fellow in overalls and a blue shirt. He was breathing hard, as if he had been running, and was muttering to himself.

Marie ran forward, and, taking him by the arm, gave him a little push toward her guests. "Frank, this is Mr. Linstrum."

Frank took off his broad straw hat and nodded to Alexandra. When he spoke to Carl, he showed a fine set of white teeth. He was burned a dull red down to his neckband, and there was a heavy three-days' stubble on his face. Even in his agitation he was handsome, but he looked a rash and violent man.

Barely saluting the callers, he turned at once to his wife and began, in an outraged tone, "I have to leave my team to drive the old woman Hiller's hogs out-a my wheat. I go to take dat old woman to de court if she ain't careful, I tell you!"

His wife spoke soothingly. "But, Frank, she has only her lame boy to help her. She does the best she can."

Alexandra looked at the excited man and offered a suggestion. "Why don't you go over there some afternoon and hog-tight her fences? You'd save time for yourself in the end."

Frank's neck stiffened. "Not-a-much, I won't. I keep my hogs home. Other peoples can do like me. See? If that Louis can mend shoes, he can mend fence."

"Maybe," said Alexandra placidly; "but I've found it sometimes pays to mend other people's fences. Good-bye, Marie. Come to see me soon."

Alexandra walked firmly down the path and Carl followed her.

Frank went into the house and threw himself on the sofa, his face to the wall, his clenched fist on his hip. Marie, having seen her guests off, came in and put her hand coaxingly on his shoulder.

"Poor Frank! You've run until you've made your head ache, now haven't you? Let me make you some coffee."

"What else am I to do?" he cried hotly in Bohemian. "Am I to let any old woman's hogs root up my wheat? Is that what I work myself to death for?"

"Don't worry about it, Frank. I'll speak to Mrs. Hiller again. But, really, she almost cried last time they got out, she was so sorry."

Frank bounced over on his other side. "That's it; you always side with them against me. They all know it. Anybody here feels free to borrow the mower and break it, or turn their hogs in on me. They know you won't care!"

Marie hurried away to make his coffee. When she came back, he was fast asleep. She sat down and looked at him for a long while, very thoughtfully. When the kitchen clock struck six she went out to get supper, closing the door gently behind her. She was always sorry for Frank when he worked himself into one of these rages, and she was sorry to have him rough and quarrelsome with his neighbors. She was perfectly aware that the neighbors had a good deal to put up with, and that they bore with Frank for her sake.

# CHAPTER VII

Marie's father, Albert Tovesky, was one of the more intelligent Bohemians who came West in the early seventies. He settled in Omaha and became a leader and adviser among his people there. Marie was his youngest child, by a second wife, and was the apple of his eye. She was barely sixteen, and was in the graduating class of the Omaha High School, when Frank Shabata arrived from the old country and set all the Bohemian girls in a flutter. He was easily the buck of the beer-gardens, and on Sunday he was a sight to see, with his silk hat and tucked shirt and blue frock-coat, wearing gloves and carrying a little wisp of a yellow cane. He was tall and fair, with splendid teeth and close-cropped yellow curls, and he wore a slightly disdainful expression, proper for a young man with high connections, whose mother had a big farm in the Elbe valley. There was often an interesting discontent in his blue eyes, and every Bohemian girl he met imagined herself the cause of that unsatisfied expression. He had a way of drawing out his cambric handkerchief slowly, by one corner, from his breast-pocket, that was melancholy and romantic in the extreme. He took a little flight with each of the more eligible Bohemian girls, but it was when he was with little Marie Tovesky that he drew his handkerchief out most slowly, and, after he had lit a fresh cigar, dropped the match most despairingly. Anyone could see, with half an eye, that his proud heart was bleeding for somebody.

One Sunday, late in the summer after Marie's graduation, she met Frank at a Bohemian picnic down the river and went rowing with him all the afternoon. When she got home that evening she went straight to her father's room and told him that she was engaged to Shabata. Old Tovesky was having a comfortable pipe before he went to bed. When he heard his daughter's announcement, he first prudently corked his beer bottle and then leaped to his feet and had a turn of temper. He characterized Frank Shabata by a Bohemian expression which is the equivalent of stuffed shirt.

"Why don't he go to work like the rest of us did? His farm in the Elbe valley, indeed! Ain't he got plenty brothers and sisters? It's his mother's farm, and why don't he stay at home and help her? Haven't I seen his mother out in the morning at five o'clock with her ladle and her big bucket on wheels, putting liquid manure on the cabbages? Don't I know the look of old Eva Shabata's hands? Like an old horse's hoofs they are—and this fellow wearing gloves and rings! Engaged, indeed! You aren't fit to be out of school, and that's what's the matter with you. I will send you off to the Sisters of the Sacred Heart in St. Louis, and they will teach you some sense, *I* guess!"

Accordingly, the very next week, Albert Tovesky took his daughter, pale and tearful, down the river to the convent. But the way to make Frank want anything was to tell him he couldn't have it. He managed to have an interview with Marie before she went away, and whereas he had been only half in love with her before, he now persuaded himself that he would not stop at anything. Marie took with her to the convent, under the canvas lining of her trunk, the results of a laborious and satisfying morning on Frank's part; no less than a dozen photographs of himself, taken in a dozen different love-lorn attitudes. There was a little round photograph for her watch-case, photographs for her wall and dresser, and even long narrow ones to be used as bookmarks. More than once the handsome gentleman was torn to pieces before the French class by an indignant nun.

Marie pined in the convent for a year, until her eighteenth birthday was passed. Then she met Frank Shabata in the Union Station in St. Louis and ran away with him. Old Tovesky forgave his daughter because there was nothing else to do, and bought her a farm in the country that she had loved so well as a child. Since then her story had been a part of the history of the Divide. She and Frank had been living there for five years when Carl Linstrum came back to pay his long deferred visit to Alexandra. Frank had, on the whole, done better than one might have expected. He had flung himself at the soil with savage energy. Once a year he went to Hastings or to Omaha, on a spree. He stayed away for a week or two, and then came home and worked like a demon. He did work; if he felt sorry for himself, that was his own affair.

# CHAPTER VIII

On the evening of the day of Alexandra's call at the Shabatas', a heavy rain set in. Frank sat up until a late hour reading the Sunday newspapers. One of the Goulds was getting a divorce, and Frank took it as a personal affront. In printing the story of the young man's marital troubles, the knowing editor gave a sufficiently colored account of his career, stating the amount of his income and the manner in which he was supposed to spend it. Frank read English slowly, and the more he read about this divorce case, the angrier he grew. At last he threw down the page with a snort. He turned to his farm-hand who was reading the other half of the paper.

"By God! if I have that young feller in de hayfield once, I show him someting. Listen here what he do wit his money." And Frank began the catalogue of the young man's reputed extravagances.

Marie sighed. She thought it hard that the Goulds, for whom she had nothing but good will, should make her so much trouble. She hated to see the Sunday newspapers come into the house. Frank was always reading about the doings of rich people and feeling outraged. He had an inexhaustible stock of stories about their crimes and follies, how they bribed the courts and shot down their butlers with impunity whenever they chose. Frank and Lou Bergson had very similar ideas, and they were two of the political agitators of the county.

The next morning broke clear and brilliant, but Frank said the ground was too wet to plough, so he took the cart and drove over to Sainte-Agnes to spend the day at Moses Marcel's saloon. After he was gone, Marie went out to the back porch to begin her butter-making. A brisk wind had come up and was driving puffy white clouds across the sky. The orchard was sparkling and rippling in the sun. Marie stood looking toward it wistfully, her hand on the lid of the churn, when she heard a sharp ring in the air, the merry sound of the whetstone on the scythe. That invitation decided her. She ran into the house, put on a short skirt and a pair of her husband's boots, caught up a tin pail and started for the orchard. Emil had already begun work and was mowing vigorously. When he saw her coming, he stopped and wiped his brow. His yellow canvas leggings and khaki trousers were splashed to the knees.

"Don't let me disturb you, Emil. I'm going to pick cherries. Isn't everything beautiful after the rain? Oh, but I'm glad to get this place mowed! When I heard it raining in the night, I thought maybe you would come and do it for me today. The wind wakened me. Didn't it blow dreadfully? Just smell the wild roses! They are always so spicy after a rain. We never had so many of them in here before. I suppose it's the wet season. Will you have to cut them, too?"

"If I cut the grass, I will," Emil said teasingly. "What's the matter with you? What makes you so flighty?"

"Am I flighty? I suppose that's the wet season, too, then. It's exciting to see everything growing so fast—and to get the grass cut! Please leave the roses till last, if you must cut them. Oh, I don't mean all of them, I mean that low place down by my tree, where there are so many. Aren't you splashed! Look at the spider-webs all over the grass. Good-bye. I'll call you if I see a snake."

She tripped away and Emil stood looking after her. In a few moments he heard the cherries dropping smartly into the pail, and he began to swing his scythe with that long, even stroke that few American boys ever learn. Marie picked cherries and sang softly to herself, stripping one glittering branch after another, shivering when she caught a shower of raindrops on her neck and hair. And Emil mowed his way slowly down toward the cherry trees.

That summer the rains had been so many and opportune that it was almost more than Shabata and his man could do to keep up with the corn; the orchard was a neglected wilderness. All sorts of weeds and herbs and flowers had grown up there; splotches of wild larkspur, pale green-and-white spikes of hoarhound, plantations of wild cotton, tangles of foxtail and wild wheat. South of the apricot trees, cornering on the wheat field, was Frank's alfalfa, where myriads of white and yellow butterflies were always fluttering above the purple blossoms. When Emil reached the lower corner by the hedge, Marie was sitting under her white mulberry tree, the pailful of cherries beside her, looking off at the gentle, tireless swelling of the wheat.

"Emil," she said suddenly—he was mowing quietly about under the tree so as not to disturb her—"what religion did the Swedes have away back, before they were Christians?"

Emil paused and straightened his back. "I don't know. About like the Germans', wasn't it?"

Marie went on as if she had not heard him. "The Bohemians, you know, were tree worshipers before the missionaries came. Father says the people in the mountains still do queer things, sometimes—they believe that trees bring good or bad luck."

Emil looked superior. "Do they? Well, which are the lucky trees? I'd like to know."

"I don't know all of them, but I know lindens are. The old people in the mountains plant lindens to purify the forest, and to do away with the spells that come from the old trees they say have lasted from heathen times. I'm a good Catholic, but I think I could get along with caring for trees, if I hadn't anything else."

"That's a poor saying," said Emil, stooping over to wipe his hands in the wet grass.

"Why is it? If I feel that way, I feel that way. I like trees because they seem more resigned to the way they have to live than other things do. I feel as if this tree knows everything I ever think of when I sit here. When I come back to it, I never have to remind it of anything; I begin just where I left off."

Emil had nothing to say to this. He reached up among the branches and began to pick the sweet, insipid fruit—long ivory-colored berries, tipped with faint pink, like white coral, that fall to the ground unheeded all summer through. He dropped a handful into her lap.

"Do you like Mr. Linstrum?" Marie asked suddenly.

"Yes. Don't you?"

"Oh, ever so much; only he seems kind of staid and school-teachery. But, of course, he is older than Frank, even. I'm sure I don't want to live to be more than thirty, do you? Do you think Alexandra likes him very much?"

"I suppose so. They were old friends."

"Oh, Emil, you know what I mean!" Marie tossed her head impatiently. "Does she really care about him? When she used to tell me about him, I always wondered whether she wasn't a little in love with him."

"Who, Alexandra?" Emil laughed and thrust his hands into his trousers pockets. "Alexandra's never been in love, you crazy!" He laughed again. "She wouldn't know how to go about it. The idea!"

Marie shrugged her shoulders. "Oh, you don't know Alexandra as well as you think you do! If you had any eyes, you would see that she is very fond of him. It would serve you all right if she walked off with Carl. I like him because he appreciates her more than you do."

Emil frowned. "What are you talking about, Marie? Alexandra's all right. She and I have always been good friends. What more do you want? I like to talk to Carl about New York and what a fellow can do there."

"Oh, Emil! Surely you are not thinking of going off there?"

"Why not? I must go somewhere, mustn't I?" The young man took up his scythe and leaned on it. "Would you rather I went off in the sand hills and lived like Ivar?"

Marie's face fell under his brooding gaze. She looked down at his wet leggings. "I'm sure Alexandra hopes you will stay on here," she murmured.

"Then Alexandra will be disappointed," the young man said roughly. "What do I want to hang around here for? Alexandra can run the farm all right, without me. I don't want to stand around and look on. I want to be doing something on my own account."

"That's so," Marie sighed. "There are so many, many things you can do. Almost anything you choose."

"And there are so many, many things I can't do." Emil echoed her tone sarcastically. "Sometimes I don't want to do anything at all, and sometimes I want to pull the four corners of the Divide together"—he threw out his arm and brought it back with a jerk—"so, like a tablecloth. I get tired of seeing men and horses going up and down, up and down."

Marie looked up at his defiant figure and her face clouded. "I wish you weren't so restless, and didn't get so worked up over things," she said sadly.

"Thank you," he returned shortly.

She sighed despondently. "Everything I say makes you cross, don't it? And you never used to be cross to me."

Emil took a step nearer and stood frowning down at her bent head. He stood in an attitude of self-defense, his feet well apart, his hands clenched and drawn up at his sides, so that the cords stood out on his bare arms. "I can't play with you like a little boy anymore," he said slowly. "That's what you miss, Marie. You'll have to get some other little boy to play with." He stopped and took a deep breath. Then he went on in a low tone, so intense that it was almost threatening: "Sometimes you seem to understand perfectly, and then sometimes you pretend you don't. You don't help things any by pretending. It's then that I want to pull the corners of the Divide together. If you *won't* understand, you know, I could make you!"

Marie clasped her hands and started up from her seat. She had grown very pale and her eyes were shining with excitement and distress. "But, Emil, if I understand, then all our good times are over, we can never do nice things together anymore. We shall have to behave like Mr. Linstrum. And, anyhow, there's nothing to understand!"

She struck the ground with her little foot fiercely. "That won't last. It will go away, and things will be just as they used to. I wish you were a Catholic. The Church helps people, indeed it does. I pray for you, but that's not the same as if you prayed yourself."

She spoke rapidly and pleadingly, looked entreatingly into his face. Emil stood defiant, gazing down at her.

"I can't pray to have the things I want," he said slowly, "and I won't pray not to have them, not if I'm damned for it."

Marie turned away, wringing her hands. "Oh, Emil, you won't try! Then all our good times are over."

"Yes; over. I never expect to have any more."

Emil gripped the handholds of his scythe and began to mow. Marie took up her cherries and went slowly toward the house, crying bitterly.

## CHAPTER IX

On Sunday afternoon, a month after Carl Linstrum's arrival, he rode with Emil up into the French country to attend a Catholic fair. He sat for most of the afternoon in the basement of the church, where the fair was held, talking to Marie Shabata, or strolled about the gravel terrace, thrown up on the hillside in front of the basement doors, where the French boys were jumping and wrestling and throwing the discus. Some of the boys were in their white baseball suits; they had just come up from a Sunday practice game down in the ball-grounds. Amedee, the newly married, Emil's best friend, was their pitcher, renowned among the country towns for his dash and skill. Amedee was a little fellow, a year younger than Emil and much more boyish in appearance; very lithe and active and neatly made, with a clear brown and white skin, and flashing white teeth. The Sainte-Agnes boys were to play the Hastings nine in a fortnight, and Amedee's lightning balls were the hope of his team. The little Frenchman seemed to get every ounce there was in him behind the ball as it left his hand.

"You'd have made the battery at the University for sure, 'Medee," Emil said as they were walking from the ball-grounds back to the church on the hill. "You're pitching better than you did in the spring."

Amedee grinned. "Sure! A married man don't lose his head no more."

He slapped Emil on the back as he caught step with him. "Oh, Emil, you wanna get married right off quick! It's the greatest thing ever!"

Emil laughed. "How am I going to get married without any girl?"

Amedee took his arm. "Pooh! There are plenty girls will have you. You wanna get some nice French girl, now. She treat you well; always be jolly. See"—he began checking off on his fingers—"there is Severine, and Alphosen, and Josephine, and Hectorine, and Louise, and Malvina—why, I could love any of them girls! Why don't you get after them? Are you stuck up, Emil, or is anything the matter with you? I never did know a boy twenty-two years old before that didn't have no girl. You wanna be a priest, maybe? Not-a for me!"

Amedee swaggered. "I bring many good Catholics into this world, I hope, and that's a way I help the Church."

Emil looked down and patted him on the shoulder. "Now you're windy, 'Medee. You Frenchies like to brag."

But Amedee had the zeal of the newly married, and he was not to be lightly shaken off. "Honest and true, Emil, don't you want *any* girl? Maybe there's some young lady in Lincoln, now, very grand"—Amedee waved his hand languidly before his face to denote the fan of heartless beauty—"and you lost your heart up there. Is that it?"

"Maybe," said Emil.

But Amedee saw no appropriate glow in his friend's face. "Bah!" he exclaimed in disgust. "I tell all the French girls to keep 'way from you. You gotta rock in there," thumping Emil on the ribs.

When they reached the terrace at the side of the church, Amedee, who was excited by his success on the ball-grounds, challenged Emil to a jumping-match, though he knew he would be beaten. They belted themselves up, and Raoul Marcel, the choir tenor and Father Duchesne's pet, and Jean Bordelau, held the string over which they vaulted. All the French boys stood round, cheering and humping themselves up when Emil or Amedee went over the wire, as if they were helping in the lift. Emil stopped at five-feet-five, declaring that he would spoil his appetite for supper if he jumped any more.

Angelique, Amedee's pretty bride, as blonde and fair as her name, who had come out to watch the match, tossed her head at Emil and said:

" 'Medee could jump much higher than you if he were as tall. And anyhow, he is much more graceful. He goes over like a bird, and you have to hump yourself all up."

"Oh, I do, do I?" Emil caught her and kissed her saucy mouth squarely, while she laughed and struggled and called, " 'Medee! 'Medee!"

"There, you see your 'Medee isn't even big enough to get you away from me. I could run away with you right now and he could only sit down and cry about it. I'll show you whether I have to hump myself!" Laughing and panting, he picked Angelique up in his arms and began running about the rectangle with her. Not until he saw Marie Shabata's tiger eyes flashing from the gloom of the basement doorway did he hand the disheveled bride over to her husband. "There, go to your graceful; I haven't the heart to take you away from him."

Angelique clung to her husband and made faces at Emil over the white shoulder of Amedee's ball-shirt. Emil was greatly amused at her air of proprietorship and at Amedee's shameless submission to it. He was delighted with his friend's good fortune. He liked to see and to think about Amedee's sunny, natural, happy love.

He and Amedee had ridden and wrestled and larked together since they were lads of twelve. On Sundays and holidays they were always arm in arm. It seemed strange that now he should have to hide the thing that Amedee was so proud of, that the feeling which gave one of them such happiness should bring the other such despair. It was like that when Alexandra tested her seed-corn in the spring, he mused. From two ears that had grown side by side, the grains of one shot up joyfully into the light, projecting themselves into the future, and the grains from the other lay still in the earth and rotted; and nobody knew why.

## CHAPTER X

While Emil and Carl were amusing themselves at the fair, Alexandra was at home, busy with her account-books, which had been neglected of late. She was almost through with her figures when she heard a cart drive up to the gate, and looking out of the window she saw her two older brothers. They had seemed to avoid her ever since Carl Linstrum's arrival, four weeks ago that day, and she hurried to the door to welcome them. She saw at once that they had come with some very definite purpose. They followed her stiffly into the sitting room. Oscar sat down, but Lou walked over to the window and remained standing, his hands behind him.

"You are by yourself?" he asked, looking toward the doorway into the parlor.

"Yes. Carl and Emil went up to the Catholic fair."

For a few moments neither of the men spoke.

Then Lou came out sharply. "How soon does he intend to go away from here?"

"I don't know, Lou. Not for some time, I hope." Alexandra spoke in an even, quiet tone that often exasperated her brothers. They felt that she was trying to be superior with them.

Oscar spoke up grimly. "We thought we ought to tell you that people have begun to talk," he said meaningly.

Alexandra looked at him. "What about?"

Oscar met her eyes blankly. "About you, keeping him here so long. It looks bad for him to be hanging on to a woman this way. People think you're getting taken in."

Alexandra shut her account-book firmly. "Boys," she said seriously, "don't let's go on with this. We won't come out anywhere. I can't take advice on such a matter. I know you mean well, but you must not feel responsible for me in things of this sort. If we go on with this talk it will only make hard feeling."

Lou whipped about from the window. "You ought to think a little about your family. You're making us all ridiculous."

"How am I?"

"People are beginning to say you want to marry the fellow."

"Well, and what is ridiculous about that?"

Lou and Oscar exchanged outraged looks. "Alexandra! Can't you see he's just a tramp and he's after your money? He wants to be taken care of, he does!"

"Well, suppose I want to take care of him? Whose business is it but my own?"

"Don't you know he'd get hold of your property?"

"He'd get hold of what I wished to give him, certainly."

Oscar sat up suddenly and Lou clutched at his bristly hair.

"Give him?" Lou shouted. "Our property, our homestead?"

"I don't know about the homestead," said Alexandra quietly. "I know you and Oscar have always expected that it would be left to your children, and I'm not sure but what you're right. But I'll do exactly as I please with the rest of my land, boys."

"The rest of your land!" cried Lou, growing more excited every minute. "Didn't all the land come out of the homestead? It was bought with money borrowed on the homestead, and Oscar and me worked ourselves to the bone paying interest on it."

"Yes, you paid the interest. But when you married we made a division of the land, and you were satisfied. I've made more on my farms since I've been alone than when we all worked together."

"Everything you've made has come out of the original land that us boys worked for, hasn't it? The farms and all that comes out of them belongs to us as a family."

Alexandra waved her hand impatiently. "Come now, Lou. Stick to the facts. You are talking nonsense. Go to the county clerk and ask him who owns my land, and whether my titles are good."

Lou turned to his brother. "This is what comes of letting a woman meddle in business," he said bitterly. "We ought to have taken things in our own hands years ago. But she liked to run things, and we humored her. We thought you had good sense, Alexandra. We never thought you'd do anything foolish."

Alexandra rapped impatiently on her desk with her knuckles. "Listen, Lou. Don't talk wild. You say you ought to have taken things into your own hands years ago. I suppose you mean before you left home. But how could you take hold of what wasn't there? I've got most of what I have now since we divided the property; I've built it up myself, and it has nothing to do with you."

Oscar spoke up solemnly. "The property of a family really belongs to the men of the family, no matter about the title. If anything goes wrong, it's the men that are held responsible."

"Yes, of course," Lou broke in. "Everybody knows that. Oscar and me have always been easygoing and we've never made any fuss. We were willing you should hold the land and have the good of it, but you got no right to part with any of it. We worked in the fields to pay for the first land you bought, and whatever's come out of it has got to be kept in the family."

Oscar reinforced his brother, his mind fixed on the one point he could see. "The property of a family belongs to the men of the family, because they are held responsible, and because they do the work."

Alexandra looked from one to the other, her eyes full of indignation. She had been impatient before, but now she was beginning to feel angry. "And what about my work?" she asked in an unsteady voice.

Lou looked at the carpet. "Oh, now, Alexandra, you always took it pretty easy! Of course we wanted you to. You liked to manage round, and we always humored you. We realize you were a great deal of help to us. There's no woman anywhere around that knows as much about business as you do, and we've always been proud of that, and thought you were pretty smart. But, of course, the real work always fell on us. Good advice is all right, but it don't get the weeds out of the corn."

"Maybe not, but it sometimes puts in the crop, and it sometimes keeps the fields for corn to grow in," said Alexandra dryly. "Why, Lou, I can remember when you and Oscar wanted to sell this homestead and all the improvements to old preacher Ericson for two thousand dollars. If I'd consented, you'd have gone down to the river and scraped along on poor farms for the rest of your lives. When I put in our first field of alfalfa you both opposed me, just because I first heard about it from a young man who had been to the University. You said I was being taken in then, and all the neighbors said so. You know as well as I do that alfalfa has been the salvation of this country. You all laughed at me when I said our land here was about ready for wheat, and I had to raise three big wheat crops before the neighbors quit putting all their land in corn. Why, I remember you cried, Lou, when we put in the first big wheat-planting, and said everybody was laughing at us."

Lou turned to Oscar. "That's the woman of it; if she tells you to put in a crop, she thinks she's put it in. It makes women conceited to meddle in business. I shouldn't think you'd want to remind us how hard you were on us, Alexandra, after the way you baby Emil."

"Hard on you? I never meant to be hard. Conditions were hard. Maybe I would never have been very soft, anyhow; but I certainly didn't choose to be the kind of girl I was. If you take even a vine and cut it back again and again, it grows hard, like a tree."

Lou felt that they were wandering from the point, and that in digression Alexandra might unnerve him. He wiped his forehead with a jerk of his handkerchief. "We never doubted you, Alexandra. We never questioned anything you did. You've always had your own way. But you can't expect us to sit like stumps and see you done out of the property by any loafer who happens along, and making yourself ridiculous into the bargain."

Oscar rose. "Yes," he broke in, "everybody's laughing to see you get took in; at your age, too. Everybody knows he's nearly five years younger than you, and is after your money. Why, Alexandra, you are forty years old!"

"All that doesn't concern anybody but Carl and me. Go to town and ask your lawyers what you can do to restrain me from disposing of my own property. And I advise you to do what they tell you; for the authority you can exert by law is the only influence you will ever have over me again." Alexandra rose. "I think I would rather not have lived to find out what I have today," she said quietly, closing her desk.

Lou and Oscar looked at each other questioningly. There seemed to be nothing to do but to go, and they walked out.

"You can't do business with women," Oscar said heavily as he clambered into the cart. "But anyhow, we've had our say, at last."

Lou scratched his head. "Talk of that kind might come too high, you know; but she's apt to be sensible. You hadn't ought to said that about her age, though, Oscar. I'm afraid that hurt her feelings; and the worst thing we can do is to make her sore at un, Sh  'l  litti  continuing."

"I only meant," said Oscar, "that she is old enough to know better, and she is. If she was going to marry, she ought to done it long ago, and not go making a fool of herself now."

Lou looked anxious, nevertheless. "Of course," he reflected hopefully and inconsistently, "Alexandra ain't much like other women-folks. Maybe it won't make her sore. Maybe she'd as soon be forty as not!"

## CHAPTER XI

Emil came home at about half-past seven o'clock that evening. Old Ivar met him at the windmill and took his horse, and the young man went directly into the house. He called to his sister and she answered from her bedroom, behind the sitting room, saying that she was lying down.

Emil went to her door.

"Can I see you for a minute?" he asked. "I want to talk to you about something before Carl comes."

Alexandra rose quickly and came to the door. "Where is Carl?"

"Lou and Oscar met us and said they wanted to talk to him, so he rode over to Oscar's with them. Are you coming out?" Emil asked impatiently.

"Yes, sit down. I'll be dressed in a moment."

Alexandra closed her door, and Emil sank down on the old slat lounge and sat with his head in his hands. When his sister came out, he looked up, not knowing whether the interval had been short or long, and he was surprised to see that the room had grown quite dark. That was just as well; it would be easier to talk if he were not under the gaze of those clear, deliberate eyes, that saw so far in some directions and were so blind in others. Alexandra, too, was glad of the dusk. Her face was swollen from crying.

Emil started up and then sat down again. "Alexandra," he said slowly, in his deep young baritone, "I don't want to go away to law school this fall. Let me put it off another year. I want to take a year off and look around. It's awfully easy to rush into a profession you don't really like, and awfully hard to get out of it. Linstrum and I have been talking about that."

"Very well, Emil. Only don't go off looking for land." She came up and put her hand on his shoulder. "I've been wishing you could stay with me this winter."

"That's just what I don't want to do, Alexandra. I'm restless. I want to go to a new place. I want to go down to the City of Mexico to join one of the University fellows who's at the head of an electrical plant. He wrote me he could give me a little job, enough to pay my way, and I could look around and see what I want to do. I want to go as soon as harvest is over. I guess Lou and Oscar will be sore about it."

"I suppose they will." Alexandra sat down on the lounge beside him. "They are very angry with me, Emil. We have had a quarrel. They will not come here again."

Emil scarcely heard what she was saying; he did not notice the sadness of her tone. He was thinking about the reckless life he meant to live in Mexico.

"What about?" he asked absently.

"About Carl Linstrum. They are afraid I am going to marry him, and that some of my property will get away from them."

Emil shrugged his shoulders. "What nonsense!" he murmured. "Just like them."

Alexandra drew back. "Why nonsense, Emil?"

"Why, you've never thought of such a thing, have you? They always have to have something to fuss about."

"Emil," said his sister slowly, "you ought not to take things for granted. Do you agree with them that I have no right to change my way of living?"

Emil looked at the outline of his sister's head in the dim light. They were sitting close together and he somehow felt that she could hear his thoughts.

He was silent for a moment, and then said in an embarrassed tone, "Why, no, certainly not. You ought to do whatever you want to. I'll always back you."

"But it would seem a little bit ridiculous to you if I married Carl?"

Emil fidgeted. The issue seemed to him too far-fetched to warrant discussion. "Why, no. I should be surprised if you wanted to. I can't see exactly why. But that's none of my business. You ought to do as you please. Certainly you ought not to pay any attention to what the boys say."

Alexandra sighed. "I had hoped you might understand, a little, why I do want to. But I suppose that's too much to expect. I've had a pretty lonely life, Emil. Besides Marie, Carl is the only friend I have ever had."

Emil was awake now; a name in her last sentence roused him. He put out his hand and took his sister's awkwardly. "You ought to do just as you wish, and I think Carl's a fine fellow. He and I would always get on. I don't believe any of the things the boys say about him, honest I don't. They are suspicious of him because he's intelligent. You know their way. They've been sore at me ever since you let me go away to college. They're always trying to catch me up. If I were you, I wouldn't pay any attention to them. There's nothing to get upset about. Carl's a sensible fellow. He won't mind them."

"I don't know. If they talk to him the way they did to me, I think he'll go away."

Emil grew more and more uneasy. "Think so? Well, Marie said it would serve us all right if you walked off with him."

"Did she? Bless her little heart! *She* would." Alexandra's voice broke.

Emil began unlacing his leggings. "Why don't you talk to her about it? There's Carl, I hear his horse. I guess I'll go upstairs and get my boots off. No, I don't want any supper. We had supper at five o'clock, at the fair."

Emil was glad to escape and get to his own room. He was a little ashamed for his sister, though he had tried not to show it. He felt that there was something indecorous in her proposal, and she did seem to him somewhat ridiculous. There was trouble enough in the world, he reflected, as he threw himself upon his bed, without people who were forty years old imagining they wanted to get married. In the darkness and silence Emil was not likely to think long about Alexandra. Every image slipped away but one. He had seen Marie in the crowd that afternoon. She sold candy at the fair. *Why* had she ever run away with Frank Shabata, and how could she go on laughing and working and taking an interest in things? Why did she like so many people, and why had she seemed pleased when all the French and Bohemian boys, and the priest himself, crowded round her candy stand? Why did she care about anyone but him? Why could he never, never find the thing he looked for in her playful, affectionate eyes?

Then he fell to imagining that he looked once more and found it there, and what it would be like if she loved him—she who, as Alexandra said, could give her whole heart. In that dream he could lie for hours, as if in a trance. His spirit went out of his body and crossed the fields to Marie Shabata.

At the University dances the girls had often looked wonderingly at the tall young Swede with the fine head, leaning against the wall and frowning, his arms folded, his eyes fixed on the ceiling or the floor. All the girls were a little afraid of him. He was distinguished-looking, and not the jollying kind. They felt that he was too intense and preoccupied. There was something queer about him. Emil's fraternity rather prided itself upon its dances, and sometimes he did his duty and danced every dance. But whether he was on the floor or brooding in a corner, he was always thinking about Marie Shabata. For two years the storm had been gathering in him.

## CHAPTER XII

Carl came into the sitting room while Alexandra was lighting the lamp. She looked up at him as she adjusted the shade. His sharp shoulders stooped as if he were very tired, his face was pale, and there were bluish shadows under his dark eyes. His anger had burned itself out and left him sick and disgusted.

"You have seen Lou and Oscar?" Alexandra asked.

"Yes." His eyes avoided hers.

Alexandra took a deep breath. "And now you are going away. I thought so."

Carl threw himself into a chair and pushed the dark lock back from his forehead with his white, nervous hand. "What a hopeless position you are in, Alexandra!" he exclaimed feverishly. "It is your fate to be always surrounded by little men. And I am no better than the rest. I am too little to face the criticism of even such men as Lou and Oscar. Yes, I am going away; tomorrow. I cannot even ask you to give me a promise until I have something to offer you. I thought, perhaps, I could do that; but I find I can't."

"What good comes of offering people things they don't need?" Alexandra asked sadly. "I don't need money. But I have needed you for a great many years. I wonder why I have been permitted to prosper, if it is only to take my friends away from me."

"I don't deceive myself," Carl said frankly. "I know that I am going away on my own account. I must make the usual effort. I must have something to show for myself. To take what you would give me, I should have to be either a very large man or a very small one, and I am only in the middle class."

Alexandra sighed. "I have a feeling that if you go away, you will not come back. Something will happen to one of us, or to both. People have to snatch at happiness when they can, in this world. It is always easier to lose than to find. What I have is yours, if you care enough about me to take it."

Carl rose and looked up at the picture of John Bergson. "But I can't, my dear, I can't! I will go North at once. Instead of idling about in California all winter, I shall be getting my bearings up there. I won't waste another week. Be patient with me, Alexandra. Give me a year!"

"As you will," said Alexandra wearily. "All at once, in a single day, I lose everything; and I do not know why. Emil, too, is going away." Carl was still studying John Bergson's face and Alexandra's eyes followed his. "Yes," she said, "if he could have seen all that would come of the task he gave me, he would have been sorry. I hope he does not see me now. I hope that he is among the old people of his blood and country, and that tidings do not reach him from the New World."

## PART III. WINTER MEMORIES

### CHAPTER I

Winter has settled down over the Divide again; the season in which Nature recuperates, in which she sinks to sleep between the fruitfulness of autumn and the passion of spring. The birds have gone. The teeming life that goes on down in the long grass is exterminated. The prairie dog keeps his hole. The rabbits run chivering from one frozen garden patch to another and are hard put to it to find frost-bitten cabbage stalks. At night the coyotes roam the wintry waste, howling for food. The variegated fields are all one color now; the pastures, the stubble, the roads, the sky are the same leaden gray. The hedgerows and trees are scarcely perceptible against the bare earth, whose slaty hue they have taken on. The ground is frozen so hard that it bruises the foot to walk in the roads or in the ploughed fields. It is like an iron country, and the spirit is oppressed by its rigor and melancholy. One could easily believe that in that dead landscape the germs of life and fruitfulness were extinct forever.

Alexandra has settled back into her old routine. There are weekly letters from Emil. Lou and Oscar she has not seen since Carl went away. To avoid awkward encounters in the presence of curious spectators, she has stopped going to the Norwegian Church and drives up to the Reform Church at Hanover, or goes with Marie Shabata to the Catholic Church, locally known as "the French Church." She has not told Marie about Carl, or her differences with her brothers. She was never very communicative about her own affairs, and when she came to the point, an instinct told her that about such things she and Marie would not understand one another.

Old Mrs. Lee had been afraid that family misunderstandings might deprive her of her yearly visit to Alexandra. But on the first day of December Alexandra telephoned Annie that tomorrow she would send Ivar over for her mother, and the next day the old lady arrived with her bundles. For twelve years Mrs. Lee had always entered Alexandra's sitting room with the same exclamation, "Now we be yust-a like old times!" She enjoyed the liberty Alexandra gave her, and hearing her own language about her all day long. Here she could wear her nightcap and sleep with all her windows shut, listen to Ivar reading the Bible, and here she could run about among the stables in a pair of Emil's old boots. Though she was bent almost double, she was as spry as a gopher. Her face was as brown as if it had been varnished, and as full of wrinkles as a washerwoman's hands. She had three jolly old teeth left in the front of her mouth, and when she grinned she looked very knowing, as if when you found out how to take it, life wasn't half bad. While she and Alexandra patched and pieced and quilted, she talked incessantly about stories she read in a Swedish family paper, telling the plots in great detail; or about her life on a dairy farm in Gottland when she was a girl. Sometimes she forgot which were the printed stories and which were the real stories, it all seemed so far away. She loved to take a little brandy, with hot water and sugar, before she went to bed, and Alexandra always had it ready for her. "It sends good dreams," she would say with a twinkle in her eye.

When Mrs. Lee had been with Alexandra for a week, Marie Shabata telephoned one morning to say that Frank had gone to town for the day, and she would like them to come over for coffee in the afternoon. Mrs. Lee hurried to wash out and iron her new cross-stitched apron, which she had finished only the night before; a checked gingham apron worked with a design ten inches broad across the bottom; a hunting scene, with fir trees and a stag and dogs and huntsmen. Mrs. Lee was firm with herself at dinner, and refused a second helping of apple dumplings. "I ta-ank I save up," she said with a giggle.

At two o'clock in the afternoon Alexandra's cart drove up to the Shabatas' gate, and Marie saw Mrs. Lee's red shawl come bobbing up the path. She ran to the door and pulled the old woman into the house with a hug, helping her to take off her wraps while Alexandra blanketed the horse outside. Mrs. Lee had put on her best black satine dress—she abominated woolen stuffs, even in winter—and a crocheted collar, fastened with a big pale gold pin, containing faded daguerreotypes of her father and mother. She had not worn her apron for fear of rumpling it, and now she shook it out and tied it round her waist with a conscious air. Marie drew back and threw up her hands, exclaiming, "Oh, what a beauty! I've never seen this one before, have I, Mrs. Lee?"

The old woman giggled and ducked her head. "No, yust las' night I ma-ake. See dis tread; verra strong, no wa-ash out, no fade. My sister send from Sveden. I yust-a ta-ank you like dis."

Marie ran to the door again. "Come in, Alexandra. I have been looking at Mrs. Lee's apron. Do stop on your way home and show it to Mrs. Hiller. She's crazy about cross-stitch."

While Alexandra removed her hat and veil, Mrs. Lee went out to the kitchen and settled herself in a wooden rocking-chair by the stove, looking with great interest at the table, set for three, with a white cloth, and a pot of pink geraniums in the middle. "My, a-an't you gotta fine plants; such-a much flower. How you keep from freeze?"

She pointed to the window-shelves, full of blooming fuchsias and geraniums.

"I keep the fire all night, Mrs. Lee, and when it's very cold I put them all on the table, in the middle of the room. Other nights I only put newspapers behind them. Frank laughs at me for fussing, but when they don't bloom he says, 'What's the matter with the darned things?'—What do you hear from Carl, Alexandra?"

"He got to Dawson before the river froze, and now I suppose I won't hear any more until spring. Before he left California he sent me a box of orange flowers, but they didn't keep very well. I have brought a bunch of Emil's letters for you." Alexandra came out from the sitting room and pinched Marie's cheek playfully. "You don't look as if the weather ever froze you up. Never have colds, do you? That's a good girl. She had dark red cheeks like this when she was a little girl, Mrs. Lee. She looked like some queer foreign kind of a doll. I've never forgot the first time I saw you in Mieklejohn's store, Marie, the time father was lying sick. Carl and I were talking about that before he went away."

"I remember, and Emil had his kitten along. When are you going to send Emil's Christmas box?"

"It ought to have gone before this. I'll have to send it by mail now, to get it there in time."

Marie pulled a dark purple silk necktie from her workbasket. "I knit this for him. It's a good color, don't you think? Will you please put it in with your things and tell him it's from me, to wear when he goes serenading."

Alexandra laughed. "I don't believe he goes serenading much. He says in one letter that the Mexican ladies are said to be very beautiful, but that don't seem to me very warm praise."

Marie tossed her head. "Emil can't fool me. If he's bought a guitar, he goes serenading. Who wouldn't, with all those Spanish girls dropping flowers down from their windows! I'd sing to them every night, wouldn't you, Mrs. Lee?"

The old lady chuckled. Her eyes lit up as Marie bent down and opened the oven door. A delicious hot fragrance blew out into the tidy kitchen. "My, somet'ing smell good!" She turned to Alexandra with a wink, her three yellow teeth making a brave show, "I ta-ank dat stop my yaw from ache no more!" she said contentedly.

Marie took out a pan of delicate little rolls, stuffed with stewed apricots, and began to dust them over with powdered sugar. "I hope you'll like these, Mrs. Lee; Alexandra does. The Bohemians always like them with their coffee. But if you don't, I have a coffee-cake with nuts and poppy seeds. Alexandra, will you get the cream jug? I put it in the window to keep cool."

"The Bohemians," said Alexandra, as they drew up to the table, "certainly know how to make more kinds of bread than any other people in the world. Old Mrs. Hiller told me once at the church supper that she could make seven kinds of fancy bread, but Marie could make a dozen."

Mrs. Lee held up one of the apricot rolls between her brown thumb and forefinger and weighed it critically. "Yust like-a fedders," she pronounced with satisfaction. "My, a-an't dis nice!" she exclaimed as she stirred her coffee. "I yust ta-ake a liddle yelly now, too, I ta-ank."

Alexandra and Marie laughed at her forehandedness, and fell to talking of their own affairs. "I was afraid you had a cold when I talked to you over the telephone the other night, Marie. What was the matter, had you been crying?"

"Maybe I had," Marie smiled guiltily. "Frank was out late that night. Don't you get lonely sometimes in the winter, when everybody has gone away?"

"I thought it was something like that. If I hadn't had company, I'd have run over to see for myself. If you get down-hearted, what will become of the rest of us?" Alexandra asked.

"I don't, very often. There's Mrs. Lee without any coffee!"

Later, when Mrs. Lee declared that her powers were spent, Marie and Alexandra went upstairs to look for some crochet patterns the old lady wanted to borrow. "Better put on your coat, Alexandra. It's cold up there, and I have no idea where those patterns are. I may have to look through my old trunks." Marie caught up a shawl and opened the stair door, running up the steps ahead of her guest. "While I go through the bureau drawers, you might look in those hat-boxes on the closet-shelf, over where Frank's clothes hang. There are a lot of odds and ends in them."

She began tossing over the contents of the drawers, and Alexandra went into the clothes-closet. Presently she came back, holding a slender elastic yellow stick in her hand.

"What in the world is this, Marie? You don't mean to tell me Frank ever carried such a thing?"

Marie blinked at it with astonishment and sat down on the floor. "Where did you find it? I didn't know he had kept it. I haven't seen it for years."

"It really is a cane, then?"

"Yes. One he brought from the old country. He used to carry it when I first knew him. Isn't it foolish? Poor Frank!"

Alexandra twirled the stick in her fingers and laughed. "He must have looked funny!"

Marie was thoughtful. "No, he didn't, really. It didn't seem out of place. He used to be awfully gay like that when he was a young man. I guess people always get what's hardest for them, Alexandra."

Marie gathered the shawl closer about her and still looked hard at the cane. "Frank would be all right in the right place," she said reflectively. "He ought to have a different kind of wife, for one thing. Do you know, Alexandra, I could pick out exactly the right sort of woman for Frank—now. The trouble is you almost have to marry a man before you can find out the sort of wife he needs; and usually it's exactly the sort you are not. Then what are you going to do about it?" she asked candidly.

Alexandra confessed she didn't know. "However," she added, "it seems to me that you get along with Frank about as well as any woman I've ever seen or heard of could."

Marie shook her head, pursing her lips and blowing her warm breath softly out into the frosty air. "No; I was spoiled at home. I like my own way, and I have a quick tongue. When Frank brags, I say sharp things, and he never forgets. He goes over and over it in his mind; I can feel him. Then I'm too giddy. Frank's wife ought to be timid, and she ought not to care about another living thing in the world but just Frank! I didn't, when I married him, but I suppose I was too young to stay like that." Marie sighed.

Alexandra had never heard Marie speak so frankly about her husband before, and she felt that it was wiser not to encourage her. No good, she reasoned, ever came from talking about such things, and while Marie was thinking aloud, Alexandra had been steadily searching the hat-boxes. "Aren't these the patterns, Maria?"

Maria sprang up from the floor. "Sure enough, we were looking for patterns, weren't we? I'd forgot about everything but Frank's other wife. I'll put that away."

She poked the cane behind Frank's Sunday clothes, and though she laughed, Alexandra saw there were tears in her eyes.

When they went back to the kitchen, the snow had begun to fall, and Marie's visitors thought they must be getting home. She went out to the cart with them, and tucked the robes about old Mrs. Lee while Alexandra took the blanket off her horse. As they drove away, Marie turned and went slowly back to the house. She took up the package of letters Alexandra had brought, but she did not read them. She turned them over and looked at the foreign stamps, and then sat watching the flying snow while the dusk deepened in the kitchen and the stove sent out a red glow.

Marie knew perfectly well that Emil's letters were written more for her than for Alexandra. They were not the sort of letters that a young man writes to his sister. They were both more personal and more painstaking; full of descriptions of the gay life in the old Mexican capital in the days when the strong hand of Porfirio Diaz was still strong. He told about bullfights and cockfights, churches and *fiestas*, the flower-markets and the fountains, the music and dancing, the people of all nations he met in the Italian restaurants on San Francisco Street. In short, they were the kind of letters a young man writes to a woman when he wishes himself and his life to seem interesting to her, when he wishes to enlist her imagination in his behalf.

Marie, when she was alone or when she sat sewing in the evening, often thought about what it must be like down there where Emil was; where there were flowers and street bands everywhere, and carriages rattling up and down, and where there was a little blind boot-black in front of the cathedral who could play any tune you asked for by dropping the lids of blacking-boxes on the stone steps. When everything is done and over for one at twenty-three, it is pleasant to let the mind wander forth and follow a young adventurer who has life before him. "And if it had not been for me," she thought, "Frank might still be free like that, and having a good time making people admire him. Poor Frank, getting married wasn't very good for him either. I'm afraid I do set people against him, as he says. I seem, somehow, to give him away all the time. Perhaps he would try to be agreeable to people again, if I were not around. It seems as if I always make him just as bad as he can be."

Later in the winter, Alexandra looked back upon that afternoon as the last satisfactory visit she had had with Marie. After that day the younger woman seemed to shrink more and more into herself. When she was with Alexandra she was not spontaneous and frank as she used to be. She seemed to be brooding over something, and holding something back. The weather had a good deal to do with their seeing less of each other than usual. There had not been such snowstorms in twenty years, and the path across the fields was drifted deep from Christmas until March. When the two neighbors went to see each other, they had to go round by the wagon-road, which was twice as far. They telephoned each other almost every night, though in January there was a stretch of three weeks when the wires were down, and when the postman did not come at all.

Marie often ran in to see her nearest neighbor, old Mrs. Hiller, who was crippled with rheumatism and had only her son, the lame shoemaker, to take care of her; and she went to the French Church, whatever the weather. She was a sincerely devout girl. She prayed for herself and for Frank, and for Emil, among the temptations of that gay, corrupt old city. She found more comfort in the Church that winter than ever before. It seemed to come closer to her, and to fill an emptiness that ached in her heart. She tried to be patient with her husband. He and his hired man usually played California Jack in the evening. Marie sat sewing or crocheting and tried to take a friendly interest in the game, but she was always thinking about the wide fields outside, where the snow was drifting over the fences; and about the orchard, where the snow was falling and packing, crust over crust. When she went out into the dark kitchen to fix her plants for the night, she used to stand by the window and look out at the white fields, or watch the currents of snow whirling over the orchard. She seemed to feel the weight of all the snow that lay down there. The branches had become so hard that they wounded your hand if you but tried to break a twig. And yet, down under the frozen crusts, at the roots of the trees, the secret of life was still safe, warm as the blood in one's heart; and the spring would come again! Oh, it would come again!

## CHAPTER II

If Alexandra had had much imagination she might have guessed what was going on in Marie's mind, and she would have seen long before what was going on in Emil's. But that, as Emil himself had more than once reflected, was Alexandra's blind side, and her life had not been of the kind to sharpen her vision. Her training had all been toward the end of making her proficient in what she had undertaken to do. Her personal life, her own realization of herself, was almost a subconscious existence; like an underground river that came to the surface only here and there, at intervals months apart, and then sank again to flow on under her own fields. Nevertheless, the underground stream was there, and it was because she had so much personality to put into her enterprises and succeeded in putting it into them so completely, that her affairs prospered better than those of her neighbors.

There were certain days in her life, outwardly uneventful, which Alexandra remembered as peculiarly happy; days when she was close to the flat, fallow world about her, and felt, as it were, in her own body the joyous germination in the soil. There were days, too, which she and Emil had spent together, upon which she loved to look back. There had been such a day when they were down on the river in the dry year, looking over the land. They had made an early start one morning and had driven a long way before noon. When Emil said he was hungry, they drew back from the road, gave Brigham his oats among the bushes, and climbed up to the top of a grassy bluff to eat their lunch under the shade of some little elm trees. The river was clear there, and shallow, since there had been no rain, and it ran in ripples over the sparkling sand. Under the overhanging willows of the opposite bank there was an inlet where the water was deeper and flowed so slowly that it seemed to sleep in the sun. In this little bay a single wild duck was swimming and diving and preening her feathers, disporting herself very happily in the flickering light and shade. They sat for a long time, watching the solitary bird take its pleasure. No living thing had ever seemed to Alexandra as beautiful as that wild duck. Emil must have felt about it as she did, for afterward, when they were at home, he used sometimes to say, "Sister, you know our duck down there—" Alexandra remembered that day as one of the happiest in her life. Years afterward she thought of the duck as still there, swimming and diving all by herself in the sunlight, a kind of enchanted bird that did not know age or change.

Most of Alexandra's happy memories were as impersonal as this one; yet to her they were very personal. Her mind was a white book, with clear writing about weather and beasts and growing things. Not many people would have cared to read it; only a happy few. She had never been in love, she had never indulged in sentimental reveries. Even as a girl she had looked upon men as work-fellows. She had grown up in serious times.

There was one fancy indeed, which persisted through her girlhood. It most often came to her on Sunday mornings, the one day in the week when she lay late abed listening to the familiar morning sounds; the windmill singing in the brisk breeze, Emil whistling as he blacked his boots down by the kitchen door. Sometimes, as she lay thus luxuriously idle, her eyes closed, she used to have an illusion of being lifted up bodily and carried lightly by someone very strong. It was a man, certainly, who carried her, but he was like no man she knew; he was much larger and stronger and swifter, and he carried her as easily as if she were a sheaf of wheat. She never saw him, but, with eyes closed, she could feel that he was yellow like the sunlight, and there was the smell of ripe cornfields about him. She could feel him approach, bend over her and lift her, and then she could feel herself being carried swiftly off across the fields. After such a reverie she would rise hastily, angry with herself, and go down to the bath-house that was partitioned off the kitchen shed. There she would stand in a tin tub and prosecute her bath with vigor, finishing it by pouring buckets of cold well-water over her gleaming white body which no man on the Divide could have carried very far.

As she grew older, this fancy more often came to her when she was tired than when she was fresh and strong. Sometimes, after she had been in the open all day, overseeing the branding of the cattle or the loading of the pigs, she would come in chilled, take a concoction of spices and warm home-made wine, and go to bed with her body actually aching with fatigue. Then, just before she went to sleep, she had the old sensation of being lifted and carried by a strong being who took from her all her bodily weariness.

## PART IV. THE WHITE MULBERRY TREE

## CHAPTER I

The French Church, properly the Church of Sainte-Agnes, stood upon a hill. The high, narrow, red-brick building, with its tall steeple and steep roof, could be seen for miles across the wheat fields, though the little town of Sainte-Agnes was completely hidden away at the foot of the hill. The church looked powerful and triumphant there on its eminence, so high above the rest of the landscape, with miles of warm color lying at its feet, and by its position and setting it reminded one of some of the churches built long ago in the wheat-lands of middle France.

Late one June afternoon Alexandra Bergson was driving along one of the many roads that led through the rich French farming country to the big church. The sunlight was shining directly in her face, and there was a blaze of light all about the red church on the hill. Beside Alexandra lounged a strikingly exotic figure in a tall Mexican hat, a silk sash, and a black velvet jacket sewn with silver buttons. Emil had returned only the night before, and his sister was so proud of him that she decided at once to take him up to the church supper, and to make him wear the Mexican costume he had brought home in his trunk. "All the girls who have stands are going to wear fancy costumes," she argued, "and some of the boys. Marie is going to tell fortunes, and she sent to Omaha for a Bohemian dress her father brought back from a visit to the old country. If you wear those clothes, they will all be pleased. And you must take your guitar. Everybody ought to do what they can to help along, and we have never done much. We are not a talented family."

The supper was to be at six o'clock, in the basement of the church, and afterward there would be a fair, with charades and an auction. Alexandra had set out from home early, leaving the house to Signa and Nelse Jensen, who were to be married next week. Signa had shyly asked to have the wedding put off until Emil came home.

Alexandra was well satisfied with her brother. As they drove through the rolling French country toward the westering sun and the stalwart church, she was thinking of that time long ago when she and Emil drove back from the river valley to the still unconquered Divide. Yes, she told herself, it had been worth while; both Emil and the country had become what she had hoped. Out of her father's children there was one who was fit to cope with the world, who had not been tied to the plow, and who had a personality apart from the soil. And that, she reflected, was what she had worked for. She felt well satisfied with her life.

When they reached the church, a score of teams were hitched in front of the basement doors that opened from the hillside upon the sanded terrace, where the boys wrestled and had jumping-matches. Amedee Chevalier, a proud father of one week, rushed out and embraced Emil. Amedee was an only son—hence he was a very rich young man—but he meant to have twenty children himself, like his uncle Xavier. "Oh, Emil," he cried, hugging his old friend rapturously, "why ain't you been up to see my boy? You come tomorrow, sure? Emil, you wanna get a boy right off! It's the greatest thing ever! No, no, no! Angel not sick at all. Everything just fine. That boy he come into this world laughin', and he been laughin' ever since. You come an' see!" He pounded Emil's ribs to emphasize each announcement.

Emil caught his arms. "Stop, Amedee. You're knocking the wind out of me. I brought him cups and spoons and blankets and moccasins enough for an orphan asylum. I'm awful glad it's a boy, sure enough!"

The young men crowded round Emil to admire his costume and to tell him in a breath everything that had happened since he went away. Emil had more friends up here in the French country than down on Norway Creek. The French and Bohemian boys were spirited and jolly, liked variety, and were as much predisposed to favor anything new as the Scandinavian boys were to reject it. The Norwegian and Swedish lads were much more self-centered, apt to be egotistical and jealous. They were cautious and reserved with Emil because he had been away to college, and were prepared to take him down if he should try to put on airs with them. The French boys liked a bit of swagger, and were always delighted to hear about anything new: new clothes, new games, new songs, new dances. Now they carried Emil off to show him the club room they had just fitted up over the post-office, down in the village. They ran down the hill in a drove, all laughing and chattering at once, some in French, some in English.

Alexandra went into the cool, whitewashed basement where the women were setting the tables. Marie was standing on a chair, building a little tent of shawls where she was to tell fortunes. She sprang down and ran toward Alexandra, stopping short and looking at her in disappointment. Alexandra nodded to her encouragingly.

"Oh, he will be here, Marie. The boys have taken him off to show him something. You won't know him. He is a man now, sure enough. I have no boy left. He smokes terrible-smelling Mexican cigarettes and talks Spanish. How pretty you look, child. Where did you get those beautiful earrings?"

"They belonged to father's mother. He always promised them to me. He sent them with the dress and said I could keep them."

Marie wore a short red skirt of stoutly woven cloth, a white bodice and kirtle, a yellow silk turban wound low over her brown curls, and long coral pendants in her ears. Her ears had been pierced against a piece of cork by her great-aunt when she was seven years old. In those germless days she had worn bits of broom-straw, plucked from the common sweeping-broom, in the lobes until the holes were healed and ready for little gold rings.

When Emil came back from the village, he lingered outside on the terrace with the boys. Marie could hear him talking and strumming on his guitar while Raoul Marcel sang falsetto. She was vexed with him for staying out there. It made her very nervous to hear him and not to see him; for, certainly, she told herself, she was not going out to look for him. When the supper bell rang and the boys came trooping in to get seats at the first table, she forgot all about her annoyance and ran to greet the tallest of the crowd, in his conspicuous attire. She didn't mind showing her embarrassment at all. She blushed and laughed excitedly as she gave Emil her hand, and looked delightedly at the black velvet coat that brought out his fair skin and fine blond head. Marie was incapable of being lukewarm about anything that pleased her. She simply did not know how to give a half-hearted response. When she was delighted, she was as likely as not to stand on her tiptoes and clap her hands. If people laughed at her, she laughed with them.

"Do the men wear clothes like that every day, in the street?" She caught Emil by his sleeve and turned him about. "Oh, I wish I lived where people wore things like that! Are the buttons real silver? Put on the hat, please. What a heavy thing! How do you ever wear it? Why don't you tell us about the bullfights?"

She wanted to wring all his experiences from him at once, without waiting a moment. Emil smiled tolerantly and stood looking down at her with his old, brooding gaze, while the French girls fluttered about him in their white dresses and ribbons, and Alexandra watched the scene with pride. Several of the French girls, Marie knew, were hoping that Emil would take them to supper, and she was relieved when he took only his sister. Marie caught Frank's arm and dragged him to the same table, managing to get seats opposite the Bergsons, so that she could hear what they were talking about. Alexandra made Emil tell Mrs. Xavier Chevalier, the mother of the twenty, about how he had seen a famous matador killed in the bullring. Marie listened to every word, only taking her eyes from Emil to watch Frank's plate and keep it filled. When Emil finished his account—bloody enough to satisfy Mrs. Xavier and to make her feel thankful that she was not a matador—Marie broke out with a volley of questions. How did the women dress when they went to bullfights? Did they wear mantillas? Did they never wear hats?

After supper the young people played charades for the amusement of their elders, who sat gossiping between their guesses. All the shops in Sainte-Agnes were closed at eight o'clock that night, so that the merchants and their clerks could attend the fair. The auction was the liveliest part of the entertainment, for the French boys always lost their heads when they began to bid, satisfied that their extravagance was in a good cause. After all the pincushions and sofa pillows and embroidered slippers were sold, Emil precipitated a panic by taking out one of his turquoise shirt studs, which everyone had been admiring, and handing it to the auctioneer. All the French girls clamored for it, and their sweethearts bid against each other recklessly. Marie wanted it, too, and she kept making signals to Frank, which he took a sour pleasure in disregarding. He didn't see the use of making a fuss over a fellow just because he was dressed like a clown. When the turquoise went to Malvina Sauvage, the French banker's daughter, Marie shrugged her shoulders and betook herself to her little tent of shawls, where she began to shuffle her cards by the light of a tallow candle, calling out, "Fortunes, fortunes!"

The young priest, Father Duchesne, went first to have his fortune read. Marie took his long white hand, looked at it, and then began to run off her cards. "I see a long journey across water for you, Father. You will go to a town all cut up by water; built on islands, it seems to be, with rivers and green fields all about. And you will visit an old lady with a white cap and gold hoops in her ears, and you will be very happy there."

*"Mais, oui,"* said the priest, with a melancholy smile. *"C'est L'Isle-Adam, chez ma mere. Vous etes tres savante, ma fille."* He patted her yellow turban, calling, *"Venez donc, mes garcons! Il y a ici une veritable clairvoyante!"*

Marie was clever at fortune-telling, indulging in a light irony that amused the crowd. She told old Brunot, the miser, that he would lose all his money, marry a girl of sixteen, and live happily on a crust. Sholte, the fat Russian boy, who lived for his stomach, was to be disappointed in love, grow thin, and shoot himself from despondency. Amedee was to have twenty children, and nineteen of them were to be girls. Amedee slapped Frank on the back and asked him why he didn't see what the fortune-teller would promise him. But Frank shook off his friendly hand and grunted, "She tell my fortune long ago; bad enough!" Then he withdrew to a corner and sat glowering at his wife.

Frank's case was all the more painful because he had no one in particular to fix his jealousy upon. Sometimes he could have thanked the man who would bring him evidence against his wife. He had discharged a good farm-boy, Jan Smirka, because he thought Marie was fond of him; but she had not seemed to miss Jan when he was gone, and she had been just as kind to the next boy. The farmhands would always do anything for Marie; Frank couldn't find one so surly that he would not make an effort to please her. At the bottom of his heart Frank knew well enough that if he could once give up his grudge, his wife would come back to him. But he could never in the world do that. The grudge was fundamental. Perhaps he could not have given it up if he had tried. Perhaps he got more satisfaction out of feeling himself abused than he would have got out of being loved. If he could once have made Marie thoroughly unhappy, he might have relented and raised her from the dust. But she had never humbled herself. In the first days of their love she had been his slave; she had admired him abandonedly. But the moment he began to bully her and to be unjust, she began to draw away; at first in tearful amazement, then in quiet, unspoken disgust. The distance between them had widened and hardened. It no longer contracted and brought them suddenly together. The spark of her life went somewhere else, and he was always watching to surprise it. He knew that somewhere she must get a feeling to live upon, for she was not a woman who could live without loving. He wanted to prove to himself the wrong he felt. What did she hide in her heart? Where did it go? Even Frank had his churlish delicacies; he never reminded her of how much she had once loved him. For that Marie was grateful to him.

While Marie was chattering to the French boys, Amedee called Emil to the back of the room and whispered to him that they were going to play a joke on the girls. At eleven o'clock, Amedee was to go up to the switchboard in the vestibule and turn off the electric lights, and every boy would have a chance to kiss his sweetheart before Father Duchesne could find his way up the stairs to turn the current on again. The only difficulty was the candle in Marie's tent; perhaps, as Emil had no sweetheart, he would oblige the boys by blowing out the candle. Emil said he would undertake to do that.

At five minutes to eleven he sauntered up to Marie's booth, and the French boys dispersed to find their girls. He leaned over the card-table and gave himself up to looking at her. "Do you think you could tell my fortune?" he murmured. It was the first word he had had alone with her for almost a year. "My luck hasn't changed any. It's just the same."

Marie had often wondered whether there was anyone else who could look his thoughts to you as Emil could. Tonight, when she met his steady, powerful eyes, it was impossible not to feel the sweetness of the dream he was dreaming; it reached her before she could shut it out, and hid itself in her heart. She began to shuffle her cards furiously. "I'm angry with you, Emil," she broke out with petulance. "Why did you give them that lovely blue stone to sell? You might have known Frank wouldn't buy it for me, and I wanted it awfully!"

Emil laughed shortly. "People who want such little things surely ought to have them," he said dryly. He thrust his hand into the pocket of his velvet trousers and brought out a handful of uncut turquoises, as big as marbles. Leaning over the table he dropped them into her lap. "There, will those do? Be careful, don't let anyone see them. Now, I suppose you want me to go away and let you play with them?"

Marie was gazing in rapture at the soft blue color of the stones. "Oh, Emil! Is everything down there beautiful like these? How could you ever come away?"

At that instant Amedee laid hands on the switchboard. There was a shiver and a giggle, and everyone looked toward the red blur that Marie's candle made in the dark. Immediately that, too, was gone. Little shrieks and currents of soft laughter ran up and down the dark hall. Marie started up—directly into Emil's arms. In the same instant she felt his lips. The veil that had hung uncertainly between them for so long was dissolved. Before she knew what she was doing, she had committed herself to that kiss that was at once a boy's and a man's, as timid as it was tender; so like Emil and so unlike anyone else in the world. Not until it was over did she realize what it meant. And Emil, who had so often imagined the shock of this first kiss, was surprised at its gentleness and naturalness. It was like a sigh which they had breathed together; almost sorrowful, as if each were afraid of wakening something in the other.

When the lights came on again, everybody was laughing and shouting, and all the French girls were rosy and shining with mirth. Only Marie, in her little tent of shawls, was pale and quiet. Under her yellow turban the red coral pendants swung against white cheeks. Frank was still staring at her, but he seemed to see nothing. Years ago, he himself had had the power to take the blood from her cheeks like that. Perhaps he did not remember—perhaps he had never noticed! Emil was already at the other end of the hall, walking about with the shoulder-motion he had acquired among the Mexicans, studying the floor with his intent, deep-set eyes. Marie began to take down and fold her shawls. She did not glance up again. The young people drifted to the other end of the hall where the guitar was sounding. In a moment she heard Emil and Raoul singing:

"Across the Rio Grand-e, There lies a sunny land-e, My bright-eyed Mexico!"

Alexandra Bergson came up to the card booth. "Let me help you, Marie. You look tired."

She placed her hand on Marie's arm and felt her shiver. Marie stiffened under that kind, calm hand. Alexandra drew back, perplexed and hurt.

There was about Alexandra something of the impervious calm of the fatalist, always disconcerting to very young people, who cannot feel that the heart lives at all unless it is still at the mercy of storms; unless its strings can scream to the touch of pain.

## CHAPTER II

Signa's wedding supper was over. The guests, and the tiresome little Norwegian preacher who had performed the marriage ceremony, were saying good-night.

Old Ivar was hitching the horses to the wagon to take the wedding presents and the bride and groom up to their new home, on Alexandra's north quarter. When Ivar drove up to the gate, Emil and Marie Shabata began to carry out the presents, and Alexandra went into her bedroom to bid Signa good-bye and to give her a few words of good counsel. She was surprised to find that the bride had changed her slippers for heavy shoes and was pinning up her skirts. At that moment Nelse appeared at the gate with the two milk cows that Alexandra had given Signa for a wedding present.

Alexandra began to laugh. "Why, Signa, you and Nelse are to ride home. I'll send Ivar over with the cows in the morning."

Signa hesitated and looked perplexed. When her husband called her, she pinned her hat on resolutely. "I ta-ank I better do yust like he say," she murmured in confusion.

Alexandra and Marie accompanied Signa to the gate and saw the party set off, old Ivar driving ahead in the wagon and the bride and groom following on foot, each leading a cow. Emil burst into a laugh before they were out of hearing.

"Those two will get on," said Alexandra as they turned back to the house. "They are not going to take any chances. They will feel safer with those cows in their own stable. Marie, I am going to send for an old woman next. As soon as I get the girls broken in, I marry them off."

"I've no patience with Signa, marrying that grumpy fellow!" Marie declared. "I wanted her to marry that nice Smirka boy who worked for us last winter. I think she liked him, too."

"Yes, I think she did," Alexandra assented, "but I suppose she was too much afraid of Nelse to marry anyone else. Now that I think of it, most of my girls have married men they were afraid of. I believe there is a good deal of the cow in most Swedish girls. You high-strung Bohemian can't understand us. We're a terribly practical people, and I guess we think a cross man makes a good manager."

Marie shrugged her shoulders and turned to pin up a lock of hair that had fallen on her neck. Somehow Alexandra had irritated her of late. Everybody irritated her. She was tired of everybody. "I'm going home alone, Emil, so you needn't get your hat," she said as she wound her scarf quickly about her head. "Good-night, Alexandra," she called back in a strained voice, running down the gravel walk.

Emil followed with long strides until he overtook her. Then she began to walk slowly. It was a night of warm wind and faint starlight, and the fireflies were glimmering over the wheat.

"Marie," said Emil after they had walked for a while, "I wonder if you know how unhappy I am?"

Marie did not answer him. Her head, in its white scarf, drooped forward a little.

Emil kicked a clod from the path and went on:

"I wonder whether you are really shallow-hearted, like you seem? Sometimes I think one boy does just as well as another for you. It never seems to make much difference whether it is me or Raoul Marcel or Jan Smirka. Are you really like that?"

"Perhaps I am. What do you want me to do? Sit round and cry all day? When I've cried until I can't cry anymore, then—then I must do something else."

"Are you sorry for me?" he persisted.

"No, I'm not. If I were big and free like you, I wouldn't let anything make me unhappy. As old Napoleon Brunot said at the fair, I wouldn't go lovering after no woman. I'd take the first train and go off and have all the fun there is."

"I tried that, but it didn't do any good. Everything reminded me. The nicer the place was, the more I wanted you." They had come to the stile and Emil pointed to it persuasively. "Sit down a moment, I want to ask you something." Marie sat down on the top step and Emil drew nearer. "Would you tell me something that's none of my business if you thought it would help me out? Well, then, tell me, *please* tell me, why you ran away with Frank Shabata!"

Marie drew back. "Because I was in love with him," she said firmly.

"Really?" he asked incredulously.

"Yes, indeed. Very much in love with him. I think I was the one who suggested our running away. From the first it was more my fault than his."

Emil turned away his face.

"And now," Marie went on, "I've got to remember that. Frank is just the same now as he was then, only then I would see him as I wanted him to be. I would have my own way. And now I pay for it."

"You don't do all the paying."

"That's it. When one makes a mistake, there's no telling where it will stop. But you can go away; you can leave all this behind you."

"Not everything. I can't leave you behind. Will you go away with me, Marie?"

Marie started up and stepped across the stile. "Emil! How wickedly you talk! I am not that kind of a girl, and you know it. But what am I going to do if you keep tormenting me like this!" she added plaintively.

"Marie, I won't bother you anymore if you will tell me just one thing. Stop a minute and look at me. No, nobody can see us. Everybody's asleep. That was only a firefly. Marie, *stop* and tell me!"

Emil overtook her and catching her by the shoulders shook her gently, as if he were trying to awaken a sleepwalker.

Marie hid her face on his arm. "Don't ask me anything more. I don't know anything except how miserable I am. And I thought it would be all right when you came back. Oh, Emil," she clutched his sleeve and began to cry, "what am I to do if you don't go away? I can't go, and one of us must. Can't you see?"

Emil stood looking down at her, holding his shoulders stiff and stiffening the arm to which she clung. Her white dress looked gray in the darkness. She seemed like a troubled spirit, like some shadow out of the earth, clinging to him and entreating him to give her peace. Behind her the fireflies were weaving in and out over the wheat. He put his hand on her bent head. "On my honor, Marie, if you will say you love me, I will go away."

She lifted her face to his. "How could I help it? Didn't you know?"

Emil was the one who trembled, through all his frame. After he left Marie at her gate, he wandered about the fields all night, till morning put out the fireflies and the stars.

## CHAPTER III

One evening, a week after Signa's wedding, Emil was kneeling before a box in the sitting room, packing his books. From time to time he rose and wandered about the house, picking up stray volumes and bringing them listlessly back to his box. He was packing without enthusiasm. He was not very sanguine about his future. Alexandra sat sewing by the table. She had helped him pack his trunk in the afternoon. As Emil came and went by her chair with his books, he thought to himself that it had not been so hard to leave his sister since he first went away to school. He was going directly to Omaha, to read law in the office of a Swedish lawyer until October, when he would enter the law school at Ann Arbor. They had planned that Alexandra was to come to Michigan—a long journey for her—at Christmas time, and spend several weeks with him. Nevertheless, he felt that this leave-taking would be more final than his earlier ones had been; that it meant a definite break with his old home and the beginning of something new—he did not know what. His ideas about the future would not crystallize; the more he tried to think about it, the vaguer his conception of it became. But one thing was clear, he told himself; it was high time that he made good to Alexandra, and that ought to be incentive enough to begin with.

As he went about gathering up his books he felt as if he were uprooting things. At last he threw himself down on the old slat lounge where he had slept when he was little, and lay looking up at the familiar cracks in the ceiling.

"Tired, Emil?" his sister asked.

"Lazy," he murmured, turning on his side and looking at her. He studied Alexandra's face for a long time in the lamplight. It had never occurred to him that his sister was a handsome woman until Marie Shabata had told him so. Indeed, he had never thought of her as being a woman at all, only a sister. As he studied her bent head, he looked up at the picture of John Bergson above the lamp. "No," he thought to himself, "she didn't get it there. I suppose I am more like that."

"Alexandra," he said suddenly, "that old walnut secretary you use for a desk was father's, wasn't it?"

Alexandra went on stitching. "Yes. It was one of the first things he bought for the old log house. It was a great extravagance in those days. But he wrote a great many letters back to the old country. He had many friends there, and they wrote to him up to the time he died. No one ever blamed him for grandfather's disgrace. I can see him now, sitting there on Sundays, in his white shirt, writing pages and pages, so carefully. He wrote a fine, regular hand, almost like engraving. Yours is something like his, when you take pains."

"Grandfather was really crooked, was he?"

"He married an unscrupulous woman, and then—then I'm afraid he was really crooked. When we first came here father used to have dreams about making a great fortune and going back to Sweden to pay back to the poor sailors the money grandfather had lost."

Emil stirred on the lounge. "I say, that would have been worth while, wouldn't it? Father wasn't a bit like Lou or Oscar, was he? I can't remember much about him before he got sick."

"Oh, not at all!" Alexandra dropped her sewing on her knee. "He had better opportunities; not to make money, but to make something of himself. He was a quiet man, but he was very intelligent. You would have been proud of him, Emil."

Alexandra felt that he would like to know there had been a man of his kin whom he could admire. She knew that Emil was ashamed of Lou and Oscar, because they were bigoted and self-satisfied. He never said much about them, but she could feel his disgust. His brothers had shown their disapproval of him ever since he first went away to school. The only thing that would have satisfied them would have been his failure at the University. As it was, they resented every change in his speech, in his dress, in his point of view; though the latter they had to conjecture, for Emil avoided talking to them about any but family matters. All his interests they treated as affectations.

Alexandra took up her sewing again. "I can remember father when he was quite a young man. He belonged to some kind of a musical society, a male chorus, in Stockholm. I can remember going with mother to hear them sing. There must have been a hundred of them, and they all wore long black coats and white neckties. I was used to seeing father in a blue coat, a sort of jacket, and when I recognized him on the platform, I was very proud. Do you remember that Swedish song he taught you, about the ship boy?"

"Yes. I used to sing it to the Mexicans. They like anything different." Emil paused. "Father had a hard fight here, didn't he?" he added thoughtfully.

"Yes, and he died in a dark time. Still, he had hope. He believed in the land."

"And in you, I guess," Emil said to himself. There was another period of silence; that warm, friendly silence, full of perfect understanding, in which Emil and Alexandra had spent many of their happiest half-hours.

At last Emil said abruptly, "Lou and Oscar would be better off if they were poor, wouldn't they?"

Alexandra smiled. "Maybe. But their children wouldn't. I have great hopes of Milly."

Emil shivered. "I don't know. Seems to me it gets worse as it goes on. The worst of the Swedes is that they're never willing to find out how much they don't know. It was like that at the University. Always so pleased with themselves! There's no getting behind that conceited Swedish grin. The Bohemians and Germans were so different."

"Come, Emil, don't go back on your own people. Father wasn't conceited, Uncle Otto wasn't. Even Lou and Oscar weren't when they were boys."

Emil looked incredulous, but he did not dispute the point. He turned on his back and lay still for a long time, his hands locked under his head, looking up at the ceiling. Alexandra knew that he was thinking of many things. She felt no anxiety about Emil. She had always believed in him, as she had believed in the land. He had been more like himself since he got back from Mexico; seemed glad to be at home, and talked to her as he used to do. She had no doubt that his wandering fit was over, and that he would soon be settled in life.

"Alexandra," said Emil suddenly, "do you remember the wild duck we saw down on the river that time?"

His sister looked up. "I often think of her. It always seems to me she's there still, just like we saw her."

"I know. It's queer what things one remembers and what things one forgets." Emil yawned and sat up. "Well, it's time to turn in."

He rose, and going over to Alexandra stooped down and kissed her lightly on the cheek. "Good-night, sister. I think you did pretty well by us."

Emil took up his lamp and went upstairs. Alexandra sat finishing his new nightshirt, that must go in the top tray of his trunk.

## CHAPTER IV

The next morning Angelique, Amedee's wife, was in the kitchen baking pies, assisted by old Mrs. Chevalier. Between the mixing-board and the stove stood the old cradle that had been Amedee's, and in it was his black-eyed son. As

Angelique, flushed and excited, with flour on her hands, stopped to smile at the baby, Emil Bergson rode up to the kitchen door on his mare and dismounted.

"'Medee is out in the field, Emil," Angelique called as she ran across the kitchen to the oven. "He begins to cut his wheat today; the first wheat ready to cut anywhere about here. He bought a new header, you know, because all the wheat's so short this year. I hope he can rent it to the neighbors, it cost so much. He and his cousins bought a steam thresher on shares. You ought to go out and see that header work. I watched it an hour this morning, busy as I am with all the men to feed. He has a lot of hands, but he's the only one that knows how to drive the header or how to run the engine, so he has to be everywhere at once. He's sick, too, and ought to be in his bed."

Emil bent over Hector Baptiste, trying to make him blink his round, bead-like black eyes. "Sick? What's the matter with your daddy, kid? Been making him walk the floor with you?"

Angelique sniffed. "Not much! We don't have that kind of babies. It was his father that kept Baptiste awake. All night I had to be getting up and making mustard plasters to put on his stomach. He had an awful colic. He said he felt better this morning, but I don't think he ought to be out in the field, overheating himself."

Angelique did not speak with much anxiety, not because she was indifferent, but because she felt so secure in their good fortune. Only good things could happen to a rich, energetic, handsome young man like Amedee, with a new baby in the cradle and a new header in the field.

Emil stroked the black fuzz on Baptiste's head. "I say, Angelique, one of 'Medee's grandmothers, 'way back, must have been a squaw. This kid looks exactly like the Indian babies."

Angelique made a face at him, but old Mrs. Chevalier had been touched on a sore point, and she let out such a stream of fiery *patois* that Emil fled from the kitchen and mounted his mare.

Opening the pasture gate from the saddle, Emil rode across the field to the clearing where the thresher stood, driven by a stationary engine and fed from the header boxes. As Amedee was not on the engine, Emil rode on to the wheat field, where he recognized, on the header, the slight, wiry figure of his friend, coatless, his white shirt puffed out by the wind, his straw hat stuck jauntily on the side of his head. The six big work-horses that drew, or rather pushed, the header, went abreast at a rapid walk, and as they were still green at the work they required a good deal of management on Amedee's part; especially when they turned the corners, where they divided, three and three, and then swung round into line again with a movement that looked as complicated as a wheel of artillery. Emil felt a new thrill of admiration for his friend, and with it the old pang of envy at the way in which Amedee could do with his might what his hand found to do, and feel that, whatever it was, it was the most important thing in the world. "I'll have to bring Alexandra up to see this thing work," Emil thought; "it's splendid!"

When he saw Emil, Amedee waved to him and called to one of his twenty cousins to take the reins. Stepping off the header without stopping it, he ran up to Emil who had dismounted. "Come along," he called. "I have to go over to the engine for a minute. I gotta green man running it, and I gotta to keep an eye on him."

Emil thought the lad was unnaturally flushed and more excited than even the cares of managing a big farm at a critical time warranted. As they passed behind a last year's stack, Amedee clutched at his right side and sank down for a moment on the straw.

"Ouch! I got an awful pain in me, Emil. Something's the matter with my insides, for sure."

Emil felt his fiery cheek. "You ought to go straight to bed, 'Medee, and telephone for the doctor; that's what you ought to do."

Amedee staggered up with a gesture of despair. "How can I? I got no time to be sick. Three thousand dollars' worth of new machinery to manage, and the wheat so ripe it will begin to shatter next week. My wheat's short, but it's gotta grand full berries. What's he slowing down for? We haven't got header boxes enough to feed the thresher, I guess."

Amedee started hot-foot across the stubble, leaning a little to the right as he ran, and waved to the engineer not to stop the engine.

Emil saw that this was no time to talk about his own affairs. He mounted his mare and rode on to Sainte-Agnes, to bid his friends there good-bye. He went first to see Raoul Marcel, and found him innocently practicing the "Gloria" for the big confirmation service on Sunday while he polished the mirrors of his father's saloon.

As Emil rode homewards at three o'clock in the afternoon, he saw Amedee staggering out of the wheat field, supported by two of his cousins. Emil stopped and helped them put the boy to bed.

## CHAPTER V

When Frank Shabata came in from work at five o'clock that evening, old Moses Marcel, Raoul's father, telephoned him that Amedee had had a seizure in the wheat field, and that Doctor Paradis was going to operate on him as soon as the Hanover doctor got there to help. Frank dropped a word of this at the table, bolted his supper, and rode off to Sainte-Agnes, where there would be sympathetic discussion of Amedee's case at Marcel's saloon.

As soon as Frank was gone, Marie telephoned Alexandra. It was a comfort to hear her friend's voice. Yes, Alexandra knew what there was to be known about Amedee. Emil had been there when they carried him out of the field, and had stayed with him until the doctors operated for appendicitis at five o'clock. They were afraid it was too late to do much good; it should have been done three days ago. Amedee was in a very bad way. Emil had just come home, worn out and sick himself. She had given him some brandy and put him to bed.

Marie hung up the receiver. Poor Amedee's illness had taken on a new meaning to her, now that she knew Emil had been with him. And it might so easily have been the other way—Emil who was ill and Amedee who was sad! Marie looked about the dusky sitting room. She had seldom felt so utterly lonely. If Emil was asleep, there was not even a chance of his coming; and she could not go to Alexandra for sympathy. She meant to tell Alexandra everything, as soon as Emil went away. Then whatever was left between them would be honest.

But she could not stay in the house this evening. Where should she go? She walked slowly down through the orchard, where the evening air was heavy with the smell of wild cotton. The fresh, salty scent of the wild roses had given way before this more powerful perfume of midsummer. Wherever those ashes-of-rose balls hung on their milky stalks, the air about them was saturated with their breath. The sky was still red in the west and the evening star hung directly over the Bergsons' windmill. Marie crossed the fence at the wheat field corner, and walked slowly along the path that led to Alexandra's. She could not help feeling hurt that Emil had not come to tell her about Amedee. It seemed to her most unnatural that he should not have come. If she were in trouble, certainly he was the one person in the world she would want to see. Perhaps he wished her to understand that for her he was as good as gone already.

Marie stole slowly, flutteringly, along the path, like a white night-moth out of the fields. The years seemed to stretch before her like the land; spring, summer, autumn, winter, spring; always the same patient fields, the patient little trees, the patient lives; always the same yearning, the same pulling at the chain—until the instinct to live had torn itself and bled and weakened for the last time, until the chain secured a dead woman, who might cautiously be released. Marie walked on, her face lifted toward the remote, inaccessible evening star.

When she reached the stile she sat down and waited. How terrible it was to love people when you could not really share their lives!

Yes, in so far as she was concerned, Emil was already gone. They couldn't meet anymore. There was nothing for them to say. They had spent the last penny of their small change; there was nothing left but gold. The day of love-tokens was past. They had now only their hearts to give each other. And Emil being gone, what was her life to be like? In some ways, it would be easier. She would not, at least, live in perpetual fear. If Emil were once away and settled at work, she would not have the feeling that she was spoiling his life. With the memory he left her, she could be as rash as she chose. Nobody could be the worse for it but herself; and that, surely, did not matter. Her own case was clear. When a girl had loved one man, and then loved another while that man was still alive, everybody knew what to think of her. What happened to her was of little consequence, so long as she did not drag other people down with her. Emil once away, she could let everything else go and live a new life of perfect love.

Marie left the stile reluctantly. She had, after all, thought he might come. And how glad she ought to be, she told herself, that he was asleep. She left the path and went across the pasture. The moon was almost full. An owl was hooting somewhere in the fields. She had scarcely thought about where she was going when the pond glittered before her, where Emil had shot the ducks. She stopped and looked at it. Yes, there would be a dirty way out of life, if one chose to take it. But she did not want to die. She wanted to live and dream—a hundred years, forever! As long as this sweetness welled up in her heart, as long as her breast could hold this treasure of pain! She felt as the pond must feel when it held the moon like that; when it encircled and swelled with that image of gold.

In the morning, when Emil came down-stairs, Alexandra met him in the sitting room and put her hands on his shoulders. "Emil, I went to your room as soon as it was light, but you were sleeping so sound I hated to wake you. There was nothing you could do, so I let you sleep. They telephoned from Sainte-Agnes that Amedee died at three o'clock this morning."

## CHAPTER VI

The Church has always held that life is for the living. On Saturday, while half the village of Sainte-Agnes was mourning for Amedee and preparing the funeral black for his burial on Monday, the other half was busy with white dresses and white veils for the great confirmation service tomorrow, when the bishop was to confirm a class of one hundred boys and girls. Father Duchesne divided his time between the living and the dead. All day Saturday the church was a scene of bustling activity, a little hushed by the thought of Amedee. The choir were busy rehearsing a mass of Rossini, which they had studied and practised for this occasion. The women were trimming the altar, the boys and girls were bringing flowers.

On Sunday morning the bishop was to drive overland to Sainte-Agnes from Hanover, and Emil Bergson had been asked to take the place of one of Amedee's cousins in the cavalcade of forty French boys who were to ride across country to meet the bishop's carriage. At six o'clock on Sunday morning the boys met at the church. As they stood holding their horses by the bridle, they talked in low tones of their dead comrade. They kept repeating that Amedee had always been a good boy, glancing toward the red-brick church which had played so large a part in Amedee's life, had been the scene of his most serious moments and of his happiest hours. He had played and wrestled and sung and courted under its shadow. Only three weeks ago he had proudly carried his baby there to be christened. They could not doubt that that invisible arm was still about Amedee; that through the church on earth he had passed to the church triumphant, the goal of the hopes and faith of so many hundred years.

When the word was given to mount, the young men rode at a walk out of the village; but once out among the wheat fields in the morning sun, their horses and their own youth got the better of them. A wave of zeal and fiery enthusiasm swept over them. They longed for a Jerusalem to deliver. The thud of their galloping hoofs interrupted many a country breakfast and brought many a woman and child to the door of the farmhouses as they passed. Five miles east of Sainte-Agnes they met the bishop in his open carriage, attended by two priests. Like one man the boys swung off their hats in a broad salute, and bowed their heads as the handsome old man lifted his two fingers in the episcopal blessing. The horsemen closed about the carriage like a guard, and whenever a restless horse broke from control and shot down the road ahead of the body, the bishop laughed and rubbed his plump hands together. "What fine boys!" he said to his priests. "The Church still has her cavalry."

As the troop swept past the graveyard half a mile east of the town—the first frame church of the parish had stood there—old Pierre Seguin was already out with his pick and spade, digging Amedee's grave. He knelt and uncovered as the bishop passed. The boys with one accord looked away from old Pierre to the red church on the hill, with the gold cross flaming on its steeple.

Mass was at eleven. While the church was filling, Emil Bergson waited outside, watching the wagons and buggies drive up the hill. After the bell began to ring, he saw Frank Shabata ride up on horseback and tie his horse to the hitch-bar. Marie, then, was not coming. Emil turned and went into the church. Amedee's was the only empty pew, and he sat down in it. Some of Amedee's cousins were there, dressed in black and weeping. When all the pews were full, the old men and boys packed the open space at the back of the church, kneeling on the floor. There was scarcely a family in town that was not represented in the confirmation class, by a cousin, at least. The new communicants, with their clear, reverent faces, were beautiful to look upon as they entered in a body and took the front benches reserved for them. Even before the Mass began, the air was charged with feeling. The choir had never sung so well and Raoul Marcel, in the "Gloria," drew even the bishop's eyes to the organ loft. For the offertory he sang Gounod's "Ave Maria"—always spoken of in Sainte-Agnes as "the Ave Maria."

Emil began to torture himself with questions about Marie. Was she ill? Had she quarreled with her husband? Was she too unhappy to find comfort even here? Had she, perhaps, thought that he would come to her? Was she waiting for him? Overtaxed by excitement and sorrow as he was, the rapture of the service took hold upon his body and mind. As he listened to Raoul, he seemed to emerge from the conflicting emotions which had been whirling him about and sucking him under. He felt as if a clear light broke upon his mind, and with it a conviction that good was, after all, stronger than evil, and that good was possible to men. He seemed to discover that there was a kind of rapture in which he could love forever without faltering and without sin. He looked across the heads of the people at Frank Shabata with calmness. That rapture was for those who could feel it; for people who could not, it was non-existent. He coveted nothing that was Frank Shabata's. The spirit he had met in music was his own. Frank Shabata had never found it; would never find it if he lived beside it a thousand years; would have destroyed it if he had found it, as Herod slew the innocents, as Rome slew the martyrs.

*San—cta Mari-i-i-a,*

wailed Raoul from the organ loft;

*O—ra pro no-o-bis!*

And it did not occur to Emil that anyone had ever reasoned thus before, that music had ever before given a man this equivocal revelation.

The confirmation service followed the Mass. When it was over, the congregation thronged about the newly confirmed. The girls, and even the boys, were kissed and embraced and wept over. All the aunts and grandmothers wept with joy. The housewives had much ado to tear themselves away from the general rejoicing and hurry back to their kitchens. The country parishioners were staying in town for dinner, and nearly every house in Sainte-Agnes entertained visitors that day. Father Duchesne, the bishop, and the visiting priests dined with Fabien Sauvage, the banker. Emil and Frank Shabata were both guests of old Moise Marcel. After dinner Frank and old Moise retired to the rear room of the saloon to play California Jack and drink their cognac, and Emil went over to the banker's with Raoul, who had been asked to sing for the bishop.

At three o'clock, Emil felt that he could stand it no longer. He slipped out under cover of "The Holy City," followed by Malvina's wistful eye, and went to the stable for his mare. He was at that height of excitement from which everything is foreshortened, from which life seems short and simple, death very near, and the soul seems to soar like an eagle. As he rode past the graveyard he looked at the brown hole in the earth where Amedee was to lie, and felt no horror. That, too, was beautiful, that simple doorway into forgetfulness. The heart, when it is too much alive, aches for that brown earth, and ecstasy has no fear of death. It is the old and the poor and the maimed who shrink from that brown hole; its wooers are found among the young, the passionate, the gallant-hearted. It was not until he had passed the graveyard that Emil realized where he was going. It was the hour for saying good-bye. It might be the last time that he would see her alone, and today he could leave her without rancor, without bitterness.

Everywhere the grain stood ripe and the hot afternoon was full of the smell of the ripe wheat, like the smell of bread baking in an oven. The breath of the wheat and the sweet clover passed him like pleasant things in a dream. He could feel nothing but the sense of diminishing distance. It seemed to him that his mare was flying, or running on wheels, like a railway train. The sunlight, flashing on the window-glass of the big red barns, drove him wild with joy. He was like an arrow shot from the bow. His life poured itself out along the road before him as he rode to the Shabata farm.

When Emil alighted at the Shabatas' gate, his horse was in a lather. He tied her in the stable and hurried to the house. It was empty. She might be at Mrs. Hiller's or with Alexandra. But anything that reminded him of her would be enough, the orchard, the mulberry tree . . . When he reached the orchard the sun was hanging low over the wheat field. Long fingers of light reached through the apple branches as through a net; the orchard was riddled and shot with gold; light was the reality, the trees were merely interferences that reflected and refracted light. Emil went softly down between the cherry trees toward the wheat field. When he came to the corner, he stopped short and put his hand over his mouth. Marie was lying on her side under the white mulberry tree, her face half hidden in the grass, her eyes closed, her hands lying limply where they had happened to fall. She had lived a day of her new life of perfect love, and it had left her like this. Her breast rose and fell faintly, as if she were asleep. Emil threw himself down beside her and took her in his arms. The blood came back to her cheeks, her amber eyes opened slowly, and in them Emil saw his own face and the orchard and the sun. "I was dreaming this," she whispered, hiding her face against him, "don't take my dream away!"

## CHAPTER VII

When Frank Shabata got home that night, he found Emil's mare in his stable. Such an impertinence amazed him. Like everybody else, Frank had had an exciting day. Since noon he had been drinking too much, and he was in a bad temper. He talked bitterly to himself while he put his own horse away, and as he went up the path and saw that the house was dark he felt an added sense of injury. He approached quietly and listened on the doorstep. Hearing nothing, he opened the kitchen door and went softly from one room to another. Then he went through the house again, upstairs and down, with no better result. He sat down on the bottom step of the box stairway and tried to get his wits together. In that unnatural quiet there was no sound but his own heavy breathing. Suddenly an owl began to hoot out in the fields. Frank lifted his head. An idea flashed into his mind, and his sense of injury and outrage grew. He went into his bedroom and took his murderous 405 Winchester from the closet.

When Frank took up his gun and walked out of the house, he had not the faintest purpose of doing anything with it. He did not believe that he had any real grievance. But it gratified him to feel like a desperate man. He had got into the habit of seeing himself always in desperate straits. His unhappy temperament was like a cage; he could never get out of it; and he felt that other people, his wife in particular, must have put him there. It had never more than dimly occurred to Frank that he made his own unhappiness. Though he took up his gun with dark projects in his mind, he would have been paralyzed with fright had he known that there was the slightest probability of his ever carrying any of them out.

Frank went slowly down to the orchard gate, stopped and stood for a moment lost in thought. He retraced his steps and looked through the barn and the hayloft. Then he went out to the road, where he took the foot-path along the outside of the orchard hedge. The hedge was twice as tall as Frank himself, and so dense that one could see through it only by peering closely between the leaves. He could see the empty path a long way in the moonlight. His mind traveled ahead to the stile, which he always thought of as haunted by Emil Bergson. But why had he left his horse?

At the wheat field corner, where the orchard hedge ended and the path led across the pasture to the Bergsons', Frank stopped. In the warm, breathless night air he heard a murmuring sound, perfectly inarticulate, as low as the sound of water coming from a spring, where there is no fall, and where there are no stones to fret it. Frank strained his ears. It ceased. He held his breath and began to tremble. Resting the butt of his gun on the ground, he parted the mulberry leaves softly with his fingers and peered through the hedge at the dark figures on the grass, in the shadow of the mulberry tree. It seemed to him that they must feel his eyes, that they must hear him breathing. But they did not. Frank, who had always wanted to see things blacker than they were, for once wanted to believe less than he saw. The woman lying in the shadow might so easily be one of the Bergsons' farm-girls . . . Again the murmur, like water welling out of the ground. This time he heard it more distinctly, and his blood was quicker than his brain. He began to act, just as a man who falls into the fire begins to act. The gun sprang to his shoulder, he sighted mechanically and fired three times without stopping, stopped without knowing why. Either he shut his eyes or he had vertigo. He did not see anything while he was firing. He thought he heard a cry simultaneous with the second report, but he was not sure. He peered again through the hedge, at the two dark figures under the tree. They had fallen a little apart from each other, and were perfectly still—no, not quite; in a white patch of light, where the moon shone through the branches, a man's hand was plucking spasmodically at the grass.

Suddenly the woman stirred and uttered a cry, then another, and another. She was living! She was dragging herself toward the hedge! Frank dropped his gun and ran back along the path, shaking, stumbling, gasping. He had never imagined such horror. The cries followed him. They grew fainter and thicker, as if she were choking. He dropped on his knees beside the hedge and crouched like a rabbit, listening; fainter, fainter; a sound like a whine; again—a moan—another—silence. Frank scrambled to his feet and ran on, groaning and praying. From habit he went toward the house, where he was used to being soothed when he had worked himself into a frenzy, but at the sight of the black, open door, he started back. He knew that he had murdered somebody, that a woman was bleeding and moaning in the orchard, but he had not realized before that it was his wife. The gate stared him in the face. He threw his hands over his head. Which way to turn? He lifted his tormented face and looked at the sky. "Holy Mother of God, not to suffer! She was a good girl—not to suffer!"

Frank had been wont to see himself in dramatic situations; but now, when he stood by the windmill, in the bright space between the barn and the house, facing his own black doorway, he did not see himself at all. He stood like the hare when the dogs are approaching from all sides. And he ran like a hare, back and forth about that moonlit space, before he could make up his mind to go into the dark stable for a horse. The thought of going into a doorway was terrible to him. He caught Emil's horse by the bit and led it out. He could not have buckled a bridle on his own. After two or three attempts, he lifted himself into the saddle and started for Hanover. If he could catch the one o'clock train, he had money enough to get as far as Omaha.

While he was thinking dully of this in some less sensitized part of his brain, his acuter faculties were going over and over the cries he had heard in the orchard. Terror was the only thing that kept him from going back to her, terror that she might still be she, that she might still be suffering. A woman, mutilated and bleeding in his orchard—it was because it was a woman that he was so afraid. It was inconceivable that he should have hurt a woman. He would rather be eaten by wild beasts than see her move on the ground as she had moved in the orchard. Why had she been so careless? She knew he was like a crazy man when he was angry. She had more than once taken that gun away from him and held it, when he was angry with other people. Once it had gone off while they were struggling over it. She was never afraid. But, when she knew him, why hadn't she been more careful? Didn't she have all summer before her to love Emil Bergson in, without taking such chances? Probably she had met the Smirka boy, too, down there in the orchard. He didn't care. She could have met all the men on the Divide there, and welcome, if only she hadn't brought this horror on him.

There was a wrench in Frank's mind. He did not honestly believe that of her. He knew that he was doing her wrong. He stopped his horse to admit this to himself the more directly, to think it out the more clearly. He knew that he was to blame. For three years he had been trying to break her spirit. She had a way of making the best of things that seemed to him a sentimental affectation. He wanted his wife to resent that he was wasting his best years among these stupid and unappreciative people; but she had seemed to find the people quite good enough. If he ever got rich he meant to buy her pretty clothes and take her to California in a Pullman car, and treat her like a lady; but in the mean time he wanted her to feel that life was as ugly and as unjust as he felt it. He had tried to make her life ugly. He had refused to share any of the little pleasures she was so plucky about making for herself. She could be gay about the least thing in the world; but she must be gay! When she first came to him, her faith in him, her adoration—Frank struck the mare with his fist. Why had Marie made him do this thing; why had she brought this upon him? He was overwhelmed by sickening misfortune. All at once he heard her cries again—he had forgotten for a moment. "Maria," he sobbed aloud, "Maria!"

When Frank was halfway to Hanover, the motion of his horse brought on a violent attack of nausea. After it had passed, he rode on again, but he could think of nothing except his physical weakness and his desire to be comforted by his wife. He wanted to get into his own bed. Had his wife been at home, he would have turned and gone back to her meekly enough.

# CHAPTER VIII

When old Ivar climbed down from his loft at four o'clock the next morning, he came upon Emil's mare, jaded and lather-stained, her bridle broken, chewing the scattered tufts of hay outside the stable door. The old man was thrown into a fright at once. He put the mare in her stall, threw her a measure of oats, and then set out as fast as his bow-legs could carry him on the path to the nearest neighbor.

"Something is wrong with that boy. Some misfortune has come upon us. He would never have used her so, in his right senses. It is not his way to abuse his mare," the old man kept muttering, as he scuttled through the short, wet pasture grass on his bare feet.

While Ivar was hurrying across the fields, the first long rays of the sun were reaching down between the orchard boughs to those two dew-drenched figures. The story of what had happened was written plainly on the orchard grass, and on the white mulberries that had fallen in the night and were covered with dark stain. For Emil the chapter had been short. He was shot in the heart, and had rolled over on his back and died. His face was turned up to the sky and his brows were drawn in a frown, as if he had realized that something had befallen him. But for Marie Shabata it had not been so easy. One ball had torn through her right lung, another had shattered the carotid artery. She must have started up and gone toward the hedge, leaving a trail of blood. There she had fallen and bled. From that spot there was another trail, heavier than the first, where she must have dragged herself back to Emil's body. Once there, she seemed not to have struggled anymore. She had lifted her head to her lover's breast, taken his hand in both her own, and bled quietly to death. She was lying on her right side in an easy and natural position, her cheek on Emil's shoulder. On her face there was a look of ineffable content. Her lips were parted a little; her eyes were lightly closed, as if in a daydream or a light slumber. After she lay down there, she seemed not to have moved an eyelash. The hand she held was covered with dark stains, where she had kissed it.

But the stained, slippery grass, the darkened mulberries, told only half the story. Above Marie and Emil, two white butterflies from Frank's alfalfa field were fluttering in and out among the interlacing shadows; diving and soaring, now close together, now far apart; and in the long grass by the fence the last wild roses of the year opened their pink hearts to die.

When Ivar reached the path by the hedge, he saw Shabata's rifle lying in the way. He turned and peered through the branches, falling upon his knees as if his legs had been mowed from under him. "Merciful God!" he groaned.

Alexandra, too, had risen early that morning, because of her anxiety about Emil. She was in Emil's room upstairs when, from the window, she saw Ivar coming along the path that led from the Shabatas'. He was running like a spent man, tottering and lurching from side to side. Ivar never drank, and Alexandra thought at once that one of his spells had come upon him, and that he must be in a very bad way indeed. She ran downstairs and hurried out to meet him, to hide his infirmity from the eyes of her household. The old man fell in the road at her feet and caught her hand, over which he bowed his shaggy head. "Mistress, mistress," he sobbed, "it has fallen! Sin and death for the young ones! God have mercy upon us!"

# PART V. ALEXANDRA

## CHAPTER I

Ivar was sitting at a cobbler's bench in the barn, mending harness by the light of a lantern and repeating to himself the 101st Psalm. It was only five o'clock of a mid-October day, but a storm had come up in the afternoon, bringing black clouds, a cold wind and torrents of rain. The old man wore his buffalo-skin coat, and occasionally stopped to warm his fingers at the lantern. Suddenly a woman burst into the shed, as if she had been blown in, accompanied by a shower of rain-drops. It was Signa, wrapped in a man's overcoat and wearing a pair of boots over her shoes. In time of trouble Signa had come back to stay with her mistress, for she was the only one of the maids from whom Alexandra would accept much personal service. It was three months now since the news of the terrible thing that had happened in Frank Shabata's orchard had first run like a fire over the Divide. Signa and Nelse were staying on with Alexandra until winter.

"Ivar," Signa exclaimed as she wiped the rain from her face, "do you know where she is?"

The old man put down his cobbler's knife. "Who, the mistress?"

"Yes. She went away about three o'clock. I happened to look out of the window and saw her going across the fields in her thin dress and sun-hat. And now this storm has come on. I thought she was going to Mrs. Hiller's, and I telephoned as soon as the thunder stopped, but she had not been there. I'm afraid she is out somewhere and will get her death of cold."

Ivar put on his cap and took up the lantern. *"Ja, ja,* we will see. I will hitch the boy's mare to the cart and go."

Signa followed him across the wagon-shed to the horses' stable. She was shivering with cold and excitement. "Where do you suppose she can be, Ivar?"

The old man lifted a set of single harness carefully from its peg. "How should I know?"

"But you think she is at the graveyard, don't you?" Signa persisted. "So do I. Oh, I wish she would be more like herself! I can't believe it's Alexandra Bergson come to this, with no head about anything. I have to tell her when to eat and when to go to bed."

"Patience, patience, sister," muttered Ivar as he settled the bit in the horse's mouth. "When the eyes of the flesh are shut, the eyes of the spirit are open. She will have a message from those who are gone, and that will bring her peace. Until then we must bear with her. You and I are the only ones who have weight with her. She trusts us."

"How awful it's been these last three months." Signa held the lantern so that he could see to buckle the straps. "It don't seem right that we must all be so miserable. Why do we all have to be punished? Seems to me like good times would never come again."

Ivar expressed himself in a deep sigh, but said nothing. He stooped and took a sandburr from his toe.

"Ivar," Signa asked suddenly, "will you tell me why you go barefoot? All the time I lived here in the house I wanted to ask you. Is it for a penance, or what?"

"No, sister. It is for the indulgence of the body. From my youth up I have had a strong, rebellious body, and have been subject to every kind of temptation. Even in age my temptations are prolonged. It was necessary to make some allowances; and the feet, as I understand it, are free members. There is no divine prohibition for them in the Ten Commandments. The hands, the tongue, the eyes, the heart, all the bodily desires we are commanded to subdue; but the feet are free members. I indulge them without harm to anyone, even to trampling in filth when my desires are low. They are quickly cleaned again."

Signa did not laugh. She looked thoughtful as she followed Ivar out to the wagon-shed and held the shafts up for him, while he backed in the mare and buckled the hold-backs. "You have been a good friend to the mistress, Ivar," she murmured.

"And you, God be with you," replied Ivar as he clambered into the cart and put the lantern under the oilcloth lap-cover. "Now for a ducking, my girl," he said to the mare, gathering up the reins.

As they emerged from the shed, a stream of water, running off the thatch, struck the mare on the neck. She tossed her head indignantly, then struck out bravely on the soft ground, slipping back again and again as she climbed the hill to the main road. Between the rain and the darkness Ivar could see very little, so he let Emil's mare have the rein, keeping her head in the right direction. When the ground was level, he turned her out of the dirt road upon the sod, where she was able to trot without slipping.

Before Ivar reached the graveyard, three miles from the house, the storm had spent itself, and the downpour had died into a soft, dripping rain. The sky and the land were a dark smoke color, and seemed to be coming together, like two waves. When Ivar stopped at the gate and swung out his lantern, a white figure rose from beside John Bergson's white stone.

The old man sprang to the ground and shuffled toward the gate calling, "Mistress, mistress!"

Alexandra hurried to meet him and put her hand on his shoulder. *"Tyst!* Ivar. There's nothing to be worried about. I'm sorry if I've scared you all. I didn't notice the storm till it was on me, and I couldn't walk against it. I'm glad you've come. I am so tired I didn't know how I'd ever get home."

Ivar swung the lantern up so that it shone in her face. *"Gud!* You are enough to frighten us, mistress. You look like a drowned woman. How could you do such a thing!"

Groaning and mumbling he led her out of the gate and helped her into the cart, wrapping her in the dry blankets on which he had been sitting.

Alexandra smiled at his solicitude. "Not much use in that, Ivar. You will only shut the wet in. I don't feel so cold now; but I'm heavy and numb. I'm glad you came."

Ivar turned the mare and urged her into a sliding trot. Her feet sent back a continual spatter of mud.

Alexandra spoke to the old man as they jogged along through the sullen gray twilight of the storm. "Ivar, I think it has done me good to get cold clear through like this, once. I don't believe I shall suffer so much anymore. When you get so near the dead, they seem more real than the living. Worldly thoughts leave one. Ever since Emil died, I've suffered so when it rained. Now that I've been out in it with him, I shan't dread it. After you once get cold clear through, the feeling of the rain on you is sweet. It seems to bring back feelings you had when you were a baby. It carries you back into the dark, before you were born; you can't see things, but they come to you, somehow, and you know them and aren't afraid of them. Maybe it's like that with the dead. If they feel anything at all, it's the old things, before they were born, that comfort people like the feeling of their own bed does when they are little."

"Mistress," said Ivar reproachfully, "those are bad thoughts. The dead are in Paradise."

Then he hung his head, for he did not believe that Emil was in Paradise.

When they got home, Signa had a fire burning in the sitting room stove. She undressed Alexandra and gave her a hot footbath, while Ivar made ginger tea in the kitchen. When Alexandra was in bed, wrapped in hot blankets, Ivar came in with his tea and saw that she drank it. Signa asked permission to sleep on the slat lounge outside her door. Alexandra endured their attentions patiently, but she was glad when they put out the lamp and left her. As she lay alone in the dark, it occurred to her for the first time that perhaps she was actually tired of life. All the physical operations of life seemed difficult and painful. She longed to be free from her own body, which ached and was so heavy. And longing itself was heavy: she yearned to be free of that.

As she lay with her eyes closed, she had again, more vividly than for many years, the old illusion of her girlhood, of being lifted and carried lightly by someone very strong. He was with her a long while this time, and carried her very far, and in his arms she felt free from pain. When he laid her down on her bed again, she opened her eyes, and, for the first time in her life, she saw him, saw him clearly, though the room was dark, and his face was covered. He was standing in the doorway of her room. His white cloak was thrown over his face, and his head was bent a little forward. His shoulders seemed as strong as the foundations of the world. His right arm, bared from the elbow, was dark and gleaming, like bronze, and she knew at once that it was the arm of the mightiest of all lovers. She knew at last for whom it was she had waited, and where he would carry her. That, she told herself, was very well. Then she went to sleep.

Alexandra wakened in the morning with nothing worse than a hard cold and a stiff shoulder. She kept her bed for several days, and it was during that time that she formed a resolution to go to Lincoln to see Frank Shabata. Ever since she last saw him in the courtroom, Frank's haggard face and wild eyes had haunted her. The trial had lasted only three days. Frank had given himself up to the police in Omaha and pleaded guilty of killing without malice and without premeditation. The gun was, of course, against him, and the judge had given him the full sentence—ten years. He had now been in the State Penitentiary for a month.

Frank was the only one, Alexandra told herself, for whom anything could be done. He had been less in the wrong than any of them, and he was paying the heaviest penalty. She often felt that she herself had been more to blame than poor Frank. From the time the Shabatas had first moved to the neighboring farm, she had omitted no opportunity of throwing Marie and Emil together. Because she knew Frank was surly about doing little things to help his wife, she was always sending Emil over to spade or plant or carpenter for Marie. She was glad to have Emil see as much as possible of an intelligent, city-bred girl like their neighbor; she noticed that it improved his manners. She knew that Emil was fond of Marie, but it had never occurred to her that Emil's feeling might be different from her own. She wondered at herself now, but she had never thought of danger in that direction. If Marie had been unmarried—oh, yes! Then she would have kept her eyes open. But the mere fact that she was Shabata's wife, for Alexandra, settled everything. That she was beautiful, impulsive, barely two years older than Emil, these facts had had no weight with Alexandra. Emil was a good boy, and only bad boys ran after married women.

Now, Alexandra could in a measure realize that Marie was, after all, Marie; not merely a "married woman." Sometimes, when Alexandra thought of her, it was with an aching tenderness. The moment she had reached them in the orchard that morning, everything was clear to her. There was something about those two lying in the grass, something in the way Marie had settled her cheek on Emil's shoulder, that told her everything. She wondered then how they could have helped loving each other; how she could have helped knowing that they must. Emil's cold, frowning face, the girl's content—Alexandra had felt awe of them, even in the first shock of her grief.

The idleness of those days in bed, the relaxation of body which attended them, enabled Alexandra to think more calmly than she had done since Emil's death. She and Frank, she told herself, were left out of that group of friends who had been overwhelmed by disaster. She must certainly see Frank Shabata. Even in the courtroom her heart had grieved for him. He was in a strange country, he had no kinsmen or friends, and in a moment he had ruined his life. Being what he was, she felt, Frank could not have acted otherwise. She could understand his behavior more easily than she could understand Marie's. Yes, she must go to Lincoln to see Frank Shabata.

The day after Emil's funeral, Alexandra had written to Carl Linstrum; a single page of notepaper, a bare statement of what had happened. She was not a woman who could write much about such a thing, and about her own feelings she could never write very freely. She knew that Carl was away from post-offices, prospecting somewhere in the interior. Before he started he had written her where he expected to go, but her ideas about Alaska were vague. As the weeks went by and she heard nothing from him, it seemed to Alexandra that her heart grew hard against Carl. She began to wonder whether she would not do better to finish her life alone. What was left of life seemed unimportant.

## CHAPTER II

Late in the afternoon of a brilliant October day, Alexandra Bergson, dressed in a black suit and traveling-hat, alighted at the Burlington depot in Lincoln. She drove to the Lindell Hotel, where she had stayed two years ago when she came up for Emil's Commencement. In spite of her usual air of sureness and self-possession, Alexandra felt ill at ease in hotels, and she was glad, when she went to the clerk's desk to register, that there were not many people in the lobby. She had her supper early, wearing her hat and black jacket down to the dining room and carrying her handbag. After supper she went out for a walk.

It was growing dark when she reached the university campus. She did not go into the grounds, but walked slowly up and down the stone walk outside the long iron fence, looking through at the young men who were running from one building to another, at the lights shining from the armory and the library. A squad of cadets were going through their drill behind the armory, and the commands of their young officer rang out at regular intervals, so sharp and quick that Alexandra could not understand them. Two stalwart girls came down the library steps and out through one of the iron gates. As they passed her, Alexandra was pleased to hear them speaking Bohemian to each other. Every few moments a boy would come running down the flagged walk and dash out into the street as if he were rushing to announce some wonder to the world. Alexandra felt a great tenderness for them all. She wished one of them would stop and speak to her. She wished she could ask them whether they had known Emil.

As she lingered by the south gate she actually did encounter one of the boys. He had on his drill cap and was swinging his books at the end of a long strap. It was dark by this time; he did not see her and ran against her. He snatched off his cap and stood bareheaded and panting. "I'm awfully sorry," he said in a bright, clear voice, with a rising inflection, as if he expected her to say something.

"Oh, it was my fault!" said Alexandra eagerly. "Are you an old student here, may I ask?"

"No, ma'am. I'm a Freshie, just off the farm. Cherry County. Were you hunting somebody?"

"No, thank you. That is—" Alexandra wanted to detain him. "That is, I would like to find some of my brother's friends. He graduated two years ago."

"Then you'd have to try the Seniors, wouldn't you? Let's see; I don't know any of them yet, but there'll be sure to be some of them around the library. That red building, right there," he pointed.

"Thank you, I'll try there," said Alexandra lingeringly.

"Oh, that's all right! Good-night." The lad clapped his cap on his head and ran straight down Eleventh Street. Alexandra looked after him wistfully.

She walked back to her hotel unreasonably comforted. "What a nice voice that boy had, and how polite he was. I know Emil was always like that to women." And again, after she had undressed and was standing in her nightgown, brushing her long, heavy hair by the electric light, she remembered him and said to herself, "I don't think I ever heard a nicer voice than that boy had. I hope he will get on well here. Cherry County; that's where the hay is so fine, and the coyotes can scratch down to water."

At nine o'clock the next morning Alexandra presented herself at the warden's office in the State Penitentiary. The warden was a German, a ruddy, cheerful-looking man who had formerly been a harness-maker. Alexandra had a letter to him from the German banker in Hanover. As he glanced at the letter, Mr. Schwartz put away his pipe.

"That big Bohemian, is it? Sure, he's gettin' along fine," said Mr. Schwartz cheerfully.

"I am glad to hear that. I was afraid he might be quarrelsome and get himself into more trouble. Mr. Schwartz, if you have time, I would like to tell you a little about Frank Shabata, and why I am interested in him."

The warden listened genially while she told him briefly something of Frank's history and character, but he did not seem to find anything unusual in her account.

"Sure, I'll keep an eye on him. We'll take care of him all right," he said, rising. "You can talk to him here, while I go to see to things in the kitchen. I'll have him sent in. He ought to be done washing out his cell by this time. We have to keep 'em clean, you know."

The warden paused at the door, speaking back over his shoulder to a pale young man in convicts' clothes who was seated at a desk in the corner, writing in a big ledger.

"Bertie, when 1037 is brought in, you just step out and give this lady a chance to talk."

The young man bowed his head and bent over his ledger again.

When Mr. Schwartz disappeared, Alexandra thrust her black-edged handkerchief nervously into her handbag. Coming out on the streetcar she had not had the least dread of meeting Frank. But since she had been here the sounds and smells in the corridor, the look of the men in convicts' clothes who passed the glass door of the warden's office, affected her unpleasantly.

The warden's clock ticked, the young convict's pen scratched busily in the big book, and his sharp shoulders were shaken every few seconds by a loose cough which he tried to smother. It was easy to see that he was a sick man. Alexandra looked at him timidly, but he did not once raise his eyes. He wore a white shirt under his striped jacket, a high collar, and a necktie, very carefully tied. His hands were thin and white and well cared for, and he had a seal ring on his little finger. When he heard steps approaching in the corridor, he rose, blotted his book, put his pen in the rack, and left the room without raising his eyes. Through the door he opened a guard came in, bringing Frank Shabata.

"You the lady that wanted to talk to 1037? Here he is. Be on your good behavior, now. He can set down, lady," seeing that Alexandra remained standing. "Push that white button when you're through with him, and I'll come."

The guard went out and Alexandra and Frank were left alone.

Alexandra tried not to see his hideous clothes. She tried to look straight into his face, which she could scarcely believe was his. It was already bleached to a chalky gray. His lips were colorless, his fine teeth looked yellowish. He glanced at Alexandra sullenly, blinked as if he had come from a dark place, and one eyebrow twitched continually. She felt at once that this interview was a terrible ordeal to him. His shaved head, showing the conformation of his skull, gave him a criminal look which he had not had during the trial.

Alexandra held out her hand. "Frank," she said, her eyes filling suddenly, "I hope you'll let me be friendly with you. I understand how you did it. I don't feel hard toward you. They were more to blame than you."

Frank jerked a dirty blue handkerchief from his trousers pocket. He had begun to cry. He turned away from Alexandra. "I never did mean to do not'ing to dat woman," he muttered. "I never mean to do not'ing to dat boy. I ain't had not'ing ag'in' dat boy. I always like dat boy fine. An' then I find him—" He stopped. The feeling went out of his face and eyes. He dropped into a chair and sat looking stolidly at the floor, his hands hanging loosely between his knees, the handkerchief lying across his striped leg. He seemed to have stirred up in his mind a disgust that had paralyzed his faculties.

"I haven't come up here to blame you, Frank. I think they were more to blame than you." Alexandra, too, felt benumbed.

Frank looked up suddenly and stared out of the office window. "I guess dat place all go to hell what I work so hard on," he said with a slow, bitter smile. "I not care a damn." He stopped and rubbed the palm of his hand over the light bristles on his head with annoyance. "I no can t'ink without my hair," he complained. "I forget English. We not talk here, except swear."

Alexandra was bewildered. Frank seemed to have undergone a change of personality. There was scarcely anything by which she could recognize her handsome Bohemian neighbor. He seemed, somehow, not altogether human. She did not know what to say to him.

"You do not feel hard to me, Frank?" she asked at last.

Frank clenched his fist and broke out in excitement. "I not feel hard at no woman. I tell you I not that kind-a man. I never hit my wife. No, never I hurt her when she devil me something awful!"

He struck his fist down on the warden's desk so hard that he afterward stroked it absently. A pale pink crept over his neck and face. "Two, t'ree years I know dat woman don' care no more 'bout me, Alexandra Bergson. I know she after some other man. I know her, oo-oo! An' I ain't never hurt her. I never would-a done dat, if I ain't had dat gun along. I don' know what in hell make me take dat gun. She always say I ain't no man to carry gun. If I been in dat house, where she ought-a been—but das a foolish talk."

Frank rubbed his head and stopped suddenly, as he had stopped before. Alexandra felt that there was something strange in the way he chilled off, as if something came up in him that extinguished his power of feeling or thinking.

"Yes, Frank," she said kindly. "I know you never meant to hurt Marie."

Frank smiled at her queerly. His eyes filled slowly with tears. "You know, I most forgit dat woman's name. She ain't got no name for me no more. I never hate my wife, but dat woman what make me do dat—honest to God, but I hate her! I no man to fight. I don' want to kill no boy and no woman. I not care how many men she take under dat tree. I no care for not'ing but dat fine boy I kill, Alexandra Bergson. I guess I go crazy sure 'nough."

Alexandra remembered the little yellow cane she had found in Frank's clothes-closet. She thought of how he had come to this country a gay young fellow, so attractive that the prettiest Bohemian girl in Omaha had run away with him. It seemed unreasonable that life should have landed him in such a place as this. She blamed Marie bitterly. And why, with her happy, affectionate nature, should she have brought destruction and sorrow to all who had loved her, even to poor old Joe Tovesky, the uncle who used to carry her about so proudly when she was a little girl? That was the strangest thing of all. Was there, then, something wrong in being warm-hearted and impulsive like that? Alexandra hated to think so. But there was Emil, in the Norwegian graveyard at home, and here was Frank Shabata. Alexandra rose and took him by the hand.

"Frank Shabata, I am never going to stop trying until I get you pardoned. I'll never give the Governor any peace. I know I can get you out of this place."

Frank looked at her distrustfully, but he gathered confidence from her face. "Alexandra," he said earnestly, "if I git out-a here, I not trouble dis country no more. I go back where I come from; see my mother."

Alexandra tried to withdraw her hand, but Frank held on to it nervously. He put out his finger and absently touched a button on her black jacket. "Alexandra," he said in a low tone, looking steadily at the button, "you ain' t'ink I use dat girl awful bad before—"

"No, Frank. We won't talk about that," Alexandra said, pressing his hand. "I can't help Emil now, so I'm going to do what I can for you. You know I don't go away from home often, and I came up here on purpose to tell you this."

The warden at the glass door looked in inquiringly. Alexandra nodded, and he came in and touched the white button on his desk. The guard appeared, and with a sinking heart Alexandra saw Frank led away down the corridor. After a few words with Mr. Schwartz, she left the prison and made her way to the street-car. She had refused with horror the warden's cordial invitation to "go through the institution." As the car lurched over its uneven roadbed, back toward Lincoln, Alexandra thought of how she and Frank had been wrecked by the same storm and of how, although she could come out into the sunlight, she had not much more left in her life than he. She remembered some lines from a poem she had liked in her schooldays:

> Henceforth the world will only be
> A wider prison-house to me—

and sighed. A disgust of life weighed upon her heart; some such feeling as had twice frozen Frank Shabata's features while they talked together. She wished she were back on the Divide.

When Alexandra entered her hotel, the clerk held up one finger and beckoned to her. As she approached his desk, he handed her a telegram. Alexandra took the yellow envelope and looked at it in perplexity, then stepped into the elevator without opening it. As she walked down the corridor toward her room, she reflected that she was, in a manner, immune from evil tidings. On reaching her room she locked the door, and sitting down on a chair by the dresser, opened the telegram. It was from Hanover, and it read:

> Arrived Hanover last night. Shall wait here until you come.
> Please hurry. *Carl Linstrum.*

Alexandra put her head down on the dresser and burst into tears.

## CHAPTER III

The next afternoon Carl and Alexandra were walking across the fields from Mrs. Hiller's. Alexandra had left Lincoln after midnight, and Carl had met her at the Hanover station early in the morning. After they reached home, Alexandra had gone over to Mrs. Hiller's to leave a little present she had bought for her in the city. They stayed at the old lady's door but a moment, and then came out to spend the rest of the afternoon in the sunny fields.

Alexandra had taken off her black traveling suit and put on a white dress; partly because she saw that her black clothes made Carl uncomfortable and partly because she felt oppressed by them herself. They seemed a little like the prison where she had worn them yesterday, and to be out of place in the open fields. Carl had changed very little. His cheeks were browner and fuller. He looked less like a tired scholar than when he went away a year ago, but no one, even now, would have taken him for a man of business. His soft, lustrous black eyes, his whimsical smile, would be less against him in the Klondike than on the Divide. There are always dreamers on the frontier.

Carl and Alexandra had been talking since morning. Her letter had never reached him. He had first learned of her misfortune from a San Francisco paper, four weeks old, which he had picked up in a saloon, and which contained a brief account of Frank Shabata's trial. When he put down the paper, he had already made up his mind that he could reach Alexandra as quickly as a letter could; and ever since he had been on the way; day and night, by the fastest boats and trains he could catch. His steamer had been held back two days by rough weather.

As they came out of Mrs. Hiller's garden they took up their talk again where they had left it.

"But could you come away like that, Carl, without arranging things? Could you just walk off and leave your business?" Alexandra asked.

Carl laughed. "Prudent Alexandra! You see, my dear, I happen to have an honest partner. I trust him with everything. In fact, it's been his enterprise from the beginning, you know. I'm in it only because he took me in. I'll have to go back in the spring. Perhaps you will want to go with me then. We haven't turned up millions yet, but we've got a start that's worth following. But this winter I'd like to spend with you. You won't feel that we ought to wait longer, on Emil's account, will you, Alexandra?"

Alexandra shook her head. "No, Carl; I don't feel that way about it. And surely you needn't mind anything Lou and Oscar say now. They are much angrier with me about Emil, now, than about you. They say it was all my fault. That I ruined him by sending him to college."

"No, I don't care a button for Lou or Oscar. The moment I knew you were in trouble, the moment I thought you might need me, it all looked different. You've always been a triumphant kind of person."

Carl hesitated, looking sidewise at her strong, full figure. "But you do need me now, Alexandra?"

She put her hand on his arm. "I needed you terribly when it happened, Carl. I cried for you at night. Then everything seemed to get hard inside of me, and I thought perhaps I should never care for you again. But when I got your telegram yesterday, then—then it was just as it used to be. You are all I have in the world, you know."

Carl pressed her hand in silence. They were passing the Shabatas' empty house now, but they avoided the orchard path and took one that led over by the pasture pond.

"Can you understand it, Carl?" Alexandra murmured. "I have had nobody but Ivar and Signa to talk to. Do talk to me. Can you understand it? Could you have believed that of Marie Tovesky? I would have been cut to pieces, little by little, before I would have betrayed her trust in me!"

Carl looked at the shining spot of water before them. "Maybe she was cut to pieces, too, Alexandra. I am sure she tried hard; they both did. That was why Emil went to Mexico, of course. And he was going away again, you tell me, though he had only been home three weeks. You remember that Sunday when I went with Emil up to the French Church fair? I thought that day there was some kind of feeling, something unusual, between them. I meant to talk to you about it. But on my way back I met Lou and Oscar and got so angry that I forgot everything else. You mustn't be hard on them, Alexandra. Sit down here by the pond a minute. I want to tell you something."

They sat down on the grass-tufted bank and Carl told her how he had seen Emil and Marie out by the pond that morning, more than a year ago, and how young and charming and full of grace they had seemed to him. "It happens like that in the world sometimes, Alexandra," he added earnestly. "I've seen it before. There are women who spread ruin around them through no fault of theirs, just by being too beautiful, too full of life and love. They can't help it. People come to them as people go to a warm fire in winter. I used to feel that in her when she was a little girl. Do you remember how all the Bohemians crowded round her in the store that day, when she gave Emil her candy? You remember those yellow sparks in her eyes?"

Alexandra sighed. "Yes. People couldn't help loving her. Poor Frank does, even now, I think; though he's got himself in such a tangle that for a long time his love has been bitterer than his hate. But if you saw there was anything wrong, you ought to have told me, Carl."

Carl took her hand and smiled patiently. "My dear, it was something one felt in the air, as you feel the spring coming, or a storm in summer. I didn't *see* anything. Simply, when I was with those two young things, I felt my blood go quicker, I felt—how shall I say it?—an acceleration of life. After I got away, it was all too delicate, too intangible, to write about."

Alexandra looked at him mournfully. "I try to be more liberal about such things than I used to be. I try to realize that we are not all made alike. Only, why couldn't it have been Raoul Marcel, or Jan Smirka? Why did it have to be my boy?"

"Because he was the best there was, I suppose. They were both the best you had here."

The sun was dropping low in the west when the two friends rose and took the path again. The straw-stacks were throwing long shadows, the owls were flying home to the prairie dog town. When they came to the corner where the pastures joined, Alexandra's twelve young colts were galloping in a drove over the brow of the hill.

"Carl," said Alexandra, "I should like to go up there with you in the spring. I haven't been on the water since we crossed the ocean, when I was a little girl. After we first came out here I used to dream sometimes about the shipyard where father worked, and a little sort of inlet, full of masts." Alexandra paused. After a moment's thought she said, "But you would never ask me to go away for good, would you?"

"Of course not, my dearest. I think I know how you feel about this country as well as you do yourself." Carl took her hand in both his own and pressed it tenderly.

"Yes, I still feel that way, though Emil is gone. When I was on the train this morning, and we got near Hanover, I felt something like I did when I drove back with Emil from the river that time, in the dry year. I was glad to come back to it. I've lived here a long time. There is great peace here, Carl, and freedom . . . I thought when I came out of that prison, where poor Frank is, that I should never feel free again. But I do, here." Alexandra took a deep breath and looked off into the red west.

"You belong to the land," Carl murmured, "as you have always said. Now more than ever."

"Yes, now more than ever. You remember what you once said about the graveyard, and the old story writing itself over? Only it is we who write it, with the best we have."

They paused on the last ridge of the pasture, overlooking the house and the windmill and the stables that marked the site of John Bergson's homestead. On every side the brown waves of the earth rolled away to meet the sky.

"Lou and Oscar can't see those things," said Alexandra suddenly. "Suppose I do will my land to their children, what difference will that make? The land belongs to the future, Carl; that's the way it seems to me. How many of the names on the county clerk's plat will be there in fifty years? I might as well try to will the sunset over there to my brother's children. We come and go, but the land is always here. And the people who love it and understand it are the people who own it—for a little while."

Carl looked at her wonderingly. She was still gazing into the west, and in her face there was that exalted serenity that sometimes came to her at moments of deep feeling. The level rays of the sinking sun shone in her clear eyes.

"Why are you thinking of such things now, Alexandra?"

"I had a dream before I went to Lincoln—but I will tell you about that afterward, after we are married. It will never come true, now, in the way I thought it might." She took Carl's arm and they walked toward the gate. "How many times we have walked this path together, Carl. How many times we will walk it again! Does it seem to you like coming back to your own place? Do you feel at peace with the world here? I think we shall be very happy. I haven't any fears. I think when friends marry, they are safe. We don't suffer like—those young ones." Alexandra ended with a sigh.

They had reached the gate. Before Carl opened it, he drew Alexandra to him and kissed her softly, on her lips and on her eyes.

She leaned heavily on his shoulder. "I am tired," she murmured. "I have been very lonely, Carl."

They went into the house together, leaving the Divide behind them, under the evening star. Fortunate country, that is one day to receive hearts like Alexandra's into its bosom, to give them out again in the yellow wheat, in the rustling corn, in the shining eyes of youth!

# The Lone Star Ranger

## Zane Grey

## TO CAPTAIN JOHN HUGHES
## AND HIS TEXAS RANGERS

It may seem strange to you that out of all the stories I heard on the Rio Grande I should choose as first that of Buck Duane—outlaw and gunman. But, indeed, Ranger Coffee's story of the last of the Duanes has haunted me, and I have given full rein to imagination and have retold it in my own way. It deals with the old law—the old border days—therefore it is better first. Soon, perchance, I shall have the pleasure of writing of the border of today, which in Joe Sitter's laconic speech, "Shore is 'most as bad an' wild as ever!"

In the North and East there is a popular idea that the frontier of the West is a thing long past, and remembered now only in stories. As I think of this I remember Ranger Sitter when he made that remark, while he grimly stroked an unhealed bullet wound. And I remember the giant Vaughn, that typical son of stalwart Texas, sitting there quietly with bandaged head, his thoughtful eye boding ill to the outlaw who had ambushed him. Only a few months have passed since then—when I had my memorable sojourn with you—and yet, in that short time, Russell and Moore have crossed the Divide, like Rangers.

Gentlemen—I have the honor to dedicate this book to you, and the hope that it shall fall to my lot to tell the world the truth about a strange, unique, and misunderstood body of men—the Texas Rangers—who made the great Lone Star State habitable, who never know peaceful rest and sleep, who are passing, who surely will not be forgotten and will someday come into their own.

ZANE GREY

# BOOK I. THE OUTLAW

## CHAPTER I

So it was in him, then—an inherited fighting instinct, a driving intensity to kill. He was the last of the Duanes, that old fighting stock of Texas. But not the memory of his dead father, nor the pleading of his soft-voiced mother, nor the warning of this uncle who stood before him now, had brought to Buck Duane so much realization of the dark passionate strain in his blood. It was the recurrence, a hundred-fold increased in power, of a strange emotion that for the last three years had arisen in him.

"Yes, Cal Bain's in town, full of bad whisky an' huntin' for you," repeated the elder man, gravely.

"It's the second time," muttered Duane, as if to himself.

"Son, you can't avoid a meetin'. Leave town till Cal sobers up. He ain't got it in for you when he's not drinkin'."

"But what's he want me for?" demanded Duane. "To insult me again? I won't stand that twice."

"He's got a fever that's rampant in Texas these days, my boy. He wants gunplay. If he meets you he'll try to kill you."

Here it stirred in Duane again, that bursting gush of blood, like a wind of flame shaking all his inner being, and subsiding to leave him strangely chilled.

"Kill me! What for?" he asked.

"Lord knows there ain't any reason. But what's that to do with most of the shootin' these days? Didn't five cowboys over to Everall's kill one another dead all because they got to jerkin' at a quirt among themselves? An' Cal has no reason to love you. His girl was sweet on you."

"I quit when I found out she was his girl."

"I reckon she ain't quit. But never mind her or reasons. Cal's here, just drunk enough to be ugly. He's achin' to kill somebody. He's one of them four-flush gunfighters. He'd like to be thought bad. There's a lot of wild cowboys who're ambitious for a reputation. They talk about how quick they are on the draw. They ape Bland an' King Fisher an' Hardin an' all the big outlaws. They make threats about joinin' the gangs along the Rio Grande. They laugh at the sheriffs an' brag about how they'd fix the rangers. Cal's sure not much for you to bother with, if you only keep out of his way."

"You mean for me to run?" asked Duane, in scorn.

"I reckon I wouldn't put it that way. Just avoid him. Buck, I'm not afraid Cal would get you if you met down there in town. You've your father's eye an' his slick hand with a gun. What I'm most afraid of is that you'll kill Bain."

Duane was silent, letting his uncle's earnest words sink in, trying to realize their significance.

"If Texas ever recovers from that fool war an' kills off these outlaws, why, a young man will have a lookout," went on the uncle. "You're twenty-three now, an' a powerful sight of a fine fellow, barrin' your temper. You've a chance in life. But if you go gunfightin', if you kill a man, you're ruined. Then you'll kill another. It'll be the same old story. An' the rangers would make you an outlaw. The rangers mean law an' order for Texas. This even-break business doesn't work with them. If you resist arrest they'll kill you. If you submit to arrest, then you go to jail, an' mebbe you hang."

"I'd never hang," muttered Duane, darkly.

"I reckon you wouldn't," replied the old man. "You'd be like your father. He was ever ready to draw—too ready. In times like these, with the Texas Rangers enforcin' the law, your Dad would have been driven to the river. An', son, I'm afraid you're a chip off the old block. Can't you hold in—keep your temper—run away from trouble? Because it'll only result in you gettin' the worst of it in the end. Your father was killed in a street-fight. An' it was told of him that he shot twice after a bullet had passed through his heart. Think of the terrible nature of a man to be able to do that. If you have any such blood in you, never give it a chance."

"What you say is all very well, uncle," returned Duane, "but the only way out for me is to run, and I won't do it. Cal Bain and his outfit have already made me look like a coward. He says I'm afraid to come out and face him. A man simply can't stand that in this country. Besides, Cal would shoot me in the back someday if I didn't face him."

"Well, then, what're you goin' to do?" inquired the elder man.

"I haven't decided—yet."

"No, but you're comin' to it mighty fast. That damned spell is workin' in you. You're different today. I remember how you used to be moody an' lose your temper an' talk wild. Never was much afraid of you then. But now you're gettin' cool an' quiet, an' you think deep, an' I don't like the light in your eye. It reminds me of your father."

"I wonder what Dad would say to me today if he were alive and here," said Duane.

"What do you think? What could you expect of a man who never wore a glove on his right hand for twenty years?"

"Well, he'd hardly have said much. Dad never talked. But he would have done a lot. And I guess I'll go downtown and let Cal Bain find me."

Then followed a long silence, during which Duane sat with downcast eyes, and the uncle appeared lost in sad thought of the future. Presently he turned to Duane with an expression that denoted resignation, and yet a spirit which showed wherein they were of the same blood.

"You've got a fast horse—the fastest I know of in this country. After you meet Bain hurry back home. I'll have a saddle-bag packed for you and the horse ready."

With that he turned on his heel and went into the house, leaving Duane to revolve in his mind his singular speech. Buck wondered presently if he shared his uncle's opinion of the result of a meeting between himself and Bain. His thoughts were vague. But on the instant of final decision, when he had settled with himself that he would meet Bain, such a storm of passion assailed him that he felt as if he was being shaken with ague. Yet it was all internal, inside his breast, for his hand was like a rock and, for all he could see, not a muscle about him quivered. He had no fear of Bain or of any other man; but a vague fear of himself, of this strange force in him, made him ponder and shake his head. It was as if he had not all to say in this matter. There appeared to have been in him a reluctance to let himself go, and some voice, some spirit from a distance, something he was not accountable for, had compelled him. That hour of Duane's life was like years of actual living, and in it he became a thoughtful man.

He went into the house and buckled on his belt and gun. The gun was a Colt .45, six-shot, and heavy, with an ivory handle. He had packed it, on and off, for five years. Before that it had been used by his father. There were a number of notches filed in the bulge of the ivory handle. This gun was the one his father had fired twice after being shot through the heart, and his hand had stiffened so tightly upon it in the death-grip that his fingers had to be pried open. It had never been drawn upon any man since it had come into Duane's possession. But the cold, bright polish of the weapon showed how it had been used. Duane could draw it with inconceivable rapidity, and at twenty feet he could split a card pointing edgewise toward him.

Duane wished to avoid meeting his mother. Fortunately, as he thought, she was away from home. He went out and down the path toward the gate. The air was full of the fragrance of blossoms and the melody of birds. Outside in the road a neighbor woman stood talking to a countryman in a wagon; they spoke to him; and he heard, but did not reply. Then he began to stride down the road toward the town.

Wellston was a small town, but important in that unsettled part of the great state because it was the trading-center of several hundred miles of territory. On the main street there were perhaps fifty buildings, some brick, some frame, mostly adobe, and one-third of the lot, and by far the most prosperous, were saloons. From the road Duane turned into this street. It was a wide thoroughfare lined by hitching-rails and saddled horses and vehicles of various kinds. Duane's eye ranged down the street, taking in all at a glance, particularly persons moving leisurely up and down. Not a cowboy was in sight. Duane slackened his stride, and by the time he reached Sol White's place, which was the first saloon, he was walking slowly. Several people spoke to him and turned to look back after they had passed. He paused at the door of White's saloon, took a sharp survey of the interior, then stepped inside.

The saloon was large and cool, full of men and noise and smoke. The noise ceased upon his entrance, and the silence ensuing presently broke to the clink of Mexican silver dollars at a monte table. Sol White, who was behind the bar, straightened up when he saw Duane; then, without speaking, he bent over to rinse a glass. All eyes except those of the Mexican gamblers were turned upon Duane; and these glances were keen, speculative, questioning. These men knew Bain was looking for trouble; they probably had heard his boasts. But what did Duane intend to do? Several of the cowboys and ranchers present exchanged glances. Duane had been weighed by unerring Texas instinct, by men who all packed guns. The boy was the son of his father. Whereupon they greeted him and returned to their drinks and cards. Sol White stood with his big red hands out upon the bar; he was a tall, raw-boned Texan with a long mustache waxed to sharp points.

"Howdy, Buck," was his greeting to Duane. He spoke carelessly and averted his dark gaze for an instant.

"Howdy, Sol," replied Duane, slowly. "Say, Sol, I hear there's a gent in town looking for me bad."

"Reckon there is, Buck," replied White. "He came in heah aboot an hour ago. Shore he was some riled an' a-roarin' for gore. Told me confidential a certain party had given you a white silk scarf, an' he was hell-bent on wearin' it home spotted red."

"Anybody with him?" queried Duane.

"Burt an' Sam Outcalt an' a little cowpuncher I never seen before. They-all was coaxin' trim to leave town. But he's looked on the flowin' glass, Buck, an' he's heah for keeps."

"Why doesn't Sheriff Oaks lock him up if he's that bad?"

"Oaks went away with the rangers. There's been another raid at Flesher's ranch. The King Fisher gang, likely. An' so the town's shore wide open."

Duane stalked outdoors and faced down the street. He walked the whole length of the long block, meeting many people—farmers, ranchers, clerks, merchants, Mexicans, cowboys, and women. It was a singular fact that when he turned to retrace his steps the street was almost empty. He had not returned a hundred yards on his way when the street was wholly deserted. A few heads protruded from doors and around corners. That main street of Wellston saw some such situation every few days. If it was an instinct for Texans to fight, it was also instinctive for them to sense with remarkable quickness the signs of a coming gunplay. Rumor could not fly so swiftly. In less than ten minutes everybody who had been on the street or in the shops knew that Buck Duane had come forth to meet his enemy.

Duane walked on. When he came to within fifty paces of a saloon he swerved out into the middle of the street, stood there for a moment, then went ahead and back to the sidewalk. He passed on in this way the length of the block. Sol White was standing in the door of his saloon.

"Buck, I'm a-tippin' you off," he said, quick and low-voiced. "Cal Bain's over at Everall's. If he's a-huntin' you bad, as he brags, he'll show there."

Duane crossed the street and started down. Notwithstanding White's statement Duane was wary and slow at every door. Nothing happened, and he traversed almost the whole length of the block without seeing a person. Everall's place was on the corner.

Duane knew himself to be cold, steady. He was conscious of a strange fury that made him want to leap ahead. He seemed to long for this encounter more than anything he had ever wanted. But, vivid as were his sensations, he felt as if in a dream.

Before he reached Everall's he heard loud voices, one of which was raised high. Then the short door swung outward as if impelled by a vigorous hand. A bow-legged cowboy wearing wooley chaps burst out upon the sidewalk. At sight of Duane he seemed to bound into the air, and he uttered a savage roar.

Duane stopped in his tracks at the outer edge of the sidewalk, perhaps a dozen rods from Everall's door.

If Bain was drunk he did not show it in his movement. He swaggered forward, rapidly closing up the gap. Red, sweaty, disheveled, and hatless, his face distorted and expressive of the most malignant intent, he was a wild and sinister figure. He had already killed a man, and this showed in his demeanor. His hands were extended before him, the right hand a little lower than the left. At every step he bellowed his rancor in speech mostly curses. Gradually he slowed his walk, then halted. A good twenty-five paces separated the men.

"Won't nothin' make you draw, you—!" he shouted, fiercely.

"I'm waitin' on you, Cal," replied Duane.

Bain's right hand stiffened—moved. Duane threw his gun as a boy throws a ball underhand—a draw his father had taught him. He pulled twice, his shots almost as one. Bain's big Colt boomed while it was pointed downward and he was falling. His bullet scattered dust and gravel at Duane's feet. He fell loosely, without contortion.

In a flash all was reality for Duane. He went forward and held his gun ready for the slightest movement on the part of Bain. But Bain lay upon his back, and all that moved were his breast and his eyes. How strangely the red had left his face—and also the distortion! The devil that had showed in Bain was gone. He was sober and conscious. He tried to speak, but failed. His eyes expressed something pitifully human. They changed—rolled—set blankly.

Duane drew a deep breath and sheathed his gun. He felt calm and cool, glad the fray was over. One violent expression burst from him. "The fool!"

When he looked up there were men around him.

"Plumb center," said one.

Another, a cowboy who evidently had just left the gaming table, leaned down and pulled open Bain's shirt. He had the ace of spades in his hand. He laid it on Bain's breast, and the black figure on the card covered the two bullet holes just over Bain's heart.

Duane wheeled and hurried away. He heard another man say:

"Reckon Cal got what he deserved. Buck Duane's first gunplay. Like father like son!"

## CHAPTER II

A thought kept repeating itself to Duane, and it was that he might have spared himself concern through his imagining how awful it would be to kill a man. He had no such feeling now. He had rid the community of a drunken, bragging, quarrelsome cowboy.

When he came to the gate of his home and saw his uncle there with a mettlesome horse, saddled, with canteen, rope, and bags all in place, a subtle shock pervaded his spirit. It had slipped his mind—the consequence of his act. But sight of the horse and the look of his uncle recalled the fact that he must now become a fugitive. An unreasonable anger took hold of him.

"The d—d fool!" he exclaimed, hotly. "Meeting Bain wasn't much, Uncle Jim. He dusted my boots, that's all. And for that I've got to go on the dodge."

"Son, you killed him—then?" asked the uncle, huskily.

"Yes. I stood over him—watched him die. I did as I would have been done by."

"I knew it. Long ago I saw it comin'. But now we can't stop to cry over spilt blood. You've got to leave town an' this part of the country."

"Mother!" exclaimed Duane.

"She's away from home. You can't wait. I'll break it to her—what she always feared."

Suddenly Duane sat down and covered his face with his hands.

"My God! Uncle, what have I done?" His broad shoulders shook.

"Listen, son, an' remember what I say," replied the elder man, earnestly.

"Don't ever forget. You're not to blame. I'm glad to see you take it this way, because maybe you'll never grow hard an' callous. You're not to blame. This is Texas. You're your father's son. These are wild times. The law as the rangers are laying it down now can't change life all in a minute. Even your mother, who's a good, true woman, has had her share in making you what you are this moment. For she was one of the pioneers—the fightin' pioneers of this state. Those years of wild times, before you was born, developed in her instinct to fight, to save her life, her children, an' that instinct has cropped out in you. It will be many years before it dies out of the boys born in Texas."

"I'm a murderer," said Duane, shuddering.

"No, son, you're not. An' you never will be. But you've got to be an outlaw till time makes it safe for you to come home."

"An outlaw?"

"I said it. If we had money an' influence we'd risk a trial. But we've neither. An' I reckon the scaffold or jail is no place for Buckley Duane. Strike for the wild country, an' wherever you go an' whatever you do—be a man. Live honestly, if that's possible. If it isn't, be as honest as you can. If you have to herd with outlaws try not to become bad. There are outlaws who 're not all bad—many who have been driven to the river by such a deal as this you had. When you get among these men avoid brawls. Don't drink; don't gamble. I needn't tell you what to do if it comes to gunplay, as likely it will. You can't come home. When this thing is lived down, if that time ever comes, I'll get word into the unsettled country. It'll reach you someday. That's all. Remember, be a man. Goodby."

Duane, with blurred sight and contracting throat, gripped his uncle's hand and bade him a wordless farewell. Then he leaped astride the black and rode out of town.

As swiftly as was consistent with a care for his steed, Duane put a distance of fifteen or eighteen miles behind him. With that he slowed up, and the matter of riding did not require all his faculties. He passed several ranches and was seen by men. This did not suit him, and he took an old trail across country. It was a flat region with a poor growth of mesquite and prickly-pear cactus. Occasionally he caught a glimpse of low hills in the distance. He had hunted often in that section, and knew where to find grass and water. When he reached this higher ground he did not, however, halt at the first favorable camping-spot, but went on and on. Once he came out upon the brow of a hill and saw a considerable stretch of country beneath him. It had the gray sameness characterizing all that he had traversed. He seemed to want to see wide spaces—to get a glimpse of the great wilderness lying somewhere beyond to the southwest. It was sunset when he decided to camp at a likely spot he came across. He led the horse to water, and then began searching through the shallow valley for a suitable place to camp. He passed by old campsites that he well remembered. These, however, did not strike his fancy this time, and the significance of the change in him did not occur at the moment. At last he found a secluded spot, under cover of thick mesquites and oaks, at a goodly distance from the old trail. He took saddle and pack off the horse. He looked among his effects for a hobble, and, finding that his uncle had failed to put one in, he suddenly remembered that he seldom used a hobble, and never on this horse. He cut a few feet off the end of his lasso and used that. The horse, unused to such hampering of his free movements, had to be driven out upon the grass.

Duane made a small fire, prepared and ate his supper. This done, ending the work of that day, he sat down and filled his pipe. Twilight had waned into dusk. A few wan stars had just begun to show and brighten. Above the low continuous hum of insects sounded the evening carol of robins. Presently the birds ceased their singing, and then the quiet was more noticeable. When night set in and the place seemed all the more isolated and lonely for that Duane had a sense of relief.

It dawned upon him all at once that he was nervous, watchful, sleepless. The fact caused him surprise, and he began to think back, to take note of his late actions and their motives. The change one day had wrought amazed him. He who had always been free, easy, happy, especially when out alone in the open, had become in a few short hours bound, serious, preoccupied. The silence that had once been sweet now meant nothing to him except a medium whereby he might the better hear the sounds of pursuit. The loneliness, the night, the wild, that had always been beautiful to him, now only conveyed a sense of safety for the present. He watched, he listened, he thought. He felt tired, yet had no inclination to rest. He intended to be off by dawn, heading toward the southwest. Had he a destination? It was vague as his knowledge of that great waste of mesquite and rock bordering the Rio Grande. Somewhere out there was a refuge. For he was a fugitive from justice, an outlaw.

This being an outlaw then meant eternal vigilance. No home, no rest, no sleep, no content, no life worth the living! He must be a lone wolf or he must herd among men obnoxious to him. If he worked for an honest living he still must hide his identity and take risks of detection. If he did not work on some distant outlying ranch, how was he to live? The idea of stealing was repugnant to him. The future seemed gray and somber enough. And he was twenty-three years old.

Why had this hard life been imposed upon him?

The bitter question seemed to start a strange iciness that stole along his veins. What was wrong with him? He stirred the few sticks of mesquite into a last flickering blaze. He was cold, and for some reason he wanted some light.

The black circle of darkness weighed down upon him, closed in around him. Suddenly he sat bolt upright and then froze in that position. He had heard a step. It was behind him—no—on the side. Someone was there. He forced his hand down to his gun, and the touch of cold steel was another icy shock. Then he waited. But all was silent—silent as only a wilderness arroyo can be, with its low murmuring of wind in the mesquite. Had he heard a step? He began to breathe again.

But what was the matter with the light of his campfire? It had taken on a strange green luster and seemed to be waving off into the outer shadows. Duane heard no step, saw no movement; nevertheless, there was another present at that campfire vigil. Duane saw him. He lay there in the middle of the green brightness, prostrate, motionless, dying. Cal Bain! His features were wonderfully distinct, clearer than any cameo, more sharply outlined than those of any picture. It was a hard face softening at the threshold of eternity. The red tan of sun, the coarse signs of drunkenness, the ferocity and hate so characteristic of Bain were no longer there. This face represented a different Bain, showed all that was human in him fading, fading as swiftly as it blanched white. The lips wanted to speak, but had not the power. The eyes held an agony of thought. They revealed what might have been possible for this man if he lived—that he saw his mistake too late. Then they rolled, set blankly, and closed in death.

That haunting visitation left Duane sitting there in a cold sweat, a remorse gnawing at his vitals, realizing the curse that was on him. He divined that never would he be able to keep off that phantom. He remembered how his father had been eternally pursued by the furies of accusing guilt, how he had never been able to forget in work or in sleep those men he had killed.

The hour was late when Duane's mind let him sleep, and then dreams troubled him. In the morning he bestirred himself so early that in the gray gloom he had difficulty in finding his horse. Day had just broken when he struck the old trail again.

He rode hard all morning and halted in a shady spot to rest and graze his horse. In the afternoon he took to the trail at an easy trot. The country grew wilder. Bald, rugged mountains broke the level of the monotonous horizon. About three in the afternoon he came to a little river which marked the boundary line of his hunting territory.

The decision he made to travel upstream for a while was owing to two facts: the river was high with quicksand bars on each side, and he felt reluctant to cross into that region where his presence alone meant that he was a marked man. The bottomlands through which the river wound to the southwest were more inviting than the barrens he had traversed. The rest of that day he rode leisurely up-stream. At sunset he penetrated the brakes of willow and cottonwood to spend the night. It seemed to him that in this lonely cover he would feel easy and content. But he did not. Every feeling, every imagining he had experienced the previous night returned somewhat more vividly and accentuated by newer ones of the same intensity and color.

In this kind of travel and camping he spent three more days, during which he crossed a number of trails, and one road where cattle—stolen cattle, probably—had recently passed. Thus time exhausted his supply of food, except salt, pepper, coffee, and sugar, of which he had a quantity. There were deer in the brakes; but, as he could not get close enough to kill them with a revolver, he had to satisfy himself with a rabbit. He knew he might as well content himself with the hard fare that assuredly would be his lot.

Somewhere up this river there was a village called Huntsville. It was distant about a hundred miles from Wellston, and had a reputation throughout southwestern Texas. He had never been there. The fact was this reputation was such that honest travelers gave the town a wide berth. Duane had considerable money for him in his possession, and he concluded to visit Huntsville, if he could find it, and buy a stock of provisions.

The following day, toward evening, he happened upon a road which he believed might lead to the village. There were a good many fresh horse-tracks in the sand, and these made him thoughtful. Nevertheless, he followed the road, proceeding cautiously. He had not gone very far when the sound of rapid hoofbeats caught his ears. They came from his rear. In the darkening twilight he could not see any great distance back along the road. Voices, however, warned him that these riders, whoever they were, had approached closer than he liked. To go farther down the road was not to be thought of, so he turned a little way in among the mesquites and halted, hoping to escape being seen or heard. As he was now a fugitive, it seemed every man was his enemy and pursuer.

The horsemen were fast approaching. Presently they were abreast of Duane's position, so near that he could hear the creak of saddles, the clink of spurs.

"Shore he crossed the river below," said one man.

"I reckon you're right, Bill. He's slipped us," replied another.

Rangers or a posse of ranchers in pursuit of a fugitive! The knowledge gave Duane a strange thrill. Certainly they could not have been hunting him. But the feeling their proximity gave him was identical to what it would have been had he been this particular hunted man. He held his breath; he clenched his teeth; he pressed a quieting hand upon his horse. Suddenly he became aware that these horsemen had halted. They were whispering. He could just make out a dark group closely massed. What had made them halt so suspiciously?

"You're wrong, Bill," said a man, in a low but distinct voice.

"The idee of hearin' a hoss heave. You're wuss'n a ranger. And you're hell-bent on killin' that rustler. Now I say let's go home and eat."

"Wal, I'll just take a look at the sand," replied the man called Bill.

Duane heard the clink of spurs on steel stirrup and the thud of boots on the ground. There followed a short silence which was broken by a sharply breathed exclamation.

Duane waited for no more. They had found his trail. He spurred his horse straight into the brush. At the second crashing bound there came yells from the road, and then shots. Duane heard the hiss of a bullet close by his ear, and as it struck a branch it made a peculiar singing sound. These shots and the proximity of that lead missile roused in Duane a quick, hot resentment which mounted into a passion almost ungovernable. He must escape, yet it seemed that he did not care whether he did or not. Something grim kept urging him to halt and return the fire of these men. After running a couple of hundred yards he raised himself from over the pommel, where he had bent to avoid the stinging branches, and tried to guide his horse. In the dark shadows under mesquites and cottonwoods he was hard put to it to find open passage; however, he succeeded so well and made such little noise that gradually he drew away from his pursuers. The sound of their horses crashing through the thickets died away. Duane reined in and listened. He had distanced them. Probably they would go into camp till daylight, then follow his tracks. He started on again, walking his horse, and peered sharply at the ground, so that he might take advantage of the first trail he crossed. It seemed a long while until he came upon one. He followed it until a late hour, when, striking the willow brakes again and hence the neighborhood of the river, he picketed his horse and lay down to rest. But he did not sleep. His mind bitterly revolved the fate that had come upon him. He made efforts to think of other things, but in vain.

Every moment he expected the chill, the sense of loneliness that yet was ominous of a strange visitation, the peculiarly imagined lights and shades of the night—these things that presaged the coming of Cal Bain. Doggedly Duane fought against the insidious phantom. He kept telling himself that it was just imagination, that it would wear off in time. Still in his heart he did not believe what he hoped. But he would not give up; he would not accept the ghost of his victim as a reality.

Gray dawn found him in the saddle again headed for the river. Half an hour of riding brought him to the dense chaparral and willow thickets. These he threaded to come at length to the ford. It was a gravel bottom, and therefore an easy crossing. Once upon the opposite shore he reined in his horse and looked darkly back. This action marked his acknowledgment of his situation: he had voluntarily sought the refuge of the outlaws; he was beyond the pale.

A bitter and passionate curse passed his lips as he spurred his horse into the brakes on that alien shore.

He rode perhaps twenty miles, not sparing his horse nor caring whether or not he left a plain trail.

"Let them hunt me!" he muttered.

When the heat of the day began to be oppressive, and hunger and thirst made themselves manifest, Duane began to look about him for a place to halt for the noon-hours. The trail led into a road which was hard packed and smooth from the tracks of cattle. He doubted not that he had come across one of the roads used by border raiders. He headed into it, and had scarcely traveled a mile when, turning a curve, he came point-blank upon a single horseman riding toward him. Both riders wheeled their mounts sharply and were ready to run and shoot back. Not more than a hundred paces separated them. They stood then for a moment watching each other.

"Mawnin', stranger," called the man, dropping his hand from his hip.

"Howdy," replied Duane, shortly.

They rode toward each other, closing half the gap, then they halted again.

"I seen you ain't no ranger," called the rider, "an' shore I ain't none."

He laughed loudly, as if he had made a joke.

"How'd you know I wasn't a ranger?" asked Duane, curiously. Somehow he had instantly divined that his horseman was no officer, or even a rancher trailing stolen stock.

"Wal," said the fellow, starting his horse forward at a walk, "a ranger'd never git ready to run the other way from one man."

He laughed again. He was small and wiry, slouchy of attire, and armed to the teeth, and he bestrode a fine bay horse. He had quick, dancing brown eyes, at once frank and bold, and a coarse, bronzed face. Evidently he was a good-natured ruffian.

Duane acknowledged the truth of the assertion, and turned over in his mind how shrewdly the fellow had guessed him to be a hunted man.

"My name's Luke Stevens, an' I hail from the river. Who're you?" said this stranger.

Duane was silent.

"I reckon you're Buck Duane," went on Stevens. "I heerd you was a damn bad man with a gun."

This time Duane laughed, not at the doubtful compliment, but at the idea that the first outlaw he met should know him. Here was proof of how swiftly facts about gunplay traveled on the Texas border.

"Wal, Buck," said Stevens, in a friendly manner, "I ain't presumin' on your time or company. I see you're headin' fer the river. But will you stop long enough to stake a feller to a bite of grub?"

"I'm out of grub, and pretty hungry myself," admitted Duane.

"Been pushin' your hoss, I see. Wal, I reckon you'd better stock up before you hit thet stretch of country."

He made a wide sweep of his right arm, indicating the southwest, and there was that in his action which seemed significant of a vast and barren region.

"Stock up?" queried Duane, thoughtfully.

"Shore. A feller has jest got to eat. I can rustle along without whisky, but not without grub. Thet's what makes it so embarrassin' travelin' these parts dodgin' your shadow. Now, I'm on my way to Mercer. It's a little two-bit town up the river a ways. I'm goin' to pack out some grub."

Stevens's tone was inviting. Evidently he would welcome Duane's companionship, but he did not openly say so. Duane kept silence, however, and then Stevens went on.

"Stranger, in this here country two's a crowd. It's safer. I never was much on this lone-wolf dodgin', though I've done it of necessity. It takes a damn good man to travel alone any length of time. Why, I've been thet sick I was jest achin' fer some ranger to come along an' plug me. Give me a pardner any day. Now, mebbe you're not thet kind of a feller, an' I'm shore not presumin' to ask. But I just declares myself sufficient."

"You mean you'd like me to go with you?" asked Duane.

Stevens grinned. "Wal, I should smile. I'd be particular proud to be braced with a man of your reputation."

"See here, my good fellow, that's all nonsense," declared Duane, in some haste.

"Shore I think modesty becomin' to a youngster," replied Stevens. "I hate a brag. An' I've no use fer these four-flush cowboys thet 're always lookin' fer trouble an' talkin' gunplay. Buck, I don't know much about you. But every man who's lived along the Texas border remembers a lot about your Dad. It was expected of you, I reckon, an' much of your rep was established before you thronged your gun. I jest heerd thet you was lightnin' on the draw, an' when you cut loose with a gun, why the figger on the ace of spades would cover your cluster of bullet holes. Thet's the word thet's gone down the border. It's the kind of reputation most sure to fly far an' swift ahead of a man in this country. An' the safest, too; I'll gamble on thet. It's the land of the draw. I see now you're only a boy, though you're shore a strappin' husky one. Now, Buck, I'm not a spring chicken, an' I've been long on the dodge. Mebbe a little of my society won't hurt you none. You'll need to learn the country."

There was something sincere and likable about this outlaw.

"I dare say you're right," replied Duane, quietly. "And I'll go to Mercer with you."

Next moment he was riding down the road with Stevens. Duane had never been much of a talker, and now he found speech difficult. But his companion did not seem to mind that. He was a jocose, voluble fellow, probably glad now to hear the sound of his own voice. Duane listened, and sometimes he thought with a pang of the distinction of name and heritage of blood his father had left to him.

## CHAPTER III

Late that day, a couple of hours before sunset, Duane and Stevens, having rested their horses in the shade of some mesquites near the town of Mercer, saddled up and prepared to move.

"Buck, as we're lookin' fer grub, an' not trouble, I reckon you'd better hang up out here," Stevens was saying, as he mounted. "You see, towns an' sheriffs an' rangers are always lookin' fer new fellers gone bad. They sort of forget most of the old boys, except those as are plumb bad. Now, nobody in Mercer will take notice of me. Reckon there's been a thousand men run into the river country to become outlaws since yours truly. You jest wait here an' be ready to ride hard. Mebbe my besettin' sin will go operatin' in spite of my good intentions. In which case there'll be—"

His pause was significant. He grinned, and his brown eyes danced with a kind of wild humor

"Stevens, have you got any money?" asked Duane.

"Money!" exclaimed Luke, blankly. "Say, I haven't owned a two-bit piece since—wal, fer some time."

"I'll furnish money for grub," returned Duane. "And for whisky, too, providing you hurry back here—without making trouble."

"Shore you're a downright good pard," declared Stevens, in admiration, as he took the money. "I give my word, Buck, an' I'm here to say I never broke it yet. Lay low, an' look fer me back quick."

With that he spurred his horse and rode out of the mesquites toward the town. At that distance, about a quarter of a mile, Mercer appeared to be a cluster of low adobe houses set in a grove of cottonwoods. Pastures of alfalfa were dotted by horses and cattle. Duane saw a sheep-herder driving in a meager flock.

Presently Stevens rode out of sight into the town. Duane waited, hoping the outlaw would make good his word. Probably not a quarter of an hour had elapsed when Duane heard the clear reports of a Winchester rifle, the clatter of rapid hoof-beats, and yells unmistakably the kind to mean danger for a man like Stevens. Duane mounted and rode to the edge of the mesquites.

He saw a cloud of dust down the road and a bay horse running fast. Stevens apparently had not been wounded by any of the shots, for he had a steady seat in his saddle and his riding, even at that moment, struck Duane as admirable. He carried a large pack over the pommel, and he kept looking back. The shots had ceased, but the yells increased. Duane saw several men running and waving their arms. Then he spurred his horse and got into a swift stride, so Stevens would not pass him. Presently the outlaw caught up with him. Stevens was grinning, but there was now no fun in the dancing eyes. It was a devil that danced in them. His face seemed a shade paler.

"Was jest comin' out of the store," yelled Stevens. "Run plumb into a rancher—who knowed me. He opened up with a rifle. Think they'll chase us."

They covered several miles before there were any signs of pursuit, and when horsemen did move into sight out of the cottonwoods Duane and his companion steadily drew farther away.

"No hosses in thet bunch to worry us," called out Stevens.

Duane had the same conviction, and he did not look back again. He rode somewhat to the fore, and was constantly aware of the rapid thudding of hoofs behind, as Stevens kept close to him. At sunset they reached the willow brakes and the river. Duane's horse was winded and lashed with sweat and lather. It was not until the crossing had been accomplished that Duane halted to rest his animal. Stevens was riding up the low, sandy bank. He reeled in the saddle. With an exclamation of surprise Duane leaped off and ran to the outlaw's side.

Stevens was pale, and his face bore beads of sweat. The whole front of his shirt was soaked with blood.

"You're shot!" cried Duane.

"Wal, who 'n hell said I wasn't? Would you mind givin' me a lift—on this here pack?"

Duane lifted the heavy pack down and then helped Stevens to dismount. The outlaw had a bloody foam on his lips, and he was spitting blood.

"Oh, why didn't you say so!" cried Duane. "I never thought. You seemed all right."

"Wal, Luke Stevens may be as gabby as an old woman, but sometimes he doesn't say anythin'. It wouldn't have done no good."

Duane bade him sit down, removed his shirt, and washed the blood from his breast and back. Stevens had been shot in the breast, fairly low down, and the bullet had gone clear through him. His ride, holding himself and that heavy pack in the saddle, had been a feat little short of marvelous. Duane did not see how it had been possible, and he felt no hope for the outlaw. But he plugged the wounds and bound them tightly.

"Feller's name was Brown," Stevens said. "Me an' him fell out over a hoss

I stole from him over in Huntsville. We had a shootin'-scrape then. Wal, as I was straddlin' my hoss back there in Mercer I seen this Brown, an' seen him before he seen me. Could have killed him, too. But I wasn't breakin' my word to you. I kind of hoped he wouldn't spot me. But he did—an' fust shot he got me here. What do you think of this hole?"

"It's pretty bad," replied Duane; and he could not look the cheerful outlaw in the eyes.

"I reckon it is. Wal, I've had some bad wounds I lived over. Guess mebbe I can stand this one. Now, Buck, get me some place in the brakes, leave me some grub an' water at my hand, an' then you clear out."

"Leave you here alone?" asked Duane, sharply.

"Shore. You see, I can't keep up with you. Brown an' his friends will foller us across the river a ways. You've got to think of number one in this game."

"What would you do in my case?" asked Duane, curiously.

"Wal, I reckon I'd clear out an' save my hide," replied Stevens.

Duane felt inclined to doubt the outlaw's assertion. For his own part he decided his conduct without further speech. First he watered the horses, filled canteens and water bag, and then tied the pack upon his own horse. That done, he lifted Stevens upon his horse, and, holding him in the saddle, turned into the brakes, being careful to pick out hard or grassy ground that left little signs of tracks. Just about dark he ran across a trail that Stevens said was a good one to take into the wild country.

"Reckon we'd better keep right on in the dark—till I drop," concluded Stevens, with a laugh.

All that night Duane, gloomy and thoughtful, attentive to the wounded outlaw, walked the trail and never halted till daybreak. He was tired then and very hungry. Stevens seemed in bad shape, although he was still spirited and cheerful. Duane made camp. The outlaw refused food, but asked for both whisky and water. Then he stretched out.

"Buck, will you take off my boots?" he asked, with a faint smile on his pallid face.

Duane removed them, wondering if the outlaw had the thought that he did not want to die with his boots on. Stevens seemed to read his mind.

"Buck, my old daddy used to say thet I was born to be hanged. But I wasn't—an' dyin' with your boots on is the next wust way to croak."

"You've a chance to—to get over this," said Duane.

"Shore. But I want to be correct about the boots—an' say, pard, if I do go over, jest you remember thet I was appreciatin' of your kindness."

Then he closed his eyes and seemed to sleep.

Duane could not find water for the horses, but there was an abundance of dew-wet grass upon which he hobbled them. After that was done he prepared himself a much-needed meal. The sun was getting warm when he lay down to sleep, and when he awoke it was sinking in the west. Stevens was still alive, for he breathed heavily. The horses were in sight. All was quiet except the hum of insects in the brush. Duane listened awhile, then rose and went for the horses.

When he returned with them he found Stevens awake, bright-eyed, cheerful as usual, and apparently stronger.

"Wal, Buck, I'm still with you an' good fer another night's ride," he said. "Guess about all I need now is a big pull on thet bottle. Help me, will you? There! thet was bully. I ain't swallowin' my blood this evenin'. Mebbe I've bled all there was in me."

While Duane got a hurried meal for himself, packed up the little outfit, and saddled the horses Stevens kept on talking. He seemed to be in a hurry to tell Duane all about the country. Another night ride would put them beyond fear of pursuit, within striking distance of the Rio Grande and the hiding-places of the outlaws.

When it came time for mounting the horses Stevens said, "Reckon you can pull on my boots once more." In spite of the laugh accompanying the words Duane detected a subtle change in the outlaw's spirit.

On this night travel was facilitated by the fact that the trail was broad enough for two horses abreast, enabling Duane to ride while upholding Stevens in the saddle.

The difficulty most persistent was in keeping the horses in a walk. They were used to a trot, and that kind of gait would not do for Stevens. The red died out of the west; a pale afterglow prevailed for a while; darkness set in; then the broad expanse of blue darkened and the stars brightened. After a while Stevens ceased talking and drooped in his saddle. Duane kept the horses going, however, and the slow hours wore away. Duane thought the quiet night would never break to dawn, that there was no end to the melancholy, brooding plain. But at length a grayness blotted out the stars and mantled the level of mesquite and cactus.

Dawn caught the fugitives at a green camping-site on the bank of a rocky little stream. Stevens fell a dead weight into Duane's arms, and one look at the haggard face showed Duane that the outlaw had taken his last ride. He knew it, too. Yet that cheerfulness prevailed.

"Buck, my feet are orful tired packin' them heavy boots," he said, and seemed immensely relieved when Duane had removed them.

This matter of the outlaw's boots was strange, Duane thought. He made Stevens as comfortable as possible, then attended to his own needs. And the outlaw took up the thread of his conversation where he had left off the night before.

"This trail splits up a ways from here, an' every branch of it leads to a hole where you'll find men—a few, mebbe, like yourself—some like me—an' gangs of no-good hoss-thieves, rustlers, an' such. It's easy livin', Buck. I reckon, though, that you'll not find it easy. You'll never mix in. You'll be a lone wolf. I seen that right off. Wal, if a man can stand the loneliness, an' if he's quick on the draw, mebbe lone-wolfin' it is the best. Shore I don't know. But these fellers in here will be suspicious of a man who goes it alone. If they get a chance they'll kill you."

Stevens asked for water several times. He had forgotten or he did not want the whisky. His voice grew perceptibly weaker.

"Be quiet," said Duane. "Talking uses up your strength."

"Aw, I'll talk till—I'm done," he replied, doggedly. "See here, pard, you can gamble on what I'm tellin' you. An' it'll be useful. From this camp we'll—you'll meet men right along. An' none of them will be honest men. All the same, some are better'n others. I've lived along the river fer twelve years. There's three big gangs of outlaws. King Fisher—you know him, I reckon, fer he's half the time livin' among respectable folks. King is a pretty good feller. It'll do to tie up with him ant his gang. Now, there's Cheseldine, who hangs out in the Rim Rock way up the river. He's an outlaw chief. I never seen him, though I stayed once right in his camp. Late years he's got rich an' keeps back pretty well hid. But Bland—I knowed Bland fer years. An' I haven't any use fer him. Bland has the biggest gang. You ain't likely to miss strikin' his place sometime or other. He's got a regular town, I might say. Shore there's some gamblin' an' gunfightin' goin' on at Bland's camp all the time. Bland has killed some twenty men, an' thet's not countin' greasers."

Here Stevens took another drink and then rested for a while.

"You ain't likely to get on with Bland," he resumed, presently. "You're too strappin' big an' good-lookin' to please the chief. Fer he's got women in his camp. Then he'd be jealous of your possibilities with a gun. Shore I reckon he'd be careful, though. Bland's no fool, an' he loves his hide. I reckon any of the other gangs would be better fer you when you ain't goin' it alone."

Apparently that exhausted the fund of information and advice Stevens had been eager to impart. He lapsed into silence and lay with closed eyes. Meanwhile the sun rose warm; the breeze waved the mesquites; the birds came down to splash in the shallow stream; Duane dozed in a comfortable seat. By and by something roused him. Stevens was once more talking, but with a changed tone.

"Feller's name—was Brown," he rambled. "We fell out—over a hoss I stole from him—in Huntsville. He stole it fuss. Brown's one of them sneaks—afraid of the open—he steals an' pretends to be honest. Say, Buck, mebbe you'll meet Brown someday—you an' me are pards now."

"I'll remember, if I ever meet him," said Duane.

That seemed to satisfy the outlaw. Presently he tried to lift his head, but had not the strength. A strange shade was creeping across the bronzed rough face.

"My feet are pretty heavy. Shore you got my boots off?"

Duane held them up, but was not certain that Stevens could see them. The outlaw closed his eyes again and muttered incoherently. Then he fell asleep. Duane believed that sleep was final. The day passed, with Duane watching and waiting. Toward sundown Stevens awoke, and his eyes seemed clearer. Duane went to get some fresh water, thinking his comrade would surely want some. When he returned Stevens made no sign that he wanted anything. There was something bright about him, and suddenly Duane realized what it meant.

"Pard, you—stuck—to me!" the outlaw whispered.

Duane caught a hint of gladness in the voice; he traced a faint surprise in the haggard face. Stevens seemed like a little child.

To Duane the moment was sad, elemental, big, with a burden of mystery he could not understand.

Duane buried him in a shallow arroyo and heaped up a pile of stones to mark the grave. That done, he saddled his comrade's horse, hung the weapons over the pommel; and, mounting his own steed, he rode down the trail in the gathering twilight.

# CHAPTER IV

Two days later, about the middle of the forenoon, Duane dragged the two horses up the last ascent of an exceedingly rough trail and found himself on top of the Rim Rock, with a beautiful green valley at his feet, the yellow, sluggish Rio Grande shining in the sun, and the great, wild, mountainous barren of Mexico stretching to the south.

Duane had not fallen in with any travelers. He had taken the likeliest-looking trail he had come across. Where it had led him he had not the slightest idea, except that here was the river, and probably the enclosed valley was the retreat of some famous outlaw.

No wonder outlaws were safe in that wild refuge! Duane had spent the last two days climbing the roughest and most difficult trail he had ever seen. From the looks of the descent he imagined the worst part of his travel was yet to come. Not improbably it was two thousand feet down to the river. The wedge-shaped valley, green with alfalfa and cottonwood, and nestling down amid the bare walls of yellow rock, was a delight and a relief to his tired eyes.

Eager to get down to a level and to find a place to rest, Duane began the descent.

The trail proved to be the kind that could not be descended slowly. He kept dodging rocks which his horses loosed behind him. And in a short time he reached the valley, entering at the apex of the wedge. A stream of clear water tumbled out of the rocks here, and most of it ran into irrigation-ditches. His horses drank thirstily. And he drank with that fullness and gratefulness common to the desert traveler finding sweet water. Then he mounted and rode down the valley wondering what would be his reception.

The valley was much larger than it had appeared from the high elevation. Well watered, green with grass and tree, and farmed evidently by good hands, it gave Duane a considerable surprise. Horses and cattle were everywhere. Every clump of cottonwoods surrounded a small adobe house. Duane saw Mexicans working in the fields and horsemen going to and fro. Presently he passed a house bigger than the others with a porch attached. A woman, young and pretty he thought, watched him from a door. No one else appeared to notice him.

Presently the trail widened into a road, and that into a kind of square lined by a number of adobe and log buildings of rudest structure. Within sight were horses, dogs, a couple of steers, Mexican women with children, and white men, all of whom appeared to be doing nothing. His advent created no interest until he rode up to the white men, who were lolling in the shade of a house. This place evidently was a store and saloon, and from the inside came a lazy hum of voices.

As Duane reined to a halt one of the loungers in the shade rose with a loud exclamation:

"Bust me if thet ain't Luke's hoss!"

The others accorded their interest, if not assent, by rising to advance toward Duane.

"How about it, Euchre? Ain't thet Luke's bay?" queried the first man.

"Plain as your nose," replied the fellow called Euchre.

"There ain't no doubt about thet, then," laughed another, "fer Bosomer's nose is shore plain on the landscape."

These men lined up before Duane, and as he coolly regarded them he thought they could have been recognized anywhere as desperadoes. The man called Bosomer, who had stepped forward, had a forbidding face which showed yellow eyes, an enormous nose, and a skin the color of dust, with a thatch of sandy hair.

"Stranger, who are you an' where in the hell did you git thet bay hoss?" he demanded. His yellow eyes took in Stevens's horse, then the weapons hung on the saddle, and finally turned their glinting, hard light upward to Duane.

Duane did not like the tone in which he had been addressed, and he remained silent. At least half his mind seemed busy with curious interest in regard to something that leaped inside him and made his breast feel tight. He recognized it as that strange emotion which had shot through him often of late, and which had decided him to go out to the meeting with Bain. Only now it was different, more powerful.

"Stranger, who are you?" asked another man, somewhat more civilly.

"My name's Duane," replied Duane, curtly.

"An' how'd you come by the hoss?"

Duane answered briefly, and his words were followed by a short silence, during which the men looked at him. Bosomer began to twist the ends of his beard.

"Reckon he's dead, all right, or nobody'd hev his hoss an' guns," presently said Euchre.

"Mister Duane," began Bosomer, in low, stinging tones, "I happen to be Luke Stevens's side-pardner."

Duane looked him over, from dusty, worn-out boots to his slouchy sombrero. That look seemed to inflame Bosomer.

"An' I want the hoss an' them guns," he shouted.

"You or anybody else can have them, for all I care. I just fetched them in. But the pack is mine," replied Duane. "And say, I befriended your pard. If you can't use a civil tongue you'd better cinch it."

"Civil? Haw, haw!" rejoined the outlaw. "I don't know you. How do we know you didn't plug Stevens, an' stole his hoss, an' jest happened to stumble down here?"

"You'll have to take my word, that's all," replied Duane, sharply.

"I ain't takin' your word! Savvy thet? An' I was Luke's pard!"

With that Bosomer wheeled and, pushing his companions aside, he stamped into the saloon, where his voice broke out in a roar.

Duane dismounted and threw his bridle.

"Stranger, Bosomer is shore hot-headed," said the man Euchre. He did not appear unfriendly, nor were the others hostile.

At this juncture several more outlaws crowded out of the door, and the one in the lead was a tall man of stalwart physique. His manner proclaimed him a leader. He had a long face, a flaming red beard, and clear, cold blue eyes that fixed in close scrutiny upon Duane. He was not a Texan; in truth, Duane did not recognize one of these outlaws as native to his state.

"I'm Bland," said the tall man, authoritatively. "Who're you and what're you doing here?"

Duane looked at Bland as he had at the others. This outlaw chief appeared to be reasonable, if he was not courteous. Duane told his story again, this time a little more in detail.

"I believe you," replied Bland, at once. "Think I know when a fellow is lying."

"I reckon you're on the right trail," put in Euchre. "Thet about Luke wantin' his boots took off—thet satisfies me. Luke hed a mortal dread of dyin' with his boots on."

At this sally the chief and his men laughed.

"You said Duane—Buck Duane?" queried Bland. "Are you a son of that Duane who was a gunfighter some years back?"

"Yes," replied Duane.

"Never met him, and glad I didn't," said Bland, with a grim humor. "So you got in trouble and had to go on the dodge? What kind of trouble?"

"Had a fight."

"Fight? Do you mean gunplay?" questioned Bland. He seemed eager, curious, speculative.

"Yes. It ended in gunplay, I'm sorry to say," answered Duane.

"Guess I needn't ask the son of Duane if he killed his man," went on Bland, ironically. "Well, I'm sorry you bucked against trouble in my camp. But as it is, I guess you'd be wise to make yourself scarce."

"Do you mean I'm politely told to move on?" asked Duane, quietly.

"Not exactly that," said Bland, as if irritated. "If this isn't a free place there isn't one on earth. Every man is equal here. Do you want to join my band?"

"No, I don't."

"Well, even if you did I imagine that wouldn't stop Bosomer. He's an ugly fellow. He's one of the few gunmen I've met who wants to kill somebody all the time. Most men like that are four-flushes. But Bosomer is all one color, and that's red. Merely for your own sake I advise you to hit the trail."

"Thanks. But if that's all I'll stay," returned Duane. Even as he spoke he felt that he did not know himself.

Bosomer appeared at the door, pushing men who tried to detain him, and as he jumped clear of a last reaching hand he uttered a snarl like an angry dog. Manifestly the short while he had spent inside the saloon had been devoted to drinking and talking himself into a frenzy. Bland and the other outlaws quickly moved aside, letting Duane stand alone. When Bosomer saw Duane standing motionless and watchful a strange change passed quickly in him. He halted in his tracks, and as he did that the men who had followed him out piled over one another in their hurry to get to one side.

Duane saw all the swift action, felt intuitively the meaning of it, and in Bosomer's sudden change of front. The outlaw was keen, and he had expected a shrinking, or at least a frightened antagonist. Duane knew he was neither. He felt like iron, and yet thrill after thrill ran through him. It was almost as if this situation had been one long familiar to him. Somehow he understood this yellow-eyed Bosomer. The outlaw had come out to kill him. And now, though somewhat checked by the stand of a stranger, he still meant to kill. Like so many desperadoes of his ilk, he was victim of a passion to kill for the sake of killing. Duane divined that no sudden animosity was driving Bosomer. It was just his chance. In that moment murder would have been joy to him. Very likely he had forgotten his pretext for a quarrel. Very probably his faculties were absorbed in conjecture as to Duane's possibilities.

But he did not speak a word. He remained motionless for a long moment, his eyes pale and steady, his right hand like a claw.

That instant gave Duane a power to read in his enemy's eyes the thought that preceded action. But Duane did not want to kill another man. Still he would have to fight, and he decided to cripple Bosomer. When Bosomer's hand moved Duane's gun was spouting fire. Two shots only—both from Duane's gun—and the outlaw fell with his right arm shattered. Bosomer cursed harshly and floundered in the dust, trying to reach the gun with his left hand. His comrades, however, seeing that Duane would not kill unless forced, closed in upon Bosomer and prevented any further madness on his part.

## CHAPTER V

Of the outlaws present Euchre appeared to be the one most inclined to lend friendliness to curiosity; and he led Duane and the horses away to a small adobe shack. He tied the horses in an open shed and removed their saddles. Then, gathering up Stevens's weapons, he invited his visitor to enter the house.

It had two rooms—windows without coverings—bare floors. One room contained blankets, weapons, saddles, and bridles; the other a stone fireplace, rude table and bench, two bunks, a box cupboard, and various blackened utensils.

"Make yourself to home as long as you want to stay," said Euchre. "I ain't rich in this world's goods, but I own what's here, an' you're welcome."

"Thanks. I'll stay awhile and rest. I'm pretty well played out," replied Duane.

Euchre gave him a keen glance.

"Go ahead an' rest. I'll take your horses to grass." Euchre left Duane alone in the house. Duane relaxed then, and mechanically he wiped the sweat from his face. He was laboring under some kind of a spell or shock which did not pass off quickly. When it had worn away he took off his coat and belt and made himself comfortable on the blankets. And he had a thought that if he rested or slept what difference would it make on the morrow? No rest, no sleep could change the gray outlook of the future. He felt glad when Euchre came bustling in, and for the first time he took notice of the outlaw.

Euchre was old in years. What little hair he had was gray, his face clean-shaven and full of wrinkles; his eyes were half shut from long gazing through the sun and dust. He stooped. But his thin frame denoted strength and endurance still unimpaired.

"Hev a drink or a smoke?" he asked.

Duane shook his head. He had not been unfamiliar with whisky, and he had used tobacco moderately since he was sixteen. But now, strangely, he felt a disgust at the idea of stimulants. He did not understand clearly what he felt. There was that vague idea of something wild in his blood, something that made him fear himself.

Euchre wagged his old head sympathetically. "Reckon you feel a little sick. When it comes to shootin' I run. What's your age?"

"I'm twenty-three," replied Duane.

Euchre showed surprise. "You're only a boy! I thought you thirty anyways. Buck, I heard what you told Bland, an' puttin' thet with my own figgerin', I reckon you're no criminal yet. Throwin' a gun in self-defense—thet ain't no crime!"

Duane, finding relief in talking, told more about himself.

"Huh," replied the old man. "I've been on this river fer years, an' I've seen hundreds of boys come in on the dodge. Most of them, though, was no good. An' thet kind don't last long. This river country has been an' is the refuge fer criminals from all over the states. I've bunked with bank cashiers, forgers, plain thieves, an' out-an'-out murderers, all of which had no bizness on the T... border. Fellers like Bland are exceptions. He's no Texan—you seen thet. The gang he rules here come from all over, an' they're tough cusses, you can bet on thet. They live fat an' easy. If it wasn't fer the fightin' among themselves they'd shore grow populous. The Rim Rock is no place for a peaceable, decent feller. I heard you tell Bland you wouldn't join his gang. Thet'll not make him take a likin' to you. Have you any money?"

"Not much," replied Duane.

"Could you live by gamblin'? Are you any good at cards?"

"No."

"You wouldn't steal hosses or rustle cattle?"

"No."

"When your money's gone how'n hell will you live? There ain't any work a decent feller could do. You can't herd with greasers. Why, Bland's men would shoot at you in the fields. What'll you do, son?"

"God knows," replied Duane, hopelessly. "I'll make my money last as long as possible—then starve."

"Wal, I'm pretty pore, but you'll never starve while I got anythin'."

Here it struck Duane again—that something human and kind and eager which he had seen in Stevens. Duane's estimate of outlaws had lacked this quality. He had not accorded them any virtues. To him, as to the outside world, they had been merely vicious men without one redeeming feature.

"I'm much obliged to you, Euchre," replied Duane. "But of course I won't live with anyone unless I can pay my share."

"Have it any way you like, my son," said Euchre, good-humoredly. "You make a fire, an' I'll set about gettin' grub. I'm a sourdough, Buck. Thet man doesn't live who can beat my bread."

"How do you ever pack supplies in here?" asked Duane, thinking of the almost inaccessible nature of the valley.

"Some comes across from Mexico, an' the rest down the river. Thet river trip is a bird. It's more'n five hundred miles to any supply point. Bland has mozos, greaser boatmen. Sometimes, too, he gets supplies in from downriver. You see, Bland sells thousands of cattle in Cuba. An' all this stock has to go down by boat to meet the ships."

"Where on earth are the cattle driven down to the river?" asked Duane.

"Thet's not my secret," replied Euchre, shortly. "Fact is, I don't know. I've rustled cattle for Bland, but he never sent me through the Rim Rock with them."

Duane experienced a sort of pleasure in the realization that interest had been stirred in him. He was curious about Bland and his gang, and glad to have something to think about. For every once in a while he had a sensation that was almost like a pang. He wanted to forget. In the next hour he did forget, and enjoyed helping in the preparation and eating of the meal. Euchre, after washing and hanging up the several utensils, put on his hat and turned to go out.

"Come along or stay here, as you want," he said to Duane.

"I'll stay," rejoined Duane, slowly.

The old outlaw left the room and trudged away, whistling cheerfully.

Duane looked around him for a book or paper, anything to read; but all the printed matter he could find consisted of a few words on cartridge-boxes and an advertisement on the back of a tobacco-pouch. There seemed to be nothing for him to do. He had rested; he did not want to lie down anymore. He began to walk to and fro, from one end of the room to the other. And as he walked he fell into the lately acquired habit of brooding over his misfortune.

Suddenly he straightened up with a jerk. Unconsciously he had drawn his gun. Standing there with the bright cold weapon in his hand, he looked at it in consternation. How had he come to draw it? With difficulty he traced his thoughts backward, but could not find any that was accountable for his act. He discovered, however, that he had a remarkable tendency to drop his hand to his gun. That might have come from the habit long practice in drawing had given him. Likewise, it might have come from a subtle sense, scarcely thought of at all, of the late, close, and inevitable relation between that weapon and himself. He was amazed to find that, bitter as he had grown at fate, the desire to live burned strong in him. If he had been as unfortunately situated, but with the difference that no man wanted to put him in jail or take his life, he felt that this burning passion to be free, to save himself, might not have been so powerful. Life certainly held no bright prospects for him. Already he had begun to despair of ever getting back to his home. But to give up like a white-hearted coward, to let himself be handcuffed and jailed, to run from a drunken, bragging cowboy, or be shot in cold blood by some border brute who merely wanted to add another notch to his gun—these things were impossible for Duane because there was in him the temper to fight. In that hour he yielded only to fate and the spirit inborn in him. Hereafter this gun must be a living part of him. Right then and there he returned to a practice he had long discontinued—the draw. It was now a stern, bitter, deadly business with him. He did not need to fire the gun, for accuracy was a gift and had become assured. Swiftness on the draw, however, could be improved, and he set himself to acquire the limit of speed possible to any man. He stood still in his tracks; he paced the room; he sat down, lay down, put himself in awkward positions; and from every position he practiced throwing his gun—practiced it till he was hot and tired and his arm ached and his hand burned. That practice he determined to keep up every day. It was one thing, at least, that would help pass the weary hours.

Later he went outdoors to the cooler shade of the cottonwoods. From this point he could see a good deal of the valley. Under different circumstances Duane felt that he would have enjoyed such a beautiful spot. Euchre's shack sat against the first rise of the slope of the wall, and Duane, by climbing a few rods, got a view of the whole valley. Assuredly it was an outlaw settlement. He saw a good many Mexicans, who, of course, were hand and glove with Bland. Also he saw enormous flatboats, crude of structure, moored along the banks of the river. The Rio Grande rolled away between high bluffs. A cable, sagging deep in the middle, was stretched over the wide yellow stream, and an old scow, evidently used as a ferry, lay anchored on the far shore.

The valley was an ideal retreat for an outlaw band operating on a big scale. Pursuit scarcely need be feared over the broken trails of the Rim Rock. And the open end of the valley could be defended against almost any number of men coming down the river. Access to Mexico was easy and quick. What puzzled Duane was how Bland got cattle down to the river, and he wondered if the rustler really did get rid of his stolen stock by use of boats.

Duane must have idled considerable time up on the hill, for when he returned to the shack Euchre was busily engaged around the campfire.

"Wal, glad to see you ain't so pale about the gills as you was," he said, by way of greeting. "Pitch in an' we'll soon have grub ready. There's shore one consolin' fact round this here camp."

"What's that?" asked Duane.

"Plenty of good juicy beef to eat. An' it doesn't cost a short bit."

"But it costs hard rides and trouble, bad conscience, and life, too, doesn't it?"

"I ain't shore about the bad conscience. Mine never bothered me none. An' as for life, why, thet's cheap in Texas."

"Who is Bland?" asked Duane, quickly changing the subject. "What do you know about him?"

"We don't know who he is or where he hails from," replied Euchre. "Thet's always been somethin' to interest the gang. He must have been a young man when he struck Texas. Now he's middle-aged. I remember how years ago he was soft-spoken an' not rough in talk or act like he is now. Bland ain't likely his right name. He knows a lot. He can doctor you, an' he's shore a knowin' feller with tools. He's the kind thet rules men. Outlaws are always ridin' in here to join his gang, an' if it hadn't been fer the gamblin' an' gunplay he'd have a thousand men around him."

"How many in his gang now?"

"I reckon there's short of a hundred now. The number varies. Then Bland has several small camps up an' down the river. Also he has men back on the cattle-ranges."

"How does he control such a big force?" asked Duane. "Especially when his band's composed of bad men. Luke Stevens said he had no use for Bland. And I heard once somewhere that Bland was a devil."

"Thet's it. He is a devil. He's as hard as flint, violent in temper, never made any friends except his right-hand men, Dave Rugg an' Chess Alloway. Bland'll shoot at a wink. He's killed a lot of fellers, an' some fer nothin'. The reason thet outlaws gather round him an' stick is because he's a safe refuge, an' then he's well heeled. Bland is rich. They say he has a hundred thousand pesos hid somewhere, an' lots of gold. But he's free with money. He gambles when he's not off with a shipment of cattle. He throws money around. An' the fact is there's always plenty of money where he is. Thet's what holds the gang. Dirty, bloody money!"

"It's a wonder he hasn't been killed. All these years on the border!" exclaimed Duane.

"Wal," replied Euchre, dryly, "he's been quicker on the draw than the other fellers who hankered to kill him, thet's all."

Euchre's reply rather chilled Duane's interest for the moment. Such remarks always made his mind revolve round facts pertaining to himself.

"Speakin' of this here swift wrist game," went on Euchre, "there's been considerable talk in camp about your throwin' of a gun. You know, Buck, thet among us fellers—us hunted men—there ain't anythin' calculated to rouse respect like a slick hand with a gun. I heard Bland say this afternoon—an' he said it serious-like an' speculative—thet he'd never seen your equal. He was watchin' of you close, he said, an' just couldn't follow your hand when you drawed. All the fellers who seen you meet Bosomer had somethin' to say. Bo was about as handy with a gun as any man in this camp, barrin' Chess Alloway an' mebbe Bland himself. Chess is the captain with a Colt—or he was. An' he shore didn't like the references made about your speed. Bland was honest in acknowledgin' it, but he didn't like it, neither. Some of the fellers allowed your draw might have been just accident. But most of them figgered different. An' they all shut up when Bland told who an' what your Dad was. 'Pears to me I once seen your Dad in a gunscrape over at Santone, years ago. Wal, I put my oar in today among the fellers, an' I says: 'What ails you locoed gents? Did young Duane budge an inch when Bo came roarin' out, blood in his eye? Wasn't he cool an' quiet, steady of lips, an' weren't his eyes readin' Bo's mind? An' thet lightnin' draw—can't you-all see thet's a family gift?'"

Euchre's narrow eyes twinkled, and he gave the dough he was rolling a slap with his flour-whitened hand. Manifestly he had proclaimed himself a champion and partner of Duane's, with all the pride an old man could feel in a young one whom he admired.

"Wal," he resumed, presently, "thet's your introduction to the border, Buck. An' your card was a high trump. You'll be let severely alone by real gunfighters an' men like Bland, Alloway, Rugg, an' the bosses of the other gangs. After all, these real men are men, you know, an' onless you cross them they're no more likely to interfere with you than you are with them. But there's a sight of fellers like Bosomer in the river country. They'll all want your game. An' every town you ride into will scare up some cowpuncher full of booze or a long-haired four-flush gunman or a sheriff—an' these men will be playin' to the crowd an' yellin' for your blood. Thet's the Texas of it. You'll have to hide fer ever in the brakes or you'll have to *kill* such men. Buck, I reckon this ain't cheerful news to a decent chap like you. I'm only tellin' you because I've taken a likin' to you, an' I seen right off thet you ain't border-wise. Let's eat now, an' afterward we'll go out so the gang can see you're not hidin'."

When Duane went out with Euchre the sun was setting behind a blue range of mountains across the river in Mexico. The valley appeared to open to the southwest. It was a tranquil, beautiful scene. Somewhere in a house near at hand a woman was singing. And in the road Duane saw a little Mexican boy driving home some cows, one of which wore a bell. The sweet, happy voice of a woman and a whistling barefoot boy—these seemed utterly out of place here.

Euchre presently led to the square and the row of rough houses Duane remembered. He almost stepped on a wide imprint in the dust where Bosomer had confronted him. And a sudden fury beset him that he should be affected strangely by the sight of it.

"Let's have a look in here," said Euchre.

Duane had to bend his head to enter the door. He found himself in a very large room enclosed by adobe walls and roofed with brush. It was full of rude benches, tables, seats. At one corner a number of kegs and barrels lay side by side in a rack. A Mexican boy was lighting lamps hung on posts that sustained the log rafters of the roof.

"The only feller who's goin' to put a close eye on you is Benson," said Euchre. "He runs the place an' sells drinks. The gang calls him Jackrabbit Benson, because he's always got his eye peeled an' his ear cocked. Don't notice him if he looks you over, Buck. Benson is scared to death of every newcomer who rustles into Bland's camp. An' the reason, I take it, is because he's done somebody dirt. He's hidin'. Not from a sheriff or ranger! Men who hide from them don't act like Jackrabbit Benson. He's hidin' from some guy who's huntin' him to kill him. Wal, I'm always expectin' to see some feller ride in here an' throw a gun on Benson. Can't say I'd be grieved."

Duane casually glanced in the direction indicated, and he saw a spare, gaunt man with a face strikingly white beside the red and bronze and dark skins of the men around him. It was a cadaverous face. The black mustache hung down; a heavy lock of black hair dropped down over the brow; deep-set, hollow, staring eyes looked out piercingly. The man had a restless, alert, nervous manner. He put his hands on the board that served as a bar and stared at Duane. But when he met Duane's glance he turned hurriedly to go on serving out liquor.

"What have you got against him?" inquired Duane, as he sat down beside Euchre. He asked more for something to say than from real interest. What did he care about a mean, haunted, craven-faced criminal?

"Wal, mebbe I'm cross-grained," replied Euchre, apologetically. "Shore an outlaw an' rustler such as me can't be touchy. But I never stole nothin' but cattle from some rancher who never missed 'em anyway. Thet sneak Benson—he was the means of puttin' a little girl in Bland's way."

"Girl?" queried Duane, now with real attention.

"Shore. Bland's great on women. I'll tell you about this girl when we get out of here. Some of the gang are goin' to be sociable, an' I can't talk about the chief."

During the ensuing half-hour a number of outlaws passed by Duane and Euchre, halted for a greeting or sat down for a moment. They were all gruff, loud-voiced, merry, and good-natured. Duane replied civilly and agreeably when he was personally addressed; but he refused all invitations to drink and gamble. Evidently he had been accepted, in a way, as one of their clan. No one made any hint of an allusion to his affair with Bosomer. Duane saw readily that Euchre was well liked. One outlaw borrowed money from him: another asked for tobacco.

By the time it was dark the big room was full of outlaws and Mexicans, most of whom were engaged at monte. These gamblers, especially the Mexicans, were intense and quiet. The noise in the place came from the drinkers, the loungers. Duane had seen gambling-resorts—some of the famous ones in San Antonio and El Paso, a few in border towns where license went unchecked. But this place of Jackrabbit Benson's impressed him as one where guns and knives were accessories to the game. To his perhaps rather distinguishing eye the most prominent thing about the gamesters appeared to be their weapons. On several of the tables were piles of silver—Mexican pesos—as large and high as the crown of his hat. There were also piles of gold and silver in United States coin. Duane needed no experienced eyes to see that betting was heavy and that heavy sums exchanged hands. The Mexicans showed a sterner obsession, an intenser passion. Some of the Americans staked freely, nonchalantly, as befitted men to whom money was nothing. These latter were manifestly winning, for there were brother outlaws there who wagered coin with grudging, sullen, greedy eyes. Boisterous talk and laughter among the drinking men drowned, except at intervals, the low, brief talk of the gamblers. The clink of coin sounded incessantly; sometimes just low, steady musical rings; and again, when a pile was tumbled quickly, there was a silvery crash. Here an outlaw pounded on a table with the butt of his gun; there another noisily palmed a roll of dollars while he studied his opponent's face. The noises, however, in Benson's den did not contribute to any extent to the sinister aspect of the place. That seemed to come from the grim and reckless faces, from the bent, intent heads, from the dark lights and shades. There were bright lights, but these served only to make the shadows. And in the shadows lurked unrestrained lust of gain, a spirit ruthless and reckless, a something at once suggesting lawlessness, theft, murder, and hell.

"Bland's not here tonight," Euchre was saying. "He left today on one of his trips, takin' Alloway an' some others. But his other man, Rugg, he's here. See him standin' with them three fellers, all close to Benson. Rugg's the little bow-legged man with the half of his face shot off. He's one-eyed. But he can shore see out of the one he's got. An', darn me! there's Hardin. You know him? He's got an outlaw gang as big as Bland's. Hardin is standin' next to Benson. See how quiet an' unassumin' he looks. Yes, thet's Hardin. He comes here once in a while to see Bland. They're friends, which's shore strange. Do you see thet greaser there—the one with gold an' lace on his sombrero?

Thet's Manuel, a Mexican bandit. He's a great gambler. Comes here often to drop his coin. Next to him is Bill Marr—the feller with the bandana round his head. Bill rode in the other day with some fresh bullet holes. He's been shot more'n any feller I ever heard of. He's full of lead. Funny, because Bill's no troublehunter, an', like me, he'd rather run than shoot. But he's the best rustler Bland's got—a grand rider, an' a wonder with cattle. An' see the tow-headed youngster. Thet's Kid Fuller, the kid of Bland's gang. Fuller has hit the pace hard, an' he won't last the year out on the border. He killed his sweetheart's father, got run out of Staceytown, took to stealin' hosses. An' next he's here with Bland. Another boy gone wrong, an' now shore a hard nut."

Euchre went on calling Duane's attention to other men, just as he happened to glance over them. Any one of them would have been a marked man in a respectable crowd. Here each took his place with more or less distinction, according to the record of his past wild prowess and his present possibilities. Duane, realizing that he was tolerated there, received in careless friendly spirit by this terrible class of outcasts, experienced a feeling of revulsion that amounted almost to horror. Was his being there not an ugly dream? What had he in common with such ruffians? Then in a flash of memory came the painful proof—he was a criminal in sight of Texas law; he, too, was an outcast.

For the moment Duane was wrapped up in painful reflections; but Euchre's heavy hand, clapping with a warning hold on his arm, brought him back to outside things.

The hum of voices, the clink of coin, the loud laughter had ceased. There was a silence that manifestly had followed some unusual word or action sufficient to still the room. It was broken by a harsh curse and the scrape of a bench on the floor. Some man had risen.

"You stacked the cards, you—!"

"Say that twice," another voice replied, so different in its cool, ominous tone from the other.

"I'll say it twice," returned the first gamester, in hot haste. "I'll say it three times. I'll whistle it. Are you deaf? You light-fingered gent! You stacked the cards!"

Silence ensued, deeper than before, pregnant with meaning. For all that Duane saw, not an outlaw moved for a full moment. Then suddenly the room was full of disorder as men rose and ran and dived everywhere.

"Run or duck!" yelled Euchre, close to Duane's ear. With that he dashed for the door. Duane leaped after him. They ran into a jostling mob. Heavy gunshots and hoarse yells hurried the crowd Duane was with pell-mell out into the darkness. There they all halted, and several peeped in at the door.

"Who was the Kid callin'?" asked one outlaw.

"Bud Marsh," replied another.

"I reckon them fust shots was Bud's. Adios Kid. It was comin' to him," went on yet another.

"How many shots?"

"Three or four, I counted."

"Three heavy an' one light. Thet light one was the Kid's .38. Listen! There's the Kid hollerin' now. He ain't cashed, anyway."

At this juncture most of the outlaws began to file back into the room. Duane thought he had seen and heard enough in Benson's den for one night and he started slowly down the walk. Presently Euchre caught up with him.

"Nobody hurt much, which's shore some strange," he said. "The Kid— young Fuller thet I was tellin' you about—he was drinkin' an' losin'. Lost his nut, too, callin' Bud Marsh thet way. Bud's as straight at cards as any of 'em. Somebody grabbed Bud, who shot into the roof. An' Fuller's arm was knocked up. He only hit a greaser."

## CHAPTER VI

Next morning Duane found that a moody and despondent spell had fastened on him. Wishing to be alone, he went out and walked a trail leading round the river bluff. He thought and thought. After a while he made out that the trouble with him probably was that he could not resign himself to his fate. He abhorred the possibility chance seemed to hold in store for him. He could not believe there was no hope. But what to do appeared beyond his power to tell.

Duane had intelligence and keenness enough to see his peril—the danger threatening his character as a man, just as much as that which threatened his life. He cared vastly more, he discovered, for what he considered honor and integrity than he did for life. He saw that it was bad for him to be alone. But, it appeared, lonely months and perhaps years inevitably must be his. Another thing puzzled him. In the bright light of day he could not recall the state of mind that was his at twilight or dusk or in the dark night. By day these visitations became to him what they really were—phantoms of his conscience. He could dismiss the thought of them then. He could scarcely remember or believe that this strange feat of fancy or imagination had troubled him, pained him, made him sleepless and sick.

That morning Duane spent an unhappy hour wrestling decision out of the unstable condition of his mind. But at length he determined to create interest in all that he came across and so forget himself as much as possible.

He had an opportunity now to see just what the outlaw's life really was. He meant to force himself to be curious, sympathetic, clear-sighted. And he would stay there in the valley until its possibilities had been exhausted or until circumstances sent him out upon his uncertain way.

When he returned to the shack Euchre was cooking dinner.

"Say, Buck, I've news for you," he said; and his tone conveyed either pride in his possession of such news or pride in Duane. "Feller named Bradley rode in this mornin'. He's heard some about you. Told about the ace of spades they put over the bullet holes in thet cowpuncher Bain you plugged. Then there was a rancher shot at a water-hole twenty miles south of Wellston. Reckon you didn't do it?"

"No, I certainly did not," replied Duane.

"Wal, you get the blame. It ain't nothin' for a feller to be saddled with gunplays he never made. An', Buck, if you ever get famous, as seems likely, you'll be blamed for many a crime. The border'll make an outlaw an' murderer out of you. Wal, that's enough of thet. I've more news. You're goin' to be popular."

"Popular? What do you mean?"

"I met Bland's wife this mornin'. She seen you the other day when you rode in. She shore wants to meet you, an' so do some of the other women in camp. They always want to meet the new fellers who've just come in. It's lonesome for women here, an' they like to hear news from the towns."

"Well, Euchre, I don't want to be impolite, but I'd rather not meet any women," rejoined Duane.

"I was afraid you wouldn't. Don't blame you much. Women are hell. I was hopin', though, you might talk a little to thet poor lonesome kid."

"What kid?" inquired Duane, in surprise.

"Didn't I tell you about Jennie—the girl Bland's holdin' here—the one Jackrabbit Benson had a hand in stealin'?"

"You mentioned a girl. That's all. Tell me now," replied Duane, abruptly.

"Wal, I got it this way. Mebbe it's straight, an' mebbe it ain't. Some years ago Benson made a trip over the river to buy mescal an' other drinks. He'll sneak over there once in a while. An' as I get it he run across a gang of greasers with some gringo prisoners. I don't know, but I reckon there was some barterin', perhaps murderin'. Anyway, Benson fetched the girl back. She was more dead than alive. But it turned out she was only starved an' scared half to death. She hadn't been harmed. I reckon she was then about fourteen years old. Benson's idee, he said, was to use her in his den sellin' drinks an' the like. But I never went much on Jackrabbit's word. Bland seen the kid right off and took her—bought her from Benson. You can gamble Bland didn't do thet from notions of chivalry. I ain't gainsayin, however, but thet Jennie was better off with Kate Bland. She's been hard on Jennie, but she's kept Bland an' the other men from treatin' the kid shameful. Late Jennie has growed into an all-fired pretty girl, an' Kate is powerful jealous of her. I can see hell brewin' over there in Bland's cabin. Thet's why I wish you'd come over with me. Bland's hardly ever home. His wife's invited you. Shore, if she gets sweet on you, as she has on—wal, thet 'd complicate matters. But you'd get to see Jennie, an' mebbe you could help her. Mind, I ain't hintin' nothin'. I'm just wantin' to put her in your way. You're a man an' can think fer yourself. I had a baby girl once, an' if she'd lived she be as big as Jennie now, an', by Gawd, I wouldn't want her here in Bland's camp."

"I'll go, Euchre. Take me over," replied Duane. He felt Euchre's eyes upon him. The old outlaw, however, had no more to say.

In the afternoon Euchre set off with Duane, and soon they reached Bland's cabin. Duane remembered it as the one where he had seen the pretty woman watching him ride by. He could not recall what she looked like. The cabin was the same as the other adobe structures in the valley, but it was larger and pleasantly located rather high up in a grove of cottonwoods. In the windows and upon the porch were evidences of a woman's hand. Through the open door Duane caught a glimpse of bright Mexican blankets and rugs.

Euchre knocked upon the side of the door.

"Is that you, Euchre?" asked a girl's voice, low, hesitatingly. The tone of it, rather deep and with a note of fear, struck Duane. He wondered what she would be like.

"Yes, it's me, Jennie. Where's Mrs. Bland?" answered Euchre.

"She went over to Deger's. There's somebody sick," replied the girl.

Euchre turned and whispered something about luck. The snap of the outlaw's eyes was added significance to Duane.

"Jennie, come out or let us come in. Here's the young man I was tellin' you about," Euchre said.

"Oh, I can't! I look so—so—"

"Never mind how you look," interrupted the outlaw, in a whisper. "It ain't no time to care fer thet. Here's young Duane. Jennie, he's no rustler, no thief. He's different. Come out, Jennie, an' mebbe he'll—"

Euchre did not complete his sentence. He had spoken low, with his glance shifting from side to side.

But what he said was sufficient to bring the girl quickly. She appeared in the doorway with downcast eyes and a stain of red in her white cheek. She had a pretty, sad face and bright hair.

"Don't be bashful, Jennie," said Euchre. "You an' Duane have a chance to talk a little. Now I'll go fetch Mrs. Bland, but I won't be hurryin'."

With that Euchre went away through the cottonwoods.

"I'm glad to meet you, Miss—Miss Jennie," said Duane. "Euchre didn't mention your last name. He asked me to come over to—"

Duane's attempt at pleasantry halted short when Jennie lifted her lashes to look at him. Some kind of a shock went through Duane. Her gray eyes were beautiful, but it had not been beauty that cut short his speech. He seemed to see a tragic struggle between hope and doubt that shone in her piercing gaze. She kept looking, and Duane could not break the silence. It was no ordinary moment.

"What did you come here for?" she asked, at last.

"To see you," replied Duane, glad to speak.

"Why?"

"Well—Euchre thought—he wanted me to talk to you, cheer you up a bit," replied Duane, somewhat lamely. The earnest eyes embarrassed him.

"Euchre's good. He's the only person in this awful place who's been good to me. But he's afraid of Bland. He said you were different. Who are you?"

Duane told her.

"You're not a robber or rustler or murderer or some bad man come here to hide?"

"No, I'm not," replied Duane, trying to smile.

"Then why are you here?"

"I'm on the dodge. You know what that means. I got in a shooting-scrape at home and had to run off. When it blows over I hope to go back."

"But you can't be honest here?"

"Yes, I can."

"Oh, I know what these outlaws are. Yes, you're different." She kept the strained gaze upon him, but hope was kindling, and the hard lines of her youthful face were softening.

Something sweet and warm stirred deep in Duane as he realized the unfortunate girl was experiencing a birth of trust in him.

"O God! Maybe you're the man to save me—to take me away before it's too late."

Duane's spirit leaped.

"Maybe I am," he replied, instantly.

She seemed to check a blind impulse to run into his arms. Her cheek flamed, her lips quivered, her bosom swelled under her ragged dress. Then the glow began to fade; doubt once more assailed her.

"It can't be. You're only—after me, too, like Bland—like all of them."

Duane's long arms went out and his hands clasped her shoulders. He shook her.

"Look at me—straight in the eye. There are decent men. Haven't you a father—a brother?"

"They're dead—killed by raiders. We lived in Dimmit County. I was carried away," Jennie replied, hurriedly. She put up an appealing hand to him. "Forgive me. I believe—I know you're good. It was only—I live so much in fear—I'm half crazy—I've almost forgotten what good men are like, Mister Duane, you'll help me?"

"Yes, Jennie, I will. Tell me how. What must I do? Have you any plan?"

"Oh no. But take me away."

"I'll try," said Duane, simply. "That won't be easy, though. I must have time to think. You must help me. There are many things to consider. Horses, food, trails, and then the best time to make the attempt. Are you watched—kept prisoner?"

"No. I could have run off lots of times. But I was afraid. I'd only have fallen into worse hands. Euchre has told me that. Mrs. Bland beats me, half starves me, but she has kept me from her husband and these other dogs. She's been as good as that, and I'm grateful. She hasn't done it for love of me, though. She always hated me. And lately she's growing jealous. There was a man came here by the name of Spence—so he called himself. He tried to be kind to me. But she wouldn't let him. She was in love with him. She's a bad woman. Bland finally shot Spence, and that ended that. She's been jealous ever since. I hear her fighting with Bland about me. She swears she'll kill me before he gets me. And Bland laughs in her face. Then I've heard Chess Alloway try to persuade Bland to give me to him. But Bland doesn't laugh then. Just lately before Bland went away things almost came to a head. I couldn't sleep. I wished Mrs. Bland would kill me. I'll certainly kill myself if they ruin me. Duane, you must be quick if you'd save me."

"I realize that," replied he, thoughtfully. "I think my difficulty will be to fool Mrs. Bland. If she suspected me she'd have the whole gang of outlaws on me at once."

"She would that. You've got to be careful—and quick."

"What kind of woman is she?" inquired Duane.

"She's—she's brazen. I've heard her with her lovers. They get drunk sometimes when Bland's away. She's got a terrible temper. She's vain. She likes flattery. Oh, you could fool her easy enough if you'd lower yourself to—to—"

"To make love to her?" interrupted Duane.

Jennie bravely turned shamed eyes to meet his.

"My girl, I'd do worse than that to get you away from here," he said, bluntly.

"But—Duane," she faltered, and again she put out the appealing hand. "Bland will kill you."

Duane made no reply to this. He was trying to still a rising strange tumult in his breast. The old emotion—the rush of an instinct to kill! He turned cold all over.

"Chess Alloway will kill you if Bland doesn't," went on Jennie, with her tragic eyes on Duane's.

"Maybe he will," replied Duane. It was difficult for him to force a smile. But he achieved one.

"Oh, better take me off at once," she said. "Save me without risking so much—without making love to Mrs. Bland!"

"Surely, if I can. There! I see Euchre coming with a woman."

"That's her. Oh, she mustn't see me with you."

"Wait—a moment," whispered Duane, as Jennie slipped indoors. "We've settled it. Don't forget. I'll find some way to get word to you, perhaps through Euchre. Meanwhile keep up your courage. Remember I'll save you somehow. We'll try strategy first. Whatever you see or hear me do, don't think less of me—"

Jennie checked him with a gesture and a wonderful gray flash of eyes.

"I'll bless you with every drop of blood in my heart," she whispered, passionately.

It was only as she turned away into the room that Duane saw she was lame and that she wore Mexican sandals over bare feet.

He sat down upon a bench on the porch and directed his attention to the approaching couple. The trees of the grove were thick enough for him to make reasonably sure that Mrs. Bland had not seen him talking to Jennie. When the outlaw's wife drew near Duane saw that she was a tall, strong, full-bodied woman, rather good-looking with a full-blown, bold attractiveness. Duane was more concerned with her expression than with her good looks; and as she appeared unsuspicious he felt relieved. The situation then took on a singular zest.

Euchre came up on the porch and awkwardly introduced Duane to Mrs. Bland. She was young, probably not over twenty-five, and not quite so prepossessing at close range. Her eyes were large, rather prominent, and brown in color. Her mouth, too, was large, with the lips full, and she had white teeth.

Duane took her proffered hand and remarked frankly that he was glad to meet her.

Mrs. Bland appeared pleased; and her laugh, which followed, was loud and rather musical.

"Mr. Duane—Buck Duane, Euchre said, didn't he?" she asked.

"Buckley," corrected Duane. "The nickname's not of my choosing."

"I'm certainly glad to meet you, Buckley Duane," she said, as she took the seat Duane offered her. "Sorry to have been out. Kid Fuller's lying over at Deger's. You know he was shot last night. He's got fever today. When Bland's away I have to nurse all these shot-up boys, and it sure takes my time. Have you been waiting here alone? Didn't see that slattern girl of mine?"

She gave him a sharp glance. The woman had an extraordinary play of feature, Duane thought, and unless she was smiling was not pretty at all.

"I've been alone," replied Duane. "Haven't seen anybody but a sick-looking girl with a bucket. And she ran when she saw me."

"That was Jen," said Mrs. Bland. "She's the kid we keep here, and she sure hardly pays her keep. Did Euchre tell you about her?"

"Now that I think of it, he did say something or other."

"What did he tell you about me?" bluntly asked Mrs. Bland.

"Wal, Kate," replied Euchre, speaking for himself, "you needn't worry none, for I told Buck nothin' but compliments."

Evidently the outlaw's wife liked Euchre, for her keen glance rested with amusement upon him.

"As for Jen, I'll tell you her story someday," went on the woman. "It's a common enough story along this river. Euchre here is a tender-hearted old fool, and Jen has taken him in."

"Wal, seein' as you've got me figgered correct," replied Euchre, dryly, "I'll go in an' talk to Jennie if I may."

"Certainly. Go ahead. Jen calls you her best friend," said Mrs. Bland, amiably. "You're always fetching some Mexican stuff, and that's why, I guess."

When Euchre had shuffled into the house Mrs. Bland turned to Duane with curiosity and interest in her gaze.

"Bland told me about you."

"What did he say?" queried Duane, in pretended alarm.

"Oh, you needn't think he's done you dirt; Bland's not that kind of a man. He said: 'Kate, there's a young fellow in camp—rode in here on the dodge. He's no criminal, and he refused to join my band. Wish he would. Slickest hand with a gun I've seen for many a day! I'd like to see him and Chess meet out there in the road.' Then Bland went on to tell how you and Bosomer came together."

"What did you say?" inquired Duane, as she paused.

"Me? Why, I asked him what you looked like," she replied, gayly.

"Well?" went on Duane.

"Magnificent chap, Bland said. Bigger than any man in the valley. Just a great blue-eyed sunburned boy!"

"Humph!" exclaimed Duane. "I'm sorry he led you to expect somebody worth seeing."

"But I'm not disappointed," she returned, archly. "Duane, are you going to stay long here in camp?"

"Yes, till I run out of money and have to move. Why?"

Mrs. Bland's face underwent one of the singular changes. The smiles and flushes and glances, all that had been coquettish about her, had lent her a certain attractiveness, almost beauty and youth. But with some powerful emotion she changed and instantly became a woman of discontent, Duane imagined, of deep, violent nature.

"I'll tell you, Duane," she said, earnestly, "I'm sure glad if you mean to bide here awhile. I'm a miserable woman, Duane. I'm an outlaw's wife, and I hate him and the life I have to lead. I come of a good family in Brownsville. I never knew Bland was an outlaw till long after he married me. We were separated at times, and I imagined he was away on business. But the truth came out. Bland shot my own cousin, who told me. My family cast me off, and I had to flee with Bland. I was only eighteen then. I've lived here since. I never see a decent woman or man. I never hear anything about my old home or folks or friends. I'm buried here—buried alive with a lot of thieves and murderers. Can you blame me for being glad to see a young fellow—a gentleman—like the boys I used to go with? I tell you it makes me feel full—I want to cry. I'm sick for somebody to talk to. I have no children, thank God! If I had I'd not stay here. I'm sick of this hole. I'm lonely—"

There appeared to be no doubt about the truth of all this. Genuine emotion checked, then halted the hurried speech. She broke down and cried. It seemed strange to Duane that an outlaw's wife—and a woman who fitted her consort and the wild nature of their surroundings—should have weakness enough to weep. Duane believed and pitied her.

"I'm sorry for you," he said.

"Don't be *sorry* for me," she said. "That only makes me see the—the difference between you and me. And don't pay any attention to what these outlaws say about me. They're ignorant. They couldn't understand me. You'll hear that Bland killed men who ran after me. But that's a lie. Bland, like all the other outlaws along this river, is always looking for somebody to kill. He *swears* not, but I don't believe him. He explains that gunplay gravitates to men who are the real thing—that it is provoked by the four-flushes, the bad men. I don't know. All I know is that somebody is being killed every other day. He hated Spence before Spence ever saw me."

"Would Bland object if I called on you occasionally?" inquired Duane.

"No, he wouldn't. He likes me to have friends. Ask him yourself when he comes back. The trouble has been that two or three of his men fell in love with me, and when half drunk got to fighting. You're not going to do that."

"I'm not going to get half drunk, that's certain," replied Duane.

He was surprised to see her eyes dilate, then glow with fire. Before she could reply Euchre returned to the porch, and that put an end to the conversation.

Duane was content to let the matter rest there, and had little more to say. Euchre and Mrs. Bland talked and joked, while Duane listened. He tried to form some estimate of her character. Manifestly she had suffered a wrong, if not worse, at Bland's hands. She was bitter, morbid, overemotional. If she was a liar, which seemed likely enough, she was a frank one, and believed herself. She had no cunning. The thing which struck Duane so forcibly was that she thirsted for respect. In that, better than in her weakness of vanity, he thought he had discovered a trait through which he could manage her.

Once, while he was revolving these thoughts, he happened to glance into the house, and deep in the shadow of a corner he caught a pale gleam of Jennie's face with great, staring eyes on him. She had been watching him, listening to what he said. He saw from her expression that she had realized what had been so hard for her to believe. Watching his chance, he flashed a look at her; and then it seemed to him the change in her face was wonderful.

Later, after he had left Mrs. Bland with a meaning *"Adios—mañana,"* and was walking along beside the old outlaw, he found himself thinking of the girl instead of the woman, and of how he had seen her face blaze with hope and gratitude.

## CHAPTER VII

That night Duane was not troubled by ghosts haunting his waking and sleeping hours. He awoke feeling bright and eager, and grateful to Euchre for having put something worthwhile into his mind. During breakfast, however, he was unusually thoughtful, working over the idea of how much or how little he would confide in the outlaw. He was aware of Euchre's scrutiny.

"Wal," began the old man, at last, "how'd you make out with the kid?"

"Kid?" inquired Duane, tentatively.

"Jennie, I mean. What'd you an' she talk about?"

"We had a little chat. You know you wanted me to cheer her up."

Euchre sat with coffee-cup poised and narrow eyes studying Duane.

"Reckon you cheered her, all right. What I'm afeared of is mebbe you done the job too well."

"How so?"

"Wal, when I went in to Jen last night I thought she was half crazy. She was burstin' with excitement, an' the look in her eyes hurt me. She wouldn't tell me a darn word you said. But she hung onto my hands, an' showed every way without speakin' how she wanted to thank me fer bringin' you over. Buck, it was plain to me thet you'd either gone the limit or else you'd been kinder prodigal of cheer an' hope. I'd hate to think you'd led Jennie to hope more'n ever would come true."

Euchre paused, and, as there seemed no reply forthcoming, he went on:

"Buck, I've seen some outlaws whose word was good. Mine is. You can trust me. I trusted you, didn't I, takin' you over there an' puttin' you wise to my tryin' to help thet poor kid?"

Thus enjoined by Euchre, Duane began to tell the conversations with Jennie and Mrs. Bland word for word. Long before he had reached an end Euchre set down the coffee-cup and began to stare, and at the conclusion of the story his face lost some of its red color and beads of sweat stood out thickly on his brow.

"Wal, if thet doesn't floor me!" he ejaculated, blinking at Duane. "Young man, I figgered you was some swift, an' sure to make your mark on this river; but I reckon I missed your real caliber. So thet's what it means to be a man! I guess I'd forgot. Wal, I'm old, an' even if my heart was in the right place I never was built fer big stunts. Do you know what it'll take to do all you promised Jen?"

"I haven't any idea," replied Duane, gravely.

"You'll have to pull the wool over Kate Bland's eyes, ant even if she falls in love with you, which's shore likely, thet won't be easy. An' she'd kill you in a minnit, Buck, if she ever got wise. You ain't mistaken her none, are you?"

"Not me, Euchre. She's a woman. I'd fear her more than any man."

"Wal, you'll have to kill Bland an' Chess Alloway an' Rugg, an' mebbe some others, before you can ride off into the hills with thet girl."

"Why? Can't we plan to be nice to Mrs. Bland and then at an opportune time sneak off without any gunplay?"

"Don't see how on earth," returned Euchre, earnestly. "When Bland's away he leaves all kinds of spies an' scouts watchin' the valley trails. They've all got rifles. You couldn't git by them. But when the boss is home there's a difference. Only, of course, him an' Chess keep their eyes peeled. They both stay to home pretty much, except when they're playin' monte or poker over at Benson's. So I say the best bet is to pick out a good time in the afternoon, drift over careless-like with a couple of hosses, choke Mrs. Bland or knock her on the head, take Jennie with you, an' make a rush to git out of the valley. If you had luck you might pull thet stunt without throwin' a gun. But I reckon the best figgerin' would include dodgin' some lead an' leavin' at least Bland or Alloway dead behind you. I'm figgerin', of course, thet when they come home an' find out you're visitin' Kate frequent they'll jest naturally look fer results. Chess don't like you, fer no reason except you're swift on the draw—mebbe swifter 'n him. Thet's the hell of this gunplay business. No one can ever tell who's the swifter of two gunmen till they meet. Thet fact holds a fascination mebbe you'll learn someday. Bland would treat you civil onless there was reason not to, an' then I don't believe he'd invite himself to a meetin' with you. He'd set Chess or Rugg to put you out of the way. Still Bland's no coward, an' if you came across him at a bad moment you'd have to be quicker 'n you was with Bosomer."

"All right. I'll meet what comes," said Duane, quickly. "The great point is to have horses ready and pick the right moment, then rush the trick through."

"Thet's the *only* chance fer success. An' you can't do it alone."

"I'll have to. I wouldn't ask you to help me. Leave you behind!"

"Wal, I'll take my chances," replied Euchre, gruffly. "I'm goin' to help Jennie, you can gamble your last peso on thet. There's only four men in this camp who would shoot me—Bland, an' his right-hand pards, an' thet rabbit-faced Benson. If you happened to put out Bland and Chess, I'd stand a good show with the other two. Anyway, I'm old an' tired—what's the difference if I do git plugged? I can risk as much as you, Buck, even if I am afraid of gun-play. You said correct, 'Hosses ready, the right minnit, then rush the trick.' Thet much 's settled. Now let's figger all the little details."

They talked and planned, though in truth it was Euchre who planned, Duane who listened and agreed. While awaiting the return of Bland and his lieutenants it would be well for Duane to grow friendly with the other outlaws, to sit in a few games of monte, or show a willingness to spend a little money. The two schemers were to call upon Mrs. Bland every day—Euchre to carry messages of cheer and warning to Jennie, Duane to blind the elder woman at any cost. These preliminaries decided upon, they proceeded to put them into action.

No hard task was it to win the friendship of the most of those good-natured outlaws. They were used to men of a better order than theirs coming to the hidden camps and sooner or later sinking to their lower level. Besides, with them everything was easy come, easy go. That was why life itself went on so carelessly and usually ended so cheaply. There were men among them, however, that made Duane feel that terrible inexplicable wrath rise in his breast. He could not bear to be near them. He could not trust himself. He felt that any instant a word, a deed, something might call too deeply to that instinct he could no longer control. Jackrabbit Benson was one of these men. Because of him and other outlaws of his ilk Duane could scarcely ever forget the reality of things. This was a hidden valley, a robbers' den, a rendezvous for murderers, a wild place stained red by deeds of wild men. And because of that there was always a charged atmosphere. The merriest, idlest, most careless moment might in the flash of an eye end in ruthless and tragic action. In an assemblage of desperate characters it could not be otherwise. The terrible thing that Duane sensed was this. The valley was beautiful, sunny, fragrant, a place to dream in; the mountaintops were always blue or gold rimmed, the yellow river slid slowly and majestically by, the birds sang in the cottonwoods, the horses grazed and pranced, children played and women longed for love, freedom, happiness; the outlaws rode in and out, free with money and speech; they lived comfortably in their adobe homes, smoked, gambled, talked, laughed, whiled away the idle hours—and all the time life there was wrong, and the simplest moment might be precipitated by that evil into the most awful of contrasts. Duane felt rather than saw a dark, brooding shadow over the valley.

Then, without any solicitation or encouragement from Duane, the Bland woman fell passionately in love with him. His conscience was never troubled about the beginning of that affair. She launched herself. It took no great perspicuity on his part to see that. And the thing which evidently held her in check was the newness, the strangeness, and for the moment the all-satisfying fact of his respect for her. Duane exerted himself to please, to amuse, to interest, to fascinate her, and always with deference. That was his strong point, and it had made his part easy so far. He believed he could carry the whole scheme through without involving himself any deeper.

He was playing at a game of love—playing with life and death. Sometimes he trembled, not that he feared Bland or Alloway or any other man, but at the deeps of life he had come to see into. He was carried out of his old mood. Not once since this daring motive had stirred him had he been haunted by the phantom of Bain beside his bed. Rather had he been haunted by Jennie's sad face, her wistful smile, her eyes. He never was able to speak a word to her. What little communication he had with her was through Euchre, who carried short messages. But he caught glimpses of her every time he went to the Bland house. She contrived somehow to pass door or window, to give him a look when chance afforded. And Duane discovered with surprise that these moments were more thrilling to him than any with Mrs. Bland. Often Duane knew Jennie was sitting just inside the window, and then he felt inspired in his talk, and it was all made for her. So at least she came to know him while as yet she was almost a stranger. Jennie had been instructed by Euchre to listen, to understand that this was Duane's only chance to help keep her mind from constant worry, to gather the import of every word which had a double meaning.

Euchre said that the girl had begun to wither under the strain, to burn up with intense hope which had flamed within her. But all the difference Duane could see was a paler face and darker, more wonderful eyes. The eyes seemed to be entreating him to hurry, that time was flying, that soon it might be too late. Then there was another meaning in them, a light, a strange fire wholly inexplicable to Duane. It was only a flash gone in an instant. But he remembered it because he had never seen it in any other woman's eyes. And all through those waiting days he knew that Jennie's face, and especially the warm, fleeting glance she gave him, was responsible for a subtle and gradual change in him. This change he fancied, was only that through remembrance of her he got rid of his pale, sickening ghosts.

One day a careless Mexican threw a lighted cigarette up into the brush matting that served as a ceiling for Benson's den, and there was a fire which left little more than the adobe walls standing. The result was that while repairs were being made there was no gambling and drinking. Time hung very heavily on the hands of some two-score outlaws. Days passed by without a brawl, and Bland's valley saw more successive hours of peace than ever before. Duane, however, found the hours anything but empty. He spent more time at Mrs. Bland's; he walked miles on all the trails leading out of the valley; he had a care for the condition of his two horses.

Upon his return from the latest of these tramps Euchre suggested that they go down to the river to the boat landing.

"Ferry couldn't run ashore this mornin'," said Euchre. "River gettin' low an' sandbars makin' it hard fer hosses. There's a greaser freight wagon stuck in the mud. I reckon we might hear news from the freighters. Bland's supposed to be in Mexico."

Nearly all the outlaws in camp were assembled on the riverbank, lolling in the shade of the cottonwoods. The heat was oppressive. Not an outlaw offered to help the freighters, who were trying to dig a heavily freighted wagon out of the quicksand. Few outlaws would work for themselves, let alone for the despised Mexicans.

Duane and Euchre joined the lazy group and sat down with them. Euchre lighted a black pipe, and, drawing his hat over his eyes, lay back in comfort after the manner of the majority of the outlaws. But Duane was alert, observing, thoughtful. He never missed anything. It was his belief that any moment an idle word might be of benefit to him. Moreover, these rough men were always interesting.

"Bland's been chased across the river," said one.

"New, he's deliverin' cattle to thet Cuban ship," replied another.

"Big deal on, hey?"

"Some big. Rugg says the boss hed an order fer fifteen thousand."

"Say, that order'll take a year to fill."

"New. Hardin is in cahoots with Bland. Between 'em they'll fill orders bigger 'n thet."

"Wondered what Hardin was rustlin' in here fer."

Duane could not possibly attend to all the conversation among the outlaws. He endeavored to get the drift of talk nearest to him.

"Kid Fuller's goin' to cash," said a sandy-whiskered little outlaw.

"So Jim was tellin' me. Blood-poison, ain't it? Thet hole wasn't bad. But he took the fever," rejoined a comrade.

"Deger says the Kid might pull through if he hed nursin'."

"Wal, Kate Bland ain't nursin' any shot-up boys these days. She hasn't got time."

A laugh followed this sally; then came a penetrating silence. Some of the outlaws glanced good-naturedly at Duane. They bore him no ill will. Manifestly they were aware of Mrs. Bland's infatuation.

"Pete, 'pears to me you've said thet before."

"Shore. Wal, it's happened before."

This remark drew louder laughter and more significant glances at Duane. He did not choose to ignore them any longer.

"Boys, poke all the fun you like at me, but don't mention any lady's name again. My hand is nervous and itchy these days."

He smiled as he spoke, and his speech was drawled; but the good humor in no wise weakened it. Then his latter remark was significant to a class of men who from inclination and necessity practiced at gun-drawing until they wore callous and sore places on their thumbs and inculcated in the very deeps of their nervous organization a habit that made even the simplest and most innocent motion of the hand end at or near the hip. There was something remarkable about a gunfighter's hand. It never seemed to be gloved, never to be injured, never out of sight or in an awkward position.

There were grizzled outlaws in that group, some of whom had many notches on their gun-handles, and they, with their comrades, accorded Duane silence that carried conviction of the regard in which he was held.

Duane could not recall any other instance where he had let fall a familiar speech to these men, and certainly he had never before hinted of his possibilities. He saw instantly that he could not have done better.

"Orful hot, ain't it?" remarked Bill Black, presently. Bill could not keep quiet for long. He was a typical Texas desperado, had never been anything else. He was stoop-shouldered and bow-legged from much riding; a wiry little man, all muscle, with a square head, a hard face partly black from scrubby beard and red from sun, and a bright, roving, cruel eye. His shirt was open at the neck, showing a grizzled breast.

"Is there any guy in this heah outfit sport enough to go swimmin'?" he asked.

"My Gawd, Bill, you ain't agoin' to wash!" exclaimed a comrade.

This raised a laugh in which Black joined. But no one seemed eager to join him in a bath.

"Laziest outfit I ever rustled with," went on Bill, discontentedly. "Nuthin' to do! Say, if nobody wants to swim maybe some of you'll gamble?"

He produced a dirty pack of cards and waved them at the motionless crowd.

"Bill, you're too good at cards," replied a lanky outlaw.

"Now, Jasper, you say thet powerful sweet, an' you look sweet, er I might take it to heart," replied Black, with a sudden change of tone.

Here it was again—that upflashing passion. What Jasper saw fit to reply would mollify the outlaw or it would not. There was an even balance.

"No offense, Bill," said Jasper, placidly, without moving.

Bill grunted and forgot Jasper. But he seemed restless and dissatisfied. Duane knew him to be an inveterate gambler. And as Benson's place was out of running-order, Black was like a fish on dry land.

"Wal, if you-all are afraid of the cairds, what will you bet on?" he asked, in disgust.

"Bill, I'll play you a game of mumbly peg fer two bits." replied one.

Black eagerly accepted. Betting to him was a serious matter. The game obsessed him, not the stakes. He entered into the mumbly peg contest with a thoughtful mien and a corded brow. He won. Other comrades tried their luck with him and lost. Finally, when Bill had exhausted their supply of two-bit pieces or their desire for that particular game, he offered to bet on anything.

"See thet turtle-dove there?" he said, pointing. "I'll bet he'll scare at one stone or he won't. Five pesos he'll fly or he won't fly when someone chucks a stone. Who'll take me up?"

That appeared to be more than the gambling spirit of several outlaws could withstand.

"Take thet. Easy money," said one.

"Who's goin' to chuck the stone?" asked another.

"Anybody," replied Bill.

"Wal, I'll bet you I can scare him with one stone," said the first outlaw.

"We're in on thet, Jim to fire the darnick," chimed in the others.

The money was put up, the stone thrown. The turtle-dove took flight, to the great joy of all the outlaws except Bill.

"I'll bet you-all he'll come back to thet tree inside of five minnits," he offered, imperturbably.

Hereupon the outlaws did not show any laziness in their alacrity to cover Bill's money as it lay on the grass. Somebody had a watch, and they all sat down, dividing attention between the timepiece and the tree. The minutes dragged by to the accompaniment of various jocular remarks anent a fool and his money. When four and three-quarter minutes had passed a turtledove alighted in the cottonwood. Then ensued an impressive silence while Bill calmly pocketed the fifty dollars.

"But it hadn't the same dove!" exclaimed one outlaw, excitedly. "This 'n is smaller, dustier, not so purple."

Bill eyed the speaker loftily.

"Wal, you'll have to ketch the other one to prove thet. *Sabe*, pard? Now I'll bet any gent heah the fifty I won thet I can scare thet dove with one stone."

No one offered to take his wager.

"Wal, then, I'll bet any of you even money thet you *can't* scare him with one stone."

Not proof against this chance, the outlaws made up a purse, in no wise disconcerted by Bill's contemptuous allusions to their banding together. The stone was thrown. The dove did not fly. Thereafter, in regard to that bird, Bill was unable to coax or scorn his comrades into any kind of wager.

He tried them with a multiplicity of offers, and in vain. Then he appeared at a loss for some unusual and seductive wager. Presently a little ragged Mexican boy came along the river trail, a particularly starved and poor-looking little fellow. Bill called to him and gave him a handful of silver coins. Speechless, dazed, he went his way hugging the money.

"I'll bet he drops some before he gits to the road," declared Bill. "I'll bet he runs. Hurry, you four-flush gamblers."

Bill failed to interest any of his companions, and forthwith became sullen and silent. Strangely his good humor departed in spite of the fact that he had won considerable.

Duane, watching the disgruntled outlaw, marveled at him and wondered what was in his mind. These men were more variable than children, as unstable as water, as dangerous as dynamite.

"Bill, I'll bet you ten you can't spill whatever's in the bucket thet peon's packin'," said the outlaw called Jim.

Black's head came up with the action of a hawk about to swoop.

Duane glanced from Black to the road, where he saw a crippled peon carrying a tin bucket toward the river. This peon was a half-witted Indian who lived in a shack and did odd jobs for the Mexicans. Duane had met him often.

"Jim, I'll take you up," replied Black.

Something, perhaps a harshness in his voice, caused Duane to whirl. He caught a leaping gleam in the outlaw's eye.

"Aw, Bill, thet's too fur a shot," said Jasper, as Black rested an elbow on his knee and sighted over the long, heavy Colt. The distance to the peon was about fifty paces, too far for even the most expert shot to hit a moving object so small as a bucket.

Duane, marvelously keen in the alignment of sights, was positive that Black held too high. Another look at the hard face, now tense and dark with blood, confirmed Duane's suspicion that the outlaw was not aiming at the bucket at all. Duane leaped and struck the leveled gun out of his hand. Another outlaw picked it up.

Black fell back astounded. Deprived of his weapon, he did not seem the same man, or else he was cowed by Duane's significant and formidable front. Sullenly he turned away without even asking for his gun.

## CHAPTER VIII

What a contrast, Duane thought, the evening of that day presented to the state of his soul!

The sunset lingered in golden glory over the distant Mexican mountains; twilight came slowly; a faint breeze blew from the river cool and sweet; the late cooing of a dove and the tinkle of a cowbell were the only sounds; a serene and tranquil peace lay over the valley.

Inside Duane's body there was strife. This third facing of a desperate man had thrown him off his balance. It had not been fatal, but it threatened so much. The better side of his nature seemed to urge him to die rather than to go on fighting or opposing ignorant, unfortunate, savage men. But the perversity of him was so great that it dwarfed reason, conscience. He could not resist it. He felt something dying in him. He suffered. Hope seemed far away. Despair had seized upon him and was driving him into a reckless mood when he thought of Jennie.

He had forgotten her. He had forgotten that he had promised to save her. He had forgotten that he meant to snuff out as many lives as might stand between her and freedom. The very remembrance sheered off his morbid introspection. She made a difference. How strange for him to realize that! He felt grateful to her. He had been forced into outlawry; she had been stolen from her people and carried into captivity. They had met in the river fastness, he to instill hope into her despairing life, she to be the means, perhaps, of keeping him from sinking to the level of her captors. He became conscious of a strong and beating desire to see her, talk with her.

These thoughts had run through his mind while on his way to Mrs. Bland's house. He had let Euchre go on ahead because he wanted more time to compose himself. Darkness had about set in when he reached his destination. There was no light in the house. Mrs. Bland was waiting for him on the porch.

She embraced him, and the sudden, violent, unfamiliar contact sent such a shock through him that he all but forgot the deep game he was playing. She, however, in her agitation did not notice his shrinking. From her embrace and the tender, incoherent words that flowed with it he gathered that Euchre had acquainted her of his action with Black.

"He might have killed you," she whispered, more clearly; and if Duane had ever heard love in a voice he heard it then. It softened him. After all, she was a woman, weak, fated through her nature, unfortunate in her experience of life, doomed to unhappiness and tragedy. He met her advance so far that he returned the embrace and kissed her. Emotion such as she showed would have made any woman sweet, and she had a certain charm. It was easy, even pleasant, to kiss her; but Duane resolved that, whatever her abandonment might become, he would not go further than the lie she made him act.

"Buck, you love me?" she whispered.

"Yes—yes," he burst out, eager to get it over, and even as he spoke he caught the pale gleam of Jennie's face through the window. He felt a shame he was glad she could not see. Did she remember that she had promised not to misunderstand any action of his? What did she think of him, seeing him out there in the dusk with this bold woman in his arms? Somehow that dim sight of Jennie's pale face, the big dark eyes, thrilled him, inspired him to his hard task of the present.

"Listen, dear," he said to the woman, and he meant his words for the girl. "I'm going to take you away from this outlaw den if I have to kill Bland, Alloway, Rugg—anybody who stands in my path. You were dragged here. You are good—I know it. There's happiness for you somewhere—a home among good people who will care for you. Just wait till—"

His voice trailed off and failed from excess of emotion. Kate Bland closed her eyes and leaned her head on his breast. Duane felt her heart beat against his, and conscience smote him a keen blow. If she loved him so much! But memory and understanding of her character hardened him again, and he gave her such commiseration as was due her sex, and no more.

"Boy, that's good of you," she whispered, "but it's too late. I'm done for. I can't leave Bland. All I ask is that you love me a little and stop your gun-throwing."

The moon had risen over the eastern bulge of dark mountain, and now the valley was flooded with mellow light, and shadows of cottonwoods wavered against the silver.

Suddenly the clip-clop, clip-clop of hoofs caused Duane to raise his head and listen. Horses were coming down the road from the head of the valley. The hour was unusual for riders to come in. Presently the narrow, moonlit lane was crossed at its far end by black moving objects. Two horses Duane discerned.

"It's Bland!" whispered the woman, grasping Duane with shaking hands. "You must run! No, he'd see you. That 'd be worse. It's Bland! I know his horse's trot."

"But you said he wouldn't mind my calling here," protested Duane. "Euchre's with me. It'll be all right."

"Maybe so," she replied, with visible effort at self-control. Manifestly she had a great fear of Bland. "If I could only think!"

Then she dragged Duane to the door, pushed him in.

"Euchre, come out with me! Duane, you stay with the girl! I'll tell Bland you're in love with her. Jen, if you give us away I'll wring your neck."

The swift action and fierce whisper told Duane that Mrs. Bland was herself again. Duane stepped close to Jennie, who stood near the window. Neither spoke, but her hands were outstretched to meet his own. They were small, trembling hands, cold as ice. He held them close, trying to convey what he felt—that he would protect her. She leaned against him, and they looked out of the window. Duane felt calm and sure of himself. His most pronounced feeling besides that for the frightened girl was a curiosity as to how Mrs. Bland would rise to the occasion. He saw the riders dismount down the lane and wearily come forward. A boy led away the horses. Euchre, the old fox, was talking loud and with remarkable ease, considering what he claimed was his natural cowardice.

"—that was way back in the sixties, about the time of the war," he was saying. "Rustlin' cattle wasn't nuthin' then to what it is now. An' times is rougher these days. This gun-throwin' has come to be a disease. Men have an itch for the draw same as they used to have fer poker. The only real gambler outside of greasers we ever had here was Bill, an' I presume Bill is burnin' now."

The approaching outlaws, hearing voices, halted a rod or so from the porch. Then Mrs. Bland uttered an exclamation, ostensibly meant to express surprise, and hurried out to meet them. She greeted her husband warmly and gave welcome to the other man. Duane could not see well enough in the shadow to recognize Bland's companion, but he believed it was Alloway.

"Dog-tired we are and starved," said Bland, heavily. "Who's here with you?"

"That's Euchre on the porch. Duane is inside at the window with Jen," replied Mrs. Bland.

"Duane!" he exclaimed. Then he whispered low—something Duane could not catch.

"Why, I asked him to come," said the chief's wife. She spoke easily and naturally and made no change in tone. "Jen has been ailing. She gets thinner and whiter every day. Duane came here one day with Euchre, saw Jen, and went loony over her pretty face, same as all you men. So I let him come."

Bland cursed low and deep under his breath. The other man made a violent action of some kind and apparently was quieted by a restraining hand.

"Kate, you let Duane make love to Jennie?" queried Bland, incredulously.

"Yes, I did," replied the wife, stubbornly. "Why not? Jen's in love with him. If he takes her away and marries her she can be a decent woman."

Bland kept silent a moment, then his laugh pealed out loud and harsh.

"Chess, did you get that? Well, by God! what do you think of my wife?"

"She's lyin' or she's crazy," replied Alloway, and his voice carried an unpleasant ring.

Mrs. Bland promptly and indignantly told her husband's lieutenant to keep his mouth shut.

"Ho, ho, ho!" rolled out Bland's laugh.

Then he led the way to the porch, his spurs clinking, the weapons he was carrying rattling, and he flopped down on a bench.

"How are you, boss?" asked Euchre.

"Hello, old man. I'm well, but all in."

Alloway slowly walked on to the porch and leaned against the rail. He answered Euchre's greeting with a nod. Then he stood there a dark, silent figure.

Mrs. Bland's full voice in eager questioning had a tendency to ease the situation. Bland replied briefly to her, reporting a remarkably successful trip.

Duane thought it time to show himself. He had a feeling that Bland and Alloway would let him go for the moment. They were plainly nonplussed, and Alloway seemed sullen, brooding. "Jennie," whispered Duane, "that was clever of Mrs. Bland. We'll keep up the deception. Any day now be ready!"

She pressed close to him, and a barely audible "Hurry!" came breathing into his ear.

"Good night, Jennie," he said, aloud. "Hope you feel better tomorrow."

Then he stepped out into the moonlight and spoke. Bland returned the greeting, and, though he was not amiable, he did not show resentment.

"Met Jasper as I rode in," said Bland, presently. "He told me you made Bill Black mad, and there's liable to be a fight. What did you go off the handle about?"

Duane explained the incident. "I'm sorry I happened to be there," he went on. "It wasn't my business."

"Scurvy trick that 'd been," muttered Bland. "You did right. All the same, Duane, I want you to stop quarreling with my men. If you were one of us—that'd be different. I can't keep my men from fighting. But I'm not called on to let an outsider hang around my camp and plug my rustlers."

"I guess I'll have to be hitting the trail for somewhere," said Duane.

"Why not join my band? You've got a bad start already, Duane, and if I know this border you'll never be a respectable citizen again. You're a born killer. I know every bad man on this frontier. More than one of them have told me that something exploded in their brain, and when sense came back there lay another dead man. It's not so with me. I've done a little shooting, too, but I never wanted to kill another man just to rid myself of the last one. My dead men don't sit on my chest at night. That's the gunfighter's trouble. He's crazy. He has to kill a new man—he's driven to it to forget the last one."

"But I'm no gunfighter," protested Duane. "Circumstances made me—"

"No doubt," interrupted Bland, with a laugh. "Circumstances made me a rustler. You don't know yourself. You're young; you've got a temper; your father was one of the most dangerous men Texas ever had. I don't see any other career for you. Instead of going it alone—a lone wolf, as the Texans say—why not make friends with other outlaws? You'll live longer."

Euchre squirmed in his seat.

"Boss, I've been givin' the boy egzactly thet same line of talk. Thet's why I took him in to bunk with me. If he makes pards among us there won't be any more trouble. An' he'd be a grand feller fer the gang. I've seen Wild Bill Hickok throw a gun, an' Billy the Kid, an' Hardin, an' Chess here—all the fastest men on the border. An' with apologies to present company, I'm here to say Duane has them all skinned. His draw is different. You can't see how he does it."

Euchre's admiring praise served to create an effective little silence. Alloway shifted uneasily on his feet, his spurs jangling faintly, and did not lift his head. Bland seemed thoughtful.

"That's about the only qualification I have to make me eligible for your band," said Duane, easily.

"It's good enough," replied Bland, shortly. "Will you consider the idea?"

"I'll think it over. Good night."

He left the group, followed by Euchre. When they reached the end of the lane, and before they had exchanged a word, Bland called Euchre back. Duane proceeded slowly along the moonlit road to the cabin and sat down under the cottonwoods to wait for Euchre. The night was intense and quiet, a low hum of insects giving the effect of a congestion of life. The beauty of the soaring moon, the ebony cañons of shadow under the mountain, the melancholy serenity of the perfect night, made Duane shudder in the realization of how far aloof he now was from enjoyment of these things. Never again so long as he lived could he be natural. His mind was clouded. His eye and ear henceforth must register impressions of nature, but the joy of them had fled.

Still, as he sat there with a foreboding of more and darker work ahead of him there was yet a strange sweetness left to him, and it lay in thought of Jennie. The pressure of her cold little hands lingered in his. He did not think of her as a woman, and he did not analyze his feelings. He just had vague, dreamy thoughts and imaginations that were interspersed in the constant and stern revolving of plans to save her.

A shuffling step roused him. Euchre's dark figure came crossing the moonlit grass under the cottonwoods. The moment the outlaw reached him Duane saw that he was laboring under great excitement. It scarcely affected Duane. He seemed to be acquiring patience, calmness, strength.

"Bland kept you pretty long," he said.

"Wait till I git my breath," replied Euchre. He sat silent a little while, fanning himself with a sombrero, though the night was cool, and then he went into the cabin to return presently with a lighted pipe.

"Fine night," he said; and his tone further acquainted Duane with Euchre's quaint humor. "Fine night for love-affairs, by gum!"

"I'd noticed that," rejoined Duane, dryly.

"Wal, I'm a son of a gun if I didn't stand an' watch Bland choke his wife till her tongue stuck out an' she got black in the face."

"No!" ejaculated Duane.

"Hope to die if I didn't. Buck, listen to this here yarn. When I got back to the porch I seen Bland was wakin' up. He'd been too fagged out to figger much. Alloway an' Kate had gone in the house, where they lit up the lamps. I heard Kate's high voice, but Alloway never chirped. He's not the talkin' kind, an' he's damn dangerous when he's thet way. Bland asked me some questions right from the shoulder. I was ready for them, an' I swore the moon was green cheese. He was satisfied. Bland always trusted me, an' liked me, too, I reckon. I hated to lie black thet way. But he's a hard man with bad intentions toward Jennie, an' I'd double-cross him any day.

"Then we went into the house. Jennie had gone to her little room, an' Bland called her to come out. She said she was undressin'. An' he ordered her to put her clothes back on. Then, Buck, his next move was some surprisin'. He deliberately thronged a gun on Kate. Yes sir, he pointed his big blue Colt right at her, an' he says:

"'I've a mind to blow out your brains.'

"'Go ahead,' says Kate, cool as could be.

"'You lied to me,' he roars.

"Kate laughed in his face. Bland slammed the gun down an' made a grab fer her. She fought him, but wasn't a match fer him, an' he got her by the throat. He choked her till I thought she was strangled. Alloway made him stop. She flopped down on the bed an' gasped fer a while. When she come to them hardshelled cusses went after her, trying to make her give herself away. I think Bland was jealous. He suspected she'd got thick with you an' was foolin' him. I reckon thet's a sore feelin' fer a man to have—to guess pretty nice, but not to *be* sure. Bland gave it up after a while. An' then he cussed an' raved at her. One sayin' of his is worth pinnin' in your sombrero: 'It ain't nuthin' to kill a man. I don't need much fer thet. But I want to *know*, you hussy!'

"Then he went in an' dragged poor Jen out. She'd had time to dress. He was so mad he hurt her sore leg. You know Jen got thet injury fightin' off one of them devils in the dark. An' when I seen Bland twist her—hurt her—I had a queer hot feelin' deep down in me, an' fer the only time in my life I wished I was a gunfighter.

"Wal, Jen amazed me. She was whiter'n a sheet, an' her eyes were big and stary, but she had nerve. Fust time I ever seen her show any.

"'Jennie,' he said, 'my wife said Duane came here to see you. I believe she's lyin'. I think she's been carryin' on with him, an' I want to *know*. If she's been an' you tell me the truth I'll let you go. I'll send you out to Huntsville, where you can communicate with your friends. I'll give you money.'

"Thet must hev been a hell of a minnit fer Kate Bland. If evet I seen death in a man's eye I seen it in Bland's. He loves her. Thet's the strange part of it.

"'Has Duane been comin' here to see my wife?' Bland asked, fierce-like.

"'No,' said Jennie.

"'He's been after you?'

"'Yes.'

"'He has fallen in love with you? Kate said thet.'

"'I—I'm not—I don't know—he hasn't told me.'

"'But you're in love with him?'

"'Yes,' she said; an', Buck, if you only could have seen her! She thronged up her head, an' her eyes were full of fire. Bland seemed dazed at sight of her. An' Alloway, why, thet little skunk of an outlaw cried right out. He was hit plumb center. He's in love with Jen. An' the look of her then was enough to make any feller quit. He jest slunk out of the room. I told you, mebbe, thet he'd been tryin' to git Bland to marry Jen to him. So even a tough like Alloway can love a woman!

"Bland stamped up an' down the room. He sure was dyin' hard.

"'Jennie,' he said, once more turnin' to her. 'You swear in fear of your life thet you're tellin' truth. Kate's not in love with Duane? She's let him come to see you? There's been nuthin' between them?'

"'No. I swear,' answered Jennie; an' Bland sat down like a man licked.

"'Go to bed, you white-faced—' Bland choked on some word or other—a bad one, I reckon—an' he positively shook in his chair.

"Jennie went then, an' Kate began to have hysterics. An' your Uncle Euchre ducked his nut out of the door an' come home."

Duane did not have a word to say at the end of Euchre's long harangue. He experienced relief. As a matter of fact, he had expected a good deal worse. He thrilled at the thought of Jennie perjuring herself to save that abandoned woman. What mysteries these feminine creatures were!

"Wal, there's where our little deal stands now," resumed Euchre, meditatively. "You know, Buck, as well as me thet if you'd been some feller who hadn't shown he was a wonder with a gun you'd now be full of lead. If you'd happen to kill Bland an' Alloway, I reckon you'd be as safe on this here border as you would in Santone. Such is gun fame in this land of the draw."

## CHAPTER IX

Both men were awake early, silent with the premonition of trouble ahead, thoughtful of the fact that the time for the long-planned action was at hand. It was remarkable that a man as loquacious as Euchre could hold his tongue so long; and this was significant of the deadly nature of the intended deed. During breakfast he said a few words customary in the service of food. At the conclusion of the meal he seemed to come to an end of deliberation.

"Buck, the sooner the better now," he declared, with a glint in his eye. "The more time we use up now the less surprised Bland'll be."

"I'm ready when you are," replied Duane, quietly, and he rose from the table.

"Wal, saddle up, then," went on Euchre, gruffly. "Tie on them two packs I made, one fer each saddle. You can't tell—mebbe either hoss will be carryin' double. It's good they're both big, strong hosses. Guess thet wasn't a wise move of your Uncle Euchre's—bringin' in your hosses an' havin' them ready?"

"Euchre, I hope you're not going to get in bad here. I'm afraid you are. Let me do the rest now," said Duane.

The old outlaw eyed him sarcastically.

"Thet 'd be turrible now, wouldn't it? If you want to know, why, I'm in bad already. I didn't tell you thet Alloway called me last night. He's gettin' wise pretty quick."

"Euchre, you're going with me?" queried Duane, suddenly divining the truth.

"Wal, I reckon. Either to hell or safe over the mountain! I wisht I was a gunfighter. I hate to leave here without takin' a peg at Jackrabbit Benson. Now, Buck, you do some hard figgerin' while I go nosin' round. It's pretty early, which 's all the better."

Euchre put on his sombrero, and as he went out Duane saw that he wore a gun-and-cartridge belt. It was the first time Duane had ever seen the outlaw armed.

Duane packed his few belongings into his saddlebags, and then carried the saddles out to the corral. An abundance of alfalfa in the corral showed that the horses had fared well. They had gotten almost fat during his stay in the valley. He watered them, put on the saddles loosely cinched, and then the bridles. His next move was to fill the two canvas water-bottles. That done, he returned to the cabin to wait.

At the moment he felt no excitement or agitation of any kind. There was no more thinking and planning to do. The hour had arrived, and he was ready. He understood perfectly the desperate chances he must take. His thoughts became confined to Euchre and the surprising loyalty and goodness in the hardened old outlaw. Time passed slowly. Duane kept glancing at his watch. He hoped to start the thing and get away before the outlaws were out of their beds. Finally he heard the shuffle of Euchre's boots on the hard path. The sound was quicker than usual.

When Euchre came around the corner of the cabin Duane was not so astounded as he was concerned to see the outlaw white and shaking. Sweat dripped from him. He had a wild look.

"Luck ours—so-fur, Buck!" he panted.

"You don't look it," replied Duane.

"I'm turrible sick. Jest killed a man. Fust one I ever killed!"

"Who?" asked Duane, startled.

"Jackrabbit Benson. An' sick as I am, I'm gloryin' in it. I went nosin' round up the road. Saw Alloway goin' into Deger's. He's thick with the Degers. Reckon he's askin' questions. Anyway, I was sure glad to see him away from Bland's. An' he didn't see me. When I dropped into Benson's there wasn't nobody there but Jackrabbit an' some greasers he was startin' to work. Benson never had no use fer me. An' he up an' said he wouldn't give a two-bit piece fer my life. I asked him why.

"'You're double-crossin' the boss an' Chess,' he said.

"'Jack, what 'd you give fer your own life?' I asked him.

"He straightened up surprised an' mean-lookin'. An' I let him have it, plumb center! He wilted, an' the greasers run. I reckon I'll never sleep again, But I had to do it."

Duane asked if the shot had attracted any attention outside.

"I didn't see anybody but the greasers, an' I sure looked sharp. Comin' back I cut across through the cottonwoods past Bland's cabin. I meant to keep out of sight, but somehow I had an idee I might find out if Bland was awake yet. Sure enough I run plumb into Beppo, the boy who tends Bland's hosses. Beppo likes me. An' when I inquired of his boss he said Bland had been up all night fightin' with the señora. An', Buck, here's how I figger. Bland couldn't let up last night. He was sore, an' he went after Kate again, tryin' to wear her down. Jest as likely he might have went after Jennie, with wuss intentions. Anyway, he an' Kate must have had it hot an' heavy. We're pretty lucky."

"It seems so. Well, I'm going," said Duane, tersely.

"Lucky! I should smile! Bland's been up all night after a most draggin' ride home. He'll be fagged out this mornin', sleepy, sore, an' he won't be expectin' hell before breakfast. Now, you walk over to his house. Meet him how you like. Thet's your game. But I'm suggestin', if he comes out an' you want to parley, you can jest say you'd thought over his proposition an' was ready to join his band, or you ain't. You'll have to kill him, an' it 'd save time to go fer your gun on sight. Might be wise, too, fer it's likely he'll do thet same."

"How about the horses?"

"I'll fetch them an' come along about two minnits behind you. 'Pears to me you ought to have the job done an' Jennie outside by the time I git there. Once on them hosses, we can ride out of camp before Alloway or anybody else gits into action. Jennie ain't much heavier than a rabbit. Thet big black will carry you both."

"All right. But once more let me persuade you to stay—not to mix any more in this," said Duane, earnestly.

"Nope. I'm goin'. You heard what Benson told me. Alloway wouldn't give me the benefit of any doubts. Buck, a last word—look out fer thet Bland woman!"

Duane merely nodded, and then, saying that the horses were ready, he strode away through the grove. Accounting for the short cut across grove and field, it was about five minutes' walk up to Bland's house. To Duane it seemed long in time and distance, and he had difficulty in restraining his pace. As he walked there came a gradual and subtle change in his feelings. Again he was going out to meet a man in conflict. He could have avoided this meeting. But despite the fact of his courting the encounter he had not as yet felt that hot, inexplicable rush of blood. The motive of this deadly action was not personal, and somehow that made a difference.

No outlaws were in sight. He saw several Mexican herders with cattle. Blue columns of smoke curled up over some of the cabins. The fragrant smell of it reminded Duane of his home and cutting wood for the stove. He noted a cloud of creamy mist rising above the river, dissolving in the sunlight.

Then he entered Bland's lane.

While yet some distance from the cabin he heard loud, angry voices of man and woman. Bland and Kate still quarreling! He took a quick survey of the surroundings. There was now not even a Mexican in sight. Then he hurried a little. Halfway down the lane he turned his head to peer through the cottonwoods. This time he saw Euchre coming with the horses. There was no indication that the old outlaw might lose his nerve at the end. Duane had feared this.

Duane now changed his walk to a leisurely saunter. He reached the porch and then distinguished what was said inside the cabin.

"If you do, Bland, by Heaven I'll fix you and her!" That was panted out in Kate Bland's full voice.

"Let me looser I'm going in there, I tell you!" replied Bland, hoarsely. "What for?"

"I want to make a little love to her. Ha! Ha! It'll be fun to have the laugh on her new lover."

"You lie!" cried Kate Bland.

"I'm not saying what I'll do to her *afterward!*" His voice grew hoarser with passion. "Let me go now!"

"No! no! I won't let you go. You'll choke the—the truth out of her—you'll kill her."

"The *truth!*" hissed Bland.

"Yes. I lied. Jen lied. But she lied to save me. You needn't—murder her—for that."

Bland cursed horribly. Then followed a wrestling sound of bodies in violent straining contact—the scrape of feet—the jangle of spurs—a crash of sliding table or chair, and then the cry of a woman in pain.

Duane stepped into the open door, inside the room. Kate Bland lay half across a table where she had been flung, and she was trying to get to her feet. Bland's back was turned. He had opened the door into Jennie's room and had one foot across the threshold. Duane caught the girl's low, shuddering cry. Then he called out loud and clear.

With cat-like swiftness Bland wheeled, then froze on the threshold. His sight, quick as his action, caught Duane's menacing unmistakable position.

Bland's big frame filled the door. He was in a bad place to reach for his gun. But he would not have time for a step. Duane read in his eyes the desperate calculation of chances. For a fleeting instant Bland shifted his glance to his wife. Then his whole body seemed to vibrate with the swing of his arm.

Duane shot him. He fell forward, his gun exploding as it hit into the floor, and dropped loose from stretching fingers. Duane stood over him, stooped to turn him on his back. Bland looked up with clouded gaze, then gasped his last.

"Duane, you've killed him!" cried Kate Bland, huskily. "I knew you'd have to!"

She staggered against the wall, her eyes dilating, her strong hands clenching, her face slowly whitening. She appeared shocked, half stunned, but showed no grief.

"Jennie!" called Duane, sharply.

"Oh—Duane!" came a halting reply.

"Yes. Come out. Hurry!"

She came out with uneven steps, seeing only him, and she stumbled over Bland's body. Duane caught her arm, swung her behind him. He feared the woman when she realized how she had been duped. His action was protective, and his movement toward the door equally as significant.

"Duane," cried Mrs. Bland.

It was no time for talk. Duane edged on, keeping Jennie behind him. At that moment there was a pounding of iron-shod hoofs out in the lane. Kate Bland bounded to the door. When she turned back her amazement was changing to realization.

"Where 're you taking Jen?" she cried, her voice like a man's.

"Get out of my way," replied Duane. His look perhaps, without speech, was enough for her. In an instant she was transformed into a fury.

"You hound! All the time you were fooling me! You made love to me! You let me believe—you swore you loved me! Now I see what was queer about you. All for that girl! But you can't have her. You'll never leave here alive. Give me that girl! Let me—get at her! She'll never win any more men in this camp."

She was a powerful woman, and it took all Duane's strength to ward off her onslaughts. She clawed at Jennie over his upheld arm. Every second her fury increased.

*"Help! Help! Help!"* she shrieked, in a voice that must have penetrated to the remotest cabin in the valley.

"Let go! Let go!" cried Duane, low and sharp. He still held his gun in his right hand, and it began to be hard for him to ward the woman off. His coolness had gone with her shriek for help. "Let go!" he repeated, and he shoved her fiercely.

Suddenly she snatched a rifle off the wall and backed away, her strong hands fumbling at the lever. As she jerked it down, throwing a shell into the chamber and cocking the weapon, Duane leaped upon her. He struck up the rifle as it went off, the powder burning his face.

"Jennie, run out! Get on a horse!" he said.

Jennie flashed out of the door.

With an iron grasp Duane held to the rifle barrel. He had grasped it with his left hand, and he gave such a pull that he swung the crazed woman off the floor. But he could not loose her grip. She was as strong as he.

"Kate! Let go!"

He tried to intimidate her. She did not see his gun thrust in her face, or reason had given way to such an extent to passion that she did not care. She cursed. Her husband had used the same curses, and from her lips they seemed strange, unsexed, more deadly. Like a tigress she fought him; her face no longer resembled a woman's. The evil of that outlaw life, the wildness and rage, the meaning to kill, was even in such a moment terribly impressed upon Duane.

He heard a cry from outside—a man's cry, hoarse and alarming.

It made him think of loss of time. This demon of a woman might yet block his plan.

"Let go!" he whispered, and felt his lips stiff. In the grimness of that instant he relaxed his hold on the rifle barrel.

With sudden, redoubled, irresistible strength she wrenched the rifle down and discharged it. Duane felt a blow—a shock—a burning agony tearing through his breast. Then in a frenzy he jerked so powerfully upon the rifle that he threw the woman against the wall. She fell and seemed stunned.

Duane leaped back, whirled, flew out of the door to the porch. The sharp cracking of a gun halted him. He saw Jennie holding to the bridle of his bay horse. Euchre was astride the other, and he had a Colt leveled, and he was firing down the lane. Then came a single shot, heavier, and Euchre's ceased. He fell from the horse.

A swift glance back showed to Duane a man coming down the lane. Chess Alloway! His gun was smoking. He broke into a run. Then in an instant he saw Duane, and tried to check his pace as he swung up his arm. But that slight pause was fatal. Duane shot, and Alloway was falling when his gun went off. His bullet whistled close to Duane and thudded into the cabin.

Duane bounded down to the horses. Jennie was trying to hold the plunging bay. Euchre lay flat on his back, dead, a bullet hole in his shirt, his face set hard, and his hands twisted round gun and bridle.

"Jennie, you've nerve, all right!" cried Duane, as he dragged down the horse she was holding. "Up with you now! There! Never mind—long stirrups! Hang on somehow!"

He caught his bridle out of Euchre's clutching grip and leaped astride. The frightened horses jumped into a run and thundered down the lane into the road. Duane saw men running from cabins. He heard shouts. But there were no shots fired. Jennie seemed able to stay on her horse, but without stirrups she was thrown about so much that Duane rode closer and reached out to grasp her arm.

Thus they rode through the valley to the trail that led up over the steep and broken Rim Rock. As they began to climb Duane looked back. No pursuers were in sight.

"Jennie, we're going to get away!" he cried, exultation for her in his voice.

She was gazing horror-stricken at his breast, as in turning to look back he faced her.

"Oh, Duane, your shirt's all bloody!" she faltered, pointing with trembling fingers.

With her words Duane became aware of two things—the hand he instinctively placed to his breast still held his gun, and he had sustained a terrible wound.

Duane had been shot through the breast far enough down to give him grave apprehension of his life. The clean-cut hole made by the bullet bled freely both at its entrance and where it had come out, but with no signs of hemorrhage. He did not bleed at the mouth; however, he began to cough up a reddish-tinged foam.

As they rode on, Jennie, with pale face and mute lips, looked at him.

"I'm badly hurt, Jennie," he said, "but I guess I'll stick it out."

"The woman—did she shoot you?"

"Yes. She was a devil. Euchre told me to look out for her. I wasn't quick enough."

"You didn't have to—to—" shivered the girl.

"No! No!" he replied.

They did not stop climbing while Duane tore a scarf and made compresses, which he bound tightly over his wounds. The fresh horses made fast time up the rough trail. From open places Duane looked down. When they surmounted the steep ascent and stood on top of the Rim Rock, with no signs of pursuit down in the valley, and with the wild, broken fastnesses before them, Duane turned to the girl and assured her that they now had every chance of escape.

"But—your—wound!" she faltered, with dark, troubled eyes. "I see—the blood—dripping from your back!"

"Jennie, I'll take a lot of killing," he said.

Then he became silent and attended to the uneven trail. He was aware presently that he had not come into Bland's camp by this route. But that did not matter; any trail leading out beyond the Rim Rock was safe enough. What he wanted was to get far away into some wild retreat where he could hide till he recovered from his wound. He seemed to feel a fire inside his breast, and his throat burned so that it was necessary for him to take a swallow of water every little while. He began to suffer considerable pain, which increased as the hours went by and then gave way to a numbness. From that time on he had need of his great strength and endurance. Gradually he lost his steadiness and his keen sight; and he realized that if he were to meet foes, or if pursuing outlaws should come up with him, he could make only a poor stand. So he turned off on a trail that appeared seldom traveled.

Soon after this move he became conscious of a further thickening of his senses. He felt able to hold on to his saddle for a while longer, but he was failing. Then he thought he ought to advise Jennie, so in case she was left alone she would have some idea of what to do.

"Jennie, I'll give out soon," he said. "No—I don't mean—what you think. But I'll drop soon. My strength's going. If I die—you ride back to the main trail. Hide and rest by day. Ride at night. That trail goes to water. I believe you could get across the Nueces, where some rancher will take you in."

Duane could not get the meaning of her incoherent reply. He rode on, and soon he could not see the trail or hear his horse. He did not know whether they traveled a mile or many times that far. But he was conscious when the horse stopped, and had a vague sense of falling and feeling Jennie's arms before all became dark to him.

When consciousness returned he found himself lying in a little hut of mesquite branches. It was well built and evidently some years old. There were two doors or openings, one in front and the other at the back. Duane imagined it had been built by a fugitive—one who meant to keep an eye both ways and not to be surprised. Duane felt weak and had no desire to move. Where was he, anyway? A strange, intangible sense of time, distance, of something far behind weighed upon him. Sight of the two packs Euchre had made brought his thought to Jennie. What had become of her? There was evidence of her work in a smoldering fire and a little blackened coffee-pot. Probably she was outside looking after the horses or getting water. He thought he heard a step and listened, but he felt tired, and presently his eyes closed and he fell into a doze.

Awakening from this, he saw Jennie sitting beside him. In some way she seemed to have changed. When he spoke she gave a start and turned eagerly to him.

"Duane!" she cried.

"Hello. How're you, Jennie, and how am I?" he said, finding it a little difficult to talk.

"Oh, I'm all right," she replied. "And you've come to—your wound's healed; but you've been sick. Fever, I guess. I did all I could."

Duane saw now that the difference in her was a whiteness and tightness of skin, a hollowness of eye, a look of strain.

"Fever? How long have we been here?" he asked.

She took some pebbles from the crown of his sombrero and counted them.

"Nine Nine days," she answered.

"Nine days!" he exclaimed, incredulously. But another look at her assured him that she meant what she said. "I've been sick all the time? You nursed me?"

"Yes."

"Bland's men didn't come along here?"

"No."

"Where are the horses?"

"I keep them grazing down in a gorge back of here. There's good grass and water."

"Have you slept any?"

"A little. Lately I couldn't keep awake."

"Good Lord! I should think not. You've had a time of it sitting here day and night nursing me, watching for the outlaws. Come, tell me all about it."

"There's nothing much to tell."

"I want to know, anyway, just what you did—how you felt."

"I can't remember very well," she replied, simply. "We must have ridden forty miles that day we got away. You bled all the time. Toward evening you lay on your horse's neck. When we came to this place you fell out of the saddle. I dragged you in here and stopped your bleeding. I thought you'd die that night. But in the morning I had a little hope. I had forgotten the horses. But luckily they didn't stray far. I caught them and kept them down in the gorge. When your wounds closed and you began to breathe stronger I thought you'd get well quick. It was fever that put you back. You raved a lot, and that worried me, because I couldn't stop you. Anybody trailing us could have heard you a good ways. I don't know whether I was scared most then or when you were quiet, and it was so dark and lonely and still all around. Every day I put a stone in your hat."

"Jennie, you saved my life," said Duane.

"I don't know. Maybe. I did all I knew how to do," she replied. "You saved mine—more than my life."

Their eyes met in a long gaze, and then their hands in a close clasp.

"Jennie, we're going to get away," he said, with gladness. "I'll be well in a few days. You don't know how strong I am. We'll hide by day and travel by night. I can get you across the river."

"And then?" she asked.

"We'll find some honest rancher."

"And then?" she persisted.

"Why," he began, slowly, "that's as far as my thoughts ever got. It was pretty hard, I tell you, to assure myself of so much. It means your safety. You'll tell your story. You'll be sent to some village or town and taken care of until a relative or friend is notified."

"And you?" she inquired, in a strange voice.

Duane kept silence.

"What will you do?" she went on.

"Jennie, I'll go back to the brakes. I daren't show my face among respectable people. I'm an outlaw."

"You're no criminal!" she declared, with deep passion.

"Jennie, on this border the little difference between an outlaw and a criminal doesn't count for much."

"You won't go back among those terrible men? You, with your gentleness and sweetness—all that's good about you? Oh, Duane, don't—don't go!"

"I can't go back to the outlaws, at least not Bland's band. No, I'll go alone. I'll lone-wolf it, as they say on the border. What else can I do, Jennie?"

"Oh, I don't know. Couldn't you hide? Couldn't you slip out of Texas—go far away?"

"I could never get out of Texas without being arrested. I could hide, but a man must live. Never mind about me, Jennie."

In three days Duane was able with great difficulty to mount his horse.

During daylight, by short relays, he and Jennie rode back to the main trail, where they hid again till he had rested. Then in the dark they rode out of the cañons and gullies of the Rim Rock, and early in the morning halted at the first water to camp.

From that point they traveled after nightfall and went into hiding during the day. Once across the Nueces River, Duane was assured of safety for her and great danger for himself. They had crossed into a country he did not know. Somewhere east of the river there were scattered ranches. But he was as liable to find the rancher in touch with the outlaws as he was likely to find him honest. Duane hoped his good fortune would not desert him in this last service to Jennie. Next to the worry of that was realization of his condition. He had gotten up too soon; he had ridden too far and hard, and now he felt that any moment he might fall from his saddle. At last, far ahead over a barren mesquite-dotted stretch of dusty ground, he espied a patch of green and a little flat, red ranch house. He headed his horse for it and turned a face he tried to make cheerful for Jennie's sake. She seemed both happy and sorry.

When near at hand he saw that the rancher was a thrifty farmer. And thrift spoke for honesty. There were fields of alfalfa, fruit-trees, corrals, windmill pumps, irrigation-ditches, all surrounding a neat little adobe house. Some children were playing in the yard. The way they ran at sight of Duane hinted of both the loneliness and the fear of their isolated lives. Duane saw a woman come to the door, then a man. The latter looked keenly, then stepped outside. He was a sandy-haired, freckled Texan.

"Howdy, stranger," he called, as Duane halted. "Get down, you an' your woman. Say, now, air you sick or shot or what? Let me—"

Duane, reeling in his saddle, bent searching eyes upon the rancher. He thought he saw good will, kindness, honesty. He risked all on that one sharp glance. Then he almost plunged from the saddle.

The rancher caught him, helped him to a bench.

"Martha, come out here!" he called. "This man's sick. No; he's shot, or I don't know bloodstains."

Jennie had slipped off her horse and to Duane's side. Duane appeared about to faint.

"Air you his wife?" asked the rancher.

"No. I'm only a girl he saved from outlaws. Oh, he's so paler! Duane, Duane!"

"Buck Duane!" exclaimed the rancher, excitedly. "The man who killed Bland an' Alloway? Say, I owe him a good turn, an' I'll pay it, young woman."

The rancher's wife came out, and with a manner at once kind and practical essayed to make Duane drink from a flask. He was not so far gone that he could not recognize its contents, which he refused, and weakly asked for water. When that was given him he found his voice.

"Yes, I'm Duane. I've only overdone myself—just all in. The wounds I got at Bland's are healing. Will you take this girl in—hide her awhile till the excitement's over among the outlaws?"

"I shore will," replied the Texan.

"Thanks. I'll remember you—I'll square it."

"What 're you goin' to do?"

"I'll rest a bit—then go back to the brakes."

"Young man, you ain't in any shape to travel. See here—any rustlers on your trail?"

"I think we gave Bland's gang the slip."

"Good. I'll tell you what. I'll take you in along with the girl, an' hide both of you till you get well. It'll be safe. My nearest neighbor is five miles off. We don't have much company."

"You risk a great deal. Both outlaws and rangers are hunting me," said Duane.

"Never seen a ranger yet in these parts. An' have always got along with outlaws, mebbe exceptin' Bland. I tell you I owe you a good turn."

"My horses might betray you," added Duane.

"I'll hide them in a place where there's water an' grass. Nobody goes to it. Come now, let me help you indoors."

Duane's last fading sensations of that hard day were the strange feel of a bed, a relief at the removal of his heavy boots, and of Jennie's soft, cool hands on his hot face.

He lay ill for three weeks before he began to mend, and it was another week then before he could walk out a little in the dusk of the evenings. After that his strength returned rapidly. And it was only at the end of this long siege that he recovered his spirits. During most of his illness he had been silent, moody.

"Jennie, I'll be riding off soon," he said, one evening. "I can't impose on this good man Andrews much longer. I'll never forget his kindness. His wife, too—she's been so good to us. Yes, Jennie, you and I will have to say good-by very soon."

"Don't hurry away," she replied.

Lately Jennie had appeared strange to him. She had changed from the girl he used to see at Mrs. Bland's house. He took her reluctance to say good-by as another indication of her regret that he must go back to the brakes. Yet somehow it made him observe her more closely. She wore a plain, white dress made from material Mrs. Andrews had given her. Sleep and good food had improved her. If she had been pretty out there in the outlaw den now she was more than that. But she had the same paleness, the same strained look, the same dark eyes full of haunting shadows. After Duane's realization of the change in her he watched her more, with a growing certainty that he would be sorry not to see her again.

"It's likely we won't ever see each other again," he said. "That's strange to think of. We've been through some hard days, and I seem to have known you a long time."

Jennie appeared shy, almost sad, so Duane changed the subject to something less personal.

Andrews returned one evening from a several days' trip to Huntsville.

"Duane, everybody's talkin' about how you cleaned up the Bland outfit," he said, important and full of news. "It's some exaggerated, accordin' to what you told me; but you've shore made friends on this side of the Nueces. I reckon there ain't a town where you wouldn't find people to welcome you. Huntsville, you know, is some divided in its ideas. Half the people are crooked. Likely enough, all them who was so loud in praise of you are the crookedest. For instance, I met King Fisher, the boss outlaw of these parts. Well, King thinks he's a decent citizen. He was tellin' me what a grand job yours was for the border an' honest cattlemen. Now that Bland and Alloway are done for, King Fisher will find rustlin' easier. There's talk of Hardin movin' his camp over to Bland's. But I don't know how true it is. I reckon there ain't much to it. In the past when a big outlaw chief went under, his band almost always broke up an' scattered. There's no one left who could run thet outfit."

"Did you hear of any outlaws huntin' me?" asked Duane.

"Nobody from Bland's outfit is huntin' you, thet's shore," replied Andrews. "Fisher said there never was a hoss straddled to go on your trail. Nobody had any use for Bland. Anyhow, his men would be afraid to trail you. An' you could go right in to Huntsville, where you'd be some popular. Reckon you'd be safe, too, except when some of them fool saloon loafers or bad cowpunchers would try to shoot you for the glory in it. Them kind of men will bob up everywhere you go, Duane."

"I'll be able to ride and take care of myself in a day or two," went on Duane. "Then I'll go—I'd like to talk to you about Jennie."

"She's welcome to a home here with us."

"Thank you, Andrews. You're a kind man. But I want Jennie to get farther away from the Rio Grande. She'd never be safe here. Besides, she may be able to find relatives. She has some, though she doesn't know where they are."

"All right, Duane. Whatever you think best. I reckon now you'd better take her to some town. Go north an' strike for Shelbyville or Crockett. Them's both good towns. I'll tell Jennie the names of men who'll help her. You needn't ride into town at all."

"Which place is nearer, and how far is it?"

"Shelbyville. I reckon about two days' ride. Poor stock country, so you ain't liable to meet rustlers. All the same, better hit the trail at night an' go careful."

At sunset two days later Duane and Jennie mounted their horses and said good-by to the rancher and his wife. Andrews would not listen to Duane's thanks.

"I tell you I'm beholden to you yet," he declared.

"Well, what can I do for you?" asked Duane. "I may come along here again someday."

"Get down an' come in, then, or you're no friend of mine. I reckon there ain't nothin' I can think of—I just happen to remember—" Here he led Duane out of earshot of the women and went on in a whisper. "Buck, I used to be well-to-do. Got skinned by a man named Brown—Rodney Brown. He lives in Huntsville, an' he's my enemy. I never was much on fightin', or I'd fixed him. Brown ruined me—stole all I had. He's a hoss an' cattle thief, an' he has pull enough at home to protect him. I reckon I needn't say any more."

"Is this Brown a man who shot an outlaw named Stevens?" queried Duane, curiously.

"Shore, he's the same. I heard thet story. Brown swears he plugged Stevens through the middle. But the outlaw rode off, an' nobody ever knew for shore."

"Luke Stevens died of that shot. I buried him," said Duane.

Andrews made no further comment, and the two men returned to the women.

"The main road for about three miles, then where it forks take the left-hand road and keep on straight. That what you said, Andrews?"

"Shore. An' good luck to you both!"

Duane and Jennie trotted away into the gathering twilight. At the moment an insistent thought bothered Duane. Both Luke Stevens and the rancher Andrews had hinted to Duane to kill a man named Brown. Duane wished with all his heart that they had not mentioned it, let alone taken for granted the execution of the deed. What a bloody place Texas was! Men who robbed and men who were robbed both wanted murder. It was in the spirit of the country. Duane certainly meant to avoid ever meeting this Rodney Brown. And that very determination showed Duane how dangerous he really was—to men and to himself. Sometimes he had a feeling of how little stood between his sane and better self and a self utterly wild and terrible. He reasoned that only intelligence could save him—only a thoughtful understanding of his danger and a hold upon some ideal.

Then he fell into low conversation with Jennie, holding out hopeful views of her future, and presently darkness set in. The sky was overcast with heavy clouds; there was no air moving; the heat and oppression threatened storm. By and by Duane could not see a rod in front of him, though his horse had no difficulty in keeping to the road. Duane was bothered by the blackness of the night. Traveling fast was impossible, and any moment he might miss the road that led off to the left. So he was compelled to give all his attention to peering into the thick shadows ahead. As good luck would have it, he came to higher ground where there was less mesquite, and therefore not such impenetrable darkness; and at this point he came to where the road split.

Once headed in the right direction, he felt easier in mind. To his annoyance, however, a fine, misty rain set in. Jennie was not well dressed for wet weather; and, for that matter, neither was he. His coat, which in that dry warm climate he seldom needed, was tied behind his saddle, and he put it on Jennie.

They traveled on. The rain fell steadily; if anything, growing thicker. Duane grew uncomfortably wet and chilly. Jennie, however, fared somewhat better by reason of the heavy coat. The night passed quickly despite the discomfort, and soon a gray, dismal, rainy dawn greeted the travelers.

Jennie insisted that he find some shelter where a fire could be built to dry his clothes. He was not in a fit condition to risk catching cold. In fact, Duane's teeth were chattering. To find a shelter in that barren waste seemed a futile task. Quite unexpectedly, however, they happened upon a deserted adobe cabin situated a little off the road. Not only did it prove to have a dry interior, but also there was firewood. Water was available in pools everywhere; however, there was no grass for the horses.

A good fire and hot food and drink changed the aspect of their condition as far as comfort went. And Jennie lay down to sleep. For Duane, however, there must be vigilance. This cabin was no hiding place. The rain fell harder all the time, and the wind changed to the north. "It's a norther, all right," muttered Duane. "Two or three days." And he felt that his extraordinary luck had not held out. Still one point favored him, and it was that travelers were not likely to come along during the storm. Jennie slept while Duane watched. The saving of this girl meant more to him than any task he had ever assumed. First it had been partly from a human feeling to succor an unfortunate woman, and partly a motive to establish clearly to himself that he was no outlaw. Lately, however, had come a different sense, a strange one, with something personal and warm and protective in it.

As he looked down upon her, a slight, slender girl with bedraggled dress and disheveled hair, her face, pale and quiet, a little stern in sleep, and her long, dark lashes lying on her cheek, he seemed to see her fragility, her prettiness, her femininity as never before. But for him she might at that very moment have been a broken, ruined girl lying back in that cabin of the Blands'. The fact gave him a feeling of his importance in this shifting of her destiny. She was unharmed, still young; she would forget and be happy; she would live to be a good wife and mother. Somehow the thought swelled his heart. His act, death-dealing as it had been, was a noble one, and helped him to hold on to his drifting hopes. Hardly once since Jennie had entered into his thought had those ghosts returned to torment him.

Tomorrow she would be gone among good, kind people with a possibility of finding her relatives. He thanked God for that; nevertheless, he felt a pang.

She slept more than half the day. Duane kept guard, always alert, whether he was sitting, standing, or walking. The rain pattered steadily on the roof and sometimes came in gusty flurries through the door. The horses were outside in a shed that afforded poor shelter, and they stamped restlessly. Duane kept them saddled and bridled.

About the middle of the afternoon Jennie awoke. They cooked a meal and afterward sat beside the little fire. She had never been, in his observation of her, anything but a tragic figure, an unhappy girl, the farthest removed from serenity and poise. That characteristic capacity for agitation struck him as stronger in her this day. He attributed it, however, to the long strain, the suspense nearing an end. Yet sometimes when her eyes were on him she did not seem to be thinking of her freedom, of her future.

"This time tomorrow you'll be in Shelbyville," he said.

"Where will you be?" she asked, quickly.

"Me? Oh, I'll be making tracks for some lonesome place," he replied.

The girl shuddered.

"I've been brought up in Texas. I remember what a hard lot the men of my family had. But poor as they were, they had a roof over their heads, a hearth with a fire, a warm bed—somebody to love them. And you, Duane—oh, my God! What must your life be? You must ride and hide and watch eternally. No decent food, no pillow, no friendly word, no clean clothes, no woman's hand! Horses, guns, trails, rocks, holes—these must be the important things in your life. You must go on riding, hiding, killing until you meet—"

She ended with a sob and dropped her head on her knees. Duane was amazed, deeply touched.

"My girl, thank you for that thought of me," he said, with a tremor in his voice. "You don't know how much that means to me."

She raised her face, and it was tear-stained, eloquent, beautiful.

"I've heard tell—the best of men go to the bad out there. You won't. Promise me you won't. I never—knew any man—like you. I—I—we may never see each other again—after today. I'll never forget you. I'll pray for you, and I'll never give up trying to—to do something. Don't despair. It's never too late. It was my hope that kept me alive—out there at Bland's—before you came. I was only a poor weak girl. But if I could hope—so can you. Stay away from men. Be a lone wolf. Fight for your life. Stick out your exile—and maybe—someday—"

Then she lost her voice. Duane clasped her hand and with feeling as deep as hers promised to remember her words. In her despair for him she had spoken wisdom—pointed out the only course.

Duane's vigilance, momentarily broken by emotion, had no sooner reasserted itself than he discovered the bay horse, the one Jennie rode, had broken his halter and gone off. The soft wet earth had deadened the sound of his hoofs. His tracks were plain in the mud. There were clumps of mesquite in sight, among which the horse might have strayed. It turned out, however, that he had not done so.

Duane did not want to leave Jennie alone in the cabin so near the road. So he put her up on his horse and bade her follow. The rain had ceased for the time being, though evidently the storm was not yet over. The tracks led up a wash to a wide flat where mesquite, prickly pear, and thorn-bush grew so thickly that Jennie could not ride into it. Duane was thoroughly concerned. He must have her horse. Time was flying. It would soon be night. He could not expect her to scramble quickly through that brake on foot. Therefore he decided to risk leaving her at the edge of the thicket and go in alone.

As he went in a sound startled him. Was it the breaking of a branch he had stepped on or thrust aside? He heard the impatient pound of his horse's hoofs. Then all was quiet. Still he listened, not wholly satisfied. He was never satisfied in regard to safety; he knew too well that there never could be safety for him in this country.

The bay horse had threaded the ulules of the thicket. Duane wondered what had drawn him there. Certainly it had not been grass, for there was none. Presently he heard the horse tramping along, and then he ran. The mud was deep, and the sharp thorns made going difficult. He came up with the horse, and at the same moment crossed a multitude of fresh horse tracks.

He bent lower to examine them, and was alarmed to find that they had been made very recently, even since it had ceased raining. They were tracks of well-shod horses. Duane straightened up with a cautious glance all around. His instant decision was to hurry back to Jennie. But he had come a goodly way through the thicket, and it was impossible to rush back. Once or twice he imagined he heard crashings in the brush, but did not halt to make sure. Certain he was now that some kind of danger threatened.

Suddenly there came an unmistakable thump of horses' hoofs off somewhere to the fore. Then a scream rent the air. It ended abruptly. Duane leaped forward, tore his way through the thorny brake. He heard Jennie cry again—an appealing call quickly hushed. It seemed more to his right, and he plunged that way. He burst into a glade where a smoldering fire and ground covered with footprints and tracks showed that campers had lately been. Rushing across this, he broke his passage out to the open. But he was too late.

His horse had disappeared. Jennie was gone. There were no riders in sight. There was no sound. There was a heavy trail of horses going north. Jennie had been carried off—probably by outlaws. Duane realized that pursuit was out of the question—that Jennie was lost.

## CHAPTER X

A hundred miles from the haunts most familiar with Duane's deeds, far up where the Nueces ran a trickling clear stream between yellow cliffs, stood a small deserted shack of covered mesquite poles. It had been made long ago, but was well preserved. A door faced the overgrown trail, and another faced down into a gorge of dense thickets. On the border fugitives from law and men who hid in fear of someone they had wronged never lived in houses with only one door.

It was a wild spot, lonely, not fit for human habitation except for the outcast. He, perhaps, might have found it hard to leave for most of the other wild nooks in that barren country. Down in the gorge there was never-failing sweet water, grass all the year round, cool, shady retreats, deer, rabbits, turkeys, fruit, and miles and miles of narrow-twisting, deep cañon full of broken rocks and impenetrable thickets. The scream of the panther was heard there, the squall of the wildcat, the cough of the jaguar. Innumerable bees buzzed in the spring blossoms, and, it seemed, scattered honey to the winds. All day there was continuous song of birds, that of the mocking-bird loud and sweet and mocking above the rest.

On clear days—and rare indeed were cloudy days—with the subsiding of the wind at sunset a hush seemed to fall around the little hut. Far-distant dim blue mountains stood gold-rimmed gradually to fade with the shading of light.

At this quiet hour a man climbed up out of the gorge and sat in the westward door of the hut. This lonely watcher of the west and listener to the silence was Duane. And this hut was the one where, three years before, Jennie had nursed him back to life.

The killing of a man named Sellers, and the combination of circumstances that had made the tragedy a memorable regret, had marked, if not a change, at least a cessation in Duane's activities. He had trailed Sellers to kill him for the supposed abducting of Jennie. He had trailed him long after he had learned Sellers traveled alone. Duane wanted absolute assurance of Jennie's death. Vague rumors, a few words here and there, unauthenticated stories, were all Duane had gathered in years to substantiate his belief—that Jennie died shortly after the beginning of her second captivity. But Duane did not know surely. Sellers might have told him. Duane expected, if not to force it from him at the end, to read it in his eyes. But the bullet went too unerringly; it locked his lips and fixed his eyes.

After that meeting Duane lay long at the ranch house of a friend, and when he recovered from the wound Sellers had given him he started with two horses and a pack for the lonely gorge on the Nueces. There he had been hidden for months, a prey to remorse, a dreamer, a victim of phantoms.

It took work for him to find subsistence in that rocky fastness. And work, action, helped to pass the hours. But he could not work all the time, even if he had found it to do. Then in his idle moments and at night his task was to live with the hell in his mind.

The sunset and the twilight hour made all the rest bearable. The little hut on the rim of the gorge seemed to hold Jennie's presence. It was not as if he felt her spirit. If it had been he would have been sure of her death. He hoped Jennie had not survived her second misfortune; and that intense hope had burned into belief, if not surety. Upon his return to that locality, on the occasion of his first visit to the hut, he had found things just as they had left them, and a poor, faded piece of ribbon Jennie had used to tie around her bright hair. No wandering outlaw or traveler had happened upon the lonely spot, which further endeared it to Duane.

A strange feature of this memory of Jennie was the freshness of it—the failure of years, toil, strife, death-dealing to dim it—to deaden the thought of what might have been. He had a marvelous gift of visualization. He could shut his eyes and see Jennie before him just as clearly as if she had stood there in the flesh. For hours he did that, dreaming, dreaming of life he had never tasted and now never would taste. He saw Jennie's slender, graceful figure, the old brown ragged dress in which he had seen her first at Bland's, her little feet in Mexican sandals, her fine hands coarsened by work, her round arms and swelling throat, and her pale, sad, beautiful face with its staring dark eyes. He remembered every look she had given him, every word she had spoken to him, every time she had touched him. He thought of her beauty and sweetness, of the few things which had come to mean to him that she must have loved him; and he trained himself to think of these in preference to her life at Bland's, the escape with him, and then her recapture, because such memories led to bitter, fruitless pain. He had to fight suffering because it was eating out his heart.

Sitting there, eyes wide open, he dreamed of the old homestead and his white-haired mother. He saw the old home life, sweetened and filled by dear new faces and added joys, go on before his eyes with him a part of it.

Then in the inevitable reaction, in the reflux of bitter reality, he would send out a voiceless cry no less poignant because it was silent: "Poor fool! No,

I shall never see mother again—never go home—never have a home. I am Duane, the Lone Wolf! Oh, God! I wish it were over! These dreams torture me! What have I to do with a mother, a home, a wife? No bright-haired boy, no dark-eyed girl will ever love me. I am an outlaw, an outcast, dead to the good and decent world. I am alone—alone. Better be a callous brute or better dead! I shall go mad thinking! Man, what is left to you? A hiding-place like a wolf's—lonely silent days, lonely nights with phantoms! Or the trail and the road with their bloody tracks, and then the hard ride, the sleepless, hungry ride to some hole in rocks or brakes. What hellish thing drives me? Why can't I end it all? What is left? Only that damned unquenchable spirit of the gunfighter to live—to hang on to miserable life—to have no fear of death, yet to cling like a leach—to die as gunfighters seldom die, with boots off! Bain, you were first, and you're long avenged. I'd change with you. And Sellers, you were last, and you're avenged. And you others—you're avenged. Lie quiet in your graves and give me peace!"

But they did not lie quiet in their graves and give him peace.

A group of specters trooped out of the shadows of dusk and, gathering round him, escorted him to his bed.

When Duane had been riding the trails passion-bent to escape pursuers, or passion-bent in his search, the constant action and toil and exhaustion made him sleep. But when in hiding, as time passed, gradually he required less rest and sleep, and his mind became more active. Little by little his phantoms gained hold on him, and at length, but for the saving power of his dreams, they would have claimed him utterly.

How many times he had said to himself: "I am an intelligent man. I'm not crazy. I'm in full possession of my faculties. All this is fancy—imagination—conscience. I've no work, no duty, no ideal, no hope—and my mind is obsessed, thronged with images. And these images naturally are of the men with whom I have dealt. I can't forget them. They come back to me, hour after hour; and when my tortured mind grows weak, then maybe I'm not just right till the mood wears out and lets me sleep."

So he reasoned as he lay down in his comfortable camp. The night was star-bright above the cañon-walls, darkly shadowing down between them. The insects hummed and chirped and thrummed a continuous thick song, low and monotonous. Slow-running water splashed softly over stones in the streambed. From far down the cañon came the mournful hoot of an owl. The moment he lay down, thereby giving up action for the day, all these things weighed upon him like a great heavy mantle of loneliness. In truth, they did not constitute loneliness.

And he could no more have dispelled thought than he could have reached out to touch a cold, bright star.

He wondered how many outcasts like him lay under this star-studded, velvety sky across the fifteen hundred miles of wild country between El Paso and the mouth of the river. A vast wild territory—a refuge for outlaws! Somewhere he had heard or read that the Texas Rangers kept a book with names and records of outlaws—three thousand known outlaws. Yet these could scarcely be half of that unfortunate horde which had been recruited from all over the states. Duane had traveled from camp to camp, den to den, hiding place to hiding place, and he knew these men. Most of them were hopeless criminals; some were avengers; a few were wronged wanderers; and among them occasionally was a man, human in his way, honest as he could be, not yet lost to good.

But all of them were akin in one sense—their outlawry; and that starry night they lay with their dark faces up, some in packs like wolves, others alone like the gray wolf who knew no mate. It did not make much difference in Duane's thought of them that the majority were steeped in crime and brutality, more often than not stupid from rum, incapable of a fine feeling, just lost wild dogs.

Duane doubted that there was a man among them who did not realize his moral wreck and ruin. He had met poor, half-witted wretches who knew it. He believed he could enter into their minds and feel the truth of all their lives—the hardened outlaw, coarse, ignorant, bestial, who murdered as Bill Black had murdered, who stole for the sake of stealing, who craved money to gamble and drink, defiantly ready for death, and, like that terrible outlaw, Helm, who cried out on the scaffold, "Let her rip!"

The wild youngsters seeking notoriety and reckless adventure; the cowboys with a notch on their guns, with boastful pride in the knowledge that they were marked by rangers; the crooked men from the North, defaulters, forgers, murderers, all pale-faced, flat-chested men not fit for that wilderness and not surviving; the dishonest cattlemen, hand and glove with outlaws, driven from their homes; the old grizzled, bow-legged genuine rustlers—all these Duane had come in contact with, had watched and known, and as he felt with them he seemed to see that as their lives were bad, sooner or later to end dismally or tragically, so they must pay some kind of earthly penalty—if not of conscience, then of fear; if not of fear, then of that most terrible of all things to restless, active men—pain, the pang of flesh and bone.

Duane knew, for he had seen them pay. Best of all, moreover, he knew the internal life of the gunfighter of that select but by no means small class of which he was representative. The world that judged him and his kind judged him as a machine, a killing-machine, with only mind enough to hunt, to meet, to slay another man. It had taken three endless years for Duane to understand his own father. Duane knew beyond all doubt that the gunfighters like

Bland, like Alloway, like Sellers, men who were evil and had no remorse, no spiritual accusing Nemesis, had something far more torturing to mind, more haunting, more murderous of rest and sleep and peace; and that something was abnormal fear of death. Duane knew this, for he had shot these men; he had seen the quick, dark shadow in eyes, the presentiment that the will could not control, and then the horrible certainty. These men must have been in agony at every meeting with a possible or certain foe—more agony than the hot rend of a bullet. They were haunted, too, haunted by this fear, by every victim calling from the grave that nothing was so inevitable as death, which lurked behind every corner, hid in every shadow, lay deep in the dark tube of every gun. These men could not have a friend; they could not love or trust a woman. They knew their one chance of holding on to life lay in their own distrust, watchfulness, dexterity, and that hope, by the very nature of their lives, could not be lasting. They had doomed themselves. What, then, could possibly have dwelt in the depths of their minds as they went to their beds on a starry night like this, with mystery in silence and shadow, with time passing surely, and the dark future and its secret approaching every hour—what, then, but hell?

The hell in Duane's mind was not fear of man or fear of death. He would have been glad to lay down the burden of life, providing death came naturally. Many times he had prayed for it. But that overdeveloped, superhuman spirit of defense in him precluded suicide or the inviting of an enemy's bullet. Sometimes he had a vague, scarcely analyzed idea that this spirit was what had made the Southwest habitable for the white man.

Every one of his victims, singly and collectively, returned to him forever, it seemed, in cold, passionless, accusing domination of these haunted hours. They did not accuse him of dishonor or cowardice or brutality or murder; they only accused him of death. It was as if they knew more than when they were alive, had learned that life was a divine mysterious gift not to be taken. They thronged about him with their voiceless clamoring, drifted around him with their fading eyes.

## CHAPTER XI

After nearly six months in the Nueces gorge the loneliness and inaction of his life drove Duane out upon the trails seeking anything rather than to hide longer alone, a prey to the scourge of his thoughts. The moment he rode into sight of men a remarkable transformation occurred in him. A strange warmth stirred in him—a longing to see the faces of people, to hear their voices—a pleasurable emotion sad and strange. But it was only a precursor of his old bitter, sleepless, and eternal vigilance. When he hid alone in the brakes he was safe from all except his deeper, better self; when he escaped from this into the haunts of men his force and will went to the preservation of his life.

Mercer was the first village he rode into. He had many friends there. Mercer claimed to owe Duane a debt. On the outskirts of the village there was a grave overgrown by brush so that the rude-lettered post which marked it was scarcely visible to Duane as he rode by. He had never read the inscription. But he thought now of Hardin, no other than the erstwhile ally of Bland. For many years Hardin had harassed the stockmen and ranchers in and around Mercer. On an evil day for him he or his outlaws had beaten and robbed a man who once succored Duane when sore in need. Duane met Hardin in the little plaza of the village, called him every name known to border men, taunted him to draw, and killed him in the act.

Duane went to the house of one Jones, a Texan who had known his father, and there he was warmly received. The feel of an honest hand, the voice of a friend, the prattle of children who were not afraid of him or his gun, good wholesome food, and change of clothes—these things for the time being made a changed man of Duane. To be sure, he did not often speak. The price of his head and the weight of his burden made him silent. But eagerly he drank in all the news that was told him. In the years of his absence from home he had never heard a word about his mother or uncle. Those who were his real friends on the border would have been the last to make inquiries, to write or receive letters that might give a clue to Duane's whereabouts.

Duane remained all day with this hospitable Jones, and as twilight fell was loath to go and yielded to a pressing invitation to remain overnight. It was seldom indeed that Duane slept under a roof. Early in the evening, while Duane sat on the porch with two awed and hero-worshiping sons of the house, Jones returned from a quick visit down to the post office. Summarily he sent the boys off. He labored under intense excitement.

"Duane, there's rangers in town," he whispered. "It's all over town, too, that you're here. You rode in long after sunup. Lots of people saw you. I don't believe there's a man or boy that 'd squeal on you. But the women might. They gossip, and these rangers are handsome fellows—devils with the women."

"What company of rangers?" asked Duane, quickly.

"Company A, under Captain MacNelly, that new ranger. He made a big name in the war. And since he's been in the ranger service he's done wonders. He's cleaned up some bad places south, and he's working north."

"MacNelly. I've heard of him. Describe him to me."

"Slight-built chap, but wiry and tough. Clean face, black mustache and hair. Sharp black eyes. He's got a look of authority. MacNelly's a fine man, Duane. Belongs to a good Southern family. I'd hate to have him look you up."

Duane did not speak.

"MacNelly's got nerve, and his rangers are all experienced men. If they find out you're here they'll come after you. MacNelly's no gunfighter, but he wouldn't hesitate to do his duty, even if he faced sure death. Which he would in this case. Duane, you mustn't meet Captain MacNelly. Your record is clean, if it is terrible. You never met a ranger or any officer except a rotten sheriff now and then, like Rod Brown."

Still Duane kept silence. He was not thinking of danger, but of the fact of how fleeting must be his stay among friends.

"I've already fixed up a pack of grub," went on Jones. "I'll slip out to saddle your horse. You watch here."

He had scarcely uttered the last word when soft, swift footsteps sounded on the hard path. A man turned in at the gate. The light was dim, yet clean enough to disclose an unusually tall figure. When it appeared nearer he was seen to be walking with both arms raised, hands high. He slowed his stride.

"Does Burt Jones live here?" he asked, in a low, hurried voice.

"I reckon. I'm Burt. What can I do for you?" replied Jones.

The stranger peered around, stealthily came closer, still with his hands up.

"It is known that Buck Duane is here. Captain MacNelly's camping on the river just out of town. He sends word to Duane to come out there after dark."

The stranger wheeled and departed as swiftly and strangely as he had come.

"Bust me! Duane, whatever do you make of that?" exclaimed Jones.

"A new one on me," replied Duane, thoughtfully.

"First fool thing I ever heard of MacNelly doing. Can't make head nor tails of it. I'd have said offhand that MacNelly wouldn't double-cross anybody. He struck me as a square man, sand all through. But, hell! he must mean treachery. I can't see anything else in that deal."

"Maybe the Captain wants to give me a fair chance to surrender without bloodshed," observed Duane. "Pretty decent of him, if he meant that."

"He *invites you* out to his camp *after dark*. Something strange about this, Duane. But MacNelly's a new man out here. He does some queer things. Perhaps he's getting a swelled head. Well, whatever his intentions, his presence around Mercer is enough for us. Duane, you hit the road and put some miles between you the amiable Captain before daylight. Tomorrow I'll go out there and ask him what in the devil he meant."

"That messenger he sent—he was a ranger," said Duane.

"Sure he was, and a nervy one! It must have taken sand to come bracing you that way. Duane, the fellow didn't pack a gun. I'll swear to that. Pretty odd, this trick. But you can't trust it. Hit the road, Duane."

A little later a black horse with muffled hoofs, bearing a tall, dark rider who peered keenly into every shadow, trotted down a pasture lane back of Jones's house, turned into the road, and then, breaking into swifter gait, rapidly left Mercer behind.

Fifteen or twenty miles out Duane drew rein in a forest of mesquite, dismounted, and searched about for a glade with a little grass. Here he staked his horse on a long lariat; and, using his saddle for a pillow, his saddle-blanket for covering, he went to sleep.

Next morning he was off again, working south. During the next few days he paid brief visits to several villages that lay in his path. And in each some one particular friend had a piece of news to impart that made Duane profoundly thoughtful. A ranger had made a quiet, unobtrusive call upon these friends and left this message, "Tell Buck Duane to ride into Captain MacNelly's camp sometime after night."

Duane concluded, and his friends all agreed with him, that the new ranger's main purpose in the Nueces country was to capture or kill Buck Duane, and that this message was simply an original and striking ruse, the daring of which might appeal to certain outlaws.

But it did not appeal to Duane. His curiosity was aroused; it did not, however, tempt him to any foolhardy act. He turned southwest and rode a hundred miles until he again reached the sparsely settled country. Here he heard no more of rangers. It was a barren region he had never but once ridden through, and that ride had cost him dear. He had been compelled to shoot his way out. Outlaws were not in accord with the few ranchers and their cowboys who ranged there. He learned that both outlaws and Mexican raiders had long been at bitter enmity with these ranchers. Being unfamiliar with roads and trails, Duane had pushed on into the heart of this district, when all the time he really believed he was traveling around it. A rifle shot from a ranch house, a deliberate attempt to kill him because he was an unknown rider in those parts, discovered to Duane his mistake; and a hard ride to get away persuaded him to return to his old methods of hiding by day and traveling by night.

He got into rough country, rode for three days without covering much ground, but believed that he was getting on safer territory. Twice he came to a wide bottomland green with willow and cottonwood and thick as chaparral, somewhere through the middle of which ran a river he decided must be the lower Nueces.

One evening, as he stole out from a covert where he had camped, he saw the lights of a village. He tried to pass it on the left, but was unable to because the brakes of this bottomland extended in almost to the outskirts of the village, and he had to retrace his steps and go round to the right. Wire fences and horses in pasture made this a task, so it was well after midnight before he accomplished it. He made ten miles or more then by daylight, and after that proceeded cautiously along a road which appeared to be well worn from travel. He passed several thickets where he would have halted to hide during the day but for the fact that he had to find water.

He was a long while in coming to it, and then there was no thicket or clump of mesquite near the waterhole that would afford him covert. So he kept on.

The country before him was ridgy and began to show cottonwoods here and there in the hollows and yucca and mesquite on the higher ground. As he mounted a ridge he noted that the road made a sharp turn, and he could not see what was beyond it. He slowed up and was making the turn, which was down-hill between high banks of yellow clay, when his mettlesome horse heard something to frighten him or shied at something and bolted.

The few bounds he took before Duane's iron arm checked him were enough to reach the curve. One flashing glance showed Duane the open once more, a little valley below with a wide, shallow, rocky stream, a clump of cottonwoods beyond, a somber group of men facing him, and two dark, limp, strangely grotesque figures hanging from branches.

The sight was common enough in southwest Texas, but Duane had never before found himself so unpleasantly close.

A hoarse voice pealed out: "By hell! There's another one!"

"Stranger, ride down an' account fer yourself!" yelled another.

"Hands up!"

"Thet's right, Jack; don't take no chances. Plug him!"

These remarks were so swiftly uttered as almost to be continuous. Duane was wheeling his horse when a rifle cracked. The bullet struck his left forearm and he thought broke it, for he dropped the rein. The frightened horse leaped. Another bullet whistled past Duane. Then the bend in the road saved him probably from certain death. Like the wind his fleet steed wend down the long hill.

Duane was in no hurry to look back. He knew what to expect. His chief concern of the moment was for his injured arm. He found that the bones were still intact; but the wound, having been made by a soft bullet, was an exceedingly bad one. Blood poured from it. Giving the horse his head, Duane wound his scarf tightly round the holes, and with teeth and hand tied it tightly. That done, he looked back over his shoulder.

Riders were making the dust fly on the hillside road. There were more coming round the cut where the road curved. The leader was perhaps a quarter of a mile back, and the others strung out behind him. Duane needed only one glance to tell him that they were fast and hard-riding cowboys in a land where all riders were good. They would not have owned any but strong, swift horses. Moreover, it was a district where ranchers had suffered beyond all endurance the greed and brutality of outlaws. Duane had simply been so unfortunate as to run right into a lynching party at a time of all times when any stranger would be in danger and any outlaw put to his limit to escape with his life.

Duane did not look back again till he had crossed the ridgy piece of ground and had gotten to the level road. He had gained upon his pursuers. When he ascertained this he tried to save his horse, to check a little that killing gait. This horse was a magnificent animal, big, strong, fast; but his endurance had never been put to a grueling test. And that worried Duane. His life had made it impossible to keep one horse very long at a time, and this one was an unknown quantity.

Duane had only one plan—the only plan possible in this case—and that was to make the river bottoms, where he might elude his pursuers in the willow brakes. Fifteen miles or so would bring him to the river, and this was not a hopeless distance for any good horse if not too closely pressed. Duane concluded presently that the cowboys behind were losing a little in the chase because they were not extending their horses. It was decidedly unusual for such riders to save their mounts. Duane pondered over this, looking backward several times to see if their horses were stretched out. They were not, and the fact was disturbing. Only one reason presented itself to Duane's conjecturing, and it was that with him headed straight on that road his pursuers were satisfied not to force the running. He began to hope and look for a trail or a road turning off to right or left. There was none. A rough, mesquite-dotted and yucca-spired country extended away on either side. Duane believed that he would be compelled to take to this hard going. One thing was certain—he had to go round the village. The river, however, was on the outskirts of the village; and once in the willows, he would be safe.

Dust clouds far ahead caused his alarm to grow. He watched with his eyes strained; he hoped to see a wagon, a few stray cattle. But no, he soon descried several horsemen. Shots and yells behind him attested to the fact that his pursuers likewise had seen these newcomers on the scene. More than a mile separated these two parties, yet that distance did not keep them from soon understanding each other. Duane waited only to see this new factor show signs of sudden quick action, and then, with a muttered curse, he spurred his horse off the road into the brush.

He chose the right side, because the river lay nearer that way. There were patches of open sandy ground between clumps of cactus and mesquite, and he found that despite a zigzag course he made better time. It was impossible for him to locate his pursuers. They would come together, he decided, and take to his tracks.

What, then, was his surprise and dismay to run out of a thicket right into a low ridge of rough, broken rock, impossible to get a horse over. He wheeled to the left along its base. The sandy ground gave place to a harder soil, where his horse did not labor so. Here the growths of mesquite and cactus became scanter, affording better travel but poor cover. He kept sharp eyes ahead, and, as he had expected, soon saw moving dust-clouds and the dark figures of horses. They were half a mile away, and swinging obliquely across the flat, which fact proved that they had entertained a fair idea of the country and the fugitive's difficulty.

Without an instant's hesitation Duane put his horse to his best efforts, straight ahead. He had to pass those men. When this was seemingly made impossible by a deep wash from which he had to turn, Duane began to feel cold and sick. Was this the end? Always there had to be an end to an outlaw's career. He wanted then to ride straight at these pursuers. But reason outweighed instinct. He was fleeing for his life; nevertheless, the strongest instinct at the time was his desire to fight.

He knew when these three horsemen saw him, and a moment afterward he lost sight of them as he got into the mesquite again. He meant now to try to reach the road, and pushed his mount severely, though still saving him for a final burst. Rocks, thickets, bunches of cactus, washes—all operated against his following a straight line. Almost he lost his bearings, and finally would have ridden toward his enemies had not good fortune favored him in the matter of an open burned-over stretch of ground.

Here he saw both groups of pursuers, one on each side and almost within gun-shot. Their sharp yells, as much as his cruel spurs, drove his horse into that pace which now meant life or death for him. And never had Duane bestrode a gamer, swifter, stancher beast. He seemed about to accomplish the impossible. In the dragging sand he was far superior to any horse in pursuit, and on this sandy open stretch he gained enough to spare a little in the brush beyond. Heated now and thoroughly terrorized, he kept the pace through thickets that almost tore Duane from his saddle. Something weighty and grim eased off Duane. He was going to get out in front! The horse had speed, fire, stamina.

Duane dashed out into another open place dotted by few trees, and here, right in his path, within pistol range, stood horsemen waiting. They yelled, they spurred toward him, but did not fire at him. He turned his horse—faced to the right. Only one thing kept him from standing his ground to fight it out. He remembered those dangling limp figures hanging from the cottonwoods. These ranchers would rather hang an outlaw than do anything. They might draw all his fire and then capture him. His horror of hanging was so great as to be all out of proportion compared to his gunfighter's instinct of self-preservation.

A race began then, a dusty, crashing drive through gray mesquite. Duane could scarcely see, he was so blinded by stinging branches across his eyes. The hollow wind roared in his ears. He lost his sense of the nearness of his pursuers. But they must have been close. Did they shoot at him? He imagined he heard shots. But that might have been the cracking of dead snags. His left arm hung limp, almost useless; he handled the rein with his right; and most of the time he hung low over the pommel. The gray walls flashing by him, the whip of twigs, the rush of wind, the heavy, rapid pound of hoofs, the violent motion of his horse—these vied in sensation with the smart of sweat in his eyes, the rack of his wound, the cold, sick cramp in his stomach. With these also was dull, raging fury. He had to run when he wanted to fight. It took all his mind to force back that bitter hate of himself, of his pursuers, of this race for his useless life.

Suddenly he burst out of a line of mesquite into the road. A long stretch of lonely road! How fiercely, with hot, strange joy, he wheeled his horse upon it! Then he was sweeping along, sure now that he was out in front. His horse still had strength and speed, but showed signs of breaking. Presently Duane looked back. Pursuers—he could not count how many—were loping along in his rear. He paid no more attention to them, and with teeth set he faced ahead, grimmer now in his determination to foil them.

He passed a few scattered ranch houses where horses whistled from corrals, and men curiously watched him fly past. He saw one rancher running, and he felt intuitively that this fellow was going to join in the chase. Duane's steed pounded on, not noticeably slower, but with a lack of former smoothness, with a strained, convulsive, jolting stride which showed he was almost done.

Sight of the village ahead surprised Duane. He had reached it sooner than he expected. Then he made a discovery—he had entered the zone of wire fences. As he dared not turn back now, he kept on, intending to ride through the village. Looking backward, he saw that his pursuers were half a mile distant, too far to alarm any villagers in time to intercept him in his flight. As he rode by the first houses his horse broke and began to labor. Duane did not believe he would last long enough to go through the village.

Saddled horses in front of a store gave Duane an idea, not by any means new, and one he had carried out successfully before. As he pulled in his heaving mount and leaped off, a couple of ranchers came out of the place, and one of them stepped to a clean-limbed, fiery bay. He was about to get into his saddle when he saw Duane, and then he halted, a foot in the stirrup.

Duane strode forward, grasped the bridle of this man's horse.

"Mine's done—but not killed," he panted. "Trade with me."

"Wal, stranger, I'm shore always ready to trade," drawled the man. "But ain't you a little swift?"

Duane glanced back up the road. His pursuers were entering the village.

"I'm Duane—Buck Duane," he cried, menacingly. "Will you trade? Hurry!"

The rancher, turning white, dropped his foot from the stirrup and fell back.

"I reckon I'll trade," he said.

Bounding up, Duane dug spurs into the bay's flanks. The horse snorted in fright, plunged into a run. He was fresh, swift, half wild. Duane flashed by the remaining houses on the street out into the open. But the road ended at that village or else led out from some other quarter, for he had ridden straight into the fields and from them into rough desert. When he reached the cover of mesquite once more he looked back to find six horsemen within rifle shot of him, and more coming behind them.

His new horse had not had time to get warm before Duane reached a high sandy bluff below which lay the willow brakes. As far as he could see extended an immense flat strip of red-tinged willow. How welcome it was to his eye! He felt like a hunted wolf that, weary and lame, had reached his hole in the rocks. Zigzagging down the soft slope, he put the bay to the dense wall of leaf and branch. But the horse balked.

There was little time to lose. Dismounting, he dragged the stubborn beast into the thicket. This was harder and slower work than Duane cared to risk. If he had not been rushed he might have had better success. So he had to abandon the horse—a circumstance that only such sore straits could have driven him to. Then he went slipping swiftly through the narrow aisles.

He had not gotten under cover any too soon. For he heard his pursuers piling over the bluff, loud-voiced, confident, brutal. They crashed into the willows.

"Hi, Sid! Heah's your hoss!" called one, evidently to the man Duane had forced into a trade.

"Say, if you locoed gents'll hold up a little I'll tell you somethin'," replied a voice from the bluff.

"Come on, Sid! We got him corralled," said the first speaker.

"Wal, mebbe, an' if you hev it's liable to be damn hot. *Thet feller was Buck Duane!*"

Absolute silence followed that statement. Presently it was broken by a rattling of loose gravel and then low voices.

"He can't git across the river, I tell you," came to Duane's ears. "He's corralled in the brake. I know thet hole."

Then Duane, gliding silently and swiftly through the willows, heard no more from his pursuers. He headed straight for the river. Threading a passage through a willow brake was an old task for him. Many days and nights had gone to the acquiring of a skill that might have been envied by an Indian.

The Rio Grande and its tributaries for the most of their length in Texas ran between wide, low, flat lands covered by a dense growth of willow. Cottonwood, mesquite, prickly pear, and other growths mingled with the willow, and altogether they made a matted, tangled copse, a thicket that an inexperienced man would have considered impenetrable. From above, these wild brakes looked green and red; from the inside they were gray and yellow—a striped wall. Trails and glades were scarce. There were a few deer-runways and sometimes little paths made by peccaries—the jabali, or wild pigs, of Mexico. The ground was clay and unusually dry, sometimes baked so hard that it left no imprint of a track. Where a growth of cottonwood had held back the encroachment of the willows there usually was thick grass and underbrush. The willows were short, slender poles with stems so close together that they almost touched, and with the leafy foliage forming a thick covering. The depths of this brake Duane had penetrated was a silent, dreamy, strange place. In the middle of the day the light was weird and dim. When a breeze fluttered the foliage, then slender shafts and spears of sunshine pierced the green mantle and danced like gold on the ground.

Duane had always felt the strangeness of this kind of place, and likewise he had felt a protecting, harboring something which always seemed to him to be the sympathy of the brake for a hunted creature. Any unwounded creature, strong and resourceful, was safe when he had glided under the low, rustling green roof of this wild covert. It was not hard to conceal tracks; the springy soil gave forth no sound; and men could hunt each other for weeks, pass within a few yards of each other and never know it. The problem of sustaining life was difficult; but, then, hunted men and animals survived on very little.

Duane wanted to cross the river if that was possible, and, keeping in the brake, work his way upstream till he had reached country more hospitable. Remembering what the man had said in regard to the river, Duane had his doubts about crossing. But he would take any chance to put the river between him and his hunters. He pushed on. His left arm had to be favored, as he could scarcely move it. Using his right to spread the willows, he slipped sideways between them and made fast time. There were narrow aisles and washes and holes low down and paths brushed by animals, all of which he took advantage of, running, walking, crawling, stooping any way to get along. To keep in a straight line was not easy—he did it by marking some bright sunlit stem or tree ahead, and when he reached it looked straight on to mark another. His progress necessarily grew slower, for as he advanced the brake became wilder, denser, darker. Mosquitoes began to whine about his head. He kept on without pause. Deepening shadows under the willows told him that the afternoon was far advanced. He began to fear he had wandered in a wrong direction. Finally a strip of light ahead relieved his anxiety, and after a toilsome penetration of still denser brush he broke through to the bank of the river.

He faced a wide, shallow, muddy stream with brakes on the opposite bank extending like a green and yellow wall. Duane perceived at a glance the futility of his trying to cross at this point. Everywhere the sluggish water raved quicksand bars. In fact, the bed of the river was all quicksand, and very likely there was not a foot of water anywhere. He could not swim; he could not crawl; he could not push a log across. Any solid thing touching that smooth yellow sand would be grasped and sucked down. To prove this he seized a long pole and, reaching down from the high bank, thrust it into the stream. Right there near shore there apparently was no bottom to the treacherous quicksand. He abandoned any hope of crossing the river. Probably for miles up and down it would be just the same as here. Before leaving the bank he tied his hat upon the pole and lifted enough water to quench his thirst. Then he worked his way back to where thinner growth made advancement easier, and kept on up-stream till the shadows were so deep he could not see. Feeling around for a place big enough to stretch out on, he lay down. For the time being he was as safe there as he would have been beyond in the Rim Rock. He was tired, though not exhausted, and in spite of the throbbing pain in his arm he dropped at once into sleep.

## CHAPTER XII

Sometime during the night Duane awoke. A stillness seemingly so thick and heavy as to have substance blanketed the black willow brake. He could not see a star or a branch or tree trunk or even his hand before his eyes. He lay there waiting, listening, sure that he had been awakened by an unusual sound. Ordinary noises of the night in the wilderness never disturbed his rest. His faculties, like those of old fugitives and hunted creatures, had become trained to a marvelous keenness. A long low breath of slow wind moaned through the willows, passed away; some stealthy, soft-footed beast trotted by him in the darkness; there was a rustling among dry leaves; a fox barked lonesomely in the distance. But none of these sounds had broken his slumber.

Suddenly, piercing the stillness, came a bay of a bloodhound. Quickly Duane sat up, chilled to his marrow. The action made him aware of his crippled arm. Then came other bays, lower, more distant. Silence enfolded him again, all the more oppressive and menacing in his suspense. Bloodhounds had been put on his trail, and the leader was not far away. All his life Duane had been familiar with bloodhounds; and he knew that if the pack surrounded him in this impenetrable darkness he would be held at bay or dragged down as wolves dragged a stag. Rising to his feet, prepared to flee as best he could, he waited to be sure of the direction he should take.

The leader of the hounds broke into cry again, a deep, full-toned, ringing bay, strange, ominous, terribly significant in its power. It caused a cold sweat to ooze out all over Duane's body. He turned from it, and with his uninjured arm outstretched to feel for the willows he groped his way along. As it was impossible to pick out the narrow passages, he had to slip and squeeze and plunge between the yielding stems. He made such a crashing that he no longer heard the baying of the hounds. He had no hope to elude them. He meant to climb the first cottonwood that he stumbled upon in his blind flight. But it appeared he never was going to be lucky enough to run against one. Often he fell, sometimes flat, at others upheld by the willows. What made the work so hard was the fact that he had only one arm to open a clump of close-growing stems and his feet would catch or tangle in the narrow crotches, holding him fast. He had to struggle desperately. It was as if the willows were clutching hands, his enemies, fiendishly impeding his progress. He tore his clothes on sharp branches and his flesh suffered many a prick. But in a terrible earnestness he kept on until he brought up hard against a cottonwood tree.

There he leaned and rested. He found himself as nearly exhausted as he had ever been, wet with sweat, his hands torn and burning, his breast laboring, his legs stinging from innumerable bruises. While he leaned there to catch his breath he listened for the pursuing hounds. For a long time there was no sound from them. This, however, did not deceive him into any hopefulness. There were bloodhounds that bayed often on a trail, and others that ran mostly silent. The former were more valuable to their owner and the latter more dangerous to the fugitive. Presently Duane's ears were filled by a chorus of short ringing yelps. The pack had found where he had slept, and now the trail was hot. Satisfied that they would soon overtake him, Duane set about climbing the cottonwood, which in his condition was difficult of ascent.

It happened to be a fairly large tree with a fork about fifteen feet up, and branches thereafter in succession. Duane climbed until he got above the enshrouding belt of blackness. A pale gray mist hung above the brake, and through it shone a line of dim lights. Duane decided these were bonfires made along the bluff to render his escape more difficult on that side. Away round in the direction he thought was north he imagined he saw more fires, but, as the mist was thick, he could not be sure. While he sat there pondering the matter, listening for the hounds, the mist and the gloom on one side lightened; and this side he concluded was east and meant that dawn was near. Satisfying himself on this score, he descended to the first branch of the tree.

His situation now, though still critical, did not appear to be so hopeless as it had been. The hounds would soon close in on him, and he would kill them or drive them away. It was beyond the bounds of possibility that any men could have followed running hounds through that brake in the night. The thing that worried Duane was the fact of the bonfires. He had gathered from the words of one of his pursuers that the brake was a kind of trap, and he began to believe there was only one way out of it, and that was along the bank where he had entered, and where obviously all night long his pursuers had kept fires burning. Further conjecture on this point, however, was interrupted by a crashing in the willows and the rapid patter of feet.

Underneath Duane lay a gray, foggy obscurity. He could not see the ground, nor any object but the black trunk of the tree. Sight would not be needed to tell him when the pack arrived. With a pattering rush through the willows the hounds reached the tree; and then high above crash of brush and thud of heavy paws rose a hideous clamor. Duane's pursuers far off to the south would hear that and know what it meant. And at daybreak, perhaps before, they would take a short cut across the brake, guided by the baying of hounds that had treed their quarry.

It wanted only a few moments, however, till Duane could distinguish the vague forms of the hounds in the gray shadow below. Still he waited. He had no shots to spare. And he knew how to treat bloodhounds. Gradually the obscurity lightened, and at length Duane had good enough sight of the hounds for his purpose. His first shot killed the huge brute leader of the pack. Then, with unerring shots, he crippled several others. That stopped the baying. Piercing howls arose. The pack took fright and fled, its course easily marked by the howls of the crippled members. Duane reloaded his gun, and, making certain all the hounds had gone, he descended to the ground and set off at a rapid pace to the northward.

The mist had dissolved under a rising sun when Duane made his first halt some miles north of the scene where he had waited for the hounds. A barrier to further progress, in shape of a precipitous rocky bluff, rose sheer from the willow brake. He skirted the base of the cliff, where walking was comparatively easy, around in the direction of the river. He reached the end finally to see there was absolutely no chance to escape from the brake at that corner. It took extreme labor, attended by some hazard and considerable pain to his arm, to get down where he could fill his sombrero with water. After quenching his thirst he had a look at his wound. It was caked over with blood and dirt. When washed off the arm was seen to be inflamed and swollen around the bullet hole. He bathed it, experiencing a soothing relief in the cool water. Then he bandaged it as best he could and arranged a sling round his neck. This mitigated the pain of the injured member and held it in a quiet and restful position, where it had a chance to begin mending.

As Duane turned away from the river he felt refreshed. His great strength and endurance had always made fatigue something almost unknown to him. However, tramping on foot day and night was as unusual to him as to any other riders of the Southwest, and it had begun to tell on him. Retracing his steps, he reached the point where he had abruptly come upon the bluff, and here he determined to follow along its base in the other direction until he found a way out or discovered the futility of such effort.

Duane covered ground rapidly. From time to time he paused to listen. But he was always listening, and his eyes were ever roving. This alertness had become second nature with him, so that except in extreme cases of caution he performed it while he pondered his gloomy and fateful situation. Such habit of alertness and thought made time fly swiftly.

By noon he had rounded the wide curve of the brake and was facing south. The bluff had petered out from a high, mountainous wall to a low abutment of rock, but it still held to its steep, rough nature and afforded no crack or slope where quick ascent could have been possible. He pushed on, growing warier as he approached the danger zone, finding that as he neared the river on this side it was imperative to go deeper into the willows. In the afternoon he reached a point where he could see men pacing to and fro on the bluff. This assured him that whatever place was guarded was one by which he might escape. He headed toward these men and approached to within a hundred paces of the bluff where they were. There were several men and several boys, all armed and, after the manner of Texans, taking their task leisurely. Farther down Duane made out black dots on the horizon of the bluff line, and these he concluded were more guards stationed at another outlet. Probably all the available men in the district were on duty. Texans took a grim pleasure in such work. Duane remembered that upon several occasions he had served such duty himself.

Duane peered through the branches and studied the lay of the land. For several hundred yards the bluff could be climbed. He took stock of those careless guards. They had rifles, and that made vain any attempt to pass them in daylight. He believed an attempt by night might be successful; and he was swiftly coming to a determination to hide there till dark and then try it, when the sudden yelping of a dog betrayed him to the guards on the bluff.

The dog had likely been placed there to give an alarm, and he was lustily true to his trust. Duane saw the men run together and begin to talk excitedly and peer into the brake, which was a signal for him to slip away under the willows. He made no noise, and he assured himself he must be invisible. Nevertheless, he heard shouts, then the cracking of rifles, and bullets began to zip and swish through the leafy covert. The day was hot and windless, and Duane concluded that whenever he touched a willow stem, even ever so slightly, it vibrated to the top and sent a quiver among the leaves. Through this the guards had located his position. Once a bullet hissed by him; another thudded into the ground before him. This shooting loosed a rage in Duane. He had to fly from these men, and he hated them and himself because of it. Always in the fury of such moments he wanted to give back shot for shot. But he slipped on through the willows, and at length the rifles ceased to crack.

He sheered to the left again, in line with the rocky barrier, and kept on, wondering what the next mile would bring.

It brought worse, for he was seen by sharp-eyed scouts, and a hot fusillade drove him to run for his life, luckily to escape with no more than a bullet-creased shoulder.

Later that day, still undaunted, he sheered again toward the trap-wall, and found that the nearer he approached to the place where he had come down into the brake the greater his danger. To attempt to run the blockade of that trail by day would be fatal. He waited for night, and after the brightness of the fires had somewhat lessened he assayed to creep out of the brake. He succeeded in reaching the foot of the bluff, here only a bank, and had begun to crawl stealthily up under cover of a shadow when a hound again betrayed his position. Retreating to the willows was as perilous a task as had ever confronted Duane, and when he had accomplished it, right under what seemed a hundred blazing rifles, he felt that he had indeed been favored by Providence. This time men followed him a goodly ways into the brake, and the ripping of lead through the willows sounded on all sides of him.

When the noise of pursuit ceased Duane sat down in the darkness, his mind clamped between two things—whether to try again to escape or wait for possible opportunity. He seemed incapable of decision. His intelligence told him that every hour lessened his chances for escape. He had little enough chance in any case, and that was what made another attempt so desperately hard. Still it was not love of life that bound him. There would come an hour, sooner or later, when he would wrench decision out of this chaos of emotion and thought. But that time was not yet. He had remained quiet long enough to cool off and recover from his run he found that he was tired. He stretched out to rest. But the swarms of vicious mosquitoes prevented sleep. This corner of the brake was low and near the river, a breeding ground for the bloodsuckers. They sang and hummed and whined around him in an ever-increasing horde. He covered his head and hands with his coat and lay there patiently. That was a long and wretched night. Morning found him still strong physically, but in a dreadful state of mind.

First he hurried for the river. He could withstand the pangs of hunger, but it was imperative to quench thirst. His wound made him feverish, and therefore more than usually hot and thirsty. Again he was refreshed. That morning he was hard put to it to hold himself back from attempting to cross the river. If he could find a light log it was within the bounds of possibility that he might ford the shallow water and bars of quicksand. But not yet! Wearily, doggedly he faced about toward the bluff.

All that day and all that night, all the next day and all the next night, he stole like a hunted savage from river to bluff; and every hour forced upon him the bitter certainty that he was trapped.

Duane lost track of days, of events. He had come to an evil pass. There arrived an hour when, closely pressed by pursuers at the extreme southern corner of the brake, he took to a dense thicket of willows, driven to what he believed was his last stand.

If only these human bloodhounds would swiftly close in on him! Let him fight to the last bitter gasp and have it over! But these hunters, eager as they were to get him, had care of their own skins. They took few risks. They had him cornered.

It was the middle of the day, hot, dusty, oppressive, threatening storm. Like a snake Duane crawled into a little space in the darkest part of the thicket and lay still. Men had cut him off from the bluff, from the river, seemingly from all sides. But he heard voices only from in front and toward his left. Even if his passage to the river had not been blocked, it might just as well have been.

"Come on fellers—down hyar," called one man from the bluff.

"Got him corralled at last," shouted another.

"Reckon ye needn't be too shore. We thought thet more 'n once," taunted another.

"I seen him, I tell you."

"Aw, thet was a deer."

"But Bill found fresh tracks an' blood on the willows."

"If he's winged we needn't hurry."

"Hold on thar, you boys," came a shout in authoritative tones from farther up the bluff. "Go slow. You-all air gittin' foolish at the end of a long chase."

"Thet's right, Colonel. Hold 'em back. There's nothin' shorer than somebody'll be stoppin' lead pretty quick. He'll be huntin' us soon!"

"Let's surround this corner an' starve him out."

"Fire the brake."

How clearly all this talk pierced Duane's ears! In it he seemed to hear his doom. This, then, was the end he had always expected, which had been close to him before, yet never like now.

"By God!" whispered Duane, "the thing for me to do now—is go out—meet them!"

That was prompted by the fighting, the killing instinct in him. In that moment it had almost superhuman power. If he must die, that was the way for him to die. What else could be expected of Buck Duane? He got to his knees and drew his gun. With his swollen and almost useless hand he held what spare ammunition he had left. He ought to creep out noiselessly to the edge of the willows, suddenly face his pursuers, then, while there was a beat left in his heart, kill, kill, kill. These men all had rifles. The fight would be short. But the marksmen did not live on earth who could make such a fight go wholly against him. Confronting them suddenly he could kill a man for every shot in his gun.

Thus Duane reasoned. So he hoped to accept his fate—to meet this end. But when he tried to step forward something checked him. He forced himself; yet he could not go. The obstruction that opposed his will was as insurmountable as it had been physically impossible for him to climb the bluff.

Slowly he fell back, crouched low, and then lay flat. The grim and ghastly dignity that had been his a moment before fell away from him. He lay there stripped of his last shred of self-respect. He wondered was he afraid; had he, the last of the Duanes—had he come to feel fear? No! Never in all his wild life had he so longed to go out and meet men face to face. It was not fear that held him back. He hated this hiding, this eternal vigilance, this hopeless life. The damnable paradox of the situation was that if he went out to meet these men there was absolutely no doubt of his doom. If he clung to his covert there was a chance, a merest chance, for his life. These pursuers, dogged and unflagging as they had been, were mortally afraid of him. It was his fame that made them cowards. Duane's keenness told him that at the very darkest and most perilous moment there was still a chance for him. And the blood in him, the temper of his father, the years of his outlawry, the pride of his unsought and hated career, the nameless, inexplicable something in him made him accept that slim chance.

Waiting then became a physical and mental agony. He lay under the burning sun, parched by thirst, laboring to breathe, sweating and bleeding. His uncared-for wound was like a red-hot prong in his flesh. Blotched and swollen from the never-ending attack of flies and mosquitoes his face seemed twice its natural size, and it ached and stung.

On one side, then, was this physical torture; on the other the old hell, terribly augmented at this crisis, in his mind. It seemed that thought and imagination had never been so swift. If death found him presently, how would it come? Would he get decent burial or be left for the peccaries and the coyotes? Would his people ever know where he had fallen? How wretched, how miserable his state! It was cowardly, it was monstrous for him to cling longer to this doomed life. Then the hate in his heart, the hellish hate of these men on his trail—that was like a scourge. He felt no longer human. He had degenerated into an animal that could think. His heart pounded, his pulse beat, his breast heaved; and this internal strife seemed to thunder into his ears. He was now enacting the tragedy of all crippled, starved, hunted wolves at bay in their dens. Only his tragedy was infinitely more terrible because he had mind enough to see his plight, his resemblance to a lonely wolf, bloody-fanged, dripping, snarling, fire-eyed in a last instinctive defiance.

Mounted upon the horror of Duane's thought was a watching, listening intensity so supreme that it registered impressions which were creations of his imagination. He heard stealthy steps that were not there; he saw shadowy moving figures that were only leaves. A hundred times when he was about to pull trigger he discovered his error. Yet voices came from a distance, and steps and crackings in the willows, and other sounds real enough. But Duane could not distinguish the real from the false. There were times when the wind which had arisen sent a hot, pattering breath down the willow aisles, and Duane heard it as an approaching army.

This straining of Duane's faculties brought on a reaction which in itself was a respite. He saw the sun darkened by thick slow spreading clouds. A storm appeared to be coming. How slowly it moved! The air was like steam. If there broke one of those dark, violent storms common though rare to the country, Duane believed he might slip away in the fury of wind and rain. Hope, that seemed unquenchable in him, resurged again. He hailed it with a bitterness that was sickening.

Then at a rustling step he froze into the old strained attention. He heard a slow patter of soft feet. A tawny shape crossed a little opening in the thicket. It was that of a dog. The moment while that beast came into full view was an age. The dog was not a bloodhound, and if he had a trail or a scent he seemed to be at fault on it. Duane waited for the inevitable discovery. Any kind of a hunting-dog could have found him in that thicket. Voices from outside could be heard urging on the dog. Rover they called him. Duane sat up at the moment the dog entered the little shaded covert. Duane expected a yelping, a baying, or at least a bark that would tell of his hiding-place. A strange relief swiftly swayed over Duane. The end was near now. He had no further choice. Let them come—a quick fierce exchange of shots—and then this torture past! He waited for the dog to give the alarm.

But the dog looked at him and trotted by into the thicket without a yelp. Duane could not believe the evidence of his senses. He thought he had suddenly gone deaf. He saw the dog disappear, heard him running to and fro among the willows, getting farther and farther away, till all sound from him ceased.

"Thar's Rover," called a voice from the bluff-side. "He's been through thet black patch."

"Nary a rabbit in there," replied another.

"Bah! Thet pup's no good," scornfully growled another man. "Put a hound at thet clump of willows."

"Fire's the game. Burn the brake before the rain comes."

The voices droned off as their owners evidently walked up the ridge.

Then upon Duane fell the crushing burden of the old waiting, watching, listening spell. After all, it was not to end just now. His chance still persisted—looked a little brighter—led him on, perhaps, to forlorn hope.

All at once twilight settled quickly down upon the willow brake, or else Duane noted it suddenly. He imagined it to be caused by the approaching storm. But there was little movement of air or cloud, and thunder still muttered and rumbled at a distance. The fact was the sun had set, and at this time of overcast sky night was at hand.

Duane realized it with the awakening of all his old force. He would yet elude his pursuers. That was the moment when he seized the significance of all these fortunate circumstances which had aided him. Without haste and without sound he began to crawl in the direction of the river. It was not far, and he reached the bank before darkness set in. There were men up on the bluff carrying wood to build a bonfire. For a moment he half yielded to a temptation to try to slip along the river shore, close in under the willows. But when he raised himself to peer out he saw that an attempt of this kind would be liable to failure. At the same moment he saw a rough-hewn plank lying beneath him, lodged against some willows. The end of the plank extended in almost to a point beneath him. Quick as a flash he saw where a desperate chance invited him. Then he tied his gun in an oilskin bag and put it in his pocket.

The bank was steep and crumbly. He must not break off any earth to splash into the water. There was a willow growing back some few feet from the edge of the bank. Cautiously he pulled it down, bent it over the water so that when he released it there would be no springing back. Then he trusted his weight to it, with his feet sliding carefully down the bank. He went into the water almost up to his knees, felt the quicksand grip his feet; then, leaning forward till he reached the plank, he pulled it toward him and lay upon it.

Without a sound one end went slowly under water and the farther end appeared lightly braced against the overhanging willows. Very carefully then Duane began to extricate his right foot from the sucking sand. It seemed as if his foot was incased in solid rock. But there was a movement upward, and he pulled with all the power he dared use. It came slowly and at length was free. The left one he released with less difficulty. The next few moments he put all his attention on the plank to ascertain if his weight would sink it into the sand. The far end slipped off the willows with a little splash and gradually settled to rest upon the bottom. But it sank no farther, and Duane's greatest concern was relieved. However, as it was manifestly impossible for him to keep his head up for long he carefully crawled out upon the plank until he could rest an arm and shoulder upon the willows.

When he looked up it was to find the night strangely luminous with fires. There was a bonfire on the extreme end of the bluff, another a hundred paces beyond. A great flare extended over the brake in that direction. Duane heard a roaring on the wind, and he knew his pursuers had fired the willows. He did not believe that would help them much. The brake was dry enough, but too green to burn readily. And as for the bonfires he discovered that the men, probably having run out of wood, were keeping up the light with oil and stuff from the village. A dozen men kept watch on the bluff scarcely fifty paces from where Duane lay concealed by the willows. They talked, cracked jokes, sang songs, and manifestly considered this outlaw hunting a great lark. As long as the bright light lasted Duane dared not move. He had the patience and the endurance to wait for the breaking of the storm, and if that did not come, then the early hour before dawn when the gray fog and gloom were over the river.

Escape was now in his grasp. He felt it. And with that in his mind he waited, strong as steel in his conviction, capable of withstanding any strain endurable by the human frame.

The wind blew in puffs, grew wilder, and roared through the willows, carrying bright sparks upward. Thunder rolled down over the river, and lightning began to flash. Then the rain fell in heavy sheets, but not steadily. The flashes of lightning and the broad flares played so incessantly that Duane could not trust himself out on the open river. Certainly the storm rather increased the watchfulness of the men on the bluff. He knew how to wait, and he waited, grimly standing pain and cramp and chill. The storm wore away as desultorily as it had come, and the long night set in. There were times when Duane thought he was paralyzed, others when he grew sick, giddy, weak from the strained posture. The first paling of the stars quickened him with a kind of wild joy. He watched them grow paler, dimmer, disappear one by one. A shadow hovered down, rested upon the river, and gradually thickened. The bonfire on the bluff showed as through a foggy veil. The watchers were mere groping dark figures.

Duane, aware of how cramped he had become from long inaction, began to move his legs and uninjured arm and body, and at length overcame a paralyzing stiffness. Then, digging his hand in the sand and holding the plank with his knees, he edged it out into the river. Inch by inch he advanced until clear of the willows. Looking upward, he saw the shadowy figures of the men on the bluff. He realized they ought to see him, feared that they would. But he kept on, cautiously, noiselessly, with a heart-numbing slowness. From time to time his elbow made a little gurgle and splash in the water. Try as he might, he could not prevent this. It got to be like the hollow roar of a rapid filling his ears with mocking sound. There was a perceptible current out in the river, and it hindered straight advancement. Inch by inch he crept on, expecting to hear the bang of rifles, the spattering of bullets. He tried not to look backward, but failed. The fire appeared a little dimmer, the moving shadows a little darker.

Once the plank stuck in the sand and felt as if it were settling. Bringing feet to aid his hand, he shoved it over the treacherous place. This way he made faster progress. The obscurity of the river seemed to be enveloping him. When he looked back again the figures of the men were coalescing with the surrounding gloom, the fires were streaky, blurred patches of light. But the sky above was brighter. Dawn was not far off.

To the west all was dark. With infinite care and implacable spirit and waning strength Duane shoved the plank along, and when at last he discerned the black border of bank it came in time, he thought, to save him. He crawled out, rested till the gray dawn broke, and then headed north through the willows.

## CHAPTER XIII

How long Duane was traveling out of that region he never knew. But he reached familiar country and found a rancher who had before befriended him. Here his arm was attended to; he had food and sleep; and in a couple of weeks he was himself again.

When the time came for Duane to ride away on his endless trail his friend reluctantly imparted the information that some thirty miles south, near the village of Shirley, there was posted at a certain cross-road a reward for Buck Duane dead or alive. Duane had heard of such notices, but he had never seen one. His friend's reluctance and refusal to state for what particular deed this reward was offered roused Duane's curiosity. He had never been any closer to Shirley than this rancher's home. Doubtless some post-office burglary, some gun-shooting scrape had been attributed to him. And he had been accused of worse deeds. Abruptly Duane decided to ride over there and find out who wanted him dead or alive, and why.

As he started south on the road he reflected that this was the first time he had ever deliberately hunted trouble. Introspection awarded him this knowledge; during that last terrible flight on the lower Nueces and while he lay abed recuperating he had changed. A fixed, immutable, hopeless bitterness abided with him. He had reached the end of his rope. All the power of his mind and soul were unavailable to turn him back from his fate.

That fate was to become an outlaw in every sense of the term, to be what he was credited with being—that is to say, to embrace evil. He had never committed a crime. He wondered now was crime close to him? He reasoned finally that the desperation of crime had been forced upon him, if not its motive; and that if driven, there was no limit to his possibilities. He understood now many of the hitherto inexplicable actions of certain noted outlaws—why they had returned to the scene of the crime that had outlawed them; why they took such strangely fatal chances; why life was no more to them than a breath of wind; why they rode straight into the jaws of death to confront wronged men or hunting rangers, vigilantes, to laugh in their very faces. It was such bitterness as this that drove these men.

Toward afternoon, from the top of a long hill, Duane saw the green fields and trees and shining roofs of a town he considered must be Shirley. And at the bottom of the hill he came upon an intersecting road. There was a placard nailed on the crossroad sign-post. Duane drew rein near it and leaned close to read the faded print. *$1000 Reward for Buck Duane Dead or Alive.* Peering closer to read the finer, more faded print, Duane learned that he was wanted for the murder of Mrs. Jeff Aiken at her ranch near Shirley. The month September was named, but the date was illegible. The reward was offered by the woman's husband, whose name appeared with that of a sheriff's at the bottom of the placard.

Duane read the thing twice. When he straightened he was sick with the horror of his fate, wild with passion at those misguided fools who could believe that he had harmed a woman. Then he remembered Kate Bland, and, as always when she returned to him, he quaked inwardly. Years before word had gone abroad that he had killed her, and so it was easy for men wanting to fix a crime to name him. Perhaps it had been done often. Probably he bore on his shoulders a burden of numberless crimes.

A dark, passionate fury possessed him. It shook him like a storm shakes the oak. When it passed, leaving him cold, with clouded brow and piercing eye, his mind was set. Spurring his horse, he rode straight toward the village.

Shirley appeared to be a large, pretentious country town. A branch of some railroad terminated there. The main street was wide, bordered by trees and commodious houses, and many of the stores were of brick. A large plaza shaded by giant cottonwood trees occupied a central location.

Duane pulled his running horse and halted him, plunging and snorting, before a group of idle men who lounged on benches in the shade of a spreading cottonwood. How many times had Duane seen just that kind of lazy shirt-sleeved Texas group! Not often, however, had he seen such placid, lolling, good-natured men change their expression, their attitude so swiftly. His advent apparently was momentous. They evidently took him for an unusual visitor. So far as Duane could tell, not one of them recognized him, had a hint of his identity.

He slid off his horse and threw the bridle.

"I'm Buck Duane," he said. "I saw that placard—out there on a sign-post. It's a damn lie! Somebody find this man Jeff Aiken. I want to see him."

His announcement was taken in absolute silence. That was the only effect he noted, for he avoided looking at these villagers. The reason was simple enough; Duane felt himself overcome with emotion. There were tears in his eyes. He sat down on a bench, put his elbows on his knees and his hands to his face. For once he had absolutely no concern for his fate. This ignominy was the last straw.

Presently, however, he became aware of some kind of commotion among these villagers. He heard whisperings, low, hoarse voices, then the shuffle of rapid feet moving away. All at once a violent hand jerked his gun from its holster. When Duane rose a gaunt man, livid of face, shaking like a leaf, confronted him with his own gun.

"Hands up, thar, you Buck Duane!" he roared, waving the gun.

That appeared to be the cue for pandemonium to break loose. Duane opened his lips to speak, but if he had yelled at the top of his lungs he could not have made himself heard. In weary disgust he looked at the gaunt man, and then at the others, who were working themselves into a frenzy. He made no move, however, to hold up his hands. The villagers surrounded him, emboldened by finding him now unarmed. Then several men lay hold of his arms and pinioned them behind his back. Resistance was useless even if Duane had had the spirit. Some one of them fetched his halter from his saddle, and with this they bound him helpless.

People were running now from the street, the stores, the houses. Old men, cowboys, clerks, boys, ranchers came on the trot. The crowd grew. The increasing clamor began to attract women as well as men. A group of girls ran up, then hung back in fright and pity.

The presence of cowboys made a difference. They split up the crowd, got to Duane, and lay hold of him with rough, businesslike hands. One of them lifted his fists and roared at the frenzied mob to fall back, to stop the racket. He beat them back into a circle; but it was some little time before the hubbub quieted down so a voice could be heard.

"Shut up, will you-all?" he was yelling. "Give us a chance to hear somethin'. Easy now—soho. There ain't nobody goin' to be hurt. Thet's right; everybody quiet now. Let's see what's come off."

This cowboy, evidently one of authority, or at least one of strong personality, turned to the gaunt man, who still waved Duane's gun.

"Abe, put the gun down," he said. "It might go off. Here, give it to me. Now, what's wrong? Who's this roped gent, an' what's he done?"

The gaunt fellow, who appeared now about to collapse, lifted a shaking hand and pointed.

"Thet thar feller—he's Buck Duane!" he panted.

An angry murmur ran through the surrounding crowd.

"The rope! The rope! Throw it over a branch! String him up!" cried an excited villager.

"Buck Duane! Buck Duane!"

"Hang him!"

The cowboy silenced these cries.

"Abe, how do you know this fellow is Buck Duane?" he asked, sharply.

"Why—he said so," replied the man called Abe.

"What!" came the exclamation, incredulously.

"It's a tarnal fact," panted Abe, waving his hands importantly. He was an old man and appeared to be carried away with the significance of his deed. "He like to rid' his hoss right over us-all. Then he jumped off, says he was Buck Duane, an' he wanted to see Jeff Aiken bad."

This speech caused a second commotion as noisy though not so enduring as the first. When the cowboy, assisted by a couple of his mates, had restored order again someone had slipped the noose-end of Duane's rope over his head.

"Up with him!" screeched a wild-eyed youth.

The mob surged closer was shoved back by the cowboys.

"Abe, if you ain't drunk or crazy tell thet over," ordered Abe's interlocutor.

With some show of resentment and more of dignity Abe reiterated his former statement.

"If he's Buck Duane how'n hell did you get hold of his gun?" bluntly queried the cowboy.

"Why—he set down thar—an' he kind of hid his face on his hand. An' I grabbed his gun an' got the drop on him."

What the cowboy thought of this was expressed in a laugh. His mates likewise grinned broadly. Then the leader turned to Duane.

"Stranger, I reckon you'd better speak up for yourself," he said.

That stilled the crowd as no command had done.

"I'm Buck Duane, all right," said Duane, quietly. "It was this way—"

The big cowboy seemed to vibrate with a shock. All the ruddy warmth left his face; his jaw began to bulge; the corded veins in his neck stood out in knots. In an instant he had a hard, stern, strange look. He shot out a powerful hand that fastened in the front of Duane's blouse.

"Somethin' queer here. But if you're Duane you're sure in bad. Any fool ought to know that. You mean it, then?"

"Yes."

"Rode in to shoot up the town, eh? Same old stunt of you gunfighters? Meant to kill the man who offered a reward? Wanted to see Jeff Aiken bad, huh?"

"No," replied Duane. "Your citizen here misrepresented things. He seems a little off his head."

"Reckon he is. Somebody is, that's sure. You claim Buck Duane, then, an' all his doings?"

"I'm Duane; yes. But I won't stand for the blame of things I never did. That's why I'm here. I saw that placard out there offering the reward. Until now I never was within half a day's ride of this town. I'm blamed for what I never did. I rode in here, told who I was, asked somebody to send for Jeff Aiken."

"An' then you set down an' let this old guy throw your own gun on you?" queried the cowboy in amazement.

"I guess that's it," replied Duane.

"Well, it's powerful strange, if you're really Buck Duane."

A man elbowed his way into the circle.

"It's Duane. I recognize him. I seen him in more'n one place," he said. "Sibert, you can rely on what I tell you. I don't know if he's locoed or what. But I do know he's the genuine Buck Duane. Anyone who'd ever seen him onct would never forget him."

"What do you want to see Aiken for?" asked the cowboy Sibert.

"I want to face him, and tell him I never harmed his wife."

"Why?"

"Because I'm innocent, that's all."

"Suppose we send for Aiken an' he hears you an' doesn't believe you; what then?"

"If he won't believe me—why, then my case's so bad—I'd be better off dead."

A momentary silence was broken by Sibert.

"If this isn't a queer deal! Boys, reckon we'd better send for Jeff."

"Somebody went fer him. He'll be comin' soon," replied a man.

Duane stood a head taller than that circle of curious faces. He gazed out above and beyond them. It was in this way that he chanced to see a number of women on the outskirts of the crowd. Some were old, with hard faces, like the men. Some were young and comely, and most of these seemed agitated by excitement or distress. They cast fearful, pitying glances upon Duane as he stood there with that noose round his neck. Women were more human than men, Duane thought. He met eyes that dilated, seemed fascinated at his gaze, but were not averted. It was the old women who were voluble, loud in expression of their feelings.

Near the trunk of the cottonwood stood a slender woman in white. Duane's wandering glance rested upon her. Her eyes were riveted upon him. A soft-hearted woman, probably, who did not want to see him hanged!

"Thar comes Jeff Aiken now," called a man, loudly.

The crowd shifted and trampled in eagerness.

Duane saw two men coming fast, one of whom, in the lead, was of stalwart build. He had a gun in his hand, and his manner was that of fierce energy.

The cowboy Sibert thrust open the jostling circle of men.

"Hold on, Jeff," he called, and he blocked the man with the gun. He spoke so low Duane could not hear what he said, and his form hid Aiken's face. At that juncture the crowd spread out, closed in, and Aiken and Sibert were caught in the circle. There was a pushing forward, a pressing of many bodies, hoarse cries and flinging hands—again the insane tumult was about to break out—the demand for an outlaw's blood, the call for a wild justice executed a thousand times before on Texas's bloody soil.

Sibert bellowed at the dark encroaching mass. The cowboys with him beat and cuffed in vain.

"Jeff, will you listen?" broke in Sibert, hurriedly, his hand on the other man's arm.

Aiken nodded coolly. Duane, who had seen many men in perfect control of themselves under circumstances like these, recognized the spirit that dominated Aiken. He was white, cold, passionless. There were lines of bitter grief deep round his lips. If Duane ever felt the meaning of death he felt it then.

"Sure this 's your game, Aiken," said Sibert. "But hear me a minute. Reckon there's no doubt about this man bein' Buck Duane. He seen the placard out at the cross-roads. He rides in to Shirley. He says he's Buck Duane an' he's lookin' for Jeff Aiken. That's all clear enough. You know how these gunfighters go lookin' for trouble. But here's what stumps me. Duane sits down there on the bench and lets old Abe Strickland grab his gun ant get the drop on him. More'n that, he gives me some strange talk about how, if he couldn't make you believe he's innocent, he'd better be dead. You see for yourself Duane ain't drunk or crazy or locoed. He doesn't strike me as a man who rode in here huntin' blood. So I reckon you'd better hold on till you hear what he has to say."

Then for the first time the drawn-faced, hungry-eyed giant turned his gaze upon Duane. He had intelligence which was not yet subservient to passion. Moreover, he seemed the kind of man Duane would care to have judge him in a critical moment like this.

"Listen," said Duane, gravely, with his eyes steady on Aiken's, "I'm Buck Duane. I never lied to any man in my life. I was forced into outlawry. I've never had a chance to leave the country. I've killed men to save my own life. I never intentionally harmed any woman. I rode thirty miles today— deliberately to see what this reward was, who made it, what for. When I read the placard I went sick to the bottom of my soul. So I rode in here to find you—to tell you this: I never saw Shirley before today. It was impossible for me to have—killed your wife. Last September I was two hundred miles north of here on the upper Nueces. I can prove that. Men who know me will tell you I couldn't murder a woman. I haven't any idea why such a deed should be laid at my hands. It's just that wild border gossip. I have no idea what reasons you have for holding me responsible. I only know—you're wrong. You've been deceived. And see here, Aiken. You understand I'm a miserable man. I'm about broken, I guess. I don't care any more for life, for anything. If you can't look me in the eyes, man to man, and believe what I say—why, by God! You can kill me!"

Aiken heaved a great breath.

"Buck Duane, whether I'm impressed or not by what you say needn't matter. You've had accusers, justly or unjustly, as will soon appear. The thing is we can prove you innocent or guilty. My girl Lucy saw my wife's assailant."

He motioned for the crowd of men to open up.

"Somebody—you, Sibert—go for Lucy. That'll settle this thing."

Duane heard as a man in an ugly dream. The faces around him, the hum of voices, all seemed far off. His life hung by the merest thread. Yet he did not think of that so much as of the brand of a woman-murderer which might be soon sealed upon him by a frightened, imaginative child.

The crowd trooped apart and closed again. Duane caught a blurred image of a slight girl clinging to Sibert's hand. He could not see distinctly. Aiken lifted the child, whispered soothingly to her not to be afraid. Then he fetched her closer to Duane.

"Lucy, tell me. Did you ever see this man before?" asked Aiken, huskily and low. "Is he the one—who came in the house that day—struck you down—and dragged mama—?"

Aiken's voice failed.

A lightning flash seemed to clear Duane's blurred sight. He saw a pale, sad face and violet eyes fixed in gloom and horror upon his. No terrible moment in Duane's life ever equaled this one of silence—of suspense.

"It's ain't him!" cried the child.

Then Sibert was flinging the noose off Duane's neck and unwinding the bonds round his arms. The spellbound crowd awoke to hoarse exclamations.

"See there, my locoed gents, how easy you'd hang the wrong man," burst out the cowboy, as he made the rope-end hiss. "You-all are a lot of wise rangers. Haw! Haw!"

He freed Duane and thrust the bone-handled gun back in Duane's holster.

"You Abe, there. Reckon you pulled a stunt! But don't try the like again. And, men, I'll gamble there's a hell of a lot of bad work Buck Duane's named for—which all he never done. Clear away there. Where's his hoss? Duane, the road's open out of Shirley."

Sibert swept the gaping watchers aside and pressed Duane toward the horse, which another cowboy held. Mechanically Duane mounted, felt a lift as he went up. Then the cowboy's hard face softened in a smile.

"I reckon it ain't uncivil of me to say—hit that road quick!" he said, frankly.

He led the horse out of the crowd. Aiken joined him, and between them they escorted Duane across the plaza. The crowd appeared irresistibly drawn to follow.

Aiken paused with his big hand on Duane's knee. In it, unconsciously probably, he still held the gun.

"Duane, a word with you," he said. "I believe you're not so black as you've been painted. I wish there was time to say more. Tell me this, anyway. Do you know the Ranger Captain MacNelly?"

"I do not," replied Duane, in surprise.

"I met him only a week ago over in Fairfield," went on Aiken, hurriedly. "He declared you never killed my wife. I didn't believe him—argued with him. We almost had hard words over it. Now—I'm sorry. The last thing he said was: 'If you ever see Duane don't kill him. Send him into my camp after dark!' He meant something strange. What—I can't say. But he was right, and I was wrong. If Lucy had batted an eye I'd have killed you. Still, I wouldn't advise you to hunt up MacNelly's camp. He's clever. Maybe he believes there's no treachery in his new ideas of ranger tactics. I tell you for all it's worth. Good-by. May God help you further as he did this day!"

Duane said good-by and touched the horse with his spurs.

"So long, Buck!" called Sibert, with that frank smile breaking warm over his brown face; and he held his sombrero high.

## CHAPTER XIV

When Duane reached the crossing of the roads the name Fairfield on the sign-post seemed to be the thing that tipped the oscillating balance of decision in favor of that direction.

He answered here to unfathomable impulse. If he had been driven to hunt up Jeff Aiken, now he was called to find this unknown ranger captain. In Duane's state of mind clear reasoning, common sense, or keenness were out of the question. He went because he felt he was compelled.

Dusk had fallen when he rode into a town which inquiry discovered to be Fairfield. Captain MacNelly's camp was stationed just out of the village limits on the other side.

No one except the boy Duane questioned appeared to notice his arrival. Like Shirley, the town of Fairfield was large and prosperous, compared to the innumerable hamlets dotting the vast extent of southwestern Texas. As Duane rode through, being careful to get off the main street, he heard the tolling of a church-bell that was a melancholy reminder of his old home.

There did not appear to be any camp on the outskirts of the town. But as Duane sat his horse, peering around and undecided what further move to make, he caught the glint of flickering lights through the darkness. Heading toward them, he rode perhaps a quarter of a mile to come upon a grove of mesquite. The brightness of several fires made the surrounding darkness all the blacker. Duane saw the moving forms of men and heard horses. He advanced naturally, expecting any moment to be halted.

"Who goes there?" came the sharp call out of the gloom.

Duane pulled his horse. The gloom was impenetrable.

"One man—alone," replied Duane.

"A stranger?"

"Yes."

"What do you want?"

"I'm trying to find the ranger camp."

"You've struck it. What's your errand?"

"I want to see Captain MacNelly."

"Get down and advance. Slow. Don't move your hands. It's dark, but I can see."

Duane dismounted, and, leading his horse, slowly advanced a few paces. He saw a dully bright object—a gun—before he discovered the man who held it. A few more steps showed a dark figure blocking the trail. Here Duane halted.

"Come closer, stranger. Let's have a look at you," the guard ordered, curtly.

Duane advanced again until he stood before the man. Here the rays of light from the fires flickered upon Duane's face.

"Reckon you're a stranger, all right. What's your name and your business with the Captain?"

Duane hesitated, pondering what best to say.

"Tell Captain MacNelly I'm the man he's been asking to ride into his camp—after dark," finally said Duane.

The ranger bent forward to peer hard at this night visitor. His manner had been alert, and now it became tense.

"Come here, one of you men, quick," he called, without turning in the least toward the campfire.

"Hello! What's up, Pickens?" came the swift reply. It was followed by a rapid thud of boots on soft ground. A dark form crossed the gleams from the firelight. Then a ranger loomed up to reach the side of the guard. Duane heard whispering, the purport of which he could not catch. The second ranger swore under his breath. Then he turned away and started back.

"Here, ranger, before you go, understand this. My visit is peaceful—friendly if you'll let it be. Mind, I was asked to come here—after dark."

Duane's clear, penetrating voice carried far. The listening rangers at the campfire heard what he said.

"Ho, Pickens! Tell that fellow to wait," replied an authoritative voice. Then a slim figure detached itself from the dark, moving group at the campfire and hurried out.

"Better be foxy, Cap," shouted a ranger, in warning.

"Shut up—all of you," was the reply.

This officer, obviously Captain MacNelly, soon joined the two rangers who were confronting Duane. He had no fear. He strode straight up to Duane.

"I'm MacNelly," he said. "If you're my man, don't mention your name—yet."

All this seemed so strange to Duane, in keeping with much that had happened lately.

"I met Jeff Aiken today," said Duane. "He sent me—"

"You've met Aiken!" exclaimed MacNelly, sharp, eager, low. "By all that's bully!" Then he appeared to catch himself, to grow restrained.

"Men, fall back, leave us alone a moment."

The rangers slowly withdrew.

"Buck Duane! It's you?" he whispered, eagerly.

"Yes."

"If I give my word you'll not be arrested—you'll be treated fairly—will you come into camp and consult with me?"

"Certainly."

"Duane, I'm sure glad to meet you," went on MacNelly; and he extended his hand.

Amazed and touched, scarcely realizing this actuality, Duane gave his hand and felt no unmistakable grip of warmth.

"It doesn't seem natural, Captain MacNelly, but I believe I'm glad to meet you," said Duane, soberly.

"You will be. Now we'll go back to camp. Keep your identity mum for the present."

He led Duane in the direction of the campfire.

"Pickers, go back on duty," he ordered, "and, Beeson, you look after this horse."

When Duane got beyond the line of mesquite, which had hid a good view of the camp-site, he saw a group of perhaps fifteen rangers sitting around the fires, near a long low shed where horses were feeding, and a small adobe house at one side.

"We've just had grub, but I'll see you get some. Then we'll talk," said MacNelly. "I've taken up temporary quarters here. Have a rustler job on hand. Now, when you've eaten, come right into the house."

Duane was hungry, but he hurried through the ample supper that was set before him, urged on by curiosity and astonishment. The only way he could account for his presence there in a ranger's camp was that MacNelly hoped to get useful information out of him. Still that would hardly have made this captain so eager. There was a mystery here, and Duane could scarcely wait for it to be solved. While eating he had bent keen eyes around him. After a first quiet scrutiny the rangers apparently paid no more attention to him. They were all veterans in service—Duane saw that—and rugged, powerful men of iron constitution. Despite the occasional joke and sally of the more youthful members, and a general conversation of campfire nature, Duane was not deceived about the fact that his advent had been an unusual and striking one, which had caused an undercurrent of conjecture and even consternation among them. These rangers were too well trained to appear openly curious about their captain's guest. If they had not deliberately attempted to be oblivious of his presence Duane would have concluded they thought him an ordinary visitor, somehow of use to MacNelly. As it was, Duane felt a suspense that must have been due to a hint of his identity.

He was not long in presenting himself at the door of the house.

"Come in and have a chair," said MacNelly, motioning for the one other occupant of the room to rise. "Leave us, Russell, and close the door. I'll be through these reports right off."

MacNelly sat at a table upon which was a lamp and various papers. Seen in the light he was a fine-looking, soldierly man of about forty years, dark-haired and dark-eyed, with a bronzed face, shrewd, stern, strong, yet not wanting in kindliness. He scanned hastily over some papers, fussed with them, and finally put them in envelopes. Without looking up he pushed a cigar case toward Duane, and upon Duane's refusal to smoke he took a cigar, rose to light it at the lamp chimney, and then, settling back in his chair, he faced Duane, making a vain attempt to hide what must have been the fulfillment of a long-nourished curiosity.

"Duane, I've been hoping for this for two years," he began.

Duane smiled a little—a smile that felt strange on his face. He had never been much of a talker. And speech here seemed more than ordinarily difficult.

MacNelly must have felt that.

He looked long and earnestly at Duane, and his quick, nervous manner changed to grave thoughtfulness.

"I've lots to say, but where to begin," he mused. "Duane, you've had a hard life since you went on the dodge. I never met you before, don't know what you looked like as a boy. But I can see what—well, even ranger life isn't all roses."

He rolled his cigar between his lips and puffed clouds of smoke.

"Ever hear from home since you left Wellston?" he asked, abruptly.

"No."

"Never a word?"

"Not one," replied Duane, sadly.

"That's tough. I'm glad to be able to tell you that up to just lately your mother, sister, uncle—all your folks, I believe—were well. I've kept posted. But haven't heard lately."

Duane averted his face a moment, hesitated till the swelling left his throat, and then said, "It's worth what I went through today to hear that."

"I can imagine how you feel about it. When I was in the war—but let's get down to the business of this meeting."

He pulled his chair close to Duane's.

"You've had word more than once in the last two years that I wanted to see you?"

"Three times, I remember," replied Duane.

"Why didn't you hunt me up?"

"I supposed you imagined me one of those gunfighters who couldn't take a dare and expected me to ride up to your camp and be arrested."

"That was natural, I suppose," went on MacNelly. "You didn't know me, otherwise you would have come. I've been a long time getting to you. But the nature of my job, as far as you're concerned, made me cautious. Duane, you're aware of the hard name you bear all over the Southwest?"

"Once in a while I'm jarred into realizing," replied Duane.

"It's the hardest, barring Murrell and Cheseldine, on the Texas border. But there's this difference. Murrell in his day was known to deserve his infamous name. Cheseldine in his day also. But I've found hundreds of men in southwest Texas who're your friends, who swear you never committed a crime. The farther south I get the clearer this becomes. What I want to know is the truth. Have you ever done anything criminal? Tell me the truth, Duane. It won't make any difference in my plan. And when I say crime I mean what I would call crime, or any reasonable Texan."

"That way my hands are clean," replied Duane.

"You never held up a man, robbed a store for grub, stole a horse when you needed him bad—never anything like that?"

"Somehow I always kept out of that, just when pressed the hardest."

"Duane, I'm damn glad!" MacNelly exclaimed, gripping Duane's hand. "Glad for you mother's sake! But, all the same, in spite of this, you are a Texas outlaw accountable to the state. You're perfectly aware that under existing circumstances, if you fell into the hands of the law, you'd probably hang, at least go to jail for a long term."

"That's what kept me on the dodge all these years," replied Duane.

"Certainly." MacNelly removed his cigar. His eyes narrowed and glittered. The muscles along his brown cheeks set hard and tense. He leaned closer to Duane, laid sinewy, pressing fingers upon Duane's knee.

"Listen to this," he whispered, hoarsely. "If I place a pardon in your hand—make you a free, honest citizen once more, clear your name of infamy, make your mother, your sister proud of you—will you swear yourself to a service, *any* service I demand of you?"

Duane sat stock still, stunned.

Slowly, more persuasively, with show of earnest agitation, Captain MacNelly reiterated his startling query.

"My God!" burst from Duane. "What's this? MacNelly, you *can't* be in earnest!"

"Never more so in my life. I've a deep game. I'm playing it square. What do you say?"

He rose to his feet. Duane, as if impelled, rose with him. Ranger and outlaw then locked eyes that searched each other's souls. In MacNelly's Duane read truth, strong, fiery purpose, hope, even gladness, and a fugitive mounting assurance of victory.

Twice Duane endeavored to speak, failed of all save a hoarse, incoherent sound, until, forcing back a flood of speech, he found a voice.

"Any service? Every service! MacNelly, I give my word," said Duane.

A light played over MacNelly's face, warming out all the grim darkness. He held out his hand. Duane met it with his in a clasp that men unconsciously give in moments of stress.

When they unclasped and Duane stepped back to drop into a chair MacNelly fumbled for another cigar—he had bitten the other into shreds—and, lighting it as before, he turned to his visitor, now calm and cool. He had the look of a man who had justly won something at considerable cost. His next move was to take a long leather case from his pocket and extract from it several folded papers.

"Here's your pardon from the Governor," he said, quietly. "You'll see, when you look it over, that it's conditional. When you sign this paper I have here the condition will be met."

He smoothed out the paper, handed Duane a pen, ran his forefinger along a dotted line.

Duane's hand was shaky. Years had passed since he had held a pen. It was with difficulty that he achieved his signature. Buckley Duane—how strange the name looked!

"Right here ends the career of Buck Duane, outlaw and gunfighter," said MacNelly; and, seating himself, he took the pen from Duane's fingers and wrote several lines in several places upon the paper. Then with a smile he handed it to Duane.

"That makes you a member of Company A, Texas Rangers."

"So that's it!" burst out Duane, a light breaking in upon his bewilderment. "You want me for ranger service?"

"Sure. That's it," replied the Captain, dryly. "Now to hear what that service is to be. I've been a busy man since I took this job, and, as you may have heard, I've done a few things. I don't mind telling you that political influence put me in here and that up Austin way there's a good deal of friction in the Department of State in regard to whether or not the ranger service is any good—whether it should be discontinued or not. I'm on the party side who's defending the ranger service. I contend that it's made Texas habitable. Well, it's been up to me to produce results. So far I have been successful. My great ambition is to break up the outlaw gangs along the river. I have never ventured in there yet because I've been waiting to get the lieutenant I needed. You, of course, are the man I had in mind. It's my idea to start way up the Rio Grande and begin with Cheseldine. He's the strongest, the worst outlaw of the times. He's more than rustler. It's Cheseldine and his gang who are operating on the banks. They're doing bank robbing. That's my private opinion, but it's not been backed up by any evidence. Cheseldine doesn't leave evidences. He's intelligent, cunning. No one seems to have seen him—to know what he looks like. I assume, of course, that you are a stranger to the country he dominates. It's five hundred miles west of your ground. There's a little town over there called Fairdale. It's the nest of a rustler gang. They rustle and murder at will. Nobody knows who the leader is. I want you to find out. Well, whatever way you decide is best you will proceed to act upon. You are your own boss. You know such men and how they can be approached. You will take all the time needed, if it's months. It will be necessary for you to communicate with me, and that will be a difficult matter. For Cheseldine dominates several whole counties. You must find some way to let me know when I and my rangers are needed. The plan is to break up Cheseldine's gang. It's the toughest job on the border. Arresting him alone isn't to be heard of. He couldn't be brought out. Killing him isn't much better, for his select men, the ones he operates with, are as dangerous to the community as he is. We want to kill or jail this choice selection of robbers and break up the rest of the gang. To find them, to get among them somehow, to learn their movements, to lay your trap for us rangers to spring—that, Duane, is your service to me, and God knows it's a great one!"

"I have accepted it," replied Duane.

"Your work will be secret. You are now a ranger in my service. But no one except the few I choose to tell will know of it until we pull off the job. You will simply be Buck Duane till it suits our purpose to acquaint Texas with the fact that you're a ranger. You'll see there's no date on that paper. No one will ever know just when you entered the service. Perhaps we can make it appear that all or most of your outlawry has really been good service to the state. At that, I'll believe it'll turn out so."

MacNelly paused a moment in his rapid talk, chewed his cigar, drew his brows together in a dark frown, and went on. "No man on the border knows so well as you the deadly nature of this service. It's a thousand to one that you'll be killed. I'd say there was no chance at all for any other man beside you. Your reputation will go far among the outlaws. Maybe that and your nerve and your gunplay will pull you through. I'm hoping so. But it's a long, long chance against your ever coming back."

"That's not the point," said Duane. "But in case I get killed out there—what—"

"Leave that to me," interrupted Captain MacNelly. "Your folks will know at once of your pardon and your ranger duty. If you lose your life out there I'll see your name cleared—the service you render known. You can rest assured of that."

"I am satisfied," replied Duane. "That's so much more than I've dared to hope."

"Well, it's settled, then. I'll give you money for expenses. You'll start as soon as you like—the sooner the better. I hope to think of other suggestions, especially about communicating with me."

Long after the lights were out and the low hum of voices had ceased round the campfire Duane lay wide awake, eyes staring into the blackness, marveling over the strange events of the day. He was humble, grateful to the depths of his soul. A huge and crushing burden had been lifted from his heart. He welcomed this hazardous service to the man who had saved him. Thought of his mother and sister and Uncle Jim, of his home, of old friends came rushing over him the first time in years that he had happiness in the memory. The disgrace he had put upon them would now be removed; and in the light of that, his wasted life of the past, and its probable tragic end in future service as atonement changed their aspects. And as he lay there, with the approach of sleep finally dimming the vividness of his thought, so full of mystery, shadowy faces floated in the blackness around him, haunting him as he had always been haunted.

It was broad daylight when he awakened. MacNelly was calling him to breakfast. Outside sounded voices of men, crackling of fires, snorting and stamping of horses, the barking of dogs. Duane rolled out of his blankets and made good use of the soap and towel and razor and brush near by on a bench—things of rare luxury to an outlaw on the ride. The face he saw in the mirror was as strange as the past he had tried so hard to recall. Then he stepped to the door and went out.

The rangers were eating in a circle round a tarpaulin spread upon the ground.

"Fellows," said MacNelly, "shake hands with Buck Duane. He's on secret ranger service for me. Service that'll likely make you all hump soon! Mind you, keep mum about it."

The rangers surprised Duane with a roaring greeting, the warmth of which he soon divined was divided between pride of his acquisition to their ranks and eagerness to meet that violent service of which their captain hinted. They were jolly, wild fellows, with just enough gravity in their welcome to show Duane their respect and appreciation, while not forgetting his lone-wolf record. When he had seated himself in that circle, now one of them, a feeling subtle and uplifting pervaded him.

After the meal Captain MacNelly drew Duane aside.

"Here's the money. Make it go as far as you can. Better strike straight for El Paso, snook around there and hear things. Then go to Valentine. That's near the river and within fifty miles or so of the edge of the Rim Rock. Somewhere up there Cheseldine holds fort. Somewhere to the north is the town Fairdale. But he doesn't hide all the time in the rocks. Only after some daring raid or holdup. Cheseldine's got border towns on his staff, or scared of him, and these places we want to know about, especially Fairdale. Write me care of the adjutant at Austin. I don't have to warn you to be careful where you mail letters. Ride a hundred, two hundred miles, if necessary, or go clear to El Paso."

MacNelly stopped with an air of finality, and then Duane slowly rose.

"I'll start at once," he said, extending his hand to the Captain. "I wish—I'd like to thank you."

"Hell, man! Don't thank me!" replied MacNelly, crushing the proffered hand. "I've sent a lot of good men to their deaths, and maybe you're another. But, as I've said, you've one chance in a thousand. And, by Heaven! I'd hate to be Cheseldine or any other man you were trailing. No, not good-by—Adios, Duane! May we meet again!"

# BOOK II. THE RANGER

## CHAPTER XV

West of the Pecos River, Texas extended a vast wild region, barren in the north where the Llano Estacado spread its shifting sands, fertile in the south along the Rio Grande. A railroad marked an undeviating course across five hundred miles of this country, and the only villages and towns lay on or near this line of steel. Unsettled as was this western Texas, and despite the acknowledged dominance of the outlaw bands, the pioneers pushed steadily into it. First had come the lone rancher; then his neighbors in near and far valleys; then the hamlets; at last the railroad and the towns. And still the pioneers came, spreading deeper into the valleys, farther and wider over the plains. It was mesquite-dotted, cactus-covered desert, but rich soil upon which water acted like magic. There was little grass to an acre, but there were millions of acres. The climate was wonderful. Cattle flourished and ranchers prospered.

The Rio Grande flowed almost due south along the western boundary for a thousand miles, and then, weary of its course, turned abruptly north, to make what was called the Big Bend. The railroad, running west, cut across this bend, and all that country bounded on the north by the railroad and on the south by the river was as wild as the Staked Plains. It contained not one settlement. Across the face of this Big Bend, as if to isolate it, stretched the Ord mountain range, of which Mount Ord, Cathedral Mount, and Elephant Mount raised bleak peaks above their fellows. In the valleys of the foothills and out across the plains were ranches, and farther north villages, and the towns of Alpine and Marfa.

Like other parts of the great Lone Star State, this section of Texas was a world in itself—a world where the riches of the rancher were ever enriching the outlaw. The village closest to the gateway of this outlaw-infested region was a little place called Ord, named after the dark peak that loomed some miles to the south. It had been settled originally by Mexicans—there were still the ruins of adobe missions—but with the advent of the rustler and outlaw many inhabitants were shot or driven away, so that at the height of Ord's prosperity and evil sway there were but few Mexicans living there, and these had their choice between holding hand-and-glove with the outlaws or furnishing target practice for that wild element.

Toward the close of a day in September a stranger rode into Ord, and in a community where all men were remarkable for one reason or another he excited interest. His horse, perhaps, received the first and most engaging attention—horses in that region being apparently more important than men.

This particular horse did not attract with beauty. At first glance he seemed ugly. But he was a giant, black as coal, rough despite the care manifestly bestowed upon him, long of body, ponderous of limb, huge in every way. A bystander remarked that he had a grand head. True, if only his head had been seen he would have been a beautiful horse. Like men, horses show what they are in the shape, the size, the line, the character of the head. This one denoted fire, speed, blood, loyalty, and his eyes were as soft and dark as a woman's. His face was solid black, except in the middle of his forehead, where there was a round spot of white.

"Say mister, mind tellin' me his name?" asked a ragged urchin, with born love of a horse in his eyes.

"Bullet," replied the rider.

"Thet there's fer the white mark, ain't it?" whispered the youngster to another. "Say, ain't he a whopper? Biggest hoss I ever seen."

Bullet carried a huge black silver-ornamented saddle of Mexican make, a lariat and canteen, and a small pack rolled into a tarpaulin.

This rider apparently put all care of appearances upon his horse. His apparel was the ordinary jeans of the cowboy without vanity, and it was torn and travel-stained. His boots showed evidence of an intimate acquaintance with cactus. Like his horse, this man was a giant in stature, but rangier, not so heavily built. Otherwise the only striking thing about him was his somber face with its piercing eyes, and hair white over the temples. He packed two guns, both low down—but that was too common a thing to attract notice in the Big Bend. A close observer, however, would have noted a singular fact— this rider's right hand was more bronzed, more weather-beaten than his left. He never wore a glove on that right hand!

He had dismounted before a ramshackle structure that bore upon its wide, high-boarded front the sign, "Hotel." There were horsemen coming and going down the wide street between its rows of old stores, saloons, and houses. Ord certainly did not look enterprising. Americans had manifestly assimilated much of the leisure of the Mexicans. The hotel had a wide platform in front, and this did duty as porch and sidewalk. Upon it, and leaning against a hitching rail, were men of varying ages, most of them slovenly in old jeans and slouched sombreros. Some were booted, belted, and spurred. No man there wore a coat, but all wore vests. The guns in that group would have outnumbered the men.

It was a crowd seemingly too lazy to be curious. Good nature did not appear to be wanting, but it was not the frank and boisterous kind natural to the cowboy or rancher in town for a day. These men were idlers; what else, perhaps, was easy to conjecture. Certainly to this arriving stranger, who flashed a keen eye over them, they wore an atmosphere never associated with work.

Presently a tall man, with a drooping, sandy mustache, leisurely detached himself from the crowd.

"Howdy, stranger," he said.

The stranger had bent over to loosen the cinches; he straightened up and nodded. Then: "I'm thirsty!"

That brought a broad smile to faces. It was characteristic greeting. One and all trooped after the stranger into the hotel. It was a dark, ill-smelling barn of a place, with a bar as high as a short man's head. A bartender with a scarred face was serving drinks.

"Line up, gents," said the stranger.

They piled over one another to get to the bar, with coarse jests and oaths and laughter. None of them noted that the stranger did not appear so thirsty as he had claimed to be. In fact, though he went through the motions, he did not drink at all.

"My name's Jim Fletcher," said the tall man with the drooping, sandy mustache. He spoke laconically, nevertheless there was a tone that showed he expected to be known. Something went with that name. The stranger did not appear to be impressed.

"My name might be Blazes, but it ain't," he replied. "What do you call this burg?"

"Stranger, this heah me-tropoles bears the handle Ord. Is thet new to you?"

He leaned back against the bar, and now his little yellow eyes, clear as crystal, flawless as a hawk's, fixed on the stranger. Other men crowded close, forming a circle, curious, ready to be friendly or otherwise, according to how the tall interrogator marked the new-comer.

"Sure, Ord's a little strange to me. Off the railroad some, ain't it? Funny trails hereabouts."

"How fur was you goin'?"

"I reckon I was goin' as far as I could," replied the stranger, with a hard laugh.

His reply had subtle reaction on that listening circle. Some of the men exchanged glances. Fletcher stroked his drooping mustache, seemed thoughtful, but lost something of that piercing scrutiny.

"Wal, Ord's the jumpin'-off place," he said, presently. "Sure you've heerd of the Big Bend country?"

"I sure have, an' was makin' tracks fer it," replied the stranger.

Fletcher turned toward a man in the outer edge of the group. "Knell, come in heah."

This individual elbowed his way in and was seen to be scarcely more than a boy, almost pale beside those bronzed men, with a long, expressionless face, thin and sharp.

"Knell, this heah's—" Fletcher wheeled to the stranger. "What'd you call yourself?"

"I'd hate to mention what I've been callin' myself lately."

This sally fetched another laugh. The stranger appeared cool, careless, indifferent. Perhaps he knew, as the others present knew, that this show of Fletcher's, this pretense of introduction, was merely talk while he was looked over.

Knell stepped up, and it was easy to see, from the way Fletcher relinquished his part in the situation, that a man greater than he had appeared upon the scene.

"Any business here?" he queried, curtly. When he spoke his expressionless face was in strange contrast with the ring, the quality, the cruelty of his voice. This voice betrayed an absence of humor, of friendliness, of heart.

"Nope," replied the stranger.

"Know anybody hereabouts?"

"Nary one."

"Jest ridin' through?"

"Yep."

"Slopin' fer back country, eh?"

There came a pause. The stranger appeared to grow a little resentful and drew himself up disdainfully.

"Wal, considerin' you-all seem so damn friendly an' oncurious down here in this Big Bend country, I don't mind sayin' yes—I am in on the dodge," he replied, with deliberate sarcasm.

"From west of Ord—out El Paso way, mebbe?"

"Sure."

"A-huh! Thet so?" Knell's words cut the air, stilled the room. "You're from way down the river. Thet's what they say down there—'on the dodge.' Stranger, you're a liar!"

With swift clink of spur and thump of boot the crowd split, leaving Knell and the stranger in the center.

Wild breed of that ilk never made a mistake in judging a man's nerve. Knell had cut out with the trenchant call, and stood ready. The stranger suddenly lost his every semblance to the rough and easy character before manifest in him. He became bronze. That situation seemed familiar to him. His eyes held a singular piercing light that danced like a compass-needle.

"Sure I lied," he said; "so I ain't takin' offense at the way you called me. I'm lookin' to make friends, not enemies. You don't strike me as one of them four-flushes, achin' to kill somebody. But if you are—go ahead an' open the ball . . . You see, I never throw a gun on them fellers till they go fer theirs."

Knell coolly eyed his antagonist, his strange face not changing in the least. Yet somehow it was evident in his look that here was metal which rang differently from what he had expected. Invited to start a fight or withdraw, as he chose, Knell proved himself big in the manner characteristic of only the genuine gunman.

"Stranger, I pass," he said, and, turning to the bar, he ordered liquor.

The tension relaxed, the silence broke, the men filled up the gap; the incident seemed closed. Jim Fletcher attached himself to the stranger, and now both respect and friendliness tempered his asperity.

"Wal, fer want of a better handle I'll call you Dodge," he said.

"Dodge's as good as any . . . Gents, line up again—an' if you can't be friendly, be careful!"

Such was Buck Duane's debut in the little outlaw hamlet of Ord.

Duane had been three months out of the Nueces country. At El Paso he bought the finest horse he could find, and, armed and otherwise outfitted to suit him, he had taken to unknown trails. Leisurely he rode from town to town, village to village, ranch to ranch, fitting his talk and his occupation to the impression he wanted to make upon different people whom he met. He was in turn a cowboy, a rancher, a cattleman, a stock-buyer, a boomer, a land-hunter; and long before he reached the wild and inhospitable Ord he had acted the part of an outlaw, drifting into new territory. He passed on leisurely because he wanted to learn the lay of the country, the location of villages and ranches, the work, habit, gossip, pleasures, and fears of the people with whom he came in contact. The one subject most impelling to him—outlaws—he never mentioned; but by talking all around it, sifting the old ranch and cattle story, he acquired a knowledge calculated to aid his plot. In this game time was of no moment; if necessary he would take years to accomplish his task. The stupendous and perilous nature of it showed in the slow, wary preparation. When he heard Fletcher's name and faced Knell he knew he had reached the place he sought. Ord was a hamlet on the fringe of the grazing country, of doubtful honesty, from which, surely, winding trails led down into that free and never-disturbed paradise of outlaws—the Big Bend.

Duane made himself agreeable, yet not too much so, to Fletcher and several other men disposed to talk and drink and eat; and then, after having a care for his horse, he rode out of town a couple of miles to a grove he had marked, and there, well hidden, he prepared to spend the night. This proceeding served a double purpose—he was safer, and the habit would look well in the eyes of outlaws, who would be more inclined to see in him the lone-wolf fugitive.

Long since Duane had fought out a battle with himself, won a hard-earned victory. His outer life, the action, was much the same as it had been; but the inner life had tremendously changed. He could never become a happy man, he could never shake utterly those haunting phantoms that had once been his despair and madness; but he had assumed a task impossible for any man save one like him, he had felt the meaning of it grow strangely and wonderfully, and through that flourished up consciousness of how passionately he now clung to this thing which would blot out his former infamy. The iron fetters no more threatened his hands; the iron door no more haunted his dreams. He never forgot that he was free. Strangely, too, along with this feeling of new manhood there gathered the force of imperious desire to run these chief outlaws to their dooms. He never called them outlaws—but rustlers, thieves, robbers, murderers, criminals. He sensed the growth of a relentless driving passion, and sometimes he feared that, more than the newly acquired zeal and pride in this ranger service, it was the old, terrible inherited killing instinct lifting its hydra-head in new guise. But of that he could not be sure. He dreaded the thought. He could only wait.

Another aspect of the change in Duane, neither passionate nor driving, yet not improbably even more potent of new significance to life, was the imperceptible return of an old love of nature dead during his outlaw days.

For years a horse had been only a machine of locomotion, to carry him from place to place, to beat and spur and goad mercilessly in flight; now this giant black, with his splendid head, was a companion, a friend, a brother, a loved thing, guarded jealously, fed and trained and ridden with an intense appreciation of his great speed and endurance. For years the daytime, with its birth of sunrise on through long hours to the ruddy close, had been used for sleep or rest in some rocky hole or willow brake or deserted hut, had been hated because it augmented danger of pursuit, because it drove the fugitive to lonely, wretched hiding; now the dawn was a greeting, a promise of another day to ride, to plan, to remember, and sun, wind, cloud, rain, sky—all were joys to him, somehow speaking his freedom. For years the night had been a black space, during which he had to ride unseen along the endless trails, to peer with cat-eyes through gloom for the moving shape that ever pursued him; now the twilight and the dusk and the shadows of grove and cañon darkened into night with its train of stars, and brought him calm reflection of the day's happenings, of the morrow's possibilities, perhaps a sad, brief procession of the old phantoms, then sleep. For years cañons and valleys and mountains had been looked at as retreats that might be dark and wild enough to hide even an outlaw; now he saw these features of the great desert with something of the eyes of the boy who had once burned for adventure and life among them.

This night a wonderful afterglow lingered long in the west, and against the golden-red of clear sky the bold, black head of Mount Ord reared itself aloft, beautiful but aloof, sinister yet calling. Small wonder that Duane gazed in fascination upon the peak! Somewhere deep in its corrugated sides or lost in a rugged cañon was hidden the secret stronghold of the master outlaw Cheseldine. All down along the ride from El Paso Duane had heard of Cheseldine, of his band, his fearful deeds, his cunning, his widely separated raids, of his flitting here and there like a jack-o'-lantern; but never a word of his den, never a word of his appearance.

Next morning Duane did not return to Ord. He struck off to the north, riding down a rough, slow-descending road that appeared to have been used occasionally for cattle driving. As he had ridden in from the west, this northern direction led him into totally unfamiliar country. While he passed on, however, he exercised such keen observation that in the future he would know whatever might be of service to him if he chanced that way again.

The rough, wild, brush-covered slope down from the foothills gradually leveled out into plain, a magnificent grazing country, upon which till noon of that day Duane did not see a herd of cattle or a ranch. About that time he made out smoke from the railroad, and after a couple of hours' riding he entered a town which inquiry discovered to be Bradford. It was the largest town he had visited since Marfa, and he calculated must have a thousand or fifteen hundred inhabitants, not including Mexicans. He decided this would be a good place for him to hold up for a while, being the nearest town to Ord, only forty miles away. So he hitched his horse in front of a store and leisurely set about studying Bradford.

It was after dark, however, that Duane verified his suspicions concerning Bradford. The town was awake after dark, and there was one long row of saloons, dance halls, gambling resorts in full blast. Duane visited them all, and was surprised to see wildness and license equal to that of the old river camp of Bland's in its palmiest days. Here it was forced upon him that the farther west one traveled along the river the sparser the respectable settlements, the more numerous the hard characters, and in consequence the greater the element of lawlessness. Duane returned to his lodging-house with the conviction that MacNelly's task of cleaning up the Big Bend country was a stupendous one. Yet, he reflected, a company of intrepid and quick-shooting rangers could have soon cleaned up this Bradford.

The innkeeper had one other guest that night, a long black-coated and wide-sombreroed Texan who reminded Duane of his grandfather. This man had penetrating eyes, a courtly manner, and an unmistakable leaning toward companionship and mint juleps. The gentleman introduced himself as Colonel Webb, of Marfa, and took it as a matter of course that Duane made no comment about himself.

"Sir, it's all one to me," he said, blandly, waving his hand. "I have traveled.

Texas is free, and this frontier is one where it's healthier and just as friendly for a man to have no curiosity about his companion. You might be Cheseldine, of the Big Bend, or you might be Judge Little, of El Paso—it's all one to me. I enjoy drinking with you anyway."

Duane thanked him, conscious of a reserve and dignity that he could not have felt or pretended three months before. And then, as always, he was a good listener. Colonel Webb told, among other things, that he had come out to the Big Bend to look over the affairs of a deceased brother who had been a rancher and a sheriff of one of the towns, Fairdale by name.

"Found no affairs, no ranch, not even his grave," said Colonel Webb. "And I tell you, sir, if hell's any tougher than this Fairdale I don't want to expiate my sins there."

"Fairdale . . . I imagine sheriffs have a hard row to hoe out here," replied Duane, trying not to appear curious.

The Colonel swore lustily.

"My brother was the only honest sheriff Fairdale ever had. It was wonderful how long he lasted. But he had nerve, he could throw a gun, and he was on the square. Then he was wise enough to confine his work to offenders of his own town and neighborhood. He let the riding outlaws alone, else he wouldn't have lasted at all . . . What this frontier needs, sir, is about six companies of Texas Rangers."

Duane was aware of the Colonel's close scrutiny.

"Do you know anything about the service?" he asked.

"I used to. Ten years ago when I lived in San Antonio. A fine body of men, sir, and the salvation of Texas."

"Governor Stone doesn't entertain that opinion," said Duane.

Here Colonel Webb exploded. Manifestly the governor was not his choice for a chief executive of the great state. He talked politics for a while, and of the vast territory west of the Pecos that seemed never to get a benefit from Austin. He talked enough for Duane to realize that here was just the kind of intelligent, well-informed, honest citizen that he had been trying to meet. He exerted himself thereafter to be agreeable and interesting; and he saw presently that here was an opportunity to make a valuable acquaintance, if not a friend.

"I'm a stranger in these parts," said Duane, finally. "What is this outlaw situation you speak of?"

"It's damnable, sir, and unbelievable. Not rustling any more, but just wholesale herd stealing, in which some big cattlemen, supposed to be honest, are equally guilty with the outlaws. On this border, you know, the rustler has always been able to steal cattle in any numbers. But to get rid of big bunches— that's the hard job. The gang operating between here and Valentine evidently have not this trouble. Nobody knows where the stolen stock goes. But I'm not alone in my opinion that most of it goes to several big stockmen. They ship to San Antonio, Austin, New Orleans, also to El Paso. If you travel the stock road between here and Marfa and Valentine you'll see dead cattle all along the line and stray cattle out in the scrub. The herds have been driven fast and far, and stragglers are not rounded up."

"Wholesale business, eh?" remarked Duane. "Who are these—er—big stock buyers?"

Colonel Webb seemed a little startled at the abrupt query. He bent his penetrating gaze upon Duane and thoughtfully stroked his pointed beard.

"Names, of course, I'll not mention. Opinions are one thing, direct accusation another. This is not a healthy country for the informer."

When it came to the outlaws themselves Colonel Webb was disposed to talk freely. Duane could not judge whether the Colonel had a hobby of that subject or the outlaws were so striking in personality and deed that any man would know all about them. The great name along the river was Cheseldine, but it seemed to be a name detached from an individual. No person of veracity known to Colonel Webb had ever seen Cheseldine, and those who claimed that doubtful honor varied so diversely in descriptions of the chief that they confused the reality and lent to the outlaw only further mystery. Strange to say of an outlaw leader, as there was no one who could identify him, so there was no one who could prove he had actually killed a man. Blood flowed like water over the Big Bend country, and it was Cheseldine who spilled it. Yet the fact remained there were no eyewitnesses to connect any individual called Cheseldine with these deeds of violence. But in striking contrast to this mystery was the person, character, and cold-blooded action of Poggin and Knell, the chief's lieutenants. They were familiar figures in all the towns within two hundred miles of Bradford. Knell had a record, but as gunman with an incredible list of victims Poggin was supreme. If Poggin had a friend no one ever heard of him. There were a hundred stories of his nerve, his wonderful speed with a gun, his passion for gambling, his love of a horse—his cold, implacable, inhuman wiping out of his path any man that crossed it.

"Cheseldine is a name, a terrible name," said Colonel Webb. "Sometimes I wonder if he's not only a name. In that case where does the brains of this gang come from? No; there must be a master craftsman behind this border pillage; a master capable of handling those terrors Poggin and Knell. Of all the thousands of outlaws developed by western Texas in the last twenty years these three are the greatest. In southern Texas, down between the Pecos and the Nueces, there have been and are still many bad men. But I doubt if any outlaw there, possibly excepting Buck Duane, ever equaled Poggin. You've heard of this Duane?"

"Yes, a little," replied Duane, quietly. "I'm from southern Texas. Buck Duane then is known out here?"

"Why, man, where isn't his name known?" returned Colonel Webb. "I've kept track of his record as I have all the others. Of course, Duane, being a lone outlaw, is somewhat of a mystery also, but not like Cheseldine. Out here there have drifted many stories of Duane, horrible some of them. But despite them a sort of romance clings to that Nueces outlaw. He's killed three great outlaw leaders, I believe—Bland, Hardin, and the other I forgot. Hardin was known in the Big Bend, had friends there. Bland had a hard name at Del Rio."

"Then this man Duane enjoys rather an unusual repute west of the Pecos?" inquired Duane.

"He's considered more of an enemy to his kind than to honest men. I understand Duane had many friends, that whole counties swear by him—secretly, of course, for he's a hunted outlaw with rewards on his head. His fame in this country appears to hang on his matchless gunplay and his enmity toward outlaw chiefs. I've heard many a rancher say: 'I wish to God that Buck Duane would drift out here! I'd give a hundred pesos to see him and Poggin meet.' It's a singular thing, stranger, how jealous these great outlaws are of each other."

"Yes, indeed, all about them is singular," replied Duane. "Has Cheseldine's gang been busy lately?"

"No. This section has been free of rustling for months, though there's unexplained movements of stock. Probably all the stock that's being shipped now was rustled long ago. Cheseldine works over a wide section, too wide for news to travel inside of weeks. Then sometimes he's not heard of at all for a spell. These lulls are pretty surely indicative of a big storm sooner or later. And Cheseldine's deals, as they grow fewer and farther between, certainly get bigger, more daring. There are some people who think Cheseldine had nothing to do with the bank-robberies and train holdups during the last few years in this country. But that's poor reasoning. The jobs have been too well done, too surely covered, to be the work of greasers or ordinary outlaws."

"What's your view of the outlook? How's all this going to wind up? Will the outlaw ever be driven out?" asked Duane.

"Never. There will always be outlaws along the Rio Grande. All the armies in the world couldn't comb the wild brakes of that fifteen hundred miles of river. But the sway of the outlaw, such as is enjoyed by these great leaders, will sooner or later be past. The criminal element flock to the Southwest. But not so thick and fast as the pioneers. Besides, the outlaws kill themselves, and the ranchers are slowly rising in wrath, if not in action. That will come soon. If they only had a leader to start the fight! But that will come. There's talk of vigilantes, the same that were organized in California and are now in force in Idaho. So far it's only talk. But the time will come. And the days of Cheseldine and Poggin are numbered."

Duane went to bed that night exceedingly thoughtful. The long trail was growing hot. This voluble colonel had given him new ideas. It came to Duane in surprise that he was famous along the upper Rio Grande. Assuredly he would not long be able to conceal his identity. He had no doubt that he would soon meet the chiefs of this clever and bold rustling gang. He could not decide whether he would be safer unknown or known. In the latter case his one chance lay in the fatality connected with his name, in his power to look it and act it. Duane had never dreamed of any sleuth-hound tendency in his nature, but now he felt something like one. Above all others his mind fixed on Poggin—Poggin the brute, the executor of Cheseldine's will, but mostly upon Poggin the gunman. This in itself was a warning to Duane. He felt terrible forces at work within him. There was the stern and indomitable resolve to make MacNelly's boast good to the governor of the state—to break up Cheseldine's gang. Yet this was not in Duane's mind before a strange grim and deadly instinct—which he had to drive away for fear he would find in it a passion to kill Poggin, not for the state, nor for his word to MacNelly, but for himself. Had his father's blood and the hard years made Duane the kind of man who instinctively wanted to meet Poggin? He was sworn to MacNelly's service, and he fought himself to keep that, and that only, in his mind.

Duane ascertained that Fairdale was situated two days' ride from Bradford toward the north. There was a stage which made the journey twice a week.

Next morning Duane mounted his horse and headed for Fairdale. He rode leisurely, as he wanted to learn all he could about the country. There were few ranches. The farther he traveled the better grazing he encountered, and, strange to note, the fewer herds of cattle.

It was just sunset when he made out a cluster of adobe houses that marked the halfway point between Bradford and Fairdale. Here, Duane had learned, was stationed a comfortable inn for wayfarers.

When he drew up before the inn the landlord and his family and a number of loungers greeted him laconically.

"Beat the stage in, hey?" remarked one.

"There she comes now," said another. "Joel shore is drivin' tonight."

Far down the road Duane saw a cloud of dust and horses and a lumbering coach. When he had looked after the needs of his horse he returned to the group before the inn. They awaited the stage with that interest common to isolated people. Presently it rolled up, a large mud-bespattered and dusty vehicle, littered with baggage on top and tied on behind. A number of passengers alighted, three of whom excited Duane's interest. One was a tall, dark, striking-looking man, and the other two were ladies, wearing long gray ulsters and veils. Duane heard the proprietor of the inn address the man as Colonel Longstreth, and as the party entered the inn Duane's quick ears caught a few words which acquainted him with the fact that Longstreth was the Mayor of Fairdale.

Duane passed inside himself to learn that supper would soon be ready. At table he found himself opposite the three who had attracted his attention.

"Ruth, I envy the lucky cowboys," Longstreth was saying.

Ruth was a curly-headed girl with gray or hazel eyes.

"I'm crazy to ride bronchos," she said.

Duane gathered she was on a visit to western Texas. The other girl's deep voice, sweet like a bell, made Duane regard her closer. She had beauty as he had never seen it in another woman. She was slender, but the development of her figure gave Duane the impression she was twenty years old or more. She had the most exquisite hands Duane had ever seen. She did not resemble the Colonel, who was evidently her father. She looked tired, quiet, even melancholy. A finely chiseled oval face; clear, olive-tinted skin, long eyes set wide apart and black as coal, beautiful to look into; a slender, straight nose that had something nervous and delicate about it which made Duane think of a thoroughbred; and a mouth by no means small, but perfectly curved; and hair like jet—all these features proclaimed her beauty to Duane. Duane believed her a descendant of one of the old French families of eastern Texas. He was sure of it when she looked at him, drawn by his rather persistent gaze. There were pride, fire, and passion in her eyes. Duane felt himself blushing in confusion. His stare at her had been rude, perhaps, but unconscious. How many years had passed since he had seen a girl like her! Thereafter he kept his eyes upon his plate, yet he seemed to be aware that he had aroused the interest of both girls.

After supper the guests assembled in a big sitting room where an open fire place with blazing mesquite sticks gave out warmth and cheery glow. Duane took a seat by a table in the corner, and, finding a paper, began to read. Presently when he glanced up he saw two dark-faced men, strangers who had not appeared before, and were peering in from a doorway. When they saw Duane had observed them they stepped back out of sight.

It flashed over Duane that the strangers acted suspiciously. In Texas in the seventies it was always bad policy to let strangers go unheeded. Duane pondered a moment. Then he went out to look over these two men. The doorway opened into a patio, and across that was a little dingy, dim-lighted barroom. Here Duane found the innkeeper dispensing drinks to the two strangers. They glanced up when he entered, and one of them whispered. He imagined he had seen one of them before. In Texas, where outdoor men were so rough, bronzed, bold, and sometimes grim of aspect, it was no easy task to pick out the crooked ones. But Duane's years on the border had augmented a natural instinct or gift to read character, or at least to sense the evil in men; and he knew at once that these strangers were dishonest.

"Hey somethin'?" one of them asked, leering. Both looked Duane up and down.

"No thanks, I don't drink," Duane replied, and returned their scrutiny with interest. "How's tricks in the Big Bend?"

Both men stared. It had taken only a close glance for Duane to recognize a type of ruffian most frequently met along the river. These strangers had that stamp, and their surprise proved he was right. Here the innkeeper showed signs of uneasiness, and seconded the surprise of his customers. No more was said at the instant, and the two rather hurriedly went out.

"Say, boss, do you know those fellows?" Duane asked the innkeeper.

"Nope."

"Which way did they come?"

"Now I think of it, them fellers rid in from both corners today," he replied, and he put both hands on the bar and looked at Duane. "They nooned heah, comin' from Bradford, they said, an' trailed in after the stage."

When Duane returned to the sitting-room Colonel Longstreth was absent, also several of the other passengers. Miss Ruth sat in the chair he had vacated, and across the table from her sat Miss Longstreth. Duane went directly to them.

"Excuse me," said Duane, addressing them. "I want to tell you there are a couple of rough-looking men here. I've just seen them. They mean evil. Tell your father to be careful. Lock your doors—bar your windows tonight."

"Oh!" cried Ruth, very low. "Ray, do you hear?"

"Thank you; we'll be careful," said Miss Longstreth, gracefully. The rich color had faded in her cheek. "I saw those men watching you from that door. They had such bright black eyes. Is there really danger—here?"

"I think so," was Duane's reply.

Soft swift steps behind him preceded a harsh voice: "Hands up!"

No man quicker than Duane to recognize the intent in those words! His hands shot up. Miss Ruth uttered a little frightened cry and sank into her chair. Miss Longstreth turned white, her eyes dilated. Both girls were staring at someone behind Duane.

"Turn around!" ordered the harsh voice.

The big, dark stranger, the bearded one who had whispered to his comrade in the barroom and asked Duane to drink, had him covered with a cocked gun. He strode forward, his eyes gleaming, pressed the gun against him, and with his other hand dove into his inside coat pocket and tore out his roll of bills. Then he reached low at Duane's hip, felt his gun, and took it. Then he slapped the other hip, evidently in search of another weapon. That done, he backed away, wearing an expression of fiendish satisfaction that made Duane think he was only a common thief, a novice at this kind of game.

His comrade stood in the door with a gun leveled at two other men, who stood there frightened, speechless.

"Git a move on, Bill," called this fellow; and he took a hasty glance backward. A stamp of hoofs came from outside. Of course the robbers had horses waiting. The one called Bill strode across the room, and with brutal, careless haste began to prod the two men with his weapon and to search them. The robber in the doorway called "Rustle!" and disappeared.

Duane wondered where the innkeeper was, and Colonel Longstreth and the other two passengers. The bearded robber quickly got through with his searching, and from his growls Duane gathered he had not been well remunerated. Then he wheeled once more. Duane had not moved a muscle, stood perfectly calm with his arms high. The robber strode back with his bloodshot eyes fastened upon the girls. Miss Longstreth never flinched, but the little girl appeared about to faint.

"Don't yap, there!" he said, low and hard. He thrust the gun close to Ruth. Then Duane knew for sure that he was no knight of the road, but a plain cutthroat robber. Danger always made Duane exult in a kind of cold glow. But now something hot worked within him. He had a little gun in his pocket. The robber had missed it. And he began to calculate chances.

"Any money, jewelry, diamonds!" ordered the ruffian, fiercely.

Miss Ruth collapsed. Then he made at Miss Longstreth. She stood with her hands at her breast. Evidently the robber took this position to mean that she had valuables concealed there. But Duane fancied she had instinctively pressed her hands against a throbbing heart.

"Come out with it!" he said, harshly, reaching for her.

"Don't dare touch me!" she cried, her eyes ablaze. She did not move. She had nerve.

It made Duane thrill. He saw he was going to get a chance. Waiting had been a science with him. But here it was hard. Miss Ruth had fainted, and that was well. Miss Longstreth had fight in her, which fact helped Duane, yet made injury possible to her. She eluded two lunges the man made at her. Then his rough hand caught her waist, and with one pull ripped it asunder, exposing her beautiful shoulder, white as snow.

She cried out. The prospect of being robbed or even killed had not shaken Miss Longstreth's nerve as had this brutal tearing off of half her waist.

The ruffian was only turned partially away from Duane. For himself he could have waited no longer. But for her! That gun was still held dangerously upward close to her. Duane watched only that. Then a bellow made him jerk his head. Colonel Longstreth stood in the doorway in a magnificent rage. He had no weapon. Strange how he showed no fear! He bellowed something again.

Duane's shifting glance caught the robber's sudden movement. It was a kind of start. He seemed stricken. Duane expected him to shoot Longstreth. Instead the hand that clutched Miss Longstreth's torn waist loosened its hold. The other hand with its cocked weapon slowly dropped till it pointed to the floor. That was Duane's chance.

Swift as a flash he drew his gun and fired. *Thud!* went his bullet, and he could not tell on the instant whether it hit the robber or went into the ceiling. Then the robber's gun boomed harmlessly. He fell with blood spurting over his face. Duane realized he had hit him, but the small bullet had glanced.

Miss Longstreth reeled and might have fallen had Duane not supported her. It was only a few steps to a couch, to which he half led, half carried her. Then he rushed out of the room, across the patio, through the bar to the yard. Nevertheless, he was cautious. In the gloom stood a saddled horse, probably the one belonging to the fellow he had shot. His comrade had escaped. Returning to the sitting-room, Duane found a condition approaching pandemonium.

The innkeeper rushed in, pitchfork in hands. Evidently he had been out at the barn. He was now shouting to find out what had happened. Joel, the stage-driver, was trying to quiet the men who had been robbed. The woman, wife of one of the men, had come in, and she had hysterics. The girls were still and white. The robber Bill lay where he had fallen, and Duane guessed he had made a fair shot, after all. And, lastly, the thing that struck Duane most of all was Longstreth's rage. He never saw such passion. Like a caged lion Longstreth stalked and roared. There came a quieter moment in which the innkeeper shrilly protested:

"Man, what're you ravin' aboot? Nobody's hurt, an' thet's lucky. I swear to God I hadn't nothin' to do with them fellers!"

"I ought to kill you anyhow!" replied Longstreth. And his voice now astounded Duane, it was so full of power.

Upon examination Duane found that his bullet had furrowed the robber's temple, torn a great piece out of his scalp, and, as Duane had guessed, had glanced. He was not seriously injured, and already showed signs of returning consciousness.

"Drag him out of here!" ordered Longstreth; and he turned to his daughter.

Before the innkeeper reached the robber Duane had secured the money and gun taken from him; and presently recovered the property of the other men. Joel helped the innkeeper carry the injured man somewhere outside.

Miss Longstreth was sitting white but composed upon the couch, where lay Miss Ruth, who evidently had been carried there by the Colonel. Duane did not think she had wholly lost consciousness, and now she lay very still, with eyes dark and shadowy, her face pallid and wet. The Colonel, now that he finally remembered his women-folk, seemed to be gentle and kind. He talked soothingly to Miss Ruth, made light of the adventure, said she must learn to have nerve out here where things happened.

"Can I be of any service?" asked Duane, solicitously.

"Thanks; I guess there's nothing you can do. Talk to these frightened girls while I go see what's to be done with that thick-skulled robber," he replied, and, telling the girls that there was no more danger, he went out.

Miss Longstreth sat with one hand holding her torn waist in place; the other she extended to Duane. He took it awkwardly, and he felt a strange thrill.

"You saved my life," she said, in grave, sweet seriousness.

"No, no!" Duane exclaimed. "He might have struck you, hurt you, but no more."

"I saw murder in his eyes. He thought I had jewels under my dress. I couldn't bear his touch. The beast! I'd have fought. Surely my life was in peril."

"Did you kill him?" asked Miss Ruth, who lay listening.

"Oh no. He's not badly hurt."

"I'm very glad he's alive," said Miss Longstreth, shuddering.

"My intention was bad enough," Duane went on. "It was a ticklish place for me. You see, he was half drunk, and I was afraid his gun might go off. Fool careless he was!"

"Yet you say you didn't save me," Miss Longstreth returned, quickly.

"Well, let it go at that," Duane responded. "I saved you something."

"Tell me all about it?" asked Miss Ruth, who was fast recovering.

Rather embarrassed, Duane briefly told the incident from his point of view.

"Then you stood there all the time with your hands up thinking of nothing—watching for nothing except a little moment when you might draw your gun?" asked Miss Ruth.

"I guess that's about it," he replied.

"Cousin," said Miss Longstreth, thoughtfully, "it was fortunate for us that this gentleman happened to be here. Papa scouts—laughs at danger. He seemed to think there was no danger. Yet he raved after it came."

"Go with us all the way to Fairdale—please?" asked Miss Ruth, sweetly offering her hand. "I am Ruth Herbert. And this is my cousin, Ray Longstreth."

"I'm traveling that way," replied Duane, in great confusion. He did not know how to meet the situation.

Colonel Longstreth returned then, and after bidding Duane a good night, which seemed rather curt by contrast to the graciousness of the girls, he led them away.

Before going to bed Duane went outside to take a look at the injured robber and perhaps to ask him a few questions. To Duane's surprise, he was gone, and so was his horse. The innkeeper was dumfounded. He said that he left the fellow on the floor in the barroom.

"Had he come to?" inquired Duane.

"Sure. He asked for whisky."

"Did he say anything else?"

"Not to me. I heard him talkin' to the father of them girls."

"You mean Colonel Longstreth?"

"I reckon. He sure was some riled, wasn't he? Jest as if I was to blame fer that two-bit of a holdup!"

"What did you make of the old gent's rage?" asked Duane, watching the innkeeper. He scratched his head dubiously. He was sincere, and Duane believed in his honesty.

"Wal, I'm doggoned if I know what to make of it. But I reckon he's either crazy or got more nerve than most Texans."

"More nerve, maybe," Duane replied. "Show me a bed now, innkeeper."

Once in bed in the dark, Duane composed himself to think over the several events of the evening. He called up the details of the holdup and carefully revolved them in mind. The Colonel's wrath, under circumstances where almost any Texan would have been cool, nonplussed Duane, and he put it down to a choleric temperament. He pondered long on the action of the robber when Longstreth's bellow of rage burst in upon him. This ruffian, as bold and mean a type as Duane had ever encountered, had, from some cause or other, been startled. From whatever point Duane viewed the man's strange indecision he could come to only one conclusion—his start, his check, his fear had been that of recognition. Duane compared this effect with the suddenly acquired sense he had gotten of Colonel Longstreth's powerful personality. Why had that desperate robber lowered his gun and stood paralyzed at sight and sound of the Mayor of Fairdale? This was not answerable. There might have been a number of reasons, all to Colonel Longstreth's credit, but Duane could not understand. Longstreth had not appeared to see danger for his daughter, even though she had been roughly handled, and had advanced in front of a cocked gun. Duane probed deep into this singular fact, and he brought to bear on the thing all his knowledge and experience of violent Texas life. And he found that the instant Colonel Longstreth had appeared on the scene there was no further danger threatening his daughter. Why? That likewise Duane could not answer. Then his rage, Duane concluded, had been solely at the idea of *his* daughter being assaulted by a robber. This deduction was indeed a thought-disturber, but Duane put it aside to crystallize and for more careful consideration.

Next morning Duane found that the little town was called Sanderson. It was larger than he had at first supposed. He walked up the main street and back again. Just as he arrived some horsemen rode up to the inn and dismounted. And at this juncture the Longstreth party came out. Duane heard Colonel Longstreth utter an exclamation. Then he saw him shake hands with a tall man. Longstreth looked surprised and angry, and he spoke with force; but Duane could not hear what it was he said. The fellow laughed, yet somehow he struck Duane as sullen, until suddenly he espied Miss Longstreth. Then his face changed, and he removed his sombrero. Duane went closer.

"Floyd, did you come with the teams?" asked Longstreth, sharply.

"Not me. I rode a horse, good and hard," was the reply.

"Humph! I'll have a word to say to you later." Then Longstreth turned to his daughter. "Ray, here's the cousin I've told you about. You used to play with him ten years ago—Floyd Lawson. Floyd, my daughter—and my niece, Ruth Herbert."

Duane always scrutinized everyone he met, and now with a dangerous game to play, with a consciousness of Longstreth's unusual and significant personality, he bent a keen and searching glance upon this Floyd Lawson.

He was under thirty, yet gray at his temples—dark, smooth-shaven, with lines left by wildness, dissipation, shadows under dark eyes, a mouth strong and bitter, and a square chin—a reckless, careless, handsome, sinister face strangely losing the hardness when he smiled. The grace of a gentleman clung round him, seemed like an echo in his mellow voice. Duane doubted not that he, like many a young man, had drifted out to the frontier, where rough and wild life had wrought sternly but had not quite effaced the mark of good family.

Colonel Longstreth apparently did not share the pleasure of his daughter and his niece in the advent of this cousin. Something hinged on this meeting. Duane grew intensely curious, but, as the stage appeared ready for the journey, he had no further opportunity to gratify it.

# CHAPTER XVI

Duane followed the stage through the town, out into the open, on to a wide, hard-packed road showing years of travel. It headed northwest. To the left rose a range of low, bleak mountains he had noted yesterday, and to the right sloped the mesquite-patched sweep of ridge and flat. The driver pushed his team to a fast trot, which gait surely covered ground rapidly.

The stage made three stops in the forenoon, one at a place where the horses could be watered, the second at a chuck wagon belonging to cowboys who were riding after stock, and the third at a small cluster of adobe and stone houses constituting a hamlet the driver called Longstreth, named after the Colonel. From that point on to Fairdale there were only a few ranches, each one controlling great acreage.

Early in the afternoon from a ridgetop Duane sighted Fairdale, a green patch in the mass of gray. For the barrens of Texas it was indeed a fair sight. But he was more concerned with its remoteness from civilization than its beauty. At that time, in the early seventies, when the vast western third of Texas was a wilderness, the pioneer had done wonders to settle there and establish places like Fairdale.

It needed only a glance for Duane to pick out Colonel Longstreth's ranch. The house was situated on the only elevation around Fairdale, and it was not high, nor more than a few minutes' walk from the edge of the town. It was a low, flat-roofed structure made of red adobe bricks, and covered what appeared to be fully an acre of ground. All was green about it, except where the fenced corrals and numerous barns or sheds showed gray and red.

Duane soon reached the shady outskirts of Fairdale, and entered the town with mingled feelings of curiosity, eagerness, and expectation. The street he rode down was a main one, and on both sides of the street was a solid row of saloons, resorts, hotels. Saddled horses stood hitched all along the sidewalk in two long lines, with a buckboard and team here and there breaking the continuity. This block was busy and noisy.

From all outside appearances Fairdale was no different from other frontier towns, and Duane's expectations were scarcely realized. As the afternoon was waning he halted at a little inn. A boy took charge of his horse. Duane questioned the lad about Fairdale and gradually drew to the subject most in mind.

"Colonel Longstreth has a big outfit, eh?"

"Reckon he has," replied the lad. "Doan know how many cowboys. They're always comin' and goin'. I ain't acquainted with half of them."

"Much movement of stock these days?"

"Stock's always movin'," he replied, with a queer look.

"Rustlers?"

But he did not follow up that look with the affirmative Duane expected.

"Lively place, I hear—Fairdale is?"

"Ain't so lively as Sanderson, but it's bigger."

"Yes, I heard it was. Fellow down there was talking about two cowboys who were arrested."

"Sure. I heered all about that. Joe Bean an' Brick Higgins—they belong heah, but they ain't heah much. Longstreth's boys."

Duane did not want to appear over-inquisitive, so he turned the talk into other channels.

After getting supper Duane strolled up and down the main street. When darkness set in he went into a hotel, bought cigars, sat around, and watched. Then he passed out and went into the next place. This was of rough crude exterior, but the inside was comparatively pretentious and ablaze with lights. It was full of men coming and going—a dusty-booted crowd that smelled of horses and smoke. Duane sat down for a while, with wide eyes and open ears. Then he hunted up the bar, where most of the guests had been or were going. He found a great square room lighted by six huge lamps, a bar at one side, and all the floor-space taken up by tables and chairs. This was the only gambling place of any size in southern Texas in which he had noted the absence of Mexicans. There was some card-playing going on at this moment. Duane stayed in there for a while, and knew that strangers were too common in Fairdale to be conspicuous. Then he returned to the inn where he had engaged a room.

Duane sat down on the steps of the dingy little restaurant. Two men were conversing inside, and they had not noticed Duane.

"Laramie, what's the stranger's name?" asked one.

"He didn't say," replied the other.

"Sure was a strappin' big man. Struck me a little odd, he did. No cattleman, him. How'd you size him?"

"Well, like one of them cool, easy, quiet Texans who's been lookin' for a man for years—to kill him when he found him."

"Right you are, Laramie; and, between you an' me, I hope he's lookin' for Long—"

"'S—sh!" interrupted Laramie. "You must be half drunk, to go talkin' that way."

Thereafter they conversed in too low a tone for Duane to hear, and presently Laramie's visitor left. Duane went inside, and, making himself agreeable, began to ask casual questions about Fairdale. Laramie was not communicative.

Duane went to his room in a thoughtful frame of mind. Had Laramie's visitor meant he hoped someone had come to kill Longstreth? Duane inferred just that from the interrupted remark. There was something wrong about the Mayor of Fairdale. Duane felt it. And he felt also, if there was a crooked and dangerous man, it was this Floyd Lawson. The innkeeper Laramie would be worth cultivating. And last in Duane's thoughts that night was Miss Longstreth. He could not help thinking of her—how strangely the meeting with her had affected him. It made him remember that long-past time when girls had been a part of his life. What a sad and dark and endless void lay between that past and the present! He had no right even to dream of a beautiful woman like Ray Longstreth. That conviction, however, did not dispel her; indeed, it seemed perversely to make her grow more fascinating. Duane grew conscious of a strange, unaccountable hunger, a something that was like a pang in his breast.

Next day he lounged about the inn. He did not make any overtures to the taciturn proprietor. Duane had no need of hurry now. He contented himself with watching and listening. And at the close of that day he decided Fairdale was what MacNelly had claimed it to be, and that he was on the track of an unusual adventure. The following day he spent in much the same way, though on one occasion he told Laramie he was looking for a man. The innkeeper grew a little less furtive and reticent after that. He would answer casual queries, and it did not take Duane long to learn that Laramie had seen better days—that he was now broken, bitter, and hard. Someone had wronged him.

Several days passed. Duane did not succeed in getting any closer to Laramie, but he found the idlers on the corners and in front of the stores unsuspicious and willing to talk. It did not take him long to find out that Fairdale stood parallel with Huntsville for gambling, drinking, and fighting. The street was always lined with dusty, saddled horses, the town full of strangers. Money appeared more abundant than in any place Duane had ever visited; and it was spent with the abandon that spoke forcibly of easy and crooked acquirement. Duane decided that Sanderson, Bradford, and Ord were but notorious outposts to this Fairdale, which was a secret center of rustlers and outlaws. And what struck Duane strangest of all was the fact that Longstreth was mayor here and held court daily. Duane knew intuitively, before a chance remark gave him proof, that this court was a sham, a farce. And he wondered if it were not a blind. This wonder of his was equivalent to suspicion of Colonel Longstreth, and Duane reproached himself. Then he realized that the reproach was because of the daughter. Inquiry had brought him the fact that Ray Longstreth had just come to live with her father. Longstreth had originally been a planter in Louisiana, where his family had remained after his advent in the West. He was a rich rancher; he owned half of Fairdale; he was a cattle buyer on a large scale. Floyd Lawson was his lieutenant and associate in deals.

On the afternoon of the fifth day of Duane's stay in Fairdale he returned to the inn from his usual stroll, and upon entering was amazed to have a rough-looking young fellow rush by him out of the door. Inside Laramie was lying on the floor, with a bloody bruise on his face. He did not appear to be dangerously hurt.

"Bo Snecker! He hit me and went after the cash-drawer," said Laramie, laboring to his feet.

"Are you hurt much?" queried Duane.

"I guess not. But Bo needn't to have soaked me. I've been robbed before without that."

"Well, I'll take a look after Bo," replied Duane.

He went out and glanced down the street toward the center of the town. He did not see anyone he could take for the innkeeper's assailant. Then he looked up the street, and he saw the young fellow about a block away, hurrying along and gazing back.

Duane yelled for him to stop and started to go after him. Snecker broke into a run. Then Duane set out to overhaul him. There were two motives in Duane's action—one of anger, and the other a desire to make a friend of this man Laramie, whom Duane believed could tell him much.

Duane was light on his feet, and he had a giant stride. He gained rapidly upon Snecker, who, turning this way and that, could not get out of sight. Then he took to the open country and ran straight for the green hill where Longstreth's house stood. Duane had almost caught Snecker when he reached the shrubbery and trees and there eluded him. But Duane kept him in sight, in the shade, on the paths, and up the road into the courtyard, and he saw Snecker go straight for Longstreth's house.

Duane was not to be turned back by that, singular as it was. He did not stop to consider. It seemed enough to know that fate had directed him to the path of this rancher Longstreth. Duane entered the first open door on that side of the court. It opened into a corridor which led into a plaza. It had wide, smooth stone porches, and flowers and shrubbery in the center. Duane hurried through to burst into the presence of Miss Longstreth and a number of young people. Evidently she was giving a little party.

Lawson stood leaning against one of the pillars that supported the porch roof; at sight of Duane his face changed remarkably, expressing amazement, consternation, then fear.

In the quick ensuing silence Miss Longstreth rose white as her dress. The young women present stared in astonishment, if they were not equally perturbed. There were cowboys present who suddenly grew intent and still. By these things Duane gathered that his appearance must be disconcerting. He was panting. He wore no hat or coat. His big gun sheath showed plainly at his hip.

Sight of Miss Longstreth had an unaccountable effect upon Duane. He was plunged into confusion. For the moment he saw no one but her.

"Miss Longstreth—I came—to search—your house," panted Duane.

He hardly knew what he was saying, yet the instant he spoke he realized that that should have been the last thing for him to say. He had blundered. But he was not used to women, and this dark-eyed girl made him thrill and his heart beat thickly and his wits go scattering.

"Search my house!" exclaimed Miss Longstreth; and red succeeded the white in her cheeks. She appeared astonished and angry. "What for? Why, how dare you! This is unwarrantable!"

"A man—Bo Snecker—assaulted and robbed Jim Laramie," replied Duane, hurriedly. "I chased Snecker here—saw him run into the house."

"Here? Oh, sir, you must be mistaken. We have seen no one. In the absence of my father I'm mistress here. I'll not permit you to search."

Lawson appeared to come out of his astonishment. He stepped forward.

"Ray, don't be bothered now," he said, to his cousin. "This fellow's making a bluff. I'll settle him. See here, Mister, you clear out!"

"I want Snecker. He's here, and I'm going to get him," replied Duane, quietly.

"Bah! That's all a bluff," sneered Lawson. "I'm on to your game. You just wanted an excuse to break in here—to see my cousin again. When you saw the company you invented that excuse. Now, be off, or it'll be the worse for you."

Duane felt his face burn with a tide of hot blood. Almost he felt that he was guilty of such motive. Had he not been unable to put this Ray Longstreth out of his mind? There seemed to be scorn in her eyes now. And somehow that checked his embarrassment.

"Miss Longstreth, will you let me search the house?" he asked.

"No."

"Then—I regret to say—I'll do so without your permission."

"You'll not dare!" she flashed. She stood erect, her bosom swelling.

"Pardon me, yes, I will."

"Who are you?" she demanded, suddenly.

"I'm a Texas Ranger," replied Duane.

"*A Texas Ranger!*" she echoed.

Floyd Lawson's dark face turned pale.

"Miss Longstreth, I don't need warrants to search houses," said Duane. "I'm sorry to annoy you. I'd prefer to have your permission. A ruffian has taken refuge here—in your father's house. He's hidden somewhere. May I look for him?"

"If you are indeed a ranger."

Duane produced his papers. Miss Longstreth haughtily refused to look at them.

"Miss Longstreth, I've come to make Fairdale a safer, cleaner, better place for women and children. I don't wonder at your resentment. But to doubt me—insult me. Someday you may be sorry."

Floyd Lawson made a violent motion with his hands.

"All stuff! Cousin, go on with your party. I'll take a couple of cowboys and go with this—this Texas Ranger."

"Thanks," said Duane, coolly, as he eyed Lawson. "Perhaps you'll be able to find Snecker quicker than I could."

"What do you mean?" demanded Lawson, and now he grew livid. Evidently he was a man of fierce quick passions.

"Don't quarrel," said Miss Longstreth. "Floyd, you go with him. Please hurry. I'll be nervous till—the man's found or you're sure there's not one."

They started with several cowboys to search the house. They went through the rooms searching, calling out, peering into dark places. It struck Duane more than forcibly that Lawson did all the calling. He was hurried, too, tried to keep in the lead. Duane wondered if he knew his voice would be recognized by the hiding man. Be that as it might, it was Duane who peered into a dark corner and then, with a gun leveled, said, "Come out!"

He came forth into the flare—a tall, slim, dark-faced youth, wearing sombrero, blouse and trousers. Duane collared him before any of the others could move and held the gun close enough to make him shrink. But he did not impress Duane as being frightened just then; nevertheless, he had a clammy face, the pallid look of a man who had just gotten over a shock. He peered into Duane's face, then into that of the cowboy next to him, then into Lawson's, and if ever in Duane's life he beheld relief it was then. That was all Duane needed to know, but he meant to find out more if he could.

"Who're you?" asked Duane, quietly.

"Bo Snecker," he said.

"What'd you hide here for?"

He appeared to grow sullen.

"Reckoned I'd be as safe in Longstreth's as anywheres."

"Ranger, what'll you do with him?" Lawson queried, as if uncertain, now the capture was made.

"I'll see to that," replied Duane, and he pushed Snecker in front of him out into the court.

Duane had suddenly conceived the idea of taking Snecker before Mayor Longstreth in the court.

When Duane arrived at the hall where court was held there were other men there, a dozen or more, and all seemed excited; evidently, news of Duane had preceded him. Longstreth sat at a table up on a platform. Near him sat a thick-set grizzled man, with deep eyes, and this was Hanford Owens, county judge. To the right stood a tall, angular, yellow-faced fellow with a drooping sandy mustache. Conspicuous on his vest was a huge silver shield. This was Gorsech, one of Longstreth's sheriffs. There were four other men whom Duane knew by sight, several whose faces were familiar, and half a dozen strangers, all dusty horsemen.

Longstreth pounded hard on the table to be heard. Mayor or not, he was unable at once to quell the excitement. Gradually, however, it subsided, and from the last few utterances before quiet was restored Duane gathered that he had intruded upon some kind of a meeting in the hall.

"What'd you break in here for?" demanded Longstreth.

"Isn't this the court? Aren't you the Mayor of Fairdale?" interrogated Duane. His voice was clear and loud, almost piercing.

"Yes," replied Longstreth. Like flint he seemed, yet Duane felt his intense interest.

"I've arrested a criminal," said Duane.

"Arrested a criminal!" ejaculated Longstreth. "You? Who're you?"

"I'm a ranger," replied Duane.

A significant silence ensued.

"I charge Snecker with assault on Laramie and attempted robbery—if not murder. He's had a shady past here, as this court will know if it keeps a record."

"What's this I hear about you, Bo? Get up and speak for yourself," said Longstreth, gruffly.

Snecker got up, not without a furtive glance at Duane, and he had shuffled forward a few steps toward the Mayor. He had an evil front, but not the boldness even of a rustler.

"It ain't so, Longstreth," he began, loudly. "I went in Laramie's place fer grub. Some feller I never seen before come in from the hall an' hit Laramie an' wrestled him on the floor. I went out. Then this big ranger chased me an' fetched me here. I didn't do nothin'. This ranger's hankerin' to arrest somebody. Thet's my hunch, Longstreth."

Longstreth said something in an undertone to Judge Owens, and that worthy nodded his great bushy head.

"Bo, you're discharged," said Longstreth, bluntly. "Now the rest of you clear out of here."

He absolutely ignored the ranger. That was his rebuff to Duane—his slap in the face to an interfering ranger service. If Longstreth was crooked he certainly had magnificent nerve. Duane almost decided he was above suspicion. But his nonchalance, his air of finality, his authoritative assurance— these to Duane's keen and practiced eyes were in significant contrast to a certain tenseness of line about his mouth and a slow paling of his olive skin. In that momentary lull Duane's scrutiny of Longstreth gathered an impression of the man's intense curiosity.

Then the prisoner, Snecker, with a cough that broke the spell of silence, shuffled a couple of steps toward the door.

"Hold on!" called Duane. The call halted Snecker, as if it had been a bullet.

"Longstreth, I saw Snecker attack Laramie," said Duane, his voice still ringing. "What has the court to say to that?"

"The court has this to say. West of the Pecos we'll not aid any ranger service. We don't want you out here. Fairdale doesn't need you."

"That's a lie, Longstreth," retorted Duane. "I've letters from Fairdale citizens all begging for ranger service."

Longstreth turned white. The veins corded at his temples. He appeared about to burst into rage. He was at a loss for quick reply.

Floyd Lawson rushed in and up to the table. The blood showed black and thick in his face; his utterance was incoherent, his uncontrollable outbreak of temper seemed out of all proportion to any cause he should reasonably have had for anger. Longstreth shoved him back with a curse and a warning glare.

"Where's your warrant to arrest Snecker?" shouted Longstreth.

"I don't need warrants to make arrests. Longstreth, you're ignorant of the power of Texas Rangers."

"You'll come none of your damned ranger stunts out here. I'll block you."

That passionate reply of Longstreth's was the signal Duane had been waiting for. He had helped on the crisis. He wanted to force Longstreth's hand and show the town his stand.

Duane backed clear of everybody.

"Men! I call on you all!" cried Duane, piercingly. "I call on you to witness the arrest of a criminal prevented by Longstreth, Mayor of Fairdale. It will be recorded in the report to the Adjutant-General at Austin. Longstreth, you'll never prevent another arrest."

Longstreth sat white with working jaw.

"Longstreth, you've shown your hand," said Duane, in a voice that carried far and held those who heard. "Any honest citizen of Fairdale can now see what's plain—yours is a damn poor hand! You're going to hear me call a spade a spade. In the two years you've been Mayor you've never arrested one rustler. Strange, when Fairdale's a nest for rustlers! You've never sent a prisoner to Del Rio, let alone to Austin. You have no jail. There have been nine murders during your office—innumerable street fights and holdups. Not one arrest! But you have ordered arrests for trivial offenses, and have punished these out of all proportion. There have been lawsuits in your court suits over water rights, cattle deals, property lines. Strange how in these lawsuits you or Lawson or other men close to you were always involved! Strange how it seems the law was stretched to favor your interest!"

Duane paused in his cold, ringing speech. In the silence, both outside and inside the hall, could be heard the deep breathing of agitated men. Longstreth was indeed a study. Yet did he betray anything but rage at this interloper?

"Longstreth, here's plain talk for you and Fairdale," went on Duane. "I don't accuse you and your court of dishonesty. I say *strange!* Law here has been a farce. The motive behind all this laxity isn't plain to me—yet. But I call your hand!"

## CHAPTER XVII

Duane left the hall, elbowed his way through the crowd, and went down the street. He was certain that on the faces of some men he had seen ill-concealed wonder and satisfaction. He had struck some kind of a hot trait, and he meant to see where it led. It was by no means unlikely that Cheseldine might be at the other end. Duane controlled a mounting eagerness. But ever and anon it was shot through with a remembrance of Ray Longstreth. He suspected her father of being not what he pretended. He might, very probably would, bring sorrow and shame to this young woman. The thought made him smart with pain. She began to haunt him, and then he was thinking more of her beauty and sweetness than of the disgrace he might bring upon her. Some strange emotion, long locked inside Duane's heart, knocked to be heard, to be let out. He was troubled.

Upon returning to the inn he found Laramie there, apparently none the worse for his injury.

"How are you, Laramie?" he asked.

"Reckon I'm feelin' as well as could be expected," replied Laramie. His head was circled by a bandage that did not conceal the lump where he had been struck. He looked pale, but was bright enough.

"That was a good crack Snecker gave you," remarked Duane.

"I ain't accusin' Bo," remonstrated Laramie, with eyes that made Duane thoughtful.

"Well, I accuse him. I caught him—took him to Longstreth's court. But they let him go."

Laramie appeared to be agitated by this intimation of friendship.

"See here, Laramie," went on Duane, "in some parts of Texas it's policy to be close-mouthed. Policy and health-preserving! Between ourselves, I want you to know I lean on your side of the fence."

Laramie gave a quick start. Presently Duane turned and frankly met his gaze. He had startled Laramie out of his habitual set taciturnity; but even as he looked the light that might have been amaze and joy faded out of his face, leaving it the same old mask. Still Duane had seen enough. Like a bloodhound he had a scent.

"Talking about work, Laramie, who'd you say Snecker worked for?"

"I didn't say."

"Well, say so now, can't you? Laramie, you're powerful peevish today. It's that bump on your head. Who does Snecker work for?"

"When he works at all, which sure ain't often, he rides for Longstreth."

"Humph! Seems to me that Longstreth's the whole circus round Fairdale. I was some sore the other day to find I was losing good money at Longstreth's faro game. Sure if I'd won I wouldn't have been sore—ha, ha! But I was surprised to hear someone say Longstreth owned the Hope So joint."

"He owns considerable property hereabouts," replied Laramie, constrainedly.

"Humph again! Laramie, like every other fellow I meet in this town, you're afraid to open your trap about Longstreth. Get me straight, Laramie. I don't care a damn for Colonel Mayor Longstreth. And for cause I'd throw a gun on him just as quick as on any rustler in Pecos."

"Talk's cheap," replied Laramie, making light of his bluster, but the red was deeper in his face.

"Sure. I know that," Duane said. "And usually I don't talk. Then it's not well known that Longstreth owns the Hope So?"

"Reckon it's known in Pecos, all right. But Longstreth's name isn't connected with the Hope So. Blandy runs the place."

"That Blandy. His faro game's crooked, or I'm a locoed bronch. Not that we don't have lots of crooked faro dealers. A fellow can stand for them. But Blandy's mean, back-handed, never looks you in the eyes. That Hope So place ought to be run by a good fellow like you, Laramie."

"Thanks," replied he; and Duane imagined his voice a little husky. "Didn't you hear I used to run it?"

"No. Did you?" Duane said, quickly.

"I reckon. I built the place, made additions twice, owned it for eleven years."

"Well, I'll be doggoned." It was indeed Duane's turn to be surprised, and with the surprise came a glimmering. "I'm sorry you're not there now. Did you sell out?"

"No. Just lost the place."

Laramie was bursting for relief now—to talk, to tell. Sympathy had made him soft.

"It was two years ago—two years last March," he went on. "I was in a big cattle deal with Longstreth. We got the stock—an' my share, eighteen hundred head, was rustled off. I owed Longstreth. He pressed me. It come to a lawsuit—an' I—was ruined."

It hurt Duane to look at Laramie. He was white, and tears rolled down his cheeks. Duane saw the bitterness, the defeat, the agony of the man. He had failed to meet his obligations; nevertheless, he had been swindled. All that he suppressed, all that would have been passion had the man's spirit not been broken, lay bare for Duane to see. He had now the secret of his bitterness. But the reason he did not openly accuse Longstreth, the secret of his reticence and fear—these Duane thought best to try to learn at some later time.

"Hard luck! It certainly was tough," Duane said. "But you're a good loser. And the wheel turns! Now, Laramie, here's what. I need your advice. I've got a little money. But before I lose it I want to invest some. Buy some stock, or buy an interest in some rancher's herd. What I want you to steer me on is a good square rancher. Or maybe a couple of ranchers, if there happen to be two honest ones. Ha, ha! No deals with ranchers who ride in the dark with rustlers! I've a hunch Fairdale is full of them. Now, Laramie, you've been here for years. Sure you must know a couple of men above suspicion."

"Thank God I do," he replied, feelingly. "Frank Morton an' Si Zimmer, my friends an' neighbors all my prosperous days, an' friends still. You can gamble on Frank and Si. But if you want advice from me—don't invest money in stock now."

"Why?"

"Because any new feller buyin' stock these days will be rustled quicker 'n he can say Jack Robinson. The pioneers, the new cattlemen—these are easy pickin' for the rustlers. Lord knows all the ranchers are easy enough pickin'. But the new fellers have to learn the ropes. They don't know anythin' or anybody. An' the old ranchers are wise an' sore. They'd fight if they—"

"What?" Duane put in, as he paused. "If they knew who was rustling the stock?"

"Nope."

"If they had the nerve?"

"Not thet so much."

"What then? What'd make them fight?"

"A leader!"

"Howdy thar, Jim," boomed a big voice.

A man of great bulk, with a ruddy, merry face, entered the room.

"Hello, Morton," replied Laramie. "I'd introduce you to my guest here, but I don't know his name."

"Haw! Haw! Thet's all right. Few men out hyar go by their right names."

"Say, Morton," put in Duane, "Laramie gave me a hunch you'd be a good man to tie to. Now, I've a little money and before I lose it I'd like to invest it in stock."

Morton smiled broadly.

"I'm on the square," Duane said, bluntly. "If you fellows never size up your neighbors any better than you have sized me—well, you won't get any richer."

It was enjoyment for Duane to make his remarks to these men pregnant with meaning. Morton showed his pleasure, his interest, but his faith held aloof.

"I've got some money. Will you let me in on some kind of deal? Will you start me up as a stockman with a little herd all my own?"

"Wal, stranger, to come out flat-footed, you'd be foolish to buy cattle now. I don't want to take your money an' see you lose out. Better go back across the Pecos where the rustlers ain't so strong. I haven't had more'n twenty-five hundred herd of stock for ten years. The rustlers let me hang on to a breedin' herd. Kind of them, ain't it?"

"Sort of kind. All I hear is rustlers, Morton," replied Duane, with impatience. "You see, I haven't ever lived long in a rustler-run county. Who heads the gang, anyway?"

Morton looked at Duane with a curiously amused smile, then snapped his big jaw as if to shut in impulsive words.

"Look here, Morton. It stands to reason, no matter how strong these rustlers are, how hidden their work, however involved with supposedly honest men—they *can't* last."

"They come with the pioneers, an' they'll last till thar's a single steer left," he declared.

"Well, if you take that view of circumstances I just figure you as one of the rustlers."

Morton looked as if he were about to brain Duane with the butt of his whip. His anger flashed by then, evidently as unworthy of him, and, something striking him as funny, he boomed out a laugh.

"It's not so funny," Duane went on. "If you're going to pretend a yellow streak, what else will I think?"

"Pretend?" he repeated.

"Sure. I know men of nerve. And here they're not any different from those in other places. I say if you show anything like a lack of sand it's all bluff. By nature you've got nerve. There are a lot of men around Fairdale who're afraid of their shadows—afraid to be out after dark—afraid to open their mouths. But you're not one. So I say if you claim these rustlers will last you're pretending lack of nerve just to help the popular idea along. For they *can't* last. What you need out here is some new blood. Savvy what I mean?"

"Wal, I reckon I do," he replied, looking as if a storm had blown over him. "Stranger, I'll look you up the next time I come to town."

Then he went out.

Laramie had eyes like flint striking fire.

He breathed a deep breath and looked around the room before his gaze fixed again on Duane.

"Wal," he replied, speaking low. "You've picked the right men. Now, who in the hell are you?"

Reaching into the inside pocket of his buckskin vest, Duane turned the lining out. A star-shaped bright silver object flashed as he shoved it, pocket and all, under Jim's hard eyes.

"*Ranger!*" he whispered, cracking the table with his fist. "You sure rung true to me."

"Laramie, do you know who's boss of this secret gang of rustlers hereabouts?" asked Duane, bluntly. It was characteristic of him to come sharp to the point. His voice—something deep, easy, cool about him—seemed to steady Laramie.

"No," replied Laramie.

"Does anybody know?" went on Duane.

"Wal, I reckon there's not one honest native who *knows*."

"But you have your suspicions?"

"We have."

"Give me your idea about this crowd that hangs round the saloons—the regulars."

"Jest a bad lot," replied Laramie, with the quick assurance of knowledge. "Most of them have been here years. Others have drifted in. Some of them work, odd times. They rustle a few steers, steal, rob, anythin' for a little money to drink an' gamble. Jest a bad lot!"

"Have you any idea whether Cheseldine and his gang are associated with this gang here?"

"Lord knows. I've always suspected them the same gang. None of us ever seen Cheseldine—an' thet's strange, when Knell, Poggin, Panhandle Smith, Blossom Kane, and Fletcher, they all ride here often. No, Poggin doesn't come often. But the others do. For thet matter, they're around all over west of the Pecos."

"Now I'm puzzled over this," said Duane. "Why do men—apparently honest men—seem to be so close-mouthed here? Is that a fact, or only my impression?"

"It's a sure fact," replied Laramie, darkly. "Men have lost cattle an' property in Fairdale—lost them honestly or otherwise, as hasn't been proved. An' in some cases when they talked—hinted a little—they was found dead. Apparently held up an robbed. But dead. Dead men don't talk! Thet's why we're close-mouthed."

Duane felt a dark, somber sternness. Rustling cattle was not intolerable. Western Texas had gone on prospering, growing in spite of the hordes of rustlers ranging its vast stretches; but a cold, secret, murderous hold on a little struggling community was something too strange, too terrible for men to stand long.

The ranger was about to speak again when the clatter of hoofs interrupted him. Horses halted out in front, and one rider got down. Floyd Lawson entered. He called for tobacco.

If his visit surprised Laramie he did not show any evidence. But Lawson showed rage as he saw the ranger, and then a dark glint flitted from the eyes that shifted from Duane to Laramie and back again. Duane leaned easily against the counter.

"Say, that was a bad break of yours," Lawson said. "If you come fooling round the ranch again there'll be hell."

It seemed strange that a man who had lived west of the Pecos for ten years could not see in Duane something which forbade that kind of talk. It certainly was not nerve Lawson showed; men of courage were seldom intolerant. With the matchless nerve that characterized the great gunmen of the day there was a cool, unobtrusive manner, a speech brief, almost gentle, certainly courteous. Lawson was a hot-headed Louisianian of French extraction; a man, evidently, who had never been crossed in anything, and who was strong, brutal, passionate, which qualities in the face of a situation like this made him simply a fool.

"I'm saying again, you used your ranger bluff just to get near Ray Longstreth," Lawson sneered. "Mind you, if you come up there again there'll be hell."

"You're right. But not the kind you think," Duane retorted, his voice sharp and cold.

"Ray Longstreth wouldn't stoop to know a dirty blood-tracker like you," said Lawson, hotly. He did not seem to have a deliberate intention to rouse Duane; the man was simply rancorous, jealous. "I'll call you right. You cheap bluffer! You four-flush! You damned interfering, conceited ranger!"

"Lawson, I'll not take offense, because you seem to be championing your beautiful cousin," replied Duane, in slow speech. "But let me return your compliment. You're a fine Southerner! Why, you're only a cheap four-flush— damned, bull-headed *rustler!*"

Duane hissed the last word. Then for him there was the truth in Lawson's working passion-blackened face.

Lawson jerked, moved, meant to draw. But how slow! Duane lunged forward. His long arm swept up. And Lawson staggered backward, knocking table and chairs, to fall hard, in a half-sitting posture against the wall.

"Don't draw!" warned Duane.

"Lawson, git away from your gun!" yelled Laramie.

But Lawson was crazed with fury. He tugged at his hip, his face corded with purple welts, malignant, murderous. Duane kicked the gun out of his hand. Lawson got up, raging, and rushed out.

Laramie lifted his shaking hands.

"What'd you wing him for?" he wailed. "He was drawin' on you. Kickin' men like him won't do out here."

"That bull-headed fool will roar and butt himself with all his gang right into our hands. He's just the man I've needed to meet. Besides, shooting him would have been murder."

"Murder!" exclaimed Laramie.

"Yes, for me," replied Duane.

"That may be true—whoever you are—but if Lawson's the man you think he is he'll begin thet secret underground bizness. Why, Lawson won't sleep of nights now. He an' Longstreth have always been after me."

"Laramie, what are your eyes for?" demanded Duane. "Watch out. And now here. See your friend Morton. Tell him this game grows hot. Together you approach four or five men you know well and can absolutely trust. I may need your help."

Then Duane went from place to place, corner to corner, bar to bar, watching, listening, recording. The excitement had preceded him, and speculation was rife. He thought best to keep out of it. After dark he stole up to Longstreth's ranch. The evening was warm; the doors were open; and in the twilight the only lamps that had been lit were in Longstreth's big sitting room, at the far end of the house. When a buckboard drove up and Longstreth and Lawson alighted, Duane was well hidden in the bushes, so well screened that he could get but a fleeting glimpse of Longstreth as he went in. For all Duane could see, he appeared to be a calm and quiet man, intense beneath the surface, with an air of dignity under insult. Duane's chance to observe Lawson was lost. They went into the house without speaking and closed the door.

At the other end of the porch, close under a window, was an offset between step and wall, and there in the shadow Duane hid. So Duane waited there in the darkness with patience born of many hours of hiding.

Presently a lamp was lit; and Duane heard the swish of skirts.

"Something's happened surely, Ruth," he heard Miss Longstreth say, anxiously. "Papa just met me in the hall and didn't speak. He seemed pale, worried."

"Cousin Floyd looked like a thundercloud," said Ruth. "For once he didn't try to kiss me. Something's happened. Well, Ray, this had been a bad day."

"Oh, dear! Ruth, what can we do? These are wild men. Floyd makes life miserable for me. And he teases you unmer—"

"I don't call it teasing. Floyd wants to spoon," declared Ruth, emphatically. "He'd run after any woman."

"A fine compliment to me, Cousin Ruth," laughed Ray.

"I don't care," replied Ruth, stubbornly, "it's so. He's mushy. And when he's been drinking and tries to kiss me—I hate him!"

There were steps on the hall floor.

"Hello, girls!" sounded out Lawson's voice, minus its usual gaiety.

"Floyd, what's the matter?" asked Ray, presently. "I never saw papa as he is tonight, nor you so—so worried. Tell me, what has happened?"

"Well, Ray, we had a jar today," replied Lawson, with a blunt, expressive laugh.

"Jar?" echoed both the girls, curiously.

"We had to submit to a damnable outrage," added Lawson, passionately, as if the sound of his voice augmented his feeling. "Listen, girls; I'll tell you-all about it." He coughed, cleared his throat in a way that betrayed he had been drinking.

Duane sunk deeper into the shadow of his covert, and, stiffening his muscles for a protected spell of rigidity, prepared to listen with all acuteness and intensity. Just one word from this Lawson, inadvertently uttered in a moment of passion, might be the word Duane needed for his clue.

"It happened at the town hall," began Lawson, rapidly. "Your father and Judge Owens and I were there in consultation with three ranchers from out of town. Then that damned ranger stalked in dragging Snecker, the fellow who hid here in the house. He had arrested Snecker for alleged assault on a restaurant-keeper named Laramie. Snecker being obviously innocent, he was discharged. Then this ranger began shouting his insults. Law was a farce in Fairdale. The court was a farce. There was no law. Your father's office as mayor should be impeached. He made arrests only for petty offenses. He was afraid of the rustlers, highwaymen, murderers. He was afraid or—he just let them alone. He used his office to cheat ranchers and cattlemen in lawsuits. All this the ranger yelled for everyone to hear. A damnable outrage. Your father, Ray, insulted in his own court by a rowdy ranger!"

"Oh!" cried Ray Longstreth, in mingled distress and anger.

"The ranger service wants to rule western Texas," went on Lawson. "These rangers are all a low set, many of them worse than the outlaws they hunt. Some of them were outlaws and gunfighters before they became rangers. This is one of the worst of the lot. He's keen, intelligent, smooth, and that makes him more to be feared. For he is to be feared. He wanted to kill. He would kill. If your father had made the least move he would have shot him. He's a cold-nerved devil—the born gunman. My God, any instant I expected to see your father fall dead at my feet!"

"Oh, Floyd! The unspeakable ruffian!" cried Ray Longstreth, passionately.

"You see, Ray, this fellow, like all rangers, seeks notoriety. He made that play with Snecker just for a chance to rant against your father. He tried to inflame all Fairdale against him. That about the lawsuits was the worst! Damn him! He'll make us enemies."

"What do you care for the insinuations of such a man?" said Ray Longstreth, her voice now deep and rich with feeling. "After a moment's thought no one will be influenced by them. Do not worry, Floyd. Tell papa not to worry. Surely after all these years he can't be injured in reputation by—by an adventurer."

"Yes, he can be injured," replied Floyd, quickly. "The frontier is a queer place. There are many bitter men here—men who have failed at ranching.

And your father has been wonderfully successful. The ranger has dropped poison, and it'll spread."

## CHAPTER XVIII

Strangers rode into Fairdale; and other hard-looking customers, new to Duane if not to Fairdale, helped to create a charged and waiting atmosphere. The saloons did unusual business and were never closed. Respectable citizens of the town were awakened in the early dawn by rowdies carousing in the streets.

Duane kept pretty close under cover during the day. He did not entertain the opinion that the first time he walked down-street he would be a target for guns. Things seldom happened that way; and when they did happen so, it was more accident than design. But at night he was not idle. He met Laramie, Morton, Zimmer, and others of like character; a secret club had been formed; and all the members were ready for action. Duane spent hours at night watching the house where Floyd Lawson stayed when he was not up at Longstreth's. At night he was visited, or at least the house was, by strange men who were swift, stealthy, mysterious—all that kindly disposed friends or neighbors would not have been. Duane had not been able to recognize any of these night visitors; and he did not think the time was ripe for a bold holding-up of one of them. Nevertheless, he was sure such an event would discover Lawson, or someone in that house, to be in touch with crooked men.

Laramie was right. Not twenty-four hours after his last talk with Duane, in which he advised quick action, he was found behind the little bar of his restaurant with a bullet hole in his breast, dead. No one could be found who had heard a shot. It had been deliberate murder, for upon the bar had been left a piece of paper rudely scrawled with a pencil: "All friends of rangers look for the same."

This roused Duane. His first move, however, was to bury Laramie. None of Laramie's neighbors evinced any interest in the dead man or the unfortunate family he had left. Duane saw that these neighbors were held in check by fear. Mrs. Laramie was ill; the shock of her husband's death was hard on her; and she had been left almost destitute with five children. Duane rented a small adobe house on the outskirts of town and moved the family into it. Then he played the part of provider and nurse and friend.

After several days Duane went boldly into town and showed that he meant business. It was his opinion that there were men in Fairdale secretly glad of a ranger's presence. What he intended to do was food for great speculation. A company of militia could not have had the effect upon the wild element of

Fairdale that Duane's presence had. It got out that he was a gunman lightning swift on the draw. It was death to face him. He had killed thirty men—wildest rumor of all—it was actually said of him he had the gun-skill of Buck Duane or of Poggin.

At first there had not only been great conjecture among the vicious element, but also a very decided checking of all kinds of action calculated to be conspicuous to a keen-eyed ranger. At the tables, at the bars and lounging-places Duane heard the remarks: "Who's thet ranger after? What'll he do fust off? Is he waitin' fer somebody? Who's goin' to draw on him fust—an' go to hell? Jest about how soon will he be found somewheres full of lead?"

When it came out somewhere that Duane was openly cultivating the honest stay-at-home citizens to array them in time against the other element, then Fairdale showed its wolf-teeth. Several times Duane was shot at in the dark and once slightly injured. Rumor had it that Poggin, the gunman, was coming to meet him. But the lawless element did not rise up in a mass to slay Duane on sight. It was not so much that the enemies of the law awaited his next move, but just a slowness peculiar to the frontier. The ranger was in their midst. He was interesting, if formidable. He would have been welcomed at card-tables, at the bars, to play and drink with the men who knew they were under suspicion. There was a rude kind of good humor even in their open hostility.

Besides, one ranger or a company of rangers could not have held the undivided attention of these men from their games and drinks and quarrels except by some decided move. Excitement, greed, appetite were rife in them. Duane marked, however, a striking exception to the usual run of strangers he had been in the habit of seeing. Snecker had gone or was under cover. Again Duane caught a vague rumor of the coming of Poggin, yet he never seemed to arrive. Moreover, the goings-on among the habitués of the resorts and the cowboys who came in to drink and gamble were unusually mild in comparison with former conduct. This lull, however, did not deceive Duane. It could not last. The wonder was that it had lasted so long.

Duane went often to see Mrs. Laramie and her children. One afternoon while he was there he saw Miss Longstreth and Ruth ride up to the door. They carried a basket. Evidently they had heard of Mrs. Laramie's trouble. Duane felt strangely glad, but he went into an adjoining room rather than meet them.

"Mrs. Laramie, I've come to see you," said Miss Longstreth, cheerfully.

The little room was not very light, there being only one window and the doors, but Duane could see plainly enough. Mrs. Laramie lay, hollow-checked and haggard, on a bed. Once she had evidently been a woman of some comeliness. The ravages of trouble and grief were there to read in her worn face; it had not, however, any of the hard and bitter lines that had characterized her husband's.

Duane wondered, considering that Longstreth had ruined Laramie, how Mrs. Laramie was going to regard the daughter of an enemy.

"So you're Granger Longstreth's girl?" queried the woman, with her bright, black eyes fixed on her visitor.

"Yes," replied Miss Longstreth, simply. "This is my cousin, Ruth Herbert. We've come to nurse you, take care of the children, help you in any way you'll let us."

There was a long silence.

"Well, you look a little like Longstreth," finally said Mrs. Laramie, "but you're not at *all* like him. You must take after your mother. Miss Longstreth, I don't know if I can—if I ought accept anything from you. Your father ruined my husband."

"Yes, I know," replied the girl, sadly. "That's all the more reason you should let me help you. Pray don't refuse. It will—mean so much to me."

If this poor, stricken woman had any resentment it speedily melted in the warmth and sweetness of Miss Longstreth's manner. Duane's idea was that the impression of Ray Longstreth's beauty was always swiftly succeeded by that of her generosity and nobility. At any rate, she had started well with Mrs. Laramie, and no sooner had she begun to talk to the children than both they and the mother were won. The opening of that big basket was an event. Poor, starved little beggars! Duane's feelings seemed too easily roused. Hard indeed would it have gone with Jim Laramie's slayer if he could have laid eyes on him then. However, Miss Longstreth and Ruth, after the nature of tender and practical girls, did not appear to take the sad situation to heart. The havoc was wrought in that household.

The needs now were cheerfulness, kindness, help, action—and these the girls furnished with a spirit that did Duane good.

"Mrs. Laramie, who dressed this baby?" presently asked Miss Longstreth. Duane peeped in to see a dilapidated youngster on her knee. That sight, if any other was needed, completed his full and splendid estimate of Ray Longstreth and wrought strangely upon his heart.

"The ranger," replied Mrs. Laramie.

"The ranger!" exclaimed Miss Longstreth.

"Yes, he's taken care of us all since—since—" Mrs. Laramie choked.

"Oh! So you've had no help but his," replied Miss Longstreth, hastily. "No women. Too bad! I'll send someone, Mrs. Laramie, and I'll come myself."

"It'll be good of you," went on the older woman. "You see, Jim had few friends—that is, right in town. And they've been afraid to help us—afraid they'd get what poor Jim—"

"That's awful!" burst out Miss Longstreth, passionately. "A brave lot of friends! Mrs. Laramie, don't you worry anymore. We'll take care of you. Here, Ruth, help me. Whatever is the matter with baby's dress?"

Manifestly Miss Longstreth had some difficulty in subduing her emotion.

"Why, it's on hind side before," declared Ruth. "I guess Mr. Ranger hasn't dressed many babies."

"He did the best he could," said Mrs. Laramie. "Lord only knows what would have become of us!"

"Then he is—is something more than a ranger?" queried Miss Longstreth, with a little break in her voice.

"He's more than I can tell," replied Mrs. Laramie. "He buried Jim. He paid our debts. He fetched us here. He bought food for us. He cooked for us and fed us. He washed and dressed the baby. He sat with me the first two nights after Jim's death, when I thought I'd die myself. He's so kind, so gentle, so patient. He has kept me up just by being near. Sometimes I'd wake from a doze, an', seeing him there, I'd know how false were all these tales Jim heard about him and believed at first. Why, he plays with the children just—just like any good man might. When he has the baby up I just can't believe he's a bloody gunman, as they say. He's good, but he isn't happy. He has such sad eyes. He looks far off sometimes when the children climb round him. They love him. His life is sad. Nobody need tell me—he sees the good in things. Once he said somebody had to be a ranger. Well, I say, 'Thank God for a ranger like him!'"

Duane did not want to hear more, so he walked into the room.

"It was thoughtful of you," Duane said. "Womankind are needed here. I could do so little. Mrs. Laramie, you look better already. I'm glad. And here's baby, all clean and white. Baby, what a time I had trying to puzzle out the way your clothes went on! Well, Mrs. Laramie, didn't I tell you—friends would come? So will the brighter side."

"Yes, I've more faith than I had," replied Mrs. Laramie. "Granger Longstreth's daughter has come to me. There for a while after Jim's death I thought I'd sink. We have nothing. How could I ever take care of my little ones? But I'm gaining courage to—"

"Mrs. Laramie, do not distress yourself anymore," said Miss Longstreth. "I shall see you are well cared for. I promise you."

"Miss Longstreth, that's fine!" exclaimed Duane. "It's what I'd have—expected of you."

It must have been sweet praise to her, for the whiteness of her face burned out in a beautiful blush.

"And it's good of you, too, Miss Herbert, to come," added Duane. "Let me thank you both. I'm glad I have you girls as allies in part of my lonely task here. More than glad for the sake of this good woman and the little ones. But both of you be careful about coming here alone. There's risk. And now I'll be going. Good-by, Mrs. Laramie. I'll drop in again tonight. Good-by."

"Mr. Ranger, wait!" called Miss Longstreth, as he went out. She was white and wonderful. She stepped out of the door close to him.

"I have wronged you," she said, impulsively.

"Miss Longstreth! How can you say that?" he returned.

"I believed what my father and Floyd Lawson said about you. Now I see—I wronged you."

"You make me very glad. But, Miss Longstreth, please don't speak of wronging me. I have been a—a gunman, I am a ranger—and much said of me is true. My duty is hard on others—sometimes on those who are innocent, alas! But God knows that duty is hard, too, on me."

"I did wrong you. If you entered my home again I would think it an honor. I—"

"Please—please don't, Miss Longstreth," interrupted Duane.

"But, sir, my conscience flays me," she went on. There was no other sound like her voice. "Will you take my hand? Will you forgive me?"

She gave it royally, while the other was there pressing at her breast. Duane took the proffered hand. He did not know what else to do.

Then it seemed to dawn upon him that there was more behind this white, sweet, noble intensity of her than just the making amends for a fancied or real wrong. Duane thought the man did not live on earth who could have resisted her then.

"I honor you for your goodness to this unfortunate woman," she said, and now her speech came swiftly. "When she was all alone and helpless you were her friend. It was the deed of a man. But Mrs. Laramie isn't the only unfortunate woman in the world. I, too, am unfortunate. Ah, how I may soon need a friend! Will you be my friend? I'm so alone. I'm terribly worried. I fear—I fear—oh, surely I'll need a friend soon—soon. Oh, I'm afraid of what you'll find out sooner or later. I want to help you. Let us save life if not honor. Must I stand alone—all alone? Will you—will you be—" Her voice failed.

It seemed to Duane that she must have discovered what he had begun to suspect—that her father and Lawson were not the honest ranchers they pretended to be. Perhaps she knew more! Her appeal to Duane shook him deeply. He wanted to help her more than he had ever wanted anything. And with the meaning of the tumultuous sweetness she stirred in him there came realization of a dangerous situation.

"I must be true to my duty," he said, hoarsely.

"If you knew me you'd know I could never ask you to be false to it."

"Well, then—I'll do anything for you."

"Oh, thank you! I'm ashamed that I believed my cousin Floyd! He lied—he lied. I'm all in the dark, strangely distressed. My father wants me to go back home. Floyd is trying to keep me here. They've quarreled. Oh, I know something dreadful will happen. I know I'll need you if—if—will you help me?"

"Yes," replied Duane, and his look brought the blood to her face.

## CHAPTER XIX

After supper Duane stole out for his usual evening's spying. The night was dark, without starlight, and a stiff wind rustled the leaves. Duane bent his steps toward the Longstreths' ranchhouse. He had so much to think about that he never knew where the time went. This night when he reached the edge of the shrubbery he heard Lawson's well-known footsteps and saw Longstreth's door open, flashing a broad bar of light in the darkness. Lawson crossed the threshold, the door closed, and all was dark again outside. Not a ray of light escaped from the window.

Little doubt there was that his talk with Longstreth would be interesting to Duane. He tiptoed to the door and listened, but could hear only a murmur of voices. Besides, that position was too risky. He went round the corner of the house.

This side of the big adobe house was of much older construction than the back and larger part. There was a narrow passage between the houses, leading from the outside through to the patio.

This passage now afforded Duane an opportunity, and he decided to avail himself of it in spite of the very great danger. Crawling on very stealthily, he got under the shrubbery to the entrance of the passage. In the blackness a faint streak of light showed the location of a crack in the wall. He had to slip in sidewise. It was a tight squeeze, but he entered without the slightest noise. As he progressed the passage grew a very little wider in that direction, and that fact gave rise to the thought that in case of a necessary and hurried exit he would do best by working toward the patio. It seemed a good deal of time was consumed in reaching a vantage-point. When he did get there the crack he had marked was a foot over his head. There was nothing to do but find toe-holes in the crumbling walls, and by bracing knees on one side, back against the other, hold himself up. Once with his eye there he did not care what risk he ran. Longstreth appeared disturbed; he sat stroking his mustache; his brow was clouded. Lawson's face seemed darker, more sullen, yet lighted by some indomitable resolve.

"We'll settle both deals tonight," Lawson was saying. "That's what I came for."

"But suppose I don't choose to talk here?" protested Longstreth, impatiently. "I never before made my house a place to—"

"We've waited long enough. This place's as good as any. You've lost your nerve since that ranger hit the town. First now, will you give Ray to me?"

"Floyd; you talk like a spoiled boy. Give Ray to you! Why, she's a woman, and I'm finding out that she's got a mind of her own. I told you I was willing for her to marry you. I tried to persuade her. But Ray hasn't any use for you now. She liked you at first. But now she doesn't. So what can I do?"

"You can make her marry me," replied Lawson.

"Make that girl do what she doesn't want to? It couldn't be done even if I tried. And I don't believe I'll try. I haven't the highest opinion of you as a prospective son-in-law, Floyd. But if Ray loved you I would consent. We'd all go away together before this damned miserable business is out. Then she'd never know. And maybe you might be more like you used to be before the West ruined you. But as matters stand, you fight your own game with her. And I'll tell you now you'll lose."

"What'd you want to let her come out here for?" demanded Lawson, hotly. "It was a dead mistake. I've lost my head over her. I'll have her or die. Don't you think if she was my wife I'd soon pull myself together? Since she came we've none of us been right. And the gang has put up a holler. No, Longstreth, we've got to settle things tonight."

"Well, we can settle what Ray's concerned in, right now," replied Longstreth, rising. "Come on; we'll ask her. See where you stand."

They went out, leaving the door open. Duane dropped down to rest himself and to wait. He would have liked to hear Miss Longstreth's answer. But he could guess what it would be. Lawson appeared to be all Duane had thought him, and he believed he was going to find out presently that he was worse.

The men seemed to be absent a good while, though that feeling might have been occasioned by Duane's thrilling interest and anxiety. Finally he heard heavy steps. Lawson came in alone. He was leaden-faced, humiliated. Then something abject in him gave place to rage. He strode the room; he cursed. Then Longstreth returned, now appreciably calmer. Duane could not but decide that he felt relief at the evident rejection of Lawson's proposal.

"Don't fuss about it, Floyd," he said. "You see I can't help it. We're pretty wild out here, but I can't rope my daughter and give her to you as I would an unruly steer."

"Longstreth, I can *make* her marry me," declared Lawson, thickly.

"How?"

"You know the hold I got on you—the deal that made you boss of this rustler gang?"

"It isn't likely I'd forget," replied Longstreth, grimly.

"I can go to Ray, tell her that, make her believe I'd tell it broadcast—tell this ranger—unless she'd marry me."

Lawson spoke breathlessly, with haggard face and shadowed eyes. He had no shame. He was simply in the grip of passion. Longstreth gazed with dark, controlled fury at this relative. In that look Duane saw a strong, unscrupulous man fallen into evil ways, but still a man. It betrayed Lawson to be the wild and passionate weakling. Duane seemed to see also how during all the years of association this strong man had upheld the weak one. But that time had gone forever, both in intent on Longstreth's part and in possibility. Lawson, like the great majority of evil and unrestrained men on the border, had reached a point where influence was futile. Reason had degenerated. He saw only himself.

"But, Floyd, Ray's the one person on earth who must never know I'm a rustler, a thief, a red-handed ruler of the worst gang on the border," replied Longstreth, impressively.

Floyd bowed his head at that, as if the significance had just occurred to him. But he was not long at a loss.

"She's going to find it out sooner or later. I tell you she knows now there's something wrong out here. She's got eyes. Mark what I say."

"Ray has changed, I know. But she hasn't any idea yet that her daddy's a boss rustler. Ray's concerned about what she calls my duty as mayor. Also I think she's not satisfied with my explanations in regard to certain property."

Lawson halted in his restless walk and leaned against the stone mantelpiece. He had his hands in his pockets. He squared himself as if this was his last stand. He looked desperate, but on the moment showed an absence of his usual nervous excitement.

"Longstreth, that may well be true," he said. "No doubt all you say is true. But it doesn't help me. I want the girl. If I don't get her—I reckon we'll all go to hell!"

He might have meant anything, probably meant the worst. He certainly had something more in mind. Longstreth gave a slight start, barely perceptible, like the switch of an awakening tiger. He sat there, head down, stroking his mustache. Almost Duane saw his thought. He had long experience in reading men under stress of such emotion. He had no means to vindicate his judgment, but his conviction was that Longstreth right then and there decided that the thing to do was to kill Lawson. For Duane's part he wondered that Longstreth had not come to such a conclusion before. Not improbably the advent of his daughter had put Longstreth in conflict with himself.

Suddenly he threw off a somber cast of countenance, and he began to talk. He talked swiftly, persuasively, yet Duane imagined he was talking to smooth Lawson's passion for the moment. Lawson no more caught the fateful significance of a line crossed, a limit reached, a decree decided than if he had not been present. He was obsessed with himself. How, Duane wondered, had a man of his mind ever lived so long and gone so far among the exacting conditions of the Southwest? The answer was, perhaps, that Longstreth had guided him, upheld him, protected him. The coming of Ray Longstreth had been the entering-wedge of dissension.

"You're too impatient," concluded Longstreth. "You'll ruin any chance of happiness if you rush Ray. She might be won. If you told her who I am she'd hate you forever. She might marry you to save me, but she'd hate you. That isn't the way. Wait. Play for time. Be different with her. Cut out your drinking. She despises that. Let's plan to sell out here—stock, ranch, property—and leave the country. Then you'd have a show with her."

"I told you we've got to stick," growled Lawson. "The gang won't stand for our going. It can't be done unless you want to sacrifice everything."

"You mean double-cross the men? Go without their knowing? Leave them here to face whatever comes?"

"I mean just that."

"I'm bad enough, but not that bad," returned Longstreth. "If I can't get the gang to let me off, I'll stay and face the music. All the same, Lawson, did it ever strike you that most of the deals the last few years have been *yours?*"

"Yes. If I hadn't rung them in there wouldn't have been any. You've had cold feet, and especially since this ranger has been here."

"Well, call it cold feet if you like. But I call it sense. We reached our limit long ago. We began by rustling a few cattle—at a time when rustling was laughed at. But as our greed grew so did our boldness. Then came the gang, the regular trips, the one thing and another till, before we knew it—before I knew it—we had shady deals, holdups, and *murders* on our record. Then we *had* to go on. Too late to turn back!"

"I reckon we've all said that. None of the gang wants to quit. They all think, and I think, we can't be touched. We may be blamed, but nothing can be proved. We're too strong."

"There's where you're dead wrong," rejoined Longstreth, emphatically. "I imagined that once, not long ago. I was bullheaded. Who would ever connect Granger Longstreth with a rustler gang? I've changed my mind. I've begun to think. I've reasoned out things. We're crooked, and we can't last. It's the nature of life, even here, for conditions to grow better. The wise deal for us would be to divide equally and leave the country, all of us."

"But you and I have all the stock—all the gain," protested Lawson.

"I'll split mine."

"I won't—that settles that," added Lawson, instantly.

Longstreth spread wide his hands as if it was useless to try to convince this man. Talking had not increased his calmness, and he now showed more than impatience. A dull glint gleamed deep in his eyes.

"Your stock and property will last a long time—do you lots of good when this ranger—"

"Bah!" hoarsely croaked Lawson. The ranger's name was a match applied to powder. "Haven't I told you he'd be dead soon—any time—same as Laramie is?"

"Yes, you mentioned the—the supposition," replied Longstreth, sarcastically. "I inquired, too, just how that very desired event was to be brought about."

"The gang will lay him out."

"Bah!" retorted Longstreth, in turn. He laughed contemptuously.

"Floyd, don't be a fool. You've been on the border for ten years. You've packed a gun and you've used it. You've been with rustlers when they killed their men. You've been present at many fights. But you never in all that time saw a man like this ranger. You haven't got sense enough to see him right if you had a chance. Neither have any of you. The only way to get rid of him is for the gang to draw on him, all at once. Then he's going to drop some of them."

"Longstreth, you say that like a man who wouldn't care much if he did drop some of them," declared Lawson; and now he was sarcastic.

"To tell you the truth, I wouldn't," returned the other, bluntly. "I'm pretty sick of this mess."

Lawson cursed in amazement. His emotions were all out of proportion to his intelligence. He was not at all quick-witted. Duane had never seen a vainer or more arrogant man.

"Longstreth, I don't like your talk," he said.

"If you don't like the way I talk you know what you can do," replied Longstreth, quickly. He stood up then, cool and quiet, with flash of eyes and set of lips that told Duane he was dangerous.

"Well, after all, that's neither here nor there," went on Lawson, unconsciously cowed by the other. "The thing is, do I get the girl?"

"Not by any means except her consent."

"You'll not make her marry me?"

"No. No," replied Longstreth, his voice still cold, low-pitched.

"All right. Then I'll make her."

Evidently Longstreth understood the man before him so well that he wasted no more words. Duane knew what Lawson never dreamed of, and that was that Longstreth had a gun somewhere within reach and meant to use it. Then heavy footsteps sounded outside tramping upon the porch. Duane might have been mistaken, but he believed those footsteps saved Lawson's life.

"There they are," said Lawson, and he opened the door.

Five masked men entered. They all wore coats hiding any weapons. A big man with burly shoulders shook hands with Longstreth, and the others stood back.

The atmosphere of that room had changed. Lawson might have been a nonentity for all he counted. Longstreth was another man—a stranger to Duane. If he had entertained a hope of freeing himself from this band, of getting away to a safer country, he abandoned it at the very sight of these men. There was power here, and he was bound.

The big man spoke in low, hoarse whispers, and at this all the others gathered around him close to the table. There were evidently some signs of membership not plain to Duane. Then all the heads were bent over the table. Low voices spoke, queried, answered, argued. By straining his ears Duane caught a word here and there. They were planning, and they were brief. Duane gathered they were to have a rendezvous at or near Ord.

Then the big man, who evidently was the leader of the present convention, got up to depart. He went as swiftly as he had come, and was followed by his comrades. Longstreth prepared for a quiet smoke. Lawson seemed uncommunicative and unsociable. He smoked fiercely and drank continually. All at once he straightened up as if listening.

"What's that?" he called, suddenly.

Duane's strained ears were pervaded by a slight rustling sound.

"Must be a rat," replied Longstreth.

The rustle became a rattle.

"Sounds like a rattlesnake to me," said Lawson.

Longstreth got up from the table and peered round the room.

Just at that instant Duane felt an almost inappreciable movement of the adobe wall which supported him. He could scarcely credit his senses. But the rattle inside Longstreth's room was mingling with little dull thuds of falling dirt. The adobe wall, merely dried mud, was crumbling. Duane distinctly felt a tremor pass through it. Then the blood gushed back to his heart.

"What in the hell!" exclaimed Longstreth.

"I smell dust," said Lawson, sharply.

That was the signal for Duane to drop down from his perch, yet despite his care he made a noise.

"Did you hear a step?" queried Longstreth.

No one answered. But a heavy piece of the adobe wall fell with a thud. Duane heard it crack, felt it shake.

"There's somebody between the walls!" thundered Longstreth.

Then a section of the wall fell inward with a crash. Duane began to squeeze his body through the narrow passage toward the patio.

"Hear him!" yelled Lawson. "This side!"

"No, he's going that way," yelled Longstreth.

The tramp of heavy boots lent Duane the strength of desperation. He was not shirking a fight, but to be cornered like a trapped coyote was another matter. He almost tore his clothes off in that passage. The dust nearly stifled him. When he burst into the patio it was not a single instant too soon. But one deep gasp of breath revived him and he was up, gun in hand, running for the outlet into the court. Thumping footsteps turned him back. While there was a chance to get away he did not want to fight. He thought he heard someone running into the patio from the other end. He stole along, and coming to a door, without any idea of where it might lead, he softly pushed it open a little way and slipped in.

# CHAPTER XX

A low cry greeted Duane. The room was light. He saw Ray Longstreth sitting on her bed in her dressing gown. With a warning gesture to her to be silent he turned to close the door. It was a heavy door without bolt or bar, and when Duane had shut it he felt safe only for the moment. Then he gazed around the room. There was one window with blind closely drawn. He listened and seemed to hear footsteps retreating, dying away.

Then Duane turned to Miss Longstreth. She had slipped off the bed, half to her knees, and was holding out trembling hands. She was as white as the pillow on her bed. She was terribly frightened. Again with warning hand commanding silence, Duane stepped softly forward, meaning to reassure her.

"Oh!" she whispered, wildly; and Duane thought she was going to faint. When he got close and looked into her eyes he understood the strange, dark expression in them. She was terrified because she believed he meant to kill her, or do worse, probably worse. Duane realized he must have looked pretty hard and fierce bursting into her room with that big gun in hand.

The way she searched Duane's face with doubtful, fearful eyes hurt him.

"Listen. I didn't know this was your room. I came here to get away—to save my life. I was pursued. I was spying on—on your father and his men. They heard me, but did not see me. They don't know who was listening. They're after me now."

Her eyes changed from blank gulfs to dilating, shadowing, quickening windows of thought.

Then she stood up and faced Duane with the fire and intelligence of a woman in her eyes.

"Tell me now. You were spying on my father?"

Briefly Duane told her what had happened before he entered her room, not omitting a terse word as to the character of the men he had watched.

"My God! So it's that? I knew something was terribly wrong here—with him—with the place—the people. And right off I hated Floyd Lawson. Oh, it'll kill me if—if—it's so much worse than I dreamed. What shall I do?"

The sound of soft steps somewhere near distracted Duane's attention, reminded him of her peril, and now, what counted more with him, made clear the probability of being discovered in her room.

"I'll have to get out of here," whispered Duane.

"Wait," she replied. "Didn't you say they were hunting for you?"

"They sure are," he returned, grimly.

"Oh, then you mustn't go. They might shoot you before you got away. Stay. If we hear them you can hide. I'll turn out the light. I'll meet them at the door. You can trust me. Wait till all quiets down, if we have to wait till morning. Then you can slip out."

"I oughtn't to stay. I don't want to—I won't," Duane replied, perplexed and stubborn.

"But you must. It's the only safe way. They won't come here."

"Suppose they should? It's an even chance Longstreth'll search every room and corner in this old house. If they found me here I couldn't start a fight. You might be hurt. Then—the fact of my being here—"

Duane did not finish what he meant, but instead made a step toward the door. White of face and dark of eye, she took hold of him to detain him. She was as strong and supple as a panther. But she need not have been either resolute or strong, for the clasp of her hand was enough to make Duane weak.

"Up yet, Ray?" came Longstreth's clear voice, too strained, too eager to be natural.

"No. I'm in bed reading. Good night," instantly replied Miss Longstreth, so calmly and naturally that Duane marveled at the difference between man and woman. Then she motioned for Duane to hide in the closet. He slipped in, but the door would not close altogether.

"Are you alone?" went on Longstreth's penetrating voice.

"Yes," she replied. "Ruth went to bed."

The door swung inward with a swift scrape and jar. Longstreth half entered, haggard, flaming-eyed. Behind him Duane saw Lawson, and indistinctly another man.

Longstreth barred Lawson from entering, which action showed control as well as distrust. He wanted to see into the room. When he had glanced around he went out and closed the door.

Then what seemed a long interval ensued. The house grew silent once more. Duane could not see Miss Longstreth, but he heard her quick breathing. How long did she mean to let him stay hidden there? Hard and perilous as his life had been, this was a new kind of adventure. He had divined the strange softness of his feeling as something due to the magnetism of this beautiful woman. It hardly seemed possible that he, who had been outside the pale for so many years, could have fallen in love. Yet that must be the secret of his agitation.

Presently he pushed open the closet door and stepped forth. Miss Longstreth had her head lowered upon her arms and appeared to be in distress. At his touch she raised a quivering face.

"I think I can go now—safely," he whispered.

"Go then, if you must, but you may stay till you're safe," she replied.

"I—I couldn't thank you enough. It's been hard on me—this finding out— and you his daughter. I feel strange. I don't understand myself well. But I want you to know—if I were not an outlaw—a ranger—I'd lay my life at your feet."

"Oh! You have seen so—so little of me," she faltered.

"All the same it's true. And that makes me feel more the trouble my coming caused you."

"You will not fight my father?"

"Not if I can help it. I'm trying to get out of his way.'

"But you spied upon him."

"I am a ranger, Miss Longstreth."

"And oh! I am a rustler's daughter," she cried. "That's so much more terrible than I'd suspected. It was tricky cattle deals I imagined he was engaged in. But only tonight I had strong suspicions aroused."

"How? Tell me."

"I overheard Floyd say that men were coming tonight to arrange a meeting for my father at a rendezvous near Ord. Father did not want to go. Floyd taunted him with a name."

"What name?" queried Duane.

"It was Cheseldine."

"*Cheseldine!* My God! Miss Longstreth, why did you tell me that?"

"What difference does that make?"

"Your father and Cheseldine are one and the same," whispered Duane, hoarsely.

"I gathered so much myself," she replied, miserably. "But Longstreth is father's real name."

Duane felt so stunned he could not speak at once. It was the girl's part in this tragedy that weakened him. The instant she betrayed the secret Duane realized perfectly that he did love her. The emotion was like a great flood.

"Miss Longstreth, all this seems so unbelievable," he whispered. "Cheseldine is the rustler chief I've come out here to get. He's only a name. Your father is the real man. I've sworn to get him. I'm bound by more than law or oaths. I can't break what binds me. And I must disgrace you—wreck your lifer. Why, Miss Longstreth, I believe I—I love you. It's all come in a rush. I'd die for you if I could. How fatal—terrible—this is! How things work out!"

She slipped to her knees, with her hands on his.

"You won't kill him?" she implored. "If you care for me—you won't kill him?"

"No. That I promise you."

With a low moan she dropped her head upon the bed.

Duane opened the door and stealthily stole out through the corridor to the court.

When Duane got out into the dark, where his hot face cooled in the wind, his relief equaled his other feelings.

The night was dark, windy, stormy, yet there was no rain. Duane hoped as soon as he got clear of the ranch to lose something of the pain he felt. But long after he had tramped out into the open there was a lump in his throat and an ache in his breast. All his thought centered around Ray Longstreth. What a woman she had turned out to be! He seemed to have a vague, hopeless hope that there might be, there must be, some way he could save her.

## CHAPTER XXI

Before going to sleep that night Duane had decided to go to Ord and try to find the rendezvous where Longstreth was to meet his men. These men Duane wanted even more than their leader. If Longstreth, or Cheseldine, was the brains of that gang, Poggin was the executor. It was Poggin who needed to be found and stopped. Poggin and his right-hand men! Duane experienced a strange, tigerish thrill. It was thought of Poggin more than thought of success for MacNelly's plan. Duane felt dubious over this emotion.

Next day he set out for Bradford. He was glad to get away from Fairdale for a while. But the hours and the miles in no wise changed the new pain in his heart. The only way he could forget Miss Longstreth was to let his mind dwell upon Poggin, and even this was not always effective.

He avoided Sanderson, and at the end of the day and a half he arrived at Bradford.

The night of the day before he reached Bradford, No. 6, the mail and express train going east, was held up by train-robbers, the Wells-Fargo messenger killed over his safe, the mail-clerk wounded, the bags carried away. The engine of No. 6 came into town minus even a tender, and engineer and fireman told conflicting stories. A posse of railroad men and citizens, led by a sheriff Duane suspected was crooked, was made up before the engine steamed back to pick up the rest of the train. Duane had the sudden inspiration that he had been cudgeling his mind to find; and, acting upon it, he mounted his horse again and left Bradford unobserved. As he rode out into the night, over a dark trail in the direction of Ord, he uttered a short, grim, sardonic laugh at the hope that he might be taken for a train robber.

He rode at an easy trot most of the night, and when the black peak of Ord Mountain loomed up against the stars he halted, tied his horse, and slept until dawn. He had brought a small pack, and now he took his time cooking breakfast. When the sun was well up he saddled Bullet, and, leaving the trail where his tracks showed plain in the ground, he put his horse to the rocks and brush. He selected an exceedingly rough, roundabout, and difficult course to Ord, hid his tracks with the skill of a long-hunted fugitive, and arrived there with his horse winded and covered with lather. It added considerable to his arrival that the man Duane remembered as Fletcher and several others saw him come in the back way through the lots and jump a fence into the road.

Duane led Bullet up to the porch where Fletcher stood wiping his beard. He was hatless, vestless, and evidently had just enjoyed a morning drink.

"Howdy, Dodge," said Fletcher, laconically.

Duane replied, and the other man returned the greeting with interest.

"Jim, my hoss 's done up. I want to hide him from any chance tourists as might happen to ride up curious-like."

"Haw! Haw! Haw!"

Duane gathered encouragement from that chorus of coarse laughter.

"Wal, if them tourists ain't too durned snooky the hoss'll be safe in the 'dobe shack back of Bill's here. Feed thar, too, but you'll hev to rustle water."

Duane led Bullet to the place indicated, had care of his welfare, and left him there. Upon returning to the tavern porch Duane saw the group of men had been added to by others, some of whom he had seen before. Without comment Duane walked along the edge of the road, and wherever one of the tracks of his horse showed he carefully obliterated it. This procedure was attentively watched by Fletcher and his companions.

"Wal, Dodge," remarked Fletcher, as Duane returned, "thet's safer 'n prayin' fer rain."

Duane's reply was a remark as loquacious as Fletcher's, to the effect that a long, slow, monotonous ride was conducive to thirst. They all joined him, unmistakably friendly. But Knell was not there, and most assuredly not Poggin. Fletcher was no common outlaw, but, whatever his ability, it probably lay in execution of orders. Apparently at that time these men had nothing to do but drink and lounge around the tavern. Evidently they were poorly supplied with money, though Duane observed they could borrow a peso occasionally from the bartender. Duane set out to make himself agreeable and succeeded. There was card playing for small stakes, idle jests of coarse nature, much bantering among the younger fellows, and occasionally a mild quarrel. All morning men came and went, until, all told, Duane calculated he had seen at least fifty. Toward the middle of the afternoon a young fellow burst into the saloon and yelled one word:

"Posse!"

From the scramble to get outdoors Duane judged that word and the ensuing action was rare in Ord.

"What the hell!" muttered Fletcher, as he gazed down the road at a dark, compact bunch of horses and riders. "Fust time I ever seen thet in Ord! We're gettin' popular like them camps out of Valentine. Wish Phil was here or Poggy. Now all you gents keep quiet. I'll do the talkin'."

The posse entered the town, trotted up on dusty horses, and halted in a bunch before the tavern. The party consisted of about twenty men, all heavily armed, and evidently in charge of a clean-cut, lean-limbed cowboy. Duane experienced considerable satisfaction at the absence of the sheriff who he had understood was to lead the posse. Perhaps he was out in another direction with a different force.

"Hello, Jim Fletcher," called the cowboy.

"Howdy," replied Fletcher.

At his short, dry response and the way he strode leisurely out before the posse Duane found himself modifying his contempt for Fletcher. The outlaw was different now.

"Fletcher, we've tracked a man to all but three miles of this place. Tracks as plain as the nose on your face. Found his camp. Then he hit into the brush, an' we lost the trail. Didn't have no tracker with us. Think he went into the mountains. But we took a chance an' rid over the rest of the way, seein' Ord was so close. Anybody come in here late last night or early this mornin'?"

"Nope," replied Fletcher.

His response was what Duane had expected from his manner, and evidently the cowboy took it as a matter of course. He turned to the others of the posse, entering into a low consultation. Evidently there was difference of opinion, if not real dissension, in that posse.

"Didn't I tell ye this was a wild-goose chase, comin' way out here?" protested an old hawk-faced rancher. "Them hoss tracks we follored ain't like any of them we seen at the water-tank where the train was held up."

"I'm not so sure of that," replied the leader.

"Wal, Guthrie, I've follored tracks all my life—'

"But you couldn't keep to the trail this feller made in the brush."

"Gimme time, an' I could. Thet takes time. An' heah you go hell-bent fer election! But it's a wrong lead out this way. If you're right this road agent, after he killed his pals, would hev rid back right through town. An' with them mailbags! Supposin' they was greasers? Some greasers has sense, an' when it comes to thievin' they're shore cute."

"But we ain't got any reason to believe this robber who murdered the greasers is a greaser himself. I tell you it was a slick job done by no ordinary sneak. Didn't you hear the facts? One greaser hopped the engine an' covered the engineer an' fireman. Another greaser kept flashin' his gun outside the train. The big man who shoved back the car-door an' did the killin'—he was the real gent, an' don't you forget it."

Some of the posse sided with the cowboy leader and some with the old cattleman. Finally the young leader disgustedly gathered up his bridle.

"Aw, hell! Thet sheriff shoved you off this trail. Mebbe he hed reasons. Savvy thet? If I hed a bunch of cowboys with me—I tell you what—I'd take a chance an' clean up this hole!"

All the while Jim Fletcher stood quietly with his hands in his pockets.

"Guthrie, I'm shore treasurin' up your friendly talk," he said. The menace was in the tone, not the content of his speech.

"You can—an' be damned to you, Fletcher!" called Guthrie, as the horses started.

Fletcher, standing out alone before the others of his clan, watched the posse out of sight.

"Luck fer you-all thet Poggy wasn't here," he said, as they disappeared. Then with a thoughtful mien he strode up on the porch and led Duane away from the others into the barroom. When he looked into Duane's face it was somehow an entirely changed scrutiny.

"Dodge, where'd you hide the stuff? I reckon I git in on this deal, seein' I staved off Guthrie."

Duane played his part. Here was his opportunity, and like a tiger after prey he seized it. First he coolly eyed the outlaw and then disclaimed any knowledge whatever of the train-robbery other than Fletcher had heard himself. Then at Fletcher's persistence and admiration and increasing show of friendliness he laughed occasionally and allowed himself to swell with pride, though still denying. Next he feigned a lack of consistent willpower and seemed to be wavering under Fletcher's persuasion and grew silent, then surly. Fletcher, evidently sure of ultimate victory, desisted for the time being; however, in his solicitous regard and close companionship for the rest of that day he betrayed the bent of his mind.

Later, when Duane started up announcing his intention to get his horse and make for camp out in the brush, Fletcher seemed grievously offended.

"Why don't you stay with me? I've got a comfortable 'dobe over here. Didn't I stick by you when Guthrie an' his bunch come up? Supposin' I hedn't showed down a cold hand to him? You'd be swingin' somewheres now. I tell you, Dodge, it ain't square."

"I'll square it. I pay my debts," replied Duane. "But I can't put up here all night. If I belonged to the gang it 'd be different."

"What gang?" asked Fletcher, bluntly.

"Why, Cheseldine's."

Fletcher's beard nodded as his jaw dropped.

Duane laughed. "I run into him the other day. Knowed him on sight. Sure, he's the kingpin rustler. When he seen me an' asked me what reason I had for bein' on earth or some such like—why, I up an' told him."

Fletcher appeared staggered.

"Who in all-fired hell air you talkin' about?"

"Didn't I tell you once? Cheseldine. He calls himself Longstreth over there."

All of Fletcher's face not covered by hair turned a dirty white. "Cheseldine—Longstreth!" he whispered, hoarsely. "Gord Almighty! You braced the—" Then a remarkable transformation came over the outlaw. He gulped; he straightened his face; he controlled his agitation. But he could not send the healthy brown back to his face. Duane, watching this rude man, marveled at the change in him, the sudden checking movement, the proof of a wonderful fear and loyalty. It all meant Cheseldine, a master of men!

"Who air you?" queried Fletcher, in a queer, strained voice.

"You gave me a handle, didn't you? Dodge. Thet's as good as any. Shore it hits me hard. Jim, I've been pretty lonely for years, an' I'm gettin' in need of pals. Think it over, will you? See you mañana."

The outlaw watched Duane go off after his horse, watched him as he returned to the tavern, watched him ride out into the darkness—all without a word.

Duane left the town, threaded a quiet passage through cactus and mesquite to a spot he had marked before, and made ready for the night. His mind was so full that he found sleep aloof. Luck at last was playing his game. He sensed the first slow heave of a mighty crisis. The end, always haunting, had to be sternly blotted from thought. It was the approach that needed all his mind.

He passed the night there, and late in the morning, after watching trail and road from a ridge, he returned to Ord. If Jim Fletcher tried to disguise his surprise the effort was a failure. Certainly he had not expected to see Duane again. Duane allowed himself a little freedom with Fletcher, an attitude hitherto lacking.

That afternoon a horseman rode in from Bradford, an outlaw evidently well known and liked by his fellows, and Duane heard him say, before he could possibly have been told the train-robber was in Ord, that the loss of money in the holdup was slight. Like a flash Duane saw the luck of this report. He pretended not to have heard.

In the early twilight at an opportune moment he called Fletcher to him, and, linking his arm within the outlaw's, he drew him off in a stroll to a log bridge spanning a little gully. Here after gazing around, he took out a roll of bills, spread it out, split it equally, and without a word handed one half to Fletcher. With clumsy fingers Fletcher ran through the roll.

"Five hundred!" he exclaimed. "Dodge, thet's damn handsome of you, considerin' the job wasn't—"

"Considerin' nothin'," interrupted Duane. "I'm makin' no reference to a job here or there. You did me a good turn. I split my pile. If thet doesn't make us pards, good turns an' money ain't no use in this country."

Fletcher was won.

The two men spent much time together. Duane made up a short fictitious history about himself that satisfied the outlaw, only it drew forth a laughing jest upon Duane's modesty. For Fletcher did not hide his belief that this new partner was a man of achievements. Knell and Poggin, and then Cheseldine himself, would be persuaded of this fact, so Fletcher boasted. He had influence. He would use it. He thought he pulled a stroke with Knell. But nobody on earth, not even the boss, had any influence on Poggin. Poggin was concentrated ice part of the time; all the rest he was bursting hell. But Poggin loved a horse. He never loved anything else. He could be won with that black horse Bullet. Cheseldine was already won by Duane's monumental nerve; otherwise he would have killed Duane.

Little by little the next few days Duane learned the points he longed to know; and how indelibly they etched themselves in his memory! Cheseldine's hiding place was on the far slope of Mount Ord, in a deep, high-walled valley. He always went there just before a contemplated job, where he met and planned with his lieutenants. Then while they executed he basked in the sunshine before one or another of the public places he owned. He was there in the Ord den now, getting ready to plan the biggest job yet. It was a bank-robbery; but where, Fletcher had not as yet been advised.

Then when Duane had pumped the now amenable outlaw of all details pertaining to the present he gathered data and facts and places covering a period of ten years Fletcher had been with Cheseldine. And herewith was unfolded a history so dark in its bloody regime, so incredible in its brazen daring, so appalling in its proof of the outlaw's sweep and grasp of the country from Pecos to Rio Grande, that Duane was stunned. Compared to this Cheseldine of the Big Bend, to this rancher, stock buyer, cattle speculator, property holder, all the outlaws Duane had ever known sank into insignificance. The power of the man stunned Duane; the strange fidelity given him stunned Duane; the intricate inside working of his great system was equally stunning. But when Duane recovered from that the old terrible passion to kill consumed him, and it raged fiercely and it could not be checked. If that red-handed Poggin, if that cold-eyed, dead-faced Knell had only been at Ord! But they were not, and Duane with help of time got what he hoped was the upper hand of himself.

# CHAPTER XXII

Again inaction and suspense dragged at Duane's spirit. Like a leashed hound with a keen scent in his face Duane wanted to leap forth when he was bound. He almost fretted. Something called to him over the bold, wild brow of Mount Ord. But while Fletcher stayed in Ord waiting for Knell and Poggin, or for orders, Duane knew his game was again a waiting one.

But one day there were signs of the long quiet of Ord being broken. A messenger strange to Duane rode in on a secret mission that had to do with Fletcher. When he went away Fletcher became addicted to thoughtful moods and lonely walks. He seldom drank, and this in itself was a striking contrast to former behavior. The messenger came again. Whatever communication he brought, it had a remarkable effect upon the outlaw. Duane was present in the tavern when the fellow arrived, saw the few words whispered, but did not hear them. Fletcher turned white with anger or fear, perhaps both, and he cursed like a madman. The messenger, a lean, dark-faced, hard-riding fellow reminding Duane of the cowboy Guthrie, left the tavern without even a drink and rode away off to the west. This west mystified and fascinated Duane as much as the south beyond Mount Ord. Where were Knell and Poggin? Apparently they were not at present with the leader on the mountain. After the messenger left Fletcher grew silent and surly. He had presented a variety of moods to Duane's observation, and this latest one was provocative of thought. Fletcher was dangerous. It became clear now that the other outlaws of the camp feared him, kept out of his way. Duane let him alone, yet closely watched him.

Perhaps an hour after the messenger had left, not longer, Fletcher manifestly arrived at some decision, and he called for his horse. Then he went to his shack and returned. To Duane the outlaw looked in shape both to ride and to fight. He gave orders for the men in camp to keep close until he returned. Then he mounted.

"Come here, Dodge," he called.

Duane went up and laid a hand on the pommel of the saddle. Fletcher walked his horse, with Duane beside him, till they reached the log bridge, when he halted.

"Dodge, I'm in bad with Knell," he said. "An' it 'pears I'm the cause of friction between Knell an' Poggy. Knell never had any use fer me, but Poggy's been square, if not friendly. The boss has a big deal on, an' here it's been held up because of this scrap. He's waitin' over there on the mountain to give orders to Knell or Poggy, an' neither one's showin' up. I've got to stand in the breach, an' I ain't enjoyin' the prospects."

"What's the trouble about, Jim?" asked Duane.

"Reckon it's a little about you, Dodge," said Fletcher, dryly. "Knell hadn't any use fer you thet day. He ain't got no use fer a man onless he can rule him. Some of the boys here hev blabbed before I edged in with my say, an' there's hell to pay. Knell claims to know somethin' about you thet'll make both the boss an' Poggy sick when he springs it. But he's keepin' quiet. Hard man to figger, thet Knell. Reckon you'd better go back to Bradford fer a day or so, then camp out near here till I come back."

"Why?"

"Wal, because there ain't any use fer you to git in bad, too. The gang will ride over here any day. If they're friendly, I'll light a fire on the hill there, say three nights from tonight. If you don't see it thet night you hit the trail. I'll do what I can. Jim Fletcher sticks to his pals. So long, Dodge."

Then he rode away.

He left Duane in a quandary. This news was black. Things had been working out so well. Here was a setback. At the moment Duane did not know which way to turn, but certainly he had no idea of going back to Bradford. Friction between the two great lieutenants of Cheseldine! Open hostility between one of them and another of the chief's right-hand men! Among outlaws that sort of thing was deadly serious. Generally such matters were settled with guns. Duane gathered encouragement even from disaster. Perhaps the disintegration of Cheseldine's great band had already begun. But what did Knell know? Duane did not circle around the idea with doubts and hopes; if Knell knew anything it was that this stranger in Ord, this new partner of Fletcher's, was no less than Buck Duane. Well, it was about time, thought Duane, that he made use of his name if it were to help him at all. That name had been MacNelly's hope. He had anchored all his scheme to Duane's fame. Duane was tempted to ride off after Fletcher and stay with him. This, however, would hardly be fair to an outlaw who had been fair to him. Duane concluded to await developments and when the gang rode in to Ord, probably from their various hiding-places, he would be there ready to be denounced by Knell. Duane could not see any other culmination of this series of events than a meeting between Knell and himself. If that terminated fatally for Knell there was all probability of Duane's being in no worse situation than he was now. If Poggin took up the quarrel! Here Duane accused himself again—tried in vain to revolt from a judgment that he was only reasoning out excuses to meet these outlaws.

Meanwhile, instead of waiting, why not hunt up Cheseldine in his mountain retreat? The thought no sooner struck Duane than he was hurrying for his horse.

He left Ord, ostensibly toward Bradford, but, once out of sight, he turned off the road, circled through the brush, and several miles south of town he struck a narrow grass-grown trail that Fletcher had told him led to Cheseldine's camp. The horse tracks along this trail were not less than a week old, and very likely much more. It wound between low, brush-covered foothills, through arroyos and gullies lined with mesquite, cottonwood, and scrub-oak.

In an hour Duane struck the slope of Mount Ord, and as he climbed he got a view of the rolling, black-spotted country, partly desert, partly fertile, with long, bright lines of dry streambeds winding away to grow dim in the distance. He got among broken rocks and cliffs, and here the open, downward-rolling land disappeared, and he was hard put to it to find the trail. He lost it repeatedly and made slow progress. Finally he climbed into a region of all rock benches, rough here, smooth there, with only an occasional scratch of iron horseshoe to guide him. Many times he had to go ahead and then work to right or left till he found his way again. It was slow work; it took all day; and night found him halfway up the mountain. He halted at a little side-cañon with grass and water, and here he made camp. The night was clear and cool at that height, with a dark blue sky and a streak of stars blinking across. With this day of action behind him he felt better satisfied than he had been for some time. Here, on this venture, he was answering to a call that had so often directed his movements, perhaps his life, and it was one that logic or intelligence could take little stock of. And on this night, lonely like the ones he used to spend in the Nueces gorge, and memorable of them because of a likeness to that old hiding-place, he felt the pressing return of old haunting things—the past so long ago, wild flights, dead faces—and the places of these were taken by one quiveringly alive, white, tragic, with its dark, intent, speaking eyes—Ray Longstreth's.

That last memory he yielded to until he slept.

In the morning, satisfied that he had left still fewer tracks than he had followed up this trail, he led his horse up to the head of the cañon, there a narrow crack in low cliffs, and with branches of cedar fenced him in. Then he went back and took up the trail on foot.

Without the horse he made better time and climbed through deep clefts, wide cañons, over ridges, up shelving slopes, along precipices—a long, hard climb—till he reached what he concluded was a divide. Going down was easier, though the farther he followed this dim and winding trail the wider the broken battlements of rock. Above him he saw the black fringe of piñon and pine, and above that the bold peak, bare, yellow, like a desert butte. Once, through a wide gateway between great escarpments, he saw the lower country beyond the range, and beyond this, vast and clear as it lay in his sight, was the great river that made the Big Bend. He went down and down, wondering how a horse could follow that broken trail, believing there must be another better one somewhere into Cheseldine's hiding place.

He rounded a jutting corner, where view had been shut off, and presently came out upon the rim of a high wall. Beneath, like a green gulf seen through blue haze, lay an amphitheater walled in on the two sides he could see. It lay perhaps a thousand feet below him; and, plain as all the other features of that wild environment, there shone out a big red stone or adobe cabin, white water shining away between great borders, and horses and cattle dotting the levels. It was a peaceful, beautiful scene. Duane could not help grinding his teeth at the thought of rustlers living there in quiet and ease.

Duane worked halfway down to the level, and, well hidden in a niche, he settled himself to watch both trail and valley. He made note of the position of the sun and saw that if anything developed or if he decided to descend any farther there was small likelihood of his getting back to his camp before dark. To try that after nightfall he imagined would be vain effort.

Then he bent his keen eyes downward. The cabin appeared to be a crude structure. Though large in size, it had, of course, been built by outlaws.

There was no garden, no cultivated field, no corral. Excepting for the rude pile of stones and logs plastered together with mud, the valley was as wild, probably, as on the day of discovery. Duane seemed to have been watching for a long time before he saw any sign of man, and this one apparently went to the stream for water and returned to the cabin.

The sun went down behind the wall, and shadows were born in the darker places of the valley. Duane began to want to get closer to that cabin. What had he taken this arduous climb for? He held back, however, trying to evolve further plans.

While he was pondering the shadows quickly gathered and darkened. If he was to go back to camp he must set out at once. Still he lingered. And suddenly his wide-roving eye caught sight of two horsemen riding up the valley. They must have entered at a point below, round the huge abutment of rock, beyond Duane's range of sight. Their horses were tired and stopped at the stream for a long drink.

Duane left his perch, took to the steep trail, and descended as fast as he could without making noise. It did not take him long to reach the valley floor. It was almost level, with deep grass, and here and there clumps of bushes. Twilight was already thick down there. Duane marked the location of the trail, and then began to slip like a shadow through the grass and from bush to bush. He saw a bright light before he made out the dark outline of the cabin. Then he heard voices, a merry whistle, a coarse song, and the clink of iron cooking utensils. He smelled fragrant wood-smoke. He saw moving dark figures cross the light. Evidently there was a wide door, or else the fire was out in the open.

Duane swerved to the left, out of direct line with the light, and thus was able to see better. Then he advanced noiselessly but swiftly toward the back of the house. There were trees close to the wall. He would make no noise, and he could scarcely be seen—if only there was no watchdog! But all his outlaw days he had taken risks with only his useless life at stake; now, with that changed, he advanced stealthy and bold as an Indian. He reached the cover of the trees, knew he was hidden in their shadows, for at few paces' distance he had been able to see only their tops. From there he slipped up to the house and felt along the wall with his hands.

He came to a little window where light shone through. He peeped in. He saw a room shrouded in shadows, a lamp turned low, a table, chairs. He saw an open door, with bright flare beyond, but could not see the fire. Voices came indistinctly. Without hesitation Duane stole farther along—all the way to the end of the cabin. Peeping round, he saw only the flare of light on bare ground. Retracing his cautious steps, he paused at the crack again, saw that no man was in the room, and then he went on round that end of the cabin. Fortune favored him. There were bushes, an old shed, a woodpile, all the cover he needed at that corner. He did not even need to crawl.

Before he peered between the rough corner of wall and the bush growing close to it Duane paused a moment. This excitement was different from that he had always felt when pursued. It had no bitterness, no pain, no dread. There was as much danger here, perhaps more, yet it was not the same. Then he looked.

He saw a bright fire, a red-faced man bending over it, whistling, while he handled a steaming pot. Over him was a roofed shed built against the wall, with two open sides and two supporting posts. Duane's second glance, not so blinded by the sudden bright light, made out other men, three in the shadow, two in the flare, but with backs to him.

"It's a smoother trail by long odds, but ain't so short as this one right over the mountain," one outlaw was saying.

"What's eatin' you, Panhandle?" ejaculated another. "Blossom an' me rode from Faraway Springs, where Poggin is with some of the gang."

"Excuse me, Phil. Shore I didn't see you come in, an' Boldt never said nothin'."

"It took you a long time to get here, but I guess that's just as well," spoke up a smooth, suave voice with a ring in it.

Longstreth's voice—Cheseldine's voice!

Here they were—Cheseldine, Phil Knell, Blossom Kane, Panhandle Smith, Boldt—how well Duane remembered the names!—all here, the big men of Cheseldine's gang, except the biggest—Poggin. Duane had holed them, and his sensations of the moment deadened sight and sound of what was before him. He sank down, controlled himself, silenced a mounting exultation, then from a less-strained position he peered forth again.

The outlaws were waiting for supper. Their conversation might have been that of cowboys in camp, ranchers at a roundup. Duane listened with eager ears, waiting for the business talk that he felt would come. All the time he watched with the eyes of a wolf upon its quarry. Blossom Kane was the lean-limbed messenger who had so angered Fletcher. Boldt was a giant in stature, dark, bearded, silent. Panhandle Smith was the red-faced cook, merry, profane, a short, bow-legged man resembling many rustlers Duane had known, particularly Luke Stevens. And Knell, who sat there, tall, slim, like a boy in build, like a boy in years, with his pale, smooth, expressionless face and his cold, gray eyes. And Longstreth, who leaned against the wall, handsome, with his dark face and beard like an aristocrat, resembled many a rich Louisiana planter Duane had met. The sixth man sat so much in the shadow that he could not be plainly discerned, and, though addressed, his name was not mentioned.

Panhandle Smith carried pots and pans into the cabin, and cheerfully called out: "If you gents air hungry fer grub, don't look fer me to feed you with a spoon."

The outlaws piled inside, made a great bustle and clatter as they sat to their meal. Like hungry men, they talked little.

Duane waited there awhile, then guardedly got up and crept round to the other side of the cabin. After he became used to the dark again he ventured to steal along the wall to the window and peeped in. The outlaws were in the first room and could not be seen.

Duane waited. The moments dragged endlessly. His heart pounded. Longstreth entered, turned up the light, and, taking a box of cigars from the table, he carried it out.

"Here, you fellows, go outside and smoke," he said. "Knell, come on in now. Let's get it over."

He returned, sat down, and lighted a cigar for himself. He put his booted feet on the table.

Duane saw that the room was comfortably, even luxuriously furnished.

There must have been a good trail, he thought, else how could all that stuff have been packed in there. Most assuredly it could not have come over the trail he had traveled. Presently he heard the men go outside, and their voices became indistinct. Then Knell came in and seated himself without any of his chief's ease. He seemed preoccupied and, as always, cold.

"What's wrong, Knell? Why didn't you get here sooner?" queried Longstreth.

"Poggin, damn him! We're on the outs again."

"What for?"

"Aw, he needn't have got sore. He's breakin' a new hoss over at Faraway, an' you know him where a hoss 's concerned. That kept him, I reckon, more than anythin'."

"What else? Get it out of your system so we can go on to the new job."

"Well, it begins back a ways. I don't know how long ago—weeks—a stranger rode into Ord an' got down easy-like as if he owned the place. He seemed familiar to me. But I wasn't sure. We looked him over, an' I left, tryin' to place him in my mind."

"What'd he look like?"

"Rangy, powerful man, white hair over his temples, still, hard face, eyes like knives. The way he packed his guns, the way he walked an' stood an' swung his right hand showed me what he was. You can't fool me on the gun-sharp. An' he had a grand horse, a big black."

"I've met your man," said Longstreth.

"No!" exclaimed Knell. It was wonderful to hear surprise expressed by this man that did not in the least show it in his strange physiognomy. Knell laughed a short, grim, hollow laugh. "Boss, this here big gent drifts into Ord again an' makes up to Jim Fletcher. Jim, you know, is easy led. He likes men. An' when a posse come along trailin' a blind lead, huntin' the wrong way for the man who held up No. 6, why, Jim—he up an' takes this stranger to be the fly road-agent an' cottons to him. Got money out of him sure. An' that's what stumps me more. What's this man's game? I happen to know, boss, that he couldn't have held up No. 6."

"How do you know?" demanded Longstreth.

"Because I did the job myself."

A dark and stormy passion clouded the chief's face.

"Damn you, Knell! You're incorrigible. You're unreliable. Another break like that queers you with me. Did you tell Poggin?"

"Yes. That's one reason we fell out. He raved. I thought he was goin' to kill me."

"Why did you tackle such a risky job without help or plan?"

"It offered, that's all. An' it was easy. But it was a mistake. I got the country an' the railroad hollerin' for nothin'. I just couldn't help it. You know what idleness means to one of us. You know also that this very life breeds fatality. It's wrong—that's why. I was born of good parents, an' I know what's right. We're wrong, an' we can't beat the end, that's all. An' for my part I don't care a damn when that comes."

"Fine wise talk from you, Knell," said Longstreth, scornfully. "Go on with your story."

"As I said, Jim cottons to the pretender, an' they get chummy. They're together all the time. You can gamble Jim told all he knew an' then some. A little liquor loosens his tongue. Several of the boys rode over from Ord, an' one of them went to Poggin an' says Jim Fletcher has a new man for the gang. Poggin, you know, is always ready for any new man. He says if one doesn't turn out good he can be shut off easy. He rather liked the way this new pard of Jim's was boosted. Jim an' Poggin always hit it up together. So until I got on the deal Jim's pard was already in the gang, without Poggin or you ever seein' him. Then I got to figurin' hard. Just where had I ever seen that chap? As it turned out, I never had seen him, which accounts for my bein' doubtful. I'd never forget any man I'd seen. I dug up a lot of old papers from my kit an' went over them. Letters, pictures, clippin's, an' all that. I guess I had a pretty good notion what I was lookin' for an' who I wanted to make sure of. At last I found it. An' I knew my man. But I didn't spring it on Poggin. Oh no! I want to have some fun with him when the time comes. He'll be wilder than a trapped wolf. I sent Blossom over to Ord to get word from Jim, an' when he verified all this talk I sent Blossom again with a message calculated to make Jim hump. Poggin got sore, said he'd wait for Jim, an' I could come over here to see you about the new job. He'd meet me in Ord."

Knell had spoken hurriedly and low, now and then with passion. His pale eyes glinted like fire in ice, and now his voice fell to a whisper.

"Who do you think Fletcher's new man is?"

"Who?" demanded Longstreth.

*"Buck Duane!"*

Down came Longstreth's boots with a crash, then his body grew rigid.

"That Nueces outlaw? That two-shot ace-of-spades gun-thrower who killed Bland, Alloway—?"

"An' Hardin." Knell whispered this last name with more feeling than the apparent circumstance demanded.

"Yes; and Hardin, the best one of the Rim Rock fellows—Buck Duane!"

Longstreth was so ghastly white now that his black mustache seemed outlined against chalk. He eyed his grim lieutenant. They understood each other without more words. It was enough that Buck Duane was there in the Big Bend. Longstreth rose presently and reached for a flask, from which he drank, then offered it to Knell. He waved it aside.

"Knell," began the chief, slowly, as he wiped his lips, "I gathered you have some grudge against this Buck Duane."

"Yes."

"Well, don't be a fool now and do what Poggin or almost any of you men would—don't meet this Buck Duane. I've reason to believe he's a Texas Ranger now."

"The hell you say!" exclaimed Knell.

"Yes. Go to Ord and give Jim Fletcher a hunch. He'll get Poggin, and they'll fix even Buck Duane."

"All right. I'll do my best. But if I run into Duane—"

"Don't run into him!" Longstreth's voice fairly rang with the force of its passion and command. He wiped his face, drank again from the flask, sat down, resumed his smoking, and, drawing a paper from his vest pocket he began to study it.

"Well, I'm glad that's settled," he said, evidently referring to the Duane matter. "Now for the new job. This is October the eighteenth. On or before the twenty-fifth there will be a shipment of gold reach the Rancher's Bank of Val Verde. After you return to Ord give Poggin these orders. Keep the gang quiet. You, Poggin, Kane, Fletcher, Panhandle Smith, and Boldt to be in on the secret and the job. Nobody else. You'll leave Ord on the twenty-third, ride across country by the trail till you get within sight of Mercer. It's a hundred miles from Bradford to Val Verde—about the same from Ord. Time your travel to get you near Val Verde on the morning of the twenty-sixth. You won't have to more than trot your horses. At two o'clock in the afternoon, sharp, ride into town and up to the Rancher's Bank. Val Verde's a pretty big town. Never been any holdups there. Town feels safe. Make it a clean, fast, daylight job. That's all. Have you got the details?"

Knell did not even ask for the dates again.

"Suppose Poggin or me might be detained?" he asked.

Longstreth bent a dark glance upon his lieutenant.

"You never can tell what'll come off," continued Knell. "I'll do my best."

"The minute you see Poggin tell him. A job on hand steadies him. And I say again—look to it that nothing happens. Either you or Poggin carry the job through. But I want both of you in it. Break for the hills, and when you get up in the rocks where you can hide your tracks head for Mount Ord. When all's quiet again I'll join you here. That's all. Call in the boys."

Like a swift shadow and as noiseless Duane stole across the level toward the dark wall of rock. Every nerve was a strung wire. For a little while his mind was cluttered and clogged with whirling thoughts, from which, like a flashing scroll, unrolled the long, baffling order of action. The game was now in his hands. He must cross Mount Ord at night. The feat was improbable, but it might be done. He must ride into Bradford, forty miles from the foothills before eight o'clock next morning. He must telegraph MacNelly to be in Val Verde on the twenty-fifth. He must ride back to Ord, to intercept Knell, face him be denounced, kill him, and while the iron was hot strike hard to win Poggin's half-won interest as he had wholly won Fletcher's. Failing that last, he must let the outlaws alone to bide their time in Ord, to be free to ride on to their new job in Val Verde. In the meantime he must plan to arrest Longstreth. It was a magnificent outline, incredible, alluring, unfathomable in its nameless certainty. He felt like fate. He seemed to be the iron consequences falling upon these doomed outlaws.

Under the wall the shadows were black, only the tips of trees and crags showing, yet he went straight to the trail. It was merely a grayness between borders of black. He climbed and never stopped. It did not seem steep. His feet might have had eyes. He surmounted the wall, and, looking down into the ebony gulf pierced by one point of light, he lifted a menacing arm and shook it. Then he strode on and did not falter till he reached the huge shelving cliffs. Here he lost the trail; there was none; but he remembered the shapes, the points, the notches of rock above. Before he reached the ruins of splintered ramparts and jumbles of broken walls the moon topped the eastern slope of the mountain, and the mystifying blackness he had dreaded changed to magic silver light. It seemed as light as day, only soft, mellow, and the air held a transparent sheen. He ran up the bare ridges and down the smooth slopes, and, like a goat, jumped from rock to rock. In this light he knew his way and lost no time looking for a trail. He crossed the divide and then had all downhill before him. Swiftly he descended, almost always sure of his memory of the landmarks. He did not remember having studied them in the ascent, yet here they were, even in changed light, familiar to his sight. What he had once seen was pictured on his mind. And, true as a deer striking for home, he reached the cañon where he had left his horse.

Bullet was quickly and easily found. Duane threw on the saddle and pack, cinched them tight, and resumed his descent. The worst was now to come. Bare downward steps in rock, sliding, weathered slopes, narrow black gullies, a thousand openings in a maze of broken stone—these Duane had to descend in fast time, leading a giant of a horse. Bullet cracked the loose fragments, sent them rolling, slid on the scaly slopes, plunged down the steps, followed like a faithful dog at Duane's heels.

Hours passed as moments. Duane was equal to his great opportunity. But he could not quell that self in him which reached back over the lapse of lonely, searing years and found the boy in him. He who had been worse than dead was now grasping at the skirts of life—which meant victory, honor, happiness. Duane knew he was not just right in part of his mind. Small wonder that he was not insane, he thought! He tramped on downward, his marvelous faculty for covering rough ground and holding to the true course never before even in flight so keen and acute. Yet all the time a spirit was keeping step with him. Thought of Ray Longstreth as he had left her made him weak. But now, with the game clear to its end, with the trap to spring, with success strangely haunting him, Duane could not dispel memory of her. He saw her white face, with its sweet sad lips and the dark eyes so tender and tragic. And time and distance and risk and toil were nothing.

The moon sloped to the west. Shadows of trees and crags now crossed to the other side of him. The stars dimmed. Then he was out of the rocks, with the dim trail pale at his feet. Mounting Bullet, he made short work of the long slope and the foothills and the rolling land leading down to Ord. The little outlaw camp, with its shacks and cabins and row of houses, lay silent and dark under the paling moon. Duane passed by on the lower trail, headed into the road, and put Bullet to a gallop. He watched the dying moon, the waning stars, and the east. He had time to spare, so he saved the horse. Knell would be leaving the rendezvous about the time Duane turned back toward Ord. Between noon and sunset they would meet.

The night wore on. The moon sank behind low mountains in the west. The stars brightened for a while, then faded. Gray gloom enveloped the world, thickened, lay like smoke over the road. Then shade by shade it lightened, until through the transparent obscurity shone a dim light.

Duane reached Bradford before dawn. He dismounted some distance from the tracks, tied his horse, and then crossed over to the station. He heard the clicking of the telegraph instrument, and it thrilled him. An operator sat inside reading. When Duane tapped on the window he looked up with startled glance, then went swiftly to unlock the door.

"Hello. Give me paper and pencil. Quick," whispered Duane.

With trembling hands the operator complied. Duane wrote out the message he had carefully composed.

"Send this—repeat it to make sure—then keep mum. I'll see you again. Good-by."

The operator stared, but did not speak a word.

Duane left as stealthily and swiftly as he had come. He walked his horse a couple miles back on the road and then rested him till break of day. The east began to redden, Duane turned grimly in the direction of Ord.

When Duane swung into the wide, grassy square on the outskirts of Ord he saw a bunch of saddled horses hitched in front of the tavern. He knew what that meant. Luck still favored him. If it would only hold! But he could ask no more. The rest was a matter of how greatly he could make his power felt. An open conflict against odds lay in the balance. That would be fatal to him, and to avoid it he had to trust to his name and a presence he must make terrible. He knew outlaws. He knew what qualities held them. He knew what to exaggerate.

There was not an outlaw in sight. The dusty horses had covered distance that morning. As Duane dismounted he heard loud, angry voices inside the tavern. He removed coat and vest, hung them over the pommel. He packed two guns, one belted high on the left hip, the other swinging low on the right side. He neither looked nor listened, but boldly pushed the door and stepped inside.

The big room was full of men, and every face pivoted toward him. Knell's pale face flashed into Duane's swift sight; then Boldt's, then Blossom Kane's, then Panhandle Smith's, then Fletcher's, then others that were familiar, and last that of Poggin. Though Duane had never seen Poggin or heard him described, he knew him. For he saw a face that was a record of great and evil deeds.

There was absolute silence. The outlaws were lined back of a long table upon which were papers, stacks of silver coin, a bundle of bills, and a huge gold-mounted gun.

"Are you gents lookin' for me?" asked Duane. He gave his voice all the ringing force and power of which he was capable. And he stepped back, free of anything, with the outlaws all before him.

Knell stood quivering, but his face might have been a mask. The other outlaws looked from him to Duane. Jim Fletcher flung up his hands.

"My Gawd, Dodge, what'd you bust in here fer?" he said, plaintively, and slowly stepped forward. His action was that of a man true to himself. He meant he had been sponsor for Duane and now he would stand by him.

"Back, Fletcher!" called Duane, and his voice made the outlaw jump.

"Hold on, Dodge, an' you-all, everybody," said Fletcher. "Let me talk, seein' I'm in wrong here."

His persuasions did not ease the strain.

"Go ahead. Talk," said Poggin.

Fletcher turned to Duane. "Pard, I'm takin' it on myself thet you meet enemies here when I swore you'd meet friends. It's my fault. I'll stand by you if you let me."

"No, Jim," replied Duane.

"But what'd you come fer without the signal?" burst out Fletcher, in distress. He saw nothing but catastrophe in this meeting.

"Jim, I ain't pressin' my company none. But when I'm wanted bad—"

Fletcher stopped him with a raised hand. Then he turned to Poggin with a rude dignity.

"Poggy, he's my pard, an' he's riled. I never told him a word thet'd make him sore. I only said Knell hadn't no more use fer him than fer me. Now, what you say goes in this gang. I never failed you in my life. Here's my pard. I vouch fer him. Will you stand fer me? There's goin' to be hell if you don't. An' us with a big job on hand!"

While Fletcher toiled over his slow, earnest persuasion Duane had his gaze riveted upon Poggin. There was something leonine about Poggin. He was tawny. He blazed. He seemed beautiful as fire was beautiful. But looked at closer, with glance seeing the physical man, instead of that thing which shone from him, he was of perfect build, with muscles that swelled and rippled, bulging his clothes, with the magnificent head and face of the cruel, fierce, tawny-eyed jaguar.

Looking at this strange Poggin, instinctively divining his abnormal and hideous power, Duane had for the first time in his life the inward quaking fear of a man. It was like a cold-tongued bell ringing within him and numbing his heart. The old instinctive firing of blood followed, but did not drive away that fear. He knew. He felt something here deeper than thought could go. And he hated Poggin.

That individual had been considering Fletcher's appeal.

"Jim, I ante up," he said, "an' if Phil doesn't raise us out with a big hand—why, he'll get called, an' your pard can set in the game."

Every eye shifted to Knell. He was dead white. He laughed, and anyone hearing that laugh would have realized his intense anger equally with an assurance which made him master of the situation.

"Poggin, you're a gambler, you are—the ace-high, straight-flush hand of the Big Bend," he said, with stinging scorn. "I'll bet you my roll to a greaser peso that I can deal you a hand you'll be afraid to play."

"Phil, you're talkin' wild," growled Poggin, with both advice and menace in his tone.

"If there's anythin' you hate it's a man who pretends to be somebody else when he's not. Thet so?"

Poggin nodded in slow-gathering wrath.

"Well, Jim's new pard—this man Dodge—he's not who he seems. Oh-ho! He's a hell of a lot different. But *I* know him. An' when I spring his name on you, Poggin, you'll freeze to your gizzard. Do you get me? You'll freeze, an' your hand'll be stiff when it ought to be lightnin'—all because you'll realize you've been standin' there five minutes—five minutes *alive* before him!"

If not hate, then assuredly great passion toward Poggin manifested itself in Knell's scornful, fiery address, in the shaking hand he thrust before Poggin's face. In the ensuing silent pause Knell's panting could be plainly heard. The other men were pale, watchful, cautiously edging either way to the wall, leaving the principals and Duane in the center of the room.

"Spring his name, then, you—" said Poggin, violently, with a curse.

Strangely Knell did not even look at the man he was about to denounce. He leaned toward Poggin, his hands, his body, his long head all somewhat expressive of what his face disguised.

*"Buck Duane!"* he yelled, suddenly.

The name did not make any great difference in Poggin. But Knell's passionate, swift utterance carried the suggestion that the name ought to bring Poggin to quick action. It was possible, too, that Knell's manner, the import of his denunciation, the meaning back of all his passion held Poggin bound more than the surprise. For the outlaw certainly was surprised, perhaps staggered at the idea that he, Poggin, had been about to stand sponsor with Fletcher for a famous outlaw hated and feared by all outlaws.

Knell waited a long moment, and then his face broke its cold immobility in an extraordinary expression of devilish glee. He had hounded the great Poggin into something that gave him vicious, monstrous joy.

*"Buck Duane!* Yes," he broke out, hotly. "The Nueces gunman! That two-shot, ace-of-spades lone wolf! You an' I—we've heard a thousand times of him—talked about him often. An' here he *in front* of you! Poggin, you were backin' Fletcher's new pard, Buck Duane. An' he'd fooled you both but for me. But *I* know him. An' I know why he drifted in here. To flash a gun on Cheseldine—on you—on me! Bah! Don't tell me he wanted to join the gang. You know a gunman, for you're one yourself. Don't you always want to kill another man? An' don't you always want to meet a real man, not a four-flush? It's the madness of the gunman, an' I know it. Well, Duane faced you—called you! An' when I sprung his name, what ought you have done? What would the boss—anybody—have expected of Poggin? Did you throw your gun, swift, like you have so often? Naw; you froze. An' why? Because here's a man with the kind of nerve you'd love to have. Because he's great—meetin' us here alone. Because you know he's a wonder with a gun an' you love life. Because you an' I an' every damned man here had to take his front, each to himself. If we all drew we'd kill him. Sure! But who's goin' to lead? Who was goin' to be first? Who was goin' to make him draw? Not you, Poggin! You leave that for a lesser man—me—who've lived to see you a coward. It comes once to every gunman. You've met your match in Buck Duane. An', by God, I'm glad! Here's once I show you up!"

The hoarse, taunting voice failed. Knell stepped back from the comrade he hated. He was wet, shaking, haggard, but magnificent.

"Buck Duane, do you remember Hardin?" he asked, in scarcely audible voice.

"Yes," replied Duane, and a flash of insight made clear Knell's attitude.

"You met him—forced him to draw—killed him?"

"Yes."

"Hardin was the best pard I ever had."

His teeth clicked together tight, and his lips set in a thin line.

The room grew still. Even breathing ceased. The time for words had passed. In that long moment of suspense Knell's body gradually stiffened, and at last the quivering ceased. He crouched. His eyes had a soul-piercing fire.

Duane watched them. He waited. He caught the thought—the breaking of Knell's muscle-bound rigidity. Then he drew.

Through the smoke of his gun he saw two red spurts of flame. Knell's bullets thudded into the ceiling. He fell with a scream like a wild thing in agony.

Duane did not see Knell die. He watched Poggin. And Poggin, like a stricken and astounded man, looked down upon his prostrate comrade.

Fletcher ran at Duane with hands aloft.

"Hit the trail, you liar, or you'll hev to kill me!" he yelled.

With hands still up, he shouldered and bodied Duane out of the room.

Duane leaped on his horse, spurred, and plunged away.

## CHAPTER XXIII

Duane returned to Fairdale and camped in the mesquite till the twenty-third of the month. The few days seemed endless. All he could think of was that the hour in which he must disgrace Ray Longstreth was slowly but inexorably coming. In that waiting time he learned what love was and also duty. When the day at last dawned he rode like one possessed down the rough slope, hurdling the stones and crashing through the brush, with a sound in his ears that was not all the rush of the wind. Something dragged at him.

Apparently one side of his mind was unalterably fixed, while the other was a hurrying conglomeration of flashes of thought, reception of sensations. He could not get calmness. By and by, almost involuntarily, he hurried faster on. Action seemed to make his state less oppressive; it eased the weight. But the farther he went on the harder it was to continue. Had he turned his back upon love, happiness, perhaps on life itself?

There seemed no use to go on farther until he was absolutely sure of himself. Duane received a clear warning thought that such work as seemed haunting and driving him could never be carried out in the mood under which he labored. He hung on to that thought. Several times he slowed up, then stopped, only to go on again. At length, as he mounted a low ridge, Fairdale lay bright and green before him not far away, and the sight was a conclusive check. There were mesquites on the ridge, and Duane sought the shade beneath them. It was the noon hour, with hot, glary sun and no wind. Here Duane had to have out his fight. Duane was utterly unlike himself; he could not bring the old self back; he was not the same man he once had been. But he could understand why. It was because of Ray Longstreth. Temptation assailed him. To have her his wife! It was impossible. The thought was insidiously alluring. Duane pictured a home. He saw himself riding through the cotton and rice and cane, home to a stately old mansion, where long-eared hounds bayed him welcome, and a woman looked for him and met him with happy and beautiful smile. There might—there would be children. And something new, strange, confounding with its emotion, came to life deep in Duane's heart. There would be children! Ray their mother! The kind of life a lonely outcast always yearned for and never had! He saw it all, felt it all.

But beyond and above all other claims came Captain MacNelly's. It was then there was something cold and death-like in Duane's soul. For he knew, whatever happened, of one thing he was sure—he would have to kill either Longstreth or Lawson. Longstreth might be trapped into arrest; but Lawson had no sense, no control, no fear. He would snarl like a panther and go for his gun, and he would have to be killed. This, of all consummations, was the one to be calculated upon.

Duane came out of it all bitter and callous and sore—in the most fitting of moods to undertake a difficult and deadly enterprise. He had fallen upon his old strange, futile dreams, now rendered poignant by reason of love. He drove away those dreams. In their places came the images of the olive-skinned Longstreth with his sharp eyes, and the dark, evil-faced Lawson, and then returned tenfold more thrilling and sinister the old strange passion to meet Poggin.

It was about one o'clock when Duane rode into Fairdale. The streets for the most part were deserted. He went directly to find Morton and Zimmer. He found them at length, restless, somber, anxious, but unaware of the part he had played at Ord. They said Longstreth was home, too. It was possible that Longstreth had arrived home in ignorance.

Duane told them to be on hand in town with their men in case he might need them, and then with teeth locked he set off for Longstreth's ranch.

Duane stole through the bushes and trees, and when nearing the porch he heard loud, angry, familiar voices. Longstreth and Lawson were quarreling again. How Duane's lucky star guided him! He had no plan of action, but his brain was equal to a hundred lightning-swift evolutions. He meant to take any risk rather than kill Longstreth. Both of the men were out on the porch. Duane wormed his way to the edge of the shrubbery and crouched low to watch for his opportunity.

Longstreth looked haggard and thin. He was in his shirt-sleeves, and he had come out with a gun in his hand. This he laid on a table near the wall. He wore no belt.

Lawson was red, bloated, thick-lipped, all fiery and sweaty from drink, though sober on the moment, and he had the expression of a desperate man in his last stand. It was his last stand, though he was ignorant of that.

"What's your news? You needn't be afraid of my feelings," said Lawson.

"Ray confessed to an interest in this ranger," replied Longstreth.

Duane thought Lawson would choke. He was thick-necked anyway, and the rush of blood made him tear at the soft collar of his shirt. Duane awaited his chance, patient, cold, all his feelings shut in a vise.

"But why should your daughter meet this ranger?" demanded Lawson, harshly.

"She's in love with him, and he's in love with her."

Duane reveled in Lawson's condition. The statement might have had the force of a juggernaut. Was Longstreth sincere? What was his game?

Lawson, finding his voice, cursed Ray, cursed the ranger, then Longstreth.

"You damned selfish fool!" cried Longstreth, in deep bitter scorn. "All you think of is yourself—your loss of the girl. Think once of *me*—my home—my life!"

Then the connection subtly put out by Longstreth apparently dawned upon the other. Somehow through this girl her father and cousin were to be betrayed. Duane got that impression, though he could not tell how true it was. Certainly Lawson's jealousy was his paramount emotion.

"To hell with you!" burst out Lawson, incoherently. He was frenzied. "I'll have her, or nobody else will!"

"You never will," returned Longstreth, stridently. "So help me God I'd rather see her the ranger's wife than yours!"

While Lawson absorbed that shock Longstreth leaned toward him, all of hate and menace in his mien.

"Lawson, you made me what I am," continued Longstreth. "I backed you—shielded you. *You're* Cheseldine—if the truth is told! Now it's ended. I quit you. I'm done!"

Their gray passion-corded faces were still as stones.

*"Gentlemen!"* Duane called in far-reaching voice as he stepped out. *"You're both done!"*

They wheeled to confront Duane.

"Don't move! Not a muscle! Not a finger!" he warned.

Longstreth read what Lawson had not the mind to read. His face turned from gray to ashen.

"What d'ye mean?" yelled Lawson, fiercely, shrilly. It was not in him to obey a command, to see impending death.

All quivering and strung, yet with perfect control, Duane raised his left hand to turn back a lapel of his open vest. The silver star flashed brightly.

Lawson howled like a dog. With barbarous and insane fury, with sheer impotent folly, he swept a clawing hand for his gun. Duane's shot broke his action.

Before Lawson ever tottered, before he loosed the gun, Longstreth leaped behind him, clasped him with left arm, quick as lightning jerked the gun from both clutching fingers and sheath. Longstreth protected himself with the body of the dead man. Duane saw red flashes, puffs of smoke; he heard quick reports. Something stung his left arm. Then a blow like wind, light of sound yet shocking in impact, struck him, staggered him. The hot rend of lead followed the blow. Duane's heart seemed to explode, yet his mind kept extraordinarily clear and rapid.

Duane heard Longstreth work the action of Lawson's gun. He heard the hammer click, fall upon empty shells. Longstreth had used up all the loads in Lawson's gun. He cursed as a man cursed at defeat. Duane waited, cool and sure now. Longstreth tried to lift the dead man, to edge him closer toward the table where his own gun lay. But, considering the peril of exposing himself, he found the task beyond him. He bent peering at Duane under Lawson's arm, which flopped out from his side. Longstreth's eyes were the eyes of a man who meant to kill. There was never any mistaking the strange and terrible light of eyes like those. More than once Duane had a chance to aim at them, at the top of Longstreth's head, at a strip of his side.

Longstreth flung Lawson's body off. But even as it dropped, before Longstreth could leap, as he surely intended, for the gun, Duane covered him, called piercingly to him:

"Don't jump for the gun! Don't! I'll kill you! Sure as God I'll kill you!"

Longstreth stood perhaps ten feet from the table where his gun lay. Duane saw him calculating chances. He was game. He had the courage that forced Duane to respect him. Duane just saw him measure the distance to that gun. He was magnificent. He meant to do it. Duane would have to kill him.

"Longstreth, listen," cried Duane, swiftly. "The game's up. You're done. But think of your daughter! I'll spare your life—I'll try to get you freedom on one condition. For her sake! I've got you nailed—all the proofs. There lies Lawson. You're alone. I've Morton and men to my aid. Give up. Surrender. Consent to demands, and I'll spare you. Maybe I can persuade MacNelly to let you go free back to your old country. It's for Ray's sake! Her life, perhaps her happiness, can be saved! Hurry, man! Your answer!"

"Suppose I refuse?" he queried, with a dark and terrible earnestness.

"Then I'll kill you in your tracks! You can't move a hand! Your word or death! Hurry, Longstreth! Be a man! For her sake! Quick! Another second now—I'll kill you!"

"All right, Buck Duane, I give my word," he said, and deliberately walked to the chair and fell into it.

Longstreth looked strangely at the bloody blot on Duane's shoulder.

"There come the girls!" he suddenly exclaimed. "Can you help me drag Lawson inside? They mustn't see him."

Duane was facing down the porch toward the court and corrals. Miss Longstreth and Ruth had come in sight, were swiftly approaching, evidently alarmed. The two men succeeded in drawing Lawson into the house before the girls saw him.

"Duane, you're not hard hit?" said Longstreth.

"Reckon not," replied Duane.

"I'm sorry. If only you could have told me sooner! Lawson, damn him! Always I've split over him!"

"But the last time, Longstreth."

"Yes, and I came near driving you to kill me, too. Duane, you talked me out of it. For Ray's sake! She'll be in here in a minute. This'll be harder than facing a gun."

"Hard now. But I hope it'll turn out all right."

"Duane, will you do me a favor?" he asked, and he seemed shamefaced.

"Sure."

"Let Ray and Ruth think Lawson shot you. He's dead. It can't matter. Duane, the old side of my life is coming back. It's been coming. It'll be here just about when she enters this room. And, by God, I'd change places with Lawson if I could!"

"Glad you—said that, Longstreth," replied Duane. "And sure—Lawson plugged me. It's our secret."

Just then Ray and Ruth entered the room. Duane heard two low cries, so different in tone, and he saw two white faces. Ray came to his side. She lifted a shaking hand to point at the blood upon his breast. White and mute, she gazed from that to her father.

"Papa!" cried Ray, wringing her hands.

"Don't give way," he replied, huskily. "Both you girls will need your nerve. Duane isn't badly hurt. But Floyd is—is dead. Listen. Let me tell it quick. There's been a fight. It—it was Lawson—it was Lawson's gun that shot Duane. Duane let me off. In fact, Ray, he saved me. I'm to divide my property—return so far as possible what I've stolen—leave Texas at once with Duane, under arrest. He says maybe he can get MacNelly, the ranger captain, to let me go. For your sake!"

She stood there, realizing her deliverance, with the dark and tragic glory of her eyes passing from her father to Duane.

"You must rise above this," said Duane to her. "I expected this to ruin you. But your father is alive. He will live it down. I'm sure I can promise you he'll be free. Perhaps back there in Louisiana the dishonor will never be known. This country is far from your old home. And even in San Antonio and Austin a man's evil repute means little. Then the line between a rustler and a rancher is hard to draw in these wild border days. Rustling is stealing cattle, and I once heard a well-known rancher say that all rich cattlemen had done a little stealing. Your father drifted out here, and, like a good many others, he succeeded. It's perhaps just as well not to split hairs, to judge him by the law and morality of a civilized country. Some way or other he drifted in with bad men. Maybe a deal that was honest somehow tied his hands. This matter of land, water, a few stray head of stock had to be decided out of court. I'm sure in his case he never realized where he was drifting. Then one thing led to another, until he was face to face with dealing that took on crooked form. To protect himself he bound men to him. And so the gang developed. Many powerful gangs have developed that way out here. He could not control them. He became involved with them. And eventually their dealings became deliberately and boldly dishonest. That meant the inevitable spilling of blood sooner or later, and so he grew into the leader because he was the strongest. Whatever he is to be judged for, I think he could have been infinitely worse."

## CHAPTER XXIV

On the morning of the twenty-sixth Duane rode into Bradford in time to catch the early train. His wounds did not seriously incapacitate him. Longstreth was with him. And Miss Longstreth and Ruth Herbert would not be left behind. They were all leaving Fairdale forever. Longstreth had turned over the whole of his property to Morton, who was to divide it as he and his comrades believed just. Duane had left Fairdale with his party by night, passed through Sanderson in the early hours of dawn, and reached Bradford as he had planned.

That fateful morning found Duane outwardly calm, but inwardly he was in a tumult. He wanted to rush to Val Verde. Would Captain MacNelly be there with his rangers, as Duane had planned for them to be? Memory of that tawny Poggin returned with strange passion. Duane had borne hours and weeks and months of waiting, had endured the long hours of the outlaw, but now he had no patience. The whistle of the train made him leap.

It was a fast train, yet the ride seemed slow.

Duane, disliking to face Longstreth and the passengers in the car, changed his seat to one behind his prisoner. They had seldom spoken. Longstreth sat with bowed head, deep in thought. The girls sat in a seat near by and were pale but composed. Occasionally the train halted briefly at a station. The latter half of that ride Duane had observed a wagon-road running parallel with the railroad, sometimes right alongside, at others near or far away. When the train was about twenty miles from Val Verde Duane espied a dark group of horsemen trotting eastward. His blood beat like a hammer at his temples. The gang! He thought he recognized the tawny Poggin and felt a strange inward contraction. He thought he recognized the clean-cut Blossom Kane, the black-bearded giant Boldt, the red-faced Panhandle Smith, and Fletcher. There was another man strange to him. Was that Knell? No! It could not have been Knell.

Duane leaned over the seat and touched Longstreth on the shoulder.

"Look!" he whispered. Cheseldine was stiff. He had already seen.

The train flashed by; the outlaw gang receded out of range of sight.

"Did you notice Knell wasn't with them?" whispered Duane.

Duane did not speak to Longstreth again till the train stopped at Val Verde.

They got off the car, and the girls followed as naturally as ordinary travelers. The station was a good deal larger than that at Bradford, and there was considerable action and bustle incident to the arrival of the train.

Duane's sweeping gaze searched faces, rested upon a man who seemed familiar. This fellow's look, too, was that of one who knew Duane, but was waiting for a sign, a cue. Then Duane recognized him—MacNelly, clean-shaven. Without mustache he appeared different, younger.

When MacNelly saw that Duane intended to greet him, to meet him, he hurried forward. A keen light flashed from his eyes. He was glad, eager, yet suppressing himself, and the glances he sent back and forth from Duane to Longstreth were questioning, doubtful. Certainly Longstreth did not look the part of an outlaw.

"Duane! Lord, I'm glad to see you," was the Captain's greeting. Then at closer look into Duane's face his warmth fled—something he saw there checked his enthusiasm, or at least its utterance.

"MacNelly, shake hand with Cheseldine," said Duane, low-voiced.

The ranger captain stood dumb, motionless. But he saw Longstreth's instant action, and awkwardly he reached for the outstretched hand.

"Any of your men down here?" queried Duane, sharply.

"No. They're uptown."

"Come. MacNelly, you walk with him. We've ladies in the party. I'll come behind with them."

They set off uptown. Longstreth walked as if he were with friends on the way to dinner. The girls were mute. MacNelly walked like a man in a trance. There was not a word spoken in four blocks.

Presently Duane espied a stone building on a corner of the broad street. There was a big sign, "Rancher's Bank."

"There's the hotel," said MacNelly. "Some of my men are there. We've scattered around."

They crossed the street, went through office and lobby, and then Duane asked MacNelly to take them to a private room. Without a word the Captain complied. When they were all inside Duane closed the door, and, drawing a deep breath as if of relief, he faced them calmly.

"Miss Longstreth, you and Miss Ruth try to make yourselves comfortable now," he said. "And don't be distressed." Then he turned to his captain. "MacNelly, this girl is the daughter of the man I've brought to you, and this one is his niece."

Then Duane briefly related Longstreth's story, and, though he did not spare the rustler chief, he was generous.

"When I went after Longstreth," concluded Duane, "it was either to kill him or offer him freedom on conditions. So I chose the latter for his daughter's sake. He has already disposed of all his property. I believe he'll live up to the conditions. He's to leave Texas never to return. The name Cheseldine has been a mystery, and now it'll fade."

A few moments later Duane followed MacNelly to a large room, like a hall, and here were men reading and smoking. Duane knew them—rangers!

MacNelly beckoned to his men.

"Boys, here he is."

"How many men have you?" asked Duane.

"Fifteen."

MacNelly almost embraced Duane, would probably have done so but for the dark grimness that seemed to be coming over the man. Instead he glowed, he sputtered, he tried to talk, to wave his hands. He was beside himself. And his rangers crowded closer, eager, like hounds ready to run. They all talked at once, and the word most significant and frequent in their speech was "outlaws."

MacNelly clapped his fist in his hand.

"This'll make the adjutant sick with joy. Maybe we won't have it on the Governor! We'll show them about the ranger service. Duane! How'd you ever do it?"

"Now, Captain, not the half nor the quarter of this job's done. The gang's coming down the road. I saw them from the train. They'll ride into town on the dot—two-thirty."

"How many?" asked MacNelly.

"Poggin, Blossom Kane, Panhandle Smith, Boldt, Jim Fletcher, and another man I don't know. These are the picked men of Cheseldine's gang. I'll bet they'll be the fastest, hardest bunch you rangers ever faced."

"Poggin—that's the hard nut to crack! I've heard their records since I've been in Val Verde. Where's Knell? They say he's a boy, but hell and blazes!"

"Knell's dead."

"Ah!" exclaimed MacNelly, softly. Then he grew businesslike, cool, and of harder aspect. "Duane, it's your game today. I'm only a ranger under orders. We're all under your orders. We've absolute faith in you. Make your plan quick, so I can go around and post the boys who're not here."

"You understand there's no sense in trying to arrest Poggin, Kane, and that lot?" queried Duane.

"No, I don't understand that," replied MacNelly, bluntly.

"It can't be done. The drop can't be got on such men. If you meet them they shoot, and mighty quick and straight. Poggin! That outlaw has no equal with a gun—unless—he's got to be killed quick. They'll all have to be killed. They're all bad, desperate, know no fear, are lightning in action."

"Very well, Duane; then it's a fight. That'll be easier, perhaps. The boys are spoiling for a fight. Out with your plan, now."

"Put one man at each end of this street, just at the edge of town. Let him hide there with a rifle to block the escape of any outlaw that we might fail to get. I had a good look at the bank building. It's well situated for our purpose. Put four men up in that room over the bank—four men, two at each open window. Let them hide till the game begins. They want to be there so in case these foxy outlaws get wise before they're down on the ground or inside the bank. The rest of your men put inside behind the counters, where they'll hide. Now go over to the bank, spring the thing on the bank officials, and don't let them shut up the bank. You want their aid. Let them make sure of their gold. But the clerks and cashier ought to be at their desks or window when Poggin rides up. He'll glance in before he gets down. They make no mistakes, these fellows. We must be slicker than they are, or lose. When you get the bank people wise, send your men over one by one. No hurry, no excitement, no unusual thing to attract notice in the bank."

"All right. That's great. Tell me, where do you intend to wait?"

Duane heard MacNelly's question, and it struck him peculiarly. He had seemed to be planning and speaking mechanically. As he was confronted by the fact it nonplussed him somewhat, and he became thoughtful, with lowered head.

"Where'll you wait, Duane?" insisted MacNelly, with keen eyes speculating.

"I'll wait in front, just inside the door," replied Duane, with an effort.

"Why?" demanded the Captain.

"Well," began Duane, slowly, "Poggin will get down first and start in. But the others won't be far behind. They'll not get swift till inside. The thing is— they *mustn't* get clear inside, because the instant they do they'll pull guns. That means death to somebody. If we can we want to stop them just at the door."

"But will you hide?" asked MacNelly.

"Hide!" The idea had not occurred to Duane.

"There's a wide-open doorway, a sort of round hall, a vestibule, with steps leading up to the bank. There's a door in the vestibule, too. It leads somewhere. We can put men in there. You can be there."

Duane was silent.

"See here, Duane," began MacNelly, nervously. "You shan't take any undue risk here. You'll hide with the rest of us?"

"No!" The word was wrenched from Duane.

MacNelly stared, and then a strange, comprehending light seemed to flit over his face.

"Duane, I can give you no orders today," he said, distinctly. "I'm only offering advice. Need you take any more risks? You've done a grand job for the service—already. You've paid me a thousand times for that pardon. You've redeemed yourself. The Governor, the adjutant-general—the whole state will rise up and honor you. The game's almost up. We'll kill these outlaws, or enough of them to break forever their power. I say, as a ranger, need you take more risk than your captain?"

Still Duane remained silent. He was locked between two forces. And one, a tide that was bursting at its bounds, seemed about to overwhelm him. Finally that side of him, the retreating self, the weaker, found a voice.

"Captain, you want this job to be sure?" he asked.

"Certainly."

"I've told you the way I alone know the kind of men to be met. Just *what* I'll do or *where* I'll be I can't say yet. In meetings like this the moment decides. But I'll be there!"

MacNelly spread wide his hands, looked helplessly at his curious and sympathetic rangers, and shook his head.

"Now you've done your work—laid the trap—is this strange move of yours going to be fair to Miss Longstreth?" asked MacNelly, in significant low voice.

Like a great tree chopped at the roots Duane vibrated to that. He looked up as if he had seen a ghost.

Mercilessly the ranger captain went on: "You can win her, Duane! Oh, you can't fool me. I was wise in a minute. Fight with us from cover—then go back to her. You will have served the Texas Rangers as no other man has. I'll accept your resignation. You'll be free, honored, happy. That girl loves you! I saw it in her eyes. She's—"

But Duane cut him short with a fierce gesture. He lunged up to his feet, and the rangers fell back. Dark, silent, grim as he had been, still there was a transformation singularly more sinister, stranger.

"Enough. I'm done," he said, somberly. "I've planned. Do we agree—or shall I meet Poggin and his gang alone?"

MacNelly cursed and again threw up his hands, this time in baffled chagrin. There was deep regret in his dark eyes as they rested upon Duane.

Duane was left alone.

Never had his mind been so quick, so clear, so wonderful in its understanding of what had heretofore been intricate and elusive impulses of his strange nature. His determination was to meet Poggin; meet him before anyone else had a chance—Poggin first—and then the others! He was as unalterable in that decision as if on the instant of its acceptance he had become stone.

Why? Then came realization. He was not a ranger now. He cared nothing for the state. He had no thought of freeing the community of a dangerous outlaw, of ridding the country of an obstacle to its progress and prosperity. He wanted to kill Poggin. It was significant now that he forgot the other outlaws. He was the gunman, the gun-thrower, the gunfighter, passionate and terrible. His father's blood, that dark and fierce strain, his mother's spirit, that strong and unquenchable spirit of the surviving pioneer—these had been in him; and the killings, one after another, the wild and haunted years, had made him, absolutely in spite of his will, the gunman. He realized it now, bitterly, hopelessly. The thing he had intelligence enough to hate he had become. At last he shuddered under the driving, ruthless inhuman bloodlust of the gunman. Long ago he had seemed to seal in a tomb that horror of his kind—the need, in order to forget the haunting, sleepless presence of his last victim, to go out and kill another. But it was still there in his mind, and now it stalked out, worse, more powerful, magnified by its rest, augmented by the violent passions peculiar and inevitable to that strange, wild product of the Texas frontier—the gunfighter. And those passions were so violent, so raw, so base, so much lower than what ought to have existed in a thinking man. Actual pride of his record! Actual vanity in his speed with a gun. Actual jealousy of any rival!

Duane could not believe it. But there he was, without a choice. What he had feared for years had become a monstrous reality. Respect for himself, blindness, a certain honor that he had clung to while in outlawry—all, like scales, seemed to fall away from him. He stood stripped bare, his soul naked—the soul of Cain. Always since the first brand had been forced and burned upon him he had been ruined. But now with conscience flayed to the quick, yet utterly powerless over this tiger instinct, he was lost. He said it. He admitted it. And at the utter abasement the soul he despised suddenly leaped and quivered with the thought of Ray Longstreth.

Then came agony. As he could not govern all the chances of this fatal meeting—as all his swift and deadly genius must be occupied with Poggin, perhaps in vain—as hard-shooting men whom he could not watch would be close behind, this almost certainly must be the end of Buck Duane. That did not matter. But he loved the girl. He wanted her. All her sweetness, her fire, and pleading returned to torture him.

At that moment the door opened, and Ray Longstreth entered.

"Duane," she said, softly. "Captain MacNelly sent me to you."

"But you shouldn't have come," replied Duane.

"As soon as he told me I would have come whether he wished it or not. You left me—all of us—stunned. I had no time to thank you. Oh, I do— with all my soul. It was noble of you. Father is overcome. He didn't expect so much. And he'll be true. But, Duane, I was told to hurry, and here I'm selfishly using time."

"Go, then—and leave me. You mustn't unnerve me now, when there's a desperate game to finish."

"Need it be desperate?" she whispered, coming close to him.

"Yes; it can't be else."

MacNelly had sent her to weaken him; of that Duane was sure. And he felt that she had wanted to come. Her eyes were dark, strained, beautiful, and they shed a light upon Duane he had never seen before.

"You're going to take some mad risk," she said. "Let me persuade you not to. You said—you cared for me—and I—oh, Duane—don't you—know—?"

The low voice, deep, sweet as an old chord, faltered and broke and failed.

Duane sustained a sudden shock and an instant of paralyzed confusion of thought.

She moved, she swept out her hands, and the wonder of her eyes dimmed in a flood of tears.

"My God! You can't care for me?" he cried, hoarsely.

Then she met him, hands outstretched.

"But I do—I do!"

Swift as light Duane caught her and held her to his breast. He stood holding her tight, with the feel of her warm, throbbing breast and the clasp of her arms as flesh and blood realities to fight a terrible fear. He felt her, and for the moment the might of it was stronger than all the demons that possessed him. And he held her as if she had been his soul, his strength on earth, his hope of Heaven, against his lips.

The strife of doubt all passed. He found his sight again. And there rushed over him a tide of emotion unutterably sweet and full, strong like an intoxicating wine, deep as his nature, something glorious and terrible as the blaze of the sun to one long in darkness. He had become an outcast, a wanderer, a gunman, a victim of circumstances; he had lost and suffered worse than death in that loss; he had gone down the endless bloody trail, a killer of men, a fugitive whose mind slowly and inevitably closed to all except the instinct to survive and a black despair; and now, with this woman in his arms, her swelling breast against his, in this moment almost of resurrection, he bent under the storm of passion and joy possible only to him who had endured so much.

"Do you care—a little?" he whispered, unsteadily.

He bent over her, looking deep into the dark wet eyes.

She uttered a low laugh that was half sob, and her arms slipped up to his neck.

"A little! Oh, Duane—Duane—a great deal!"

Their lips met in their first kiss. The sweetness, the fire of her mouth seemed so new, so strange, so irresistible to Duane. His sore and hungry heart throbbed with thick and heavy beats. He felt the outcast's need of love. And he gave up to the enthralling moment. She met him half-way, returned kiss for kiss, clasp for clasp, her face scarlet, her eyes closed, till, her passion and strength spent, she fell back upon his shoulder.

Duane suddenly thought she was going to faint. He divined then that she had understood him, would have denied him nothing, not even her life, in that moment. But she was overcome, and he suffered a pang of regret at his unrestraint.

Presently she recovered, and she drew only the closer, and leaned upon him with her face upturned. He felt her hands on his, and they were soft, clinging, strong, like steel under velvet. He felt the rise and fall, the warmth of her breast. A tremor ran over him. He tried to draw back, and if he succeeded a little her form swayed with him, pressing closer. She held her face up, and he was compelled to look. It was wonderful now: white, yet glowing, with the red lips parted, and dark eyes alluring. But that was not all. There was passion, unquenchable spirit, woman's resolve deep and mighty.

"I love you, Duane!" she said. "For my sake don't go out to meet this outlaw face to face. It's something wild in you. Conquer it if you love me."

Duane became suddenly weak, and when he did take her into his arms again he scarcely had strength to lift her to a seat beside him. She seemed more than a dead weight. Her calmness had fled. She was throbbing, palpitating, quivering, with hot wet cheeks and arms that clung to him like vines. She lifted her mouth to his, whispering, "Kiss me!" She meant to change him, hold him.

Duane bent down, and her arms went round his neck and drew him close. With his lips on hers he seemed to float away. That kiss closed his eyes, and he could not lift his head. He sat motionless holding her, blind and helpless, wrapped in a sweet dark glory. She kissed him—one long endless kiss—or else a thousand times. Her lips, her wet cheeks, her hair, the softness, the fragrance of her, the tender clasp of her arms, the swell of her breast—all these seemed to enclose him.

Duane could not put her from him. He yielded to her lips and arms, watching her, involuntarily returning her caresses, sure now of her intent, fascinated by the sweetness of her, bewildered, almost lost. This was what it was to be loved by a woman. His years of outlawry had blotted out any boyish love he might have known. This was what he had to give up—all this wonder of her sweet person, this strange fire he feared yet loved, this mate his deep and tortured soul recognized. Never until that moment had he divined the meaning of a woman to a man. That meaning was physical inasmuch that he learned what beauty was, what marvel in the touch of quickening flesh; and it was spiritual in that he saw there might have been for him, under happier circumstances, a life of noble deeds lived for such a woman.

"Don't go! Don't go!" she cried, as he started violently.

"I must. Dear, good-by! Remember I loved you."

He pulled her hands loose from his, stepped back.

"Ray, dearest—I believe—I'll come back!" he whispered.

These last words were falsehood.

He reached the door, gave her one last piercing glance, to fix for ever in memory that white face with its dark, staring, tragic eyes.

*"Duane!"*

He fled with that moan like thunder, death, hell in his ears.

To forget her, to get back his nerve, he forced into mind the image of Poggin—Poggin, the tawny-haired, the yellow-eyed, like a jaguar, with his rippling muscles. He brought back his sense of the outlaw's wonderful presence, his own unaccountable fear and hate. Yes, Poggin had sent the cold sickness of fear to his marrow. Why, since he hated life so? Poggin was his supreme test. And this abnormal and stupendous instinct, now deep as the very foundation of his life, demanded its wild and fatal issue. There was a horrible thrill in his sudden remembrance that Poggin likewise had been taunted in fear of him.

So the dark tide overwhelmed Duane, and when he left the room he was fierce, implacable, steeled to any outcome, quick like a panther, somber as death, in the thrall of his strange passion.

There was no excitement in the street. He crossed to the bank corner. A clock inside pointed the hour of two. He went through the door into the vestibule, looked around, passed up the steps into the bank. The clerks were at their desks, apparently busy. But they showed nervousness. The cashier paled at sight of Duane. There were men—the rangers—crouching down behind the low partition. All the windows had been removed from the iron grating before the desks. The safe was closed. There was no money in sight. A customer came in, spoke to the cashier, and was told to come tomorrow.

Duane returned to the door. He could see far down the street, out into the country. There he waited, and minutes were eternities. He saw no person near him; he heard no sound. He was insulated in his unnatural strain.

At a few minutes before half past two a dark, compact body of horsemen appeared far down, turning into the road. They came at a sharp trot—a group that would have attracted attention anywhere at any time. They came a little faster as they entered town; then faster still; now they were four blocks away, now three, now two. Duane backed down the middle of the vestibule, up the steps, and halted in the center of the wide doorway.

There seemed to be a rushing in his ears through which pierced sharp, ringing clip-clop of iron hoofs. He could see only the corner of the street. But suddenly into that shot lean-limbed dusty bay horses. There was a clattering of nervous hoofs pulled to a halt.

Duane saw the tawny Poggin speak to his companions. He dismounted quickly. They followed suit. They had the manner of ranchers about to conduct some business. No guns showed. Poggin started leisurely for the bank door, quickening step a little. The others, close together, came behind him. Blossom Kane had a bag in his left hand. Jim Fletcher was left at the curb, and he had already gathered up the bridles.

Poggin entered the vestibule first, with Kane on one side, Boldt on the other, a little in his rear.

As he strode in he saw Duane.

"Hell's fire!" he cried.

Something inside Duane burst, piercing all of him with cold. Was it that fear?

"Buck Duane!" echoed Kane.

One instant Poggin looked up and Duane looked down.

Like a striking jaguar Poggin moved. Almost as quickly Duane threw his arm.

The guns boomed almost together.

Duane felt a blow just before he pulled trigger. His thoughts came fast, like the strange dots before his eyes. His rising gun had loosened in his hand. Poggin had drawn quicker! A tearing agony encompassed his breast. He pulled—pulled—at random. Thunder of booming shots all about him! Red flashes, jets of smoke, shrill yells! He was sinking. The end; yes, the end! With fading sight he saw Kane go down, then Boldt. But supreme torture, bitterer than death, Poggin stood, mane like a lion's, back to the wall, bloody-faced, grand, with his guns spouting red!

All faded, darkened. The thunder deadened. Duane fell, seemed floating. There it drifted—Ray Longstreth's sweet face, white, with dark, tragic eyes, fading from his sight . . . fading . . . fading . . .

# CHAPTER XXV

Light shone before Duane's eyes—thick, strange light that came and went. For a long time dull and booming sounds rushed by, filling all. It was a dream in which there was nothing; a drifting under a burden; darkness, light, sound, movement; and vague, obscure sense of time—time that was very long. There was fire—creeping, consuming fire. A dark cloud of flame enveloped him, rolled him away.

He saw then, dimly, a room that was strange, strange people moving about over him, with faint voices, far away, things in a dream. He saw again, clearly, and consciousness returned, still unreal, still strange, full of those vague and far-away things. Then he was not dead. He lay stiff, like a stone, with a weight ponderous as a mountain upon him and all his bound body racked in slow, dull-beating agony.

A woman's face hovered over him, white and tragic-eyed, like one of his old haunting phantoms, yet sweet and eloquent. Then a man's face bent over him, looked deep into his eyes, and seemed to whisper from a distance: "Duane—Duane! Ah, he knew me!"

After that there was another long interval of darkness. When the light came again, clearer this time, the same earnest-faced man bent over him. It was MacNelly. And with recognition the past flooded back.

Duane tried to speak. His lips were weak, and he could scarcely move them.

"Poggin!" he whispered. His first real conscious thought was for Poggin. Ruling passion—eternal instinct!

"Poggin is dead, Duane; shot to pieces," replied MacNelly, solemnly. "What a fight he made! He killed two of my men, wounded others. God! He was a tiger. He used up three guns before we downed him."

"Who—got—away?"

"Fletcher, the man with the horses. We downed all the others. Duane, the job's done—it's done! Why, man, you're—"

"What of—of—*her?*"

"Miss Longstreth has been almost constantly at your bedside. She helped the doctor. She watched your wounds. And, Duane, the other night, when you sank low—so low—I think it was her spirit that held yours back. Oh, she's a wonderful girl. Duane, she never gave up, never lost her nerve for a moment. Well, we're going to take you home, and she'll go with us. Colonel Longstreth left for Louisiana right after the fight. I advised it. There was great excitement. It was best for him to leave."

"Have I—a—chance—to recover?"

"Chance? Why, man," exclaimed the Captain, "you'll get well! You'll pack a sight of lead all your life. But you can stand that. Duane, the whole Southwest knows your story. You need never again be ashamed of the name Buck Duane. The brand outlaw is washed out. Texas believes you've been a secret ranger all the time. You're a hero. And now think of home, your mother, of this noble girl—of your future."

The rangers took Duane home to Wellston.

A railroad had been built since Duane had gone into exile. Wellston had grown. A noisy crowd surrounded the station, but it stilled as Duane was carried from the train.

A sea of faces pressed close. Some were faces he remembered—schoolmates, friends, old neighbors. There was an upflinging of many hands. Duane was being welcomed home to the town from which he had fled. A deadness within him broke. This welcome hurt him somehow, quickened him; and through his cold being, his weary mind, passed a change. His sight dimmed.

Then there was a white house, his old home. How strange, yet how real! His heart beat fast. Had so many, many years passed? Familiar yet strange it was, and all seemed magnified.

They carried him in, these ranger comrades, and laid him down, and lifted his head upon pillows. The house was still, though full of people. Duane's gaze sought the open door.

Someone entered—a tall girl in white, with dark, wet eyes and a light upon her face. She was leading an old lady, gray-haired, austere-faced, somber and sad. His mother! She was feeble, but she walked erect. She was pale, shaking, yet maintained her dignity.

The someone in white uttered a low cry and knelt by Duane's bed. His mother flung wide her arms with a strange gesture.

"This man! They've not brought back my boy. This man's his father! Where is my son? My son—oh, my son!"

When Duane grew stronger it was a pleasure to lie by the west window and watch Uncle Jim whittle his stick and listen to his talk. The old man was broken now. He told many interesting things about people Duane had known—people who had grown up and married, failed, succeeded, gone away, and died. But it was hard to keep Uncle Jim off the subject of guns, outlaws, fights. He could not seem to divine how mention of these things hurt Duane. Uncle Jim was childish now, and he had a great pride in his nephew. He wanted to hear of all of Duane's exile. And if there was one thing more than another that pleased him it was to talk about the bullets which Duane carried in his body.

"Five bullets, ain't it?" he asked, for the hundredth time.

"Five in that last scrap! By gum! And you had six before?"

"Yes, uncle," replied Duane.

"Five and six. That makes eleven. By gum! A man's a man, to carry all that lead. But, Buck, you could carry more. There's that nigger Edwards, right here in Wellston. He's got a ton of bullets in him. Doesn't seem to mind them none. And there's Cole Miller. I've seen him. Been a bad man in his day. They say he packs twenty-three bullets. But he's bigger than you—got more flesh . . . Funny, wasn't it, Buck, about the doctor only bein' able to cut one bullet out of you—that one in your breastbone? It was a forty-one caliber, an unusual cartridge. I saw it, and I wanted it, but Miss Longstreth wouldn't part with it. Buck, there was a bullet left in one of Poggin's guns, and that bullet was the same kind as the one cut out of you. By gum! Boy, it'd have killed you if it'd stayed there."

"It would indeed, uncle," replied Duane, and the old, haunting, somber mood returned.

But Duane was not often at the mercy of childish old hero-worshiping Uncle Jim. Miss Longstreth was the only person who seemed to divine Duane's gloomy mood, and when she was with him she warded off all suggestion.

One afternoon, while she was there at the west window, a message came for him. They read it together.

You have saved the ranger service to the Lone Star State.

MacNelly

Ray knelt beside him at the window, and he believed she meant to speak then of the thing they had shunned. Her face was still white, but sweeter now, warm with rich life beneath the marble; and her dark eyes were still intent, still haunted by shadows, but no longer tragic.

"I'm glad for MacNelly's sake as well as the state's," said Duane.

She made no reply to that and seemed to be thinking deeply. Duane shrank a little.

"The pain—is it any worse today?" she asked, instantly.

"No; it's the same. It will always be the same. I'm full of lead, you know. But I don't mind a little pain."

"Then—it's the old mood—the fear?" she whispered. "Tell me."

"Yes. It haunts me. I'll be well soon—able to go out. Then that—that hell will come back!"

"No, no!" she said, with emotion.

"Some drunken cowboy, some fool with a gun, will hunt me out in every town, wherever I go," he went on, miserably. "Buck Duane! To kill Buck Duane!"

"Hush! Don't speak so. Listen. You remember that day in Val Verde, when I came to you—plead with you not to meet Poggin? Oh, that was a terrible hour for me. But it showed me the truth. I saw the struggle between your passion to kill and your love for me. I could have saved you then had I known what I know now. Now I understand that—that thing which haunts you. But you'll never have to draw again. You'll never have to kill another man, thank God!"

Like a drowning man he would have grasped at straws, but he could not voice his passionate query.

She put tender arms round his neck. "Because you'll have me with you always," she replied. "Because always I shall be between you and that—that terrible thing."

It seemed with the spoken thought absolute assurance of her power came to her. Duane realized instantly that he was in the arms of a stronger woman that she who had plead with him that fatal day.

"We'll—we'll be married and leave Texas," she said, softly, with the red blood rising rich and dark in her cheeks.

"Ray!"

"Yes we will, though you're laggard in asking me, sir."

"But, dear—suppose," he replied, huskily, "suppose there might be—be children—a boy. A boy with his father's blood!"

"I pray God there will be. I do not fear what you fear. But even so—he'll be half my blood."

Duane felt the storm rise and break in him. And his terror was that of joy quelling fear. The shining glory of love in this woman's eyes made him weak as a child. How could she love him—how could she so bravely face a future with him? Yet she held him in her arms, twining her hands round his neck, and pressing close to him. Her faith and love and beauty—these she meant to throw between him and all that terrible past. They were her power, and she meant to use them all. He dared not think of accepting her sacrifice.

"But Ray—you dear, noble girl—I'm poor. I have nothing. And I'm a cripple."

"Oh, you'll be well someday," she replied. "And listen. I have money. My mother left me well off. All she had was her father's—do you understand? We'll take Uncle Jim and your mother. We'll go to Louisiana—to my old home. It's far from here. There's a plantation to work. There are horses and cattle—a great cypress forest to cut. Oh, you'll have much to do. You'll forget there. You'll learn to love my home. It's a beautiful old place. There are groves where the gray moss blows all day and the nightingales sing all night."

"My darling!" cried Duane, brokenly. "No, no, no!"

Yet he knew in his heart that he was yielding to her, that he could not resist her a moment longer. What was this madness of love?

"We'll be happy," she whispered. "Oh, I know. Come! Come! Come!"

Her eyes were closing, heavy-lidded, and she lifted sweet, tremulous, waiting lips.

With bursting heart Duane bent to them. Then he held her, close pressed to him, while with dim eyes he looked out over the line of low hills in the west, down where the sun was setting gold and red, down over the Nueces and the wild brakes of the Rio Grande which he was never to see again.

It was in this solemn and exalted moment that Duane accepted happiness and faced a new life, trusting this brave and tender woman to be stronger than the dark and fateful passion that had shadowed his past.

It would come back—that wind of flame, that madness to forget, that driving, relentless instinct for blood. It would come back with those pale, drifting, haunting faces and the accusing fading eyes, but all his life, always between them and him, rendering them powerless, would be the faith and love and beauty of this noble woman.

# THE MYSTERIOUS RIDER

## Zane Grey

## CHAPTER I

A September sun, losing some of its heat if not its brilliance, was dropping low in the west over the black Colorado range. Purple haze began to thicken in the timbered notches. Gray foothills, round and billowy, rolled down from the higher country. They were smooth, sweeping, with long velvety slopes and isolated patches of aspens that blazed in autumn gold. Splotches of red vine colored the soft gray of sage. Old White Slides, a mountain scarred by avalanche, towered with bleak rocky peak above the valley, sheltering it from the north.

A girl rode along the slope, with gaze on the sweep and range and color of the mountain fastness that was her home. She followed an old trail which led to a bluff overlooking an arm of the valley. Once it had been a familiar lookout for her, but she had not visited the place of late. It was associated with serious hours of her life. Here seven years before, when she was twelve, she had made a hard choice to please her guardian—the old rancher whom she loved and called father, who had indeed been a father to her. That choice had been to go to school in Denver. Four years she had lived away from her beloved gray hills and black mountains. Only once since her return had she climbed to this height, and that occasion, too, was memorable as an unhappy hour. It had been three years ago. Today girlish ordeals and griefs seemed back in the past: she was a woman at nineteen and face to face with the first great problem in her life.

The trail came up back of the bluff, through a clump of aspens with white trunks and yellow fluttering leaves, and led across a level bench of luxuriant grass and wild flowers to the rocky edge.

She dismounted and threw the bridle. Her mustang, used to being petted, rubbed his sleek, dark head against her and evidently expected like demonstration in return, but as none was forthcoming he bent his nose to the grass and began grazing. The girl's eyes were intent upon some waving, slender, white-and-blue flowers. They smiled up wanly, like pale stars, out of the long grass that had a tinge of gold.

"Columbines," she mused, wistfully, as she plucked several of the flowers and held them up to gaze wonderingly at them, as if to see in them some revelation of the mystery that shrouded her birth and her name. Then she stood with dreamy gaze upon the distant ranges.

"Columbine! . . . So they named me—those miners who found me—a baby—lost in the woods—asleep among the columbines." She spoke aloud, as if the sound of her voice might convince her.

So much of the mystery of her had been revealed that day by the man she had always called father. Vaguely she had always been conscious of some mystery, something strange about her childhood, some relation never explained.

"No name but Columbine," she whispered, sadly, and now she understood a strange longing of her heart.

Scarcely an hour back, as she ran down the wide porch of White Slides ranch house, she had encountered the man who had taken care of her all her life. He had looked upon her as kindly and fatherly as of old, yet with a difference. She seemed to see him as old Bill Belllounds, pioneer and rancher, of huge frame and broad face, hard and scarred and grizzled, with big eyes of blue fire.

"Collie," the old man had said, "I reckon hyar's news. A letter from Jack . . . He's comin' home."

Belllounds had waved the letter. His huge hand trembled as he reached to put it on her shoulder. The hardness of him seemed strangely softened. Jack was his son. Buster Jack, the range had always called him, with other terms, less kind, that never got to the ears of his father. Jack had been sent away three years ago, just before Columbine's return from school. Therefore she had not seen him for over seven years. But she remembered him well—a big, rangy boy, handsome and wild, who had made her childhood almost unendurable.

"Yes—my son—Jack—he's comin' home," said Belllounds, with a break in his voice. "An', Collie—now I must tell you somethin'."

"Yes, dad," she had replied, with strong clasp of the heavy hand on her shoulder.

"Thet's just it, lass. I ain't your dad. I've tried to be a dad to you an' I've loved you as my own. But you're not flesh an' blood of mine. An' now I must tell you."

The brief story followed. Seventeen years ago miners working a claim of Belllounds's in the mountains above Middle Park had found a child asleep in the columbines along the trail. Near that point Indians, probably Arapahoes coming across the mountains to attack the Utes, had captured or killed the occupants of a prairie-schooner. There was no other clue. The miners took the child to their camp, fed and cared for it, and, after the manner of their kind, named it Columbine. Then they brought it to Belllounds.

"Collie," said the old rancher, "it needn't never have been told, an' wouldn't but fer one reason. I'm gettin' old. I reckon I'd never split my property between you an' Jack. So I mean you an' him to marry. You always steadied Jack. With a wife like you'll be—wal, mebbe Jack'll—"

"Dad!" burst out Columbine. "Marry Jack! . . . Why I—I don't even remember him!"

"Haw! Haw!" laughed Belllounds. "Wal, you dog-gone soon will. Jack's in Kremmlin', an' he'll be hyar tonight or tomorrow."

"But—I—I don't l-love him," faltered Columbine.

The old man lost his mirth; the strong-lined face resumed its hard cast; the big eyes smoldered. Her appealing objection had wounded him. She was reminded of how sensitive the old man had always been to any reflection cast upon his son.

"Wal, thet's onlucky"; he replied, gruffly. "Mebbe you'll change. I reckon no girl could help a boy much, onless she cared for him. Anyway, you an' Jack will marry."

He had stalked away and Columbine had ridden her mustang far up the valley slope where she could be alone. Standing on the verge of the bluff, she suddenly became aware that the quiet and solitude of her lonely resting-place had been disrupted. Cattle were bawling below her and along the slope of Old White Slides and on the grassy uplands above. She had forgotten that the cattle were being driven down into the lowlands for the fall roundup. A great red-and-white-spotted herd was milling in the park just beneath her. Calves and yearlings were making the dust fly along the mountain slope; wild old steers were crashing in the sage, holding level, unwilling to be driven down; cows were running and lowing for their lost ones. Melodious and clear rose the clarion calls of the cowboys. The cattle knew those calls and only the wild steers kept up-grade.

Columbine also knew each call and to which cowboy it belonged. They sang and yelled and swore, but it was all music to her. Here and there along the slope, where the aspen groves clustered, a horse would flash across an open space; the dust would fly, and a cowboy would peal out a lusty yell that rang along the slope and echoed under the bluff and lingered long after the daring rider had vanished in the steep thickets.

"I wonder which is Wils," murmured Columbine, as she watched and listened, vaguely conscious of a little difference, a strange check in her remembrance of this particular cowboy. She felt the change, yet did not understand. One after one she recognized the riders on the slopes below, but Wilson Moore was not among them. He must be above her, then, and she turned to gaze across the grassy bluff, up the long, yellow slope, to where the gleaming aspens half hid a red bluff of mountain, towering aloft. Then from far to her left, high up a scrubby ridge of the slope, rang down a voice that thrilled her: *"Go—aloong— you-ooooo."* Red cattle dashed pell-mell down the slope, raising the dust, tearing the brush, rolling rocks, and letting out hoarse bawls.

*"Whoop-ee!"* High-pitched and pealing came a clearer yell.

Columbine saw a white mustang flash out on top of the ridge, silhouetted against the blue, with mane and tail flying. His gait on that edge of steep slope proved his rider to be a reckless cowboy for whom no heights or depths had terrors. She would have recognized him from the way he rode, if she had not known the slim, erect figure. The cowboy saw her instantly. He pulled the mustang, about to plunge down the slope, and lifted him, rearing and wheeling. Then Columbine waved her hand. The cowboy spurred his horse along the crest of the ridge, disappeared behind the grove of aspens, and came in sight again around to the right, where on the grassy bench he slowed to a walk in descent to the bluff.

The girl watched him come, conscious of an unfamiliar sense of uncertainty in this meeting, and of the fact that she was seeing him differently from any other time in the years he had been a playmate, a friend, almost like a brother. He had ridden for Belllounds for years, and was a cowboy because he loved cattle well and horses better, and above all a life in the open. Unlike most cowboys, he had been to school; he had a family in Denver that objected to his wild range life, and often importuned him to come home; he seemed aloof sometimes and not readily understood.

While many thoughts whirled through Columbine's mind she watched the cowboy ride slowly down to her, and she became more concerned with a sudden restraint. How was Wilson going to take the news of this forced change about to come in her life? That thought leaped up. It gave her a strange pang. But she and he were only good friends. As to that, she reflected, of late they had not been the friends and comrades they formerly were. In the thrilling uncertainty of this meeting she had forgotten his distant manner and the absence of little attentions she had missed.

By this time the cowboy had reached the level, and with the lazy grace of his kind slipped out of the saddle. He was tall, slim, round-limbed, with the small hips of a rider, and square, though not broad shoulders. He stood straight like an Indian. His eyes were hazel, his features regular, his face bronzed. All men of the open had still, lean, strong faces, but added to this in him was a steadiness of expression, a restraint that seemed to hide sadness.

"Howdy, Columbine!" he said. "What are you doing up here? You might get run over."

"Hello, Wils!" she replied, slowly. "Oh, I guess I can keep out of the way."

"Some bad steers in that bunch. If any of them run over here Pronto will leave you to walk home. That mustang hates cattle. And he's only half broke, you know."

"I forgot you were driving today," she replied, and looked away from him. There was a moment's pause—long, it seemed to her.

"What'd you come for?" he asked, curiously.

"I wanted to gather columbines. See." She held out the nodding flowers toward him. "Take one . . . Do you like them?"

"Yes. I like columbine," he replied, taking one of them. His keen hazel eyes, softened, darkened. "Colorado's flower."

"Columbine! . . . It is my name."

"Well, could you have a better? It sure suits you."

"Why?" she asked, and she looked at him again.

"You're slender—graceful. You sort of hold your head high and proud. Your skin is white. Your eyes are blue. Not bluebell blue, but columbine blue—and they turn purple when you're angry."

"Compliments! Wilson, this is new kind of talk for you," she said.

"You're different today."

"Yes, I am." She looked across the valley toward the westering sun, and the slight flush faded from her cheeks. "I have no right to hold my head proud. No one knows who I am—where I came from."

"As if that made any difference!" he exclaimed.

"Belllounds is not my dad. I have no dad. I was a waif. They found me in the woods—a baby—lost among the flowers. Columbine Belllounds I've always been. But that is not my name. No one can tell what my name really is."

"I knew your story years ago, Columbine," he replied, earnestly. "Everybody knows. Old Bill ought to have told you long before this. But he loves you. So does—everybody. You must not let this knowledge sadden you . . . I'm sorry you've never known a mother or a sister. Why, I could tell you of many orphans who—whose stories were different."

"You don't understand. I've been happy. I've not longed for any—anyone except a mother. It's only—"

"What don't I understand?"

"I've not told you all."

"No? Well, go on," he said, slowly.

Meaning of the hesitation and the restraint that had obstructed her thought now flashed over Columbine. It lay in what Wilson Moore might think of her prospective marriage to Jack Belllounds. Still she could not guess why that should make her feel strangely uncertain of the ground she stood on or how it could cause a constraint she had to fight herself to hide. Moreover, to her annoyance, she found that she was evading his direct request for the news she had withheld.

"Jack Belllounds is coming home tonight or tomorrow," she said. Then, waiting for her companion to reply, she kept an unseeing gaze upon the scanty pines fringing Old White Slides. But no reply appeared to be forthcoming from Moore. His silence compelled her to turn to him. The cowboy's face had subtly altered; it was darker with a tinge of red under the bronze; and his lower lip was released from his teeth, even as she looked. He had his eyes intent upon the lasso he was coiling. Suddenly he faced her and the dark fire of his eyes gave her a shock.

"I've been expecting that shorthorn back for months," he said, bluntly.

"You—never—liked Jack?" queried Columbine, slowly. That was not what she wanted to say, but the thought spoke itself.

"I should smile I never did."

"Ever since you and he fought—long ago—all over—"

His sharp gesture made the coiled lasso loosen.

"Ever since I licked him good—don't forget that," interrupted Wilson. The red had faded from the bronze.

"Yes, you licked him," mused Columbine. "I remember that. And Jack's hated you ever since."

"There's been no love lost."

"But, Wils, you never before talked this way—spoke out so—against Jack," she protested.

"Well, I'm not the kind to talk behind a fellow's back. But I'm not mealy-mouthed, either, and—and—"

He did not complete the sentence and his meaning was enigmatic. Altogether Moore seemed not like himself. The fact disturbed Columbine. Always she had confided in him. Here was a most complex situation—she burned to tell him, yet somehow feared to—she felt an incomprehensible satisfaction in his bitter reference to Jack—she seemed to realize that she valued Wilson's friendship more than she had known, and now for some strange reason it was slipping from her.

"We—we were such good friends—pards," said Columbine, hurriedly and irrelevantly.

"Who?" He stared at her.

"Why, you—and me."

"Oh!" His tone softened, but there was still disapproval in his glance. "What of that?"

"Something has happened to make me think I've missed you—lately—that's all."

"Ahuh!" His tone held finality and bitterness, but he would not commit himself. Columbine sensed a pride in him that seemed the cause of his aloofness.

"Wilson, why have you been different lately?" she asked, plaintively.

"What's the good to tell you now?" he queried, in reply.

That gave her a blank sense of actual loss. She had lived in dreams and he in realities. Right now she could not dispel her dream—see and understand all that he seemed to. She felt like a child, then, growing old swiftly. The strange past longing for a mother surged up in her like a strong tide. Some one to lean on, someone who loved her, someone to help her in this hour when fatality knocked at the door of her youth—how she needed that!

"It might be bad for me—to tell me, but tell me, anyhow," she said, finally, answering as someone older than she had been an hour ago—to something feminine that leaped up. She did not understand this impulse, but it was in her.

"No!" declared Moore, with dark red staining his face. He slapped the lasso against his saddle, and tied it with clumsy hands. He did not look at her. His tone expressed anger and amaze.

"Dad says I must marry Jack," she said, with a sudden return to her natural simplicity.

"I heard him tell that months ago," snapped Moore.

"You did! Was that—why?" she whispered.

"It was," he answered, ringingly.

"But that was no reason for you to be—be—to stay away from me," she declared, with rising spirit.

He laughed shortly.

"Wils, didn't you like me any more after dad said that?" she queried.

"Columbine, a girl nineteen years and about to—to get married—ought not be a fool," he replied, with sarcasm.

"I'm not a fool," she rejoined, hotly.

"You ask fool questions."

"Well, you *didn't* like me afterward or you'd never have mistreated me."

"If you say I mistreated you—you say what's untrue," he replied, just as hotly.

They had never been so near a quarrel before. Columbine experienced a sensation new to her—a commingling of fear, heat, and pang, it seemed, all in one throb. Wilson was hurting her. A quiver ran all over her, along her veins, swelling and tingling.

"You mean I lie?" she flashed.

"Yes, I do—if—"

But before he could conclude she slapped his face. It grew pale then, while she began to tremble.

"Oh—I didn't intend that. Forgive me," she faltered.

He rubbed his cheek. The hurt had not been great, so far as the blow was concerned. But his eyes were dark with pain and anger.

"Oh, don't distress yourself," he burst out. "You slapped me before—once, years ago—for kissing you. I—I apologize for saying you lied. You're only out of your head. So am I."

That poured oil upon the troubled waters. The cowboy appeared to be hesitating between sudden flight and the risk of staying longer.

"Maybe that's it," replied Columbine, with a half-laugh. She was not far from tears and fury with herself. "Let us make up—be friends again."

Moore squared around aggressively. He seemed to fortify himself against something in her. She felt that. But his face grew harder and older than she had ever seen it.

"Columbine, do you know where Jack Belllounds has been for these three years?" he asked, deliberately, entirely ignoring her overtures of friendship.

"No. Somebody said Denver. Someone else said Kansas City. I never asked dad, because I knew Jack had been sent away. I've supposed he was working—making a man of himself."

"Well, I hope to Heaven—for your sake—what you suppose comes true," returned Moore, with exceeding bitterness.

"Do *you* know where he has been?" asked Columbine. Some strange feeling prompted that. There was a mystery here. Wilson's agitation seemed strange and deep.

"Yes, I do." The cowboy bit that out through closing teeth, as if locking them against an almost overmastering temptation.

Columbine lost her curiosity. She was woman enough to realize that there might well be facts which would only make her situation harder.

"Wilson," she began, hurriedly, "I owe all I am to dad. He has cared for me—sent me to school. He has been so good to me. I've loved him always. It would be a shabby return for all his protection and love if—if I refused—"

"Old Bill is the best man ever," interrupted Moore, as if to repudiate any hint of disloyalty to his employer. "Everybody in Middle Park and all over owes Bill something. He's sure good. There never was anything wrong with him except his crazy blindness about his son. Buster Jack—the—the—"

Columbine put a hand over Moore's lips.

"The man I must marry," she said, solemnly.

"You must—you will?" he demanded.

"Of course. What else could I do? I never thought of refusing."

"Columbine!" Wilson's cry was so poignant, his gesture so violent, his dark eyes so piercing that Columbine sustained a shock that held her trembling and mute. "How can you love Jack Belllounds? You were twelve years old when you saw him last. How can you love him?"

"I don't" replied Columbine.

"Then how could you marry him?"

"I owe dad obedience. It's his hope that I can steady Jack."

*"Steady Jack!"* exclaimed Moore, passionately. "Why, you girl—you white-faced flower! *You* with your innocence and sweetness steady that damned pup! My Heavens! He was a gambler and a drunkard. He—"

"Hush!" implored Columbine.

"He cheated at cards," declared the cowboy, with a scorn that placed that vice as utterly base.

"But Jack was only a wild boy," replied Columbine, trying with brave words to champion the son of the man she loved as her father. "He has been sent away to work. He'll have outgrown that wildness. He'll come home a man."

"Bah!" cried Moore, harshly.

Columbine felt a sinking within her. Where was her strength? She, who could walk and ride so many miles, to become sick with an inward quaking! It was childish. She struggled to hide her weakness from him.

"It's not like you to be this way," she said. "You used to be generous. Am I to blame? Did I choose my life?"

Moore looked quickly away from her, and, standing with a hand on his horse, he was silent for a moment. The squaring of his shoulders bore testimony to his thought. Presently he swung up into the saddle. The mustang snorted and champed the bit and tossed his head, ready to bolt.

"Forget my temper," begged the cowboy, looking down upon Columbine. "I take it all back. I'm sorry. Don't let a word of mine worry you. I was only jealous."

"Jealous!" exclaimed Columbine, wonderingly.

"Yes. That makes a fellow see red and green. Bad medicine! You never felt it."

"What were you jealous of?" asked Columbine.

The cowboy had himself in hand now and he regarded her with a grim amusement.

"Well, Columbine, it's like a story," he replied. "I'm the fellow disowned by his family—a wanderer of the wilds—no good—and no prospects . . . Now our friend Jack, he's handsome and rich. He has a doting old dad. Cattle, horses—ranches! He wins the girl. See!"

Spurring his mustang, the cowboy rode away. At the edge of the slope he turned in the saddle. "I've got to drive in this bunch of cattle. It's late. You hurry home." Then he was gone. The stones cracked and rolled down under the side of the bluff.

Columbine stood where he had left her: dubious, yet with the blood still hot in her cheeks.

"Jealous? . . . He wins the girl?" she murmured in repetition to herself. "Whatever could he have meant? He didn't mean—he didn't—"

The simple, logical interpretation of Wilson's words opened Columbine's mind to a disturbing possibility of which she had never dreamed. That he might love her! If he did, why had he not said so? Jealous, maybe, but he did not love her! The next throb of thought was like a knock at a door of her heart—a door never yet opened, inside which seemed a mystery of feeling, of hope, despair, unknown longing, and clamorous voices. The woman just born in her, instinctive and self-preservative, shut that door before she had more than a glimpse inside. But then she felt her heart swell with its nameless burdens.

Pronto was grazing near at hand. She caught him and mounted. It struck her then that her hands were numb with cold. The wind had ceased fluttering the aspens, but the yellow leaves were falling, rustling. Out on the brow of the slope she faced home and the west.

A glorious Colorado sunset had just reached the wonderful height of its color and transformation. The sage slopes below her seemed rosy velvet; the golden aspens on the farther reaches were on fire at the tips; the foothills rolled clear and mellow and rich in the light; the gulf of distance on to the great black range was veiled in mountain purple; and the dim peaks beyond the range stood up, sunset-flushed and grand. The narrow belt of blue sky between crags and clouds was like a river full of fleecy sails and wisps of silver. Above towered a pall of dark cloud, full of the shades of approaching night.

"Oh, beautiful!" breathed the girl, with all her worship of nature. That wild world of sunset grandeur and loneliness and beauty was hers. Over there, under a peak of the black range, was the place where she had been found, a baby, lost in the forest. She belonged to that, and so it belonged to her. Strength came to her from the glory of light on the hills.

Pronto shot up his ears and checked his trot.

"What is it, boy?" called Columbine. The trail was getting dark. Shadows were creeping up the slope as she rode down to meet them. The mustang had keen sight and scent. She reined him to a halt.

All was silent. The valley had begun to shade on the far side and the rose and gold seemed fading from the nearer. Below, on the level floor of the valley, lay the rambling old ranch house, with the cabins nestling around, and the corrals leading out to the soft hay fields, misty and gray in the twilight. A single light gleamed. It was like a beacon.

The air was cold with a nip of frost. From far on the other side of the ridge she had descended came the bawls of the last straggling cattle of the roundup. But surely Pronto had not shot up his ears for them. As if in answer a wild sound pealed down the slope, making the mustang jump. Columbine had heard it before.

"Pronto, it's only a wolf," she soothed him.

The peal was loud, rather harsh at first, then softened to a mourn, wild, lonely, haunting. A pack of coyotes barked in angry answer, a sharp, staccato, yelping chorus, the more piercing notes biting on the cold night air. These mountain mourns and yelps were music to Columbine. She rode on down the trail in the gathering darkness, less afraid of the night and its wild denizens than of what awaited her at White Slides Ranch.

# CHAPTER II

Darkness settled down like a black mantle over the valley. Columbine rather hoped to find Wilson waiting to take care of her horse, as used to be his habit, but she was disappointed. No light showed from the cabin in which the cowboys lived; he had not yet come in from the roundup. She unsaddled, and turned Pronto loose in the pasture.

The windows of the long, low ranch house were bright squares in the blackness, sending cheerful rays afar. Columbine wondered in trepidation if Jack Belllounds had come home. It required effort of will to approach the house. Yet since she must meet him, the sooner the ordeal was over the better. Nevertheless she tiptoed past the bright windows, and went all the length of the long porch, and turned around and went back, and then hesitated, fighting a slow drag of her spirit, an oppression upon her heart. The door was crude and heavy. It opened hard.

Columbine entered a big room lighted by a lamp on the upper table and by blazing logs in a huge stone fireplace. This was the living room, rather gloomy in the corners, and bare, but comfortable, for all simple needs. The logs were new and the chinks between them filled with clay, still white, showing that the house was of recent build.

The rancher, Belllounds, sat in his easy chair before the fire, his big, horny hands extended to the warmth. He was in his shirtsleeves, a gray, bold-faced man, of over sixty years, still muscular and rugged.

At Columbine's entrance he raised his drooping head, and so removed the suggestion of sadness in his posture.

"Wal, lass, hyar you are," was his greeting. "Jake has been hollerin' thet chuck was ready. Now we can eat."

"Dad—did—did your son come?" asked Columbine.

"No. I got word jest at sundown. One of Baker's cowpunchers from up the valley. He rode up from Kremmlin' an' stopped to say Jack was celebratin' his arrival by too much red liquor. Reckon he won't be home tonight. Mebbe tomorrow."

Belllounds spoke in an even, heavy tone, without any apparent feeling. Always he was mercilessly frank and never spared the truth. But Columbine, who knew him well, felt how this news flayed him. Resentment stirred in her toward the wayward son, but she knew better than to voice it.

"Natural like, I reckon, fer Jack to feel gay on gettin' home. I ain't holdin' thet ag'in' him. These last three years must have been gallin' to thet boy."

Columbine stretched her hands to the blaze.

"It's cold, dad," she averred. "I didn't dress warmly, so I nearly froze. Autumn is here and there's frost in the air. Oh, the hills were all gold and red—the aspen leaves were falling. I love autumn, but it means winter is so near."

"Wal, wal, time flies," sighed the old man. "Where'd you ride?"

"Up the west slope to the bluff. It's far. I don't go there often."

"Meet any of the boys? I sent the outfit to drive stock down from the mountain. I've lost a good many head lately. They're eatin' some weed thet poisons them. They swell up an' die. Wuss this year than ever before."

"Why, that is serious, dad! Poor things! That's worse than eating loco . . . Yes, I met Wilson Moore driving down the slope."

"Ahuh! Wal, let's eat."

They took seats at the table which the cook, Jake, was loading with steaming victuals. Supper appeared to be a rather sumptuous one this evening, in honor of the expected guest, who had not come. Columbine helped the old man to his favorite dishes, stealing furtive glances at his lined and shadowed face. She sensed a subtle change in him since the afternoon, but could not see any sign of it in his look or demeanor. His appetite was as hearty as ever.

"So you met Wils. Is he still makin' up to you?" asked Belllounds, presently.

"No, he isn't. I don't see that he ever did—that—dad," she replied.

"You're a kid in mind an' a woman in body. Thet cowpuncher has been lovesick over you since you were a little girl. It's what kept him hyar ridin' fer me."

"Dad, I don't believe it," said Columbine, feeling the blood at her temples. "You always imagined such things about Wilson, and the other boys as well."

"Ahuh! I'm an old fool about wimmen, hey? Mebbe I was years ago. But I can see now . . . Didn't Wils always get ory-eyed when any of the other boys shined up to you?"

"I can't remember that he did," replied Columbine. She felt a desire to laugh, yet the subject was anything but amusing to her.

"Wal, you've always been innocent-like. Thank the Lord you never leaned to tricks of most pretty lasses, makin' eyes at all the men. Anyway, a matter of three months ago I told Wils to keep away from you—thet you were not fer any poor cowpuncher."

"You never liked him. Why? Was it fair, taking him as boys come?"

"Wal, I reckon it wasn't," replied Belllounds, and as he looked up his broad face changed to ruddy color. "Thet boy's the best rider an' roper I've had in years. He ain't the bronco-bustin' kind. He never drank. He was honest an' willin'. He saves his money. He's good at handlin' stock. Thet boy will be a rich rancher someday."

"Strange, then, you never liked him," murmured Columbine. She felt ashamed of the good it did her to hear Wilson praised.

"No, it ain't strange. I have my own reasons," replied Belllounds, gruffly, as he resumed eating.

Columbine believed she could guess the cause of the old rancher's unreasonable antipathy for this cowboy. Not improbably it was because Wilson had always been superior in every way to Jack Belllounds. The boys had been natural rivals in everything pertaining to life on the range. What Bill Belllounds admired most in men was paramount in Wilson and lacking in his own son.

"Will you put Jack in charge of your ranches, now?" asked Columbine.

"Not much. I reckon I'll try him hyar at White Slides as foreman. An' if he runs the outfit, then I'll see."

"Dad, he'll never run the White Slides outfit," asserted Columbine.

"Wal, it is a hard bunch, I'll agree. But I reckon the boys will stay, exceptin', mebbe, Wils. An' it'll be jest as well fer him to leave."

"It's not good business to send away your best cowboy. I've heard you complain lately of lack of men."

"I sure do need men," replied Belllounds, seriously. "Stock gettin' more 'n we can handle. I sent word over the range to Meeker, hopin' to get some men there. What I need most jest now is a fellar who knows dogs an' who'll hunt down the wolves an' lions an' bears thet're livin' off my cattle."

"Dad, you need a whole outfit to handle the packs of hounds you've got. Such an assortment of them! There must be a hundred. Only yesterday some man brought a lot of mangy, long-eared canines. It's funny. Why, dad, you're the laughingstock of the range!'

"Yes, an' the range'll be thankin' me when I rid it of all these varmints," declared Belllounds. "Lass, I swore I'd buy every dog fetched to me, until I had enough to kill off the coyotes an' lofers an' lions. I'll do it, too. But I need a hunter."

"Why not put Wilson Moore in charge of the hounds? He's a hunter."

"Wal, lass, thet might be a good idee," replied the rancher, nodding his grizzled head. "Say, you're sort of wantin' me to keep Wils on."

"Yes, dad."

"Why? Do you like him so much?"

"I like him—of course. He has been almost a brother to me."

"Ahuh! Wal, are you sure you don't like him more'n you ought—considerin' what's in the wind?"

"Yes, I'm sure I don't," replied Columbine, with tingling cheeks.

"Wal, I'm glad of thet. Reckon it'll be no great matter whether Wils stays or leaves. If he wants to I'll give him a job with the hounds."

That evening Columbine went to her room early. It was a cozy little blanketed nest which she had arranged and furnished herself. There was a little square window cut through the logs and through which many a night the snow had blown in upon her bed. She loved her little isolated refuge. This night it was cold, the first time this autumn, and the lighted lamp, though brightening the room, did not make it appreciably warmer. There was a stone fireplace, but as she had neglected to bring in wood she could not start a fire. So she undressed, blew out the lamp, and went to bed. Columbine was soon warm, and the darkness of her little room seemed good to her. Sleep she felt never would come that night. She wanted to think; she could not help but think; and she tried to halt the whirl of her mind. Wilson Moore occupied the foremost place in her varying thoughts—a fact quite remarkable and unaccountable. She tried to change it. In vain! Wilson persisted—on his white mustang flying across the ridge-top—coming to her as never before— with his anger and disapproval—his strange, poignant cry, "Columbine!" that haunted her—with his bitter smile and his resignation and his mocking talk of jealousy. He persisted and grew with the old rancher's frank praise.

"I must not think of him," she whispered. "Why, I'll be—be married soon . . . Married!"

That word transformed her thought, and where she had thrilled she now felt cold. She revolved the fact in mind.

"It's true, I'll be married, because I ought—I must," she said, half aloud. "Because I can't help myself. I ought to want to—for dad's sake . . . But I don't—I don't."

She longed above all things to be good, loyal, loving, helpful, to show her gratitude for the home and the affection that had been bestowed upon a nameless waif. Bill Belllounds had not been under any obligation to succor a strange, lost child. He had done it because he was big, noble. Many splendid deeds had been laid at the old rancher's door. She was not of an ungrateful nature. She meant to pay. But the significance of the price began to dawn upon her.

"It will change my whole life," she whispered, aghast.

But how? Columbine pondered. She must go over the details of that change. No mother had ever taught her. The few women that had been in the Belllounds home from time to time had not been sympathetic or had not stayed long enough to help her much. Even her school life in Denver had left her still a child as regarded the serious problems of women.

"If I'm his wife," she went on, "I'll have to be with him—I'll have to give up this little room—I'll never be free—alone—happy, anymore."

That was the first detail she enumerated. It was also the last. Realization came with a sickening little shudder. And that moment gave birth to the nucleus of an unconscious revolt.

The coyotes were howling. Wild, sharp, sweet notes! They soothed her troubled, aching head, lulled her toward sleep, reminded her of the gold-and-purple sunset, and the slopes of sage, the lonely heights, and the beauty that would never change. On the morrow, she drowsily thought, she would persuade Wilson not to kill all the coyotes; to leave a few, because she loved them.

\* \* \* \* \*

Bill Belllounds had settled in Middle Park in 1860. It was wild country, a home of the Ute Indians, and a natural paradise for elk, deer, antelope, buffalo. The mountain ranges harbored bear. These ranges sheltered the rolling valley land which some explorer had named Middle Park in earlier days.

Much of this enclosed tableland was prairie, where long grass and wildflowers grew luxuriantly. Belllounds was a cattleman, and he saw the possibilities there. To which end he sought the friendship of Piah, chief of the Utes. This noble red man was well disposed toward the white settlers, and his tribe, during those troublous times, kept peace with these invaders of their mountain home.

In 1868 Belllounds was instrumental in persuading the Utes to relinquish Middle Park. The slopes of the hills were heavily timbered; gold and silver had been found in the mountains. It was a country that attracted prospectors, cattlemen, lumbermen. The summer season was not long enough to grow grain, and the nights too frosty for corn; otherwise Middle Park would have increased rapidly in population.

In the years that succeeded the departure of the Utes Bill Belllounds developed several cattle ranches and acquired others. White Slides Ranch lay some twenty-odd miles from Middle Park, being a winding arm of the main valley land. Its development was a matter of later years, and Belllounds lived there because the country was wilder. The rancher, as he advanced in years, seemed to want to keep the loneliness that had been his in earlier days. At the time of the return of his son to White Slides Belllounds was rich in cattle and land, but he avowed frankly that he had not saved any money, and probably never would. His hand was always open to every man and he never remembered an obligation. He trusted everyone. A proud boast of his was that neither white man nor red man had ever betrayed his trust. His cowboys took advantage of him, his neighbors imposed upon him, but none were there who did not make good their debts of service or stock. Belllounds was one of the great pioneers of the frontier days to whom the West owed its settlement; and he was finer than most, because he proved that the Indians, if not robbed or driven, would respond to friendliness.

* * * * *

Belllounds was not seen at his customary tasks on the day he expected his son. He walked in the fields and around the corrals; he often paced up and down the porch, scanning the horizon below, where the road from Kremmling showed white down the valley; and part of the time he stayed indoors.

It so happened that early in the afternoon he came out in time to see a buckboard, drawn by dust-and-lather-stained horses, pull into the yard. And then he saw his son. Some of the cowboys came running. There were greetings to the driver, who appeared well known to them.

Jack Belllounds did not look at them. He threw a bag out of the buckboard and then clambered down slowly, to go toward the porch.

"Wal, Jack—my son—I'm sure glad you're back home," said the old rancher, striding forward. His voice was deep and full, singularly rich. But that was the only sign of feeling he showed.

"Howdy—dad!" replied the son, not heartily, as he put out his hand to his father's.

Jack Belllounds's form was tall, with a promise of his father's bulk. But he did not walk erect; he slouched a little. His face was pale, showing he had not of late been used to sun and wind. Any stranger would have seen the resemblance of boy to man would have granted the handsome boldness, but denied the strength. The lower part of Jack Belllounds's face was weak.

The constraint of this meeting was manifest mostly in the manner of the son. He looked ashamed, almost sullen. But if he had been under the influence of liquor at Kremmling, as reported the day before, he had entirely recovered.

"Come on in," said the rancher.

When they got into the big living room, and Belllounds had closed the doors, the son threw down his baggage and faced his father aggressively.

"Do they all know where I've been?" he asked, bitterly. Broken pride and shame flamed in his face.

"Nobody knows. The secret's been kept." replied Belllounds.

Amaze and relief transformed the young man. "Aw, now, I'm—glad—" he exclaimed, and he sat down, half covering his face with shaking hands.

"Jack, we'll start over," said Belllounds, earnestly, and his big eyes shone with a warm and beautiful light. "Right hyar. We'll never speak of where you've been these three years. Never again!"

Jack gazed up, then, with all the sullenness and shadow gone.

"Father, you were wrong about—doing me good. It's done me harm. But now, if nobody knows—why, I'll try to forget it."

"Mebbe I blundered," replied Belllounds, pathetically. "Yet, God knows I meant well. You sure were—But thet's enough palaver . . . You'll go to work as foreman of White Slides. An' if you make a success of it I'll be only too glad to have you boss the ranch. I'm gettin' along in years, son. An' the last year has made me poorer. Hyar's a fine range, but I've less stock this year than last. There's been some rustlin' of cattle, an a big loss from wolves an' lions an' poison-weed . . . What d'you say, son?"

"I'll run White Slides," replied Jack, with a wave of his hand. "I hadn't hoped for such a chance. But it's due me. Who's in the outfit I know?"

"Reckon no one, except Wils Moore."

"Is that cowboy here yet? I don't want him."

"Wal, I'll put him to chasin' varmints with the hounds. An' say, son, this outfit is bad. You savvy—it's bad. You can't run that bunch. The only way you can handle them is to get up early an' come back late. Sayin' little, but sawin' wood. Hard work."

Jack Belllounds did not evince any sign of assimilating the seriousness of his father's words.

"I'll show them," he said. "They'll find out who's boss. Oh, I'm aching to get into boots and ride and tear around."

Belllounds stroked his grizzled beard and regarded his son with mingled pride and doubt. Not at this moment, most assuredly, could he get away from the wonderful fact that his only son was home.

"Thet's all right, son. But you've been off the range fer three years. You'll need advice. Now listen. Be gentle with hosses. You used to be mean with a hoss. Some cowboys jam their hosses around an' make 'em pitch an' bite. But it ain't the best way. A hoss has got sense. I've some fine stock, an' don't want it spoiled. An' be easy an' quiet with the boys. It's hard to get help these days. I'm short on hands now . . . You'd do best, son, to stick to your dad's ways with hosses an' men."

"Dad, I've seen you kick horses an' shoot at men," replied Jack.

"Right, you have. But them was particular bad cases. I'm not advisin' thet way . . . Son, it's close to my heart—this hope I have thet you'll—"

The full voice quavered and broke. It would indeed have been a hardened youth who could not have felt something of the deep and unutterable affection in the old man. Jack Belllounds put an arm around his father's shoulder.

"Dad, I'll make you proud of me yet. Give me a chance. And don't be sore if I can't do wonders right at first."

"Son, you shall have every chance. An' thet reminds me. Do you remember Columbine?"

"I should say so," replied Jack, eagerly. "They spoke of her in Kremmling. Where is she?"

"I reckon somewheres about. Jack, you an' Columbine are to marry."

"Marry! Columbine and me?" he ejaculated.

"Yes. You're my son an' she's my adopted daughter. I won't split my property. An' it's right she had a share. A fine, strong, quiet, pretty lass, Jack, an' she'll make a good wife. I've set my heart on the idee."

"But Columbine always hated me."

"Wal, she was a kid then an' you teased her. Now she's a woman, an' willin' to please me. Jack, you'll not buck ag'in' this deal?"

"That depends," replied Jack. "I'd marry 'most any girl you wanted me to. But if Columbine were to flout me as she used to—why, I'd buck sure enough . . . Dad, are you sure she knows nothing, suspects nothing of where you—you sent me?"

"Son, I swear she doesn't."

"Do you mean you'd want us to marry soon?"

"Wal, yes, as soon as Collie would think reasonable. Jack, she's shy an' strange, an' deep, too. If you ever win her heart you'll be richer than if you owned all the gold in the Rockies. I'd say go slow. But contrariwise, it'd mebbe be surer to steady you, keep you home, if you married right off."

"Married right off!" echoed Jack, with a laugh. "It's like a story. But wait till I see her."

\* \* \* \* \*

At that very moment Columbine was sitting on the topmost log of a high corral, deeply interested in the scene before her.

Two cowboys were in the corral with a saddled mustang. One of them carried a canvas sack containing tools and horseshoes. As he dropped it with a metallic clink the mustang snorted and jumped and rolled the whites of his eyes. He knew what that clink meant.

"Miss Collie, air you-all goin' to sit up thar?" inquired the taller cowboy, a lean, supple, and powerful fellow, with a rough, red-blue face, hard as a rock, and steady, bright eyes.

"I sure am, Jim," she replied, imperturbably.

"But we've gotta hawg-tie him," protested the cowboy.

"Yes, I know. And you're going to be gentle about it."

Jim scratched his sandy head and looked at his comrade, a little gnarled fellow, like the bleached root of a tree. He seemed all legs.

"You hear, you Wyomin' galoot," he said to Jim. "Them shoes goes on Whang right gentle."

Jim grinned, and turned to speak to his mustang. "Whang, the law's laid down an' we wanta see how much hoss sense you hev."

The shaggy mustang did not appear to be favorably impressed by this speech. It was a mighty distrustful look he bent upon the speaker.

"Jim, seein' as how this here job's aboot the last Miss Collie will ever boss us on, we gotta do it without Whang turnin' a hair," drawled the other cowboy.

"Lem, why is this the last job I'll ever boss you boys?" demanded Columbine, quickly.

Jim gazed quizzically at her, and Lem assumed that blank, innocent face Columbine always associated with cowboy deviltry.

"Wal, Miss Collie, we reckon the new boss of White Slides rode in today."

"You mean Jack Belllounds came home," said Columbine. "Well, I'll boss you boys the same as always."

"Thet'd be mighty fine for us, but I'm feared it ain't writ in the fatal history of White Slides," replied Jim.

"Buster Jack will run over the ole man an' marry you," added Lem.

"Oh, so that's your idea," rejoined Columbine, lightly. "Well, if such a thing did come to pass I'd be your boss more than ever."

"I reckon no, Miss Collie, for we'll not be ridin' fer White Sides," said Jim, simply.

Columbine had sensed this very significance long before when the possibility of Buster Jack's return had been rumored. She knew cowboys. As well try to change the rocks of the hills!

"Boys, the day you leave White Slides will be a sad one for me," sighed Columbine.

"Miss Collie, we 'ain't gone yet," put in Lem, with awkward softness. "Jim has long hankered fer Wyomin' an' he jest talks thet way."

Then the cowboys turned to the business in hand. Jim removed the saddle, but left the bridle on. This move, of course, deceived Whang. He had been broken to stand while his bridle hung, and, like a horse that would have been good if given a chance, he obeyed as best he could, shaking in every limb. Jim, apparently to hobble Whang, roped his forelegs together, low down, but suddenly slipped the rope over the knees. Then Whang knew he had been deceived. He snorted fire, let out a scream, and, rearing on his hind legs, he pawed the air savagely. Jim hauled on the rope while Whang screamed and fought with his forefeet high in the air. Then Jim, with a powerful jerk, pulled Whang down and threw him, while Lem, seizing the bridle, hauled him over on his side and sat upon his head. Whereupon Jim slipped the loop off one front hoof and pulled the other leg back across one of the hind ones, where both were secured by a quick hitch. Then the lasso was wound and looped around front and back hoofs together. When this had been done the mustang was rolled over on his other side, his free front hoof lassoed and pulled back to the hind one, where both were secured, as had been the others. This rendered the mustang powerless, and the shoeing proceeded.

Columbine hated to sit by and watch it, but she always stuck to her post, when opportunity afforded, because she knew the cowboys would not be brutal while she was there.

"Wal, he'll step high to-morrer," said Lem, as he got up from his seat on the head of Whang.

"Ahuh! An', like a mule, he'll be my friend fer twenty years jest to get a chance to kick me." replied Jim.

For Columbine, the most interesting moment of this incident was when the mustang raised his head to look at his legs, in order to see what had been done to them. There was something almost human in that look. It expressed intelligence and fear and fury.

The cowboys released his legs and let him get up. Whang stamped his iron-shod hoofs.

"It was a mean trick, Whang," said Columbine. "If I owned you that'd never be done to you."

"I reckon you can have him fer the askin'," said Jim, as he threw on the saddle. "Nobody but me can ride him. Do you want to try?"

"Not in these clothes," replied Columbine, laughing.

"Wal, Miss Collie, you're shore dressed up fine today, fer some reason or other," said Lem, shaking his head, while he gathered up the tools from the ground.

"Ahuh! An' here comes the reason," exclaimed Jim, in low, hoarse whisper.

Columbine heard the whisper and at the same instant a sharp footfall on the gravel road. She quickly turned, almost losing her balance. And she recognized Jack Belllounds. The boy Buster Jack she remembered so well was approaching, now a young man, taller, heavier, older, with paler face and bolder look. Columbine had feared this meeting, had prepared herself for it. But all she felt when it came was annoyance at the fact that he had caught her sitting on top of the corral fence, with little regard for dignity. It did not occur to her to jump down. She merely sat straight, smoothed down her skirt, and waited.

Jim led the mustang out of the corral and Lem followed. It looked as if they wanted to avoid the young man, but he prevented that.

"Howdy, boys! I'm Jack Belllounds," he said, rather loftily. But his manner was nonchalant. He did not offer to shake hands.

Jim mumbled something, and Lem said, "Hod do."

"That's an ornery-looking bronc," went on Belllounds, and he reached with careless hand for the mustang. Whang jerked so hard that he pulled Jim half over.

"Wal, he ain't a bronc, but I reckon he's all the rest," drawled Jim.

Both cowboys seemed slow, careless. They were neither indifferent nor responsive. Columbine saw their keen, steady glances go over Belllounds. Then she took a second and less hasty look at him. He wore high-heeled, fancy-topped boots, tight-fitting trousers of dark material, a heavy belt with silver buckle, and a white, soft shirt, with wide collar, open at the neck. He was bareheaded.

"I'm going to run White Slides," he said to the cowboys. "What're your names?"

Columbine wanted to giggle, which impulse she smothered. The idea of anyone asking Jim his name! She had never been able to find out.

"My handle is Lemuel Archibawld Billings," replied Lem, blandly. The middle name was an addition no one had ever heard.

Belllounds then directed his glance and steps toward the girl. The cowboys dropped their heads and shuffled on their way.

"There's only one girl on the ranch," said Belllounds, "so you must be Columbine."

"Yes. And you're Jack," she replied, and slipped off the fence. "I'm glad to welcome you home."

She offered her hand, and he held it until she extricated it. There was genuine surprise and pleasure in his expression.

"Well, I'd never have known you," he said, surveying her from head to foot. "It's funny. I had the clearest picture of you in mind. But you're not at all like I imagined. The Columbine I remember was thin, white-faced, and all eyes."

"It's been a long time. Seven years," she replied. "But I knew you. You're older, taller, bigger, but the same Buster Jack."

"I hope not," he said, frankly condemning that former self. "Dad needs me. He wants me to take charge here—to be a man. I'm back now. It's good to be home. I never was worth much. Lord! I hope I don't disappoint him again."

"I hope so, too," she murmured. To hear him talk frankly, seriously, like this counteracted the unfavorable impression she had received. He seemed earnest. He looked down at the ground, where he was pushing little pebbles with the toe of his boot. She had a good opportunity to study his face, and availed herself of it. He did look like his father, with his big, handsome head, and his blue eyes, bolder perhaps from their prominence than from any direct gaze or fire. His face was pale, and shadowed by worry or discontent. It seemed as though a repressed character showed there. His mouth and chin were undisciplined. Columbine could not imagine that she despised anything she saw in the features of this young man. Yet there was something about him that held her aloof. She had made up her mind to do her part unselfishly. She would find the best in him, like him for it, be strong to endure and to help. Yet she had no power to control her vague and strange perceptions. Why was it that she could not feel in him what she liked in Jim Montana or Lem or Wilson Moore?

"This was my second long stay away from home," said Belllounds. "The first was when I went to school in Kansas City. I liked that. I was sorry when they turned me out—sent me home . . . But the last three years were hell."

His face worked, and a shade of dark blood rippled over it.

"Did you work?" queried Columbine.

"Work! It was worse than work . . . Sure I worked," he replied.

Columbine's sharp glance sought his hands. They looked as soft and unscarred as her own. What kind of work had he done, if he told the truth?

"Well, if you work hard for dad, learn to handle the cowboys, and never take up those old bad habits—"

"You mean drink and cards? I swear I'd forgotten them for three years—until yesterday. I reckon I've the better of them."

"Then you'll make dad and me happy. You'll be happy, too."

Columbine thrilled at the touch of fineness coming out in him. There was good in him, whatever the mad, wild pranks of his boyhood.

"Dad wants us to marry," he said, suddenly, with shyness and a strange, amused smile. "Isn't that funny? You and me—who used to fight like cat and dog! Do you remember the time I pushed you into the old mud-hole? And you lay in wait for me, behind the house, to hit me with a rotten cabbage?"

"Yes, I remember," replied Columbine, dreamily. "It seems so long ago."

"And the time you ate my pie, and how I got even by tearing off your little dress, so you had to run home almost without a stitch on?"

"Guess I've forgotten that," replied Columbine, with a blush. "I must have been very little then."

"You were a little devil . . . Do you remember the fight I had with Moore—about you?"

She did not answer, for she disliked the fleeting expression that crossed his face. He remembered too well.

"I'll settle that score with Moore," he went on. "Besides, I won't have him on the ranch."

"Dad needs good hands," she said, with her eyes on the gray sage slopes. Mention of Wilson Moore augmented the aloofness in her. An annoyance pricked along her veins.

"Before we get any farther I'd like to know something. Has Moore ever made love to you?"

Columbine felt that prickling augment to a hot, sharp wave of blood. Why was she at the mercy of strange, quick, unfamiliar sensations? Why did she hesitate over that natural query from Jack Belllounds?

"No. He never has," she replied, presently.

"That's damn queer. You used to like him better than anybody else. You sure hated me . . . Columbine, have you outgrown that?"

"Yes, of course," she answered. "But I hardly hated you."

"Dad said you were willing to marry me. Is that so?"

Columbine dropped her head. His question, kindly put, did not affront her, for it had been expected. But his actual presence, the meaning of his words, stirred in her an unutterable spirit of protest. She had already in her will consented to the demand of the old man; she was learning now, however, that she could not force her flesh to consent to a surrender it did not desire.

"Yes, I'm willing," she replied, bravely.

"Soon?" he flashed, with an eager difference in his voice.

"If I had my way it'd not be—too soon," she faltered. Her downcast eyes had seen the stride he had made closer to her, and she wanted to run.

"Why? Dad thinks it'd be good for me," went on Belllounds, now, with strong, self-centered thought. "It'd give me responsibility. I reckon I need it. Why not soon?"

"Wouldn't it be better to wait awhile?" she asked. "We do not know each other—let alone care—"

"Columbine, I've fallen in love with you," he declared, hotly.

"Oh, how could you!" cried Columbine, incredulously.

"Why, I always was moony over you—when we were kids," he said. "And now to meet you grown up like this—so pretty and sweet—such a—a healthy, blooming girl . . . And dad's word that you'd be my wife soon—*mine*—why, I just went off my head at sight of you."

Columbine looked up at him and was reminded of how, as a boy, he had always taken a quick, passionate longing for things he must and would have. And his father had not denied him. It might really be that Jack had suddenly fallen in love with her.

"Would you want to take me without my—my love?" she asked, very low. "I don't love you now. I might sometime, if you were good—if you made dad happy—if you conquered—"

"Take you! I'd take you if you—if you hated me," he replied, now in the grip of passion.

"I'll tell dad how I feel," she said, faintly, "and—and marry you when he says."

He kissed her, would have embraced her had she not put him back.

"Don't! Some—someone will see."

"Columbine, we're engaged," he asserted, with a laugh of possession. "Say, you needn't look so white and scared. I won't eat you. But I'd like to . . . Oh, you're a sweet girl! Here I was hating to come home. And look at my luck!"

Then with a sudden change, that seemed significant of his character, he lost his ardor, dropped the half-bold, half-masterful air, and showed the softer side.

"Collie, I never was any good," he said. "But I want to be better. I'll prove it. I'll make a clean breast of everything. I won't marry you with any secret between us. You might find out afterward and hate me . . . Do you have any idea where I've been these last three years?"

"No," answered Columbine.

"I'll tell you right now. But you must promise never to mention it to anyone—or throw it up to me—ever."

He spoke hoarsely, and had grown quite white. Suddenly Columbine thought of Wilson Moore! He had known where Jack had spent those years. He had resisted a strong temptation to tell her. That was as noble in him as the implication of Jack's whereabouts had been base.

"Jack, that is big of you," she replied, hurriedly. "I respect you—like you for it. But you needn't tell me. I'd rather you didn't. I'll take the will for the deed."

Belllounds evidently experienced a poignant shock of amaze, of relief, of wonder, of gratitude. In an instant he seemed transformed.

"Collie, if I hadn't loved you before I'd love you now. That was going to be the hardest job I ever had—to tell you my—my story. I meant it. And now I'll not have to feel your shame for me and I'll not feel I'm a cheat or a liar . . . But I will tell you this—if you love me you'll make a man of me!"

## CHAPTER III

The rancher thought it best to wait till after the roundup before he turned over the foremanship to his son. This was wise, but Jack did not see it that way. He showed that his old, intolerant spirit had, if anything, grown during his absence. Belllounds patiently argued with him, explaining what certainly should have been clear to a young man brought up in Colorado. The fall roundup was the most important time of the year, and during the strenuous drive the appointed foreman should have absolute control. Jack gave in finally with a bad grace.

It was unfortunate that he went directly from his father's presence out to the corrals. Some of the cowboys who had ridden all the day before and stood guard all night had just come in. They were begrimed with dust, weary, and sleepy-eyed.

"This hyar outfit won't see my tracks no more," said one, disgustedly. "I never kicked on doin' two men's work. But when it comes to rustlin' day and night, all the time, I'm a-goin' to pass."

"Turn in, boys, and sleep till we get back with the chuck-wagon," said Wilson Moore. "We'll clean up that bunch today."

"Ain't you tired, Wils?" queried Bludsoe, a squat, bow-legged cowpuncher who appeared to be crippled or very lame.

"Me? Naw!" grunted Moore, derisively. "Blud, you sure ask fool questions... Why, you—mahogany-colored, stump-legged, biped of a cowpuncher, I've had three hours' sleep in four nights!"

"What's a biped?" asked Bludsoe, dubiously.

Nobody enlightened him.

"Wils, you-all air the only eddicated cowman I ever loved, but I'm a son-of-a-gun if we ain't agoin' to come to blows someday," declared Bludsoe.

"He shore can sling English," drawled Lem Billings. "I reckon he swallowed a dictionary onct."

"Wal, he can sling a rope, too, an' thet evens up," added Jim Montana.

Just at this moment Jack Belllounds appeared upon the scene. The cowboys took no notice of him. Jim was bandaging a leg of his horse; Bludsoe was wearily gathering up his saddle and trappings; Lem was giving his tired mustang a parting slap that meant much. Moore evidently awaited a fresh mount. A Mexican lad had come in out of the pasture leading several horses, one of which was the mottled white mustang that Moore rode most of the time.

Belllounds lounged forward with interest as Moore whistled, and the mustang showed his pleasure. Manifestly he did not like the Mexican boy and he did like Moore.

"Spottie, it's drag yearlings around for you today," said the cowboy, as he caught the mustang. Spottie tossed his head and stepped high until the bridle was on. When the saddle was thrown and strapped in place the mustang showed to advantage. He was beautiful, but not too graceful or sleek or fine-pointed or prancing to prejudice any cowboy against his qualities for work.

Jack Belllounds admiringly walked all around the mustang a little too close to please Spottie.

"Moore, he's a fair-to-middling horse," said Belllounds, with the air of judge of horseflesh. "What's his name?"

"Spottie," replied Moore, shortly, as he made ready to mount.

"Hold on, will you!" ordered Jack, peremptorily. "I like this horse. I want to look him over."

When he grasped the bridle reins out of the cowboy's hand Spottie jumped as if he had been shot at. Belllounds jerked at him and went closer. The mustang reared, snorting, plunging to get loose. Then Jack Belllounds showed the sudden temper for which he was noted. Red stained his pale cheeks.

"Damn you—come down!" he shouted, infuriated at the mustang, and with both hands he gave a powerful lunge. Spottie came down, and stood there, trembling all over, his ears laid back, his eyes showing fright and pain. Blood dripped from his mouth where the bit had cut him.

"I'll teach you to stand," said Belllounds, darkly. "Moore, lend me your spurs. I want to try him out."

"I don't lend my spurs—or my horse, either," replied the cowboy, quietly, with a stride that put him within reach of Spottie.

The other cowboys had dropped their trappings and stood at attention, with intent gaze and mute lips.

"Is he your horse?" demanded Jack, with a quick flush.

"I reckon so," replied Moore, slowly. "No one but me ever rode him."

"Does my father own him or do you own him."

"Well, if that's the way you figure—he belongs to White Slides," returned the cowboy. "I never bought him. I only raised him from a colt, broke him, and rode him."

"I thought so. Moore, he's mine, and I'm going to ride him now. Lend me spurs, one of you cowpunchers."

Nobody made any motion to comply. There seemed to be a suspense at hand that escaped Belllounds.

"I'll ride him without spurs," he declared, presently, and again he turned to mount the mustang.

"Belllounds, it'd be better for you not to ride him now," said Moore, coolly.

"Why, I'd like to know?" demanded Belllounds, with the temper of one who did not tolerate opposition.

"He's the only horse left for me to ride," answered the cowboy. "We're branding today. Hudson was hurt yesterday. He was foreman, and he appointed me to fill his place. I've got to rope yearlings. Now, if you get up on Spottie you'll excite him. He's high-strung, nervous. That'll be bad for him, as he hates cutting-out and roping."

The reasonableness of this argument was lost upon Belllounds.

"Moore, maybe it'd interest you to know that I'm foreman of White Slides," he asserted, not without loftiness.

His speech manifestly decided something vital for the cowboy.

"Ahuh! . . . I'm sure interested this minute," replied Moore, and then, stepping to the side of the mustang, with swift hands he unbuckled the cinch, and with one sweep he drew saddle and blanket to the ground.

The action surprised Belllounds. He stared. There seemed something boyish in his lack of comprehension. Then his temper flamed.

"What do you mean by that?" he demanded, with a strident note in his voice. "Put that saddle back."

"Not much. It's my saddle. Cost sixty dollars at Kremmling last year. Good old hard-earned saddle! . . . And you can't ride it. Savvy?"

"Yes, I savvy," replied Belllounds, violently. "Now you'll savvy what I say. I'll have you discharged."

"Nope. Too late," said Moore, with cool, easy scorn. "I figured that. And I quit a minute ago—when you showed what little regard you had for a horse."

"You quit! . . . Well, it's damned good riddance. I wouldn't have you in the outfit."

"You couldn't have kept me, Buster Jack."

The epithet must have been an insult to Belllounds. "Don't you dare call me that," he burst out, furiously.

Moore pretended surprise. "Why not? It's your range name. We all get a handle, whether we like it or not. There's Montana and Blud and Lemme Two Bits. They call me Professor. Why should you kick on yours?"

"I won't stand it now. Not from anyone—especially not you."

"Ahuh! Well, I'm afraid it'll stick," replied Moore, with sarcasm. "It sure suits you. Don't you bust everything you monkey with? Your old dad will sure be glad to see you bust the roundup today—and I reckon the outfit tomorrow."

"You insolent cowpuncher!" shouted Belllounds, growing beside himself with rage. "If you don't shut up I'll bust your face."

"Shut up! . . . Me? Nope. It can't be did. This is a free country, Buster Jack." There was no denying Moore's cool, stinging repetition of the epithet that had so affronted Belllounds.

"I always hated you!" he rasped out, hoarsely. Striking hard at Moore, he missed, but a second effort landed a glancing blow on the cowboy's face.

Moore staggered back, recovered his balance, and, hitting out shortly, he returned the blow. Belllounds fell against the corral fence, which upheld him.

"Buster Jack—you're crazy!" cried the cowboy, his eyes flashing. "Do you think you can lick me—after where you've been these three years?"

Like a maddened boy Belllounds leaped forward, this time his increased violence and wildness of face expressive of malignant rage. He swung his arms at random. Moore avoided his blows and planted a fist squarely on his adversary's snarling mouth. Belllounds fell with a thump. He got up with clumsy haste, but did not rush forward again. His big, prominent eyes held a dark and ugly look. His lower jaw wabbled as he panted for breath and speech at once.

"Moore—I'll kill—you!" he hissed, with glance flying everywhere for a weapon. From ground to cowboys he looked. Bludsoe was the only one packing a gun. Belllounds saw it, and he was so swift in bounding forward that he got a hand on it before Bludsoe could prevent.

"Let go! Give me—that gun! By God! I'll fix him!" yelled Belllounds, as Bludsoe grappled with him.

There was a sharp struggle. Bludsoe wrenched the other's hands free, and, pulling the gun, he essayed to throw it. But Belllounds blocked his action and the gun fell at their feet.

"Grab it!" sang out Bludsoe, ringingly. "Quick, somebody! The damned fool'll kill Wils."

Lem, running in, kicked the gun just as Belllounds reached for it. When it rolled against the fence Jim was there to secure it. Lem likewise grappled with the struggling Belllounds.

"Hyar, you Jack Belllounds," said Lem, "couldn't you see Wils wasn't packin' no gun? A-r'arin' like thet! . . . Stop your rantin' or we'll sure handle you rough."

"The old man's comin'," called Jim, warningly.

The rancher appeared. He strode swiftly, ponderously. His gray hair waved. His look was as stern as that of an eagle.

"What the hell's goin' on?" he roared.

The cowboys released Jack. That worthy, sullen and downcast, muttering to himself, stalked for the house.

"Jack, stand your ground," called old Belllounds.

But the son gave no heed. Once he looked back over his shoulder, and his dark glance saw no one save Moore.

"Boss, thar's been a little argyment," explained Jim, as with swift hand he hid Bludsoe's gun. "Nuthin' much."

"Jim, you're a liar," replied the old rancher.

"Aw!" exclaimed Jim, crestfallen.

"What're you hidin'? . . . You've got somethin' there. Gimme thet gun."

Without more ado Jim handed the gun over.

"It's mine, boss," put in Bludsoe.

"Ahuh? Wal, what was Jim hidin' it fer?" demanded Belllounds.

"Why, I jest tossed it to him—when I—sort of j'ined in with the argyment. We was tusslin' some an' I didn't want no gun."

How characteristic of cowboys that they lied to shield Jack Belllounds! But it was futile to attempt to deceive the old rancher. Here was a man who had been forty years dealing with all kinds of men and events.

"Bludsoe, you can't fool me," said old Bill, calmly. He had roared at them, and his eyes still flashed like blue fire, but he was calm and cool. Returning the gun to its owner, he continued: "I reckon you'd spare my feelin's an' lie about some trick of Jack's. Did he bust out?"

"Wal, tolerable like," replied Bludsoe, dryly.

"Ahuh! Tell me, then—an' no lies."

Belllounds's shrewd eyes had rested upon Wilson Moore. The cowboy's face showed the red marks of battle and the white of passion.

"I'm not going to lie, you can bet on that," he declared, forcefully.

"Ahuh! I might hev knowed you an' Jack'd clash," said Belllounds, gruffly. "What happened?"

"He hurt my horse. If it hadn't been for that there'd been no trouble."

A light leaped up in the old man's bold eyes. He was a lover of horses. Many hard words, and blows, too, he had dealt cowboys for being brutal.

"What'd he do?"

"Look at Spottie's mouth."

The rancher's way of approaching a horse was singularly different from his son's, notwithstanding the fact that Spottie knew him and showed no uneasiness. The examination took only a moment.

"Tongue cut bad. Thet's a damn shame. Take thet bridle off . . . There. If it'd been an ornery hoss, now . . . Moore, how'd this happen?"

"We just rode in," replied Wilson, hurriedly. "I was saddling Spottie when Jack came up. He took a shine to the mustang and wanted to ride him. When Spottie reared—he's shy with strangers—why, Jack gave a hell of a jerk on the bridle. The bit cut Spottie . . . Well, that made me mad, but I held in. I objected to Jack riding Spottie. You see, Hudson was hurt yesterday and he appointed me foreman for today. I needed Spottie. But your son couldn't see it, and that made me sore. Jack said the mustang was his—"

"His?" interrupted Belllounds.

"Yes. He claimed Spottie. Well, he wasn't really mine, so I gave in. When I threw off the saddle, which *was* mine, Jack began to roar. He said he was foreman and he'd have me discharged. But I said I'd quit already. We both kept getting sorer and I called him Buster Jack . . . He hit me first. Then we fought. I reckon I was getting the best of him when he made a dive for Bludsoe's gun. And that's all."

"Boss, as sure as I'm a born cowman," put in Bludsoe, "he'd hev plugged Wils if he'd got my gun. At thet he damn near got it!"

The old man stroked his scant gray beard with his huge, steady hand, apparently not greatly concerned by the disclosure.

"Montana, what do you say?" he queried, as if he held strong store by that quiet cowboy's opinion.

"Wal, boss," replied Jim, reluctantly, "Buster Jack's temper was bad onct, but now it's plumb wuss."

Whereupon Belllounds turned to Moore with a gesture and a look of a man who, in justice to something in himself, had to speak.

"Wils, it's onlucky you clashed with Jack right off," he said. "But thet was to be expected. I reckon Jack was in the wrong. Thet hoss was yours by all a cowboy holds right an' square. Mebbe by law Spottie belonged to White Slides Ranch—to me. But he's yours now, fer I give him to you."

"Much obliged, Belllounds. I sure do appreciate that," replied Moore, warmly. "It's what anybody'd gamble Bill Belllounds would do."

"Ahuh! An' I'd take it as a favor if you'd stay on today an' get thet brandin' done."

"All right, I'll do that for you," replied Moore. "Lem, I guess you won't get your sleep till tonight. Come on."

"Awl," sighed Lem, as he picked up his bridle.

* * * * *

Late that afternoon Columbine sat upon the porch, watching the sunset. It had been a quiet day for her, mostly indoors. Once only had she seen Jack, and then he was riding by toward the pasture, whirling a lasso round his head. Jack could ride like one born to the range, but he was not an adept in the use of a rope. Nor had Columbine seen the old rancher since breakfast. She had heard his footsteps, however, pacing slowly up and down his room.

She was watching the last rays of the setting sun rimming with gold the ramparts of the mountain eastward, and burning a crown for Old White Slides peak. A distant bawl and bellow of cattle had died away. The branding was over for that fall. How glad she felt! The wind, beginning to grow cold as the sun declined, cooled her hot face. In the solitude of her room Columbine had cried enough that day to scald her cheeks.

Presently, down the lane between the pastures, she saw a cowboy ride into view. Very slowly he came, leading another horse. Columbine recognized Lem a second before she saw that he was leading Pronto. That struck her as strange. Another glance showed Pronto to be limping. Apparently he could just get along, and that was all. Columbine ran out in dismay, reaching the corral gate before Lem did. At first she had eyes only for her beloved mustang.

"Oh, Lem—Pronto's hurt!" she cried.

"Wal, I should smile he is," replied Lem.

But Lem was not smiling. And when he wore a serious face for Columbine something had indeed happened. The cowboy was the color of dust and so tired that he reeled.

"Lem, he's all bloody!" exclaimed Columbine, as she ran toward Pronto.

"Hyar, you jest wait," ordered Lem, testily. "Pronto's all cut up, an' you gotta hustle some linen an' salve."

Columbine flew away to do his bidding, and so quick and violent was she that when she got back to the corral she was out of breath. Pronto whinnied as she fell, panting, on her knees beside Lem, who was examining bloody gashes on the legs of the mustang.

"Wal, I reckon no great harm did," said Lem, with relief. "But he shore hed a close shave. Now you help me doctor him up."

"Yes—I'll help," panted Columbine. "I've done this kind—of thing often—but never—to Pronto . . . Oh, I was afraid—he'd been gored by a steer."

"Wal, he come damn near bein'," replied Lem, grimly. "An' if it hedn't been fer ridin' you don't see every day, why thet ornery Texas steer'd hev got him."

"Who was riding? Lem, was it you? Oh, I'll never be able to do enough for you!"

"Wuss luck, it weren't me," said Lem.

"No? Who, then?"

"Wal, it was Wils, an' he made me swear to tell you nuthin'—leastways about him."

"Wils! Did he save Pronto? . . . And didn't want you to tell me? Lem, something has happened. You're not like yourself."

"Miss Collie, I reckon I'm nigh all in," replied Lem, wearily. "When I git this bandagin' done I'll fall right off my hoss."

"But you're on the ground now, Lem," said Columbine, with a nervous laugh. "What happened?"

"Did you hear about the argyment this mawnin'?"

"No. What—who—"

"You can ask Ole Bill aboot thet. The way Pronto was hurt come off like this. Buster Jack rode out to where we was brandin' an' jumped his hoss over a fence into the pasture. He hed a rope an' he got to chasin' some hosses over thar. One was Pronto, an' the son-of-a-gun somehow did git the noose over Pronto's head. But he couldn't hold it, or didn't want to, fer Pronto broke loose an' jumped the fence. This wasn't so bad as far as it went. But one of them bad steers got after Pronto. He run an' sure stepped on the rope, an' fell. The big steer nearly piled on him. Pronto broke some records then. He shore was scared. Howsoever he picked out rough ground an' run plumb into some dead brush. Reckon thar he got cut up. We was all a good ways off. The steer went bawlin' an' plungin' after Pronto. Wils yelled fer a rifle, but nobody hed one. Nor a six-shooter, either . . . I'm goin' back to packin' a gun. Wal, Wils did some ridin' to git over thar in time to save Pronto."

"Lem, that is not all," said Columbine, earnestly, as the cowboy concluded. Her knowledge of the range told her that Lem had narrated nothing so far which could have been cause for his cold, grim, evasive manner; and her woman's intuition divined a catastrophe.

"Nope . . . Wils's hoss fell on him."

Lem broke that final news with all a cowboy's bluntness.

"Was he hurt—*Lem!*" cried Columbine.

"Say, Miss Collie," remonstrated Lem, "we're doctorin' up your hoss. You needn't drop everythin' an' grab me like thet. An' you're white as a sheet, too. It ain't nuthin' much fer a cowboy to hev a hoss fall on him."

"Lem Billings, I'll hate you if you don't tell me quick," flashed Columbine, fiercely.

"Ahuh! So thet's how the land lays," replied Lem, shrewdly. "Wal, I'm sorry to tell you thet Wils was bad hurt. Now, not *real* bad! . . . The hoss fell on his leg an' broke it. I cut off his boot. His foot was all smashed. But thar wasn't any other hurt—honest! They're takin' him to Kremmlin'."

"Ah!" Columbine's low cry sounded strangely in her ears, as if someone else had uttered it.

"Buster Jack made two bursts this hyar day," concluded Lem, reflectively. "Miss Collie, I ain't shore how you're regardin' thet individool, but I'm tellin' you this, fer your own good. He's bad medicine. He has his old man's temper thet riles up at nuthin' an' never felt a halter. Wusser'n thet, he's spoiled an' he acts like a colt thet'd tasted loco. The idee of his ropin' Pronto right thar near the roundup! Anyone would think he jest come West. Old Bill is no fool. But he wears blinders when he looks at his son. I'm predictin' bad days fer White Slides Ranch."

## CHAPTER IV

Only one man at Meeker appeared to be attracted by the news that Rancher Bill Belllounds was offering employment. This was a little cadaverous-looking fellow, apparently neither young nor old, who said his name was Bent Wade. He had drifted into Meeker with two poor horses and a pack.

"Whar you from?" asked the innkeeper, observing how Wade cared for his horses before he thought of himself. The query had to be repeated.

"Cripple Creek. I was cook for some miners an' I panned gold between times," was the reply.

"Humph! Thet oughter been a better-payin' job than any to be hed hereabouts."

"Yes, got big pay there," said Wade, with a sigh.

"What'd you leave fer?"

"We hed a fight over the diggin's an' I was the only one left. I'll tell you . . ." Whereupon Wade sat down on a box, removed his old sombrero, and began to talk. An idler sauntered over, attracted by something. Then a miner happened by to halt and join the group.

Next, old Kemp, the patriarch of the village, came and listened attentively. Wade seemed to have a strange magnetism, a magic tongue.

He was small of stature, but wiry and muscular. His garments were old, soiled, worn. When he removed the wide-brimmed sombrero he exposed a remarkable face. It was smooth except for a drooping mustache, and pallid, with drops of sweat standing out on the high, broad forehead; gaunt and hollow-cheeked, with an enormous nose, and cavernous eyes set deep under shaggy brows. These features, however, were not so striking in themselves. Long, sloping, almost invisible lines of pain, the shadow of mystery and gloom in the deep-set, dark eyes, a sad harmony between features and expression, these marked the man's face with a record no keen eye could miss.

Wade told a terrible tale of gold and blood and death. It seemed to relieve him. His face changed, and lost what might have been called its tragic light, its driven intensity.

His listeners shook their heads in awe. Hard tales were common in Colorado, but this one was exceptional. Two of the group left without comment. Old Kemp stared with narrow, half-recognizing eyes at the newcomer.

"Wal! Wal!" ejaculated the innkeeper. "It do beat hell what can happen! . . . Stranger, will you put up your hosses an' stay?"

"I'm lookin' for work," replied Wade.

It was then that mention was made of Belllounds sending to Meeker for hands.

"Old Bill Belllounds thet settled Middle Park an' made friends with the Utes," said Wade, as if certain of his facts.

"Yep, you have Bill to rights. Do you know him?"

"I seen him once twenty years ago."

"Ever been to Middle Park? Belllounds owns ranches there," said the innkeeper.

"He ain't livin' in the Park now," interposed Kemp. "He's at White Slides, I reckon, these last eight or ten years. Thet's over the Gore Range."

"Prospected all through that country," said Wade.

"Wal, it's a fine part of Colorado. Hay an' stock country—too high fer grain. Did you mean you'd been through the Park?"

"Once—long ago," replied Wade, staring with his great, cavernous eyes into space. Some memory of Middle Park haunted him.

"Wal, then, I won't be steerin' you wrong," said the innkeeper. "I like thet country. Some people don't. An' I say if you can cook or pack or punch cows or 'most anythin' you'll find a bunk with Old Bill. I understand he was needin' a hunter most of all. Lions an' wolves bad! Can you hunt?"

"Hey?" queried Wade, absently, as he inclined his ear. "I'm deaf on one side."

"Are you a good man with dogs an' guns?" shouted his questioner.

"Tolerable," replied Wade.

"Then you're sure of a job."

"I'll go. Much obliged to you."

"Not a-tall. I'm doin' Belllounds a favor. Reckon you'll put up here tonight?"

"I always sleep out. But I'll buy feed an' supplies," replied Wade, as he turned to his horses.

Old Kemp trudged down the road, wagging his gray head as if he was contending with a memory sadly failing him. An hour later when Bent Wade rode out of town he passed Kemp, and hailed him. The old-timer suddenly slapped his leg: "By Golly! I knowed I'd met him before!"

Later, he said with a show of gossipy excitement to his friend the innkeeper, "Thet fellar was Bent Wade!"

"So he told me," returned the other.

"But didn't you never hear of him? *Bent Wade?*"

"Now you tax me, thet name do 'pear familiar. But dash take it, I can't remember. I knowed he was somebody, though. Hope I didn't wish a gunfighter or outlaw on Old Bill. Who was he, anyhow?"

"They call him Hell-Bent Wade. I seen him in Wyomin', whar he were a stage-driver. But I never heerd who he was an' what he was till years after. Thet was onct I dropped down into Boulder. Wade was thar, all shot up, bein' nussed by Sam Coles. Sam's dead now. He was a friend of Wade's an' knowed him fer long. Wal, I heerd all thet anybody ever heerd about him, I reckon. Accordin' to Coles this hyar Hell-Bent Wade was a strange, wonderful sort of fellar. He had the most amazin' ways. He could do anythin' under the sun better'n anyone else. Bad with guns! He never stayed in one place fer long. He never hunted trouble, but trouble follered him. As I remember Coles, thet was Wade's queer idee—he couldn't shake trouble. No matter whar he went, always thar was hell. Thet's what gave him the name Hell-Bent . . . An' Coles swore thet Wade was the whitest man he ever knew. Heart of gold, he said. Always savin' somebody, helpin' somebody, givin' his money or time—never thinkin' of himself a-tall . . . When he began to tell thet story about Cripple Creek then my ole head begun to ache with rememberin'. Fer I'd heerd Bent

Wade talk before. Jest the same kind of story he told hyar, only wuss. Lordy! but thet fellar has seen times. An' queerest of all is thet idee he has how hell's on his trail an' everywhere he roams it ketches up with him, an' thar he meets the man who's got to hear his tale!"

* * * * *

Sunset found Bent Wade far up the valley of White River under the shadow of the Flat Top Mountains. It was beautiful country. Grassy hills, with colored aspen groves, swelled up on his left, and across the brawling stream rose a league-long slope of black spruce, above which the bare red-and-gray walls of the range towered, glorious with the blaze of sinking sun. White patches of snow showed in the sheltered nooks. Wade's gaze rested longest on the colored heights.

By and by the narrow valley opened into a park, at the upper end of which stood a log cabin. A few cattle and horses grazed in an enclosed pasture. The trail led by the cabin. As Wade rode up a bushy-haired man came out of the door, rifle in hand. He might have been going out to hunt, but his scrutiny of Wade was that of a lone settler in a wild land.

"Howdy, stranger!" he said.

"Good evenin'," replied Wade. "Reckon you're Blair an' I'm nigh the headwaters of this river?"

"Yep, a matter of three miles to Trapper's Lake."

"My name's Wade. I'm packin' over to take a job with Bill Belllounds."

"Git down an' come in," returned Blair. "Bill's man stopped with me some time ago."

"Obliged, I'm sure, but I'll be goin' on," responded Wade. "Do you happen to have a hunk of deer meat? Game powerful scarce comin' up this valley."

"Lots of deer an' elk higher up. I chased a bunch of more'n thirty, I reckon, right out of my pasture this mornin'."

Blair crossed to an open shed near by and returned with half a deer haunch, which he tied upon Wade's packhorse.

"My ole woman's ailin'. Do you happen to hev some terbaccer?

"I sure do—both smokin' an' chewin', an' I can spare more chewin'. A little goes a long ways with me."

"Wal, gimme some of both, most chewin'," replied Blair, with evident satisfaction.

"You acquainted with Belllounds?" asked Wade, as he handed over the tobacco.

"Wal, yes, everybody knows Bill. You'd never find a whiter boss in these hills."

"Has he any family?"

"Now, I can't say as to thet," replied Blair. "I heerd he lost a wife years ago. Mebbe he married ag'in. But Bill's gittin' along."

"Good day to you, Blair," said Wade, and took up his bridle.

"Good day an' good luck. Take the right-hand trail. Better trot up a bit, if you want to make camp before dark."

Wade soon entered the spruce forest. Then he came to a shallow, roaring river. The horses drank the water, foaming white and amber around their knees, and then with splash and thump they forded it over the slippery rocks. As they cracked out upon the trail a covey of grouse whirred up into the low branches of spruce-trees. They were tame.

"That's somethin' like," said Wade. "First birds I've seen this fall. Reckon I can have stew any day."

He halted his horse and made a move to dismount, but with his eyes on the grouse he hesitated. "Tame as chickens, an' they sure are pretty."

Then he rode on, leading his packhorse. The trail was not steep, although in places it had washed out, thus hindering a steady trot. As he progressed the forest grew thick and darker, and the fragrance of pine and spruce filled the air. A dreamy roar of water rushing over rocks rang in the traveler's ears. It receded at times, then grew louder. Presently the forest shade ahead lightened and he rode out into a wide space where green moss and flags and flowers surrounded a wonderful spring-hole. Sunset gleams shone through the trees to color the wide, round pool. It was shallow all along the margin, with a deep, large green hole in the middle, where the water boiled up. Trout were feeding on gnats and playing on the surface, and some big ones left wakes behind them as they sped to deeper water. Wade had an appreciative eye for all this beauty, his gaze lingering longest upon the flowers.

"Wild woods is the place for me," he soliloquized, as the cool wind fanned his cheeks and the sweet tang of evergreen tingled his nostrils. "But sure I'm most haunted in these lonely, silent places."

Bent Wade had the look of a haunted man. Perhaps the consciousness he confessed was part of his secret.

Twilight had come when again he rode out into the open. Trapper's Lake lay before him, a beautiful sheet of water, mirroring the black slopes and the fringed spruces and the flat peaks. Over all its gray, twilight-softened surface showed little swirls and boils and splashes where the myriads of trout were rising. The trail led out over open grassy shores, with a few pines straggling down to the lake, and clumps of spruces raising dark blurs against the background of gleaming lake. Wade heard a sharp crack of hoofs on rock, and he knew he had disturbed deer at their drinking; also he heard a ring of horns on the branch of a tree, and was sure an elk was slipping off through the woods. Across the lake he saw a campfire and a pale, sharp-pointed object that was a trapper's tent or an Indian's tepee.

Selecting a campsite for himself, he unsaddled his horse, threw the pack off the other, and, hobbling both animals, he turned them loose. His roll of bedding, roped in canvas tarpaulin, he threw under a spruce-tree. Then he opened his oxhide-covered packs and laid out utensils and bags, little and big. All his movements were methodical, yet swift, accurate, habitual. He was not thinking about what he was doing. It took him some little time to find a suitable log to split for firewood, and when he had started a blaze night had fallen, and the light as it grew and brightened played fantastically upon the isolating shadows.

Lid and pot of the little Dutch oven he threw separately upon the sputtering fire, and while they heated he washed his hands, mixed the biscuits, cut slices of meat off the deer haunch, and put water on to boil. He broiled his meat on the hot, red coals, and laid it near on clean pine chips, while he waited for bread to bake and coffee to boil. The smell of wood-smoke and odorous steam from pots and the fragrance of spruce mingled together, keen, sweet, appetizing. Then he ate his simple meal hungrily, with the content of the man who had fared worse.

After he had satisfied himself he washed his utensils and stowed them away, with the bags. Whereupon his movements acquired less dexterity and speed. The rest hour had come. Still, like the long-experienced man in the open, he looked around for more to do, and his gaze fell upon his weapons, lying on his saddle. His rifle was a Henry—shiny and smooth from long service and care. His small gun was a Colt's 45. It had been carried in a saddle holster. Wade rubbed the rifle with his hands, and then with a greasy rag which he took from the sheath. After that he held the rifle to the heat of the fire. A squall of rain had overtaken him that day, wetting his weapons. A subtle and singular difference seemed to show in the way he took up the Colt's. His action was slow, his look reluctant. The small gun was not merely a thing of steel and powder and ball. He dried it and rubbed it with care, but not with love, and then he stowed it away.

Next Wade unrolled his bed under the spruce, with one end of the tarpaulin resting on the soft mat of needles. On top of that came the two woolly sheepskins, which he used to lie upon, then his blankets, and over all the other end of the tarpaulin.

This ended his tasks for the day. He lighted his pipe and composed himself beside the campfire to smoke and rest awhile before going to bed. The silence of the wilderness enfolded lake and shore; yet presently it came to be a silence accentuated by near and distant sounds, faint, wild, lonely—the low hum of falling water, the splash of tiny waves on the shore, the song of insects, and the dismal hoot of owls.

"Bill Belllounds—an' he needs a hunter," soliloquized Bent Wade, with gloomy, penetrating eyes, seeing far through the red embers. "That will suit me an' change my luck, likely. Livin' in the woods, away from people—I could stick to a job like that . . . But if this White Slides is close to the old trail I'll never stay."

He sighed, and a darker shadow, not from flickering fire, overspread his cadaverous face. Eighteen years ago he had driven the woman he loved away from him, out into the world with her baby girl. Never had he rested beside a campfire that that old agony did not recur! Jealous fool! Too late he had discovered his fatal blunder; and then had begun a search over Colorado, ending not a hundred miles across the wild mountains from where he brooded that lonely hour—a search ended by news of the massacre of a wagon-train by Indians.

That was Bent Wade's secret.

And no earthly sufferings could have been crueler than his agony and remorse, as through the long years he wandered on and on. The very good that he tried to do seemed to foment evil. The wisdom that grew out of his suffering opened pitfalls for his wandering feet. The wildness of men and the passion of women somehow waited with incredible fatality for that hour when chance led him into their lives. He had toiled, he had given, he had fought, he had sacrificed, he had killed, he had endured for the human nature which in his savage youth he had betrayed. Yet out of his supreme and endless striving to undo, to make reparation, to give his life, to find God, had come, it seemed to Wade in his abasement, only a driving torment.

But though his thought and emotion fluctuated, varying, wandering, his memory held a fixed and changeless picture of a woman, fair and sweet, with eyes of nameless blue, and face as white as a flower.

"Baby would have been—let's see—'most nineteen years old now—if she'd lived," he said. "A big girl, I reckon, like her mother . . . Strange how, as I grow older, I remember better!"

The night wind moaned through the spruces; dark clouds scudded across the sky, blotting out the bright stars; a steady, low roar of water came from the outlet of the lake. The campfire flickered and burned out, so that no sparks blew into the blackness, and the red embers glowed and paled and crackled. Wade at length got up and made ready for bed. He threw back tarpaulin and blankets, and laid his rifle alongside where he could cover it. His coat served for a pillow and he put the Colt's gun under that; then pulling off his boots, he slipped into bed, dressed as he was, and, like all men in the open, at once fell asleep.

For Wade, and for countless men like him, who for many years had roamed the West, this sleeping alone in wild places held both charm and peril. But the fascination of it was only a vague realization, and the danger was laughed at.

Over Bent Wade's quiet form the shadows played, the spruce boughs waved, the piny needles rustled down, the wind moaned louder as the night advanced. By and by the horses rested from their grazing; the insects ceased to hum; and the continuous roar of water dominated the solitude. If wild animals passed Wade's camp they gave it a wide berth.

* * * * *

Sunrise found Wade on the trail, climbing high up above the lake, making for the pass over the range. He walked, leading his horses up a zigzag trail that bore the tracks of recent travelers. Although this country was sparsely settled, yet there were men always riding from camp to camp or from one valley town to another. Wade never tarried on a well-trodden trail.

As he climbed higher the spruce trees grew smaller, no longer forming a green aisle before him, and at length they became dwarfed and stunted, and at last failed altogether. Soon he was above timberline and out upon a flat-topped mountain range, where in both directions the land rolled and dipped, free of tree or shrub, colorful with grass and flowers. The elevation exceeded eleven thousand feet. A whipping wind swept across the plain-land. The sun was pale-bright in the east, slowly being obscured by gray clouds. Snow began to fall, first in scudding, scanty flakes, but increasing until the air was full of a great, fleecy swirl. Wade rode along the rim of a mountain wall, watching a beautiful snowstorm falling into the brown gulf beneath him. Once as he headed round a break he caught sight of mountain sheep cuddled under a protecting shelf. The snow squall blew away, like a receding wall, leaving grass and flowers wet. As the dark clouds parted, the sun shone warmer out of the blue. Gray peaks, with patches of white, stood up above their black-timbered slopes.

Wade soon crossed the flat-topped pass over the range and faced a descent, rocky and bare at first, but yielding gradually to the encroachment of green. He left the cold winds and bleak trails above him. In an hour, when he was half down the slope, the forest had become warm and dry, fragrant and still. At length he rode out upon the brow of a last wooded bench above a grassy valley, where a bright, winding stream gleamed in the sun. While the horses rested Wade looked about him. Nature never tired him. If he had any peace it emanated from the silent places, the solemn hills, the flowers and animals of the wild and lonely land.

A few straggling pines shaded this last low hill above the valley. Grass grew luxuriantly there in the open, but not under the trees, where the brown needle-mats jealously obstructed the green. Clusters of columbines waved their graceful, sweet, pale-blue flowers that Wade felt a joy in seeing. He loved flowers—columbines, the glory of Colorado, came first, and next the many-hued purple asters, and then the flaunting spikes of paint-brush, and after them the nameless and numberless wildflowers that decked the mountain meadows and colored the grass of the aspen groves and peeped out of the edge of snow fields.

"Strange how it seems good to live—when I look at a columbine—or watch a beaver at his work—or listen to the bugle of an elk!" mused Bent Wade. He wondered why, with all his life behind him, he could still find comfort in these things.

Then he rode on his way. The grassy valley, with its winding stream, slowly descended and widened, and left foothill and mountain far behind. Far across a wide plain rose another range, black and bold against the blue. In the afternoon Wade reached Elgeria, a small hamlet, but important by reason of its being on the main stage line, and because here miners and cattlemen bought supplies. It had one street, so wide it appeared to be a square, on which faced a line of bold board houses with high, flat fronts. Wade rode to the inn where the stagecoaches made headquarters. It suited him to feed and rest his horses there, and partake of a meal himself, before resuming his journey.

The proprietor was a stout, pleasant-faced little woman, loquacious and amiable, glad to see a stranger for his own sake rather than from considerations of possible profit. Though Wade had never before visited Elgeria, he soon knew all about the town, and the miners up in the hills, and the only happenings of moment—the arrival and departure of stages.

"Prosperous place," remarked Wade. "I saw that. An' it ought to be growin'."

"Not so prosperous fer me as it uster be," replied the lady. "We did well when my husband was alive, before our competitor come to town. He runs a hotel where miners can drink an' gamble. I don't . . . But I reckon I've no cause to complain. I live."

"Who runs the other hotel?"

"Man named Smith. Reckon thet's not his real name. I've had people here who—but it ain't no matter."

"Men change their names," replied Wade.

"Stranger, air you packin' through or goin' to stay?"

"On my way to White Slides Ranch, where I'm goin' to work for Belllounds. Do you know him?"

"Know Belllounds? Me? Wal, he's the best friend I ever had when I was at Kremmlin'. I lived there several years. My husband had stock there. In fact, Bill started us in the cattle business. But we got out of there an' come here, where Bob died, an' I've been stuck ever since."

"Everybody has a good word for Belllounds," observed Wade.

"You'll never hear a bad one," replied the woman, with cheerful warmth. "Bill never had but one fault, an' people loved him fer thet."

"What was it?"

"He's got a wild boy thet he thinks the sun rises an' sets in. Buster Jack, they call him. He used to come here often. But Bill sent him away somewhere. The boy was spoiled. I saw his mother years ago—she's dead this long time—an' she was no wife fer Bill Belllounds. Jack took after her. An' Bill was thet woman's slave. When she died all his big heart went to the son, an' thet accounts. Jack will never be any good."

Wade thoughtfully nodded his head, as if he understood, and was pondering other possibilities.

"Is he the only child?"

"There's a girl, but she's not Bill's kin. He adopted her when she was a baby. An' Jack's mother hated this child—jealous, we used to think, because it might grow up an' get some of Bill's money.'

"What's the girl's name?" asked Wade.

"Columbine. She was over here last summer with Old Bill. They stayed with me. It was then Bill had hard words with Smith across the street. Bill was resentin' somethin' Smith put in my way. Wal, the lass's the prettiest I ever seen in Colorado, an' as good as she's pretty. Old Bill hinted to me he'd likely make a match between her an' his son Jack. An' I ups an' told him, if Jack hadn't turned over a new leaf when he comes home, thet such a marriage would be tough on Columbine. Whew, but Old Bill was mad. He jest can't stand a word ag'in' thet Buster Jack."

"Columbine Belllounds," mused Wade. "Queer name."

"Oh, I've knowed three girls named Columbine. Don't you know the flower? It's common in these parts. Very delicate, like a sago lily, only paler."

"Were you livin' in Kremmlin' when Belllounds adopted the girl?" asked Wade.

"Laws no!" was the reply. "Thet was long before I come to Middle Park. But I heerd all about it. The baby was found by gold-diggers up in the mountains. Must have got lost from a wagon-train thet Indians set on soon after—so the miners said. Anyway, Old Bill took the baby an' raised her as his own."

"How old is she now?" queried Wade, with a singular change in his tone.

"Columbine's around nineteen."

Bent Wade lowered his head a little, hiding his features under the old, battered, wide-brimmed hat. The amiable innkeeper did not see the tremor that passed over him, nor the slight stiffening that followed, nor the gray pallor of his face. She went on talking until someone called her.

Wade went outdoors, and with bent head walked down the street, across a little river, out into green pasture-land. He struggled with an amazing possibility. Columbine Belllounds might be his own daughter. His heart leaped with joy. But the joy was short-lived. No such hope in this world for Bent Wade! This coincidence, however, left him with a strange, prophetic sense in his soul of a tragedy coming to White Slides Ranch. Wade possessed some power of divination, some strange gift to pierce the veil of the future. But he could not exercise this power at will; it came involuntarily, like a messenger of trouble in the dark night. Moreover, he had never yet been able to draw away from the fascination of this knowledge. It lured him on. Always his decision had been to go on, to meet this boding circumstance, or to remain and meet it, in the hope that he might take someone's burden upon his shoulders. He sensed it now, in the keen, poignant clairvoyance of the moment—the tangle of life that he was about to enter. Old Bill Belllounds, big and fine, victim of love for a wayward son; Buster Jack, the waster, the tearer-down, the destroyer, the wild youth at a wild time; Columbine, the girl of unknown birth, good and loyal, subject to a condition sure to ruin her. Wade's strange mind revolved a hundred outcomes to this conflict of characters, but not one of them was the one that was written. That remained dark. Never had he received so strong a call out of the unknown, nor had he ever felt such intense curiosity. Hope had long been dead in him, except the one that he might atone in some way for the wrong he had done his wife. So the pangs of emotion that recurred, in spite of reason and bitterness, were not recognized by him as lingering hopes. Wade denied the human in him, but he thrilled at the thought of meeting Columbine Belllounds. There was something here beyond all his comprehension.

"It *might*—be true!" he whispered. "I'll know when I see her."

Then he walked back toward the inn. On the way he looked into the barroom of the hotel run by Smith. It was a hard-looking place, half full of idle men, whose faces were as open pages to Bent Wade. Curiosity did not wholly control the impulse that made him wait at the door till he could have a look at the man Smith. Somewhere, at some time, Wade had met most of the veterans of western Colorado. So much he had traveled! But the impulse that held him was answered and explained when Smith came in—a burly man, with an ugly scar marring one eye. Bent Wade recognized Smith. He recognized the scar. For that scar was his own mark, dealt to this man, whose name was not Smith, and who had been as evil as he looked, and whose nomadic life was not due to remorse or love of travel.

Wade passed on without being seen. This recognition meant less to him than it would have ten years ago, as he was not now the kind of man who hunted old enemies for revenge or who went to great lengths to keep out of their way. Men there were in Colorado who would shoot at him on sight. There had been more than one that had shot to his cost.

* * * * *

That night Wade camped in the foothills east of Elgeria, and upon the following day, at sunrise, his horses were breaking the frosty grass and ferns of the timbered range. This he crossed, rode down into a valley where a lonely cabin nestled, and followed an old, blazed trail that wound up the course of a brook. The water was of a color that made rock and sand and moss seem like gold. He saw no signs or tracks of game. A gray jay now and then screeched his approach to unseen denizens of the woods. The stream babbled past him over mossy ledges, under the dark shade of clumps of spruces, and it grew smaller as he progressed toward its source. At length it was lost in a swale of high, rank grass, and the blazed trail led on through heavy pine woods. At noon he reached the crest of the divide, and, halting upon an open, rocky eminence, he gazed down over a green and black forest, slow-descending to a great irregular park that was his destination for the night.

Wade needed meat, and to that end, as he went on, he kept a sharp lookout for deer, especially after he espied fresh tracks crossing the trail. Slipping along ahead of his horses, that followed him almost too closely to permit of his noiseless approach to game, he hunted all the way down to the great open park without getting a shot.

This park was miles across and miles long, covered with tall, waving grass, and it had straggling arms that led off into the surrounding belt of timber. It sloped gently toward the center, where a round, green acreage of grass gave promise of water. Wade rode toward this, keeping somewhat to the right, as he wanted to camp at the edge of the woods. Soon he rode out beyond one of the projecting peninsulas of forest to find the park spreading wider in that direction. He saw horses grazing with elk, and far down at the notch, where evidently the park had outlet in a narrow valley, he espied the black, hump-shaped, shaggy forms of buffalo. They bobbed off out of sight. Then the elk saw or scented him, and they trotted away, the antlered bulls ahead of the cows. Wade wondered if the horses were wild. They showed great interest, but no fear. Beyond them was a rising piece of ground, covered with pine, and it appeared to stand aloft from the forest on the far side as well as upon that by which he was approaching. Riding a mile or so farther he ascertained that this bit of wooded ground resembled an island in a lake. Presently he saw smoke arising above the treetops.

A tiny brook welled out of the green center of the park and meandered around to pass near the island of pines. Wade saw unmistakable signs of prospecting along this brook, and farther down, where he crossed it, he found tracks made that day.

The elevated plot of ground appeared to be several acres in extent, covered with small-sized pines, and at the far edge there was a little log cabin. Wade expected to surprise a lone prospector at his evening meal. As he rode up a dog ran out of the cabin, barking furiously. A man, dressed in fringed buckskin, followed. He was tall, and had long, iron-gray hair over his shoulders. His bronzed and weather-beaten face was a mass of fine wrinkles where the grizzled hair did not hide them, and his shining, red countenance proclaimed an honest, fearless spirit.

"Howdy, stranger!" he called, as Wade halted several rods distant. His greeting was not welcome, but it was civil. His keen scrutiny, however, attested to more than his speech.

"Evenin', friend," replied Wade. "Might I throw my pack here?"

"Sure. Get down," answered the other. "I calkilate I never seen you in these diggin's."

"No. I'm Bent Wade, an' on my way to White Slides to work for Belllounds."

"Glad to meet you. I'm new hereabouts, myself, but I know Belllounds. My name's Lewis. I was jest cookin' grub. An' it'll burn, too, if I don't rustle. Turn your hosses loose an' come in."

Wade presented himself with something more than his usual methodical action. He smelled buffalo steak, and he was hungry. The cabin had been built years ago, and was a ramshackle shelter at best. The stone fireplace, however, appeared well preserved. A bed of red coals glowed and cracked upon the hearth.

"Reckon I sure smelled buffalo meat," observed Wade, with much satisfaction. "It's long since I chewed a hunk of that."

"All ready. Now pitch in . . . Yes, thar's some buffalo left in here. Not hunted much. Thar's lots of elk an' herds of deer. After a little snow you'd think a drove of sheep had been trackin' around. An' some bear."

Wade did not waste many words until he had enjoyed that meal. Later, while he helped his host, he recurred to the subject of game.

"If there's so many deer then there's lions an' wolves."

"You bet. I see tracks every day. Had a shot at a lofer not long ago. Missed him. But I reckon thar's more varmints over in the Troublesome country back of White Slides."

"Troublesome! Do they call it that?" asked Wade, with a queer smile.

"Sure. An' it *is* troublesome. Belllounds has been tryin' to hire a hunter. Offered me big wages to kill off the wolves an' lions."

"That's the job I'm goin' to take."

"Good!" exclaimed Lewis. "I'm sure glad. Belllounds is a nice fellar. I felt sort of cheap till I told him I wasn't really a hunter. You see, I'm prospectin' up here, an' pretendin' to be a hunter."

"What do you make that bluff for?" queried Wade.

"You couldn't fool anyone who'd ever prospected for gold. I saw your signs out here."

"Wal, you've sharp eyes, thet's all. Wade, I've some ondesirable neighbors over here. I'd just as lief they didn't see me diggin' gold. Lately I've had a hunch they're rustlin' cattle. Anyways, they've sold cattle in Kremmlin' thet came from over around Elgeria."

"Wherever there's cattle there's sure to be some stealin'," observed Wade.

"Wal, you needn't say anythin' to Belllounds, because mebbe I'm wrong. An' if I found out I was right I'd go down to White Slides an' tell it myself. Belllounds done some favors."

"How far to White Slides?" asked Wade, with a puff on his pipe.

"Roundabout trail, an' rough, but you'll make it in one day, easy. Beautiful country. Open, big peaks an' ranges, with valleys an' lakes. Never seen such grass!"

"Did you ever see Belllounds's son?"

"No. Didn't know he hed one. But I seen his gal the fust day I was thar. She was nice to me. I went thar to be fixed up a bit. Nearly chopped my hand off. The gal—Columbine, she's called—doctored me up. Fact is, I owe considerable to thet White Slides Ranch. There's a cowboy, Wils somethin', who rode up here with some medicine fer me—some they didn't have when I was thar. You'll like thet boy. I seen he was sweet on the gal an' I sure couldn't blame him."

Bent Wade removed his pipe and let out a strange laugh, significant with its little note of grim confirmation.

"What's funny about thet?" demanded Lewis, rather surprised.

"I was only laughin'," replied Wade. "What you said about the cowboy bein' sweet on the girl popped into my head before you told it. Well, boys will be boys. I was young once an' had my day."

Lewis grunted as he bent over to lift a red coal to light his pipe, and as he raised his head he gave Wade a glance of sympathetic curiosity.

"Wal, I hope I'll see more of you," he said, as his guest rose, evidently to go.

"Reckon you will, as I'll be chasin' hounds all over. An' I want a look at them neighbors you spoke of that might be rustlers . . . I'll turn in now. Good night."

## CHAPTER V

Bent Wade rode out of the forest to look down upon the White Slides country at the hour when it was most beautiful.

"Never seen the beat of that!" he exclaimed, as he halted.

The hour was sunset, with the golden rays and shadows streaking ahead of him down the rolling sage hills, all rosy and gray with rich, strange softness. Groves of aspens stood isolated from one another—here crowning a hill with blazing yellow, and there fringing the brow of another with gleaming gold, and lower down reflecting the sunlight with brilliant red and purple. The valley seemed filled with a delicate haze, almost like smoke. White Slides Ranch was hidden from sight, as it lay in the bottomland. The gray old peak towered proud and aloof, clear-cut and sunset-flushed against the blue. The eastern slope of the valley was a vast sweep of sage and hill and grassy bench and aspen bench, on fire with the colors of autumn made molten by the last flashing of the sun. Great black slopes of forest gave sharp contrast, and led up to the red-walled ramparts of the mountain range.

Wade watched the scene until the fire faded, the golden shafts paled and died, the rosy glow on sage changed to cold steel gray. Then he rode out upon the foothills. The trail led up and down slopes of sage. Grass grew thicker as he descended. Once he startled a great flock of prairie chickens, or sage hens, large gray birds, lumbering, swift fliers, that whirred up, and soon plumped down again into the sage. Twilight found him on a last long slope of the foothills, facing the pasture-land of the valley, with the ranch still five miles distant, now showing misty and dim in the gathering shadows.

Wade made camp where a brook ran near an aspen thicket. He had no desire to hurry to meet events at White Slides Ranch, although he longed to see this girl that belonged to Belllounds. Night settled down over the quiet foothills. A pack of roving coyotes visited Wade, and sat in a half-circle in the shadows back of the campfire. They howled and barked. Nevertheless sleep visited Wade's tired eyelids the moment he lay down and closed them.

\* \* \* \* \*

Next morning, rather late, Wade rode down to White Slides Ranch. It looked to him like the property of a rich rancher who held to the old and proven customs of his generation. The corrals were new, but their style was old. Wade reflected that it would be hard for rustlers or horse-thieves to steal out of those corrals. A long lane led from the pasture-land, following the brook that ran through the corrals and by the back door of the rambling, comfortable-looking cabin. A cowboy was leading horses across a wide square between the main ranch house and a cluster of cabins and sheds. He saw the visitor and waited.

"Mornin'," said Wade, as he rode up.

"Hod do," replied the cowboy.

Then these two eyed each other, not curiously nor suspiciously, but with that steady, measuring gaze common to Western men.

"My name's Wade," said the traveler. "Come from Meeker way. I'm lookin' for a job with Belllounds."

"I'm Lem Billings," replied the other. "Ridin' fer White Slides fer years. Reckon the boss'll be glad to take you on."

"Is he around?"

"Sure. I jest seen him," replied Billings, as he haltered his horses to a post. "I reckon I ought to give you a hunch."

"I'd take that as a favor."

"Wal, we're short of hands," said the cowboy. "Jest got the roundup over. Hudson was hurt an' Wils Moore got crippled. Then the boss's son has been put on as foreman. Three of the boys quit. Couldn't stand him. This hyar son of Belllounds is a son-of-a-gun! Me an' pards of mine, Montana an' Bludsoe, are stickin' on—wal, fer reasons thet ain't egzactly love fer the boss. But Old Bill's the best of bosses . . . Now the hunch is—thet if you git on hyar you'll hev to do two or three men's work."

"Much obliged," replied Wade. "I don't shy at that."

"Wal, git down an' come in," added Billings, heartily.

He led the way across the square, around the corner of the ranch house, and up on a long porch, where the arrangement of chairs and blankets attested to the hand of a woman. The first door was open, and from it issued voices; first a shrill, petulant boy's complaint, and then a man's deep, slow, patient reply.

Lem Billings knocked on the doorjamb.

"Wal, what's wanted?" called Belllounds.

"Boss, thar's a man wantin' to see you," replied Lem.

Heavy steps approached the doorway and it was filled with the large figure of the rancher. Wade remembered Belllounds and saw only a gray difference in years.

"Good mornin', Lem, an' good moinin' to you, stranger," was the rancher's greeting, his bold, blue glance, honest and frank and keen, with all his long experience of men, taking Wade in with one flash.

Lem discreetly walked to the end of the porch as another figure, that of the son who resembled the father, filled the doorway, with eyes less kind, bent upon the visitor.

"My name's Wade. I'm over from Meeker way, hopin' to find a job with you," said Wade.

"Glad to meet you," replied Belllounds, extending his huge hand to shake Wade's. "I need you, sure bad. What's your special brand of work?"

"I reckon any kind."

"Set down, stranger," replied Belllounds, pulling up a chair. He seated himself on a bench and leaned against the log wall. "Now, when a boy comes an' says he can do anythin', why I jest *haw! haw!* at him. But you're a man,

Wade, an' one as has been there. Now I'm hard put fer hands. Jest speak out now fer yourself. No one else can speak fer you, thet's sure. An' this is bizness."

"Any work with stock, from punchin' steers to doctorin' horses," replied Wade, quietly. "Am fair carpenter an' mason. Good packer. Know farmin'. Can milk cows an' make butter. I've been cook in many outfits. Read an' write an' not bad at figures. Can do work on saddles an' harness, an'—"

"Hold on!" yelled Belllounds, with a hearty laugh. "I ain't imposin' on no man, no matter how I need help. You're sure a jack of all range trades. An' I wish you was a hunter."

"I was comin' to that. You didn't give me time."

"Say, do you know hounds?" queried Belllounds, eagerly.

"Yes. Was raised where everybody had packs. I'm from Kentucky. An' I've run hounds off an' on for years. I'll tell you—"

Belllounds interrupted Wade.

"By all that's lucky! An' last, can you handle guns? We 'ain't had a good shot on this range fer Lord knows how long. I used to hit plumb center with a rifle. My eyes are pore now. An' my son can't hit a flock of haystacks. An' the cowpunchers are 'most as bad. Sometimes right hyar where you could hit elk with a club we're out of fresh meat."

"Yes, I can handle guns," replied Wade, with a quiet smile and a lowering of his head. "Reckon you didn't catch my name."

"Wal— no, I didn't," slowly replied Belllounds, and his pause, with the keener look he bestowed upon Wade, told how the latter's query had struck home.

"Wade—Bent Wade," said Wade, with quiet distinctness.

"*Not Hell-Bent Wade!*" ejaculated Belllounds.

"The same . . . I ain't proud of the handle, but I never sail under false colors."

"Wal, I'll be damned!" went on the rancher. "Wade, I've heerd of you fer years. Some bad, but most good, an' I reckon I'm jest as glad to meet you as if you'd been somebody else."

"You'll give me the job?"

"I should smile."

"I'm thankin' you. Reckon I was some worried. Jobs are hard for me to get an' harder to keep."

"Thet's not onnatural, considerin' the hell which's said to camp on your trail," replied Belllounds, dryly. "Wade, I can't say I take a hell of a lot of stock in such talk. Fifty years I've been west of the Missouri. I know the West an' I know men. Talk flies from camp to ranch, from diggin's to town, an' always someone adds a little more. Now I trust my judgment an' I trust men. No one ever betrayed me yet."

"I'm that way, too," replied Wade. "But it doesn't pay, an' yet I still kept on bein' that way . . . Belllounds, my name's as bad as good all over western Colorado. But as man to man I tell you—I never did a low-down trick in my life . . . Never but once."

"An' what was thet?" queried the rancher, gruffly.

"I killed a man who was innocent," replied Wade, with quivering lips, "an'—an' drove the woman I loved to her death."

"Aw! We all make mistakes sometime in our lives," said Belllounds, hurriedly. "I made 'most as big a one as yours—so help me God! . . ."

"I'll tell you—" interrupted Wade.

"You needn't tell me anythin'," said Belllounds, interrupting in his turn. "But at thet some time I'd like to hear about the Lascelles outfit over on the Gunnison. I knowed Lascelles. An' a pardner of mine down in Middle Park came back from the Gunnison with the dog-gondest story I ever heerd. Thet was five years ago this summer. Of course I knowed your name long before, but this time I heerd it powerful strong. You got in thet mix-up to your neck . . . Wal, what consarns me now is this. Is there any sense in the talk thet wherever you land there's hell to pay?"

"Belllounds, there's no sense in it, but a lot of truth," confessed Wade, gloomily.

"Ahuh! . . . Wal, Hell-Bent Wade, I'll take a chance on you," boomed the rancher's deep voice, rich with the intent of his big heart. "I've gambled all my life. An' the best friends I ever made were men I'd helped . . . What wages do you ask?"

"I'll take what you offer."

"I'm payin' the boys forty a month, but thet's not enough fer you."

"Yes, that'll do."

"Good, it's settled," concluded Belllounds, rising. Then he saw his son standing inside the door. "Say, Jack, shake hands with Bent Wade, hunter an' all-around man. Wade, this's my boy. I've jest put him on as foreman of the outfit, an' while I'm at it I'll say thet you'll take orders from me an' not from him."

Wade looked up into the face of Jack Belllounds, returned his brief greeting, and shook his limp hand. The contact sent a strange chill over Wade. Young Belllounds's face was marred by a bruise and shaded by a sullen light.

"Get Billin's to take you out to thet new cabin an' sheds I jest had put up," said the rancher. "You'll bunk in the cabin . . . Aw, I know. Men like you sleep in the open. But you can't do thet under Old White Slides in winter. Not much! Make yourself to home, an' I'll walk out after a bit an' we'll look over the dog outfit. When you see thet outfit you'll holler fer help."

Wade bowed his thanks, and, putting on his sombrero, he turned away. As he did so he caught a sound of light, quick footsteps on the far end of the porch.

"Hello, you-all!" cried a girl's voice, with melody in it that vibrated piercingly upon Wade's sensitive ears.

"Mornin', Columbine," replied the rancher.

Bent Wade's heart leaped up. This girlish voice rang upon the chord of memory. Wade had not the strength to look at her then. It was not that he could not bear to look, but that he could not bear the disillusion sure to follow his first glimpse of this adopted daughter of Belllounds. Sweet to delude himself! Ah! the years were bearing sterner upon his head! The old dreams persisted, sadder now for the fact that from long use they had become half-realities! Wade shuffled slowly across the green square to where the cowboy waited for him. His eyes were dim, and a sickness attended the sinking of his heart.

"Wade, I ain't a bettin' fellar, but I'll bet Old Bill took you up," vouchsafed Billings, with interest.

"Glad to say he did," replied Wade. "You're to show me the new cabin where I'm to bunk."

"Come along," said Lem, leading off. "Air you agoin' to handle stock or chase coyotes?"

"My job's huntin'."

"Wal, it may be thet from sunup to sundown, but between times you'll be sure busy otherwise, I opine," went on Lem. "Did you meet the boss's son?"

"Yes, he was there. An' Belllounds made it plain I was to take orders from him an' not from his son."

"Thet'll make your job a million times easier," declared Lem, as if to make up for former hasty pessimism. He led the way past some log cabins, and sheds with dirt roofs, and low, flat-topped barns, out across another brook where willow-trees were turning yellow. Then the new cabin came into view. It was small, with one door and one window, and a porch across the front. It stood on a small elevation, near the swift brook, and overlooking the ranch house perhaps a quarter of a mile below. Above it, and across the brook, had been built a high fence constructed of aspen poles laced closely together. The sounds therefrom proclaimed this stockade to be the dog-pen.

Lem helped Wade unpack and carry his outfit into the cabin. It contained one room, the corner of which was filled with blocks and slabs of pine, evidently left there after the construction of the cabin, and meant for firewood. The ample size of the stone fireplace attested to the severity of the winters.

"Real sawed boards on the floor!" exclaimed Lem, meaning to impress the newcomer. "I call this a plumb good bunk."

"Much too good for me," replied Wade.

"Wal, I'll look after your hosses," said Lem. "I reckon you'll fix up your bunk. Take my hunch an' ask Miss Collie to find you some furniture an' sich like. She's Ole Bill's daughter, an' she makes up fer—fer—wal, fer a lot we hev to stand. I'll fetch the boys over later."

"Do you smoke?" asked Wade. "I've somethin' fine I fetched up from Leadville."

"Smoke! Me? I'll give you a hoss right now for a cigar. I git one onct a year, mebbe."

"Here's a box I've been packin' for long," replied Wade, as he handed it up to Billings. "They're Spanish, all right. Too rich for my blood!"

A box of gold could not have made that cowboy's eyes shine any brighter.

"*Whoop-ee!*" he yelled. "Why, man, you're like the fairy in the kid's story! Won't I make the outfit wild? Aw, I forgot. Thar's only Jim an' Blud left. Wal, I'll divvy with them. Sure, Wade, you hit me right. I was dyin' fer a real smoke. An' I reckon what's mine is yours."

Then he strode out of the cabin, whistling a merry cowboy tune.

Wade was left sitting in the middle of the room on his roll of bedding, and for a long time he remained there motionless, with his head bent, his worn hands idly clasped. A heavy footfall outside aroused him from his meditation.

"Hey, Wade!" called the cheery voice of Belllounds. Then the rancher appeared at the door. "How's this bunk suit you?"

"Much too fine for an old-timer like me," replied Wade.

"Old-timer! Say, you're young yet. Look at me. Sixty-eight last birthday! Wal, every dog has his day . . . What're you needin' to fix this bunk comfortable like?"

"Reckon I don't need much."

"Wal, you've beddin' an' cook outfit. Go get a table, an' a chair an' a bench from thet first cabin. The boys thet had it are gone. Somethin' with a back to it, a rockin'-chair, if there's one. You'll find tools, an' boxes, an' stuff in the workshop, if you want to make a cupboard or anythin'."

"How about a lookin'-glass?" asked Wade. "I had a piece, but I broke it."

"Haw! Haw! Mebbe we can rustle thet, too. My girl's good on helpin' the boys fix up. Woman-like, you know. An' she'll fetch you some decorations on her own hook. Now let's take a look at the hounds."

Belllounds led the way out toward the crude dog-corral, and the way he leaped the brook bore witness to the fact that he was still vigorous and spry. The door of the pen was made of boards hung on wire. As Belllounds opened it there came a pattering rush of many padded feet, and a chorus of barks and whines. Wade's surprised gaze took in forty or fifty dogs, mostly hounds, browns and blacks and yellows, all sizes—a motley, mangy, hungry pack, if he had ever seen one.

"I swore I'd buy every hound fetched to me, till I'd cleaned up the varmints around White Slides. An' sure I was imposed on," explained the rancher.

"Some good-lookin' hounds in the bunch," replied Wade. "An' there's hardly too many. I'll train two packs, so I can rest one when the other's huntin'."

"Wal, I'll be dog-goned!" ejaculated Belllounds, with relief. "I sure thought you'd roar. All this rabble to take care of!"

"No trouble after I've got acquainted," said Wade. "Have they been hunted any?"

"Some of the boys took out a bunch. But they split on deer tracks an' elk tracks an' Lord knows what all. Never put up a lion! Then again Billings took some out after a pack of coyotes, an' gol darn me if the coyotes didn't lick the hounds. An' wuss! Jack, my son, got it into his head thet he was a hunter. The other mornin' he found a fresh lion track back of the corral. An' he ups an' puts the whole pack of hounds on the trail. I had a good many more hounds in the pack than you see now. Wal, anyway, it was great to hear the noise thet pack made. Jack lost every blamed hound of them. Thet night an' next day an' the followin' they straggled in. But twenty some never did come back."

Wade laughed. "They may come yet. I reckon, though, they've gone home where they came from. Are any of these hounds recommended?"

"Every consarned one of them," declared Belllounds.

"That's funny. But I guess it's natural. Do you know for sure whether you bought any good dogs?"

"Yes, I gave fifty dollars for two hounds. Got them of a friend in Middle Park whose pack killed off the lions there. They're good dogs, trained on lion, wolf, an' bear."

"Pick 'em out," said Wade.

With a throng of canines crowding and fawning round him, and snapping at one another, it was difficult for the rancher to draw the two particular ones apart so they could be looked over. At length he succeeded, and Wade drove back the rest of the pack.

"The big fellar's Sampson an' the other's Jim," said Belllounds.

Sampson was a huge hound, gray and yellow, with mottled black marks, very long ears, and big, solemn eyes. Jim, a good-sized dog, but small in comparison with the other, was black all over, except around the nose and eyes. Jim had many scars. He was old, yet not past a vigorous age, and he seemed a quiet, dignified, wise hound, quite out of his element in that mongrel pack.

"If they're as good as they look we're lucky," said Wade, as he tied the ends of his rope round their necks. "Now are there any more you know are good?"

"Denver, come hyar!" yelled Belllounds. A white, yellow-spotted hound came wagging his tail. "I'll swear by Denver. An' there's one more—Kane.

He's half bloodhound, a queer, wicked kind of dog. He keeps to himself . . . Kane! Come hyar!"

Belllounds tramped around the corral, and finally found the hound in question, asleep in a dusty hole. Kane was the only beautiful dog in the lot. If half of him was bloodhound the other half was shepherd, for his black and brown hair was inclined to curl, and his head had the fine thoroughbred contour of the shepherd. His ears, long and drooping and thin, betrayed the hound in him. Kane showed no disposition to be friendly. His dark eyes, sad and mournful, burned with the fires of doubt.

Wade haltered Kane, Jim, and Sampson, which act almost precipitated a fight, and led them out of the corral. Denver, friendly and glad, followed at the rancher's heels.

"I'll keep them with me an' make lead dogs out of them," said Wade. "Belllounds, that bunch hasn't had enough to eat. They're half starved."

"Wal, thet's worried me more'n you'll guess," declared Belllounds, with irritation. "What do a lot of cowpunchin' fellars know about dogs? Why, they nearly ate Bludsoe up. He wouldn't feed 'em. An' Wils, who seemed good with dogs, was taken off bad hurt the other day. Lem's been tryin' to rustle feed fer them. Now we'll give back the dogs you don't want to keep, an' thet way thin out the pack."

"Yes, we won't need 'em all. An' I reckon I'll take the worry of this dog-pack off your mind."

"Thet's your job, Wade. My orders are fer you to kill off the varmints. Lions, wolves, coyotes. An' every fall some ole silvertip gits bad, an' now an' then other bears. Whatever you need in the way of supplies jest ask fer. We send regular to Kremmlin'. You can hunt fer two months yet, barrin' an onusual early winter . . . I'm askin' you—if my son tramps on your toes—I'd take it as a favor fer you to be patient. He's only a boy yet, an' coltish."

Wade divined that was a favor difficult for Belllounds to ask. The old rancher, dominant and forceful and self-sufficient all his days, had begun to feel an encroachment of opposition beyond his control. If he but realized it, the favor he asked of Wade was an appeal.

"Belllounds, I get along with everybody," Wade assured him. "An' maybe I can help your son. Before I'd reached here I'd heard he was wild, an' so I'm prepared."

"If you'd do thet—wal, I'd never forgit it," replied the rancher, slowly. "Jack's been away fer three years. Only got back a week or so ago. I calkilated he'd be sobered, steadied, by—thet—thet work I put him to. But I'm not sure. He's changed. When he gits his own way he's all I could ask. But thet way he wants ain't always what it ought to be. An' so thar's been clashes. But Jack's a fine young man. An' he'll outgrow his temper an' crazy notions. Work'll do it."

"Boys will be boys," replied Wade, philosophically. "I've not forgotten when I was a boy."

"Neither hev I. Wal, I'll be goin', Wade. I reckon Columbine will be up to call on you. Bein' the only woman-folk in my house, she sort of runs it. An' she's sure interested in thet pack of hounds."

Belllounds trudged away, his fine old head erect, his gray hair shining in the sun.

Wade sat down upon the step of his cabin, pondering over the rancher's remarks about his son. Recalling the young man's physiognomy, Wade began to feel that it was familiar to him. He had seen Jack Belllounds before. Wade never made mistakes in faces, though he often had a task to recall names. And he began to go over the recent past, recalling all that he could remember of Meeker, and Cripple Creek, where he had worked for several months, and so on, until he had gone back as far as his last trip to Denver.

"Must have been there," mused Wade, thoughtfully, and he tried to recall all the faces he had seen. This was impossible, of course, yet he remembered many. Then he visualized the places in Denver that for one reason or another had struck him particularly. Suddenly into one of these flashed the pale, sullen, bold face of Jack Belllounds.

"It was *there!*" he exclaimed, incredulously. "Well! . . . If thet's not the strangest yet! Could I be mistaken? No. I saw him . . . Belllounds must have known it—must have let him stay there , , , Maybe put him there! He's just the kind of a man to go to extremes to reform his son."

Singular as was this circumstance, Wade dwelt only momentarily on it. He dismissed it with the conviction that it was another strange happening in the string of events that had turned his steps toward White Slides Ranch. Wade's mind stirred to the probability of an early sight of Columbine Belllounds. He would welcome it, both as interesting and pleasurable, and surely as a relief. The sooner a meeting with her was over the better. His life had been one long succession of shocks, so that it seemed nothing the future held could thrill him, amaze him, torment him. And yet how well he knew that his heart was only the more responsive for all it had withstood! Perhaps here at White Slides he might meet with an experience dwarfing all others. It was possible; it was in the nature of events. And though he repudiated such a possibility, he fortified himself against a subtle divination that he might at last have reached the end of his long trail, where anything might happen.

Three of the hounds lay down at Wade's feet. Kane, the bloodhound, stood watching this new master, after the manner of a dog who was a judge of men. He sniffed at Wade. He grew a little less surly.

Wade's gaze, however, was on the path that led down along the border of the brook to disappear in the willows. Above this clump of yellowing trees could be seen the ranch house. A girl with fair hair stepped off the porch. She appeared to be carrying something in her arms, and shortly disappeared behind the willows. Wade saw her and surmised that she was coming to his cabin. He did not expect any more or think any more. His faculties condensed to the objective one of sight.

The girl, when she reappeared, was perhaps a hundred yards distant. Wade bent on her one keen, clear glance. Then his brain and his blood beat wildly. He saw a slender girl in riding-costume, lithe and strong, with the free step of one used to the open. It was this form, this step that struck Wade. "My— God! How like Lucy!" he whispered, and he tried to pierce the distance to see her face. It gleamed in the sunshine. Her fair hair waved in the wind. She was coming, but so slowly! All of Wade that was physical and emotional seemed to wait—clamped. The moment was age-long, with nothing beyond it. While she was still at a distance her face became distinct. And Wade sustained a terrible shock . . . Then, as one in a dream, as in a blur of strained peering into a maze, he saw the face of his sweetheart, his wife, the Lucy of his early manhood. It moved him out of the past. Closer! Pang on pang quivered in his heart. Was this only a nightmare? Or had he at last gone mad! This girl raised her head. She was looking—she saw him. Terror mounted upon Wade's consciousness.

"That's Lucy's face!" he gasped. "So help—me, God! . . . It's for this—I wandered here! She's my flesh an' blood—my Lucy's child—my own!"

Fear and presentiment and blank amaze and stricken consciousness left him in the lightning-flash of divination that was recognition as well. A shuddering cataclysm enveloped him, a passion so stupendous that it almost brought oblivion.

The three hounds leaped up with barks and wagging tails. They welcomed this visitor. Kane lost still more of his canine aloofness.

Wade's breast heaved. The blue sky, the gray hills, the green willows, all blurred in his sight, that seemed to hold clear only the face floating closer.

"I'm Columbine Belllounds," said a voice.

It stilled the storm in Wade. It was real. It was a voice of twenty years ago. The burden on his breast lifted. Then flashed the spirit, the old self-control of a man whose life had held many terrible moments.

"Mornin', miss. I'm glad to meet you," he replied, and there was no break, no tone unnatural in his greeting.

So they gazed at each other, she with that instinctive look peculiar to women in its intuitive powers, but common to all persons who had lived far from crowds and to whom a newcomer was an event. Wade's gaze, intense and all-embracing, found that face now closer in resemblance to the imagined Lucy's—a pretty face, rather than beautiful, but strong and sweet—its striking qualities being a colorless fairness of skin that yet held a rose and golden tint, and the eyes of a rare and exquisite shade of blue.

"Oh! Are you feeling ill?" she asked. "You look so—so pale."

"No. I'm only tuckered out," replied Wade, easily, as he wiped the clammy drops from his brow. "It was a long ride to get here."

"I'm the lady of the house," she said, with a smile. "I'm glad to welcome you to White Slides, and hope you'll like it."

"Well, Miss Columbine, I reckon I will," he replied, returning the smile. "Now if I was younger I'd like it powerful much."

She laughed at that. "Men are all alike, young or old."

"Don't ever think so," said Wade, earnestly.

"No? I guess you're right about that. I've fetched you up some things for your cabin. May I peep in?"

"Come in," replied Wade, rising. "You must excuse my manners. It's long indeed since I had a lady caller."

She went in, and Wade, standing on the threshold, saw her survey the room with a woman's sweeping glance.

"I told dad to put some—"

"Miss, your dad told me to go get them, an' I've not done it yet. But I will presently."

"Very well. I'll leave these things and come back later," she replied, depositing a bundle upon the floor. "You won't mind if I try to to make you a little comfortable. It's dreadful the way outdoor men live when they do get indoors."

"I reckon I'll be slow in lettin' you see what a good housekeeper I am," he replied. "Because then, maybe, I'll see more of you."

"Weren't you a sad flatterer in your day?" she queried, archly.

Her intonation, the tilt of her head, gave Wade such a pang that he could not answer. And to hide his momentary restraint he turned back to the hounds. Then she came out upon the porch.

"I love hounds," she said, patting Denver, which caress immediately made Jim and Sampson jealous. "I've gotten on pretty well with these, but that Kane won't make up. Isn't he splendid? But he's afraid—no, not afraid of me, but he doesn't like me."

"It's mistrust. He's been hurt. I reckon he'll get over that after a while."

"You don't beat dogs?" she asked, eagerly.

"No, miss. That's not the way to get on with hounds or horses."

Her glance was a blue flash of pleasure.

"How glad that makes me! Why, I quit coming here to see and feed the dogs because somebody was always kicking them around."

Wade handed the rope to her. "You hold them, so when I come out with some meat they won't pile over me." He went inside, took all that was left of the deer haunch out of his pack, and, picking up his knife, returned to the porch. The hounds saw the meat and yelped. They pulled on the rope.

"You hounds behave," ordered Wade, as he sat down on the step and began to cut the meat. "Jim, you're the oldest an' hungriest. Here . . . Now you, Sampson. Here!" . . . The big hound snapped at the meat. Whereupon Wade slapped him. "Are you a pup or a wolf that you grab for it? Here." Sampson was slower to act, but he snapped again. Whereupon Wade hit him again, with open hand, not with violence or rancor, but a blow that meant Sampson must obey.

Next time the hound did not snap. Denver had to be cuffed several times before he showed deference to this new master. But the bloodhound Kane refused to take any meat out of Wade's hand. He growled and showed his teeth, and sniffed hungrily.

"Kane will have to be handled carefully," observed Wade. "He'd bite pretty quick."

"But, he's so splendid," said the girl. "I don't like to think he's mean. You'll be good to him—try to win him?"

"I'll do my best with him."

"Dad's full of glee that he has a real hunter at White Slides at last. Now I'm glad, and sorry, too. I hate to think of little calves being torn and killed by lions and wolves. And it's dreadful to know bears eat grown-up cattle. But I love the mourn of a wolf and the yelp of a coyote. I can't help hoping you don't kill them all—quite."

"It's not likely, miss," he replied. "I'll be pretty sure to clean out the lions an' drive off the bears. But the wolf family can't be exterminated. No animal so cunnin' as a wolf! . . . I'll tell you . . . Some years ago I went to cook on a ranch north of Denver, on the edge of the plains. An' right off I began to hear stories about a big lobo—a wolf that was an old residenter. He'd been known for long, an' he got meaner an' wiser as he was hunted. His specialty got to be yearlings, an' the ranchers all over rose up in arms against him. They hired all the old hunters an' trappers in the country to kill him. No good! Old Lobo went right on pullin' down yearlings. Every night he'd get one or more. An' he was so cute an' so swift that he'd work on different ranches on different nights. Finally he killed eleven yearlings for my boss on one night. Eleven! Think of that. An' then I said to my boss, 'I reckon you'd better let me go kill that gray butcher.' An' my boss laughed at me. But he let me go. He'd have tried anythin'. I took a hunk of meat, a blanket, my gun, an' a pair of snow-shoes, an' I set out on old Lobo's tracks . . . An', Miss Columbine, I *walked* old Lobo to death in the snow!"

"Why, how wonderful!" exclaimed the girl, breathless and glowing with interest. "Oh, it seems a pity such a splendid brute should be killed. Wild animals are cruel. I wish it were different."

"Life is cruel, miss, an' I echo your wish," replied Wade, sadly.

"You have had great experiences. Dad said to me, 'Collie, here at last is a man who can tell you enough stories!' . . . But I don't believe you ever could."

"You like stories?" asked Wade, curiously.

"Love them. All kinds, but I like adventure best. *I* should have been a boy. Isn't it strange, I can't hurt anything myself or bear to see even a steer slaughtered? But you can't tell too bloody and terrible stories for me. Except I hate Indian stories. The very thought of Indians makes me shudder . . . Someday I'll tell you a story."

Wade could not find his tongue readily.

"I must go now," she continued, and moved off the porch. Then she hesitated, and turned with a smile that was wistful and impulsive. "I—I believe we'll be good friends."

"Miss Columbine, we sure will, if I can live up to my part," replied Wade.

Her smile deepened, even while her gaze grew unconsciously penetrating. Wade felt how subtly they were drawn to each other. But she had no inkling of that.

"It takes two to make a bargain," she replied, seriously. "I've my part. Good-by."

Wade watched her lithe stride, and as she drew away the restraint he had put upon himself loosened. When she disappeared his feeling burst all bounds. Dragging the dogs inside, he closed the door. Then, like one broken and spent, he fell face against the wall, with the hoarsely whispered words, "I'm thankin' God!"

## CHAPTER VI

September's glory of gold and red and purple began to fade with the autumnal equinox. It rained enough to soak the frost-bitten leaves, and then the mountain winds sent them flying and fluttering and scurrying to carpet the dells and spot the pools in the brooks and color the trails. When the weather cleared and the sun rose bright again many of the aspen thickets were leafless and bare, and the willows showed stark against the gray sage hills, and the vines had lost their fire. Hills and valleys had sobered with subtle change that left them nonetheless beautiful.

A mile or more down the road from White Slides, in a protected nook, nestled two cabins belonging to a cattleman named Andrews, who had formerly worked for Belllounds and had recently gone into the stock business for himself. He had a rather young wife, and several children, and a brother who rode for him. These people were the only neighbors of Belllounds for some ten miles on the road toward Kremmling.

Columbine liked Mrs. Andrews and often rode or walked down there for a little visit and a chat with her friend and a romp with the children.

Toward the end of September Columbine found herself combating a strong desire to go down to the Andrews ranch and try to learn some news about Wilson Moore. If anything had been heard at White Slides it certainly had not been told her. Jack Belllounds had ridden to Kremmling and back in one day, but Columbine would have endured much before asking him for information.

She did, however, inquire of the freighter who hauled Belllounds's supplies, and the answer she got was awkwardly evasive. That nettled Columbine. Also it raised a suspicion which she strove to subdue. Finally it seemed apparent that Wilson Moore's name was not to be mentioned to her.

First, in her growing resentment, she had an impulse to go to her new friend, the hunter Wade, and confide in him not only her longing to learn about Wilson, but also other matters that were growing daily more burdensome. How strange for her to feel that in some way Jack Belllounds had come between her and the old man she loved and called father! Columbine had not divined that until lately. She felt it now in the fact that she no longer sought the rancher as she used to, and he had apparently avoided her. But then, Columbine reflected, she might be entirely wrong, for when Belllounds did meet her at mealtimes, or anywhere, he seemed just as affectionate as of old. Still he was not the same man. A chill, an atmosphere of shadow, had pervaded the once wholesome ranch. And so, feeling not yet well enough acquainted with Wade to confide so intimately in him, she stifled her impulses and resolved to make some effort herself to find out what she wanted to know.

As luck would have it, when she started out to walk down to the Andrews ranch she encountered Jack Belllounds.

"Where are you going?" he inquired, inquisitively.

"I'm going to see Mrs. Andrews," she replied.

"No, you're not!" he declared, quickly, with a flash.

Columbine felt a queer sensation deep within her, a hot little gathering that seemed foreign to her physical being, and ready to burst out. Of late it had stirred in her at words or acts of Jack Belllounds. She gazed steadily at him, and he returned her look with interest. What he was thinking she had no idea of, but for herself it was a recurrence and an emphasis of the fact that she seemed growing farther away from this young man she had to marry. The weeks since his arrival had been the most worrisome she could remember.

"I *am* going," she replied, slowly.

"No!" he replied, violently. "I won't have you running off down there to—to gossip with that Andrews woman."

"Oh, *you* won't?" inquired Columbine, very quietly. How little he understood her!

"That's what I said."

"You're not my boss yet, Mister Jack Belllounds," she flashed, her spirit rising. He could irritate her as no one else.

"I soon will be. And what's a matter of a week or a month?" he went on, calming down a little.

"I've promised, yes," she said, feeling her face blanch, "and I keep my promises . . . But I didn't say when. If you talk like that to me it might be a good many weeks—or—or months before I name the day."

*"Columbine!"* he cried, as she turned away. There was genuine distress in his voice. Columbine felt again an assurance that had troubled her. No matter how she was reacting to this new relation, it seemed a fearful truth that Jack was really falling in love with her. This time she did not soften.

"I'll call dad to *make* you stay home," he burst out again, his temper rising.

Columbine wheeled as on a pivot.

"If you do you've got less sense than I thought."

Passion claimed him then.

"I know why you're going. It's to see that club-footed cowboy Moore! . . . Don't let me catch you with him!"

Columbine turned her back upon Belllounds and swung away, every pulse in her throbbing and smarting. She hurried on into the road. She wanted to run, not to get out of sight or hearing, but to fly from something, she knew not what.

"Oh! it's more than his temper!" she cried, hot tears in her eyes. "He's mean—*mean—mean!* What's the use of me denying that—anymore—just because I love dad? . . . My life will be wretched . . . It *is* wretched!"

Her anger did not last long, nor did her resentment. She reproached herself for the tart replies that had inflamed Jack. Never again would she forget herself!

"But he—he makes me furious," she cried, in sudden excuse for herself. "What did he say? 'That club-footed cowboy Moore'! . . . Oh, that was vile. He's heard, then, that poor Wilson has a bad foot, perhaps permanently crippled . . . If it's true . . . But why should he yell that he knew I wanted to see Wilson? . . . I did *not!* I *do* not . . . Oh, but I do, I do!"

And then Columbine was to learn straightway that she would forget herself again, that she had forgotten, and that a sadder, stranger truth was dawning upon her—she was discovering another Columbine within herself, a wilful, passionate, different creature who would no longer be denied.

Almost before Columbine realized that she had started upon the visit she was within sight of the Andrews ranch. So swiftly had she walked! It behooved her to hide such excitement as had dominated her. And to that end she slowed her pace, trying to put her mind on other matters.

The children saw her first and rushed upon her, so that when she reached the cabin door she could not well have been otherwise than rosy and smiling. Mrs. Andrews, ruddy and strong, looked the pioneer rancher's hard-working wife. Her face brightened at the advent of Columbine, and showed a little surprise and curiosity as well.

"Laws, but it's good to see you, Columbine," was her greeting. "You 'ain't been here for a long spell."

"I've been coming, but just put it off," replied Columbine.

And so, after the manner of women neighbors, they began to talk of the fall roundup, and the near approach of winter with its loneliness, and the children, all of which naturally led to more personal and interesting topics.

"An' is it so, Columbine, that you're to marry Jack Belllounds?" asked Mrs. Andrews, presently.

"Yes, I guess it is," replied Columbine, smiling.

"Humph! I'm no relative of yours or even a particular, close friend, but I'd like to say—"

"Please don't," interposed Columbine.

"All right, my girl. I guess it's better I don't say anythin'. It's a pity, though, onless you love this Buster Jack. An' you never used to do that, I'll swan."

"No, I don't love Jack—yet—as I ought to love a husband. But I'll try, and if—if I—I never do—still, it's my duty to marry him."

"Some woman ought to talk to Bill Belllounds," declared Mrs. Andrews with a grimness that boded ill for the old rancher.

"Did you know we had a new man up at the ranch?" asked Columbine, changing the subject.

"You mean the hunter, Hell-Bent Wade?"

"Yes. But I hate that ridiculous name," said Columbine.

"It's queer, like lots of names men get in these parts. An' it'll stick. Wade's been here twice; once as he was passin' with the hounds, an' the other night. I like him, Columbine. He's true-blue, for all his strange name. My men-folks took to him like ducks to water."

"I'm glad. I took to him almost like that," rejoined Columbine. "He has the saddest face I ever saw."

"Sad? Wal, yes. That man has seen a good deal of what they tacked on to his name. I laughed when I seen him first. Little lame fellar, crooked-legged an' ragged, with thet awful homely face! But I forgot how he looked next time he came."

"That's just it. He's not much to look at, but you forget his homeliness right off," replied Columbine, warmly. "You feel something behind all his—his looks."

"Wal, you an' me are women, an' we feel different," replied Mrs. Andrews. "Now my men-folks take much store on what Wade can *do*. He fixed up Tom's gun, that's been out of whack for a year. He made our clock run ag'in, an' run better than ever. Then he saved our cow from that poison-weed. An' Tom gave her up to die."

"The boys up home were telling me Mr. Wade had saved some of our cattle. Dad was delighted. You know he's lost a good many head of stock from this poison-weed. I saw so many dead steers on my last ride up the mountain. It's too bad our new man didn't get here sooner to save them. I asked him how he did it, and he said he was a doctor."

"A cow-doctor," laughed Mrs. Andrews. "Wal, that's a new one on me. Accordin' to Tom, this here Wade, when he seen our sick cow, said she'd eat poison-weed—larkspur, I think he called it—an' then when she drank water it formed a gas in her stomach an' she swelled up turrible. Wade jest stuck his knife in her side a little an' let the gas out, and she got well."

"Ughh! . . . What cruel doctoring! But if it saves the cattle, then it's good."

"It'll save them if they can be got to right off," replied Mrs. Andrews.

"Speaking of doctors," went on Columbine, striving to make her query casual, "do you know whether or not Wilson Moore had his foot treated by a doctor at Kremmling?"

"He did not, answered Mrs. Andrews. "Wasn't no doctor there. They'd had to send to Denver, an', as Wils couldn't take that trip or wait so long, why, Mrs. Plummer fixed up his foot. She made a good job of it, too, as I can testify."

"Oh, I'm—very thankful!" murmured Columbine. "He'll not be crippled or—or club-footed, then?"

"I reckon not. You can see for yourself. For Wils's here. He was drove up night before last an' is stayin' with my brother-in-law—in the other cabin there."

Mrs. Andrews launched all this swiftly, with evident pleasure, but with more of woman's subtle motive. Her eyes were bent with shrewd kindness upon the younger woman.

"Here!" exclaimed Columbine, with a start, and for an instant she was at the mercy of conflicting surprise and joy and alarm. Alternately she flushed and paled.

"Sure he's here," replied Mrs. Andrews, now looking out of the door. "He ought to be in sight somewheres. He's walkin' with a crutch."

"Crutch!" cried Columbine, in dismay.

"Yes, crutch, an' he made it himself . . . I don't see him nowheres. Mebbe he went in when he see you comin'. For he's powerful sensitive about that crutch."

"Then—if he's so—so sensitive, perhaps I'd better go," said Columbine, struggling with embarrassment and discomfiture. What if she happened to meet him! Would he imagine her purpose in coming there? Her heart began to beat unwontedly.

"Suit yourself, lass," replied Mrs. Andrews, kindly. "I know you and Wils quarreled, for he told me. An' it's a pity . . . Wal, if you must go, I hope you'll come again before the snow flies. Good-by."

Columbine bade her a hurried good-by and ventured forth with misgivings. And almost around the corner of the second cabin, which she had to pass, and before she had time to recover her composure, she saw Wilson Moore, hobbling along on a crutch, holding a bandaged foot off the ground. He had seen her; he was hurrying to avoid a meeting, or to get behind the corrals there before she observed him.

"Wilson!" she called, involuntarily. The instant the name left her lips she regretted it. But too late! The cowboy halted, slowly turned.

Then Columbine walked swiftly up to him, suddenly as brave as she had been fearful. Sight of him had changed her.

"Wilson Moore, you meant to avoid me," she said, with reproach.

"Howdy, Columbine!" he drawled, ignoring her words.

"Oh, I was so sorry you were hurt!" she burst out. "And now I'm so glad—you're—you're . . . Wilson, you're thin and pale—you've suffered!"

"It pulled me down a bit," he replied.

Columbine had never before seen his face anything except bronzed and lean and healthy, but now it bore testimony to pain and strain and patient endurance. He looked older. Something in the fine, dark, hazel eyes hurt her deeply.

"You never sent me word," she went on, reproachfully. "No one would tell me anything. The boys said they didn't know. Dad was angry when I asked him. I'd never have asked Jack. And the freighter who drove up—he lied to me. So I came down here today purposely to ask news of you, but I never dreamed you were here . . . Now I'm glad I came."

What a singular, darkly kind, yet strange glance he gave her!

"That was like you, Columbine," he said. "I knew you'd feel badly about my accident. But how could I send word to you?"

"You saved—Pronto," she returned, with a strong tremor in her voice. "I can't thank you enough."

"That was a funny thing. Pronto went out of his head. I hope he's all right."

"He's almost well. It took some time to pick all the splinters out of him. He'll be all right soon—none the worse for that—that cowboy trick of Mister Jack Belllounds."

Columbine finished bitterly. Moore turned his thoughtful gaze away from her.

"I hope Old Bill is well," he remarked, lamely.

"Have you told your folks of your accident?" asked Columbine, ignoring his remark.

"No."

"Oh, Wilson, you ought to have sent for them, or have written at least."

"Me? To go crying for them when I got in trouble? I couldn't see it that way."

"Wilson, you'll be going—home—soon—to Denver—won't you?" she faltered.

"No," he replied, shortly.

"But what will you do? Surely you can't work—not so soon?"

"Columbine, I'll never—be able to ride again—like I used to," he said, tragically. "I'll ride, yes, but never the old way."

"Oh!" Columbine's tone, and the exquisite softness and tenderness with which she placed a hand on the rude crutch would have been enlightening to anyone but these two absorbed in themselves. "I can't bear to believe that."

"I'm afraid it's true. Bad smash, Columbine! I just missed being club-footed."

"You should have care. You should have . . . Wilson, do you intend to stay here with the Andrews?"

"Not much. They have troubles of their own. Columbine, I'm going to homestead one hundred and sixty acres."

"Homestead!" she exclaimed, in amaze. "Where?"

"Up there under Old White Slides. I've long intended to. You know that pretty little valley under the red bluff. There's a fine spring. You've been there with me. There by the old cabin built by prospectors?"

"Yes, I know. It's a pretty place—fine valley, but Wils, you can't *live* there," she expostulated.

"Why not, I'd like to know?"

"That little cubby-hole! It's only a tiny one-room cabin, roof all gone, chinks open, chimney crumbling . . . Wilson, you don't mean to tell me you want to live there alone?"

"Sure. What'd you think?" he replied, with sarcasm. "Expect me to *marry* some girl? Well, I wouldn't, even if anyone would have a cripple."

"Who—who will take care of you?" she asked, blushing furiously.

"I'll take care of myself," he declared. "Good Lord! Columbine, I'm not an invalid yet. I've got a few friends who'll help me fix up the cabin. And that reminds me. There's a lot of my stuff up in the bunkhouse at White Slides. I'm going to drive up soon to haul it away."

"Wilson Moore, do you mean it?" she asked, with grave wonder. "Are you going to homestead near White Slides Ranch—and *live* there—when—"

She could not finish. An overwhelming disaster, for which she had no name, seemed to be impending.

"Yes, I am," he replied. "Funny how things turn out, isn't it?"

"It's very—very funny," she said, dazedly, and she turned slowly away without another word.

"Good-by, Columbine," he called out after her, with farewell, indeed, in his voice.

All the way home Columbine was occupied with feelings that swayed her to the exclusion of rational consideration of the increasing perplexity of her situation. And to make matters worse, when she arrived at the ranch it was to meet Jack Belllounds with a face as black as a thundercloud.

"The old man wants to see you," he announced, with an accent that recalled his threat of a few hours back.

"Does he?" queried Columbine, loftily. "From the courteous way you speak I imagine it's important."

Belllounds did not deign to reply to this. He sat on the porch, where evidently he had awaited her return, and he looked anything but happy.

"Where is dad?" continued Columbine.

Jack motioned toward the second door, beyond which he sat, the one that opened into the room the rancher used as a kind of office and storeroom. As Columbine walked by Jack he grasped her skirt.

"Columbine! You're angry?" he said, appealingly.

"I reckon I am," replied Columbine.

"Don't go in to dad when you're that way," implored Jack. "He's angry, too—and—and—it'll only make matters worse."

From long experience Columbine could divine when Jack had done something in the interest of self and then had awakened to possible consequences. She pulled away from him without replying, and knocked on the office door.

"Come in," called the rancher.

Columbine went in. "Hello, dad! Do you want me?"

Belllounds sat at an old table, bending over a soiled ledger, with a stubby pencil in his huge hand. When he looked up Columbine gave a little start.

"Where've you been?" he asked, gruffly.

"I've been calling on Mrs. Andrews," replied Columbine.

"Did you go thar to see her?"

"Why—certainly!" answered Columbine, with a slow break in her speech.

"You didn't go to meet Wilson Moore?"

"No."

"An' I reckon you'll say you hadn't heerd he was there?"

"I had not," flashed Columbine.

"Wal, *did* you see him?"

"Yes, sir, I did, but quite by accident."

"Ahuh! Columbine, are you lyin' to me?"

The hot blood flooded to Columbine's cheeks, as if she had been struck a blow.

*"Dad!"* she cried, in hurt amaze.

Belllounds seemed thick, imponderable, as if something had forced a crisis in him and his brain was deeply involved. The habitual, cool, easy, bold, and frank attitude in the meeting of all situations seemed to have been encroached upon by a break, a bewilderment, a lessening of confidence.

"Wal, are you lyin'?" he repeated, either blind to or unaware of her distress.

"I could not—lie to you," she faltered, "even—if—I wanted to."

The heavy, shadowed gaze of his big eyes was bent upon her as if she had become a new and perplexing problem.

"But you seen Moore?"

"Yes—sir." Columbine's spirit rose.

"An' talked with him?"

"Of course."

"Lass, I ain't likin' thet, an' I ain't likin' the way you look an' speak."

"I am sorry. I can't help either."

"What'd this cowboy say to you?"

"We talked mostly about his injured foot."

"An' what else?" went on Belllounds, his voice rising.

"About—what he meant to do now."

"Ahuh! An' thet's homesteadin' the Sage Creek Valley?"

"Yes, sir."

"Did you want him to do thet?"

"I! Indeed I didn't."

"Columbine, not so long ago you told me this fellar wasn't sweet on you. An' do you still say that to me—are you still insistin' he ain't in love with you?"

"He never said so—I never believed it . . . and now I'm sure—he isn't!"

"Ahuh! Wal, thet same day you was jest as sure you didn't care anythin' particular fer him. Are you thet sure now?"

"No!" whispered Columbine, very low. She trembled with a suggestion of unknown forces. Not to save a new and growing pride would she evade any question from this man upon whom she had no claim, to whom she owed her life and her bringing up. But something cold formed in her.

Belllounds, self-centered and serious as he strangely was, seemed to check his probing, either from fear of hearing more from her or from an awakening of former kindness. But her reply was a shock to him, and, throwing down his pencil with the gesture of a man upon whom decision was forced, he rose to tower over her.

"You've been like a daughter to me. I've done all I knowed how fer you. I've lived up to the best of my lights. An' I've loved you," he said, sonorously and pathetically. "You know what my hopes are—fer the boy—an' fer you . . . We needn't waste any more talk. From this minnit you're free to do as you like. Whatever you do won't make any change in my carin' fer you . . . But you gotta decide. Will you marry Jack or not?"

"I promised you—I would. I'll keep my word," replied Columbine, steadily.

"So far so good," went on the rancher. "I'm respectin' you fer what you say . . . An' now, *when* will you marry him?"

The little room drifted around in Columbine's vague, blank sight. All seemed to be drifting. She had no solid anchor.

"Any—day you say—the sooner the—better," she whispered.

"Wal, lass, I'm thankin' you," he replied, with voice that sounded afar to her. "An' I swear, if I didn't believe it's best fer Jack an' you, why I'd never let you marry . . . So we'll set the day. October first! Thet's the day you was fetched to me a baby—more'n seventeen years ago."

"October—first—then, dad," she said, brokenly, and she kissed him as if in token of what she knew she owed him. Then she went out, closing the door behind her.

Jack, upon seeing her, hastily got up, with more than concern in his pale face.

"Columbine!" he cried, hoarsely. "How you look! . . . Tell me. What happened? Girl, don't tell me you've—you've—"

"Jack Belllounds," interrupted Columbine, in tragic amaze at this truth about to issue from her lips, "I've promised to marry you—on October first."

He let out a shout of boyish exultation and suddenly clasped her in his arms. But there was nothing boyish in the way he handled her, in the almost savage evidence of possession. "Collie, I'm mad about you," he began, ardently. "You never let me tell you. And I've grown worse and worse. Today I—when I saw you going down there—where that Wilson Moore is—I got terribly jealous. I was sick. I'd been glad to kill him! . . . It made me see how I loved you. Oh, I didn't know. But now . . . Oh, I'm mad for you!" He crushed her to him, unmindful of her struggles; his face and neck were red; his eyes on fire. And he began trying to kiss her mouth, but failed, as she struggled desperately. His kisses fell upon cheek and ear and hair.

"Let me—go!" panted Columbine. "You've no—no—oh, you might have waited." Breaking from him, she fled, and got inside her room with the door almost closed, when his foot intercepted it.

Belllounds was half laughing his exultation, half furious at her escape, and altogether beside himself.

"No," she replied, so violently that it appeared to awake him to the fact that there was someone besides himself to consider.

"Aw!" He heaved a deep sigh. "All right. I won't try to get in. Only listen . . . Collie, don't mind my—my way of showing you how I felt. Fact is, I went plumb off my head. Is that any wonder, you—you darling—when I've been so scared you'd never have me? Collie, I've felt that you were the one thing in the world I wanted most and would never get. But now . . . October first! Listen. I promise you I'll not drink any more—nor gamble—nor nag dad for money. I don't like his way of running the ranch, but I'll do it, as long as he lives. I'll even try to tolerate that club-footed cowboy's brass in homesteading a ranch right under my nose. I'll—I'll do anything you ask of me."

"Then—please—go away!" cried Columbine, with a sob.

When he was gone Columbine barred the door and threw herself upon her bed to shut out the light and to give vent to her surcharged emotions. She wept like a girl whose youth was ending; and after the paroxysm had passed, leaving her weak and strangely changed, she tried to reason out what had happened to her. Over and over again she named the appeal of the rancher, the sense of her duty, the decision she had reached, and the disgust and terror inspired in her by Jack Belllounds's reception of her promise. These were facts of the day and they had made of her a palpitating, unhappy creature, who nevertheless had been brave to face the rancher and confess that which she had scarce confessed to herself. But now she trembled and cringed on the verge of a catastrophe that withheld its whole truth.

"I begin to see now," she whispered, after the thought had come and gone and returned to change again. "If Wilson had—cared for me I—I might have—cared, too . . . But I do—care—something. I couldn't lie to dad. Only I'm not sure—how much. I never dreamed of—of *loving* him, or anyone. It's so strange. All at once I feel old. And I can't understand these—these feelings that shake me."

So Columbine brooded over the trouble that had come to her, never regretting her promise to the old rancher, but growing keener in the realization of a complexity in her nature that sooner or later would separate the life of her duty from the life of her desire. She seemed all alone, and when this feeling possessed her a strange reminder of the hunter Wade flashed up. She stifled another impulse to confide in him. Wade had the softness of a woman, and his face was a record of the trials and travails through which he had come unhardened, unembittered. Yet how could she tell her troubles to him? A stranger, a rough man of the wilds, whose name had preceded him, notorious and deadly, with that vital tang of the West in its meaning! Nevertheless, Wade drew her, and she thought of him until the recurring memory of Jack Belllounds's rude clasp again crept over her with an augmenting disgust and fear. Must she submit to that? Had she promised that? And then Columbine felt the dawning of realities.

## CHAPTER VII

Columbine was awakened in the gray dawn by the barking of coyotes. She dreaded the daylight thus heralded. Never before in her life had she hated the rising of the sun. Resolutely she put the past behind her and faced the future, believing now that with the great decision made she needed only to keep her mind off what might have been, and to attend to her duty.

At breakfast she found the rancher in better spirits than he had been for weeks. He informed her that Jack had ridden off early for Kremmling, there to make arrangements for the wedding on October first.

"Jack's out of his head," said Belllounds. "Wal, thet comes only onct in a man's life. I remember . . . Jack's goin' to drive you to Kremmlin' an' ther take stage fer Denver. I allow you'd better put in your best licks on fixin' up an' packin' the clothes you'll need. Women-folk naturally want to look smart on weddin'-trips."

"Dad!" exclaimed Columbine, in dismay. "I never thought of clothes. And I don't want to leave White Slides."

"But, lass, you're goin' to be married!" expostulated Belllounds.

"Didn't it occur to Jack to take me to Kremmling? I can't make new dresses out of old ones."

"Wal, I reckon neither of us thought of thet. But you can buy what you like in Denver."

Columbine resigned herself. After all, what did it matter to her? The vague, haunting dreams of girlhood would never come true. So she went to her wardrobe and laid out all her wearing apparel. Taking stock of it this way caused her further dismay, for she had nothing fit to wear in which either to be married or to take a trip to Denver. There appeared to be nothing to do but take the rancher's advice, and Columbine set about refurbishing her meager wardrobe. She sewed all day.

What with self-control and work and the passing of hours, Columbine began to make some approach to tranquility. In her simplicity she even began to hope that being good and steadfast and dutiful would earn her a little meed of happiness. Some haunting doubt of this flashed over her mind like a swift shadow of a black wing, but she dispelled that as she had dispelled the fear and disgust which often rose up in her mind.

To Columbine's surprise and to the rancher's concern the prospective bridegroom did not return from Kremmling on the second day. When night came Belllounds reluctantly gave up looking for him.

Jack's non-appearance suited Columbine, and she would have been glad to be let alone until October first, which date now seemed appallingly close. On the afternoon of Jack's third day of absence from the ranch Columbine rode out for some needed exercise. Pronto not being available, she rode another mustang and one that kept her busy. On the way back to the ranch she avoided the customary trail which led by the cabins of Wade and the cowboys. Columbine had not seen one of her friends since the unfortunate visit to the Andrews ranch. She particularly shrank from meeting Wade, which feeling was in strange contrast to her former impulses.

As she rode around the house she encountered Wilson Moore seated in a light wagon. Her mustang reared, almost unseating her. But she handled him roughly, being suddenly surprised and angry at this unexpected meeting with the cowboy.

"Howdy, Columbine!" greeted Wilson, as she brought the mustang to his feet. "You're sure learning to handle a horse—since I left this here ranch. Wonder who's teaching you! I never could get you to rake even a bronc!"

The cowboy had drawled out his admiring speech, half amused and half satiric.

"I'm—mad!" declared Columbine. "That's why."

"What're you mad at?" queried Wilson.

She did not reply, but kept on gazing steadily at him. Moore still looked pale and drawn, but he had improved since last she saw him.

"Aren't you going to speak to a fellow?" he went on.

"How are you, Wils?" she asked.

"Pretty good for a club-footed has-been cowpuncher."

"I wish you wouldn't call yourself such names," rejoined Columbine, peevishly. "You're not a club-foot. I hate that word!"

"Me, too. Well, joking aside, I'm better. My foot is fine. Now, if I don't hurt it again I'll sure never be a club-foot."

"You must be careful," she said, earnestly.

"Sure. But it's hard for me to be idle. Think of me lying still all day with nothing to do but read! That's what knocked me out. I wouldn't have minded the pain if I could have gotten about . . . Columbine, I've moved in!"

"What! Moved in?" she queried, blankly.

"Sure. I'm in my cabin on the hill. It's plumb great. Tom Andrews and Bert and your hunter Wade fixed up the cabin for me. That Wade is sure a good fellow. And say! What he can do with his hands! He's been kind to me. Took an interest in me, and between you and me he sort of cheered me up."

"Cheered you up! Wils, were you unhappy?" she asked, directly.

"Well, rather. What'd you expect of a cowboy who'd crippled himself—and lost his girl?"

Columbine felt the smart of tingling blood in her face, and she looked from Wilson to the wagon. It contained saddles, blankets, and other cowboy accoutrements for which he had evidently come.

"That's a double misfortune," she replied, evenly. "It's too bad both came at once. It seems to me if I were a cowboy and—and felt so toward a girl, I'd have let her know."

"This girl I mean knew, all right," he said, nodding his head.

"She didn't—she didn't!" cried Columbine.

"How do you know?" he queried, with feigned surprise. He was bent upon torturing her.

"You meant me. I'm the girl you lost!"

"Yes, you are—God help me!" replied Moore, with genuine emotion.

"But you—you never told me—you never told me," faltered Columbine, in distress.

"Never told you what? That you were my girl?"

"No—no. But that you—you cared—"

"Columbine Bellounds, I told you—let you see—in every way under the sun," he flashed at her.

"Let me see—what?" faltered Columbine, feeling as if the world were about to end.

"That I loved you."

"Oh! . . . Wilson!" whispered Columbine, wildly.

"Yes—loved you. Could you have been so innocent—so blind you never knew? I can't believe it."

"But I never dreamed you—you—" She broke off dazedly, overwhelmed by a tragic, glorious truth.

"Collie! . . . Would it have made any difference?"

"Oh, all the difference in the world!" she wailed.

"What difference?" he asked, passionately.

Columbine gazed wide-eyed and helpless at the young man. She did not know how to tell him what all the difference in the world really was.

Suddenly Wilson turned away from her to listen. Then she heard rapid beating of hoofs on the road.

"That's Buster Jack," said the cowboy. "Just my luck! There wasn't anyone here when I arrived. Reckon I oughtn't have stayed. Columbine, you look pretty much upset."

"What do I care how I look!" she exclaimed, with a sharp resentment attending this abrupt and painful break in her agitation.

Next moment Jack Belllounds galloped a foam-lashed horse into the courtyard and hauled up short with a recklessness he was noted for. He swung down hard and violently cast the reins from him.

"Ahuh! I gambled on just this," he declared, harshly.

Columbine's heart sank. His gaze was fixed on her face, with its telltale evidences of agitation.

"What've you been crying about?" he demanded.

"I haven't been," she retorted.

His bold and glaring eyes, hot with sudden temper, passed slowly from her to the cowboy. Columbine became aware then that Jack was under the influence of liquor. His heated red face grew darker with a sneering contempt.

"Where's dad?" he asked, wheeling toward her.

"I don't know. He's not here," replied Columbine, dismounting. The leap of thought and blood to Jack's face gave her a further sinking of the heart. The situation unnerved her.

Wilson Moore had grown a shade paler. He gathered up his reins, ready to drive off.

"Belllounds, I came up after my things I'd left in the bunk," he said, coolly. "Happened to meet Columbine and stopped to chat a minute."

"That's what *you* say," sneered Belllounds. "You were making love to Columbine. I saw that in her face. You know it—and she knows it—and I know it You're a liar!"

"Belllounds, I reckon I am," replied Moore, turning white. "I did tell Columbine what I thought she knew—what I ought to have told long ago."

"Ahuh! Well, I don't want to hear it. But I'm going to search that wagon."

"What!" ejaculated the cowboy, dropping his reins as if they stung him.

"You just hold on till I see what you've got in there," went on Belllounds, and he reached over into the wagon and pulled at a saddle.

"Say, do you mean anything? . . . This stuff's mine, every strap of it. Take your hands off."

Belllounds leaned on the wagon and looked up with insolent, dark intent.

"Moore, I wouldn't trust you. I think you'd steal anything you got your hands on."

Columbine uttered a passionate little cry of shame and protest.

"Jack, how dare you!"

"You shut up! Go in the house!" he ordered.

"You insult me," she replied, in bitter humiliation.

"Will you go in?" he shouted.

"No, I won't."

"All right, look on, then. I'd just as lief have you." Then he turned to the cowboy. "Moore, show up that wagon-load of stuff unless you want me to throw it out in the road."

"Belllounds, you know I can't do that," replied Moore, coldly. "And I'll give you a hunch. You'd better shut up yourself and let me drive on . . . If not for her sake, then for your own."

Belllounds grasped the reins, and with a sudden jerk pulled them out of the cowboy's hands.

"You damn club-foot! Your gift of gab doesn't go with me," yelled Belllounds, as he swung up on the hub of the wheel. But it was manifest that his desire to search the wagon was only a pretense, for while he pulled at this and that his evil gaze was on the cowboy, keen to meet any move that might give excuse for violence. Moore evidently read this, for, gazing at Columbine, he shook his head, as if to acquaint her with a situation impossible to help.

"Columbine, please hand me up the reins," he said. "I'm lame, you know. Then I'll be going."

Columbine stepped forward to comply, when Belllounds, leaping down from the wheel, pushed her back with masterful hand. Opposition to him was like waving a red flag in the face of a bull. Columbine recoiled from his look as well as touch.

"You keep out of this or I'll teach you who's boss here," he said, stridently.

"You're going too far!" burst out Columbine.

Meanwhile Wilson had laboriously climbed down out of the wagon, and, utilizing his crutch, he hobbled to where Belllounds had thrown the reins, and stooped to pick them up. Belllounds shoved Columbine farther back, and then he leaped to confront the cowboy.

"I've got you now, Moore," he said, hoarse and low. Stripped of all pretense, he showed the ungovernable nature of his temper. His face grew corded and black. The hand he thrust out shook like a leaf. "You smooth-tongued liar! I'm on to your game. I know you'd put her against me. I know you'd try to win her—less than a week before her wedding-day . . . But it's not for that I'm going to beat hell out of you! It's because I hate you! Ever since I can remember my father held you up to me! And he sent me to—to—he sent me away because of you. By God! that's why I hate you!"

All that was primitive and violent and base came out with strange frankness in Belllounds's tirade. Only when calm could his mind be capable of hidden calculation. The devil that was in him now seemed rampant.

"Belllounds, you're mighty brave to stack up this way against a one-legged man," declared the cowboy, with biting sarcasm.

"If you had two club-feet I'd only be the gladder," yelled Belllounds, and swinging his arm, he slapped Moore so that it nearly toppled him over. Only the injured foot, coming down hard, saved him.

When Columbine saw that, and then how Wilson winced and grew deathly pale, she uttered a low cry, and she seemed suddenly rooted to the spot, weak, terrified at what was now inevitable, and growing sick and cold and faint.

"It's a damn lucky thing for you I'm not packing a gun," said Moore, grimly. "But you knew—or you'd never hit me—you coward."

"I'll make you swallow that," snarled Belllounds, and this time he swung his fist, aiming a heavy blow at Moore.

Then the cowboy whirled aloft the heavy crutch. "If you hit at me again I'll let out what little brains you've got. God knows that's little enough! . . . Belllounds, I'm going to call you to your face—before this girl your bat-eyed old man means to give you. You're not drunk. You're only ugly—mean. You've got a chance now to lick me because I'm crippled. And you're going to make the most of it. Why, you cur, I could come near licking you with only one leg. But if you touch me again I'll brain you! . . . You never were any good. You're no good now. You never will be anything but Buster Jack—half dotty, selfish as hell, bull-headed and mean! . . . And that's the last word I'll ever waste on you."

"I'll kill you!" bawled Belllounds, black with fury.

Moore wielded the crutch menacingly, but as he was not steady on his feet he was at the disadvantage his adversary had calculated upon. Belllounds ran around the cowboy, and suddenly plunged in to grapple with him. The crutch descended, but to little purpose. Belllounds's heavy onslaught threw Moore to the ground. Before he could rise Belllounds pounced upon him.

Columbine saw all this dazedly. As Wilson fell she closed her eyes, fighting a faintness that almost overcame her. She heard wrestling, threshing sounds, and sodden thumps, and a scattering of gravel. These noises seemed at first distant, then grew closer. As she gazed again with keener perception, Moore's horse plunged away from the fiercely struggling forms that had rolled almost under his feet. During the ensuing moments it was an equal battle so far as Columbine could tell. Repelled, yet fascinated, she watched. They beat each other, grappled and rolled over, first one on top, then the other. But the advantage of being uppermost presently was Belllounds's. Moore was weakening. That became noticeable more and more after each time he had wrestled and rolled about. Then Belllounds, getting this position, lay with his weight upon Moore, holding him down, and at the same time kicking with all his might. He was aiming to disable the cowboy by kicking the injured foot. And he was succeeding. Moore let out a strangled cry, and struggled desperately. But he was held and weighted down. Belllounds raised up now and, looking backward, he deliberately and furiously kicked Moore's bandaged foot; once, twice, again and again, until the straining form under him grew limp. Columbine, slowly freezing with horror, saw all this. She could not move. She could not scream. She wanted to rush in and drag Jack off of Wilson, to hurt him, to kill him, but her muscles were paralyzed. In her agony she could not even look away. Belllounds got up astride his prostrate adversary and began to beat him brutally, swinging heavy, sodden blows. His face then was terrible to see. He meant murder.

Columbine heard approaching voices and the thumping of hasty feet. That unclamped her cloven tongue. Wildly she screamed. Old Bill Belllounds appeared, striding off the porch. And the hunter Wade came running down the path.

"Dad! He's killing Wilson!" cried Columbine.

"Hyar, you devil!" roared the rancher.

Jack Belllounds got up. Panting, disheveled, with hair ruffled and face distorted, he was not a pleasant sight for even the father. Moore lay unconscious, with ghastly, bloody features, and his bandaged foot showed great splotches of red.

"My Gawd, son!" gasped Old Bill. "You didn't pick on this hyar crippled boy?"

The evidence was plain, in Moore's quiet, pathetic form, in the panting, purple-faced son. Jack Belllounds did not answer. He was in the grip of a passion that had at last been wholly unleashed and was still unsatisfied. Yet a malignant and exultant gratification showed in his face.

"That—evens us—up, Moore," he panted, and stalked away.

By this time Wade reached the cowboy and knelt beside him. Columbine came running to fall on her knees. The old rancher seemed stricken.

"Oh—oh! It was terrible—" cried Columbine. "Oh—he's so white—and the blood—"

"Now, lass, that's no way for a woman," said Wade, and there was something in his kind tone, in his look, in his presence, that calmed Columbine. "I'll look after Moore. You go get some water an' a towel."           —

Columbine rose to totter into the house. She saw a red stain on the hand she had laid upon the cowboy's face, and with a strange, hot, bursting sensation, strong and thrilling, she put that red place to her lips. Running out with the things required by Wade, she was in time to hear the rancher say, "Looks hurt bad, to me."

"Yes, I reckon," replied Wade.

While Columbine held Moore's head upon her lap the hunter bathed the bloody face. It was battered and bruised and cut, and in some places, as fast as Wade washed away the red, it welled out again.

Columbine watched that quiet face, while her heart throbbed and swelled with emotions wholly beyond her control and understanding. When at last Wilson opened his eyes, fluttering at first, and then wide, she felt a surge that shook her whole body. He smiled wanly at her, and at Wade, and then his gaze lifted to Belllounds.

"I guess—he licked me," he said, in weak voice. "He kept kicking my sore foot—till I fainted. But he licked me—all right."

"Wils, mebbe he did lick you," replied the old rancher, brokenly, "but I reckon he's damn little to be proud of—lickin' a crippled man—thet way."

"Boss, Jack'd been drinking," said Moore, weakly. "And he sure had—some excuse for going off his head. He caught me—talking sweet to Columbine . . . and then—I called him all the names—I could lay my tongue to."

"Ahuh!" The old man seemed at a loss for words, and presently he turned away, sagging in the shoulders, and plodded into the house.

The cowboy, supported by Wade on one side, with Columbine on the other, was helped to an upright position, and with considerable difficulty was gotten into the wagon. He tried to sit up, but made a sorry showing of it.

"I'll drive him home an' look after him," said Wade. "Now, Miss Collie, you're upset, which ain't no wonder. But now you brace. It might have been worse. Just you go to your room till you're sure of yourself again."

Moore smiled another wan smile at her. "I'm sorry," he said.

"What for? Me?" she asked.

"I mean I'm sorry I was so infernal unlucky—running into you—and bringing all this distress—to you. It was my fault. If I'd only kept—my mouth shut!"

"You need not be sorry you met me," she said, with her eyes straight upon his. "I'm glad . . . But oh! If your foot is badly hurt I'll never—never—"

"Don't say it," interrupted Wilson.

"Lass, you're bent on doin' somethin'," said Wade, in his gentle voice.

"Bent?" she echoed, with something deep and rich in her voice. "Yes, I'm bent—*bent* like your name—to speak my mind!"

Then she ran toward the house and up on the porch, to enter the living room with heaving breast and flashing eyes. Manifestly the rancher was berating his son. The former gaped at sight of her and the latter shrank.

"Jack Belllounds," she cried, "you're not half a man . . . You're a coward and a brute!"

One tense moment she stood there, lightning scorn and passion in her gaze, and then she rushed out, impetuously, as she had come.

## CHAPTER VIII

Columbine did not leave her room anymore that day. What she suffered there she did not want anyone to know. What it cost her to conquer herself again she had only a faint conception of. She did conquer, however, and that night made up the sleep she had lost the night before.

Strangely enough, she did not feel afraid to face the rancher and his son. Recent happenings had not only changed her, but had seemed to give her strength. When she presented herself at the breakfast-table Jack was absent. The old rancher greeted her with more than usual solicitude.

"Jack's sick," he remarked, presently.

"Indeed," replied Columbine.

"Yes. He said it was the drinkin' he's not accustomed to. Wal, I reckon it was what you called him. He didn't take much store on what I called him, which was wuss . . . I tell you, lass, Jack's set his heart so hard on you thet it's turrible."

"Queer way he has of showing the—the affections of his heart," replied Columbine, shortly.

"Thet was the drink," remonstrated the old man, pathetic and earnest in his motive to smooth over the quarrel.

"But he promised me he would not drink anymore."

Belllounds shook his gray old head sadly.

"Ahuh! Jack fires up an' promises anythin'. He means it at the time. But the next hankerin' thet comes over him wipes out the promise. I know . . . But he's had good excuse fer this break. The boys in town began celebratin' fer October first. Great wonder Jack didn't come home clean drunk."

"Dad, you're as good as gold," said Columbine, softening. How could she feel hard toward him?

"Collie, then you're not agoin' back on the ole man?"

"No."

"I was afeared you'd change your mind about marryin' Jack."

"When I promised I meant it. I didn't make it on conditions."

"But, lass, promises can be broke," he said, with the sonorous roll in his voice.

"I never yet broke one of mine."

"Wal, I hev. Not often, mebbe, but I hev . . . An', lass, it's reasonable. Thar's times when a man jest can't live up to what he swore by. An' fer a girl—why, I can see how easy she'd change an' grow overnight. It's only fair fer me to say that no matter what you think you owe me you couldn't be blamed now fer dislikin' Jack."

"Dad, if by marrying Jack I can help him to be a better son to you, and more of a man, I'll be glad," she replied.

"Lass, I'm beginnin' to see how big an' fine you are," replied Belllounds, with strong feeling. "An' it's worryin' me . . . My neighbors hev always accused me of seein' only my son. Only Buster Jack! I was blind an' deaf as to him! . . . Wal, I'm not so damn blind as I used to be. The scales are droppin' off my ole eyes . . . But I've got one hope left as far as Jack's concerned. Thet's marryin' him to you. An' I'm stickin' to it."

"So will I stick to it, dad," she replied. "I'll go through with October first!"

Columbine broke off, vouchsafing no more, and soon left the breakfast table, to take up the work she had laid out to do. And she accomplished it, though many times her hands dropped idle and her eyes peered out of her window at the drab slides of the old mountain.

Later, when she went out to ride, she saw the cowboy Lem working in the blacksmith shop.

"Wal, Miss Collie, air you-all still hangin' round this hyar ranch?" he asked, with welcoming smile.

"Lem, I'm almost ashamed now to face my good friends, I've neglected them so long," she replied.

"Aw, now, what're friends fer but to go to? . . . You're lookin' pale, I reckon. More like thet thar flower I see so much on the hills."

"Lem, I want to ride Pronto. Do you think he's all right, now?"

"I reckon some movin' round will do Pronto good. He's eatin' his haid off."

The cowboy went with her to the pasture gate and whistled Pronto up. The mustang came trotting, evidently none the worse for his injuries, and eager to resume the old climbs with his mistress. Lem saddled him, paying particular attention to the cinch.

"Reckon we'd better not cinch him tight," said Lem. "You jest be careful an' remember your saddle's loose."

"All right, Lem," replied Columbine, as she mounted. "Where are the boys this morning?"

"Blud an' Jim air repairin' fence up the crick."

"And where's Ben?"

"Ben? Oh, you mean Wade. Wal, I 'ain't seen him since yestidday. He was skinnin' a lion then, over hyar on the ridge. Thet was in the mawnin'. I reckon he's around, fer I seen some of the hounds."

"Then, Lem—you haven't heard about the fight yesterday between Jack and Wilson Moore?"

Lem straightened up quickly. "Nope, I 'ain't heerd a word."

"Well, they fought, all right," said Columbine, hurriedly. "I saw it. I was the only one there. Wilson was badly used up before dad and Ben got there. Ben drove off with him."

"But, Miss Collie, how'd it come off? I seen Wils the other day. Was up to his homestead. An' the boy jest manages to rustle round on a crutch. He couldn't fight."

"That was just it. Jack saw his opportunity, and he forced Wilson to fight— accused him of stealing. Wils tried to avoid trouble. Then Jack jumped him.

Wilson fought and held his own until Jack began to kick his injured foot. Then Wilson fainted and—and Jack beat him."

Lem dropped his head, evidently to hide his expression. "Wal, dog-gone me!" he ejaculated. "Thet's too bad."

Columbine left the cowboy and rode up the lane toward Wade's cabin. She did not analyze her deliberate desire to tell the truth about that fight, but she would have liked to proclaim it to the whole range and to the world. Once clear of the house she felt free, unburdened, and to talk seemed to relieve some congestion of her thoughts.

The hounds heralded Columbine's approach with a deep and booming chorus. Sampson and Jim lay upon the porch, unleashed. The other hounds were chained separately in the aspen grove a few rods distant. Sampson thumped the boards with his big tail, but he did not get up, which laziness attested to the fact that there had been a lion chase the day before and he was weary and stiff. If Wade had been at home he would have come out to see what had occasioned the clamor. As Columbine rode by she saw another fresh lion-pelt pegged upon the wall of the cabin.

She followed the brook. It had cleared since the rains and was shining and sparkling in the rough, swift places, and limpid and green in the eddies. She passed the dam made by the solitary beaver that inhabited the valley. Freshly cut willows showed how the beaver was preparing for the long winter ahead. Columbine remembered then how greatly pleased Wade had been to learn about this old beaver; and more than once Wade had talked about trapping some younger beavers and bringing them there to make company for the old fellow.

The trail led across the brook at a wide, shallow place, where the splashing made by Pronto sent the trout scurrying for deeper water. Columbine kept to that trail, knowing that it led up into Sage Valley, where Wilson Moore had taken up the homestead property. Fresh horse tracks told her that Wade had ridden along there some time earlier. Pronto shied at the whirring of sage hens. Presently Columbine ascertained they were flushed by the hound Kane, that had broken loose and followed her. He had done so before, and the fact had not displeased her.

"Kane! Kane! Come here!" she called. He came readily, but halted a rod or so away, and made an attempt at wagging his tail, a function evidently somewhat difficult for him. When she resumed trotting he followed her.

Old White Slides had lost all but the drabs and dull yellows and greens, and of course those pale, light slopes that had given the mountain its name. Sage Valley was only one of the valleys at its base. It opened out half a mile wide, dominated by the looming peak, and bordered on the far side by an aspen-thicketed slope. The brook babbled along under the edge of this thicket.

Cattle and horses grazed here and there on the rich, grassy levels, Columbine was surprised to see so many cattle and wondered to whom they belonged. All of Belllounds's stock had been driven lower down for the winter. There among the several horses that whistled at her approach she espied the white mustang Belllounds had given to Moore. It thrilled her to see him. And next, she suffered a pang to think that perhaps his owner might never ride him again. But Columbine held her emotions in abeyance.

The cabin stood high upon a level terrace, with clusters of aspens behind it, and was sheltered from winter blasts by a gray cliff, picturesque and crumbling, with its face overgrown by creeping vines and colorful shrubs, Wilson Moore could not have chosen a more secluded and beautiful valley for his homesteading adventure. The little gray cabin, with smoke curling from the stone chimney, had lost its look of dilapidation and disuse, yet there was nothing new that Columbine could see. The last quarter of the ascent of the slope, and the few rods across the level terrace, seemed extraordinarily long to Columbine. As she dismounted and tied Pronto her heart was beating and her breath was coming fast.

The door of the cabin was open. Kane trotted past the hesitating Columbine and went in.

"You son-of-a-hound-dog!" came to Columbine's listening ears in Wade's well-known voice. "I'll have to beat you—sure as you're born."

"I heard a horse," came in a lower voice, that was Wilson's.

"Darn me if I'm not gettin' deafer every day," was the reply.

Then Wade appeared in the doorway.

"It's nobody but Miss Collie," he announced, as he made way for her to enter.

"Good morning!" said Columbine, in a voice that had more than cheerfulness in it.

"*Collie!* . . . Did you come to see me?"

She heard this incredulous query just an instant before she saw Wilson at the far end of the room, lying under the light of a window. The inside of the cabin seemed vague and unfamiliar.

"I surely did," she replied, advancing. "How are you?"

"Oh, I'm all right. Tickled to death, right now. Only, I hate to have you see this battered mug of mine."

"You needn't—care," said Columbine, unsteadily. And indeed, in that first glance she did not see him clearly. A mist blurred her sight and there was a lump in her throat. Then, to recover herself, she looked around the cabin.

"Well—Wils Moore—if this isn't fine!" she ejaculated, in amaze and delight. Columbine sustained an absolute surprise. A magic hand had transformed the interior of that rude old prospector's abode. A carpenter and a mason and a decorator had been wonderfully at work. From one end to the other Columbine gazed; from the big window under which Wilson lay on a blanketed couch to the open fireplace where Wade grinned she looked and looked, and then up to the clean, aspen-poled roof and down to the floor, carpeted with deer hides. The chinks between the logs of the walls were plastered with red clay; the dust and dirt were gone; the place smelled like sage and wood-smoke and fragrant, frying meat. Indeed, there were a glowing bed of embers and a steaming kettle and a smoking pot; and the way the smoke and steam curled up into the gray old chimney attested to its splendid draught. In each corner hung a deer-head, from the antlers of which depended accoutrements of a cowboy—spurs, ropes, belts, scarfs, guns. One corner contained cupboard, ceiling high, with new, clean doors of wood, neatly made; and next to it stood a table, just as new. On the blank wall beyond that were pegs holding saddles, bridles, blankets, clothes.

"He did it—all this inside," burst out Moore, delighted with her delight. "Quicker than a flash! Collie, isn't this great? I don't mind being down on my back. And he says they call him Hell-Bent Wade. I call him Heaven-Sent Wade!"

When Columbine turned to the hunter, bursting with her pleasure and gratitude, he suddenly dropped the forked stick he used as a lift, and she saw his hand shake when he stooped to recover it. How strangely that struck her!

"Ben, it's perfectly possible that you've been sent by Heaven," she remarked, with a humor which still held gravity in it.

"Me! A good angel? That'd be a new job for Bent Wade," he replied, with a queer laugh. "But I reckon I'd try to live up to it."

There were small sprigs of golden aspen leaves and crimson oak leaves on the wall above the foot of Wilson's bed. Beneath them, on pegs, hung a rifle. And on the windowsill stood a glass jar containing columbines. They were fresh. They had just been picked. They waved gently in the breeze, sweetly white and blue, strangely significant to the girl.

Moore laughed defiantly.

"Wade thought to fetch these flowers in," he explained. "They're his favorites as well as mine. It won't be long now till the frost kills them . . . and I want to be happy while I may!"

Again Columbine felt that deep surge within her, beyond her control, beyond her understanding, but now gathering and swelling, soon to be reckoned with. She did not look at Wilson's face then. Her downcast gaze saw that his right hand was bandaged, and she touched it with an unconscious tenderness.

"Your hand! Why is it all wrapped up?"

The cowboy laughed with grim humor.

"Have you seen Jack this morning?"

"No," she replied, shortly.

"Well, if you had, you'd know what happened to my fist."

"Did you hurt it on him?" she asked, with a queer little shudder that was not unpleasant.

"Collie, I busted that fist on his handsome face."

"Oh, it was dreadful!" she murmured. "Wilson, he meant to kill you."

"Sure. And I'd cheerfully have killed him."

"You two must never meet again," she went on.

"I hope to Heaven we never do," replied Moore, with a dark earnestness that meant more than his actual words.

"Wilson, will you avoid him—for my sake?" implored Columbine, unconsciously clasping the bandaged hand.

"I will. I'll take the back trails. I'll sneak like a coyote. I'll hide and I'll watch... But, Columbine Belllounds, if he ever corners me again—"

"Why, you'll leave him to Hell-Bent Wade," interrupted the hunter, and he looked up from where he knelt, fixing those great, inscrutable eyes upon the cowboy. Columbine saw something beyond his face, deeper than the gloom, a passion and a spirit that drew her like a magnet. "An' now, Miss Collie," he went on, "I reckon you'll want to wait on our invalid. He's got to be fed."

"I surely will," replied Columbine, gladly, and she sat down on the edge of the bed. "Ben, you fetch that box and put his dinner on it."

While Wade complied, Columbine, shyly aware of her nearness to the cowboy, sought to keep up conversation. "Couldn't you help yourself with your left hand?" she inquired.

"That's one worse," he answered, taking it from under the blanket, where it had been concealed.

"Oh!" cried Columbine, in dismay.

"Broke two bones in this one," said Wilson, with animation. "Say, Collie, our friend Wade is a doctor, too. Never saw his beat!"

"And a cook, too, for here's your dinner. You must sit up," ordered Columbine.

"Fold that blanket and help me up on it," replied Moore.

How strange and disturbing for Columbine to bend over him, to slip her arms under him and lift him! It recalled a long-forgotten motherliness of her doll-playing days. And her face flushed hot.

"Can't you move?" she asked, suddenly becoming aware of how dead a weight the cowboy appeared.

"Not—very much," he replied. Drops of sweat appeared on his bruised brow. It must have hurt him to move.

"You said your foot was all right."

"It is," he returned. "It's still on my leg, as I know darned well."

"Oh!" exclaimed Columbine, dubiously. Without further comment she began to feed him.

"It's worth getting licked to have this treat," he said.

"Nonsense!" she rejoined.

"I'd stand it again—to have you come here and feed me . . . But not from *him.*"

"Wilson, I never knew you to be facetious before. Here, take this."

Apparently he did not see her outstretched hand.

"Collie, you've changed. You're older. You're a woman, now—and the prettiest—"

"Are you going to eat?" demanded Columbine.

"Huh!" exclaimed the cowboy, blankly. "Eat? Oh yes, sure. I'm powerful hungry. And maybe Heaven-Sent Wade can't cook!"

But Columbine had trouble in feeding him. What with his helplessness, and his propensity to watch her face instead of her hands, and her own mounting sensations of a sweet, natural joy and fitness in her proximity to him, she was hard put to it to show some dexterity as a nurse. And all the time she was aware of Wade, with his quiet, forceful presence, hovering near. Could he not see her hands trembling? And would he not think that weakness strange? Then driftingly came the thought that she would not shrink from Wade's reading her mind. Perhaps even now he understood her better than she understood herself.

"I can't—eat any more," declared Moore, at last.

"You've done very well for an invalid," observed Columbine. Then, changing the subject, she asked, "Wilson, you're going to stay here—winter here, dad would call it?"

"Yes."

"Are those your cattle down in the valley?"

"Sure. I've got near a hundred head. I saved my money and bought cattle."

"That's a good start for you. I'm glad. But who's going to take care of you and your stock until you can work again?"

"Why, my friend there, Heaven-Sent Wade," replied Moore, indicating the little man busy with the utensils on the table, and apparently hearing nothing.

"Can I fetch you anything to eat—or read?" she inquired.

"Fetch yourself," he replied, softly.

"But, boy, how could I fetch you anything without fetching myself?"

"Sure, that's right. Then fetch me some jam and a book—tomorrow. Will you?"

"I surely will."

"That's a promise. I know your promises of old."

"Then good-by till tomorrow. I must go. I hope you'll be better."

"I'll stay sick in bed till you stop coming."

Columbine left rather precipitously, and when she got outdoors it seemed that the hills had never been so softly, dreamily gray, nor their loneliness so sweet, nor the sky so richly and deeply blue. As she untied Pronto the hunter came out with Kane at his heels.

"Miss Collie, if you'll go easy I'll ketch my horse an' ride down with you," he said.

She mounted, and walked Pronto out to the trail, and slowly faced the gradual descent. It was really higher up there than she had surmised. And the view was beautiful. The gray, rolling foothills, so exquisitely colored at that hour, and the black-fringed ranges, one above the other, and the distant peaks, sunset-flushed across the purple, all rose open and clear to her sight, so wildly and splendidly expressive of the Colorado she loved.

At the foot of the slope Wade joined her.

"Lass, I'm askin' you not to tell Belllounds that I'm carin' for Wils," he said, in his gentle, persuasive way.

"I won't. But why not tell dad? He wouldn't mind. He'd do that sort of thing himself."

"Reckon he would. But this deal's out of the ordinary. An' Wils's not in as good shape as he thinks. I'm not takin' any chances. I don't want to lose my job, an' I don't want to be hindered from attendin' to this boy."

They had ridden as far as the first aspen grove when Wade concluded this remark. Columbine halted her horse, causing her companion to do likewise. Her former misgivings were augmented by the intelligence of Wade's sad, lined face.

"Ben, tell me," she whispered, with a hand going to his arm.

"Miss Collie, I'm a sort of doctor in my way. I studied some medicine an' surgery. An' I know. I wouldn't tell you this if it wasn't that I've got to rely on you to help me."

"I will—but go on—tell me," interposed Columbine trying to fortify herself.

"Wils's foot is all messed up. Buster Jack kicked it all out of shape. An' it's a hundred times worse than ever. I'm afraid of blood-poisonin' an' gangrene. You know gangrene is a dyin' an' rottin' of the flesh . . . I told the boy straight out that he'd better let me cut his foot off. An' he swore he'd keep his foot or die! Well, if gangrene does set in we can't save his leg, an' maybe not his life."

"Oh, it can't be as bad as all that!" cried Columbine. "Oh, I knew—I knew there was something . . . Ben, you mean even at best now—he'll be a—" She broke off, unable to finish.

"Miss Collie, in any case Wils'll never ride again—not like a cowboy."

That for Columbine seemed the worst and the last straw. Hot tears blinded her, hot blood gushed over her, hot heart-beats throbbed in her throat.

"Poor boy! That'll—ruin him," she cried. "He loved—a horse. He loved to ride. He was the—best rider of them all. And now he's ruined! He'll be lame—a cripple—club-footed! . . . All because of that Jack Belllounds! The brute—the coward! I hate him! Oh, I *hate* him! . . . And I've got to marry him—on October first! Oh, God pity me!"

Blindly Columbine reeled out of her saddle and slowly dropped to the grass, where she burst into a violent storm of sobs and tears. It shook her every fiber. It was hopeless, terrible grief. The dry grass received her flood of tears and her incoherent words.

Wade dismounted and, kneeling beside her, placed a gentle hand upon her heaving shoulder, but he spoke no word. By and by, when the storm had begun to subside, he raised her head.

"Lass, nothin' is ever so bad as it seems," he said, softly. "Come, sit up. Let me talk to you."

"Oh, Ben, something terrible *has* happened," she cried. "It's in *me!* I don't know what it is. But it'll kill me."

"I know," he replied, as her head fell upon his shoulder. "Miss Collie, I'm an old fellow that's had everythin' happen to him, an' I'm livin' yet, tryin' to help people along. No one dies so easy. Why, you're a fine, strong girl—an' somethin' tells me you was made for happiness. I know how things turn out. Listen—"

"But, Ben—you don't know—about me," she sobbed. "I've told you—I— hate Jack Belllounds. But I've—got to marry him! . . . His father raised me— from a baby. He brought me up. I owe him—my life . . . I've no relation—no mother—no father! No one loves me—for myself!"

"Nobody loves you!" echoed Wade, with an exquisite tone of repudiation. "Strange how people fool themselves! Lass, you're huggin' your troubles too hard. An' you're wrong. Why, everybody loves you! Lem an' Jim—why you just brighten the hard world they live in. An' that poor, hot-headed Jack—he loves you as well as he can love anythin'. An' the old man—no daughter could be loved more . . . An' I—I love you, lass, just like—as if you—might have been my own. I'm goin' to be the friend—the brother you need. An' I reckon I can come somewheres near bein' a mother, if you'll let me."

Something, some subtle power or charm, stole over Columbine, assuaging her terrible sense of loss, of grief. There was tenderness in this man's hands, in his voice, and through them throbbed strong and passionate life and spirit.

"Do you really love me—*love* me?" she whispered, somehow comforted, somehow feeling that what he offered was what she had missed as a child. "And you want to be all that for me?"

"Yes, lass, an' I reckon you'd better try me."

"Oh, how good you are! I felt that—the very first time I was with you. I've wanted to come to you—to tell you my troubles. I love dad and he loves me, but he doesn't understand. Dad is wrapped up in his son. I've had no one. I never had anyone."

"You have someone now," returned Wade, with a rich, deep mellowness in his voice that soothed Columbine and made her wonder. "An' because I've been through so much I can tell you what'll help you . . . Lass, if a woman isn't big an' brave, how will a man ever be? There's more in women than in men. Life has given you a hard knock, placin' you here—no real parents—an' makin' you responsible to a man whose only fault is blinded love for his son. Well, you've got to meet it, face it, with what a woman has more of than any man. Courage! Suppose you do hate this Buster Jack. Suppose you do love this poor, crippled Wilson Moore . . . Lass, don't look like that! Don't deny. You do love that boy . . . Well, it's hell. But you can never tell what'll happen when you're honest and square. If you feel it your duty to pay your debt to the old man you call dad—to pay it by marryin' his son, why do it, an' be a woman. There's nothin' as great as a woman can be. There's happiness that comes in strange, unheard-of ways. There's more in this life than what you want most. *You* didn't place yourself in this fix. So if you meet it with courage an' faithfulness to yourself, why, it'll not turn out as you dread . . . Someday, if you ever think you're broken-hearted, I'll tell you my story. An' then you'll not think your lot so hard. For I've had a broken heart an' ruined life, an' yet I've lived on an' on, findin' happiness I never dreamed would come, fightin' or workin'. An' how I found the world beautiful, an' how I love the flowers an' hills an' wild things so well—that, just that would be enough to live for! . . . An' think, lass, of what a wonderful happiness will come to me in showin' all this to you. That'll be the crownin' glory. An' if it's that much to me, then you be sure there's nothin' on earth I won't do for you."

Columbine lifted her tear-stained face with a light of inspiration.

"Oh, Wilson was right!" she murmured. "You are Heaven-sent! And I'm going to love you!"

## CHAPTER IX

A new spirit, or a liberation of her own, had fired Columbine, and was now burning within her, unquenchable and unutterable. Some divine spark had penetrated into that mysterious depth of her, to inflame and to illumine, so that when she arose from this hour of calamity she felt that to the tenderness and sorrow and fidelity in her soul had been added the lightning flash of passion.

"Oh, Ben—shall I be able to hold onto this?" she cried, flinging wide her arms, as if to embrace the winds of heaven.

"This what, lass?" he asked.

"This—this *woman!*" she answered, passionately, with her hands sweeping back to press her breast.

"No woman who wakes ever goes back to a girl again," he said, sadly.

"I wanted to die—and now I want to live—to fight . . . Ben, you've uplifted me. I was little, weak, miserable . . . But in my dreams, or in some state I can't remember or understand, I've waited for your very words. I was ready. It's as if I knew you in some other world, before I was born on this earth; and when you spoke to me here, so wonderfully—as my mother might have spoken— my heart leaped up in recognition of you and your call to my womanhood! . . . Oh, how strange and beautiful!"

"Miss Collie," he replied, slowly, as he bent to his saddle-straps, "you're young, an' you've no understandin' of what's strange an' terrible in life. An' beautiful, too, as you say . . . Who knows? Maybe in some former state I was somethin' to you. I believe in that. Reckon I can't say how or what. Maybe we were flowers or birds. I've a weakness for that idea."

"Birds! I like the thought, too," replied Columbine. "I love most birds. But there are hawks, crows, buzzards!"

"I reckon. Lass, there's got to be balance in nature. If it weren't for the ugly an' the evil, we wouldn't know the beautiful an' good . . . An' now let's ride home. It's gettin' late."

"Ben, ought I not go back to Wilson right now?" she asked, slowly.

"What for?"

"To tell him—something—and why I can't come tomorrow, or ever afterward," she replied, low and tremulously.

Wade pondered over her words. It seemed to Columbine that her sharpened faculties sensed something of hostility, of opposition in him.

"Reckon tomorrow would be better," he said, presently. "Wilson's had enough excitement for one day."

"Then I'll go tomorrow," she returned.

In the gathering, cold twilight they rode down the trail in silence.

"Good night, lass," said Wade, as he reached his cabin. "An' remember you're not alone anymore."

"Good night, my friend," she replied, and rode on.

Columbine encountered Jim Montana at the corrals, and it was not too dark for her to see his foam-lashed horse. Jim appeared non-committal, almost surly. But Columbine guessed that he had ridden to Kremmling and back in one day, on some order of Jack's.

"Miss Collie, I'll tend to Pronto," he offered. "An' yore supper'll be waitin'."

A bright fire blazed on the living room hearth. The rancher was reading by its light.

"Hello, rosy-cheeks!" greeted the rancher, with unusual amiability. "Been ridin' ag'in' the wind, hey? Wal, if you ain't pretty, then my eyes are pore!"

"It's cold, dad," she replied, "and the wind stings. But I didn't ride fast nor far . . . I've been up to see Wilson Moore."

"Ahuh! Wal, how's the boy?" asked Belllounds, gruffly.

"He said he was all right, but—but I guess that's not so," responded Columbine.

"Any friends lookin' after him?"

"Oh yes—he must have friends—the Andrewses and others. I'm glad to say his cabin is comfortable. He'll be looked after."

"Wal, I'm glad to hear thet. I'll send Lem or Wade up thar an' see if we can do anythin' fer the boy."

"Dad—that's just like you," replied Columbine, with her hand seeking his broad shoulder.

"Ahuh! Say, Collie, hyar's letters from 'most everybody in Kremmlin' wantin' to be invited up fer October first. How about askin' 'em?"

"The more the merrier," replied Columbine.

"Wal, I reckon I'll not ask anybody."

"Why not, dad?"

"No one can gamble on thet son of mine, even on his weddin'-day," replied Belllounds, gloomily.

"Dad, what'd Jack do today?"

"I'm not sayin' he did anythin'," answered the rancher

"Dad, you can gamble on me."

"Wal, I should smile," he said, putting his big arm around her. "I wish you was Jack an' Jack was you."

At that moment the young man spoken of slouched into the room, with his head bandaged, and took a seat at the supper table.

"Wal, Collie, let's go an' get it," said the rancher, cheerily. "I can always eat, anyhow."

"I'm hungry as a bear," rejoined Columbine, as she took her seat, which was opposite Jack.

"Where 'ye you been?" he asked, curiously.

"Why, good evening, Jack! Did you finally notice me? . . . I've been riding Pronto, the first time since he was hurt. Had a lovely ride—up through Sage Valley."

Jack glowered at her with the one unbandaged eye, and growled something under his breath, and then began to stab meat and potatoes with his fork.

"What's the matter, Jack? Aren't you well?" asked Columbine, with a solicitude just a little too sweet to be genuine.

"Yes, I'm well," snapped Jack.

"But you look sick. That is, what I can see of your face looks sick. Your mouth droops at the corners. You're very pale—and red in spots. And your one eye glows with unearthly woe, as if you were not long for this world!"

The amazing nature of this speech, coming from the girl who had always been so sweet and quiet and backward, was attested to by the consternation of Jack and the mirth of his father.

"Are you making fun of me?" demanded Jack.

"Why, Jack! Do you think I would make fun of you? I only wanted to say how queer you look . . . Are you going to be married with one eye?"

Jack collapsed at that, and the old man, after a long stare of open-mouthed wonder, broke out: "Haw! Haw! Haw! . . . By Golly! Lass—I'd never believed thet was in you . . . Jack, be game an' take your medicine . . . An' both of you forgive an' forget. Thar'll be quarrels enough, mebbe, without rakin' over the past."

When alone again Columbine reverted to a mood vastly removed from her apparent levity with the rancher and his son. A grave and inward-searching thought possessed her, and it had to do with the uplift, the spiritual advance, the rise above mere personal welfare, that had strangely come to her through Bent Wade. From their first meeting he had possessed a singular attraction for her that now, in the light of the meaning of his life, seemed to Columbine to be the man's nobility and wisdom, arising out of his travail, out of the terrible years that had left their record upon his face.

And so Columbine strove to bind forever in her soul the spirit which had arisen in her, interpreting from Wade's rude words of philosophy that which she needed for her own light and strength.

She appreciated her duty toward the man who had been a father to her. Whatever he asked that would she do. And as for the son she must live with the rest of her life, her duty there was to be a good wife, to bear with his faults, to strive always to help him by kindness, patience, loyalty, and such affection as was possible to her. Hate had to be reckoned with, and hate, she knew, had no place in a good woman's heart. It must be expelled, if that were humanly possible. All this was hard, would grow harder, but she accepted it, and knew her mind.

Her soul was her own, unchangeable through any adversity. She could be with that alone always, aloof from the petty cares and troubles common to people. Wade's words had thrilled her with their secret, with their limitless hope of an unknown world of thought and feeling. Happiness, in the ordinary sense, might never be hers. Alas for her dreams! But there had been given her a glimpse of something higher than pleasure and contentment. Dreams were but dreams. But she could still dream of what had been, of what might have been, of the beauty and mystery of life, of something in nature that called sweetly and irresistibly to her. Who could rob her of the rolling, gray, velvety hills, and the purple peaks and the black ranges, among which she had been found a waif, a little lost creature, born like a columbine under the spruces?

Love, sudden-dawning, inexplicable love, was her secret, still tremulously new, and perilous in its sweetness. That only did she fear to realize and to face, because it was an unknown factor, a threatening flame. Her sudden knowledge of it seemed inextricably merged with the mounting, strong, and steadfast stream of her spirit.

"I'll go to him. I'll tell him," she murmured. "He shall have *that!* . . . Then I must bid him—good-by—forever!"

To tell Wilson would be sweet; to leave him would be bitter. Vague possibilities haunted her. What might come of the telling? How dark loomed the bitterness! She could not know what hid in either of these acts until they were fulfilled. And the hours became long, and sleep far off, and the quietness of the house a torment, and the melancholy wail of coyotes a reminder of happy girlhood, never to return.

* * * * *

When next day the long-deferred hour came Columbine selected a horse that she could run, and she rode up the winding valley swift as the wind. But at the aspen grove, where Wade's keen, gentle voice had given her secret life, she suffered a reaction that made her halt and ascend the slope very slowly and with many stops.

Sight of Wade's horse haltered near the cabin relieved Columbine somewhat of a gathering might of emotion. The hunter would be inside and so she would not be compelled at once to confess her secret. This expectancy gave impetus to her lagging steps. Before she reached the open door she called out.

"Collie, you're late," answered Wilson, with both joy and reproach, as she entered. The cowboy lay upon his bed, and he was alone in the room.

"Oh! . . . Where is Ben?" exclaimed Columbine.

"He was here. He cooked my dinner. We waited, but you never came. The dinner got cold. I made sure you'd backed out—weren't coming at all—and I couldn't eat . . . Wade said he knew you'd come. He went off with the hounds, somewhere . . . and oh, Collie, it's all right now!"

Columbine walked to his bedside and looked down upon him with a feeling as if some giant hand was tugging at her heart. He looked better. The swelling and redness of his face were less marked. And at that moment no pain shadowed his eyes. They were soft, dark, eloquent. If Columbine had not come with her avowed resolution and desire to unburden her heart she would have found that look in his eyes a desperately hard one to resist. Had it ever shone there before? Blind she had been.

"You're better," she said, happily.

"Sure—*now*. But I had a bad night. Didn't sleep till near daylight. Wade found me asleep . . . Collie, it's good of you to come. You look so—so wonderful! I never saw your face glow like that. And your eyes—oh!"

"You think I'm pretty, then?" she asked, dreamily, not occupied at all with that thought.

He uttered a contemptuous laugh.

"Come closer," he said, reaching for her with a clumsy bandaged hand.

Down upon her knees Columbine fell. Both hands flew to cover her face. And as she swayed forward she shook violently, and there escaped her lips a little, muffled sound.

"Why—Collie!" cried Moore, astounded. "Good Heavens! Don't cry! I—I didn't mean anything. I only wanted to feel you—touch your hand."

"Here," she answered, blindly holding out her hand, groping for his till she found it. Her other was still pressed to her eyes. One moment longer would Columbine keep her secret—hide her eyes—revel in the unutterable joy and sadness of this crisis that could come to a woman only once.

"What in the world?" ejaculated the cowboy, now bewildered. But he possessed himself of the trembling hand offered. "Collie, you act so strange . . . You're not crying! . . . Am I only locoed, or flighty, or what? Dear, look at me."

Columbine swept her hand from her eyes with a gesture of utter surrender.

"Wilson, I'm ashamed—and sad—and gloriously happy," she said, with swift breathlessness.

"Why?" he asked.

"Because of—of something I have to tell you," she whispered.

"What is that?"

She bent over him.

"Can't you guess?"

He turned pale, and his eyes burned with intense fire.

"I won't guess . . . I daren't guess."

"It's something that's been true for years—forever, it seems—something I never dreamed of till last night," she went on, softly.

"Collie!" he cried. "Don't torture me!"

"Do you remember long ago—when we quarreled so dreadfully—because you kissed me?" she asked.

"Do you think I could kiss *you*—and live to forget?"

"I love you!" she whispered, shyly, feeling the hot blood burn her.

That whisper transformed Wilson Moore. His arm flashed round her neck and pulled her face down to his, and, holding her in a close embrace, he kissed her lips and cheeks and wet eyes, and then again her lips, passionately and tenderly.

Then he pressed her head down upon his breast.

"My God! I can't believe! Say it again!" he cried, hoarsely.

Columbine buried her flaming face in the blanket covering him, and her hands clutched it tightly. The wildness of his joy, the strange strength and power of his kisses, utterly changed her. Upon his breast she lay, without desire to lift her face. All seemed different, wilder, as she responded to his appeal: "Yes, I love you! Oh, I love—love—love you!"

"Dearest! . . . Lift your face . . . It's true now. I know. It's proved. But let me look at you."

Columbine lifted herself as best she could. But she was blinded by tears and choked with utterance that would not come, and in the grip of a shuddering emotion that was realization of loss in a moment when she learned the supreme and imperious sweetness of love.

"Kiss me, Columbine," he demanded.

Through blurred eyes she saw his face, white and rapt, and she bent to it, meeting his lips with her first kiss which was her last.

"Again, Collie—again!" he begged.

"No—no more," she whispered, very low, and encircling his neck with her arms she hid her face and held him convulsively, and stifled the sobs that shook her.

Then Moore was silent, holding her with his free hand, breathing hard, and slowly quieting down. Columbine felt then that he knew that there was something terribly wrong, and that perhaps he dared not voice his fear. At any rate, he silently held her, waiting. That silent wait grew unendurable for Columbine. She wanted to prolong this moment that was to be all she could ever surrender. But she dared not do so, for she knew if he ever kissed her again her duty to Belllounds would vanish like mist in the sun.

To release her hold upon him seemed like a tearing of her heartstrings. She sat up, she wiped the tears from her eyes, she rose to her feet, all the time striving for strength to face him again.

A loud voice ringing from the cliffs outside, startled Columbine. It came from Wade calling the hounds. He had returned, and the fact stirred her.

"I'm to marry Jack Belllounds on October first."

The cowboy raised himself up as far as he was able. It was agonizing for Columbine to watch the changing and whitening of his face!

"No—no!" he gasped.

"Yes, it's true," she replied, hopelessly.

"No!" he exclaimed, hoarsely.

"But, Wilson, I tell you yes. I came to tell you. It's true—oh, it's true!"

"But, girl, you said you love me," he declared, transfixing her with dark, accusing eyes.

"That's just as terribly true."

He softened a little, and something of terror and horror took the place of anger.

Just then Wade entered the cabin with his soft tread, hesitated, and then came to Columbine's side. She could not unrivet her gaze from Moore to look at her friend, but she reached out with trembling hand to him. Wade clasped it in a horny palm.

Wilson fought for self-control in vain.

"Collie, if you love me, how can you marry Jack Belllounds?" he demanded.

"I must."

"Why must you?"

"I owe my life and my bringing up to his father. He wants me to do it. His heart is set upon my helping Jack to become a man . . . Dad loves me, and I love him. I must stand by him. I must repay him. It is my duty."

"You've a duty to yourself—as a woman!" he rejoined, passionately. "Belllounds is wrapped up in his son. He's blind to the shame of such a marriage. But you're not."

"Shame?" faltered Columbine.

"Yes. The shame of marrying one man when you love another. You can't love two men . . . You'll give yourself. You'll be his *wife!* Do you understand what that means?"

"I—I think—I do," replied Columbine, faintly. Where had vanished all her wonderful spirit? This fire-eyed boy was breaking her heart with his reproach.

"But you'll bear his children," cried Wilson. "Mother of—them—when you love me! . . . Didn't you think of that?"

"Oh no—I never did—I never did!" wailed Columbine.

"Then you'll think before it's too late?" he implored, wildly. "Dearest Collie, think! You won't ruin yourself! You won't? Say you won't!"

"But—oh, Wilson, what can I say? I've got to marry him."

"Collie, I'll kill him before he gets you."

"You mustn't talk so. If you fought again—if anything terrible happened, it'd kill me."

"You'd be better off!" he flashed, white as a sheet.

Columbine leaned against Wade for support. She was fast weakening in strength, although her spirit held. She knew what was inevitable. But Wilson's agony was rending her.

"Listen," began the cowboy again. "It's your life—your happiness—your soul . . . Belllounds is crazy over that spoiled boy. He thinks the sun rises and sets in him . . . But Jack Belllounds is no good on this earth! Collie dearest, don't think that's my jealousy. I am horribly jealous. But I know him. He's not worth you! No man is—and he the least. He'll break your heart, drag you down, ruin your health—kill you, as sure as you stand there. I want you to know I could prove to you what he is. But don't make me. Trust me, Collie. Believe me."

"Wilson, I do believe you," cried Columbine. "But it doesn't make any difference. It only makes my duty harder."

"He'll treat you like he treats a horse or a dog. He'll beat you—"

"He never will! If he ever lays a hand on me—"

"If not that, he'll tire of you. Jack Belllounds never stuck to anything in his life, and never will. It's not in him. He wants what he can't have. If he gets it, then right off he doesn't want it. Oh, I've known him since he was a kid . . . Columbine, you've a mistaken sense of duty. No girl need sacrifice her all because some man found her a lost baby and gave her a home. A woman owes more to herself than to anyone."

"Oh, that's true, Wilson. I've thought it all . . . But you're unjust—hard. You make no allowance for—for some possible good in everyone. Dad swears I can reform Jack. Maybe I can. I'll pray for it."

"Reform Jack Belllounds! How can you save a bad egg? That damned coward! Didn't he prove to you what he was when he jumped on me and kicked my broken foot till I fainted? . . . What do you want?"

"Don't say any more—please," cried Columbine. "Oh, I'm so sorry . . . I oughtn't have come . . . Ben, take me home."

"But, Collie, I love you," frantically urged Wilson. "And he—he may love you—but he's—Collie—he's been—"

Here Moore seemed to bite his tongue, to hold back speech, to fight something terrible and desperate and cowardly in himself.

Columbine heard only his impassioned declaration of love, and to that she vibrated.

"You speak as if this was one-sided," she burst out, as once more the gush of hot blood surged over her. "You don't love me any more than I love you. Not as much, for I'm a woman! . . . I love with all my heart and soul!"

Moore fell back upon the bed, spent and overcome.

"Wade, my friend, for God's sake do something," he whispered, appealing to the hunter as if in a last hope. "Tell Collie what it'll mean for her to marry Belllounds. If that doesn't change her, then tell her what it'll mean to me. I'll never go home. I'll never leave here. If she hadn't told me she loved me then, I might have stood anything. But now I can't. It'll kill me, Wade."

"Boy, you're talkin' flighty again," replied Wade. "This mornin' when I come you were dreamin' an' talkin'—clean out of your head . . . Well, now, you an' Collie listen. You're right an' she's right. I reckon I never run across a deal with two people fixed just like you. But that doesn't hinder me from feelin' the same about it as I'd feel about somethin' I was used to."

He paused, and, gently releasing Columbine, he went to Moore, and retied his loosened bandage, and spread out the disarranged blankets. Then he sat down on the edge of the bed and bent over a little, running a roughened hand through the scant hair that had begun to silver upon his head. Presently he looked up, and from that sallow face, with its lines and furrows, and from the deep, inscrutable eyes, there fell a light which, however sad and wise in its infinite understanding of pain and strife, was still ruthless and unquenchable in its hope.

"Wade, for God's sake save Columbine!" importuned Wilson.

"Oh, if you only could!" cried Columbine, impelled beyond her power to resist by that prayer.

"Lass, you stand by your convictions," he said, impressively. "An' Moore, you be a man an' don't make it so hard for her. Neither of you can do anythin' . . . Now there's old Belllounds—he'll never change. He might r'ar up for this or that, but he'll never change his cherished hopes for his son . . . But Jack might change! Lookin' back over all the years I remember many boys like this Buster Jack, an' I remember how in the nature of their doin's they just hanged themselves. I've a queer foresight about people whose trouble I've made my own. It's somethin' that never fails. When their trouble's goin' to turn out bad then I feel a terrible yearnin' to tell the story of Hell-Bent Wade. That foresight of trouble gave me my name . . . But it's not operatin' here . . . An' so, my young friends, you can believe me when I say somethin' will happen. As far as October first is concerned, or any time near, Collie isn't goin' to marry Jack Belllounds."

## CHAPTER X

One day Wade remarked to Belllounds: "You can never tell what a dog is until you know him. Dogs are like men. Some of 'em look good, but they're really bad. An' that works the other way round. If a dog's born to run wild an' be a sheep-killer, that's what he'll be. I've known dogs that loved men as no humans could have loved them. It doesn't make any difference to a dog if his master is a worthless scamp."

"Wal, I reckon most of them hounds I bought had no good masters, judgin' from the way they act," replied the rancher.

"I'm developin' a first-rate pack," said Wade. "Jim hasn't any faults exceptin' he doesn't bay enough. Sampson's not as true-nosed as Jim, but he'll follow Jim, an' he has a deep, heavy bay you can hear for miles. So that makes up for Jim's one fault. These two hounds hang together, an' with them I'm developin' others. Denver will split off of bear or lion tracks when he jumps a deer. I reckon he's not young enough to be cured of that. Some of the younger hounds are comin' on fine. But there's two dogs in the bunch that beat me all hollow."

"Which ones?" asked Belllounds.

"There's that bloodhound, Kane," replied the hunter. "He's sure a queer dog. I can't win him. He minds me now because I licked him, an' once good an' hard when he bit me . . . But he doesn't cotton to me worth a damn. He's gettin' fond of Miss Columbine, an' I believe might make a good watchdog for her. Where'd he come from, Belllounds?"

"Wal, if I don't disremember he was born in a prairie-schooner, comin' across the plains. His mother was a full-blood, an' come from Louisiana."

"That accounts for an instinct I see croppin' out in Kane," rejoined Wade. "He likes to trail a man. I've caught him doin' it. An' he doesn't take to huntin' lions or bear. Why, the other day, when the hounds treed a lion an' went howlin' wild, Kane came up, an' he looked disgusted an' went off by himself. He hunts by himself, anyhow. First off I thought he might be a sheep-killer. But I reckon not. He can trail men, an' that's about all the good he is. His mother must have been a slave-hunter, an' Kane inherits that trailin' instinct."

"Ahuh! Wal, train him on trailin' men, then. I've seen times when a dog like thet'd come handy. An' if he takes to Collie an' you approve of him, let her have him. She's been coaxin' me fer a dog."

"That isn't a bad idea. Miss Collie walks an' rides alone a good deal, an' she never packs a gun."

"Tummy about thet," said Belllounds. "Collie is game in most ways, but she'd never kill anythin' . . . Wade, you ain't thinkin' she ought to stop them lonesome walks an' rides?"

"No, sure not, so long as she doesn't go too far away."

"Ahuh! Wal, supposin' she rode up out of the valley, west on the Black Range?"

"That won't do, Belllounds," replied Wade, seriously. "But Miss Collie's not goin' to, for I've cautioned her. Fact is I've run across some hard-lookin' men between here an' Buffalo Park. They're not hunters or prospectors or cattlemen or travelers."

"Wal, you don't say!" rejoined Belllounds. "Now, Wade, are you connectin' up them strangers with the stock I missed on this last roundup?"

"Reckon I can't go as far as that," returned Wade. "But I didn't like their looks."

"Thet comin' from you, Wade, is like the findin's of a jury . . . It's gettin' along toward October. Snow'll be flyin' soon. You don't reckon them strangers will winter in the woods?"

"No, I don't. Neither does Lewis. You recollect him?"

"Yes, thet prospector who hangs out around Buffalo Park, lookin' fer gold. He's been hyar. Good fellar, but crazy on gold."

"I've met Lewis several times, one place and another. I lost the hounds day before yesterday. They treed a lion an' Lewis heard the racket, an' he stayed with them till I come up. Then he told me some interestin' news. You see he's been worryin' about this gang thet's rangin' around Buffalo Park, an' he's tried to get a line on them. Somebody took a shot at him in the woods. He couldn't swear it was one of that outfit, but he could swear he wasn't near shot by accident. Now Lewis says these men pack to an' fro from Elgeria, an' he has a hunch they're in cahoots with Smith, who runs a place there. You know Smith?"

"No, I don't, an' haven't any wish to," declared Belllounds, shortly. "He always looked shady to me. An' he's not been square with friends of mine in Elgeria. But no one ever proved him crooked, whatever was thought. Fer my part, I never missed a guess in my life. Men don't have scars on their face like his fer nothin'."

"Boss, I'm confidin' what I want kept under your hat," said Wade, quietly. "I knew Smith. He's as bad as the West makes them. I gave him that scar . . . An' when he sees me he's goin' for his gun."

"Wal, I'll be darned! Doesn't surprise me. It's a small world . . . Wade, I'll keep my mouth shut, sure. But what's your game?"

"Lewis an' I will find out if there is any connection between Smith an' this gang of strangers—an' the occasional loss of a few head of stock."

"Ahuh! Wal, you have my good will, you bet . . . Sure thar's been some rustlin' of cattle. Not enough to make any rancher holler, an' I reckon there never will be any more of thet in Colorado. Still, if we get the drop on some outfit we sure ought to corral them."

"Boss, I'm tellin' you—"

"Wade, you ain't agoin' to start thet tellin' hell-bent happenin's to come hyar at White Slides?" interrupted Belllounds, plaintively.

"No, I reckon I've no hunch like that now," responded Wade, seriously. "But I was about to say that if Smith is in on any rustlin' of cattle he'll be hard to catch, an' if he's caught there'll be shootin' to pay. He's cunnin' an' has had long experience. It's not likely he'd work openly, as he did years ago. If he's stealin' stock or buyin' an' sellin' stock that someone steals for him, it's only on a small scale, an' it'll be hard to trace."

"Wal, he might be deep," said Belllounds, reflectively. "But men like thet, no matter how deep or cunnin' they are, always come to a bad end. Jest works out natural . . . Had you any grudge ag'in' Smith?"

"What I give him was for somebody else, an' was sure little enough. He's got the grudge against me."

"Ahuh! Wal, then, don't you go huntin' fer trouble. Try an' make White

Slides one place thet'll disprove your name. All the same, don't shy at sight of anythin' suspicious round the ranch."

The old man plodded thoughtfully away, leaving the hunter likewise in a brown study.

"He's gettin' a hunch that I'll tell him of some shadow hoverin' black over White Slides," soliloquized Wade. "Maybe—maybe so. But I don't see any yet . . . Strange how a man will say what he didn't start out to say. Now, I started to tell him about that amazin' dog Fox."

Fox was the great dog of the whole pack, and he had been absolutely overlooked, which fact Wade regarded with contempt for himself. Discovery of this particular dog came about by accident. Somewhere in the big corral there was a hole where the smaller dogs could escape, but Wade had been unable to find it. For that matter the corral was full of holes, not any of which, however, it appeared to Wade, would permit anything except a squirrel to pass in and out.

One day when the hunter, very much exasperated, was prowling around and around inside the corral, searching for this mysterious vent, a rather small dog, with short gray and brown woolly hair, and shaggy brows half hiding big, bright eyes, came up wagging his stump of a tail.

"Well, what do you know about it?" demanded Wade. Of course he had noticed this particular dog, but to no purpose. On this occasion the dog repeated so unmistakably former overtures of friendship that Wade gave him close scrutiny. He was neither young nor comely nor thoroughbred, but there was something in his intelligent eyes that struck the hunter significantly. "Say, maybe I overlooked somethin'? But there's been a heap of dogs round here an' you're no great shucks for looks. Now, if you're talkin' to me come an' find that hole."

Whereupon Wade began another search around the corral. It covered nearly an acre of ground, and in some places the fence-poles had been sunk near rocks. More than once Wade got down upon his hands and knees to see if he could find the hole. The dog went with him, watching with knowing eyes that the hunter imagined actually laughed at him. But they were glad eyes, which began to make an appeal. Presently, when Wade came to a rough place, the dog slipped under a shelving rock, and thence through a half-concealed hole in the fence; and immediately came back through to wag his stump of a tail and look as if the finding of that hole was easy enough.

"You old fox," declared Wade, very much pleased, as he patted the dog. "You found it for me, didn't you? Good dog! Now I'll fix that hole, an' then you can come to the cabin with me. An' your name's Fox."

That was how Fox introduced himself to Wade, and found his opportunity. The fact that he was not a hound had operated against his being taken out hunting, and therefore little or no attention had been paid him. Very shortly Fox showed himself to be a dog of superior intelligence. The hunter had lived much with dogs and had come to learn that the longer he lived with them the more there was to marvel at and love.

Fox insisted so strongly on being taken out to hunt with the hounds that Wade, vowing not to be surprised at anything, let him go. It happened to be a particularly hard day on hounds because of old tracks and cross-tracks and difficult ground. Fox worked out a labyrinthine trail that Sampson gave up and Jim failed on. This delighted Wade, and that night he tried to find out from Andrews, who sold the dog to Belllounds, something about Fox. All the information obtainable was that Andrews suspected the fellow from whom he had gotten Fox had stolen him. Belllounds had never noticed him at all. Wade kept the possibilities of Fox to himself and reserved his judgment, and every day gave the dog another chance to show what he knew.

Long before the end of that week Wade loved Fox and decided that he was a wonderful animal. Fox liked to hunt, but it did not matter what he hunted. That depended upon the pleasure of his master. He would find hobbled horses that were hiding out and standing still to escape detection. He would trail cattle. He would tree squirrels and point grouse. Invariably he suited his mood to the kind of game he hunted. If put on an elk track, or that of deer, he would follow it, keeping well within sight of the hunter, and never uttering a single bark or yelp; and without any particular eagerness he would stick until he had found the game or until he was called off. Bear and cat tracks, however, roused the savage instinct in him, and transformed him. He yelped at every jump on a trail, and whenever his yelp became piercing and continuous Wade well knew the quarry was in sight. He fought bear like a wise old dog that knew when to rush in with a snap and when to keep away. When lions or wildcats were treed Fox lost much of his ferocity and interest. Then the matter of that particular quarry was ended. His most valuable characteristic, however, was his ability to stick on the track upon which he was put. Wade believed if he put Fox on the trail of a rabbit, and if a bear or lion were to cross that trail ahead of him, Fox would stick to the rabbit. Even more remarkable was it that Fox would not steal a piece of meat and that he would fight the other dogs for being thieves.

Fox and Kane, it seemed to the hunter in his reflective foreshadowing of events at White Slides, were destined to play most important parts.

\* \* \* \* \*

Upon a certain morning, several days before October first—which date rankled in the mind of Wade—he left Moore's cabin, leading a packhorse. The hounds he had left behind at the ranch, but Fox accompanied him.

"Wade, I want some elk steak," old Belllounds had said the day before. "Nothin' like a good rump steak! I was raised on elk meat. Now hyar, more'n a week ago I told you I wanted some. There's elk all around. I heerd a bull whistle at sunup today. Made me wish I was young ag'in! . . . You go pack in an elk."

"I haven't run across any bulls lately," Wade had replied, but he did not mention that he had avoided such a circumstance. The fact was Wade admired and loved the elk above all horned wild animals. So strange was his attitude toward elk that he had gone meat-hungry many a time with these great stags bugling near his camp.

As he climbed the yellow, grassy mountain-side, working round above the valley, his mind was not centered on the task at hand, but on Wilson Moore, who had come to rely on him with the unconscious tenacity of a son whose faith in his father was unshakable. The crippled cowboy kept his hope, kept his cheerful, grateful spirit, obeyed and suffered with a patience that was fine. There had been no improvement in his injured foot. Wade worried about that much more than Moore. The thing that mostly occupied the cowboy was the near approach of October first, with its terrible possibility for him. He did not talk about it, except when fever made him irrational, but it was plain to Wade how he prayed and hoped and waited in silence. Strange how he trusted Wade to avert catastrophe of Columbine's marriage! Yet such trust seemed familiar to Wade, as he reflected over past years. Had he not wanted such trust—had he not invited it?

For twenty years no happiness had come to Wade in any sense comparable to that now secretly his, as he lived near Columbine Belllounds, divining more and more each day how truly she was his own flesh and the image of the girl he had loved and married and wronged. Columbine was his daughter. He saw himself in her. And Columbine, from being strongly attracted to him and trusting in him and relying upon him, had come to love him. That was the most beautiful and terrible fact of his life—beautiful because it brought back the past, her babyhood, and his barren years, and gave him this sudden change, where he lived transported with the sense and the joy of his possession. It was terrible because she was unhappy, because she was chained to duty and honor, because ruin faced her, and lastly because Wade began to have the vague, gloomy intimations of distant tragedy. Far off, like a cloud on the horizon, but there! Long ago he had learned the uselessness of fighting his morbid visitations. But he clung to hope, to faith in life, to the victory of the virtuous, to the defeat of evil. A thousand proofs had strengthened him in that clinging.

There were personal dread and poignant pain for Wade in Columbine Belllounds's situation. After all, he had only his subtle and intuitive assurance that matters would turn out well for her in the end. To trust that now, when the shadow began to creep over his own daughter, seemed unwise—a juggling with chance.

"I'm beginnin' to feel that I couldn't let her marry that Buster Jack," soliloquized Wade, as he rode along the grassy trail. "Fust off, seein' how strong was her sense of duty an' loyalty, I wasn't so set against it. But somethin's growin' in me. Her love for that crippled boy, now, an' his for her! Lord! They're so young an' life must be so hot an' love so sweet! I reckon that's why I couldn't let her marry Jack . . . But, on the other hand, there's the old man's faith in his son, an' there's Collie's faith in herself an' in life. Now I believe in that. An' the years have proved to me there's hope for the worst of men . . . I haven't even had a talk with this Buster Jack. I don't know him, except by hearsay. An' I'm sure prejudiced, which's no wonder, considerin' where I saw him in Denver . . . I reckon, before I go any farther, I'd better meet this Belllounds boy an' see what's in him."

\* \* \* \* \*

It was characteristic of Wade that this soliloquy abruptly ended his thoughtful considerations for the time being. This was owing to the fact that he rested upon a decision, and also because it was time he began to attend to the object of his climb.

Bench after bench he had ascended, and the higher he got the denser and more numerous became the aspen thickets and the more luxuriant the grass. Presently the long black slope of spruce confronted him, with its edge like a dark wall. He entered the fragrant forest, where not a twig stirred nor a sound pervaded the silence. Upon the soft, matted earth the hoofs of the horses made no impression and scarcely a perceptible thud.

Wade headed to the left, avoiding rough, rocky defiles of weathered cliff and wind-fallen trees, and aimed to find easy going up to the summit of the mountain bluff far above. This was new forest to him, consisting of moderate-sized spruce-trees growing so closely together that he had to go carefully to keep from snapping dead twigs. Fox trotted on in the lead, now and then pausing to look up at his master, as if for instructions.

A brightening of the dark green gloom ahead showed the hunter that he was approaching a large glade or open patch, where the sunlight fell strongly. It turned out to be a swale, or swampy place, some few acres in extent, and directly at the foot of a last steep, wooded slope. Here Fox put his nose into the air and halted.

"What're you scentin', Fox, old boy?" asked Wade, with low voice, as he peered ahead. The wind was in the wrong direction for him to approach close to game without being detected. Fox wagged his stumpy tail and looked up with knowing eyes. Wade proceeded cautiously. The swamp was a rank growth of long, weedy grasses and ferns, with here and there a green-mossed bog half hidden and a number of dwarf oak-trees. Wade's horse sank up to his knees in the mire. On the other side showed fresh tracks along the wet margin of the swale.

"It's elk, all right," said Wade, as he dismounted. "Heard us comin'. Now, Fox, stick your nose in that track. An' go slow."

With rifle ready Wade began the ascent of the slope on foot, leading his horse. An old elk trail showed a fresh track. Fox accommodated his pace to that of the toiling hunter. The ascent was steep and led up through dense forest. At intervals, when Wade halted to catch his breath and listen, he heard faint snapping of dead branches far above. At length he reached the top of the mountain, to find a wide, open space, with heavy forest in front, and a bare, ghastly, burned-over district to his right. Fox growled, and appeared about to dash forward. Then, in an opening through the forest, Wade espied a large bull elk, standing at gaze, evidently watching him. He was a gray old bull, with broken antlers. Wade made no move to shoot, and presently the elk walked out of sight.

"Too old an' tough, Fox," explained the hunter to the anxious dog. But perhaps that was not all Wade's motive in sparing him.

Once more mounted, Wade turned his attention to the burned district. It was a dreary, hideous splotch, a blackened slash in the green cover of the mountain. It sloped down into a wide hollow and up another bare slope. The ground was littered with bleached logs, trees that had been killed first by fire and then felled by wind. Here and there a lofty, spectral trunk still withstood the blasts. Across the hollow sloped a considerable area where all trees were dead and still standing—a melancholy sight. Beyond, and far round and down to the left, opened up a slope of spruce and bare ridge, where a few cedars showed dark, and then came black, spear-tipped forest again, leading the eye to the magnificent panorama of endless range on range, purple in the distance.

Wade found patches of grass where beds had been recently occupied.

"Mountain sheep, by cracky!" exclaimed the hunter. "An' fresh tracks, too!... Now I wonder if it wouldn't do to kill a sheep an' tell Belllounds I couldn't find any elk."

The hunter had no qualms about killing mountain-sheep, but he loved the lordly stags and would have lied to spare them. He rode on, with keen gaze shifting everywhere to catch a movement of something in this wilderness before him. If there was any living animal in sight it did not move. Wade crossed the hollow, wended a circuitous route through the upstanding forest of dead timber, and entered a thick woods that skirted the rim of the mountain. Presently he came out upon the open rim, from which the depths of green and gray yawned mightily. Far across, Old White Slides loomed up, higher now, with a dignity and majesty unheralded from below.

Wade found fresh sheep tracks in the yellow clay of the rim, small as little deer tracks, showing that they had just been made by ewes and lambs. Not a ram track in the group!

"Well, that lets me out," said Wade, as he peered under the bluff for sight of the sheep. They had gone over the steep rim as if they had wings. "Beats hell how sheep can go down without fallin'! An' how they can hide!"

He knew they were near at hand and he wasted time peering to spy them out. Nevertheless, he could not locate them. Fox waited impatiently for the word to let him prove how easily he could rout them out, but this permission was not forthcoming.

"We're huntin' elk, you Jack-of-all-dogs," reprovingly spoke the hunter to Fox.

So they went on around the rim, and after a couple of miles of travel came to the forest, and then open heads of hollows that widened and deepened down. Here was excellent pasture and cover for elk. Wade left the rim to ride down these slow-descending half-open ridges, where cedars grew and jack-pines stood in clumps, and little grassy-bordered brooks babbled between. He saw tracks where a big buck deer had crossed ahead of him, and then he flushed a covey of grouse that scared the horses, and then he saw where a bear had pulled a rotten log to pieces. Fox did not show any interest in these things.

By and by Wade descended to the junction of these hollows, where three tiny brooklets united to form a stream of pure, swift, clear water, perhaps a foot deep and several yards wide.

"I reckon this's the head of the Troublesome," said Wade. "Whoever named this brook had no sense . . . Yet here, at its source, it's gatherin' trouble for itself. That's the way of youth."

The grass grew thickly and luxuriantly and showed signs of recent grazing. Elk had been along the brook that morning. There were many tracks, like cow tracks, only smaller, deeper, and more oval; and there were beds where elk had lain, and torn-up places where bulls had plowed and stamped with heavy hoofs.

Fox trailed the herd to higher ground, where evidently they had entered the woods. Here Wade tied his horses, and, whispering to Fox, he proceeded stealthily through this strip of spruce. He came out to an open point, taking care, however, to keep well screened, from which he had a glimpse of a parklike hollow, grassy and watered. Working round to better vantage, he soon espied what had made Fox stand so stiff and bristling. A herd of elk were trooping up the opposite slope, scarcely a hundred yards distant. They had heard or scented him, but did not appear alarmed. They halted to look back. The hunter's quick estimate credited nearly two dozen to the herd, mostly cows. A magnificent bull, with wide-spreading antlers, and black head and shoulders and gray hind quarters, stalked out from the herd, and stood an instant, head aloft, splendidly significant of the wild. Then he trotted into the woods, his antlers noiselessly spreading the green. Others trotted off likewise. Wade raised his rifle and looked through the sight at the bull, and let him pass. Then he saw another over his rifle, and another. Reluctant and forced, he at last aimed and pulled trigger. The heavy Henry boomed out in the stillness. Fox dashed down with eager barks. When the smoke cleared away Wade saw the opposite slope bare except for one fallen elk.

Then he returned to his horses, and brought them back to where Fox perched beside the dead quarry.

"Well, Fox, that stag'll never bugle any more of a sunrise," said Wade. "Strange how we're made so we have to eat meat! I'd 'a' liked it otherwise."

He cut up the elk, and packed all the meat the horse could carry, and hung the best of what was left out of the reach of coyotes. Mounting once more, he ascended to the rim and found a slope leading down to the west. Over the basin country below he had hunted several days. This way back to the ranch was longer, he calculated, but less arduous for man and beast. His packhorse would have hard enough going in any event. From time to time Wade halted to rest the burdened pack animal. At length he came to a trail he had himself made, which he now proceeded to follow. It led out of the basin, through burned and boggy ground and down upon the forest slope, thence to the grassy and aspened uplands. One aspen grove, where he had rested before, faced the west, and, for reasons hard to guess, had suffered little from frost. All the leaves were intact, some still green, but most of them a glorious gold against the blue. It was a large grove, sloping gently, carpeted with yellow grass and such a profusion of purple asters as Wade had never seen in his flower-loving life. Here he dismounted and sat against an aspen-tree. His horses ruthlessly cropped the purple blossoms.

Nature in her strong prodigality had outdone herself here. Pale white the aspen trees shone, and above was the fluttering, quivering canopy of gold tinged with green, and below clustered the asters, thick as stars in the sky, waving, nodding, swaying gracefully to each little autumn breeze, lilac-hued and lavender and pale violet, and all the shades of exquisite purple.

Wade lingered, his senses predominating. This was one of those moments that colored his lonely wanderings. Only to see was enough. He would have shut out the encroaching thoughts of self, of others, of life, had that been wholly possible. But here, after the first few moments of exquisite riot of his senses, where fragrance of grass and blossom filled the air, and blaze of gold canopied the purple, he began to think how beautiful the earth was, how Nature hid her rarest gifts for those who loved her most, how good it was to live, if only for these blessings. And sadness crept into his meditations because all this beauty was ephemeral, all the gold would soon be gone, and the asters, so pale and pure and purple, would soon be like the glory of a dream that had passed.

Yet still followed the saving thought that frost and winter must again yield to sun, and spring, summer, autumn would return with the flowers of their season, in that perennial birth so gracious and promising. The aspen leaves would quiver and slowly gild, the grass would wave in the wind, the asters would bloom, lifting star-pale faces to the sky. Next autumn, and every year, and forever, as long as the sun warmed the earth!

It was only man who would not always return to the haunts he loved.

## CHAPTER XI

When Bent Wade desired opportunities they seemed to gravitate to him.

Upon riding into the yard of White Slides Ranch he espied Jack Belllounds sitting in idle, moping posture on the porch. Something in his dejected appearance roused Wade's pity. No one else was in sight, so the hunter took advantage of the moment.

"Hey, Belllounds, will you give me a lift with this meat?" called Wade.

"Sure," replied Jack, readily enough, and he got up. Wade led the packhorse to the door of the store cabin, which stood back of the kitchen and was joined to it by a roof. There, with Jack's assistance, he unloaded the meat and hung it up on pegs. This done, Wade set to work with knife in hand.

"I reckon a little trimmin' will improve the looks of this carcass," observed Wade.

"Wade, we never had anyone round except dad who could cut up a steer or elk," said Jack. "But you've got him beat."

"I'm pretty handy at most things."

"Handy! . . . I wish I could do just one thing as well as you. I can ride, but that's all. No one ever taught me anything."

"You're a young fellow yet, an' you've time, if you only take kindly to learnin'. I was past your age when I learned most I know."

The hunter's voice and his look, and that fascination which subtly hid in his presence, for the first time seemed to find the response of interest in young Belllounds.

"I can't stick, dad says, and he swears at me," replied Belllounds. "But I'll bet I could learn from you."

"Reckon you could. Why can't you stick to anythin'?"

"I don't know. I've been as enthusiastic over work as over riding mustangs. To ride came natural, but in work, when I do it wrong, then I hate it."

"Ahuh! That's too bad. You oughtn't to hate work. Hard work makes for what I reckon you like in a man, but don't understand. As I look back over my life—an' let me say, young fellar, it's been a tough one—what I remember most an' feel best over are the hardest jobs I ever did, an' those that cost the most sweat an' blood."

As Wade warmed to his subject, hoping to sow a good seed in Belllounds's mind, he saw that he was wasting his earnestness. Belllounds did not keep to the train of thought. His mind wandered, and now he was examining Wade's rifle.

"Old Henry forty-four," he said. "Dad has one. Also an old needle-gun. Say, can I go hunting with you?"

"Glad to have you. How do you handle a rifle?"

"I used to shoot pretty well before I went to Denver," he replied. "Haven't tried since I've been home . . . Suppose you let me take a shot at that post?" And from where he stood in the door he pointed to a big hitching post near the corral gate.

The corral contained horses, and in the pasture beyond were cattle, any of which might be endangered by such a shot. Wade saw that the young man was in earnest, that he wanted to respond to the suggestion in his mind. Consequences of any kind did not awaken after the suggestion.

"Sure. Go ahead. Shoot low, now, a little below where you want to hit," said Wade.

Belllounds took aim and fired. A thundering report shook the cabin. Dust and splinters flew from the post.

"I hit it!" he exclaimed, in delight. "I was sure I wouldn't, because I aimed 'way under."

"Reckon you did. It was a good shot."

Then a door slammed and Old Bill Belllounds appeared, his hair upstanding, his look and gait proclaiming him on the rampage.

"Jack! What'n hell are you doin'?" he roared, and he stamped up to the door to see his son standing there with the rifle in his hands. "By Heaven! If it ain't one thing it's another!"

"Boss, don't jump over the traces," said Wade. "I'll allow if I'd known the gun would let out a bellar like that I'd not have told Jack to shoot. Reckon it's because we're under the open roof that it made the racket. I'm wantin' to clean the gun while it's hot."

"Ahuh! Wal, I was scared fust, harkin' back to Indian days, an' then I was mad because I figgered Jack was up to mischief . . . Did you fetch in the meat?"

"You bet. An' I'd like a piece for myself," replied Wade.

"Help yourself, man. An' say, come down an' eat with us fer supper."

"Much obliged, boss. I sure will."

Then the old rancher trudged back to the house.

"Wade, it was bully of you!" exclaimed Jack, gratefully. "You see how quick dad's ready to jump me? I'll bet he thought I'd picked a shooting-scrape with one of the cowboys."

"Well, he's gettin' old an' testy," replied Wade. "You ought to humor him. He'll not be here always."

Belllounds answered to that suggestion with a shadowing of eyes and look of realization, affection, remorse. Feelings seemed to have a quick rise and play in him, but were not lasting. Wade casually studied him, weighing his impressions, holding them in abeyance for a sum of judgment.

"Belllounds, has anybody told you about Wils Moore bein' bad hurt?" abruptly asked the hunter.

"He is, is he?" replied Jack, and to his voice and face came sudden change. "How bad?"

"I reckon he'll be a cripple for life," answered Wade, seriously, and now he stopped in his work to peer at Belllounds. The next moment might be critical for that young man.

"Club-footed! . . . He won't lord it over the cowboys any more—or ride that white mustang!" The softer, weaker expression of his face, that which gave him some title to good looks, changed to an ugliness hard for Wade to define, since it was neither glee, nor joy, nor gratification over his rival's misfortune. It was rush of blood to eyes and skin, a heated change that somehow to Wade suggested an anxious, selfish hunger. Belllounds lacked something, that seemed certain. But it remained to be proved how deserving he was of Wade's pity.

"Belllounds, it was a dirty trick—your jumpin' Moore," declared Wade, with deliberation.

"The hell you say!" Belllounds flared up, with scarlet in his face, with sneer of amaze, with promise of bursting rage. He slammed down the gun.

"Yes, the hell I say," returned the hunter. "They call me Hell-Bent Wade!"

"Are you friends with Moore?" asked Belllounds, beginning to shake.

"Yes, I'm that with everyone. I'd like to be friends with you."

"I don't want you. And I'm giving you notice—you won't last long at White Slides."

"Neither will you!"

Belllounds turned dead white, not apparently from fury or fear, but from a shock that had its birth within the deep, mysterious, emotional reachings of his mind. He was utterly astounded, as if confronting a vague, terrible premonition of the future. Wade's swift words, like the ring of bells, had not been menacing, but prophetic.

"Young fellar, you need to be talked to, so if you've got any sense at all it'll get a wedge in your brain," went on Wade. "I'm a stranger here. But I happen to be a man who sees through things, an' I see how your dad handles you wrong. You don't know who I am an' you don't care. But if you'll listen you'll learn what might help you . . . No boy can answer to all his wild impulses without ruinin' himself. It's not natural. There are other people—people who have wills an' desires, same as you have. You've got to live with people. Here's your dad an' Miss Columbine, an' the cowboys, an' me, an' all the ranchers, so down to Kremmlin' an' other places. These are the people you've got to live with. You can't go on as you've begun, without ruinin' yourself an' your dad an' the—the girl . . . It's never too late to begin to be better. I know that. But it gets too late, sometimes, to save the happiness of others. Now I see where you're headin' as clear as if I had pictures of the future. I've got a gift that way . . . An', Belllounds, you'll not last. Unless you begin to control your temper, to forget yourself, to kill your wild impulses, to be kind, to learn what love is—you'll never last! . . . In the very nature of things, one comin' after another like your fights with Moore, an' your scarin' of Pronto, an' your drinkin' at Kremmlin', an' just now your r'arin' at me—it's in the very nature of life that goin' on so you'll sooner or later meet with hell! You've got to change, Belllounds. No halfway, spoiled-boy changin', but the straight right-about-face of a man! . . . It means you must see you're no good an' have a change of heart. Men have revolutions like that. I was no good. I did worse than you'll ever do, because you're not big enough to be really bad, an' yet I've turned out worth livin' . . . There, I'm through, an' I'm offerin' to be your friend an' to help you."

Belllounds stood with arms spread outside the door, still astounded, still pale; but as the long admonition and appeal ended he exploded stridently. "Who the hell are *you?* . . . If I hadn't been so surprised—if I'd had a chance to get a word in—I'd shut your trap! Are you a preacher masquerading here as hunter? Let me tell you, I won't be talked to like that—not by any man. Keep your advice an' friendship to yourself."

"You don't want me, then?"

"No," Belllounds snapped.

"Reckon you don't need either advice or friend, hey?"

"No, you owl-eyed, soft-voiced fool!" yelled Belllounds.

It was then Wade felt a singular and familiar sensation, a cold, creeping thing, physical and elemental, that had not visited him since he had been at White Slides.

"I reckoned so," he said, with low and gloomy voice, and he knew, if

Belllounds did not know, that he was not acquiescing with the other's harsh epithet, but only greeting the advent of something in himself.

Belllounds shrugged his burly shoulders and slouched away.

Wade finished his dressing of the meat. Then he rode up to spend an hour with Moore. When he returned to his cabin he proceeded to change his hunter garb for the best he owned. It was a proof of his unusual preoccupation that he did this before he fed the hounds. It was sunset when he left his cabin. Montana Jim and Lem hailed as he went by. Wade paused to listen to their good-natured raillery.

"See hyar, Bent, this ain't Sunday," said Lem.

"You're spruced up powerful fine. What's it fer?" added Montana.

"Boss asked me down to supper."

"Wal, you lucky son-of-a-gun! An' hyar we've no invite," returned Lem. "Say, Wade, I heerd Buster Jack roarin' at you. I was ridin' in by the storehouse . . . 'Who the hell are you?' was what collared my attention, an' I had to laugh. An' I listened to all he said. So you was offerin' him advice an' friendship?"

"I reckon."

"Wal, all I say is thet you was wastin' yore breath," declared Lem. "You're a queer fellar, Wade."

"Queer? Aw, Lem, he ain't queer," said Montana. "He's jest white. Wade, I feel the same as you. I'd like to do somethin' fer thet locoed Buster Jack."

"Montana, you're the locoed one," rejoined Lem. "Buster Jack knows what he's doin'. He can play a slicker hand of poker than you."

"Wal, mebbe. Wade, do you play poker?"

"I'd hate to take your money," replied Wade.

"You needn't be so all-fired kind about thet. Come over tonight an' take some of it. Buster Jack invited himself up to our bunk. He's itchin' fer cards. So we says shore. Blud's goin' to sit in. Now you come an' make it five-handed."

"Wouldn't young Belllounds object to me?"

"What? Buster Jack shy at gamblin' with you? Not much. He's a born gambler. He'd bet with his grandmother an' he'd cheat the coppers off a dead nigger's eyes."

"Slick with cards, eh?" inquired Wade.

"Naw, Jack's not slick. But he tries to be. An' we jest go him one slicker."

"Wouldn't Old Bill object to this card-playin'?"

"He'd be ory-eyed. But, by Golly! We're not leadin' Jack astray. An' we ain't hankerin' to play with him. All the same a little game is welcome enough."

"I'll come over," replied Wade, and thoughtfully turned away.

When he presented himself at the ranch house it was Columbine who let him in. She was prettily dressed, in a way he had never seen her before, and his heart throbbed. Her smile, her voice added to her nameless charm, that seemed to come from the past. Her look was eager and longing, as if his presence might bring something welcome to her.

Then the rancher stalked in. "Hullo, Wade! Supper's 'most ready. What's this trouble you had with Jack? He says he won't eat with you."

"I was offerin' him advice," replied Wade.

"What on?"

"Reckon on general principles."

"Humph! Wal, he told me you harangued him till you was black in the face, an'—"

"Jack had it wrong. He got black in the face," interrupted Wade.

"Did you say he was a spoiled boy an' thet he was no good an' was headin' plumb fer hell?"

"That was a little of what I said," returned Wade, gently.

"Ahuh! How'd thet come about?" queried Belllounds, gruffly. A slight stiffening and darkening overcast his face.

Wade then recalled and recounted the remarks that had passed between him and Jack; and he did not think he missed them very far. He had a great curiosity to see how Belllounds would take them, and especially the young man's scornful rejection of a sincerely offered friendship. All the time Wade was talking he was aware of Columbine watching him, and when he finished it was sweet to look at her.

"Wade, wasn't you takin' a lot on yourself?" queried the rancher, plainly displeased.

"Reckon I was. But my conscience is beholden to no man. If Jack had met me halfway that would have been better for him. An' for me, because I get good out of helpin' anyone."

His reply silenced Belllounds. No more was said before supper was announced, and then the rancher seemed taciturn. Columbine did the serving, and most all of the talking. Wade felt strangely at ease. Some subtle difference was at work in him, transforming him, but the moment had not yet come for him to question himself. He enjoyed the supper. And when he ventured to look up at Columbine, to see her strong, capable hands and her warm, blue glance, glad for his presence, sweetly expressive of their common secret and darker with a shadow of meaning beyond her power to guess, then Wade felt havoc within him, the strife and pain and joy of the truth he never could reveal. For he could never reveal his identity to her without betraying his baseness to her mother. Otherwise, to hear her call him father would have been earning that happiness with a lie. Besides, she loved Belllounds as her father, and were this trouble of the present removed she would grow still closer to the old man in his declining days. Wade accepted the inevitable, she must never know. If she might love him it must be as the stranger who came to her gates, it must be through the mysterious affinity between them and through the service he meant to render.

Wade did not linger after the meal was ended despite the fact that Belllounds recovered his cordiality. It was dark when he went out. Columbine followed him, talking cheerfully. Once outside she squeezed his hand and whispered, "How's Wilson?"

The hunter nodded his reply, and, pausing at the porch step, he pressed her hand to make his assurance stronger. His reward was instant. In the bright starlight she stood white and eloquent, staring down at him with dark, wide eyes.

Presently she whispered: "Oh, my friend! It wants only three days till October first!"

"Lass, it might be a thousand years for all you need worry," he replied, his voice low and full. Then it seemed, as she flung up her arms, that she was about to embrace him. But her gesture was an appeal to the stars, to Heaven above, for something she did not speak.

Wade bade her good night and went his way.

* * * * *

The cowboys and the rancher's son were about to engage in a game of poker when Wade entered the dimly lighted, smoke-hazed room. Montana Jim was sticking tallow candles in the middle of a rude table; Lem was searching his clothes, manifestly for money; Bludsoe shuffled a greasy deck of cards, and Jack Belllounds was filling his pipe before a fire of blazing logs on the hearth.

"Dog-gone it! I hed more money 'n thet," complained Lem. "Jim, you rode to Kremmlin' last. Did you take my money?"

"Wal, come to think of it, I reckon I did," replied Jim, in surprise at the recollection.

"An' whar's it now?"

"Pard, I 'ain't no idee. I reckon it's still in Kremmlin'. But I'll pay you back."

"I should smile you will. Pony up now."

"Bent Wade, did you come over calkilated to git skinned?" queried Bludsoe.

"Boys, I was playin' poker tolerable well in Missouri when you all was nursin'," replied Wade, imperturbably.

"I heerd he was a card-sharp," said Jim. "Wal, grab a box or a chair to set on an' let's start. Come along, Jack; you don't look as keen to play as usual."

Belllounds stood with his back to the fire and his manner did not compare favorably with that of the genial cowboys.

"I prefer to play four-handed," he said.

This declaration caused a little check in the conversation and put an end to the amiability. The cowboys looked at one another, not embarrassed, but just a little taken aback, as if they had forgotten something that they should have remembered.

"You object to my playin'?" asked Wade, quietly.

"I certainly do," replied Belllounds.

"Why, may I ask?"

"For all I know, what Montana said about you may be true," returned Belllounds, insolently.

Such a remark flung in the face of a Westerner was an insult. The cowboys suddenly grew stiff, with steady eyes on Wade. He, however, did not change in the slightest.

"I might be a card-sharp at that," he replied, coolly. "You fellows play without me. I'm not carin' about poker anymore. I'll look on."

Thus he carried over the moment that might have been dangerous. Lem gaped at him; Montana kicked a box forward to sit upon, and his action was expressive; Bludsoe slammed the cards down on the table and favored Wade with a comprehending look. Belllounds pulled a chair up to the table.

"What'll we make the limit?" asked Jim.

"Two bits," replied Lem, quickly.

Then began an argument. Belllounds was for a dollar limit. The cowboys objected.

"Why, Jack, if the ole man got on to us playin' a dollar limit he'd fire the outfit," protested Bludsoe.

This reasonable objection in no wise influenced the old man's son. He overruled the good arguments, and then hinted at the cowboys' lack of nerve. The fun faded out of their faces. Lem, in fact, grew red.

"Wal, if we're agoin' to gamble, thet's different," he said, with a cold ring in his voice, as he straddled a box and sat down. "Wade, lemme some money."

Wade slipped his hand into his pocket and drew forth a goodly handful of gold, which he handed to the cowboy. Not improbably, if this large amount had been shown earlier, before the change in the sentiment, Lem would have looked aghast and begged for mercy. As it was, he accepted it as if he were accustomed to borrowing that much every day. Belllounds had rendered futile the easy-going, friendly advances of the cowboys, as he had made it impossible to play a jolly little game for fun.

The game began, with Wade standing up, looking on. These boys did not know what a vast store of poker knowledge lay back of Wade's inscrutable eyes. As a boy he had learned the intricacies of poker in the country where it originated; and as a man he had played it with piles of yellow coins and guns on the table. His eagerness to look on here, as far as the cowboys were concerned, was mere pretense. In Belllounds's case, however, he had a profound interest. Rumors had drifted to him from time to time, since his advent at White Slides, regarding Belllounds's weakness for gambling. It might have been cowboy gossip. Wade held that there was nothing in the West as well calculated to test a boy, to prove his real character, as a game of poker.

Belllounds was a feverish better, an exultant winner, a poor loser. His understanding of the game was rudimentary. With him, the strong feeling beginning to be manifested to Wade was not the fun of matching wits and luck with his antagonists, nor a desire to accumulate money—for his recklessness disproved that—but the liberation of the gambling passion. Wade recognized that when he met it. And Jack Belllounds was not in any sense big. He was selfish and grasping in the numberless little ways common to the game, and positive about his own rights, while doubtful of the claims of others. His cheating was clumsy and crude. He held out cards, hiding them in his palm; he shuffled the deck so he left aces at the bottom, and these he would slip off to himself, and he was so blind that he could not detect his fellow player in tricks as transparent as his own. Wade was amazed and disgusted. The pity he had felt for Belllounds shifted to the old father, who believed in his son with stubborn and unquenchable faith.

"Haven't you got something to drink?" Jack asked of his companions.

"Nope. Whar'd we git it?" replied Jim.

Belllounds evidently forgot, for presently he repeated the query. The cowboys shook their heads. Wade knew they were lying, for they did have liquor in the cabin. It occurred to him, then, to offer to go to his own cabin for some, just to see what this young man would say. But he refrained.

The luck went against Belllounds and so did the gambling. He was not a lamb among wolves, by any means, but the fleecing he got suggested that. According to Wade he was getting what he deserved. No cowboys, even such good-natured and fine fellows as these, could be expected to be subjects for Belllounds's cupidity. And they won all he had.

"I'll borrow," he said, with feverish impatience. His face was pale, clammy, yet heated, especially round the swollen bruises; his eyes stood out, bold, dark, rolling and glaring, full of sullen fire. But more than anything else his mouth betrayed the weakling, the born gambler, the self-centered, spoiled, intolerant youth. It was here his bad blood showed.

"Wal, I ain't lendin' money," replied Lem, as he assorted his winnings. "Wade, here's what you staked me, an' much obliged."

"I'm out, an' I can't lend you any," said Jim.

Bludsoe had a good share of the profits of that quick game, but he made no move to lend any of it. Belllounds glared impatiently at them.

"Hell! You took my money. I'll have satisfaction," he broke out, almost shouting.

"We won it, didn't we?" rejoined Lem, cool and easy. "An' you can have all the satisfaction you want, right now or any time."

Wade held out a handful of money to Belllounds.

"Here," he said, with his deep eyes gleaming in the dim room. Wade had made a gamble with himself, and it was that Belllounds would not even hesitate to take money.

"Come on, you stingy cowpunchers," he called out, snatching the money from Wade. His action then, violent and vivid as it was, did not reveal any more than his face.

But the cowboys showed amaze, and something more. They fell straightway to gambling, sharper and fiercer than before, actuated now by the flaming spirit of this son of Belllounds. Luck, misleading and alluring, favored Jack for a while, transforming him until he was radiant, boastful, exultant. Then it changed, as did his expression. His face grew dark.

"I tell you I want drink," he suddenly demanded. "I know damn well you cowpunchers have some here, for I smelled it when I came in."

"Jack, we drank the last drop," replied Jim, who seemed less stiff than his two bunkmates.

"I've some very old rye," interposed Wade, looking at Jim, but apparently addressing all. "Fine stuff, but awful strong an' hot! . . . Makes a fellow's blood dance."

"Go get it!" Belllounds's utterance was thick and full, as if he had something in his mouth.

Wade looked down into the heated face, into the burning eyes; and through the darkness of passion that brooked no interference with its fruition he saw this youth's stark and naked soul. Wade had seen into the depths of many such abysses.

"See hyar, Wade," broke in Jim, with his quiet force, "never mind fetchin' thet red-hot rye tonight. Some other time, mebbe, when Jack wants more satisfaction. Reckon we've got a drop or so left."

"All right, boys," replied Wade, "I'll be sayin' good night."

He left them playing and strode out to return to his cabin. The night was still, cold, starlit, and black in the shadows. A lonesome coyote barked, to be answered by a wakeful hound. Wade halted at his porch, and lingered there a moment, peering up at the gray old peak, bare and star-crowned.

"I'm sorry for the old man," muttered the hunter, "but I'd see Jack Belllounds in hell before I'd let Columbine marry him."

* * * * *

October first was a holiday at White Slides Ranch. It happened to be a glorious autumn day, with the sunlight streaming gold and amber over the grassy slopes. Far off the purple ranges loomed hauntingly.

Wade had come down from Wilson Moore's cabin, his ears ringing with the crippled boy's words of poignant fear.

Fox favored his master with unusually knowing gaze. There was not going to be any lion chasing or elk hunting this day. Something was in the wind. And Fox, as a privileged dog, manifested his interest and wonder.

Before noon a buckboard with team of sweating horses halted in the yard of the ranch house. Besides the driver it contained two women whom Belllounds greeted as relatives, and a stranger, a pale man whose dark garb proclaimed him a minister.

"Come right in, folks," welcomed Belllounds, with hearty excitement.

It was Wade who showed the driver where to put the horses. Strangely, not a cowboy was in sight, an omission of duty the rancher had noted. Wade might have informed him where they were.

The door of the big living room stood open, and from it came the sound of laughter and voices. Wade, who had returned to his seat on the end of the porch, listened to them, while his keen gaze seemed fixed down the lane toward the cabins. How intent must he have been not to hear Columbine's step behind him!

"Good morning, Ben," she said.

Wade wheeled as if internal violence had ordered his movement.

"Lass, good mornin'," he replied. "You sure look sweet this October first—like the flower for which you're named."

"My friend, it *is* October first—my marriage day!" murmured Columbine.

Wade felt her intensity, and he thrilled to the brave, sweet resignation of her face. Hope and faith were unquenchable in her, yet she had fortified herself to the wreck of dreams and love.

"I'd seen you before now, but I had some job with Wils, persuadin' him that we'd not have to offer you congratulations yet awhile," replied Wade, in his slow, gentle voice.

"*Oh!*" breathed Columbine.

Wade saw her full breast swell and the leaping blood wave over her pale face. She bent to him to see his eyes. And for Wade, when she peered with straining heart and soul, all at once to become transfigured, that instant was a sweet and all-fulfilling reward for his years of pain.

"You drive me mad!" she whispered.

The heavy tread of the rancher, like the last of successive steps of fate in Wade's tragic expectancy, sounded on the porch.

"Wal, lass, hyar you are," he said, with a gladness deep in his voice. "Now, whar's the boy?"

"Dad—I've not—seen Jack since breakfast," replied Columbine, tremulously.

"Sort of a laggard in love on his weddin'-day," rejoined the rancher. His gladness and forgetfulness were as big as his heart. "Wade, have you seen Jack?"

"No—I haven't," replied the hunter, with slow, long-drawn utterance. "But—I see—him now."

Wade pointed to the figure of Jack Belllounds approaching from the direction of the cabins. He was not walking straight.

Old man Belllounds shot out his gray head like a striking eagle.

"What the hell?" he muttered, as if bewildered at this strange, uneven gait of his son. "Wade, what's the matter with Jack?"

Wade did not reply. That moment had its sorrow for him as well as understanding of the wonder expressed by Columbine's cold little hand trembling in his.

The rancher suddenly recoiled.

"So help me Gawd—he's drunk!" he gasped, in a distress that unmanned him.

Then the parson and the invited relatives came out upon the porch, with gay voices and laughter that suddenly stilled when old Belllounds cried, brokenly: "Lass—go—in—the house."

But Columbine did not move, and Wade felt her shaking as she leaned against him.

The bridegroom approached. Drunk indeed he was; not hilariously, as one who celebrated his good fortune, but sullenly, tragically, hideously drunk.

Old Belllounds leaped off the porch. His gray hair stood up like the mane of a lion. Like a giant's were his strides. With a lunge he met his reeling son, swinging a huge fist into the sodden red face. Limply Jack fell to the ground.

"Lay there, you damned prodigal!" he roared, terrible in his rage. "You disgrace me—an' you disgrace the girl who's been a daughter to me! . . . If you ever have another weddin'-day it'll not be me who sets it!"

## CHAPTER XII

November was well advanced before there came indications that winter was near at hand.

One morning, when Wade rode up to Moore's cabin, the whole world seemed obscured in a dense gray fog, through which he could not see a rod ahead of him. Later, as he left, the fog had lifted shoulder-high to the mountains, and was breaking to let the blue sky show. Another morning it was worse, and apparently thicker and grayer. As Wade climbed the trail up toward the mountain-basin, where he hunted most these days, he expected the fog to lift. But it did not. The trail under the hoofs of the horse was scarcely perceptible to him, and he seemed lost in a dense, gray, soundless obscurity.

Suddenly Wade emerged from out the fog into brilliant sunshine. In amaze he halted. This phenomenon was new to him. He was high up on the mountainside, the summit of which rose clear-cut and bold into the sky. Below him spread what resembled a white sea. It was an immense cloud bank, filling all the valleys as if with creamy foam or snow, soft, thick, motionless, contrasting vividly with the blue sky above. Old White Slides stood out, gray and bleak and brilliant, as if it were an island rock in a rolling sea of fleece. Far across this strange, level cloud floor rose the black line of the range. Wade watched the scene with a kind of rapture. He was alone on the heights. There was not a sound. The winds were stilled. But there seemed a mighty being awake all around him, in the presence of which Wade felt how little were his sorrows and hopes.

Another day brought dull gray scudding clouds, and gusts of wind and squalls of rain, and a wailing through the bare aspens. It grew colder and bleaker and darker. Rain changed to sleet and sleet to snow. That night brought winter.

Next morning, when Wade plodded up to Moore's cabin, it was through two feet of snow. A beautiful glistening white mantle covered valley and slope and mountain, transforming all into a world too dazzlingly brilliant for the unprotected gaze of man.

When Wade pushed open the door of the cabin and entered he awakened the cowboy.

"Mornin', Wils," drawled Wade, as he slapped the snow from boots and legs. "Summer has gone, winter has come, an' the flowers lay in their graves! How are you, boy?"

Moore had grown paler and thinner during his long confinement in bed. A weary shade shone in his face and a shadow of pain in his eyes. But the spirit of his smile was the same as always.

"Hello, Bent, old pard!" replied Moore. "I guess I'm fine. Nearly froze last night. Didn't sleep much."

"Well, I was worried about that," said the hunter. "We've got to arrange things somehow."

"I heard it snowing. Gee! How the wind howled! And I'm snowed in?"

"Sure are. Two feet on a level. It's good I snaked down a lot of firewood. Now I'll set to work an' cut it up an' stack it round the cabin. Reckon I'd better sleep up here with you, Wils."

"Won't Old Bill make a kick?"

"Let him kick. But I reckon he doesn't need to know anythin' about it. It is cold in here. Well, I'll soon warm it up . . . Here's some letters Lem got at Kremmlin' the other day. You read while I rustle some grub for you."

Moore scanned the addresses on the several envelopes and sighed.

"From home! I hate to read them."

"Why?" queried Wade.

"Oh, because when I wrote I didn't tell them I was hurt. I feel like a liar."

"It's just as well, Wils, because you swear you'll not go home."

"Me? I should smile not . . . Bent—I—I—hoped Collie might answer the note you took her from me."

"Not yet. Wils, give the lass time."

"Time? Heavens! It's three weeks and more."

"Go ahead an' read your letters or I'll knock you on the head with one of these chunks," ordered Wade, mildly.

The hunter soon had the room warm and cheerful, with steaming breakfast on the red-hot coals. Presently, when he made ready to serve Moore, he was surprised to find the boy crying over one of the letters.

"Wils, what's the trouble?" he asked.

"Oh, nothing. I—I—just feel bad, that's all," replied Moore.

"Ahuh! So it seems. Well, tell me about it?"

"Pard, my father—has forgiven me."

"The old son-of-a-gun! Good! What for? You never told me you'd done anythin'."

"I know—but I did—do a lot. I was sixteen then. We quarreled. And I ran off up here to punch cows. But after a while I wrote home to mother and my sister. Since then they've tried to coax me to come home. This letter's from the old man himself. Gee! . . . Well, he says he's had to knuckle. That he's ready to forgive me. But I must come home and take charge of his ranch. Isn't that great? . . . Only I can't go. And I couldn't—I couldn't ever ride a horse again—if I did go."

"Who says you couldn't?" queried Wade. "I never said so. I only said you'd never be a bronco-bustin' cowboy again. Well, suppose you're not? You'll be able to ride a little, if I can save that leg . . . Boy, your letter is damn good news. I'm sure glad. That will make Collie happy."

The cowboy had a better appetite that morning, which fact mitigated somewhat the burden of Wade's worry. There was burden enough, however, and Wade had set this day to make important decisions about Moore's injured foot. He had dreaded to remove the last dressing because conditions at that time had been unimproved. He had done all he could to ward off the threatened gangrene.

"Wils, I'm goin' to look at your foot an' tell you things," declared Wade, when the dreaded time could be put off no longer.

"Go ahead . . . And, pard, if you say my leg has to be cut off—why just pass me my gun!"

The cowboy's voice was gay and bantering, but his eyes were alight with a spirit that frightened the hunter.

"Ahuh! . . . I know how you feel. But, boy, I'd rather live with one leg an' be loved by Collie Belllounds than have nine legs for some other lass."

Wilson Moore groaned his helplessness.

"Damn you, Bent Wade! You always say what kills me! . . . Of course I would!"

"Well, lie quiet now, an' let me look at this poor, messed-up foot."

Wade's deft fingers did not work with the usual precision and speed natural to them. But at last Moore's injured member lay bare, discolored and misshapen. The first glance made the hunter quicker in his movements, closer in his scrutiny. Then he yelled his joy.

"Boy, it's better! No sign of gangrene! We'll save your leg!"

"Pard, I never feared I'd lose that. All I've feared was that I'd be club-footed . . . Let me look," replied the cowboy, and he raised himself on his elbow. Wade lifted the unsightly foot.

"My God, it's crooked!" cried Moore, passionately. "Wade, it's healed. It'll stay that way always! I can't move it! . . . Oh, but Buster Jack's ruined me!"

The hunter pushed him back with gentle hands. "Wils, it might have been worse."

"But I never gave up hope," replied Moore, in poignant grief. "I couldn't. But *now!* . . . How can you look at that—that club-foot, and not swear?"

"Well, well, boy, cussin' won't do any good. Now lay still an' let me work. You've had lots of good news this mornin'. So I think you can stand to hear a little bad news."

"What! Bad news?" queried Moore, with a start.

"I reckon. Now listen . . . The reason Collie hasn't answered your note is because she's been sick in bed for three weeks."

"Oh no!" exclaimed the cowboy, in amaze and distress.

"Yes, an' I'm her doctor," replied Wade, with pride. "First off they had Mrs. Andrews. An' Collie kept askin' for me. She was out of her head, you know. An' soon as I took charge she got better."

"Heavens! Collie ill and you never told me!" cried Moore. "I can't believe it. She's so healthy and strong. What ailed her, Bent?"

"Well, Mrs. Andrews said it was nervous breakdown. An' Old Bill was afraid of consumption. An' Jack Belllounds swore she was only shammin'."

The cowboy cursed violently.

"Here—I won't tell you any more if you're goin' to cuss that way an' jerk around," protested Wade.

"I—I'll shut up," appealed Moore.

"Well, that puddin'-head Jack is more'n you called him, if you care to hear my opinion . . . Now, Wils, the fact is that none of them know what ails Collie. But I know. She'd been under a high strain leadin' up to October first. An' the way that weddin'-day turned out—with Old Bill layin' Jack cold, an' with no marriage at all—why, Collie had a shock. An' after that she seemed pale an' tired all the time an' she didn't eat right. Well, when Buster Jack got over that awful punch he'd got from the old man he made up to Collie harder than ever. She didn't tell me then, but I saw it. An' she couldn't avoid him, except by stayin' in her room, which she did a good deal. Then Jack showed a streak of bein' decent. He surprised everybody, even Collie. He delighted Old Bill. But he didn't pull the wool over my eyes. He was like a boy spoilin' for a new toy, an' he got crazy over Collie. He's sure terribly in love with her, an' for days he behaved himself in a way calculated to make up for his drinkin' too much. It shows he can behave himself when he wants to. I mean he can control his temper an' impulse. Anyway, he made himself so good that Old Bill changed his mind, after what he swore that day, an' set another day for the weddin'. Right off, then, Collie goes down on her back . . . They didn't send for me very soon. But when I did get to see her, an' felt the way she grabbed me—as if she was drownin'—then I knew what ailed her. It was love."

"Love!" gasped Moore, breathlessly.

"Sure. Jest love for a dog-gone lucky cowboy named Wils Moore! . . . Her heart was breakin', an' she'd have died but for me! Don't imagine, Wils, that people can't die of broken hearts. They do. I know. Well, all Collie needed was me, an' I cured her ravin' and made her eat, an' now she's comin' along fine."

"Wade, I've believed in Heaven since you came down to White Slides," burst out Moore, with shining eyes. "But tell me—what did you tell her?"

"Well, my particular medicine first off was to whisper in her ear that she'd never have to marry Jack Belllounds. An' after that I gave her daily doses of talk about you."

"Pard! She loves me—still?" he whispered.

"Wils, hers is the kind that grows stronger with time. I know."

Moore strained in his intensity of emotion, and he clenched his fists and gritted his teeth.

"Oh God! This's hard on me!" he cried. "I'm a man. I love that girl more than life. And to know she's suffering for love of me—for fear of that marriage being forced upon her—to know that while I lie here a helpless cripple—it's almost unbearable."

"Boy, you've got to mend now. We've the best of hope now—for you—for her—for everythin'."

"Wade, I think I love you, too," said the cowboy. "You're saving me from madness. Somehow I have faith in you—to do whatever you want. But how could you tell Collie she'd never have to marry Buster Jack?"

"Because I know she never will," replied Wade, with his slow, gentle smile.

"You *know* that?"

"Sure."

"How on earth can you prevent it? Belllounds will never give up planning that marriage for his son. Jack will nag Collie till she can't call her soul her own. Between them they will wear her down. My friend, *how* can you prevent it?"

"Wils, fact is, I haven't reckoned out how I'm goin' to save Collie. But that's no matter. Sufficient unto the day is the evil thereof. I will do it. You can gamble on me, Wils. You must use that hope an' faith to help you get well. For we mustn't forget that you're in more danger than Collie."

"I *will* gamble on you—my life—my very soul," replied Moore, fervently. "By Heaven! I'll be the man I might have been. I'll rise out of despair. I'll even reconcile myself to being a cripple."

"An', Wils, will you rise above hate?" asked Wade, softly.

"Hate! Hate of whom?"

"Jack Belllounds."

The cowboy stared, and his lean, pale face contracted.

"Pard, you wouldn't—you couldn't expect me to—to forgive him?"

"No. I reckon not. But you needn't hate him. I don't. An' I reckon I've some reason, more than you could guess . . . Wils, hate is a poison in the blood. It's worse for him who feels it than for him against whom it rages. I know . . . Well, if you put thought of Jack out of your mind—quit broodin' over what he did to you—an' realize that he's not to blame, you'll overcome your hate. For the son of Old Bill is to be pitied. Yes, Jack Belllounds needs pity. He was ruined before he was born. He never should have been born. An' I want you to understand that, an' stop hatin' him. Will you try?"

"Wade, you're afraid I'll kill him?" whispered Moore.

"Sure. That's it. I'm afraid you might. An' consider how hard that would be for Columbine. She an' Jack were raised sister an' brother, almost. It would be hard on her. You see, Collie has a strange an' powerful sense of duty to Old Bill. If you killed Jack it would likely kill the old man, an' Collie would suffer all her life. You couldn't cure her of that. You want her to be happy."

"I do—I do. Wade, I swear I'll never kill Buster Jack. And for Collie's sake I'll try not to hate him."

"Well, that's fine. I'm sure glad to hear you promise that. Now I'll go out an' chop some wood. We mustn't let the fire go out anymore."

"Pard, I'll write another note—a letter to Collie. Hand me the blank book there. And my pencil . . . And don't hurry with the wood."

Wade went outdoors with his two-bladed ax and shovel. The wood-pile was a great mound of snow. He cleaned a wide space and a path to the side of the cabin. Working in snow was not unpleasant for him. He liked the cleanness, the whiteness, the absolute purity of new-fallen snow. The air was crisp and nipping, the frost crackled under his feet, the smoke from his pipe seemed no thicker than the steam from his breath, the ax rang on the hard aspens. Wade swung this implement like a born woodsman. The chips flew and the dead wood smelled sweet. Some logs he chopped into three-foot pieces; others he chopped and split. When he tired a little of swinging the ax he carried the cut pieces to the cabin and stacked them near the door. Now and then he would halt a moment to gaze away across the whitened slopes and rolling hills. The sense of his physical power matched something within, and his heart warmed with more than the vigorous exercise.

When he had worked thus for about two hours and had stacked a pile of wood almost as large as the cabin he considered it sufficient for the day. So he went indoors. Moore was so busily and earnestly writing that he did not hear Wade come in. His face wore an eloquent glow.

"Say, Wils, are you writin' a book?" he inquired.

"Hello! Sure I am. But I'm 'most done now . . . If Columbine doesn't answer *this* . . ."

"By the way, I'll have two letters to give her, then—for I never gave her the first one," replied Wade.

"You son-of-a-gun!"

"Well, hurry along, boy. I'll be goin' now. Here's a pole I've fetched in. You keep it there, where you can reach it, an' when the fire needs more wood you roll one of these logs on. I'll be up tonight before dark, an' if I don't fetch you a letter it'll be because I can't persuade Collie to write."

"Pard, if you bring me a letter I'll obey you—I'll lie still—I'll sleep—I'll stand anything."

"Ahuh! Then I'll fetch one," replied Wade, as he took the little book and deposited it in his pocket. "Good-by, now, an' think of your good news that come with the snow."

"Good-by, Heaven-Sent Hell-Bent Wade!" called Moore. "It's no joke of a name anymore. It's a fact."

Wade plodded down through the deep snow, stepping in his old tracks, and as he toiled on his thoughts were deep and comforting. He was thinking that if he had his life to live over again he would begin at once to find happiness in other people's happiness. Upon arriving at his cabin he set to work cleaning a path to the dog corral. The snow had drifted there and he had no easy task. It was well that he had built an enclosed house for the hounds to winter in. Such a heavy snow as this one would put an end to hunting for the time being. The ranch had ample supply of deer, bear, and elk meat, all solidly frozen this morning, that would surely keep well until used. Wade reflected that his tasks round the ranch would be feeding hounds and stock, chopping wood, and doing such chores as came along in winter-time. The pack of hounds, which he had thinned out to a smaller number, would be a care on his hands. Kane had become a much-prized possession of Columbine's and lived at the house, where he had things his own way, and always greeted Wade with a look of disdain and distrust. Kane would never forgive the hand that had hurt him. Sampson and Jim and Fox, of course, shared Wade's cabin, and vociferously announced his return.

Early in the afternoon Wade went down to the ranch house. The snow was not so deep there, having blown considerably in the open places. Someone was pounding iron in the blacksmith shop; horses were cavorting in the corrals; cattle were bawling round the hay-ricks in the barnyard.

The hunter knocked on Columbine's door.

"Come in," she called.

Wade entered, to find her alone. She was sitting up in bed, propped up with pillows, and she wore a warm, woolly jacket or dressing gown. Her paleness was now marked, and the shadows under her eyes made them appear large and mournful.

"Ben Wade, you don't care for me anymore!" she exclaimed, reproachfully.

"Why not, lass?" he asked.

"You were so long in coming," she replied, now with petulance. "I guess now I don't want you at all."

"Ahuh! That's the reward of people who worry an' work for others. Well, then, I reckon I'll go back an' not give you what I brought."

He made a pretense of leaving, and he put a hand to his pocket as if to insure the safety of some article. Columbine blushed. She held out her hands. She was repentant of her words and curious as to his.

"Why, Ben Wade, I count the minutes before you come," she said. "What'd you bring me?"

"Who's been in here?" he asked, going forward. "That's a poor fire. I'll have to fix it."

"Mrs. Andrews just left. It was good of her to drive up. She came in the sled, she said. Oh, Ben, it's winter. There was snow on my bed when I woke up. I think I am better today. Jack hasn't been in here yet!"

At this Wade laughed, and Columbine followed suit.

"Well, you look a little sassy today, which I take is a good sign," said Wade. "I've got some news that will come near to makin' you well."

"Oh, tell it quick!" she cried.

"Wils won't lose his leg. It's gettin' well. An' there was a letter from his father, forgivin' him for somethin' he never told me."

"My prayers were answered!" whispered Columbine, and she closed her eyes tight.

"An' his father wants him to come home to run the ranch," went on Wade.

"Oh!" Her eyes popped open with sudden fright. "But he can't—he won't go?"

"I reckon not. He wouldn't if he could. But someday he will, an' take you home with him."

Columbine covered her face with her hands, and was silent a moment.

"Such prophecies! They—they—" She could not conclude.

"Ahuh! I know. The strange fact is, lass, that they all come true. I wish I had all happy ones, instead of them black, croakin' ones that come like ravens . . . Well, you're better today?"

"Yes. Oh yes. Ben, what have you got for me?"

"You're in an awful hurry. I want to talk to you, an' if I show what I've got then there will be no talkin'. You say Jack hasn't been in today?"

"Not yet, thank goodness."

"How about Old Bill?"

"Ben, you never call him my dad. I wish you would. When you *don't* it always reminds me that he's really *not* my dad."

"Ahuh! Well, well!" replied Wade, with his head bowed. "It is just queer I can never remember . . . An' how was he today?"

"For a wonder he didn't mention poor me. He was full of talk about going to Kremmling. Means to take Jack along. Do you know, Ben, dad can't fool me. He's afraid to leave Jack here alone with me. So dad talked a lot about selling stock an' buying supplies, and how he needed Jack to go, and so forth. I'm mighty glad he means to take him. But my! Won't Jack be sore."

"I reckon. It's time he broke out."

"And now, dear Ben—what have you got for me? I know it's from Wilson," she coaxed.

"Lass, would you give much for a little note from Wils?" asked Wade, teasingly.

"Would I? When I've been hoping and praying for just that!"

"Well, if you'd give so much for a note, how much would you give me for a whole bookful that took Wils two hours to write?"

"Ben! Oh, I'd—I'd give—" she cried, wild with delight. "I'd *kiss* you!"

"You mean it?" he queried, waving the book aloft.

"Mean it? Come here!"

There was fun in this for Wade, but also a deep and beautiful emotion that quivered through him. Bending over her, he placed the little book in her hand. He did not see clearly, then, as she pulled him lower and kissed him on the cheek, generously, with sweet, frank gratitude and affection.

Moments strong and all-satisfying had been multiplying for Bent Wade of late. But this one magnified all. As he sat back upon the chair he seemed a little husky of voice.

"Well, well, an' so you kissed ugly old Bent Wade?"

"Yes, and I've wanted to do it before," she retorted. The dark excitation in her eyes, the flush of her pale cheeks, made her beautiful then.

"Lass, now you read your letter an' answer it. You can tear out the pages. I'll sit here an' be makin' out to be readin' aloud out of this book here, if anyone happens in sudden-like!"

"Oh, how you think of everything!"

The hunter sat beside her pretending to be occupied with the book he had taken from the table when really he was stealing glances at her face. Indeed, she was more than pretty then. Illness and pain had enhanced the sweetness of her expression. As she read on it was manifest that she had forgotten the hunter's presence. She grew pink, rosy, scarlet, radiant. And Wade thrilled with her as she thrilled, loved her more and more as she loved. Moore must have written words of enchantment. Wade's hungry heart suffered a pang of jealousy, but would not harbor it. He read in her perusal of that letter what no other dreamed of, not even the girl herself; and it was certitude of tragic and brief life for her if she could not live for Wilson Moore. Those moments of watching her were unutterably precious to Wade. He saw how some divine guidance had directed his footsteps to this home. How many years had it taken him to get there! Columbine read and read and reread—a girl with her first love letter. And for Wade, with his keen eyes that seemed to see the senses and the soul, there shone something infinite through her rapture. Never until that unguarded moment had he divined her innocence, nor had any conception been given him of the exquisite torture of her maiden fears or the havoc of love fighting for itself. He learned then much of the mystery and meaning of a woman's heart.

## CHAPTER XIII

*"Dear Wilson,*

"The note and letter from you have taken my breath away. I couldn't tell—I wouldn't dare tell, how they made me feel.

"Your good news fills me with joy. And when Ben told me you wouldn't lose your leg—that you would get well—then my eyes filled and my heart choked me, and I thanked God, who'd answered my prayers. After all the heartache and dread, it's so wonderful to find things not so terrible as they seemed. Oh, I am thankful! You have only to take care of yourself now, to lie patiently and wait, and obey Ben, and soon the time will have flown by and you will be well again. Maybe, after all, your foot will not be so bad. Maybe you can ride again, if not so wonderfully as before, then well enough to ride on your father's range and look after his stock. For, Wilson dear, you'll have to go home. It's your duty. Your father must be getting old now. He needs you. He has forgiven you—you bad boy! And you are very lucky. It almost kills me to think of your leaving White Slides. But that is selfish. I'm going to learn to be like Ben Wade. He never thinks of himself.

"Rest assured, Wilson, that I will never marry Jack Belllounds. It seems years since that awful October first. I gave my word then, and I would have lived up to it. But I've changed. I'm older. I see things differently. I love dad as well. I feel as sorry for Jack Belllounds. I still think I might help him. I still believe in my duty to his father. But I can't marry him. It would be a sin. I have no right to marry a man whom I do not love. When it comes to thought of his touching me, then I hate him. Duty toward dad is one thing, and I hold it high, but that is not reason enough for a woman to give herself. Some duty to myself is higher than that. It's hard for me to tell you—for me to understand. Love of you has opened my eyes. Still I don't think it's love of you that makes me selfish. I'm true to something in me that I never knew before. I could marry Jack, loving you, and utterly sacrifice myself, if it were right. But it would be wrong. I never realized this until you kissed me. Since then the thought of anything that approaches personal relations—any hint of intimacy with Jack fills me with disgust.

"So I'm not engaged to Jack Belllounds, and I'm never going to be. There will be trouble here. I feel it. I see it coming. Dad keeps at me persistently. He grows older. I don't think he's failing, but then there's a loss of memory, and an almost childish obsession in regard to the marriage he has set his heart on. Then his passion for Jack seems greater as he learns little by little that Jack is not all he might be. Wilson, I give you my word; I believe if dad ever really sees Jack as I see him or you see him, then something dreadful will happen. In spite of everything dad still believes in Jack. It's beautiful and terrible. That's one reason why I've wanted to help Jack. Well, it's not to be. Every day, every hour, Jack Belllounds grows farther from me. He and his father will try to persuade me to consent to this marriage. They may even try to force me. But in that way I'll be as hard and as cold as Old White Slides. No! Never! For the rest, I'll do my duty to dad. I'll stick to him. I could not engage myself to you, no matter how much I love you. And that's more every minute! . . . So don't mention taking me to your home—don't ask me again. Please, Wilson; your asking shook my very soul! Oh, how sweet that would be—your wife! . . . But if dad turns me away—I don't think he would. Yet he's so strange and like iron for all concerning Jack. If ever he turned me out I'd have no home. I'm a waif, you know. Then—then, Wilson . . .

Oh, it's horrible to be in the position I'm in. I won't say any more. You'll understand, dear.

"It's your love that awoke me, and it's Ben Wade who has saved me. Wilson, I love him almost as I do dad, only strangely. Do you know I believe he had something to do with Jack getting drunk that awful October first. I don't mean Ben would stoop to get Jack drunk. But he might have cunningly put that opportunity in Jack's way. Drink is Jack's weakness, as gambling is his passion. Well, I know that the liquor was some fine old stuff which Ben gave to the cowboys. And it's significant now how Jack avoids Ben. He hates him. He's afraid of him. He's jealous because Ben is so much with me. I've heard Jack rave to dad about this. But dad is just to others, if he can't be to his son.

"And so I want you to know that it's Ben Wade who has saved me. Since I've been sick I've learned more of Ben. He's like a woman. He understands. I never have to tell him anything. You, Wilson, were sometimes stupid or stubborn (forgive me) about little things that girls feel but can't explain. Ben knows. I tell you this because I want you to understand how and why I love him. I think I love him most for his goodness to you. Dear boy, if I hadn't loved you before Ben Wade came I'd have fallen in love with you since, just listening to his talk of you. But this will make you conceited. So I'll go on about Ben. He's our friend. Why, Wilson, that sweetness, softness, gentleness about him, the heart that makes him love us, that must be only the woman in him. I don't know what a mother would feel like, but I do know that I seem strangely happier since I've confessed my troubles to this man. It was Lem who told me how Ben offered to be a friend to Jack. And Jack flouted him. I've a queer notion that the moment Jack did this he turned his back on a better life.

"To repeat, then, Ben Wade is our friend, and to me something more that I've tried to explain. Maybe telling you this will make you think more of him and listen to his advice. I hope so. Did any boy and girl ever before so need a friend? I need that something he instils in me. If I lost it I'd be miserable. And, Wilson, I'm such a coward. I'm so weak. I have such sinkings and burnings and tossings. Oh, I'm only a woman! But I'll die fighting. That is what Ben Wade instils into me. While there was life this strange little man would never give up hope. He makes me feel that he knows more than he tells. Through him I shall get the strength to live up to my convictions, to be true to myself, to be faithful to you.

"With love,

"*Columbine.*"

\* \* \* \* \*

"December 3d.

*"Dearest Collie,*

"Your last was only a note, and I told Wade if he didn't fetch more than a note next time there would be trouble round this bunk-house. And then he brought your letter!

"I'm feeling exuberant (I think it's that) today. First time I've been up. Collie, I'm able to get up! *Whoopee!* I walk with a crutch, and don't dare put my foot down. Not that it hurts, but that my boss would have a fit! I'm glad you've stopped heaping praise upon our friend Ben. Because now I can get over my jealousy and be half decent. He's the whitest man I ever knew.

"Now listen, Collie. I've had ideas lately. I've begun to eat and get stronger and to feel good. The pain is gone. And to think I swore to Wade I'd forgive Jack Belllounds and never hate him—or kill him! . . . There, that's letting the cat out of the bag, and it's done now. But no matter. The truth is, though, that I never could stop hating Jack while the pain lasted. Now I could shake hands with him and smile at him.

"Well, as I said, I've ideas. They're great. Grab hold of the pommel now so you won't get thrown! I'm going to pitch! . . . When I get well—able to ride and go about, which Ben says will be in the spring—I'll send for my father to come to White Slides. He'll come. Then I'll tell him everything, and if Ben and I can't win him to our side then *you* can. Father never could resist you. When he has fallen in love with you, which won't take long, then we'll go to old Bill Belllounds and lay the case before him. Are you still in the saddle, Collie?

"Well, if you are, be sure to get a better hold, for I'm going to run some next. Ben Wade approved of my plan. He says Belllounds can be brought to reason. He says he can make him see the ruin for everybody were you forced to marry Jack. Strange, Collie, how Wade included himself with, you, me, Jack, and the old man, in the foreshadowed ruin! Wade is as deep as the cañon there. Sometimes when he's thoughtful he gives me a creepy feeling. At others, when he comes out with one of his easy, cool assurances that we are all right—that we will get each other—why, then something grim takes possession of me. I believe him, I'm happy, but there crosses my mind a fleeting realization—not of what our friend is now, but what he has been. And it disturbs me, chills me. I don't understand it. For, Collie, though I understand your feeling of what he is, I don't understand mine. You see, I'm a man. I've been a cowboy for ten years and more. I've seen some hard experiences and worked with a good many rough boys and men. Cowboys, Indians, Mexicans, miners, prospectors, ranchers, hunters—some of whom were bad medicine. So I've come to see men as you couldn't see them. And Bent Wade has been everything a man could be. He seems all men in one.

And despite all his kindness and goodness and hopefulness, there is the sense I have of something deadly and terrible and inevitable in him.

"It makes my heart almost stop beating to know I have this man on my side. Because I sense in him the man element, the physical—oh, I can't put it in words, but I mean something great in him that can't be beaten. What he says *must* come true! . . . And so I've already begun to dream and to think of you as my wife. If you ever are—no! *When* you are, then I will owe it to Bent Wade. No man ever owed another for so precious a gift. But, Collie, I can't help a little vague dread—of what, I don't know, unless it's a sense of the possibilities of Hell-Bent Wade . . . Dearest, I don't want to worry you or frighten you, and I can't follow out my own gloomy fancies. Don't you mind too much what I think. Only you must realize that Wade is the greatest factor in our hopes of the future. My faith in him is so unshakable that it's foolish. Next to you I love him best. He seems even dearer to me than my own people. He has made me look at life differently. Likewise he has inspired you. But you, dearest Columbine, are only a sensitive, delicate girl, a frail and tender thing like the columbine flowers of the hills. And for your own sake you must not be blind to what Wade is capable of. If you keep on loving him and idealizing him, blind to what has made him great, that is, blind to the tragic side of him, then if he did something terrible here for you and for me the shock would be bad for you. Lord knows I have no suspicions of Wade. I have no clear ideas at all. But I do know that for you he would not stop at anything. He loves you as much as I do, only differently. Such power a pale, sweet-faced girl has over the lives of men!

"Good-by for this time.

"Faithfully,

"*Wilson.*"

\* \* \* \* \*

"January 10th.

"*Dear Wilson,*

"In every letter I tell you I'm better! Why, pretty soon there'll be nothing left to say about my health. I've been up and around now for days, but only lately have I begun to gain. Since Jack has been away I'm getting fat. I eat, and that's one reason I suppose. Then I move around more.

"You ask me to tell you all I do. Goodness! I couldn't and I wouldn't. You are getting mighty bossy since you're able to hobble around, as you call it. But you can't boss *me!* However, I'll be nice and tell you a little. I don't work very much. I've helped dad with his accounts, all so hopelessly muddled since he let Jack keep the books. I read a good deal. Your letters are worn out! Then, when it snows, I sit by the window and watch. I love to see the snowflakes fall, so fleecy and white and soft! But I don't like the snowy world after the storm has passed. I shiver and hug the fire. I must have Indian in me. On moonlit nights to look out at Old White Slides, so cold and icy and grand, and over the white hills and ranges, makes me shudder. I don't know why. It's all beautiful. But it seems to me like death . . . Well, I sit idly a lot and think of you and how terribly big my love has grown, and . . . but that's all about that!

"As you know, Jack has been gone since before New Year's Day. He said he was going to Kremmling. But dad heard he went to Elgeria. Well, I didn't tell you that dad and Jack quarreled over money. Jack kept up his good behavior for so long that I actually believed he'd changed for the better. He kept at me, not so much on the marriage question, but to love him. Wilson, he nearly drove me frantic with his lovemaking. Finally I got mad and I pitched into him. Oh, I convinced him! Then he came back to his own self again. Like a flash he was Buster Jack once more. 'You can go to hell!' he yelled at me. And such a look! . . . Well, he went out, and that's when he quarreled with dad. It was about money. I couldn't help but hear some of it. I don't know whether or not dad gave Jack money, but I think he didn't. Anyway, Jack went.

"Dad was all right for a few days. Really, he seemed nicer and kinder for Jack's absence. Then all at once he sank into the glooms. I couldn't cheer him up. When Ben Wade came in after supper dad always got him to tell some of those terrible stories. You know what perfectly terrible stories Ben can tell. Well, dad had to hear the worst ones. And poor me, I didn't want to listen, but I couldn't resist. Ben *can* tell stories. And oh, what he's lived through!

"I got the idea it wasn't Jack's absence so much that made dad sit by the hour before the fire, staring at the coals, sighing, and looking so God-forsaken. My heart just aches for dad. He broods and broods. He'll break out someday, and then I don't want to be here. There doesn't seem to be any idea when Jack will come home. He might never come. But Ben says he will. He says Jack hates work and that he couldn't be gambler enough or wicked enough to support himself without working. Can't you hear Ben Wade say that? 'I'll tell you,' he begins, and then comes a prophecy of trouble or evil. And, on the other hand, think how he used to say: 'Wait! Don't give up! Nothin' is ever so bad as it seems at first! Be true to what your heart says is right! It's never too late! Love is the only good in life! Love each other and wait and trust! It'll all come right in the end!' . . . And, Wilson, I'm bound to confess that both his sense of calamity and his hope of good seem infallible. Ben Wade is supernatural. Sometimes, just for a moment, I dare to let myself believe in what he says—that our dream will come true and I'll be yours. Then oh! Oh! Oh! Joy and stars and bells and heaven! I—I . . . But what *am* I writing?

Wilson Moore, this is quite enough for today. Take care you don't believe I'm so—so *very* much in love.

"Ever,

"*Columbine.*"

\* \* \* \* \*

"February ———.

"*Dearest Collie,*

"I don't know the date, but spring's coming. Today I kicked Bent Wade with my once sore foot. It didn't hurt me, but hurt Wade's feelings. He says there'll be no holding me soon. I should say not. I'll eat you up. I'm as hungry as the mountain-lion that's been prowling round my cabin of nights. He's sure starved. Wade tracked him to a hole in the cliff.

"Collie, I can get around first rate. Don't need my crutch anymore. I can make a fire and cook a meal. Wade doesn't think so, but I do. He says if I want to hold your affection, not to let you eat anything I cook. I can rustle around, too. Haven't been far yet. My stock has wintered fairly well. This valley is sheltered, you know. Snow hasn't been too deep. Then I bought hay from Andrews. I'm hoping for spring now, and the good old sunshine on the gray sage hills. And summer, with its columbines! Wade has gone back to his own cabin to sleep. I miss him. But I'm glad to have the nights alone once more. I've got a future to plan! Read that over, Collie.

"Today, when Wade came with your letter, he asked me, sort of queer, 'Say, Wils, do you know how many letters I've fetched you from Collie?' I said, 'Lord, no, I don't, but they're a lot.' Then he said there were just forty-seven letters. Forty-seven! I couldn't believe it, and told him he was crazy. I never had such good fortune. Well, he made me count them, and, dog-gone it, he was right. Forty-seven wonderful love letters from the sweetest girl on earth! But think of Wade remembering every one! It beats me. He's beyond understanding.

"So Jack Belllounds still stays away from White Slides. Collie, I'm sure sorry for his father. What it would be to have a son like Buster Jack! My God! But for your sake I go around yelling and singing like a locoed Indian. Pretty soon spring will come. Then, you wild-flower of the hills, you girl with the sweet mouth and the sad eyes—then I'm coming after you! And all the king's horses and all the king's men can never take you away from me again!

"Your faithful

"*Wilson.*"

\* \* \* \*

"March 19th.

"*Dearest Wilson,*

"Your last letters have been read and reread, and kept under my pillow, and have been both my help and my weakness during these trying days since Jack's return.

"It has not been that I was afraid to write—though, Heaven knows, if this letter should fall into the hands of dad it would mean trouble for me, and if Jack read it—I *am* afraid to think of that! I just have not had the heart to write you. But all the time I knew I must write and that I would. Only, now, what to say tortures me. I am certain that confiding in you relieves me. That's why I've told you so much. But of late I find it harder to tell what I know about Jack Belllounds. I'm in a queer state of mind, Wilson dear. And you'll wonder, and you'll be sorry to know I haven't seen much of Ben lately—that is, not to talk to. It seems I can't *bear* his faith in me, his hope, his love—when lately matters have driven me into torturing doubt.

"But lest you might misunderstand, I'm going to try to tell you something of what is on my mind, and I want you to read it to Ben. He has been hurt by my strange reluctance to be with him.

"Jack came home on the night of March second. You'll remember that day, so gloomy and dark and dreary. It snowed and sleeted and rained. I remember how the rain roared on the roof. It roared so loud we didn't hear the horse. But we heard heavy boots on the porch outside the living room, and the swish of a slicker thrown to the floor. There was a bright fire. Dad looked up with a wild joy. All of a sudden he changed. He blazed. He recognized the heavy tread of his son. If I ever pitied and loved him it was then. I thought of the return of the Prodigal Son! . . . There came a knock on the door. Then dad recovered. He threw it open wide. The streaming light fell upon Jack Belllounds, indeed, but not as I knew him. He entered. It was the first time I ever saw Jack look in the least like a man. He was pale, haggard, much older, sullen, and bold. He strode in with a 'Howdy, folks,' and threw his wet hat on the floor, and walked to the fire. His boots were soaked with water and mud. His clothes began to steam.

"When I looked at dad I was surprised. He seemed cool and bright, with the self-contained force usual for him when something critical is about to happen.

"'Ahuh! So you come back,' he said.

"'Yes, I'm home,' replied Jack.

"'Wal, it took you quite a spell to get hyar.'

"'Do you want me to stay?'

"This question from Jack seemed to stump dad. He stared. Jack had appeared suddenly, and his manner was different from that with which he used to face dad. He had something up his sleeve, as the cowboys say. He wore an air of defiance and indifference.

"'I reckon I do,' replied dad, deliberately. 'What do you mean by askin' me thet?'

"'I'm of age, long ago. You can't make me stay home. I can do as I like.'

"'Ahuh! I reckon you think you can. But not hyar at White Slides. If you ever expect to get this property you'll not do as you like.'

"'To hell with that. I don't care whether I ever get it or not.'

"Dad's face went as white as a sheet. He seemed shocked. After a moment he told me I'd better go to my room. I was about to go when Jack said: 'No, let her stay. She'd best hear now what I've got to say. It concerns her.'

"'So ho! Then you've got a heap to say?' exclaimed dad, queerly. 'All right, you have your say first.'

"Jack then began to talk in a level and monotonous voice, so unlike him that I sat there amazed. He told how early in the winter, before he left the ranch, he had found out that he was honestly in love with me. That it had changed him—made him see he had never been any good—and inflamed him with the resolve to be better. He had tried. He had succeeded. For six weeks he had been all that could have been asked of any young man. I am bound to confess that he was! . . . Well, he went on to say how he had fought it out with himself until he absolutely *knew* he could control himself. The courage and inspiration had come from his love for me. That was the only good thing he'd ever felt. He wanted dad and he wanted me to understand absolutely, without any doubt, that he had found a way to hold on to his good intentions and good feelings. And that was for *me!* . . . I was struck all a-tremble at the truth. It was true! Well, then he forced me to a decision. Forced me, without ever hinting of this change, this possibility in him. I had told him I *couldn't* love him. Never! Then he said I could go to hell and he gave up. Failing to get money from dad he stole it, without compunction and without regret! He had gone to Kremmling, then to Elgeria.

"'I let myself go,' he said, without shame, 'and I drank and gambled. When I was drunk I didn't remember Collie. But when I was sober I did. And she haunted me. That grew worse all the time. So I drank to forget her . . . The money lasted a great deal longer than I expected. But that was because I won as much as I lost, until lately. Then I borrowed a good deal from those men I gambled with, but mostly from ranchers who knew my father would be responsible . . . I had a shooting-scrape with a man named Elbert, in Smith's place at Elgeria. We quarreled over cards. He cheated. And when I hit him he drew on me. But he missed. Then I shot him . . . He lived three days—and died. That sobered me. And once more there came to me truth of what I might have been. I went back to Kremmling. And I tried myself out again. I worked awhile for Judson, who was the rancher I had borrowed most from. At night I went into town and to the saloons, where I met my gambling cronies. I put myself in the atmosphere of drink and cards. And I resisted both. I could make myself indifferent to both. As soon as I was sure of myself I decided to come home. And here I am.'

"This long speech of Jack's had a terrible effect upon me. I was stunned and sick. But if it did that to me *what* did it do to dad? Heaven knows, I can't tell you. Dad gave a lurch, and a great heave, as if at the removal of a rope that had all but strangled him.

"'Ahuh-huh!' he groaned. 'An' now you're hyar—what's thet mean?'

"'It means that it's not yet too late,' replied Jack. 'Don't misunderstand me. I'm not repenting with that side of me which is bad. But I've sobered up. I've had a shock. I see my ruin. I still love you, dad, despite—the cruel thing you did to me. I'm your son and I'd like to make up to you for all my shortcomings. And so help me Heaven! I can do that, and will do it, if Collie will marry me. Not only marry me—that'd not be enough—but love me—I'm crazy for her love. It's terrible.'

"'You spoiled weaklin'!' thundered dad. 'How 'n hell can I believe you?'

"'Because I know it,' declared Jack, standing right up to his father, white and unflinching.

"Then dad broke out in such a rage that I sat there scared so stiff I could not move. My heart beat thick and heavy. Dad got livid of face, his hair stood up, his eyes rolled. He called Jack every name I ever heard anyone call him, and then a thousand more. Then he cursed him. Such dreadful curses! Oh, how sad and terrible to hear dad!

"'Right you are!' cried Jack, bitter and hard and ringing of voice. 'Right, by God! But am I all to blame? Did I bring myself here on this earth! . . . There's something wrong in me that's not all my fault . . . You can't shame me or scare me or hurt me. I could fling in your face those damned three years of hell you sent me to! But what's the use for you to roar at me or for me to reproach you? I'm ruined unless you give me Collie—make her love me. That will save me. And I want it for your sake and hers—not for my own. Even if I do love her madly I'm not wanting her for that. I'm no good. I'm not fit to touch her . . . I've just come to tell you the truth. I feel for Collie—I'd do for Collie—as you did for my mother! Can't you understand? I'm your son. I've some of you in me. And I've found out what it is. Do you and Collie want to take me at my word?'

"I think it took dad longer to read something strange and convincing in Jack than it took me. Anyway, dad got the stunning consciousness that Jack *knew* by some divine or intuitive power that his reformation was inevitable, if I loved him. Never have I had such a distressing and terrible moment as that revelation brought to me! I felt the truth. I could save Jack Belllounds. No woman is ever fooled at such critical moments of life. Ben Wade once said that I could have reformed Jack were it possible to love him. Now the truth of that came home to me, and somehow it was overwhelming.

"Dad received this truth—and it was beyond me to realize what it meant to him. He must have seen all his earlier hopes fulfilled, his pride vindicated, his shame forgotten, his love rewarded. Yet he must have seen all that, as would a man leaning with one foot over a bottomless abyss. He looked transfigured, yet conscious of terrible peril. His great heart seemed to leap to meet this last opportunity, with all forgiveness, with all gratitude; but his will yielded with a final and irrevocable resolve. A resolve dark and sinister!

"He raised his huge fists higher and higher, and all his body lifted and strained, towering and trembling, while his face was that of a righteous and angry god.

"'My son, I take your word!' he rolled out, his voice filling the room and reverberating through the house. 'I give you Collie! . . . She will be yours! . . . But, by the love I bore your mother—I swear—if you ever steal again—I'll kill you!'

"I can't say any more—

*"Columbine."*

# CHAPTER XIV

Spring came early that year at White Slides Ranch. The snow melted off the valleys, and the wildflowers peeped from the greening grass while yet the mountain domes were white. The long stone slides were glistening wet, and the brooks ran full-banked, noisy and turbulent and roily.

Soft and fresh of color the gray old sage slopes came out from under their winter mantle; the bleached tufts of grass waved in the wind and showed tiny blades of green at the roots; the aspens and oaks, and the vines on fences and cliffs, and the round-clumped, brook-bordering willows took on a hue of spring.

The mustangs and colts in the pastures snorted and ran and kicked and cavorted; and on the hillsides the cows began to climb higher, searching for the tender greens, bawling for the newborn calves. Eagles shrieked the release of the snow-bound peaks, and the elks bugled their piercing calls. The grouse-cocks spread their gorgeous brown plumage in parade before their twittering mates, and the jays screeched in the woods, and the sage hens sailed along the bosom of the gray slopes.

Black bears, and browns, and grizzlies came out of their winter's sleep, and left huge, muddy tracks on the trails; the timber wolves at dusk mourned their hungry calls for life, for meat, for the wildness that was passing; the coyotes yelped at sunset, joyous and sharp and impudent.

But winter yielded reluctantly its hold on the mountains. The black, scudding clouds, and the squalls of rain and sleet and snow, whitening and melting and vanishing, and the cold, clear nights, with crackling frost, all retarded the work of the warming sun. The day came, however, when the greens held their own with the grays; and this was the assurance of nature that spring could not be denied, and that summer would follow.

\* \* \* \* \*

Bent Wade was hiding in the willows along the trail that followed one of the brooks. Of late, on several mornings, he had skulked like an Indian under cover, watching for someone. On this morning, when Columbine Belllounds came riding along, he stepped out into the trail in front of her.

"Oh, Ben! You startled me!" she exclaimed, as she held hard on the frightened horse.

"Good mornin', Collie," replied Wade. "I'm sorry to scare you, but I'm particular anxious to see you. An' considerin' how you avoid me these days, I had to waylay you in regular road-agent style."

Wade gazed up searchingly at her. It had been some time since he had been given the privilege and pleasure of seeing her close at hand. He needed only one look at her to confirm his fears. The pale, sweet, resolute face told him much.

"Well, now you've waylaid me, what do you want?" she queried, deliberately.

"I'm goin' to take you to see Wils Moore," replied Wade, watching her closely.

"No!" she cried, with the red staining her temples.

"Collie, see here. Did I ever oppose anythin' you wanted to do?"

"Not—yet," she said.

"I reckon you expect me to?"

She did not answer that. Her eyes drooped, and she nervously twisted the bridle reins.

"Do you doubt my—my good intentions toward you—my love for you?" he asked, in gentle and husky voice.

"Oh, Ben! No! No! It's that I'm afraid of your love for me! I can't bear— what I have to bear—if I see you, if I listen to you."

"Then you've weakened? You're no proud, high-strung, thoroughbred girl anymore? You're showin' yellow?"

"Ben Wade, I deny that," she answered, spiritedly, with an uplift of her head. "It's not weakness, but strength I've found."

"Ahuh! Well, I reckon I understand. Collie, listen. Wils let me read your last letter to him."

"I expected that. I think I told him to. Anyway, I wanted you to know—what—what ailed me."

"Lass, it was a fine, brave letter—written by a girl facin' an upheaval of conscience an' soul. But in your own trouble you forget the effect that letter might have on Wils Moore."

"Ben! . . . I—I've lain awake at night—oh, was he hurt?"

"Collie, I reckon if you don't see Wils he'll kill himself or kill Buster Jack," replied Wade, gravely.

"I'll see—him!" she faltered. "But oh, Ben—you don't mean that Wilson would be so base—so cowardly?"

"Collie, you're a child. You don't realize the depths to which a man can sink. Wils has had a long, hard pull this winter. My nursin' an' your letters have saved his life. He's well, now, but that long, dark spell of mind left its shadow on him. He's morbid."

"What does he—want to see me—for?" asked Columbine, tremulously. There were tears in her eyes. "It'll only cause more pain—make matters worse."

"Reckon I don't agree with you. Wils just wants an' needs to *see* you. Why, he appreciated your position. I've heard him cry like a woman over it an' our helplessness. What ails him is lovesickness, the awful feelin' which comes to a man who believes he has lost his sweetheart's love."

"Poor boy! So he imagines I don't love him anymore? Good Heavens! How stupid men are! . . . I'll see him, Ben. Take me to him."

For answer, Wade grasped the bridle of her horse and, turning him, took a course leading away behind the hill that lay between them and the ranch house. The trail was narrow and brushy, making it necessary for him to walk ahead of the horse. So the hunter did not speak to her or look at her for some time. He plodded on with his eyes downcast. Something tugged at Wade's mind, an old, familiar, beckoning thing, vague and mysterious and black, a presage of catastrophe. But it was only an opening wedge into his mind. It had not entered. Gravity and unhappiness occupied him. His senses, nevertheless, were alert. He heard the low roar of the flooded brook, the whir of rising grouse ahead, the hoofs of deer on stones, the song of spring birds. He had an eye also for the wan wildflowers in the shaded corners. Presently he led the horse out of the willows into the open and up a low-swelling, long slope of fragrant sage. Here he dropped back to Columbine's side and put his hand upon the pommel of her saddle. It was not long until her own hand softly fell upon his and clasped it. Wade thrilled under the warm touch. How well he knew her heart! When she ceased to love anyone to whom she had given her love then she would have ceased to breathe.

"Lass, this isn't the first mornin' I've waited for you," he said, presently. "An' when I had to go back to Wils without you—well, it was hard."

"Then he wants to see me—so badly?" she asked.

"Reckon you've not thought much about him or me lately," said Wade.

"No. I've tried to put you out of my mind. I've had so much to think of— why, even the sleepless nights have flown!"

"Are you goin' to confide in me—as you used to?"

"Ben, there's nothing to confide. I'm just where I left off in that letter to Wilson. And the more I think the more muddled I get."

Wade greeted this reply with a long silence. It was enough to feel her hand upon his and to have the glad comfort and charm of her presence once more. He seemed to have grown older lately. The fragrant breath of the sage slopes came to him as something precious he must feel and love more. A haunting transience mocked him from these rolling gray hills. Old White Slides loomed gray and dark up into the blue, grim and stern reminder of age and of fleeting time. There was a cloud on Wade's horizon.

"Wils is waitin' down there," said Wade, pointing to a grove of aspens below. "Reckon it's pretty close to the house, an' a trail runs along there. But Wils can't ride very well yet, an' this appeared to be the best place."

"Ben, I don't care if dad or Jack know I've met Wilson. I'll tell them," said Columbine.

"Ahuh! Well, if I were you I wouldn't," he replied.

They went down the slope and entered the grove. It was an open, pretty spot, with grass and wildflowers, and old, bleached logs, half sunny and half shady under the newborn, fluttering aspen leaves. Wade saw Moore sitting on his horse. And it struck the hunter significantly that the cowboy should be mounted when an hour back he had left him sitting disconsolately on a log. Moore wanted Columbine to see him first, after all these months of fear and dread, mounted upon his horse. Wade heard Columbine's glad little cry, but he did not turn to look at her then. But when they reached the spot where Moore stood Wade could not resist the desire to see the meeting between the lovers.

Columbine, being a woman, and therefore capable of hiding agitation, except in moments of stress, met that trying situation with more apparent composure than the cowboy. Moore's long, piercing gaze took the rose out of Columbine's cheeks.

"Oh, Wilson! I'm so happy to see you on your horse again!" she exclaimed. "It's too good to be true. I've prayed for that more than anything else. Can you get up into your saddle like you used to? Can you ride well again? . . . Let me see your foot."

Moore held out a bulky foot. He wore a shoe, and it was slashed.

"I can't wear a boot," he explained.

"Oh, I see!" exclaimed Columbine, slowly, with her glad smile fading. "You can't put that—that foot in a stirrup, can you?"

"No."

"But—it—it will—you'll be able to wear a boot soon," she implored.

"Never again, Collie," he said, sadly.

And then Wade perceived that, like a flash, the old spirit leaped up in Columbine. It was all he wanted to see.

"Now, folks," he said, "I reckon two's company an' three's a crowd. I'll go off a little ways an' keep watch."

"Ben, you stay here," replied Columbine, hurriedly.

"Why, Collie? Are you afraid—or ashamed to be with me alone?" asked Moore, bitterly.

Columbine's eyes flashed. It was seldom they lost their sweet tranquility. But now they had depth and fire.

"No, Wilson, I'm neither afraid nor ashamed to be with you alone," she declared. "But I can be as natural—as much myself with Ben here as I could be alone. Why can't you be? If dad and Jack heard of our meeting the fact of Ben's presence might make it look different to them. And why should I heap trouble upon my shoulders?"

"I beg pardon, Collie," said the cowboy. "I've just been afraid of—of things."

"My horse is restless," returned Columbine. "Let's get off and talk."

So they dismounted. It warmed Wade's gloomy heart to see the woman-look in Columbine's eyes as she watched the cowboy get off and walk. For a crippled man he did very well. But that moment was fraught with meaning for Wade. These unfortunate lovers, brave and fine in their suffering, did not realize the peril they invited by proximity. But Wade knew. He pitied them, he thrilled for them, he lived their torture with them.

"Tell me—everything," said Columbine, impulsively.

Moore, with dragging step, approached an aspen log that lay off the ground, propped by the stump, and here he leaned for support. Columbine laid her gloves on the log.

"There's nothing to tell that you don't know," replied Moore. "I wrote you all there was to write, except"—here he dropped his head—"except that the last three weeks have been hell."

"They've not been exactly heaven for me," replied Columbine, with a little laugh that gave Wade a twinge.

Then the lovers began to talk about spring coming, about horses and cattle, and feed, about commonplace ranch matters not interesting to them, but which seemed to make conversation and hide their true thoughts. Wade listened, and it seemed to him that he could read their hearts.

"Lass, an' you, Wils—you're wastin' time an' gettin' nowhere," interposed Wade. "Now let me go, so's you'll be alone."

"You stay right there," ordered Moore.

"Why, Ben, I'm ashamed to say that I actually forgot you were here," said Columbine.

"Then I'll remind you," rejoined the hunter. "Collie, tell us about Old Bill an' Jack."

"Tell you? What?"

"Well, I've seen changes in both. So has Wils, though Wils hasn't seen as much as he's heard from Lem an' Montana an' the Andrews boys."

"Oh! . . ." Columbine choked a little over her exclamation of understanding. "Dad has gotten a new lease on life, I guess. He's happy, like a boy sometimes, an' good as gold . . . It's all because of the change in Jack. That is remarkable. I've not been able to believe my own eyes. Since that night Jack came home and had the—the understanding with dad he has been another person. He has left me alone. He treats me with deference, but not a familiar word or look. He's kind. He offers the little civilities that occur, you know. But he never intrudes upon me. Not one word of the past! It is as if he would earn my respect, and have that or nothing . . . Then he works as he never worked before—on dad's books, in the shop, out on the range. He seems obsessed with some thought all the time. He talks little. All the old petulance, obstinacy, selfishness, and especially his sudden, queer impulses, and bull-headed tenacity—all gone! He has suffered physical distress, because he never was used to hard work. And more, he's suffered terribly for the want of liquor. I've heard him say to dad: 'It's hell—this burning thirst. I never knew I had it. I'll stand it, if it kills me . . . But wouldn't it be easier on me to take a drink now and then, at these bad times?' . . . And dad said: 'No, son. Break off for keeps! This taperin' off is no good way to stop drinkin'. Stand the burnin'. An' when it's gone you'll be all the gladder an' I'll be all the prouder.' . . . I have not forgotten all Jack's former failings, but I am forgetting them, little by little. For dad's sake I'm overjoyed. For Jack's I am glad. I'm convinced now that he's had his lesson—that he's sowed his wild oats—that he has become a man."

Moore listened eagerly, and when she had concluded he thoughtfully bent his head and began to cut little chips out of the log with his knife.

"Collie, I've heard a good deal of the change in Jack," he said, earnestly. "Honest Injun, I'm glad—glad for his father's sake, for his own, and for yours. The boys think Jack's locoed. But his reformation is not strange to me. If I were no good—just like he was—well, I could change as greatly for—for you."

Columbine hastily averted her face. Wade's keen eyes, apparently hidden under his old hat, saw how wet her lashes were, how her lips trembled.

"Wilson, you think then—you believe Jack will last—will stick to his new ways?" she queried, hurriedly.

"Yes, I do," he replied, nodding.

"How good of you! Oh! Wilson, it's like you to be noble—splendid. When you might have—when it'd have been so natural for you to doubt—to scorn him!"

"Collie, I'm honest about that. And now you be just as honest. Do you think Jack will stand to his colors? Never drink—never gamble—never fly off the handle again?"

"Yes, I honestly believe that—providing he gets—providing I—"

Her voice trailed off faintly.

Moore wheeled to address the hunter.

"Pard, what do you think? Tell me now. Tell us. It will help me, and Collie, too. I've asked you before, but you wouldn't—tell us now, do you believe Buster Jack will live up to his new ideals?"

Wade had long parried that question, because the time to answer it had not come till this moment.

"No," he replied, gently.

Columbine uttered a little cry.

"Why not?" demanded Moore, his face darkening.

"Reckon there are reasons that you young folks wouldn't think of, an' couldn't know."

"Wade, it's not like you to be hopeless for any man," said Moore.

"Yes, I reckon it is, sometimes," replied Wade, wagging his head solemnly. "Young folks, I'm grantin' all you say as to Jack's reformation, except that it's permanent. I'm grantin' he's sincere—that he's not playin' a part—that his vicious instincts are smothered under a noble impulse to be what he ought to be. It's no trick. Buster Jack has all but done the impossible."

"Then why isn't his sincerity and good work to be permanent?" asked Moore, impatiently, and his gesture was violent.

"Wils, his change is not moral force. It's passion."

The cowboy paled. Columbine stood silent, with intent eyes upon the hunter. Neither of them seemed to understand him well enough to make reply.

"Love can work marvels in any man," went on Wade. "But love can't change the fiber of a man's heart. A man is born so an' so. He loves an' hates an' feels accordin' to the nature. It'd be accordin' to nature for Jack Belllounds to stay reformed if his love for Collie lasted. An' that's the point. It can't last. Not in a man of his stripe."

"Why not?" demanded Moore.

"Because Jack's love will never be returned—satisfied. It takes a man of different caliber to love a woman who'll never love him. Jack's obsessed by passion now. He'd perform miracles. But that's not possible. The miracle necessary here would be for him to change his moral force, his blood, the habits of his mind. That's beyond his power."

Columbine flung out an appealing hand.

"Ben, I could pretend to love him—I might *make* myself love him, if that would give him the power."

"Lass, don't delude yourself. You can't do that," replied Wade.

"How do you know what I can do?" she queried, struggling with her helplessness.

"Why, child, I know you better than you know yourself."

"Wilson, he's right, he's right!" she cried. "That's why it's so terrible for me now. He knows my very heart. He reads my soul . . . I can *never* love Jack Belllounds. Nor *ever* pretend love!"

"Collie, if Ben knows you so well, you ought to listen to him, as you used to," said Moore, touching her hand with infinite sympathy.

Wade watched them. His pity and affection did not obstruct the ruthless expression of his opinions or the direction of his intentions.

"Lass, an' you, Wils, listen," he said, with all his gentleness. "It's bad enough without you makin' it worse. Don't blind yourselves. That's the hell with so many people in trouble. It's hard to see clear when you're sufferin' and fightin'. But *I* see clear . . . Now with just a word I could fetch this new Jack Belllounds back to his Buster Jack tricks!"

"Oh, Ben! No! No! No!" cried Columbine, in a distress that showed how his force dominated her.

Moore's face turned as white as ashes.

Wade divined then that Moore was aware of what he himself knew about Jack Belllounds. And to his love for Moore was added an infinite respect.

"I won't unless Collie forces me to," he said, significantly.

This was the critical moment, and suddenly Wade answered to it without restraint. He leaped up, startling Columbine.

"Wils, you call me pard, don't you? I reckon you never knew me. Why, the game's 'most played out, an' I haven't showed my hand! . . . I'd see Jack Belllounds in hell before I'd let him have Collie. An' if she carried out her strange an' lofty idea of duty—an' married him right this afternoon—I could an' I would part them before night!"

He ended that speech in a voice neither had ever heard him use before. And the look of him must have been in harmony with it. Columbine, wide-eyed and gasping, seemed struck to the heart. Moore's white face showed awe and fear and irresponsible primitive joy. Wade turned away from them, the better to control the passion that had mastered him. And it did not subside in an instant. He paced to and fro, his head bowed. Presently, when he faced around, it was to see what he had expected to see.

Columbine was clasped in Moore's arms.

"Collie, you didn't—you haven't—promised to marry him—again!"

"No, oh—no! I haven't! I was only—only trying to—to make up my mind. Wilson, don't look at me so terribly!"

"You'll not agree again? You'll not set another day?" demanded Moore, passionately. He strained her to him, yet held her so he could see her face, thus dominating her with both strength and will. His face was corded now, and darkly flushed. His jaw quivered. "You'll never marry Jack Belllounds! You'll not let sudden impulse—sudden persuasion or force change you? Promise! Swear you'll never marry him. Swear!"

"Oh, Wilson, I promise—I swear!" she cried. "Never! I'm yours. It would be a sin. I've been mad to—to blind myself."

"You love me! You love me!" he cried, in a sudden transport.

"Oh, yes, yes! I do."

"Say it then! Say it—so I'll never doubt—never suffer again!"

"I love you, Wilson! I—I love you—unutterably," the whispered. "I love you—so—I'm broken-hearted now. I'll never live without you. I'll die—I love you so!"

"You—you flower—you angel!" he whispered in return. "You woman! You precious creature! I've been crazed at loss of you!"

Wade paced out of earshot, and this time he remained away for a considerable time. He lived again moments of his own past, unforgettable and sad. When at length he returned toward the young couple they were sitting apart, composed once more, talking earnestly. As he neared them Columbine rose to greet him with wonderful eyes, in which reproach blended with affection.

"Ben, so this is what you've done!" she exclaimed.

"Lass, I'm only a humble instrument, an' I believe God guides me right," replied the hunter.

"I love you more, it seems, for what you make me suffer," she said, and she kissed him with a serious sweetness. "I'm only a leaf in the storm. But—let what will come . . . Take me home."

They said good-by to Wilson, who sat with head bowed upon his hands. His voice trembled as he answered them. Wade found the trail while Columbine mounted. As they went slowly down the gentle slope, stepping over the numerous logs fallen across the way, Wade caught out of the tail of his eye a moving object along the outer edge of the aspen grove above them. It was the figure of a man, skulking behind the trees. He disappeared. Wade casually remarked to Columbine that now she could spur the pony and hurry on home. But Columbine refused. When they got a little farther on, out of sight of Moore and somewhat around to the left, Wade espied the man again. He carried a rifle. Wade grew somewhat perturbed.

"Collie, you run on home," he said, sharply.

"Why? You've complained of not seeing me. Now that I want to be with you . . . Ben, you see someone!"

Columbine's keen faculties evidently sensed the change in Wade, and the direction of his uneasy glance convinced her.

"Oh, there's a man! . . . Ben, it is—yes, it's Jack," she exclaimed, excitedly.

"Reckon you'd have it better if you say Buster Jack," replied Wade, with his tragic smile.

"Ah!" whispered Columbine, as she gazed up at the aspen slope, with eyes lighting to battle.

"Run home, Collie, an' leave him to me," said Wade.

"Ben, you mean he—he saw us up there in the grove? Saw me in Wilson's arms—saw me kissing him?"

"Sure as you're born, Collie. He watched us. He saw all your love-makin'. I can tell that by the way he walks. It's Buster Jack again! Alas for the new an' noble Jack! I told you, Collie. Now you run on an' leave him to me."

Wade became aware that she turned at his last words and regarded him attentively. But his gaze was riveted on the striding form of Belllounds.

"Leave him to you? For what reason, my friend?" she asked.

"Buster Jack's on the rampage. Can't you see that? He'll insult you. He'll—"

"I will not go," interrupted Columbine, and, halting her pony, she deliberately dismounted.

Wade grew concerned with the appearance of young Belllounds, and it was with a melancholy reminder of the infallibility of his presentiments. As he and Columbine halted in the trail, Belllounds's hurried stride lengthened until he almost ran. He carried the rifle forward in a most significant manner. Black as a thundercloud was his face. Alas for the dignity and pain and resolve that had only recently showed there!

Belllounds reached them. He was frothing at the mouth. He cocked the rifle and thrust it toward Wade, holding low down.

"You—meddling sneak! If you open your trap I'll bore you!" he shouted, almost incoherently.

Wade knew when danger of life loomed imminent. He fixed his glance upon the glaring eyes of Belllounds.

"Jack, seein' I'm not packin' a gun, it'd look sorta natural, along with your other tricks, if you bored me."

His gentle voice, his cool mien, his satire, were as giant's arms to drag Belllounds back from murder. The rifle was raised, the hammer reset, the butt lowered to the ground, while Belllounds, snarling and choking, fought for speech.

"I'll get even—with you," he said, huskily. "I'm on to your game now. I'll fix you later. But—I'll do you harm now if you mix in with this!"

Then he wheeled to Columbine, and as if he had just recognized her, a change that was pitiful and shocking convulsed his face. He leaned toward her, pointing with shaking, accusing hand.

"I saw you—up there. I watched—you," he panted.

Columbine faced him, white and mute.

"It was you—wasn't it?" he yelled.

"Yes, of course it was."

She might have struck him, for the way he flinched.

"What was that—a trick—a game—a play all fixed up for my benefit?"

"I don't understand you," she replied.

"Bah! You—you white-faced cat! . . . I saw you! Saw you in Moore's arms! Saw him hug you—kiss you! . . . Then—I saw—you put up your arms—round his neck—kiss him—kiss him—kiss him! . . . I saw all that—didn't I?"

"You must have, since you say so," she returned, with perfect composure.

"But *did* you?" he almost shrieked, the blood cording and bulging red, as if about to burst the veins of temples and neck.

"Yes, I did," she flashed. There was primitive woman uppermost in her now, and a spirit no man might provoke with impunity.

*"You love him?"* he asked, very low, incredulously, with almost insane eagerness for denial in his query.

Then Wade saw the glory of her—saw her mother again in that proud, fierce uplift of face, that flamed red and then blazed white—saw hate and passion and love in all their primal nakedness.

"Love him! Love Wilson Moore? Yes, you fool! I love him! Yes! *Yes! Yes!"*

That voice would have pierced the heart of a wooden image, so Wade thought, as all his strung nerves quivered and thrilled.

Belllounds uttered a low cry of realization, and all his instinctive energy seemed on the verge of collapse. He grew limp, he sagged, he tottered. His sensorial perceptions seemed momentarily blunted.

Wade divined the tragedy, and a pang of great compassion overcame him. Whatever Jack Belllounds was in character, he had inherited his father's power to love, and he was human. Wade felt the death in that stricken soul, and it was the last flash of pity he ever had for Jack Belllounds.

"You—you—" muttered Belllounds, raising a hand that gathered speed and strength in the action. The moment of a great blow had passed, like a storm-blast through a leafless tree. Now the thousand devils of his nature leaped into ascendancy. "You—!" He could not articulate. Dark and terrible became his energy. It was like a resistless current forced through leaping thought and leaping muscle.

He struck her on the mouth, a cruel blow that would have felled her but for Wade: and then he lunged away, bowed and trembling, yet with fierce, instinctive motion, as if driven to run with the spirit of his rage.

# CHAPTER XV

Wade noticed that after her trying experience with him and Wilson and Belllounds Columbine did not ride frequently.

He managed to get a word or two with her whenever he went to the ranch house, and he needed only look at her to read her sensitive mind. All was well with Columbine, despite her trouble. She remained upheld in spirit, while yet she seemed to brood over an unsolvable problem. She had said, "But—let what will come!"—and she was waiting.

Wade hunted for more than lions and wolves these days. Like an Indian scout who scented peril or heard an unknown step upon his trail, Wade rode the hills, and spent long hours hidden on the lonely slopes, watching with somber, keen eyes. They were eyes that knew what they were looking for. They had marked the strange sight of the son of Bill Belllounds, gliding along that trail where Moore had met Columbine, sneaking and stooping, at last with many a covert glance about, to kneel in the trail and compare the horse tracks there with horseshoes he took from his pocket. That alone made Bent Wade eternally vigilant. He kept his counsel. He worked more swiftly, so that he might have leisure for his peculiar seeking. He spent an hour each night with the cowboys, listening to their recounting of the day and to their homely and shrewd opinions. He haunted the vicinity of the ranch house at night, watching and listening for that moment which was to aid him in the crisis that was impending. Many a time he had been near when Columbine passed from the living room to her corner of the house. He had heard her sigh and could almost have touched her.

Buster Jack had suffered a regurgitation of the old driving and insatiate temper, and there was gloom in the house of Belllounds. Trouble clouded the old man's eyes.

May came with the spring roundup. Wade was called to use a rope and brand calves under the order of Jack Belllounds, foreman of White Slides. That roundup showed a loss of one hundred head of stock, some branded steers, and yearlings, and many calves, in all a mixed herd. Belllounds received the amazing news with a roar. He had been ready for something to roar at. The cowboys gave as reasons winter kill, and lions, and perhaps some head stolen since the thaw. Wade emphatically denied this. Very few cattle had fallen prey to the big cats, and none, so far as he could find, had been frozen or caught in drifts. It was the young foreman who stunned them all. "Rustled," he said, darkly. "There's too many loafers and homesteaders in these hills!" And he stalked out to leave his hearers food for reflection.

Jack Belllounds drank, but no one saw him drunk, and no one could tell where he got the liquor. He rode hard and fast; he drove the cowboys one way while he went another; he had grown shifty, cunning, more intolerant than ever. Some nights he rode to Kremmling, or said he had been there, when next day the cowboys found another spent and broken horse to turn out. On other nights he coaxed and bullied them into playing poker. They won more of his money than they cared to count.

Columbine confided to Wade, with mournful whisper, that Jack paid no attention to her whatever, and that the old rancher attributed this coldness, and Jack's backsliding, to her irresponsiveness and her tardiness in setting the wedding-day that must be set. To this Wade had whispered in reply, "Don't ever forget what I said to you an' Wils that day!"

So Wade upheld Columbine with his subtle dominance, and watched over her, as it were, from afar. No longer was he welcome in the big living room. Belllounds reacted to his son's influence.

Twice in the early mornings Wade had surprised Jack Belllounds in the blacksmith shop. The meetings were accidental, yet Wade ever remembered how coincidence beckoned him thither and how circumstance magnified strange reflections. There was no reason why Jack should not be tinkering in the blacksmith shop early of a morning. But Wade followed an uncanny guidance. Like his hound Fox, he never split on trails. When opportunity afforded he went into the shop and looked it over with eyes as keen as the nose of his dog. And in the dust of the floor he had discovered little circles with dots in the middle, all uniform in size. Sight of them did not shock him until they recalled vividly the little circles with dots in the earthen floor of Wilson Moore's cabin. Little marks made by the end of Moore's crutch! Wade grinned then like a wolf showing his fangs. And the vitals of a wolf could no more strongly have felt the instinct to rend.

For Wade, the cloud on his horizon spread and darkened, gathered sinister shape of storm, harboring lightning and havoc. It was the cloud in his mind, the foreshadowing of his soul, the prophetic sense of like to like. Where he wandered there the blight fell!

\* \* \* \* \*

Significant was the fact that Belllounds hired new men. Bludsoe had quit. Montana Jim grew surly these days and packed a gun. Lem Billings had threatened to leave. New and strange hands for Jack Belllounds to direct had a tendency to release a strain and tide things over.

Every time the old rancher saw Wade he rolled his eyes and wagged his head, as if combating superstition with an intelligent sense of justice. Wade knew what troubled Belllounds, and it strengthened the gloomy mood that, like a poison lichen, seemed finding root.

Every day Wade visited his friend Wilson Moore, and most of their conversation centered round that which had become a ruling passion for both. But the time came when Wade deviated from his gentleness of speech and leisure of action.

"Bent, you're not like you were," said Moore, once, in surprise at the discovery. "You're losing hope and confidence."

"No. I've only somethin' on my mind."

"What?"

"I reckon I'm not goin' to tell you now."

"You've got *hell* on your mind!" flashed the cowboy, in grim inspiration.

Wade ignored the insinuation and turned the conversation to another subject.

"Wils, you're buyin' stock right along?"

"Sure am. I saved some money, you know. And what's the use to hoard it? I'll buy cheap. In five years I'll have five hundred, maybe a thousand head. Wade, my old dad will be pleased to find out I've made the start I have."

"Well, it's a fine start, I'll allow. Have you picked up any unbranded stock?"

"Sure I have. Say, pard, are you worrying about this two-bit rustler work that's been going on?"

"Wils, it ain't two bits anymore. I reckon it's gettin' into the four-bit class."

"I've been careful to have my business transactions all in writing," said Moore. "It makes these fellows sore, because some of them can't write. And they're not used to it. But I'm starting this game in my own way."

"Have you sold any stock?"

"Not yet. But the Andrews boys are driving some thirty-odd head to Kremmling for me to be sold."

"Ahuh! Well, I'll be goin'," Wade replied, and it was significant of his state of mind that he left his young friend sorely puzzled. Not that Wade did not see Moore's anxiety! But the drift of events at White Slides had passed beyond the stage where sympathetic and inspiring hope might serve Wade's purpose. Besides, his mood was gradually changing as these events, like many fibers of a web, gradually closed in toward a culminating knot.

That night Wade lounged with the cowboys and new hands in front of the little storehouse where Belllounds kept supplies for all. He had lounged there before in the expectation of seeing the rancher's son. And this time anticipation was verified. Jack Belllounds swaggered over from the ranch house. He met civility and obedience now where formerly he had earned but ridicule and opposition. So long as he worked hard himself the cowboys endured. The subtle change in him seemed of sterner stuff. The talk, as usual, centered round the stock subjects and the banter and gossip of ranch hands. Wade selected an interval when there was a lull in the conversation, and with eyes that burned under the shadow of his broad-brimmed sombrero he watched the son of Belllounds.

"Say, boys, Wils Moore has begun sellin' cattle," remarked Wade, casually. "The Andrews brothers are drivin' for him."

"Wal, so Wils's spread-eaglin' into a real rancher!" ejaculated Lem Billings. "Mighty glad to hear it. Thet boy shore will git rich."

Wade's remark incited no further expressions of interest. But it was Jack Belllounds's secret mind that Wade wished to pierce. He saw the leaping of a thought that was neither interest nor indifference nor contempt, but a creative thing which lent a fleeting flash to the face, a slight shock to the body. Then Jack Belllounds bent his head, lounged there for a little while longer, lost in absorption, and presently he strolled away.

Whatever that mounting thought of Jack Belllounds's was it brought instant decision to Wade. He went to the ranch house and knocked upon the living room door. There was a light within, sending rays out through the windows into the semi-darkness. Columbine opened the door and admitted Wade. A bright fire crackled in the hearth. Wade flashed a reassuring look at Columbine.

"Evenin', Miss Collie. Is your dad in?"

"Oh, it's you, Ben!" she replied, after her start. "Yes, dad's here."

The old rancher looked up from his reading. "Howdy, Wade! What can I do fer you?"

"Belllounds, I've cleaned out the cats an' most of the varmints on your range. An' my work, lately, has been all sorts, not leavin' me any time for little jobs of my own. An' I want to quit."

"Wade, you've clashed with Jack!" exclaimed the rancher, jerking erect.

"Nothin' of the kind. Jack an' me haven't had words a good while. I'm not denyin' we might, an' probably would clash sooner or later. But that's not my reason for quittin'."

Manifestly this put an entirely different complexion upon the matter. Belllounds appeared immensely relieved.

"Wal, all right. I'll pay you at the end of the month. Let's see, thet's not long now. You can lay off tomorrow."

Wade thanked him and waited for further remarks. Columbine had fixed big, questioning eyes upon Wade, which he found hard to endure. Again he tried to flash her a message of reassurance. But Columbine did not lose her look of blank wonder and gravity.

"Ben! Oh, you're not going to leave White Slides?" she asked.

"Reckon I'll hang around yet awhile," he replied.

Belllounds was wagging his head regretfully and ponderingly.

"Wal, I remember the day when no man quit me. Wal, wal! Times change. I'm an old man now. Mebbe, mebbe I'm testy. An' then thar's thet boy!"

With a shrug of his broad shoulders he dismissed what seemed an encroachment of pessimistic thought.

"Wade, you're packin' off, then, on the trail? Always on the go, eh?"

"No, I'm not hurryin' off," replied Wade.

"Wal, might I ask what you're figgerin' on?"

"Sure. I'm considerin' a cattle deal with Moore. He's a pretty keen boy an' his father has big ranchin' interests. I've saved a little money an' I'm no spring chicken anymore. Wils has begun to buy an' sell stock, so I reckon I'll go in with him."

"Ahuh!" Belllounds gave a grunt of comprehension. He frowned, and his big eyes set seriously upon the blazing fire. He grasped complications in this information.

"Wal, it's a free country," he said at length, and evidently his personal anxieties were subjected to his sense of justice. "Owin' to the peculiar circumstances hyar at my range, I'd prefer thet Moore an' you began somewhar else. Thet's natural. But you've my good will to start on an' I hope I've yours."

"Belllounds, you've every man's good will," replied Wade. "I hope you won't take offense at my leavin'. You see I'm on Wils Moore's side in—in what you called these peculiar circumstances. He's got nobody else. An' I reckon you can look back an' remember how you've taken sides with some poor devil an' stuck to him. Can't you?"

"Wal, I reckon I can. An' I'm not thinkin' less of you fer speakin' out like thet."

"All right. Now about the dogs. I turn the pack over to you, an' it's a good one. I'd like to buy Fox."

"Buy nothin', man. You can have Fox, an' welcome."

"Much obliged," returned the hunter, as he turned to go. "Fox will sure be help for me. Belllounds, I'm goin' to round up this outfit that's rustlin' your cattle. They're gettin' sort of bold."

"Wade, you'll do thet on your own hook?" asked the rancher, in surprise.

"Sure. I like huntin' men more than other varmints. Then I've a personal interest. You know the hint about homesteaders hereabouts reflects some on Wils Moore."

"Stuff!" exploded the rancher, heartily. "Do you think any cattleman in these hills would believe Wils Moore a rustler?"

"The hunch has been whispered," said Wade. "An' you know how all ranchers say they rustled a little on the start."

"Aw, hell! Thet's different. Every new rancher drives in a few unbranded calves an' keeps them. But stealin' stock—thet's different. An' I'd as soon suspect my own son of rustlin' as Wils Moore."

Belllounds spoke with a sincere and frank ardor of defense for a young man once employed by him and known to be honest. The significance of the comparison he used had not struck him. His was the epitome of a successful rancher, sure in his opinions, speaking proudly and unreflectingly of his own son, and being just to another man.

Wade bowed and backed out of the door. "Sure that's what I'd reckon you'd say, Belllounds . . . I'll drop in on you if I find any sign in the woods. Good night."

Columbine went with him to the end of the porch, as she had used to go before the shadow had settled over the lives of the Belllounds.

"Ben, you're up to something," she whispered, seizing him with hands that shook.

"Sure. But don't you worry," he whispered back.

"Do they hint that Wilson is a rustler?" she asked, intensely.

"Somebody did, Collie."

"How vile! Who? Who?" she demanded, and her face gleamed white.

"Hush, lass! You're all a-tremble," he returned, warily, and he held her hands.

"Ben, they're pressing me hard to set another wedding-day. Dad is angry with me now. Jack has begun again to demand. Oh, I'm afraid of him! He has no respect for me. He catches at me with hands like claws. I have to jerk away . . . Oh, Ben, Ben! Dear friend, what on earth shall I do?"

"Don't give in. Fight Jack! Tell the old man you must have time. Watch your chance when Jack is away an' ride up the Buffalo Park trail an' look for me."

Wade had to release his hands from her clasp and urge her gently back. How pale and tragic her face gleamed!

* * * * *

Wade took his horses, his outfit, and the dog Fox, and made his abode with Wilson Moore. The cowboy hailed Wade's coming with joy and pestered him with endless questions.

From that day Wade haunted the hills above White Slides, early and late, alone with his thoughts, his plans, more and more feeling the suspense of happenings to come. It was on a June day when Jack Belllounds rode to Kremmling that Wade met Columbine on the Buffalo Park trail. She needed to see him, to find comfort and strength. Wade far exceeded his own confidence in his effort to uphold her. Columbine was in a strange state, not of vacillation between two courses, but of a standstill, as if her will had become obstructed and waited for some force to upset the hindrance. She did not inquire as to the welfare of Wilson Moore, and Wade vouchsafed no word of him. But she importuned the hunter to see her every day or no more at all. And Wade answered her appeal and her need by assuring her that he would see her, come what might. So she was to risk more frequent rides.

During the second week of June Wade rode up to visit the prospector, Lewis, and learned that which complicated the matter of the rustlers. Lewis had been suspicious, and active on his own account. According to the best of his evidence and judgment there had been a gang of rough men come of late to Gore Peak, where they presumably were prospecting. This gang was composed of strangers to Lewis. They had ridden to his cabin, bought and borrowed of him, and, during his absence, had stolen from him. He believed they were in hiding, probably being guilty of some depredation in another locality. They gave both Kremmling and Elgeria a wide berth. On the other hand, the Smith gang from Elgeria rode to and fro, like ranchers searching for lost horses. There were only three in this gang, including Smith. Lewis had seen these men driving unbranded stock. And lastly, Lewis casually imparted the information, highly interesting to Wade, that he had seen Jack Belllounds riding through the forest. The prospector did not in the least, however, connect the appearance of the son of Belllounds with the other facts so peculiarly interesting to Wade. Cowboys and hunters rode trails across the range, and though they did so rather infrequently, there was nothing unusual about encountering them.

Wade remained all night with Lewis, and next morning rode six miles along the divide, and then down into a valley, where at length he found a cabin described by the prospector. It was well hidden in the edge of the forest, where a spring gushed from under a low cliff. But for water and horse tracks Wade would not have found it easily. Rifle in hand, and on foot, he slipped around in the woods, as a hunter might have, to stalk drinking deer. There were no smoke, no noise, no horses anywhere round the cabin, and after watching awhile Wade went forward to look at it. It was an old ramshackle hunter's or prospector's cabin, with dirt floor, a crumbling fireplace and chimney, and a bed platform made of boughs. Including the door, it had three apertures, and the two smaller ones, serving as windows, looked as if they had been intended for portholes as well. The inside of the cabin was large and unusually well lighted, owing to the windows and to the open chinks between the logs. Wade saw a deck of cards lying bent and scattered in one corner, as if a violent hand had flung them against the wall. Strange that Wade's memory returned a vivid picture of Jack Belllounds in just that act of violence! The only other thing around the place which earned scrutiny from Wade was a number of horseshoe tracks outside, with the left front shoe track familiar to him. He examined the clearest imprints very carefully. If they had not been put there by Wilson Moore's white mustang, Spottie, then they had been made by a horse with a strangely similar hoof and shoe. Spottie had a hoof malformed, somewhat in the shape of a triangle, and the iron shoe to fit it always had to be bent, so that the curve was sharp and the ends closer together than those of his other shoes.

Wade rode down to White Slides that day, and at the evening meal he casually asked Moore if he had been riding Spottie of late.

"Sure. What other horse could I ride? Do you think I'm up to trying one of those broncs?" asked Moore, in derision.

"Reckon you haven't been leavin' any tracks up Buffalo Park way?"

The cowboy slammed down his knife. "Say, Wade, are you growing dotty? Good Lord! If I'd ridden that far—if I was able to do it—wouldn't you hear me yell?"

"Reckon so, come to think of it. I just saw a track like Spottie's, made two days ago."

"Well, it wasn't his, you can gamble on that," returned the cowboy.

* * * * *

Wade spent four days hiding in an aspen grove, on top of one of the highest foothills above White Slides Ranch. There he lay at ease, like an Indian, calm and somber, watching the trails below, waiting for what he knew was to come.

On the fifth morning he was at his post at sunrise. A casual remark of one of the new cowboys the night before accounted for the early hour of Wade's reconnoiter. The dawn was fresh and cool, with sweet odor of sage on the air; the jays were squalling their annoyance at this early disturber of their grove; the east was rosy above the black range and soon glowed with gold and then changed to fire. The sun had risen. All the mountain world of black range and gray hill and green valley, with its shining stream, was transformed as if by magic color. Wade sat down with his back to an aspen tree, his gaze down upon the ranch house and the corrals. A lazy column of blue smoke curled up toward the sky, to be lost there. The burros were braying, the calves were bawling, the colts were whistling. One of the hounds bayed full and clear.

The scene was pastoral and beautiful. Wade saw it clearly and whole. Peace and plenty, a happy rancher's home, the joy of the dawn and the birth of summer, the rewards of toil—all seemed significant there. But Wade pondered on how pregnant with life that scene was—nature in its simplicity and freedom and hidden cruelty, and the existence of people, blindly hating, loving, sacrificing, mostly serving some noble aim, and yet with baseness among them, the lees with the wine, evil intermixed with good.

By and by the cowboys appeared on their spring mustangs, and in twos and threes they rode off in different directions. But none rode Wade's way. The sun rose higher, and there was warmth in the air. Bees began to hum by Wade, and fluttering moths winged uncertain flight over him.

At the end of another hour Jack Belllounds came out of the house, gazed around him, and then stalked to the barn where he kept his horses. For a little while he was not in sight; then he reappeared, mounted on a white horse, and he rode into the pasture, and across that to the hay-field, and along the edge of this to the slope of the hill. Here he climbed to a small clump of aspens. This grove was not so far from Wilson Moore's cabin; in fact, it marked the boundary line between the rancher's range and the acres that Moore had acquired. Jack vanished from sight here, but not before Wade had made sure he was dismounting.

"Reckon he kept to that grassy ground for a reason of his own—and plainer to me than any tracks," soliloquized Wade, as he strained his eyes. At length Belllounds came out of the grove, and led his horse round to where Wade knew there was a trail leading to and from Moore's cabin. At this point Jack mounted and rode west. Contrary to his usual custom, which was to ride hard and fast, he trotted the white horse as a cowboy might have done when going out on a day's work. Wade had to change his position to watch Belllounds, and his somber gaze followed him across the hill, down the slope, along the willow-bordered brook, and so on to the opposite side of the great valley, where Jack began to climb in the direction of Buffalo Park.

After Belllounds had disappeared and had been gone for an hour, Wade went down on the other side of the hill, found his horse where he had left him, in a thicket, and, mounting, he rode around to strike the trail upon which Belllounds had ridden. The imprint of fresh horse tracks showed clear in the soft dust. And the left front track had been made by a shoe crudely triangular in shape, identical with that peculiar to Wilson Moore's horse.

"Ahuh!" muttered Wade, in greeting to what he had expected to see. "Well, Buster Jack, it's a plain trail now—damn your crooked soul!"

The hunter took up that trail, and he followed it into the woods. There he hesitated. Men who left crooked trails frequently ambushed them, and Belllounds had made no effort to conceal his tracks. Indeed, he had chosen the soft, open ground, even after he had left the trail to take to the grassy, wooded benches. There were cattle here, but not as many as on the more open aspen slopes across the valley. After deliberating a moment, Wade decided that he must risk being caught trailing Belllounds. But he would go slowly, trusting to eye and ear, to outwit this strangely acting foreman of White Slides Ranch.

To that end he dismounted and took the trail. Wade had not followed it far before he became convinced that Belllounds had been looking in the thickets for cattle; and he had not climbed another mile through the aspens and spruce before he discovered that Belllounds was driving cattle. Thereafter Wade proceeded more cautiously. If the long grass had not been wet he would have encountered great difficulty in trailing Belllounds. Evidence was clear now that he was hiding the tracks of the cattle by keeping to the grassy levels and slopes which, after the sun had dried them, would not leave a trace. There were stretches where even the keen-eyed hunter had to work to find the direction taken by Belllounds. But here and there, in other localities, there showed faint signs of cattle and horse tracks.

The morning passed, with Wade slowly climbing to the edge of the black timber. Then, in a hollow where a spring gushed forth, he saw the tracks of a few cattle that had halted to drink, and on top of these the tracks of a horse with a crooked left front shoe. The rider of this horse had dismounted. There was an imprint of a cowboy's boot, and near it little sharp circles with dots in the center.

"Well, I'll be damned!" ejaculated Wade. "I call that mighty cunnin'. Here they are—proofs as plain as writin'—that Wils Moore rustled Old Bill's cattle! . . . Buster Jack, you're not such a fool as I thought . . . He's made somethin' like the end of Wils's crutch. An' knowin' how Wils uses that every time he gets off his horse, why, the dirty pup carried his instrument with him an' made these tracks!"

Wade left the trail then, and, leading his horse to a covert of spruce, he sat down to rest and think. Was there any reason for following Belllounds farther? It did not seem needful to take the risk of being discovered. The forest above was open. No doubt Belllounds would drive the cattle somewhere and turn them over to his accomplices.

"Buster Jack's outbusted himself this time, sure," soliloquized Wade. "He's double-crossin' his rustler friends, same as he is Moore. For he's goin' to blame this cattle-stealin' onto Wils. An' to do that he's layin' his tracks so he can follow them, or so any good trailer can. It doesn't concern me so much now who're his pards in this deal. Reckon it's Smith an' some of his gang."

Suddenly it dawned upon Wade that Jack Belllounds was stealing cattle from his father. "Whew!" he whistled softly. "Awful hard on the old man! Who's to tell him when all this comes out? Aw, I'd hate to do it. I wouldn't. There's some things even I'd not tell."

Straightway this strange aspect of the case confronted Wade and gripped his soul. He seemed to feel himself changing inwardly, as if a gray, gloomy, sodden hand, as intangible as a ghostly dream, had taken him bodily from himself and was now leading him into shadows, into drear, lonely, dark solitude, where all was cold and bleak; and on and on over naked shingles that marked the world of tragedy. Here he must tell his tale, and as he plodded on his relentless leader forced him to tell his tale anew.

Wade recognized this as his black mood. It was a morbid dominance of the mind. He fought it as he would have fought a devil. And mastery still was his. But his brow was clammy and his heart was leaden when he had wrested that somber, mystic control from his will.

"Reckon I'd do well to take up this trail tomorrow an' see where it leads," he said, and as a gloomy man, burdened with thought, he retraced his way down the long slope, and over the benches, to the grassy slopes and aspen groves, and thus to the sage hills.

It was dark when he reached the cabin, and Moore had supper almost ready.

"Well, old-timer, you look fagged out," called out the cowboy, cheerily. "Throw off your boots, wash up, and come and get it!"

"Pard Wils, I'm not reboundin' as natural as I'd like. I reckon I've lived some years before I got here, an' a lifetime since."

"Wade, you have a queer look, lately," observed Moore, shaking his head solemnly. "Why, I've seen a dying man look just like you—now—round the mouth—but most in the eyes!"

"Maybe the end of the long trail is White Slides Ranch," replied Wade, sadly and dreamily, as if to himself.

"If Collie heard you say that!" exclaimed Moore, in anxious concern.

"Collie an' you will hear me say a lot before long," returned Wade. "But, as it's calculated to make you happy—why, all's well. I'm tired an' hungry."

Wade did not choose to sit round the fire that night, fearing to invite interrogation from his anxious friend, and for that matter from his other inquisitively morbid self.

Next morning, though Wade felt rested, and the sky was blue and full of fleecy clouds, and the melody of birds charmed his ear, and over all the June air seemed thick and beating with the invisible spirit he loved, he sensed the oppression, the nameless something that presaged catastrophe.

Therefore, when he looked out of the door to see Columbine swiftly riding up the trail, her fair hair flying and shining in the sunlight, he merely ejaculated, "Ahuh!"

"What's that?" queried Moore, sharp to catch the inflection.

"Look out," replied Wade, as he began to fill his pipe.

"Heavens! It's Collie! Look at her riding! Uphill, too!"

Wade followed him outdoors. Columbine was not long in arriving at the cabin, and she threw the bridle and swung off in the same motion, landing with a light thud. Then she faced them, pale, resolute, stern, all the sweetness gone to bitter strength—another and a strange Columbine.

"I've not slept a wink!" she said. "And I came as soon as I could get away."

Moore had no word for her, not even a greeting. The look of her had stricken him. It could have only one meaning.

"Mornin', lass," said the hunter, and he took her hand. "I couldn't tell you looked sleepy, for all you said. Let's go into the cabin."

So he led Columbine in, and Moore followed. The girl manifestly was in a high state of agitation, but she was neither trembling nor frightened nor sorrowful. Nor did she betray any lack of an unflinching and indomitable spirit. Wade read the truth of what she imagined was her doom in the white glow of her, in the matured lines of womanhood that had come since yesternight, in the sustained passion of her look.

"Ben! Wilson! The worst has come!" she announced.

Moore could not speak. Wade held Columbine's hand in both of his.

"Worst! Now, Collie, that's a terrible word. I've heard it many times. An' all my life the worst's been comin'. An' it hasn't come yet. You—only twenty years old—talkin' wild—the worst has come! . . . Tell me your trouble now an' I'll tell you where you're wrong."

"Jack's a thief—a cattle thief!" rang Columbine's voice, high and clear.

"Ahuh! Well, go on," said Wade.

"Jack has taken money from rustlers—*for cattle stolen from his father!*"

Wade felt the lift of her passion, and he vibrated to it.

"Reckon that's no news to me," he replied.

Then she quivered up to a strong and passionate delivery of the thing that had transformed her.

*"I'm going to marry Jack Belllounds!"*

Wilson Moore leaped toward her with a cry, to be held back by Wade's hand.

"Now, Collie," he soothed, "tell us all about it."

Columbine, still upheld by the strength of her spirit, related how she had ridden out the day before, early in the afternoon, in the hope of meeting Wade. She rode over the sage hills, along the edges of the aspen benches, everywhere that she might expect to meet or see the hunter, but as he did not appear, and as she was greatly desirous of talking with him, she went on up into the woods, following the line of the Buffalo Park trail, though keeping aside from it. She rode very slowly and cautiously, remembering Wade's instructions. In this way she ascended the aspen benches, and the spruce-bordered ridges, and then the first rise of the black forest. Finally she had gone farther than ever before and farther than was wise.

When she was about to turn back she heard the thud of hoofs ahead of her. Pronto shot up his ears. Alarmed and anxious, Columbine swiftly gazed about her. It would not do for her to be seen. Yet, on the other hand, the chances were that the approaching horse carried Wade. It was lucky that she was on Pronto, for he could be trusted to stand still and not neigh. Columbine rode into a thick clump of spruces that had long, shelving branches, reaching down. Here she hid, holding Pronto motionless.

Presently the sound of hoofs denoted the approach of several horses. That augmented Columbine's anxiety. Peering out of her covert, she espied three horsemen trotting along the trail, and one of them was Jack Belllounds. They appeared to be in strong argument, judging from gestures and emphatic movements of their heads. As chance would have it they halted their horses not half a dozen rods from Columbine's place of concealment. The two men with Belllounds were rough-looking, one of them, evidently a leader, having a dark face disfigured by a horrible scar.

Naturally they did not talk loud, and Columbine had to strain her ears to catch anything. But a word distinguished here and there, and accompanying actions, made transparent the meaning of their presence and argument. The big man refused to ride any farther. Evidently he had come so far without realizing it. His importunities were for "more head of stock." His scorn was for a "measly little bunch not worth the risk." His anger was for Belllounds's foolhardiness in "leavin' a trail." Belllounds had little to say, and most of that was spoken in a tone too low to be heard. His manner seemed indifferent, even reckless. But he wanted "money." The scar-faced man's name was "Smith." Then Columbine gathered from Smith's dogged and forceful gestures, and his words, "no money" and "bigger bunch," that he was unwilling to pay what had been agreed upon unless Belllounds promised to bring a larger number of cattle. Here Belllounds roundly cursed the rustler, and apparently argued that course "next to impossible." Smith made a sweeping movement with his arm, pointing south, indicating some place afar, and part of his speech was "Gore Peak." The little man, companion of Smith, got into the argument, and, dismounting from his horse, he made marks upon the smooth earth of the trail. He was drawing a rude map showing direction and locality. At length, when Belllounds nodded as if convinced or now informed, this third member of the party remounted, and seemed to have no more to say. Belllounds pondered sullenly. He snatched a switch from off a bough overhead and flicked his boot and stirrup with it, an action that made his horse restive. Smith leered and spoke derisively, of which speech Columbine heard, "Aw hell!" and "yellow streak," and "no one'd ever," and "son of Bill Belllounds," and "rustlin' stock." Then this scar-faced man drew out a buckskin bag. Either the contempt or the gold, or both, overbalanced vacillation in the weak mind of Jack Belllounds, for he lifted his head, showing his face pale and malignant, and without trace of shame or compunction he snatched the bag of gold, shouted a hoarse, "All right, damn you!" and, wheeling the white mustang, he spurred away, quickly disappearing.

The rustlers sat their horses, gazing down the trail, and Smith wagged his dark head doubtfully. Then he spoke quite distinctly, "I ain't a-trustin' thet Belllounds pup!" and his comrade replied, "Boss, we ain't stealin' the stock, so what th' hell!" Then they turned their horses and trotted out of sight and hearing up the timbered slope.

Columbine was so stunned, and so frightened and horrified, that she remained hidden there for a long time before she ventured forth. Then, heading homeward, she skirted the trail and kept to the edge of the forest, making a wide detour over the hills, finally reaching the ranch at sunset. Jack did not appear at the evening meal. His father had one of his spells of depression and seemed not to have noticed her absence. She lay awake all night thinking and praying.

Columbine concluded her narrative there, and, panting from her agitation and hurry, she gazed at the bowed figure of Moore, and then at Wade.

"I *had* to tell you this shameful secret," she began again. "I'm forced. If you do not help me, if something is not done, there'll be a horrible—end to all!"

"We'll help you, but how?" asked Moore, raising a white face.

"I don't know yet. I only *feel*—I only *feel* what may happen, if I don't prevent it . . . Wilson, you must go home—at least for a while."

"It'll not look right for Wils to leave White Slides now," interposed Wade, positively.

"But why? Oh, I fear—"

"Never mind now, lass. It's a good reason. An' you mustn't fear anythin'. I agree with you—we've got to prevent this—this that's goin' to happen."

"Oh, Ben, my dear friend, we must prevent it—you *must!*"

"Ahuh! . . . So I was figurin'."

"Ben, you must go to Jack an' tell him—show him the peril—frighten him terribly—so that he will not do—do this shameful thing again."

"Lass, I reckon I could scare Jack out of his skin. But what good would that do?"

"It'll stop this—this madness . . . Then I'll marry him—and keep him safe—after that!"

"Collie, do you think marryin' Buster Jack will stop his bustin' out?"

"Oh, I *know* it will. He had conquered over the evil in him. I saw that. I felt it. He conquered over his baser nature for love of me. Then—when he heard—from my own lips—that I loved Wilson—why, then he fell. He didn't care. He drank again. He let go. He sank. And now he'll ruin us all. Oh, it looks as if he meant it that way! . . . But I can change him. I will marry him. I will love him—or I will *live a lie!* I will make him think I love him!"

Wilson Moore, deadly pale, faced her with flaming eyes.

"Collie, *why?* For God's sake, explain why you will shame your womanhood and ruin me—all for that coward—that thief?"

Columbine broke from Wade and ran to Wilson, as if to clasp him, but something halted her and she stood before him.

"Because dad will kill him!" she cried.

"My God! What are you saying?" exclaimed Moore, incredulously. "Old Bill would roar and rage, but hurt that boy of his—never!"

"Wils, I reckon Collie is right. You haven't got Old Bill figured. I know," interposed Wade, with one of his forceful gestures.

"Wilson, listen, and don't set your heart against me. For I *must* do this thing," pleaded Columbine. "I heard dad swear he'd kill Jack. Oh, I'll never forget! He was terrible! If he ever finds out that Jack stole from his own father—stole cattle like a common rustler, and sold them for gold to gamble and drink with—he will kill him! . . . That's as true as fate . . . Think how horrible that would be for me! Because I'm to blame here, mostly. I fell in love with *you*, Wilson Moore, otherwise I could have saved Jack already.

"But it's not that I think of myself. Dad has loved me. He has been as a father to me. You know he's not my real father. Oh, if I only had a real one! . . . And I owe him so much. But then it's not because I owe him or because I love him. It's because of his own soul! . . . That splendid, noble old man, who has been so good to everyone—who had only one fault, and that love of his son—must he be let go in blinded and insane rage at the failure of his life, the ruin of his son—must he be allowed to kill his own flesh and blood? . . . It would be murder! It would damn dad's soul to everlasting torment. No! No! I'll not let that be!"

"Collie—how about—your own soul?" whispered Moore, lifting himself as if about to expend a tremendous breath.

"That doesn't matter," she replied.

"Collie—Collie—" he stammered, but could not go on.

Then it seemed to Wade that they both turned to him unconscious of the inevitableness of his relation to this catastrophe, yet looking to him for the spirit, the guidance that became habitual to them. It brought the warm blood back to Wade's cold heart. It was his great reward. How intensely and implacably did his soul mount to that crisis!

"Collie, I'll never fail you," he said, and his gentle voice was deep and full. "If Jack can be scared into haltin' in his mad ride to hell—then I'll do it. I'm not promisin' so much for him. But I'll swear to you that Old Belllounds's hands will never be stained with his son's blood!"

"Oh, Ben! Ben!" she cried, in passionate gratitude. "I'll love you—bless you all my life!"

"Hush, lass! I'm not one to bless . . . An' now you must do as I say. Go home an' tell them you'll marry Jack in August. Say August thirteenth."

"So long! Oh, why put it off? Wouldn't it be better—safer, to settle it all—once and forever?"

"No man can tell everythin'. But that's my judgment."

"Why August thirteenth?" she queried, with strange curiosity. "An unlucky date!"

"Well, it just happened to come to my mind—that date," replied Wade, in his slow, soft voice of reminiscence. "I was married on August thirteenth—twenty-one years ago . . . An', Collie, my wife looked somethin' like you. Isn't that strange, now? It's a little world . . . An' she's been gone eighteen years!"

"Ben, I never dreamed you ever had a wife," said Columbine, softly, with her hands going to his shoulder. "You must tell me of her someday . . . But now—if you want time—if you think it best—I'll not marry Jack till August thirteenth."

"That'll give me time," replied Wade. "I'm thinkin' Jack ought to be—reformed, let's call it—before you marry him. If all you say is true—why we can turn him round. Your promise will do most . . . So, then, it's settled?"

"Yes—dear—friends," faltered the girl, tremulously, on the verge of a breakdown, now that the ordeal was past.

Wilson Moore stood gazing out of the door, his eyes far away on the gray slopes.

"Queer how things turn out," he said, dreamily. "August thirteenth! . . . That's about the time the columbines blow on the hills . . . And I always meant columbine-time—"

Here he sharply interrupted himself, and the dreamy musing gave way to passion. "But I mean it yet! I'll—I'll die before I give up hope of you!"

## CHAPTER XVI

Wade, watching Columbine ride down the slope on her homeward way, did some of the hardest thinking he had yet been called upon to do. It was not necessary to acquaint Wilson Moore with the deeper and more subtle motives that had begun to actuate him. It would not utterly break the cowboy's spirit to live in suspense. Columbine was safe for the present. He had insured her against fatality. Time was all he needed. Possibility of an actual consummation of her marriage to Jack Belllounds did not lodge for an instant in Wade's consciousness. In Moore's case, however, the present moment seemed critical. What should he tell Moore—what should he conceal from him?

"Son, come in here," he called to the cowboy.

"Pard, it looks—bad!" said Moore, brokenly.

Wade looked at the tragic face and cursed under his breath.

"Buck up! It's never as bad as it looks. Anyway, we *know* now what to expect, an' that's well."

Moore shook his head. "Couldn't you see how like steel Collie was? . . . But I'm on to you, Wade. You think by persuading Collie to put that marriage off that we'll gain time. You're gambling with time. You swear Buster Jack will hang himself. You won't quit fighting this deal."

"Buster Jack has slung the noose over a tree, an' he's about ready to slip his head into it," replied Wade.

"Bah! . . . You drive me wild," cried Moore, passionately. "How can you? Where's all that feeling you seemed to have for me? You nursed me—you saved my leg—and my life. You must have cared about me. But now—you talk about that dolt—that spoiled old man's pet—that damned cur, as if you believed he'd ruin himself. No such luck! no such hope! . . . Every day things grow worse. Yet the worse they grow the stronger you seem! It's all out of proportion. It's dreams. Wade, I hate to say it, but I'm sure you're not always—just right in your mind."

"Wils, now ain't that queer?" replied Wade, sadly. "I'm agreein' with you."

"Aw!" Moore shook himself savagely and laid an affectionate and appealing arm on his friend's shoulder. "Forgive me, pard! . . . It's me who's out of his head . . . But my heart's broken."

"That's what you think," rejoined Wade, stoutly. "But a man's heart can't break in a day. I know . . . An' the God's truth is Buster Jack will hang himself!"

Moore raised his head sharply, flinging himself back from his friend so as to scrutinize his face. Wade felt the piercing power of that gaze.

"Wade, what do you mean?"

"Collie told us some interestin' news about Jack, didn't she? Well, she didn't know what I know. Jack Belllounds had laid a cunnin' an' devilish trap to prove you guilty of rustlin' his father's cattle."

"Absurd!" ejaculated Moore, with white lips.

"I'd never given him credit for brains to hatch such a plot," went on Wade. "Now listen. Not long ago Buster Jack made a remark in front of the whole outfit, includin' his father, that the homesteaders on the range were rustlin' cattle. It fell sort of flat, that remark. But no one could calculate on his infernal cunnin'. I quit workin' for Belllounds that night, an' I've put my time in spyin' on the boy. In my day I've done a good deal of spyin', but I've never run across anyone slicker than Buster Jack. To cut it short—he got himself a white-speckled mustang that's a dead ringer for Spottie. He measured the tracks of your horse's left front foot—the bad hoof, you know, an' he made a shoe exactly the same as Spottie wears. Also, he made some kind of a contraption that's like the end of your crutch. These he packs with him. I saw him ride across the pasture to hide his tracks, climb up the sage for the same reason, an' then hide in that grove of aspens over there near the trail you use. Here, you can bet, he changed shoes on the left front foot of his horse. Then he took to the trail, an' he left tracks for a while, an' then he was careful to hide them again. He stole his father's stock an' drove it up over the grassy benches where even you or I couldn't track him next day. But up on top, when it suited him, he left some horse tracks, an' in the mud near a spring-hole he gets off his horse, steppin' with one foot—an' makin' little circles with dots like those made by the end of your crutch. Then 'way over in the woods there's a cabin where he meets his accomplices. Here he leaves the same horse tracks an' crutch tracks . . . Simple as A B C, Wils, when you see how he did it. But I'll tell you straight—if I hadn't been suspicious of Buster Jack—that trick of his would have made you a rustler!"

"Damn him!" hissed the cowboy, in utter consternation and fury.

"Ahuh! That's my sentiment exactly."

"I swore to Collie I'd never kill him!"

"Sure you did, son. An' you've got to keep that oath. I pin you down to it. You can't break faith with Collie . . . An' you don't want his bad blood on your hands."

"No! No!" he replied, violently. "Of course I don't. I won't. But God! How sweet it would be to tear out his lying tongue—to—"

"I reckon it would. Only don't talk about that," interrupted Wade, bluntly. "You see, now, don't you, how he's about hanged himself."

"No, pard, I don't. We can't squeal that on him, any more than we can squeal what Collie told us."

"Son, you're young in dealin' with crooked men. You don't get the drift of motives. Buster Jack is not only robbin' his father an' hatchin' a dirty trap for you, but he's double-crossin' the rustlers he's sellin' the cattle to. He's riskin' their necks. He's goin' to find *your* tracks, showin' you dealt with them. Sure, he won't give them away, an' he's figurin' on their gettin' out of it, maybe by leavin' the range, or a shootin'-fray, or some way. The big thing with Jack is that he's goin' to accuse you of rustlin' an' show your tracks to his father. Well, that's a risk he's given the rustlers. It happens that I know this scar-face Smith. We've met before. Now it's easy to see from what Collie heard that Smith is not trustin' Buster Jack. So, all underneath this Jack Belllounds's game, there's forces workin' unbeknown to him, beyond his control, an' sure to ruin him."

"I see. I see. By Heaven! Wade, nothing else but ruin seems possible! . . . But suppose it works out his way! . . . What then? What of Collie?"

"Son, I've not got that far along in my reckonin'," replied Wade.

"But for my sake—think. If Buster Jack gets away with his trick—if he doesn't hang himself by some blunder or fit of temper or spree—what then of Collie?"

Wade could not answer this natural and inevitable query for the reason that he had found it impossible of consideration.

"Sufficient unto the day is the evil thereof," he replied.

"Wade, you've said that before. It helped me. But now I need more than a few words from the Bible. My faith is low. I . . . oh, I tried to pray because Collie told me she had prayed! But what are prayers? We're dealing with a stubborn, iron-willed old man who idolizes his son; we're dealing with a crazy boy, absolutely self-centered, crafty, and vicious, who'll stop at nothing. And, lastly, we're dealing with a girl who's so noble and high-souled that she'll sacrifice her all—her life to pay her debt. If she were really Bill Belllounds's daughter she'd *never* marry Jack, saying, of course, that he was not her brother . . . Do you know that it will *kill* her, if she marries him?"

"Ahuh! I reckon it would," replied Wade, with his head bowed. Moore roused his gloomy forebodings. He did not care to show this feeling or the effect the cowboy's pleading had upon him.

"Ah! So you admit it? Well, then, what of Collie?"

"*If* she marries him—she'll have to die, I suppose," replied Wade.

Then Wilson Moore leaped at his friend and with ungentle hands lifted him, pushed him erect.

"Damn you, Wade! You're not square with me! You don't tell me all!" he cried, hoarsely.

"Now, Wils, you're set up. I've told you all I know. I swear that."

"But you couldn't stand the thought of Collie dying for that brute! You couldn't! Oh, I know. I can feel some things that are hard to tell. So, you're either out of your head or you've something up your sleeve. It's hard to explain how you affect me. One minute I'm ready to choke you for that damned strangeness—whatever it is. The next minute I feel it—I trust it, myself . . . Wade, you're not—you *can't* be infallible!"

"I'm only a man, Wils, an' your friend. I reckon you do find me queer. But that's no matter. Now let's look at this deal—each from his own side of the fence. An' each actin' up to his own lights! You do what your conscience dictates, always thinkin' of Collie—not of yourself! An' I'll live up to my principles. Can we do more?"

"No, indeed, Wade, we can't," replied Moore, eloquently.

"Well, then, here's my hand. I've talked too much, I reckon. An' the time for talkin' is past."

In silence Moore gripped the hand held out to him, trying to read Wade's mind, apparently once more uplifted and strengthened by that which he could not divine.

* * * * *

Wade's observations during the following week brought forth the fact that Jack Belllounds was not letting any grass grow under his feet. He endeavored to fulfill his agreement with Smith, and drove a number of cattle by moonlight. These were part of the stock that the rancher had sold to buyers at Kremmling, and which had been collected and held in the big, fenced pasture down the valley next to the Andrews ranch. The loss was not discovered until the cattle had been counted at Kremmling. Then they were credited to loss by straying. In driving a considerable herd of half-wild steers, with an inadequate force of cowboys, it was no unusual thing to lose a number.

Wade, however, was in possession of the facts not later than the day after this midnight steal in the moonlight. He was forced to acknowledge that no one would have believed it possible for Jack Belllounds to perform a feat which might well have been difficult for the best of cowboys. But Jack accomplished it and got back home before daylight. And Wade was bound to admit that circumstantial evidence against Wilson Moore, which, of course, Jack Belllounds would soon present, would be damning and apparently irrefutable.

Waiting for further developments, Wade closely watched the ranch house, which duty interfered with his attention to the outlying trails. What he did not want to miss was being present when Jack Belllounds accused Wilson Moore of rustling cattle.

So it chanced that Wade was chatting with the cowboys one Sunday afternoon when Jack, accompanied by three strangers, all mounted on dusty, tired horses, rode up to the porch and dismounted.

Lem Billings manifested unusual excitement.

"Montana, ain't thet Sheriff Burley from Kremmlin'?" he queried.

"Shore looks like him . . . Yep, thet's him. Now, what's doin'?"

The cowboys exchanged curious glances, and then turned to Wade.

"Bent, what do you make of thet?" asked Lem, as he waved his hand toward the house. "Buster Jack ridin' up with Sheriff Burley."

The rancher, Belllounds, who was on the porch, greeted the visitors, and then they all went into the house.

"Boys, it's what I've been lookin' for," replied Wade.

"Shore. Reckon we all have idees. An' if my idee is correct I'm agoin' to git pretty damn sore pronto," declared Lem.

They were all silent for a few moments, meditating over this singular occurrence, and watching the house. Presently Old Bill Belllounds strode out upon the porch, and, walking out into the court, he peered around as if looking for someone. Then he espied the little group of cowboys.

"Hey!" he yelled. "One of you boys ride up an' fetch Wils Moore down hyar!"

"All right, boss," called Lem, in reply, as he got up and gave a hitch to his belt.

The rancher hurried back, head down, as if burdened.

"Wade, I reckon you want to go fetch Wils?" queried Lem.

"If it's all the same to you. I'd rather not," replied Wade.

"By Golly! I don't blame you. Boys, shore'n hell, Burley's after Wils."

"Wal, suppos'n' he is," said Montana. "You can gamble Wils ain't agoin' to run. I'd jest like to see him face thet outfit. Burley's a pretty square fellar. An' he's no fool."

"It's as plain as your nose, Montana, an' thet's shore big enough," returned Lem, with a hard light in his eyes. "Buster Jack's busted out, an' he's figgered Wils in some deal thet's rung in the sheriff. Wal, I'll fetch Wils." And, growling to himself, the cowboy slouched off after his horse.

Wade got up, deliberate and thoughtful, and started away.

"Say, Bent, you're shore goin' to see what's up?" asked Montana, in surprise.

"I'll be around, Jim," replied Wade, and he strolled off to be alone. He wanted to think over this startling procedure of Jack Belllounds's. Wade was astonished. He had expected that an accusation would be made against Moore by Jack, and an exploitation of such proofs as had been craftily prepared, but he had never imagined Jack would be bold enough to carry matters so far. Sheriff Burley was a man of wide experience, keen, practical, shrewd. He was also one of the countless men Wade had rubbed elbows with in the eventful past. It had been Wade's idea that Jack would be satisfied to face his father with the accusation of Moore, and thus cover his tracks. Whatever Old Belllounds might have felt over the loss of a few cattle, he would never have hounded and arrested a cowboy who had done well by him. Burley, however, was a sheriff, and a conscientious one, and he happened to be particularly set against rustlers.

Here was a complication of circumstances. What would Jack Belllounds insist upon? How would Columbine take this plot against the honor and liberty of Wilson Moore? How would Moore himself react to it? Wade confessed that he was helpless to solve these queries, and there seemed to be a further one, insistent and gathering—what was to be his own attitude here? That could not be answered, either, because only a future moment, over which he had no control, and which must decide events, held that secret. Worry beset Wade, but he still found himself proof against the insidious gloom ever hovering near, like his shadow.

He waited near the trail to intercept Billings and Moore on their way to the ranch house; and to his surprise they appeared sooner than it would have been reasonable to expect them. Wade stepped out of the willows and held up his hand. He did not see anything unusual in Moore's appearance.

"Wils, I reckon we'd do well to talk this over," said Wade.

"Talk what over?" queried the cowboy, sharply.

"Why, Old Bill's sendin' for you, an' the fact of Sheriff Burley bein' here."

"Talk nothing. Let's see what they want, and then talk. Pard, you remember the agreement we made not long ago?"

"Sure. But I'm sort of worried, an' maybe——"

"You needn't worry about me. Come on," interrupted Moore. "I'd like you to be there. And, Lem, fetch the boys."

"I shore will, an' if you need any backin' you'll git it."

When they reached the open Lem turned off toward the corrals, and Wade walked beside Moore's horse up to the house.

Belllounds appeared at the door, evidently having heard the sound of hoofs.

"Hello, Moore! Get down an' come in," he said, gruffly.

"Belllounds, if it's all the same to you I'll take mine in the open," replied the cowboy, coolly.

The rancher looked troubled. He did not have the ease and force habitual to him in big moments.

"Come out hyar, you men," he called in the door.

Voices, heavy footsteps, the clinking of spurs, preceded the appearance of the three strangers, followed by Jack Belllounds. The foremost was a tall man in black, sandy-haired and freckled, with clear gray eyes, and a drooping mustache that did not hide stern lips and rugged chin. He wore a silver star on his vest, packed a gun in a greasy holster worn low down on his right side, and under his left arm he carried a package.

It suited Wade, then, to step forward; and if he expected surprise and pleasure to break across the sheriff's stern face he certainly had not reckoned in vain.

"Wal, I'm a son-of-a-gun!" ejaculated Burley, bending low, with quick movement, to peer at Wade.

"Howdy, Jim. How's tricks?" said Wade, extending his hand, and the smile that came so seldom illumined his sallow face.

"Hell-Bent Wade, as I'm a born sinner!" shouted the sheriff, and his hand leaped out to grasp Wade's and grip it and wring it. His face worked. "My Gawd! I'm glad to see you, old-timer! Wal, you haven't changed at all! . . . Ten years! How time flies! An' it's shore you?"

"Same, Jim, an' powerful glad to meet you," replied Wade.

"Shake hands with Bridges an' Lindsay," said Burley, indicating his two comrades. "Stockmen from Grand Lake . . . Boys, you've heerd me talk about him. Wade an' I was both in the old fight at Blair's ranch on the Gunnison.

An' I've shore reason to recollect him! . . . Wade, what're you doin' up in these diggin's?"

"Drifted over last fall, Jim, an' have been huntin' varmints for Belllounds," replied Wade. "Cleaned the range up fair to middlin'. An' since I quit Belllounds I've been hangin' round with my young pard here, Wils Moore, an' interestin' myself in lookin' up cattle tracks."

Burley's back was toward Belllounds and his son, so it was impossible for them to see the sudden little curious light that gleamed in his eyes as he looked hard at Wade, and then at Moore.

"Wils Moore. How d'ye do? I reckon I remember you, though I don't ride up this way much of late years."

The cowboy returned the greeting civilly enough, but with brevity.

Belllounds cleared his throat and stepped forward. His manner showed he had a distasteful business at hand.

"Moore, I sent for you on a serious matter, I'm sorry to say."

"Well, here I am. What is it?" returned the cowboy, with clear, hazel eyes, full of fire, steady on the old rancher's.

"Jack, you know, is foreman of White Slides now. An' he's made a charge against you."

"Then let him face me with it," snapped Moore.

Jack Belllounds came forward, hands in his pockets, self-possessed, even a little swaggering, and his pale face and bold eyes showed the gravity of the situation and his mastery over it.

Wade watched this meeting of the rivals and enemies with an attention powerfully stimulated by the penetrating scrutiny Burley laid upon them. Jack did not speak quickly. He looked hard into the tense face of Moore. Wade detected a vibration of Jack's frame and a gleam of eye that showed him not wholly in control of exultation and revenge. Fear had not struck him yet.

"Well, Buster Jack, what's the charge?" demanded Moore, impatiently.

The old name, sharply flung at Jack by this cowboy, seemed to sting and reveal and inflame. But he restrained himself as with roving glance he searched Moore's person for sight of a weapon. The cowboy was unarmed.

"I accuse you of stealing my father's cattle," declared Jack, in low, husky accents. After he got the speech out he swallowed hard.

Moore's face turned a dead white. For a fleeting instant a red and savage gleam flamed in his steady glance. Then it vanished.

The cowboys, who had come up, moved restlessly. Lem Billings dropped his head, muttering. Montana Jim froze in his tracks.

Moore's dark eyes, scornful and piercing, never moved from Jack's face. It seemed as if the cowboy would never speak again.

"You call me thief! You?" at length he exclaimed.

"Yes, I do," replied Belllounds, loudly.

"Before this sheriff and your father you accuse me of stealing cattle?"

"Yes."

"And you accuse me before this man who saved my life, who *knows* me—before Hell-Bent Wade?" demanded Moore, as he pointed to the hunter.

Mention of Wade in that significant tone of passion and wonder was not without effect upon Jack Belllounds.

"What in hell do I care for Wade?" he burst out, with the old intolerance. "Yes, I accuse you. Thief, rustler! . . . And for all I know your precious Hell-Bent Wade may be—"

He was interrupted by Burley's quick and authoritative interference.

"Hyar, young man, I'm allowin' for your natural feelin's," he said, dryly, "but I advise you to bite your tongue. I ain't acquainted with Mister Moore, but I happen to know Wade. Do you savvy? . . . Wal, then, if you've any more to say to Moore get it over."

"I've had my say," replied Belllounds, sullenly.

"On what grounds do you accuse me?" demanded Moore.

"I trailed you. I've got my proofs."

Burley stepped off the porch and carefully laid down his package.

"Moore, will you get off your hoss?" he asked. And when the cowboy had dismounted and limped aside the sheriff continued, "Is this the hoss you ride most?"

"He's the only one I have."

Burley sat down upon the edge of the porch and, carefully unwrapping the package, he disclosed some pieces of hard-baked yellow mud. The smaller ones bore the imprint of a circle with a dot in the center, very clearly defined. The larger piece bore the imperfect but reasonably clear track of a curiously shaped horseshoe, somewhat triangular. The sheriff placed these pieces upon the ground. Then he laid hold of Moore's crutch, which was carried like a rifle in a sheath hanging from the saddle, and, drawing it forth, he carefully studied the round cap on the end. Next he inserted this end into both the little circles on the pieces of mud. They fitted perfectly. The cowboys bent over to get a closer view, and Billings was wagging his head. Old Belllounds had an earnest eye for them, also. Burley's next move was to lift the left front foot of Moore's horse and expose the bottom to view. Evidently the white mustang did not like these proceedings, but he behaved himself. The iron shoe on this hoof was somewhat triangular in shape. When Burley held the larger piece of mud, with its imprint, close to the hoof, it was not possible to believe that this iron shoe had not made the triangular-shaped track.

Burley let go of the hoof and laid the pieces of mud down. Slowly the other men straightened up. Someone breathed hard.

"Moore, what do them tracks look like to you?" asked the sheriff.

"They look like mine," replied the cowboy.

"They are yours."

"I'm not denying that."

"I cut them pieces of mud from beside a water hole over hyar under Gore Peak. We'd trailed the cattle Belllounds lost, an' then we kept on trailin' them, clear to the road that goes over the ridge to Elgeria . . . Now Bridges an' Lindsay hyar bought stock lately from strange cattlemen who didn't give no clear idee of their range. Jest buyin' an' sellin', they claimed . . . I reckon the extra hoss tracks we run across at Gore Peak connects up them buyers an' sellers with whoever drove Belllounds's cattle up thar . . . Have you anythin' more to say?"

"No. Not here," replied Moore, quietly.

"Then I'll have to arrest you an' take you to Kremmlin' fer trial."

"All right. I'll go."

The old rancher seemed genuinely shocked. Red tinged his cheek and a flame flared in his eyes.

"Wils, you done me dirt," he said, wrathfully. "An' I always swore by you . . . Make a clean breast of the whole damn bizness, if you want me to treat you white. You must have been locoed or drunk, to double-cross me thet way. Come on, out with it."

"I've nothing to say," replied Moore.

"You act amazin' strange fer a cowboy I've knowed to lean toward fightin' at the drop of a hat. I tell you, speak out an' I'll do right by you . I ain't forgettin' thet White Slides gave you a hard knock. An' I was young once an' had hot blood."

The old rancher's wrathful pathos stirred the cowboy to a straining-point of his unnatural, almost haughty composure. He seemed about to break into violent utterance. Grief and horror and anger seemed at the back of his trembling lips. The look he gave Belllounds was assuredly a strange one, to come from a cowboy who was supposed to have stolen his former employer's cattle. Whatever he might have replied was cut off by the sudden appearance of Columbine.

"Dad, I heard you!" she cried, as she swept upon them, fearful and wide-eyed. "What has Wilson Moore done—that you'll do right by him?"

"Collie, go back in the house," he ordered.

"No. There's something wrong here," she said, with mounting dread in the swift glance she shot from man to man. "Oh! You're—Sheriff Burley!" she gasped.

"I reckon I am, miss, an' if young Moore's a friend of yours I'm sorry I came," replied Burley.

Wade himself reacted subtly and thrillingly to the presence of the girl.

She was alive, keen, strung, growing white, with darkening eyes of blue fire, beginning to grasp intuitively the meaning here.

"My friend! He *was* more than that—not long ago . . . What has he done? Why are you here?"

"Miss, I'm arrestin' him."

"Oh! . . . For what?"

"Rustlin' your father's cattle."

For a moment Columbine was speechless. Then she burst out, "Oh, there's a terrible mistake!"

"Miss Columbine, I shore hope so," replied Burley, much embarrassed and distressed. Like most men of his kind, he could not bear to hurt a woman. "But it looks bad fer Moore . . . See hyar! There! Look at the tracks of his hoss—left front foot-shoe all crooked. Thet's his hoss's. He acknowledges thet. An', see hyar. Look at the little circles an' dots . . . I found these 'way over at Gore Peak, with the tracks of the stolen cattle. An' no *other* tracks, Miss Columbine!"

"Who put you on that trail?" she asked, piercingly.

"Jack, hyar. He found it fust, an' rode to Kremmlin' fer me."

"Jack! Jack Belllounds!" she cried, bursting into wild and furious laughter. Like a tigress she leaped at Jack as if to tear him to pieces. "You put the sheriff on that trail! You accuse Wilson Moore of stealing dad's cattle!"

"Yes, and I proved it," replied Jack, hoarsely.

"You! *You* proved it? So that's your revenge? . . . But you're to reckon with me, Jack Belllounds! You villain! You devil! You—" Suddenly she shrank back with a strong shudder. She gasped. Her face grew ghastly white. *"Oh, my God! . . . horrible—unspeakable!"* . . . She covered her face with her hands, and every muscle of her seemed to contract until she was stiff. Then her hands shot out to Moore.

"Wilson Moore, what have *you* to say—to this sheriff—to Jack Belllounds—to *me?"*

Moore bent upon her a gaze that must have pierced her soul, so like it was to a lightning flash of love and meaning and eloquence.

"Collie, they've got the proof. I'll take my medicine . . . Your dad is good. He'll be easy on me!'

*"You lie!"* she whispered. "And I will tell why you lie!"

Moore did not show the shame and guilt that should have been natural with his confession. But he showed an agony of distress. His hand sought Wade and dragged at him.

It did not need this mute appeal to tell Wade that in another moment Columbine would have flung the shameful truth into the face of Jack Belllounds. She was rising to that. She was terrible and beautiful to see.

"Collie," said Wade, with that voice he knew had strange power over her, with a clasp of her outflung hand, "no more! This is a man's game. It's not for a woman to judge. Not here! It's Wils's game—an' it's *mine*. I'm his friend. Whatever his trouble or guilt, I take it on my shoulders. An' it will be as if it were not!"

Moaning and wringing her hands, Columbine staggered with the burden of the struggle in her.

"I'm quite—quite mad—or dreaming. Oh, Ben!" she cried.

"Brace up, Collie. It's sure hard. Wils, your friend and playmate so many years—it's hard to believe! We all understand, Collie. Now you go in, an' don't listen to any more or look any more."

He led her down the porch to the door of her room, and as he pushed it open he whispered, "I will save you, Collie, an' Wils, an' the old man you call dad!"

Then he returned to the silent group in the yard.

"Jim, if I answer fer Wils Moore bein' in Kremmlin' the day you say, will you leave him with me?"

"Wal, I shore will, Wade," replied Burley, heartily.

"I object to that," interposed Jack Belllounds, stridently. "He confessed. He's got to go to jail."

"Wal, my hot-tempered young fellar, thar ain't any jail nearer 'n Denver. Did you know that?" returned Burley, with his dry, grim humor. "Moore's under arrest. An' he'll be as well off hyar with Wade as with me in Kremmlin', an' a damn sight happier."

The cowboy had mounted, and Wade walked beside him as he started homeward. They had not progressed far when Wade's keen ears caught the words, "Say, Belllounds, I got it figgered thet you an' your son don't savvy this fellar Wade."

"Wal, I reckon not," replied the old rancher.

And his son let out a peal of laughter, bitter and scornful and unsatisfied.


## CHAPTER XVII


Gore Peak was the highest point of the black range that extended for miles westward from Buffalo Park. It was a rounded dome, covered with timber and visible as a landmark from the surrounding country. All along the eastern slope of that range an unbroken forest of spruce and pine spread down to the edge of the valley. This valley narrowed toward its source, which was Buffalo Park. A few well-beaten trails crossed that country, one following Red Brook down to Kremmling; another crossing from the Park to White Slides; and another going over the divide down to Elgeria. The only well-known trail leading to Gore Peak was a branch-off from the valley, and it went round to the south and more accessible side of the mountain.

All that immense slope of timbered ridges, benches, ravines, and swales west of Buffalo Park was exceedingly wild and rough country. Here the buffalo took to cover from hunters, and were safe until they ventured forth into the parks again. Elk and deer and bear made this forest their home.

Bent Wade, hunter now for bigger game than wild beasts of the range, left his horse at Lewis's cabin and penetrated the dense forest alone, like a deer-stalker or an Indian in his movements. Lewis had acted as scout for Wade, and had ridden furiously down to Sage Valley with news of the rustlers. Wade had accompanied him back to Buffalo Park that night, riding in the dark. There were urgent reasons for speed. Jack Belllounds had ridden to Kremmling, and the hunter did not believe he would return by the road he had taken.

Fox, Wade's favorite dog, much to his disgust, was left behind with Lewis. The bloodhound, Kane, accompanied Wade. Kane had been ill-treated and then beaten by Jack Belllounds, and he had left White Slides to take up his home at Moore's cabin. And at last he had seemed to reconcile himself to the hunter, not with love, but without distrust. Kane never forgave; but he recognized his friend and master. Wade carried his rifle and a buckskin pouch containing meat and bread. His belt, heavily studded with shells, contained two guns, both now worn in plain sight, with the one on the right side hanging low. Wade's character seemed to have undergone some remarkable change, yet what he represented then was not unfamiliar.

He headed for the concealed cabin on the edge of the high valley, under the black brow of Gore Peak. It was early morning of a July day, with summer fresh and new to the forest. Along the park edges the birds and squirrels were holding carnival. The grass was crisp and bediamonded with sparkling frost. Tracks of game showed sharp in the white patches. Wade paused once, listening. Ah! That most beautiful of forest melodies for him—the bugle of an elk. Clear, resonant, penetrating, with these qualities held and blended by a note of wildness, it rang thrillingly through all Wade's being. The hound listened, but was not interested. He kept close beside the hunter or at his heels, a stealthily stepping, warily glancing hound, not scenting the four-footed denizens of the forest. He expected his master to put him on the trail of men.

The distance from the Park to Gore Peak, as a crow would have flown, was not great. But Wade progressed slowly; he kept to the dense parts of the forest; he avoided the open aisles, the swales, the glades, the high ridges, the rocky ground. When he came to the Elgeria trail he was not disappointed to find it smooth, untrodden by any recent travel. Half a mile farther on through the forest, however, he encountered tracks of three horses, made early the day before. Still farther on he found cattle and horse tracks, now growing old and dim. These tracks, pointed toward Elgeria, were like words of a printed page to Wade.

About noon he climbed a rocky eminence that jutted out from a slow-descending ridge, and from this vantage point he saw down the wavering black and green bosom of the mountain slope. A narrow valley, almost hidden, gleamed yellow in the sunlight. At the edge of this valley a faint column of blue smoke curled upward.

"Ahuh!" muttered the hunter, as he looked. The hound whined and pushed a cool nose into Wade's hand.

Then Wade resumed his noiseless and stealthy course through the woods. He began a descent, leading off somewhat to the right of the point where the smoke had arisen. The presence of the rustlers in the cabin was of importance, yet not so paramount as another possibility. He expected Jack Belllounds to be with them or meet them there, and that was the thing he wanted to ascertain. When he got down below the little valley he swung around to the left to cross the trail that came up from the main valley, some miles still farther down. He found it, and was not surprised to see fresh horse tracks, made that morning. He recognized those tracks. Jack Belllounds was with the rustlers, come, no doubt, to receive his pay.

Then the change in Wade, and the actions of a trailer of men, became more singularly manifest. He reverted to some former habit of mind and body. He was as slow as a shadow, absolutely silent, and the gaze that roved ahead and all around must have taken note of every living thing, of every moving leaf or fern or bough. The hound, with hair curling up stiff on his back, stayed close to Wade, watching, listening, and stepping with him. Certainly Wade expected the rustlers to have someone of their number doing duty as an outlook. So he kept uphill, above the cabin, and made his careful way through the thicket coverts, which at that place were dense and matted clumps of jack pine and spruce. At last he could see the cabin and the narrow, grassy valley just beyond. To his relief the horses were unsaddled and grazing. No man was in sight. But there might be a dog. The hunter, in his slow advance, used keen and unrelaxing vigilance, and at length he decided that if there had been a dog he would have been tied outside to give an alarm.

Wade had now reached his objective point. He was some eighty paces from the cabin, in line with an open aisle down which he could see into the cleared space before the door. On his left were thick, small spruces, with low-spreading branches, and they extended all the way to the cabin on that side, and in fact screened two walls of it. Wade knew exactly what he was going to do. No longer did he hesitate. Laying down his rifle, he tied the hound to a little spruce, patting him and whispering for him to stay there and be still.

Then Wade's action in looking to his belt-guns was that of a man who expected to have recourse to them speedily and by whom the necessity was neither regretted nor feared. Stooping low, he entered the thicket of spruces. The soft, spruce-matted ground, devoid of brush or twig, did not give forth the slightest sound of step, nor did the brushing of the branches against his body. In some cases he had to bend the boughs. Thus, swiftly and silently, with the gliding steps of an Indian, he approached the cabin till the brown-barked logs loomed before him, shutting off the clearer light.

He smelled a mingling of wood and tobacco smoke; he heard low, deep voices of men; the shuffling and patting of cards; the musical click of gold. Resting on his knees a moment the hunter deliberated. All was exactly as he had expected. Luck favored him. These gamblers would be absorbed in their game. The door of the cabin was just around the corner, and he could glide noiselessly to it or gain it in a few leaps. Either method would serve. But which he must try depended upon the position of the men inside and that of their weapons.

Rising silently, Wade stepped up to the wall and peeped through a chink between the logs. The sunshine streamed through windows and door. Jack Belllounds sat on the ground, full in its light, back to the wall. He was in his shirtsleeves. The gambling fever and the grievous soreness of a loser shone upon his pale face. Smith sat with back to Wade, opposite Belllounds. The other men completed the square. All were close enough together to reach comfortably for the cards and gold before them. Wade's keen eyes took this in at a single glance, and then steadied searchingly for smaller features of the scene. Belllounds had no weapon. Smith's belt and gun lay in the sunlight on the hard, clay floor, out of reach except by violent effort. The other two rustlers both wore their weapons. Wade gave a long scrutiny to the faces of these comrades of Smith, and evidently satisfied himself as to what he had to expect from them.

Wade hesitated; then stooping low, he softly swept aside the intervening boughs of spruce, glided out of the thicket into the open. Two noiseless bounds! Another, and he was inside the door!

"Howdy, rustlers! Don't move!" he called.

The surprise of his appearance, or his voice, or both, stunned the four men. Belllounds dropped his cards, and his jaw dropped at the same instant. These were absolutely the only visible movements.

"I'm in talkin' humor, an' the longer you listen the longer you'll have to live," said Wade. "But don't move!"

"We ain't movin'," burst out Smith. "Who're you, an' what d'ye want?"

It was singular that the rustler leader had not had a look at Wade, whose movements had been swift and who now stood directly behind him. Also it was obvious that Smith was sitting very stiff-necked and straight. Not improbably he had encountered such situations before.

"Who're you?" he shouted, hoarsely.

"You ought to know me." The voice was Wade's, gentle, cold, with depth and ring in it.

"I've heerd your voice somewhars—I'll gamble on thet."

"Sure. You ought to recognize my voice, Cap," returned Wade.

The rustler gave a violent start—a start that he controlled instantly.

"Cap! You callin' me thet?"

"Sure. We're old friends—*Cap Folsom!*"

In the silence, then, the rustler's hard breathing could be heard; his neck bulged red; only the eyes of his two comrades moved; Belllounds began to recover somewhat from his consternation. Fear had clamped him also, but not fear of personal harm or peril. His mind had not yet awakened to that.

"You've got me pat! But who're you?" said Folsom, huskily.

Wade kept silent.

"Who'n hell is thet man?" yelled the rustler It was not a query to his comrades any more than to the four winds. It was a furious questioning of a memory that stirred and haunted, and as well a passionate and fearful denial.

"His name's Wade," put in Belllounds, harshly. "He's the friend of Wils Moore. He's the hunter I told you about—worked for my father last winter."

"Wade? . . . What? *Wade!* You never told me his name. It ain't—it ain't—"

"Yes, it is, Cap," interrupted Wade. "It's the old boy that spoiled your handsome mug—long ago."

"*Hell-Bent Wade!*" gasped Folsom, in terrible accents. He shook all over. An ashen paleness crept into his face. Instinctively his right hand jerked toward his gun; then, as in his former motion, froze in the very act.

"Careful, Cap!" warned Wade. "It'd be a shame not to hear me talk a little . . . Turn around now an' greet an old pard of the Gunnison days."

Folsom turned as if a resistless, heavy force was revolving his head.

"By Gawd! . . . Wade!" he ejaculated. The tone of his voice, the light in his eyes, must have been a spiritual acceptance of a dreadful and irrefutable fact—perhaps the proximity of death. But he was no coward. Despite the hunter's order, given as he stood there, gun drawn and ready, Folsom wheeled back again, savagely to throw the deck of cards in Belllounds's face. He cursed horribly . . . "You spoiled brat of a rich rancher! Why'n hell didn't you tell me thet varmint-hunter was Wade."

"I did tell you," shouted Belllounds, flaming of face.

"You're a liar! You never said Wade—W-a-d-e, right out, so I'd hear it. An' I'd never passed by Hell-Bent Wade."

"Aw, that name made me tired," replied Belllounds, contemptuously.

"Haw! Haw! Haw!" bawled the rustler. "Made you tired, hey? Think you're funny? Wal, if you knowed how many men thet name's made tired—an' tired fer keeps—you'd not think it so damn funny."

"Say, what're you giving me? That Sheriff Burley tried to tell me and dad a lot of rot about this Wade. Why, he's only a little, bow-legged, big-nosed meddler—a man with a woman's voice—a sneaking cook and camp-doctor and cow-milker, and God only knows what else."

"Boy, you're correct. God only knows what else! . . . It's the *else* you've got to learn. An' I'll gamble you'll learn it . . . Wade, have you changed or grown old thet you let a pup like this yap such talk?"

"Well, Cap, he's very amusin' just now, an' I want you-all to enjoy him. Because, if you don't force my hand I'm goin' to tell you some interestin' stuff about this Buster Jack . . . Now, will you be quiet an' listen—an' answer for your pards?"

"Wade, I answer fer no man. But, so far as I've noticed, my pards ain't hankerin' to make any loud noise," Folsom replied, indicating his comrades, with sarcasm.

The red-bearded one, a man of large frame and gaunt face, wicked and wild-looking, spoke out, "Say, Smith, or whatever the hell's yore right handle—is this hyar a game we're playin'?"

"I reckon. An' if you turn a trick you'll be damn lucky," growled Folsom.

The other rustler did not speak. He was small, swarthy-faced, with sloe-black eyes and matted hair, evidently a white man with Mexican blood. Keen, strung, furtive, he kept motionless, awaiting events.

"Buster Jack, these new pards of yours are low-down rustlers, an' one of them's worse, as I could prove," said Wade, "but compared with you they're all gentlemen."

Belllounds leered. But he was losing his bravado. Something began to dawn upon his obtuse consciousness.

"What do I care for you or your gabby talk?" he flashed, sullenly.

"You'll care when I tell these rustlers how you double-crossed them."

Belllounds made a spring, like that of a wolf in a trap; but when halfway up he slipped. The rustler on his right kicked him, and he sprawled down again, back to the wall.

"Buster, look into this!" called Wade, and he leveled the gun that quivered momentarily, like a compass needle, and then crashed fire and smoke. The bullet spat into a log. But it had cut the lobe of Belllounds's ear, bringing blood. His face turned a ghastly, livid hue. All in a second terror possessed him—shuddering, primitive terror of death.

Folsom haw-hawed derisively and in crude delight. "Say, Buster Jack, don't get any idee thet my ole pard Wade was shootin' at your head. Aw, no!"

The other rustlers understood then, if Belllounds had not, that the situation was in control of a man not in any sense ordinary.

"Cap, did you know Buster Jack accused my friend, Wils Moore, of stealin' these cattle you're sellin'?" asked Wade, deliberately.

"What cattle did you say?" asked the rustler, as if he had not heard aright.

"The cattle Buster Jack stole from his father an' sold to you."

"Wal, now! Bent Wade at his old tricks! I might have knowed it, once I seen you . . . Naw, I'd no idee Belllounds blamed thet stealin' on to anyone."

"He did."

"Ahuh! Wal, who's this Wils Moore?"

"He's a cowboy, as fine a youngster as ever straddled a horse. Buster Jack hates him. He licked Jack a couple of times an' won the love of a girl that Jack wants."

"Ho! Ho! Quite romantic, I declare . . . Say, thar's some damn queer notions I'm gettin' about you, Buster Jack."

Belllounds lay propped against the wall, sagging there, laboring of chest, sweating of face. The boldness of brow held, because it was fixed, but that of his eyes had gone; and his mouth and chin showed craven weakness. He stared in dread suspense at Wade.

"Listen. An' all of you sit tight," went on Wade, swiftly. "Jack stole the cattle from his father. He's a thief at heart. But he had a double motive. He left a trail—he left tracks behind. He made a crooked horseshoe, like that Wils Moore's horse wears, an' he put that on his own horse. An' he made a contraption—a little iron ring with a dot in it, an' he left the crooked shoe tracks, an' he left the little ring tracks—"

"By Gawd! I seen them funny tracks!" ejaculated Folsom. "At the water hole an' right hyar in front of the cabin. I seen them. I knowed Jack made them, somehow, but I didn't think. His white hoss has a crooked left front shoe."

"Yes, he has, when Jack takes off the regular shoe an' nails on the crooked one . . . Men, I followed those tracks They lead up here to your cabin. Belllounds made them with a purpose . . . An' he went to Kremmlin' to get Sheriff Burley. An' he put him wise to the rustlin' of cattle to Elgeria. An' he fetched him up to White Slides to accuse Wils Moore. An' he trailed his own tracks up here, showin' Burley the crooked horse track an' the little circle—that was supposed to be made by the end of Moore's crutch—an' he led Burley with his men right to this cabin an' to the trail where you drove the cattle over the divide . . . An' then he had Burley dig out some cakes of mud holdin' these tracks, an' they fetched them down to White Slides. Buster Jack blamed the stealin' on to Moore. An' Burley arrested Moore. The trial comes off next week at Kremmlin'."

"Damn me!" exclaimed Folsom, wonderingly. "A man's never too old to learn! I knowed this pup was stealin' from his own father, but I reckoned he was jest a natural-born, honest rustler, with a hunch fer drink an' cards."

"Well, he's double-crossed you, Cap. An' if I hadn't rounded you up your chances would have been good for swingin'."

"Ahuh! Wade, I'd sure preferred them chances of swingin' to your over-kind interferin' in my bizness. Allus interferin', Wade, thet's your weakness! . . . But gimmie a gun!"

"I reckon not, Cap."

"Gimme a gun!" roared the rustler. "Lemme sit hyar an' shoot the eyes outen this—lyin' pup of a Belllounds! . . . Wade, put a gun in my hand—a gun with two shells—or only one. You can stand with your gun at my head . . . Let me kill this skunk!"

For all Belllounds could tell, death was indeed close. No trace of a Belllounds was apparent about him then, and his face was a horrid spectacle for a man to be forced to see. A froth foamed over his hanging lower lip.

"Cap, I ain't trustin' you with a gun just this particular minute," said Wade.

Folsom then bawled his curses to his comrades.

"——! Kill him! Throw your guns an' bore him—right in them bulgin' eyes! . . . I'm tellin' you—we've gotta fight, anyhow. We're agoin' to cash right hyar. But kill him first!"

Neither of Folsom's lieutenants yielded to the fierce exhortation of their leader or to their own evilly expressed passions. It was Wade who dominated them. Then ensued a silence fraught with suspense, growing more charged every long instant. The balance here seemed about to be struck.

"Wade, I've been a gambler all my life, an' a damn smart one, if I do say it myself," declared the rustler leader, his voice inharmonious with the facetiousness of his words. "An' I'll make a last bet."

"Go ahead, Cap. What'll you bet?" answered the cold voice, still gentle, but different now in its inflection.

"By Gawd! I'll bet all the gold hyar that Hell-Bent Wade wouldn't shoot any man in the back!"

"You win!"

Slowly and stiffly the rustler rose to his feet. When he reached his height he deliberately swung his leg to kick Belllounds in the face.

"Thar! I'd like to have a reckonin' with you, Buster Jack," he said. "I ain't dealin' the cards hyar. But somethin' tells me thet, shaky as I am in my boots, I'd liefer be in mine than yours."

With that, and expelling a heavy breath, he wrestled around to confront the hunter.

"Wade. I've no hunch to your game, but it's slower'n I recollect you."

"Why, Cap, I was in a talkin' humor," replied Wade.

"Hell! You're up to some dodge. What'd you care fer my learnin' thet pup had double-crossed me? You won't let me kill him."

"I reckon I wanted him to learn what real men thought of him."

"Ahuh! Wal, an' now I've onlightened him, what's the next deal?"

"You'll all go to Kremmlin' with me an' I'll turn you over to Sheriff Burley."

That was the gauntlet thrown down by Wade. It was not unexpected, and acceptance seemed a relief. Folsom's eyeballs became living fire with the desperate gleam of the reckless chances of life. Cutthroat he might have been, but he was brave, and he proved the significance of Wade's attitude.

"Pards, hyar's to luck!" he rang out, hoarsely, and with pantherish quickness he leaped for his gun.

A tense, surcharged instant—then all four men, as if released by some galvanized current of rapidity, flashed into action. Guns boomed in unison. Spurts of red, clouds of smoke, ringing reports, and hoarse cries filled the cabin. Wade had fired as he leaped. There was a thudding patter of lead upon the walls. The hunter flung himself prostrate behind the bough framework that had served as bedstead. It was made of spruce boughs, thick and substantial. Wade had not calculated falsely in estimating it as a bulwark of defense. Pulling his second gun, he peeped from behind the covert.

Smoke was lifting, and drifting out of door and windows. The atmosphere cleared. Belllounds sagged against the wall, pallid, with protruding eyes of horror on the scene before him. The dark-skinned little man lay writhing. All at once a tremor stilled his convulsions. His body relaxed limply. As if by magic his hand loosened on the smoking gun. Folsom was on his knees, reeling and swaying, waving his gun, peering like a drunken man for some lost object. His temple appeared half shot away, a bloody and horrible sight.

"Pards, I got him!" he said, in strange, half-strangled whisper. "I got him! . . . Hell-Bent Wade! My respects! I'll meet you—thar!"

His reeling motion brought his gaze in line with Belllounds. The violence of his start sent drops of blood flying from his gory temple.

"Ahuh! The cards run—my way. Belllounds, hyar's to your—lyin' eyes!"

The gun wavered and trembled and circled. Folsom strained in last terrible effort of will to aim it straight. He fired. The bullet tore hair from Belllounds's head, but missed him. Again the rustler aimed, and the gun wavered and shook. He pulled trigger. The hammer clicked upon an empty chamber. With low and gurgling cry of baffled rage Folsom dropped the gun and sank face forward, slowly stretching out.

The red-bearded rustler had leaped behind the stone chimney that all but hid his body. The position made it difficult for him to shoot because his gun-hand was on the inside, and he had to press his body tight to squeeze it behind the corner of ragged stone. Wade had the advantage. He was lying prone with his right hand round the corner of the framework. An overhang of the bough-ends above protected his head when he peeped out. While he watched for a chance to shoot he loaded his empty gun with his left hand. The rustler strained and writhed his body, twisting his neck, and suddenly darting out his head and arm, he shot. His bullet tore the overhang of boughs above Wade's face. And Wade's answering shot, just a second too late, chipped the stone corner where the rustler's face had flashed out. The bullet, glancing, hummed out of the window. It was a close shave. The rustler let out a hissing, inarticulate cry. He was trapped. In his effort to press in closer he projected his left elbow beyond the corner of the chimney. Wade's quick shot shattered his arm.

There was no asking or offering of quarter here. This was the old feud of the West—of the vicious and the righteous in strife—both reared in the same stern school. The rustler gave his body such contortion that he was twisted almost clear around, with his right hand over his left shoulder. He punched the muzzle of his gun into a crack between two stones, and he pried to open them. The dry clay cement crumbled, the crack widened. Sighting along the barrel he aimed it with the narrow strip of Wade's shoulder that was visible above the framework. Then he shot and hit. Wade shrank flatter and closer, hiding himself to better advantage. The rustler made his great blunder then, for in that moment he might have rushed out and killed his adversary. But, instead, he shot again—another time—a third. And his heavy bullets tore and splintered the boughs dangerously close to the hunter's head. Then came an awkward, almost hopeless task for the rustler, in maintaining his position while reloading his gun. He did it, and his panting attested to the labor and pain it cost him.

So much, in fact, that he let his knee protrude. Wade fired, breaking that knee. The rustler sagged in his tracks, his hip stuck out to afford a target for the remorseless Wade. Still the doomed man did not cry out, though it was evident that he could not now keep his body from sagging into sight of the hunter. Then with a desperate courage worthy of a better cause, and with a spirit great in its defeat, the rustler plunged out from his hiding place, gun extended. His red beard, his gaunt face, fierce and baleful, his wabbling plunge that was really a fall, made a sight which was terrible. He hopped out of that fall. His gun began to blaze. But it only matched the blazes of Wade's. And the rustler pitched headlong over the framework, falling heavily against the wall beyond.

Then there was silence for a long moment. Wade stirred, as if to look around. Belllounds also stirred, and gulped, as if to breathe. The three prostrate rustlers lay inert, their positions singularly tragic and settled. The smoke again began to lift, to float out of the door and windows. In another moment the big room seemed less hazy.

Wade rose, not without effort, and he had a gun in each hand. Those hands were bloody; there was blood on his face, and his left shoulder was red. He approached Belllounds.

Wade was terrible then—terrible with a ruthlessness that was no pretense. To Belllounds it must have represented death—a bloody death which he was not prepared to meet.

"Come out of your trance, you pup rustler!" yelled Wade.

"For God's sake, don't kill me!" implored Belllounds, stricken with terror.

"Why not? Look around! My busy day, Buster! . . . An' for that Cap Folsom it's been ten years comin' . . . I'm goin' to shoot you in the belly an' watch you get sick to your stomach!"

Belllounds, with whisper, and hands, and face, begged for his life in an abjectness of sheer panic.

"What!" roared the hunter. "Didn't you know I come to kill you?"

"Yes—yes! I've seen—that. It's awful! . . . I never harmed you . . . Don't kill me! Let me live, Wade. I swear to God I'll—I'll never do it again . . . For dad's sake—for Collie's sake—don't kill me!"

"I'm Hell-Bent Wade! . . . You wouldn't listen to them——when they wanted to tell you who I am!"

Every word of Wade's drove home to this boy the primal meaning of sudden death. It inspired him with an unutterable fear. That was what clamped his brow in a sweaty band and upreared his hair and rolled his eyeballs. His magnified intelligence, almost ghastly, grasped a hope in Wade's apparent vacillation and in the utterance of the name of Columbine. Intuition, a subtle sense, inspired him to beg in that name.

"Swear you'll give up Collie!" demanded Wade, brandishing his guns with bloody hands.

"Yes—yes! My God, I'll do anything!" moaned Belllounds.

"Swear you'll tell your father you'd had a change of heart. You'll give Collie up! . . . Let Moore have her!"

"I swear! . . . But if you tell dad—I stole his cattle—he'll do for me!"

"We won't squeal that. I'll save you if you give up the girl. Once more, Buster Jack—try an' make me believe you'll square the deal."

Belllounds had lost his voice. But his mute, fluttering lips were infinite proof of the vow he could not speak. The boyishness, the stunted moral force, replaced the manhood in him then. He was only a factor in the lives of others, protected even from this Nemesis by the greatness of his father's love.

"Get up, an' take my scarf," said Wade, "an' bandage these bullet holes I got."

## CHAPTER XVIII

Wade's wounds were not in any way serious, and with Belllounds's assistance he got to the cabin of Lewis, where weakness from loss of blood made it necessary that he remain. Belllounds went home.

The next day Wade sent Lewis with packhorse down to the rustler's cabin, to bury the dead men and fetch back their effects. Lewis returned that night, accompanied by Sheriff Burley and two deputies, who had been busy on their own account. They had followed horse tracks from the water hole under Gore Peak to the scene of the fight, and had arrived to find Lewis there. Burley had appropriated the considerable amount of gold, which he said could be identified by cattlemen who had bought the stolen cattle.

When opportunity afforded Burley took advantage of it to speak to Wade when the others were out of earshot.

"Thar was another man in thet cabin when the fight come off," announced the sheriff. "An' he come up hyar with you."

"Jim, you're locoed," replied Wade.

The sheriff laughed, and his shrewd eyes had a kindly, curious gleam.

"Next you'll be givin' me a hunch thet you're in a fever an' out of your head."

"Jim, I'm not as clear-headed as I might be."

"Wal, tell me or not, jest as you like. I seen his tracks—follered them. An' Wade, old pard, I've reckoned long ago thar's a nigger in the woodpile."

"Sure. An' you know me. I'd take it friendly of you to put Moore's trial off fer a while—till I'm able to ride to Krernmlin'. Maybe then I can tell you a story."

Burley threw up his hands in genuine apprehension. "Not much! You ain't agoin' to tell *me* no story! . . . But I'll wait on you, an' welcome. Reckon I owe you a good deal on this rustler roundup. Wade, thet must have been a man-sized fight, even fer you. I picked up twenty-six empty shells. An' the little half-breed had one empty shell an' five loaded ones in his gun. You must have got him quick. Hey?"

"Jim, I'm observin' you're a heap more curious than ever, an' you always was an inquisitive cuss," complained Wade. "I don't recollect what happened."

"Wal, wal, have it your own way," replied Burley, with good nature. "Now, Wade, I'll pitch camp hyar in the park tonight, an' to-morrer I'll ride down to White Slides on my way to Kremmlin'. What're you wantin' me to tell Belllounds?"

The hunter pondered a moment.

"Reckon it's just as well that you tell him somethin' . . . You can say the rustlers are done for an' that he'll get his stock back. I'd like you to tell him that the rustlers were more to blame than Wils Moore. Just say that an' nothin' else about Wils. Don't mention about your suspectin' there was another man around when the fight come off . . . Tell the cowboys that I'll be down in a few days. An' if you happen to get a chance for a word alone with Miss Collie, just say I'm not bad hurt an' that all will be well."

"Ahuh!" Burley grunted out the familiar exclamation. He did not say any more then, but he gazed thoughtfully down upon the pale hunter, as if that strange individual was one infinitely to respect, but never to comprehend.

* * * * *

Wade's wounds healed quickly; nevertheless, it was more than several days before he felt spirit enough to undertake the ride. He had to return to White Slides, but he was reluctant to do so. Memory of Jack Belllounds dragged at him, and when he drove it away it continually returned. This feeling was almost equivalent to an augmentation of his gloomy foreboding, which ever hovered on the fringe of his consciousness. But one morning he started early, and, riding very slowly, with many rests, he reached the Sage Valley cabin before sunset. Moore saw him coming, yelled his delight and concern, and almost lifted him off the horse. Wade was too tired to talk much, but he allowed himself to be fed and put to bed and worked over.

"Boot's on the other foot now, pard," said Moore, with delight at the prospect of returning service. "Say, you're all shot up! And it's I who'll be nurse!"

"Wils, I'll be around tomorrow," replied the hunter. "Have you heard any news from down below?"

"Sure. I've met Lem every night."

Then he related Burley's version of Wade's fight with the rustlers in the cabin. From the sheriff's lips the story gained much. Old Bill Belllounds had received the news in a singular mood; he offered no encomiums to the victor; contrary to his usual custom of lauding every achievement of labor or endurance, he now seemed almost to regret the affray. Jack Belllounds had returned from Kremmling and he was present when Burley brought news of the rustlers. What he thought none of the cowboys vouchsafed to say, but he was drunk the next day, and he lost a handful of gold to them. Never had he gambled so recklessly. Indeed, it was as if he hated the gold he lost. Little had been seen of Columbine, but little was sufficient to make the cowboys feel concern.

Wade made scarcely any comment upon this news from the ranch; next day, however, he was up, and caring for himself, and he told Moore about the fight and how he had terrorized Belllounds and exhorted the promises from him.

"Never in God's world will Buster Jack live up to those promises!" cried Moore, with absolute conviction. "I know him, Ben. He meant them when he made them. He'd swear his soul away—then next day he'd lie or forget or betray."

"I'm not believin' that till I know," replied the hunter, gloomily. "But I'm afraid of him . . . I've known bad men to change. There's a grain of good in all men—somethin' divine. An' it comes out now an' then. Men rise on steppin'-stones of their dead selves to higher things! . . . This is Belllounds's chance for the good in him. If it's not there he will do as you say. If it is—that scare he had will be the turnin'-point in his life. I'm hopin', but I'm afraid."

"Ben, you wait and see," said Moore, earnestly. "Heaven knows I'm not one to lose hope for my fellowmen—hope for the higher things you've taught me . . . But human nature is human nature. Jack *can't* give Collie up, just the same as I *can't*. That's self-preservation as well as love."

\* \* \* \* \*

The day came when Wade walked down to White Slides. There seemed to be a fever in his blood, which he tried to convince himself was a result of his wounds instead of the condition of his mind. It was Sunday, a day of sunshine and squall, of azure-blue sky, and great, sailing, purple clouds. The sage of the hills glistened and there was a sweetness in the air.

The cowboys made much of Wade. But the old rancher, seeing him from the porch, abruptly went into the house. No one but Wade noticed this omission of courtesy. Directly, Columbine appeared, waving her hand, and running to meet him.

"Dad saw you. He told me to come out and excuse him . . . Oh, Ben, I'm so happy to see you! You don't look hurt at all. What a fight you had! . . . Oh, I was sick! But let me forget that . . . How are you? And how's Wils?"

Thus she babbled until out of breath.

"Collie, it's sure good to see you," said Wade, feeling the old, rich thrill at her presence. "I'm comin' on tolerable well. I wasn't bad hurt, but I bled a lot. An' I reckon I'm older 'n I was when packin' gunshot holes was nothin'. Every year tells. Only a man doesn't know till after . . . An' how are you, Collie?"

Her blue eyes clouded, and a tremor changed the expression of her sweet lips.

"I am unhappy, Ben," she said. "But what could we expect? It might be worse. For instance, you might have been killed. I've much to be thankful for."

"I reckon so. We all have . . . I fetched a message from Wils, but I oughtn't tell it."

"Please do," she begged, wistfully.

"Well, Wils says, tell Collie I love her every day more an' more, an' that my love keeps up my courage an' my belief in God, an' if she ever marries Jack Belllounds she can come up to visit my grave among the columbines on the hill."

Strange how Wade experienced comfort in thus torturing her! She was rosy at the beginning of his speech and white at its close. "Oh, it's true! It's true!" she whispered. "It'll kill him, as it will me!"

"Cheer up, Columbine," said Wade. "It's a long time till August thirteenth . . . An' now tell me, why did Old Bill run when he saw me comin'?"

"Ben, I suspect dad has the queerest notion you want to tell him some awful bloody story about the rustlers."

"Ahuh! Well, not yet . . . An' how's Jack Belllounds actin' these days?"

Wade felt the momentousness of that query, but it seemed her face had been telltale enough, without confirmation of words.

"My friend, somehow I hate to tell you. You're always so hopeful, so ready to think good instead of evil . . . But Jack has been rough with me, almost brutal. He was drunk once. Every day he drinks, sometimes a little, sometimes more. But drink changes him. And it's dragging dad down. Dad doesn't say so, yet I feel he's afraid of what will come next . . . Jack has nagged me to marry him right off. He wanted to the day he came back from Kremmling. He's eager to leave White Slides. Dad knows that, also, and it worries him. But of course I refused."

The presence of Columbine, so vivid and sweet and stirring, and all about her the sunlight, the golden gleams on the sage hills, and Wade's heart and brain and spirit sustained a subtle transformation. It was as if what had been beautiful with light had suddenly, strangely darkened. Then Wade imagined he stood alone in a gloomy house, which was his own heart, and he was listening to the arrival of a tragic messenger whose foot sounded heavy on the stairs, whose hand turned slowly upon the knob, whose gray presence opened the door and crossed the threshold.

"Buster Jack didn't break off with you, Collie?" asked the hunter.

"Break off with me! . . . No, indeed! Whatever possessed you to say that?"

"An' he didn't offer to give you up to Wils Moore?"

"Ben, are you crazy?" cried Columbine.

"Collie; listen. I'll tell you." The old urge knocked at Wade's mind. "Buster Jack was in the cabin, gamblin' with the rustlers, when I cornered them. You remember I meant to scare Buster Jack within an inch of his life? Well, I made use of my opportunity. I worked up the rustlers. Then I told Jack I'd give away his secret. He made to jump an' run, I reckon. But he hadn't the nerve. I shot a piece out of his ear, just to begin the fun. An' then I told the rustlers how Jack had double-crossed them. Folsom, the boss rustler, roared like a mad steer. He was wild to kill Jack. He begged for a gun to shoot out Jack's eyes. An' so were the other rustlers burnin' to kill him. Bad outfit. There was a fight, which, I'm bound to confess, was not short an' sweet. There was a lot of shootin'. An' in a cabin gun-shots almost lift the roof. Folsom was on his knees, dyin', wavin' his gun, whisperin' in fiendish glee that he had done for me. When he saw Jack an' remembered he shook so with fury that he scattered blood all over. An' he took long aim at Jack, tryin' to steady his gun. He couldn't, an' he missed, an' then fell over dead with his head on Jack's knees. That left the red-bearded rustler, who had hid behind the chimney. Jack watched the rest of that fight, an' for a youngster it must have been nerve-rackin'. I broke the rustler's arm, an' then his knee, an' then I got him in the hip two more times before he hobbled out to his finish. He'd shot me up considerable, so that when I braced Jack I must have been a hair-raisin' sight. I made Jack believe I meant to murder him. He begged an' cried, an' he got to prayin' for his life for your sake. It was sickenin', but it was what I wanted. So then I made him swear he'd free you an' give you up to Moore."

"Oh! Oh, Ben, how awful!" whispered Columbine, shuddering. "How *could* you tell me such a horrible story?"

"Reckon I wanted you to know how Jack come to make the promises an' what they were."

"Promises! What are promises or oaths to Jack Belllounds?" she cried, in passionate contempt. "You wasted your breath. Coward—liar that he is!"

"Ahuh!" Wade looked straight ahead of him as if he saw some expected and unpleasant thing far in the distance. Then with irresistible steps, neither swift nor slow, but ponderous, he strode to the porch and mounted the steps.

"Why, Ben, where are you going?" called Columbine, in surprise, as she followed him.

He did not answer. He approached the closed door of the living room.

"Ben!" cried Columbine, in alarm.

But he had no reply for her—indeed, no thought of her. Without knocking, he opened the door with rude and powerful hand, and, striding in, closed it after him.

Bill Belllounds was standing, back against the great stone chimney, arms folded, a stolid and grim figure, apparently fortified against an intrusion he had expected.

"Wal, what do you want?" he asked, gruffly. He had sensed catastrophe in the first sight of the hunter.

"Belllounds, I reckon I want a hell of a lot," replied Wade. "An' I'm askin' you to see we're not disturbed."

"Bar the door."

Wade dropped the bar in place, and then, removing his sombrero, he wiped his moist brow.

"Do you see an enemy in me?" he asked, curiously.

"Speakin' out fair, Wade, there ain't any reason I can see that you're an enemy to me," replied Belllounds. "But I feel somethin'. It ain't because I'm takin' my son's side. It's more than that. A queer feelin', an' one I never had before. I got it first when you told the story of the Gunnison feud."

"Belllounds, we can't escape our fates. An' it was written long ago I was to tell you a worse an' harder story than that."

"Wal, mebbe I'll listen an' mebbe I won't. I ain't promisin', these days."

"Are you goin' to make Collie marry Jack?" demanded the hunter.

"She's willin'."

"You know that's not true. Collie's willin' to sacrifice love, honor, an' life itself, to square her debt to you."

The old rancher flushed a burning red, and in his eyes flared a spirit of earlier years.

"Wade, you can go too far," he warned. "I'm appreciatin' your good-heartedness. It sort of warms me toward you . . . But this is my business. You've no call to interfere. You've done that too much already. An' I'm reckonin' Collie would be married to Jack now if it hadn't been for you."

"Ahuh! . . . That's why I'm thankin' God I happened along to White Slides. Belllounds, your big mistake is thinkin' your son is good enough for this girl. An' you're makin' mistakes about me. I've interfered here, an' you may take my word for it I had the right."

"Strange talk, Wade, but I'll make allowances."

"You needn't. I'll back my talk . . . But, first, I'm askin' you—an' if this talk hurts, I'm sorry—why don't you give some of your love for your no-good Buster Jack to Collie?"

Belllounds clenched his huge fists and glared. Anger leaped within him. He recognized in Wade an outspoken, bitter adversary to his cherished hopes for his son and his stubborn, precious pride.

"By Heaven! Wade, I'll—"

"Belllounds, I can make you swallow that kind of talk," interrupted Wade. "It's man to man now. An' I'm a match for you any day. Savvy? . . . Do you think I'm damn fool enough to come here an' brace you unless I knew that. Talk to me as you'd talk about some other man's son."

"It ain't possible," rejoined the rancher, stridently.

"Then listen to me first . . . Your son Jack, to say the least, will ruin Collie. Do you see that?"

"By Gawd! I'm afraid so," groaned Belllounds, big in his humiliation. "But it's my one last bet, an' I'm goin' to play it."

"Do you know marryin' him will *kill* her?"

"What! . . . You're overdoin' your fears, Wade. Women don't die so easy."

"Some of them die, an' Collie's one that will, *if* she ever marries Jack."

"*If!* . . . Wal, she's goin' to."

"We don't agree," said Wade, curtly.

"Are you runnin' my family?"

"No. But I'm runnin' a large-sized *if* in this game. You'll admit that presently . . . Belllounds, you make me mad. You don't meet me man to man. You're not the Bill Belllounds of old. Why, all over this state of Colorado you're known as the whitest of the white. Your name's a byword for all that's square an' big an' splendid. But you're so blinded by your worship of that wild boy that you're another man in all pertainin' to him. I don't want to harp on his short-comm's. I'm for the girl. She doesn't love him. She can't. She will only drag herself down an' die of a broken heart . . . Now, I'm askin' you, before it's too late—give up this marriage."

"Wade! I've shot men for less than you've said!" thundered the rancher, beside himself with rage and shame.

"Ahuh! I reckon you have. But not men like me . . . I tell you, straight to your face, it's a fool deal you're workin'—a damn selfish one—a dirty job, to put on an innocent, sweet girl—an' as sure as you stand there, if you do it, you'll ruin four lives!"

"Four!" exclaimed Belllounds. But any word would have expressed his humiliation.

"I should have said three, leavin' Jack out. I meant Collie's an' yours an' Wils Moore's."

"Moore's is about ruined already, I've a hunch."

"You can get hunches you never dreamed of, Belllounds, old as you are. An' I'll give you one presently . . . But we drift off. Can't you keep cool?"

"Cool! With you rantin' hell-bent for election? Haw! Haw! . . . Wade, you're locoed. You always struck me queer . . . An' if you'll excuse me, I'm gettin' tired of this talk. We're as far apart as the poles. An' to save what good feelin's we both have, let's quit."

"You don't love Collie, then?" queried Wade, imperturbably.

"Yes, I do. That's a fool idee of yours. It puts me out of patience."

"Belllounds, you're not her real father."

The rancher gave a start, and he stared as he had stared before, fixedly and perplexedly at Wade.

"No, I'm not."

"If she *were* your real daughter—your own flesh an' blood—an' Jack Belllounds was *my* son, would you let her marry him?"

"Wal, Wade, I reckon I wouldn't."

"Then how can you expect my consent to her marriage with your son?"

"*What!*" Belllounds lunged over to Wade, leaned down, shaken by overwhelming amaze.

"Collie is my daughter!"

A loud expulsion of breath escaped Belllounds. Lower he leaned, and looked with piercing gaze into the face and eyes that in this moment bore strange resemblance to Columbine.

"So help me Gawd! . . . That's the secret? . . . Hell-Bent Wade! An' you've been on my trail!"

He staggered to his big chair and fell into it. No trace of doubt showed in his face. The revelation had struck home because of its very greatness.

Wade took the chair opposite. His likeness to Columbine had faded now. It had been love, a spirit, a radiance, a glory. It was gone. And Wade's face became the emblem of tragedy.

"Listen, Belllounds. I'll tell you! . . . The ways of God are inscrutable. I've been twenty years tryin' to atone for the wrong I did Collie's mother. I've been a prospector for the trouble of others. I've been a bearer of their burdens. An' if I can save Collie's happiness an' her soul, I reckon I won't be denied the peace of meetin' her mother in the other world . . . I recognized Collie the moment I laid eyes on her. She favors her mother in looks, an' she has her mother's sensitiveness, her fire an' pride, an' she even has her voice. It's low an' sweet—alto, they used to call it . . . But I'd recognized Collie as my own if I'd been blind an' deaf . . . It's over eighteen years ago that we had the trouble. I was no boy, but I was terribly in love with Lucy. An' she loved me with a passion I never learned till too late. We came West from Missouri. She was born in Texas. I had a rovin' disposition an' didn't stick long at any kind of work. But I was lookin' for a ranch. My wife had some money an' I had high hopes. We spent our first year of married life travelin' through Kansas. At Dodge I got tied up for a while. You know, in them days Dodge was about the wildest camp on the plains. My wife's brother run a place there. He wasn't much good. But she thought he was perfect. Strange how blood relations can't see the truth about their own people! Anyway, her brother Spencer had no use for me, because I could tell how slick he was with the cards an' beat him at his own game. Spencer had a gamblin' pard, a cowboy run out of Texas, one Cap Fol—but no matter about his name. One night they were fleecin' a stranger an' I broke into the game, winnin' all they had. The game ended in a fight, with bloodshed, but nobody killed. That set Spencer an' his pard Cap against me. The stranger was a planter from Louisiana. He'd been an officer in the rebel army. A high-strung, handsome Southerner, fond of wine an' cards an' women. Well, he got to payin' my wife a good deal of attention when I was away, which happened to be often. She never told me. I was jealous those days.

"My little girl you call Columbine was born there durin' a long absence of mine. When I got home Lucy an' the baby were gone. Also the Southerner! . . . Spencer an' his pard Cap, an' others they had in the deal, proved to me, so it seemed, that the little girl was not really mine! . . . An' so I set out on a hunt for my wife an' her lover. I found them. An' I killed him before her eyes. But she was innocent, an' so was he, as came out too late. He'd been, indeed, her friend. She scorned me. She told me how her brother Spencer an' his friends had established guilt of mine that had driven her from me.

"I went back to Dodge to have a little quiet smoke with these men who had ruined me. They were gone. The trail led to Colorado. Nearly a year later I rounded them all up in a big wagon-train post north of Denver. Another brother of my wife's, an' her father, had come West, an' by accident or fate we all met there. We had a family quarrel. My wife would not forgive me—would not speak to me, an' her people backed her up. I made the great mistake to take her father an' other brothers to belong to the same brand as Spencer. In this I wronged them an' her.

"What I did to them, Belllounds, is one story I'll never tell to any man who might live to repeat it. But it drove my wife near crazy. An' it made me Hell-Bent Wade! . . . She ran off from me there, an' I trailed her all over Colorado. An' the end of that trail was not a hundred miles from where we stand now. The last trace I had was of the burnin' of a prairie-schooner by Arapahoes as they were goin' home from a foray on the Utes . . . The little girl might have toddled off the trail. But I reckon she was hidden or dropped by her mother, or someone fleein' for life. Your men found her in the columbines."

Belllounds drew a long, deep breath.

"What a man never expects always comes true . . . Wade, the lass is yours. I can see it in the way you look at me. I can feel it . . . She's been like my own. I've done my best, accordin' to my conscience. An' I've loved her, for all they say I couldn't see aught but Jack . . . You'll take her away from me?"

"No. Never," was the melancholy reply.

"What! Why not?"

"Because she loves you . . . I could never reveal myself to Collie. I couldn't win her love with a lie. An' I'd have to lie, to be false as hell . . . False to her mother an' to Collie an' to all I hold high! I'd have to tell Collie the truth—the wrong I did her mother—the *hell* I visited upon her mother's people . . . She'd fear me."

"Ahuh! . . . An' you'll never change—I reckon that!" exclaimed Belllounds.

"No. I changed once, eighteen years ago. I can't go back . . . I can't undo all I hoped was good."

"You think Collie'd fear you?"

"She'd never *love* me as she does you, or as she loves me even now. That is my rock of refuge."

"She'd hate you, Wade."

"I reckon. An' so she must never know."

"Ahuh! . . . Wal, wal, life is a hell of a deal! Wade, if you could live yours over again, knowin' what you know now, an' that you'd love an' suffer the same—would you want to do it?"

"Yes. I love life, with all it brings. I wouldn't have the joy without the pain. But I reckon only men who've come to our years would want it over again."

"Wal, I'm with you thar. I'd take what came. Rain an' sun! . . . But all this you tell, an' the hell you hint at, ain't changin' this hyar deal of Jack's an' Collie's. Not one jot! . . . If she remains my adopted daughter she marries my son . . . Wade, I'm haltered like the north star in that."

"Belllounds, will you take a day to think it over?" appealed Wade.

"Ahuh! But that won't change me."

"Won't it change you to know that if you force this marriage you'll lose all?"

"All! Ain't that more queer talk?"

"I mean lose all—your son, your adopted daughter—his chance of reformin', her hope of happiness. These ought to be all in life left to you."

"Wal, they are. But I can't see your argument. You're beyond me, Wade. You're holdin' back, like you did with your hell-bent story."

Ponderously, as if the burden and the doom of the world weighed him down, the hunter got up and fronted Belllounds.

"When I'm driven to tell I'll come . . . But, once more, old man, choose between generosity an' selfishness. Between blood tie an' noble loyalty to your good deed in its beginnin' . . . Will you give up this marriage for your son—so that Collie can have the man she loves?"

"You mean your young pard an' two-bit of a rustler—Wils Moore?"

"Wils Moore, yes. My friend, an' a man, Belllounds, such as you or I never was."

"No!" thundered the rancher, purple in the face.

With bowed head and dragging step Wade left the room.

\* \* \* \* \*

By slow degrees of plodding steps, and periods of abstracted lagging, the hunter made his way back to Moore's cabin. At his entrance the cowboy leaped up with a startled cry.

"Oh, Wade! . . . Is Collie dead?" he cried.

Such was the extent of calamity he imagined from the somber face of Wade.

"No. Collie's well."

"Then, man, what on earth's happened?"

"Nothin' yet . . . But somethin' is goin' on in my mind . . . Moore, I'd like you to let me alone."

At sunset Wade was pacing the aspen grove on the hill. There was sunlight and shade under the trees, a rosy gold on the sage slopes, a purple-and-violet veil between the black ranges and the sinking sun.

Twilight fell. The stars came out white and clear. Night cloaked the valley with dark shadows and the hills with its obscurity. The blue vault overhead deepened and darkened. The hunter patrolled his beat, and hours were moments to him. He heard the low hum of the insects, the murmur of running water, the rustle of the wind. A coyote cut the keen air with high-keyed, staccato cry. The owls hooted, with dismal and weird plaint, one to the other. Then a wolf mourned. But these sounds only accentuated the loneliness and wildness of the silent night.

Wade listened to them, to the silence. He felt the wildness and loneliness of the place, the breathing of nature; he peered aloft at the velvet blue of the mysterious sky with its deceiving stars. All that had been of help to him through days of trial was now as if it had never been. When he lifted his eyes to the great, dark peak, so bold and clear-cut against the sky, it was not to receive strength again. Nature in its cruelty mocked him. His struggle had to do with the most perfect of nature's works—man.

Wade was now in passionate strife with the encroaching mood that was a mocker of his idealism. Many times during the strange, long martyrdom of his penance had he faced this crisis, only to go down to defeat before elemental instincts. His soul was steeped in gloom, but his intelligence had not yet succumbed to passion. The beauty of Columbine's character and the nobility of Moore's were not illusions to Wade. They were true. These two were of the finest fiber of human nature. They loved. They represented youth and hope—a progress through the ages toward a better race. Wade believed in the good to be, in the future of men. Nevertheless, all that was fine and worthy in Columbine and Moore was to go unrewarded, unfulfilled, because of the selfish pride of an old man and the evil passion of the son. It was a conflict as old as life. Of what avail were Columbine's high sense of duty, Moore's fine manhood, the many victories they had won over the headlong and imperious desires of love? What avail were Wade's good offices, his spiritual teaching, his eternal hope in the order of circumstances working out to good? These beautiful characteristics of virtue were not so strong as the unchangeable passion of old Belllounds and the vicious depravity of his son. Wade could not imagine himself a god, proving that the wages of sin was death. Yet in his life he had often been an impassive destiny, meting out terrible consequences. Here he was incalculably involved. This was the cumulative end of years of mounting plots, tangled and woven into the web of his pain and his remorse and his ideal. But hope was dying. That was his strife-realization against the morbid clairvoyance of his mind. He could not help Jack Belllounds to be a better man. He could not inspire the old rancher to a forgetfulness of selfish and blinded aims. He could not prove to Moore the truth of the reward that came from unflagging hope and unassailable virtue. He could not save Columbine with his ideals.

The night wore on, and Wade plodded under the rustling aspens. The insects ceased to hum, the owls to hoot, the wolves to mourn. The shadows of the long spruces gradually merged into the darkness of night. Above, infinitely high, burned the pale stars, wise and cold, aloof and indifferent, eyes of other worlds of mystery.

In those night hours something in Wade died, but his idealism, unquenchable and inexplicable, the very soul of the man, saw its justification and fulfillment in the distant future.

The gray of the dawn stole over the eastern range, and before its opaque gloom the blackness of night retreated, until valley and slope and grove were shrouded in spectral light, where all seemed unreal.

And with it the gray-gloomed giant of Wade's mind, the morbid and brooding spell, had gained its long-encroaching ascendancy. He had again found the man to whom he must tell his story. Tragic and irrevocable decree! It was his life that forced him, his crime, his remorse, his agony, his endless striving. How true had been his steps! They had led, by devious and tortuous paths, to the home of his daughter.

Wade crouched under the aspens, accepting this burden as a man being physically loaded with tremendous weights. His shoulders bent to them. His breast was sunken and labored. All his muscles were cramped. His blood flowed sluggishly. His heart beat with slow, muffled throbs in his ears. There was a creeping cold in his veins, ice in his marrow, and death in his soul. The giant that had been shrouded in gray threw off his cloak, to stand revealed, black and terrible. And it was he who spoke to Wade, in dreadful tones, like knells. Bent Wade—man of misery—who could find no peace on earth— whose presence unknit the tranquil lives of people and poisoned their blood and marked them for doom! Wherever he wandered there followed the curse! Always this had been so. He was the harbinger of catastrophe. He who preached wisdom and claimed to be taught by the flowers, who loved life and hated injustice, who mingled with his kind, ever searching for that one who needed him, he must become the woe and the bane and curse of those he would only serve! Insupportable and pitiful fate! The fiends of the past mocked him, like wicked ghouls, voiceless and dim. The faces of the men he had killed were around him in the gray gloom, pale, drifting visages of distortion, accusing him, claiming him. Likewise, these gleams of faces were specters of his mind, a procession eternal, mournful, and silent, wending their way on and on through the regions of his thought. All were united, all drove him, all put him on the trail of catastrophe. They foreshadowed the future, they inclosed events, they lured him with his endless illusions. He was in the vortex of a vast whirlpool, not of water or of wind, but of life. Alas! he seemed indeed the very current of that whirlpool, a monstrous force, around which evil circled and lurked and conquered. Wade—who had the ill-omened croak of the raven—Wade—who bent his driven steps toward hell!

\* \* \* \* \*

In the brilliant sunlight of the summer morning Wade bent his resistless steps down toward White Slides Ranch. The pendulum had swung. The hours were propitious. Seemingly, events that already cast their shadows waited for him. He saw Jack Belllounds going out on the fast and furious ride which had become his morning habit.

Columbine intercepted Wade. The shade of woe and tragedy in her face were the same as he had pictured there in his gloomy vigil of the night.

"My friend, I was coming to you . . . Oh, I can bear no more!"

Her hair was disheveled, her dress disordered, the hands she tremblingly held out bore discolored marks. Wade led her into the seclusion of the willow trail.

"Oh, Ben! . . . He fought me—like—a beast!" she panted.

"Collie, you needn't tell me more," said Wade, gently. "Go up to Wils. Tell him."

"But I must tell you. I can bear—no more . . . He fought me—hurt me—and when dad heard us—and came—Jack lied . . . Oh, the dog! . . . Ben, his father believed—when Jack swore he was only mad—only trying to shake me—for my indifference and scorn . . . But, my God! Jack meant . . ."

"Collie, go up to Wils," interposed the hunter.

"I want to see Wils. I need to—I must. But I'm afraid . . . Oh, it will make things worse!"

"Go!"

She turned away, actuated by more than her will.

"Collie!" came the call, piercingly and strangely after her. Bewildered, startled by the wildness of that cry, she wheeled. But Wade was gone. The shaking of the willows attested to his hurry.

\* \* \* \* \*

Old Belllounds braced his huge shoulders against the wall in the attitude of a man driven to his last stand.

"Ahuh!" he rolled, sonorously. "So hyar you are again? . . . Wal, tell your worst, Hell-Bent Wade, an' let's have an end to your croakin'."

Belllounds had fortified himself, not with convictions or with illusions, but with the last desperate courage of a man true to himself.

"I'll tell you . . ." began the hunter.

And the rancher threw up his hands in a mockery that was furious, yet with outward shrinking.

"Just now, when Buster Jack fought with Collie, he meant bad by her!"

"Aw, no! . . . He was jest rude—tryin' to be masterful . . . An' the lass's like a wild filly. She needs a tamin' down."

Wade stretched forth a lean and quivering hand that seemed the symbol of presaged and tragic truth.

"Listen, Belllounds, an' I'll tell you . . . No use tryin' to hatch a rotten egg! There's no good in your son. His good intentions he paraded for virtues, believin' himself that he'd changed. But a flip of the wind made him Buster Jack again . . . Collie would sacrifice her life for duty to you—whom she loves as her father. Wils Moore sacrificed his honor for Collie—rather than let you learn the truth . . . But they call me Hell-Bent Wade, an' I will tell you!"

The straining hulk of Belllounds crouched lower, as if to gather impetus for a leap. Both huge hands were outspread as if to ward off attack from an unseen but long-dreaded foe. The great eyes rolled. And underneath the terror and certainty and tragedy of his appearance seemed to surge the resistless and rising swell of a dammed-up, terrible rage.

"I'll tell you . . ." went on the remorseless voice. "I watched your Buster Jack. I watched him gamble an' drink. I trailed him. I found the little circles an' the crooked horse tracks—made to trap Wils Moore . . . A damned cunnin' trick! . . . Burley suspects a nigger in the woodpile. Wils Moore knows the truth. He lied for Collie's sake an' yours. He'd have stood the trial—an' gone to jail to save Collie from what she dreaded . . . Belllounds, your son was in the cabin gamblin' with the rustlers when I cornered them . . . I offered to keep Jack's secret if he'd swear to give Collie up. He swore on his knees, beggin' in her name! . . . An' he comes back to bully her, an' worse . . . Buster Jack! . . . He's the thorn in your heart, Belllounds. He's the rustler who stole your cattle! . . . Your pet son—a sneakin' thief!"

# CHAPTER XIX

Jack Belllounds came riding down the valley trail. His horse was in a lather of sweat. Both hair and blood showed on the long spurs this son of a great pioneer used in his pleasure rides. He had never loved a horse.

At a point where the trail met the brook there were thick willow patches, with open, grassy spots between. As Belllounds reached this place a man stepped out of the willows and laid hold of the bridle. The horse shied and tried to plunge, but an iron arm held him.

"Get down, Buster," ordered the man.

It was Wade.

Belllounds had given as sharp a start as his horse. He was sober, though the heated red tinge of his face gave indication of a recent use of the bottle. That color quickly receded. Events of the last month had left traces of the hardening and lowering of Jack Belllounds's nature.

"Wha-at? . . . Let go of that bridle!" he ejaculated.

Wade held it fast, while he gazed up into the prominent eyes, where fear shone and struggled with intolerance and arrogance and quickening gleams of thought.

"You an' I have somethin' to talk over," said the hunter.

Belllounds shrank from the low, cold, even voice, that evidently reminded him of the last time he had heard it.

"No, we haven't," he declared, quickly. He seemed to gather assurance with his spoken thought, and conscious fear left him. "Wade, you took advantage of me that day—when you made me swear things. I've changed my mind . . . And as for that deal with the rustlers, I've got my story. It's as good as yours. I've been waiting for you to tell my father. You've got some reason for not telling him. I've a hunch it's Collie. I'm on to you, and I've got my nerve back. You can gamble I—"

He had grown excited when Wade interrupted him.

"Will you get off that horse?"

"No, I won't," replied Belllounds, bluntly.

With swift and powerful lunge Wade pulled Belllounds down, sliding him shoulders first into the grass. The released horse shied again and moved away. Buster Jack raised himself upon his elbow, pale with rage and alarm. Wade kicked him, not with any particular violence.

"Get up!" he ordered.

The kick had brought out the rage in Belllounds at the expense of the amaze and alarm.

"Did you kick *me?*" he shouted.

"Buster, I was only handin' you a bunch of flowers—some columbines, as your taste runs," replied Wade, contemptuously.

"I'll—I'll—" returned Buster Jack, wildly, bursting for expression. His hand went to his gun.

"Go ahead, Buster. Throw your gun on me. That'll save maybe a hell of a lot of talk."

It was then Jack Belllounds's face turned livid. Comprehension had dawned upon him.

"You—you want me to fight you?" he queried, in hoarse accents.

"I reckon that's what I meant."

No affront, no insult, no blow could have affected Buster Jack as that sudden knowledge.

"Why—why—you're crazy! Me fight you—a gunman," he stammered. "No—no. It wouldn't be fair. Not an even break! . . . No, I'd have no chance on earth!"

"I'll give you first shot," went on Wade, in his strange, monotonous voice.

"Bah! You're lying to me," replied Belllounds, with pale grimace. "You just want me to get a gun in my hand—then you'll drop me, and claim an even break."

"No. I'm square. You saw me play square with your rustler pard. He was a lifelong enemy of mine. An' a gunfighter to boot! . . . Pull your gun an' let drive. I'll take my chances."

Buster Jack's eyes dilated. He gasped huskily. He pulled his gun, but actually did not have strength or courage enough to raise it. His arm shook so that the gun rattled against his chaps.

"No nerve, hey? Not half a man! . . . Buster Jack, why don't you finish game? Make up for your low-down tricks. At the last try to be worthy of your dad. In his day he was a real man . . . Let him have the consolation that you faced Hell-Bent Wade an' died in your boots!"

"I— can't—fight you!" panted Belllounds. "I know now! . . . I saw you throw a gun! It wouldn't be fair!"

"But I'll make you fight me," returned Wade, in steely tones. "I'm givin' you a chance to dig up a little manhood. Askin' you to meet me man to man! Handin' you a little the best of it to make the odds even! . . . Once more, will you be game?"

"Wade, I'll not fight—I'm going—" replied Belllounds, and he moved as if to turn.

"Halt! . . ." Wade leaped at the white Belllounds. "If you run I'll break a leg for you—an' then I'll beat your miserable brains out! . . . Have you no sense? Can't you recognize what's comin'? . . . *I'm goin' to kill you, Buster Jack!*"

"My God!" whispered the other, understanding fully at last.

"Here's where you pay for your dirty work. The time comes to every man. You've a choice, not to live—for you'll never get away from Hell-Bent Wade— but to rise above yourself at last."

"But what for? Why do you want to kill me? I never harmed you."

"Columbine is my daughter!" replied the hunter.

"Ah!" breathed Belllounds.

"She loves Wils Moore, who's as white a man as you are black."

Across the pallid, convulsed face of Belllounds spread a slow, dull crimson.

"Aha, Buster Jack! I struck home there," flashed Wade, his voice rising. "That gives your eyes the ugly look . . . I hate them lyin', bulgin' eyes of yours. An' when my time comes to shoot I'm goin' to put them both out."

"By Heaven! Wade, you'll have to kill me if you ever expect that club-foot Moore to get Collie!"

"He'll get her," replied Wade, triumphantly. "Collie's with him now. I sent her. I told her to tell Wils how you tried to force her—"

Belllounds began to shake all over. A torture of jealous hate and deadly terror convulsed him.

"Buster, did you ever think you'd get her kisses—as Wils's gettin' right now?" queried the hunter. "Good Lord! The conceit of some men! . . . Why, you poor, weak-minded, cowardly pet of a blinded old man—you conceited ass—you selfish an' spoiled boy! . . . Collie never had any use for you. An' now she hates you."

"It was you who made her!" yelled Belllounds, foaming at the mouth.

"Sure," went on the deliberate voice, ringing with scorn. "An' only a little while ago she called you a dog . . . I reckon she meant a different kind of a dog than the hounds over there. For to say they were like you would be an insult to them . . . Sure she hates you, an' I'll gamble right now she's got her arms around Wils's neck!"

"——!" hissed Belllounds.

"Well, you've got a gun in your hand," went on the taunting voice. "Ahuh! . . . Have it your way. I'm warmin' up now, an' I'd like to tell you . . ."

"Shut up!" interrupted the other, frantically. The blood in him was rising to a fever heat. But fear still clamped him. He could not raise the gun and he seemed in agony.

"Your father knows you're a thief," declared Wade, with remorseless, deliberate intent. "I told him how I watched you—trailed you—an' learned the plot you hatched against Wils Moore . . . Buster Jack busted himself at last, stealin' his own father's cattle . . . I've seen some ragin' men in my day, but Old Bill had them beaten. You've disgraced him—broken his heart— embittered the end of his life . . . An' he'd mean for you what I mean now!"

"He'd never—harm me!" gasped Buster Jack, shuddering.

"He'd kill you—you white-livered pup!" cried Wade, with terrible force. "Kill you before he'd let you go to worse dishonor! . . . An' I'm goin' to save him stainin' his hands."

"I'll kill *you*!" burst out Belllounds, ending in a shriek. But this was not the temper that always produced heedless action in him. It was hate. He could not raise the gun. His intelligence still dominated his will. Yet fury had mitigated his terror.

"You'll be doin' me a service, Buster . . . But you're mighty slow at startin'. I reckon I'll have to play my last trump to make you fight. Oh, by God! I can tell you! . . . Belllounds, there're dead men callin' me now. Callin' me not to murder you in cold blood! I killed one man once—a man who wouldn't fight—an innocent man! I killed him with my bare hands, an' if I tell you my story—an' how I killed him—an' that I'll do the same for you . . . You'll save me that, Buster. No man with a gun in his hands could face what he knew . . . But save me more. Save me the tellin'!"

"No! No! I won't listen!"

"Maybe I won't have to," replied Wade, mournfully. He paused, breathing heavily. The sober calm was gone.

Belllounds lowered the half-raised gun, instantly answering to the strange break in Wade's strained dominance.

"Don't tell me—any more! I'll not listen! . . . I won't fight! Wade, you're crazy! Let me off an' I swear—"

"Buster, I told Collie you were three years in jail!" suddenly interrupted Wade.

A mortal blow dealt Belllounds would not have caused such a shock of amaze, of torture. The secret of the punishment meted out to him by his father! The hideous thing which, instead of reforming, had ruined him! All of hell was expressed in his burning eyes.

"Ahuh! . . . I've known it long!" cried Wade, tragically. "Buster Jack, you're the man who must hear my story . . . I'll tell you . . ."

\* \* \* \* \*

In the aspen grove up the slope of Sage Valley Columbine and Wilson were sitting on a log. Whatever had been their discourse, it had left Moore with head bowed in his hands, and with Columbine staring with sad eyes that did not see what they looked at. Columbine's mind then seemed a dull blank. Suddenly she started.

"Wils!" she cried. "Did you hear—anything?"

"No," he replied, wearily raising his head.

"I thought I heard a shot," said Columbine. "It—it sort of made me jump. I'm nervous."

Scarcely had she finished speaking when two clear, deep detonations rang out. Gun-shots!

"There! . . . Oh, Wils! Did you hear?"

"Hear!" whispered Moore. He grew singularly white. "Yes—yes! . . . Collie—"

"Wils," she interrupted, wildly, as she began to shake. "Just a little bit ago—I saw Jack riding down the trail!"

"Collie! . . . Those two shots came from Wade's guns I'd know it among a thousand! . . . Are you sure you heard a shot before?"

"Oh, something dreadful has happened! Yes, I'm sure. Perfectly sure. A shot not so loud or heavy."

"My God!" exclaimed Moore, staring aghast at Columbine.

"Maybe that's what Wade meant. I never saw through him."

"Tell me. Oh, I don't understand!" wailed Columbine, wringing her hands.

Moore did not explain what he meant. For a crippled man, he made quick time in getting to his horse and mounting.

"Collie, I'll ride down there. I'm afraid something has happened . . . I never understood him! . . . I forgot he was Hell-Bent Wade! If there's been a—a fight or any trouble—I'll ride back and meet you."

Then he rode down the trail.

Columbine had come without her horse, and she started homeward on foot. Her steps dragged. She knew something dreadful had happened. Her heart beat slowly and painfully; there was an oppression upon her breast; her brain whirled with contending tides of thought. She remembered Wade's face. How blind she had been! It exhausted her to walk, though she went so slowly. There seemed to be a chill and a darkening in the atmosphere, an unreality in the familiar slopes and groves, a strangeness and shadow upon White Slides Valley.

Moore did not return to meet her. His white horse grazed in the pasture opposite the first clump of willows, where Sage Valley merged into the larger valley. Then she saw other horses, among them Lem Billings's bay mustang. Columbine faltered on, when suddenly she recognized the horse Jack had ridden—a sorrel, spent and foam-covered, standing saddled, with bridle down and riderless—then certainty of something awful clamped her with horror. Men's husky voices reached her throbbing ears. Someone was running. Footsteps thudded and died away. Then she saw Lem Billings come out of the willows, look her way, and hurry toward her. His awkward, cowboy gait seemed too slow for his earnestness. Columbine felt the piercing gaze of his eyes as her own became dim.

"Miss Collie, thar's been—turrible fight!" he panted.

"Oh, Lem! . . . I know. It was Ben—and Jack," she cried.

"Shore. Your hunch's correct. An' it couldn't be no wuss!"

Columbine tried to see his face, the meaning that must have accompanied his hoarse voice; but she seemed going blind.

"Then—then—" she whispered, reaching out for Lem.

"Hyar, Miss Collie," he said, in great concern, as he took kind and gentle hold of her. "Reckon you'd better wait. Let me take you home."

"Yes. But tell—tell me first," she cried, frantically. She could not bear suspense, and she felt her senses slipping away from her.

"My Gawd! Who'd ever have thought such hell would come to White Slides!" exclaimed Lem, with strong emotion. "Miss Collie, I'm powerful sorry fer you. But mebbe it's best so . . . They're both dead! . . . Wade just died with his head on Wils's lap. But Jack never knowed what hit him. He was shot plumb center—both his eyes shot out! . . . Wade was shot low down . . . Montana an' me agreed thet Jack throwed his gun first an' Wade killed him after bein' mortal shot himself."

* * * * *

Late that afternoon, as Columbine lay upon her bed, the strange stillness of the house was disturbed by a heavy tread. It passed out of the living room and came down the porch toward her door. Then followed a knock.

"Dad!" she called, swiftly rising.

Belllounds entered, leaving the door ajar. The sunlight streamed in.

"Wal, Collie, I see you're bracin' up," he said.

"Oh yes, dad, I'm—I'm all right," she replied, eager to help or comfort him.

The old rancher seemed different from the man of the past months. The pallor of a great shock, the havoc of spent passion, the agony of terrible hours, showed in his face. But Old Bill Belllounds had come into his own again—back to the calm, iron pioneer who had lived all events, over whom storm of years had broken, whose great spirit had accepted this crowning catastrophe as it had all the others, who saw his own life clearly, now that its bitterest lesson was told.

"Are you strong enough to bear another shock, my lass, an' bear it now—so to make an end—so to-morrer we can begin anew?" he asked, with the voice she had not heard for many a day. It was the voice that told of consideration for her.

"Yes, dad," she replied, going to him.

"Wal, come with me. I want you to see Wade."

He led her out upon the porch, and thence into the living room, and from there into the room where lay the two dead men, one on each side. Blankets covered the prone, quiet forms.

Columbine had meant to beg to see Wade once before he was laid away forever. She dreaded the ordeal, yet strangely longed for it. And here she was self-contained, ready for some nameless shock and uplift, which she divined was coming as she had divined the change in Belllounds.

Then he stripped back the blanket, disclosing Wade's face. Columbine thrilled to the core of her heart. Death was there, white and cold and merciless, but as it had released the tragic soul, the instant of deliverance had been stamped on the rugged, cadaverous visage, by a beautiful light; not of peace, nor of joy, nor of grief, but of hope! Hope had been the last emotion of Hell-Bent Wade.

"Collie, listen," said the old rancher, in deep and trembling tones. "When a man's dead, what he's been comes to us with startlin' truth. Wade was the whitest man I ever knew. He had a queer idee—a twist in his mind—an' it was thet his steps were bent toward hell. He imagined thet everywhere he traveled there he fetched hell. But he was wrong. His own trouble led him to the trouble of others. He saw through life. An' he was as big in his hope fer the good as he was terrible in his dealin' with the bad. I never saw his like . . . He loved you, Collie, better than you ever knew. Better than Jack, or Wils, or me! You know what the Bible says about him who gives his life fer his friend. Wal, Wade was my friend, an' Jack's, only we never could see! . . . An' he was Wils's friend. An' to you he must have been more than words can tell . . . We all know what child's play it would have been fer Wade to kill Jack without bein' hurt himself. But he wouldn't do it. So he spared me an' Jack, an' I reckon himself. Somehow he made Jack fight an' die like a man. God only knows how he did that. But it saved me from—from hell—an' you an' Wils from misery . . . Wade could have taken you from me an' Jack. He had only to tell you his secret, an' he wouldn't. He saw how you loved me, as if you were my real child . . . But. Collie, lass, it was *he* who was your father!"

With bursting heart Columbine fell upon her knees beside that cold, still form.

Belllounds softly left the room and closed the door behind him.


## CHAPTER XX

Nature was prodigal with her colors that autumn. The frosts came late, so that the leaves did not gradually change their green. One day, as if by magic, there was gold among the green, and in another there was purple and red. Then the hilltops blazed with their crowns of aspen groves; and the slopes of sage shone mellow gray in the sunlight; and the vines on the stone fences straggled away in lines of bronze; and the patches of ferns under the cliffs faded fast; and the great rock slides and black-timbered reaches stood out in their somber shades.

Columbines bloomed in all the dells among the spruces, beautiful stalks with heavy blossoms, the sweetest and palest of blue-white flowers. Motionless they lifted their faces to the light. Out in the aspen groves, where the grass was turning gold, the columbines blew gracefully in the wind, nodding and swaying. The most exquisite and finest of these columbines hid in the shaded nooks, star-sweet in the silent gloom of the woods.

Wade's last few whispered words to Moore had been interpreted that the hunter desired to be buried among the columbines in the aspen grove on the slope above Sage Valley. Here, then, had been made his grave.

\* \* \* \* \*

One day Belllounds sent Columbine to fetch Moore down to White Slides. It was a warm, Indian-summer afternoon, and the old rancher sat out on the porch in his shirt-sleeves. His hair was white now, but no other change was visible in him. No restraint attended his greeting to the cowboy.

"Wils, I reckon I'd be glad if you'd take your old job as foreman of White Slides," he said.

"Are you asking me?" queried Moore, eagerly.

"Wal, I reckon so."

"Yes, I'll come," replied the cowboy.

"What'll your dad say?"

"I don't know. That worries me. He's coming to visit me. I heard from him again lately, and he means to take stage for Kremmling soon."

"Wal, that's fine. I'll be glad to see him . . . Wils, you're goin' to be a big cattleman before you know it. Hey, Collie?"

"If you say so, dad, it'll come true," replied Columbine with her hand on his shoulder.

"Wils, you'll be runnin' White Slides Ranch before long, unless Collie runs you. Haw! Haw!"

Collie could not reply to this startling announcement from the old rancher, and Moore appeared distressed with embarrassment.

"Wal, I reckon you young folks had better ride down to Kremmlin' an' get married."

This kindly, matter-of-fact suggestion completely stunned the cowboy, and all Columbine could do was to gaze at the rancher.

"Say, I hope I ain't intrudin' my wishes on a young couple that's got over dyin' fer each other," dryly continued Belllounds, with his huge smile.

"Dad!" cried Columbine, and then she threw her arms around him and buried her head on his shoulder.

"Wal, wal, I reckon that answers that," he said, holding her close. "Moore, she's yours, with my blessin' an' all I have . . . An' you must understand I'm glad things have worked out to your good an' to Collie's happiness . . . Life's not over fer me yet. But I reckon the storms are past, thank God! . . . We learn as we live. I'd hold it onworthy not to look forward an' to hope. I'm wantin' peace an' quiet now, with grandchildren around me in my old age . . . So ride along to Kremmlin' an' hurry home."

\* \* \* \* \*

The evening of the day Columbine came home to White Slides the bride of Wilson Moore she slipped away from the simple festivities in her honor and climbed to the aspen grove on the hill to spend a little while beside the grave of her father.

The afterglow of sunset burned dull gold and rose in the western sky, rendering glorious the veil of purple over the ranges. Down in the lowlands twilight had come, softly gray. The owls were hooting; a coyote barked; from far away floated the mourn of a wolf.

Under the aspens it was silent and lonely and sad. The leaves quivered without any sound of rustling. Columbine's heart was full of a happiness that she longed to express somehow, there beside this lonely grave. It was what she owed the strange man who slept here in the shadows. Grief abided with her, and always there would be an eternal remorse and regret. Yet she had loved him. She had been his, all unconsciously. His life had been terrible, but it had been great. As the hours of quiet thinking had multiplied, Columbine had grown in her divination of Wade's meaning. His had been the spirit of man lighting the dark places; his had been the ruthless hand against all evil, terrible to destroy.

Her father! After all, how closely was she linked to the past! How closely protected, even in the hours of most helpless despair! Thus she understood him. Love was the food of life, and hope was its spirituality, and beauty was its reward to the seeing eye. Wade had lived these great virtues, even while he had earned a tragic name.

"I will live them. I will have faith and hope and love, for I am his daughter," she said. A faint, cool breeze strayed through the aspens, rustling the leaves whisperingly, and the slender columbines, gleaming pale in the twilight, lifted their sweet faces.

# GUNMAN'S
# RECKONING

## Max Brand

### CHAPTER I

The fifty empty freights danced and rolled and rattled on the rough road
bed and filled Jericho Pass with thunder; the big engine was laboring
and grunting at the grade, but five cars back the noise of the locomotive
was lost. Yet there is a way to talk above the noise of a freight train just as
there is a way to whistle into the teeth of a stiff wind. This freight-car talk
is pitched just above the ordinary tone—it is an overtone of conversation,
one might say—and it is distinctly nasal. The brakie could talk above the
racket, and so, of course, could Lefty Joe. They sat about in the center of
the train, on the forward end of one of the cars. No matter how the train
lurched and staggered over that fearful road bed, these two swayed in their
places as easily and as safely as birds on swinging perches. The brakie had
watched Lefty Joe for two dollars; he had secured fifty cents; and since the
vigor of Lefty's oaths had convinced him that this was all the money the
tramp had, the two now sat elbow to elbow and killed the distance with
their talk.

"It's like old times to have you here," said the brakie. "You used to play this
line when you jumped from coast to coast."

"Sure," said Lefty Joe, and he scowled at the mountains on either side of
the pass. The train was gathering speed, and the peaks lurched eastward in a
confused, ragged procession. "And a durned hard ride it's been many a time."

"Kind of queer to see you," continued the brakie. "Heard you was rising
in the world."

He caught the face of the other with a rapid side glance, but Lefty Joe was
sufficiently concealed by the dark.

"Heard you were the main guy with a whole crowd behind you," went on
the brakie.

"Yeh?"

"Sure. Heard you was riding the cushions, and all that."

"Yeh?"

"But I guess it was all bunk; here you are back again, anyway."

"Yep," agreed Lefty.

The brakie scratched his head, for the silence of the tramp convinced him that there had been, after all, a good deal of truth in the rumor. He ran back on another tack and slipped about Lefty.

"I never laid much on what they said," he averred. "I know you, Lefty; you can do a lot, but when it comes to leading a whole gang, like they said you was, and all that—well, I knew it was a lie. Used to tell 'em that."

"You talked foolish, then," burst out Lefty suddenly. "It was all straight."

The brakie could hear the click of his companion's teeth at the period to this statement, as though he regretted his outburst.

"Well, I'll be hanged," murmured the brakie innocently.

Ordinarily, Lefty was not easily lured, but this night he apparently was in the mood for talk.

"Kennebec Lou, the Clipper, and Suds. Them and a lot more. They was all with me; they was all under me; I was the Main Guy!"

What a ring in his voice as he said it! The beaten general speaks thus of his past triumphs. The old man remembered his youth in such a voice. The brakie was impressed; he repeated the three names.

"Even Suds?" he said. "Was even Suds with you?"

"Even Suds!"

The brakie stirred a little, wabbling from side to side as he found a more comfortable position; instead of looking straight before him, he kept a sideglance steadily upon his companion, and one could see that he intended to remember what was said on this night.

"Even Suds," echoed the brakie. "Good heavens, and ain't he a man for you?"

"He was a man," replied Lefty Joe with an indescribable emphasis.

"Huh?"

"He ain't a man anymore."

"Get bumped off?"

"No. Busted."

The brakie considered this bit of news and rolled it back and forth and tried its flavor against his gossiping palate.

"Did you fix him after he left you?"

"No."

"I see. You busted him while he was still with you. Then Kennebec Lou and the Clipper get sore at the way you treat Suds. So here you are back on the road with your gang all gone bust. Hard luck, Lefty."

But Lefty whined with rage at this careless diagnosis of his downfall.

"You're all wrong," he said. "You're all wrong. You don't know nothin'."

The brakie waited, grinning securely into the night, and preparing his mind for the story. But the story consisted of one word, flung bitterly into the rushing air.

"Donnegan!"

"Him?" cried the brakie, starting in his place.

"Donnegan!" cried Lefty, and his voice made the word into a curse.

The brakie nodded.

"Them that get tangled with Donnegan don't last long. You ought to know that."

At this the grief, hate, and rage in Lefty Joe were blended and caused an explosion.

"Confound Donnegan. Who's Donnegan? I ask you, who's Donnegan?"

"A guy that makes trouble," replied the brakie, evidently hard put to it to find a definition.

"Oh, don't he make it, though? Confound him!"

"You ought to of stayed shut of him, Lefty."

"Did I hunt him up, I ask you? Am I a nut? No, I ain't. Do I go along stepping on the tail of a rattlesnake? No more do I look up Donnegan."

He groaned as he remembered.

"I was going fine. Nothing could of been better. I had the boys together. We was doing so well that I was riding the cushions and I went around planning the jobs. Nice, clean work. No cans tied to it. But one day I had to meet Suds down in the Meriton Jungle. You know?"

"I've heard plenty," said the brakie.

"Oh, it ain't so bad—the Meriton. I've seen a lot worse. Found Suds there, and Suds was playing Black Jack with an old gink. He was trimmin' him close. Get Suds going good and he could read 'em three down and bury 'em as fast as they came under the bottom card. Takes a hand to do that sort of work. And that's the sort of work Suds was doing for the old man. Pretty soon the game was over and the old man was busted. He took up his pack and beat it, saying nothing and looking sick. I started talking to Suds.

"And while he was talking, along comes a bo and gives us a once-over. He knew me. 'Is this here a friend of yours, Lefty?' he says.

"'Sure,' says I.

"'Then, he's in Dutch. He trimmed that old dad, and the dad is one of Donnegan's pals. Wait till Donnegan hears how your friend made the cards talk while he was skinning the old boy!

"He passes me the wink and goes on. Made me sick. I turned to Suds, and the fool hadn't batted an eye. Never even heard of Donnegan. You know how it is? Half the road never heard of it; part of the roads don't know nothin' else. He's like a jumping tornado; hits every ten miles and don't bend a blade of grass in between.

"Took me about five minutes to tell Suds about Donnegan. Then Suds let out a grunt and started down the trail for the old dad. Missed him. Dad had got out of the Jungle and copped a rattler. Suds come back half green and half yeller.

"'I've done it; I've spilled the beans,' he says.

"'That ain't half sayin' it,' says I.

"Well, we lit out after that and beat it down the line as fast as we could. We got the rest of the boys together; I had a swell job planned up. Everything staked. Then, the first news come that Donnegan was after Suds.

"News just dropped on us out of the sky. Suds, you know how he is. Strong bluff. Didn't bat an eye. Laughed at this Donnegan. Got a hold of an old pal of his, named Levine, and he is a mighty hot scrapper. From a knife to a toenail, they was nothing that Levine couldn't use in a fight. Suds sent him out to cross Donnegan's trail.

"He crossed it, well enough. Suds got a telegram a couple days later saying that Levine had run into a wild cat and was considerable chawed and would Suds send him a stake to pay the doctor?

"Well, after that Suds got sort of nervous. Didn't take no interest in his work no more. Kept a weather eye out watching for the coming of Donnegan. And pretty soon he up and cleaned out of camp.

"Next day, sure enough, along comes Donnegan and asks for Suds. We kept still—all but Kennebec Lou. Kennebec is some fighter himself. Two hundred pounds of mule muscle with the brain of a devil to tell what to do— yes, you can lay it ten to one that Kennebec is some fighter. That day he had a good edge from a bottle of rye he was trying for a friend.

"He didn't need to go far to find trouble in Donnegan. A wink and a grin was all they needed for a password, and then they went at each other's throats. Kennebec made the first pass and hit thin air; and before he got back on his heels, Donnegan had hit him four times. Then Kennebec jumped back and took a fresh start with a knife."

Here Lefty Joe paused and sighed.

He continued, after a long interval: "Five minutes later we was all busy tyin' up what was left of Kennebec; Donnegan was down the road whistlin' like a bird. And that was the end of my gang. What with Kennebec Lou and Suds both gone, what chance did I have to hold the boys together?"

# CHAPTER II

The brakie heard this recital with the keenest interest, nodding from time to time.

"What beats me, Lefty," he said at the end of the story, "is why you didn't knife into the fight yourself and take a hand with Donnegan."

At this Lefty was silent. It was rather the silence of one which cannot tell whether or not it is worthwhile to speak than it was the silence of one who needs time for thought.

"I'll tell you why, bo. It's because when I take a trail like that it only has one end I'm going to bump off the other bird or he's going to bump off me."

The brakie cleared his throat.

"Look here," he said, "looks to me like a queer thing that you're on this train."

"Does it" queried Lefty softly "Why?"

"Because Donnegan is two cars back, asleep."

"The devil you say!"

The brakie broke into laughter.

"Don't kid yourself along," he warned. "Don't do it. It ain't wise—with me."

"What you mean?"

"Come on, Lefty. Come clean. You better do a fade off this train."

"Why, you fool—"

"It don't work, Joe. Why, the minute I seen you I knew why you was here. I knew you meant to croak Donnegan."

"Me croak him? Why should I croak him?"

"Because you been trailing him two thousand miles. Because you ain't got the nerve to meet him face to face and you got to sneak in and take a crack at him while he's lying asleep. That's you, Lefty Joe!"

He saw Lefty sway toward him; but, all stories aside, it is a very bold tramp that cares for argument of a serious nature with a brakie. And even Lefty Joe was deterred from violent action. In the darkness his upper lip twitched, but he carefully smoothed his voice.

"You don't know nothing, pal," he declared.

"Don't I?"

"Nothing," repeated Lefty.

He reached into his clothes and produced something which rustled in the rush of wind. He fumbled, and finally passed a scrap of the paper into the hand of the brakie.

"My heavens," drawled the latter. "D'you think you can fix me with a buck for a job like this? You can't bribe me to stand around while you bump off Donnegan. Can't be done, Lefty!"

"One buck, did you say?"

Lefty Joe expertly lighted a match in spite of the roaring wind, and by this wild light the brakie read the denomination of the bill with a gasp. He rolled up his face and was in time to catch the sneer on the face of Lefty before a gust snatched away the light of the match.

They had topped the highest point in Jericho Pass and now the long train dropped into the down grade with terrific speed. The wind became a hurricane. But to the brakie all this was no more than a calm night. His thoughts were raging in him, and if he looked back far enough he remembered the dollar which Donnegan had given him; and how he had promised Donnegan to give the warning before anything went wrong. He thought of this, but rustling against the palm of his right hand was the bill whose denomination he had read, and that figure ate into his memory, ate into his brain.

After all what was Donnegan to him? What was Donnegan but a worthless tramp? Without any answer to that last monosyllabic query, the brakie hunched forward, and began to work his way up the train.

The tramp watched him go with laughter. It was silent laughter. In the most quiet room it would not have sounded louder than a continual, light hissing noise. Then he, in turn, moved from his place, and worked his way along the train in the opposite direction to that in which the brakie had disappeared.

He went expertly, swinging from car to car with apelike clumsiness—and surety. Two cars back. It was not so easy to reach the sliding side door of that empty car. Considering the fact that it was night, that the train was bucking furiously over the old roadbed, Lefty had a not altogether simple task before him. But he managed it with the same apelike adroitness. He could climb with his feet as well as his hands. He would trust a ledge as well as he would trust the rung of a ladder.

Under his discreet manipulations from above the door loosened and it became possible to work it back. But even this the tramp did with considerable care. He took advantage of the lurching of the train, and every time the car jerked he forced the door to roll a little, so that it might seem for all the world as though the motion of the train alone were operating it.

For suppose that Donnegan wakened out of his sound sleep and observed the motion of the door; he would be suspicious if the door opened in a single continued motion; but if it worked in these degrees he would be hypersuspicious if he dreamed of danger. So the tramp gave five whole minutes to that work.

When it was done he waited for a time, another five minutes, perhaps, to see if the door would be moved back. And when it was not disturbed, but allowed to stand open, he knew that Donnegan still slept.

It was time then for action, and Lefty Joe prepared for the descent into the home of the enemy. Let it not be thought that he approached this moment with a fallen heart, and with a cringing, snaky feeling as a man might be expected to feel when he approached to murder a sleeping foeman. For that was not Lefty's emotion at all. Rather he was overcome by a tremendous happiness. He could have sung with joy at the thought that he was about to rid himself of this pest.

True, the gang was broken up. But it might rise again. Donnegan had fallen upon it like a blight. But with Donnegan out of the way would not Suds come back to him instantly? And would not Kennebec Lou himself return in admiration of a man who had done what he, Kennebec, could not do? With those two as a nucleus, how greatly might he not build!

Justice must be done to Lefty Joe. He approached this murder as a statesman approaches the removal of a foe from the path of public prosperity. There was no more rancor in his attitude. It was rather the blissful largeness of the heart that comes to the politician when he unearths the scandal which will blight the race of his rival.

With the peaceful smile of a child, therefore, Lefty Joe lay stretched at full length along the top of the car and made his choice of weapons. On the whole, his usual preference, day or night, was for a revolver. Give him a gat and Lefty was at home in any company. But he had reasons for transferring his alliance on this occasion. In the first place, a boxcar which is reeling and pitching to and fro, from side to side, is not a very good shooting platform— even for a snapshot like Lefty Joe. Also, the pitch darkness in the car would be a further annoyance to good aim. And in the third and most decisive place, if he were to miss his first shot he would not be extremely apt to place his second bullet. For Donnegan had a reputation with his own revolver. Indeed, it was said that he rarely carried the weapon, because when he did he was always tempted too strongly to use it. So that the chances were large that Donnegan would not have the gun now. Yet if he did have it—if he, Lefty, did miss his first shot—then the story would be brief and bitter indeed.

On the other hand, a knife offered advantages almost too numerous to be listed. It gave one the deadly assurance which only comes with the knowledge of an edge of steel in one's hand. And when the knife reaches its mark it ends a battle at a stroke.

Of course these doubts and considerations pro and con went through the mind of the tramp in about the same space of time that it requires for a dog to waken, snap at a fly, and drowse again. Eventually, he took out his knife. It was a sheath knife which he wore from a noose of silk around his throat, and it always lay closest to his heart. The blade of the knife was of the finest Spanish steel, in the days when Spanish smiths knew how to draw out steel to a streak of light; the handle of the knife was from Milan. On the whole, it was a delicate and beautiful weapon—and it had the durable suppleness of—say—hatred itself.

Lefty Joe, like a pirate in a tale, took this weapon between his teeth; allowed his squat, heavy bulk to swing down and dangle at arm's length for an instant, and then he swung himself a little and landed softly on the floor of the car.

Who has not heard snow drop from the branch upon other snow beneath? That was the way Lefty Joe dropped to the floor of the car. He remained as he had fallen; crouched, alert, with one hand spread out on the boards to balance him and give him a leverage and a start in case he should wish to spring in any direction.

Then he began to probe the darkness in every direction; with every glance he allowed his head to dart out a little. The movement was like a chicken pecking at imaginary grains of corn. But eventually he satisfied himself that his quarry lay in the forward end of the car; that he was prone; that he, Lefty, had accomplished nine-tenths of his purpose by entering the place of his enemy unobserved.

## CHAPTER III

But even though this major step was accomplished successfully, Lefty Joe was not the man to abandon caution in the midst of an enterprise. The roar of the train would have covered sounds ten times as loud as those of his snaky approach, yet he glided forward with as much care as though he were stepping on old stairs in a silent house. He could see a vague shadow— Donnegan; but chiefly he worked by that peculiar sense of direction which some people possess in a dim light. The blind, of course, have that sense in a high degree of sensitiveness, but even those who are not blind may learn to trust the peculiar and inverted sense of direction.

With this to aid him, Lefty Joe went steadily, slowly across the first and most dangerous stage of his journey. That is, he got away from the square of the open door, where the faint starlight might vaguely serve to silhouette his body. After this, it was easier work.

Of course, when he alighted on the floor of the car, the knife had been transferred from his teeth to his left hand; and all during his progress forward the knife was being balanced delicately, as though he were not yet quite sure of the weight of the weapon. Just as a prizefighter keeps his deadly, poised hands in play, moving them as though he fears to lose his intimate touch with them.

This stalking had occupied a matter of split seconds. Now Lefty Joe rose slowly. He was leaning very far forward, and he warded against the roll of the car by spreading out his right hand close to the floor; his left hand he poised with the knife, and he began to gather his muscles for the leap. He had already taken the last preliminary movement—he had swung himself to the right side a little and, lightening his left foot, had thrown all his weight upon the right—in fact, his body was literally suspended in the instant of springing, catlike, when the shadow which was Donnegan came to life.

The shadow convulsed as shadows are apt to swirl in a green pool when a stone is dropped into it; and a bit of board two feet long and some eight inches wide cracked against the shins of Lefty Joe.

It was about the least dramatic weapon that could have been chosen under those circumstances, but certainly no other defense could have frustrated Lefty's spring so completely. Instead of launching out in a compact mass whose point of contact was the reaching knife, Lefty crawled stupidly forward upon his knees, and had to throw out his knife hand to save his balance.

It is a singular thing to note how important balance is to men. Animals fight, as a rule, just as well on their backs as they do on their feet. They can lie on their sides and bite; they can swing their claws even while they are dropping through the air. But man needs poise and balance before he can act. What is speed in a fighter? It is not so much an affair of the muscles as it is the power of the brain to adapt itself instantly to each new move and put the body in a state of balance. In the prize ring speed does not mean the ability to strike one lightning blow, but rather that, having finished one drive, the fighter is in position to hit again, and then again, so that no matter where the impetus of his last lunge has placed him he is ready and poised to shoot all his weight behind his fist again and drive it accurately at a vulnerable spot. Individually the actions may be slow; but the series of efforts seem rapid. That is why a superior boxer seems to hypnotize his antagonist with movements which to the spectator seem perfectly easy, slow, and sure.

But if Lefty lacked much in agility, he had an animal-like sense of balance. Sprawling, helpless, he saw the convulsed shadow that was Donnegan take form as a straight shooting body that plunged through the air above him. Lefty Joe dug his left elbow into the floor of the car and whirled back upon his shoulders, bunching his knees high over his stomach. Nine chances out of ten, if Donnegan had fallen flatwise upon this alert enemy, he would have received those knees in the pit of his own stomach and instantly been paralyzed. But in the jumping, rattling car even Donnegan was capable of making mistakes. His mistake in this instance saved his life, for springing too far, he came down not in reaching distance of Lefty's throat, but with his chest on the knees of the older tramp.

As a result, Donnegan was promptly kicked head over heels and tumbled the length of the car. Lefty was on his feet and plunging after the tumbling form in the twinkling of an eye, literally speaking, and he was only kept from burying his knife in the flesh of his foe by a sway of the car that staggered him in the act of striking. Donnegan, the next instant, was beyond reach. He had struck the end of the car and rebounded like a ball of rubber at a tangent. He slid into the shadows, and Lefty, putting his own shoulders to the wall, felt for his revolver and knew that he was lost. He had failed in his first surprise attack, and without surprise to help him now he was gone. He weighed his revolver, decided that it would be madness to use it, for if he missed, Donnegan would instantly be guided by the flash to shoot him full of holes.

Something slipped by the open door—something that glimmered faintly; and Lefty Joe knew that it was the red head of Donnegan. Donnegan, soft-footed as a shadow among shadows. Donnegan on a blood trail. It lowered the heartbeat of Lefty Joe to a tremendous, slow pulse. In that moment he gave up hope and, resigning himself to die, determined to fight to the last gasp, as became one of his reputation and national celebrity on "the road."

Yet Lefty Joe was no common man and no common fighter. No, let the shade of Rusty Dick, whom Lefty met and beat in his glorious prime—let this shade arise and speak for the prowess of Lefty Joe. In fact it was because he was such a good fighter himself that he recognized his helplessness in the hands of Donnegan.

The faint glimmer of color had passed the door. It was dissolved in deeper shadows at once, and soundlessly; Lefty knew that Donnegan was closer and closer.

Of one thing he felt more and more confident, that Donnegan did not have his revolver with him. Otherwise, he would have used it before. For what was darkness to this devil, Donnegan. He walked like a cat, and most likely he could see like a cat in the dark. Instinctively the older tramp braced himself with his right hand held at a guard before his breast and the knife poised in his left, just as a man would prepare to meet the attack of a panther. He even took to probing the darkness in a strange hope to catch the glimmer of the eyes of Donnegan as he moved to the attack. If there were a hair's breadth of light, then Donnegan himself must go down. A single blow would do it.

But the devil had instructed his favorite Donnegan how to fight. He did not come lunging through the shadows to meet the point of that knife. Instead, he had worked a snaky way along the floor and now he leaped in and up at Lefty, taking him under the arms.

A dozen hands, it seemed, laid hold on Lefty. He fought like a demon and tore himself away, but the multitude of hands pursued him. They were small hands. Where they closed they tore the clothes and bit into his very flesh. Once a hand had him by the throat, and when Lefty jerked himself away it was with a feeling that his flesh had been seared by five points of red-hot iron. All this time his knife was darting; once it ripped through cloth, but never once did it find the target. And half a second later Donnegan got his hold. The flash of the knife as Lefty raised it must have guided the other. He shot his right hand up behind the left shoulder of the other and imprisoned the wrist. Not only did it make the knife hand helpless, but by bearing down with his own weight Donnegan could put his enemy in most exquisite torture.

For an instant they whirled; then they went down, and Lefty was on top. Only for a moment. The impetus which had sent him to the floor was used by Donnegan to turn them over, and once fairly on top his left hand was instantly at the throat of Lefty.

Twice Lefty made enormous efforts, but then he was done. About his body the limbs of Donnegan were twisted, tightening with incredible force; just as hot iron bands sink resistlessly into place. The stranglehold cut away life at its source. Once he strove to bury his teeth in the arm of Donnegan. Once, as the horror caught at him, he strove to shriek for help. All he succeeded in doing was in raising an awful, sobbing whisper. Then, looking death in the face, Lefty plunged into the great darkness.

## CHAPTER IV

When he wakened, he jumped at a stride into the full possession of his faculties. He had been placed near the open door, and the rush of night air had done its work in reviving him. But Lefty, drawn back to life, felt only a vague wonder that his life had not been taken. Perhaps he was being reserved by the victor for an Indian death of torment. He felt cautiously and found that not only were his hands free, but his revolver had not been taken from him. A familiar weight was on his chest—the very knife had been returned to its sheath.

Had Donnegan returned these things to show how perfectly he despised his enemy?

"He's gone!" groaned the tramp, sitting up quickly.

"He's here," said a voice that cut easily through the roar of the train. "Waiting for you, Lefty."

The tramp was staggered again. But then, who had ever been able to fathom the ways of Donnegan?

"Donnegan!" he cried with a sudden recklessness.

"Yes?"

"You're a fool!"

"Yes?"

"For not finishing the job."

Donnegan began to laugh. In the uproar of the train it was impossible really to hear the sound, but Lefty caught the pulse of it. He fingered his bruised throat; swallowing was a painful effort. And an indescribable feeling came over him as he realized that he sat armed to the teeth within a yard of the man he wanted to kill, and yet he was as effectively rendered helpless as though iron shackles had been locked on his wrists and legs. The night light came through the doorway, and he could make out the slender outline of Donnegan and again he caught the faint luster of that red hair; and out of the shadowy form a singular power emanated and sapped his strength at the root.

Yet he went on viciously: "Sooner or later, Donnegan, I'll get you!"

The red head of Donnegan moved, and Lefty Joe knew that the younger man was laughing again.

"Why are you after me?" he asked at length.

It was another blow in the face of Lefty. He sat for a time blinking with owlish stupidity.

"Why?" he echoed. And he spoke his astonishment from the heart.

"Why am I after you?" he said again. "Why, confound you, ain't you Donnegan?"

"Yes."

"Don't the whole road know that I'm after you and you after me?"

"The whole road is crazy. I'm not after you."

Lefty choked.

"Maybe I been dreaming. Maybe you didn't bust up the gang? Maybe you didn't clean up on Suds and Kennebec?"

"Suds? Kennebec? I sort of remember meeting them."

"You sort of—the devil!" Lefty Joe sputtered the words. "And after you cleaned up my crowd, ain't it natural and good sense for you to go on and try to clean up on me?"

"Sounds like it."

"But I figured to beat you to it. I cut in on your trail, Donnegan, and before I leave it you'll know a lot more about me."

"You're warning me ahead of time?"

"You've played this game square with me; I'll play square with you. Next time there'll be no slips, Donnegan. I dunno why you should of picked on me, though. Just the natural devil in you."

"I haven't picked on you," said Donnegan.

"What?"

"I'll give you my word."

A tingle ran through the blood of Lefty Joe. Somewhere he had heard, in rumor, that the word of Donnegan was as good as gold. He recalled that rumor now and something of dignity in the manner with which Donnegan made his announcement carried a heavy weight. As a rule, the tramps vowed with many oaths; here was one of the knights of the road who made his bare word sufficient. And Lefty Joe heard with great wonder.

"All I ask," he said, "is why you hounded my gang, if you wasn't after me?"

"I didn't hound them. I ran into Suds by accident. We had trouble. Then Levine. Then Kennebec Lou tried to take a fall out of me."

A note of whimsical protest crept into the voice of Donnegan.

"Somehow there's always a fight wherever I go," he said. "Fights just sort of grow up around me."

Lefty Joe snarled.

"You didn't mean nothing by just 'happening' to run into three of my boys one after another?"

"Not a thing."

Lefty rocked himself back and forth in an ecstasy of impatience.

"Why don't you stay put?" he complained. "Why don't you stake out your own ground and stay put in it? You cut in on every guy's territory. There ain't any privacy anymore since you hit the road. What you got? A roving commission?"

Donnegan waited for a moment before he answered. And when he spoke his voice had altered. Indeed, he had remarkable ability to pitch his voice into the roar of the freight train, and above or beneath it, and give it a quality such as he pleased.

"I'm following a trail, but not yours," he admitted at length. "I'm following *a* trail. I've been at it these two years and nothing has come of it."

"Who you after?"

"A man with red hair."

"That tells me a lot."

Donnegan refused to explain.

"What you got against him—the color of his hair?"

And Lefty roared contentedly at his own stale jest.

"It's no good," replied Donnegan. "I'll never get on the trail."

Lefty broke in: "You mean to say you've been working two solid years and all on a trail that you ain't even found?"

The silence answered him in the affirmative.

"Ain't nobody been able to tip you off to him?" went on Lefty, intensely interested.

"Nobody. You see, he's a hard sort to describe. Red hair, that's all there was about him for a clue. But if any one ever saw him stripped they'd remember him by a big blotchy birthmark on his left shoulder."

"Eh?" grunted Lefty Joe.

He added: "What was his name?"

"Don't know. He changed monikers when he took to the road."

"What was he to you?"

"A man I'm going to find."

"No matter where the trail takes you?"

"No matter where."

At this Lefty was seized with unaccountable laughter. He literally strained his lungs with that Homeric outburst. When he wiped the tears from his eyes, at length, the shadow on the opposite side of the doorway had disappeared. He found his companion leaning over him, and this time he could catch the dull glint of starlight on both hair and eyes.

"What d'you know?" asked Donnegan.

"How do you stand toward this bird with the birthmark and the red hair?" queried Lefty with caution.

"What d'you know?" insisted Donnegan.

All at once passion shook him; he fastened his grip in the shoulder of the larger man, and his fingertips worked toward the bone.

"What do you know?" he repeated for the third time, and now there was no hint of laughter in the hard voice of Lefty.

"You fool, if you follow that trail you'll go to the devil. It was Rusty Dick; and he's dead!"

His triumphant laughter came again, but Donnegan cut into it.

"Rusty Dick was the one you—killed!"

"Sure. What of it? We fought fair and square."

"Then Rusty wasn't the man I want. The man I want would of eaten two like you, Lefty."

"What about the birthmark? It sure was on his shoulder; Donnegan."

"Heavens!" whispered Donnegan.

"What's the matter?"

"Rusty Dick," gasped Donnegan. "Yes, it must have been he."

"Sure it was. What did you have against him?"

"It was a matter of blood—between us," stammered Donnegan.

His voice rose in a peculiar manner, so that Lefty shrank involuntarily.

"You killed Rusty?"

"Ask any of the boys. But between you and me, it was the booze that licked Rusty Dick. I just finished up the job and surprised everybody."

The train was out of the mountains and in a country of scattering hills, but here it struck a steep grade and settled down to a grind of slow labor; the rails hummed, and suspense filled the freight car.

"Hey," cried Lefty suddenly. "You fool, you'll do a flop out the door in about a minute!"

He even reached out to steady the toppling figure, but Donnegan pitched straight out into the night. Lefty craned his neck from the door, studying the roadbed, but at that moment the locomotive topped the little rise and the whole train lurched forward.

"After all," murmured Lefty Joe, "it sounds like Donnegan. Hated a guy so bad that he hadn't any use for livin' when he heard the other guy was dead. But I'm never goin' to cross his path again, I hope."

## CHAPTER V

But Donnegan had leaped clear of the roadbed, and he struck almost to the knees in a drift of sand. Otherwise, he might well have broken his legs with that foolhardy chance. As it was, the fall whirled him over and over, and by the time he had picked himself up the lighted caboose of the train was rocking past him. Donnegan watched it grow small in the distance, and then, when it was only a red, uncertain star far down the track, he turned to the vast country around him.

The mountains were to his right, not far away, but caught up behind the shadows so that it seemed a great distance. Like all huge, half-seen things they seemed in motion toward him. For the rest, he was in bare, rolling country. The skyline everywhere was clean; there was hardly a sign of a tree. He knew, by a little reflection, that this must be cattle country, for the brakie had intimated as much in their talk just before dusk. Now it was early night, and a wind began to rise, blowing down the valley with a keen motion and a rapidly lessening temperature, so that Donnegan saw he must get to a shelter. He could, if necessary, endure any privation, but his tastes were for luxurious comfort. Accordingly he considered the landscape with gloomy disapproval. He was almost inclined to regret his plunge from the lumbering freight train. Two things had governed him in making that move. First, when he discovered that the long trail he followed was definitely fruitless, he was filled with a great desire to cut himself away from his past and make a new start. Secondly, when he learned that Rusty Dick had been killed by Joe, he wanted desperately to get the throttle of the latter under his thumb. If ever a man risked his life to avoid a sin, it was Donnegan jumping from the train to keep from murder.

He stooped to sight along the ground, for this is the best way at night and often horizon lights are revealed in this manner. But now Donnegan saw nothing to serve as a guide. He therefore drew in his belt until it fitted snug about his gaunt waist, settled his cap firmly, and headed straight into the wind.

Nothing could have shown his character more distinctly.

When in doubt, head into the wind.

With a jaunty, swinging step he sauntered along, and this time, at least, his tactics found an early reward. Topping the first large rise of ground, he saw in the hollow beneath him the outline of a large building. And as he approached it, the wind clearing a high blowing mist from the stars, he saw a jumble of outlying houses. Sheds, barns, corrals—it was the nucleus of a big ranch. It is a maxim that, if you wish to know a man look at his library and if you wish to know a rancher, look at his barn. Donnegan made a small detour to the left and headed for the largest of the barns.

He entered it by the big, sliding door, which stood open; he looked up, and saw the stars shining through a gap in the roof. And then he stood quietly for a time, listening to the voices of the wind in the ruin. Oddly enough, it was pleasant to Donnegan. His own troubles and sorrow had poured upon him so thickly in the past hour or so that it was soothing to find evidence of the distress of others. But perhaps this meant that the entire establishment was deserted.

He left the barn and went toward the house. Not until he was close under its wall did he come to appreciate its size. It was one of those great, rambling, two-storied structures which the cattle kings of the past generation were fond of building. Standing close to it, he heard none of the intimate sounds of the storm blowing through cracks and broken walls; no matter into what disrepair the barns had fallen, the house was still solid; only about the edges of the building the storm kept murmuring.

Yet there was not a light, neither above nor below. He came to the front of the house. Still no sign of life. He stood at the door and knocked loudly upon it, and though, when he tried the knob, he found that the door was latched, yet no one came in response. He knocked again, and putting his ear close he heard the echoes walk through the interior of the building.

After this, the wind rose in sudden strength and deafened him with rattlings; above him, a shutter was swung open and then crashed to, so that the opening of the door was a shock of surprise to Donnegan. A dim light from a source which he could not direct suffused the interior of the hall; the door itself was worked open a matter of inches and Donnegan was aware of two keen old eyes glittering out at him. Beyond this he could distinguish nothing.

"Who are you?" asked a woman's voice. "And what do you want?"

"I'm a stranger, and I want something to eat and a place to sleep. This house looks as if it might have spare rooms."

"Where d'you come from?"

"Yonder," said Donnegan, with a sufficiently noncommittal gesture.

"What's your name?"

"Donnegan."

"I don't know you. Be off with you, Mr. Donnegan!"

He inserted his foot in the closing crack of the door.

"Tell me where I'm to go?" he persisted.

At this her voice rose in pitch, with squeaky rage.

"I'll raise the house on you!"

"Raise 'em. Call down the man of the house. I can talk to him better than I can to you; but I won't walk off like this. If you can feed me, I'll pay you for what I eat."

A shrill cackling—he could not make out the words. And since patience was not the first of Donnegan's virtues, he seized on the knob of the door and deliberately pressed it wide. Standing in the hall, now, and closing the door slowly behind him, he saw a woman with old, keen eyes shrinking away toward the staircase. She was evidently in great fear, but there was something infinitely malicious in the manner in which she kept working her lips soundlessly. She was shrinking, and half turned away, yet there was a suggestion that in an instant she might whirl and fly at his face. The door now clicked, and with the windstorm shut away Donnegan had a queer feeling of being trapped.

"Now call the man of the house," he repeated. "See if I can't come to terms with him."

"He'd make short work of you if he came," she replied. She broke into a shrill laughter, and Donnegan thought he had never seen a face so ugly. "If he came," she said, "you'd rue the day."

"Well, I'll talk to you, then. I'm not asking charity. I want to pay for what I get."

"This ain't a hotel. You go on down the road. Inside eight miles you'll come to the town."

"Eight miles!"

"That's nothing for a man to ride."

"Not at all, if I had something to ride."

"You ain't got a horse?"

"No."

"Then how do you come here?"

"I walked."

If this sharpened her suspicions, it sharpened her fear also. She put one foot on the lowest step of the stairs.

"Be off with you, Mr. Donnegally, or whatever your outlandish name is. You'll get nothing here. What brings you—"

A door closed and a footstep sounded lightly on the floor above. And Donnegan, already alert in the strange atmosphere of this house, gave back a pace so as to get an honest wall behind him. He noted that the step was quick and small, and preparing himself to meet a wisp of manhood—which, for that matter, was the type he was most inclined to fear—Donnegan kept a corner glance upon the old woman at the foot of the stairs and steadily surveyed the shadows at the head of the rise.

Out of that darkness a foot slipped; not even a boy's foot—a very child's. The shock of it made Donnegan relax his caution for an instant, and in that instant she came into the reach of the light. It was a wretched light at best, for it came from a lamp with smoky chimney which the old hag carried, and at the raising and lowering of her hand the flame jumped and died in the throat of the chimney and set the hall awash with shadows. Falling away to a point of yellow, the lamp allowed the hall to assume a certain indefinite dignity of height and breadth and calm proportions; but when the flame rose Donnegan could see the broken balusters of the balustrade, the carpet, faded past any design and worn to rattiness, wall paper which had rotted or dried away and hung in crisp tatters here and there, and on the ceiling an irregular patch from which the plaster had fallen and exposed the lathwork. But at the coming of the girl the old woman had turned, and as she did the flame tossed up in the lamp and Donnegan could see the newcomer distinctly.

Once before his heart had risen as it rose now. It had been the fag end of a long party, and Donnegan, rousing from a drunken sleep, staggered to the window. Leaning there to get the freshness of the night air against his hot face, he had looked up, and saw the white face of the moon going up the sky; and a sudden sense of the blackness and loathing against the city had come upon Donnegan, and the murky color of his own life; and when he turned away from the window he was sober. And so it was that he now stared up at the girl. At her breast she held a cloak together with one hand and the other hand touched the railing of the stairs. He saw one foot suspended for the next step, as though the sight of him kept her back in fear. To the miserable soul of Donnegan she seemed all that was lovely, young, and pure; and her hair, old gold in the shadow and pale gold where the lamp struck it, was to Donnegan like a miraculous light about her face.

Indeed, that little pause was a great and awful moment. For considering that Donnegan, who had gone through his whole life with his eyes ready either to mock or hate, and who had rarely used his hand except to make a fist of it; Donnegan who had never, so far as is known, had a companion; who had asked the world for action, not kindness; this Donnegan now stood straight with his back against the wall, and poured out the story of his wayward life to a mere slip of a girl.

## CHAPTER VI

Even the old woman, whose eyes were sharpened by her habit of looking constantly for the weaknesses and vices of men, could not guess what was going on behind the thin, rather ugly face of Donnegan; the girl, perhaps, may have seen more. For she caught the glitter of his active eyes even at that distance. The hag began to explain with vicious gestures that set the light flaring up and down.

"He ain't come from nowhere, Lou," she said. "He ain't going nowhere; he wants to stay here for the night."

The foot which had been suspended to take the next step was now withdrawn. Donnegan, remembered at last, whipped off his cap, and at once the light flared and burned upon his hair. It was a wonderful red; it shone, and it had a terrible blood tinge so that his face seemed pale beneath it. There were three things that made up the peculiar dominance of Donnegan's countenance. The three things were the hair, the uneasy, bright eyes, and the rather thin, compressed lips. When Donnegan slept he seemed about to waken from a vigorous dream; when he sat down he seemed about to leap to his feet; and when he was standing he gave that impression of a poise which is ready for anything. It was no wonder that the girl, seeing that face and that alert, aggressive body, shrank a little on the stairs. Donnegan, that instant, knew that these two women were really alone in the house as far as fighting men were concerned.

And the fact disturbed him more than a leveled gun would have done. He went to the foot of the stairs, even past the old woman, and, raising his head, he spoke to the girl.

"My name's Donnegan. I came over from the railroad—walked. I don't want to walk that other eight miles unless there's a real need for it. I—" Why did he pause? "I'll pay for anything I get here."

His voice was not too certain; behind his teeth there was knocking a desire to cry out to her the truth. "I am Donnegan. Donnegan the tramp. Donnegan the shiftless. Donnegan the fighter. Donnegan the killer. Donnegan the penniless, worthless. But for heaven's sake let me stay until morning and let me look at you—from a distance!"

But, after all, perhaps he did not need to say all these things. His clothes were rags, upon his face there was a stubble of unshaven red, which made the pallor about his eyes more pronounced. If the girl had been half blind she must have felt that here was a man of fire. He saw her gather the wrap a little closer about her shoulders, and that sign of fear made him sick at heart.

"Mr. Donnegan," said the girl. "I am sorry. We cannot take you into the house. Eight miles—"

Did she expect to turn a sinner from the gates of heaven with a mere phrase? He cast out his hand, and she winced as though he had shaken his fist at her.

"Are you afraid?" cried Donnegan.

"I don't control the house."

He paused, not that her reply had baffled him, but the mere pleasure of hearing her speak accounted for it. It was one of those low, light voices which are apt to have very little range or volume, and which break and tremble absurdly under any stress of emotion; and often they become shrill in a higher register; but inside conversational limits, if such a term may be used, there is no fiber so delightful, so purely musical. Suppose the word "velvet" applied to a sound. That voice came soothingly and delightfully upon the ear of Donnegan, from which the roar and rattle of the empty freight train had not quite departed. He smiled at her.

"But," he protested, "this is west of the Rockies—and I don't see any other way out."

The girl, all this time, was studying him intently, a little sadly, he thought. Now she shook her head, but there was more warmth in her voice.

"I'm sorry. I can't ask you to stay without first consulting my father."

"Go ahead. Ask him."

She raised her hand a little; the thought seemed to bring her to the verge of trembling, as though he were asking a sacrilege.

"Why not?" he urged.

She did not answer, but, instead, her eyes sought the old, woman, as if to gain her interposition; she burst instantly into speech.

"Which there's no good talking anymore," declared the ancient vixen. "Are you wanting to make trouble for her with the colonel? Be off, young man. It ain't the first time I've told you you'd get nowhere in this house!"

There was no possible answer left to Donnegan, and he did as usual the surprising thing. He broke into laughter of such clear and ringing tone—such infectious laughter—that the old woman blinked in the midst of her wrath as though she were seeing a new man, and he saw the lips of the girl parted in wonder.

"My father is an invalid," said the girl. "And he lives by strict rules. I could not break in on him at this time of the evening."

"If that's all"—Donnegan actually began to mount the steps—"I'll go in and talk to your father myself."

She had retired one pace as he began advancing, but as the import of what he said became clear to her she was rooted to one position by astonishment.

"Colonel Macon—my father—" she began. Then: "Do you really wish to see him?"

The hushed voice made Donnegan smile—it was such a voice as one boy uses when he asks the other if he really dares enter the pasture of the red bull. He chuckled again, and this time she smiled, and her eyes were widened, partly by fear of his purpose and partly from his nearness. They seemed to be suddenly closer together. As though they were on one side against a common enemy, and that enemy was her father. The old woman was cackling sharply from the bottom of the stairs, and then bobbing in pursuit and calling on Donnegan to come back. At length the girl raised her hand and silenced her with a gesture.

Donnegan was now hardly a pace away; and he saw that she lived up to all the promise of that first glance. Yet still she seemed unreal. There is a quality of the unearthly about a girl's beauty; it is, after all, only a gay moment between the formlessness of childhood and the hardness of middle age. This girl was pale, Donnegan saw, and yet she had color. She had the luster, say, of a white rose, and the same bloom. Lou, the old woman had called her, and Macon was her father's name. Lou Macon—the name fitted her, Donnegan thought. For that matter, if her name had been Sally Smith, Donnegan would probably have thought it beautiful. The keener a man's mind is and the more he knows about men and women and the ways of the world, the more apt he is to be intoxicated by a touch of grace and thoughtfulness; and all these age-long seconds the perfume of girlhood had been striking up to Donnegan's brain.

She brushed her timidity away and with the same gesture accepted Donnegan as something more than a dangerous vagrant. She took the lamp from the hands of the crone and sent her about her business, disregarding the mutterings and the warnings which trailed behind the departing form. Now she faced Donnegan, screening the light from her eyes with a cupped hand and by the same device focusing it upon the face of Donnegan. He mutely noted the small maneuver and gave her credit, but for the pleasure of seeing the white of her fingers and the way they tapered to a pink transparency at the tips, he forgot the poor figure he must make with his soiled, ragged shirt, his unshaven face, his gaunt cheeks.

Indeed, he looked so straight at her that in spite of her advantage with the light she had to avoid his glance.

"I am sorry," said Lou Macon, "and ashamed because we can't take you in. The only house on the range where you wouldn't be welcome, I know. But my father leads a very close life; he has set ways. The ways of an invalid, Mr. Donnegan."

"And you're bothered about speaking to him of me?"

"I'm almost afraid of letting you go in yourself."

"Let me take the risk."

She considered him again for a moment, and then turned with a nod and he followed her up the stairs into the upper hall. The moment they stepped into it he heard her clothes flutter and a small gale poured on them. It was criminal to allow such a building to fall into this ruinous condition. And a gloomy picture rose in Donnegan's mind of the invalid, thin-faced, sallow-eyed, white-haired, lying in his bed listening to the storm and silently gathering bitterness out of the pain of living. Lou Macon paused again in the hall, close to a door on the right.

"I'm going to send you in to speak to my father," she said gravely. "First I have to tell you that he's different."

Donnegan replied by looking straight at her, and this time she did not wince from the glance. Indeed, she seemed to be probing him, searching with a peculiar hope. What could she expect to find in him? What that was useful to her? Not once in all his life had such a sense of impotence descended upon Donnegan. Her father? Bah! Invalid or no invalid he would handle that fellow, and if the old man had an acrid temper, Donnegan at will could file his own speech to a point. But the girl! In the meager hand which held the lamp there was a power which all the muscles of Donnegan could not compass; and in his weakness he looked wistfully at her.

"I hope your talk will be pleasant. I hope so." She laid her hand on the knob of the door and withdrew it hastily; then, summoning great resolution, she opened the door and showed Donnegan in.

"Father," she said, "this is Mr. Donnegan. He wishes to speak to you."

The door closed behind Donnegan, and hearing that whishing sound which the door of a heavy safe will make, he looked down at this, and saw that it was actually inches thick! Once more the sense of being in a trap descended upon him.


# CHAPTER VII

He found himself in a large room which, before he could examine a single feature of it, was effectively curtained from his sight. Straight into his face shot a current of violent white light that made him blink. There was the natural recoil, but in Donnegan recoils were generally protected by several strata of willpower and seldom showed in any physical action. On the present occasion his first dismay was swiftly overwhelmed by a cold anger at the insulting trick. This was not the trick of a helpless invalid; Donnegan could not see a single thing before him, but he obeyed a very deep instinct and advanced straight into the current of light.

He was glad to see the light switched away. The comparative darkness washed across his eyes in a pleasant wave and he was now able to distinguish a few things in the room. It was, as he had first surmised, quite large. The ceiling was high; the proportions comfortably spacious; but what astounded Donnegan was the real elegance of the furnishings. There was no mistaking the deep, silken texture of the rug upon which he stepped; the glow of light barely reached the wall, and there showed faintly in streaks along yellowish hangings. Beside a table which supported a big reading lamp—gasoline, no doubt, from the intensity of its light—sat Colonel Macon with a large volume spread across his knees. Donnegan saw two highlights—fine silver hair that covered the head of the invalid and a pair of white hands fallen idly upon the surface of the big book, for if the silver hair suggested age the smoothly finished hands suggested perennial youth. They were strong, carefully tended, complacent hands. They suggested to Donnegan a man sufficient unto himself.

"Mr. Donnegan, I am sorry that I cannot rise to receive you. Now, what pleasant accident has brought me the favor of this call?"

Donnegan was taken aback again, and this time more strongly than by the flare of light against his eyes. For in the voice he recognized the quality of the girl—the same softness, the same velvety richness, though the pitch was a bass. In the voice of this man there was the same suggestion that the tone would crack if it were forced either up or down. With this great difference, one could hardly conceive of a situation which would push that man's voice beyond its monotone. It flowed with deadly, all-embracing softness. It clung about one; it fascinated and baffled the mind of the listener.

But Donnegan was not in the habit of being baffled by voices. Neither was he a lover of formality. He looked about for a place to sit down, immediately discovered that while the invalid sat in an enormous easy-chair bordered by shelves and supplied with wheels for raising and lowering the back and for propelling the chair about the room on its rubber tires, it was the only chair in the room which could make any pretensions toward comfort. As a matter of fact, aside from this one immense chair, devoted to the pleasure of the invalid, there was nothing in the room for his visitors to sit upon except two or three miserable backless stools.

But Donnegan was not long taken aback. He tucked his cap under his arm, bowed profoundly in honor of the colonel's compliments, and brought one of the stools to a place where it was no nearer the rather ominous circle of the lamplight than was the invalid himself. With his eyes accustomed to the new light, Donnegan could now take better stock of his host. He saw a rather handsome face, with eyes exceedingly blue, young, and active; but the features of Macon as well as his body were blurred and obscured by a great fatness. He was truly a prodigious man, and one could understand the stoutness with which the invalid chair was made. His great wrist dimpled like the wrist of a healthy baby, and his face was so enlarged with superfluous flesh that the lower part of it quite dwarfed the upper. He seemed, at first glance, a man with a low forehead and bright, careless eyes and a body made immobile by flesh and sickness. A man whose spirits despised and defied pain. Yet a second glance showed that the forehead was, after all, a nobly proportioned one, and for all the bulk of that figure, for all the cripple-chair, Donnegan would not have been surprised to see the bulk spring lightly out of the chair to meet him.

For his own part, sitting back on the stool with his cap tucked under his arm and his hands folded about one knee, he met the faint, cold smile of the colonel with a broad grin of his own.

"I can put it in a nutshell," said Donnegan. "I was tired; dead beat; needed a handout, and rapped at your door. Along comes a mystery in the shape of an ugly-looking woman and opens the door to me. Tries to shut me out; I decided to come in. She insists on keeping me outside; all at once I see that I have to get into the house. I am brought in; your daughter tries to steer me off, sees that the job is more than she can get away with, and shelves me off upon you. And that, Colonel Macon, is the pleasant accident which brings you the favor of this call."

It would have been a speech both stupid and pert in the mouth of another; but Donnegan knew how to flavor words with a touch of mockery of himself as well as another. There were two manners in which this speech could have been received—with a wink or with a smile. But it would have been impossible to hear it and grow frigid. As for the colonel, he smiled.

It was a tricky smile, however, as Donnegan felt. It spread easily upon that vast face and again went out and left all to the dominion of the cold, bright eyes.

"A case of curiosity," commented the colonel.

"A case of hunger," said Donnegan.

"My dear Mr. Donnegan, put it that way if you wish!"

"And a case of blankets needed for one night."

"Really? Have you ventured into such a country as this without any equipment?"

"Outside of my purse, my equipment is of the invisible kind."

"Wits," suggested the colonel.

"Thank you."

"Not at all. You hinted at it yourself."

"However, a hint is harder to take than to make."

The colonel raised his faultless right hand—and oddly enough his great corpulence did not extend in the slightest degree to his hand, but stopped short at the wrists—and stroked his immense chin. His skin was like Lou Macon's, except that in place of the white-flower bloom his was a parchment, dead pallor. He lowered his hand with the same slow precision and folded it with the other, all the time probing Donnegan with his difficult eyes.

"Unfortunately—most unfortunately, it is impossible for me to accommodate you, Mr. Donnegan."

The reply was not flippant, but quick. "Not at all. I am the easiest person in the world to accommodate."

The big man smiled sadly.

"My fortune has fallen upon evil days, sir. It is no longer what it was. There are in this house three habitable rooms; this one; my daughter's apartment; the kitchen where old Haggie sleeps. Otherwise you are in a rat trap of a place."

He shook his head, a slow, decisive motion.

"A spare blanket," said Donnegan, "will be enough."

There was another sigh and another shake of the head.

"Even a corner of a rug to roll up in will do perfectly."

"You see, it is impossible for me to entertain you."

"Bare boards will do well enough for me, Colonel Macon. And if I have a piece of bread, a plate of cold beans—anything—I can entertain myself."

"I am sorry to see you so compliant, Mr. Donnegan, because that makes my refusal seem the more unkind. But I cannot have you sleeping on the bare floor. Not on such a night. Pneumonia comes on one like a cat in the dark in such weather. It is really impossible to keep you here, sir."

"H'm-m," said Donnegan. He began to feel that he was stumped, and it was a most unusual feeling for him.

"Besides, for a young fellow like you, with your agility, what is eight miles? Walk down the road and you will come to a place where you will be made at home and fed like a king."

"Eight miles, that's not much! But on such a night as this?"

There was a faint glint in the eyes of the colonel; was he not sharpening his wits for his contest of words, and enjoying it?

"The wind will be at your back and buoy your steps. It will shorten the eight miles to four."

Very definitely Donnegan felt that the other was reading him. What was it that he saw as he turned the pages?

"There is one thing you fail to take into your accounting."

"Ah?"

"I have an irresistible aversion to walking."

"Ah?" repeated Macon.

"Or exercise in any form."

"Then you are unfortunate to be in this country without a horse."

"Unfortunate, perhaps, but the fact is that I'm here. Very sorry to trouble you, though, colonel."

"I am rarely troubled," said the colonel coldly. "And since I have no means of accommodation, the laws of hospitality rest light on my shoulders."

"Yet I have an odd thought," replied Donnegan.

"Well? You have expressed a number already, it seems to me."

"It's this: that you've already made up your mind to keep me here."

## CHAPTER VIII

The colonel stiffened in his chair, and under his bulk even those ponderous timbers quaked a little. Once more Donnegan gained an impression of chained activity ready to rise to any emergency. The colonel's jaw set and the last vestige of the smile left his eyes. Yet it was not anger that showed in its place. Instead, it was rather a hungry searching. He looked keenly into the face and the soul of Donnegan as a searchlight sweeps over waters by night.

"You are a mind reader, Mr. Donnegan."

"No more of a mind reader than a Chinaman is."

"Ah, they are great readers of mind, my friend."

Donnegan grinned, and at this the colonel frowned.

"A great and mysterious people, sir. I keep evidences of them always about me. Look!"

He swept the shaft of the reading light up and it fell upon a red vase against the yellow hangings. Even Donnegan's inexperienced eye read a price into that shimmering vase.

"Queer color," he said.

"Dusty claret. Ah, they have the only names for their colors. Think! Peach bloom—liquid dawn—ripe cherry—oil green—green of powdered tea—blue of the sky after rain—what names for color! What other land possesses such a tongue that goes straight to the heart!"

The colonel waved his faultless hands and then dropped them back upon the book with the tenderness of a benediction.

"And their terms for texture—pear's rind—lime peel—millet seed! Do not scoff at China, Mr. Donnegan. She is the fairy godmother, and we are the poor children."

He changed the direction of the light; Donnegan watched him, fascinated.

"But what convinced you that I wished to keep you here?"

"To amuse you, Colonel Macon."

The colonel exposed gleaming white teeth and laughed in that soft, smooth-flowing voice.

"Amuse me? For fifteen years I have sat in this room and amused myself by taking in what I would and shutting out the rest of the world. I have made the walls thick and padded them to keep out all sound. You observe that there is no evidence here of the storm that is going on tonight. Amuse me? Indeed!"

And Donnegan thought of Lou Macon in her old, drab dress, huddling the poor cloak around her shoulders to keep out the cold, while her father lounged here in luxury. He could gladly have buried his lean fingers in that fat throat. From the first he had had an aversion to this man.

"Very well, I shall go. It has been a pleasant chat, colonel."

"Very pleasant. And thank you. But before you go, taste this whisky. It will help you when you enter the wind."

He opened a cabinet in the side of the chair and brought out a black bottle and a pair of glasses and put them on the broad arm of the chair. Donnegan sauntered back.

"You see," he murmured, "you will not let me go."

At this the colonel raised his head suddenly and glared into the eyes of his guest, and yet so perfect was his muscular and nerve control that he did not interrupt the thin stream of amber which trickled into one of the glasses. Looking down again, he finished pouring the drinks. They pledged each other with a motion, and drank. It was very old, very oily. And Donnegan smiled as he put down the empty glass.

"Sit down," said the colonel in a new voice.

Donnegan obeyed.

"Fate," went on the colonel, "rules our lives. We give our honest endeavors, but the deciding touch is the hand of Fate."

He garnished this absurd truism with a wave of his hand so solemn that Donnegan was chilled; as though the fat man were artfully conversant with the Three Sisters.

"Fate has brought you to me; therefore, I intend to keep you."

"Here?"

"In my service. I am about to place a great mission and a great trust in your hands."

"In the hands of a man you know nothing about?"

"I know you as if I had raised you."

Donnegan smiled, and shaking his head, the red hair flashed and shimmered.

"As long as there is no work attached to the mission, it may be agreeable to me."

"But there is work."

"Then the contract is broken before it is made."

"You are rash. But I had rather begin with a dissent and then work upward."

Donnegan waited.

"To balance against work—"

"Excuse me. Nothing balances against work for me."

"To balance against work," continued the colonel, raising a white hand and by that gesture crushing the protest of Donnegan, "there is a great reward."

"Colonel Macon, I have never worked for money before and I shall not work for it now."

"You trouble me with interruptions. Who mentioned money? You shall not have a penny!"

"No?"

"The reward shall grow out of the work."

"And the work?"

"Is fighting."

At this Donnegan narrowed his eyes and searched the fat man thoroughly. It sounded like the talk of a charlatan, and yet there was a crispness to these sentences that made him suspect something underneath. For that matter, in certain districts his name and his career were known. He had never dreamed that that reputation could have come within a thousand miles of this part of the mountain desert.

"You should have told me in the first place," he said with some anger, "that you knew me."

"Mr. Donnegan, upon my honor, I never heard your name before my daughter uttered it."

Donnegan waited soberly.

"I despise charlatanry as much as the next man. You shall see the steps by which I judged you. When you entered the room I threw a strong light upon you. You did not blanch; you immediately walked straight into the shaft of light although you could not see a foot before you."

"And that proved?"

"A combative instinct, and coolness; not the sort of brute vindictiveness that fights for a rage, for a cool-minded love of conflict. Is that clear?"

Donnegan shrugged his shoulders.

"And above all, I need a fighter. Then I watched your eyes and your hands. The first were direct and yet they were alert. And your hands were perfectly steady."

"Qualifications for a fighter, eh?"

"Do you wish further proof?"

"Well?"

"What of the fight to the death which you went through this same night?"

Donnegan started. It was a small movement, that flinching, and he covered it by continuing the upward gesture of his hand to his coat; he drew out tobacco and cigarette papers and commenced to roll his smoke. Looking up, he saw that the eyes of Colonel Macon were smiling, although his face was grave.

A glint of understanding passed between the two men, but not a spoken word.

"I assure you, there was no death tonight," said Donnegan at length.

"Tush! Of course not! But the tear on the shoulder of your coat—ah, that is too smooth edged for a tear, too long for the bite of a scissors. Am I right? Tush! Not a word!"

The colonel beamed with an almost tender pride, and Donnegan, knowing that the fat man looked upon him as a murderer, newly come from a death, considered the beaming face and thought many things in silence.

"So it was easy to see that in coolness, courage, fighting instinct, skill, you were probably what I want. Yet something more than all these qualifications is necessary for the task which lies ahead of you."

"You pile up the bad features, eh?"

"To entice you, Donnegan. For one man, paint a rosy beginning, and once under way he will manage the hard parts. For you, show you the hard shell and you will trust it contains the choice flesh. I was saying, that I waited to see other qualities in you; qualities of the judgment. And suddenly you flashed upon me a single glance; I felt it clash against my willpower. I felt your look go past my guard like a rapier slipping around my blade. I, Colonel Macon, was for the first time outfaced, out-maneuvered. I admit it, for I rejoice in meeting such a man. And the next instant you told me that I should keep you here out of my own wish! Admirable!"

The admiration of the colonel, indeed, almost overwhelmed Donnegan, but he saw that in spite of the genial smile, the face suffused with warmth, the colonel was watching him every instant, flinty eyed. Donnegan did as he had done on the stairs; he burst into laughter.

When he had done, the colonel was leaning forward in his chair with his fingers interlacing, examining his guest from beneath somber brows. As he sat lurched forward he gave a terrible impression of that reserved energy which Donnegan had sensed before.

"Donnegan," said the colonel, "I shall talk no more nonsense to you. You are a terrible fellow!"

And Donnegan knew that, for the first time in the colonel's life, he was meeting another man upon equal ground.


## CHAPTER IX

In a way, it was an awful tribute, for one great fact grew upon him: that the colonel represented almost perfectly the power of absolute evil. Donnegan was not a squeamish sort, but the fat, smiling face of Macon filled him with unutterable aversion. A dozen times he would have left the room, but a silken thread held him back, the thought of Lou.

"I shall be terse and entirely frank," said the colonel, and at once Donnegan reared triple guard and balanced himself for attack or defense.

"Between you and me," went on the fat man, "deceptive words are folly. A waste of energy." He flushed a little. "You are, I believe, the first man who has ever laughed at me." The click of his teeth as he snapped them on this sentence seemed to promise that he should also be the last.

"So I tear away the veils which made me ridiculous, I grant you. Donnegan, we have met each other just in time."

"True," said Donnegan, "you have a task for me that promises a lot of fighting; and in return I get lodgings for the night."

"Wrong, wrong! I offer you much more. I offer you a career of action in which you may forget the great sorrow which has fallen upon you: and in the battles which lie before you, you will find oblivion for the sad past which lies behind you."

Here Donnegan sprang to his feet with his hand caught at his breast; and he stood quivering, in an agony. Pain worked him as anger would do, and, his slender frame swelling, his muscles taut, he stood like a panther enduring the torture because knows it is folly to attempt to escape.

"You are a human devil!" Donnegan said at last, and sank back upon his stool. For a moment he was overcome, his head falling upon his breast, and even when he looked up his face was terribly pale, and his eyes dull. His expression, however, cleared swiftly, and aside from the perspiration which shone on his forehead it would have been impossible ten seconds later to discover that the blow of the colonel had fallen upon him.

All of this the colonel had observed and noted with grim satisfaction. Not once did he speak until he saw that all was well.

"I am sorry," he said at length in a voice almost as delicate as the voice of Lou Macon. "I am sorry, but you forced me to say more than I wished to say."

Donnegan brushed the apology aside.

His voice became low and hurried. "Let us get on in the matter. I am eager to learn from you, colonel."

"Very well. Since it seems that there is a place for both our interests in this matter, I shall run on in my tale and make it, as I promised you before, absolutely frank and curt. I shall not descend into small details. I shall give you a main sketch of the high points; for all men of mind are apt to be confused by the face of a thing, whereas the heart of it is perfectly clear to them."

He settled into his narrative.

"You have heard of The Corner? No? Well, that is not strange; but a few weeks ago gold was found in the sands where the valleys of Young Muddy and Christobel Rivers join. The Corner is a long, wide triangle of sand, and the sand is filled with a gold deposit brought down from the headwaters of both rivers and precipitated here, where one current meets the other and reduces the resultant stream to sluggishness. The sands are rich—very rich!"

He had become a trifle flushed as he talked, and now, perhaps to cover his emotion, he carefully selected a cigarette from the humidor beside him and lighted it without haste before he spoke another word.

"Long ago I prospected over that valley; a few weeks ago it was brought to my attention again. I determined to stake some claims and work them. But I could not go myself. I had to send a trustworthy man. Whom should I select? There was only one possible. Jack Landis is my ward. A dozen years ago his parents died and they sent him to my care, for my fortune was then comfortable. I raised him with as much tenderness as I could have shown my own son; I lavished on him the affection and—"

Here Donnegan coughed lightly; the fat man paused, and observing that this hypocrisy did not draw the veil over the bright eyes of his guest, he continued: "In a word, I made him one of my family. And when the need for a man came I turned to him. He is young, strong, active, able to take care of himself."

At this Donnegan pricked his ears.

"He went, accordingly, to The Corner and staked the claims and filed them as I directed. I was right. There was gold. Much gold. It panned out in nuggets."

He made an indescribable gesture, and through his strong fingers Donnegan had a vision of yellow gold pouring.

"But there is seldom a discovery of importance claimed by one man alone. This was no exception. A villain named William Lester, known as a scoundrel over the length and breadth of the cattle country, claimed that he had made the discovery first. He even went so far as to claim that I had obtained my information from him and he tried to jump the claims staked by Jack Landis, whereupon Jack, very properly, shot Lester down. Not dead, unfortunately, but slightly wounded.

"In the meantime the rush for The Corner started. In a week there was a village; in a fortnight there was a town; in a month The Corner had become the talk of the ranges. Jack Landis found in the claims a mint. He sent me back a mere souvenir."

The fat man produced from his vest pocket a little chunk of yellow and with a dexterous motion whipped it at Donnegan. It was done so suddenly, so unexpectedly that the wanderer was well-nigh taken by surprise. But his hand flashed up and caught the metal before it struck his face. He found in the palm of his hand a nugget weighing perhaps five ounces, and he flicked it back to the colonel.

"He sent me the souvenir, but that was all. Since that time I have waited.

Nothing has come. I sent for word, and I learned that Jack Landis had betrayed his trust, fallen in love with some undesirable woman of the mining camp, denied my claim to any of the gold to which I had sent him. Unpleasant news? Yes. Ungrateful boy? Yes. But my mind is hardened against adversity.

"Yet this blow struck me close to the heart. Because Landis is engaged to marry my daughter, Lou. At first I could hardly believe in his disaffection. But the truth has at length been borne home to me. The scoundrel has abandoned both Lou and me!"

Donnegan repeated slowly: "Your daughter loves this chap?"

The colonel allowed his glance to narrow, and he could do this the more safely because at this moment Donnegan's eyes were wandering into the distance. In that unguarded second Donnegan was defenseless and the colonel read something that set him beaming.

"She loves him, of course," he said, "and he is breaking her heart with his selfishness."

"He is breaking her heart?" echoed Donnegan.

The colonel raised his hand and stroked his enormous chin. Decidedly he believed that things were getting on very well.

"This is the position," he declared. "Jack Landis was threatened by the wretch Lester, and shot him down. But Lester was not single-handed. He belongs to a wild crew, led by a mysterious fellow of whom no one knows very much, a deadly fighter, it is said, and a keen organizer and handler of men. Red-haired, wild, smooth. A bundle of contradictions. They call him Lord Nick because he has the pride of a nobleman and the cunning of the devil. He has gathered a few chosen spirits and cool fighters—the Pedlar, Joe Rix, Harry Masters—all celebrated names in the cattle country.

"They worship Lord Nick partly because he is a genius of crime and partly because he understands how to guide them so that they may rob and even kill with impunity. His peculiarity is his ability to keep within the bounds of the law. If he commits a robbery he always first establishes marvelous alibis and throws the blame toward someone else; if it is the case of a killing, it is always the other man who is the aggressor. He has been before a jury half a dozen times, but the devil knows the law and pleads his own case with a tongue that twists the hearts out of the stupid jurors. You see? No common man. And this is the leader of the group of which Lester is one of the most debased members. He had no sooner been shot than Lord Nick himself appeared. He had his followers with him. He saw Jack Landis, threatened him with death, and made Jack swear that he would hand over half of the profits of the mines to the gang—of which, I suppose, Lester gets his due proportion. At the same time, Lord Nick attempted to persuade Jack that I, his adopted father, you might say, was really in the wrong, and that I had stolen the claims from this wretched Lester!"

He waved this disgusting accusation into a mist and laughed with hateful softness.

"The result is this: Jack Landis draws a vast revenue from the mines. Half of it he turns over to Lord Nick, and Lord Nick in return gives him absolute freedom and backing in the camp, where he is, and probably will continue the dominant factor. As for the other half, Landis spends it on this woman with whom he has become infatuated. And not a penny comes through to me!"

Colonel Macon leaned back in his chair and his eyes became fixed upon a great distance. He smiled, and the blood turned cold in the veins of Donnegan.

"Of course this adventuress, this Nelly Lebrun, plays hand in glove with Lord Nick and his troupe; unquestionably she shares her spoils, so that nine-tenths of the revenue from the mines is really flowing back through the hands of Lord Nick and Jack Landis has become a silly figurehead. He struts about the streets of The Corner as a great mine owner, and with the power of Lord Nick behind him, not one of the people of the gambling houses and dance halls dares cross him. So that Jack has come to consider himself a great man. Is it clear?"

Donnegan had not yet drawn his gaze entirely back from the distance.

"This is the possible solution," went on the colonel. "Jack Landis must be drawn away from the influence of this Nelly Lebrun. He must be brought back to us and shown his folly both as regards the adventuress and Lord Nick; for so long as Nelly has a hold on him, just so long Lord Nick will have his hand in Jack's pocket. You see how beautifully their plans and their work dovetail? How, therefore, am I to draw him from Nelly? There is only one way: send my daughter to the camp—send Lou to The Corner and let one glimpse of her beauty turn the shabby prettiness of this woman to a shadow! Lou is my last hope!"

At this Donnegan wakened. His sneer was not a pleasant thing to see.

"Send her to a new mining camp. Colonel Macon, you have the gambling spirit; you are willing to take great chances!"

"So! So!" murmured the colonel, a little taken aback. "But I should never send her except with an adequate protector."

"An adequate protector even against these celebrated gunmen who run the camp as you have already admitted?"

"An adequate protector—you are the man!"

Donnegan shivered.

"I? I take your daughter to the camp and play her against Nelly Lebrun to win back Jack Landis? Is that the scheme?"

"It is."

"Ah," murmured Donnegan. And he got up and began to walk the room, white-faced; the colonel watched him in a silent agony of anxiety.

"She truly loves this Landis?" asked Donnegan, swallowing.

"A love that has grown out of their long intimacy together since they were children."

"Bah! Calf love! Let the fellow go and she will forget him. Hearts are not broken in these days by disappointments in love affairs."

The colonel writhed in his chair.

"But Lou—you do not know her heart!" he suggested. "If you looked closely at her you would have seen that she is pale. She does not suspect the truth, but I think she is wasting away because Jack hasn't written for weeks."

He saw Donnegan wince under the whip.

"It is true," murmured the wanderer. "She is not like others, heaven knows!" He turned. "And what if I fail to bring over Jack Landis with the sight of Lou?"

The colonel relaxed; the great crisis was past and Donnegan would undertake the journey.

"In that case, my dear lad, there is an expedient so simple that you astonish me by not perceiving it. If there is no way to wean Landis away from the woman, then get him alone and shoot him through the heart. In that way you remove from the life of Lou a man unworthy of her and you also make the mines come to the heir of Jack Landis—namely, myself. And in the latter case, Mr. Donnegan, be sure—oh, be sure that I should not forget who brought the mines into my hands!"

## CHAPTER X

Fifty miles over any sort of going is a stiff march. Fifty miles uphill and down and mostly over districts where there was only a rough cow path in lieu of a road made a prodigious day's work; and certainly it was an almost incredible feat for one who professed to hate work with a consuming passion and who had looked upon an eight-mile jaunt the night before as an insuperable burden. Yet such was the distance which Donnegan had covered, and now he drove the pack mule out on the shoulder of the hill in full view of The Corner with the triangle of the Young Muddy and Christobel Rivers embracing the little town. Even the gaunt, leggy mule was tired to the dropping point, and the tough buckskin which trailed up behind went with downward head. When Louise Macon turned to him, he had reached the point where he swung his head around first and then grudgingly followed the movement with his body. The girl was tired, also, in spite of the fact that she had covered every inch of the distance in the saddle. There was that violet shade of weariness under her eyes and her shoulders slumped forward. Only Donnegan, the hater of labor, was fresh.

They had started in the first dusk of the coming day; it was now the yellow time of the slant afternoon sunlight; between these two points there had been a body of steady plodding. The girl had looked askance at that gaunt form of Donnegan's when they began; but before three hours, seeing that the spring never left his step nor the swinging rhythm his stride, she began to wonder. This afternoon, nothing he did could have surprised her. From the moment he entered the house the night before he had been a mystery. Till her death day she would not forget the fire with which he had stared up at her from the foot of the stairs. But when he came out of her father's room—not cowed and whipped as most men left it—he had looked at her with a veiled glance, and since that moment there had always been a mist of indifference over his eyes when he looked at her.

In the beginning of that day's march all she knew was that her father trusted her to this stranger, Donnegan, to take her to The Corner, where he was to find Jack Landis and bring Jack back to his old allegiance and find what he was doing with his time and his money. It was a quite natural proceeding, for Jack was a wild sort, and he was probably gambling away all the gold that was dug in his mines. It was perfectly natural throughout, except that she should have been trusted so entirely to a stranger. That was a remarkable thing, but, then, her father was a remarkable man, and it was not the first time that his actions had been inscrutable, whether concerning her or the affairs of other people. She had heard men come into their house cursing Colonel Macon with death in their faces; she had seen them sneak out after a soft-voiced interview and never appear again. In her eyes, her father was invincible, all-powerful. When she thought of superlatives, she thought of him. Her conception of mystery was the smile of the colonel, and her conception of tenderness was bounded by the gentle voice of the same man. Therefore, it was entirely sufficient to her that the colonel had said: "Go, and trust everything to Donnegan. He has the power to command you and you must obey—until Jack comes back to you."

That was odd, for, as far as she knew, Jack had never left her. But she had early discarded any will to question her father. Curiosity was a thing which the fat man hated above all else.

Therefore, it was really not strange to her that throughout the journey her guide did not speak half a dozen words to her. Once or twice when she attempted to open the conversation he had replied with crushing monosyllables, and there was an end. For the rest, he was always swinging down the trail ahead of her at a steady, unchanging, rapid stride. Uphill and down it never varied. And so they came out upon the shoulder of the hill and saw the storm center of The Corner. They were in the hills behind the town; two miles would bring them into it. And now Donnegan came back to her from the mule. He took off his hat and shook the dust away; he brushed a hand across his face. He was still unshaven. The red stubble made him hideous, and the dust and perspiration covered his face as with a mask. Only his eyes were rimmed with white skin.

"You'd better get off the horse, here," said Donnegan.

He held her stirrup, and she obeyed without a word.

"Sit down."

She sat down on the flat-topped boulder which he designated, and, looking up, observed the first sign of emotion in his face. He was frowning, and his face was drawn a little.

"You are tired," he stated.

"A little."

"You are tired," said the wanderer in a tone that implied dislike of any denial. Therefore she made no answer. "I'm going down into the town to look things over. I don't want to parade you through the streets until I know where Landis is to be found and how he'll receive you. The Corner is a wild town; you understand?"

"Yes," she said blankly, and noted nervously that the reply did not please him. He actually scowled at her.

"You'll be all right here. I'll leave the pack mule with you; if anything should happen—but nothing is going to happen, I'll be back in an hour or so. There's a pool of water. You can get a cold drink there and wash up if you want to while I'm gone. But don't go to sleep!"

"Why not?"

"A place like this is sure to have a lot of stragglers hunting around it. Bad characters. You understand?"

She could not understand why he should make a mystery of it; but then, he was almost as strange as her father. His careful English and his ragged clothes were typical of him inside and out.

"You have a gun there in your holster. Can you use it?"

"Yes."

"Try it."

It was a thirty-two, a woman's light weapon. She took it out and balanced it in her hand.

"The blue rock down the hillside. Let me see you chip it."

Her hand went up, and without pausing to sight along the barrel, she fired; fire flew from the rock, and there appeared a white, small scar. Donnegan sighed with relief.

"If you squeezed the butt rather than pulled the trigger," he commented, "you would have made a bull's-eye that time. Now, I don't mean that in any likelihood you'll have to defend yourself. I simply want you to be aware that there's plenty of trouble around The Corner."

"Yes," said the girl.

"You're not afraid?"

"Oh, no."

Donnegan settled his hat a little more firmly upon his head. He had been on the verge of attributing her gentleness to a blank, stupid mind; he began to realize that there was metal under the surface. He felt that some of the qualities of the father were echoed faintly, and at a distance, in the child. In a way, she made him think of an unawakened creature. When she was roused, if the time ever came, it might be that her eye could become a thing alternately of fire and ice, and her voice might carry with a ring.

"This business has to be gotten through quickly," he went on. "One meeting with Jack Landis will be enough."

She wondered why he set his jaw when he said this, but he was wondering how deeply the colonel's ward had fallen into the clutches of Nelly Lebrun. If that first meeting did not bring Landis to his senses, what followed? One of two things. Either the girl must stay on in The Corner and try her hand with her fiancé again, or else the final brutal suggestion of the colonel must be followed; he must kill Landis. It was a cold-blooded suggestion, but Donnegan was a cold-blooded man. As he looked at the girl, where she sat on the boulder, he knew definitely, first and last, that he loved her, and that he would never again love any other woman. Every instinct drew him toward the necessity of destroying Landis. There was his stumbling block. But what if she truly loved Landis?

He would have to wait in order to find that out. And as he stood there with the sun shining on the red stubble on his face he made a resolution the more profound because it was formed in silence: if she truly loved Landis he would serve her hand and foot until she had her will.

But all he said was simply: "I shall be back before it's dark."

"I shall be comfortable here," replied the girl, and smiled farewell at him.

And while Donnegan went down the slope full of darkness he thought of that smile.

The Corner spread more clearly before him with every step he made. It was a type of the gold-rush town. Of course most of the dwellings were tents—dog tents many of them; but there was a surprising sprinkling of wooden shacks, some of them of considerable size. Beginning at the very edge of the town and spread over the sand flats were the mines and the black sprinkling of laborers. And the town itself was roughly jumbled around one street. Over to the left the main road into The Corner crossed the wide, shallow ford of the Young Muddy River and up this road he saw half a dozen wagons coming, wagons of all sizes; but nothing went out of The Corner. People who came stayed there, it seemed.

He dropped over the lower hills, and the voice of the gold town rose to him. It was a murmur like that of an army preparing for battle. Now and then a blast exploded, for what purpose he could not imagine in this school of mining. But as a rule the sounds were subdued by the distance. He caught the muttering of many voices, in which laughter and shouts were brought to the level of a whisper at close hand; and through all this there was a persistent clangor of metallic sounds. No doubt from the blacksmith shops where picks and other implements were made or sharpened and all sorts of repairing carried on. But the predominant tone of the voice of The Corner was this persistent ringing of metal. It suggested to Donnegan that here was a town filled with men of iron and all the gentler parts of their natures forgotten. An odd place to bring such a woman as Lou Macon, surely!

He reached the level, and entered the town.

## CHAPTER XI

Hunting for news, he went naturally to the news emporium which took the place of the daily paper—namely, he went to the saloons. But on the way he ran through a liberal cross-section of The Corner's populace. First of all, the tents and the ruder shacks. He saw little sheet-iron stoves with the tin dishes piled, unwashed, upon the tops of them when the miners rushed back to their work; broken handles of picks and shovels; worn-out shirts and overalls lay where they had been tossed; here was a flat strip of canvas supported by four four-foot poles and without shelter at the sides, and the belongings of one careless miner tumbled beneath this miserable shelter; another man had striven for some semblance of a home and he had framed a five-foot walk leading up to the closed flap of his tent with stones of a regular size. But nowhere was there a sign of life, and would not be until semidarkness brought the unwilling workers back to the tents.

Out of this district he passed quickly onto the main street, and here there was a different atmosphere. The first thing he saw was a man dressed as a cowpuncher from belt to spurs—spurs on a miner—but above the waist he blossomed in a frock coat and a silk hat. Around the coat he had fastened his belt, and the shirt beneath the coat was common flannel, open at the throat. He walked, or rather staggered, on the arm of an equally strange companion who was arrayed in a white silk shirt, white flannel trousers, white dancing pumps, and a vast sombrero! But as if this was not sufficient protection for his head, he carried a parasol of the most brilliant green silk and twirled it above his head. The two held a wavering course and went blindly past Donnegan.

It was sufficiently clear that the storekeeper had followed the gold.

He noted a cowboy sitting in his saddle while he rolled a cigarette. Obviously he had come in to look things over rather than to share in the mining, and he made the one sane, critical note in the carnival of noise and color. Donnegan began to pass stores. There was the jeweler's; the gent's furnishing; a real estate office—what could real estate be doing on the Young Muddy's desert? Here was the pawnshop, the windows of which were already packed. The blacksmith had a great establishment, and the roar of the anvils never died away; feed and grain and a dozen lunch-counter restaurants. All this had come to The Corner within six weeks.

Liquor seemed to be plentiful, too. In the entire length of the street he hardly saw a sober man, except the cowboy. Half a dozen in one group pitched silver dollars at a mark. But he was in the saloon district now, and dominant among the rest was the big, unpainted front of a building before which hung an enormous sign:

LEBRUN'S JOY EMPORIUM

Donnegan turned in under the sign.

It was one big room. The bar stretched completely around two sides of it. The floor was dirt, but packed to the hardness of wood. The low roof was supported by a scattering of wooden pillars, and across the floor the gaming tables were spread. At that vast bar not ten men were drinking now; at the crowding tables there were not half a dozen players; yet behind the bar stood a dozen tenders ready to meet the evening rush from the mines. And at the tables waited an equal number of the professional gamblers of the house.

From the door Donnegan observed these things with one sweeping glance, and then proceeded to transform himself. One jerk at the visor of his cap brought it down over his eyes and covered his face with shadow; a single shrug bunched the ragged coat high around his shoulders, and the shoulders themselves he allowed to drop forward. With his hands in his pockets he glided slowly across the room toward the bar, for all the world a picture of the guttersnipe who had been kicked from pillar to post until self-respect is dead in him. And pausing in his advance, he leaned against one of the pillars and looked hungrily toward the bar.

He was immediately hailed from behind the bar with: "Hey, you. No tramps in here. Pay and stay in Lebrun's!"

The command brought an immediate protest. A big fellow stepped from the bar, his sombrero pushed to the back of his head, his shirt sleeves rolled to the elbow away from vast hairy forearms. One of his long arms swept out and brought Donnegan to the bar.

"I ain't no prophet," declared the giant, "but I can spot a man that's dry. What'll you have, bud?" And to the bartender he added: "Leave him be, pardner, unless you're all set for considerable noise in here."

"Long as his drinks are paid for," muttered the bartender, "here he stays. But these floaters do make me tired!"

He jabbed the bottle across the bar at Donnegan and spun a glass noisily at him, and the "floater" observed the angry bartender with a frightened side glance, and then poured his drink gingerly. When the glass was half full he hesitated and sought the face of the bartender again, for permission to go on.

"Fill her up!" commanded the giant. "Fill her up, lad, and drink hearty."

"I never yet," observed the bartender darkly, "seen a beggar that wasn't a hog."

At this Donnegan's protector shifted his belt so that the holster came a little more forward on his thigh.

"Son," he said, "how long you been in these parts?"

"Long enough," declared the other, and lowered his black brows. "Long enough to be sick of it."

"Maybe, maybe," returned the cowpuncher-miner, "meantime you tie to this. We got queer ways out here. When a gent drinks with us he's our friend. This lad here is my pardner, just now. If I was him I would of knocked your head off before now for what you've said——"

"I don't want no trouble," Donnegan said whiningly.

At this the bartender chuckled, and the miner showed his teeth in his disgust.

"Every gent has got his own way," he said sourly. "But while you drink with Hal Stern you drink with your chin up, bud. And don't forget it. And them that tries to run over you got to run over me."

Saying this, he laid his large left hand on the bar and leaned a little toward the bartender, but his right hand remained hanging loosely at his side. It was near the holster, as Donnegan noticed. And the bartender, having met the boring glance of the big man for a moment, turned surlily away. The giant looked to Donnegan and observed: "Know a good definition of the word, skunk?"

"Nope," said Donnegan, brightening now that the stern eye, of the bartender was turned away.

"Here's one that might do. A skunk is a critter that bites when your back is turned and runs when you look it in the eye. Here's how!"

He drained his own glass, and Donnegan dexterously followed the example.

"And what might you be doing around these parts?" asked the big man, veiling his contempt under a mild geniality.

"Me? Oh, nothing."

"Looking for a job, eh?"

Donnegan shrugged.

"Work ain't my line," he confided.

"H'm-m-m," said Hal Stern. "Well, you don't make no bones about it."

"But just now," continued Donnegan, "I thought maybe I'd pick up some sort of a job for a while." He looked ruefully at the palms of his hands which were as tender as the hands of a woman. "Heard a fellow say that Jack Landis was a good sort to work for—didn't rush his men none. They said I might find him here."

The big man grunted.

"Too early for him. He don't circulate around much till the sun goes down. Kind of hard on his skin, the sun, maybe. So you're going to work for him?"

"I was figuring on it."

"Well, tie to this, bud. If you work for him you won't have him over you."

"No?"

"No, you'll have"—he glanced a little uneasily around him—"Lord Nick."

"Who's he?"

"Who's he?" The big man started in astonishment. "Sufferin' catamounts! Who is he?" He laughed in a disagreeable manner. "Well, son, you'll find out, right enough!"

"The way you talk, he don't sound none too good."

Hal Stern grew anxious. "The way I talk? Have I said anything agin' him? Not a word! He's—he's—well, there ain't ever been trouble between us and there never ain't going to be." He flushed and looked steadily at Donnegan. "Maybe he sent you to talk to me?" he asked coldly.

But Donnegan's eyes took on a childish wideness.

"Why, I never seen him," he declared. Hall Stern allowed the muscles of his face to relax. "All right," he said, "they's no harm done. But Lord Nick is a name that ain't handled none too free in these here parts. Remember that!"

"But how," pondered Donnegan, "can I be working for Lord Nick when I sign up to work under Jack Landis?"

"I'll tell you how. Nick and Lebrun work together. Split profits. And Nelly Lebrun works Landis for his dust. So the stuff goes in a circle—Landis to Nelly to Lebrun to Nick. That clear?"

"I don't quite see it," murmured Donnegan.

"I didn't think you would," declared the other, and snorted his disgust. "But that's all I'm going to say. Here come the boys—and dead dry!"

For the afternoon was verging upon evening, and the first drift of laborers from the mines was pouring into The Corner. One thing at least was clear to Donnegan: that everyone knew how infatuated Landis had become with Nelly Lebrun and that Landis had not built up an extraordinarily good name for himself.

# CHAPTER XII

By the time absolute darkness had set in, Donnegan, in the new role of lady's chaperon, sat before a dying fire with Louise Macon beside him. He had easily seen from his talk with Stern that Landis was a public figure, whether from the richness of his claims or his relations with Lord Nick and Lebrun, or because of all these things; but as a public figure it would be impossible to see him alone in his own tent, and unless Louise could meet him alone half her power over him—supposing that she still retained any—would be lost. Better by far that Landis should come to her than that she should come to him, so Donnegan had rented two tents by the day at an outrageous figure from the enterprising real estate company of The Corner and to this new home he brought the girl.

She accepted the arrangement with surprising equanimity. It seemed that her father's training had eliminated from her mind any questioning of the motives of others. She became even cheerful as she set about arranging the pack which Donnegan put in her tent. Afterward she cooked their supper over the fire which he built for her. Never was there such a quick house-settling. And by the time it was absolutely dark they had washed the dishes and sat before Lou's tent looking over the night lights of The Corner and hearing the voice of its Great White Way opening.

She had not even asked why he did not bring her straight to Jack Landis. She had looked into Donnegan's tent, furnished with a single blanket and his canvas kit, and had offered to share her pack with him. And now they sat side by side before the tent and still she asked no questions about what was to come.

Her silence was to Donnegan the dropping of the water upon the hard rock. He was crumbling under it, and a wild hatred for the colonel rose in him. No doubt that spirit of evil had foreseen all this; and he knew that every moment spent with the girl would drive Donnegan on closer to the accomplishment of the colonel's great purpose—the death of Jack Landis. For the colonel, as Jack's next of kin, would take over all his mining interests and free them at a stroke from the silent partnership which apparently existed with Lord Nick and Lester. One bullet would do all this: and with Jack dead, who else stood close to the girl? It was only necessary that she should not know who sped the bullet home.

A horrible fancy grew up in Donnegan, as he sat there, that between him and the girl lay a dead body.

He was glad when the time came and he could tell her that he was going down to The Corner to find Jack Landis and bring him to her. She rose to watch him go and he heard her say "Come soon!"

It shocked Donnegan into realization that for all her calm exterior she was perfectly aware of the danger of her position in the wild mining camp. She must know, also, that her reputation would be compromised; yet never once had she winced, and Donnegan was filled with wonder as he went down the hill toward the camp which was spread beneath him; for their tents were a little detached from the main body of the town. Behind her gentle eyes, he now felt, and under the softness of her voice, there was the same iron nerve that was in her father. Her hatred could be a deathless passion, and her love also; and the great question to be answered now was, did she truly love Jack Landis?

The Corner at night was like a scene at a circus. There was the same rush of people, the same irregular flush of lights, the same glimmer of lanterns through canvas, the same air of impermanence. Once, in one of those hushes which will fall upon every crowd, he heard a coyote wailing sharply and far away, as though the desert had sent out this voice to mock at The Corner and all it contained.

He had only to ask once to discover where Landis was: Milligan's dance hall. Before Milligan's place a bonfire burned from the beginning of dusk to the coming of day; and until the time when that fire was quenched with buckets of water, it was a sign to all that the merriment was under way in the dance hall. If Lebrun's was the sun of the amusement world in The Corner, Milligan's was the moon. Everybody who had money to lose went to Lebrun's. Every one who was out for gayety went to Milligan's. Milligan was a plunger. He had brought up an orchestra which demanded fifteen dollars a day and he paid them that and more. He not only was able to do this, but he established a bar at the entrance from which all who entered were served with a free drink. The entrance, also, was not subject to charge. The initial drink at the door was spiced to encourage thirst, so Milligan made money as fast, and far more easily, than if he had been digging it out of the ground.

To the door of this pleasure emporium came Donnegan. He had transformed himself into the ragged hobo by the jerking down of his cap again, and the hunching of his shoulders. And shrinking past the bar with a hungry sidewise glance, as one who did not dare present himself for free liquor, he entered Milligan's.

That is, he had put his foot across the threshold when he was caught roughly by the shoulder and dragged to one side. He found himself looking up into the face of a strapping fellow who served Milligan as bouncer. Milligan had an eye for color. Andy Lewis was tolerably well known as a fighting man of parts, who not only wore two guns but could use them both at once, which is much more difficult than is generally understood. But far more than for his fighting parts Milligan hired his bouncer for the sake of his face. It was a countenance made to discourage troublemakers. A mule had kicked Lewis in the chin, and a great white welt deformed his lower lip. Scars of smallpox added to his decorative effect, and he had those extremely bushy brows which for some reason are generally considered to denote ferocity. Now, Donnegan was not above middle height at best, and in his present shrinking attitude he found himself looking up a full head into the formidable face of the bouncer.

"And what are you doing in here?" asked the genial Andy. "Don't you know this joint is for white folks?"

"I ain't colored," murmured Donnegan.

"You took considerable yaller to me," declared Lewis. He straightway chuckled, and his own keen appreciation of his wit softened his expression. "What you want?"

Donnegan shivered under his rags.

"I want to see Jack Landis," he said.

It had a wonderful effect upon the doorkeeper. Donnegan found that the very name of Landis was a charm of power in The Corner.

"You want to see him?" he queried in amazement. "You?"

He looked Donnegan over again, and then grinned broadly, as if in anticipation. "Well, go ahead. There he sits—no, he's dancing."

The music was in full swing; it was chiefly brass; but now and then, in softer moments, one could hear a violin squeaking uncertainly. At least it went along with a marked, regular rhythm, and the dancers swirled industriously around the floor. A very gay crowd; color was apparently appreciated in The Corner. And Donnegan, standing modestly out of sight behind a pillar until the dance ended, noted twenty phases of life in twenty faces. And Donnegan saw the flushes of liquor, and heard the loud voices of happy fellows who had made their "strikes"; but in all that brilliant crew he had no trouble in picking out Jack Landis and Nelly Lebrun.

They danced together, and where they passed, the others steered a little off so as to give them room on the dance floor, as if the men feared that they might cross the formidable Landis, and as if the women feared to be brought into too close comparison with Nelly Lebrun. She was, indeed, a brilliant figure. She had eyes of the Creole duskiness, a delicate olive skin, with a pastel coloring. The hand on the shoulder of Landis was a thing of fairy beauty. And her eyes had that peculiar quality of seeming to see everything, and rest on every face particularly. So that, as she whirled toward Donnegan, he winced, feeling that she had found him out among the shadows.

She had a glorious partner to set her off. And Donnegan saw bitterly why Lou Macon could love him. Height without clumsiness, bulk and a light foot at once, a fine head, well poised, blond hair and a Grecian profile—such was Jack Landis. He wore a vest of fawn skin; his boots were black in the foot and finished with the softest red leather for the leg. And he had yellow buckskin trousers, laced in a Mexican fashion with silver at the sides; a narrow belt, a long, red silk handkerchief flying from behind his neck in cowboy fashion. So much flashing splendor, even in that gay assembly, would have been childishly conspicuous on another man. But in big Jack Landis there was patently a great deal of the unaffected child. He was having a glorious time on this evening, and his eye roved the room challenging admiration in a manner that was amusing rather than offensive. He was so overflowingly proud of having the prettiest girl in The Corner upon his arm and so conscious of being himself probably the finest-looking man that he escaped conceit, it might almost be said, by his very excess of it.

Upon this splendid individual, then, the obscure Donnegan bent his gaze. He saw the dancers pause and scatter as the music ended, saw them drift to the tables along the edges of the room, saw the scurry of waiters hurrying drinks up in the interval, saw Nelly Lebrun sip a lemonade, saw Jack Landis toss off something stronger. And then Donnegan skirted around the room and came to the table of Jack Landis at the very moment when the latter was tossing a gold piece to the waiter and giving a new order.

Prodigal sons in the distance of thought are apt to be both silly: and disgusting, but at close hand they usually dazzle the eye. Even the cold brain of Donnegan was daunted a little as he drew near.

He came behind the chair of the tall master of The Corner, and while Nelly Lebrun stopped her glass halfway to her lips and stared at the ragged stranger, Donnegan was whispering in the ear of Jack Landis: "I've got to see you alone."

Landis turned his head slowly and his eye darkened a little as he met the reddish, unshaven face of the stranger. Then, with a careless shrug of distaste, he drew out a few coins and poured them into Donnegan's palm; the latter pocketed them.

"Lou Macon," said Donnegan.

Jack Landis rose from his chair, and it was not until he stood so close to Donnegan that the latter realized the truly Herculean proportions of the young fellow. He bowed his excuses to Nelly Lebrun, not without grace of manner, and then huddled Donnegan into a corner with a wave of his vast arm.

"Now what do you want? Who are you? Who put that name in your mouth?"

"She's in The Corner," said Donnegan, and he dwelt upon the face of Jack Landis with feverish suspense. A moment later a great weight had slipped from his heart. If Lou Macon loved Landis it was beyond peradventure that Landis was not breaking his heart because of the girl. For at her name he flushed darkly, and then, that rush of color fading, he was left with a white spot in the center of each cheek.

## CHAPTER XIII

First his glance plunged into vacancy; then it flicked over his shoulder at Nelly Lebrun and he bit his lip. Plainly, it was not the most welcome news that Jack Landis had ever heard.

"Where is she?" he asked nervously of Donnegan, and he looked over the ragged fellow again.

"I'll take you to her."

The big man swayed back and forth from foot to foot, balancing in his hesitation. "Wait a moment."

He strode to Nelly Lebrun and bent over her; Donnegan saw her eyes flash up—oh, heart of the south, what eyes of shadow and fire! Jack Landis trembled under the glance; yes, he was deeply in love with the girl. And Donnegan watched her face shade with suspicion, stiffen with cold anger, warm and soften again under the explanations of Jack Landis.

Donnegan, looking from the distance, could read everything; it is nearness that bewitches a man when he talks to a woman. When Odysseus talked to Circe, no doubt he stood on the farther side of the room!

When Landis came again, he was perspiring from the trial of fire through which he had just passed.

"Come," he ordered, and set out at a sweeping stride.

Plainly he was anxious to get this matter done with as soon as possible. As for Donnegan, he saw a man whom Landis had summoned to take his place sit down at the table with Nelly Lebrun. She was laughing with the newcomer as though nothing troubled her at all, but over his shoulder her glance probed the distance and followed Jack Landis. She wanted to see the messenger again, the man who had called her companion away; but in this it was fox challenging fox. Donnegan took note and was careful to place between him and the girl every pillar and every group of people. As far as he was concerned, her first glance must do to read and judge and remember him by.

Outside Landis shot several questions at him in swift succession; he wanted to know how the girl had happened to make the trip. Above all, what the colonel was thinking and doing and if the colonel himself had come. But Donnegan replied with monosyllables, and Landis, apparently reconciling himself to the fact that the messenger was a fool, ceased his questions. They kept close to a run all the way out of the camp and up the hillside to the two detached tents where Donnegan and the girl slept that night. A lantern burned in both the tents.

"She has made things ready for me," thought Donnegan, his heart opening. "She has kept house for me!"

He pointed out Lou's tent to his companion and the big man, with a single low word of warning, threw open the flap of the tent and strode in.

There was only the split part of a second between the rising and the fall of the canvas, but in that swift interval, Donnegan saw the girl starting up to receive Landis. Her calm was broken at last. Her cheeks were flushed; her eyes were starry with what? Expectancy? Love?

It stopped Donnegan like a blow in the face and turned his heart to lead; and then, shamelessly, he glided around the tent and dropped down beside it to eavesdrop. After all, there was some excuse. If she loved the man he, Donnegan, would let him live; if she did not love him, he, Donnegan, would kill him like a worthless rat under heel. That is, if he could. No wonder that the wanderer listened with heart and soul!

He missed the first greeting. It was only a jumble of exclamations, but now he heard: "But, Lou, what a wild idea. Across the mountains—with whom?"

"The man who brought you here."

"Who's he?"

"I don't know."

"You don't know? He looks like a shifty little rat to me."

"He's big enough, Jack."

Such small praise was enough to set Donnegan's heart thumping.

"Besides, father told me to go with him, to trust him."

"Ah!" There was an abrupt chilling and lowering of Landis' voice. "The colonel knows him? He's one of the colonel's men?"

Plainly the colonel was to him as the rod to the child.

"Why didn't you come directly to me?"

"We thought it would be better not to."

"H'm-m. Your guide—well, what was the colonel's idea in sending you here? Heavens above, doesn't he know that a mining camp is no place for a young girl? And you haven't a sign of a chaperon, Lou! What the devil can I do? What was in his mind?"

"You haven't written for a long time."

"Good Lord! Written! Letters! Does he think I have time for letters?" The lie came smoothly enough. "Working day and night?"

Donnegan smoothed his whiskers and grinned into the night. Landis might prove better game than he had anticipated.

"He worried," said the girl, and her voice was as even as ever. "He worried, and sent me to find out if anything is wrong."

Then: "Nonsense! What is there to worry about? Lou, I'm half inclined to think that the colonel doesn't trust me!"

She did not answer. Was she reading beneath the boisterous assurance of Landis?

"One thing is clear to me—and to you, too, I hope. The first thing is to send you back in a hurry."

Still no answer.

"Lou, do you distrust me?"

At length she managed to speak, but it was with some difficulty: "There is another reason for sending me."

"Tell me."

"Can't you guess, Jack?"

"I'm not a mind reader."

"The cad," said Donnegan through his teeth.

"It's the old reason."

"Money?"

"Yes."

A shadow swept across the side of the tent; it was Landis waving his arm carelessly.

"If that's all, I can fix you up and send you back with enough to carry the colonel along. Look here—why, I have five hundred with me. Take it, Lou. There's more behind it, but the colonel mustn't think that there's as much money in the mines as people say. No idea how much living costs up here. Heavens, no! And the prices for labor! And then they shirk the job from dawn to dark. I have to watch 'em every minute, I tell you!"

He sighed noisily.

"But the end of it is, dear"—how that small word tore into the heart of Donnegan, who crouched outside—"that you must go back tomorrow morning. I'd send you tonight, if I could. As a matter of fact, I don't trust the red-haired rat who—"

The girl interrupted while Donnegan still had control of his hair-trigger temper.

"You forget, Jack. Father sent me here, but he did not tell me to come back."

At this Jack Landis burst into an enormous laughter.

"You don't mean, Lou, that you actually intend to stay on?"

"What else can I mean?"

"Of course it makes it awkward if the colonel didn't expressly tell you just what to do. I suppose he left it to my discretion, and I decide definitely that you must go back at once."

"I can't do it."

"Lou, don't you hear me saying that I'll take the responsibility? If your father blames you let him tell me—"

He broke down in the middle of his sentence and another of those uncomfortable little pauses ensued. Donnegan knew that their eyes were miserably upon each other; the man tongue-tied by his guilt; the girl wretchedly guessing at the things which lay behind her fiancé's words.

"I'm sorry you don't want me here."

"It isn't that, but—"

He apparently expected to be interrupted, but she waited coolly for him to finish the sentence, and, of course, he could not. After all, for a helpless girl she had a devilish effective way of muzzling Landis. Donnegan chuckled softly in admiration.

All at once she broke through the scene; her voice did not rise or harden, but it was filled with finality, as though she were weary of the interview.

"I'm tired out; it's been a hard ride, Jack. You go home now and look me up again any time tomorrow."

"I—Lou—I feel mighty bad about having you up here in this infernal tent, when the camp is full, and—"

"You can't lie across the entrance to my tent and guard me, Jack. Besides, I don't need you for that. The man who's with me will protect me."

"He doesn't look capable of protecting a cat!"

"My father said that in any circumstances he would be able to take care of me."

This reply seemed to overwhelm Landis.

"The colonel trusts him as far as all that?" he muttered. "Then I suppose you're safe enough. But what about comfort, Lou?"

"I've done without comfort all my life. Run along, Jack. And take this money with you. I can't have it."

"But, didn't the colonel send—"

"You can express it through to him. To me it's—not pleasant to take it."

"Why, Lou, you don't mean—"

"Good night, Jack. I don't mean anything, except that I'm tired."

The shadow swept along the wall of the tent again. Donnegan, with a shaking pulse, saw the profile of the girl and the man approach as he strove to take her in his arms and kiss her good night. And then one slender bar of shadow checked Landis.

"Not tonight."

"Lou, you aren't angry with me?"

"No. But you know I have queer ways. Just put this down as one of them. I can't explain."

There was a muffled exclamation and Landis went from the tent and strode down the hill; he was instantly lost in the night. But Donnegan, turning to the entrance flap, called softly. He was bidden to come in, and when he raised the flap he saw her sitting with her hands clasped loosely and resting upon her knees. Her lips were a little parted, and colorless; her eyes were dull with a mist; and though she rallied herself a little, the wanderer could see that she was only half-aware of him.

The face which he saw was a milestone in his life. For he had loved her jealously, fiercely before; but seeing her now, dazed, hurt, and uncomplaining, tenderness came into Donnegan. It spread to his heart with a strange pain and made his hands tremble.

All that he said was: "Is there anything you need?"

"Nothing," she replied, and he backed out and away.

But in that small interval he had turned out of the course of his gay, selfish life. If Jack Landis had hurt her like this—if she loved him so truly—then Jack Landis she should have.

There was an odd mixture of emotions in Donnegan; but he felt most nearly like the poor man from whose hand his daughter tugs back and looks wistfully, hopelessly, into the bright window at all the toys. What pain is there greater than the pain that comes to the poor man in such a time? He huddles his coat about him, for his heart is as cold as a Christmas day; and if it would make his child happy, he would pour out his heart's blood on the snow.

Such was the grief of Donnegan as he backed slowly out into the night. Though Jack Landis were fixed as high as the moon he would tear him out of his place and give him to the girl.

## CHAPTER XIV

The lantern went out in the tent; she was asleep; and when he knew that, Donnegan went down into The Corner. He had been trying to think out a plan of action, and finding nothing better than to thrust a gun stupidly under Landis' nose and make him mark time, Donnegan went into Lebrun's place. As if he hoped the bustle there would supply him with ideas.

Lebrun's was going full blast. It was not filled with the shrill mirth of Milligan's. Instead, all voices were subdued to a point here. The pitch was never raised. If a man laughed, he might show his teeth but he took good care that he did not break into the atmosphere of the room. For there was a deadly undercurrent of silence which would not tolerate more than murmurs on the part of others. Men sat grim-faced over the cards, the man who was winning, with his cold, eager eye; the chronic loser of the night with his iron smile; the professional, ever debonair, with the dull eye which comes from looking too often and too closely into the terrible face of chance. A very keen observer might have observed a resemblance between those men and Donnegan.

Donnegan roved swiftly here and there. The calm eye and the smooth play of an obvious professional in a linen suit kept him for a moment at one table, looking on; then he went to the games, and after changing the gold which Jack Landis had given as alms to silver dollars, he lost it with precision upon the wheel.

He went on, from table to table, from group to group. In Lebrun's his clothes were not noticed. It was no matter whether he played or did not play, whether he won or lost; they were too busy to notice. But he came back, at length, to the man who wore the linen coat and who won so easily. Something in his method of dealing appeared to interest Donnegan greatly.

It was jackpot; the chips were piled high; and the man in the linen coat was dealing again. How deftly he mixed the cards!

Indeed, all about him was elegant, from the turn of his black cravat to the cut of the coat. An inebriate passed, shouldered and disturbed his chair, and rising to put it straight again, the gambler was seen to be about the height and build of Donnegan.

Donnegan studied him with the interest of an artist. Here was a man, harking back to Nelly Lebrun and her love of brilliance, who would probably win her preference over Jack Landis for the simple reason that he was different. That is, there was more in his cravat to attract astonished attention in The Corner than there was in all the silver lace of Landis. And he was a man's man, no doubt of that. On the inebriate he had flashed one glance of fire, and his lean hand had stirred uneasily toward the breast of his coat. Donnegan, who missed nothing, saw and understood.

Interested? He was fascinated by this man because he recognized the kinship which existed between them. They might almost have been blood brothers, except for differences in the face. He knew, for instance, just what each glance of the man in the linen coat meant, and how he was weighing his antagonists. As for the others, they were cool players themselves, but here they had met their master. It was the difference between the amateur and the professional. They played good chancey poker, but the man in the linen coat did more—he stacked the cards!

For the first moment Donnegan was not sure; it was not until there was a slight faltering in the deal—an infinitely small hesitation which only a practiced eye like that of Donnegan's could have noticed—that he was sure. The winner was crooked. Yet the hand was interesting for all that. He had done the master trick, not only giving himself the winning hand but also giving each of the others a fine set of cards.

And the betting was wild on that historic pot! To begin with the smallest hand was three of a kind; and after the draw the weakest was a straight. And they bet furiously. The stranger had piqued them with his consistent victories. Now they were out for blood. Chips having been exhausted, solid gold was piled up on the table—a small fortune!

The man in the linen coat, in the middle of the hand, called for drinks. They drank. They went on with the betting. And then at last came the call.

Donnegan could have clapped his hands to applaud the smooth rascal. It was not an affair of breaking the others who sat in. They were all prosperous mine owners, and probably they had been carefully selected according to the size of purse, in preparation for the sacrifice. But the stakes were swept into the arms and then the canvas bag of the winner. If it was not enough to ruin the miners it was at least enough to clean them out of ready cash and discontinue the game on that basis. They rose; they went to the bar for a drink; but while the winner led the way, two of the losers dropped back a trifle and fell into earnest conversation, frowning. Donnegan knew perfectly what the trouble was. They had noticed that slight faltering in the deal; they were putting their mental notes on the game together.

But the winner, apparently unconscious of suspicion, lined up his victims at the bar. The first drink went hastily down; the second was on the way—it was standing on the bar. And here he excused himself; he broke off in the very middle of a story, and telling them that he would be back any moment, stepped into a crowd of newcomers.

The moment he disappeared, Donnegan saw the other four put their heads close together, and saw a sudden darkening of faces; but as for the genial winner, he had no sooner passed to the other side of the crowd and out of view, than he turned directly toward the door. His careless saunter was exchanged for a brisk walk; and Donnegan, without making himself conspicuous, was hard pressed to follow that pace.

At the door he found that the gambler, with his canvas sack under his arm, had turned to the right toward the line of saddle horses which stood in the shadow; and no sooner did he reach the gloom at the side of the building than he broke into a soft, swift run. He darted down the line of horses until he came to one which was already mounted. This Donnegan saw as he followed somewhat more leisurely and closer to the horses to avoid observance. He made out that the man already on horseback was a big Negro and that he had turned his own mount and a neighboring horse out from the rest of the horses, so that they were both pointing down the street of The Corner. Donnegan saw the Negro throw the lines of his lead horse into the air. In exchange he caught the sack which the runner tossed to him, and then the gambler leaped into his saddle.

It was a simple but effective plan. Suppose he were caught in the midst of a cheat; his play would be to break away to the outside of the building, shooting out the lights, if possible—trusting to the confusion to help him—and there he would find his horse held ready for him at a time when a second might be priceless. On this occasion no doubt the clever rascal had sensed the suspicion of the others.

At any rate, he lost no time. He waited neither to find his stirrups nor grip the reins firmly, but the same athletic leap which carried him into the saddle set the horse in motion, and from a standing start the animal broke into a headlong gallop. He received, however, an additional burden at once.

For Donnegan, from the second time he saw the man of the linen coat, had been revolving a daring plan, and during the poker game the plan had slowly matured. The moment he made sure that the gambler was heading for a horse, he increased his own speed. Ordinarily he would have been noted, but now, no doubt, the gambler feared no pursuit except one accompanied by a hue and cry. He did not hear the shadow-footed Donnegan racing over the soft ground behind him; but when he had gained the saddle, Donnegan was close behind with the impetus of his run to aid him. It was comparatively simple, therefore, to spring high in the air, and he struck fairly and squarely behind the saddle of the man in the linen coat. When he landed his revolver was in his hand and the muzzle jabbed into the back of the gambler.

The other made one frantic effort to twist around, then recognized the pressure of the revolver and was still. The horses, checking their gallops in unison, were softly dog-trotting down the street.

"Call off your man!" warned Donnegan, for the big Negro had reined back; the gun already gleamed in his hand.

A gesture from the gambler sent the gun into obscurity, yet still the fellow continued to fall back.

"Tell him to ride ahead."

"Keep in front, George."

"And not too far."

"Very well. And now?"

"We'll talk later. Go straight on, George, to the clump of trees beyond the end of the street. And ride straight. No dodging!"

"It was a good hand you played," continued Donnegan; taking note that of the many people who were now passing them none paid the slightest attention to two men riding on one horse and chatting together as they rode. "It was a good hand, but a bad deal. Your thumb slipped on the card, eh?"

"You saw, eh?" muttered the other.

"And two of the others saw it. But they weren't sure till afterward."

"I know. The blockheads! But I spoiled their game for them. Are you one of us, pal?"

But Donnegan smiled to himself. For once at least the appeal of gambler to gambler should fail.

"Keep straight on," he said. "We'll talk later on."

## CHAPTER XV

Before Donnegan gave the signal to halt in a clear space where the starlight was least indistinct, they reached the center of the trees.

"Now, George," he said, "drop your gun to the ground."

There was a flash and faint thud.

"Now the other gun."

"They ain't anymore, sir."

"Your other gun," repeated Donnegan.

A little pause. "Do what he tells you, George," said the gambler at length, and a second weapon fell.

"Now keep on your horse and keep a little off to the side," went on Donnegan, "and remember that if you try to give me the jump I might miss you in this light, but I'd be sure to hit your horse. So don't take chances, George. Now, sir, just hold your hands over your head and then dismount."

He had already gone through the gambler and taken his weapons; he was now obeyed. The man of the linen coat tossed up his arms, flung his right leg over the horn of the saddle, and slipped to the ground.

Donnegan joined his captive. "I warn you first," he said gently, "that I am quite expert with a revolver, and that it will be highly dangerous to attempt to trick me. Lower your arms if you wish, but please be careful of what you do with your hands. There are such things as knife throwing, I know, but it takes a fast wrist to flip a knife faster than a bullet. We understand each other?"

"Perfectly," agreed the other. "By the way, my name is Godwin. And suppose we become frank. You are in temporary distress. It was impossible for you to make a loan at the moment and you are driven to this forced— touch. Now, if half—"

"Hush," said Donnegan. "You are too generous. But the present question is not one of money. I have long since passed over that. The money is now mine. Steady!" This to George, who lurched in the saddle; but Godwin was calm as stone. "It is not the question of the money that troubles me, but the question of the men. I could easily handle one of you. But I fear to allow both of you to go free. You would return on my trail; there are such things as waylayings by night, eh? And so, Mr. Godwin, I think my best way out is to shoot you through the head. When your body is found it will be taken for granted that the servant killed the master for the sake of the money which he won by crooked card play. I think that's simple. Put your hands up, George, or, by heck, I'll let the starlight shine through you!"

The huge arms of George were raised above his head; Godwin, in the meantime, had not spoken.

"I almost think you mean it," he said after a short pause.

"Good," said Donnegan. "I do not wish to kill you unprepared."

There was a strangled sound deep in the throat of Godwin; then he was able to speak again, but now his voice was made into a horrible jumble by fear.

"Pal," he said, "you're dead wrong. George here—he's a devil. If you let him live he'll kill you—as sure as you're standing here. You don't know him. He's George Green. He's got a record as long as my arm and as bad as the devil's name. He—he's the man to get rid of. Me? Why, man, you and I could team it together. But George—not—"

Donnegan began to laugh, and the gambler stammered to a halt.

"I knew you when I laid eyes on you for the first time," said Donnegan. "You have the hands of a craftsman, but your eyes are put too close together. A coward's eyes—a cur's face, Godwin. But you, George—have you heard what he said?"

No answer from George but a snarl.

"It sounds logical what he said, eh, George?"

Dead silence.

"But," said Donnegan, "there are flaws in the plan. Godwin, get out of your clothes."

The other fell on his knees.

"For heaven's sake," he pleaded.

"Shut up," commanded Donnegan. "I'm not going to shoot you. I never intended to, you fool. But I wanted to see if you were worth splitting the coin with. You're not. Now get out of your clothes."

He was obeyed in fumbling haste and while that operation went on, he succeeded in jumping out of his own rags and still kept the two fairly steadily under the nose of his gun. He tossed this bundle to Godwin, who accepted it with a faint oath; and Donnegan stepped calmly and swiftly into the clothes of his victim.

"A perfect fit," he said at length, "and to show that I'm pleased, here's your purse back. Must be close to two hundred in that, from the weight."

Godwin muttered some unintelligible curse.

"Tush. Now, get out! If you show your face in The Corner again, some of those miners will spot you, and they'll dress you in tar and feathers."

"You fool. If they see you in my clothes?"

"They'll never see these after tonight, probably. You have other clothes in your packs, Godwin. Lots of 'em. You're the sort who knows how to dress, and I'll borrow your outfit. Get out!"

The other made no reply; a weight seemed to have fallen upon him along with his new outfit, and he slunk into the darkness. George made a move to follow; there was a muffled shriek from Godwin, who fled headlong; and then a sharp command from Donnegan stopped the big man.

"Come here," said Donnegan.

George Washington Green rode slowly closer.

"If I let you go what would you do?"

There was a glint of teeth.

"I'd find him."

"And break him in two, eh? Instead, I'm going to take you home, where you'll have a chance of breaking me in two instead. There's something about the cut of your shoulders and your head that I like, Green; and if you don't murder me in the first hour or so, I think we'll get on very well together. You hear?"

The silence of George Washington Green was a tremendous thing.

"Now ride ahead of me. I'll direct you how to go."

He went first straight back through the town and up the hill to the two tents. He made George go before him into the tent and take up the roll of bedding; and then, with George and the bedding leading the way, and Donnegan leading the two horses behind, they went across the hillside to a shack which he had seen vacated that evening. It certainly could not be rented again before morning, and in the meantime Donnegan would be in possession, which was a large part of the law in The Corner, as he knew.

A little lean-to against the main shack served as a stable; the creek down the hillside was the watering trough. And Donnegan stood by while the big Negro silently tended to the horses—removing the packs and preparing them for the night. Still in silence he produced a small lantern and lighted it. It showed his face for the first time—the skin ebony black and polished over the cheekbones, but the rest of the face almost handsome, except that the slight flare of his nostrils gave him a cast of inhuman ferocity. And the fierceness was given point by a pair of arms of gorilla length; broad shoulders padded with rolling muscles, and the neck of a bull. On the whole, Donnegan, a connoisseur of fighting men, had never seen such promise of strength.

At his gesture, George led the way into the house. It was more commodious than most of the shacks of The Corner. In place of a single room this had two compartments—one for the kitchen and another for the living room. In vacating the hut, the last occupants had left some of the furnishings behind them. There was a mirror, for instance, in the corner; and beneath the mirror a cheap table in whose open drawer appeared a tumble of papers. Donnegan dropped the heavy sack of Godwin's winnings to the floor, and while George hung the lantern on a nail on the wall, Donnegan crossed to the table and appeared to run through the papers.

He was humming carelessly while he did it, but all the time he watched with catlike intensity the reflection of George in the mirror above him. He saw—rather dimly, for the cheap glass showed all its images in waves—that George turned abruptly after hanging up the lantern, paused, and then whipped a hand into his coat pocket and out again.

Donnegan leaped lightly to one side, and the knife, hissing past his head, buried itself in the wall, and its vibrations set up a vicious humming. As for Donnegan, the leap that carried him to one side whirled him about also; he faced the big man, who was now crouched in the very act of following the knife cast with the lunge of his powerful body. There was no weapon in Donnegan's hand, and yet George hesitated, balanced—and then slowly drew himself erect.

He was puzzled. An outburst of oaths, the flash of a gun, and he would have been at home in the brawl, but the silence, the smile of Donnegan and the steady glance were too much for him. He moistened his lips, and yet he could not speak. And Donnegan knew that what paralyzed George was the manner in which he had received warning. Evidently the simple explanation of the mirror did not occur to the fellow; and the whole incident took on supernatural colorings. A phrase of explanation and Donnegan would become again an ordinary human being; but while the small link was a mystery the brain and body of George were numb. It was necessary above all to continue inexplicable. Donnegan, turning, drew the knife from the wall with a jerk. Half the length of the keen blade had sunk into the wood—a mute tribute to the force and speed of George's hand—and now Donnegan took the bright little weapon by the point and gave it back to the other.

"If you throw for the body instead of the head," said Donnegan, "you have a better chance of sending the point home."

He turned his back again upon the gaping giant, and drawing up a broken box before the open door he sat down to contemplate the night. Not a sound behind him. It might be that the big fellow had regained his nerve and was stealing up for a second attempt; but Donnegan would have wagered his soul that George Washington Green had his first and last lesson and that he would rather play with bare lightning than ever again cross his new master.

At length: "When you make down the bunks," said Donnegan, "put mine farthest from the kitchen. You had better do that first."

"Yes—sir," came the deep bass murmur behind him.

And the heart of Donnegan stirred, for that "sir" meant many things.

Presently George crossed the floor with a burden; there was the "whish" of the blankets being unrolled—and then a slight pause. It seemed to him that he could hear a heavier breathing. Why? And searching swiftly back through his memory he recalled that his other gun, a stub-nosed thirty-eight, was in the center of his blanket roll.

And he knew that George had the weapon in his big hand. One pressure of the trigger would put an end to Donnegan; one bullet would give George the canvas sack and its small treasure.

"When you clean my gun," said Donnegan, "take the action to pieces and go over every part."

He could actually feel the start of George.

Then: "Yes, sir," in a subdued whisper.

If the escape from the knife had startled George, this second incident had convinced him that his new master possessed eyes in the back of his head.

And Donnegan, paying no further heed to him, looked steadily across the hillside to the white tent of Lou Macon, fifty yards away.

## CHAPTER XVI

His plan, grown to full stature so swiftly, and springing out of nothing, well nigh, had come out of his first determination to bring Jack Landis back to Lou Macon; for he could interpret those blank, misty eyes with which she had sat after the departure of Landis in only one way. Yet to rule even the hand of big Jack Landis would be hard enough and to rule his heart was quite another story. Remembering Nelly Lebrun, he saw clearly that the only way in which he could be brought back to Lou was first to remove Nelly as a possibility in his eyes. But how remove Nelly as long as it was her cue from her father to play Landis for his money? How remove her, unless it were possible to sweep Nelly off her feet with another man? She might, indeed, be taken by storm, and if she once slighted Landis for the sake of another, his boyish pride would probably do the rest, and his next step would be to return to Lou Macon.

All this seemed logical, but where find the man to storm the heart of Nelly and dazzle her bright, clever eyes? His own rags had made him shrug his shoulders; and it was the thought of clothes which had made him fasten his attention so closely on the man of the linen suit in Lebrun's. Donnegan with money, with well-fitted clothes, and with a few notorious escapades behind him—yes, Donnegan with such a flying start might flutter the heart of Nelly Lebrun for a moment. But he must have the money, the clothes, and then he must deliberately set out to startle The Corner, make himself a public figure, talked of, pointed at, known, feared, respected, and even loved by at least a few. He must accomplish all these things beginning at a literal zero.

It was the impossible nature of this that tempted Donnegan. But the paradoxical picture of the ragged skulker in Milligan's actually sitting at the same table with Nelly Lebrun and receiving her smiles stayed with him. He intended to rise, literally Phoenixlike, out of ashes. And the next morning, in the red time of the dawn, he sat drinking the coffee which George Washington Green had made for him and considering the details of the problem. Clothes, which had been a main obstacle, were now accounted for, since, as he had suspected, the packs of Godwin contained a luxurious wardrobe of considerable compass. At that moment, for instance, Donnegan was wrapped in a dressing gown of padded silk and his feet were encased in slippers.

But clothes were the least part of his worries. To startle The Corner, and thereby make himself attractive in the eyes of Nelly Lebrun, overshadowing Jack Landis—that was the thing! But to startle The Corner, where gold strikes were events of every twenty-four hours, just now—where robberies were common gossip, and where the killings now averaged nearly three a day— to startle The Corner was like trying to startle the theatrical world with a sensational play. Indeed, this parallel could have been pursued, for Donnegan was the nameless actor and the mountain desert was the stage on which he intended to become a headliner. No wonder, then, that his lean face was compressed in thought. Yet no one could have guessed it by his conversation. At the moment he was interrupted, his talk ran somewhat as follows.

"George, Godwin taught you how to make coffee?"

"Yes, sir," from George. Since the night before he had appeared totally subdued. Never once did he venture a comment. And ever Donnegan was conscious of big, bright eyes watching him in a reverent fear not untinged by superstition. Once, in the middle of the night, he had wakened and seen the vast shadow of George's form leaning over the sack of money. Murder by stealth in the dark had been in the giant's mind, no doubt. But when, after that, he came and leaned over Donnegan's bunk, the master closed his eyes and kept on breathing regularly, and finally George returned to his own place— softly as a gigantic cat. Even in the master's sleep he found something to be dreaded, and Donnegan knew that he could now trust the fellow through anything. In the morning, at the first touch of light, he had gone to the stores and collected provisions. And a comfortable breakfast followed.

"Godwin," resumed Donnegan, "was talented in many ways."

The big man showed his teeth in silence; for since Godwin proposed the sacrifice of the servant to preserve himself, George had apparently altered his opinion of the gambler.

"A talented man, George, but he knew nothing about coffee. It should never boil. It should only begin to cream through the crust. Let that happen; take the pot from the fire; put it back and let the surface cream again. Do this three times, and then pour the liquid from the grounds and you have the right strength and the right heating. You understand?"

"Yes, sir."

"And concerning the frying of bacon—"

At this point the interruption came in the shape of four men at the open door; and one of these Donnegan recognized as the real estate dealer, who had shrewdly set up tents and shacks on every favorable spot in The Corner and was now reaping a rich harvest. Gloster was his name. It was patent that he did not see in the man in the silk dressing robe the unshaven miscreant of the day before who had rented the two tents.

"How'dee," he said, standing on the threshold, with the other three in the background.

Donnegan looked at him and through him.

"My name is Gloster. I own this shack and I've come to find out why you're in it."

"George," said Donnegan, "speak to him. Tell him that I know houses are scarce in The Corner; that I found this place by accident vacant; that I intend to stay in it on purpose."

George Washington Green instantly rose to the situation; he swallowed a vast grin and strode to the door. And though Mr. Gloster's face crimsoned with rage at such treatment he controlled his voice. In The Corner manhood was apt to be reckoned by the pound, and George was a giant.

"I heard what your boss said, buddie," said Gloster. "But I've rented this cabin and the next one to these three gents and their party, and they want a home. Nothing to do but vacate. Which speed is the thing I want. Thirty minutes will—"

"Thirty minutes don't change nothing," declared George in his deep, soft voice.

The real estate man choked. Then: "You tell your boss that jumping a cabin is like jumping a claim. They's a law in The Corner for gents like him."

George made a gesture of helplessness; but Gloster turned to the three.

"Both shacks or none at all," said the spokesman. "One ain't big enough to do us any good. But if this bird won't vamoose—"

He was a tolerably rough-appearing sort and he was backed by two of a kind. No doubt dangerous action would have followed had not George shown himself capable of rising to a height. He stepped from the door; he approached Gloster and said in a confidential whisper that reached easily to the other three: "They ain't any call for a quick play, mister. Watch yo'selves. Maybe you don't know who the boss is?"

"And what's more, I don't care," said Gloster defiantly but with his voice instinctively lowered. He stared past George, and behold, the man in the dressing gown still sat in quiet and sipped his coffee.

"It's Donnegan," whispered George.

"Don—who's he?"

"You don't know Donnegan?"

The mingled contempt and astonishment of George would have moved a thing of stone. It certainly troubled Gloster. And he turned to the three.

"Gents," he said, "they's two things we can do. Try the law—and law's a lame lady in these parts—or throw him out. Say which?"

The three looked from Gloster to the shack; from the shack to Donnegan, absently sipping his coffee; from Donnegan to George, who stood exhibiting a broad grin of anticipated delight. The contrast was too much for them.

There is one great and deep-seated terror in the mountain desert, and that is for the man who may be other than he seems. The giant with the rough voice and the boisterous ways is generally due for a stormy passage west of the Rockies; but the silent man with the gentle manners receives respect. Traditions live of desperadoes with exteriors of womanish calm and the action of devils. And Donnegan sipping his morning coffee fitted into the picture which rumor had painted. The three looked at one another, declared that they had not come to fight for a house but to rent one, that the real estate agent could go to the devil for all of them, and that they were bound elsewhere. So they departed and left Gloster both relieved and gloomy.

"Now," said Donnegan to George, "tell him that we'll take both the shacks, and he can add fifty percent to his old price."

The bargain was concluded on the spot; the money was paid by George. Gloster went down the hill to tell The Corner that a mystery had hit the town and George brought the canvas bag back to Donnegan with the top still untied—as though to let it be seen that he had not pocketed any of the gold

"I don't want to count it," said Donnegan. "Keep the bag, George. Keep money in your pocket. Treat both of us well. And when that's gone I'll get more."

If the manner in which Donnegan had handled the renting of the cabins had charmed George, he was wholly entranced by this last touch of free spending. To serve a man who was his master was one thing; to serve one who trusted him so completely was quite another. To live under the same roof with a man who was a riddle was sufficiently delightful; but to be allowed actually to share in the mystery was a superhappiness. He was singing when he started to wash the dishes, and Donnegan went across the hill to the tent of Lou Macon.

She was laying the fire before the tent; and the morning freshness had cleared from her face any vestige of the trouble of the night before; and in the slant light her hair was glorious, all ruffling gold, semitransparent. She did not smile at him; but she could give the effect of smiling while her face remained grave; it was her inward calm content of which people were aware.

"You missed me?"

"Yes."

"You were worried?"

"No."

He felt himself put quietly at a distance. So he took her up the hill to her new home—the shack beside his own; and George cooked her breakfast. When she had been served, Donnegan drew the big man to one side.

"She's your mistress," said Donnegan. "Everything you do for her is worth two things you do for me. Watch her as if she were in your eye. And if a hair of her head is ever harmed—you see that fire burning yonder—the bed of coals?"

"Sir?"

"I'll catch you and make a fire like that and feed you into it—by inches!"

And the pale face of Donnegan became for an instant the face of a demon. George Washington Green saw, and never forgot.

Afterward, in order that he might think, Donnegan got on one of the horses he had taken from Godwin and rode over the hills. They were both leggy chestnuts, with surprising signs of blood and all the earmarks of sprinters; but in Godwin's trade sharp getaways were probably often necessary. The pleasure he took in the action of the animal kept him from getting into his problem.

How to startle The Corner? How follow up the opening gun which he had fired at the expense of Gloster and the three miners?

He broke off, later in the day, to write a letter to Colonel Macon, informing him that Jack Landis was tied hard and fast by Nelly Lebrun and that for the present nothing could be done except wait, unless the colonel had suggestions to offer.

The thought of the colonel, however, stimulated Donnegan. And before midafternoon he had thought of a thing to do.

## CHAPTER XVII

The bar in Milligan's was not nearly so pretentious an affair as the bar in Lebrun's, but it was of a far higher class. Milligan had even managed to bring in a few bottles of wine, and he had dispensed cheap claret at two dollars a glass when the miners wished to celebrate a rare occasion. There were complaints, not of the taste, but of the lack of strength. So Milligan fortified his liquor with pure alcohol and after that the claret went like a sweet song in The Corner. Among other things, he sold mint juleps; and it was the memory of the big sign proclaiming this fact that furnished Donnegan with his idea.

He had George Washington Green put on his town clothes—a riding suit in which Godwin had had him dress for the sake of formal occasions. Resplendent in black boots, yellow riding breeches, and blue silk shirt, the big man came before Donnegan for instructions.

"Go down to Milligan's," said the master. "They don't allow colored people to enter the door, but you go to the door and start for the bar. They won't let you go very far. When they stop you, tell them you come from Donnegan and that you have to get me some mint for a julep. Insist. The bouncer will start to throw you out."

George showed his teeth.

"No fighting back. Don't lift your hand. When you find that you can't get in, come back here. Now, ride."

So George mounted the horse and went. Straight to Milligan's he rode and dismounted; and half of The Corner's scant daytime population came into the street to see the brilliant horseman pass.

Scar-faced Lewis met the big man at the door. And size meant little to Andy, except an easier target.

"Well, confound my soul," said Lewis, blocking the way. "A Negro in Milligan's? Get out!"

Big George did not move.

"I been sent, mister," he said mildly. "I been sent for enough mint to make a julep."

"You been sent to the wrong place," declared Andy, hitching at his cartridge belt. "Ain't you seen that sign?"

And he pointed to the one which eliminated colored patrons.

"Signs don't mean nothin' to my boss," said George.

"Who's he?"

"Donnegan."

"And who's Donnegan?"

It puzzled George. He scratched his head in bewilderment seeking for an explanation. "Donnegan is—Donnegan," he explained.

"I heard Gloster talk about him," offered someone in the rapidly growing group. "He's the gent that rented the two places on the hill."

"Tell him to come himse'f," said Andy Lewis. "We don't play no favorites at Milligan's."

"Mister," said big George, "I don't want to bring no trouble on this heah place, but—don't make me go back and bring Donnegan."

Even Andy Lewis was staggered by this assurance.

"Rules is rules," he finally decided. "And out you go."

Big George stepped from the doorway and mounted his horse.

"I call on all you gen'lemen," he said to the assembled group, "to say that I done tried my best to do this peaceable. It ain't me that's sent for Donnegan; it's him!"

He rode away, leaving Scar-faced Lewis biting his long mustaches in anxiety. He was not exactly afraid, but he waited in the suspense which comes before a battle. Moreover, an audience was gathering. The word went about as only a rumor of mischief can travel. New men had gathered. The few day gamblers tumbled out of Lebrun's across the street to watch the fun. The storekeepers were in their doors. Lebrun himself, withered and dark and yellow of eye, came to watch. And here and there through the crowd there was a spot of color where the women of the town appeared. And among others, Nelly Lebrun with Jack Landis beside her. On the whole it was not a large crowd, but what it lacked in size it made up in intense interest.

For though The Corner had had its share of troubles of fist and gun, most of them were entirely impromptu affairs. Here was a fight in the offing for which the stage was set, the actors set in full view of a conveniently posted audience, and all the suspense of a curtain rising. The waiting bore in upon Andy Lewis. Without a doubt he intended to kill his man neatly and with dispatch, but the possibility of missing before such a crowd as this sent a chill up and down his spine. If he failed now his name would be a sign for laughter ever after in The Corner.

A hum passed down the street; it rose to a chuckle, and then fell away to sudden silence, for Donnegan was coming.

He came on a prancing chestnut horse which sidled uneasily on a weaving course, as though it wished to show off for the benefit of the rider and the crowd at once. It was a hot afternoon and Donnegan's linen riding suit shone an immaculate white. He came straight down the street, as unaware of the audience which awaited him as though he rode in a park where crowds were the common thing. Behind him came George Green, just a careful length back. Rumor went before the two with a whisper on either side.

"That's Donnegan. There he comes!"

"Who's Donnegan?"

"Gloster's man. The one who bluffed out Gloster and three others."

"He pulled his shooting iron and trimmed the whiskers of one of 'em with a chunk of lead."

"D'you mean that?"

"What's that kind of a gent doing in The Corner?"

"Come to buy, I guess. He looks like money."

"Looks like a confounded dude."

"We'll see his hand in a minute."

Donnegan was now opposite the dance hall, and Andy Lewis had his hand touching the butt of his gun, but though Donnegan was looking straight at him, he kept his reins in one hand and his heavy riding crop in the other. And without a move toward his own gun, he rode straight up to the door of the dance hall, with Andy in front of it. George drew rein behind him and turned upon the crowd one broad, superior grin.

As who should say: "I promised you lightning; now watch it strike!"

If the crowd had been expectant before, it was now reduced to wire-drawn tenseness.

"Are you the fellow who turned back my man?" asked Donnegan.

His quiet voice fell coldly upon the soul of Andy. He strove to warm himself by an outbreak of temper.

"They ain't any poor fool dude can call me a fellow!" he shouted.

The crowd blinked; but when it opened its eyes the gunplay had not occurred. The hand of Andy was relaxing from the butt of his gun and an expression of astonishment and contempt was growing upon his face.

"I haven't come to curse you," said the rider, still occupying his hands with crop and reins. "I've come to ask you a question and get an answer. Are you the fellow who turned back my man?"

"I guess you ain't the kind I was expectin' to call on me," drawled Andy, his fear gone, and he winked at the crowd. But the others were not yet ready to laugh. Something about the calm face of Donnegan had impressed them. "Sure, I'm the one that kicked him out. He ain't allowed in there."

"It's the last of my thoughts to break in upon a convention in your city," replied the grave rider, "but my man was sent on an errand and therefore he had a right to expect courtesy. George, get off your horse and go into Milligan's place. I want that mint!"

For a moment Andy was too stunned to answer. Then his voice came harshly and he swayed from side to side, gathering and summoning his wrath

"Keep out boy! Keep out, or you're buzzard meat. I'm warnin'—"

For the first time his glance left the rider to find George, and that instant was fatal. The hand of Donnegan licked out as the snake's tongue darts—the loaded quirt slipped over in his hand, and holding it by the lash he brought the butt of it thudding on the head of Andy.

Even then the instinct to fight remained in the stunned man; while he fell, he was drawing the revolver; he lay in a crumpling heap at the feet of Donnegan's horse with the revolver shoved muzzle first into the sand.

Donnegan's voice did not rise.

"Go in and get that mint, George," he ordered. "And hurry. This rascal has kept me waiting until I'm thirsty."

Big George hesitated only one instant—it was to sweep the crowd for the second time with his confident grin—and he strode through the door of the dance hall. As for Donnegan, his only movement was to swing his horse around and shift riding crop and reins into the grip of his left hand. His other hand was dropped carelessly upon his hip. Now, both these things were very simple maneuvers, but The Corner noted that his change of face had enabled Donnegan to bring the crowd under his eye, and that his right hand was now ready for a more serious bit of work if need be. Moreover, he was probing faces with his glance. And every armed man in that group felt that the eye of the rider was directed particularly toward him.

There had been one brief murmur; then the silence lay heavily again, for it was seen that Andy had been only slightly stunned—knocked out, as a boxer might be. Now his sturdy brains were clearing. His body stiffened into a human semblance once more; he fumbled, found the butt of his gun with his first move. He pushed his hat straight: and so doing he raked the welt which the blow had left on his head. The pain finished clearing the mist from his mind; in an instant he was on his feet, maddened with shame. He saw the semicircle of white faces, and the whole episode flashed back on him. He had been knocked down like a dog.

For a moment he looked into the blank faces of the crowd; someone noted that there was no gun strapped at the side of Donnegan. A voice shouted a warning.

"Stop, Lewis. The dude ain't got a gun. It's murder!"

It was now that Lewis saw Donnegan sitting the saddle directly behind him, and he whirled with a moan of fury. It was a twist of his body—in his eagerness—rather than a turning upon his feet. And he was half around before the rider moved. Then he conjured a gun from somewhere in his clothes. There was the flash of the steel, an explosion, and Scar-faced Lewis was on his knees with a scream of pain holding his right forearm with his left hand.

The crowd hesitated still for a second, as though it feared to interfere; but Donnegan had already put up his weapon. A wave of the curious spectators rushed across the street and gathered around the injured man. They found that he had been shot through the fleshy part of the thumb, and the bullet, ranging down the arm, had sliced a furrow to the bone all the way to the elbow. It was a grisly wound.

Big George Washington Green came running to the door of the dance hall with a sprig of something green in his hand; one glance assured him that all was well; and once more that wide, confident grin spread upon his face. He came to the master and offered the mint; and Donnegan, raising it to his face, inhaled the scent deeply.

"Good," he said. "And now for a julep, George! Let's go home!"

Across the street a dark-eyed girl had clasped the arm of her companion in hysterical excitement.

"Did you see?" she asked of her tall companion.

"I saw a murderer shoot down a man; he ought to be hung for it!"

"But the mint! Did you see him smile over it? Oh, what a devil he is; and what a man!"

Jack Landis flashed a glance of suspicion down at her, but her dancing eyes had quite forgotten him. They were following the progress of Donnegan down the street. He rode slowly, and George kept that formal distance, just a length behind.

## CHAPTER XVIII

Before Milligan's the crowd began to buzz like murmuring hornets around a nest that has been tapped, when they pour out and cannot find the disturber. It was a rather helpless milling around the wounded man, and Nelly Lebrun was the one who worked her way through the crowd and came to Andy Lewis. She did not like Andy. She had been known to refer to him as a cowardly hawk of a man; but now she bullied the crowd in a shrill voice and made them bring water and cloth. Then she cleansed and bandaged the wound in Andy Lewis' arm and had some of them take him away.

By this time the outskirts of the crowd had melted away; but those who had really seen all parts of the little drama remained to talk. The subject was a real one. Had Donnegan aimed at the hand of Andy and risked his own life on his ability to disable the other without killing him? Or had he fired at Lewis' body and struck the hand and arm only by a random lucky chance?

If the second were the case, he was only a fair shot with plenty of nerve and a great deal of luck. If the first were true, then this was a nerve of ice-tempered steel, an eye vulture-sharp, and a hand, miraculous, fast, and certain. To strike that swinging hand with a snap shot, when a miss meant a bullet fired at his own body at deadly short range  truly it would take a credulous man to believe that Donnegan had coldly planned to disable his man without killing him.

"A murderer by intention," exclaimed Milligan. He had hunted long and hard before he found a man with a face like that of Lewis, capable of maintaining order by a glance; now he wanted revenge. "A murder by intention!" he cried to the crowd, standing beside the place where the imprint of Andy's knees was still in the sand. "And like a murderer he ought to be treated. He aimed to kill Andy; he had luck and only broke his hand. Now, boys, I say it ain't so much what he's done as the way he's done it. He's given us the laugh. He's come in here in his dude clothes and tried to walk over us. But it don't work. Not in The Corner. If Andy was dead, I'd say lynch the dude. But he ain't, and all I say is: Run him out of town."

Here there was a brief outburst of applause, but when it ended, it was observed that there was a low, soft laughter. The crowd gave way between Milligan and the mocker. It was seen that he who laughed was old Lebrun, rubbing his olive-skinned hands together and showing his teeth in his mirth. There was no love lost between Lebrun and Milligan, even if Nelly was often in the dance hall and the center of its merriment.

"It takes a thief to catch a thief," said Lebrun enigmatically, when he saw that he had the ear of the crowd, "and it takes a man to catch a man."

"What the devil do you mean by that?" a dozen voices asked.

"I mean, that if you got men enough to run out this man Donnegan, The Corner is a better town than I think."

It brought a growl, but no answer. Lebrun had never been seen to lift his hand, but he was more dreaded than a rattler.

"We'll try," said Milligan dryly. "I ain't much of a man myself"—there were dark rumors about Milligan's past and the crowd chuckled at this modesty—"but I'll try my hand agin' him with a bit of backing. And first I want to tell you boys that they ain't any danger of him having aimed at Andy's hand. I tell you, it ain't possible, hardly, for him to have planned to hit a swingin' target like that. Maybe some could do it. I dunno."

"How about Lord Nick?"

"Sure, Lord Nick might do anything. But Donnegan ain't Lord Nick."

"Not by twenty pounds and three inches."

This brought a laugh. And by comparison with the terrible and familiar name of Lord Nick, Donnegan became a smaller danger. Besides, as Milligan said, it was undoubtedly luck. And when he called for volunteers, three or four stepped up at once. The others made a general milling, as though each were trying to get forward and each were prevented by the crowd in front. But in the background big Jack Landis was seriously trying to get to the firing line. He was encumbered with the clinging weight of Nelly Lebrun.

"Don't go, Jack," she pleaded. "Please! Please! Be sensible. For my sake!"

She backed this appeal with a lifting of her eyes and a parting of her lips, and Jack Landis paused.

"You won't go, dear Jack?"

Now, Jack knew perfectly well that the girl was only half sincere. It is the peculiar fate of men that they always know when a woman is playing with them, but, from Samson down, they always go to the slaughter with open eyes, hoping each moment that the girl has been seriously impressed at last. As for Jack Landis, his slow mind did not readily get under the surface of the arts of Nelly, but he knew that there was at least a tinge of real concern in the girl's desire to keep him from the posse which Milligan was raising.

"But they's something about him that I don't like, Nelly. Something sort of familiar that I don't like." For naturally enough he did not recognize the transformed Donnegan, and the name he had never heard before. "A gunfighter, that's what he is!"

"Why, Jack, sometimes they call you the same thing; say that you hunt for trouble now and then!"

"Do they say that?" asked the young chap quickly, flushing with vanity. "Oh,

I aim to take care of myself. And I'd like to take a hand with this murdering Donnegan."

"Jack, listen! Don't go; keep away from him!"

"Why do you look like that? As if I was a dead one already."

"I tell you, Jack, he'd kill you!"

Something in her terrible assurance whitened the cheeks of Landis, but he was also angered. When a very young man becomes both afraid and angry he is apt to be dangerous. "What do you know of him?" he asked suspiciously.

"You silly! But I saw his face when he lifted that mint. He'd already forgotten about the man he had just shot down. He was thinking of nothing but the scent of the mint. And did you notice his giant servant? He never had a moment's doubt of Donnegan's ability to handle the entire crowd. I tell you, it gave me a chill of ghosts to see the big black fellow's eyes. He knew that Donnegan would win. And Donnegan won! Jack, you're a big man and a strong man and a brave man, and we all know it. But don't be foolish. Stay away from Donnegan!"

He wavered just an instant. If she could have sustained her pleading gaze a moment longer she would have won him, but at the critical instant her gaze became distant. She was seeing the calm face of Donnegan as he raised the mint. And as though he understood, Jack Landis hardened.

"I'm glad you don't want me shot up, Nelly," he said coldly. "Mighty good of you to watch out for me. But—I'm going to run this Donnegan out of town!"

"He's never harmed you; why—"

"I don't like his looks. For a man like me that's enough!"

And he strode away toward Milligan. He was greeted by a cheer just as the girl reached the side of her father.

"Jack is going," she said. "Make him come back!"

But the old man was still rubbing his hands; there seemed to be a perpetual chill in the tips of the fingers.

"He is a jackass. The moment I first saw his face I knew that he was meant for gun fodder—buzzard food! Let him go. Bah!"

The girl shivered. "And then the mines?" she asked, changing her tactics.

"Ah, yes. The mines! But leave that to Lord Nick. He'll handle it well enough!"

So Jack Landis strode up the hill first and foremost of the six stalwart men who wished to correct the stranger's apparent misunderstandings of the status of The Corner. They were each armed to the teeth and each provided with enough bullets to disturb a small city. All this in honor of Donnegan.

They found the shack wrapped in the warm, mellow light of the late afternoon; and on a flat-topped rock outside it big George sat whittling a stick into a grotesque imitation of a snake coiled. He did not rise when the posse approached. He merely rocked back upon the rock, embraced his knees in both of his enormous arms, and, in a word, transformed himself into a round ball of mirth. But having hugged away his laughter he was able to convert his joy into a vast grin. That smile stopped the posse. When a mob starts for a scene of violence the least exhibition of fear incenses it, but mockery is apt to pour water on its flames of anger.

Decidedly the fury of the posse was chilled by the grin of George. Milligan, who had lived south of the Mason-Dixon line, stepped up to impress George properly.

"Boy," he said, frowning, "go in and tell your man that we've come for him. Tell him to step right out here and get ready to talk. We don't mean him no harm less'n he can't explain one or two things. Hop along!"

The "boy" did not stir. Only he shifted his eyes from face to face and his grin broadened. Ripples of mirth waved along his chest and convulsed his face, but still he did not laugh. "Go in and tell them things to Donnegan," he said. "But don't ask me to wake him up. He's sleepin' soun' an' fas'. Like a baby; mostly, he sleeps every day to get rested up for the night. Now, can't you-all wait till Donnegan wakes up tonight? No? Then step right in, gen'lemen; but if you-all is set on wakin' him up now, George will jus' step over the hill, because he don't want to be near the explosion."

At this, he allowed his mirth free rein. His laughter shook up to his throat, to his enormous mouth; it rolled and bellowed across the hillside; and the posse stood, each man in his place, and looked frigidly upon one another. But having been laughed at, they felt it necessary to go on, and do or die. So they strode across the hill and were almost to the door when another phenomenon occurred. A girl in a cheap calico dress of blue was seen to run out of a neighboring shack and spring up before the door of Donnegan's hut. When she faced the crowd it stopped again.

The soft wind was blowing the blue dress into lovely, long, curving lines; about her throat a white collar of some sheer stuff was being lifted into waves, or curling against her cheek; and the golden hair, in disorder, was tousled low upon her forehead.

Whirling thus upon the crowd, she shocked them to a pause, with her parted lips, her flare of delicate color.

"Have you come here," she cried, "for—for Donnegan?"

"Lady," began someone, and then looked about for Jack Landis, who was considered quite a hand with the ladies. But Jack Landis was discovered fading out of view down the hillside. One glance at that blue dress had quite routed him, for now he remembered the red-haired man who had escorted Lou Macon to The Corner—and the colonel's singular trust in this fellow. It explained much, and he fled before he should be noticed.

Before the spokesman could continue his speech, the girl had whipped inside the door. And the posse was dumbfounded. Milligan saw that the advance was ruined. "Boys," he said, "we came to fight a man; not to storm a house with a woman in it. Let's go back. We'll tend to Donnegan later on."

"We'll drill him clean!" muttered the others furiously, and straightway the posse departed down the hill.

But inside the girl had found, to her astonishment, that Donnegan was stretched upon his bunk wrapped again in the silken dressing gown and with a smile upon his lips. He looked much younger, as he slept, and perhaps it was this that made the girl steal forward upon tiptoe and touch his shoulder so gently.

He was up on his feet in an instant. Alas, vanity, vanity! Donnegan in shoes was one thing, for his shoes were of a particular kind; but Donnegan in his slippers was a full two inches shorter. He was hardly taller than the girl; he was, if the bitter truth must be known, almost a small man. And Donnegan was furious at having been found by her in such careless attire— and without those dignity-building shoes. First he wanted to cut the throat of big George.

"What have you done, what have you done?" cried the girl, in one of those heart-piercing whispers of fear. "They have come for you—a whole crowd—of armed men—they're outside the door! What have you done? It was something done for me, I know!"

Donnegan suddenly transferred his wrath from big George to the mob.

"Outside my door?" he asked. And as he spoke he slipped on a belt at which a heavy holster tugged down on one side, and buckled it around him.

"Oh, no, no, no!" she pleaded, and caught him in her arms.

Donnegan allowed her to stop him with that soft power for a moment, until his face went white—as if with pain. Then he adroitly gathered both her wrists into one of his bony hands; and having rendered her powerless, he slipped by her and cast open the door.

It was an empty scene upon which they looked, with big George rocking back and forth upon a rock, convulsed with silent laughter. Donnegan looked sternly at the girl and swallowed. He was fearfully susceptible to mockery.

"There seems to have been a jest?" he said.

But she lifted him a happy, tearful face.

"Ah, thank heaven!" she cried gently.

Oddly enough, Donnegan at this set his teeth and turned upon his heel, and the girl stole out the door again, and closed it softly behind her. As a matter of fact, not even the terrible colonel inspired in her quite the fear which Donnegan instilled.

# CHAPTER XIX

"Big Landis lost his nerve and sidestepped at the last minute, and then the whole gang faded."

That was the way the rumors of the affair always ended at each repetition in Lebrun's and Milligan's that night. The Corner had had many things to talk about during its brief existence, but nothing to compare with a man who entered a shooting scrape with such a fellow as Scar-faced Lewis all for the sake of a spray of mint. And the main topic of conversation was: Did Donnegan aim at the body or the hand of the bouncer?

On the whole, it was an excellent thing for Milligan's. The place was fairly well crowded, with a few vacant tables. For everyone wanted to hear Milligan's version of the affair. He had a short and vigorous one, trimmed with neat oaths. It was all the girl in the blue calico dress, according to him. The posse couldn't storm a house with a woman in it or even conduct a proper lynching in her presence. And no one was able to smile when Milligan said this. Neither was anyone nervy enough to question the courage of Landis. It looked strange, that sudden flight of his, but then, he was a proven man. Everyone remembered the affair of Lester. It had been a clean-cut fight, and Jack Landis had won cleanly on his merits.

Nevertheless some of the whispers had not failed to come to the big man, and his brow was black.

The most terribly heartless and selfish passion of all is shame in a young man. To repay the sidelong glances which he met on every side, Jack Landis would have willingly crowded every living soul in The Corner into one house and touched a match to it. And chiefly because he felt the injustice of the suspicion. He had no fear of Donnegan.

He had a theory that little men had little souls. Not that he ever formulated the theory in words, but he vaguely felt it and adhered to it. He had more fear of one man of six two than a dozen under five ten. He reserved in his heart of hearts a place of awe for one man whom he had never seen. That was for Lord Nick, for that celebrated character was said to be as tall and as finely built as Jack Landis himself. But as for Donnegan—Landis wished there were three Donnegans instead of one.

Tonight his cue was surly silence. For Nelly Lebrun had been warned by her father, and she was making desperate efforts to recover any ground she might have lost. Besides, to lose Jack Landis would be to lose the most spectacular fellow in The Corner, to say nothing of the one who held the largest and the choicest of the mines. The blond, good looks of Landis made a perfect background for her dark beauty. With all these stakes to play for, Nelly outdid herself. If she were attractive enough ordinarily, when she exerted herself to fascinate, Nelly was intoxicating. What chance had poor Jack Landis against her? He did not call for her that night but went to play gloomily at Lebrun's until Nelly walked into Lebrun's and drew him away from a table. Half an hour later she had him whirling through a dance in Milligan's and had danced the gloom out of his mind for the moment. Before the evening was well under way, Landis was making love to her openly, and Nelly was in the position of one who had roused the bear.

It was a dangerous flirtation and it was growing clumsy. In any place other than The Corner it would have been embarrassing long ago; and when Jack Landis, after a dance, put his one big hand over both of Nelly's and held her moveless while he poured out a passionate declaration, Nelly realized that something must be done. Just what she could not tell.

And it was at this very moment that a wave of silence, beginning at the door, rushed across Milligan's dance floor. It stopped the bartenders in the act of mixing drinks; it put the musicians out of key, and in the midst of a waltz phrase they broke down and came to a discordant pause.

What was it?

The men faced the door, wondering, and then the swift rumor passed from lip to lip—almost from eye to eye, so rapidly it sped—Donnegan is coming! Donnegan, and big George with him.

"Someone tell Milligan!"

But Milligan had already heard; he was back of the bar giving directions; guns were actually unlimbering. What would happen?

"Shall I get you out of this?" Landis asked the girl.

"Leave now?" She laughed fiercely and silently. "I'm just beginning to live! Miss Donnegan in action? No, sir!"

She would have given a good deal to retract that sentence, for it washed the face of Landis white with jealousy.

Surely Donnegan had built greater than he knew.

And suddenly he was there in the midst of the house. No one had stopped him— at least, no one had interfered with his servant. Big George had on a white suit and a dappled green necktie; he stood directly behind his master and made him look like a small boy. For Donnegan was in black, and he had a white neckcloth wrapped as high and stiffly as an old-fashioned stock. Altogether he was a queer, drab figure compared with the brilliant Donnegan of that afternoon. He looked older, more weary. His lean face was pale; and his hair flamed with redoubled ardor on that account. Never was hair as red as that, not even the hair of Lord Nick, said the people in Milligan's this night.

He was perfectly calm even in the midst of that deadly silence. He stood looking about him. He saw Gloster, the real estate man, and bowed to him deliberately.

For some reason that drew a gasp.

Then he observed a table which was apparently to his fancy and crossed the floor with a light, noiseless step, big George padding heavily behind him. At the little round table he waited until George had drawn out the chair for him and then he sat down. He folded his arms lightly upon his breast and once more surveyed the scene, and big George drew himself up behind Donnegan. Just once his eyes rolled and flashed savagely in delight at the sensation that they were making, then the face of George was once again impassive.

If Donnegan had not carried it off with a certain air, the whole entrance would have seemed decidedly stagey, but The Corner, as it was, found much to wonder at and little to criticize. And in the West grown men are as shrewd judges of affectation as children are in other places.

"Putting on a lot of style, eh?" said Jack Landis, and with fierce intensity he watched the face of Nelly Lebrun.

For once she was unguarded.

"He's superb!" she exclaimed. "The big fellow is going to bring a drink for him."

She looked up, surprised by the silence of Landis, and found that his face was actually yellow.

"I'll tell you something. Do you remember the little red-headed tramp who came in here the other night and spoke to me?"

"Very well. You seemed to be bothered."

"Maybe. I dunno. But that's the man—the one who's sitting over there now all dressed up—the man The Corner is talking about—Donnegan! A tramp!"

She caught her breath.

"Is that the one?" A pause. "Well, I believe it. He's capable of anything!"

"I think you like him all the better for knowing that."

"Jack, you're angry."

"Why should I be? I hate to see you fooled by the bluff of a tramp, though."

"Tush! Do you think I'm fooled by it? But it's an interesting bluff, Jack, don't you think?"

"Nelly, he's interesting enough to make you blush; by heaven, the hound is lookin' right at you now, Nelly!"

He had pressed her suddenly against the wall and she struck back desperately in self-defense.

"By the way, what did he want to see you about?"

It spiked the guns of Landis for the time being, at least. And the girl followed by striving to prove that her interest in Donnegan was purely impersonal.

"He's clever," she ran on, not daring to look at the set face of her companion. "See how he fails to notice that he's making a sensation? You'd think he was in a big restaurant in a city. He takes the drink off the tray from that fellow as if it were a common thing to be waited on by a body-servant in The Corner. Jack, I'll wager that there's something crooked about him. A professional gambler, say!"

Jack Landis thawed a little under this careless chatter. He still did not quite trust her.

"Do you know what they're whispering? That I was afraid to face him!"

She tilted her head back, so that the light gleamed on her young throat, and she broke into laughter.

"Why, Jack, that's foolish. You proved yourself when you first came to The Corner. Maybe some of the newcomers may have said something, but all the old-timers know you had some different reason for leaving the rest of them. By the way, what was the reason?"

She sent a keen little glance at him from the corner of her eyes, but the moment she saw that he was embarrassed and at sea because of the query she instantly slipped into a fresh tide of careless chatter and covered up his confusion for him.

"See how the girls are making eyes at him."

"I'll tell you why," Jack replied. "A girl likes to be with the man who's making the town talk." He added pointedly: "Oh, I've found that out!"

She shrugged that comment away.

"He isn't paying the slightest attention to any of them," she murmured. "He's queer! Has he just come here hunting trouble?"

## CHAPTER XX

It should be understood that before this the men in Milligan's had reached a subtly unspoken agreement that red-haired Donnegan was not one of them. In a word, they did not like him because he made a mystery of himself. And, also, because he was different. Yet there was a growing feeling that the shooting of Lewis through the hand had not been an accident, for the whole demeanor of Donnegan composed the action of a man who is a professional trouble maker. There was no reason why he should go to Milligan's and take his servant with him unless he wished a fight. And why a man should wish to fight the entire Corner was something no one could guess.

That he should have done all this merely to focus all eyes upon him, and particularly the eyes of a girl, did not occur to anyone. It looked rather like the bravado of a man who lived for the sake of fighting. Now, men who hunt trouble in the mountain desert generally find all that they may desire, but for the time being everyone held back, wolfishly, waiting for another to take the first step toward Donnegan. Indeed, there was an unspoken conviction that the man who took the first step would probably not live to take another. In the meantime both men and women gave Donnegan the lion's share of their attention. There was only one who was clever enough to conceal it, and that one was the pair of eyes to which the red-haired man was playing—Nelly Lebrun. She confined herself strictly to Jack Landis.

So it was that when Milligan announced a tag dance and the couples swirled onto the floor gayly, Donnegan decided to take matters into his own hands and offer the first overt act. It was clumsy; he did not like it; but he hated this delay. And he knew that every moment he stayed on there with big George behind his chair was another red rag flaunted in the face of The Corner.

He saw the men who had no girl with them brighten at the announcement of the tag dance. And when the dance began he saw the prettiest girls tagged quickly, one after the other. All except Nelly Lebrun. She swung securely around the circle in the big arms of Jack Landis. She seemed to be set apart and protected from the common touch by his size, and by his formidable, challenging eye. Donnegan felt as never before the unassailable position of this fellow; not only from his own fighting qualities, but because he had behind him the whole unfathomable power of Lord Nick and his gang.

Nelly approached in the arms of Landis in making the first circle of the dance floor; her eyes, grown dull as she surrendered herself wholly to the rhythm of the waltz, saw nothing. They were blank as unlighted charcoal. She came opposite Donnegan, her back was toward him; she swung in the arms of Landis, and then, past the shoulder of her partner, she flashed a glance at Donnegan. The spark had fallen on the charcoal, and her eyes were aflame. Aflame to Donnegan; the next instant the veil had dropped across her face once more.

She was carried on, leaving Donnegan tingling.

A wise man upon whom that look had fallen might have seen, not Nelly Lebrun in the cheap dance hall, but Helen of Sparta and all Troy's dead. But Donnegan was clever, not wise. And he saw only Nelly Lebrun and the broad shoulders of Jack Landis.

Let the critic deal gently with Donnegan. He loved Lou Macon with all his heart and his soul, and yet because another beautiful girl had looked at him, there he sat at his table with his jaw set and the devil in his eye. And while she and Landis were whirling through the next circumference of the room, Donnegan was seeing all sides of the problem. If he tagged Landis it would be casting the glove in the face of the big man—and in the face of old Lebrun—and in the face of that mysterious and evil power, Lord Nick himself. And consider, that besides these he had already insulted all of The Corner.

Why not let things go on as they were? Suppose he were to allow Landis to plunge deeper into his infatuation? Suppose he were to bring Lou Macon to this place and let her see Landis sitting with Nelly, making love to her with every tone in his voice, every light in his eye? Would not that cure Lou? And would not that open the door to Donnegan?

And remember, in considering how Donnegan was tempted, that he was not a conscientious man. He was in fact what he seemed to be—a wanderer, a careless vagrant, living by his wits. For all this, he had been touched by the divine fire—a love that is greater than self. And the more deeply he hated Landis, the more profoundly he determined that he should be discarded by Nelly and forced back to Lou Macon. In the meantime, Nelly and Jack were coming again. They were close; they were passing; and this time her eye had no spark for Donnegan.

Yet he rose from his table, reached the floor with a few steps, and touched Landis lightly on the shoulder. The challenge was passed. Landis stopped abruptly and turned his head; his face showed merely dull astonishment. The current of dancers split and washed past on either side of the motionless trio, and on every face there was a glittering curiosity. What would Landis do?

Nothing. He was too stupefied to act. He, Jack Landis, had actually been tagged while he was dancing with the woman which all The Corner knew to be his girl! And before his befogged senses cleared the girl was in the arms of the red-haired man and was lost in the crowd.

What a buzz went around the room! For a moment Landis could no more move than he could think; then he sent a sullen glance toward the girl and retreated to their table. A childish sullenness clouded his face while he sat there; only one decision came clearly to him: he must kill Donnegan!

In the meantime people noted two things. The first was that Donnegan danced very well with Nelly Lebrun; and his red hair beside the silken black of the girl's was a startling contrast. It was not a common red. It flamed, as though with phosphoric properties of its own. But they danced well; and the eyes of both of them were gleaming. Another thing: men did not tag Donnegan anymore than they had offered to tag Landis. One or two slipped out from the outskirts of the floor, but something in the face of Donnegan discouraged them and made them turn elsewhere as though they had never started for Nelly Lebrun in the first place. Indeed, to a two-year-old child it would have been apparent that Nelly and the red-headed chap were interested in each other.

As a matter of fact they did not speak a single syllable until they had gone around the floor one complete turn and the dance was coming toward an end.

It was he who spoke first, gloomily: "I shouldn't have done it; I shouldn't have tagged him!"

At this she drew back a little so that she could meet his eyes.

"Why not?"

"The whole crew will be on my trail."

"What crew?"

"Beginning with Lord Nick!"

This shook her completely out of the thrall of the dance.

"Lord Nick? What makes you think that?"

"I know he's thick with Landis. It'll mean trouble."

He was so simple about it that she began to laugh. It was not such a voice as Lou Macon's. It was high and light, and one could suspect that it might become shrill under a stress.

"And yet it looks as though you've been hunting trouble," she said.

"I couldn't help it," said Donnegan naively.

It was a very subtle flattery, this frankness from a man who had puzzled all The Corner. Nelly Lebrun felt that she was about to look behind the scenes and she tingled with delight.

"Tell me," she said. "Why not?"

"Well," said Donnegan. "I had to make a noise because I wanted to be noticed."

She glanced about her; every eye was upon them.

"You've made your point," she murmured. "The whole town is talking of nothing else."

"I don't care an ounce of lead about the rest of the town."

"Then—"

She stopped abruptly, seeing toward what he was tending. And the heart of Nelly Lebrun fluttered for the first time in many a month. She believed him implicitly. It was for her sake that he had made all this commotion; to draw her attention. For every lovely girl, no matter how cool-headed, has a foolish belief in the power of her beauty. As a matter of fact Donnegan had told her the truth. It had all been to win her attention, from the fight for the mint to the tagging for the dance. How could she dream that it sprang out of anything other than a wild devotion to her? And while Donnegan coldly calculated every effect, Nelly Lebrun began to see in him the man of a dream, a spirit out of a dead age, a soul of knightly, reckless chivalry. In that small confession he cast a halo about himself which no other hand could ever remove entirely so far as Nelly Lebrun was concerned.

"You understand?" he was saying quietly.

She countered with a question as direct as his confession.

"What are you, Mr. Donnegan?"

"A wanderer," said Donnegan instantly, "and an avoider of work."

At that they laughed together. The strain was broken and in its place there was a mutual excitement. She saw Landis in the distance watching their laughter with a face contorted with anger, but it only increased her unreasoning happiness.

"Mr. Donnegan, let me give you friendly advice. I like you: I know you have courage; and I saw you meet Scar-faced Lewis. But if I were you I'd leave The Corner tonight and never come back. You've set every man against you. You've stepped on the toes of Landis and he's a big man here. And even if you were to prove too much for Jack you'd come against Lord Nick, as you say yourself. Do you know Nick?"

"No."

"Then, Mr. Donnegan, leave The Corner!"

The music, ending, left them face to face as he dropped his arm from about her. And she could appreciate now, for the first time, that he was smaller than he had seemed at a distance, or while he was dancing. He seemed a frail figure indeed to face the entire banded Corner—and Lord Nick.

"Don't you see," said Donnegan, "that I can't stop now?"

There was a double meaning that sent her color flaring.

He added in a low, tense voice, "I've gone too far. Besides, I'm beginning to hope!"

She paused, then made a little gesture of abandon.

"Then stay, stay!" she whispered with eyes on fire. "And good luck to you, Mr. Donnegan!"

## CHAPTER XXI

As they went back, toward Nelly's table, where Jack Landis was trying to appear carelessly at ease, the face of Donnegan was pale. One might have thought that excitement and fear caused his pallor; but as a matter of fact it was in him an unfailing sign of happiness and success. Landis had manners enough to rise as they approached. He found himself being presented to the smaller man. He heard the cool, precise voice of Donnegan acknowledging the introduction; and then the red-headed man went back to his table; and Jack Landis was alone with Nelly Lebrun again.

He scowled at her, and she tried to look repentant, but since she could not keep the dancing light out of her eyes, she compromised by looking steadfastly down at the table. Which convinced Landis that she was thinking of her late partner. He made a great effort, swallowed, and was able to speak smoothly enough.

"Looked as if you were having a pretty good time with that—tramp."

The color in her cheeks was anger; Landis took it for shame.

"He dances beautifully," she replied.

"Yeh; he's pretty smooth. Take a gent like that, it's hard for a girl to see through him."

"Let's not talk about him, Jack."

"All right. Is he going to dance with you again?"

"I promised him the third dance after this."

For a time Landis could not trust his voice. Then: "Kind of sorry about that. Because I'll be going home before then."

At this she raised her eyes for the first time. He was astonished and a little horrified to see that she was not in the least flustered, but very angry.

"You'll go home before I have a chance for that dance?" she asked. "You're acting like a two-year-old, Jack. You are!"

He flushed. Burning would be too easy a death for Donnegan.

"He's making a laughingstock out of me; look around the room!"

"Nobody's thinking about you at all, Jack. You're just self-conscious."

Of course, it was pouring acid upon an open wound. But she was past the point of caution.

"Maybe they ain't," said Landis, controlling his rage. "I don't figure that I amount to much. But I rate myself as high as a skunk like him!"

It may have been a smile that she gave him. At any rate, he caught the glint of teeth, and her eyes were as cold as steel points. If she had actually defended the stranger she would not have infuriated Landis so much.

"Well, what does he say about himself?"

"He says frankly that he's a vagrant."

"And you don't believe him?"

She did not speak.

"Makin' a play for sympathy. Confound a man like that, I say!"

Still she did not answer; and now Landis became alarmed.

"D'you really like him, Nelly?"

"I liked him well enough to introduce him to you, Jack."

"I'm sorry I talked so plain if you put it that way," he admitted heavily. "I didn't know you picked up friends so fast as all that!" He could not avoid adding this last touch of the poison point.

His back was to Donnegan, and consequently the girl, facing him, could look straight across the room at the red-headed man. She allowed herself one brief glance, and she saw that he was sitting with his elbow on the table, his chin in his hand, looking fixedly at her. It was the gaze of one who forgets all else and wraps himself in a dream. Other people in the room were noting that changeless stare and the whisper buzzed more and more loudly, but Donnegan had forgotten the rest of the world, it seemed. It was a very cunning piece of acting, not too much overdone, and once more the heart of Nelly Lebrun fluttered.

She remembered that in spite of his frankness he had not talked with insolent presumption to her. He had merely answered her individual questions with an astonishing, childlike frankness. He had laid his heart before her, it seemed. And now he sat at a distance looking at her with the white, intense face of one who sees a dream.

Nelly Lebrun was recalled by the heavy breathing of Jack Landis and she discovered that she had allowed her eyes to rest too long on the red-headed stranger. She had forgotten; her eyes had widened; and even Jack Landis was able to look into her mind and see things that startled him. For the first time he sensed that this was more than a careless flirtation. And he sat stiffly at the table, looking at her and through her with a fixed smile. Nelly, horrified, strove to cover her tracks.

"You're right, Jack," she said. "I—I think there was something brazen in the way he tagged you. And—let's go home together!"

Too late. The mind of Landis was not oversharp, but now jealousy gave it a point. He nodded his assent, and they got up, but there was no increase in his color. She read as plain as day in his face that he intended murder this night and Nelly was truly frightened.

So she tried different tactics. All the way to the substantial little house which Lebrun had built at a little distance from the gambling hall, she kept up a running fire of steady conversation. But when she said good night to him, his face was still set. She had not deceived him. When he turned, she saw him go back into the night with long strides, and within half an hour she knew, as clearly as if she were remembering the picture instead of foreseeing it, that Jack and Donnegan would face each other gun in hand on the floor of Milligan's dance hall.

Still, she was not foolish enough to run after Jack, take his arm, and make a direct appeal. It would be too much like begging for Donnegan, and even if Jack forgave her for this interest in his rival, she had sense enough to feel that Donnegan himself never would. Something, however, must be done to prevent the fight, and she took the straightest course.

She went as fast as a run would carry her straight behind the intervening houses and came to the back entrance to the gaming hall. There she entered and stepped into the little office of her father. Black Lebrun was not there. She did not want him. In his place there sat the Pedlar and Joe Rix; they were members of Lord Nick's chosen crew, and since Nick's temporary alliance with Lebrun for the sake of plundering Jack Landis, Nick's men were Nelly's men. Indeed, this was a formidable pair. They were the kind of men about whom many whispers and no facts circulate: and yet the facts are far worse than the whispers. It was said that Joe Rix, who was a fat little man with a great aversion to a razor and a pair of shallow, pale blue eyes, was in reality a merciless fiend. He was; and he was more than that, if there be a stronger superlative. If Lord Nick had dirty work to be done, there was the man who did it with a relish. The Pedlar, on the other hand, was an exact opposite. He was long, lean, raw-boned, and prodigiously strong in spite of his lack of flesh. He had vast hands, all loose skin and outstanding tendons; he had a fleshless face over which his smile was capable of extending limitlessly. He was the sort of a man from whom one would expect shrewdness, some cunning, stubbornness, a dry humor, and many principles. All of which, except the last, was true of the Pedlar.

There was this peculiarity about the Pedlar. In spite of his broad grins and his wise, bright eyes, none, even of Lord Nick's gang, extended a friendship or familiarity toward him. When they spoke of the Pedlar they never used his name. They referred to him as "him" or they indicated him with gestures. If he had a fondness for any living creature it was for fat Joe Rix.

Yet on seeing this ominous pair, Nelly Lebrun cried out softly in delight. She ran to them, and dropped a hand on the bony shoulder of the Pedlar and one on the plump shoulder of Joe Rix, whose loose flesh rolled under her fingertips.

"It's Jack Landis!" she cried. "He's gone to Milligan's to fight the new man. Stop him!"

"Donnegan?" said Joe, and did not rise.

"Him?" said the Pedlar, and moistened his broad lips like one on the verge of starvation.

"Are you going to sit here?" she cried. "What will Lord Nick say if he finds out you've let Jack get into a fight?"

"We ain't nursin' mothers," declared the Pedlar. "But I'd kind of like to look on!"

And he rose. Unkinking joint after joint, straightening his legs, his back, his shoulders, his neck, he soared up and up until he stood a prodigious height. The girl controlled a shudder of disgust.

"Joe!" she appealed.

"You want us to clean up Donnegan?" he asked, rising, but without interest in his voice.

To his surprise, she slipped back to the door and blocked it with her outcast arms.

"Not a hair of his head!" she said fiercely. "Swear that you won't harm him, boys!"

"What the devil!" ejaculated Joe, who was a blunt man in spite of his fat. "You want us to keep Jack from fightin', but you don't want us to hurt the other gent. What you want? Hogtie 'em both?"

"Yes, yes; keep Jack out of Milligan's; but for heaven's sake don't try to put a hand on Donnegan."

"Why not?"

"For your sakes; he'd kill you, Joe!"

At this they both gaped in unison, and as one man they drawled in vast admiration: "Good heavens!"

"But go, go, go!" cried the girl.

And she shoved them through the door and into the night.

## CHAPTER XXII

To the people in Milligan's it had been most incredible that Jack Landis should withdraw from a competition of any sort. And though the girls were able to understand his motives in taking Nelly Lebrun away they were not able to explain this fully to their men companions. For one and all they admitted that Jack was imperiling his hold on the girl in question if he allowed her to stay near this red-headed fiend. But one and all they swore that Jack Landis had ruined himself with her by taking her away. And this was a paradox which made masculine heads in The Corner spin. The main point was that Jack Landis had backed down before a rival; and this fact was stunning enough. Donnegan, however, was not confused. He sent big George to ask Milligan to come to him for a moment.

Milligan, at this, cursed George, but he was drawn by curiosity to consent. A moment later he was seated at Donnegan's table, drinking his own liquor as it was served to him from the hands of big George. If the first emotions of the dance-hall proprietor were anger and intense curiosity, his second emotion was that never-failing surprise which all who came close to the wanderer felt. For he had that rare faculty of seeming larger when in action, even when actually near much bigger men. Only when one came close to Donnegan one stepped, as it were, through a veil, and saw the almost fragile reality. When Milligan had caught his breath and adjusted himself, he began as follows:

"Now, Bud," he said, "you've made a pretty play. Not bad at all. But no more bluffs in Milligan's."

"Bluff!" Donnegan repeated gently.

"About your servant. I let it pass for one night, but not for another."

"My dear Mr. Milligan! However"—changing the subject easily—"what I wish to speak to you about is a bit of trouble which I foresee. I think, sir, that Jack Landis is coming back."

"What makes you think that?"

"It's a feeling I have. I have queer premonitions, Mr. Milligan, I'm sure he's coming and I'm sure he's going to attempt a murder."

Milligan's thick lips framed his question but he did not speak: fear made his face ludicrous.

"Right here?"

"Yes."

"A shootin' scrape here! You?"

"He has me in mind. That's why I'm speaking to you."

"Don't wait to speak to me about it. Get up and get out!"

"Mr. Milligan, you're wrong. I'm going to stay here and you're going to protect me."

"Well, confound your soul! They ain't much nerve about you, is there?"

"You run a public place. You have to protect your patrons from insult."

"And who began it, then? Who started walkin' on Jack's toes? Now you come whinin' to me! By heck, I hope Jack gets you!"

"You're a genial soul," said Donnegan. "Here's to you!"

But something in his smile as he sipped his liquor made Milligan sit straighter in his chair.

As for Donnegan, he was thinking hard and fast. If there were a shooting affair and he won, he would nevertheless run a close chance of being hung by a mob. He must dispose that mob to look upon him as the defendant and Landis as the aggressor. He had not foreseen the crisis until it was fairly upon him. He had thought of Nelly playing Landis along more gradually and carefully, so that, while he was slowly learning that she was growing cold to him, he would have a chance to grow fond of Lou Macon once more. But even across the width of the room he had seen the girl fire up, and from that moment he knew the result. Landis already suspected him; Landis, with the feeling that he had been robbed, would do his best to kill the thief. He might take a chance with Landis, if it came to a fight, just as he had taken a chance with Lewis. But how different this case would be! Landis was no dull-nerved ruffian and drunkard. He was a keen boy with a hair-trigger balance, and in a gunplay he would be apt to beat the best of them all. Of all this Donnegan was fully aware. Either he must place his own life in terrible hazard or else he must shoot to kill; and if he killed, what of Lou Macon?

While he smiled into the face of Milligan, perspiration was bursting out under his armpits.

"Mr. Milligan, I implore you to give me your aid."

"What's the difference?" Milligan asked in a changed tone. "If he don't fight you here he'll fight you later."

"You're wrong, Mr. Milligan. He isn't the sort to hold malice. He'll come here tonight and try to get at me like a bulldog straining on a leash. If he is kept away he'll get over his bad temper."

Milligan pushed back his chair.

"You've tried to force yourself down the throat of The Corner," he said, "and now you yell for help when you see the teeth."

He had raised his voice. Now he got up and strode noisily away. Donnegan waited until he was halfway across the dance floor and then rose in turn.

"Gentlemen," he said.

The quiet voice cut into every conversation; the musicians lowered the instruments.

"I have just told Mr. Milligan that I am sure Jack Landis is coming back here to try to kill me. I have asked for his protection. He has refused it. I intend to stay here and wait for him, Jack Landis. In the meantime I ask any able-bodied man who will do so, to try to stop Landis when he enters."

He sat down, raised his glass, and sipped the drink. Two hundred pairs of eyes were fastened with hawklike intensity upon him, and they could perceive no quiver of his hand.

The sipping of his liquor was not an affectation. For he was drinking, at incredible cost, liquors from Milligan's store of rareties.

The effect of Donnegan's announcement was first a silence, then a hum, then loud voices of protest, curiosity—and finally a scurrying toward the doors.

Yet really very few left. The rest valued a chance to see the fight beyond the fear of random slugs of lead which might fly their way. Besides, where such men as Donnegan and big Jack Landis were concerned, there was not apt to be much wild shooting. The dancing stopped, of course. The finish was ordered by Milligan to play, in a frantic endeavor to rouse custom again; but the music of its own accord fell away in the middle of the piece. For the musicians could not watch the notes and the door at the same time.

As for Donnegan, he found that it was one thing to wait and another to be waited for. He, too, wished to turn and watch that door until it should be filled by the bulk of Jack Landis. Yet he fought the desire.

And in the midst of this torturing suspense an idea came to him, and at the same instant Jack Landis entered the doorway. He stood there looking vast against the night. One glance around was sufficient to teach him the meaning of the silence. The stage was set, and the way opened to Donnegan. Without a word, big George stole to one side.

Straight to the middle of the dance floor went Jack Landis, red-faced, with long, heavy steps. He faced Donnegan.

"You skunk!" shouted Landis. "I've come for you!"

And he went for his gun. Donnegan, too, stirred. But when the revolver leaped into the hand of Landis, it was seen that the hands of Donnegan rose past the line of his waist, past his shoulders, and presently locked easily behind his head. A terrible chance, for Landis had come within a breath of shooting. So great was the impulse that, as he checked the pressure of his forefinger, he stumbled a whole pace forward. He walked on.

"You need cause to fight?" he cried, striking Donnegan across the face with the back of his left hand, jerking up the muzzle of the gun in his right.

Now a dark trickle was seen to come from the broken lips of Donnegan, yet he was smiling faintly.

Jack Landis muttered a curse and said sneeringly: "Are you afraid?"

There were sick faces in that room; men turned their heads, for nothing is so ghastly as the sight of a man who is taking water.

"Hush," said Donnegan. "I'm going to kill you, Jack. But I want to kill you fairly and squarely. There's no pleasure, you see, in beating a youngster like you to the draw. I want to give you a fighting chance. Besides"—he removed one hand from behind his head and waved it carelessly to where the men of The Corner crouched in the shadow—"you people have seen me drill one chap already, and I'd like to shoot you in a new way. Is that agreeable?"

Two terrible, known figures detached themselves from the gloom near the door.

"Hark to this gent sing," said one, and his name was the Pedlar. "Hark to him sing, Jack, and we'll see that you get fair play."

"Good," said his friend, Joe Rix. "Let him take his try, Jack."

As a matter of fact, had Donnegan reached for a gun, he would have been shot before even Landis could bring out a weapon, for the steady eye of Joe Rix, hidden behind the Pedlar, had been looking down a revolver barrel at the forehead of Donnegan, waiting for that first move. But something about the coolness of Donnegan fascinated them.

"Don't shoot, Joe," the Pedlar had said. "That bird is the chief over again. Don't plug him!"

And that was why Donnegan lived.

## CHAPTER XXII

If he had taken the eye of the hardened Rix and the still harder Pedlar, he had stunned the men of The Corner. And breathlessly they waited for his proposal to Jack Landis.

He spoke with his hands behind his head again, after he had slowly taken out a handkerchief and wiped his chin.

"I'm a methodical fellow, Landis," he said. "I hate to do an untidy piece of work. I have been disgusted with myself since my little falling out with Lewis. I intended to shoot him cleanly through the hand, but instead of that I tore up his whole forearm. Sloppy work, Landis. I don't like it. Now, in meeting you, I want to do a clean, neat, precise job. One that I'll be proud of."

A moaning voice was heard faintly in the distance. It was the Pedlar, who had wrapped himself in his gaunt arms and was crooning softly, with unspeakable joy: "Hark to him sing! Hark to him sing! A ringer for the chief!"

"Why should we be in such a hurry?" continued Donnegan. "You see that clock in the corner? Tut, tut! Turn your head and look. Do you think I'll drop you while you look around?"

Landis flung one glance over his shoulder at the big clock, whose pendulum worked solemnly back and forth.

"In five minutes," said Donnegan, "it will be eleven o'clock. And when it's eleven o'clock the clock will chime. Now, Landis, you and I shall sit down here like gentlemen and drink our liquor and think our last thoughts. Heavens, man, is there anything more disagreeable than being hurried out of life? But when the clock chimes, we draw our guns and shoot each other through the heart—the brain—wherever we have chosen. But, Landis, if one of us should inadvertently—or through nervousness—beat the clock's chime by the split part of a second, the good people of The Corner will fill that one of us promptly full of lead."

He turned to the crowd.

"Gentlemen, is it a good plan?"

As well as a Roman crowd if it wanted to see a gladiator die, the mayor history of The Corner responded to the stimulus of this delightful entertainment. There was a joyous chorus of approval.

"When the clock strikes, then," said Landis, and flung himself down in a chair, setting his teeth over his rage.

Donnegan smiled benevolently upon him; then he turned again and beckoned to George. The big man strode closer and leaned.

"George," he said. "I'm not going to kill this fellow."

"No, sir; certainly, sir," whispered the other. "George can kill him for you, sir."

Donnegan smiled wanly.

"I'm not going to kill him, George, on account of the girl on the hill. You know? And the reason is that she's fond of the lubber. I'll try to break his nerve, George, and drill him through the arm, say. No, I can't take chances like that. But if I have him shaking in time, I'll shoot him through the right shoulder, George.

"But if I miss and he gets me instead, mind you, never raise a hand against him. If you so much as touch his skin, I'll rise out of my grave and haunt you. You hear? Good-by, George."

But big George withdrew without a word, and the reason for his speechlessness was the glistening of his eyes.

"If I live," said Donnegan, "I'll show that George that I appreciate him."

He went on aloud to Landis: "So glum, my boy? Tush! We have still four minutes left. Are you going to spend your last four minutes hating me?"

He turned: "Another liqueur, George. Two of them."

The big man brought the drinks, and having put one on the table of Donnegan, he was directed to take the other to Landis.

"It's really good stuff," said Donnegan. "I'm not an expert on these matters; but I like the taste. Will you try it?"

It seemed that Landis dared not trust himself to speech. As though a vast and deadly hatred were gathered in him, and he feared lest it should escape in words the first time he parted his teeth.

He took the glass of liqueur and slowly poured it upon the floor. From the crowd there was a deep murmur of disapproval. And Landis, feeling that he had advanced the wrong foot in the matter, glowered scornfully about him and then stared once more at Donnegan.

"Just as you please," said Donnegan, sipping his glass. "But remember this, my young friend, that a fool is a fool, drunk or sober."

Landis showed his teeth, but made no other answer. And Donnegan anxiously flashed a glance at the clock. He still had three minutes. Three minutes in which he must reduce this stalwart fellow to a trembling, nervous wreck. Otherwise, he must shoot to kill, or else sit there and become a certain sacrifice for the sake of Lou Macon. Yet he controlled the muscles of his face and was still able to smile as he turned again to Landis.

"Three minutes left," he said. "Three minutes for you to compose yourself, Landis. Think of it, man! All the good life behind you. Have you nothing to remember? Nothing to soften your mind? Why die, Landis, with a curse in your heart and a scowl on your lips?"

Once more Landis stirred his lips; but there was only the flash of his teeth; he maintained his resolute silence.

"Ah," murmured Donnegan, "I am sorry to see this. And before all your admirers, Landis. Before all your friends. Look at them scattered there under the lights and in the shadows. No farewell word for them? Nothing kindly to say? Are you going to leave them without a syllable of goodfellowship?"

"Confound you!" muttered Landis.

There was another hum from the crowd; it was partly wonder, partly anger. Plainly they were not pleased with Jack Landis on this day.

Donnegan shook his head sadly.

"I hoped," he said, "that I could teach you how to die. But I fail. And yet you should be grateful to me for one thing, Jack. I have kept you from being a murderer in cold blood. I kept you from killing a defenseless man as you intended to do when you walked up to me a moment ago."

He smiled genially in mockery, and there was a scowl on the face of Landis. "Two minutes," said Donnegan.

Leaning back in his chair, he yawned. For a whole minute he did not stir. "One minute?" he murmured inquisitively.

And there was a convulsive shudder through the limbs of Landis. It was the first sign that he was breaking down under the strain. There remained only one minute in which to reduce him to a nervous wreck!

The strain was telling in other places. Donnegan turned and saw in the shadow and about the edges of the room a host of drawn, tense faces and burning eyes. Never while they lived would they forget that scene.

"And now that the time is close," said Donnegan, "I must look to my gun."

He made a gesture; how it was, no one was swift enough of eye to tell, but a gun appeared in his hand. At the flash of it, Landis' weapon leaped up to the mark and his face convulsed. But Donnegan calmly spun the cylinder of his revolver and held it toward Landis, dangling from his forefinger under the guard.

"You see?" he said to Landis. "Clean as a whistle, and easy as a girl's smile. I hate a stiff action, Jack."

And Landis slowly allowed the muzzle of his own gun to sink. For the first time his eyes left the eyes of Donnegan, and sinking, inch by inch, stared fascinated at the gun in the hand of the enemy.

"Thirty seconds," said Donnegan by way of conversation.

Landis jerked up his head and his eyes once more met the eyes of Donnegan, but this time they were wide, and the pointed glance of Donnegan sank into them. The lips of Landis parted. His tongue tremblingly moistened them.

"Keep your nerve," said Donnegan in an undertone.

"You hound!" gasped Landis.

"I knew it," said Donnegan sadly. "You'll die with a curse on your lips."

He added: "Ten seconds, Landis!"

And then he achieved his third step toward victory, for Landis jerked his head around, saw the minute hand almost upon its mark, and swung back with a shudder toward Donnegan. From the crowd there was a deep breath.

And then Landis was seen to raise the muzzle of his gun again, and crouch over it, leveling it straight at Donnegan. He, at least, would send his bullet straight to the mark when that first chime went humming through the big room.

But Donnegan? He made his last play to shatter the nerve of Landis. With the minute hand on the very mark, he turned carelessly, the revolver still dangling by the trigger guard, and laughed toward the crowd.

And out of the crowd there came a deep, sobbing breath of heartbreaking suspense.

It told on Landis. Out of the corner of his eye Donnegan saw the muscles of the man's face sag and tremble; saw him allow his gun to fall, in imitation of Donnegan, to his side; and saw the long arm quivering.

And then the chime rang, with a metallic, sharp click and then a long and reverberant clanging.

With a gasp Landis whipped up his gun and fired. Once, twice, again, the weapon crashed. And, to the eternal wonder of all who saw it, at a distance of five paces Landis three times missed his man. But Donnegan, sitting back with a smile, raised his own gun almost with leisure, unhurried, dropped it upon the mark, and sent a forty-five slug through the right shoulder of Jack Landis.

The blow of the slug, like the punch of a strong man's fist, knocked the victim out of his chair to the floor. He lay clutching at his shoulder.

"Gentlemen," said Donnegan, rising, "is there a doctor here?"

## CHAPTER XXIV

That was the signal for the rush that swept across the floor and left a flood of marveling men around the fallen Landis. On the outskirts of this tide, Donnegan stepped up to two men, Joe Rix and the Pedlar. They greeted him with expectant glances.

"Gentlemen," said Donnegan, "will you step aside?"

They followed him to a distance from the clamoring group.

"I have to thank you," said Donnegan.

"For what?"

"For changing your minds," said Donnegan, and left them.

And afterward the Pedlar murmured with an oddly twisted face: "Cat-eye, Joe. He can see in the dark! But I told you he was worth savin'."

"Speakin' in general," said Joe, "which you ain't hardly ever wrong when you get stirred up about a thing."

"He's something new," the Pedlar said wisely.

"Ay, he's rare."

"But talkin' aside, suppose he was to meet up with Lord Nick?"

The smile of Joe Rix was marvelously evil.

"You got a great mind for great things," he declared. "You ought to of been in politics."

In the meantime the doctor had been found. The wound had been cleansed. It was a cruel one, for the bullet had torn its way through flesh and sinew, and for many a week the fighting arm of Jack Landis would be useless. It had, moreover, carried a quantity of cloth into the wound, and it was almost impossible to cleanse the hole satisfactorily. As for the bullet itself, it had whipped cleanly through, at that short distance making nothing of its target.

A door was knocked off its hinges. But before the wounded man was placed upon it, Lebrun appeared at the door into Milligan's. He was never a very cheery fellow in appearance, and now he looked like a demoniac. He went straight to Joe Rix and the skeleton form of the Pedlar. He raised one finger as he looked at them.

"I've heard," said Lebrun. "Lord Nick likewise shall hear."

Joe Rix changed color. He bustled about, together with the Pedlar, and lent a hand in carrying the wounded man to the house of Lebrun, for Nelly Lebrun was to be the nurse of Landis.

In the meantime, Donnegan went up the hill with big George behind him. Already he was a sinisterly marked man. Working through the crowd near Lebrun's gambling hall, a drunkard in the midst of a song stumbled against him. But the sight of the man with whom he had collided, sobered him as swiftly as the lash of a whip across his face. It was impossible for him, in that condition, to grow pale. But he turned a vivid purple.

"Sorry, Mr. Donnegan."

Donnegan, with a shrug of his shoulders, passed on. The crowd split before him, for they had heard his name. There were brave men, he knew, among them. Men who would fight to the last drop of blood rather than be shamed, but they shrank from Donnegan without shame, as they would have shrunk from the coming of a rattler had their feet been bare. So he went easily through the crowd with big George in his wake, walking proudly.

For George had stood to one side and watched Donnegan indomitably beat down the will of Jack Landis, and the sight would live in his mind forever. Indeed, if Donnegan had bidden the sun to stand in the heavens, the big man would have looked for obedience. That the forbearance of Donnegan should have been based on a desire to serve a girl certainly upset the mind of George, but it taught him an amazing thing—that Donnegan was capable of affection.

The terrible Donnegan went on. In his wake the crowd closed slowly, for many had paused to look after the little man. Until they came to the outskirts of the town and climbed the hill toward the two shacks. The one was, of course, dark. But the shack in which Lou Macon lived burst with light. Donnegan paused to consider this miracle. He listened, and he heard voices—the voice of a man, laughing loudly. Thinking something was wrong, he hurried forward and called loudly.

What he saw when he was admitted made him speechless. Colonel Macon, ensconced in his invalid chair, faced the door, and near him was Lou Macon. Lou rose, half-frightened by the unexpected interruption, but the liquid laughter of the colonel set all to rights at once.

"Come in, Donnegan. Come in, lad," said the colonel.

"I heard a man's voice," Donnegan said half apologetically. The sick color began to leave his face, and relief swept over it slowly. "I thought something might be wrong. I didn't think of you." And looking down, as all men will in moments of relaxation from a strain, he did not see the eyes of Lou Macon grow softly luminous as they dwelt upon him.

"Come in, George," went on the colonel, "and make yourself comfortable in the kitchen. Close the door. Sit down, Donnegan. When your letter came I saw that I was needed here. Lou, have you looked into our friend's cabin? No? Nothing like a woman's touch to give a man the feeling of homeliness, Lou. Step over to Donnegan's cabin and put it to rights. Yes, I know that George takes care of it, but George is one thing, and your care will be another. Besides, I must be alone with him for a moment. Man talk confuses a girl, Lou. You shouldn't listen to it."

She withdrew with that faint, dreamy smile with which she so often heard the instructions of her father; as though she were only listening with half of her mind. When she was gone, though the door to the kitchen stood wide open, and big George was in it, the colonel lowered his bass voice so successfully that it was as safe as being alone with Donnegan.

"And now for facts," he began.

"But," said Donnegan, "how—that chair—how in the world have you come here?"

The colonel shook his head.

"My dear boy, you grieve and disappoint me. The manner in which a thing is done is not important. Mysteries are usually simply explained. As for my small mystery—a neighbor on the way to The Corner with a wagon stopped in, and I asked him to take me along. So here I am. But now for your work here, lad?"

"Bad," said Donnegan.

"I gathered you had been unfortunate. And now you have been fighting?"

"You have heard?"

"I see it in your eye, Donnegan. When a man has been looking fear in the face for a time, an image of it remains in his eyes. They are wider, glazed with the other thing."

"It was forced on me," said Donnegan. "I have shot Landis."

He was amazed to see the colonel was vitally affected. His lips remained parted over his next word, and one eyelid twitched violently. But the spasm passed over quickly. When he raised his perfect hands and pressed them together just under his chin. He smiled in a most winning manner that made the blood of Donnegan run cold.

"Donnegan," he said softly, "I see that I have misjudged you. I underestimated you. I thought, indeed, that your rare qualities were qualified by painful weaknesses. But now I see that you are a man, and from this moment we shall act together with open minds. So you have done it? Tush, then I need not have taken my trip. The work is done; the mines come to me as the heir of Jack. And yet, poor boy, I pity him! He misjudged me; he should not have ventured to this deal with Lord Nick and his compatriots!"

"Wait," exclaimed Donnegan. "You're wrong; Landis is not dead."

Once more the colonel was checked, but this time the alteration in his face was no more than a comma's pause in a long balanced sentence. It was impossible to obtain more than one show of emotion from him in a single conversation.

"Not dead? Well, Donnegan, that is unfortunate. And after you had punctured him you had no chance to send home the finishing shot?"

Donnegan merely watched the colonel and tapped his bony finger against the point of his chin.

"Ah," murmured the colonel, "I see another possibility. It is almost as good—it may even be better than his death. You have disabled him, and having done this you at once take him to a place where he shall be under your surveillance—this, in fact, is a very comfortable outlook—for me and my interests. But for you, Donnegan, how the devil do you benefit by having Jack flat on his back, sick, helpless, and in a perfect position to excite all the sympathies of Lou?"

Now, Donnegan had known cold-blooded men in his day, but that there existed such a man as the colonel had never come into his mind. He looked upon the colonel, therefore, with neither disgust nor anger, but with a distant and almost admiring wonder. For perfect evil always wins something akin to admiration from more common people.

"Well," continued the colonel, a little uneasy under this silent scrutiny— silence was almost the only thing in the world that could trouble him—"well, Donnegan, my lad, this is your plan, is it not?"

"To shoot down Landis, then take possession of him and while I nurse him back to health hold a gun—metaphorically speaking—to his head and make him do as I please: sign some lease, say, of the mines to you?"

The colonel shifted himself to a more comfortable position in his chair, brought the tips of his fingers together under his vast chin, and smiled benevolently upon Donnegan.

"It is as I thought," he murmured. "Donnegan, you are rare; you are exquisite!"

"And you," said Donnegan, "are a scoundrel."

"Exactly. I am very base." The colonel laughed. "You and I alone can speak with intimate knowledge of me." His chuckle shook all his body, and set the folds of his face quivering. His mirth died away when he saw Donnegan come to his feet.

"Eh?" he called.

"Good-by," said Donnegan.

"But where—Landis—Donnegan, what devil is in your eye?"

"A foolish devil, Colonel Macon. I surrender the benefits of all my work for you and go to make sure that you do not lay your hands upon Jack Landis."

The colonel opened and closed his lips foolishly like a fish gasping silently out of water. It was rare indeed for the colonel to appear foolish.

"In heaven's name, Donnegan!"

The little man smiled. He had a marvelously wicked smile, which came from the fact that his lips could curve while his eyes remained bright and straight, and malevolently unwrinkled. He laid his hand on the knob of the door.

"Donnegan," cried the colonel, gray of face, "give me one minute."

## CHAPTER XXV

Donnegan stepped to a chair and sat down. He took out his watch and held it in his hand, studying the dial, and the colonel knew that his time limit was taken literally.

"I swear to you," he said, "that if you can help me to the possession of Landis while he is ill, I shall not lay a finger upon him or harm him in any way."

"You swear?" said Donnegan with that ugly smile.

"My dear boy, do you think I am reckless enough to break a promise I have given to you?"

The cynical glance of Donnegan probed the colonel to the heart, but the eyes of the fat man did not wince. Neither did he speak again, but the two calmly stared at each other. At the end of the minute, Donnegan slipped the watch into his pocket.

"I am ready to listen to reason," he said. And the colonel passed one of his strong hands across his forehead.

"Now," and he sighed, "I feel that the crisis is passed. With a man of your caliber, Donnegan, I fear a snap judgment above all things. Since you give me a chance to appeal to your reason I feel safe. As from the first, I shall lay my cards upon the table. You are fond of Lou. I took it for granted that you would welcome a chance to brush Landis out of your path. It appears that I am wrong. I admit my error. Only fools cling to convictions; wise men are ready to meet new viewpoints. Very well. You wish to spare Landis for reasons of your own which I do not pretend to fathom. Perhaps, you pity him; I cannot tell. Now, you wonder why I wish to have Landis in my care if I do not intend to put an end to him and thereby become owner of his mines? I shall tell you frankly. I intend to own the mines, if not through the death of Jack, then through a legal act signed by the hand of Jack."

"A willing signature?" asked Donnegan, calmly.

A shadow came and went across the face of the colonel, and Donnegan caught his breath. There were times when he felt that if the colonel possessed strength of body as well as strength of mind even he, Donnegan, would be afraid of the fat man.

"Willing or unwilling," said the colonel, "he shall do as I direct!"

"Without force?"

"Listen to me," said the colonel. "You and I are not children, and therefore we know that ordinary men are commanded rather by fear of what may happen to them than by being confronted with an actual danger. I have told you that I shall not so much as raise the weight of a finger against Jack Landis. I shall not. But a whisper adroitly put in his ear may accomplish the same ends." He added with a smile. "Personally, I dislike physical violence. In that, Mr. Donnegan, we belong to opposite schools of action."

The picture came to Donnegan of Landis, lying in the cabin of the colonel, his childish mind worked upon by the devilish insinuation of the colonel. Truly, if Jack did not go mad under the strain he would be very apt to do as the colonel wished.

"I have made a mess of this from the beginning," said Donnegan, quietly. "In the first place, I intended to play the role of the self-sacrificing. You don't understand? I didn't expect that you would. In short, I intended to send Landis back to Lou by making a flash that would dazzle The Corner, and dazzle Nelly Lebrun as well—win her away from Landis, you see? But the fool, as soon as he saw that I was flirting with the girl, lowered his head and charged at me like a bull. I had to strike him down in self-defense.

"But now you ask me to put him wholly in your possession. Colonel, you omit one link in your chain of reasoning. The link is important—to me. What am I to gain by placing him within the range of your whispering?"

"Tush! Do I need to tell you? I still presume you are interested in Lou, though you attempted to do so much to give Landis back to her. Well, Donnegan, you must know that when she learns it was a bullet from your gun that struck down Landis, she'll hate you, my boy, as if you were a snake. But if she knows that after all you were forced into the fight, and that you took the first opportunity to bring Jack into my—er—paternal care—her sentiments may change. No, they will change."

Donnegan left his chair and began to pace the floor. He was no more self-conscious in the presence of the colonel than a man might be in the presence of his own evil instincts. And it was typical of the colonel's insight that he made no attempt to influence the decision of Donnegan after this point was reached. He allowed him to work out the matter in his own way. At length, Donnegan paused.

"What's the next step?" he asked.

The colonel sighed, and by that sigh he admitted more than words could tell.

"A reasonable man," he said, "is the delight of my heart. The next step, Donnegan, is to bring Jack Landis to this house."

"Tush!" said Donnegan. "Bring him away from Lebrun? Bring him away from the tigers of Lord Nick's gang? I saw them at Milligan's place tonight. A bad set, Colonel Macon."

"A set you can handle," said the colonel, calmly.

"Ah?"

"The danger will in itself be the thing that tempts you," he went on. "To go among those fellows, wild as they are, and bring Jack Landis away to this house."

"Bring him here," said Donnegan with indescribable bitterness, "so that she may pity his wounds? Bring him here where she may think of him and tend him and grow to hate me?"

"Grow to fear you," said the colonel.

"An excellent thing to accomplish," said Donnegan coldly.

"I have found it so," remarked the colonel, and lighted a cigarette.

He drew the smoke so deep that when it issued again from between his lips it was a most transparent, bluish vapor. Fear came upon Donnegan. Not fear, surely, of the fat man, helpless in his invalid's chair, but fear of the mind working ceaselessly behind those hazy eyes. He turned without a word and went to the door. The moment it opened under his hand, he felt a hysterical impulse to leap out of the room swiftly and slam the door behind him—to put a bar between him and the eye of the colonel, just as a child leaps from the dark room into the lighted and closes the door quickly to keep out the following night. He had to compel himself to move with proper dignity.

When outside, he sighed; the quiet of the night was like a blessing compared with the ordeal of the colonel's devilish coldness. Macon's advice had seemed almost logical the moment before. Win Lou Macon by the power of fear, well enough, for was not fear the thing which she had followed all her life? Was it not through fear that the colonel himself had reduced her to such abject, unquestioning obedience?

He went thoughtfully to his own cabin, and, down-headed in his musings, he became aware with a start of Lou Macon in the hut. She had changed the room as her father had bidden her to do. Just wherein the difference lay, Donnegan could not tell. There was a touch of evergreen in one corner; she had laid a strip of bright cloth over the rickety little table, and in ten minutes she had given the hut a semblance of permanent livableness. Donnegan saw her now, with some vestige of the smile of her art upon her face; but she immediately smoothed it to perfect gravity. He had never seen such perfect self-command in a woman.

"Is there anything more that I can do?" she asked, moving toward the door.

"Nothing."

"Good night."

"Wait."

She still seemed to be under the authority which the colonel had delegated to Donnegan when they started for The Corner. She turned, and without a word came back to him. And a pang struck through Donnegan. What would he not have given if she had come at his call not with these dumb eyes, but with a spark of kindliness? Instead, she obeyed him as a soldier obeys a commander.

"There has been trouble," said Donnegan.

"Yes?" she said, but there was no change in her face.

"It was forced upon me." Then he added: "It amounted to a shooting affair."

There was a change in her face now, indeed. A glint came in her eyes, and the suggestion of the colonel which he had once or twice before sensed in her, now became more vivid than ever before. The same contemptuous heartlessness, which was the colonel's most habitual expression, now looked at Donnegan out of the lovely face of the girl.

"They were fools to press you to the wall," she said. "I have no pity for them."

For a moment Donnegan only stared at her; on what did she base her confidence in his prowess as a fighting man?

"It was only one man," he said huskily.

Ah, there he had struck her home! As though the words were a burden, she shrank from him; then she slipped suddenly close to him and caught both his hands. Her head was raised far back; she had pressed close to him; she seemed in every line of her body to plead with him against himself, and all the veils which had curtained her mind from him dropped away. He found himself looking down into eyes full of fire and shadow; and eager lips; and the fiber of her voice made her whole body tremble.

"It isn't Jack?" she pleaded. "It isn't Jack that you've fought with?"

And he said to himself: "She loves him with all her heart and soul!"

"It is he," said Donnegan in an agony. Pain may be like a fire that tempers some strong men; and now Donnegan, because he was in torment, smiled, and his eye was as cold as steel.

The girl flung away his hands.

"You bought murderer!" she cried at him.

"He is not dead."

"But you shot him down!"

"He attacked me; it was self-defense."

She broke into a low-pitched, mirthless laughter. Where was the filmy-eyed girl he had known? The laughter broke off short—like a sob.

"Don't you suppose I've known?" she said. "That I've read my father? That I knew he was sending a bloodhound when he sent you? But, oh, I thought you had a touch of the other thing!"

He cringed under her tone.

"I'll bring him to you," said Donnegan desperately. "I'll bring him here so that you can take care of him."

"You'll take him away from Lord Nick—and Lebrun—and the rest?" And it was the cold smile of her father with which she mocked him.

"I'll do it."

"You play a deep game," said the girl bitterly. "Why would you do it?"

"Because," said Donnegan faintly, "I love you."

Her hand had been on the knob of the door; now she twitched it open and was gone; and the last that Donnegan saw was the width of the startled eyes.

"As if I were a leper," muttered Donnegan. "By heaven, she looked at me as if I were unclean!"

But once outside the door, the girl stood with both hands pressed to her face, stunned. When she dropped them, they folded against her breast, and her face tipped up.

Even by starlight, had Donnegan been there to look, he would have seen the divinity which comes in the face of a woman when she loves.

## CHAPTER XXVI

Had he been there to see, even in the darkness he would have known, and he could have crossed the distance between their lives with a single step, and taken her into his heart. But he did not see. He had thrown himself upon his bunk and lay face down, his arms stretched rigidly out before him, his teeth set, his eyes closed.

For what Donnegan had wanted in the world, he had taken; by force when he could, by subtlety when he must. And now, what he wanted most of all was gone from him, he felt, forever. There was no power in his arms to take that part of her which he wanted; he had no craft which could encompass her.

Big George, stealing into the room, wondered at the lithe, slender form of the man in the bed. Seeing him thus, it seemed that with the power of one hand, George could crush him. But George would as soon have closed his fingers over a rattler. He slipped away into the kitchen and sat with his arms wrapped around his body, as frightened as though he had seen a ghost.

But Donnegan lay on the bed without moving for hours and hours, until big George, who sat wakeful and terrified all that time, was sure that he slept. Then he stole in and covered Donnegan with a blanket, for it was the chill, gray time of the night.

But Donnegan was not asleep, and when George rose in the morning, he found the master sitting at the table with his arms folded tightly across his breast and his eyes burning into vacancy.

He spent the day in that chair.

It was the middle of the afternoon when George came with a scared face and a message that a "gen'leman who looks riled, sir," wanted to see him. There was no answer, and George perforce took the silence as acquiescence. So he opened the door and announced: "Mr. Lester to see you, sir."

Into the fiery haze of Donnegan's vision stepped a raw-boned fellow with sandy hair and a disagreeably strong jaw.

"You're the gent that's here with the colonel, ain't you?" said Lester.

Donnegan did not reply.

"You're the gent that cleaned up on Landis, ain't you?" continued the sandy-haired man.

There was still the same silence, and Lester burst out: "It don't work, Donnegan. You've showed you're man-sized several ways since you been in The Corner. Now I come to tell you to get out from under Colonel Macon. Why? Because he's crooked, because we know he's crooked; because he played crooked with me. You hear me talk?"

Still Donnegan considered him without a word.

"We're goin' to run him out, Donnegan. We want you on our side if we can get you; if we can't get you, then we'll run you out along with the colonel."

He began to talk with difficulty, as though Donnegan's stare unnerved him. He even took a step back toward the door.

"You can't bluff me out, Donnegan. I ain't alone. They's others behind me. I don't need to name no names. Here's another thing: you ain't alone yourself. You got a woman and a cripple on your hands. Now, Donnegan, you're a fast man with a gun and you're a fast man at thinkin', but I ask you personal: have you got a chance runnin' under that weight?"

He added fiercely: "I'm through. Now, talk turkey, Donnegan, or you're done!"

For the first time Donnegan moved. It was to make to big George a significant signal with his thumb, indicating the visitor. However, Lester did not wait to be thrown bodily from the cabin. One enormous oath exploded from his lips, and he backed sullenly through the door and slammed it after him.

"It kind of looks," said big George, "like a war, sir."

And still Donnegan did not speak, until the afternoon was gone, and the evening, and the full black of the night had swallowed up the hills around The Corner.

Then he left the chair, shaved, and dressed carefully, looked to his revolver, stowed it carefully and invisibly away among his clothes, and walked leisurely down the hill. An outbreak of cursing, stamping, hair-tearing, shooting could not have affected big George as this quiet departure did. He followed, unordered, but as he stepped across the threshold of the hut he rolled up his eyes to the stars.

"Oh, heavens above," muttered George, "have mercy on Mr. Donnegan. He ain't happy."

And he went down the hill, making sure that he was fit for battle with knife and gun.

He had sensed Donnegan's mental condition accurately enough. The heart of the little man was swelled to the point of breaking. A twenty-hour vigil had whitened his face, drawn in his cheeks, and painted his eyes with shadow; and now he wanted action. He wanted excitement, strife, competition; something to fill his mind. And naturally enough he had two places in mind—Lebrun's and Milligan's.

It is hard to relate the state of Donnegan's mind at this time. Chiefly, he was conscious of a peculiar and cruel pain that made him hollow; it was like homesickness raised to the $n$th degree. Vaguely he realized that in some way, somehow, he must fulfill his promise to the girl and bring Jack Landis home. The colonel dared not harm the boy for fear of Donnegan; and the girl would be happy. For that very reason Donnegan wanted to tear Landis to shreds.

It is not extremely heroic for a man tormented with sorrow to go to a gambling hall and then to a dance hall to seek relief. But Donnegan was not a hero. He was only a man, and, since his heart was empty, he wanted something that might fill it. Indeed, like most men, suffering made him a good deal of a boy.

So the high heels of Donnegan tapped across the floor of Lebrun's. A murmur went before him whenever he appeared now, and a way opened for him. At the roulette wheel he stopped, placed fifty on red, and watched it double three times. George, at a signal from the master, raked in the winnings. And Donnegan sat at a faro table and won again, and again rose disconsolately and went on. For when men do not care how luck runs it never fails to favor them. The devotees of fortune are the ones she punishes.

In the meantime the whisper ran swiftly through The Corner.

"Donnegan is out hunting trouble."

About the good that is in men rumor often makes mistakes, but for evil she has an infallible eye and at once sets all of her thousand tongues wagging. Indeed, any man with half an eye could not fail to get the meaning of his fixed glance, his hard set jaw, and the straightness of his mouth. If he had been a ghost, men could not have avoided him more sedulously, and the giant servant who stalked at his back. Not that The Corner was peopled with cowards. The true Westerner avoids trouble, but cornered, he will fight like a wildcat.

So people watched from the corner of their eyes as Donnegan passed.

He left Lebrun's. There was no competition. Luck blindly favored him, and Donnegan wanted contest, excitement. He crossed to Milligan's. Rumor was there before him. A whisper conveyed to a pair of mighty-limbed cow-punchers that they were sitting at the table which Donnegan had occupied the night before, and they wisely rose without further hint and sought other chairs. Milligan, anxious-eyed, hurried to the orchestra, and with a blast of sound they sought to cover up the entry of the gunman.

As a matter of fact that blare of horns only served to announce him. Something was about to happen; the eyes of men grew shadowy; the eyes of women brightened. And then Donnegan appeared, with George behind him, and crossed the floor straight to his table of the night before. Not that he had forethought in going toward it, but he was moving absentmindedly.

Indeed, he had half forgotten that he was a public figure in The Corner, and sitting sipping the cordial which big George brought him at once, he let his glance rove swiftly around the room. The eye of more than one brave man sank under that glance; the eye of more than one woman smiled back at him; but where the survey of Donnegan halted was on the face of Nelly Lebrun.

She was crossing the farther side of the floor alone, unescorted except for the whisper about her, but seeing Donnegan she stopped abruptly. Donnegan instantly rose. She would have gone on again in a flurry; but that would have been too pointed.

A moment later Donnegan was threading his way across the dance floor to Nelly Lebrun, with all eyes turned in his direction. He had his hat under his arm; and in his black clothes, with his white stock, he made an old-fashioned figure as he bowed before the girl and straightened again.

"Did you send for me?" Donnegan inquired.

Nelly Lebrun was frankly afraid; and she was also delighted. She felt that she had been drawn into the circle of intense public interest which surrounded the red-headed stranger; she remembered on the other hand that her father would be furious if she exchanged two words with the man. And for that very reason she was intrigued. Donnegan, being forbidden fruit, was irresistible. So she let the smile come to her lips and eyes, and then laughed outright in her excitement.

"No," she said with her lips, while her eyes said other things.

"I've come to ask a favor: to talk with you one minute."

"If I should—what would people say?"

"Let's find out."

"It would be—daring," said Nelly Lebrun. "After last night."

"It would be delightful," said Donnegan. "Here's a table ready for us."

She went a pace closer to it with him.

"I think you've frightened the poor people away from it. I mustn't sit down with you, Mr. Donnegan."

And she immediately slipped into the chair.

## CHAPTER XXVII

She qualified her surrender, of course, by sitting on the very edge of the chair. She had on a wine-colored dress, and, with the excitement whipping color into her cheeks and her eyes dancing, Nelly Lebrun was a lovely picture.

"I must go at once," said Nelly.

"Of course, I can't expect you to stay."

She dropped one hand on the edge of the table. One would have thought that she was in the very act of rising.

"Do you know that you frighten me?"

"I?" said Donnegan, with appropriate inflection.

"As if I were a man and you were angry."

"But you see?" And he made a gesture with both of his palms turned up. "People have slandered me. I am harmless."

"The minute is up, Mr. Donnegan. What is it you wish?"

"Another minute."

"Now you laugh at me."

"No, no!"

"And in the next minute?"

"I hope to persuade you to stay till the third minute."

"Of course, I can't."

"I know; it's impossible."

"Quite." She settled into the chair. "See how people stare at me! They remember poor Jack Landis and they think—the whole crowd—"

"A crowd is always foolish. In the meantime, I'm happy."

"You?"

"To be here; to sit close to you; to watch you."

Her glance was like the tip of a rapier, searching him through for some iota of seriousness under this banter.

"Ah?" and Nelly Lebrun laughed.

"Don't you see that I mean it?"

"You can watch me from a distance, Mr. Donnegan."

"May I say a bold thing?"

"You have said several."

"No one can really watch you from a distance."

She canted her head a little to one side; such an encounter of personal quips was a seventh heaven to her.

"That's a riddle, Mr. Donnegan."

"A simple one. The answer is, because there's too much to watch."

He joined her when she laughed, but the laughter of Donnegan made not a sound, and he broke in on her mirth suddenly.

"Ah, don't you see I'm serious?"

Her glance flicked on either side, as though she feared someone might have read his lips.

"Not a soul can hear me," murmured Donnegan, "and I'm going to be bolder still, and tell you the truth."

"It's the last thing I dare stay to hear."

"You are too lovely to watch from a distance, Nelly Lebrun."

He was so direct that even Nelly Lebrun, expert in flirtations, was given pause, and became sober. She shook her head and raised a cautioning finger. But Donnegan was not shaken.

"Because there is a glamour about a beautiful girl," he said gravely. "One has to step into the halo to see her, to know her. Are you contented to look at a flower from a distance? That's an old comparison, isn't it? But there is something like a fragrance about you, Nelly Lebrun. Don't be afraid. No one can hear; no one shall ever dream I've said such bold things to you. In the meantime, we have a truth party. There is a fragrance, I say. It must be breathed. There is a glow which must touch one. As it touches me now, you see?"

Indeed, there was a faint color in his cheeks. And the girl flushed more deeply; her eyes were still bright, but they no longer sharpened to such a penetrating point. She was believing at least a little part of what he said, and her disbelief only heightened her joy in what was real in this strangest of lovemakings.

"I shall stay here to learn one thing," she said. "What deviltry is behind all this talk, Mr. Donnegan?"

"Is that fair to me? Besides, I only follow a beaten trail in The Corner."

"And that?"

"Toward Nelly Lebrun."

"A beaten trail? You?" she cried, with just a touch of anger. "I'm not a child, Mr. Donnegan!"

"You are not; and that's why I am frank."

"You have done all these things—following this trail you speak of?"

"Remember," said Donnegan soberly. "What have I done?"

"Shot down two men; played like an actor on a stage a couple of times at least, if I must be blunt; hunted danger like—like a reckless madman; dared all The Corner to cross you; flaunted the red rag in the face of the bull. Those are a few things you have done, sir! And all on one trail? That trail you spoke of?"

"Nelly Lebrun—"

"I'm listening; and do you know I'm persuading myself to believe you?"

"It's because you feel the truth before I speak it. Truth speaks for itself, you know."

"I have closed my eyes—you see? I have stepped into a masquerade. Now you can talk."

"Masquerades are exciting," murmured Donnegan.

"And they are sometimes beautiful."

"But this sober truth of mine—"

"Well?"

"I came here unknown—and I saw you, Nelly Lebrun."

He paused; she was looking a little past him.

"I came in rags; no friends; no following. And I saw that I should have to make you notice me."

"And why? No, I shouldn't have asked that."

"You shouldn't ask that," agreed Donnegan. "But I saw you the queen of The Corner, worshiped by all men. What could I do? I am not rich. I am not big. You see?"

He drew her attention to his smallness with a flush which never failed to touch the face of Donnegan when he thought of his size; and he seemed to swell and grow greater in the very instant she glanced at him.

"What could I do? One thing; fight. I have fought. I fought to get the eye of The Corner, but most of all to attract your attention. I came closer to you. I saw that one man blocked the way—mostly. I decided to brush him aside. How?"

"By fighting?" She had not been carried away by his argument. She was watching him like a lynx every moment.

"Not by that. By bluffing. You see, I was not fool enough to think that you would—particularly notice a fighting bully."

He laid his open hand on the table. It was like exposing both strength and weakness; and into such a trap it would have been a singularly hard-minded woman who might not have stepped. Nelly Lebrun leaned a little closer. She forgot to criticize.

"It was bluff. I saw that Landis was big and good-looking. And what was I beside him? Nothing. I could only hope that he was hollow; yellow—you see? So I tried the bluff. You know about it. The clock, and all that claptrap. But Landis wasn't yellow. He didn't crumble. He lasted long enough to call my bluff, and I had to shoot in self-defense. And then, when he lay on the floor, I saw that I had failed."

"Failed?"

He lowered his eyes for fear that she would catch the glitter of them.

"I knew that you would hate me for what I had done because I had only proved that Landis was a brave youngster with enough nerve for nine out of ten. And I came tonight—to ask you to forgive me. No, not that—only to ask you to understand. Do you?"

He raised his glance suddenly at that, and their eyes met with one of these electric shocks which will go tingling through two people. And when the lips of Nelly Lebrun parted a little, he knew that she was in the trap. He closed his hand that lay on the table—curling the fingers slowly. In that way he expressed all his exultation.

"There is something wrong," said the girl, in a tone of one who argues with herself. "It's all too logical to be real."

"Ah?"

"Was that your only reason for fighting Jack Landis?"

"Do I have to confess even that?"

She smiled in the triumph of her penetration, but it was a brief, unhappy smile. One might have thought that she would have been glad to be deceived.

"I came to serve a girl who was unhappy," said Donnegan. "Her fiancé had left her; her fiancé was Jack Landis. And she's now in a hut up the hill waiting for him. And I thought that if I ruined him in your eyes he'd go back to a girl who wouldn't care so much about bravery. Who'd forgive him for having left her. But you see what a fool I was and how clumsily I worked? My bluff failed, and I only wounded him, put him in your house, under your care, where he'll be happiest, and where there'll never be a chance for this girl to get him back."

Nelly Lebrun, with her folded hands under her chin, studied him.

"Mr. Donnegan," she said, "I wish I knew whether you are the most chivalrous, self-sacrificing of men, or simply the most gorgeous liar in the desert."

"And it's hardly fair," said Donnegan, "to expect me to tell you that."

# CHAPTER XXVIII

It gave them both a welcome opportunity to laugh, welcome to the girl because it broke into an excitement which was rapidly telling upon her, and welcome to Donnegan because the strain of so many distortions of the truth was telling upon him as well. They laughed together. One hasty glance told Donnegan that half the couples in the room were whispering about Donnegan and Nelly Lebrun; but when he looked across the table he saw that Nelly Lebrun had not a thought for what might be going on in the minds of others. She was quite content.

"And the girl?" she said.

Donnegan rested his forehead upon his hand in thought. He dared not let Nelly see his face at this moment, for the mention of Lou Macon had poured the old flood of sorrow back upon him And therefore, when he looked up, he was sneering.

"You know these blond, pretty girls?" he said.

"Oh, they are adorable!"

"With dull eyes," said Donnegan coldly, and a twinkle came into the responsive eye of Nelly Lebrun. "The sort of a girl who sees a hero in such a fellow as Jack Landis."

"And Jack is brave."

"I shouldn't have said that."

"Never mind. Brave, but such a boy."

"Are you serious?"

She looked questioningly at Donnegan and they smiled together, slowly.

"I—I'm glad it's that way," and Donnegan sighed.

"And did you really think it could be any other way?"

"I didn't know. I'm afraid I was blind."

"But the poor girl on the hill; I wish I could see her."

She was watching Donnegan very sharply again.

"A good idea. Why don't you?"

"You seem to like her?"

"Yes," said Donnegan judiciously. "She has an appealing way; I'm very sorry for her. But I've done my best; I can't help her."

"Isn't there some way?"

"Of what?"

"Of helping her."

Donnegan laughed. "Go to your father and persuade him to send Landis back to her."

She shook her head.

"Of course, that wouldn't do. There's business mixed up in all this, you know."

"Business? Well, I guessed at that."

"My part in it wasn't very pleasant," she remarked sadly.

Donnegan was discreetly silent, knowing that silence extracts secrets.

"They made me—flirt with poor Jack. I really liked him!"

How much the past tense may mean!

"Poor fellow," murmured the sympathetic Donnegan. "But why," with gathering heat, "couldn't you help me to do the thing I can't do alone? Why couldn't you get him away from the house?"

"With Joe Rix and the Pedlar guarding him?"

"They'll be asleep in the middle of the night."

"But Jack would wake up and make a noise."

"There are things that would make him sleep through anything."

"But how could he be moved?"

"On a horse litter kept ready outside."

"And how carried to the litter?"

"I would carry him." The girl looked at him with a question and then with a faint smile beginning. "Easily," said Donnegan, stiffening in his chair. "Very easily."

It pleased her to find this weakness in the pride of the invincible Donnegan. It gave her a secure feeling of mastery. So she controlled her smile and looked with a sort of superior kindliness upon the red-headed little man.

"It's no good," Nelly Lebrun said with a sigh. "Even if he were taken away—and then it would get you into a bad mess."

"Would it? Worse than I'm in?"

"Hush! Lord Nick is coming to The Corner; and no matter what you've done so far—I think I could quiet him. But if you were to take Landis away—then nothing could stop him."

Donnegan sneered.

"I begin to think Lord Nick is a bogie," he said. "Everyone whispers when they speak of him." He leaned forward. "I should like to meet him, Nelly Lebrun!"

It staggered Nelly. "Do you mean that?" she cried softly.

"I do."

She caught her breath and then a spark of deviltry gleamed. "I wonder!" said Nelly Lebrun, and her glance weighed Donnegan.

"All I ask is a fair chance," he said.

"He is a big man," said the girl maliciously.

The never-failing blush burned in the face of Donnegan.

"A large target is more easily hit," he said through his teeth.

Her thoughts played back and forth in her eyes.

"I can't do it," she said.

Donnegan played a random card.

"I was mistaken," he said darkly. "Jack was not the man I should have faced. Lord Nick!"

"No, no, no, Mr. Donnegan!"

"You can't persuade me. Well, I was a fool not to guess it!"

"I really think," said the girl gloomily, "that as soon as Lord Nick comes, you'll hunt him out!"

He bowed to her with cold politeness. "In spite of his size," said Donnegan through his teeth once more.

And at this the girl's face softened and grew merry.

"I'm going to help you to take Jack away," she said, "on one condition."

"And that?"

"That you won't make a step toward Lord Nick when he comes."

"I shall not avoid him," said Donnegan.

"You're unreasonable! Well, not avoid him, but simply not provoke him. I'll arrange it so that Lord Nick won't come hunting trouble."

"And he'll let Jack stay with the girl and her father?"

"Perhaps he'll persuade them to let him go of their own free will."

Donnegan thought of the colonel and smiled.

"In that case, of course, I shouldn't care at all." He added: "But do you mean all this?"

"You shall see."

They talked only a moment longer and then Donnegan left the hall with the girl on his arm. Certainly the thoughts of all in Milligan's followed that pair; and it was seen that Donnegan took her to the door of her house and then went away through the town and up the hill. And big George followed him like a shadow cast from a lantern behind a man walking in a fog.

In the hut on the hill, Donnegan put George quickly to work, and with a door and some bedding, a litter was hastily constructed and swung between the two horses. In the meantime, Donnegan climbed higher up the hill and watched steadily over the town until, in a house beneath him, two lights were shown. He came back at that and hurried down the hill with George behind and around the houses until they came to the pretentious cabin of the gambler, Lebrun.

Once there, Donnegan went straight to an unlighted window, tapped; and it was opened from within, softly. Nelly Lebrun stood within.

"It's done," she said. "Joe and the Pedlar are sound asleep. They drank too much."

"Your father."

"Hasn't come home."

"And Jack Landis?"

"No matter what you do, he won't wake up; but be careful of his shoulder. It's badly torn. How can you carry him?"

She could not see Donnegan's flush, but she heard his teeth grit. And he slipped through the window, gesturing to George to come close. It was still darker inside the room—far darker than the starlit night outside. And the one path of lighter gray was the bed of Jack Landis. His heavy breathing was the only sound. Donnegan kneeled beside him and worked his arms under the limp figure.

And while he kneeled there a door in the house was opened and closed softly. Donnegan stood up.

"Is the door locked?"

"No," whispered the girl.

"Quick!"

"Too late. It's father, and he'd hear the turning of the key."

They waited, while the light, quick step came down the hall of the cabin. It came to the door, it went past; and then the steps retraced and the door was opened gently.

There was a light in the hall; the form of Lebrun was outlined black and distinct.

"Jack!" he whispered.

No sound; he made as if to enter, and then he heard the heavy breathing of the sleeper, apparently.

"Asleep, poor fool," murmured the gambler, and closed the door.

The door was no sooner closed than Donnegan had raised the body of the sleeper. Once, as he rose, straining, it nearly slipped from his arms; and when he stood erect he staggered. But once he had gained his equilibrium, he carried the wounded man easily enough to the window through which George reached his long arms and lifted out the burden.

"You see?" said Donnegan, panting, to the girl.

"Yes; it was really wonderful!"

"You are laughing, now."

"I? But hurry. My father has a fox's ear for noises."

"He will not hear this, I think." There was a swift scuffle, very soft of movement.

"Nelly!" called a far-off voice.

"Hurry, hurry! Don't you hear?"

"You forgive me?"

"No—yes—but hurry!"

"You will remember me?"

"Mr. Donnegan!"

"Adieu!"

She caught a picture of him sitting in the window for the split part of a second, with his hat off, bowing to her. Then he was gone. And she went into the hall, panting with excitement.

"Heavens!" Nelly Lebrun murmured. "I feel as if I had been hunted, and I must look it. What if he—" Whatever the thought was she did not complete it. "It may have been for the best," added Nelly Lebrun.

## CHAPTER XXIX

It is your phlegmatic person who can waken easily in the morning, but an active mind readjusts itself slowly to the day. So Nelly Lebrun roused herself with an effort and scowled toward the door at which the hand was still rapping.

"Yes?" she called drowsily.

"This is Nick. May I come in?"

"This is who?"

The name had brought her instantly into complete wakefulness; she was out of the bed, had slipped her feet into her slippers and whipped a dressing gown around her while she was asking the question. It was a luxurious little boudoir which she had managed to equip. Skins of the lynx, cunningly matched, had been sewn together to make her a rug, and the soft fur of the wildcat was the outer covering of her bed. She threw back the tumbled bedclothes, tossed half a dozen pillows into place, transforming it into a day couch, and ran to the mirror.

And in the meantime, the deep voice outside the door was saying: "Yes, Nick. May I come in?"

She gave a little ecstatic cry, but while it was still tingling on her lips, she was winding her hair into shape with lightning speed; had dipped the tips of her fingers in cold water and rubbed her eyes awake and brilliant, and with one circular rub had brought the color into her cheeks.

Scarcely ten seconds from the time when she first answered the knock, Nelly was opening the door and peeping out into the hall.

The rest was done by the man without; he cast the door open with the pressure of his foot, caught the girl in his arms, and kissed her; and while he closed the door the girl slipped back and stood with one hand pressed against her face, and her face held that delightful expression halfway between laughter and embarrassment. As for Lord Nick, he did not even smile. He was not, in fact, a man who was prone to gentle expressions, but having been framed by nature for a strong dominance over all around him, his habitual expression was a proud self-containment. It would have been insolence in another man; in Lord Nick it was rather leonine.

He was fully as tall as Jack Landis, but he carried his height easily, and was so perfectly proportioned that unless he was seen beside another man he did not look large. The breadth of his shoulders was concealed by the depth of his chest; and the girth of his throat was made to appear quite normal by the lordly size of the head it supported. To crown and set off his magnificent body there was a handsome face; and he had the combination of active eyes and red hair, which was noticeable in Donnegan, too. In fact, there was a certain resemblance between the two men; in the set of the jaw for instance, in the gleam of the eye, and above all in an indescribable ardor of spirit, which exuded from them both. Except, of course, that in Donnegan, one was conscious of all spirit and very little body, but in Lord Nick hand and eye were terribly mated. Looking upon so splendid a figure, it was no wonder that the mountain desert had forgiven the crimes of Lord Nick because of the careless insolence with which he treated the law. It requires an exceptional man to make a legal life attractive and respected; it takes a genius to make law-breaking glorious.

No wonder that Nelly Lebrun stood with her hand against her cheek, looking him over, smiling happily at him, and questioning him about his immediate past all in the same glance. He waved her back to her couch, and she hesitated. Then, as though she remembered that she now had to do with Lord Nick in person, she obediently curled up on the lounge, and waited expectantly.

"I hear you've been raising the devil," said this singularly frank admirer.

The girl merely looked at him.

"Well?" he insisted.

"I haven't done a thing," protested Nelly rather childishly.

"No?" One felt that he could have crushed her with evidence to the contrary but that he was restraining himself. It was not worthwhile to bother with such a girl seriously. "Things have fallen into a tangle since I left, old Satan Macon is on the spot and your rat of a father has let Landis get away. What have you been doing, Nelly, while all this was going on? Sitting with your eyes closed?"

He took a chair and lounged back in it gracefully.

"How could I help it? I'm not a watchdog."

He was silent for a time. "Well," he said, "if you told me the truth I suppose I shouldn't love you, my girl. But this time I'm in earnest. Landis is a mint, silly child. If we let him go we lose the mint."

"I suppose you'll get him back?"

"First, I want to find out how he got away."

"I know how."

"Ah?"

"Donnegan."

"Donnegan, Donnegan, Donnegan!" burst out Lord Nick, and though he did not raise the pitch of his voice, he allowed its volume to swell softly so that it filled the room like the humming of a great, angry tiger. "Nobody says three words without putting in the name of Donnegan as one of them! You, too!"

She shrugged her shoulders.

"Donnegan thrills The Corner!" went on the big man in the same terrible voice. "Donnegan wears queer clothes; Donnegan shoots Scar-faced Lewis; Donnegan pumps the nerve out of poor Jack Landis and then drills him. Why, Nelly, it looks as though I'll have to kill this intruding fool!"

She blanched at this, but did not appear to notice.

"It's a long time since you've killed a man, isn't it?" she asked coldly.

"It's an awful business," declared Lord Nick. "Always complications; have to throw the blame on the other fellow. And even these blockheads are beginning to get tired of my self-defense pleas."

"Well," murmured the girl, "don't cross that bridge until you come to it; and you'll never come to it."

"Never. Because I don't want him killed."

"Ah," Lord Nick murmured. "And why?"

"Because he's in love—with me."

"Tush!" said Lord Nick. "I see you, my dear. Donnegan seems to be a rare fellow, but he couldn't have gotten Landis out of this house without help. Rix and the Pedlar may have been a bit sleepy, but Donnegan had to find out when they fell asleep. He had a confederate. Who? Not Rix; not the Pedlar; not Lebrun. They all know me. It had to be someone who doesn't fear me. Who? Only one person in the world. Nelly, you're the one!"

She hesitated a breathless instant.

"Yes," she said. "I am."

She added, as he stared calmly at her, considering: "There's a girl in the case. She came up here to get Landis; seems he was in love with her once. And I pitied her. I sent him back to her. Suppose he is a mint; haven't we coined enough money out of him? Besides, I couldn't have kept on with it."

"No?"

"He was getting violent, and he talked marriage all day, every day. I haven't any nerves, you say, but he began to put me on edge. So I got rid of him."

"Nelly, are you growing a conscience?"

She flushed and then set her teeth.

"But I'll have to teach you business methods, my dear. I have to bring him back."

"You'll have to go through Donnegan to do it."

"I suppose so."

"You don't understand, Nick. He's different."

"Eh?"

"He's like you."

"What are you driving at?"

"Nick, I tell you upon my word of honor, no matter what a terrible fighter you may be, Donnegan will give you trouble. He has your hair and your eyes and he moves like a cat. I've never seen such a man—except you. I'd rather see you fight the plague than fight Donnegan!"

For the first time Lord Nick showed real emotion; he leaned a little forward.

"Just what does he mean to you?" he asked. "I've stood for a good deal, Nelly; I've given you absolute freedom, but if I ever suspect you—"

The lion was up in him unmistakably now. And the girl shrank.

"If it were serious, do you suppose I'd talk like this?"

"I don't know. You're a clever little devil, Nell. But I'm clever, too. And I begin to see through you. Do you still want to save Donnegan?"

"For your own sake."

He stood up.

"I'm going up the hill today. If Donnegan's there, I'll go through him; but I'm going to have Landis back!"

She, also, rose.

"There's only one way out and I'll take that way. I'll get Donnegan to leave the house."

"I don't care what you do about that."

"And if he isn't there, will you give me your word that you won't hunt him out afterward?"

"I never make promises, Nell."

"But I'll trust you, Nick."

"Very well. I start up the hill in an hour. You have that long."

## CHAPTER XXX

The air was thin and chilly; snow had fallen in the mountains to the north, and the wind was bringing the cold down to The Corner. Nelly Lebrun noted this as she dressed and made up her mind accordingly. She sent out two messages: one to the cook to send breakfast to her room, which she ate while she finished dressing with care; and the other to the gambling house, summoning one of the waiters. When he came, she gave him a note for Donnegan. The fellow flashed a glance at her as he took the envelope. There was no need to give that name and address in The Corner, and the girl tingled under the glance.

She finished her breakfast and then concentrated in polishing up her appearance. From all of which it may be gathered that Nelly Lebrun was in love with Donnegan, but she really was not. But he had touched in her that cord of romance which runs through every woman; whenever it is touched the vibration is music, and Nelly was filled with the sound of it. And except for

Lord Nick, there is no doubt that she would have really lost her head; for she kept seeing the face of Donnegan, as he had leaned toward her across the little table in Milligan's. And that, as anyone may know, is a dangerous symptom.

Her glances were alternating between her mirror and her watch, and the hands of the latter pointed to the fact that fifty minutes of her hour had elapsed when a message came up that she was waited for in the street below. So Nelly Lebrun went down in her riding costume, the corduroy swishing at each step, and tapping her shining boots with the riding crop. Her own horse she found at the hitching rack, and beside it Donnegan was on his chestnut horse. It was a tall horse, and he looked more diminutive than ever before, pitched so high in the saddle.

He was on the ground in a flash with the reins tucked under one arm and his hat under the other; she became aware of gloves and white-linen stock, and pale, narrow face. Truly Donnegan made a natty appearance.

"There's no day like a cool day for riding," she said, "and I thought you might agree with me."

He untethered her horse while he murmured an answer. But for his attitude she cared little so long as she had him riding away from that house on the hill where Lord Nick in all his terror would appear in some few minutes. Besides, as they swung up the road—the chestnut at a long-strided canter and Nelly's black at a soft and choppy pace—the wind of the gallop struck into her face; Nelly was made to enjoy things one by one and not two by two. They hit over the hills, and when the first impulse of the ride was done they were a mile or more away from The Corner—and Lord Nick.

The resemblance between the two men was less striking now that she had Donnegan beside her. He seemed more wizened, paler, and intense as a violin string screwed to the snapping point; there was none of the lordly tolerance of Nick about him; he was like a bull terrier compared with a stag hound. And only the color of his eyes and his hair made her make the comparison at all.

"What could be better?" she said when they checked their horses on a hilltop to look over a gradual falling of the ground below. "What could be better?" The wind flattened a loose curl of hair against her cheek, and overhead the wild geese were flying and crying, small and far away.

"One thing better," said Donnegan, "and that is to sit in a chair and see this."

She frowned at such frankness; it was almost blunt discourtesy.

"You see, I'm a lazy man."

"How long has it been," the girl asked sharply, "since you have slept?"

"Two days, I think."

"What's wrong?"

He lifted his eyes slowly from a glittering, distant rock, and brought his glance toward her by degrees. He had a way of exciting people even in the most commonplace conversation, and the girl felt a thrill under his look.

"That," said Donnegan, "is a dangerous question."

And he allowed such hunger to come into his eye that she caught her breath. The imp of perversity made her go on.

"And why dangerous?"

It was an excellent excuse for an outpouring of the heart from Donnegan, but, instead, his eyes twinkled at her.

"You are not frank," he remarked.

She could not help laughing, and her laughter trailed away musically in her excitement.

"Having once let down the bars I cannot keep you at arm's length. After last night I suppose I should never have let you see me for—days and days."

"That's why I'm curious," said Donnegan, "and not flattered. I'm trying to find what purpose you have in taking me riding."

"I wonder," she said thoughtfully, "if you will."

And since such fencing with the wits delighted her, she let all her delight come with a sparkle in her eyes.

"I have one clue."

"Yes?"

"And that is that you may have the old-woman curiosity to find out how many ways a man can tell her that he's fond of her."

Though she flushed a little she kept her pulse admirably.

"I suppose that is part of my interest," she admitted.

"I can think of a great many ways of saying it," said Donnegan. "I am the dry desert, you are the rain, and yet I remain dry and produce no grass."

"A very pretty comparison," said the girl with a smile.

"A very green one," and Donnegan smiled. "I am the wind and you are the wild geese, and yet I keep on blowing after you are gone and do not carry away a feather of you."

"Pretty again."

"And silly. But, really, you are very kind to me, and I shall try not to take too much advantage of it."

"Will you answer a question?"

"I had rather ask one: but go on."

"What made you so dry a desert, Mr. Donnegan?"

"There is a very leading question again."

"I don't mean it that way. For you had the same sad, hungered look the first time I saw you—when you came into Milligan's in that beggarly disguise."

"I shall confess one thing. It was not a disguise. It was the fact of me; I am a beggarly person."

"Nonsense! I'm not witless, Mr. Donnegan. You talk well. You have an education."

"In fact I have an educated taste; I disapprove of myself, you see, and long ago learned not to take myself too seriously."

"Which leads to—"

"The reason why I have wandered so much."

"Like a hunter on a trail. Hunting for what?"

"A chance to sit in a saddle—or a chair—and talk as we are talking."

"Which seems to be idly."

"Oh, you mistake me. Under the surface I am as serious as fire."

"Or ice."

At the random hit he glanced sharply at her, but she was looking a little past him, thinking.

"I have tried to get at the reason behind all your reasons," she said. "You came on me in a haphazard fashion, and yet you are not a haphazard sort."

"Do you see nothing serious about me?"

"I see that you are unhappy," said the girl gently. "And I am sorry."

Once again Donnegan was jarred, and he came within an ace of opening his mind to her, of pouring out the truth about Lou Macon. Love is a talking madness in all men and he came within an ace of confessing his troubles.

"Let's go on," she said, loosening her rein.

"Why not cut back in a semicircle toward The Corner?"

"Toward The Corner? No, no!"

There was a brightening of his eye as he noted her shudder of distaste or fear, and she strove to cover her traces.

"I'm sick of the place," she said eagerly. "Let's get as far from it as we may."

"But yonder is a very good trail leading past it."

"Of course we'll ride that way if you wish, but I'd rather go straight ahead."

If she had insisted stubbornly he would have thought nothing, but the moment she became politic he was on his guard.

"You dislike something in The Corner," he said, thinking carelessly and aloud. "You are afraid of something back there. But what could you be afraid of? Then you may be afraid of something for me. Ah, I have it! They have decided to 'get' me for taking Jack Landis away; Joe Rix and the Pedlar are waiting for me to come back!"

He looked steadily and she attempted to laugh.

"Joe Rix and the Pedlar? I would not stack ten like them against you!"

"Then it is someone else."

"I haven't said so. Of course there's no one."

She shook her rein again, but Donnegan sat still in his saddle and looked fixedly at her.

"That's why you brought me out here," he announced. "Oh, Nelly Lebrun, what's behind your mind? Who is it? By heaven, it's this Lord Nick!"

"Mr. Donnegan, you're letting your imagination run wild."

"It's gone straight to the point. But I'm not angry. I think I may get back in time."

He turned his horse, and the girl swung hers beside him and caught his arm.

"Don't go!" she pleaded. "You're right; it's Nick, and it's suicide to face him!"

The face of Donnegan set cruelly.

"The main obstacle," he said. "Come and watch me handle it!"

But she dropped her head and buried her face in her hands, and, sitting there for a long time, she heard his careless whistling blow back to her as he galloped toward The Corner.

# CHAPTER XXXI

If Nelly Lebrun had consigned him mentally to the worms, that thought made not the slightest impression upon Donnegan. A chance for action was opening before him, and above all a chance of action in the eye of Lou Macon; and he welcomed with open arms the thought that he would have an opportunity to strike for her, and keep Landis with her. He went arrowy straight and arrowy fast to the cabin on the hill, and he found ample evidence that it had become a center of attention in The Corner. There was a scattering of people in the distance, apparently loitering with no particular purpose, but undoubtedly because they awaited an explosion of some sort. He went by a group at which the chestnut shied, and as Donnegan straightened out the horse again he caught a look of both interest and pity on the faces of the men.

Did they give him up so soon as it was known that Lord Nick had entered the lists against him? Had all his display in The Corner gone for nothing as against the repute of this terrible mystery man? His vanity made him set his teeth again.

Dismounting before the cabin of the colonel, he found that worthy in his invalid chair, enjoying a sunbath in front of his house. But there was no sign of Lord Nick—no sign of Lou. A grim fear came to Donnegan that he might have to attack Nick in his own stronghold, for Jack Landis might already have been taken away to the Lebrun house.

So he went straight to the colonel, and when he came close he saw that the fat man was apparently in the grip of a chill. He had gathered a vast blanket about his shoulders and kept drawing it tighter; beneath his eyes, which looked down to the ground, there were violet shadows.

"I've lost," said Donnegan through his teeth. "Lord Nick has been here?"

The invalid lifted his eyes, and Donnegan saw a terrible thing—that the nerve of the fat man had been crushed. The folds of his face quivered as he answered huskily: "He has been here!"

"And Landis is gone?"

"No."

"Not gone? Then—"

"Nick has gone to get a horse litter. He came up just to clear the way."

"When he comes back he'll find me!"

The glance of the colonel cleared long enough to survey Donnegan slowly from head to foot, and his amusement sent the familiar hot flush over the face of the little man. He straightened to his full height, which, in his high heels, was not insignificant. But the colonel was apparently so desperate that he was willing to throw caution away.

"Compared with Lord Nick, Donnegan," he said, "you don't look half a man—even with those heels."

And he smiled calmly at Donnegan in the manner of one who, having escaped the lightning bolt itself, does not fear mere thunder.

"There is no fool like a fat fool," said Donnegan with childish viciousness. "What did Lord Nick, as you call him, do to you? He's brought out the yellow, my friend."

The colonel accepted the insult without the quiver of an eyelid. Throughout he seemed to be looking expectantly beyond Donnegan.

"My young friend," he said, "you have been very useful to me. But I must confess that you are no longer a tool equal to the task. I dismiss you. I thank you cordially for your efforts. They are worthless. You see that crowd gathering yonder? They have come to see Lord Nick prepare you for a hole in the ground. And make no mistake: if you are here when he returns that hole will have to be dug—unless they throw you out for the claws of the buzzards. In the meantime, our efforts have been wasted completely. I hadn't enough time. I had thrown the fear of sudden death into Landis, and in another hour he would have signed away his soul to me for fear of poison."

The colonel paused to chuckle at some enjoyable memory.

"Then Nick came. You see, I know all about Nick."

"And Nick knows all about you?"

For a moment the agate, catlike eyes of the colonel clouded and cleared again in their unfathomable manner.

"At moments, Donnegan," he said, "you have rare perceptions. That is exactly it—Nick knows just about everything concerning me. And so—roll your pack and climb on your horse and get away. I think you may have another five minutes before he comes."

Donnegan turned on his heel. He went to the door of the hut and threw it open. Lou sat beside Landis holding his hand, and the murmur of her voice was still pleasant as an echo through the room when she looked and saw Donnegan. At that she rose and her face hardened as she looked at him. Landis, also, lifted his head, and his face was convulsed with hatred. So Donnegan closed the door and went softly away to his own shack.

She hated him even as Landis hated him, it seemed. He should have known that he would not be thanked for bringing back her lover to her with a bullet through his shoulder. Sitting in his cabin, he took his head between his hands and thought of life and death, and made up his mind. He was afraid. If Lord Nick had been the devil himself Donnegan could not have been more afraid. But if the big stranger had been ten devils instead of one Donnegan would not have found it in his soul to run away.

Nothing remained for him in The Corner, it seemed, except his position as a man of power—a dangerous fighter. It was a less than worthless position, and yet, once having taken it up, he could not abandon it. More than one gunfighter has been in the same place, forced to act as a public menace long after he has ceased to feel any desire to fight. Of selfish motives there remained not a scruple to him, but there was still the happiness of Lou Macon. If the boy were taken back to Lebrun's, it would be fatal to her. For even if Nelly wished, she could not teach her eyes new habits, and she would ceaselessly play on the heart of the wounded man.

It was the cessation of all talk from the gathering crowd outside that made Donnegan lift his head at length, and know that Lord Nick had come. But before he had time to prepare himself, the door was cast open and into it, filling it from side to side, stepped Lord Nick.

There was no need of an introduction. Donnegan knew him by the aptness with which the name fitted that glorious figure of a man and by the calm, confident eye which now was looking him slowly over, from head to foot. Lord Nick closed the door carefully behind him.

"The colonel told me," he said in his deep, smooth voice, "that you were waiting for me here."

And Donnegan recognized the snakelike malice of the fat man in drawing him into the fight. But he dismissed that quickly from his mind. He was staring, fascinated, into the face of the other. He was a reader of men, was Donnegan; he was a reader of mind, too. In his life of battle he had learned to judge the prowess of others at a glance, just as a musician can tell the quality of a violin by the first note he hears played upon it. So Donnegan judged the quality of fighting men, and, looking into the face of Lord Nick, he knew that he had met his equal at last.

It was a great and a bitter moment to him. The sense of physical smallness he had banished a thousand times by the recollection of his speed of hand and his surety with weapons. He had looked at men muscularly great and despised them in the knowledge that a gun or a knife would make him their master. But in Lord Nick he recognized his own nerveless speed of hand, his own hair-trigger balance, his own deadly seriousness and contempt of life. The experience in battle was there, too. And he began to feel that the size of the other crushed him to the floor and made him hopeless. It was unnatural, it was wrong, that this giant in the body should be a giant in adroitness also.

Already Donnegan had died one death before he rose from his chair and stood to the full of his height ready to die again and summoning his nervous force to meet the enemy. He had seen that the big man had followed his own example and had measured him at a glance.

Indeed the history of some lives of action held less than the concentrated silence of these two men during that second's space.

And now Donnegan felt the cold eye of the other eating into his own, striving to beat him down, break his nerve. For an instant panic got hold on Donnegan. He, himself, had broken the nerve of other men by the weight of his unaided eye. Had he not reduced poor Jack Landis to a trembling wreck by five minutes of silence? And had he not seen other brave men become trembling cowards unable to face the light, and all because of that terrible power which lies in the eye of some? He fought away the panic, though perspiration was pouring out upon his forehead and beneath his armpits.

"The colonel is very kind," said Donnegan.

And that moment he sent up a prayer of thankfulness that his voice was smooth as silk, and that he was able to smile into the face of Lord Nick. The brow of the other clouded and then smoothed itself deftly. Perhaps he, too, recognized the clang of steel upon steel and knew the metal of his enemy.

"And therefore," said Lord Nick, "since most of The Corner expects business from us, it seems much as if one of us must kill the other before we part."

"As a matter of fact," said Donnegan, "I have been keeping that in mind." He added, with that deadly smile of his that never reached his eyes: "I never disappoint the public when it's possible to satisfy them."

"No," and Lord Nick nodded, "you seem to have most of the habits of an actor—including an inclination to make up for your part."

Donnegan bit his lip until it bled, and then smiled.

"I have been playing to fools," he said. "Now I shall enjoy a discriminating critic."

"Yes," remarked Lord Nick, "actors generally desire an intelligent audience for the death scene."

"I applaud your penetration and I shall speak well of you when this disagreeable duty is finished."

"Come," and Lord Nick smiled genially, "you are a game little cock!"

The telltale flush crimsoned Donnegan's face. And if the fight had begun at that moment no power under heaven could have saved Lord Nick from the frenzy of the little man.

"My size keeps me from stooping," said Donnegan, "I shall look up to you, sir, until the moment you fall."

"Well hit again! You are also a wit, I see! Donnegan, I am almost sorry for the necessity of this meeting. And if it weren't for the audience—"

"Say no more," said Donnegan, bowing. "I read your heart and appreciate all you intend."

He had touched his stock as he bowed, and now he turned to the mirror and carefully adjusted it, for it was a little awry from the ride; but in reality he used that moment to examine his own face, and the set of his jaw and the clearness of his eye reassured him. Turning again, he surprised a glint of admiration in the glance of Lord Nick.

"We are at one, sir, it appears," he said. "And there is no other way out of this disagreeable necessity?"

"Unfortunately not. I have a certain position in these parts. People are apt to expect a good deal of me. And for my part I see no way out except a gunplay—no way out between the devil and the moon!"

Astonishment swept suddenly across the face of the big man, for Donnegan, turning white as death, shrank toward the wall as though he had that moment received cold steel in his body.

"Say that again!" said Donnegan hoarsely.

"I said there was no way out," repeated Lord Nick, and though he kept his right hand in readiness, he passed his left through his red hair and stared at Donnegan with a tinge of contempt; he had seen men buckle like this at the last moment when their backs were to the wall.

"Between—" repeated Donnegan.

"The devil and the moon. Do you see a way yourself?"

He was astonished again to see Donnegan wince as if from a blow. His lips were trembling and they writhed stiffly over his words.

"Who taught you that expression?" said Donnegan.

"A gentleman," said Lord Nick.

"Ah?"

"My father, sir!"

"Oh, heaven," moaned Donnegan, catching his hands to his breast. "Oh, heaven, forgive us!"

"What the devil is in you?" asked Lord Nick.

The little man stood erect again and his eyes were now on fire.

"You are Henry Nicholas Reardon," he said.

Lord Nick set his teeth.

"Now," he said, "it is certain that you must die!"

But Donnegan cast out his arms and broke into a wild laughter.

"Oh, you fool, you fool!" he cried. "Don't you know me? I am the cripple!"

## CHAPTER XXXII

The big man crossed the floor with one vast stride, and, seizing Donnegan by both shoulders, dragged him under the full light of the window; and still the crazy laughter shook Donnegan and made him helpless.

"They tied me to a board—like a papoose," said Donnegan, "and they straightened my back—but they left me this way—wizened up." He was stammering; hysterical, and the words tumbled from his lips in a jumble. "That was a month after you ran away from home. I was going to find you. Got bigger. Took the road. Kept hunting. Then I met a yegg who told about Rusty Dick—described him like you—I thought—I thought you were dead!"

And the tears rolled down his face; he sobbed like a woman.

A strange thing happened then. Lord Nick lifted the little man in his arms as if he were a child and literally carried him in that fashion to the bunk. He put him down tenderly, still with one mighty arm around his back.

"You are Garry? You!"

"Garrison Donnegan Reardon. Aye, that's what I am. Henry, don't say that you don't know me!"

"But—your back—I thought—"

"I know—hopeless they said I was. But they brought in a young doctor. Now look at me. Little. I never grew big—but hard, Henry, as leather!"

And he sprang to his feet. And knowing that Donnegan had begun life as a cripple it was easy to appreciate certain things about his expression—a cold wistfulness, and his manner of reading the minds of men. Lord Nick was like a man in a dream. He dragged Donnegan back to the bunk and forced him to sit down with the weight of his arms. And he could not keep his hands from his younger brother. As though he were blind and had to use the sense of touch to reassure him.

"I heard lies. They said everybody was dead. I thought—"

"The fever killed them all, except me. Uncle Toby took me in. He was a devil. Helped me along, but I left him when I could. And—"

"Don't tell me anymore. All that matters is that I have you at last, Garry. Heaven knows it's a horrible thing to be kithless and kinless, but I have you now! Ah, lad, but the old pain has left its mark on you. Poor Garry!"

Donnegan shuddered.

"I've forgotten it. Don't bring it back."

"I keep feeling that you should be in that chair."

"I know. But I'm not. I'm hard as nails, I tell you."

He leaped to his feet again.

"And not so small as you might think, Henry!"

"Oh, big enough, Garry. Big enough to paralyze The Corner, from what I've heard."

"I've been playing a game with 'em, Henry. And now—if one of us could clear the road, what will we do together? Eh?"

The smile of Lord Nick showed his teeth.

"Haven't I been hungry all my life for a man like you, lad? Somebody to stand and guard my back while I faced the rest of the world?"

"And I'll do my share of the facing, too."

"You will, Garry. But I'm your elder."

"Man, man! Nobody's my elder except one that's spent half his life—as I have done!"

"We'll teach you to forget the pain. I'll make life roses for you, Garry."

"And the fools outside thought—"

Donnegan broke into a soundless laughter, and, running to the door, opened it a fraction of an inch and peeped out.

"They're standing about in a circle. I can see 'em gaping. Even from here. What will they think, Henry?"

Lord Nick ground his teeth.

"They'll think I've backed down from you," he said gloomily. "They'll think I've taken water for the first time."

"Why, confound 'em, the first man that opens his head—"

"I know, I know. You'd fill his mouth with lead, and so would I. But if it ever gets about—as it's sure to—that Lord Nick, as they call me, has been bluffed down without a fight, I'll have every Chinaman that cooks on the range talking back to me. I'll have to start all over again."

"Don't say that, Henry. Don't you see that I'll go out and explain that I'm your brother?"

"What good will that do? No, do we look alike?"

Donnegan stopped short.

"I'm not very big," he said rather coldly, "but then I'm not so very small, either. I've found myself big enough, speaking in general. Besides, we have the same hair and eyes."

"Why, man, people will laugh when they hear that we call ourselves brothers."

Donnegan ground his teeth and the old flush burned upon his face.

"I'll cut some throats if they do," he said, trembling with his passion.

"I can hear them say it. 'Lord Nick walked in on Donnegan prepared to eat him up. He measured him up and down, saw that he was a fighting wildcat in spite of his size, and decided to back out. And Donnegan was willing. They couldn't come out without a story of some kind—with the whole world expecting a death in that cabin—so they framed a crazy cock-and-bull story about being brothers.' I can hear them say that, Donnegan, and it makes me wild!"

"Do you call me Donnegan?" said Donnegan sadly.

"No, no. Garry, don't be so touchy. You've never got over that, I see. Still all pride and fire."

"You're not very humble yourself, Henry."

"Maybe not, maybe not. But I've been in a certain position around these parts, Don—Garry. And it's hard to see it go!"

Donnegan closed his eyes in deep reverie. And then he forced out the words one by one.

"Henry, I'll let everybody know that it was I who backed down. That we were about to fight." He was unable to speak; he tore the stock loose at his throat and went on: "We were about to fight; I lost my nerve; you couldn't shoot a helpless man. We began to talk. We found out we are brothers—"

"Damnation!" broke out Lord Nick, and he struck himself violently across the forehead with the back of his hand. "I'm a skunk, Garry, lad. Why, for a minute I was about to let you do it. No. No, no! A thousand times no!"

It was plain to be seen that he was arguing himself away from the temptation.

"What do I care what they say? We'll cram the words back down their throats and be hanged to 'em. Here I am worrying about myself like a selfish dog without letting myself be happy over finding you. But I am happy, Garry. Heaven knows it. And you don't doubt it, do you, old fellow?"

"Ah," said Donnegan, and he smiled to cover a touch of sadness. "I hope not. No, I don't doubt you, of course. I've spent my life wishing for you since you left us, you see. And then I followed you for three years on the road, hunting everywhere."

"You did that?"

"Yes. Three years. I liked the careless life. For to tell you the truth, I'm not worth much, Henry. I'm a loafer by instinct, and—"

"Not another word." There were tears in the eyes of Lord Nick, and he frowned them away. "Confound it, Garry, you unman me. I'll be weeping like a woman in a minute. But now, sit down. We still have some things to talk over. And we'll get to a quick conclusion."

"Ah, yes," said Donnegan, and at the emotion which had come in the face of Lord Nick, his own expression softened wonderfully. A light seemed to stand in his face. "We'll brush over the incidentals. And everything is incidental aside from the fact that we're together again. They can chisel iron chain apart, but we'll never be separated again, God willing!" He looked up as he spoke, and his face was for the moment as pure as the face of a child—Donnegan, the thief, the beggar, the liar by gift, and the man-killer by trade and artistry.

But Lord Nick in the meantime was looking down to the floor and mustering his thoughts.

"The main thing is entirely simple," he said. "You'll make one concession to my pride, Garry, boy?"

"Can you ask me?" said Donnegan softly, and he cast out his hands in a gesture that offered his heart and his soul. "Can you ask me? Anything I have is yours!"

"Don't say that," answered Lord Nick tenderly. "But this small thing—my pride, you know—I despise myself for caring what people think, but I'm weak. I admit it, but I can't help it."

"Talk out, man. You'll see if there's a bottom to things that I can give!"

"Well, it's this. Everyone knows that I came up here to get young Jack Landis and bring him back to Lebrun's—from which you stole him, you clever young devil! Well, I'll simply take him back there, Garry; and then I'll never have to ask another favor of you."

He was astonished by a sudden silence, and looking up again, he saw that Donnegan sat with his hand at his breast. It was a singularly feminine gesture to which he resorted. It was a habit which had come to him in his youth in the invalid chair, when the ceaseless torment of his crippled back became too great for him to bear.

And clearly, indeed, those days were brought home to Lord Nick as he glanced up, for Donnegan was staring at him in the same old, familiar agony, mute and helpless.

## CHAPTER XXXIII

At this Lord Nick very frankly frowned in turn. And when he frowned his face grew marvelously dark, like some wrathful god, for there was a noble, a Grecian purity to the profile of Henry Nicholas Reardon, and when he frowned he seemed to be scorning, from a distance, ignoble, earthly things which troubled him.

"I know it isn't exactly easy for you, Garry," he admitted. "You have your own pride; you have your own position here in The Corner. But I want you to notice that mine is different. You've spent a day for what you have in The Corner, here. I've spent ten years. You've played a prank, acted a part, and cast a jest for what you have. But for the place which I hold, brother mine, I've schemed with my wits, played fast and loose, and killed men. Do you hear? I've bought it with blood, and things you buy at such a price ought to stick, eh?"

He banished his frown; the smile played suddenly across his features.

"Why, I'm arguing with myself. But that look you gave me a minute ago had me worried for a little while."

At this Donnegan, who had allowed his head to fall, so that he seemed to be nodding in acquiescence, now raised his face and Lord Nick perceived the same white pain upon it. The same look which had been on the face of the cripple so often in the other days.

"Henry," said the younger brother, "I give you my oath that my pride has nothing to do with this. I'd let you drive me barefoot before you through the street yonder. I'd let every soul in The Corner know that I have no pride where you're concerned. I'll do whatever you wish—with one exception— and that one is the unlucky thing you ask. Pardner, you mustn't ask for Jack Landis! Anything else I'll work like a slave to get for you: I'll fight your battles, I'll serve you in any way you name: but don't take Landis back!"

He had talked eagerly, the words coming with a rush, and he found at the end that Lord Nick was looking at him in bewilderment.

"When a man is condemned to death," said Lord Nick slowly, "suppose somebody offers him anything in the world that he wants—palaces, riches, power—everything except his life. What would the condemned man say to a friend who made such an offer? He'd laugh at him and then call him a traitor. Eh? But I don't laugh at you, Garry. I simply explain to you why I have to have Landis back. Listen!"

He counted off his points upon the tips of his fingers, in the confident manner of a teacher who deals with a stupid child, waiting patiently for the young mind to comprehend.

"We've been bleeding Jack Landis. Do you know why? Because it was Lester who made the strike up here. He started out to file his claim. He stopped at the house of Colonel Macon. That old devil learned the location, learned everything; detained Lester with a trick, and rushed young Landis away to file the claims for himself. Then when Lester came up here he found that his claims had been jumped, and when he went to the law there was no law that could help him. He had nothing but his naked word for what he had discovered. And naturally the word of a ruffian like Lester had no weight against the word of Landis. And, you see, Landis thought that he was entirely in the right. Lester tried the other way; tried to jump the claims; and was shot down by Landis. So Lester sent for me. What was I to do? Kill Landis? The mine would go to his heirs. I tried a different way—bleeding him of his profits, after I'd explained to him that he was in the wrong. He half admitted that, but he naturally wouldn't give up the mines even after we'd almost proved to him that Lester had the first right. So Landis has been mining the gold and we've been drawing it away from him. It looks tricky, but really it's only just. And Lester and Lebrun split with me.

"But I tell you, Garry, that I'd give up everything without an afterthought. I'll give up the money and I'll make Lebrun and Lester shut up without a word. I'll make them play square and not try to knife Landis in the back. I'll do all that willingly—for you! But, Garry, I can't give up taking Landis back to Lebrun's and keeping him there until he's well. Why, man, I saw him in the hut just now. He wants to go. He's afraid of the old colonel as if he were poison—and I think he's wise in being afraid."

"The colonel won't touch him," said Donnegan.

"No?"

"No. I've told him what would happen if he does."

"Tush. Garry, Colonel Macon is the coldest-blooded murderer I've ever known. But come out in the open, lad. You see that I'm ready to listen to reason—except on one point. Tell me why you're so set on this keeping of Landis here against my will and even against the lad's own will? I'm reasonable, Garry. Do you doubt that?"

Explaining his own mildness, the voice of Lord Nick swelled again and filled the room, and he frowned on his brother. But Donnegan looked on him sadly.

"There is a girl—" he began.

"Why didn't I guess it!" exclaimed Lord Nick. "If ever you find a man unreasonable, stubborn and foolish, you'll always find a woman behind it! All this trouble because of a piece of calico?"

He leaned back, laughing thunderously in his relief.

"Come, come! I was prepared for a tragedy. Now tell me about this girl. Who and what is she?"

"The daughter of the colonel."

"You're in love with her? I'm glad to hear it, Garry. As a matter of fact I've been afraid that you were hunting in my own preserve, but if it's the colonel's daughter, you're welcome to her. So you love the girl? She's pretty, lad!"

"I love her?" said Donnegan in an indescribably tender voice. "I love her? Who am I to love her? A thief, a man-killer, a miserable play actor, a gambler, a drunkard. I love her? Bah!"

If there was one quality of the mind with which Lord Nick was less familiar than with all others, it was humbleness of spirit. He now abased his magnificent head, and resting his chin in the mighty palm of his hand, he stared with astonishment and commiseration into the face of Donnegan. He seemed to be learning new things every moment about his brother.

"Leave me out of the question," said Donnegan.

"Can't be done. If I leave you out, dear boy, there's not one of them that I care a hang about; I'd ride roughshod over the whole lot. I've done it before to better men than these!"

"Then you'll change, I know. This is the fact of the matter. She loves Landis. And if you take Landis away where will you put him?"

"Where he was stolen away. In Lebrun's."

"And what will be in Lebrun's?"

"Joe Rix to guard him and the old negress to nurse him.'"

"No, no! Nelly Lebrun will be there!"

"Eh? Are you glancing at her, now?"

"Henry, you yourself know that Landis is mad about that girl."

"Oh, she's flirted a bit with him. Turned the fool's head. He'll come out of it safe. She won't break his heart. I've seen her work on others!"

He chuckled at the memory.

"What do I care about Landis?" said Donnegan with unutterable scorn. "It's the girl. You'll break her heart, Henry; and if you do I'll never forgive you."

"Steady, lad. This is a good deal like a threat."

"No, no, no! Not a threat, heaven knows!"

"By heaven!" exclaimed Lord Nick. "I begin to be irritated to see you stick on a silly point like this. Listen to me, lad. Do you mean to say that you are making all this trouble about a slip of a girl?"

"The heart of a girl," said Donnegan calmly.

"Let Landis go; then take her in your arms and kiss her worries away. I warrant you can do it! I gather from Nell that you're not tongue-tied around women!"

"I?" echoed Donnegan, turning pale. "Don't jest at this, Henry. I'm as serious as death. She's the type of woman made to love one man, and one man only. Landis may be common as dirt; but she doesn't see it. She's fastened her heart on him. I looked in on her a little while ago. She turned white when she saw me. I brought Landis to her, but she hates me because I had to shoot him down."

"Garry," said the big man with a twinkle in his eye, "you're in love!"

It shook Donnegan to the core, but he replied instantly; "If I were in love, don't you suppose that I would have shot to kill when I met Landis?"

At this his brother blinked, frowned, and shook his head. The point was apparently plain to him and wiped out his previous convictions. Also, it eased his mind.

"Then you don't love the girl?"

"I?"

"Either way, my hands are cleared of the worry. If you want her, let me take Landis. If you don't want her, what difference does it make to you except silly sentiment?"

Donnegan made no answer.

"If she comes to Lebrun's house, I'll see that Nell doesn't bother him too much."

"Can you control her? If she wants to see this fool can you keep her away, and if she goes to him can you control her smiling?"

"Certainly," said Lord Nick, but he flushed heavily.

Donnegan smiled.

"She's a devil of a girl," admitted Henry Reardon. "But this is beside the point: which is, that you're sticking on a matter that means everything to me, and which is only a secondhand interest to you—a point of sentiment. You pity the girl. What's pity? Bah! I pity a dog in the street, but would I cross you, Garry, lad, to save the dog? Sentiment, I say, silly sentiment."

Donnegan rose.

"It was a silly sentiment," he said hoarsely, "that put me on the road following you, Henry. It was a silly sentiment that turned me into a wastrel, a wanderer, a man without a home and without friends."

"It's wrong to throw that in my face," muttered Lord Nick.

"It is. And I'm sorry for it. But I want you to see that matters of sentiment may be matters of life and death with me."

"Aye, if it were for you it would be different. I might see my way clear—but for a girl you have only a distant interest in—"

"It is a matter of whether or not her heart shall be broken."

"Come, come. Let's talk man talk. Besides, girls' hearts don't break in this country. You're old-fashioned."

"I tell you the question of her happiness is worth more than a dozen lives like yours and mine."

There had been a gathering impatience in Lord Nick. Now he, also, leaped to his feet; a giant.

"Tell me in one word: You stick on this point?"

"In one word—yes!"

"Then you deny me, Garry. You set me aside for a silly purpose of your own—a matter that really doesn't mean much to you. It shows me where I stand in your eyes—and nothing between the devil and the moon shall make me sidestep!"

They remained silent, staring at each other. Lord Nick stood with a flush of anger growing; Donnegan became whiter than ever, and he stiffened himself to his full height, which, in all who knew him well, was the danger signal.

"You take Landis?" he said softly.

"I do."

"Not," said Donnegan, "while I live!"

"You mean——" cried Lord Nick.

"I mean it!"

They had been swept back to the point at which that strangest of scenes began, but this time there was an added element—horror.

"You'd fight?"

"To the death, Henry!"

"Garry, if one of us should kill the other, he'd be cursed forever!"

"I know it."

"And she's worth even this?"

"A thousand times more! What are we? Dust in the wind; dust in the wind. But a woman like that is divine, Henry!"

Lord Nick swayed a little, setting himself in balance like an animal preparing for the leap.

"If it comes to the pinch, it is you who will die," he said.

"You've no chance against me, Garry. And I swear to you that I won't weaken. You prove that you don't care for me. You put another above me. It's my pride, my life, that you'd sacrifice to the whim of a girl!" His passion choked him.

"Are you ready?" said Donnegan.

"Yes!"

"Move first!"

"I have never formed the habit."

"Nor I! You fool, take what little advantage you can, because it won't help you in the end."

"You shall see. I have a second sight, Henry, and it shows me you dead on the floor there, looking bigger than ever, and I see the gun smoking in my hand and my heart as dead as ashes! Oh, Henry, if there were only some other way!"

They were both pale now.

"Aye," murmured Lord Nick, "if we could find a judge. My hand turns to lead when I think of fighting you, Garry."

Perspiration stood on the face of Donnegan.

"Name a judge; I'll abide by the decision."

"Some man——"

"No, no. What man could understand me? A woman, Henry!"

"Nell Lebrun."

"The girl who loves you? You want me to plead before her?"

"Put her on her honor and she'll be as straight as a string with both of us."

For a moment Donnegan considered, and at length: "She loves you, Henry. You have that advantage. You have only to let her know that this is a vital matter to you and she'll speak as you wish her to speak."

"Nonsense. You don't know her. You've seen yourself that no man can control her absolutely."

"Make a concession."

"A thousand, Garry, dear boy, if they'll get us clear from this horrible mess."

"Only this. Leave The Corner for a few hours. Give me until—tonight. Let me see Nelly during that time. You've had years to work on her. I want only this time to put my own case before her."

"Thank heaven that we're coming to see light and a way out!"

"Aye, Henry."

The big man wiped his forehead and sighed in his relief.

"A minute ago I was ready—but we'll forget all this. What will you do? How will you persuade Nelly? I almost think that you intend to make love to her, Garry!"

The little man turned paler still.

"It is exactly what I intend," he said quietly.

The brow of Lord Nick darkened solemnly, and then he forced a laugh.

"She'll be afraid to turn me down, Garry. But try your own way." He bit his lips. "Why, if you influence her that way—do it. What's a fickle jade to me? Nothing!"

"However I do it, you'll stick by her judgment, Henry?"

The perspiration had started on Lord Nick's forehead again. Doubt swayed him, but pride forced him on.

"I'll come again tonight," he said gloomily. "I'll meet you in—Milligan's?"

"In Milligan's, then."

Lord Nick, without a word of farewell, stamped across the hut and out.

As for Donnegan, he stepped backward, his legs buckled beneath him, and when big George entered, with a scared face, he found the little man half sitting on the bunk, half lying against the wall with the face and the staring eyes of a dead man.

## CHAPTER XXXIV

It was a long time before Donnegan left the hut, and when he came out the crowd which had gathered to watch the fight, or at least to mark the reports of the guns when those two terrible warriors met, was scattered. There remained before Donnegan only the colonel in his invalid's chair. Even from the distance one could see that his expression was changed, and when the little red-headed man came near the colonel looked up to him with something akin to humility.

"Donnegan," he said, stopping the other as Donnegan headed for the door of the hut, "Donnegan, don't go in there just now."

Donnegan turned and came slowly toward him.

"The reason," said the colonel, "is that you probably won't receive a very cheery reception. Unfortunate—very unfortunate. Lou has turned wrong-headed for the first time in her life and she won't listen to reason."

He chuckled softly.

"I never dreamed there was so much of my metal in her. Blood will tell, my boy; blood will tell. And when you finally get her you'll find that she's worth waiting for."

"Let me tell you a secret," said Donnegan dryly. "I am no longer waiting for her!"

"Ah?" smiled the colonel. "Of course not. This bringing of Landis to her—it was all pure self-sacrifice. It was not an attempt to soften her heart. It was not a cunning maneuver. Tush! Of course not!"

"I am about to make a profound remark," said Donnegan carelessly.

"By all means."

"You read the minds of other people through a colored glass, colonel. You see yourself everywhere."

"In other words I put my own motives into the actions and behind the actions of people? Perhaps. I am full of weaknesses. Very full. In the meantime let me tell you one important thing—if you have not made the heart of Lou tender toward you, you have at least frightened her."

The jaw on Donnegan set.

"Excellent!" he said huskily.

"Perhaps better than you think; and to keep you abreast with the times, you must know another thing. Lou has a silly idea that you are a lost soul, Donnegan, but she attributes your fall entirely to my weakness. Nothing can convince her that you did not intend to kill Landis; nothing can convince her that you did not act on my inspiration. I have tried arguing. Bah! she overwhelmed me with her scorn. You are a villain, says Lou, and I have made you one. And for the first time in my memory of her, her eyes fill with tears."

"Tears?"

"Upon my honor, and when a girl begins to weep about a man I don't need to say he is close to her heart."

"You are full of maxims, Colonel Macon."

"As a nut is full of meat. Old experience, you know. In the meantime Lou is perfectly certain that I intend to make away with Landis. Ha, ha, ha!" The laughter of the colonel was a cheery thunder, and soft as with distance. "Landis is equally convinced. He begs Lou not to fall asleep lest I should steal in on him. She hardly dares leave him to cook his food. I actually think she would have been glad to see that fiend, Lord Nick, take Landis away!"

Donnegan smiled wanly. But could he tell her, poor girl, the story of Nelly

Lebrun? Landis, in fear of his life, was no doubt at this moment pouring out protestations of deathless affection.

"And they both consider you an archdemon for keeping Lord Nick away!"

Again Donnegan winced, and coughed behind his hand to cover it.

"However," went on the colonel, "when it comes to matters with the hearts of women, I trust to time. Time alone will show her that Landis is a puppy."

"In the meantime, colonel, she keeps you from coming near Landis?"

"Not at all! You fail to understand me and my methods, dear boy. I have only to roll my chair into the room and sit and smile at Jack in order to send him into a hysteria of terror. It is amusing to watch. And I can be there while Lou is in the room and through a few careful innuendoes convey to Landis my undying determination to either remove him from my path and automatically become his heir, or else secure from him a legal transfer of his rights to the mines."

"I have learned," said Donnegan, "that Landis has not the slightest claim to them himself. And that you set him on the trail of the claims by trickery."

The colonel did not wince.

"Of course not," said the fat trickster. "Not the slightest right. My claim is a claim of superior wits, you see. And in the end all your labor shall be rewarded, for my share will go to Lou and through her it shall come to you. No?"

"Quite logical."

The colonel disregarded the other's smile.

"But I have a painful confession to make."

"Well?"

"I misjudged you, Donnegan. A moment since, when I was nearly distraught with disappointment, I said some most unpleasant things to you."

"I have forgotten them."

But the colonel raised his strong forefinger and shook his head, smiling.

"No, no, Donnegan. If you deny it, I shall know that you are harboring the most undying grudge against me. As a matter of fact, I have just had an interview with Lord Nick, and the cursed fellow put my nerves on edge."

The colonel made a wry face.

"And when you came, I saw no manner in which you could possibly thwart him."

His eyes grew wistful.

"Between friends—as a son to his future father," he said softly, "can't you tell me what the charm was that you used on. Nick to send him away? I watched him come out of the shack. He was in a fury. I could see that by the way his head thrust out between his big shoulders. And when he went down the hill he was striding like a giant, but every now and then he would stop short, and his head would go up as if he were tempted to turn around and go back, but didn't quite have the nerve. Donnegan, tell me the trick of it?"

"Willingly. I appealed to his gambling instinct."

"Which leaves me as much in the dark as ever."

But Donnegan smiled in his own peculiar and mirthless manner and he went on to the hut. Not that he expected a cheery greeting from Lou Macon, but he was drawn by the same perverse instinct which tempts a man to throw himself from a great height. At the door he paused a moment. He could distinguish no words, but he caught the murmur of Lou's voice as she talked to Jack Landis, and it had that infinitely gentle quality which only a woman's voice can have, and only when she nurses the sick. It was a pleasant torture to Donnegan to hear it. At length he summoned his resolution and tapped at the door.

The voice of Lou Macon stopped. He heard a hurried and whispered consultation. What did they expect? Then swift footfalls on the floor, and she opened the door. There was a smile of expectancy on her lips; her eyes were bright; but when she saw Donnegan her lips pinched in. She stared at him as if he were a ghost.

"I knew; I knew!" she said piteously, falling back a step but still keeping her hand upon the knob of the door as if to block the way to Donnegan. "Oh, Jack, he has killed Lord Nick and now he is here—"

To do what? To kill Landis in turn? Her horrified eyes implied as much. He saw Landis in the distance raise himself upon one elbow and his face was gray, not with pain but with dread.

"It can't be!" groaned Landis.

"Lord Nick is alive," said Donnegan. "And I have not come here to torment you; I have only come to ask that you let me speak with you alone for a moment, Lou!"

He watched her face intently. All the cabin was in deep shadow, but the golden hair of the girl glowed as if with an inherent light of its own, and the same light touched her face. Jack Landis was stricken with panic: he stammered in a dreadful eagerness of fear.

"Don't leave me, Lou. You know what it means. He wants to get you out of the way so that the colonel can be alone with me. Don't go, Lou! Don't go!"

As though she saw how hopeless it was to try to bar Donnegan by closing the door against him, she fell back to the bed. She kept her eye on the little man, as if to watch against a surprise attack, and, fumbling behind her, her hand found the hand of Landis and closed over it with the reassurance of a mother.

"Don't be afraid, Jack. I won't leave you. Not unless they carry me away by force."

"I give you my solemn word." said Donnegan in torment, "that the colonel shall not come near Landis while you're away with me."

"Your word!" murmured the girl with a sort of horrified wonder. "Your word!"

And Donnegan bowed his head.

But all at once she cast out her free hand toward him, while the other still cherished the weakness of Jack Landis.

"Oh, give them up!" she cried. "Give up my father and all his wicked plans. There is something good in you. Give him up; come with us; stand for us: and we shall be grateful all our lives!"

The little man had removed his hat, so that the sunshine burned brightly on his red hair. Indeed, there was always a flamelike quality about him. In inaction he seemed femininely frail and pale; but when his spirit was roused his eyes blazed as his hair burned in the sunlight.

"You shall learn in the end," he said to the girl, "that everything I do, I do for you."

She cried out as if he had struck her.

"It's not worthy of you," she said bitterly. "You are keeping Jack here—in peril—for my sake?"

"For your sake," said Donnegan.

She looked at him with a queer pain in her eyes.

"To keep you from needless lying," she said, "let me tell you that Jack has told me everything. I am not angry because you come and pretend that you do all these horrible things for my sake. I know my father has tempted you with a promise of a great deal of money. But in the end you will get nothing. No, he will twist everything away from you and leave you nothing! But as for me—I know everything; Jack told me."

"He has told you what? What?"

"About the woman you love."

"The woman I love?" echoed Donnegan, stupefied.

It seemed that Lou Macon could only name her with an effort that left her trembling.

"The Lebrun woman," she said. "Jack has told me."

"Did you tell her that?" he asked Landis.

"The whole town knows it," stammered the wounded man.

The cunning hypocrisy spurred Donnegan. He put his foot on the threshold of the shack, and at this the girl cried out and shrank from him; but Landis was too paralyzed to stir or speak. For a moment Donnegan was wildly tempted to pour his torrent of contempt and accusation upon Landis. To what end? To prove to the girl that the big fellow had coolly tricked her? That it was to be near Nelly Lebrun as much as to be away from the colonel that he wished so ardently to leave the shack? After all, Lou Macon was made happy by an illusion; let her keep it.

He looked at her sadly again. She stood defiant over Landis; ready to protect the helpless bulk of the man.

So Donnegan closed the door softly and turned away with ashes in his heart.

# CHAPTER XXXV

When Nelly Lebrun raised her head from her hands, Donnegan was a far figure; yet even in the distance she could catch the lilt and easy sway of his body; he rode as he walked, lightly, his feet in the stirrups half taking his weight in a semi-English fashion. For a moment she was on the verge of spurring after him, but she kept the rein taut and merely stared until he dipped away among the hills. For one thing she was quite assured that she could not overtake that hard rider; and, again, she felt that it was useless to interfere. To step between Lord Nick and one of his purposes would have been like stepping before an avalanche and commanding it to halt with a raised hand.

She watched miserably until even the dust cloud dissolved and the bare, brown hills alone remained before her. Then she turned away, and hour after hour let her black jog on.

To Nelly Lebrun this day was one of those still times which come over the life of a person, and in which they see themselves in relation to the rest of the world clearly. It would not be true to say that Nelly loved Donnegan. Certainly not as yet, for the familiar figure of Lord Nick filled her imagination. But the little man was different. Lord Nick commanded respect, admiration, obedience; but there was about Donnegan something which touched her in an intimate and disturbing manner. She had felt the will-o'-the-wisp flame which burned in him in his great moments. It was possible for her to smile at Donnegan; it was possible even to pity him for his fragility, his touchy pride about his size; to criticize his fondness for taking the center of the stage even in a cheap little mining camp like this and strutting about, the center of all attention. Yet there were qualities in him which escaped her, a possibility of metallic hardness, a pitiless fire of purpose.

To Lord Nick, he was as the bull terrier to the mastiff.

But above all she could not dislodge the memory of his strange talk with her at Lebrun's. Not that she did not season the odd avowals of Donnegan with a grain of salt, but even when she had discounted all that he said, she retained a quivering interest. Somewhere beneath his words she sensed reality.

Somewhere beneath his actions she felt a selfless willingness to throw himself away.

As she rode she was comparing him steadily with Lord Nick. And as she made the comparisons she felt more and more assured that she could pick and choose between the two. They loved her, both of them. With Nick it was an old story; with Donnegan it might be equally true in spite of its newness. And Nelly Lebrun felt rich. Not that she would have been willing to give up Lord Nick. By no means. But neither was she willing to throw away Donnegan. Diamonds in one hand and pearls in the other. Which handful must she discard?

She remained riding an unconscionable length of time, and when she drew rein again before her father's house, the black was flecked with foam from his clamped bit, and there was a thick lather under the stirrup leathers. She threw the reins to the servant who answered her call and went slowly into the house.

Donnegan, by this time, was dead. She began to feel that it would be hard to look Lord Nick in the face again. His other killings had often seemed to her glorious. She had rejoiced in the invincibility of her lover.

Now he suddenly took on the aspect of a murderer.

She found the house hushed. Perhaps everyone was at the gaming house; for now it was midafternoon. But when she opened the door to the apartment which they used as a living room she found Joe Rix and the Pedlar and Lester sitting side by side, silent. There was no whisky in sight; there were no cards in the room. Marvel of marvels, these three men were spending their time in solemn thought. A sudden thought rushed over her, and her cry told where her heart really lay, at least at this time.

"Lord Nick—has he been—"

The Pedlar lifted his gaunt head and stared at her without expression. It was Joe Rix who answered.

"Nick's upstairs."

"Safe?"

"Not a scratch."

She sank into a chair with a sigh, but was instantly on edge again with the second thought.

"Donnegan?" she whispered.

"Safe and sound," said Lester coldly.

She could not gather the truth of the statement.

"Then Nick got Landis back before Donnegan returned?"

"No."

Like any other girl, Nelly Lebrun hated a puzzle above all things in the world, at least a puzzle which affected her new friends.

"Lester, what's happened?" she demanded.

At this Lester, who had been brooding upon the floor, raised his eyes and then switched one leg over the other. He was a typical cowman, was Lester, from his crimson handkerchief knotted around his throat to his shop-made boots which fitted slenderly about his instep with the care of a gloved hand.

"I dunno what happened," said Lester. "Which looks like what counts is the things that didn't happen. Landis is still with that devil, Macon. Donnegan is loose without a scratch, and Lord Nick is in his room with a face as black as a cloudy night."

And briefly he described how Lord Nick had gone up the hill, seen the colonel, come back, taken a horse litter, and gone up the hill again, while the populace of The Corner waited for a crash. For Donnegan had arrived in the meantime. And how Nick had gone into the cabin, remained a singularly long time, and then come out, with a face half white and half red and an eye that dared anyone to ask questions. He had strode straight home to Lebrun's and gone to his room; and there he remained, never making a sound.

"But I'll give you my way of readin' the sign on that trail," said Lester. "Nick goes up the hill to clean up on Donnegan. He sees him; they size each other up in a flash; they figure that if they's a gun it means a double killin'—and they simply haul off and say a perlite fare-thee-well."

The girl paid no attention to these remarks. She was sunk in a brown study.

"There's something behind it all," she said, more to herself than to the men. "Nick is proud as the devil himself. And I can't imagine why he'd let Donnegan go. Oh, it might have been done if they'd met alone in the desert. But with the whole town looking on and waiting for Nick to clean up on Donnegan—no, it isn't possible. There must have been a showdown of some kind."

There was a grim little silence after this.

"Maybe there was," said the Pedlar dryly. "Maybe there was a showdown—and the wind-up of it is that Nick comes home meek as a six-year-old broke down in front."

She stared at him, first astonished, and then almost frightened.

"You mean that Nick may have taken water?"

The three, as one man, shrugged their shoulders, and met her glance with cold eyes.

"You fools!" cried the girl, springing to her feet. "He'd rather die!"

Joe Rix leaned forward, and to emphasize his point he stabbed one dirty forefinger into the fat palm of his other hand.

"You just start thinkin' back," he said solemnly, "and you'll remember that Donnegan has done some pretty slick things."

Lester added with a touch of contempt: "Like shootin' down Landis one day and then sittin' down and havin' a nice long chat with you the next. I dunno how he does it."

"That hunch of yours," said the girl fiercely, "ought to be roped and branded—lie! Lester, don't look at me like that. And if you think Nick has lost his grip on things you're dead wrong. Step light, Lester—and the rest of you. Or Nick may hear you walk—and think."

She flung out of the room and raced up the stairs to Lord Nick's room. There was an interval without response after her first knock. But when she rapped again he called out to know who was there. At her answer she heard his heavy stride cross the room, and the door opened slowly. His face, as she looked up to it, was so changed that she hardly knew him. His hair was unkempt, on end, where he had sat with his fingers thrust into it, buried in thought. And the marks of his palms were red upon his forehead.

"Nick," she whispered, frightened, "what is it?"

He looked down half fiercely, half sadly at her. And though his lips parted they closed again before he spoke. Fear jumped coldly in Nelly Lebrun.

"Did Donnegan—" she pleaded, white-faced. "Did he—"

"Did he bluff me out?" finished Nick. "No, he didn't. That's what everybody'll say. I know it, don't I? And that's why I'm staying here by myself, because the first fool that looks at me with a question in his face, why—I'll break him in two."

She pressed close to him, more frightened than before. That Lord Nick should have been driven to defend himself with words was almost too much for credence.

"You know I don't believe it, Nick! You know that I'm not doubting you."

But he brushed her hands roughly away.

"You want to know what it's all about? Then go over to—well, to Milligan's. Donnegan will be there. He'll explain things to you, I guess. He wants to see you. And maybe I'll come over later and join you."

Seeing Lord Nick before her, so shaken, so gray of face, so dull of eye, she pictured Donnegan as a devil in human form, cunning, resistless.

"Nick, dear—" she pleaded.

He closed the door in her face, and she heard his heavy step go back across the room. In some mysterious manner she felt the Promethean fire had been stolen from Lord Nick, and Donnegan's was the hand that had robbed him of it.

## CHAPTER XXXVI

It was fear that Nelly Lebrun felt first of all. It was fear because the impossible had happened and the immovable object had been at last moved. Going back to her own room, the record of Lord Nick flashed across her mind; one long series of thrilling deeds. He had been a great and widely known figure on the mountain desert while she herself was no more than a girl. When she first met him she had been prepared for the sight of a fire-breathing monster; and she had never quite recovered from the first thrill of finding him not devil but man.

Quite oddly, now that there seemed another man as powerful as Lord Nick or even more terrible, she felt for the big man more tenderly than ever; for like all women, there was a corner of her heart into which she wished to receive a thing she could cherish and protect. Lord Nick, the invincible, had seemed without any real need of other human beings. His love for her had seemed unreal because his need of her seemed a superficial thing. Now that he was in sorrow and defeat she suddenly visualized a Lord Nick to whom she could truly be a helpmate. Tears came to her eyes at the thought.

Yet, very contradictorily and very humanly, the moment she was in her room she began preparing her toilet for that evening at Lebrun's. Let no one think that she was already preparing to cast Lord Nick away and turn to the new star in the sky of the mountain desert. By no means. No doubt her own heart was not quite clear to Nelly. Indeed, she put on her most lovely gown with a desire for revenge. If Lord Nick had been humbled by this singular Donnegan, would it not be a perfect revenge to bring Donnegan himself to her feet? Would it not be a joy to see him turn pale under her smile, and then, when he was well-nigh on his knees, spurn the love which he offered her?

She set her teeth and her eyes gleamed with the thought. But nevertheless she went on lavishing care in the preparation for that night.

As she visioned the scene, the many curious eyes that watched her with Donnegan; the keen envy in the faces of the women; the cold watchfulness of the men, were what she pictured.

In a way she almost regretted that she was admired by such fighting men, Landis, Lord Nick, and now Donnegan, who frightened away the rank and file of other would-be admirers. But it was a pang which she could readily control and subdue.

To tell the truth the rest of the day dragged through a weary length. At the dinner table her father leaned to her and talked in his usual murmuring voice which could reach her own ear and no other by any chance.

"Nelly, there's going to be the devil to pay around The Corner. You know why. Now, be a good girl and wise girl and play your cards. Donnegan is losing his head; he's losing it over you. So play your cards."

"Turn down Nick and take up Donnegan?" she asked coldly.

"I've said enough already," said her father, and would not speak again. But it was easy to see that he already felt Lord Nick's star to be past its full glory.

Afterward, Lebrun himself took his daughter over to Milligan's and left her under the care of the dance-hall proprietor.

"I'm waiting for someone," said Nelly, and Milligan sat willingly at her table and made talk. He was like the rest of The Corner—full of the subject of the strange encounter between Lord Nick and Donnegan. What had Donnegan done to the big man? Nelly merely smiled and said they would all know in time: one thing was certain—Lord Nick had not taken water. But at this Milligan smiled behind his hand.

Ten minutes later there was that stir which announced the arrival of some public figures; and Donnegan with big George behind him came into the room. This evening he went straight to the table to Nelly Lebrun. Milligan, a little uneasy, rose. But Donnegan was gravely polite and regretted that he had interrupted.

"I have only come to ask you for five minutes of your time," he said to the girl.

She was about to put him off merely to make sure of her hold over him, but something she saw in his face fascinated her. She could not play her game. Milligan had slipped away before she knew it, and Donnegan was in his place at the table. He was as much changed as Lord Nick, she thought. Not that his clothes were less carefully arranged than ever, but in the compression of his lips and something behind his eyes she felt the difference. She would have given a great deal indeed to have learned what went on behind the door of Donnegan's shack when Lord Nick was there.

"Last time you asked for one minute and stayed half an hour," she said. "This time it's five minutes."

No matter what was on his mind he was able to answer fully as lightly.

"When I talk about myself, I'm always long-winded."

"Tonight it's someone else?"

"Yes."

She was, being a woman, intensely disappointed, but her smile was as bright as ever.

"Of course I'm listening."

"You remember what I told you of Landis and the girl on the hill?"

"She seems to stick in your thoughts, Mr. Donnegan."

"Yes, she's a lovely child."

And by his frankness he very cunningly disarmed her. Even if he had hesitated an instant she would have been on the track of the truth, but he had foreseen the question and his reply came back instantly.

He added: "Also, what I say has to do with Lord Nick."

"Ah," said the girl a little coldly.

Donnegan went on. He had chosen frankness to be his role and he played it to the full.

"It is a rather wonderful story," he went on. "You know that Lord Nick went up the hill for Landis? And The Corner was standing around waiting for him to bring the youngster down?"

"Of course."

"There was only one obstacle—which you had so kindly removed—myself."

"For your own sake, Mr. Donnegan."

"Ah, don't you suppose that I know?" And his voice touched her. "He came to kill me. And no doubt he could have done so."

Such frankness shocked her into a new attention.

Perhaps Donnegan overdid his part a little at this point, for in her heart of hearts she knew that the little man would a thousand times rather die than give way to any living man.

"But I threw my case bodily before him—the girl—her love for Landis—and the fear which revolved around your own unruly eyes, you know, if he were sent back to your father's house. I placed it all before him. At first he was for fighting at once. But the story appealed to him. He pitied the girl. And in the end he decided to let the matter be judged by a third person. He suggested a man. But I know that a man would see in my attitude nothing but foolishness. No man could have appreciated the position of that girl on the hill. I myself named another referee—yourself."

She gasped.

"And so I have come to place the question before you, because I know that you will decide honestly."

"Then I shall be honest," said the girl.

She was thinking: Why not have Landis back? It would keep the three men revolving around her. Landis on his feet and well would have been nothing; either of these men would have killed him. But Landis sick she might balance in turn against them both. Nelly had the instincts of a fencer; she loved balance.

But Donnegan was heaping up his effects. For by the shadow in her eyes he well knew what was passing through her mind, and he dared not let her speak too quickly.

"There is more hanging upon it. In the first place, if Landis is left with the girl it gives the colonel a chance to work on him, and like as not the colonel will get the young fool to sign away the mines to him—frighten him, you see, though I've made sure that the colonel will not actually harm him."

"How have you made sure? They say the colonel is a devil."

"I have spoken with him. The colonel is not altogether without sensibility to fear."

She caught the glint in the little man's eye and she believed.

"So much for that. Landis is safe, but his money may not be. Another thing still hangs upon your decision. Lord Nick wanted to know why I trusted to you? Because I felt you were honest. Why did I feel that? There was nothing to do. Besides, how could I conceal myself from such a man? I spoke frankly and told him that I trusted you because I love you."

She closed her hand hard on the edge of the table to steady herself.

"And he made no move at you?"

"He restrained himself."

"Lord Nick?" gasped the incredulous girl.

"He is a gentleman," said Donnegan with a singular pride which she could not understand.

He went on: "And unfortunately I fear that if you decide in favor of my side of the argument, I fear that Lord Nick will feel that you—that you—"

He was apparently unable to complete his sentence.

"He will feel that you no longer care for him," said Donnegan at length.

The girl pondered him with cloudy eyes.

"What is behind all this frankness?" she asked coldly.

"I shall tell you. Hopelessness is behind it. Last night I poured my heart at your feet. And I had hope. Today I have seen Lord Nick and I no longer hope."

"Ah?"

"He is worthy of a lovely woman's affection; and I—" He called her attention to himself with a deprecatory gesture.

"Do you ask me to hurt him like this?" said the girl. "His pride is the pride of the fiend. Love me? He would hate me!"

"It might be true. Still I know you would risk it, because—" he paused.

"Well?" asked the girl, whispering in her excitement.

"Because you are a lady."

He bowed to her.

"Because you are fair; because you are honest, Nelly Lebrun. Personally I think that you can win Lord Nick back with one minute of smiling. But you might not. You might alienate him forever. It will be clumsy to explain to him that you were influenced not by me, but by justice. He will make it a personal matter, whereas you and I know that it is only the right that you are seeing."

She propped her chin on the tips of her fingers, and her arm was a thing of grace. For the last moments that clouded expression had not cleared.

"If I only could read your mind," she murmured now. "There is something behind it all."

"I shall tell you what it is. It is the restraint that has fallen upon me. It is because I wish to lean closer to you across the table and speak to you of things which are at the other end of the world from Landis and the other girl. It is because I have to keep my hands gripped hard to control myself. Because, though I have given up hope, I would follow a forlorn chance, a lost cause, and tell you again and again that I love you, Nelly Lebrun!"

He had half lowered his eyes as he spoke; he had called up a vision, and the face of Lou Macon hovered dimly between him and Nelly Lebrun. If all that he spoke was a lie, let him be forgiven for it; it was the golden-haired girl whom he addressed, and it was she who gave the tremor and the fiber to his voice. And after all was he not pleading for her happiness as he believed?

He covered his eyes with his hand; but when he looked up again she could see the shadow of the pain which was slowly passing. She had never seen such emotion in any man's face, and if it was for another, how could she guess it? Her blood was singing in her veins, and the old, old question was flying back and forth through her brain like a shuttle through a loom: Which shall it be?

She called up the picture of Lord Nick, half-broken, but still terrible, she well knew. She pitied him, but when did pity wholly rule the heart of a woman? And as for Nelly Lebrun, she had the ambition of a young Caesar; she could not fill a second place. He who loved her must stand first, and she saw Donnegan as the invincible man. She had not believed half of his explanation. No, he was shielding Lord Nick; behind that shield the truth was that the big man had quailed before the small.

Of course she saw that Donnegan, pretending to be constrained by his agreement with Lord Nick, was in reality cunningly pleading his own cause. But his passion excused him. When has a woman condemned a man for loving her beyond the rules of fair play?

"Whatever you may decide," Donnegan was saying. "I shall be prepared to stand by it without a murmur. Send Landis back to your father's house and I submit: I leave The Corner and say farewell. But now, think quickly. For Lord Nick is coming to receive your answer."

## CHAPTER XXXVII

If the meeting between Lord Nick and Donnegan earlier that day had wrought up the nerves of The Corner to the point of hysteria; if the singular end of that meeting had piled mystery upon excitement; if the appearance of Donnegan, sitting calmly at the table of the girl who was known to be engaged to Nick, had further stimulated public curiosity, the appearance of Lord Nick was now a crowning burden under which The Corner staggered.

Yet not a man or a woman stirred from his chair, for everyone knew that if the long-delayed battle between these two gunfighters was at length to take place, neither bullet was apt to fly astray.

But what happened completed the wreck of The Corner's nerves, for Lord Nick walked quietly across the floor and sat down with Nelly Lebrun and his somber rival.

Oddly enough, he looked at Donnegan, not at the girl, and this token of the beaten man decided her.

"Well?" said Lord Nick.

"I have decided," said the girl. "Landis should stay where he is."

Neither of the two men stirred hand or eye. But Lord Nick turned gray. At length he rose and asked Donnegan, quietly, to step aside with him. Seeing them together, the difference between their sizes was more apparent: Donnegan seemed hardly larger than a child beside the splendid bulk of Lord Nick. But she could not overhear their talk.

"You've won," said Lord Nick, "both Landis and Nelly. And—"

"Wait," broke in Donnegan eagerly. "Henry, I've persuaded Nelly to see my side of the case, but that doesn't mean that she has turned from you to—"

"Stop!" put in Lord Nick, between his teeth. "I've not come to argue with you or ask advice or opinions. I've come to state facts. You've crawled in between me and Nelly like a snake in the grass. Very well. You're my brother. That keeps me from handling you. You've broken my reputation just as I said you would do. The bouncer at the door looked me in the eye and smiled when I came in."

He had to pause a little, breathing heavily, and avoiding Donnegan's eyes. Finally he was able to continue.

"I'm going to roll my blankets and leave The Corner and everything I have in it. You'll get my share of most things, it seems." He smiled after a ghastly, mirthless fashion. "I give you a free road. I surrender everything to you, Donnegan. But there are two things I want to warn you about. It may be that my men will not agree with me. It may be that they'll want to put up a fight for the mine. They can't get at it without getting at Macon. They can't get at him without removing you. And they'll probably try it. I warn you now.

"Another thing: from this moment there's no blood tie between us. I've found a brother and lost him in the same day. And if I ever cross you again, Donnegan, I'll shoot you on sight. Remember, I'm not threatening. I simply warn you in advance. If I were you, I'd get out of the country. Avoid me, Donnegan, as you'd avoid the devil."

And he turned on his heel. He felt the eyes of the people in the room follow him by jerks, dwelling on every one of his steps. Near the door, stepping aside to avoid a group of people coming in, he half turned and he could not avoid the sight of Donnegan and Nelly Lebrun at the other end of the room. He was leaning across the table, talking with a smile on his lips—at that distance he could not mark the pallor of the little man's face—and Nelly Lebrun was laughing. Laughing already, and oblivious of the rest of the world.

Lord Nick turned, a blur coming before his eyes, and made blindly for the door. A body collided with him; without a word he drew back his massive right fist and knocked the man down. The stunned body struck against the wall and collapsed along the floor. Lord Nick felt a great madness swell in his heart. Yet he set his teeth, controlled himself, and went on toward the house of Lebrun. He had come within an eyelash of running amuck, and the quivering hunger for action was still swelling and ebbing in him when he reached the gambler's house.

Lebrun was not in the gaming house, no doubt, at this time of night—but the rest of Nick's chosen men were there. They stood up as he entered the room—Harry Masters, newly arrived—the Pedlar—Joe Rix—three names famous in the mountain desert for deeds which were not altogether a pleasant aroma in the nostrils of the law-abiding, but whose sins had been deftly covered from legal proof by the cunning of Nick, and whose bravery itself had half redeemed them. They rose now as three wolves rise at the coming of the leader. But this time there was a question behind their eyes, and he read it in gloomy silence.

"Well?" asked Harry Masters.

In the old days not one of them would have dared to voice the question, but now things were changing, and well Lord Nick could read the change and its causes.

"Are you talking to me?" asked Nick, and he looked straight between the eyes of Masters.

The glance of the other did not falter, and it maddened Nick.

"I'm talking to you," said Masters coolly enough. "What happened between you and Donnegan?"

"What should happen?" asked Lord Nick.

"Maybe all this is a joke," said Masters bitterly. He was a square-built man, with a square face and a wrinkled, fleshy forehead. In intelligence, Nick ranked him first among the men. And if a new leader were to be chosen there was no doubt as to where the choice of the men would fall. No doubt that was why Masters put himself forward now, ready to brave the wrath of the chief. "Maybe we're fooled," went on Masters. "Maybe they ain't any call for you to fall out with Donnegan?"

"Maybe there's a call to find out this," answered Lord Nick. "Why did you leave the mines? What are you doing up here?"

The other swallowed so hard that he blinked.

"I left the mines," he declared through his set teeth, "because I was run off 'em."

"Ah," said Lord Nick, for the devil was rising in him, "I always had an idea that you might be yellow, Masters."

The right hand of Masters swayed toward his gun, hesitated, and then poised idly.

"You heard me talk?" persisted Lord Nick brutally. "I call you yellow. Why don't you draw on me? I called you yellow, you swine, and I call the rest of you yellow. You think you have me down? Why, curse you, if there were thirty of your cut, I'd say the same to you!"

There was a quick shift, the three men faced Lord Nick, but each from a different angle. And opposing them, he stood superbly indifferent, his arms folded, his feet braced. His arms were folded, but each hand, for all they knew, might be grasping the butt of a gun hidden away in his clothes. Once they flashed a glance from face to face; but there was no action. They were remembering only too well some of the wild deeds of this giant.

"You think I'm through," went on Lord Nick. "Maybe I am—through with you. You hear me talk?"

One by one, his eyes dared them, and one by one they took up the challenge, struggled, and lowered their glances. He was still their master and in that mute moment the three admitted it, the Pedlar last of all.

Masters saw fit to fall back on the last remark.

"I've swallowed a lot from you, Nick," he said gravely.

"Maybe there'll be an end to what we take one of these days. But now I'll tell you how yellow I was. A couple of gents come to me and tell me I'm through at the mine. I told them they were crazy. They said old Colonel Macon had sent them down to take charge. I laughed at 'em. They went away and came back. Who with? With the sheriff. And he flashed a paper on me. It was all drawn up clean as a whistle. Trimmed up with a lot of 'whereases' and 'as hereinbefore mentioned' and such like things. But the sheriff just gimme a look and then he tells me what it's about. Jack Landis has signed over all the mines to the colonel and the colonel has taken possession."

As he stopped, a growl came from the others.

"Lester is the man that has the complaint," said Lord Nick. "Where do the rest of you figure in it? Lester had the mines; he lost 'em because he couldn't drop Landis with his gun. He'd never have had a smell of the gold if I hadn't come in. Who made Landis see light? I did! Who worked it so that every nickel that came out of the mines went through the fingers of Landis and came back to us? I did! But I'm through with you. You can hunt for yourselves now. I've kept you together to guard one another's backs. I've kept the law off your trail. You, Masters, you'd have swung for killing the McKay brothers. Who saved you? Who was it bribed the jury that tried you for the shooting up of Derbyville, Pedlar? Who took the marshal off your trail after you'd knifed Lefty Waller, Joe Rix? I've saved you all a dozen times. Now you whine at me. I'm through with you forever!"

Stopping, he glared about him. His knuckles stung from the impact of the blow he had delivered in Milligan's place. He hungered to have one of these three stir a hand and get into action.

And they knew it. All at once they crumbled and became clay in his hands.

"Chief," said Joe Rix, the smoothest spoken of the lot, and one who was supposed to stand specially well with Lord Nick on account of his ability to bake beans, Spanish. "Chief, you've said a whole pile. You're worth more'n the rest of us all rolled together. Sure. We know that. There ain't any argument. But here's just one little point that I want to make.

"We was doing fine. The gold was running fine and free. Along comes this Donnegan. He busts up our good time. He forks in on your girl—"

A convulsion of the chief's face made Rix waver in his speech and then he went on: "He shoots Landis, and when he misses killing him—by some accident, he comes down here and grabs him out of Lebrun's own house. Smooth, eh? Then he makes Landis sign that deed to the mines. Oh, very nice work, I say. Too nice.

"'Now, speakin' man to man, they ain't any doubt that you'd like to get rid of Donnegan. Why don't you? Because everybody has a jinx, and he's yours. I ain't easy scared, maybe, but I knew an albino with white eyes once, and just to look at him made me some sick. Well, chief, they ain't nobody can say that you ever took water or ever will. But maybe the fact that this Donnegan has hair just as plumb red as yours may sort of get you off your feed. I'm just suggesting. Now, what I say is, let the rest of us take a crack at Donnegan, and you sit back and come in on the results when we've cleaned up. D'you give us a free road?"

How much went through the brain of Lord Nick? But in the end he gave his brother up to death. For he remembered how Nelly Lebrun had sat in Milligan's laughing.

"Do what you want," he said suddenly. "But I want to know none of your plans—and the man that tells me Donnegan is dead gets paid—in lead!"

## CHAPTER XXXVIII

The smile of Joe Rix was the smile of a diplomat. It could be maintained upon his face as unwaveringly as if it were wrought out of marble while Joe heard insult and lie. As a matter of fact Joe had smiled in the face of death more than once, and this is a school through which even diplomats rarely pass. Yet it was with an effort that he maintained the characteristic good-natured expression when the door to Donnegan's shack opened and he saw big George and, beyond him, Donnegan himself.

"Booze," said Joe Rix to himself instantly.

For Donnegan was a wreck. The unshaven beard—it was the middle of morning—was a reddish mist over his face. His eyes were sunken in shadow. His hair was uncombed. He sat with his shoulders hunched up like one who suffers from cold. Altogether his appearance was that of one whose energy has been utterly sapped.

"The top of the morning, Mr. Donnegan," said Joe Rix, and put his foot on the threshold.

But since big George did not move it was impossible to enter.

"Who's there?" asked Donnegan.

It was a strange question to ask, for by raising his eyes he could have seen. But Donnegan was staring down at the floor. Even his voice was a weak murmur.

"What a party! What a party he's had!" thought Joe Rix, and after all, there was cause for a celebration. Had not the little man in almost one stroke won the heart of the prettiest girl in The Corner, and also did he not probably have a working share in the richest of the diggings?

"I'm Joe Rix," he said.

"Joe Rix?" murmured Donnegan softly. "Then you're one of Lord Nick's men?"

"I was," said Joe Rix, "sort of attached to him, maybe."

Perhaps this pointed remark won the interest of Donnegan. He raised his eyes, and Joe Rix beheld the most unhappy face he had ever seen. "A bad hangover," he decided, "and that makes it bad for me!"

"Come in," said Donnegan in the same monotonous, lifeless voice.

Big George reluctantly, it seemed, withdrew to one side, and Rix was instantly in the room and drawing out a chair so that he could face Donnegan.

"I was," he proceeded "sort of tied up with Lord Nick. But"—and here he winked broadly—"it ain't much of a secret that Nick ain't altogether a lord anymore. Nope. Seems he turned out sort of common, they say."

"What fool," murmured Donnegan, "has told you that? What ass had told you that Lord Nick is a common sort?"

It shocked Joe Rix, but being a diplomat he avoided friction by changing his tactics.

"Between you and me," he said calmly enough, "I took what I heard with a grain of salt. There's something about Nick that ain't common, no matter what they say. Besides, they's some men that nobody but a fool would stand up to. It ain't hardly a shame for a man to back down from 'em."

He pointed this remark with a nod to Donnegan.

"I'll give you a bit of free information," said the little man, with his weary eyes lighted a little. "There's no man on the face of the earth who could make Lord Nick back down."

Once more Joe Rix was shocked to the verge of gaping, but again he exercised a power of marvelous self control. "About that," he remarked as pointedly as before, "I got my doubts. Because there's some things that any gent with sense will always clear away from. Maybe not one man—but say a bunch of all standin' together."

Donnegan leaned back in his chair and waited. Both of his hands remained drooping from the edge of the table, and the tired eyes drifted slowly across the face of Joe Rix.

It was obviously not the aftereffects of liquor. The astonishing possibility occurred to Joe Rix that this seemed to be a man with a broken spirit and a great sorrow. He blinked that absurdity away.

"Coming to cases," he went on, "there's yourself, Mr. Donnegan. Now, you're the sort of a man that don't sidestep nobody. Too proud to do it. But even you, I guess, would step careful if there was a whole bunch agin' you."

"No doubt," remarked Donnegan.

"I don't mean any ordinary bunch," explained Joe Rix, "but a lot of hard fellows. Gents that handle their guns like they was born with a holster on the hip."

"Fellows like Nick's crowd," suggested Donnegan quietly.

At this thrust the eyes of Joe narrowed a little.

"Yes," he admitted, "I see you get my drift."

"I think so."

"Two hard fighters would give the best man that ever pulled a gun a lot of trouble. Eh?"

"No doubt."

"And three men—they ain't any question, Mr. Donnegan—would get him ready for a hole in the ground."

"I suppose so."

"And four men would make it no fight—jest a plain butchery."

"Yes?"

"Now, I don't mean that Nick's crowd has any hard feeling about you, Mr. Donnegan."

"I'm glad to hear that."

"I knew you'd be. That's why I've come, all friendly, to talk things over. Suppose you look at it this way—"

"Joe Rix," broke in Donnegan, sighing, "I'm very tired. Won't you cut this short? Tell me in ten words just how you stand."

Joe Rix blinked once more, caught his breath, and fired his volley.

"Short talk is straight talk, mostly," he declared. "This is what Lester and the rest of us want—the mines!"

"Ah?"

"Macon stole 'em. We got 'em back through Landis. Now we've got to get 'em back through the colonel himself. But we can't get at the colonel while you're around."

"In short, you're going to start out to get me? I expected it, but it's kind of you to warn me."

"Wait, wait, wait! Don't rush along to conclusions. We ain't so much in a hurry. We don't want you out of the way. We just want you on our side."

"Shoot me up and then bring me back to life, eh?"

"Mr. Donnegan," said the other, spreading out his hands solemnly on the table, "you ain't doin' us justice. We don't hanker none for trouble with you. Any way it comes, a fight with you means somebody dead besides you. We'd get you. Four to one is too much for any man. But one or two of us might go down. Who would it be? Maybe the Pedlar, maybe Harry Masters, maybe Lester, maybe me! Oh, we know all that. No gunplay if we can keep away from it."

"You've left out the name of Lord Nick," said Donnegan.

Joe Rix winked.

"Seems like you tended to him once and for all when you got him alone in this cabin. Must have thrown a mighty big scare into him. He won't lift a hand agin' you now."

"No?" murmured Donnegan hoarsely.

"Not him! But that leaves four of us, and four is plenty, eh?"

"Perhaps."

"But I'm not here to insist on that point. No, we put a value on keepin' up good feeling between us and you, Mr. Donnegan. We ain't fools. We know a man when we see him —and the fastest gunman that ever slid a gun out of leather ain't the sort of a man that me and the rest of the boys pass over lightly. Not us! We know you, Mr. Donnegan; we respect you; we want you with us; we're going to have you with us."

"You flatter me and I thank you. But I'm glad to see that you are at last coming to the point."

"I am, and the point is five thousand dollars that's tied behind the hoss that stands outside your door."

He pushed his fat hand a little way across the table, as though the gold even then were resting in it, a yellow tide of fortune.

"For which," said Donnegan, "I'm to step aside and let you at the colonel?"

"Right."

Donnegan smiled.

"Wait," said Joe Rix. "I was makin' a first offer to see how you stood, but you're right. Five thousand ain't enough and we ain't cheapskates. Not us. Mr. Donnegan, they's ten thousand cold iron men behind that saddle out there and every cent of it belongs to you when you come over on our side."

But Donnegan merely dropped his chin upon his hand and smiled mirthlessly at Joe Rix. A wild thought came to the other man. Both of

Donnegan's hands were far from his weapons. Why not a quick draw, a snap shot, and then the glory of having killed this manslayer in single battle for Joe Rix?

The thought rushed red across his brain and then faded slowly. Something kept him back. Perhaps it was the singular calm of Donnegan; no matter how quiet he sat he suggested the sleeping cat which can leap out of dead sleep into fighting action at a touch. By the time a second thought had come to Joe Rix the idea of an attack was like an idea of suicide.

"Is that final?" he asked, though Donnegan had not said a word.

"It is."

Joe Rix stood up.

"You put it to us kind of hard. But we want you, Mr. Donnegan. And here's the whole thing in a nutshell. Come over to us. We'll stand behind you. Lord Nick is slipping. We'll put you in his place. You won't even have to face him; we'll get rid of him."

"You'll kill him and give his place to me?" asked Donnegan.

"We will. And when you're with us, you cut in on the whole amount of coin that the mines turn out—and it'll be something tidy. And right now, to show where we stand and how high we put you, I'll let you in on the rock-bottom truth. Mr. Donnegan, out there tied behind my saddle there's thirty thousand dollars in pure gold. You can take it in here and weigh it out!"

He stepped back to watch this blow take effect. To his unutterable astonishment the little man had not moved. His chin still rested upon the back of his hand, and the smile which was on the lips and not in the eyes of Donnegan remained there, fixed.

"Donnegan," muttered Joe Rix, "if we can't get you, we'll get rid of you. You understand?"

But the other continued to smile.

It gave Joe Rix a shuddering feeling that someone was stealing behind him to block his way to the door. He cast one swift glance over his shoulder and then, seeing that the way was clear, he slunk back, always keeping his face to the red-headed man. But when he came to the doorway his nerve collapsed. He whirled, covered the rest of the distance with a leap, and emerged from the cabin in a fashion ludicrously like one who has been kicked through a door.

His nerve returned as soon as the sunlight fell warmly upon him again; and he looked around hastily to see if anyone had observed his flight.

There was no one on the whole hillside except Colonel Macon in the invalid chair, and the colonel was smiling broadly, beneficently. He had his perfect hands folded across his breast and seemed to cast a prayer of peace and goodwill upon Joe Rix.

# CHAPTER XXXIX

Nelly Lebrun smelled danger. She sensed it as plainly as the deer when the puma comes between her and the wind. The many tokens that something was wrong came to her by small hints which had to be put together before they assumed any importance.

First of all, her father, who should have burst out at her in a tirade for having left Lord Nick for Donnegan said nothing at all, but kept a dark smile on his face when she was near him. He even insinuated that Nick's time was done and that another was due to supersede him.

In the second place, she had passed into a room where Masters, Joe Rix, and the Pedlar sat cheek by jowl in close conference with a hum of deep voice. But at her appearance all talk was broken off.

It was not strange that they should not invite her into their confidence if they had some dark work ahead of them; but it was exceedingly suspicious that Joe Rix attempted to pass off their whispers by immediately breaking off the soft talk and springing into the midst of a full-fledged jest; also, it was strangest of all that when the jest ended even the Pedlar, who rarely smiled, now laughed uproariously and smote Joe soundingly upon the back.

Even a child could have strung these incidents into a chain of evidence which pointed toward danger. Obviously the danger was not directly hers, but then it must be directed at someone near to her. Her father? No, he was more apt to be the prompting of their action. Lord Nick? There was nothing to gain by attacking him. Who was left? Donnegan!

As the realization came upon her it took her breath away for a moment. Donnegan was the man. At breakfast everyone had been talking about him. Lebrun had remarked that he had a face for the cards—emotionless. Joe Rix had commented upon his speed of hand, and the Pedlar had complimented the little man on his dress.

But at lunch not a word was spoken about Donnegan even after she had dexterously introduced the subject twice. Why the sudden silence? Between morning and noon Donnegan must have grievously offended them.

Fear for his sake stimulated her; but above and beyond this, indeed, there was a mighty feminine curiosity. She smelled the secret; it reeked through the house, and she was devoured by eagerness to know. She handpicked Lord Nick's gang in the hope of finding a weakness among them; some weakness upon which she could play in one of them and draw out what they were all concealing. The Pedlar was as unapproachable as a crag on a mountaintop. Masters was wise as an outlaw broncho. Lester was probably not even in the confidence of the others because since the affair with Landis his nerve had been shattered to bits and the others secretly despised him for being beaten by the youngster at the draw. There remained, therefore, only Joe Rix.

But Joe Rix was a fox of the first quality. He lied with the smoothness of silk. He could show a dozen colors in as many moments. Come to the windward of Joe Rix? It was a delicate business! But since there was nothing else to do, she fixed her mind upon it, working out this puzzle. Joe Rix wished to destroy Donnegan for reasons that were evidently connected with the mines. And she must step into his confidence to discover his plans. How should it be done? And there was a vital need for speed, for they might be within a step of executing whatever mischief it was that they were planning.

She went down from her room; they were there still, only Joe Rix was not with them. She went to the apartment where he and the other three of Nick's gang slept and rapped at the door. He maintained his smile when he saw her, but there was an uncertain quiver of his eyebrows that told her much. Plainly he was ill at ease. Suspicious? Ay, there were always clouds of suspicion drifting over the red, round face of Joe Rix. She put a tremor of excitement and trouble in her voice.

"Come into my room, Joe, where we won't be interrupted."

He followed her without a word, and since she led the way she was able to relax her expression for a necessary moment. When she closed the door behind him and faced Joe again she was once more ready to step into her part. She did not ask him to sit down. She remained for a moment with her hand on the knob and searched the face of Joe Rix eagerly.

"Do you think he can hear?" she whispered, gesturing over her shoulder.

"Who?"

"Who but Lord Nick!" she exclaimed softly.

The bewilderment of Joe clouded his face a second and then he was able to smooth it away. What on earth was the reason of her concern about Lord Nick he was obviously wondering.

"I'll tell you why," she said, answering the unspoken question at once. "He's as jealous as the devil, Joe!"

The fat little man sighed as he looked at her.

"He can't hear. Not through that log wall. But we'll talk soft, if you want."

"Yes, yes. Keep your voice down. He's already jealous of you, Joe."

"Of me?"

"He knows I like you, that I trust you; and just now he's on edge about everyone I look at."

The surprising news which the first part of this sentence contained caused Joe to gape, and the girl looked away in concern, enabling him to control his expression. For she knew well enough that men hate to appear foolishly surprised. And particularly a fox like Joe Rix.

"But what's the trouble, Nelly?" He added with a touch of venom: "I thought everything was going smoothly with you. And I thought you weren't worrying much about what Lord Nick had in his mind."

She stared at him as though astonished.

"Do you think just the same as the rest of them?" she asked sadly. "Do you mean to say that you're fooled just the same as Harry Masters and the Pedlar and the rest of those fools—including Nick himself?"

Joe Rix was by no means willing to declare himself a fool beforehand. He now mustered a look of much reserved wisdom.

"I have my own doubts, Nell, but I'm not talking about them."

He was so utterly at sea that she had to bite her lip hard to keep from breaking into ringing laughter.

"Oh, I knew that you'd seen through it, Joe," she cried softly. "You see what an awful mess I've gotten into?"

He passed a hurried hand across his forehead and then looked at her searchingly. But he could not penetrate her pretense of concern.

"No matter what I think," said Joe Rix, "you come out with it frankly. I'll listen."

"As a friend, Joe?"

She managed to throw a plea into her voice that made Joe sigh.

"Sure. You've already said that I'm your friend, and you're right."

"I'm in terrible, terrible trouble! You know how it happened. I was a fool. I tried to play with Lord Nick. And now he thinks I was in earnest."

As though the strength of his legs had given way, Joe Rix slipped down into a chair.

"Go on," he said huskily. "You were playing with Lord Nick?"

"Can't you put yourself in my place, Joe? It's always been taken for granted that I'm to marry Nick. And the moment he comes around everybody else avoids me as if I were poison. I was sick of it. And when he showed up this time it was the same old story. A man would as soon sign his own death warrant as ask me for a dance. You know how it is?"

He nodded, still at sea, but with a light beginning to dawn in his little eyes.

"I'm only a girl, Joe. I have all the weakness of other girls. I don't want to be locked up in a cage just because I—love one man!"

The avowal made Joe blink. It was the second time that day that he had been placed in an astonishing scene. But some of his old cunning remained to him.

"Nell," he said suddenly, rising from his chair and going to her. "What are you trying to do to me? Pull the wool over my eyes?"

It was too much for Nelly Lebrun. She knew that she could not face him without betraying her guilt and therefore she did not attempt it. She whirled and flung herself on her bed, face down, and began to sob violently, suppressing the sounds. And so she waited.

Presently a hand touched her shoulder lightly.

"Go away," cried Nelly in a choked voice. "I hate you, Joe Rix. You're like all the rest!"

His knee struck the floor with a soft thud.

"Come on, Nell. Don't be hard on me. I thought you were stringing me a little. But if you're playing straight, tell me what you want?"

At that she bounced upright on the bed, and before he could rise she caught him by both shoulders.

"I want Donnegan," she said fiercely.

"What?"

"I want him dead!"

Joe Rix gasped.

"Here's the cause of all my trouble. Just because I flirted with him once or twice, Nick thought I was in earnest and now he's sulking. And Donnegan puts on airs and acts as if I belonged to him. I hate him, Joe. And if he's gone Nick will come back to me. He'll come back to me, Joe; and I want him so!"

She found that Joe Rix was staring straight into her eyes, striving to probe her soul to its depths, and by a great effort she was enabled to meet that gaze. Finally the fat little man rose slowly to his feet. Her hands trailed from his shoulders as he stood up and fell helplessly upon her lap.

"Well, I'll be hanged, Nell!" exclaimed Joe Rix.

"What do you mean?"

"You're not acting a part? No, I can see you mean it. But what a cold-blooded little—" He checked himself. His face was suddenly jubilant. "Then we've got him, Nell. We've got him if you're with us. We had him anyway, but we'll make sure of him if you're with us. Look at this! You saw me put a paper in my pocket when I opened the door of my room? Here it is!"

He displayed before the astonished eyes of Nelly Lebrun a paper covered with an exact duplicate of her own swift, dainty script. And she read:

> *Nick is terribly angry and is making trouble. I have to get away. It isn't safe for me to stay here. Will you help me? Will you meet me at the shack by Donnell's ford tomorrow morning at ten o'clock?*

"But I didn't write it," cried Nelly Lebrun, bewildered.

"Nelly," Joe Rix chuckled, flushing with pleasure, "you didn't. It was me. I kind of had an idea that you wanted to get rid of this Donnegan, and I was going to do it for you and then surprise you with the good news."

"Joe, you forged it?"

"Don't bother sayin' pretty things about me and my pen," said Rix modestly. "This is nothin'! But if you want to help me, Nelly—"

His voice faded partly out of her consciousness as she fought against a tigerish desire to spring at the throat of the little fat man. But gradually it dawned on her that he was asking her to write out that note herself. Why? Because it was possible that Donnegan might have seen her handwriting and in that case, though the imitation had been good enough to deceive Nelly herself, it probably would not for a moment fool the keen eyes of Donnegan. But if she herself wrote out the note, Donnegan was already as good as dead.

"That is," concluded Joe Rix, "if he really loves you, Nell."

"The fool!" cried Nelly. "He worships the ground I walk on, Joe. And I hate him for it."

Even Joe Rix shivered, for he saw the hate in her eyes and could not dream that he himself was the cause and the object of it. There was a red haze of horror and confusion in front of her eyes, and yet she was able to smile while she copied the note for Joe Rix.

"But how are you going to work it?" she asked. "How are you going to kill him, Joe?"

"Don't bother your pretty head," said the fat man, smiling. "Just wait till we bring you the good news."

"But are you sure?" she asked eagerly. "See what he's done already. He's taken Landis away from us; he's baffled Nick himself, in some manner; and he's gathered the mines away from all of us. He's a devil, Joe, and if you want to get him you'd better take ten men for the job."

"You hate him, Nell, don't you?" queried Joe Rix, and his voice was both hard and curious. "But how has he harmed you?"

"Hasn't he taken Nick away from me? Isn't that enough?"

The fat man shivered again.

"All right. I'll tell you how it works. Now, listen!"

And he began to check off the details of his plan.

## CHAPTER XL

The day passed and the night, but how very slowly for Nelly Lebrun; she went up to her room early for she could no longer bear the meaning glances which Joe Rix cast at her from time to time. But once in her room it was still harder to bear the suspense as she waited for the noise to die away in the house. Midnight, and half an hour more went by, and then, at last, the murmurs and the laughter stopped; she alone was wakeful in Lebrun's. And when that time came she caught a scarf around her hair and her shoulders, made of a filmy material which would veil her face but through which she could see, and ventured out of her room and down the hall.

There was no particular need for such caution, however, it seemed. Nothing stirred. And presently she was outside the house and hurrying behind the houses and up the hill. Still she met nothing. If The Corner lived tonight, its life was confined to Milligan's and the gambling house.

She found Donnegan's shack and the one next to it, which the terrible colonel occupied, entirely dark, but only a moment after she tapped at the door it was opened. Donnegan, fully dressed, stood in the entrance, outlined blackly by the light which came faintly from the hooded lantern hanging on the wall. Was he sitting up all the night, unable to sleep because he waited breathlessly for that false tryst on the morrow? A great tenderness came over the heart of Nelly Lebrun.

"It is I," she whispered.

There was a soft exclamation, then she was drawn into the room.

"Is there anyone here?"

"Only big George. But he's in the kitchen and he won't hear. He never hears anything except what's meant for his ear. Take this chair!"

He was putting a blanket over the rough wood to make it more comfortable, and she submitted dumbly to his ministrations. It seemed terrible and strange to her that one so gentle should be the object of so much hate—such deadly hate as the members of Nick's gang felt for him. And now that he was sitting before her she could see that he had indeed been wakeful for a long time. His face was grimly wasted; the lips were compressed as one who has endured long pain; and his eyes gleamed at her out of a profound shadow. He remained in the gloom; the light from the lantern fell brightly upon his hands alone— meager, fleshless hands which seemed to represent hardly more strength than that of a child. Truly this man was all a creature of spirit and nerve. Therein lay his strength, as also his weakness, and again the cherishing instinct grew strong and swept over her.

"There is no one near," he said, "except the colonel and his daughter. They are up the hillside, somewhere. Did you see them?"

"No. What in the world are they out for at this time of night?"

"Because the colonel only wakes up when the sun goes down. And now he's out there humming to himself and never speaking a word to the girl. But they won't be far away. They'll stay close to see that no one comes near the cabin to get at Landis."

He added: "They must have seen you come into my cabin!"

And his lips set even harder than before. Was it fear because of her?

"They may have seen me enter, but they won't know who it was. You have the note from me?"

"Yes."

"It's a lie! It's a ruse. I was forced to write it to save you! For they're planning to murder you. Oh, my dear!"

"Hush! Hush! Murder?"

"I've been nearly hysterical all day and all the night. But, thank heaven, I'm here to warn you in time! You mustn't go. You mustn't go!"

"Who is it?"

He had drawn his chair closer: he had taken her hands, and she noted that his own were icy cold, but steady as a rock. Their pressure soothed her infinitely.

"Joe Rix, the Pedlar, Harry Masters. They'll be at the shack at ten o'clock, but not I!"

"Murder, but a very clumsy scheme. Three men leave town and commit a murder and then expect to go undetected? Not even in the mountain desert!"

"But you don't understand, you don't understand! They're wise as foxes. They'll take no risk. They don't even leave town together or travel by the same routes. Harry Masters starts first. He rides out at eight o'clock in the morning and takes the north trail. He rides down the gulch and winds out of it and strikes for the shack at the ford. At half past eight the Pedlar starts. He goes past Sandy's place and then over the trail through the marsh. You know it?"

"Yes."

"Last of all, Joe Rix starts at nine o'clock. Half an hour between them."

"How does he go to the shack?"

"By the south trail. He takes the ridge of the hills. But they'll all be at the shack long before you and they'll shoot you down from a distance as you come up to it. Plain murder, but even for cowardly murder they daren't face you except three to one."

He was thoughtful.

"Suppose they were to be met on the way?"

"You're mad to think of it!"

"But if they fail this time they'll try again. They must be taught a lesson."

"Three men? Oh, my dear, my dear! Promise!"

"Very well. I shall do nothing rash. And I shall never forget that you've come to tell me this and been in peril, Nell, for if they found you had come to me—"

"The Pedlar would cut my throat. I know him!"

"Ah! But now you must go. I'll take you down the hill, dear."

"No, no! It's much easier to get back alone. My face will be covered. But there's no way you could be disguised. You have a way of walking—good night—and God bless you!"

She was in his arms, straining him to her; and then she slipped out the door.

And sure enough, there was the colonel in his chair not fifty feet away with a girl pushing him. The moonlight was too dim for Nelly Lebrun to make out the face of Lou Macon, but even the light which escaped through the filter of clouds was enough to set her golden hair glowing. The color was not apparent, but its luster was soft silver in the night. There was a murmur of the colonel's voice as Nelly came out of the cabin.

And then, from the girl, a low cry.

It brought the blood to the cheeks of Nelly as she hurried down the hill, for she recognized the pain that was in it; and it occurred to her that if the girl was in love with Jack Landis she was strangely interested in Donnegan also.

The thought came so sharply home to her that she paused abruptly on the way down the hill. After all, this Macon girl would be a very strange sort if she were not impressed by the little red-headed man, with his gentle voice and his fiery ways, and his easy way of making himself a brilliant spectacle whenever he appeared in public. And Nelly remembered, also, with the keen suspicion of a woman in love how weakly Donnegan had responded to her embrace this night. How absent-mindedly his arms had held her, and how numbly they had fallen away when she turned at the door.

But she shook her head and made the suspicion shudder its way out of her. Lou Macon, she decided, was just the sort of girl who would think Jack Landis an ideal. Besides, she had never had an opportunity to see Donnegan in his full glory at Milligan's. And as for Donnegan? He was wearied out; his nerves relaxed; and for the deeds with which he had startled The Corner and won her own heart he was now paying the penalty in the shape of ruined nerves. Pity again swelled in her heart, and a consuming hatred for the three murderers who lived in her father's house.

And when she reached her room again her heart was filled with a singing happiness and a glorious knowledge that she had saved the man she loved.

And Donnegan himself?

He had seen Lou and her father: he had heard that low cry of pain; and now he sat bowed again over his table, his face in his hands and a raging devil in his heart.

## CHAPTER XLI

There was one complication which Nelly Lebrun might have foreseen after her pretended change of heart and her simulated confession to Joe Rix that she still loved the lionlike Lord Nick. But strangely enough she did not think of this phase: and even when her father the next morning approached her in the hall and tapping her arm whispered: "Good girl! Nick has just heard and he's hunting for you now!" Even then the full meaning did not come home to her. It was not until she saw the great form of Lord Nick stalking swiftly down the hall that she knew. He came with a glory in his face which the last day had graven with unfamiliar lines; and when he saw her he threw up his hand so that it almost brushed the ceiling, and cried out.

What could she do? Try to push him away; to explain?

There was nothing to be done. She had to submit when he swept her into his arms.

"Rix has told me. Rix has told me. Ah, Nell, you little fox!"

"Told you what, Nick?"

Was he, too, a party to the murderous plan?

But he allowed himself to be pushed away.

"I've gone through something in the last few days. Why did you do it, girl?"

She saw suddenly that she must continue to play her part.

"Some day I'll tell you why it was that I gave you up so easily, Nell. You thought I was afraid of Donnegan?" He ground his teeth and turned pale at the thought. "But that wasn't it. Some day I can tell you. But after this, the first man who comes between us—Donnegan or any other—I'll turn him into powder—under my heel!"

He ground it into the floor as he spoke. She decided that she would see how much he knew.

"It will never be Donnegan, at least," she said. "He's done for today. And I'm almost sorry for him in spite of all that he's done."

He became suddenly grave.

"What are you saying, Nell?"

"Why, Joe told you, didn't he? They've drawn Donnegan out of town, and now they're lying in wait for him. Yes, they must have him, by this time. It's ten o'clock!"

A strangely tense exclamation broke from Lord Nick. "They've gone for Donnegan?"

"Yes. Are you angry?"

The big man staggered; one would have said that he had been stunned with a blow.

"Garry!" he whispered.

"What are you saying?"

"Nell," he muttered hoarsely, "did you know about it?"

"But I did it for you, Nick. I knew you hated—"

"No, no! Don't say it!" He added bitterly, after a moment. "This is for my sins."

And then, to her: "But you knew about it and didn't warn him? You hated him all the time you were laughing with him and smiling at him? Oh, Nell! What a merciless witch of a woman you are! For the rest of them—I'll wait till they come back!"

"What are you going to do, Nick?"

"I told them I'd pay the man who killed Donnegan—with lead. Did the fools think I didn't mean it?"

Truly, no matter what shadow had passed over the big man, he was the lion again, and Nell shrank from him.

"We'll wait for them," he said. "We'll wait for them here."

And they sat down together in the room. She attempted to speak once in a shaken voice, but he silenced her with a gesture, and after that she sat and watched in quiet the singular play of varying expressions across his face. Grief, rage, tenderness, murderous hate—they followed like a puppet play.

What was Donnegan to him? And then there was a tremor of fear. Would the three suspect when they reached the shack by the ford and no Donnegan came to them? The moments stole on. Then the soft beat of a galloping horse in the sand. The horse stopped. Presently they saw Joe Rix and Harry Masters pass in front of the window. And they looked as though a cyclone had caught them up, juggled them a dizzy distance in the air, and then flung them down carelessly upon bruising rocks. Their hats were gone; and the clothes of burly Harry Masters were literally torn from his back. Joe Rix was evidently far more terribly hurt, for he leaned on the arm of Masters and they came on together, staggering.

"They've done the business!" exclaimed Lord Nick. "And now, curse them, I'll do theirs!"

But the girl could not speak. A black haze crossed before her eyes. Had Donnegan gone out madly to fight the three men in spite of her warning?

The door opened. They stood in the doorway, and if they had seemed a horrible sight passing the window, they were a deadly picture at close range. And opposite them stood Lord Nick; in spite of their wounds there was murder in his face and his revolver was out.

"You've met him? You've met Donnegan?" he asked angrily.

Masters literally carried Joe Rix to a chair and placed him in it. He had been shot through both shoulders, and though tight bandages had stanched the wound he was still in agony. Then Masters raised his head.

"We've met him," he said.

"What happened?"

But Masters, in spite of the naked gun in the hand of Lord Nick, was looking straight at Nelly Lebrun.

"We fought him."

"Then say your prayers, Masters."

"Say prayers for the Pedlar, you fool," said Masters bitterly. "He's dead, and Donnegan's still living!"

There was a faint cry from Nelly Lebrun. She sank into her chair again.

"We've been double-crossed," said Masters, still looking at the girl. "I was going down the gulch the way we planned. I come to the narrow place where the cliffs almost touch, and right off the wall above me drops a wildcat. I thought it was a cat at first. And then I found it was Donnegan.

"The way he hit me from above knocked me off the horse. Then we hit the ground. I started for my gun; he got it out of my hand; I pulled my knife. He got that away, too. His fingers work with steel springs and act like a cat's claws. Then we fought barehanded. He didn't say a word. But kept snarling in his throat. Always like a cat. And his face was devilish. Made me sick inside. Pretty soon he dived under my arms. Got me up in the air. I came down on my head.

"Of course I went out cold. When I came to there was still a mist in front of my eyes and this lump on the back of my head. He'd figured that my head was cracked and that I was dead. That's the only reason he left me. Later I climbed on my hoss and fed him the spur.

"But I was too late. I took the straight cut for the ford, and when I got there I found that Donnegan had been there before me. Joe Rix was lyin' on the floor. When he got to the shack Donnegan was waitin' for him. They went for their guns and Donnegan beat him to it. The hound didn't shoot to kill. He plugged him through both shoulders, and left him lyin' helpless. But I got a couple of bandages on him and saved him.

"Then we cut back for home and crossed the marsh. And there we found the Pedlar.

"Too late to help him. Maybe Donnegan knew that the Pedlar was something of a flash with a gun himself, and he didn't take any chances. He'd met him face to face the same way he met Joe Rix and killed him. Shot him clean between the eyes. Think of shooting for the head with a snap shot! That's what he done and Joe didn't have time to think twice after that slug hit him. His gun wasn't even fired, he was beat so bad on the draw.

"So Joe and me come back home. And we come full of questions!"

"Let me tell you something," muttered Lord Nick, putting up the weapon which he had kept exposed during all of the recital. "You've got what was coming to you. If Donnegan hadn't cleaned up on you, you'd have had to talk turkey with me. Understand?"

"Wait a minute," protested Harry Masters.

And Joe Rix, almost too far gone for speech, set his teeth over a groan and cast a look of hatred at the girl.

"Wait a minute, chief. There's one thing we all got to get straight. Somebody had tipped off Donnegan about our whole plan. Was it the Pedlar or Rix or me? I guess good sense'll tell a man that it wasn't none of us, eh? Then who was it? The only other person that knew about the plan—Nell—Nell, the crooked witch—and it's her that murdered the Pedlar—curse her!"

He thrust out his bulky arm as he spoke.

"Her that lied her way into our confidence with a lot of talk about you, Nick. Then what did she do? She goes runnin' to the gent that she said she hated. Don't you see her play? She makes fools of us—she makes a fool out of you!"

She dared not meet the glance of Lord Nick. Even now she might have acted out her part and filled in with lies, but she was totally unnerved.

"Get Rix to bed," was all he said, and he did not even glance at Nelly Lebrun.

Masters glowered at him, and then silently obeyed, lifting Joe as a helpless bulk, for the fat man was nearly fainting with pain. Not until they had gone and he had closed the door after them and upon the murmurs of the servants in the hall did Lord Nick turn to Nelly.

"Is it true?" he asked shortly.

Between relief and terror her mind was whirling.

"Is what true?"

"You haven't even sense enough to lie, Nell, eh? It's all true, then? And last night, after you'd wormed it out of Joe, you went to Donnegan?"

She could only stare miserably at him.

"And that was why you pushed me away when I kissed you a little while ago?"

Once more she was dumb. But she was beginning to be afraid. Not for herself, but for Donnegan.

"Nell, I told you I'd never let another man come between us again. I meant it. I know you're treacherous now; but that doesn't keep me from wanting you. It's Donnegan again—Donnegan still? Nell, you've killed him. As sure as if your own finger pulled the trigger when I shoot him. He's a dead one, and you've done it!"

If words would only come! But her throat was stiff and cold and aching. She could not speak.

"You've done more than kill him," said Lord Nick. "You've put a curse on me as well. And afterward I'm going to even up with you. You hear me? Nell, when I shoot Donnegan I'm doing a thing worse than if he was a girl—or a baby. You can't understand that; I don't want you to know. But some time when you're happy again and you're through grieving for Donnegan, I'll tell you the truth and make your heart black for the rest of your life."

Still words would not come. She strove to cling to him and stop him, but he cast her away with a single gesture and strode out the door.

## CHAPTER XLII

There was no crowd to block the hill at this second meeting of Donnegan and Lord Nick. There was a blank stretch of brown hillside with the wind whispering stealthily through the dead grass when Lord Nick thrust open the door of Donnegan's shack and entered.

The little man had just finished shaving and was getting back into his coat while George carried out the basin of water. And Donnegan, as he buttoned the coat, was nodding slightly to the rhythm of a song which came from the cabin of the colonel nearby. It was a clear, high music, and though the voice was light it carried the sound far. Donnegan looked up to Lord Nick; but still he kept the beat of the music.

He seemed even more fragile this morning than ever before. Yet Lord Nick was fresh from the sight of the torn bodies of the two fighting men whom this fellow had struck and left for dead, or dying, as he thought.

"Dismiss your servant," said Lord Nick.

"George, you may go out."

"And keep him out."

"Don't come back until I call for you."

Big George disappeared into the kitchen and the outside door was closed. Yet even with all the doors closed the singing of Lou Macon kept running through the cabin in a sweet and continuous thread.

> *What made the ball so fine?*
> *Robin Adair!*
> *What made the assembly shine?*
> *Robin Adair!*

And no matter what Lord Nick could say, it seemed that with half his mind Donnegan was listening to the song of the girl.

"First," said the big man, "I've broken my word."

Donnegan waved his hand and dismissed the charge. He pointed to a chair, but Lord Nick paid no heed.

"I've broken my word," he went on. "I promised that I'd give you a clear road to win over Nelly Lebrun. I gave you the road and you've won her, but now I'm taking her back!"

"Ah, Henry," said Donnegan, and a flash of eagerness came in his eyes. "You're a thousand times welcome to her."

Lord Nick quivered.

"Do you mean it?"

"Henry, don't you see that I was only playing for a purpose all the time?

And if you've opened the eyes of Nelly to the fact that you truly love her and I've been only acting out of a heartless sham—why, I'm glad of it—I rejoice, Henry, I swear I do!"

He came forward, smiling, and held out his hand; Lord Nick struck it down, and Donnegan shrank back, holding his wrist tight in the fingers of his other hand.

"Is it possible?" murmured Henry Reardon. "Is it possible that she loves a man who despises her?"

"Not that! If any other man said this to me, I'd call for an explanation of his meaning, Henry. No, no! I honor and respect her, I tell you. By heaven, Nick, she has a thread of pure, generous gold in her nature!"

"Ah?"

"She has saved my life no longer ago than this morning."

"It's perfect," said Lord Nick. And he writhed under a torment. "I am discarded for the sake of a man who despises her!"

Donnegan, frowning with thought, watched his older brother. And still the thin singing entered the room, that matchless old melody of "Robin Adair"; the day shall never come when that song does not go straight from heart to heart. But because Donnegan still listened to it, Lord Nick felt that he was contemptuously received, and a fresh spur was driven into his tender pride.

"Donnegan!" he said sharply.

Donnegan raised his hand slowly.

"Do you call me by that name?"

"Aye. You've ceased to be a brother. There's no blood tie between us now, as I warned you before."

Donnegan, very white, moved back toward the wall and rested his shoulders lightly against it, as though he needed the support. He made no answer.

"I warned you not to cross me again!" exclaimed Lord Nick.

"I have not."

"Donnegan, you've murdered my men!"

"Murder? I've met them fairly. Not murder, Henry."

"Leave out that name, I say!"

"If you wish," said Donnegan very faintly.

The sight of his resistlessness seemed to madden Lord Nick. He made one of his huge strides and came to the center of the room and dominated all that was in it, including his brother.

"You murdered my men," repeated Lord Nick. "You turned my girl against me with your lying love-making and turned her into a spy. You made her set the trap and then you saw that it was worked. You showed her how she could wind me around her finger again."

"Will you let me speak?"

"Aye, but be short."

"I swear to you, Henry, that I've never influenced her to act against you; except to win her away for just one little time, and she will return to you again. It is only a fancy that makes her interested in me. Look at us! How could any woman in her senses prefer me?"

"Are you done?"

"No, no! I have more to say: I have a thousand things!"

"I shall not hear them"

"Henry, there is a black devil in your face. Beware of it."

"Who put it there?"

"It was not I."

"What power then?"

"Something over which I have no control."

"Are you trying to mystify me?"

"Listen!" And as Donnegan raised his hand, the singing poured clear and small into the room.

"That is the power," said Donnegan.

"You're talking gibberish!" exclaimed the other pettishly.

"I suppose I shouldn't expect you to understand."

"On the other hand, what I have to say is short and to the point. A child could comprehend it. You've stolen the girl. I tried to let her go. I can't. I have to have her. Willing or unwilling she has to belong to me, Donnegan."

"If you wish, I shall promise that I shall never see her again or speak to her."

"You fool! Won't she find you out? Do you think I could trust you? Only in one place—underground."

Donnegan had clasped his hands upon his breast and his eyes were wide.

"What is it you mean, Henry?"

"I'll trust you—dead!"

"Henry!"

"That name means nothing to me; I've forgotten it. The world has forgotten it."

"Henry, I implore you to keep cool—to give me five minutes for talk—"

"No, not one. I know your cunning tongue!"

"For the sake of the days when you loved me, my brother. For the sake of the days when you used to wheel my chair and be kind to me."

"You're wasting your time. You're torturing us both for nothing. Donnegan, my will is a rock. It won't change."

And drawing closer his right hand gripped his gun and the trembling passion of the gunfighter set him shuddering.

"You're armed, Garry. Go for your gun!"

"No, no!"

"Then I'll give you cause to fight."

And as he spoke, he drew back his massive arm and with his open hand smote Donnegan heavily across the face. The weight of that blow crushed the little man against the wall.

"Your gun!" cried Lord Nick, swaying from side to side as the passion choked him.

Donnegan fell upon his knees and raised his arms.

"God have mercy on me, and on yourself!"

At that the blackness cleared slowly on the face of the big man; he thrust his revolver into the holster.

"This time," he said, "there's no death. But sooner or later we meet, Donnegan, and then, I swear by all that lives, I'll shoot you down—without mercy—like a mad dog. You've robbed me; you've hounded me: you've killed my men: you've taken the heart of the woman I love. And now nothing can save you from the end."

He turned on his heel and left the room.

And Donnegan remained kneeling, holding a stained handkerchief to his face.

All at once his strength seemed to desert him like a tree chopped at the root, and he wilted down against the wall with closed eyes.

But the music still came out of the throat and the heart of Lou, and it entered the room and came into the ears of Donnegan. He became aware that there was a strength beyond himself which had sustained him, and then he knew it had been the singing of Lou from first to last which had kept the murder out of his own heart and restrained the hand of Lord Nick.

Perhaps of all Donnegan's life, this was the first moment of true humility.


# CHAPTER XLIII

One thing was now clear. He must not remain in The Corner unless he was prepared for Lord Nick again: and in a third meeting guns must be drawn. From that greater sin he shrank, and prepared to leave. His order to George made the big man's eyes widen, but George had long since passed the point where he cared to question the decision of his master. He began to build the packs.

As for Donnegan, he could see that there was little to be won by remaining. That would save Landis to Lou Macon, to be sure, but after all, he was beginning to wonder if it were not better to let the big fellow go back to his own kind—Lebrun and the rest. For if it needed compulsion to keep him with Lou now, might it not be the same story hereafter?

Indeed, Donnegan began to feel that all his labor in The Corner had been running on a treadmill. It had all been grouped about the main purpose, which was to keep Landis with the girl. To do that now he must be prepared to face Nick again; and to face Nick meant the bringing of the guilt of fratricide upon the head of one of them. There only remained flight. He saw at last that he had been fighting blindly from the first. He had won a girl whom he did not love—though doubtless her liking was only the most fickle fancy. And she for whom he would have died he had taught to hate him. It was a grim summing up. Donnegan walked the room whistling softly to himself as he checked up his accounts.

One thing at least he had done; he had taken the joy out of his life forever.

And here, answering a rap at the door, he opened it upon Lou Macon. She wore a dress of some very soft material. It was a pale blue—faded, no doubt—but the color blended exquisitely with her hair and with the flush of her face. It came to Donnegan that it was an unnecessary cruelty of chance that made him see the girl lovelier than he had ever seen her before at the very moment when he was surrendering the last shadow of a claim upon her.

And it hurt him, also, to see the freshness of her face, the clear eyes; and to hear her smooth, untroubled voice. She had lived untouched by anything save the sunshine in The Corner.

Her glance flickered across his face, and then fluttered down, and her color increased guiltily.

"I have come to ask you a favor," she said.

"Step in," said Donnegan, recovering his poise at length.

At this, she looked past him, and her eyes widened a little. There was an imperceptible shrug of her shoulders, as though the very thought of entering this cabin horrified her. And Donnegan had to bear that look as well.

"I'll stay here; I haven't much to say. It's a small thing."

"Large or small," said Donnegan eagerly. "Tell me!"

"My father has asked me to take a letter for him down to the town and mail it. I—I understand that it would be dangerous for me to go alone. Will you walk with me?"

And Donnegan turned cold. Go down into The Corner? Where by five chances out of ten he must meet his brother in the street?

"I can do better still," he said, smiling. "I'll have George take the letter down for you."

"Thank you. But you see, father would not trust it to anyone save me. I asked him; he was very firm about it."

"Tush! I would trust George with my life."

"Yes, yes. It is not what *I* wish—but my father rarely changes his mind."

Perspiration beaded the forehead of Donnegan. Was there no way to evade this easy request?

"You see," he faltered, "I should be glad to go—"

She raised her eyes slowly.

"But I am terribly busy this morning."

She did not answer, but half of her color left her face.

"Upon my word of honor there is no danger to a woman in the town."

"But some of the ruffians of Lord Nick—"

"If they dared to even raise their voices at you, they would hear from him in a manner that they would never forget."

"Then you don't wish to go?"

She was very pale now; and to Donnegan it was more terrible than the gun in the hand of Lord Nick. Even if she thought he was slighting her why should she take it so mortally to heart? For Donnegan, who saw all things, was blind to read the face of this girl.

"It doesn't really matter," she murmured and turned away.

A gentle motion, but it wrenched the heart of Donnegan. He was instantly before her.

"Wait here a moment. I'll be ready to go down immediately."

"No. I can't take you from your—work."

What work did she assign to him in her imagination? Endless planning of deviltry no doubt.

"I shall go with you," said Donnegan. "At first—I didn't dream it could be so important. Let me get my hat."

He left her and leaped back into the cabin.

"I am going down into The Corner for a moment," he said over his shoulder to George, as he took his belt down from the wall.

The big man strode to the wall and took his hat from a nail.

"I shall not need you, George."

But George merely grinned, and his big teeth flashed at the master. And in the second place he took up a gun from the drawer and offered it to Donnegan.

"The gun in that holster ain't loaded," he said.

Donnegan considered him soberly.

"I know it. There'll be no need for a loaded gun."

But once more George grinned. All at once Donnegan turned pale.

"You dog," he whispered. "Did you listen at the door when Nick was here?"

"Me?" murmured George. "No, I just been thinking."

And so it was that while Donnegan went down the hill with Lou Macon, carrying an empty-chambered revolver, George followed at a distance of a few paces, and he carried a loaded weapon unknown to Donnegan.

It was the dull time of the day in The Corner. There were very few people in the single street, and though most of them turned to look at the little man and the girl who walked beside him, not one of them either smiled or whispered.

"You see?" said Donnegan. "You would have been perfectly safe—even from Lord Nick's ruffians. That was one of his men we passed back there."

"Yes. I'm safe with you," said the girl.

And when she looked up to him, the blood of Donnegan turned to fire.

Out of a shop door before them came a girl with a parcel under her arm. She wore a gay, semi-masculine outfit, bright-colored, jaunty, and she walked with a lilt toward them. It was Nelly Lebrun. And as she passed them, Donnegan lifted his hat ceremoniously high. She nodded to him with a smile, but the smile aimed wan and small in an instant. There was a quick widening and then a narrowing of her eyes, and Donnegan knew that she had judged Lou Macon as only one girl can judge another who is lovelier.

He glanced at Lou to see if she had noticed, and he saw her raise her head and go on with her glance proudly straight before her; but her face was very pale, and Donnegan knew that she had guessed everything that was true and far more than the truth. Her tone at the door of the post office was ice.

"I think you are right, Mr. Donnegan. There's no danger. And if you have anything else to do, I can get back home easily enough."

"I'll wait for you," murmured Donnegan sadly, and he stood as the door of the little building with bowed head.

And then a murmur came down the street. How small it was, and how sinister! It consisted of exclamations begun, and then broken sharply off. A swirl of people divided as a cloud of dust divides before a blast of wind, and through them came the gigantic figure of Lord Nick!

On he came, a gorgeous figure, a veritable king of men. He carried his hat in his hand and his red hair flamed, and he walked with great strides. Donnegan glanced behind him. The way was clear. If he turned, Lord Nick would not pursue him, he knew.

But to flee even from his brother was more than he could do; for the woman he loved would know of it and could never understand.

He touched the holster that held his empty gun—and waited!

An eternity between every step of Lord Nick. Others seemed to have sensed the meaning of this silent scene. People seemed to stand frozen in the midst of gestures. Or was that because Donnegan's own thoughts were traveling at such lightning speed that the rest of the world seemed standing still? What kept Lou Macon? If she were with him, not even Lord Nick in his madness would force on a gunplay in the presence of a woman, no doubt.

Lord Nick was suddenly close; he had paused; his voice rang over the street and struck upon Donnegan's ear as sounds come under water.

"Donnegan!"

"Aye!" called Donnegan softly.

"It's the time!"

"Aye," said Donnegan.

Then a huge body leaped before him; it was big George. And as he sprang his gun went up with his hand in a line of light. The two reports came close together as finger taps on a table, and big George, completing his spring, lurched face downward into the sand.

Dead? Not yet. All his faith and selflessness were nerving the big man. And Donnegan stood behind him, unarmed!

He reared himself upon his knees—an imposing bulk, even then, and fired again. But his hand was trembling, and the bullet shattered a sign above the head of Lord Nick. He, in his turn, it seemed to Donnegan that the motion was slow, twitched up the muzzle of his weapon and fired once more from his hip. And big George lurched back on the sand, with his face upturned to Donnegan. He would have spoken, but a burst of blood choked him; yet his eyes fixed and glazed, he mustered his last strength and offered his revolver to Donnegan.

But Donnegan let the hand fall limp to the ground. There were voices about him; steps running; but all that he clearly saw was Lord Nick with his feet braced, and his head high.

"Donnegan! Your gun!"

"Aye," said Donnegan.

"Take it then!"

But in the crisis, automatically Donnegan flipped his useless revolver out of its holster and into his hand. At the same instant the gun from Nick's hand seemed to blaze in his eyes. He was struck a crushing blow in his chest. He sank upon his knees: another blow struck his head, and Donnegan collapsed on the body of big George.


## CHAPTER XLIV

An ancient drunkard in the second story of one of the stores across the street had roused himself at the sound of the shots and now he dragged himself to the window and began to scream: "Murder! Murder!" over and over, and even The Corner shuddered at the sound of his voice.

Lord Nick, his revolver still in his hand, stalked through the film of people who now swirled about him, eager to see the dead. There was no call for the law to make its appearance, and the representatives of the law were wisely dilatory in The Corner.

He stood over the two motionless figures with a stony face.

"You saw it, boys," he said. "You know what I've borne from this fellow. The big man pulled his gun first on me. I shot in self-defense. As for—the other—it was a square fight."

"Square fight," someone answered. "You both went for your irons at the same time. Pretty work, Nick."

It was a solid phalanx of men which had collected around the moveless bodies as swiftly as mercury sinks through water. Yet none of them touched either Donnegan or George. And then the solid group dissolved at one side. It was the moan of a woman which had scattered it, and a yellow-haired girl slipped through them. She glanced once, in horror, at the mute faces of the men, and then there was a wail as she threw herself on the body of Donnegan. Somewhere she found the strength of a man to lift him and place him face upward on the sand, the gun trailing limply in his hand. And then she lay, half crouched over him, her face pressed to his heart—listening— listening for the stir of life.

Shootings were common in The Corner; the daily mortality ran high; but there had never been aftermaths like this one. Men looked at one another, and then at Lord Nick. A bright spot of color had come in his cheeks, but his face was as hard as ever.

"Get her away from him," someone murmured.

And then another man cried out, stooped, wrenched the gun from the limp hand of Donnegan and opened the cylinder. He spun it: daylight was glittering through the empty cylinder.

At this the man stiffened, and with a low bow which would have done credit to a drawing-room, he presented the weapon butt first to Lord Nick.

"Here's something the sheriff will want to see," he said, "but maybe you'll be interested, too."

But Lord Nick, with the gun in his hand, stared at it dumbly, turned the empty cylinder. And the full horror crept slowly on his mind. He had not killed his brother, he had murdered him. As his eyes cleared, he caught the glitter of the eyes which surrounded him.

And then Lou Macon was on her knees with her hands clasped at her breast and her face glorious.

"Help!" she was crying. "Help me. He's not dead, but he's dying unless you help me!"

Then Lord Nick cast away his own revolver and the empty gun of Donnegan. They heard him shout: "Garry!" and saw him stride forward.

Instantly men pressed between, hard-jawed men who meant business. It was a cordon he would have to fight his way through: but he dissolved it with a word.

"You fools! He's my brother!"

And then he was on his knees opposite Lou Macon.

"You?" she had stammered in horror.

"His brother, girl."

And ten minutes later, when the bandages had been wound, there was a strange sight of Lord Nick striding up the street with his victim in his arms. How lightly he walked; and he was talking to the calm, pale face which rested in the hollow of his shoulder.

"He will live? He will live?" Lou Macon was pleading as she hurried at the side of Lord Nick.

"God willing, he shall live!"

It was three hours before Donnegan opened his eyes. It was three days before he recovered his senses, and looking aside toward the door he saw a brilliant shaft of sunlight falling into the room. In the midst of it sat Lou Macon. She had fallen asleep in her great weariness now that the crisis was over. Behind her, standing, his great arms folded, stood the indomitable figure of Lord Nick.

Donnegan saw and wondered greatly. Then he closed his eyes dreamily. "Hush," said Donnegan to himself, as if afraid that what he saw was all a dream. "I'm in heaven, or if I'm not, it's still mighty good to be alive."

# THE UNTAMED

## Max Brand

### CHAPTER I

### PAN OF THE DESERT

Even to a high-flying bird this was a country to be passed over quickly. It was burned and brown, littered with fragments of rock, whether vast or small, as if the refuse were tossed here after the making of the world. A passing shower drenched the bald knobs of a range of granite hills and the slant morning sun set the wet rocks aflame with light. In a short time the hills lost their halo and resumed their brown. The moisture evaporated. The sun rose higher and looked sternly across the desert as if he searched for any remaining life which still struggled for existence under his burning course.

And he found life. Hardy cattle moved singly or in small groups and browsed on the withered bunch grass. Summer scorched them, winter humped their backs with cold and arched up their bellies with famine, but they were a breed schooled through generations for this fight against nature. In this junk-shop of the world, rattlesnakes were rulers of the soil. Overhead the buzzards, ominous black specks pendant against the white-hot sky, ruled the air.

It seemed impossible that human beings could live in this rock-wilderness. If so, they must be to other men what the lean, hardy cattle of the hills are to the corn-fed stabled beeves of the States.

Over the shoulder of a hill came a whistling which might have been attributed to the wind, had not this day been deathly calm. It was fit music for such a scene, for it seemed neither of heaven nor earth, but the soul of the great god Pan come back to earth to charm those nameless rocks with his wild, sweet piping. It changed to harmonious phrases loosely connected. Such might be the exultant improvisations of a master violinist.

A great wolf, or a dog as tall and rough coated as a wolf, trotted around the hillside. He paused with one foot lifted and lolling, crimson tongue, as he scanned the distance and then turned to look back in the direction from which he had come. The weird music changed to whistled notes as liquid as a flute. The sound drew closer. A horseman rode out on the shoulder and checked his mount. One could not choose him at first glance as a type of those who fight nature in a region where the thermometer moves through a scale of a hundred and sixty degrees in the year to an accompaniment of cold-stabbing winds and sweltering suns. A thin, handsome face with large brown eyes and black hair, a body tall but rather slenderly made—he might have been a descendant of some ancient family of Norman nobility; but could such proud gentry be found riding the desert in a tall-crowned sombrero with chaps on his legs and a red bandana handkerchief knotted around his throat? That first glance made the rider seem strangely out of place in such surroundings. One might even smile at the contrast, but at the second glance the smile would fade, and at the third, it would be replaced with a stare of interest. It was impossible to tell why one respected this man, but after a time there grew a suspicion of unknown strength in this lone rider, strength like that of a machine which is stopped but only needs a spark of fire to plunge it into irresistible action. Strangely enough, the youthful figure seemed in tune with that region of mighty distances, with that white, cruel sun, with that bird of prey hovering high, high in the air.

It required some study to guess at these qualities of the rider, for they were such things as a child feels more readily than a grown man; but it needed no expert to admire the horse he bestrode. It was a statue in black marble, a steed fit for a Shah of Persia! The stallion stood barely fifteen hands, but to see him was to forget his size. His flanks shimmered like satin in the sun. What promise of power in the smooth, broad hips! Only an Arab poet could run his hand over that shoulder and then speak properly of the matchless curve. Only an Arab could appreciate legs like thin and carefully drawn steel below the knees; or that flow of tail and windy mane; that generous breast with promise of the mighty heart within; that arched neck; that proud head with the pricking ears, wide forehead, and muzzle, as the Sheik said, which might drink from a pint-pot.

A rustling like dried leaves came from among the rocks and the hair rose bristling around the neck of the wolflike dog. With outstretched head he approached the rocks, sniffing, then stopped and turned shining eyes upon his master, who nodded and swung from the saddle. It was a little uncanny, this silent interchange of glances between the beast and the man. The cause of the dog's anxiety was a long rattler which now slid out from beneath a boulder, and giving its harsh warning, coiled, ready to strike. The dog backed away, but instead of growling he looked to the man.

Cowboys frequently practice with their revolvers at snakes, but one of the peculiarities of this rider was that he carried no gun, neither six-shooter nor rifle. He drew out a short knife which might be used to skin a beef or carve meat, though certainly no human being had ever used such a weapon against a five-foot rattler. He stooped and rested both hands on his thighs. His feet were not two paces from the poised head of the snake. As if marveling at this temerity, the big rattler tucked back his head and sounded the alarm again. In response the cowboy flashed his knife in the sun. Instantly the snake struck but the deadly fangs fell a few inches short of the riding boots. At the same second the man moved. No eye could follow the leap of his hand as it darted down and fastened around the snake just behind the head. The long brown body writhed about his wrist, with rattles clashing. He severed the head deftly and tossed the twisting mass back on the rocks.

Then, as if he had performed the most ordinary act, he rubbed his gloves in the sand, cleansed his knife in a similar manner, and stepped back to his horse. Contrary to the rules of horse-nature, the stallion had not flinched at sight of the snake, but actually advanced a high-headed pace or two with his short ears laid flat on his neck, and a sudden red fury in his eyes. He seemed to watch for an opportunity to help his master. As the man approached after killing the snake the stallion let his ears go forward again and touched his nose against his master's shoulder. When the latter swung into the saddle, the wolf-dog came to his side, reared, and resting his forefeet on the stirrup stared up into the rider's face. The man nodded to him, whereat, as if he understood a spoken word, the dog dropped back and trotted ahead. The rider touched the reins and galloped down the easy slope. The little episode had given the effect of a three-cornered conversation. Yet the man had been as silent as the animals.

In a moment he was lost among the hills, but still his whistling came back, fainter and fainter, until it was merely a thrilling whisper that dwelt in the air but came from no certain direction.

His course lay towards a road which looped whitely across the hills. The road twisted over a low ridge where a house stood among a grove of cottonwoods dense enough and tall enough to break the main force of any wind. On the same road, a thousand yards closer to the rider of the black stallion, was Morgan's place.

## CHAPTER II

## THE PANTHER

In the ranch house old Joseph Cumberland frowned on the floor as he heard his daughter say: "It isn't right, Dad. I never noticed it before I went away to school, but since I've come back I begin to feel that it's shameful to treat Dan in this way."

Her eyes brightened and she shook her golden head for emphasis. Her father watched her with a faintly quizzical smile and made no reply. The dignity of ownership of many thousand cattle kept the old rancher's shoulders square, and there was an antique gentility about his thin face with its white goatee. He was more like a quaint figure of the seventeenth century than a successful cattleman of the twentieth.

"It *is* shameful, Dad," she went on, encouraged by his silence, "or you could tell me some reason."

"Some reason for not letting him have a gun?" asked the rancher, still with the quizzical smile.

"Yes, yes!" she said eagerly, "and some reason for treating him in a thousand ways as if he were an irresponsible boy."

"Why, Kate, gal, you have tears in your eyes!"

He drew her onto a stool beside him, holding both her hands, and searched her face with eyes as blue and almost as bright as her own. "How does it come that you're so interested in Dan?"

"Why, Dad, dear," and she avoided his gaze, "I've always been interested in him. Haven't we grown up together?"

"Part ways you have."

"And haven't we been always just like brother and sister?"

"You're talkin' a little more'n sisterly, Kate."

"What do you mean?"

"Ay, ay! What do I mean! And now you're all red. Kate, I got an idea it's nigh onto time to let Dan start on his way."

He could not have found a surer way to drive the crimson from her face and turn it white to the lips.

"Dad!"

"Well, Kate?"

"You wouldn't send Dan away!"

Before he could answer she dropped her head against his shoulder and broke into great sobs. He stroked her head with his calloused, sunburned hand and his eyes filmed with a distant gaze.

"I might have knowed it!" he said over and over again; "I might have knowed it! Hush, my silly gal."

Her sobbing ceased with magic suddenness.

"Then you won't send him away?"

"Listen to me while I talk to you straight," said Joe Cumberland, "and accordin' to the way you take it will depend whether Dan goes or stays. Will you listen?"

"Dear Dad, with all my heart!"

"Humph!" he grunted, "that's just what I don't want. This what I'm goin' to tell you is a queer thing—a mighty lot like a fairy tale, maybe. I've kept it back from you years an' years thinkin' you'd find out the truth about Dan for yourself. But bein' so close to him has made you sort of blind, maybe! No man will criticize his own hoss."

"Go on, tell me what you mean. I won't interrupt."

He was silent for a moment, frowning to gather his thoughts.

"Have you ever seen a mule, Kate?"

"Of course!"

"Maybe you've noticed that a mule is just as strong as a horse—"

"Yes."

"—but their muscles ain't a third as big?"

"Yes, but what on earth—"

"Well, Kate, Dan is built light an' yet he's stronger than the biggest men around here."

"Are you going to send him away simply because he's strong?"

"It doesn't show nothin'," said the old man gently, "savin' that he's different from the regular run of men—an' I've seen a considerable pile of men, honey. There's other funny things about Dan maybe you ain't noticed. Take the way he has with hosses an' other animals. The wildest man-killin', spur-hatin' bronchos don't put up no fight when them long legs of Dan settle round 'em."

"Because they know fighting won't help them!"

"Maybe so, maybe so," he said quietly, "but it's kind of queer, Kate, that after most a hundred men on the best hosses in these parts had ridden in relays after Satan an' couldn't lay a rope on him, Dan could jest go out on foot with a halter an' come back in ten days leadin' the wildest devil of a mustang that ever hated men."

"It was a glorious thing to do!" she said.

Old Cumberland sighed and then shook his head.

"It shows more'n that, honey. There ain't any man but Dan that can sit the saddle on Satan. If Dan should die, Satan wouldn't be no more use to other men than a piece of haltered lightnin'. An' then tell me how Dan got hold of that wolf, Black Bart, as he calls him."

"It isn't a wolf, Dad," said Kate, "it's a dog. Dan says so himself."

"Sure he says so," answered her father, "but there was a lone wolf prowlin' round these parts for a considerable time an' raisin' Cain with the calves an' the colts. An' Black Bart comes pretty close to a description of the lone wolf. Maybe you remember Dan found his 'dog' lyin' in a gully with a bullet through his shoulder. If he was a dog how'd he come to be shot—"

"Some brute of a sheep herder may have done it. What could it prove?"

"It only proves that Dan is queer—powerful queer! Satan an' Black Bart are still as wild as they ever was, except that they got one master. An' they ain't got a thing to do with other people. Black Bart'd tear the heart out of a man that so much as patted his head."

"Why," she cried, "he'll let me do anything with him!"

"Humph!" said Cumberland, a little baffled; "maybe that's because Dan is kind of fond of you, gal, an' he has sort of introduced you to his pets, damn 'em! That's just the pint! How is he able to make his man-killers act sweet with you an' play the devil with everybody else."

"It wasn't Dan at all!" she said stoutly, "and he *isn't* queer. Satan and Black Bart let me do what I want with them because they know I love them for their beauty and their strength."

"Let it go at that," growled her father. "Kate, you're jest like your mother when it comes to arguin'. If you wasn't my little gal I'd say you was plain pig-headed. But look here, ain't you ever felt that Dan is what I call him— different? Ain't you ever seen him get mad—jest for a minute—an' watched them big brown eyes of his get all packed full of yellow light that chases a chill up and down your back like a wrigglin' snake?"

She considered this statement in a little silence.

"I saw him kill a rattler once," she said in a low voice. "Dan caught him behind the head after he had struck. He did it with his bare hand! I almost fainted. When I looked again he had cut off the head of the snake. It was—it was terrible!"

She turned to her father and caught him firmly by the shoulders.

"Look me straight in the eye, Dad, and tell me just what you mean."

"Why, Kate," said the wise old man, "you're beginnin' to see for yourself what I'm drivin' at! Haven't you got somethin' else right on the tip of your tongue?"

"There was one day that I've never told you about," she said in a low voice, looking away, "because I was afraid that if I told you, you'd shoot Black Bart. He was gnawing a big beef bone and just for fun I tried to take it away from him. He'd been out on a long trail with Dan and he was very hungry. When I put my hand on the bone he snapped. Luckily I had a thick glove on and he merely pinched my wrist. Also I think he realized what he was doing for otherwise he'd have cut through the glove as if it had been paper. He snarled fearfully and I sprang back with a cry. Dan hadn't seen what happened, but he heard the snarl and saw Black Bart's bared teeth. Then—oh, it was terrible!"

She covered her face.

"Take your time, Kate," said Cumberland softly.

"'Bart,' called Dan," she went on, "and there was such anger in his face that I think I was more afraid of him than of the big dog.

"Bart turned to him with a snarl and bared his teeth. When Dan saw that his face turned—I don't know how to say it!"

She stopped a moment and her hands tightened.

"Back in his throat there came a sound that was almost like the snarl of Black Bart. The wolf-dog watched him with a terror that was uncanny to see, the hair around his neck fairly on end, his teeth still bared, and his growl horrible.

"'Dan!' I called, 'don't go near him!'

"I might as well have called out to a whirlwind. He leaped. Black Bart sprang to meet him with eyes green with fear. I heard the loud click of his teeth as he snapped—and missed. Dan swerved to one side and caught Black Bart by the throat and drove him into the dust, falling with him.

"I couldn't move. I was weak with horror. It wasn't a struggle between a man and a beast. It was like a fight between a panther and a wolf. Black Bart was fighting hard but fighting hopelessly. Those hands were settling tighter on his throat. His big red tongue lolled out; his struggles almost ceased. Then Dan happened to glance at me. What he saw in my face sobered him. He got up, lifting the dog with him, and flung away the lifeless weight of Bart. He began to brush the dust from his clothes, looking down as if he were ashamed. He asked me if the dog had hurt me when he snapped. I could not speak for a moment. Then came the most horrible part. Black Bart, who must have been nearly killed, dragged himself to Dan on his belly, choking and whining, and licked the boots of his master!"

"Then you *do* know what I mean when I say Dan is—different?"

She hesitated and blinked, as if she were shutting her eyes on a fact. "I *don't* know. I know that he's gentle and kind and loves you more than you love him." Her voice broke a little. "Oh, Dad, you forget the time he sat up with you for many days and nights when you got sick out in the hills, and how he barely managed to get you back to the house alive!"

The old man frowned to conceal how greatly he was moved.

"I haven't forgot nothin', Kate," he said, "an' everything is for his own good. Do you know what I've been tryin' to do all these years?"

"What?"

"I've been tryin' to hide him from himself! Kate, do you remember how I found him?"

"I was too little to know. I've heard you tell a little about it. He was lost on the range. You found him twenty miles south of the house."

"Lost on the range?" repeated her father softly. "I don't think he could ever have been lost. To a hoss the corral is a home. To us our ranch is a home. To Dan Barry the whole mountain-desert is a home! This is how I found him. It was in the spring of the year when the wild geese was honkin' as they flew north. I was ridin' down a gulley about sunset and wishin' that I was closer to the ranch when I heard a funny, wild sort of whistlin' that didn't have any tune to it that I recognized. It gave me a queer feelin'. It made me think of fairy stories—an' things like that! Pretty soon I seen a figure on the crest of the hill. There was a triangle of geese away up overhead an' the boy was walkin' along lookin' up as if he was followin' the trail of the wild geese.

"He was up there walkin' between the sunset an' the stars with his head bent back, and his hands stuffed into his pockets, whistlin' as if he was goin' home from school. An' such whistlin'."

"Nobody could ever whistle like Dan," she said, and smiled.

"I rode up to him, wonderin'," went on Cumberland.

"'What're you doin' round here?' I says.

"Says he, lookin' at me casual like over his shoulder: 'I'm jest takin' a stroll an' whistlin'. Does it bother you, mister?'

"'It doesn't bother me none,' says I. 'Where do you belong, sonny?'

"'Me?' says he, lookin' sort of surprised, 'why, I belong around over there!' An' he waved his hand careless over to the settin' sun.

"There was somethin' about him that made my heart swell up inside of me. I looked down into them big brown eyes and wondered—well, I don't know what I wondered; but I remembered all at once that I didn't have no son.

"'Who's your folks?' says I, gettin' more an' more curious.

"He jest looked at me sort of bored.

"'Where does your folks live at?' says I.

"'Oh, they live around here,' says he, an' he waved his hand again, an' this time over towards the east.

"Says I: 'When do you figure on reachin' home?'

"'Oh, most any day,' says he.

"An' I looked around at them brown, naked hills with the night comin' down over them. Then I stared back at the boy an' there was something that come up in me like hunger. You see, he was lost; he was alone; the queer ring of his whistlin' was still in my ears; an' I couldn't help rememberin' that I didn't have no son.

"'Then supposin' you come along with me,' says I, 'an' I'll send you home in a buckboard tomorrow?'

"So the end of it was me ridin' home with the little kid sittin' up before me, whistlin' his heart out! When I got him home I tried to talk to him again. He couldn't tell me, or he wouldn't tell me where his folks lived, but jest kept wavin' his hand liberal to half the points of the compass. An' that's all I know of where he come from. I done all I could to find his parents. I inquired and sent letters to every rancher within a hundred miles. I advertised it through the railroads, but they said nobody'd yet been reported lost. He was still mine, at least for a while, an' I was terrible glad.

"I give the kid a spare room. I sat up late that first night listenin' to the wild geese honkin' away up in the sky an' wonderin' why I was so happy. Kate, that night there was tears in my eyes when I thought of how that kid had been out there on the hills walkin' along so happy an' independent.

"But the next mornin' he was gone. I sent my cowpunchers out to look for him.

" 'Which way shall we ride?' they asked.

"I don't know why, but I thought of the wild geese that Dan had seemed to be followin'.

" 'Ride north,' I said.

"An' sure enough, they rode north an' found him. After that I didn't have no trouble with him about runnin' away—at least not durin' the summer. An' all those months I kept plannin' how I would take care of this boy who had come wanderin' to me. It seemed like he was sort of a gift of God to make up for me havin' no son. And everythin' went well until the next fall, when the geese began to fly south.

"Sure enough, that was when Dan ran away again, and when I sent my cowpunchers south after him, they found him and brought him back. It seemed as if they'd brought back half the world to me, when I seen him. But I saw that I'd have to put a stop to this runnin' away. I tried to talk to him, but all he'd say was that he'd better be movin' on. I took the law in my hands an' told him he had to be disciplined. So I started thrashin' him with a quirt, very light. He took it as if he didn't feel the whip on his shoulders, an' he smiled. But there came up a yellow light in his eyes that made me feel as if a man was standin' right behind me with a bare knife in his hand an' smilin' jest like the kid was doin'. Finally I simply backed out of the room, an' since that day there ain't been man or beast ever has put a hand on Whistlin' Dan. To this day I reckon he ain't quite forgiven me."

"Why!" she cried, "I have never heard him mention it!"

"That's why I know he's not forgotten it. Anyway, Kate, I locked him in his room, but he wouldn't promise not to run away. Then I got an inspiration. You was jest a little toddlin' thing then. That day you was cryin' an awful lot an' I suddenly thought of puttin' you in Dan's room. I did it. I jest unlocked the door quick and then shoved you in an' locked it again. First of all you screamed terrible hard. I was afraid maybe you'd hurt yourself yellin' that way. I was about to take you out again when all at once I heard Dan start whistlin' and pretty quick your cryin' stopped. I listened an' wondered. After that I never had to lock Dan in his room. I was sure he'd stay on account of you. But now, honey, I'm gettin' to the end of the story, an' I'm goin' to give you the straight idea the way I see it.

"I've watched Dan like—like a father, almost. I think he loves me, sort of—but I've never got over being afraid of him. You see I can't forget how he smiled when I licked him! But listen to me, Kate, that fear has been with me all the time—an' it's the only time I've ever been afraid of any man. It isn't like being scared of a man, but of a panther.

"Now we'll jest nacherally add up all the points we've made about Dan— the queer way I found him without a home an' without wantin' one—that strength he has that's like the power of a mule compared with a horse—that funny control he has over wild animals so that they almost seem to know what he means when he simply looks at them (have you noticed him with Black Bart and Satan?)—then there's the yellow light that comes in his eyes when he begins to get real mad—you an' I have both seen it only once, but we don't want to see it again! More than this there's the way he handles either a knife or a gun. He hasn't practiced much with shootin' irons, but I never seen him miss a reasonable mark—or an unreasonable one either, for that matter. I've spoke to him about it. He said: 'I dunno how it is. I don't see how a feller can shoot crooked. It jest seems that when I get out a gun there's a line drawn from the barrel to the thing I'm shootin' at. All I have to do is to pull the trigger—almost with my eyes closed!' Now, Kate, do you begin to see what these here things point to?"

"Tell me what you see," she said, "and then I'll tell you what I think of it all."

"All right," he said. "I see in Dan a man who's different from the common run of us. I read in a book once that in the ages when men lived like animals an' had no weapons except sticks and stones, their muscles must have been two or three times as strong as they are now—more like the muscles of brutes. An' their hearin' an' their sight an' their quickness an' their endurance was about three times more than that of ordinary men. Kate, I think that Dan is one of those men the book described! He knows animals because he has all the powers that they have. An' I know from the way his eyes go yellow that he has the fightin' instinct of the ancestors of man. So far I've kept him away from other men. Which I may say is the main reason I bought Dan Morgan's place so's to keep fightin' men away from our Whistlin' Dan. So I've been hidin' him from himself. You see, he's my boy if he belongs to anybody. Maybe when time goes on he'll get tame. But I reckon not. It's like takin' a panther cub—or a wolf pup—an tryin' to raise it for a pet. Some day it gets the taste of blood, maybe its own blood, an' then it goes mad and becomes a killer. An' that's what I fear, Kate. So far I've kept Dan from ever havin' a single fight, but I reckon the day'll come when someone'll cross him, and then there'll be a tornado turned loose that'll jest about wreck these parts."

Her anger had grown during this speech. Now she rose.

"I won't believe you, Dad," she said. "I'd sooner trust our Dan than any man alive. I don't think you're right in a single word!"

"I was sure loco," sighed Cumberland, "to ever dream of convincin' a woman. Let it drop, Kate. We're about to get rid of Morgan's place, an' now I reckon there won't be any temptation near Dan. We'll see what time'll do for him. Let the thing drop there. Now I'm goin' over to the Bar XO outfit an' I won't be back till late tonight. There's only one thing more. I told Morgan there wasn't to be any gun-play in his place today. If you hear any shootin' go down there an' remind Morgan to take the guns off 'n the men."

Kate nodded, but her stare travelled far away, and the thing she saw was the yellow light burning in the eyes of Whistling Dan.

# CHAPTER III

## SILENT SHOOTS

It was a great day and also a sad one for Morgan. His general store and saloon had been bought out by old Joe Cumberland, who declared a determination to clear up the landscape, and thereby plunged the cowpunchers in gloom. They partially forgave Cumberland, but only because he was an old man. A younger reformer would have met armed resistance. Morgan's place was miles away from the next oasis in the desert and the closing meant dusty, thirsty leagues of added journey to every man in the neighborhood. The word "neighborhood," of course, covered a territory fifty miles square.

If the day was very sad for this important reason, it was also very glad, for rustling Morgan advertised the day of closing far and wide, and his most casual patrons dropped all business to attend the big doings. A long line of buckboards and cattle ponies surrounded the place. New comers galloped in every few moments. Most of them did not stop to tether their mounts, but simply dropped the reins over the heads of the horses and then went with rattling spurs and slouching steps into the saloon. Every man was greeted by a shout, for one or two of those within usually knew him, and when they raised a cry the others joined in for the sake of good fellowship. As a rule he responded by ordering everyone up to the bar.

One man, however, received no more greeting than the slamming of the door behind him. He was a tall, handsome fellow with tawny hair and a little smile of habit rather than mirth upon his lips. He had ridden up on a strong bay horse, a full two hands taller than the average cattle pony, and with legs and shoulders and straight back that unmistakably told of a blooded pedigree. When he entered the saloon he seemed nowise abashed by the silence, but greeted the turned heads with a wave of the hand and a good-natured "Howdy, boys!" A volley of greetings replied to him, for in the mountain-desert men cannot be strangers after the first word.

"Line up and hit the red-eye," he went on, and leaning against the bar as he spoke, his habitual smile broadened into one of actual invitation. Except for a few groups who watched the gambling in the corners of the big room, there was a general movement towards the bar.

"And make it a tall one, boys," went on the genial stranger. "This is the first time I ever irrigated Morgan's place, and from what I have heard today about the closing I suppose it will be the last time. So here's to you, Morgan!"

And he waved his glass towards the bartender. His voice was well modulated and his enunciation bespoke education. This, in connection with his careful clothes and rather modish riding-boots, might have given him the reputation of a dude, had it not been for several other essential details of his appearance. His six-gun hung so low that he would scarcely have to raise his hand to grasp the butt. He held his whisky glass in his left hand, and the right, which rested carelessly on his hip, was deeply sunburned, as if he rarely wore a glove. Moreover, his eyes were marvelously direct, and they lingered a negligible space as they touched on each man in the room. All of this the cattlemen noted instantly. What they did not see on account of his veiling fingers was that he poured only a few drops of the liquor into his glass.

In the meantime another man who had never before "irrigated" at Morgan's place, rode up. His mount, like that of the tawny-haired rider, was considerably larger and more finely built than the common range horse. In three days of hard work a cattle pony might wear down these blooded animals, but would find it impossible to either overtake or escape them in a straight run. The second stranger, short-legged, barrel-chested, and with a scrub of black beard, entered the barroom while the crowd was still drinking the health of Morgan. He took a corner chair, pushed back his hat until a mop of hair fell down his forehead, and began to roll a cigarette. The man of the tawny hair took the next seat.

"Seems to be quite a party, stranger," said the tall fellow nonchalantly.

"Sure," growled he of the black beard, and after a moment he added: "Been out on the trail long, pardner?"

"Hardly started."

"So'm I."

"As a matter of fact, I've got a lot of hard riding before me."

"So've I."

"And some long riding, too."

Perhaps it was because he turned his head suddenly towards the light, but a glint seemed to come in the eyes of the bearded man.

"Long rides," he said more amiably, "are sure hell on hosses."

"And on men, too," nodded the other, and tilted back in his chair.

The bearded man spoke again, but though a dozen cowpunchers were close by no one heard his voice except the man at his side. One side of his face remained perfectly immobile and his eyes stared straight before him drearily while he whispered from a corner of his mouth: "How long do you stay, Lee?"

"Noon," said Lee.

Once more the shorter man spoke in the manner which is learned in a penitentiary: "Me too. We must be slated for the same ride, Lee. Do you know what it is? It's nearly noon, and the chief ought to be here."

There was a loud greeting for a newcomer, and Lee took advantage of the noise to say quite openly: "If Silent said he'll come, he'll be here. But I say he's crazy to come to a place full of range riders, Bill."

"Take it easy," responded Bill. "This hangout is away off our regular beat. Nobody'll know him."

"His hide is his own and he can do what he wants with it," said Lee. "I warned him before."

"Shut up," murmured Bill, "Here's Jim now, and Hal Purvis with him!"

Through the door strode a great figure before whom the throng at the bar gave way as water rolls back from the tall prow of a ship. In his wake went a little man with a face dried and withered by the sun and small bright eyes which moved continually from side to side. Lee and Bill discovered their thirst at the same time and made towards the newcomers.

They had no difficulty in reaching them. The large man stood with his back to the bar, his elbows spread out on it, so that there was a little space left on either side of him. No one cared to press too close to this somber-faced giant. Purvis stood before him and Bill and Lee were instantly at his side. The two leaned on the bar, facing him, yet the four did not seem to make a group set apart from the rest.

"Well?" asked Lee.

"I'll tell you what it is when we're on the road," said Jim Silent. "Plenty of time, Haines."

"Who'll start first?" asked Bill.

"You can, Kilduff," said the other. "Go straight north, and go slow. Then Haines will follow you. Purvis next. I come last because I got here last. There ain't any hurry—What's this here?"

"I tell you I seen it!" called an angry voice from a corner.

"You must of been drunk an' seein' double, partner," drawled the answer.

"Look here!" said the first man, "I'm willin' to take that any way you mean it!"

"An' I'm willin'," said the other, "that you should take it any way you damn please."

Everyone in the room was grave except Jim Silent and his three companions, who were smiling grimly.

"By God, Jack," said the first man with ominous softness, "I'll take a lot from you but when it comes to doubtin' my word—"

Morgan, with popping eyes and a very red face, slapped his hand on the bar and vaulted over it with more agility than his plumpness warranted. He shouldered his way hurriedly through the crowd to the rapidly widening circle around the two disputants. They stood with their right hands resting with rigid fingers low down on their hips, and their eyes, fixed on each other, forgot the rest of the world. Morgan burst in between them.

"Look here," he thundered, "it's only by way of a favor that I'm lettin' you boys wear shootin' irons today because I promised old Cumberland there wouldn't be no fuss. If you got troubles there's enough room for you to settle them out in the hills, but there ain't none at all in here!"

The gleam went out of their eyes like four candles snuffed by the wind. Obviously they were both glad to have the tension broken. Mike wiped his forehead with a rather unsteady hand.

"I ain't huntin' for no special brand of trouble," he said, "but Jack has been ridin' the red-eye pretty hard and it's gotten into that dried up bean he calls his brain."

"Say, partner," drawled Jack, "I ain't drunk enough of the hot stuff to make me fall for the line you've been handing out."

He turned to Morgan.

"Mike, here, has been tryin' to make me believe that he knew a feller who could drill a dollar at twenty yards every time it was tossed up."

The crowd laughed, Morgan loudest of all.

"Did you anyways have Whistlin' Dan in mind?" he asked.

"No, I didn't," said Mike, "an' I didn't say this here man I was talkin' about could drill them every time. But he could do it two times out of four."

"Mike," said Morgan, and he softened his disbelief with his smile and the good-natured clap on the shoulder, "you sure must of been drinkin' when you seen him do it. I allow Whistlin' Dan could do that an' more, but he ain't human with a gun."

"How d'you know?" asked Jack, "I ain't ever seen him packin' a six-gun."

"Sure you ain't," answered Morgan, "but I have, an' I seen him use it, too. It was jest sort of by chance I saw it."

"Well," argued Mike anxiously, "then you allow it's possible if Whistlin' Dan can do it. An' I say I seen a chap who could turn the trick."

"An' who in hell is this Whistlin' Dan?" asked Jim Silent.

"He's the man that caught Satan, an' rode him," answered a bystander.

"Some man if he can ride the devil," laughed Lee Haines.

"I mean the black mustang that ran wild around here for a couple of years. Some people tell tales about him being a wonder with a gun. But Morgan's the only one who claims to have seen him work."

"Maybe you did see it, and maybe you didn't," Morgan was saying to Mike noncommittally, "but there's some pretty fair shots in this room, which I'd lay fifty bucks no man here could hit a dollar with a six-gun at twenty paces."

"While they're arguin'," said Bill Kilduff, "I reckon I'll hit the trail."

"Wait a minute," grinned Jim Silent, "an' watch me have some fun with these short-horns."

He spoke more loudly: "Are you makin' that bet for the sake of arguin', partner, or do you calculate to back it up with cold cash?"

Morgan whirled upon him with a scowl, "I ain't pulled a bluff in my life that I can't back up!" he said sharply.

"Well," said Silent, "I ain't so flush that I'd turn down fifty bucks when a kind Christian soul, as the preachers say, slides it into my glove. Not me. Lead out the dollar, pal, an' kiss it farewell!"

"Who'll hold the stakes?" asked Morgan.

"Let your friend Mike," said Jim Silent carelessly, and he placed fifty dollars in gold in the hands of the Irishman. Morgan followed suit. The crowd hurried outdoors.

A dozen bets were laid in as many seconds. Most of the men wished to place their money on the side of Morgan, but there were not a few who stood willing to risk coin on Jim Silent, stranger though he was. Something in his unflinching eye, his stern face, and the nerveless surety of his movements commanded their trust.

"How are you going, Jim?" asked Lee Haines anxiously. "Is it a safe bet? I've never seen you try a mark like this one!"

"It ain't safe," said Silent, "because I ain't mad enough to shoot my best, but it's about an even draw. Take your pick."

"Not me," said Haines, "if you had ten chances instead of one I might stack some coin on you. If the dollar were stationary I know you could do it, but a moving coin looks pretty small."

"Here you are," called Morgan, who stood at a distance of twenty paces, "are you ready?"

Silent whipped out his revolver and poised it. "Let 'er go!"

The coin whirled in the air. Silent fired as it commenced to fall—it landed untouched.

"As a kind, Christian soul," said Morgan sarcastically, "I ain't in your class, stranger. Charity always sort of interests me when I'm on the receivin' end!"

The crowd chuckled, and the sound infuriated Silent.

"Don't go back jest yet, partners," he drawled. "Mister Morgan, I got one hundred bones which holler that I can plug that dollar the second try."

"Boys," grinned Morgan, "I'm leavin' you to witness that I hate to do it, but business is business. Here you are!"

The coin whirled again. Silent, with his lips pressed into a straight line and his brows drawn dark over his eyes, waited until the coin reached the height of its rise, and then fired—missed—fired again, and sent the coin spinning through the air in a flashing semicircle. It was a beautiful piece of gun-play. In the midst of the clamor of applause Silent strode towards Morgan with his hand outstretched.

"After all," he said. "I knowed you wasn't really hard of heart. It only needed a little time and persuasion to make you dig for coin when I pass the box."

Morgan, red of face and scowling, handed over his late winnings and his own stakes.

"It took you two shots to do it," he said, "an' if I wanted to argue the pint maybe you wouldn't walk off with the coin."

"Partner," said Jim Silent gently, "I got a wanderin' hunch that you're showin' a pile of brains by not arguin' this here pint!"

There followed that little hush of expectancy which precedes trouble, but Morgan, after a glance at the set lips of his opponent, swallowed his wrath.

"I s'pose you'll tell how you did this to your kids when you're eighty," he said scornfully, "but around here, stranger, they don't think much of it. Whistlin' Dan"—he paused, as if to calculate how far he could safely exaggerate—"Whistlin' Dan can stand with his back to the coins an' when they're thrown he drills four dollars easier than you did one—an' he wouldn't waste three shots on one dollar. He ain't so extravagant!"

## CHAPTER IV

### SOMETHING YELLOW

The crowd laughed again at the excitement of Morgan, and Silent's mirth particularly was loud and long.

"An' if you're still bent on charity," he said at last, "maybe we could find somethin' else to lay a bet on!"

"Anything you name!" said Morgan hotly.

"I suppose," said Silent, "that you're some rider, eh?"

"I c'n get by with most of 'em."

"Yeh—I suppose you never pulled leather in your life?"

"Not any hoss that another man could ride straight up."

"Is that so? Well, partner, you see that roan over there?"

"That tall horse?"

"You got him. You c'n win back that hundred if you stick on his back two minutes. D'you take it?"

Morgan hesitated a moment. The big roan was footing it nervously here and there, sometimes throwing up his head suddenly after the manner of a horse of bad temper. However, the loss of that hundred dollars and the humiliation which accompanied it, weighed heavily on the saloon owner's mind.

"I'll take you," he said.

A high, thrilling whistle came faintly from the distance.

"That fellow on the black horse down the road," said Lee Haines, "I guess he's the one that can hit the four dollars? Ha! Ha! Ha!"

"Sure," grinned Silent, "listen to his whistle! We'll see if we can drag another bet out of the barkeep if the roan doesn't hurt him too bad. Look at him now!"

Morgan was having a bad time getting his foot in the stirrup, for the roan reared and plunged. Finally two men held his head and the saloon keeper swung into the saddle. There was a little silence. The roan, as if doubtful that he could really have this new burden on his back, and still fearful of the rope which had been lately tethering him, went a few short, prancing steps, and then, feeling something akin to freedom, reared straight up, snorting. The crowd yelled with delight, and the sound sent the roan back to all fours and racing down the road. He stopped with braced feet, and Morgan lurched forwards on the neck, yet he struck to his seat gamely. Whistling Dan was not a hundred yards away.

Morgan yelled and swung the quirt. The response of the roan was another race down the road at terrific speed, despite the pull of Morgan on the reins. Just as the running horse reached Whistling Dan, he stopped as short as he had done before, but this time with an added buck and a sidewise lurch all combined, which gave the effect of snapping a whip—and poor Morgan was hurled from the saddle like a stone from a sling. The crowd waved their hats and yelled with delight.

"Look out!" yelled Jim Silent. "Grab the reins!"

But though Morgan made a valiant effort the roan easily swerved past him and went racing down the road.

"My God," groaned Silent, "he's gone!"

"Saddles!" called someone. "We'll catch him!"

"Catch hell!" answered Silent bitterly. "There ain't a hoss on earth that can catch him—an' now that he ain't got the weight of a rider, he'll run away from the wind!"

"Anyway there goes Dan on Satan after him!"

"No use! The roan ain't carryin' a thing but the saddle."

"Satan never seen the day he could make the roan eat dust, anyway!"

"Look at 'em go, boys!"

"There ain't no use," said Jim Silent sadly, "he'll wind his black for nothin'— an' I've lost the best hoss on the ranges."

"I believe him," whispered one man to a neighbor, "because I've got an idea that hoss is Red Peter himself!"

His companion stared at him agape.

"Red Pete!" he said. "Why, pal, that's the hoss that Silent—"

"Maybe it is an' maybe it ain't. But why should we ask too many questions?"

"Let the marshals tend to him. He ain't ever troubled this part of the range."

"Anyway, I'm goin' to remember his face. If it's really Jim Silent, I got something that's worth tellin' to my kids when they grow up."

They both turned and looked at the tall man with an uncomfortable awe. The rest of the crowd swarmed into the road to watch the race.

The black stallion was handicapped many yards at the start before Dan could swing him around after the roan darted past with poor Morgan in ludicrous pursuit. Moreover, the roan had the inestimable advantage of an empty saddle. Yet Satan leaned to his work with a stout heart. There was no rock and pitch to his gait, no jerk and labor to his strides. Those smooth shoulders were corded now with a thousand lines where the steel muscles whipped to and fro. His neck stretched out a little—his ears laid back along the neck—his whole body settled gradually and continually down as his stride lengthened. Whistling Dan was leaning forward so that his body would break less wind. He laughed low and soft as the air whirred into his face, and now and then he spoke to his horse, no yell of encouragement, but a sound hardly louder than a whisper. There was no longer a horse and rider—the two had become one creature—a centaur—the body of a horse and the mind of a man.

For a time the roan increased his advantage, but quickly Satan began to hold him even, and then gain. First inch by inch; then at every stride the distance between them diminished. No easy task. The great roan had muscle, heart, and that empty saddle; as well, perhaps, as a thought of the free ranges which lay before him and liberty from the accursed thralldom of the bit and reins and galling spurs. What he lacked was that small whispering voice—that hand touching lightly now and then on his neck—that thrill of generous sympathy which passes between horse and rider. He lost ground steadily and more and more rapidly. Now the outstretched black head was at his tail, now at his flank, now at his girth, now at his shoulder, now they raced nose and nose. Whistling Dan shifted in the saddle. His left foot took the opposite stirrup. His right leg swung free.

The big roan swerved—the black in response to a word from his rider followed the motion—and then the miracle happened. A shadow plunged through the air; a weight thudded on the saddle of the roan; an iron hand jerked back the reins.

Red Pete hated men and feared them, but this new weight on his back was different. It was not the pressure on the reins which urged him to slow up;

he had the bit in his teeth and no human hand could pull down his head; but into the blind love, blind terror, blind rage which makes up the consciousness of a horse entered a force which he had never known before. He realized suddenly that it was folly to attempt to throw off this clinging burden. He might as well try to jump out of his skin. His racing stride shortened to a halting gallop, this to a sharp trot, and in a moment more he was turned and headed back for Morgan's place. The black, who had followed, turned at the same time like a dog and followed with jouncing bridle reins. Black Bart, with lolling red tongue, ran under his head, looking up to the stallion now and again with a comical air of proprietorship, as if he were showing the way.

It was very strange to Red Pete. He pranced sideways a little and shook his head up and down in an effort to regain his former temper, but that iron hand kept his nose down, now, and that quiet voice sounded above him—no cursing, no raking of sharp spurs to torture his tender flanks, no whir of the quirt, but a calm voice of authority and understanding. Red Pete broke into an easy canter and in this fashion they came up to Morgan in the road. Red Pete snorted and started to shy, for he recognized the clumsy, bouncing weight which had insulted his back not long before; but this quiet voiced master reassured him, and he came to a halt.

"That red devil has cost me a hundred bones and all the skin on my knees," groaned Morgan, "and I can hardly walk. Damn his eyes. But say, Dan"—and his eyes glowed with an admiration which made him momentarily forget his pains—"that was some circus stunt you done down the road there—that changin' of saddles on the run, I never seen the equal of it!"

"If you got hurt in the fall," said Dan quietly, overlooking the latter part of the speech, "why don't you climb onto Satan. He'll take you back."

Morgan laughed.

"Say, kid, I'd take a chance with Satan, but there ain't any hospital for fools handy."

"Go ahead. He won't stir a foot. Steady, Satan!"

"All right," said Morgan, "every step is sure like pullin' teeth!"

He ventured closer to the black stallion, but was stopped short. Black Bart was suddenly changed to a green-eyed devil, his hair bristling around his shoulders, his teeth bared, and a snarl that came from the heart of a killer. Satan also greeted his proposed rider with ears laid flat back on his neck and a quivering anger.

"If I'm goin' to ride Satan," declared Morgan, "I got to shoot the dog first and then blindfold the hoss."

"No you don't," said Dan. "No one else has ever had a seat on Satan, but I got an idea he'll make an exception for a sort of temporary cripple. Steady, boy. Here you, Bart, come over here an' keep your face shut!"

The dog, after a glance at his master, moved reluctantly away, keeping his eyes upon Morgan. Satan backed away with a snort. He stopped at the command of Dan, but when Morgan laid a hand on the bridle and spoke to him he trembled with fear and anger. The saloon keeper turned away.

"Thankin' you jest the same, Dan," he said, "I think I c'n walk back. I'd as soon ride a tame tornado as that hoss."

He limped on down the road with Dan riding beside him. Black Bart slunk at his heels, sniffing.

"Dan, I'm goin' to ask you a favor—an' a big one; will you do it for me?"

"Sure," said Whistling Dan. "Anything I can."

"There's a skunk down there with a bad eye an' a gun that jumps out of its leather like it had a mind of its own. He picked me for fifty bucks by nailing a dollar I tossed up at twenty yards. Then he gets a hundred because I couldn't ride this hoss of his. Which he's made a plumb fool of me, Dan. Now I was tellin' him about you—maybe I was sort of exaggeratin'—an' I said you could have your back turned when the coins was tossed an' then pick off four dollars before they hit the ground. I made it a bit high, Dan?"

His eyes were wistful.

"Nick four round boys before they hit the dust?" said Dan. "Maybe I could, I don't know. I can't try it, anyway, Morgan, because I told Dad Cumberland I'd never pull a gun while there was a crowd aroun'."

Morgan sighed; he hesitated, and then: "But you promised you'd do me a favor, Dan?"

The rider started.

"I forgot about that—I didn't think—"

"It's only to do a shootin' trick," said Morgan eagerly. "It ain't pullin' a gun on any one. Why, lad, if you'll tell me you got a ghost of a chance, I'll bet every cent in my cash drawer on you agin that skunk! You've give me your word, Dan."

Whistling Dan shrugged his shoulders.

"I've given you my word," he said, "an' I'll do it. But I guess Dad Cumberland'll be mighty sore on me."

A laugh rose from the crowd at Morgan's place, which they were nearing rapidly. It was like a mocking comment on Dan's speech. As they came closer they could see money changing hands in all directions.

"What'd you do to my hoss?" asked Jim Silent, walking out to meet them.

"He hypnotized him," said Hal Purvis, and his lips twisted over yellow teeth into a grin of satisfaction.

"Git out of the saddle damn quick," growled Silent. "It ain't nacheral he'd let you ride him like he was a plough-hoss. An' if you've tried any fancy stunts, I'll—"

"Take it easy," said Purvis as Dan slipped from the saddle without showing the slightest anger. "Take it easy. You're a bum loser. When I seen the black settle down to his work," he explained to Dan with another grin, "I knowed he'd nail him in the end an' I staked twenty on you agin my friend here! That was sure a slick change of hosses you made."

There were other losers. Money chinked on all sides to an accompaniment of laughter and curses. Jim Silent was examining the roan with a scowl, while Bill Kilduff and Hal Purvis approached Satan to look over his points. Purvis reached out towards the bridle when a murderous snarl at his feet made him jump back with a shout. He stood with his gun poised, facing Black Bart.

"Who's got any money to bet this damn wolf lives more'n five seconds?" he said savagely.

"I have," said Dan.

"Who in hell are you? What d'you mean by trailing this man-killer around?"

He turned to Dan with his gun still poised.

"Bart ain't a killer," said Dan, and the gentleness of his voice was oil on troubled waters, "but he gets peeved when a stranger comes nigh to the hoss."

"All right this time," said Purvis, slowly restoring his gun to its holster, "but if this wolf of yours looks cross-eyed at me agin he'll hit the long trail that ain't got any end, savvy?"

"Sure," said Dan, and his soft brown eyes smiled placatingly.

Purvis kept his right hand close to the butt of his gun and his eyes glinted as if he expected an answer somewhat stronger than words. At this mild acquiesence he turned away, sneering. Silent, having discovered that he could find no fault with Dan's treatment of his horse, now approached with an ominously thin-lipped smile. Lee Haines read his face and came to his side with a whisper: "Better cut out the rough stuff, Jim. This chap hasn't hurt anything but your cash, and he's already taken water from Purvis. I guess there's no call for you to make any play."

"Shut your face, Haines," responded Silent, in the same tone. "He's made a fool of me by showin' up my hoss, an' by God I'm goin' to give him a man-handlin' he'll never forget."

He whirled on Morgan.

"How about it, barkeep, is this the dead shot you was spillin' so many words about?"

Dan, as if he could not understand the broad insult, merely smiled at him with marvelous good nature.

"Keep away from him, stranger," warned Morgan. "Jest because he rode your hoss you ain't got a cause to hunt trouble with him. He's been taught not to fight."

Silent, still looking Dan over with insolent eyes, replied: "He sure sticks to his daddy's lessons. Nice an' quiet an' house broke, ain't he? In my part of the country they dress this kind of a man in gal's clothes so's nobody'll ever get sore at him an' spoil his pretty face. Better go home to your ma. This ain't any place for you. They's men aroun' here."

There was another one of those grimly expectant hushes and then a general guffaw; Dan showed no inclination to take offence. He merely stared at brawny Jim Silent with a sort of childlike wonder.

"All right," he said meekly, "if I ain't wanted around here I figger there ain't any cause why I should stay. You don't figger to be peeved at me, do you?"

The laughter changed to a veritable yell of delight. Even Silent smiled with careless contempt.

"No, kid," he answered, "if I was peeved at you, you'd learn it without askin' questions."

He turned slowly away.

"Maybe I got jaundice, boys," he said to the crowd, "but it seems to me I see something kind of yellow around here!"

The delightful subtlety of this remark roused another side-shaking burst of merriment. Dan shook his head as if the mystery were beyond his comprehension, and looked to Morgan for an explanation. The saloon-keeper approached him, struggling with a grin.

"It's all right, Dan," he said. "Don't let 'em rile you."

"You ain't got any cause to fear that," said Silent, "because it can't be done."

## CHAPTER V

### FOUR IN THE AIR

Dan looked from Morgan to Silent and back again for understanding. He felt that something was wrong, but what it was he had not the slightest idea. For many years old Joe Cumberland had patiently taught him that the last offence against God and man was to fight. The old cattleman had instilled in him the belief that if he did not cross the path of another, no one would cross his way. The code was perfect and satisfying. He would let the world alone and the world would not trouble him. The placid current of his life had never come to "white waters" of wrath.

Wherefore he gazed bewildered about him. They were laughing—they were laughing unpleasantly at him as he had seen men laugh at a fiery young colt which struggled against the rope. It was very strange. They could not mean harm. Therefore he smiled back at them rather uncertainly. Morgan slapped at his shoulder by way of good-fellowship and to hearten him, but Dan slipped away under the extended hand with a motion as subtle and swift as the twist of a snake when it flees for its hole. He had a deep aversion for contact with another man's body. He hated it as the wild horse hates the shadow of the flying rope.

"Steady up, pal," said Morgan, "the lads mean no harm. That tall man is considerable riled; which he'll now bet his sombrero agin you when it comes to shootin'."

He turned back to Silent.

"Look here, partner," he said, "this is the man I said could nail the four dollars before they hit the dust. I figger you don't think how it can be done, eh?"

"Him?" said Silent in deep disgust. "Send him back to his ma before somebody musses him all up! Why, he don't even pack a gun!"

Morgan waited a long moment so that the little silence would make his next speech impressive.

"Stranger," he said, "I've still got somewhere in the neighborhood of five hundred dollars in that cash drawer. An' every cent of it hollers that Dan can do what I said."

Silent hesitated. His code was loose, but he did not like to take advantage of a drunk or a crazy man. However, five hundred dollars was five hundred dollars. Moreover that handsome fellow who had just taken water from Hal Purvis and was now smiling foolishly at his own shame, had actually eluded Red Peter. The remembrance infuriated Silent.

"Hurry up," said Morgan confidently. "I dunno what you're thinkin', stranger. Which I'm kind of deaf an' I don't understand the way anything talks except money."

"Corral that talk, Morgan!" called a voice from the crowd, "you're plumb locoed if you think any man in the world can get away with a stunt like that! Pick four in the air!"

"You keep your jaw for yourself," said Silent angrily, "if he wants to donate a little more money to charity, let him do it. Morgan, I've got five hundred here to cover your stake."

"Make him give you odds, Morgan," said another voice, "because—"

A glance from Silent cut the suggestion short. After that there was little loud conversation. The stakes were large. The excitement made the men hush the very tones in which they spoke. Morgan moistened his white lips.

"You c'n see I'm not packin' any shootin' irons," said Dan. "Has anybody got any suggestions?"

Every gun in the crowd was instantly at his service. They were heartily tempted to despise Dan, but as one with the courage to attempt the impossible, they would help him as far as they could. He took their guns one after the other, weighed them, tried the action, and handed them back. It was almost as if there were a separate intelligence in the ends of his fingers which informed him of the qualities of each weapon.

"Nice gun," he said to the first man whose revolver he handled, "but I don't like a barrel that's quite so heavy. There's a whole ounce too much in the barrel."

"What d'you mean?" asked the cowpuncher. "I've packed that gun for pretty nigh eight years!"

"Sorry," said Dan passing on, "but I can't work right with a top-heavy gun."

The next weapon he handed back almost at once.

"What's the matter with that?" asked the owner aggressively.

"Cylinder too tight," said Dan decisively, and a moment later to another man, "Bad handle. I don't like the feel of it."

Over Jim Silent's guns he paused longer than over most of the rest, but finally he handed them back. The big man scowled.

Dan looked back to him in gentle surprise.

"You see," he explained quietly, "you got to handle a gun like a horse. If you don't treat it right it won't treat you right. That's all I know about it. Your gun ain't very clean, stranger, an' a gun that ain't kept clean gets off feet."

Silent glanced at his weapons, cursed softly, and restored them to the holsters.

"Lee," he muttered to Haines, who stood next to him, "what do you think he meant by that? D' you figger he's got somethin' up his sleeve, an' that's why he acts so like a damned woman?"

"I don't know," said Haines gravely, "he looks to me sort of queer—sort of different—damned different, chief!"

By this time Dan had secured a second gun which suited him. He whirled both guns, tried their actions alternately, and then announced that he was ready. In the dead silence, one of the men paced off the twenty yards.

Dan, with his back turned, stood at the mark, shifting his revolvers easily in his hands, and smiling down at them as if they could understand his caress.

"How you feelin', Dan?" asked Morgan anxiously.

"Everything fine," he answered.

"Are you gettin' weak?"

"No, I'm all right."

"Steady up, partner."

"Steady up? Look at my hand!"

Dan extended his arm. There was not a quiver in it.

"All right, Dan. When you're shootin', remember that I got pretty close to everything I own staked on you. There's the stranger gettin' his four dollars ready."

Silent took his place with the four dollars in his hand.

"Are you ready?" he called.

"Let her go!" said Dan, apparently without the least excitement.

Jim Silent threw the coins, and he threw them so as to increase his chances as much as possible. A little snap of his hand gave them a rapid rotary motion so that each one was merely a speck of winking light. He flung them high, for it was probable that Whistling Dan would wait to shoot until they were on the way down. The higher he threw them the more rapidly they would be travelling when they crossed the level of the markman's eye.

As a shout proclaimed the throwing of the coins, Dan whirled, and it seemed to the bystanders that a revolver exploded before he was fully turned; but one of the coins never rose to the height of the throw. There was a light "cling!" and it spun a dozen yards away. Two more shots blended almost together; two more dollars darted away in twinkling streaks of light. One coin still fell, but when it was a few inches from the earth a six-shooter barked again and the fourth dollar glanced sidewise into the dust. It takes long to describe the feat. Actually, the four shots consumed less than a second of time.

"That last dollar," said Dan, and his soft voice was the first sound out of the silence, "wasn't good. It didn't ring true. Counterfeit?"

It seemed that no one heard his words. The men were making a wild scramble for the dollars. They dived into the dust for them, rising white of face and clothes to fight and struggle over their prizes. Those dollars with the chips and neat round holes in them would confirm the truth of a story that the most credulous might be tempted to laugh to scorn. A cowpuncher offered for one of the relics—but none would part with a prize.

The moment the shooting was over Dan stepped quietly back and restored the guns to the owners. The first man seized his weapon carelessly. He was in the midst of his rush after one of the chipped coins. The other cowpuncher received his weapon almost with reverence.

"I'm thankin' you for the loan," said Dan, "an here's hopin' you always have luck with the gun."

"Luck?" said the other. "I sure *will* have luck with it. I'm goin' to oil her up and put her in a glass case back home, an' when I get grandchildren I'm goin' to point out that gun to 'em and tell 'em what men used to do in the old days. Let's go in an' surround some red-eye at my expense."

"No thanks," answered Dan, "I ain't drinkin'."

He stepped back to the edge of the circle and folded his arms. It was as if he had walked out of the picture. He suddenly seemed to be aloof from them all.

Out of the quiet burst a torrent of curses, exclamations, and shouts. Chance drew Jim Silent and his three followers together.

"My God!" whispered Lee Haines, with a sort of horror in his voice, "it wasn't human! Did you see? Did you see?"

"Am I blind?" asked Hal Purvis, "an' think of me walkin' up an' bracin' that killer like he was a two-year-old kid! I figger that's the nearest I ever come to a undeserved grave, an' I've had some close calls! 'That last dollar wasn't good! It didn't ring true,' says he when he finished. I never seen such nerve!"

"You're wrong as hell," said Silent, "a *woman* can shoot at a target, but it takes a cold *nerve* to shoot at a man—an' this feller is yellow all through!"

"Is he?" growled Bill Kilduff, "well, I'd hate to take him by surprise, so's he'd forget himself. He gets as much action out of a common six-gun as if it was a gatling. He was right about that last dollar, too. It was pure—lead!"

"All right, Haines," said Silent. "You c'n start now any time, an' the rest of us'll follow on the way I said. I'm leavin' last. I got a little job to finish up with the kid."

But Haines was staring fixedly down the road.

"I'm not leaving yet," said Haines. "Look!"

He turned to one of the cowpunchers.

"Who's the girl riding up the road, pardner?"

"That calico? She's Kate Cumberland—old Joe's gal."

"I like the name," said Haines. "She sits the saddle like a man!"

Her pony darted off from some imaginary object in the middle of the road, and she swayed gracefully, following the sudden motion. Her mount came to the sudden halt of the cattle pony and she slipped to the ground before Morgan could run out to help. Even Lee Haines, who was far quicker, could not reach her in time.

"Sorry I'm late," said Haines. "Shall I tie your horse?"

The fast ride had blown color to her face and good spirits into her eyes. She smiled up to him, and as she shook her head in refusal her eyes lingered a pardonable moment on his handsome face, with the stray lock of tawny hair fallen low across his forehead. She was used to frank admiration, but this unembarrassed courtesy was a new world to her. She was still smiling when she turned to Morgan.

"You told my father the boys wouldn't wear guns today."

He was somewhat confused.

"They seem to be wearin' them," he said weakly, and his eyes wandered about the armed circle, pausing on the ominous forms of Hal Purvis, Bill Kilduff, and especially Jim Silent, a head taller than the rest. He stood somewhat in the background, but the slight sneer with which he watched Whistling Dan dominated the entire picture.

"As a matter of fact," went on Morgan, "it would be a ten man job to take the guns away from this crew. You can see for yourself."

She glanced about the throng and started. She had seen Dan.

"How did he come here?"

"Oh, Dan?" said Morgan, "he's all right. He just pulled one of the prettiest shootin' stunts I ever seen."

"But he promised my father—" began Kate, and then stopped, flushing.

If her father was right in diagnosing Dan's character, this was the most critical day in his life, for there he stood surrounded by armed men. If there were anything wild in his nature it would be brought out that day. She was almost glad the time of trial had come.

She said: "How about the guns, Mr. Morgan?"

"If you want them collected and put away for a while," offered Lee Haines, "I'll do what I can to help you!"

Her smile of thanks set his blood tingling. His glance lingered a little too long, a little too gladly, and she colored slightly.

"Miss Cumberland," said Haines, "may I introduce myself? My name is Lee."

She hesitated. The manners she had learned in the Eastern school forbade it, but her Western instinct was truer and stronger. Her hand went out to him.

"I'm very glad to know you, Mr. Lee."

"All right, stranger," said Morgan, who in the meantime had been shifting from one foot to the other and estimating the large chances of failure in this attempt to collect the guns, "if you're going to help me corral the shootin' irons, let's start the roundup."

The girl went with them. They had no trouble in getting the weapons. The cold blue eye of Lee Haines was a quick and effective persuasion.

When they reached Jim Silent he stared fixedly upon Haines. Then he drew his guns slowly and presented them to his comrade, while his eyes shifted to Kate and he said coldly: "Lady, I hope I ain't the last one to congratulate you!"

She did not understand, but Haines scowled and colored. Dan, in the meantime, was swept into the saloon by an influx of the cowpunchers that left only Lee Haines outside with Kate. She had detained him with a gesture.


## CHAPTER VI

## LAUGHTER

"Mr. Lee," she said, "I am going to ask you to do me a favor. Will you?"

His smile was a sufficient answer, and it was in her character that she made no pretext of misunderstanding it.

"You have noticed Dan among the crowd?" she asked, "Whistling Dan?"

"Yes," he said, "I saw him do some very nice shooting."

"It's about him that I want to speak to you. Mr. Lee, he knows very little about men and their ways. He is almost a child among them. You seem—stronger—than most of the crowd here. Will you see that if trouble comes he is not imposed upon?"

She flushed a little, there was such a curious yearning in the eyes of the big man.

"If you wish it," he said simply, "I will do what I can."

As he walked beside her towards her horse, she turned to him abruptly.

"You are very different from the men I have met around here," she said.

"I am glad," he answered.

"Glad?"

"If you find me different, you will remember me, whether for better or worse."

He spoke so earnestly that she grew grave. He helped her to the saddle and she leaned a little to study him with the same gentle gravity.

"I should like to see you again, Mr. Lee," she said, and then in a little outburst, "I should like to see you a *lot!* Will you come to my house sometime?"

The directness, the sudden smile, made him flinch. His voice was a trifle unsteady when he replied.

"I *shall!*" He paused and his hand met hers. "If it is possible."

Her eyebrows raised a trifle.

"Is it so hard to do?"

"Do not ask me to explain," he said, "I am riding a long way."

"Oh, a 'long-rider'!" she laughed, "then of course—" She stopped abruptly. It may have been imagination, but he seemed to start when she spoke the phrase by which outlaws were known to each other. He was forcing his eyes to meet hers.

He said slowly: "I am going on a long journey. Perhaps I will come back. If I am able to, I shall."

He dropped his hand from hers and she remained silent, guessing at many things, and deeply moved, for every woman knows when a man speaks from his soul.

"You will not forget me?"

"I shall never forget you," she answered quietly. "Good-bye, Mr. Lee!"

Her hand touched his again, she wheeled, and rode away. He remained standing with the hand she had grasped still raised. And after a moment, as he had hoped, she turned in the saddle and waved to him. His eyes were downward and he was smiling faintly when he re-entered the saloon.

Silent sat at a table with his chin propped in his hand—his left hand, of course, for that restless right hand must always be free. He stared across the room towards Whistling Dan. The train of thoughts which kept those ominous eyes so unmoving must be broken. He sat down at the side of his chief.

"What the hell?" said the big man, "ain't you started yet?"

"Look here, Jim," said Haines cautiously, "I want you to lay off on this kid, Whistling Dan. It won't meant anything to you to raise the devil with him."

"I tell you," answered Silent, "it'll please me more'n anything in the world to push that damned girl face of his into the floor."

"Silent, I'm asking a personal favor of you!"

The leader turned upon him that untamed stare. Haines set his teeth.

"Haines," came the answer, "I'll stand more from you than from any man alive. I know you've got guts an' I know you're straight with me. But there ain't anything can keep me from man-handlin' that kid over there." He opened and shut his fingers slowly. "I sort of yearn to get at him!"

Haines recognized defeat.

"But you haven't another gun hidden on you, Jim? You won't try to shoot him up?"

"No," said Silent. "If I had a gun I don't know—but I haven't a gun. My hands'll be enough!"

All that could be done now was to get Whistling Dan out of the saloon. That would be simple. A single word would suffice to send the timid man helter-skelter homewards.

The large, lazy brown eyes turned up to Haines as the latter approached.

"Dan," he said, "hit for the timbers—get on your way—there's danger here for you!"

To his astonishment the brown eyes did not vary a shade.

"Danger?" he repeated wonderingly.

"Danger! Get up and get out if you want to save your hide!"

"What's the trouble?" said Dan, and his eyes were surprised, but not afraid.

"The biggest man in this room is after your blood."

"Is he?" said Dan wonderingly. "I'm sorry I don't feel like leavin', but I'm not tired of this place yet."

"Friend," said Haines, "if that tall man puts his hands on you, he'll break you across his knee like a rotten stick of wood!"

It was too late. Silent evidently guessed that Haines was urging his quarry to flee.

"Hey!" he roared, so that all heads turned towards him, "you over there."

Haines stepped back, sick at heart. He knew that it would be folly to meet his chief hand to hand, but he thought of his pledge to Kate, and groaned.

"What do you want of me?" asked Dan, for the pointed arm left no doubt as to whom Silent intended.

"Get up when you're spoke to" cried Silent. "Ain't you learned no manners? An' git up quick!"

Dan rose, smiling his surprise.

"Your friend has a sort of queer way of talkin'," he said to Haines.

"Don't stan' there like a fool. Trot over to the bar an' git me a jolt of red-eye. I'm dry!" thundered Silent.

"Sure!" nodded Whistling Dan amiably, "glad to!" and he went accordingly towards the bar.

The men about the room looked to each other with sick smiles. There was an excuse for acquiescence, for the figure of Jim Silent contrasted with Whistling Dan was like an oak compared with a sapling. Nevertheless such bland cowardice as Dan was showing made their flesh creep. He asked at the bar for the whisky, and Morgan spoke as Dan filled a glass nearly to the brim.

"Dan," he whispered rapidly, "I got a gun behind the bar. Say the word an' I'll take the chance of pullin' it on that big skunk. Then you make a dive for the door. Maybe I can keep him back till you get on Satan."

"Why should I beat it?" queried Dan, astonished. "I'm jest beginnin' to get interested in your place. That tall feller is sure a queer one, ain't he?"

With the same calm and wide-eyed smile of inquiry he turned away, taking the glass of liquor, and left Morgan to stare after him with a face pale with amazement, while he whispered over and over to himself: "Well, I'll be damned! Well, I'll be damned!"

Dan placed the liquor before Silent. The latter sat gnawing his lips.

"What in hell do you mean?" he said. "Did you only bring one glass? Are you too damn good to drink with me? Then drink by yourself, you white-livered coyote!"

He dashed the glass of whisky into Dan's face. Half blinded by the stinging liquor, the latter fell back a pace, sputtering, and wiping his eyes. Not a man in the room stirred. The same sick look was on each face. But the red devil broke loose in Silent's heart when he saw Dan cringe. He followed the thrown glass with his clenched fist. Dan stood perfectly still and watched the blow coming. His eyes were wide and wondering, like those of a child. The iron-hard hand struck him full on the mouth, fairly lifted him from his feet, and flung him against the wall with such violence that he recoiled again and fell forward onto his knees. Silent was making beast noises in his throat and preparing to rush on the half-prostrate figure. He stopped short.

Dan was laughing. At least that chuckling murmur was near to a laugh. Yet there was no mirth in it. It had that touch of the maniacal in it which freezes the blood. Silent halted in the midst of his rush, with his hands poised for the next blow. His mouth fell agape with an odd expression of horror as Dan stared up at him. That hideous chuckling continued. The sound defied definition. And from the shadow in which Dan was crouched his brown eyes blazed, changed, and filled with yellow fires.

"God!" whispered Silent, and at that instant the ominous crouched animal with the yellow eyes, the nameless thing which had been Whistling Dan a moment before, sprang up and forward with a leap like that of a panther.

Morgan stood behind the bar with a livid face and a fixed smile. His fingers still stiffly clutched the whisky bottle from which the last glass had been filled. Not another man in the room stirred from his place. Some sat with their cards raised in the very act of playing. Some had stopped midway a laugh. One man had been tying a bootlace. His body did not rise. Only his eyes rolled up to watch.

Dan darted under the outstretched arms of Silent, fairly heaved him up from the floor and drove him backwards. The big man half stumbled and half fell, knocking aside two chairs. He rushed back with a shout, but at sight of the white face with the thin trickle of blood falling from the lips, and at the sound of that inhuman laughter, he paused again.

Once more Dan was upon him, his hands darting out with motions too fast for the eye to follow. Jim Silent stepped back a half pace, shifted his weight, and drove his fist straight at that white face. How it happened not a man in the room could tell, but the hand did not strike home. Dan had swerved aside as lightly as a wind-blown feather and his fist rapped against Silent's ribs with a force that made the giant grunt.

Some of the horror was gone from his face and in its stead was baffled rage. He knew the scientific points of boxing, and he applied them. His eye was quick and sure. His reach was whole inches longer than his opponent's. His strength was that of two ordinary men. What did it avail him? He was like an agile athlete in the circus playing tag with a black panther. He was like a child striking futilely at a wavering butterfly. Sometimes this white-faced, laughing devil ducked under his arms. Sometimes a sidestep made his blows miss by the slightest fraction of an inch.

And for every blow he struck four rained home against him. It was impossible! It could not be! Silent telling himself that he dreamed, and those dancing fists crashed into his face and body like sledgehammers. There was no science in the thing which faced him. Had there been trained skill the second blow would have knocked Silent unconscious, and he knew it, but Dan made no effort to strike a vulnerable spot. He hit at anything which offered.

Still he laughed as he leaped back and forth. Perhaps mere weight of rushing would beat the dancing will-o'-the-wisp to the floor. Silent bored in with lowered head and clutched at his enemy. Then he roared with triumph. His outstretched hand caught Dan's shirt as the latter flicked to one side. Instantly they were locked in each other's arms! The most meaning part of the fight followed.

The moment after they grappled, Silent shifted his right arm from its crushing grip on Dan's body and clutched at the throat. The move was as swift as lightning, but the parry of the smaller man was still quicker. His left hand clutched Silent by the wrist, and that mighty sweep of arm was stopped in mid-air! They were in the middle of the room. They stood perfectly erect and close together, embraced. Their position had a ludicrous resemblance to the posture of dancers, but their bodies were trembling with effort. With every ounce of power in his huge frame Silent strove to complete his grip at the throat. He felt the right arm of Dan tightening around him closer, closer, closer! It was not a bulky arm, but it seemed to be made of linked steel which was shrinking into him, and promised to crush his very bones. The strength of this man seemed to increase. It was limitless. His breath came struggling under that pressure and the blood thundered and raged in his temples. If he could only get at that soft throat!

But his struggling right hand was held in a vice of iron. Now his numb arm gave way, slowly, inevitably. He ground his teeth and cursed. His curse was half a prayer. For answer there was the unearthly chuckle just below his ear. His hand was moved back, down, around! He was helpless as a child in the arms of its father—no, helpless as a sheep in the constricting coils of a python.

An impulse of frantic horror and shame and fear gave him redoubled strength for an instant. He tore himself clear and reeled back. Dan planted two smashes on Silent's snarling mouth. A glance showed the large man the mute, strained faces around the room. The laughing devil leaped again. Then all pride slipped like water from the heart of Jim Silent, and in its place there was only icy fear, fear not of a man, but of animal power. He caught up a heavy chair and drove it with all his desperate strength at Dan.

It cracked distinctly against his head and the weight of it fairly drove him into the floor. He fell with a limp thud on the boards. Silent, reeling and blind, staggered to and fro in the center of the room. Morgan and Lee Haines reached Dan at the same moment and kneeled beside him.

## CHAPTER VII

## THE MUTE MESSENGER

Almost at once Haines raised a hand and spoke to the crowd: "He's all right, boys. Badly cut across the head and stunned, but he'll live."

There was a deep gash on the upper part of the forehead. If the crossbar of the chair had not broken, the skull might have been injured. The impact of the blow had stunned him, and it might be many minutes before his senses returned.

As the crowd closed around Dan, a black body leaped among them, snarling hideously. They sprang back with a yell from the rush of this green-eyed fury; but Black Bart made no effort to attack them. He sat crouching before the prostrate body, licking the deathly white face, and growling horribly, and then stood over his fallen master and stared about the circle. Those who had seen a lone wolf make its stand against a pack of dogs recognized the attitude. Then without a sound, as swiftly as he had entered the room, he leaped through the door and darted off up the road. Satan, for the first time deserted by this wolfish companion, turned a high head and neighed after him, but he raced on.

The men returned to their work over Dan's body, cursing softly. There was a hair-raising unearthliness about the sudden coming and departure of Black Bart. Jim Silent and his comrades waited no longer, but took to their saddles and galloped down the road.

Within a few moments the crowd at Morgan's place began to thin out. Evening was coming on, and most of them had far to ride. They might have lingered until midnight, but this peculiar accident damped their spirits. Probably not a hundred words were spoken from the moment Silent struck Dan to the time when the last of the cattlemen took to the saddle. They avoided each other's eyes as if in shame. In a short time only Morgan remained working over Dan.

In the house of old Joe Cumberland his daughter sat fingering the keys of the only piano within many miles. The evening gloom deepened as she played with upward face and reminiscent eyes. The tune was uncertain, weird—for she was trying to recall one of those nameless airs which Dan whistled as he rode through the hills. There came a patter of swift, light footfalls in the hall, and then a heavy scratching at the door.

"Down, Bart!" she called, and went to admit him to the room.

The moment she turned the handle the door burst open and Bart fell in against her. She cried out at sight of the gleaming teeth and eyes, but he fawned about her feet, alternately whining and snarling.

"What is it, boy?" she asked, gathering her skirts close about her ankles and stepping back, for she never was without some fear of this black monster. "What do you want, Bart?"

For reply he stood stock still, raised his nose, and emitted a long wail, a mournful, a ghastly sound, with a broken-hearted quaver at the end. Kate Cumberland shrank back still farther until the wall blocked her retreat. Black Bart had never acted like this before. He followed her with a green light in his eyes, which shone phosphorescent and distinct through the growing shadows. And most terrible of all was the sound which came deep in his throat as if his brute nature was struggling to speak human words. She felt a great impulse to cry out for help, but checked herself. He was still crouching about her feet. Obviously he meant no harm to her.

He turned and ran towards the door, stopped, looked back to her, and made a sound which was nearer to the bark of a dog than anything he had ever uttered. She made a step after him. He whined with delight and moved closer to the door. Now she stopped again. He whirled and ran back, caught her dress in his teeth, and again made for the door, tugging her after him.

At last she understood and followed him. When she went towards the corral to get her horse, he planted himself in front of her and snarled so furiously that she gave up her purpose. She was beginning to be more and more afraid. A childish thought came to her that perhaps this brute was attempting to lure her away from the house, as she had seen coyotes lure dogs, and then turn his teeth against her. Nevertheless she followed. Something in the animal's eagerness moved her deeply. When he led her out to the road he released her dress and trotted ahead a short distance, looking back and whining, as if to beg her to go faster. For the first time the thought of Dan came into her mind. Black Bart was leading her down the road towards Morgan's place. What if something had happened to Dan?

She caught a breath of sharp terror and broke into a run. Bart yelped his pleasure. Yet a cold horror rose in her heart as she hurried. Had her father after all been right? What power had Dan, if he needed her, to communicate with this mute beast and send him to her? As she ran she wished for the day, the warm, clear sun—for these growing shadows of evening bred a thousand ghostly thoughts. Black Bart was running backwards and forwards before her as if he half entreated and half threatened her.

Her heart died within her as she came in sight of Morgan's place. There was only one horse before it, and that was the black stallion. Why had the others gone so soon? Breathless, she reached the door of the saloon. It was very dim within. She could make out only formless shades at first. Black Bart slid noiselessly across the floor. She followed him with her eyes, and now she saw a figure stretched straight out on the floor while another man kneeled at his side. She ran forward with a cry.

Morgan rose, stammering. She pushed him aside and dropped beside Dan. A broad white bandage circled his head. His face was almost as pale as the cloth. Her touches went everywhere over that cold face, and she moaned little syllables that had no meaning. He lived, but it seemed to her that she had found him at the legended gates of death.

"Miss Kate!" said Morgan desperately.

"You murderer!"

"You don't think that *I* did that?"

"It happened in your place—you had given Dad your word!"

Still she did not turn her head.

"Won't you hear me explain? He's jest in a sort of a trance. He'll wake up feelin' all right. Don't try to move him tonight. I'll go out an' put his hoss up in the shed. In the mornin' he'll be as good as new. Miss Kate, won't you listen to me?"

She turned reluctantly towards him. Perhaps he was right and Dan would waken from his swoon as if from a healthful sleep.

"It was that big feller with them straight eyes that done it," began Morgan.

"The one who was sneering at Dan?"

"Yes."

"Weren't there enough boys here to string him up?"

"He had three friends with him. It would of taken a hundred men to lay hands on one of those four. They were all bad ones. I'm goin' to tell you how it was, because I'm leavin' in a few minutes and ridin' south, an' I want to clear my trail before I start. This was the way it happened—"

His back was turned to the dim light which fell through the door. She could barely make out the movement of his lips. All the rest of his face was lost in shadow. As he spoke she sometimes lost his meaning and the stir of his lips became a nameless gibbering. The gray gloom settled more deeply round the room and over her heart while he talked. He explained how the difference had risen between the tall stranger and Whistling Dan. How Dan had been insulted time and again and borne it with a sort of childish stupidity. How finally the blow had been struck. How Dan had crouched on the floor, laughing, and how a yellow light gathered in his eyes.

At that, her mind went blank. When her thoughts returned she stood alone in the room. The clatter of Morgan's galloping horse died swiftly away down the road. She turned to Dan. Black Bart was crouched at watch beside him. She kneeled again—lowered her head—heard the faint but steady breathing. He seemed infinitely young—infinitely weak and helpless. The whiteness of the bandage stared up at her like an eye through the deepening gloom. All the mother in her nature came to her eyes in tears.

## CHAPTER VIII

### RED WRITING

He stirred.

"Dan—dear!"

"My head," he muttered, "it sort of aches, Kate, as if—"

He was silent and she knew that he remembered.

"You're all right now, honey. I've come here to take care of you—I won't leave you. Poor Dan!"

"How did you know?" he asked, the words trailing.

"Black Bart came for me."

"Good ol' Bart!"

The great wolf slunk closer, and licked the outstretched hand.

"Why, Kate, I'm on the floor and it's dark. Am I still in Morgan's place? Yes, I begin to see clearer."

He made an effort to rise, but she pressed him back.

"If you try to move right away you may get a fever. I'm going back to the house, and I'll bring you down some blankets. Morgan says you shouldn't attempt to move for several hours. He says you've lost a great deal of blood and that you mustn't make any effort or ride a horse till tomorrow."

Dan relaxed with a sigh.

"Kate."

"Yes, honey."

Her hand travelled lightly as blown snow across his forehead. He caught it and pressed the coolness against his cheek.

"I feel as if I'd sort of been through a fire. I seem to be still seein' red."

"Dan, it makes me feel as if I never knew you! Now you must forget all that has happened. Promise me you will!"

He was silent for a moment and then he sighed again.

"Maybe I can, Kate. Which I feel, though, as if there was somethin' inside me writ—writ in red letters—I got to try to read the writin' before I can talk much."

She barely heard him. Her hand was still against his face. A deep awe and content was creeping through her, so that she began to smile and was glad that the dark covered her face. She felt abashed before him for the first time in her life, and there was a singular sense of shame. It was as if some door in her inner heart had opened so that Dan was at liberty to look down into her soul. There was terror in this feeling, but there was also gladness.

"Kate."

"Yes—honey!"

"What were you hummin'?"

She started.

"I didn't know I was humming, Dan."

"You were, all right. It sounded sort of familiar, but I couldn't figger out where I heard it."

"I know now. It's one of your own tunes."

Now she felt a tremor so strong that she feared he would notice it.

"I must go back to the house, Dan. Maybe Dad has returned. If he has, perhaps he can arrange to have you carried back tonight."

"I don't want to think of movin', Kate. I feel mighty comfortable. I'm forgettin' all about that ache in my head. Ain't that queer? Why, Kate, what in the world are you laughin' about?"

"I don't know, Dan. I'm just happy!"

"Kate."

"Yes?"

"I like you pretty much."

"I'm so glad!"

"You an' Black Bart, an' Satan—"

"Oh!" Her tone changed.

"Why are you tryin' to take your hand away, Kate?"

"Don't you care for me any more than for your horse—and your dog?"

He drew a long breath, puzzled.

"It's some different, I figger."

"Tell me!"

"If Black Bart died—"

The wolf-dog whined, hearing his name.

"Good ol' Bart! Well, if Black Bart died maybe I'd someday have another dog I'd like almost as much."

"Yes."

"An' if Satan died—even Satan!—maybe I could sometime like another hoss pretty well—if he was a pile like Satan! But if you was to die—it'd be diff'r'nt, a considerable pile different."

"Why?"

His pauses to consider these questions were maddening.

"I don't know," he muttered at last.

Once more she was thankful for the dark to hide her smile.

"Maybe you know the reason, Kate?"

Her laughter was rich music. His hold on her hand relaxed. He was thinking of a new theme. When he laughed in turn it startled her. She had never heard that laugh before.

"What is it, Dan?"

"He was pretty big, Kate. He was bigger'n almost any man I ever seen! It was kind of funny. After he hit me I was almost glad. I didn't hate him—"

"Dear Dan!"

"I didn't hate him—I jest nacherally wanted to kill him—and wantin' to do that made me glad. Isn't that funny, Kate?"

He spoke of it as a chance traveller might point out a striking feature of the landscape to a companion.

"Dan, if you really care for me you must drop the thought of him."

His hand slipped away.

"How can I do that? That writin' I was tellin' you about—"

"Yes?"

"It's about him!"

"Ah!"

"When he hit me the first time—"

"I won't hear you tell of it!"

"The blood come down my chin—jest a little trickle of it. It was warm, Kate. That was what made me hot all through."

Her hands fell limp, cold, lifeless.

"It's as clear as the print in a book. I've got to finish him. That's the only way I can forget the taste of my own blood."

"Dan, listen to me!"

He laughed again, in the new way. She remembered that her father had dreaded the very thing that had come to Dan—this first taste of his own powers—this first taste (she shuddered) of blood!

"Dan, you've told me that you like me. You have to make a choice now, between pursuing this man, and me."

"You don't understand," he explained carefully. "I *got* to follow him. I can't help it no more'n Black Bart can help howlin' when he sees the moon."

He fell silent, listening. Far across the hills came the plaintive wail of a coyote—that shrill bodiless sound. Kate trembled.

"Dan!"

Outside, Satan whinnied softly like a call. She leaned and her lips touched his. He thrust her away almost roughly.

"They's blood on my lips, Kate! I can't kiss you till they're clean."

He turned his head.

"You must listen to me, Dan!"

"Kate, would you talk to the wind?"

"Yes, if I loved the wind!"

He turned his head.

She pleaded: "Here are my hands to cover your eyes and shut out the thoughts of this man you hate. Here are my lips, dear, to tell you that I love you unless this thirst for killing carries you away from me. Stay with me! Give me your heart to keep gentle!"

He said nothing, but even through the dark she was aware of a struggle in his face, and then, through the gloom, she began to see his eyes more clearly. They seemed to be illuminated by a light from within—they changed—there was a hint of yellow in the brown. And she spoke again, blindly, passionately.

"Give me your promise! It is so easy to do. One little word will make you safe. It will save you from yourself."

Still he answered nothing. Black Bart came and crouched at his head and stared at her fixedly.

"Speak to me!"

Only the yellow light answered her. Cold fear fought in her heart, but love still struggled against it.

"For the last time—for God's sake, Dan!"

Still that silence. She rose, shaking and weak. The changeless eyes followed her. Only fear remained now. She backed towards the door, slowly, then faster, and faster. At the threshold she whirled and plunged into the night.

Up the road she raced. Once she stumbled and fell to her knees. She cried out and glanced behind her, breathing again when she saw that nothing followed. At the house she made no pause, though she heard the voice of her father singing. She could not tell him. He should be the last in all the world to know. She went to her room and huddled into bed.

Presently a knock came at her door, and her father's voice asked if she were ill. She pleaded that she had a bad headache and wished to be alone. He asked if she had seen Dan. By a great effort she managed to reply that Dan had ridden to a neighboring ranch. Her father left the door without further question. Afterwards she heard him in the distance singing his favorite mournful ballads. It doubled her sense of woe and brought home the clinging fear. She felt that if she could weep she might live, but otherwise her heart would burst. And after hours and hours of that torture which burns the name of "woman" in the soul of a girl, the tears came. The roosters announced the dawn before she slept.

Late the next morning old Joe Cumberland knocked again at her door. He was beginning to fear that this illness might be serious. Moreover, he had a definite purpose in rousing her.

"Yes?" she called, after the second knock.

"Look out your window, honey, down to Morgan's place. You remember I said I was goin' to clean up the landscape?"

The mention of Morgan's place cleared the sleep from Kate's mind and it brought back the horror of the night before. Shivering she slipped from her bed and went to the window. Morgan's place was a mass of towering flames!

She grasped the windowsill and stared again. It could not be. It must be merely another part of the nightmare, and no reality. Her father's voice, high with exultation, came dimly to her ears, but what she saw was Dan as he had laid there the night before, hurt, helpless, too weak to move!

"There's the end of it," Joe Cumberland was saying complacently outside her door. "There ain't goin' to be even a shadow of the saloon left nor nothin' that's in it. I jest travelled down there this mornin' and touched a match to it!"

Still she stared without moving, without making a sound. She was seeing Dan as he must have wakened from a swoonlike sleep with the smell of smoke and the heat of rising flames around him. She saw him struggle, and fail to reach his feet. She almost heard him cry out—a sound drowned easily by the roar of the fire, and the crackling of the wood. She saw him drag himself with his hands across the floor, only to be beaten back by a solid wall of flame. Black Bart crouched beside him and would not leave his doomed master. Fascinated by the raging fire the black stallion Satan would break from the shed and rush into the flames!—and so the inseparable three must have perished together!

"Why don't you speak, Kate?" called her father.

"Dan!" she screamed, and pitched forward to the floor.

## CHAPTER IX

## THE PHANTOM RIDER

In the daytime the willows along the wide, level river bottom seemed an unnatural growth, for they made a streak of yellow-green across the mountain-desert when all other verdure withered and died. After nightfall they became still more dreary. Even when the air was calm there was apt to be a sound as of wind, for the tenuous, trailing branches brushed lightly together, making a guarded whispering like ghosts.

In a small clearing among these willows sat Silent and his companions. A fifth member had just arrived at this rendezvous, answered the quiet greeting with a wave of his hand, and was now busy caring for his horse. Bill Kilduff, who had a natural inclination and talent for cookery, raked up the deft dying coals of the fire over which he had cooked the supper, and set about preparing bacon and coffee for the newcomer. The latter came forward, and squatted close to the cook, watching the process with a careful eye. He made a sharp contrast with the rest of the group. From one side his profile showed the face of a good-natured boy, but when he turned his head the flicker of the firelight ran down a scar which gleamed in a jagged semi-circle from his right eyebrow to the corner of his mouth. This whole side of his countenance was drawn by the cut, the mouth stretching to a perpetual grimace. When he spoke it was as if he were attempting secrecy. The rest of the men waited in patience until he finished eating. Then Silent asked: "What news, Jordan?"

Jordan kept his regretful eyes a moment longer on his empty coffee cup.

"There ain't a pile to tell," he answered at last. "I suppose you heard about what happened to the chap you beat up at Morgan's place the other day?"

"Who knows that *I* beat him up?" asked Silent sharply.

"Nobody," said Jordan, "but when I heard the description of the man that hit Whistling Dan with the chair, I knew it was Jim Silent."

"What about Barry?" asked Haines, but Jordan still kept his eyes upon the chief.

"They was sayin' pretty general," he went on, "that you *needed* that chair, Jim. Is that right?"

The other three glanced covertly to each other. Silent's hand bunched into a great fist.

"He went loco. I had to slam him. Was he hurt bad?"

"The cut on his head wasn't much, but he was left lyin' in the saloon that night, an' the next mornin' old Joe Cumberland, not knowin' that Whistlin' Dan was in there, come down an' touched a match to the old joint. She went up in smoke an' took Dan along."

No one spoke for a moment. Then Silent cried out: "Then what was that whistlin' I've heard down the road behind us?"

Bill Kilduff broke into rolling bass laughter, and Hal Purvis chimed in with a squeaking tenor.

"We told you all along, Jim," said Purvis, as soon as he could control his voice, "that there wasn't any whistlin' behind us. We know you got powerful good hearin', Jim, but we all figger you been makin' somethin' out of nothin'. Am I right, boys?"

"You sure are," said Kilduff, "I ain't heard a thing."

Silent rolled his eyes angrily from face to face.

"I'm kind of sorry the lad got his in the fire. I was hopin' maybe we'd meet agin. There's nothin' I'd rather do than be alone five minutes with Whistlin' Dan."

His eyes dared any one to smile. The men merely exchanged glances. When he turned away they grinned broadly. Hal Purvis turned and caught Bill Kilduff by the shoulder.

"Bill," he said excitedly, "if Whistlin' Dan is dead there ain't any master for that dog!"

"What about him?" growled Kilduff.

"I'd like to try my hand with him," said Purvis, and he moistened his tight lips. "Did you see the black devil when he snarled at me in front of Morgan's place?"

"He sure didn't look too pleasant."

"Right. Maybe if I had him on a chain I could change his manners some, eh?"

"How?"

"A whip every day, damn him—a whip every time he showed his teeth at me. No eats till he whined and licked my hand."

"He'd die first. I know that kind of a dog—or a wolf."

"Maybe he'd die. Anyway I'd like to try my hand with him. Bill, I'm goin' to get hold of him some of these days if I have to ride a hundred miles an' swim a river!"

Kilduff grunted.

"Let the damn wolf be. You c'n have him, I say. What I'm thinkin' about is the hoss. Hal, do you remember the way he settled to his stride when he lighted out after Red Pete?"

Purvis shrugged his shoulders.

"You're a fool, Bill. Which no man but Barry could ever ride that hoss. I seen it in his eye. He'd cash in buckin'. He'd fight you like a man."

Kilduff sighed. A great yearning was in his eyes.

"Hal," he said softly, "they's some men go around for years an' huntin' for a girl whose picture is in their bean, cached away somewhere. When they see her they jest nacherally goes nutty. Hal, I don't give a damn for women folk, but I've travelled around a long time with a picture of a hoss in my brain, an' Satan is the hoss."

He closed his eyes.

"I c'n see him now. I c'n see them shoulders—an' that head—an', my God! them eyes—them fire eatin' eyes! Hal, if a man was to win the heart of that hoss he'd lay down his life for you—he'd run himself plumb to death! I won't never sleep tight till I get the feel of them satin sides of his between my knees."

Lee Haines heard them speak, but he said nothing. His heart also leaped when he heard of Whistling Dan's death, but he thought neither of the horse nor the dog. He was seeing the yellow hair and the blue eyes of Kate Cumberland. He approached Jordan and took a place beside him.

"Tell me some more about it, Terry," he asked.

"Some more about what?"

"About Whistling Dan's death—about the burning of the saloon," said Haines.

"What the hell! Are you still thinkin' about that?"

"I certainly am."

"Then I'll trade you news," said Terry Jordan, lowering his voice so that it would not reach the suspicious ear of Jim Silent. "I'll tell you about the burnin' if you'll tell me something about Barry's fight with Silent!"

"It's a trade," answered Haines.

"All right. Seems old Joe Cumberland had a hunch to clean up the landscape—old fool! So he jest up in the mornin' an' without sayin' a word to any one he downs to the saloon and touches a match to it. When he come back to his house he tells his girl, Kate, what he done. With that she lets out a holler an' drops in a faint."

Haines muttered.

"What's the matter?" asked Terry, a little anxiously.

"Nothin," said Haines. "She fainted, eh? Well, good!"

"Yep. She fainted an' when she come to, she told Cumberland that Dan was in the saloon, an' probably too weak to get out of the fire. They started for the place on the run. When they got there all they found was a pile of red hot coals. So everyone figures that he went up in the flames. That's all I know. Now what about the fight?"

Lee Haines sat with fixed eyes.

"There isn't much to say about the fight," he said at last.

"The hell there isn't," scoffed Terry Jordan. "From what I heard, this Whistling Dan simply cut loose and raised the devil more general than a dozen mavericks corralled with a bunch of yearlings."

"Cutting loose is right," said Haines. "It wasn't a pleasant thing to watch. One moment he was about as dangerous as an eighteen-year-old girl. The next second he was like a panther that's tasted blood. That's all there was to it, Terry. After the first blow, he was all over the chief. You know Silent's a bad man with his hands?"

"I guess we all know that," said Jordan, with a significant smile.

"Well," said Haines, "he was like a baby in the hands of Barry. I don't like to talk about it—none of us do. It makes the flesh creep."

There was a loud crackling among the underbrush several hundred yards away. It drew closer and louder.

"Start up your works agin, will you, Bill?" called Silent. "Here comes Shorty Rhinehart, an' he's overdue."

In a moment Shorty swung from his horse and joined the group. He gained his nickname from his excessive length, being taller by an inch or two than Jim Silent himself, but what he gained in height he lost in width. Even his face was monstrously long, and marked with such sad lines that the favorite name of "Shorty" was affectionately varied to "Sour-face" or "Calamity." Silent went to him at once.

"You seen Hardy?" he asked.

"I sure did," said Rhinehart, "an' it's the last time I'll make that trip to him, you can lay to that."

"Did he give you the dope?"

"No."

"What do you mean?"

"I jest want you to know that this here's my last trip to Elkhead—on *any* business."

"Why?"

"I passed three marshals on the street, an' I knew them all. They was my friends, formerly. One of them was—"

"What did they do?"

"I waved my hand to them, glad an' familiar. They jest grunted. One of them, he looked up an' down the street, an' seein' that no one was in sight, he come up to me an' without shakin' hands he says: 'I'm some surprised to see you in Elkhead, Shorty.' 'Why,' says I, 'the town's all right, ain't it?' 'It's all right,' he says, 'but you'd find it a pile more healthier out on the range.'"

"What in hell did he mean by that?" growled Silent.

"He simply meant that they're beginnin' to think a lot more about us than they used to. We've been pullin' too many jobs the last six months."

"You've said all that before, Shorty. I'm runnin' this gang. Tell me about Hardy."

"I'm comin' to that. I went into the Wells Fargo office down by the railroad, an' the clerk sent me back to find Hardy in the back room, where he generally is. When he seen me he changed color. I'd jest popped my head through the door an' sung out: 'Hello, Hardy, how's the boy?' He jumped up from the desk an' sung out so's his clerk in the outside room could hear: 'How are you, lad?' an' he pulled me quick into the room an' locked the door behind me.

"'Now what in hell have you come to Elkhead for?' says he.

"'For a drink' says I, never battin' an eye.

"'You've come a damn long ways,' says he.

"'Sure,' says I, 'that's one reason I'm so dry. Will you liquor, pal?'

"He looked like he needed a drink, all right. He begun loosening his shirt collar.

"'Thanks, but I ain't drinkin', says he. 'Look here, Shorty, are you loco to come ridin' into Elkhead this way?'

"'I'm jest beginnin' to think maybe I am,' says I.

"'Shorty,' he says in a whisper, 'they're beginnin' to get wise to the whole gang—includin' me.'

"'Take a brace,' says I. 'They ain't got a thing on you, Hardy.'

"'That don't keep 'em from thinkin' a hell of a pile,' says he, 'an' I tell you, Shorty, I'm jest about through with the whole works. It ain't worth it—not if there was a million in it. Everybody is gettin' wise to Silent, an' the rest of you. Pretty soon hell's goin' to bust loose.'

"'You've been sayin' that for two years,' says I.

"He stopped an' looked at me sort of thoughtful an' pityin'. Then he steps up close to me an' whispers in that voice: 'D'you know who's on Silent's trail now? Eh?'

"'No, an' I don't give a damn,' says I, free an' careless.

"'Tex Calder!' says he."

Silent started violently, and his hand moved instinctively to his six-gun.

"Did he say Tex Calder?"

"He said no less," answered Shorty Rhinehart, and waited to see his news take effect. Silent stood with head bowed, scowling.

"Tex Calder's a fool," he said at last. "He ought to know better'n to take to *my* trail."

"He's fast with his gun," suggested Shorty.

"Don't I know that?" said Silent. "If Alvarez, an' Bradley, an' Hunter, an' God knows how many more could come up out of their graves, they'd tell jest how quick he *is* with a six-gun. But I'm the one man on the range that's faster."

Shorty was eloquently mute.

"I ain't askin' you to take my word for it," said Jim Silent. "Now that he's after me, I'm glad of it. It had to come some day. The mountains ain't big enough for both of us to go rangin' forever. We had to lock horns some day. An' I say, God help Tex Calder!"

He turned abruptly to the rest of the men.

"Boys, I got somethin' to tell you that Shorty jest heard. Tex Calder is after us."

There came a fluent outburst of cursing.

Silent went on: "I know jest how slick Calder is. I'm bettin' on my draw to be jest the necessary half a hair quicker. He may die shootin'. I don't lay no bets that I c'n nail him before he gets his iron out of its leather, but I may be 'll be shootin' blind when he dies. Is there any one takin' that bet?"

His eyes challenged them one after another. Their glances travelled past Silent as if they were telling over and over to themselves the stories of those many men to whom Tex Calder had played the part of Fate. The leader turned back to Shorty Rhinehart.

"Now tell me what he had to say about the coin."

"Hardy says the shipment's delayed. He don't know how long."

"How'd it come to be delayed?"

"He figures that Wells Fargo got a hunch that Silent was layin' for the train that was to carry it."

"Will he let us know when it *does* come through?"

"I asked him, an' he jest hedged. He's quitting on us cold."

"I was a fool to send you, Shorty. I'm goin' myself, an' if Hardy don't come through to me—"

He broke off and announced to the rest of his gang that he intended to make the journey to Elkhead. He told Haines, who in such cases usually acted as lieutenant, to take charge of the camp. Then he saddled his roan.

In the very act of pulling up the cinch of his saddle, Silent stopped short, turned, and raised a hand for quiet. The rest were instantly still. Hal Purvis leaned his weazened face towards the ground. In this manner it was sometimes possible to detect far-off sounds which to one erect would be inaudible. In a moment, however, he straightened up, shaking his head.

"What is it?" whispered Haines.

"Shut up," muttered Silent, and the words were formed by the motion of his lips rather than through any sound. "That damned whistling again."

Every face changed. At a rustling in a near-by willow, Terry Jordan started and then cursed softly to himself. That broke the spell.

"It's the whisperin' of the willows," said Purvis.

"You lie," said Silent hoarsely. "I hear the sound growing closer."

"Barry is dead," said Haines.

Silent whipped out his revolver—and then shoved it back into the holster.

"Stand by me, boys," he pleaded. "It's his ghost come to haunt me! You can't hear it, because he ain't come for you."

They stared at him with a fascinated horror.

"How do you know it's him?" asked Shorty Rhinehart.

"There ain't no sound in the whole world like it. It's a sort of cross between the singing of a bird an' the wailin' of the wind. It's the ghost of Whistlin' Dan."

The tall roan raised his head and whinnied softly. It was an unearthly effect—as if the animal heard the sound which was inaudible to all but his master. It changed big Jim Silent into a quavering coward. Here were five practised fighters who feared nothing between heaven and hell, but what could they avail him against a bodiless spirit? The whistling stopped. He breathed again, but only for a moment.

It began again, and this time much louder and nearer. Surely the others must hear it now, or else it was certainly a ghost. The men sat with dilated eyes for an instant, and then Hal Purvis cried, "I heard it, chief! If it's a ghost, it's hauntin' me too!"

Silent cursed loudly in his relief.

"It ain't a ghost. It's Whistlin' Dan himself. An' Terry Jordan has been carryin' us lies! What in hell do you mean by it?"

"I ain't been carryin' you lies," said Jordan, hotly. "I told you what I heard. I didn't never say that there was any one seen his dead body!"

The whistling began to die out. A babble of conjecture and exclamation broke out, but Jim Silent, still sickly white around the mouth, swung up into the saddle.

"That Whistlin' Dan I'm leavin' to you, Haines," he called. "I've had his blood onct, an' if I meet him agin there's goin' to be another notch filed into my shootin' iron."

# CHAPTER X

## THE STRENGTH OF WOMEN

He rode swiftly into the dark of the willows, and the lack of noise told that he was picking his way carefully among the bended branches.

"It seems to me," said Terry Jordan, "which I'm not suggestin' anything— but it seems to me that the chief was in a considerable hurry to leave the camp."

"He was," said Hal Purvis, "an' if you seen that play in Morgan's place you wouldn't be wonderin' why. If I was the chief I'd do the same."

"Me speakin' personal," remarked Shorty Rhinehart, "I ain't layin' out to be no man-eater like the chief, but I ain't seen the man that'd make me take to the timbers that way. I don't noways expect there *is* such a man!"

"Shorty," said Haines calmly, "we all knows that you're quite a man, but you and Terry are the only ones of us who are surprised that Silent slid away. The rest of us who saw this Whistling Dan in action aren't a bit inclined to wonder. Suppose you were to meet a black panther down here in the willows?"

"I wouldn't give a damn if I had my Winchester with me."

"All right, Terry, but suppose the panther," broke in Hal Purvis, "could sling shootin' irons as well as you could—maybe *that'd* make you partic'ler pleased."

"It ain't possible," said Terry.

"Sure it ain't," grinned Purvis amiably, "an' this Barry ain't possible, either. Where you going, Lee?"

Haines turned from his task of saddling his mount.

"Private matter. Kilduff, you take my place while I'm gone. I may be back tomorrow night. The chief isn't apt to return so soon."

A few moments later Haines galloped out of the willows and headed across the hills towards old Joe Cumberland's ranch. He was remembering his promise to Kate, to keep Dan out of danger. He had failed from that promise once, but that did not mean that he had forgotten. He looked up to the yellow-bright mountain stars, and they were like the eyes of good women smiling down upon him. He guessed that she loved Barry and if he could bring her to Whistling Dan she might have strength enough to take the latter from Silent's trail. The lone rider knew well enough that to bring Dan and Kate together was to surrender his own shadowy hopes, but the golden eyes of the sky encouraged him. So he followed his impulse.

Haines could never walk that middle path which turns neither to the right nor the left, neither up nor down. He went through life with a free-swinging stride, and as the result of it he had crossed the rights of others. He might have lived a lawful life, for all his instincts were gentle. But an accident placed him in the shadow of the law. He waited for his legal trial, but when it came and false witness placed him behind the bars, the revolt came. Two days after his confinement, he broke away from his prison and went to the wilds. There he found Jim Silent, and the mountain-desert found another to add to its list of great outlaws.

Morning came as he drew close to the house, and now his reminiscences were cut short, for at a turn of the road he came upon Kate galloping swiftly over the hills. He drew his horse to a halt and raised his hand. She followed suit. They sat staring. If she had remembered his broken promise and started to reproach, he could have found answer, but her eyes were big with sorrow alone. He put out his hand without a word. She hesitated over it, her eyes questioning him mutely, and then with the ghost of a smile she touched his fingers.

"I want to explain," he said huskily.

"What?"

"You remember I gave you my word that no harm would come to Barry?"

"No man could have helped him."

"You don't hold it against me?"

A gust of wind moaned around them. She waved her arm towards the surrounding hills and her laugh blended with the sound of the wind, it was so faint. He watched her with a curious pang. She seemed among women what that morning was to the coming day—fresh, cool, aloof. It was hard to speak the words which would banish the sorrow from her eyes and make them brilliant with hope and shut him away from her thoughts with a barrier higher than mountains, and broader than seas.

"I have brought you news," he said at last, reluctantly.

She did not change.

"About Dan Barry."

Ay, she changed swiftly enough at that! He could not meet the fear and question of her glance. He looked away and saw the red rim of the sun pushing up above the hills. And color poured up the throat of Kate Cumberland, up even to her forehead beneath the blowing golden hair.

Haines jerked his sombrero lower on his head. A curse tumbled up to his lips and he had to set his teeth to keep it back.

"But I have heard his whistle."

Her lips moved but made no sound.

"Five other men heard him."

She cried out as if he had hurt her, but the hurt was happiness. He knew it and winced, for she was wonderfully beautiful.

"In the willows of the river bottom, a good twenty miles south," he said at last, "and I will show you the way, if you wish."

He watched her eyes grow large with doubt.

"Can you trust me?" he asked. "I failed you once. Can you trust me now?"

Her hand went out to him.

"With all my heart," she said. "Let us start!"

"I've given my horse a hard ride. He must have some rest."

She moaned softly in her impatience, and then: "We'll go back to the house and you can stable your horse there until you're ready to start. Dad will go with us."

"Your father cannot go," he said shortly.

"Cannot?"

"Let's start back for the ranch," he said, "and I'll tell you something about it as we go."

As they turned their horses he went on: "In order that you may reach Whistling Dan, you'll have to meet first a number of men who are camping down there in the willows."

He stopped. It became desperately difficult for him to go on.

"I am one of those men," he said, "and another of them is the one whom Whistling Dan is following."

She caught her breath and turned abruptly on him.

"What are you, Mr. Lee?"

Very slowly he forced his eyes up to meet her gaze.

"In that camp," he answered indirectly, "your father wouldn't be safe!"

It was out at last!

"Then you are—"

"Your friend."

"Forgive me. You *are* my friend!"

"The man whom Dan is following," he went on, "is the leader. If he gives the command four practised fighters pit themselves against Barry."

"It is murder!"

"You can prevent it," he said. "They know Barry is on the trail, but I think they will do nothing unless he forces them into trouble. And he will force them unless you stop him. No other human being could take him off that trail."

"I know! I know!" she muttered. "But I have already tried, and he will not listen to me!"

"But he will listen to you," insisted Haines, "when you tell him that he will be fighting not one man, but six."

"And if he doesn't listen to me?"

Haines shrugged his shoulders.

"Can't you promise that these men will not fight with him?"

"I cannot."

"But I shall plead with them myself."

He turned to her in alarm.

"No, you must not let them dream you know who they are," he warned, "for otherwise—"

Again that significant shrug of the shoulders.

He explained: "These men are in such danger that they dare not take chances. You are a woman, but if they feel that you suspect them you will no longer be a woman in their eyes."

"Then what must I do?"

"I shall ride ahead of you when we come to the willows, after I have pointed out the position of our camp. About an hour after I have arrived, for they must not know that I have brought you, you will ride down towards the camp. When you come to it I will make sure that it is I who will bring you in. You must pretend that you have simply blundered upon our fire. Whatever you do, never ask a question while you are there—and I'll be your warrant that you will come off safely. Will you try?"

He attempted no further persuasion and contented himself with merely meeting the wistful challenge of her eyes.

"I will," she said at last, and then turning her glance away she repeated softly, "I will."

He knew that she was already rehearsing what she must say to Whistling Dan.

"You are not afraid?"

She smiled.

"Do you really trust me as far as this?"

With level-eyed tenderness that took his breath, she answered: "An absolute trust, Mr. Lee."

"My name," he said in a strange voice, "is Lee Haines."

Of one accord they stopped their horses and their hands met.


## CHAPTER XI

### SILENT BLUFFS

The coming of the railroad had changed Elkhead from a mere crossing of the ways to a rather important cattle shipping point. Once a year it became a bustling town whose two streets thronged with cattlemen with pockets burdened with gold which fairly burned its way out to the open air. At other times Elkhead dropped back into a leaden-eyed sleep.

The most important citizen was Lee Hardy, the Wells Fargo agent. Office jobs are hard to find in the mountain-desert, and those who hold them win respect. The owner of a swivel chair is more lordly than the possessor of five thousand "doggies." Lee Hardy had such a swivel chair. Moreover, since large shipments of cash were often directed by Wells Fargo to Elkhead, Hardy's position was really more significant than the size of the village suggested. As a crowning stamp upon his dignity he had a clerk who handled the ordinary routine of work in the front room, while Hardy set himself up in state in a little rear office whose walls were decorated by two brilliant calendars and the colored photograph of a blond beauty advertising a toilet soap.

To this sanctuary he retreated during the heat of the day, while in the morning and evening he loitered on the small porch, chatting with passers-by. Except in the hottest part of the year he affected a soft white collar with a permanent bow tie. The leanness of his features, and his crooked neck with the prominent Adam's apple which stirred when he spoke, suggested a Yankee ancestry, but the faded blue eyes, pathetically misted, could only be found in the mountain-desert.

One morning into the inner sanctum of this dignitary stepped a man built in rectangles, a square face, square, ponderous shoulders, and even square-tipped fingers. Into the smiling haze of Hardy's face his own keen black eye sparkled like an electric lantern flashed into a dark room. He was dressed in the cowboy's costume, but there was no Western languor in his makeup. Everything about him was clear cut and precise. He had a habit of clicking his teeth as he finished a sentence. In a word, when he appeared in the doorway Lee Hardy woke up, and before the stranger had spoken a dozen words the agent was leaning forward to be sure that he would not miss a syllable.

"You're Lee Hardy, aren't you?" said he, and his eyes gave the impression of a smile, though his lips did not stir after speaking.

"I am," said the agent.

"Then you're the man I want to see. If you don't mind—"

He closed the door, pulled a chair against it, and then sat down, and folded his arms. Very obviously he meant business. Hardy switched his position in his chair, sitting a little more to the right, so that the edge of the seat would not obstruct the movement of his hand towards the holster on his right thigh.

"Well," he said good-naturedly, "I'm waitin'."

"Good," said the stranger, "I won't keep you here any longer than is necessary. In the first place my name is Tex Calder."

Hardy changed as if a slight layer of dust had been sifted over his face. He stretched out his hand.

"It's great to see you, Calder," he said, "of course I've heard about you. Everyone has. Here! I'll send over to the saloon for some red-eye. Are you dry?"

He rose, but Calder waved him back to the swivel chair.

"Not dry a bit," he said cheerily. "Not five minutes ago I had a drink of—water."

"All right," said Hardy, and settled back into his chair.

"Hardy, there's been crooked work around here."

"What in hell—"

"Get your hand away from that gun, friend."

"What the devil's the meaning of all this?"

"That's very well done," said Calder. "But this isn't the stage. Are we going to talk business like friends?"

"I've got nothing agin you," said Hardy testily, and his eyes followed Calder's right hand as if fascinated. "What do you want to say? I'll listen. I'm not very busy."

"That's exactly it," smiled Tex Calder, "I want you to get busier."

"Thanks."

"In the first place I'll be straight with you. Wells Fargo hasn't sent me here."

"Who has?"

"My conscience."

"I don't get your drift."

Through a moment of pause Calder's eyes searched the face of Hardy.

"You've been pretty flush for some time."

"I ain't been starvin'."

"There are several easy ways for you to pick up extra money."

"Yes?"

"For instance, you know all about the Wells Fargo money shipments, and there are men around here who'd pay big for what you could tell them."

The prominent Adam's apple rose and fell in Hardy's throat.

"You're quite a joker, ain't you Calder? Who, for instance?"

"Jim Silent."

"This is like a story in a book," grinned Hardy. "Go on. I suppose I've been takin' Silent's money?"

The answer came like the click of a cocked revolver.

"You have!"

"By God, Calder—"

"Steady! I have some promising evidence, partner. Would you like to hear part of it?"

"This country has its share of the world's greatest liars," said Hardy, "I don't care what you've heard."

"That saves my time. Understand me straight. I can slap you into a lock-up, if I want to, and then bring in that evidence. I'm not going to do it. I'm going to use you as a trap and through you get some of the worst of the lone riders."

"There's nothin' like puttin' your hand on the table."

"No, there isn't. I'll tell you what you're to do."

"Thanks."

The marshal drove straight on.

"I've got four good men in this town. Two of them will always be hanging around your office. Maybe you can get a job for them here, eh? I'll pay the salaries. You simply tip them off when your visitors are riders the government wants, see? You don't have to lift a hand. You just go to the door as the visitor leaves, and if he's all right you say: 'So long, we'll be meeting again before long.' But if he's a man I want, you say 'Good-bye.' That's all. My boys will see that it is good-bye."

"Go on," said the agent, "and tell the rest of the story. It starts well."

"Doesn't it?" agreed Calder, "and the way it concludes is with you reaching over and shaking hands with me and saying 'yes'!"

He leaned forward. The twinkle was gone from his eyes and he extended his hand to Hardy. The latter reached out with an impulsive gesture, wrung the proffered hand, and then slipping back into his chair broke into hysterical laughter.

"The real laugh," said Calder, watching his man narrowly, "will be on the long riders."

"Tex," said the agent. "I guess you have the dope. I won't say anything except that I'm glad as hell to be out of the rotten business at last. Once started I couldn't stop. I did one 'favor' for these devils, and after that they had me in their power. I haven't slept for months as I'm going to sleep tonight!"

He wiped his face with an agitated hand.

"A week ago," he went on, "I knew you were detailed on this work. I've been sweating ever since. Now that you've come—why, I'm glad of it!"

A faint sneer touched Calder's mouth and was gone.

"You're a wise man," he said. "Have you seen much of Jim Silent lately?"

Hardy hesitated. The role of informer was new.

"Not directly."

Calder nodded.

"Now put me right if I go off the track. The way I understand it, Jim Silent has about twenty gun fighters and long riders working in gangs under him and combining for big jobs."

"That's about it."

"The inside circle consists of Silent; Lee Haines, a man who went wrong because the law did *him* wrong; Hal Purvis, a cunning devil; and Bill Kilduff, a born fighter who loves blood for its own sake."

"Right."

"Here's something more. For Jim Silent, dead or alive, the government will pay ten thousand dollars. For each of the other three it pays five thousand. The notices aren't out yet, but they will be in a few days. Hardy, if you help me bag these men, you'll get fifty percent of the profits. Are you on?"

The hesitancy of Hardy changed to downright enthusiasm.

"Easy money, Tex. I'm your man, hand and glove."

"Don't get optimistic. This game isn't played yet, and unless I make the biggest mistake of my life we'll be guessing again before we land Silent. I've trailed some fast gunmen in my day, and I have an idea that Silent will be the hardest of the lot; but if you play your end of the game we may land him. I have a tip that he's lying out in the country near Elkhead. I'm riding out alone to get track of him. As I go out I'll tell my men that you're O.K. for this business."

He hesitated a moment with his hand on the doorknob.

"Just one thing more, Hardy. I heard a queer tale this morning about a fight in a saloon run by a man named Morgan. Do you know anything about it?"

"No."

"I was told of a fellow who chipped four dollars thrown into the air at twenty yards."

"That's a lie."

"The man who talked to me had a nicked dollar to prove his yarn."

"The devil he did!"

"And after the shooting this chap got into a fight with a tall man twice his size and fairly mopped up the floor with him. They say it wasn't a nice thing to watch. He is a frail man, but when the fight started he turned into a tiger."

"Wish I'd seen it."

"The tall man tallies to a hair with my description of Silent."

"You're wrong. I know what Silent can do with his hands. No one could beat him up. What's the name of the other?"

"Barry. Whistling Dan Barry."

Calder hesitated.

"Right or wrong, I'd like to have this Barry with me. So long."

He was gone as he had come, with a nod and a flash of the keen, black eyes. Lee Hardy stared at the door for some moments, and then went outside. The warm light of the sun had never been more welcome to him. Under that cheering influence he began to feel that with Tex Calder behind him he could safely defy the world.

His confidence received a shock that afternoon when a heavy step crossed the outside room, and his door opening without a preliminary knock, he looked up into the solemn eyes of Jim Silent. The outlaw shook his head when Hardy offered him a chair.

"What's the main idea of them two new men out in your front room, Lee?" he asked.

"Two cowpunchers that was down on their luck. I got to stand in with the boys now and then."

"I s'pose so. Shorty Rhinehart in here to see you, Lee?"

"Yep."

"You told him that the town was gettin' pretty hot."

"It is."

"You said you had no dope on when that delayed shipment was comin' through?"

Hardy made lightning calculations. A half truth would be the best way out.

"I've just got the word you want. It come this morning."

Silent's expression changed and he leaned a little closer.

"It's the nineteenth. Train number 89. Savvy? Seven o'clock at Elkhead!"

"How much? Same bunch of coin?"

"Fifty thousand!"

"That's ten more."

"Yep. A new shipment rolled in with the old one. No objections?"

Silent grinned.

"Any other news, Lee?"

"Shorty told you about Tex Calder?"

"He did. Seen him around here?"

The slightest fraction of a second in hesitation.

"No."

"Was that the straight dope you give Shorty?"

"Straighter'n hell. They're beginnin' to talk, but I guess I was jest sort of panicky when I talked with Shorty."

"This Tex Calder—"

"What about him?" This with a trace of suspicion.

"He's got a long record."

"So've you, Jim."

Once more that wolflike grin which had no mirth.

"So long, Lee. I'll be on the job. Lay to that."

He turned towards the door. Hardy followed him. A moment more, in a single word, and the job would be done. Five thousand dollars for a single word! It warmed the very heart of Lee Hardy.

Silent, as he moved away, seemed singularly thoughtful. He hesitated a moment with bowed head at the door—then whirled and shoved a six-gun under the nose of Hardy. The latter leaped back with his arms thrust above his head, straining at his hands to get them higher.

"My God, Jim!"

"You're a low-down, lyin' hound!"

Hardy's tongue clove to the roof of his mouth.

"Damn you, d'you hear me?"

"Yes! For God's sake, Jim, don't shoot!"

"Your life ain't worth a dime!"

"Give me one more chance an' I'll play square!"

A swift change came over the face of Silent, and then Hardy went hot with terror and anger. The long rider had known nothing. The gun play had been a mere bluff, but he had played into the hands of Silent, and now his life was truly worth nothing.

"You poor fool," went on Silent, his voice purring with controlled rage. "You damn blind fool! D'you think you could double cross me an' get by with it?"

"Give me a chance, Jim. One more chance, one more chance!"

Even in his terror he remembered to keep his voice low lest those in the front room should hear.

"Out with it, if you love livin'!"

"I—I can't talk while you got that gun on me!"

Silent not only lowered his gun, but actually returned it to the holster. Nothing could more clearly indicate his contempt, and Hardy, in spite of his fear, crimsoned with shame.

"It was Tex Calder," he said at last.

Silent started a little and his eyes narrowed again.

"What of him?"

"He came here a while ago an' tried to make a deal with me."

"An' made it!" said Silent ominously.

No gun pointed at him this time, but Hardy jerked his hands once more above his head and cowered against the wall.

"So help me God he didn't, Jim."

"Get your hands down."

He lowered his hands slowly.

"I told him I didn't know nothin' about you."

"What about that train? What about that shipment?"

"It's jest the way I told you, except that it's on the eighteenth instead of the nineteenth."

"I'm goin' to believe you. If you double cross me I'll have your hide. Maybe they'll get me, but there'll be enough of my boys left to get you. You can lay to that. How much did they offer you, Lee? How much am I worth to the little old U.S.A.?"

"I—I—it wasn't the money. I was afraid to stick with my game any longer."

The long rider had already turned towards the door, making no effort to keep his face to the agent. The latter, flushing again, moved his hand towards his hip, but stopped the movement. The last threat of Silent carried a deep conviction with it. He knew that the faith of lone riders to each other was an inviolable bond. Accordingly he followed at the heels of the other man into the outside room.

"So long, old timer," he called, slapping Silent on the shoulder, "I'll be seein' you agin before long."

Calder's men looked up with curious eyes. Hardy watched Silent swing onto his horse and gallop down the street. Then he went hurriedly back to his office. Once inside he dropped into the big swivel-chair, buried his face in his arms, and wept like a child.

# CHAPTER XII

# PARTNERS

Dust powdered his hat and clothes as Tex Calder trotted his horse north across the hills. His face was a sickly gray, and his black hair might have been an eighteenth-century wig, so thoroughly was it disguised. It had been a long ride. Many a long mile wound back behind him, and still the cattle pony, with hanging head, stuck to its task. Now he was drawing out on a highland, and below him stretched the light yellow-green of the willows of the bottom land. He halted his pony and swung a leg over the horn of his saddle. Then he rolled a cigarette, and while he inhaled it in long puffs he scanned the trees narrowly. Miles across, and stretching east and west farther than his eye could reach, extended the willows. Somewhere in that wilderness was the gang of Jim Silent. An army corps might have been easily concealed there.

If he was not utterly discouraged in the beginning of his search, it was merely because the rangers of the hills and plains are taught patience almost as soon as they learn to ride a horse. He surveyed the yellow-green forest calmly. In the west the low hanging sun turned crimson and bulged at the sides into a clumsy ellipse. He started down the slope at the same dog-trot which the pony had kept up all day. Just before he reached the skirts of the trees he brought his horse to a sudden halt and threw back his head. It seemed to him that he heard a faint whistling.

He could not be sure. It was so far off and unlike any whistling he had ever heard before, that he half guessed it to be the movement of a breeze through the willows, but the wind was hardly strong enough to make this sound. For a full five minutes he listened without moving his horse. Then came the thing for which he waited, a phrase of melody undoubtedly from human lips.

What puzzled him most was the nature of the music. As he rode closer to the trees it grew clearer. It was unlike any song he had ever heard. It was a strange improvisation with a touch of both melancholy and savage exultation running through it. Calder found himself nodding in sympathy with the irregular rhythm.

It grew so clear at last that he marked with some accuracy the direction from which it came. If this was Silent's camp, it must be strongly guarded, and he should approach the place more cautiously than he could possibly do on a horse. Accordingly he dismounted, threw the reins over the pony's head, and started on through the willows. The whistling became louder and louder. He moved stealthily from tree to tree, for he had not the least idea when he would run across a guard. The whistling ceased, but the marshal was now so near that he could follow the original direction without much trouble. In a few moments he might distinguish the sound of voices. If there were two or three men in the camp he might be able to surprise them and make his arrest. If the outlaws were many, at least he could lie low near the camp and perhaps learn the plans of the gang. He worked his way forward more and more carefully. At one place he thought a shadowy figure slipped through the brush a short distance away. He poised his gun, but lowered it again after a moment's thought. It must have been a stir of shadows. No human being could move so swiftly or so noiselessly.

Nevertheless the sight gave him such a start that he proceeded with even greater caution. He was crouched close to the ground. Every inch of it he scanned carefully before he set down a foot, fearful of the cracking of a fallen twig. Like most men when they hunt, he began to feel that something followed him. He tried to argue the thought out of his brain, but it persisted, and grew stronger. Half a dozen times he whirled suddenly with his revolver poised. At last he heard a stamp which could come from nothing but the hoof of a horse. The sound dispelled his fears. In another moment he would be in sight of the camp.

"Do you figger you'll find it?" asked a quiet voice behind him.

He turned and looked into the steady muzzle of a Colt. Behind that revolver was a thin, handsome face with a lock of jet-black hair falling over the forehead. Calder knew men, and now he felt a strange absence of any desire to attempt a gunplay.

"I was just taking a stroll through the willows," he said, with a mighty attempt at carelessness.

"Oh," said the other. "It appeared to me you was sort of huntin' for something. You was headed straight for my hoss."

Calder strove to find some way out. He could not. There was no waver in the hand that held that black gun. The brown eyes were decidedly discouraging to any attempt at a surprise. He felt helpless for the first time in his career.

"Go over to him, Bart," said the gentle voice of the stranger. "Stand fast!"

The last two words, directed to Calder came, with a metallic hardness, for the marshal started as a great black dog slipped from behind a tree and slunk towards him. This was the shadow which moved more swiftly and noiselessly than a human being.

"Keep back that damned wolf," he said desperately.

"He ain't goin' to hurt you," said the calm voice. "Jest toss your gun to the ground."

There was nothing else for it. Calder dropped his weapon with the butt towards Whistling Dan.

"Bring it here, Bart," said the latter.

The big animal lowered his head, still keeping his green eyes upon Calder, took up the revolver in his white fangs, and glided back to his master.

"Jest turn your back to me, an' keep your hands clear of your body," said Dan.

Calder obeyed, sweating with shame. He felt a hand pat his pockets lightly in search for a hidden weapon, and then, with his head slightly turned, he sensed the fact that Dan was dropping his revolver into its holster. He whirled and drove his clenched fist straight at Dan's face.

What happened then he would never forget to the end of his life. Calder's weapon still hung in Dan's right hand, but the latter made no effort to use it. He dropped the gun, and as Calder's right arm shot out, it was caught at the wrist, and jerked down with a force that jarred his whole body.

"Down, Bart!" shouted Dan. The great wolf checked in the midst of his leap and dropped, whining with eagerness, at Calder's feet. At the same time the marshal's left hand was seized and whipped across his body. He wrenched away with all his force. He might as well have struggled with steel manacles. He was helpless, staring into eyes which now glinted with a yellow light that sent a cold wave tingling through his blood.

The yellow gleam died; his hands were loosed; but he made no move to spring at Dan's throat. Chill horror had taken the place of his shame, and the wolf-dog still whined at his feet with lips grinned back from the long white teeth.

"Who in the name of God are you?" he gasped, and even as he spoke the truth came to him—the whistling—the panther-like speed of hand—"Whistling Dan Barry."

The other frowned.

"If you didn't know my name why were you trailin' me?"

"I wasn't after you," said Calder.

"You was crawlin' along like that jest for fun? Friend, I figger to know you. You been sent out by the tall man to lay for me."

"What tall man?" asked Calder, his wits groping.

"The one that swung the chair in Morgan's place," said Dan. "Now you're goin' to take me to your camp. I got something to say to him."

"By the Lord!" cried the marshal, "you're trailing Silent."

Dan watched him narrowly. It was hard to accuse those keen black eyes of deceit.

"I'm trailin' the man who sent you out after me," he asserted with a little less assurance.

Calder tore open the front of his shirt and pushed back one side of it. Pinned there next to his skin was his marshal's badge.

He said: "My name's Tex Calder."

It was a word to conjure with up and down the vast expanse of the mountain-desert. Dan smiled, and the change of expression made him seem ten years younger.

"Git down, Bart. Stand behind me!" The dog obeyed sullenly. "I've heard a pile of men talk about you, Tex Calder." Their hands and their eyes met. There was a mutual respect in the glances. "An' I'm a pile sorry for this."

He picked up the gun from the ground and extended it butt first to the marshal, who restored it slowly to the holster. It was the first time it had ever been forced from his grasp.

"Who was it you talked about a while ago?" asked Dan.

"Jim Silent."

Dan instinctively dropped his hand back to his revolver.

"The tall man?"

"The one you fought with in Morgan's place."

The unpleasant gleam returned to Dan's eyes.

"I thought there was only one reason why he should die, but now I see there's a heap of 'em."

Calder was all business.

"How long have you been here?" he asked.

"About a day."

"Have you seen anything of Silent here among the willows?"

"No."

"Do you think he's still here?"

"Yes."

"Why?"

"I dunno. I'll stay here till I find him among the trees or he breaks away into the open."

"How'll you know when he leaves the willows?"

Whistling Dan was puzzled.

"I dunno," he answered. "Somethin' will tell me when he gets far away from me—he an' his men."

"It's an inner sense, eh? Like the smell of the bloodhound?" said Calder, but his eyes were strangely serious.

"This day's about done," he went on. "Have you any objections to me camping with you here?"

Not a cowpuncher within five hundred miles but would be glad of such redoubted company. They went back to Calder's horse.

"We can start for my clearing," said Dan. "Bart'll bring the hoss. Fetch him in."

The wolf took the dangling bridle reins and led on the cowpony. Calder observed his performance with starting eyes, but he was averse to asking questions. In a few moments they came out on a small open space. The ground was covered with a quantity of dried bunch grass which a glorious black stallion was cropping. Now he tossed up his head so that some of his long mane fell forward between his ears and at sight of Calder his ears dropped back and his eyes blazed, but when Dan stepped from the willows the ears came forward again with a whinny of greeting. Calder watched the beautiful animal with all the enthusiasm of an expert horseman. Satan was untethered; the saddle and bridle lay in a corner of the clearing; evidently the horse was a pet and would not leave its master. He spoke gently and stepped forward to caress the velvet shining neck, but Satan snorted and started away, trembling with excitement.

"How can you keep such a wild fellow as this without hobbling him?" asked Calder.

"He ain't wild," said Dan.

"Why, he won't let me put a hand on him."

"Yes, he will. Steady, Satan!"

The stallion stood motionless with the veritable fires of hell in his eyes as Calder approached. The latter stopped.

"Not for me," he said. "I'd rather rub the moustache of the lion in the zoo than touch that black devil!"

Bart at that moment led in the cowpony and Calder started to remove the saddle. He had scarcely done so and hobbled his horse when he was startled by a tremendous snarling and snorting. He turned to see the stallion plunging hither and thither, striking with his fore-hooves, while around him, darting in and out under the driving feet, sprang the great black wolf, his teeth clashing like steel on steel. In another moment they might sink in the throat of the horse! Calder, with an exclamation of horror, whipped out his revolver, but checked himself at the very instant of firing. The master of the two animals stood with arms folded, actually smiling upon the fight!

"For God's sake!" cried the marshal. "Shoot the damned wolf, man, or he'll have your horse by the throat!"

"Leave 'em be," said Dan, without turning his head. "Satan an' Black Bart ain't got any other dogs an' hosses to run around with. They's jest playing a little by way of exercise."

Calder stood agape before what seemed the incarnate fury of the pair. Then he noticed that those snapping fangs, however close they came, always missed the flesh of the stallion, and the driving hoofs never actually endangered the leaping wolf.

"Stop 'em!" he cried at last. "It makes me nervous to watch that sort of play. It isn't natural!"

"All right," said Dan. "Stop it, boys."

He had not raised his voice, but they ceased their wild gambols instantly, the stallion, with head thrown high and arched tail and heaving sides, while the wolf, with lolling red tongue, strolled calmly towards his master.

The latter paid no further attention to them, but set about kindling a small fire over which to cook supper. Calder joined him. The marshal's mind was too full for speech, but now and again he turned a long glance of wonder upon the stallion or Black Bart. In the same silence they sat under the last light of the sunset and ate their supper. Calder, with head bent, pondered over the man of mystery and his two tamed animals. Tamed? Not one of the three was tamed, the man least of all.

He saw Dan pause from his eating to stare with wide, vacant eyes among the trees. The wolf-dog approached, looked up in his master's face, whined softly, and getting no response went back to his place and lay down, his eyes never moving from Dan. Still he stared among the trees. The gloom deepened, and he smiled faintly. He began to whistle, a low, melancholy strain so soft that it blended with the growing hush of the night. Calder listened, wholly overawed. That weird music seemed an interpretation of the vast spaces of the mountains, of the pitiless desert, of the limitless silences, and the whistler was an understanding part of the whole.

He became aware of a black shadow behind the musician. It was Satan, who rested his nose on the shoulder of the master. Without ceasing his whistling Dan raised a hand, touched the small muzzle, and Satan went at once to a side of the clearing and lay down. It was almost as if the two had said good-night! Calder could stand it no longer.

"Dan, I've got to talk to you," he began.

The whistling ceased; the wide brown eyes turned to him.

"Fire away—partner."

Ay, they had eaten together by the same fire—they had watched the coming of the night—they had shaken hands in friendship—they were partners. He knew deep in his heart that no human being could ever be the actual comrade of this man. This lord of the voiceless desert needed no human companionship; yet as the marshal glanced from the black shadow of Satan to the gleaming eyes of Bart, and then to the visionary face of Barry, he felt that he had been admitted by Whistling Dan into the mysterious company.

The thought stirred him deeply. It was as if he had made an alliance with the wandering wind. Why he had been accepted he could not dream, but he had heard the word "partner" and he knew it was meant. After all, stranger things than this happen in the mountain-desert, where man is greater and convention less. A single word has been known to estrange lifelong comrades; a single evening beside a campfire has changed foes to partners. Calder drew his mind back to business with a great effort.

"There's one thing you don't know about Jim Silent. A reward of ten thousand dollars lies on his head. The notices aren't posted yet."

Whistling Dan shrugged his shoulders.

"I ain't after money," he answered.

Calder frowned. He did not appreciate a bluff.

"Look here," he said, "if we kill him, because no power on earth will take him alive—we'll split the money."

"If you lay a hand on him," said Dan, without emotion, "we won't be friends no longer, I figger."

Calder stared.

"If you don't want to get him," he said, "why in God's name are you trailing him this way?"

Dan touched his lips. "He hit me with his fist."

He paused, and spoke again with a drawling voice that gave his words an uncanny effect.

"My blood went down from my mouth to my chin. I tasted it. Till I get him there ain't no way of me forgettin' him."

His eyes lighted with that ominous gleam.

"That's why no other man c'n put a hand on him. He's laid out all for me. Understand?"

The ring of the question echoed for a moment through Calder's mind.

"I certainly do," he said with profound conviction, "and I'll never forget it." He decided on a change of tactics. "But there are other men with Jim Silent and those men will fight to keep you from getting to him."

"I'm sorry for 'em," said Dan gently. "I ain't got nothin' agin anyone except the big man."

Calder took a long breath.

"Don't you see," he explained carefully, "if you shoot one of these men you are simply a murderer who must be apprehended by the law and punished."

"It makes it bad for me, doesn't it?" said Dan. "An' I hope I won't have to hurt more'n one or two of 'em. You see,"—he leaned forward seriously towards Calder—"I'd only shoot for their arms or their legs. I wouldn't spoil them altogether."

Calder threw up his hands in despair. Black Bart snarled at the gesture.

"I can't listen no more," said Dan. "I got to start explorin' the willows pretty soon."

"In the dark?" exclaimed Calder.

"Sure. Black Bart'll go with me. The dark don't bother him."

"I'll go along."

"I'd rather be alone. I might meet him."

"Any way you want," said Calder, "but first hear my plan—it doesn't take long to tell it."

The darkness thickened around them while he talked. The fire died out—the night swallowed up their figures.


## CHAPTER XIII

## THE LONE RIDERS ENTERTAIN

When Lee Haines rode into Silent's camp that evening no questions were asked. Questions were not popular among the long riders. He did not know more than the names of half the men who sat around the smoky fire. They were eager to forget the past, and the only allusions to former times came in chance phrases which they let fall at rare intervals. When they told an anecdote they erased all names by instinct. They would begin: "I heard about a feller over to the Circle Y outfit that was once ridin'—" etc. As a rule they themselves were "that feller over to the Circle Y outfit." Accordingly only a few grunts greeted Haines and yet he was far and away the most popular man in the group. Even solemn-eyed Jim Silent was partial to the handsome fellow.

"Heard the whistling today?" he asked.

Purvis shook his head and Terry Jordan allowed "as how it was most uncommon fortunate that this Barry feller didn't start his noise." After this Haines ate his supper in silence, his ear ready to catch the first sound of Kate's horse as it crashed through the willows and shrubs. Nevertheless it was Shorty Rhinehart who sprang to his feet first.

"They's a hoss there comin' among the willows!" he announced.

"Maybe it's Silent," remarked Haines casually.

"The chief don't make no such a noise. He picks his goin'," answered Hal Purvis.

The sound was quite audible now.

"They's been some crooked work," said Rhinehart excitedly. "Somebody's tipped off the marshals about where we're lyin'."

"All right," said Haines quietly, "you and I will investigate."

They started through the willows. Rhinehart was cursing beneath his breath.

"Don't be too fast with your six-gun," warned Haines.

"I'd rather be too early than too late."

"Maybe it isn't a marshal. If a man were looking for us he'd be a fool to come smashing along like that."

He had scarcely spoken when Kate came into view.

"A girl, by God!" said Rhinehart, with mingled relief and disgust.

"Sure thing," agreed Haines.

"Let's beat it back to the camp."

"Not a hope. She's headed straight for the camp. We'll take her in and tell her we're a bunch from the Y Circle X outfit headed north. She'll never know the difference."

"Good idea," said Rhinehart, and he added with a chuckle, "it's been nigh three months since I've talked to a piece of calico."

"Hey, there!" called Haines, and he stepped out with Rhinehart before her horse.

"Oh!" cried Kate, reining up her horse sharply. "Who are you?"

"A beaut!" muttered Rhinehart in devout admiration.

"We're from the Y Circle X outfit," said Haines glibly, "camping over here for the night. Are you lost, lady?"

"I guess I am. I thought I could get across the willows before the night fell. I'm trying to find a man who rode in this direction."

"Come on into the camp," said Haines easily. "Maybe some of the boys can put you on his track. What sort of a looking fellow is he?"

"Rides a black horse and whistles a good deal. His name is Barry. They call him Whistling Dan."

"By God!" whispered Rhinehart in the ear of Haines.

"Shut up!" answered Haines in the same tone. "Are you afraid of a girl?"

"I've trailed him south this far," went on Kate, "and a few miles away from here I lost track of him. I think he may have gone on across the willows."

"Haven't seen him," said Rhinehart amiably. "But come on to the camp, lady. Maybe one of the boys has spotted him on the way. What's your name?"

"Kate Cumberland," she answered.

He removed his hat with a broad grin and reached up a hand to her.

"I'm most certainly glad to meet you, an' my name's Shorty. This here is Lee. Want to come along with us?"

"Thank you. I'm a little worried."

"'S all right. Don't get worried. We'll show you the way out. Just follow us."

They started back through the willows, Kate following half a dozen yards behind.

"Listen here, Shorty," said Haines in a cautious voice. "You heard her name?"

"Sure."

"Well, that's the daughter of the man that raised Whistling Dan. I saw her at Morgan's place. She's probably been tipped off that he's following Silent, but she has no idea who we are."

"Sure she hasn't. She's a great looker, eh, Lee?"

"She'll do, I guess. Now get this: The girl is after Whistling Dan, and if she meets him she'll persuade him to come back to her father's place. She'll take him off our trail, and I guess none of us'll be sorry to know that he's gone, eh?"

"I begin to follow you, Lee. You've always had the head!"

"All right. Now we'll get Purvis to tell the girl that he's heard a peculiar whistling around here this evening. We'll advise her to stick around and go out when she hears the whistling again. That way she'll meet him and head him off, savvy?"

"Right," said Rhinehart.

"Then beat it ahead as fast as you can and wise up the boys."

"That's me—specially about their bein' Y Circle X fellers, eh?"

He chuckled and made ahead as fast as his long legs could carry him. Haines dropped back beside Kate.

"Everything goes finely," he assured her. "I told Rhinehart what to do. He's gone ahead to the camp. Now all you have to do is to keep your head. One of the boys will tell you that we've heard some whistling near the camp this evening. Then I'll ask you to stay around for a while in case the whistling should sound again, do you see? Remember, never ask a question!"

It was even more simple than Haines had hoped. Silent's men suspected nothing. After all, Kate's deception was a small affair, and her frankness, her laughter, and her beauty carried all before her.

The long riders became quickly familiar with her, but through their rough talk, the Westerners' reverence for a woman ran like a thread of gold over a dark cloth. Her fear lessened and almost passed away while she listened to their talk and watched their faces. The kindly human nature which had lain unexpressed in most of them for months together burst out torrent-like and flooded about her with a sense of security and power. These were conquerors of men, fighters by instinct and habit, but here they sat laughing and chattering with a helpless girl, and not a one of them but would have cut the others' throats rather than see her come to harm. The roughness of their past and the dread of their future they laid aside like an ugly cloak while they showed her what lies in the worst man's heart—a certain awe of woman. Their manners underwent a sudden change. Polite words, rusted by long disuse, were resurrected in her honour. Tremendous phrases came laboring forth. There was a general though covert rearranging of bandanas, and an interchange of self-conscious glances. Haines alone seemed impervious to her charm.

The red died slowly along the west. There was no light save the flicker of the fire, which played on Kate's smile and the rich gold of her hair, or caught out of the dark one of the lean, hard faces which circled her. Now and then it fell on the ghastly grin of Terry Jordan and Kate had to clench her hand to keep up her nerve.

It was deep night when Jim Silent rode into the clearing. Shorty Rhinehart and Hal Purvis went to him quickly to explain the presence of the girl and the fact that they were all members of the Y Circle X outfit. He responded with nods while his gloomy eyes held fast on Kate. When they presented him as the boss, Jim, he replied to her good-natured greeting in a voice that was half grunt and half growl.

## CHAPTER XIV

## DELILAH

Haines muttered at Kate's ear: "This is the man. Now keep up your courage."

"He doesn't like this," went on Haines in the same muffled voice, "but when he understands just why you're here I think he'll be as glad as any of us."

Silent beckoned to him and he went to the chief.

"What about the girl?" asked the big fellow curtly.

"Didn't Rhinehart tell you?"

"Rhinehart's a fool and so are the rest of them. Have you gone loco too, Haines, to let a girl come here?"

"Where's the harm?"

"Why, damn it, she's marked every man here."

"I let her in because she is trying to get hold of Whistling Dan."

"Which no fool girl c'n take that feller off the trail. Nothin' but lead can do that."

"I tell you," said Haines, "the boy's in love with her. I watched them at Morgan's place. She can twist him around her finger."

A faint light broke the gloom of Silent's face.

"Yaller hair an' blue eyes. They c'n do a lot. Maybe you're right. What's that?" His voice had gone suddenly husky.

A russet moon pushed slowly up through the trees. Its uncertain light fell across the clearing. For the first time the thick pale smoke of the fire was visible, rising straight up until it cleared the tops of the willows, and then caught into swift, jagging lines as the soft wind struck it. A coyote wailed from the distant hills, and before his complaint was done another sound came through the hushing of the willows, a melancholy whistling, thin with distance.

"We'll see if that's the man you want," suggested Haines.

"I'll go along," said Shorty Rhinehart.

"And me too," said a third. The whole group would have accompanied them, but the heavy voice of Jim Silent cut in: "You'll stay here, all of you except the girl and Lee."

They turned back, muttering, and Kate followed Haines into the willows.

"Well?" growled Bill Kilduff.

"What I want to know—" broke in Terry Jordan.

"Go to hell with your questions," said Silent, "but until you go there you'll do what I say, understand?"

"Look here, Jim," said Hal Purvis, "are you a king an' we jest your slaves, maybe?"

"You're goin' it a pile too hard," said Shorty Rhinehart.

Every one of these speeches came sharply out while they glared at Jim Silent. Hands were beginning to fall to the hip and fingers were curving stiffly as if for the draw. Silent leaned his broad shoulders against the side of his roan and folded his arms. His eyes went round the circle slowly, lingering an instant on each face. Under that cold stare they grew uneasy. To Shorty Rhinehart it became necessary to push back his hat and scratch his forehead. Terry Jordan found a mysterious business with his bandana. Every one of them had occasion to raise his hand from the neighborhood of his six-shooter. Silent smiled.

"A fine, hard crew you are," he said sarcastically at last. "A great bunch of long riders, lettin' a slip of a yaller-haired girl make fools of you. You over there—you, Shorty Rhinehart, you'd cut the throat of a man that looked crosswise at the Cumberland girl, wouldn't you? An' you, Purvis, you're aching to get at me, ain't you? An' you're still thinkin' of them blue eyes, Jordan?"

Before any one could speak he poured in another volley between wind and water: "One slip of a girl can make fools out of five long riders? No, you ain't long riders. All you c'n handle is hobby hosses!"

"What do you want us to do?" growled swarthy Bill Kilduff.

"Keep your face shut while I'm talkin', that's what I want you to do!"

There was a devil of rage in his eyes. His folded arms tugged at each other, and if they got free there would be gunplay. The four men shrank, and he was satisfied.

"Now I'll tell you what we're goin' to do," he went on. "We're goin' out after Haines an' the girl. If they come up with this Whistlin' Dan we're goin' to surround him an' fill him full of lead, while they're talkin'."

"Not for a million dollars!" burst in Hal Purvis.

"Not in a thousan' years!" echoed Terry Jordan.

Silent turned his watchful eyes from one to the other. They were ready to fight now, and he sensed it at once.

"Why?" he asked calmly.

"It ain't playin' square with the girl," announced Rhinehart.

"Purvis," said Silent, for he knew that the opposition centered in the figure of the venomous little gun fighter; "if you seen a mad dog that was runnin' straight at you, would you be kep' from shootin' it because a pretty girl hollered out an' asked you not to?"

Their eyes shifted rapidly from one to another, seeking a way out, and finding none.

"An' is there any difference between this hero Whistlin' Dan an' a mad dog?"

Still they were mute.

"I tell you, boys, we got a better chance of dodgin' lightnin' an' puttin' a bloodhound off our trail than we have of gettin' rid of this Whistlin' Dan. An' when he catches up with us—well, all I'm askin' is that you remember what he done to them four dollars before they hit the dust?"

"The chief's right," growled Kilduff, staring down at the ground. "It's Whistlin' Dan or us. The mountains ain't big enough to hold him an' us!"

* * * * *

Before Whistling Dan the great wolf glided among the trees. For a full hour they had wandered through the willows in this manner, and Dan had made up his mind to surrender the search when Bart, returning from one of his noiseless detours, sprang out before his master and whined softly. Dan turned, loosening his revolver in the holster, and followed Bart through the soft gloom of the tree shadows and the moonlight. His step was almost as silent as that of the slinking animal which went before. At last the wolf stopped and raised his head. Almost instantly Dan saw a man and a woman approaching through the willows. The moonlight dropped across her face. He recognized Kate, with Lee Haines walking a pace before her.

"Stand where you are," he said.

Haines leaped to one side, his revolver flashing in his hand. Dan stepped out before them while Black Bart slunk close beside him, snarling softly.

He seemed totally regardless of the gun in Haines's hand. His manner was that of a conqueror who had the outlaw at his mercy.

"You," he said, "walk over there to the side of the clearing."

"Dan!" cried Kate, as she went to him with extended arms.

He stopped her with a gesture, his eyes upon Haines, who had moved away.

"Watch him, Bart," said Dan.

The black wolf ran to Haines and crouched snarling at his feet. The outlaw restored his revolver to his holster and stood with his arms folded, his back turned. Dan looked to Kate. At the meeting of their eyes she shrank a little. She had expected a difficult task in persuading him, but not this hard aloofness. She felt suddenly as if she were a stranger to him.

"How do you come here—with him?"

"He is my friend!"

"You sure pick a queer place to go walkin' with him."

"Hush, Dan! He brought me here to find you!"

"*He* brought you here?"

"Don't you understand?"

"When I want a friend like him, I'll go huntin' for him myself; an' I'll pack a gun with me!"

That flickering yellow light played behind Dan's eyes.

"I looked into his face—an' he stared the other way."

She made a little imploring gesture, but his hand remained on his hips, and there was no softening of his voice.

"What fetched you here?"

Every word was like a hand that pushed her farther away.

"Are you dumb, Kate? What fetched you here?"

"I have come to bring you home, Dan."

"I'm home now."

"What do you mean?"

"There's the roof of my house," he jerked his hand towards the sky, "the mountain passes are my doors—an' the earth is my floor."

"No! No! We are waiting for you at the ranch."

He shrugged his shoulders.

"Dan, this wild trail has no end."

"Maybe, but I know that feller can show me the way to Jim Silent, an' now—"

He turned towards Haines as he spoke, but here a low, venomous snarl from Black Bart checked his words. Kate saw him stiffen—his lips parted to a faint smile—his head tilted back a little as if he listened intently, though she could hear nothing. She was not a yard from him, and yet she felt a thousand miles away. His head turned full upon her, and she would never forget the yellow light of his eyes.

"Dan!" she cried, but her voice was no louder than a whisper.

"Delilah!" he said, and leaped back into the shade of the willows.

Even as he sprang she saw the flash of the moonlight on his drawn revolver, and fire spat from it twice, answered by a yell of pain, the clang of a bullet on metal, and half a dozen shots from the woods behind her.

That word "Delilah!" rang in her brain to the exclusion of all the world. Vaguely she heard voices shouting—she turned a little and saw Haines facing her with his revolver in his hand, but prevented from moving by the wolf who crouched snarling at his feet. The order of his master kept him there even after that master was gone. Now men ran out into the clearing. A keen whistle sounded far off among the willows, and the wolf leaped away from his prisoner and into the shadows on the trail of Dan.

* * * * *

Tex Calder prided himself on being a light sleeper. Years spent in constant danger enabled him to keep his sense of hearing alert even when he slept. He had never been surprised. It was his boast that he never would be. Therefore when a hand dropped lightly on his shoulder he started erect from his blankets with a curse and grasped his revolver. A strong grip on his wrist paralyzed his fingers. Whistling Dan leaned above him.

"Wake up," said the latter.

"What the devil—" breathed the marshal. "You travel like a cloud shadow, Dan. You make no sound."

"Wake up and talk to me."

"I'm awake all right. What's happened?"

There was a moment of silence while Dan seemed to be trying for speech.

Black Bart, at the other side of the clearing, pointed his nose at the yellow moon and wailed. He was very close, but the sound was so controlled that it seemed to come at a great distance from some wild spirit wandering between earth and heaven.

Instead of speaking Dan jumped to his feet and commenced pacing up and down, up and down, a rapid, tireless stride; at his heels the wolf slunk, with lowered head and tail. The strange fellow was in some great trouble, Calder could see, and it stirred him mightily to know that the wild man had turned to him for help. Yet he would ask no questions.

When in doubt the cattleman rolls a cigarette, and that was what Calder did. He smoked and waited. At last the inevitable came.

"How old are you, Tex?"

"Forty-four."

"That's a good deal. You ought to know something."

"Maybe."

"About women?"

"Ah!" said Calder.

"Bronchos is cut out chiefly after one pattern," went on Dan.

"They's chiefly jest meanness. Are women the same—jest cut after one pattern?"

"What pattern, Dan?"

"The pattern of Delilah! They ain't no trust to be put in 'em?"

"A good many of us have found that out."

"I thought one woman was different from the rest."

"We all think that. Woman in particular is divine; woman in general is—hell!"

"Ay, but this one—" He stopped and set his teeth.

"What has she done?"

"She—" he hesitated, and when he spoke again his voice did not tremble; there was a deep hurt and wonder in it: "She double-crossed me!"

"When? Do you mean to say you've met a woman tonight out here among the willows? Where—how—"

"Tex—!"

"Ay, Dan."

"It's—it's hell!"

"It is now. But you'll forget her! The mountains, the desert, and above all, time—they'll cure you, my boy."

"Not in a whole century, Tex."

Calder waited curiously for the explanation. It came.

"Jest to think of her is like hearing music. Oh, God, Tex, what c'n I do to fight agin this here cold feelin' at my heart?"

Dan slipped down beside the marshal and the latter dropped a sympathetic hand over the lean, brown fingers. They returned the pressure with a bone-crushing grip.

"Fight, Dan! It will make you forget her."

"Her skin is softer'n satin, Tex."

"Ay, but you'll never touch it again, Dan."

"Her eyes are deeper'n a pool at night an' her hair is all gold like ripe corn."

"You'll never look into her eyes again, Dan, and you'll never touch the gold of that hair."

"God!"

The word was hardly more than a whisper, but it brought Black Bart leaping to his feet.

Dan spoke again: "Tex, I'm thankin' you for listenin' to me; I wanted to talk. Bein' silent was burnin' me up. There's one thing more."

"Fire it out, lad."

"This evenin' I told you I hated no man but Jim Silent."

"Yes."

"An' now they's another of his gang. Sometime—when she's standin' by— I'm goin' to take him by the throat till he don't breathe no more. Then I'll throw him down in front of her an' ask her if she c'n kiss the life back into his lips!"

Calder was actually shaking with excitement, but he was wise enough not to speak.

"Tex!"

"Ay, lad."

"But when I've choked his damned life away—"

"Yes?"

"Ay, lad."

"There'll be five more that seen her shamin' me. Tex—all hell is bustin' loose inside me!"

For a moment Calder watched, but that stare of cold hate mastered him. He turned his head.


## CHAPTER XV

## THE CROSS ROADS

As Black Bart raced away in answer to Dan's whistle, Kate recovered herself from the daze in which she stood and with a sob ran towards the willows, calling the name of Dan, but Silent sprang after her, and caught her by the arm. She cried out and struggled vainly in his grip.

"Don't follow him, boys!" called Silent. "He's a dog that can bite while he runs. Stand quiet, girl!"

Lee Haines caught him by the shoulder and jerked Silent around. His hand held the butt of his revolver, and his whole arm trembled with eagerness for the draw.

"Take your hand from her, Jim!" he said.

Silent met his eye with the same glare and while his left hand still held Kate by both her wrists his right dropped to his gun.

"Not when you tell me, Lee!"

"Damn you, I say let her go!"

"By God, Haines, I stand for too much from you!"

And still they did not draw, because each of them knew that if the crisis came it would mean death to them both. Bill Kilduff jumped between them and thrust them back.

He cried, "Ain't we got enough trouble without roundin' up work at home? Terry Jordan is shot through the arm."

Kate tugged at the restraining hand of Silent, not in an attempt to escape, but in order to get closer to Haines.

"Was this your friendship?" she said, her voice shaking with hate and sorrow, "to bring me here as a lure for Whistling Dan? Listen to me, all of you! He's escaped you now, and he'll come again. Remember him, for he shan't forget you!"

"You hear her?" said Silent to Haines.

"Is this what you want me to turn loose?"

"Silent," said Haines, "it isn't the girl alone you've double crossed. You've crooked me, and you'll pay me for it sooner or later!"

"Day or night, winter or summer, I'm willing to meet you an' fight it out. Rhinehart and Purvis, take this girl back to the clearing!"

They approached, Purvis still staring at the hand from which only a moment before his gun had been knocked by the shot of Whistling Dan. It was a thing which he could not understand—he had not yet lost a most uncomfortable sense of awe. Haines made no objection when they went off, with Kate walking between them. He knew, now that his blind anger had left him, that it was folly to draw on a fight while the rest of Silent's men stood around them.

"An' the rest of you go back to the clearin'. I got somethin' to talk over with Lee," said Silent.

The others obeyed without question, and the leader turned back to his lieutenant. For a moment longer they remained staring at each other. Then Silent moved slowly forward with outstretched hand.

"Lee," he said quietly, "I'm owin' you an apology an' I'm man enough to make it."

"I can't take your hand, Jim."

Silent hesitated.

"I guess you got cause to be mad, Lee," he said. "Maybe I played too quick a hand. I didn't think about double crossin' you. I only seen a way to get Whistlin' Dan out of our path, an' I took it without rememberin' that you was the safeguard to the girl."

Haines eyed his chief narrowly.

"I wish to God I could read your mind," he said at last, "but I'll take your word that you did it without thinking."

His hand slowly met Silent's.

"An' what about the girl now, Lee?"

"I'll send her back to her father's ranch. It will be easy to put her on the right way."

"Don't you see no reason why you can't do that?"

"Are you playing with me?"

"I'm talkin' to you as I'd talk to myself. If she's loose she'll describe us all an' set the whole range on our trail."

Haines stared.

Silent went on: "If we can't turn her loose, they's only one thing left—an' that's to take her with us wherever we go."

"On your honor, do you see no other way out?"

"Do you?"

"She may promise not to speak of it."

"There ain't no way of changin' the spots of a leopard, Lee, an' there ain't no way of keepin' a woman's tongue still."

"How can we take a girl with us."

"It ain't goin' to be for long. After we pull the job that comes on the eighteenth, we'll blow farther south an' then we'll let her go."

"And no harm will come to her while she's with us?"

"Here's my hand on it, Lee."

"How can she ride with us?"

"She won't go as a woman. I've thought of that. I brought out a new outfit for Purvis from Elkhead—trousers, chaps, shirts, an' all. He's small. They'll near fit the girl."

"There isn't any other way, Jim?"

"I leave it to you. God knows I don't want to drag any damn calico aroun' with us."

As they went back towards their clearing they arranged the details. Silent would take the men aside and explain his purpose to them. Haines could inform the girl of what she must do. Just before they reached the camp Silent stopped short and took Haines by the shoulder.

"They's one thing I can't make out, Lee, an' that's how Whistlin' Dan made his getaway. I'd of bet a thousand bones that he would be dropped before he could touch his shootin' irons. An' then what happened? Hal Purvis jest flashed a gun—and that feller shot it out'n his hand. I never seen a draw like that. His hand jest seemed to twitch—I couldn't follow the move he made—an' the next second his gun went off."

He stared at Lee with a sort of fascinated horror.

"Silent," said Haines, "can you explain how the lightning comes down out of the sky?"

"Of course not."

"Then don't ask me to explain how Whistling Dan made his getaway. One minute I heard him talkin' with the girl. The next second there was two shots and when I whirled he was gone. But he'll come back, Jim. We're not through with him. He slipped away from you and your men like water out of a sieve, but we won't slip away from him the same way."

Silent stared on again with bowed head.

"He liked the girl, Lee?"

"Anyone could see that."

"Then while she's with us he'll go pretty slow. Lee, that's another reason why she's got to stay with us. My frien', it's time we was moving out from the willows. The next time he comes up with us he won't be numb in the head. He'll be thinkin' fast an' he'll be shootin' a damn sight faster. We got two jobs ahead of us—first to get that Wells Fargo shipment, and then to get Whistling Dan. There ain't room enough in the whole world for him and me."

## CHAPTER XVI

## THE THREE OF US

In the clearing of Whistling Dan and Tex Calder the marshal had turned into his blankets once more. There was no thought of sleep in Dan's mind. When the heavy breathing of the sleeper began he rose and commenced to pace up and down on the farther side of the open space. Two pairs of glowing eyes followed him in every move. Black Bart, who trailed him up and down during the first few turns he made, now sat down and watched his master with a wistful gaze. The black stallion, who lay more like a dog than a horse on the ground, kept his ears pricked forwards, as if expecting some order. Once or twice he whinnied very softly, and finally Dan sat down beside Satan, his shoulders leaned against the satiny side and his arms flung out along the stallion's back. Several times he felt hot breath against his cheek as the horse turned a curious head towards him, but he paid no attention, even when the stallion whinnied a question in his ear. In his heart was a numb, strange feeling which made him weak. He was even blind to the fact that Black Bart at last slipped into the shadows of the willows.

Presently something cold touched his chin. He found himself staring into the yellow-green eyes of Black Bart, who panted from his run, and now dropped from his mouth something which fell into Dan's lap. It was the glove of Kate Cumberland. In the grasp of his long nervous fingers, how small it was! And yet the hand which had wrinkled the leather was strong enough to hold the heart of a man. He slipped and caught the shaggy black head of Bart between his hands. The wolf knew—in some mysterious way he knew!

The touch of sympathy unnerved him. All his sorrow and his weakness burst on his soul in a single wave. A big tear struck the shining nose of the wolf.

"Bart!" he whispered. "Did you figger on plumb bustin' my heart, pal?"

To avoid those large melancholy eyes, Bart pressed his head inside of his master's arms.

"Delilah!" whispered Dan.

After that not a sound came from the three, the horse, the dog, or the man. Black Bart curled up at the feet of his master and seemed to sleep, but every now and then an ear raised or an eye twitched open. He was on guard against a danger which he did not understand. The horse, also, with a high head scanned the circling willows, alert; but the man for whom the stallion and the wolf watched gave no heed to either. There was a vacant and dreamy expression in his eye as if he was searching his own inner heart and found there the greatest enemy of all. All night they sat in this manner, silent, moveless; the animals watching against the world, the man watching against himself. Before dawn he roused himself suddenly, crossed to the sleeping marshal, and touched him on the arm.

"It's time we hit the trail," he said, as Calder sat up in the blanket.

"What's happened? Isn't it our job to comb the willows?"

"Silent ain't in the willows."

Calder started to his feet.

"How do you know?"

"They ain't close to us, that's all I know."

Tex smiled incredulously.

"I suppose," he said good humoredly, "that your *instinct* brought you this message?"

"Instinct?" repeated Dan blankly, "I dunno."

Calder grew serious.

"We'll take a chance that you may be right. At least we can ride down the riverbank and see if there are any fresh tracks in the sand. If Silent started this morning I have an idea he'll head across the river and line out for the railroad."

In twenty minutes their breakfast was eaten and they were in the saddle. The sun had not yet risen when they came out of the willows to the broad shallow basin of the river. In spring, when the snow of the mountains melted, that river filled from bank to bank with a yellow torrent; at the dry season of the year it was a dirty little creek meandering through the sands. Down the bank they rode at a sharp trot for a mile and a half until Black Bart, who scouted ahead of them at his gliding wolf-trot, came to an abrupt stop. Dan spoke to Satan and the stallion broke into a swift gallop which left the pony of Tex Calder laboring in the rear. When they drew rein beside the wolf, they found seven distinct tracks of horses which went down the bank of the river and crossed the basin. Calder turned with a wide-eyed amazement to Dan.

"You're right again," he said, not without a touch of vexation in his voice; "but the dog stopped at these tracks. How does he know we are hunting for Silent's crew?"

"I dunno," said Dan, "maybe he jest suspects."

"They can't have a long start of us," said Calder. "Let's hit the trail. We'll get them before night."

"No," said Dan, "we won't."

"Why won't we?"

"I've seen Silent's hoss, and I've ridden him. If the rest of his gang have the same kind of hoss flesh, you c'n never catch him with that cayuse of yours."

"Maybe not today," said Calder, "but in two days we'll run him down. Seven horses can't travel as two in a long chase."

They started out across the basin, keeping to the tracks of Silent's horses. It was the marshal's idea that the outlaws would head on a fairly straight line for the railroad and accordingly when they lost the track of the seven horses they kept to this direction. Twice during the day they verified their course by information received once from a range rider and once from a man in a dusty buck-board. Both of these had sighted the fast travelling band, but each had seen it pass an hour or two before Calder and Dan arrived. Such tidings encouraged the marshal to keep his horse at an increasing speed; but in the middle of the afternoon, though black Satan showed little or no signs of fatigue, the cattle-pony was nearly blown and they were forced to reduce their pace to the ordinary dog-trot.

## CHAPTER XVII

## THE PANTHER'S PAW

Evening came and still they had not sighted the outlaws. As dark fell they drew near a house snuggled away among a group of cottonwoods. Here they determined to spend the night, for Calder's pony was now almost exhausted. A man of fifty came from the house in answer to their call and showed them the way to the horse-shed. While they unsaddled their horses he told them his name was Sam Daniels, yet he evinced no curiosity as to the identity of his guests, and they volunteered no information. His eyes lingered long and fondly over the exquisite lines of Satan. From behind, from the side, and in front, he viewed the stallion while Dan rubbed down the legs of his mount with a care which was most foreign to the ranges. Finally the cattleman reached out a hand toward the smoothly muscled shoulders.

It was Calder who stood nearest and he managed to strike up Daniels's extended arm and jerk him back from the region of danger.

"What'n hell is that for?" exclaimed Daniels.

"That horse is called Satan," said Calder, "and when any one save his owner touches him he lives up to his name and raises hell."

Before Daniels could answer, the light of his lantern fell upon Black Bart, hitherto half hidden by the deepening shadows of the night, but standing now at the entrance of the shed. The cattleman's teeth clicked together and he slapped his hand against his thigh in a reach for the gun which was not there.

"Look behind you," he said to Calder. "A wolf!"

He made a grab for the marshal's gun, but the latter forestalled him.

"Go easy, partner," he said, grinning, "that's only the running mate of the horse. He's not a wolf, at least not according to his owner—and as for being wild—look at that!"

Bart had stalked calmly into the shed and now lay curled up exactly beneath the feet of the stallion.

The two guests received a warmer welcome from Sam Daniels' wife when they reached the house. Their son, Buck, had been expected home for supper, but it was too late for them to delay the meal longer. Accordingly they sat down at once and the dinner was nearly over when Buck, having announced himself with a whoop as he rode up, entered, banging the door loudly behind him. He greeted the strangers with a careless wave of the hand and sat down at the table. His mother placed food silently before him. No explanations of his tardiness were asked and none were offered. The attitude of his father indicated clearly that the boy represented the earning power of the family. He was a big fellow with broad, thick wrists, and a straight black eye. When he had eaten, he broke into breezy conversation, and especially of a vicious mustang he had ridden on a bet the day before.

"Speakin' of hosses, Buck," said his father, "they's a black out in the shed right now that'd make your eyes jest nacherally pop out'n their sockets. No more'n fifteen hands, but a reg'lar picture. Must be greased lightnin'."

"I've heard talk of these streaks of greased lightnin'," said Buck, with a touch of scorn, "but I'll stack old Mike agin the best of them."

"An' there's a dog along with the hoss—a dog that's the nearest to a wolf of any I ever seen."

There was a sudden change in Buck—a change to be sensed rather than definitely noted with the eye. It was a stiffening of his body—an alertness of which he was at pains to make no show. For almost immediately he began to whistle softly, idly, his eyes roving carelessly across the wall while he tilted back in his chair. Dan dropped his hand close to the butt of his gun. Instantly, the eyes of Buck flashed down and centered on Dan for an instant of keen scrutiny. Certainly Buck had connected that mention of the black horse and the wolf-dog with a disturbing idea.

When they went to their room—a room in which there was no bed and they had to roll down their blankets on the floor—Dan opened the window and commenced to whistle one of his own wild tunes. It seemed to Calder that there was a break in that music here and there, and a few notes grouped together like a call. In a moment a shadowy figure leaped through the window, and Black Bart landed on the floor with soft padding feet.

Recovering from his start Calder cursed softly.

"What's the main idea?" he asked.

Dan made a signal for a lower tone.

"There ain't no idea," he answered, "but these Daniels people—do you know anything about them?"

"No. Why?"

"They interest me, that's all."

"Anything wrong?"

"I guess not."

"Why did you whistle for this infernal wolf? It makes me nervous to have him around. Get out, Bart."

The wolf turned a languid eye upon the marshal.

"Let him be," said Dan. "I don't feel no ways nacheral without havin' Bart around."

The marshal made no farther objections, and having rolled himself in his blankets was almost immediately asleep and breathing heavily. The moment Dan heard his companion draw breath with a telltale regularity, he sat up again in his blankets. Bart was instantly at his side. He patted the shaggy head lightly, and pointed towards the door.

"Guard!" he whispered.

Then he lay down and was immediately asleep. Bart crouched at his feet with his head pointed directly at the door.

In other rooms there was the sound of the Daniels family going to bed— noises distinctly heard throughout the flimsy frame of the house. After that a deep silence fell which lasted many hours, but in that darkest moment which just precedes the dawn, a light creaking came up the hall. It was very faint and it occurred only at long intervals, but at the first sound Black Bart raised his head from his paws and stared at the door with those glowing eyes which see in the dark.

Now another sound came, still soft, regular. There was a movement of the door. In the pitch dark a man could never have noticed it, but it was plainly visible to the wolf. Still more visible, when the door finally stood wide, was the form of the man who stood in the opening. In one hand he carried a lantern thoroughly hooded, but not so well wrapped that it kept back a single ray which flashed on a revolver. The intruder made a step forward, a step as light as the fall of feathers, but it was not half so stealthy as the movement of Black Bart as he slunk towards the door. He had been warned to watch that door, but it did not need a warning to tell him that a danger was approaching the sleeping master. In the crouched form of the man, in the cautious step, he recognized the unmistakable stalking of one who hunts. Another soft step the man made forward.

Then, with appalling suddenness, a blacker shadow shot up from the deep night of the floor, and white teeth gleamed before the stranger's face. He threw up his hand to save his throat. The teeth sank into his arm—a driving weight hurled him against the wall and then to the floor—the revolver and the lantern dropped clattering, and the latter, rolling from its wrapping, flooded the room with light. But neither man nor wolf uttered a sound.

Calder was standing, gun in hand, but too bewildered to act, while Dan, as if he were playing a part long rehearsed, stood covering the fallen form of Buck Daniels.

"Stand back from him, Bart!" he commanded.

The wolf slipped off a pace, whining with horrible eagerness, for he had tasted blood. Far away a shout came from Sam Daniels. Dan lowered his gun.

"Stand up," he ordered.

The big fellow picked himself up and stood against the wall with the blood streaming down his right arm. Still he said nothing and his keen eyes darted from Calder to Whistling Dan.

"Give me a strip of that old shirt over there, will you, Tex?" said Dan, "an' keep him covered while I tie up his arm."

Before Calder could move, old Daniels appeared at the door, a heavy Colt in his hand. For a moment he stood dumbfounded, but then, with a cry, jerked up his gun—a quick movement, but a fraction of a second too slow, for the hand of Dan darted out and his knuckles struck the wrist of the old cattleman. The Colt rattled on the floor. He lunged after his weapon, but the voice of Buck stopped him short.

"The game's up, Dad," he growled, "that older feller is Tex Calder."

The name, like a blow in the face, straightened old Daniels and left him white and blinking. Whistling Dan turned his back on the father and deftly bound up the lacerated arm of Buck.

"In the name o' God, Buck," moaned Sam, "what you been tryin' to do in here?"

"What you'd do if you had the guts for it. That's Tex Calder an' this is Dan Barry. They're on the trail of big Jim. I wanted to put 'em off that trail."

"Look here," said Calder, "how'd you know us?"

"I've said my little say," said Buck sullenly, "an' you'll get no more out of me between here an' any hell you can take me to."

"He knew us when his father talked about Satan an' Black Bart," said Dan to Tex. "Maybe he's one of Silent's."

"Buck, for God's sake tell 'em you know nothin' of Silent," cried old Daniels. "Boy, boy, it's hangin' for you if they get you to Elkhead an' charge you with that!"

"Dad, you're a fool," said Buck. "I ain't goin' down on my knees to 'em. Not me."

Calder, still keeping Buck covered with his gun, drew Dan a little to one side.

"What can we do with this fellow, Dan?" he said. "Shall we give up the trail and take him over to Elkhead?"

"An' break the heart of the ol' man?"

"Buck is one of the gang, that's certain."

"Get Silent an' there won't be no gang left."

"But we caught this chap in red blood—"

"He ain't very old, Tex. Maybe he could change. I think he ain't been playin' Silent's game any too long."

"We can't let him go. It isn't in reason to do that."

"I ain't thinkin' of reason. I'm thinkin' of old Sam an' his wife."

"And if we turn him loose?"

"He'll be your man till he dies."

Calder scowled.

"The whole range is filled with these silent partners of the outlaws—but maybe you're right, Dan. Look at them now!"

The father was standing close to his son and pouring out a torrent of appeal—evidently begging him in a low voice to disavow any knowledge of Silent and his crew, but Buck shook his head sullenly. He had given up hope. Calder approached them.

"Buck," he said, "I suppose you know that you could be hung for what you've tried to do tonight. If the law wouldn't hang you a lynching party would. No jail would be strong enough to keep them away from you."

Buck was silent, dogged.

"But suppose we were to let you go scot free?"

Buck started. A great flush covered his face.

"I'm taking the advice of Dan Barry in doing this," said Calder. "Barry thinks you could go straight. Tell me man to man, if I give you the chance will you break loose from Silent and his gang?"

A moment before, Buck had been steeled for the worst, but this sudden change loosened all the bonds of his pride. He stammered and choked. Calder turned abruptly away.

"Dan," he said, "here's the dawn, and it's time for us to hit the trail."

They rolled their blankets hastily and broke away from the gratitude which poured like water from the heart of old Sam. They were in their saddles when Buck came beside Dan. His pride, his shame, and his gratitude broke his voice.

"I ain't much on words," he said, "but it's you I'm thankin'!"

His hand reached up hesitatingly, and Dan caught it in a firm grip.

"Why," he said gently, "even Satan here stumbles now an' then, but that ain't no reason I should get rid of him. Good luck—partner!"

He shook the reins and the stallion leaped off after Calder's trotting pony. Buck Daniels stood motionless looking after them, and his eyes were very dim.

For an hour Dan and Tex were on the road before the sun looked over the hills. Calder halted his horse to watch.

"Dan," he said at last, "I used to think there were only two ways of handling men—one with the velvet touch and one with the touch of steel. Mine has been the way of steel, but I begin to see there's a third possibility—the touch of the panther's paw—the velvet with the steel claws hid beneath. That's your way, and I wonder if it isn't the best. I think Buck Daniels would be glad to die for you!"

He turned directly to Dan.

"But all this is aside from the point, which is that the whole country is full of these silent partners of the outlaws. The law plays a lone hand in the mountain-desert."

"You've played the lone hand and won in twenty times," said Dan.

"Ay, but the twenty-first time I may fall. The difference between success and failure in this country is just the length of time it takes to pull a trigger—and Silent is fast with a gun. He's the root of the outlaw power. We may kill a hundred men, but till he's gone we've only mowed the weeds, not pulled them. But what's the use of talking? One second will tell the tale when I stand face to face with Jim Silent and we go for our six-guns. And somewhere between that rising sun and those mountains I'll find Jim Silent and the end of things for one of us."

He started his cattle-pony into a sudden gallop, and they drove on into the bright morning.

## CHAPTER XVIII

### CAIN

Hardly a score of miles away, Jim Silent and his six companions topped a hill. He raised his hand and the others drew rein beside him. Kate Cumberland shifted her weight a little to one side of the saddle to rest and looked down from the crest on the sweep of country below. A mile away the railroad made a streak of silver light across the brown range and directly before them stood the squat station house with red-tiled roof. Just before the house, a slightly broader streak of that gleaming light showed the position of the siding rails. She turned her head towards the outlaws. They were listening to the final directions of their chief, and the darkly intent faces told their own story. She knew, from what she had gathered of their casual hints, that this was to be the scene of the train holdup.

It seemed impossible that this little group of men could hold the great fabric of a train with all its scores of passengers at their mercy. In spite of herself, half her heart wished them success. There was Terry Jordan forgetful of the wound in his arm; Shorty Rhinehart, his saturnine face longer and more calamitous than ever; Hal Purvis, grinning and nodding his head; Bill Kilduff with his heavy jaw set like a bulldog's; Lee Haines, with a lock of tawny hair blowing over his forehead, smiling faintly as he listened to Silent as if he heard a girl tell a story of love; and finally Jim Silent himself, huge, solemn, confident. She began to feel that these six men were worth six hundred.

She hated them for some reasons; she feared them for others; but the brave blood of Joe Cumberland was thick in her and she loved the danger of the coming moment. Their plans were finally agreed upon, their masks arranged, and after Haines had tied a similar visor over Kate's face, they started down the hill at a swinging gallop.

In front of the house of the station-agent they drew up, and while the others were at their horses, Lee Haines dismounted and rapped loudly at the door. It was opened by a gray-bearded man smoking a pipe. Haines covered him. He tossed up his hands and the pipe dropped from his mouth.

"Who's in the house here with you?" asked Haines.

"Not a soul!" stammered the man. "If you're lookin' for money you c'n run through the house. You won't find a thing worth takin'."

"I don't want money. I want you," said Haines; and immediately explained, "you're perfectly safe. All you have to do is to be obliging. As for the money, you just throw open that switch and flag the train when she rolls along in a few moments. We'll take care of the rest. You don't have to keep your hands up."

The hands came down slowly. For a brief instant the agent surveyed Haines and the group of masked men who sat their horses a few paces away, and then without a word he picked up his flag from behind the door and walked out of the house. Throughout the affair he never uttered a syllable. Haines walked up to the head of the siding with him while he opened the switch and accompanied him back to the point opposite the station house to see that he gave the "stop" signal correctly. In the meantime two of the other outlaws entered the little station, bound the telegrapher hand and foot, and shattered his instrument. That would prevent the sending of any call for help after the hold-up. Purvis and Jordan (since Terry could shoot with his left hand in case of need) went to the other side of the track and lay down against the grade. It was their business to open fire on the tops of the windows as the train drew to a stop. That would keep the passengers inside. The other four were distributed along the side nearest to the station house. Shorty Rhinehart and Bill Kilduff were to see that no passengers broke out from the train and attempted a flank attack. Haines would attend to having the fire box of the engine flooded. For the cracking of the safe, Silent carried the stick of dynamite.

Now the long wait began. There is a dreamlike quality about bright mornings in the open country, and everything seemed unreal to Kate. It was impossible that tragedy should come on such a day. The moments stole on. She saw Silent glance twice at his watch and scowl. Evidently the train was late and possibly they would give up the attempt. Then a light humming caught her ear.

She held her breath and listened again. It was unmistakable—a slight thing—a tremor to be felt rather than heard. She saw Haines peering under shaded eyes far down the track, and following the direction of his gaze she saw a tiny spot of haze on the horizon. The tiny puff of smoke developed to a deeper, louder note. The station agent took his place on the track.

Now the train bulked big, the engine wavering slightly to the unevenness of the roadbed. The flag of the station-agent moved. Kate closed her eyes and set her teeth. There was a rumbling and puffing and a mighty grinding—a shout somewhere—the rattle of a score of pistol shots—she opened her eyes to see the train rolling to a stop on the siding directly before her.

Kilduff and Shorty Rhinehart, crouching against the grade, were splintering the windows one by one with nicely placed shots. The baggage cars were farther up the siding than Silent calculated. He and Haines now ran towards the head of the train.

The fireman and engineer jumped from their cab, holding their arms stiffly above their heads; and Haines approached with poised revolver to make them flood the firebox. In this way the train would be delayed for some time and before it could send out the alarm the bandits would be far from pursuit. Haines had already reached the locomotive and Silent was running towards the first baggage-car when the door of that car slid open and at the entrance appeared two men with rifles at their shoulders. As they opened fire Silent pitched to the ground. Kate set her teeth and forced her eyes to stay open.

Even as the outlaw fell his revolver spoke and one of the men threw up his hands with a yell and pitched out of the open door. His companion still kept his post, pumping shots at the prone figure. Twice more the muzzle of Silent's gun jerked up and the second man crumpled on the floor of the car.

A great hissing and a jetting cloud of steam announced that Haines had succeeded in flooding the firebox. Silent climbed into the first baggage-car, stepping, as he did so, on the limp body of the Wells Fargo agent, who lay on the roadbed. A moment later he flung out the body of the second messenger. The man flopped on the ground heavily, face downwards, and then—greatest horror of all!—dragged himself to his hands and knees and began to crawl laboriously. Kate ran and dropped to her knees beside him.

"Are you hurt badly?" she pleaded. "Where? Where?"

He sagged to the ground and lay on his left side, breathing heavily.

"Where is the wound?" she repeated.

He attempted to speak, but only a bloody froth came to his lips. That was sufficient to tell her that he had been shot through the lungs.

She tore open his shirt and found two purple spots high on the chest, one to the right, and one to the left. From that on the left ran a tiny trickle of blood, but that on the right was only a small puncture in the midst of a bruise. He was far past all help.

"Speak to me!" she pleaded.

His eyes rolled and then checked on her face.

"Done for," he said in a horrible whisper, "that devil done me. Kid—cut out—this life. I've played this game—myself—an' now—I'm goin'—to hell for it!"

A great convulsion twisted his face.

"What can I do?" cried Kate.

"Tell the world—I died—game!"

His body writhed, and in the last agony his hand closed hard over hers. It was like a silent farewell, that strong clasp.

A great hand caught her by the shoulder and jerked her to her feet.

"The charge is goin' off! Jump for it!" shouted Silent in her ear.

She sprang up and at the same time there was a great boom from within the car. The side bulged out—a section of the top lifted and fell back with a crash—and Silent ran back into the smoke. Haines, Purvis, and Kilduff were instantly at the car, taking the ponderous little canvas sacks of coin as their chief handed them out.

Within two minutes after the explosion ten small sacks were deposited in the saddlebags on the horses which stood before the station-house. Silent's whistle called in Terry Jordan and Shorty Rhinehart—a sharp order forced Kate to climb into her saddle—and the train robbers struck up the hillside at a racing pace. A confused shouting rose behind them. Rifles commenced to crack where some of the passengers had taken up the weapons of the dead guards, but the bullets flew wide, and the little troop was soon safely out of range.

On the other side of the hill-top they changed their course to the right.

For half an hour the killing pace continued, and then, as there was not a sign of immediate chase, the lone riders drew down to a soberer pace. Silent called: "Keep bunched behind me. We're headed for the old Salton place—an' a long rest."

# CHAPTER XIX

## REAL MEN

Some people pointed out that Sheriff Gus Morris had never made a single important arrest in the ten years during which he had held office, and there were a few slanderers who spoke insinuatingly of the manner in which the lone riders flourished in Morris's domain. These "knockers," however, were voted down by the vast majority, who swore that the sheriff was the finest fellow who ever threw leg over saddle. They liked him for his inexhaustible good nature, the mellow baritone in which he sang the range songs at anyone's request, and perhaps more than all, for the very laxness with which he conducted his work. They had had enough of the old school of sheriffs who lived a few months gun in hand and died fighting from the saddle. The office had never seemed desirable until Gus Morris ran for it and smiled his way to a triumphant election.

Before his career as an office-holder began, he ran a combined general merchandise store, saloon, and hotel. That is to say, he ran the hostelry in name. The real executive head, general manager, clerk, bookkeeper, and cook, and sometimes even bartender was his daughter, Jacqueline. She found the place only a saloon, and a poorly patronized one at that. Her unaided energy gradually made it into a hotel, restaurant, and store. Even while her father was in office he spent most of his time around the hotel; but no matter how important he might be elsewhere, in his own house he had no voice. There the only law was the will of Jacqueline.

Out of the stable behind this hostelry Dan and Tex Calder walked on the evening of the train robbery. They had reached the place of the hold-up a full two hours after Silent's crew departed; and the fireman and engineer had been working frantically during the interim to clean out the soaked fire box and get up steam again. Tex looked at the two dead bodies, spoke to the conductor, and then cut short the voluble explanations of a score of passengers by turning his horse and riding away, followed by Dan. All that day he was gloomily silent. It was a shrewd blow at his reputation, for the outlaws had actually carried out the robbery while he was on their trail. Not till they came out of the horse-shed after stabling their horses did he speak freely.

"Dan," he said, "do you know anything about Sheriff Gus Morris?"

"No."

"Then listen to this and salt every word away. I'm an officer of the law, but I won't tell that to Morris. I hope he doesn't know me. If he does it will spoil our game. I am almost certain he is playing a close hand with the lone riders. I'll wager he'd rather see a stick of dynamite than a marshal. Remember when we get in that place that we're not after Jim Silent or any one else. We're simply travelling cowboys. No questions. I expect to learn something about the location of Silent's gang while we're here, but we'll never find out except by hints and chance remarks. We have to watch Morris like hawks. If he suspects us he'll find a way to let Silent know we're here and then the hunters will be hunted."

In the house they found a dozen cattlemen sitting down at the table in the dining room. As they entered the room the sheriff, who sat at the head of the table, waved his hand to them.

"H'ware ye, boys?" he called. "You'll find a couple of chairs right in the next room. Got two extra plates, Jac?"

As Dan followed Tex after the chairs he noticed the sheriff beckon to one of the men who sat near him. As they returned with the chairs someone was leaving the room by another door.

"Tex," he said, as they sat down side by side, "when we left the dining room for the chairs, the sheriff spoke to one of the boys and as we came back one of them was leavin' through another door. D'you think Morris knew you when you came in?"

Calder frowned thoughtfully and then shook his head.

"No," he said in a low voice. "I watched him like a hawk when we entered. He didn't bat an eye when he saw me. If he recognized me he's the greatest actor in the world, bar none! No, Dan, he doesn't know us from Adam and Abel."

"All right," said Dan, "but I don't like somethin' about this place—maybe it's the smell of the air. Tex, take my advice an' keep your gun ready for the fastest draw you ever made."

"Don't worry about me," smiled Calder. "How about yourself?"

"Hello," broke in Jacqueline from the end of the table. "Look who we've picked in the draw!"

Her voice was musical, but her accent and manner were those of a girl who has lived all her life among men and has caught their ways—with an exaggeration of that self-confidence which a woman always feels among Western men. Her blue eyes were upon Dan.

"Ain't you a long ways from home?" she went on.

The rest of the table, perceiving the drift of her badgering, broke into a rumbling bass chuckle.

"Quite a ways," said Dan, and his wide brown eyes looked seriously back at her.

A yell of delight came from the men at this naive rejoinder. Dan looked about him with a sort of childish wonder. Calder's anxious whisper came at his side: "Don't let them get you mad, Dan!" Jacqueline, having scored so heavily with her first shot, was by no means willing to give up her sport.

"With them big eyes, for a starter," she said, "all you need is long hair to be perfect. Do your folks generally let you run around like this?"

Every man canted his ear to get the answer and already they were grinning expectantly.

"I don't go out much," returned the soft voice of Dan, "an' when I do, I go with my friend, here. He takes care of me."

Another thunder of laughter broke out. Jacqueline had apparently uncovered a tenderfoot, and a rare one even for that absurd species. A sandy-haired cattle puncher who sat close to Jacqueline now took the cue from the mistress of the house.

"Ain't you a bit scared when you get around among real men?" he asked, leering up the table towards Dan.

The latter smiled gently upon him.

"I reckon maybe I am," he said amiably.

"Then you must be shakin' in your boots right now," said the other over the sound of the laughter.

"No," said Dan, "I feel sort of comfortable."

The other replied with a frown that would have intimidated a balky horse.

"What d'you mean? Ain't you jest said men made you sort of—nervous?"

He imitated the soft drawl of Dan with his last words and raised another yell of delight from the crowd. Whistling Dan turned his gentle eyes upon Jacqueline.

"Pardon me, ma'am," he began.

An instant hush fell on the men. They would not miss one syllable of the delightful remarks of this rarest of all tenderfoots, and the prelude of this coming utterance promised something that would eclipse all that had gone before.

"Talk right out, Brown-eyes," said Jacqueline, wiping the tears of delight from her eyes. "Talk right out as if you was a man. *I* won't hurt you."

"I jest wanted to ask," said Dan, "if these are real men?"

The ready laughter started, checked, and died suddenly away. The cattlemen looked at each other in puzzled surprise.

"Don't they look like it to you, honey?" asked Jacqueline curiously.

Dan allowed his eyes to pass lingeringly around the table from face to face.

"I dunno," he said at last, "they look sort of queer to me."

"For God's sake cut this short, Dan," pleaded Tex Calder in an undertone. "Let them have all the rope they want. Don't trip up our party before we get started."

"Queer?" echoed Jacqueline, and there was a deep murmur from the men.

"Sure," said Dan, smiling upon her again, "they all wear their guns so awful high."

Out of the dead silence broke the roar of the sandy-haired man: "What'n hell d'you mean by that?"

Dan leaned forward on one elbow, his right hand free and resting on the edge of the table, but still his smile was almost a caress.

"Why," he said, "maybe you c'n explain it to me. Seems to me that all these guns is wore so high they's more for ornament than use."

"You damned pup—" began Sandy.

He stopped short and stared with a peculiar fascination at Dan, who started to speak again. His voice had changed—not greatly, for its pitch was the same and the drawl was the same—but there was a purr in it that made every man stiffen in his chair and make sure that his right hand was free. The ghost of his former smile was still on his lips, but it was his eyes that seemed to fascinate Sandy.

"Maybe I'm wrong, partner," he was saying, "an' maybe you c'n prove that *your* gun ain't jest ornamental hardware?"

What followed was very strange. Sandy was a brave man and everyone at that table knew it. They waited for the inevitable to happen. They waited for Sandy's lightning move for his gun. They waited for the flash and the crack of the revolver. It did not come. There followed a still more stunning wonder.

"You c'n see," went on that caressing voice of Dan, "that everyone is waitin' for you to demonstrate—which the lady is most special interested."

And still Sandy did not move that significant right hand. It remained fixed in air a few inches above the table, the fingers stiffly spread. He moistened his white lips. Then—most strange of all!—his eyes shifted and wandered away from the face of Whistling Dan. The others exchanged incredulous glances. The impossible had happened—Sandy had taken water! The sheriff was the first to recover, though his forehead was shining with perspiration.

"What's all this stuff about?" he called. "Hey, Sandy, quit pickin' trouble with the stranger!"

Sandy seized the loophole through which to escape with his honour. He settled back in his chair.

"All right, gov'nor," he said, "I won't go spoilin' your furniture. I won't hurt him."

## CHAPTER XX

## ONE TRAIL ENDS

But this deceived no one. They had seen him palpably take water. A moment of silence followed, while Sandy stared white-faced down at the table, avoiding all eyes; but all the elements of good breeding exist under all the roughness of the West. It was Jacqueline who began with a joke which was rather old, but everyone appreciated it—at that moment—and the laughter lasted long enough to restore some of the color to Sandy's face. A general rapid fire of talk followed.

"How did you do it?" queried Calder. "I was all prepared for a gun-play."

"Why, you seen I didn't do nothin'."

"Then what in the world made Sandy freeze while his hand was on the way to his gun?"

"I dunno," sighed Dan, "but when I see his hand start movin' I sort of wanted his blood—I *wanted* him to keep right on till he got hold of his gun—and maybe he seen it in my eyes an' that sort of changed his mind."

"I haven't the least doubt that it did," said Calder grimly.

At the foot of the table Jacqueline's right hand neighbor was saying: "What happened, Jac?"

"Don't ask me," she replied. "All I know is that I don't think any less of Sandy because he backed down. I saw that stranger's face myself an' I'm still sort of weak inside."

"How did he look?"

"I dunno. Jest—jest *hungry*. Understand?"

She was silent for a time, but she was evidently thinking hard. At last she turned to the same man.

"Did you hear Brown-eyes say that the broad-shouldered feller next to him was his friend?"

"Sure. I seen them ride in together. That other one looks like a hard nut, eh?"

She returned no answer, but after a time her eyes raised slowly and rested for a long moment on Dan's face. It was towards the end of the meal when she rose and went towards the kitchen. At the door she turned, and Dan, though he was looking down at his plate, was conscious that someone was observing him. He glanced up and the moment his eyes met hers she made a significant backward gesture with her hand. He hesitated a moment and then shoved back his chair. Calder was busy talking to a table mate, so he walked out of the house without speaking to his companion. He went to the rear of the house and as he had expected she was waiting for him.

"Brown-eyes," she said swiftly, "that feller who sat beside you—is he your partner?"

"I dunno," said Dan evasively, "why are you askin'?"

Her breath was coming audibly as if from excitement.

"Have you got a fast hoss?"

"There ain't no faster."

"Believe me, he can't go none too fast with you tonight. Maybe they're after you, too."

"Who?"

"I can't tell you. Listen to me, Brown-eyes. Go get your hoss an' feed him the spur till you're a hundred miles away, an' even then don't stop runnin'."

He merely stared at her curiously.

She stamped.

"Don't stop to talk. If they're after him and you're his partner, they probably want you, too."

"I'll stay aroun'. If they're curious about me, I'll tell 'em my name—I'll even spell it for 'em. Who are they?"

"They are—hell—that's all."

"I'd like to see 'em. Maybe *they're* real men."

"They're devils. If I told you their names you'd turn stiff."

"I'll take one chance. Tell me who they are."

"I don't dare tell you."

She hesitated.

"I *will* tell you! You've made a fool out of me with them big baby eyes. Jim Silent is in that house!"

He turned and ran, but not for the horse-shed; he headed straight for the open door of the house.

\* \* \* \* \*

In the dining room two more had left the table, but the rest, lingering over their fresh filled coffee cups, sat around telling tales, and Tex Calder was among them. He was about to push back his chair when the hum of talk ceased as if at a command. The men on the opposite side of the table were staring with fascinated eyes at the door, and then a big voice boomed behind him: "Tex Calder, stan' up. You've come to the end of the trail!"

He whirled as he rose, kicking down the chair behind him, and stood face to face with Jim Silent. The great outlaw was scowling; but his gun was in its holster and his hands rested lightly on his hips. It was plain for all eyes to see that he had come not to murder but to fight a fair duel. Behind him loomed the figure of Lee Haines scarcely less imposing.

All eternity seemed poised and waiting for the second when one of the men would make the move for his gun. Not a breath was drawn in the room. Hands remained frozen in air in the midst of a gesture. Lips which had parted to speak did not close. The steady voice of the clock broke into the silence—a dying space between every tick. For the second time in his life Tex Calder knew fear.

He saw no mere man before him, but his own destiny. And he knew that if he stood before those glaring eyes another minute he would become like poor Sandy a few minutes before—a white-faced, palsied coward. The shame of the thought gave him power.

"Silent," he said, "there's a quick end to the longest trail, because—"

His hand darted down. No eye could follow the lightning speed with which he whipped out his revolver and fanned it, but by a mortal fraction of a second the convulsive jerk of Silent's hand was faster still. Two shots followed—they were rather like one drawn-out report. The woodwork splintered above the outlaw's head; Tex Calder seemed to laugh, but his lips made no sound. He pitched forward on his face.

"He fired that bullet," said Silent, "after mine hit him."

Then he leaped back through the door.

"Keep 'em back one minute, Lee, an' then after me!" he said as he ran. Haines stood in the door with folded arms. He knew that no one would dare to move a hand.

Two doors slammed at the same moment—the front door as Silent leaped into the safety of the night, and the rear door as Whistling Dan rushed into the house. He stood at the entrance from the kitchen to the dining room half crouched, and swaying from the suddenness with which he had checked his run. He saw the sprawled form of Tex Calder on the floor and the erect figure of Lee Haines just opposite him.

"For God's sake!" screamed Gus Morris, "don't shoot, Haines! He's done nothin'. Let him go!"

"My life—or his!" said Haines savagely. "He's not a man—he's a devil!"

Dan was laughing low—a sound like a croon.

"Tex," he said, "I'm goin' to take him alive for you!"

As if in answer the dying man stirred on the floor. Haines went for his gun, a move almost as lightning swift as that of Jim Silent, but now far, far too late. The revolver was hardly clear of its holster when Whistling Dan's weapon spoke. Haines, with a curse, clapped his left hand over his wounded right forearm, and then reached after his weapon as it clattered to the floor. Once more he was too late. Dan tossed his gun away with a snarl like the growl of a wolf; cleared the table at a leap, and was at Haines's throat. The bandit fought back desperately, vainly. One instant they struggled erect, swaying, the next

Haines was lifted bodily, and hurled to the floor. He writhed, but under those prisoning hands he was helpless.

The sheriff headed the rush for the scene of the struggle, but Dan stopped them.

"All you c'n do," he said, "is to bring me a piece of rope."

Jacqueline came running with a stout piece of twine which he twisted around the wrists of Haines. Then he jerked the outlaw to his feet, and stood close, his face inhumanly pale.

"If he dies," he said, pointing with a stiff arm back at the prostrate figure of Tex Calder, "you—you'll burn alive for it!"

The sheriff and two of the other men turned the body of Calder on his back. They tore open his shirt, and Jacqueline leaned over him with a basin of water trying to wipe away the ever recurrent blood which trickled down his breast. Dan brushed them away and caught the head of his companion in his arms.

"Tex!" he moaned, "Tex! Open your eyes, partner, I got him for you. I got him alive for you to look at him! Wake up!"

As if in obedience to the summons the eyes of Calder opened wide. The lids fluttered as if to clear his vision, but even then his gaze was filmed with a telltale shadow.

"Dan—Whistling Dan," he said, "I'm seeing you a long, long ways off. Partner, I'm done for."

The whole body of Dan stiffened.

"Done? Tex, you can't be! Five minutes ago you sat at that there table, smilin' an' talkin'!"

"It doesn't take five minutes. Half a second can take a man all the way to hell!"

"If you're goin', pal, if you goin', Tex, take one comfort along with you! I got the man who killed you! Come here!"

He pulled the outlaw to his knees beside the dying marshal whose face had lighted wonderfully. He strained his eyes painfully to make out the face of his slayer. Then he turned his head.

He said: "The man who killed me was Jim Silent."

Dan groaned and leaned close to Calder.

"Then I'll follow him to the end—" he began.

The feeble accent of Calder interrupted him.

"Not that way. Come close to me. I can't hear my own voice, hardly."

Dan bowed his head. A whisper murmured on for a moment, broken here and there as Dan nodded his head and said, "Yes!"

"Then hold up your hand, your right hand," said Calder at last, audibly.

Dan obeyed.

"You swear it?"

"So help me God!"

"Then here's the pledge of it!"

Calder fumbled inside his shirt for a moment, and then withdrawing his hand placed it palm down in that of Dan. The breath of the marshal was coming in a rattling gasp.

He said very faintly: "I've stopped the trails of twenty men. It took the greatest of them all to get me. He got me fair. He beat me to the draw!"

He stopped as if in awe.

"He played square—he's a better man than I. Dan, when you get him, do it the same way—face to face—with time for him to think of hell before he gets there. Partner, I'm going. Wish me luck."

"Tex—partner—good luck!"

It seemed as if that parting wish was granted, for Calder died with a smile.

When Dan rose slowly Gus Morris stepped up and laid a hand on his arm: "Look here, there ain't no use of bein' sad for Tex Calder. His business was killin' men, an' his own time was overdue."

Dan turned a face that made Morris wince.

"What's the matter?" he asked, with an attempt at bluff good nature. "Do you hate everyone because one man is dead? I'll tell you what I'll do. I'll loan you a buckboard an' a pair of hosses to take Tex back to Elkhead. As for this feller Haines, I'll take care of him."

"I sure need a buckboard," said Dan slowly, "but I'll get the loan from a—white man!"

He turned his back sharply on the sheriff and asked if any one else had a wagon they could lend him. One of the men had stopped at Morris's place on his way to Elkhead. He immediately proposed that they make the trip together.

"All right," said Morris carelessly. "I won't pick trouble with a crazy man. Come with me, Haines."

He turned to leave the room.

"Wait!" said Dan.

Haines stopped as though someone had seized him by the shoulder.

"What the devil is this now?" asked Morris furiously. "Stranger, d'you think you c'n run the world? Come on with me, Haines!"

"He stays with me," said Dan.

"By God," began Morris, "if I thought—"

"This ain't no place for you to begin thinkin'," said the man who had offered his buckboard to Dan. "This feller made the capture an' he's got the right to take him into Elkhead if he wants. They's a reward on the head of Lee Haines."

"The arrest is made in my county," said Morris stoutly, "an' I've got the say as to what's to be done with a prisoner."

"Morris," said Haines earnestly, "if I'm taken to Elkhead it'll be simply a matter of lynching. You know the crowd in that town."

"Right—right," said Morris, eagerly picking up the word. "It'd be plain lynchin'—murder—"

Dan broke in: "Haines, step over here behind me!"

For one instant Haines hesitated, and then obeyed silently.

"This is contempt of the law and an officer of the law," said Morris. "An" I'll see that you get fined so that—"

"Better cut it short there, sheriff," said one of the men. "I wouldn't go callin' the attention of folks to the way Jim Silent walked into your own house an' made his getaway without you tryin' to raise a hand. Law or no law, I'm with this stranger."

"Me too," said another; "any man who can fan a gun like him don't need no law."

The sheriff saw that the tide of opinion had set strongly against him and abandoned his position with speed if not with grace. Dan ordered Haines to walk before him outside the house. They faced each other in the dim moonlight.

"I've got one question to ask you," he said.

"Make it short," said Haines calmly. "I've got to do my talking before the lynching crowd."

"You can answer it in one word. Does Kate Cumberland—what is she to you?"

Lee Haines set his teeth.

"All the world," he said.

Even in the dim light he saw the yellow glow of Dan's eyes and he felt as if a wolf stood there trembling with eagerness to leap at his throat.

"An' what are you to her?"

"No more than the dirt under her feet!"

"Haines, you lie!"

"I tell you that if she cared for me as much as she does for the horse she rides on, I'd let the whole world know if I had to die for it the next moment."

Truth has a ring of its own.

"Haines, if I could hear that from her own lips, I'd let you go free. If you'll show me the way to Kate, I'll set you loose the minute I see her."

"I can't do it. I've given my faith to Silent and his men. Where she is, they are."

"Haines, that means death for you."

"I know it."

Another plan had come to Dan as they talked. He took Haines inside again and coming out once more, whistled for Bart. The wolf appeared as if by magic through the dark. He took out Kate's glove, which the wolf had brought to him in the willows, and allowed him to smell it. Bart whined eagerly. If he had that glove he would range the hills until he found its owner, directed to her by that strange instinct of the wild things. If Kate still loved him the glove would be more eloquent than a thousand messages. And if she managed to escape, the wolf would guide her back to his master.

He sat on his heels, caught the wolf on either side of the shaggy head, and stared into the glow of the yellow green eyes. It was as if the man were speaking to the wolf.

At last, as if satisfied, he drew a deep breath, rose, and dropped the glove. It was caught in the flashing teeth. For another moment Bart stood whining and staring up to the face of his master. Then he whirled and fled out into the night.

## CHAPTER XXI

## ONE WAY OUT

In a room of the Salton place, on the evening of the next day after Calder's death, sat Silent, with Kilduff, Rhinehart, and Jordan about him. Purvis was out scouting for the news of Haines, whose long absence commenced to worry the gang. Several times they tried to induce Kate to come out and talk with them, but she was resolute in staying alone in the room which they had assigned to her. Consequently, to while away the time, Bill Kilduff produced his mouth organ and commenced a dolorous ballad. He broke short in the midst of it and stared at the door. The others followed the direction of his eyes and saw Black Bart standing framed against the fading daylight. They started up with curses; Rhinehart drew his gun.

"Wait a minute," ordered Silent.

"Damn it!" exclaimed Jordan, "don't you see Whistling Dan's wolf? If the wolf's here, Dan isn't far behind."

Silent shook his head.

"If there's goin' to be any shootin' of that wolf leave it to Hal Purvis. He's jest nacherally set his heart on it. An' Whistlin' Dan ain't with the wolf. Look! there's a woman's glove hangin' out of his mouth. He picked that up in the willows, maybe, an' followed the girl here. Watch him!"

The wolf slunk across the room to the door which opened on Kate's apartment. Kate threw the door open—cried out at the sight of Bart—and then snatched up the glove he let drop at her feet.

"No cause for gettin' excited," said Silent. "Whistlin' Dan ain't comin' here after the wolf."

For answer she slammed the door.

At the same moment Hal Purvis entered. He stepped directly to Silent, and stood facing him with his hands resting on his hips. His smile was marvellously unpleasant.

"Well," said the chief, "what's the news? You got eloquent eyes, Hal, but I want words."

"The news is plain hell," said Purvis, "Haines—"

"What of him?"

"He's in Elkhead!"

"Elkhead?"

"Whistling Dan got him at Morris's place and took him in along with the body of Tex Calder. Jim, you got to answer for it to all of us. You went to Morris's with Lee. You come away without him and let him stay behind to be nabbed by that devil Whistlin' Dan."

"Right," said Kilduff, and his teeth clicked. "Is that playin' fair?"

"Boys," said Silent solemnly, "if I had knowed that Whistlin' Dan was there, I'd of never left Haines to stay behind. Morris said nothin' about Calder havin' a runnin' mate. Me an' Haines was in the upstairs room an' about suppertime up came a feller an' told us that Tex Calder had jest come into the dinin' room. That was all. Did Whistlin' Dan get Lee from behind?"

"He got him from the front. He beat Lee to the draw so bad that Haines hardly got his gun out of its leather!"

"The feller that told you that lied," said Silent. "Haines is as fast with his shootin' iron as I am—almost!"

The rest of the outlaws nodded to each other significantly.

Purvis went on without heeding the interruption. "After I found out about the fight I swung towards Elkhead. About five miles out of town I met up with Rogers, the deputy sheriff at Elkhead. I thought you had him fixed for us, Jim?"

"Damn his hide, I did. Is he playing us dirt now?"

"A frosty mornin' in December was nothin' to the way he talked."

"Cut all that short," said Rhinehart, "an' let's know if Rogers is goin' to be able to keep the lynching party away from Haines!"

"He says he thinks it c'n be done for a couple of days," said Purvis, "but the whole range is risin'. All the punchers are ridin' into Elkhead an' wantin' to take a look at the famous Lee Haines. Rogers says that when enough of 'em get together they'll take the law in their own hands an' nothin' can stop 'em then."

"Why don't the rotten dog give Haines a chance to make a getaway?" asked Silent. "Ain't we paid him his share ever since we started workin' these parts?"

"He don't dare take the chance," said Purvis. "He says the boys are talkin' mighty strong. They want action. They've put up a guard all around the jail an' they say that if Haines gets loose they'll string up Rogers. Everyone's wild about the killin' of Calder. Jim, ol' Saunderson, he's put up five thousand out of his own pocket to raise the price on your head!"

"An' this Whistlin' Dan," said Silent. "I s'pose they're makin' a hero out of him?"

"Rogers says every man within ten miles is talkin' about him. The whole range'll know of him in two days. He made a nice play when he got in. You know they's five thousand out on Haines's head. It was offered to him by Rogers as soon as Dan brought Lee in. What d'you think he done? Pocketed the cheque? No, he grabbed it, an' tore it up small: 'I ain't after no blood money,' he says."

"No," said Silent. "He ain't after no money—he's after me!"

"Tomorrow they bury Calder. The next day Whistlin' Dan'll be on our trail again—an' he'll be playin' the same lone hand. Rogers offered him a posse. He wouldn't take it."

"They's one pint that ain't no nearer bein' solved," said Bill Kilduff in a growl, "an' that's how you're goin' to get Haines loose. Silent, it's up to you. Which you rode away leavin' him behind."

Silent took one glance around that waiting circle. Then he nodded.

"It's up to me. Gimme a chance to think."

He started walking up and down the room, muttering. At last he stopped short.

"Boys, it can be done! They's nothin' like talkin' of a woman to make a man turn himself into a plumb fool, an' I'm goin' to make a fool out of Whistlin' Dan with this girl Kate!"

"But how in the name of God c'n you make her go out an' talk to him?" said Rhinehart.

"Son," answered Silent, "they's jest one main trouble with you—you talk a hell of a pile too much. When I've done this I'll tell you how it was figgered out!"


## CHAPTER XXII

## THE WOMAN'S WAY

It was a day later, in the morning, that a hand knocked at Kate's door and she opened it to Jim Silent. He entered, brushing off the dust of a long journey.

"Good mornin', Miss Cumberland."

He extended a hand which she overlooked.

"You still busy hatin' me?"

"I'm simply—surprised that you have come in here to talk to me."

"You look as if you seen somethin' in my face?" he said suspiciously. "What is it? Dirt?"

He brushed a hand across his forehead.

"Whatever it is," she answered, "you can't rub it away."

"I'm thinkin' of givin' you a leave of absence—if you'll promise to come back."

"Would you trust my honor?"

"In a pinch like this," he said amiably, "I would. But here's my business. Lee Haines is jailed in Elkhead. The man that put him behind the bars an' the only one that can take him out agin is Whistlin' Dan. An' the one person who can make Dan set Lee loose is you. Savvy? Will you go an' talk with Dan? This wolf of his would find him for you."

She shook her head.

"Why not?" cried Silent in a rising voice.

"The last time he saw me," she said, "he had reason to think that I tried to betray him because of Lee Haines. If I went to him now to plead for Haines he'd be sure that I was what he called me—Delilah!"

"Is that final?"

"Absolutely!"

"Now get me straight. They's a crowd of cowpunchers gatherin' in Elkhead, an' today or tomorrow they'll be strong enough to take the law into their own hands and organize a little lynchin' bee, savvy?"

She shuddered.

"It ain't pleasant, is it, the picture of big, good-lookin' Lee danglin' from the end of a rope with the crowd aroun' takin' pot-shots at him? No, it ain't, an' you're goin' to stop it. You're goin' to start from here in fifteen minutes with your hoss an' this wolf, after givin' me your promise to come back when you've seen Whistlin' Dan. You're goin' to make Dan go an' set Lee loose."

She smiled in derision.

"If Dan did that he'd be outlawed."

"You won't stir?"

"Not a step!"

"Well, kid, for everything that happens to Lee somethin' worse will happen to someone in the next room. Maybe you'd like to see him?"

He opened the door and she stepped into the entrance. Almost opposite her sat old Joe Cumberland with his hands tied securely behind his back. At sight of her he rose with a low cry. She turned on big Silent and whipped the six-gun from his hip. He barely managed to grasp her wrist and swing the heavy revolver out of line with his body.

"You little fiend," he snarled, "drop the gun, or I'll wring your neck."

"I don't fear you," she said, never wincing under the crushing grip on her wrists, "you murderer!"

He said, calmly repossessing himself of his gun, "Now take a long look at your father an' repeat all the things you was just sayin' to me."

She stared miserably at her father. When Silent caught Kate's hand Cumberland had started forward, but Kilduff and Rhinehart held him.

"What is it, Kate," he cried. "What does it mean?"

She explained it briefly: "This is Jim Silent!"

He remained staring at her with open mouth as if his brain refused to admit what his ear heard.

"There ain't no use askin' questions how an' why she's here," said Silent. "This is the pint. Lee Haines is behind the bars in Elkhead. Whistlin' Dan put him there an' maybe the girl c'n persuade Dan to bring him out again. If she don't—then everything the lynchin' gang does to Haines we're goin' to do to you. Git down on your ol' knees, Cumberland, an' beg your daughter to save your hide!"

The head of Kate dropped down.

"Untie his hands," she said. "I'll talk with Dan."

"I knew you'd see reason," grinned Silent.

"Jest one minute," said Cumberland. "Kate, is Lee Haines one of Silent's gang?"

"He is."

"An' Dan put him behind the bars?"

"Yes."

"If Dan takes him out again the boy'll be outlawed, Kate."

"Cumberland," broke in Kilduff savagely, "here's your call to stop thinkin' about Whistlin' Dan an' begin figgerin' for yourself."

"Don't you see?" said Kate, "it's your death these cowards mean."

Cumberland seemed to grow taller, he stood so stiffly erect with his chin high like a soldier.

"You shan't make no single step to talk with Dan!"

"Can't you understand that it's *you* they threaten?" she cried.

"I understan' it all," he said evenly. "I'm too old to have a young man damned for my sake."

"Shut him up!" ordered Silent. "The old fool!"

The heavy hand of Terry Jordan clapped over Joe's mouth effectually silenced him. He struggled vainly to speak again and Kate turned to Silent to shut out the sight.

"Tell your man to let him go," she said, "I will do what you wish."

"That's talkin' sense," said Silent. "Come out with me an' I'll saddle your hoss. Call the wolf."

He opened the door and in response to her whistle Black Bart trotted out and followed them out to the horse shed. There the outlaw quickly saddled Kate's pony.

He said: "Whistlin' Dan is sure headin' back in this direction because he's got an idea I'm somewhere near. Bart will find him on the way."

Silent was right. That morning Dan had started back towards Gus Morris's place, for he was sure that the outlaws were camped in that neighborhood. A little before noon he veered half a mile to the right towards a spring which welled out from a hillside, surrounded by a small grove of willows. Having found it, he drank, and watered Satan, then took off the saddle to ease the stallion, and lay down at a little distance for a ten-minute siesta, one of those half wakeful sleeps the habit of which he had learned from his wolf.

He was roused from the doze by a tremendous snorting and snarling and found Black Bart playing with Satan. It was their greeting after an absence, and they dashed about among the willows like creatures possessed. Dan brought horse and dog to a motionless stand with a single whistle, and then ran out to the edge of the willows. Down the side of the hill rode Kate at a brisk gallop. In a moment she saw him and called his name, with a welcoming wave of her arm. Now she was off her horse and running to him. He caught her hands and held her for an instant far from him like one striving to draw out the note of happiness into a song. They could not speak.

At last: "I knew you'd find a way to come."

"They let me go, Dan."

He frowned, and her eyes faltered from his.

"They sent me to you to ask you—to free Lee Haines!"

He dropped her hands, and she stood trying to find words to explain, and finding none.

"To free Haines?" he repeated heavily.

"It is Dad," she cried. "They have captured him, and they are holding him. They keep him in exchange for Haines."

"If I free Haines they'll outlaw me. You know that, Kate?"

She made a pace towards him, but he retreated.

"What can I do?" she pleaded desperately. "It is for my father—"

His face brightened as he caught at a new hope.

"Show me the way to Silent's hiding place and I'll free your father an' reach the end of this trail at the same time, Kate!"

She blenched pitifully. It was hopeless to explain.

"Dan—honey—I can't!"

She watched him miserably.

"I've given them my word to come back alone."

His head bowed. Out of the willows came Satan and Black Bart and stood beside him, the stallion nosing his shoulder affectionately.

"Dan, dear, won't you speak to me? Won't you tell me that you try to understand?"

He said at last: "Yes. I'll free Lee Haines."

The fingers of his right hand trailed slowly across the head of Black Bart. His eyes raised and looked past her far across the running curves of the hills, far away to the misty horizon.

"Kate—"

"Dan, you *do* understand?"

"I didn't know a woman could love a man the way you do Lee Haines. When I send him back to you tell him to watch himself. I'm playin' your game now, but if I meet him afterwards, I'll play my own."

All she could say was: "Will you listen to me no more, Dan?"

"Here's where we say good-bye."

He took her hand and his eyes were as unfathomable as a midnight sky. She turned to her horse and he helped her to the saddle with a steady hand.

That was all. He went back to the willows, his right arm resting on the withers of Black Satan as if upon the shoulder of a friend. As she reached the top of the hill she heard a whistling from the willows, a haunting complaint which brought the tears to her eyes. She spurred her tired horse to escape the sound.

## CHAPTER XXIII

## HELL STARTS

Between twilight and dark Whistling Dan entered Elkhead. He rose in the stirrups, on his toes, stretching the muscles of his legs. He was sensing his strength. So the pianist before he plays runs his fingers up and down the keys and sees that all is in tune and the touch perfect.

Two rival saloons faced each other at the end of the single street. At the other extremity of the lane stood the house of deputy sheriff Rogers, and a little farther was the jail. A crowd of horses stood in front of each saloon, but from the throngs within there came hardly a sound. The hush was prophetic of action; it was the lull before the storm. Dan slowed his horse as he went farther down the street.

The shadowy figure of a rider showed near the jail. He narrowed his eyes and looked more closely. Another, another, another horseman showed—four in sight on his side of the jail and probably as many more out of his vision.

Eight cattlemen guarded the place from which he must take Lee Haines, and every one of the eight, he had no doubt, was a picked man. Dan pulled up Satan to a walk and commenced to whistle softly. It was like one of those sounds of the wind, a thing to guess at rather than to know, but the effect upon Satan and Black Bart was startling.

The ears of the stallion dropped flat on his neck. He began to slink along with a gliding step which was very like the stealthy pace of Black Bart, stealing ahead. His footfall was as silent as if he had been shod with felt. Meantime Dan ran over a plan of action. He saw very clearly that he had little time for action. Those motionless guards around the jail made his task difficult enough, but there was a still greater danger. The crowds in the two saloons would be starting up the street for Haines before long. Their silence told him that.

A clatter of hoofs came behind him. He did not turn his head, but his hand dropped down to his revolver butt. The fast riding horseman swept and shot on down the street, leaving a pungent though invisible cloud of dust behind him. He stopped in front of Rogers's house and darted up the steps and through the door. Acting upon a premonition, Dan dismounted a short distance from Rogers's house and ran to the door. He opened it softly and found himself in a narrow hall dimly lighted by a smoking lamp. Voices came from the room to his right.

"What d'you mean, Hardy?" the deputy sheriff was saying.

"Hell's startin'!"

"There's a good many kinds of hell. Come out with it, Lee. I ain't no mind reader."

"They're gettin' ready for the big bust!"

"What big bust?"

"It ain't no use bluffin'. Ain't Silent told you that I'm on the inside of the game?"

"You fool!" cried Rogers. "Don't use that name!"

Dan slipped a couple of paces down the hall and flattened himself against the wall just as the door opened. Rogers looked out, drew a great breath of relief, and went back into the room. Dan resumed his former position.

"Now talk fast!" said Rogers.

"About time for you to drop that rotten bluff. Why, man, I could even tell you jest how much you've cost Jim Silent."

Rogers growled: "Tell me what's up."

"The boys are goin' for the jail tonight. They'll get out Haines an' string him up."

"It's comin' to him. He's played a hard game for a long time."

"An' so have you, Rogers, for a damn long time!"

Rogers swallowed the insult, apparently.

"What can I do?" he asked plaintively. "I'm willin' to give Silent and his gang a square deal."

"You should of done something while they was only a half-dozen cowpunchers in town. Now the town's full of riders an' they're all after blood."

"An' my blood if they don't get Haines!" broke in the deputy sheriff.

Hardy grunted.

"They sure are," he said. "I've heard 'em talk, an' they mean business. All of 'em. But how'd you answer to Jim Silent, Rogers? If you let 'em get Haines—well, Haines is Silent's partner an' Jim'll bust everything wide to get even with you."

"I c'n explain," said Rogers huskily. "I c'n show Silent how I'm helpless."

Footsteps went up and down the room.

"If they start anything," said Rogers, "I'll mark down the names of the ringleaders and I'll give 'em hell afterwards. That'll soothe Jim some."

"You won't know 'em. They'll wear masks."

Dan opened the door and stepped into the room. Rogers started up with a curse and gripped his revolver.

"I never knew you was so fond of gunplay," said Dan. "Maybe that gun of yours would be catchin' cold if you was to leave it out of the leather long?"

The sheriff restored his revolver slowly to the holster, glowering.

"An' Rogers won't be needin' you for a minute or two, went on Dan to Hardy.

They seemed to fear even his voice. The Wells Fargo agent vanished through the door and clattered down the steps.

"How long you been standin' at that door?" said Rogers, gnawing his lips.

"Jest for a breathin' space," said Dan.

Rogers squinted his eyes to make up for the dimness of the lamplight.

"By God!" he cried suddenly. "You're Whistlin' Dan Barry!"

He dropped into his chair and passed a trembling hand across his forehead.

He stammered: "Maybe you've changed your mind an' come back for that five thousand?"

"No, I've come for a man, not for money."

"A man?"

"I want Lee Haines before the crowd gets him."

"Would you really try to take Haines out?" asked Rogers with a touch of awe.

"Are there any guards in the jail?"

"Two. Lewis an' Patterson."

"Give me a written order for Haines."

The deputy wavered.

"If I do that I'm done for in this town!"

"Maybe. I want the key for Haines's handcuffs."

"Go over an' put your hoss up in the shed behind the jail," said Rogers, fighting for time, "an' when you come back I'll have the order written out an' give it to you with the key."

"Why not come over with me now?"

"I got some other business."

"In five minutes I'll be back," said Dan, and left the house.

Outside he whistled to Satan, and the stallion trotted up to him. He swung into the saddle and rode to the jail. There was not a guard in sight. He rode around to the other side of the building to reach the stable. Still he could not sight one of those shadowy horsemen who had surrounded the place a few minutes before. Perhaps the crowd had called in the guards to join the attack.

He put Satan away in the stable and as he led him into a stall he heard a roar of many voices far away. Then came the crack of half a dozen revolvers. Dan set his teeth and glanced quickly over the half-dozen horses in the little shed. He recognized the tall bay of Lee Haines at once and threw on its back the saddle which hung on a peg directly behind it. As he drew up the cinch another shout came from the street, but this time very close.

When he raced around the jail he saw the crowd pouring into the house of the deputy sheriff. He ran on till he came to the outskirts of the mob. Every man was masked, but in the excitement no one noticed that Dan's face was bare. Squirming his way through the press, Dan reached the deputy's office. It was almost filled. Rogers stood on a chair trying to argue with the cattlemen.

"No more talk, sheriff," thundered one among the cowpunchers, "we've had enough of your line of talk. Now we want some action of our own brand. For the last time: Are you goin' to order Lewis an' Patterson to give up Haines, or are you goin' to let two good men die fightin' for a damn lone rider?"

"What about the feller who's goin' to take Lee Haines out of Elkhead?" cried another.

The crowd yelled with delight.

"Yes, where is he? What about him?"

Rogers, glancing down from his position on the chair, stared into the brown eyes of Whistling Dan. He stretched out an arm that shook with excitement.

"That feller there!" he cried, "that one without a mask! Whistlin' Dan Barry is the man!"

## CHAPTER XXIV

### THE RESCUE

The throng gave back from Dan, as if from the vicinity of a panther. Dan faced the circle of scowling faces, smiling gently upon them.

"Look here, Barry," called a voice from the rear of the crowd, "why do you want to take Haines away? Throw in your cards with us. We need you."

"If it's fightin' you want," cried a joker, "maybe Lewis an' Patterson will give us all enough of it at the jail."

"I ain't never huntin' for trouble," said Dan.

"Make your play quick," said another. "We got no time to waste even on Dan Barry. Speak out, Dan. Here's a lot of good fellers aimin' to take out Haines an' give him what's due him—no more. Are you with us?"

"I'm not."

"Is that final?"

"It is."

"All right. Tie him up, boys. There ain't no other way!"

"Look out!" shouted a score of voices, for a gun flashed in Dan's hand.

He aimed at no human target. The bullet shattered the glass lamp into a thousand shivering and tinkling splinters. Thick darkness blotted the room. Instantly thereafter a blow, a groan, and the fall of a body; then a confused clamor.

"He's here!"

"Give up that gun, damn you!"

"You got the wrong man!"

"I'm Bill Flynn!"

"Guard the door!"

"Lights, for God's sake!"

"Help!"

A slender figure leaped up against the window and was dimly outlined by the starlight outside. There was a crash of falling glass, and as two or three guns exploded the figure leaped down outside the house.

"Follow him!"

"Who was that?"

"Get a light! Who's got a match?"

Half the men rushed out of the room to pursue that fleeing figure. The other half remained to see what had happened. It seemed impossible that Whistling Dan had escaped from their midst. Half a dozen sulphur matches spurted little jets of blue flame and discovered four men lying prone on the floor, most of them with the wind trampled from their bodies, but otherwise unhurt. One of them was the sheriff.

He lay with his shoulders propped against the wall. His mouth was a mass of blood.

"Who got you, Rogers?"

"Where's Barry?"

"The jail, the jail!" groaned Rogers. "Barry has gone for the jail!"

Revolvers rattled outside.

"He's gone for Haines," screamed the deputy. "Go get him, boys!"

"How can he get Haines? He ain't got the keys."

"He has, you fools! When he shot the lights out he jumped for me and knocked me off the chair. Then he went through my pockets and got the keys. Get on your way! Quick!"

The lynchers, yelling with rage, were already stamping from the room.

With the jangling bunch of keys in one hand and his revolver in the other, Dan started full speed for the jail as soon as he leaped down from the window. By the time he had covered half the intervening distance the first pursuers burst out of Rogers's house and opened fire after the shadowy fugitive. He whirled and fired three shots high in the air. No matter how impetuous, those warning shots would make the mob approach the jail with some caution.

On the door of the jail he beat furiously with the bunch of keys.

"What's up? Who's there?" cried a voice within.

"Message from Rogers. Hell's started! He's sent me with the keys!"

The door jerked open and a tall man, with a rifle slung across one arm, blocked the entrance.

"What's the message?" he asked.

"This!" said Dan, and drove his fist squarely into the other's face.

He fell without a cry and floundered on the floor, gasping. Dan picked him up and shoved him through the door, bolting it behind him. A narrow hall opened before him and ran the length of the small building. He glanced into the room on one side. It was the kitchen and eating room in one. He rushed into the one on the other side. Two men were there. One was Haines, sitting with his hands manacled. The other was the second guard, who ran for Dan, whipping his rifle to his shoulder. As flame spurted from the mouth of the gun, Dan dived at the man's knees and brought him to the floor with a crash. He rose quickly and leaned over the fallen man, who lay without moving, his arms spread wide. He had struck on his forehead when he dropped. He was stunned for the moment, but not seriously hurt. Dan ran to Haines, who stood with his hands high above his head. Far away was the shout of the coming crowd.

"Shoot and be damned!" said Haines sullenly.

For answer Dan jerked down the hands of the lone rider and commenced to try the keys on the handcuffs. There were four keys. The fourth turned the lock. Haines shouted as his hands fell free.

"After me!" cried Dan, and raced for the stable.

As they swung into their saddles outside the shed, the lynchers raced their horses around the jail.

"Straightaway!" called Dan. "Through the cottonwoods and down the lane. After me. Satan!"

The stallion leaped into a full gallop, heading straight for a tall group of cottonwoods beyond which was a lane fenced in with barbed wire. Half a dozen of the pursuers were in a position to cut them off, and now rushed for the cottonwoods, yelling to their comrades to join them. A score of lights flashed like giant fireflies as the lynchers opened fire.

"They've blocked the way!" groaned Haines.

Three men had brought their horses to a sliding stop in front of the cottonwoods and their revolvers cracked straight in the faces of Dan and Haines. There was no other way for escape. Dan raised his revolver and fired twice, aiming low. Two of the horses reared and pitched to the ground. The third rider had a rifle at his shoulder. He was holding his fire until he had drawn a careful bead. Now his gun spurted and Dan bowed far over his saddle as if he had been struck from behind.

Before the rifleman could fire again Black Bart leaped high in the air. His teeth closed on the shoulder of the lyncher and the man catapulted from his saddle to the ground. With his yell in their ears, Dan and Haines galloped through the cottonwoods, and swept down the lane.

## CHAPTER XXV

### THE LONG RIDE

A cheer of triumph came from the lynchers. In fifty yards the fugitives learned the reason, for they glimpsed a high set of bars blocking the lane. Dan pulled back beside Haines.

"Can the bay make it?" he called.

"No. I'm done for."

For answer Dan caught the bridle of Lee's horse close to the bit. They were almost to the bars. A dark shadow slid up and over them. It was Black Bart, with his head turned to look back even as he jumped, as if he were setting an example which he bid them follow. Appallingly high the bars rose directly in front of them.

"Now!" called Dan to the tall bay, and jerked up on the bit.

Satan rose like a swallow to the leap. The bay followed in gallant imitation. For an instant they hung poised in air. Then Satan pitched to the ground, landing safely and lightly on four cat-like feet. A click and a rattle behind them—the bay was also over, but his hind hoofs had knocked down the top bar. He staggered, reeled far to one side, but recovering, swept on after Satan and Dan. A yell of disappointment rang far behind.

Glancing back Haines saw the foremost of the pursuers try to imitate the feat of the fugitives, but even with the top bar down he failed. Man and horse pitched to the ground.

For almost a mile the lane held straight on, and beyond stretched the open country. They were in that free sweep of hills before the pursuers remounted beyond the bars. In daytime a mile would have been a small handicap, but with the night and the hills to cover their flight, and with such mounts as Satan and the tall bay, they were safe. In half an hour all sound of them died out, and Haines, following Dan's example, slowed his horse to an easy gallop.

The long rider was puzzled by his companion's horsemanship, for Dan rode leaning far to the right of his saddle, with his head bowed. Several times Haines was on the verge of speaking, but he refrained. He commenced to sing in the exultation of freedom. An hour before he had been in the "rat-trap" with a circle of lynchers around him, and only two terror-stricken guards to save him from the most horrible of deaths. Then came Fate and tore him away and gave him to the liberty of the boundless hills. Fate in the person of this slender, somber man. He stared at Dan with awe.

At the top of a hill his companion drew rein, reeling in the saddle with the suddenness of the halt. However, in such a horseman, this could not be. It must be merely a freak feature of his riding.

"Move," said Dan, his breath coming in pants. "Line out and get to her."

"To who?" said Haines, utterly bewildered.

"Delilah!"

"What?"

"Damn you, she's waitin' for you."

"In the name of God, Barry, why do you talk like this after you've saved me from hell?"

He stretched out his hand eagerly, but Dan reined Satan back.

"Keep your hand. I hate you worse'n hell. There ain't room enough in the world for us both. If you want to thank me do it by keepin' out of my path. Because the next time we meet you're goin' to die, Haines. It's writ in a book. Now feed your hoss the spur and run for Kate Cumberland. But remember—I'm goin' to get you again if I can."

"Kate—" began Haines. "She sent you for me?"

Only the yellow blazing eyes made answer and the wail of a coyote far away on the shadowy hill.

"Kate!" cried Haines again, but now there was a world of new meaning in his voice. He swung his horse and spurred down the slope.

At the next hillcrest he turned in the saddle, saw the motionless rider still outlined against the sky, and brought the bay to a halt. He was greatly troubled. For a reason mysterious and far beyond the horizon of his knowledge, Dan was surrendering Kate Cumberland to him.

"He's doing it while he still loves her," muttered Haines, "and am I cur enough to take her from him after he has saved me from God knows what?"

He turned his horse to ride back, but at that moment he caught the weird, the unearthly note of Dan's whistling. There was both melancholy and gladness in it. The storm wind running on the hills and exulting in the blind terror of the night had such a song as this to sing.

"If he was a man," Haines argued briefly with himself, "I'd do it. But he isn't a man. He's a devil. He has no more heart than the wolf which owns him as master. Shall I give a girl like Kate Cumberland to that wild panther? She's mine—all mine!"

Once more he turned his horse and this time galloped steadily on into the night.

When Haines dropped out of sight, Dan's whistling stopped. He looked up to the pitiless glitter of the stars. He looked down to the somber sweep of black hills. The wind was like a voice saying over and over again: "Failure." Everything was lost.

He slipped from the saddle and took off his coat. From his left shoulder the blood welled slowly, steadily. He tore a strip from his shirt and attempted to make a bandage, but he could not manage it with one hand.

The world thronged with hostile forces eager to hunt him to the death. He needed all his strength, and now that was ebbing from a wound which a child could have staunched for him, but where could he find even a friendly child? Truly all was lost! The satyr or the black panther once had less need of man's help than had Dan, but now he was hurt in body and soul. That matchless co-ordination of eye with hand and foot was gone. He saw Kate smiling into the eyes of Haines; he imagined Bill Kilduff sitting on the back of Satan, controlling all that glorious force and speed; he saw Hal Purvis fighting venomously with Bart for the mastery which eventually must belong to the man.

He turned to the wild pair. Vaguely they sensed a danger threatening their master, and their eyes mourned for his hurt. He buried his face on the strong, smooth shoulder of Satan, and groaned. There came the answering whinny and the hot breath of the horse against the side of his face. There was the whine of Black Bart behind him, then the rough tongue of the wolf touched the dripping fingers. Then he felt a hot gust of the wolf's breath against his hand.

Too late he realized what that meant. He whirled with a cry of command, but the snarl of Black Bart cut it short. The wolf stood bristling, trembling with eagerness for the kill, his great white fangs gleaming, his snarl shrill and guttural with the frenzy of his desire, for he had tasted blood. Dan understood as he stared into the yellow green fury of the wolf's eyes, yet he felt no fear, only a glory in the fierce, silent conflict. He could not move the fingers of his left hand, but those of his right curved, stiffened. He desired nothing more in the world than the contact with that great, bristling black body, to leap aside from those ominous teeth, to set his fingers in the wolf's throat. Reason might have told him the folly of such a strife, but all that remained in his mind was the love of combat—a blind passion. His eyes glowed like those of the wolf, yellow fire against the green. Black Bart crouched still lower, gathering himself for the spring, but he was held by the man's yellow gleaming eyes. They invited the battle. Fear set its icy hand on the soul of the wolf.

The man seemed to tower up thrice his normal height. His voice rang, harsh, sudden, unlike the utterance of man or beast: *"Down!"*

Fear conquered Black Bart. The fire died from his eyes. His body sank as if from exhaustion. He crawled on his belly to the feet of his master and whined an unutterable submission.

And then that hand, warm and wet with the thing whose taste set the wolf's heart on fire with the lust to kill, was thrust against his nose. He leaped back with bared teeth, growling horribly. The eyes commanded him back, commanded him relentlessly. He howled dismally to the senseless stars, yet he came; and once more that hand was thrust against his nose. He licked the fingers.

That bloodlust came hotter than before, but his fear was greater. He licked the strange hand again, whining. Then the master kneeled. Another hand, clean, and free from that horrible warm, wet sign of death, fell upon his shaggy back. The voice which he knew of old came to him, blew away the red mist from his soul, comforted him.

"Poor Bart!" said the voice, and the hand went slowly over his head. "It weren't your fault."

The stallion whinnied softly. A deep growl formed in the throat of the wolf, a mighty effort at speech. And now, like a gleam of light in a dark room, Dan remembered the house of Buck Daniels. There, at least, they could not refuse him aid. He drew on his coat, though the effort set him sweating with agony, got his foot in the stirrup with difficulty, and dragged himself to the saddle. Satan started at a swift gallop.

"Faster, Satan! Faster, partner!"

What a response! The strong body settled a little closer to the earth as the stride increased. The rhythm of the pace grew quicker, smoother. There was no adequate phrase to describe the matchless motion. And in front— always just a little in front with the plunging forefeet of the horse seeming to threaten him at every stride, ran Black Bart with his head turned as if he were the guard and guide of the fugitive.

Dan called and Black Bart yelped in answer. Satan tossed up his head and neighed as he raced along. The two replies were like human assurances that there was still a fighting chance.

The steady loss of blood was telling rapidly now. He clutched the pommel, set his teeth, and felt oblivion settle slowly and surely upon him. As his senses left him he noted the black outlines of the next high range of hills, a full ten miles away.

He only knew the pace of Satan never slackened. There seemed no effort in it. He was like one of those fabled horses, the offspring of the wind, and like the wind, tireless, eternal of motion.

A longer oblivion fell upon Dan. As he roused from it he found himself slipping in the saddle. He struggled desperately to grasp the saddlehorn and managed to draw himself up again; but the warning was sufficient to make him hunt about for some means of making himself more secure in the saddle. It was a difficult task to do anything with only one hand, but he managed to tie his left arm to the bucking-strap. If the end came, at least he was sure to die in the saddle. Vaguely he was aware as he looked around that the black hills were no longer in the distance. He was among them.

On went Satan. His breath was coming more and more labored. It seemed to Dan's dim consciousness that some of the spring was gone from that glorious stride which swept on and on with the slightest undulation, like a swallow skimming before the wind; but so long as strength remained he knew that Satan would never falter in his pace. As the delirium swept once more shadow like on his brain, he allowed himself to fall forward, and wound his fingers as closely as possible in the thick mane. His left arm jerked horribly against the bonds. Black night swallowed him once more.

Only his invincible heart kept Satan going throughout that last stretch. His ears lay flat on his neck, lifting only when the master muttered and raved in his fever. Foam flew back against his throat and breast. His breath came shorter, harder, with a rasp; but the gibbering voice of his rider urged him on, faster, and faster. They topped a small hill, and a little to the left and a mile away, rose a group of cottonwoods, and Dan, recovering consciousness, knew the house of Buck. He also knew that his last moment of consciousness was come. Surges of sleepy weakness swept over his brain. He could never guide Satan to the house.

"Bart!" he called feebly.

The wolf, whining, dropped back beside him. Dan pointed his right arm straight ahead. Black Bart leaped high into the air and his shrill yelp told that he had seen the cottonwoods and the house.

Dan summoned the last of his power and threw the reins over the head of Satan.

"Take us in, Bart," he said, and twisting his fingers into Satan's mane fell across the saddlehorn.

Satan, understanding the throwing of the reins as an order to halt, came to a sharp stop, and the body of the senseless rider sagged to one side. Black Bart caught the reins. They were bitter and salt with blood of the master.

He tugged hard. Satan whinnied his doubt, and the growl of Black Bart answered, half a threat. In a moment more they were picking their way through the brush towards the house of Buck Daniels.

Satan was far gone with exhaustion. His head drooped; his legs sprawled with every step; his eyes were glazed. Yet he staggered on with the great black wolf pulling at the reins. There was the salt taste of blood in the mouth of Black Bart; so he stalked on, saliva dripping from his mouth, and his eyes glazed with the lust to kill. His furious snarling was the threat which urged on the stallion.

## CHAPTER XXVI

### BLACK BART TURNS NURSE

It was old Mrs. Daniels who woke first at the sound of scratching and growling. She roused her husband and son, and all three went to the door, Buck in the lead with his six-gun in his hand. At sight of the wolf he started back and raised the gun, but Black Bart fawned about his feet.

"Don't shoot—it's a dog, an' there's his master!" cried Sam. "By the Lord, they's a dead man tied on that there hoss!"

Dan lay on Satan, half fallen from the saddle, with his head hanging far down, only sustained by the strength of the rein. The stallion, wholly spent, stood with his legs braced, his head low, and his breath coming in great gasps. The family ran to the rescue. Sam cut the rein and Buck lowered the limp body in his arms.

"Buck, is he dead?" whispered Mrs. Daniels.

"I don't feel no heartbeat," said Buck. "Help me fetch him into the house, Dad!"

"Look out for the hoss!" cried Sam.

Buck started back with his burden just in time, for Satan, surrendering to his exhaustion, pitched to the ground, and lay with sprawling legs like a spent dog rather than a horse.

"Let the hoss be," said Buck. "Help me with the man. He's hurt bad."

Mrs. Daniels ran ahead and lighted a lamp. They laid the body carefully upon a bed. It made a ghastly sight, the bloodless face with the black hair fallen wildly across the forehead, the mouth loosely open, and the lips black with dust.

"Dad!" said Buck. "I think I've seen this feller. God knows if he's livin' or dead."

He dropped to his knees and pressed his ear over Dan's heart.

"I can't feel no motion. Ma, get that hand mirror—"

She had it already and now held it close to the lips of the wounded man. When she drew it away their three heads drew close together.

"They's a mist on it! He's livin'!" cried Buck.

"It ain't nothing," said Sam. "The glass ain't quite clear, that's all."

Mrs. Daniels removed the last doubt by running her finger across the surface of the glass. It left an unmistakable mark.

They wasted no moment then. They brought hot and cold water, washed out his wound, cleansed away the blood; and while Mrs. Daniels and her husband fixed the bandage, Buck pounded and rubbed the limp body to restore the circulation. In a few minutes his efforts were rewarded by a great sigh from Dan.

He shouted in triumph, and then: "By God, it's Whistlin' Dan Barry."

"It is!" said Sam. "Buck, they's been devils workin' tonight. It sure took more'n one man to nail him this way."

They fell to work frantically. There was a perceptible pulse, the breathing was faint but steady, and a touch of color came in the face.

"His arm will be all right in a few days," said Mrs. Daniels, "but he may fall into a fever. He's turnin' his head from side to side and talkin'. What's he sayin', Buck?"

"He's sayin': 'Faster, Satan.'"

"That's the hoss," interpreted Sam.

"'Hold us straight, Bart!' That's what he's sayin' now."

"That's the wolf."

"'An' it's all for Delilah!' Who's Delilah, Dad?"

"Maybe it's some feller Dan knows."

"Some feller?" repeated Mrs. Daniels with scorn. "It's some worthless girl who got Whistlin' Dan into this trouble."

Dan's eyes opened but there was no understanding in them.

"Haines, I hate you worse'n hell!"

"It's Lee Haines who done this!" cried Sam.

"If it is, I'll cut out his heart!"

"It can't be Haines," broke in Mrs. Daniels. "Old man Perkins, didn't he tell us that Haines was the man that Whistlin' Dan Barry had brought down into Elkhead? How could Haines do this shootin' while he was in jail?"

"Ma," said Sam, "you watch Whistlin' Dan. Buck an' me'll take care of the hoss—that black stallion. He's pretty near all gone, but he's worth savin'. What I don't see is how he found his way to us. It's certain Dan didn't guide him all the way."

"How does the wind find its way?" said Buck. "It was the wolf that brought Dan here, but standin' here talkin' won't tell us how. Let's go out an' fix up Satan."

It was by no means an easy task. As they approached the horse he heaved himself up, snorting, and stood with legs braced, and pendant head. Even his eyes were glazed with exhaustion, but behind them it was easy to guess the dauntless anger which raged against these intruders. Yet he would have been helpless against them. It was Black Bart who interfered at this point. He stood before them, his hair bristling and his teeth bared.

Sam suggested: "Leave the door of the house open an' let him hear Whistlin' Dan's voice."

It was done. At once the delirious voice of Dan stole out to them faintly. The wolf turned his head to Satan with a plaintive whine, as if asking why the stallion remained there when that voice was audible. Then he raced for the open door and disappeared into the house.

"Hurry in, Buck!" called Sam. "Maybe the wolf'll scare Ma!"

They ran inside and found Black Bart on the bed straddling the body of Whistling Dan, and growling at poor Mrs. Daniels, who crouched in a corner of the room. It required patient work before he was convinced that they actually meant no harm to his master.

"What's the reason of it?" queried Sam helplessly. "The damn wolf let us take Dan off the hoss without makin' any fuss."

"Sure he did," assented Buck, "but he ain't sure of me yet, an' every time he comes near me he sends the cold chills up my back."

Having decided that he might safely trust them to touch Dan's body, the great wolf went the round and sniffed them carefully, his hair bristling and the forbidding growl lingering in his throat. In the end he apparently decided that they might be tolerated, though he must keep an eye upon their actions. So he sat down beside the bed and followed with an anxious eye every movement of Mrs. Daniels. The men went back to the stallion. He still stood with legs braced far apart, and head hanging low. Another mile of that long race and he would have dropped dead beneath his rider.

Nevertheless at the coming of the strangers he reared up his head a little and tried to run away. Buck caught the dangling reins near the bit. Satan attempted to strike out with his fore hoof. It was a movement as clumsy and slow as the blow of a child, and Buck easily avoided it. Realizing his helplessness Satan whinnied a heart-breaking appeal for help to his unfailing friend, Black Bart. The wail of the wolf answered dolefully from the house.

"Good Lord," groaned Buck. "Now we'll have that black devil on our hands again."

"No, we won't," chuckled Sam, "the wolf won't leave Dan. Come on along, old hoss."

Nevertheless it required hard labor to urge and drag the stallion to the stable. At the end of that time they had the saddle off and a manger full of fodder before him. They went back to the house with the impression of having done a day's work.

"Which it shows the fool nature of a hoss," moralized Sam. "That stallion would be willin' to lay right down and die for the man that's jest rode him up to the front door of death, but he wishes everlastingly that he had the strength to kick the daylight out of you an' me that's been tryin' to take care of him. You jest write this down inside your brain, Buck: a hoss is like a woman. They jest nacherally ain't no reason in 'em!"

They found Dan in a heavy sleep, his breath coming irregularly. Mrs. Daniels stated that it was the fever which she had feared and she offered to sit up with the sick man through the rest of that night. Buck lifted her from the chair and took her place beside the bed.

"No one but me is goin' to take care of Whistlin' Dan," he stated.

So the vigil began, with Buck watching Dan, and Black Bart alert, suspicious, ready at the first wrong move to leap at the throat of Buck.

## CHAPTER XXVII

## NOBODY LAUGHS

That night the power which had sent Dan into Elkhead, Jim Silent, stood his turn at watch in the narrow canyon below the old Salton place. In the house above him sat Terry Jordan, Rhinehart, and Hal Purvis playing poker, while Bill Kilduff drew a drowsy series of airs from his mouth-organ. His music was getting on the nerves of the other three, particularly Jordan and Rhinehart, for Purvis was winning steadily.

"Let up!" broke out Jordan at last, pounding on the table with his fist. "Your damn tunes are gettin' my goat. Nobody can think while you're hittin' it up like that. This ain't no prayer meetin', Bill."

For answer Kilduff removed the mouth organ to take a deep breath, blinked his small eyes, and began again in a still higher key.

"Go slow, Terry," advised Rhinehart in a soft tone. "Kilduff ain't feelin' none too well tonight."

"What's the matter with him?" growled the scar-faced man, none too anxious to start an open quarrel with the formidable Kilduff.

Rhinehart jerked his thumb over his shoulder.

"The gal in there. He don't like the game the chief has been workin' with her."

"Neither do I," said Purvis, "but I'd do worse than the chief done to get Lee Haines back."

"Get Haines back?" said Kilduff, his voice ominously deep. "There ain't no chance of that. If there was I wouldn't have no kick against the chief for what he's done to Kate."

"Maybe there's *some* chance," suggested Rhinehart.

"Chance, hell!" cried Kilduff. "One man agin a whole town full? I say all that Jim has done is to get Whistlin' Dan plugged full of lead."

"Well," said Purvis, "if that's done, ain't the game worth while?"

The rest of the men chuckled and even Kilduff smiled.

"Old Joe Cumberland is sure takin' it hard," said "Calamity" Rhinehart. "All day he's been lightin' into the girl."

"The funny part," mused Purvis, "is that the old boy really means it. I think he'd of sawed off his right hand to keep her from goin' to Whistlin' Dan."

"An' her sittin' white-faced an' starin' at nothin' an' tryin' to comfort *him!*" rumbled Kilduff, standing up under the stress of his unwonted emotion. "My God, she was apologizin' for what she done, an' tryin' to cheer him up, an' all the time her heart was bustin'."

He pulled out a violently colored bandana and wiped his forehead.

"When we all get down to hell," he said, "they'll be quite a little talkin' done about this play of Jim's—you c'n lay to that."

"Who's that singin' down the canyon?" asked Jordan. "It sounds like—"

He would not finish his sentence as if he feared to prove a false prophet. They rose as one man and stared stupidly at one another.

"Haines!" broke out Rhinehart at last.

"It ain't no ways possible!" said Kilduff. "And yet—by God, it is!"

They rushed for the door and made out two figures approaching, one on horseback, and the other on foot.

"Haines!" called Purvis, his shrill voice rising to a squeak with his excitement.

"Here I am!" rang back the mellow tones of the big lone rider, and in a moment he and Jim Silent entered the room.

Glad faces surrounded him. There was infinite wringing of his hand and much pounding on the back. Kilduff and Rhinehart pushed him back into a chair. Jordan ran for a flask of whisky, but Haines pushed the bottle away.

"I don't want anything on my breath," he said, "because I have to talk to a woman. Where's Kate?"

The men glanced at each other uneasily.

"She's here, all right," said Silent hastily. "Now tell us how you got away."

"Afterwards," said Haines. "But first Kate."

"What's your hurry to see her?" said Kilduff.

Haines laughed exultantly.

"You're jealous, Bill! Why, man, she sent for me! Sent Whistling Dan himself for me."

"Maybe she did," said Kilduff, "but that ain't no partic'lar sign I'm jealous. Tell us about the row in Elkhead."

"That's it," said Jordan. "We can't wait, Lee."

"Just one word explains it," said Haines. "Barry!"

"What did he do?" This from every throat at once.

"Broke into the jail with all Elkhead at his heels flashing their six-guns—knocked down the two guards—unlocked my bracelets (God knows where he got the key!)—shoved me onto the bay—drove away with me—shot down two men while his wolf pulled down a third—made my horse jump a set of bars as high as my head—and here I am!"

There was a general loosening of bandanas. The eyes of Jim Silent gleamed.

"And all Elkhead knows that he's the man who took you out of jail?" he asked eagerly.

"Right. He's put his mark on them," responded Haines, "but the girl, Jim!"

"By God!" said Silent. "I've got him! The whole world is agin him—the law an' the outlaws. He's done for!"

He stopped short.

"Unless you're feelin' uncommon grateful to him for what he done for you, Lee?"

"He told me he hated me like hell," said Haines. "I'm grateful to him as I'd be to a mountain lion that happened to do me a good turn. Now for Kate!"

"Let him see her," said Silent. "That's the quickest way. Call her out, Haines. We'll take a little walk while you're with her."

The moment they were gone Haines rushed to the door and knocked loudly. It was opened at once and Kate stood before him. She winced at sight of him.

"It's I, Kate!" he cried joyously. "I've come back from the dead."

She stepped from the room and closed the door behind her.

"What of Dan? Tell me! Was—was he hurt?"

"Dan?" he repeated with an impatient smile. "No, he isn't hurt. He pulled me through—got me out of jail and safe into the country. He had to drop two or three of the boys to do it."

Her head fell back a little and in the dim light, for the first time, he saw her face with some degree of clearness, and started at its pallor.

"What's the matter, Kate—dear?" he said anxiously.

"What of Dan?" she asked faintly.

"I don't know. He's outlawed. He's done for. The whole range will be against him. But why are you so worried about him, Kate? When he told me that you loved me—"

She straightened.

"Love? *You?*"

His face lengthened almost ludicrously.

"But why—Dan came for me—he said you sent him—he—" he broke down, stammering, utterly confused.

"This is why I sent him!" she answered, and throwing open the door gestured to him to enter.

He followed her and saw the lean figure of old Joe Cumberland lying on a blanket close to the wall.

"That's why!" she whispered.

"How does he come here?"

"Ask the devil in his human form! Ask your friend, Jim Silent!"

He walked into the outer room with his head low. He found the others already returned. Their carefully controlled grins spoke volumes.

"Where's Silent?" he asked heavily.

"He's gone," said Jordan.

Hal Purvis took Haines to one side.

"Take a brace," he urged.

"She hates me, Hal," said the big fellow sadly. "For God's sake, was there no other way of getting me out?"

"Not one! Pull yourself together, Lee. There ain't no one for you to hold a spite agin. Would you rather be back in Elkhead dangling from the end of a rope?"

"It seems to have been a sort of—joke," said Haines.

"Exactly. But at that sort of a joke nobody laughs!"

"And Whistling Dan Barry?"

"He's done for. We're all agin him, an' now even the rangers will help us hunt him down. Think it over careful, Haines. You're agin him because you want the girl. I want that damned wolf of his, Black Bart. Kilduff would rather get into the saddle of Satan than ride to heaven. An' Jim Silent won't never rest till he sees Dan lyin' on the ground with a bullet through his heart. Here's four of us. Each of us want something that belongs to him, from his life to his dog. Haines, I'm askin' you man to man, was there any one ever born who could get away from four men like us?"

## CHAPTER XXVIII

## WHISTLING DAN, DESPERADO

It was an urgent business which sent Silent galloping over the hills before dawn. When the first light came he was close to the place of Gus Morris. He slowed his horse to a trot, but after a careful reconnoitering, seeing no one stirring around the sheriff's house, he drew closer and commenced to whistle a range song, broken here and there with a significant phrase which sounded like a signal. Finally a cloth was waved from a window, and Silent, content, turned his back on the house, and rode away at a walk.

Within half an hour the pounding of a horse approached from behind. The plump sheriff came to a halt beside him, jouncing in the saddle with the suddenness of the stop.

"What's up?" he called eagerly.

"Whistlin' Dan."

"What's new about him? I know they're talkin' about that play he made agin Haines. They's some says he's a faster man than you, Jim!"

"They say too damned much!" snarled Silent. "This is what's new. Whistlin' Dan Barry—no less—has busted open the jail at Elkhead an' set Lee Haines free."

The sheriff could not speak.

"I fixed it, Gus. I staged the whole little game."

"*You* fixed it with Whistlin' Dan?"

"Don't ask me how I worked it. The pint is that he did the job. He got into the jail while the lynchers was guardin' it, gettin' ready for a rush. They opened fire. It was after dark last night. Haines an' Dan made a rush for it from the stable on their hosses. They was lynchers everywhere. Haines didn't have no gun. Dan wouldn't trust him with one. He did the shootin' himself. He dropped two of them with two shots. His devil of a wolf-dog brung down another."

"Shootin' at night?"

"Shootin' at night," nodded Silent. "An'' now, Gus, they's only one thing left to complete my little game—an' that's to get Whistlin' Dan Barry proclaimed an outlaw an' put a price on his head, savvy?"

"Why d'you hate him so?" asked Morris curiously.

"Morris, why d'you hate smallpox?"

"Because a man's got no chance fightin' agin it."

"Gus, that's why I hate Whistlin' Dan, but I ain't here to argue. I want you to get Dan proclaimed an outlaw."

The sheriff scowled and bit his lip.

"I can't do it, Jim."

"Why the hell can't you?"

"Don't go jumpin' down my throat. It ain't human to double cross nobody the way you're double crossin' that kid. He's clean. He fights square. He's jest done you a good turn. I can't do it, Jim."

There was an ominous silence.

"Gus," said the outlaw, "how many thousand have I given you?"

The sheriff winced.

"I dunno," he said, "a good many, Jim."

"An' now you're goin' to lay down on me?"

Another pause.

"People are gettin' pretty excited nowadays," went on Silent carelessly. "Maybe they'd get a lot more excited if they was to know jest how much I've paid you, Gus."

The sheriff struck his forehead with a pudgy hand.

"When a man's sold his soul to the devil they ain't no way of buyin' it back."

"When you're all waked up," said Silent soothingly, "they ain't no more reasonable man than you, Gus. But sometimes you get to seein' things cross-eyed. Here's my game. What do you think they'd do in Elkhead if a letter came for Dan Barry along about now?"

"The boys must be pretty hot," said the sheriff. "I suppose the letter'd be opened."

"It would," said the outlaw. "You're sure a clever feller, Gus. You c'n see a white hoss in the sunlight. Now what d'you suppose they'd think if they opened a letter addressed to Dan Barry and read something like this:

" 'Dear Dan: You made great play for L.H. None of us is going to forget it. Maybe the thing for you to do is to lay low for a while. Then join us any time you want to. We all think nobody could of worked that stunt any smoother than you done. The rest of the boys say that two thousand ain't enough for the work you've done. They vote that you get an extra thousand for it. I'm agreeable about that, and when you get short of cash just drop up and see us—you know where.

" 'That's a great bluff you've made about being on my trail. Keep it up. It'll fool everybody for a while. They'll think, maybe, that what you did for L.H. was because he was your personal friend. They won't suspect that you're now one of us. Adios,

" 'J.S.' "

Silent waited for the effect of this missive to show in Morris's face.

"Supposin' they was to read a letter like that, Gus. D'you think maybe it'd sort of peeve them?"

"He'd be outlawed inside of two days!"

"Right. Here's the letter. An' you're goin' to see that it's delivered in Elkhead, Morris."

The sheriff looked sombrely on the little square of white.

"I sort of think," he said at last, "that this here's the death warrant for Whistlin' Dan Barry."

"So do I," grinned Silent, considerably thirsty for action. "That's your chance to make one of your rarin', tarin' speeches. Then you hop into the telegraph office an' send a wire to the Governor askin' that a price be put on the head of the bloodthirsty desperado, Dan Barry, commonly known as Whistlin' Dan."

"It's like something out of a book," said the sheriff slowly. "It's like some damned horror story."

"The minute you get the reply to that telegram swear in forty deputies and announce that they's a price on Barry's head. So long, Gus. This little play'll make the boys figger you're the most efficient sheriff that never pulled a gun."

He turned his horse, laughing loudly, and the sheriff, with that laughter in his ears, rode back towards his hotel with a downward head.

* * * * *

All day at the Daniels's house the fever grew perceptibly, and that night the family held a long consultation.

"They's got to be somethin' done," said Buck. "I'm goin' to ride into town tomorrow an' get ahold of Doc Geary."

"There ain't no use of gettin' that fraud Geary," said Mrs. Daniels scornfully. "I think that if the boy c'n be saved I c'n do it as well as that doctor. But there ain't no doctor c'n help him. The trouble with Dan ain't his wound—it's his mind that's keepin' him low."

"His mind?" queried old Sam.

"Listen to him now. What's all that talkin' about Delilah?"

"If it ain't Delilah it's Kate," said Buck. "Always one of the two he's talkin' about. An' when he talks of them his fever gets worse. Who's Delilah, an' who's Kate?"

"They's one an' the same person," said Mrs. Daniels. "It do beat all how blind men are!"

"Are we now?" said her husband with some heat. "An' what good would it do even if we knowed that they was the same?"

"Because if we could locate the girl they's a big chance she'd bring him back to reason. She'd make his brain quiet, an' then his body'll take care of itself, savvy?"

"But they's a hundred Kates in the range," said Sam. "Has he said her last name, Buck, or has he given you any way of findin' out where she lives?"

"There ain't no way," brooded Buck, "except that when he talks about her sometimes he speaks of Lee Haines like he wanted to kill him. Sometimes he's dreamin' of havin' Lee by the throat. D'you honest think that havin' the girl here would do any good, ma?"

"Of course it would," she answered. "He's in love, that poor boy is, an' love is worse than bullets for some men. I don't mean you or Sam. Lord knows you wouldn't bother yourselves none about a woman."

Her eyes challenged them.

"He talks about Lee havin' the girl?" asked Sam.

"He sure does," said Buck, "which shows that he's jest ravin'. How could Lee have the girl, him bein' in jail at Elkhead?"

"But maybe Lee had her before Whistlin' Dan got him at Morris's place. Maybe she's up to Silent's camp now."

"A girl in Jim Silent's camp?" repeated Buck scornfully. "Jim'd as soon have a ton of lead hangin' on his shoulders."

"Would he though?" broke in Mrs. Daniels. "You're considerable young, Buck, to be sayin' what men'll do where they's women concerned. Where is this camp?"

"I dunno," said Buck evasively. "Maybe up in the hills. Maybe at the old Salton place. If I thought she was there, I'd risk goin' up and gettin' her— with her leave or without it!"

"Don't be talkin' fool stuff like that," said his mother anxiously. "You ain't goin' near Jim Silent agin, Buck!"

He shrugged his shoulders, with a scowl, and turned away to go back to the bedside of Whistling Dan.

In the morning Buck was hardly less haggard than Dan. His mother, with clasped hands and an anxious face, stood at the foot of the bed, but her trouble was more for her son than for Dan. Old Sam was out saddling Buck's horse, for they had decided that the doctor must be brought from Elkhead at once.

"I don't like to leave him," growled Buck. "I misdoubt what may be happenin' while I'm gone."

"Don't look at me like that," said his mother. "Why, Buck, a body would think that if he dies while you're gone you'll accuse your father an' mother of murder."

"Don't be no minute away from him," urged Buck, "that's all I ask."

"Cure his brain," said his mother monotonously, "an' his body'll take care of itself. Who's that talkin' with your dad outside?"

Very faintly they caught the sound of voices, and after a moment the departing clatter of a galloping horse. Old Sam ran into the house breathless.

"Who was it? What's the matter, pa?" asked his wife, for the old cowpuncher's face was pale even through his tan.

"Young Seaton was jest here. He an' a hundred other fellers is combin' the range an' warnin' everyone agin that Dan Barry. The bullet in his shoulder— he got it while he was breaking jail with Lee Haines. An' he shot down the hosses of two men an' his dog pulled down a third one."

"Busted jail with Lee Haines!" breathed Buck. "It ain't no ways nacheral. Which Dan hates Lee Haines!"

"He was bought off by Jim Silent," said old Sam. "They opened a letter in Elkhead, an' the letter told everything. It was signed 'J.S.' an' it thanked Dan for gettin' 'L.H.' free."

"It's a lie!" said Buck doggedly.

"Buck! Sam!" cried Mrs. Daniels, seeing the two men of her family glaring at each other with something like hate in their eyes. "Sam, have you forgot that this lad has eat your food in your house?"

Sam turned as crimson as he had been pale before.

"I forgot," he muttered. "I was scared an' forgot!"

"An' maybe you've forgot that I'd be swingin' on the end of a rope in Elkhead if it wasn't for Dan Barry?" suggested Buck.

"Buck," said his father huskily, "I'm askin' your pardon. I got sort of panicky for a minute, that's all. But what are we goin' to do with him? If he don't got help he'll be a dead man quick. An' you can't go to Elkhead for the doctor. They'd doctor Dan with six-guns, that's what they'd do."

"What could of made him do it?" said Mrs. Daniels, wiping a sudden burst of tears from her eyes.

"Oh, God," said Buck. "How'd I know why he done it? How'd I know why he turned me loose when he should of took me to Elkhead to be lynched by the mob there? The girl's the only thing to help him outside of a doctor. I'm goin' to get the girl."

"Where?"

"I dunno. Maybe I'll try the old Salton place."

"And take her away from Jim Silent?" broke in his father. "You might jest as well go an' shoot yourse'f before startin'. That'll save your hoss the long ride, an' it'll bring you to jest the same end."

"Listen!" said Buck, "they's the wolf mournin'!"

"Buck, you're loco!"

"Hush, pa!" whispered Mrs. Daniels.

She caught the hand of her brawny son.

"Buck, I'm no end proud of you, lad. If you die, it's a good death! Tell me, Buck dear, have you got a plan?"

He ground his big hand across his forehead, scowling.

"I dunno," he said, drawing a long breath. "I jest know that I got to get the girl. Words don't say what I mean. All I know is that I've got to go up there an' get that girl, and bring her back so's she can save Dan, not from the people that's huntin' him, but from himself."

"There ain't no way of changin' you?" said his father.

"Pa," said Mrs. Daniels, "sometimes you're a plumb fool!"

Buck was already in the saddle. He waved farewell, but after he set his face towards the far-away hills he never turned his head. Behind him lay the untamed three. Before him, somewhere among those naked, sunburned hills, was the woman whose love could reclaim the wild.

A dimness came before his eyes. He attempted to curse at this weakness, but in place of the blasphemy something swelled in his throat, and a still, small music filled his heart. And when at last he was able to speak his lips framed a vow like that of the old crusaders.


## CHAPTER XXIX

## "WEREWOLF"

Buck's cattle pony broke from the lope into a steady dog-trot. Now and then Buck's horse tossed his head high and jerked his ears quickly back and forth as if he were trying to shake off a fly. As a matter of fact he was bothered by his master's whistling. The only sound which he was accustomed to hear from the lips of his rider was a grunted curse now and then. This whistling made the mustang uneasy.

Buck himself did not know what the music meant, but it brought into his mind a thought of strong living and of glorious death. He had heard it whistled several times by Dan Barry when the latter lay delirious. It seemed to Buck, while he whistled this air, that the spirit of Dan traveled beside him, nerving him to the work which lay ahead, filling the messenger with his own wild strength.

As Buck dropped into a level tract of country he caught sight of a rider coming from the opposite direction. As they drew closer the other man swung his mount far to one side. Buck chuckled softly, seeing that the other evidently desired to pass without being recognized. The chuckle died when the stranger changed direction and rode straight for Buck. The latter pulled his horse to a quick stop and turned to face the oncomer. He made sure that his six-gun was loose in the holster, for it was always well to be prepared for the unusual in these chance meetings in the mountain-desert.

"Hey, Buck!" called the galloping horseman.

The hand of Daniels dropped away from his revolver, for he recognized the voice of Hal Purvis, who swiftly ranged alongside.

"What's the dope?" asked Buck, producing his tobacco and the inevitable brown papers.

"Jest lookin' the landscape over an' scoutin' around for news," answered Purvis.

"Pick up anything?"

"Yeh. Ran across some tenderfoot squatters jest out of Elkhead."

Buck grunted and lighted his cigarette.

"Which you've been sort of scarce around the outfit lately," went on Purvis.

"I'm headin' for the bunch now," said Buck.

"D'you bring along that gun of mine I left at your house?"

"Didn't think of it."

"Let's drop back to your house an' get it. Then I'll ride up to the camp with you."

Buck drew a long puff on his cigarette. He drew a quick mental picture of Purvis entering the house, finding Dan, and then—

"Sure," he said, "you c'n go back to the house an' ask pa for the gun, if you want to. I'll keep on for the hills."

"What's your hurry? It ain't more'n three miles back to your house. You won't lose no time to speak of."

"It ain't time I'm afraid of losin'," said Buck significantly.

"Then what the devil is it? I can't afford to leave that gun."

"All right," said Buck, forcing a grin of derision, "so long, Hal."

Purvis frowned at him with narrowing eyes.

"Spit it out, Buck. What's the matter with me goin' back for that gun? Ain't I apt to find it?"

"Sure. That's the point. You're apt to find *lots* of guns. Here's what I mean, Hal. Some of the cowpunchers are beginnin' to think I'm a little partial to Jim Silent's crowd. An' they're watchin' my house."

"The hell!"

"You're right. It is. That's one of the reasons I'm beatin' it for the hills."

He started his horse to a walk. "But of course if you're bound to have that gun, Hal—"

Purvis grinned mirthlessly, his lean face wrinkling to the eyes, and he swung his horse in beside Buck.

"Anyway," said Buck, "I'm glad to see you ain't a fool. How's things at the camp?"

"Rotten. They's a girl up there—"

"A girl?"

"You look sort of pleased. Sure they's a girl. Kate Cumberland, she's the one. She seen us hold up the train, an' now we don't dare let her go. She's got enough evidence to hang us all if it came to a show-down."

"Kate! Delilah."

"What you sayin'?"

"I say it's damn queer that Jim'll let a girl stay at the camp."

"Can't be helped. She's makin' us more miserable than a whole army of men. We had her in the house for a while, an' then Silent rigged up the little shack that stands a short ways—"

"I know the one you mean."

"She an' her dad is in that. We have to guard 'em at night. She ain't had no good word for any of us since she's been up there. Every time she looks at a feller she makes you feel like you was somethin' low-down—a snake, or somethin'."

"D'you mean to say none of the boys please her?" asked Buck curiously. He understood from Dan's delirious ravings that the girl was in love with Lee Haines and had deserted Barry for the outlaw. "Say, ain't Haines good-lookin' enough to please her?"

Purvis laughed unpleasantly.

"He'd like to be, but he don't quite fit her idea of a man. We'd all like to be, for that matter. She's a ravin' beauty, Buck. One of these blue-eyed, yaller-haired kind, see, with a voice like silk. Speakin' personal, I'm free to admit she's got me stopped."

Buck drew so hard on the diminishing butt of his cigarette that he burned his fingers.

"Can't do nothin' with her?" he queried.

"What you grinnin' about?" said Purvis hotly. "D'you think *you'd* have any better luck with her?"

Buck chuckled.

"The trouble with you fellers," he said complacently, "is that you're all too damned afraid of a girl. You all treat 'em like they was queens an' you was their slaves. They like a master."

The thin lips of Purvis curled.

"You're quite a man, ain't you?"

"Man enough to handle any woman that ever walked."

Purvis broke into loud laughter.

"That's what a lot of us thought," he said at last, "but she breaks all the rules. She's got her heart set on another man, an' she's that funny sort that don't never love twice. Maybe you'll guess who the man is?"

Buck frowned thoughtfully to cover his growing excitement.

"Give it up, Buck," advised Purvis. "The feller she loves is Whistlin' Dan Barry. You wouldn't think no woman would look without shiverin' at that hell-raiser. But she's goin' on a hunger strike on account of him. Since yesterday she wouldn't eat none. She says she'll starve herself to death unless we turn her loose. The hell of it is that she will. I know it an' so does the rest of the boys."

"Starve herself to death?" said Buck exuberantly. "Wait till I get hold of her!"

"*You?*"

"Me!"

Purvis viewed him with compassion.

"Me bein' your friend, Buck," he said, "take my tip an' don't try no fool stunts around that girl. Which she once belongs to Whistlin' Dan Barry an' therefore she's got the taboo mark on her for any other man. Everything he's ever owned is different, damned different!"

His voice lowered to a tone which was almost awe.

"Speakin' for myself, I don't hanker after his hoss like Bill Kilduff; or his girl, like Lee Haines; or his life, like the chief. All I want is a shot at that wolf-dog, that Black Bart!"

"You look sort of het up, Hal."

"He come near puttin' his teeth into my leg down at Morgan's place the day Barry cleaned up the chief."

"Why, any dog is apt to take a snap at a feller."

"This ain't a dog. It's a wolf. An' Whistlin' Dan—" he stopped.

"You look sort of queer, Hal. What's up?"

"You won't think I'm loco?"

"No."

"They's some folks away up north that thinks a man now an' then turns into a wolf."

Buck nodded and shrugged his shoulders. A little chill went up and down his back.

"Here's my idea, Buck. I've been thinkin'—no, it's more like dreamin' than thinkin'—that Dan Barry is a wolf turned into a man, an' Black Bart is a man turned into a wolf."

"Hal, you been drinkin'."

"Maybe."

"What made you think—" began Buck, but the long rider put spurs to his horse and once more broke into a fast gallop.


## CHAPTER XXX

### "THE MANHANDLING"

It was close to sunset time when they reached the old Salton place, where they found Silent sitting on the porch with Haines, Kilduff, Jordan, and Rhinehart.

They stood up at sight of the newcomers and shouted a welcome. Buck waved his hand, but his thoughts were not for them. The music he had heard Dan whistle formed in his throat. It reached his lips not in sound but as a smile.

At the house he swung from the saddle and shook hands with Jim Silent. The big outlaw retained Buck's fingers.

"You're comin' in mighty late," he growled, "Didn't you get the signal?"

Buck managed to meet the searching eyes.

"I was doin' better work for you by stayin' around the house," he said.

"How d'you mean?"

"I stayed there to pick up things you might want to know. It wasn't easy. The boys are beginnin' to suspect me."

"The cowpunchers is gettin' so thick around those parts," broke in Purvis, "that Buck wouldn't even let me go back to his house with him to get my gun."

The keen eyes of Silent never left the face of Daniels.

"Don't you know that Gus Morris gives us all the news we need, Buck?"

Rhinehart and Jordan, who were chatting together, stopped to listen. Buck smiled easily.

"I don't no ways doubt that Morris tells you all he knows," he said, "but the pint is that he don't know everything."

"How's that?"

"The rangers is beginnin' to look sidewise an' whisper when Morris is around. He's played his game with us too long, an' the boys are startin' to think. Thinkin' is always dangerous."

"You seem to have been doin' some tall thinkin' yourself," said Silent drily; "you guess the cowpunchers are goin' on our trail on their own hook?"

"There ain't no doubt of it."

"Where'd you hear it?"

"Young Seaton."

"He's one of them?"

"Yes."

"I'll remember him. By the way, I see you got a little token of Whistlin' Dan on your arm."

He pointed to the bandage on Buck's right forearm.

"It ain't nothin'," said Buck, shrugging his shoulders. "The cuts are all healin' up. The arm's as good as ever now."

"Anyway," said Silent, "you got somethin' comin' to you for the play you made agin that devil."

He reached into his pocket, drew out several twenty dollar gold pieces (money was never scarce with a lone rider) and passed them to Buck. The latter received the coin gingerly, hesitated, and then returned it to the hand of the chief.

"What the hell's the matter?" snarled the big outlaw. "Ain't it enough?"

"I don't want no money till I earn it," said Buck.

"Life's gettin' too peaceful for you, eh?" grinned Silent.

"Speakin' of peace," chimed in Purvis, with a liberal wink at the rest of the gang, "Buck allows he's the boy who c'n bring the dove o' the same into this camp. He says he knows the way to bring the girl over there to see reason."

Buck followed the direction of Purvis's eyes and saw Kate sitting on a rock at a little distance from the shanty in which she lived with her father. She made a pitiful figure, her chin cupped in her hand, and her eyes staring fixedly down the valley. He was recalled from her by the general laughter of the outlaws.

"You fellers laugh," he said complacently, "because you don't know no more about women than a cow knows about pictures."

"What do you think we should do with her, Solomon?" Buck met the cold blue eye of Haines.

"Maybe I ain't Solomon," he admitted genially, "but I don't need no million wives to learn all there is to know about women."

"Don't make a fool of yourself, Buck," said Silent. "There ain't no way of movin' that damn girl. She's gone on a hunger strike an' she'll die in it. We can't send her out of the valley. It's hell to have her dyin' on our hands here. But there ain't no way to make her change her mind. I've tried pleadin' with her—I've even offered her money. It don't do no good. Think of that!"

"Sure it don't," sneered Buck. "Why, you poor bunch of yearlin' calves, she don't need no coaxin'. What she needs is a manhandlin'. She wants a master, that's what she wants."

"I suppose," said Haines, "you think you're man enough to change her?"

"None of that!" broke in Silent. "D'you really think you could do somethin' with her, Buck?"

"Can I do somethin' with her?" repeated Buck scornfully. "Why, boys, there ain't nothin' I can't do with a woman."

"Is it because of your pretty face or your winnin' smile?" growled the deep bass of Bill Kilduff.

"Both!" said Buck, promptly. "The wilder they are the harder they fall for me. I've had a thirty-year old maverick eatin' out of my hand like she'd been trained for it all her life. The edyoucated ones say I'm 'different'; the old maids allow that I'm 'naive'; the pretty ones jest say I'm a 'man,' but they spell the word with capital letters."

"Daniels, you're drunk," said Haines.

"Am I? It'll take a better man than you to make me sober, Haines!"

The intervening men jumped back, but the deep voice of Silent rang out like a pistol shot: "Don't move for your six-guns, or you'll be playin' agin me!"

Haines transferred his glare to Silent, but his hand dropped from his gun. Daniels laughed.

"I ain't no mile post with a hand pointin' to trouble," he said gently. "All I say is that the girl needs excitement. Life's so damned dull for her that she ain't got no interest in livin'."

"If you're fool enough to try," said Silent, "go ahead. What are you plannin' to do?"

"You'll learn by watchin'," grinned Buck, taking the reins of his horse. "I'm goin' to ask the lady soft an' polite to step up to her cabin an' pile into some ham an' eggs. If she don't want to I'll rough her up a little, an' she'll love me for it afterwards!"

"The way she loves a snake!" growled Kilduff.

"By God, Silent," said Haines, his face white with emotion, "if Buck puts a hand on her I'll—"

"Act like a man an' not like a damn fool boy," said Silent, dropping a heavy hand on the shoulder of his lieutenant. "He won't hurt her none, Lee. I'll answer for that. Come on, Buck. Speakin' personal, I wish that calico was in hell."

Leading his horse, Buck followed Silent towards the girl. She did not move when they approached. Her eyes still held far down the valley. The steps of the big outlaw were shorter and shorter as they drew close to the girl. Finally he stopped and turned to Buck with a gesture of resignation.

"Look at her! This is what she's been doin' ever since yesterday. Buck, it's up to you to make good. There she is!"

"All right," said Buck, "it's about time for you amachoors to exit an' leave the stage clear for the big star. Now jest step back an' take notes on the way I do it. In fifteen minutes by the clock she'll be eatin' out of my hand."

Silent, expectant but baffled, retired a little. Buck removed his hat and bowed as if he were in a drawing room.

"Ma'am," he said, "I got the honor of askin' you to side-step up to the shanty with me an' tackle a plate of ham an' eggs. Are you on?"

To this Chesterfieldian outpouring of the heart, she responded with a slow glance which started at Buck's feet, travelled up to his face, and then returned to the purple distance down the canyon. In spite of himself the tell-tale crimson flooded Buck's face. Far away he caught the muffled laughter of the outlaws. He replaced his hat.

"Don't make no mistake," he went on, his gesture including the bandits in the background, and Silent particularly, "I ain't the same sort as these other fellers. I c'n understand the way you feel after bein' herded around with a lot of tin horns like these. I'm suggestin' that you take a long look at me an' notice the difference between an imitation an' a real man."

She did look at him. She even smiled faintly, and the smile made Buck's face once more grow very hot. His voice went hard.

"For the last time, I'm askin' if you'll go up to the cabin."

There was both wonder and contempt in her smile.

In an instant he was in his saddle. He swung far to one side and caught her in his arms. Vaguely he heard the yell of excitement from the outlaws. All he was vividly conscious of was the white horror of her face. She fought like a wildcat. She did not cry out. She struck him full in the face with the strength of a man, almost. He prisoned her with a stronger grip, and in so doing nearly toppled from the saddle, for his horse reared up, snorting.

A gun cracked twice and two bullets hummed close to his head. From the corner of his eye he was aware of Silent and Rhinehart flinging themselves upon Lee Haines, who struggled furiously to fire again. He drove his spurs deep and the cattle pony started a bucking course for the shanty.

"Dan!" he muttered at her ear.

The yells of the men drowned his voice. She managed to jerk her right arm free and struck him in the face. He shook her furiously.

"For Whistling Dan!" he said more loudly. "He's dying!"

She went rigid in his arms.

"Don't speak!" he panted. "Don't let them know!"

The outlaws were running after them, laughing and waving their hats.

"Dan!"

*"Faint, you fool!"*

Her eyes widened with instant comprehension. Every muscle of her body relaxed; her head fell back; she was a lifeless burden in his arms. Buck dismounted from the saddle before the shanty. He was white, shaking, but triumphant. Rhinehart and Purvis and Jordan ran up to him. Silent and Kilduff were still struggling with Haines in the distance.

Rhinehart dropped his head to listen at her breast for the heartbeat.

"She's dead!" cried Jordan.

"You're a fool," said Buck calmly. "She's jest fainted, an' when she comes to, she'll begin tellin' me what a wonderful man I am."

"She ain't dead," said Rhinehart, raising his head from her heart, "but Haines'll kill you for this, Buck!"

"Kate!" cried an agonized voice from the shanty, and old white-haired Joe Cumberland ran towards them.

"Jest a little accident happened to your daughter," explained Buck. "Never mind. I c'n carry her in all right. You fellers stay back. A crowd ain't no help. Ain't no cause to worry, Mr. Cumberland. She ain't hurt!"

He hastened on into the shanty and laid her on the bunk within. Her father hurried about to bathe her face and throat. Buck pushed the other three men out of the room.

"She ain't hurt," he said calmly, "she's jest a little fussed up. Remember I said in fifteen minutes I'd have her eatin' out of my hand. I've still got ten minutes of that time. When the ten minutes is up you all come an' take a look through that window. If you don't see the girl eatin' at that table, I'll chaw up my hat."

He crowded them through the door and shut it behind them. A cry of joy came from old Joe Cumberland and Buck turned to see Kate sitting up on the bunk.

## CHAPTER XXXI

### "LAUGH, DAMN IT!"

She brushed her father's anxious arms aside and ran to Buck.

"Shut up!" said Buck. "Talk soft. Better still, don't say nothin'!"

"Kate," stammered her father, "what has happened?"

"Listen an' you'll learn," said Buck. "But get busy first. I got to get you out of here tonight. You'll need strength for the work ahead of you. You got to eat. Get me some eggs. Eggs and ham. Got 'em? Good. You, there!" (This to Joe.) "Rake down them ashes. On the jump, Kate. Some wood here. I got only ten minutes!"

In three minutes the fire was going, and the eggs in the pan, while Joe set out some tin dishes on the rickety table, under orders from Buck, making as much noise as possible. While they worked Buck talked. By the time Kate's plate was ready his tale was done. He expected hysterics. She was merely white and steady-eyed.

"You're ready?" he concluded.

"Yes."

"Then begin by doin' what I say an' ask no questions. Silent an' his crew'll be lookin' through the window over there pretty soon. You got to be eatin' an' appearin' to enjoy talkin' to me. Get that an' don't forget it. Mix in plenty of smiles. Cumberland, you get back into the shadow an' stay there. Don't never come out into the light. Your face tells more'n a whole book, an' believe me, Jim Silent is a quick reader."

Joe retreated to a corner of the room into which the light of the lamp did not penetrate.

"Sit down at that table!" ordered Buck, and he placed a generous portion of fried eggs and ham before her.

"I can't eat. Is Dan—"

"I hear 'em at the window!"

He slipped onto a box on the opposite side of the table and leaned towards her, supporting his chin in his hands. Kate began to eat hurriedly.

"No! no!" advised Buck. "You eat as if you was scared. You want to be slow an' deliberate. Watch out! They've moved the board that covers the window!"

For he saw a group of astonished faces outside.

"Smile at me!"

Her response made even Buck forget her pallor. Outside the house there was a faint buzz of whispers.

"Keep it up!"

"I'll do my best," she said faintly.

Buck leaned back and burst into uproarious laughter.

"That's a good one!" he cried, slamming the broad palm of his hand against the table so that the tin dishes jumped. "I never heard the beat of it!" And in a whispered tone aside: *"Laugh, damn it!"*

Her laughter rang true enough, but it quavered perilously close to a sob towards the close.

"I always granted Jim Silent a lot of sense," he said, "an' has he really left you alone all this time? Damn near died of homesickness, didn't you?"

She laughed again, more confidently this time. The board was suddenly replaced at the window.

"Now I got to go out to them," he said. "After what Silent has seen he'll trust me with you. He'll let me come back."

She dropped her soft hands over his clenched fist.

"It will be soon? Minutes are greater than hours."

"I ain't forgot. Tonight's the time."

Before he reached the door she ran to him. Two arms went round his neck, two warm lips fluttered against his.

"God bless you!" she whispered.

Buck ran for the door. Outside he stood bareheaded, breathing deeply. His face was hot with shame and delight, and he had to walk up and down for a moment before he could trust himself to enter the ranch house. When he finally did so he received a greeting which made him think himself a curiosity rather than a man. Even Jim Silent regarded him with awe.

"Buck," said Jordan, "you don't never need to work no more. All you got to do is to walk into a town, pick out the swellest heiress, an' marry her."

"The trouble with girls in town," said Buck, "is that there ain't no room for a man to operate. You jest nacherally can't ride a hoss into a parlor."

Lee Haines drew Buck a little to one side.

"What message did you bring to her, Buck?" he said.

"What d'you mean?"

"Look here, friend, these other boys are too thick-headed to understand Kate Cumberland, but I know her kind."

"You're a little peeved, ain't you Lee?" grinned Buck. "It ain't my fault that she don't like you."

Haines ground his teeth.

"It was a very clever little act that you did with her, but it couldn't quite deceive me. She was too pale when she laughed."

"A jealous feller sees two things for every one that really happens, Lee."

"Who was the message from?"

"Did she ever smile at you like she done at me?"

"Was it from Dan Barry that you brought word?"

"Did she ever let her eyes go big an' soft when she looked at you?"

"Damn you."

"Did she ever lean close to you, so's you got the scent of her hair, Lee?"

"I'll kill you for this, Daniels!"

"When I left she kissed me good-bye, Lee."

In spite of his bravado, Buck was deeply anxious. He watched Haines narrowly. Only two men in the mountain-desert would have had a chance against this man in a fight, and Buck knew perfectly well that he was not one of the two.

"Watch yourself, Daniels," said Haines. "I know you're lying and I'm going to keep an eye on you."

"Thanks," grinned Buck. "I like to have a friend watchin' out for me."

Haines turned on his heel and went back to the card table, where Buck immediately joined the circle.

"Wait a minute, Lee," said Silent. "Ain't it your turn to stand guard on the Cumberlands tonight?"

"Right-o," answered Haines cheerfully, and rose from the table.

"Hold on," said Buck. "Are you goin' to spoil all the work I done today with that girl?"

"What's the matter?" asked Silent.

"Everything's the matter! Are you goin' to put a man she hates out there watchin' her."

"Damn you, Daniels," said Haines fiercely, "you're rolling up a long account, but it only takes a bullet to collect that sort of a bill!"

"If it hadn't been for Haines, would the girl's father be here?" asked Buck. "Besides, she don't like blonds."

"What type does she like?" asked Silent, enjoying the quarrel between his lieutenant and the recruit.

"Likes 'em with dark hair an' eyes," said Buck calmly. "Look at me, for instance!"

Even Haines smiled, though his lips were white with anger.

"D'you want to stand guard over her yourself?" said the chief.

"Sure," grinned Buck, "maybe she'd come out an' pass the time o' night with me."

"Go ahead and take the job," nodded Silent. "I got an idea maybe she will."

"Silent," warned Haines, "hasn't it occurred to you that there's something damned queer about the ease with which Buck slid into the favor of the girl?"

"Well?"

"All his talk about manhandling her is bunk. He had some message for her. I saw him speak to her when she was struggling in his arms. Then she conveniently fainted."

Silent turned on Buck.

"Is that straight?"

"It is," said Daniels easily.

The outlaws started and their expectant grins died out.

"By God, Buck!" roared Silent, "if you're double crossin' me—but I ain't goin' to be hasty now. What happened? Tell it yourself! What did you say to her?"

"While she was fightin' with me," said Buck, "she hollered: 'Let me go!' I says: 'I'll see you in hell first!' Then she fainted."

The roar of laughter drowned Haines's further protest.

"You win, Buck," said Silent. "Take the job."

As Buck started for the door Haines called to him:

"Hold on, Buck, if you're aboveboard you won't mind giving your word to see that no one comes up the valley and that you'll be here in the morning?"

The words set a swirling blackness before Buck's eyes. He turned slowly.

"That's reasonable," said Silent. "Speak up, Daniels."

"All right," said Buck, his voice very low. "I'll be here in the morning, and I'll see that no one comes up the valley."

There was the slightest possible emphasis on the word "up."

On a rock directly in front of the shanty Buck took up his watch. The little house behind him was black. Presently he heard the soft call of Kate: "Is it time?"

His eyes wandered to the ranch house. He could catch the drone of many voices. He made no reply.

"Is it time?" she repeated.

Still he would not venture a reply, however guarded. She called a third time, and when he made no response he heard her voice break to a moan of hopelessness. And yet he waited, waited, until the light in the ranch house went out, and there was not a sound.

"Kate!" he said, gauging his voice carefully so that it could not possibly travel to the ranch house, which all the while he carefully scanned.

For answer the front door of the shanty squeaked.

"Back!" he called. "Go back!"

The door squeaked again.

"They're asleep in the ranch house," she said. "Aren't we safe?"

"S—sh!" he warned. "Talk low! They aren't all asleep. There's one in the ranch house who'll never take his eyes off me till morning."

"What can we do?"

"Go out the back way. You won't be seen if you're careful. Haines has his eyes on me, not you. Go for the stable. Saddle your horses. Then lead them out and take the path on the other side of the house. Don't mount them until you're far below the house. Go slow all the way. Sounds travel far up this canyon."

"Aren't you coming with us?"

"No."

"But when they find us gone?"

"Think of Dan—not me!"

"God be merciful to you!"

In a moment the back door of the shanty creaked. They must be opening it by inches. When it was wide they would run for the stable. He wished now that he had warned Kate to walk, for a slow moving object catches the eye more seldom than one which travels fast. If Lee Haines was watching at that moment his attention must be held to Buck for one all important minute. He stood up, rolled a cigarette swiftly, and lighted it. The spurt and flare of the match would hold even the most suspicious eye for a short time, and in those few seconds Kate and her father might pass out of view behind the stable.

He sat down again. A muffled sneeze came from the ranch house and Buck felt his blood run cold. The forgotten cigarette between his fingers burned to a dull red and then went out. In the stable a horse stamped. He leaned back, locked his hands idly behind his head, and commenced to whistle. Now there was a snort, as of a horse when it leaves the shelter of a barn and takes the first breath of open air.

All these sounds were faint, but to Buck, straining his ears in an agony of suspense, each one came like the blast of a trumpet. Next there was a click like that of iron striking against rock. Evidently they were leading the horses around on the far side of the house. With a trembling hand he relighted his cigarette and waited, waited, waited. Then he saw them pass below the house! They were dimly stalking figures in the night, but to Buck it seemed as though they walked in the blaze of ten thousand searchlights. He held his breath in expectancy of that mocking laugh from the house—that sharp command to halt—that crack of the revolver.

Yet nothing happened. Now he caught the click of the horses' iron shoes against the rocks farther and farther down the valley. Still no sound from the ranch house. They were safe!

It was then that the great temptation seized on Buck.

It would be simple enough for him to break away. He could walk to the stable, saddle his horse, and tear past the ranch house as fast as his pony could gallop. By the time the outlaws were ready for the pursuit, he would be a mile or more away, and in the hills such a handicap was enough. One thing held him. It was frail and subtle like the invisible net of the enchanter—that word he had passed to Jim Silent, to see that nothing came up the valley and to appear in the ranch house at sunrise.

In the midst of his struggle, strangely enough, he began to whistle the music he had learned from Dan Barry, the song of the Untamed, those who hunt forever, and are forever hunted. When his whistling died away he touched his hand to his lips where Kate had kissed him, and then smiled. The sun pushed up over the eastern hills.

When he entered the ranch house the big room was a scene of much arm stretching and yawning as the outlaws dressed. Lee Haines was already dressed. Buck smiled ironically.

"I say, Lee," he said, "you look sort of used up this mornin', eh?"

The long rider scowled.

"I'd make a guess you've not had much sleep, Haines," went on Buck. "Your eyes is sort of hollow."

"Not as hollow as your damned lying heart!"

"Drop that!" commanded Silent. "You hold a grudge like a woman, Lee! How was the watch, Buck? Are you all in?"

"Nothin' come up the valley, an' here I am at sunrise," said Buck. "I reckon that speaks for itself."

"It sure does," said Silent, "but the gal and her father are kind of slow this mornin'. The old man generally has a fire goin' before dawn is fairly come. There ain't no sign of smoke now."

"Maybe he's sleepin' late after the excitement of yesterday," said Bill Kilduff. "You must of thrown some sensation into the family, Buck."

The eyes of Haines had not moved from the face of Buck.

"I think I'll go over and see what's keeping them so late in bed," he said, and left the house.

"He takes it pretty hard," said Jordan, his scarred face twisted with Satanic mirth, "but don't go rubbin' it into him, Buck, or you'll be havin' a man-sized fight on your hands. I'd jest about as soon mix with the chief as cross Haines. When he starts the undertaker does the finishin'!"

"Thanks for remindin' me," said Buck drily. Through the window he saw Haines throw open the door of the shanty.

The outcry which Buck expected did not follow. For a long moment the long rider stood there without moving. Then he turned and walked slowly back to the house, his head bent, his forehead gathered in a puzzled frown.

"What's the matter, Lee?" called Silent as his lieutenant entered the room again. "You look sort of sick. Didn't she have a bright mornin' smile for you?"

Haines raised his head slowly. The frown was not yet gone.

"They aren't there," he announced.

His eyes shifted to Buck. Everyone followed his example, Silent cursing softly.

"As a joker, Lee," said Buck coldly, "you're some Little Eva. I s'pose they jest nacherally evaporated durin' the night, maybe?"

"Haines," said Silent sharply, "are you serious?"

The latter nodded.

"Then by God, Buck, you'll have to say a lot in a few words. Lee, you suspected him all the time, but I was a fool!"

Daniels felt the color leaving his face, but help came from the quarter from which he least expected it.

"Jim, don't draw!" cried Haines.

The eyes of the chief glittered like the hawk's who sees the field mouse scurrying over the ground far below.

"He ain't your meat, Lee," he said. "It's me he's double crossed."

"Chief," said Haines, "last night while he watched the shanty, I watched *him!*"

"Well?"

"I saw him keep his post in front of the cabin all night without moving. And he was wide awake all the time."

"Then how in hell—"

"The back door of the cabin!" said Kilduff suddenly.

"By God, that's it! They sneaked out there and then went down on the other side of the house."

"If I had let them go," interposed Buck, "do you suppose I'd be here?"

The keen glance of Silent moved from Buck to Haines, and then back again. He turned his back on them.

The quiet which had fallen on the room was now broken by the usual clatter of voices, cursing, and laughter. In the midst of it Haines stepped close to Buck and spoke in a guarded voice.

"Buck," he said, "I don't know how you did it, but I have an idea—"

"Did what?"

The eyes of Haines were sad.

"I was a clean man, once," he said quietly, "and you've done a clean man's work!"

He put out his hand and that of Buck's advanced slowly to meet it.

"Was it for Dan or Kate that you did it?"

The glance of Buck roamed far away.

"I dunno," he said softly. "I think it was to save my own rotten soul!"

On the other side of the room Silent beckoned to Purvis.

"What is it?" asked Hal, coming close.

"Speak low," said Silent. "I'm talking to you, not to the crowd. I think Buck is crooked as hell. I want you to ride down to the neighborhood of his house. Scout around it day and night. You may see something worth while."

Meanwhile, in that utter blackness which precedes the dawn, Kate and her father reached the mouth of the canyon.

"Kate," said old Joe in a tremulous voice, "if I was a prayin' man I'd git down on my knees an' thank God for deliverin' you tonight."

"Thank Buck Daniels, who's left his life in pawn for us. I'll go straight for Buck's house. You must ride to Sheriff Morris and tell him that an honest man is up there in the power of Silent's gang."

"But—" he began.

She waved her hand to him, and spurring her horse to a furious gallop raced off into the night. Her father stared after her for a few moments, but then, as she had advised, rode for Gus Morris.

## CHAPTER XXXII

## THOSE WHO SEE IN THE DARK

It was still early morning when Kate swung from her horse before the house of Buck Daniels. Instinct seemed to lead her to the sickroom, and when she reached it she paid not the slightest attention to the old man and his wife, who sat nodding beside the bed. They started up when they heard the challenging growl of Black Bart, which relapsed into an eager whine of welcome as he recognized Kate.

She saw nothing but the drawn white face of Dan and his blue penciled eyelids. She ran to him. Old Sam, hardly awake, reached out to stop her. His wife held him back.

"It's Delilah!" she whispered. "I seen her face!"

Kate was murmuring soft, formless sounds which made the old man and his wife look to each other with awe. They retreated towards the door as if they had been found intruding where they had no right.

They saw the fever-bright eyes of Dan open. They heard him murmur petulantly, his glance wandering. Her hand passed across his forehead, and then her touch lingered on the bandage which surrounded his left shoulder. She cried out at that, and Dan's glance checked in its wandering and fixed upon the face which leaned above him. They saw his eyes brighten, widen, and a frown gradually contract his forehead. Then his hand went up slowly and found hers.

He whispered something.

"What did he say?" murmured Sam.

"I dunno," she answered. "I think it was 'Delilah!' See her shrink!"

"Shut up!" cautioned Sam. "Ma, he's comin' to his senses!"

There was no doubt of it now, for a meaning had come into his eyes.

"Shall I take her away?" queried Sam in a hasty whisper. "He may do the girl harm. Look at the yaller in his eyes!"

"No," said his wife softly, "it's time for us to leave 'em alone."

"But look at him now!" he muttered. "He's makin' a sound back in his throat like the growl of a wolf! I'm afeard for the gal, ma!"

"Sam, you're an old fool!"

He followed her reluctantly from the room.

"Now," said his wife, "we c'n leave the door a little open—jest a crack—an' you c'n look through and tell when she's in any reel danger."

Sam obeyed.

"Dan ain't sayin' a word," he said. "He's jest glarin' at her."

"An' what's she doin'?" asked Mrs. Daniels.

"She's got her arm around his shoulders. I never knew they could be such a pile of music in a gal's voice, ma!"

"Sam, you was always a fool!"

"He's pushin' her away to the length of his arm."

"An' she? An' she?" whispered Mrs. Daniels.

"She's talkin' quick. The big wolf is standin' close to them an' turnin' his head from one face to the other like he was wonderin' which was right in the argyment."

"The ways of lovers is as queer as the ways of the Lord, Sam!"

"Dan has caught an arm up before his face, an' he's sayin' one word over an' over. She's dropped on her knees beside the bed. She's talkin'. Why does she talk so low, ma?"

"She don't dare speak loud for fear her silly heart would bust. Oh, I know, I know! What fools all men be! What fools! She's askin' him to forgive her."

"An' he's tryin' all his might not to," whispered Mrs. Daniels in an awe-stricken voice.

"Black Bart has put his head on the lap of the gal. You c'n hear him whine! Dan looks at the wolf an' then at the girl. He seems sort of dumbfoundered. She's got her one hand on the head of Bart. She's got the other hand to her face, and she's weepin' into that hand. Martha, she's give up tryin' to persuade him."

There was a moment of silence.

"He's reachin' out his hand for Black Bart. His fingers is on those of the girl. They's both starin'."

"Ay, ay!" she said. "An' what now?"

But Sam closed the door and set his back to it, facing his wife.

"I reckon the rest of it's jest like the endin' of a book, ma," he said.

"Men is all fools!" whispered Mrs. Daniels, but there were tears in her eyes.

Sam went out to put up Kate's horse in the stable. Mrs. Daniels sat in the dining room, her hands clasped in her lap while she watched the gray dawn come up the east. When Sam entered and spoke to her, she returned no answer. He shook his head as if her mood completely baffled him, and then, worn out by the long watching, he went to bed.

For a long time Mrs. Daniels sat without moving, with the same strange smile transfiguring her. Then she heard a soft step pause at the entrance to the room, and turning saw Kate. There was something in their faces which made them strangely alike. A marvellous grace and dignity came to Mrs. Daniels as she rose.

"My dear!" she said.

"I'm so happy!" whispered Kate.

"Yes, dear! And Dan?"

"He's sleeping like a child! Will you look at him? I think the fever's gone!"

They went hand in hand—like two girls, and they leaned above the bed where Whistling Dan lay smiling as he slept. On the floor Black Bart growled faintly, opened one eye on them, and then relapsed into slumber. There was no longer anything to guard against in that house.

* * * * *

It was several days later that Hal Purvis, returning from his scouting expedition, met no less a person that Sheriff Gus Morris at the mouth of the canyon leading to the old Salton place.

"Lucky I met you, Hal," said the genial sheriff. "I've saved you from a wild-goose chase."

"How's that?"

"Silent has jest moved."

"Where?"

"He's taken the trail up the canyon an' cut across over the hills to that old shanty on Bald-eagle Creek. It stands—"

"I know where it is," said Purvis. "Why'd he move?"

"Things was gettin' too hot. I rode over to tell him that the boys was talkin' of huntin' up the canyon to see if they could get any clue of him. They knowed from Joe Cumberland that the gang was once here."

"Cumberland went to you when he got out of the valley?" queried Purvis with a grin.

"Straight."

"And then where did Cumberland go?"

"I s'pose he went home an' joined his gal."

"He didn't," said Purvis drily.

"Then where is he? An' who the hell cares where he is?"

"They're both at Buck Daniels's house."

"Look here, Purvis, ain't Buck one of your own men? Why, I seen him up at the camp jest a while ago!"

"Maybe you did, but the next time you call around he's apt to be missin'."

"D'you think—"

"He's double crossed us. I not only seen the girl an' her father at Buck's house, but I also seen a big dog hangin' around the house. Gus, it was Black Bart, an' where that wolf is you c'n lay to it that Whistlin' Dan ain't far away!"

The sheriff stared at him in dumb amazement, his mouth open.

"They's a price of ten thousand on the head of Whistlin' Dan," suggested Purvis.

The sheriff still seemed too astonished to understand.

"I s'pose," said Purvis, "that you wouldn't care special for an easy lump sum of ten thousand, what?"

"In Buck Daniels's house!" burst out the sheriff.

"Yep," nodded Purvis, "that's where the money is if you c'n get enough men together to gather in Whistlin' Dan Barry."

"D'you really think I'd get some boys together to round up Whistlin' Dan? Why, Hal, you know there ain't no real reason for that price on his head!"

"D'you always wait for 'real reasons' before you set your fat hands on a wad of money?"

The sheriff moistened his lips.

"Ten thousand dollars!"

"Ten thousand dollars!" echoed Purvis.

"By God, I'll do it! If I got him, the boys would forget all about Silent.

They're afraid of Jim, but jest the thought of Barry paralyzes them! I'll start roundin' up the boys I need today. Tonight we'll do our plannin'. Tomorrer mornin' bright an' early we'll hit the trail."

"Why not go after him tonight?"

"Because he'd have an edge on us. I got a hunch that devil c'n see in the dark."

He grinned apologetically for this strange idea, but Purvis nodded with perfect sympathy, and then turned his horse up the canyon. The sheriff rode home whistling. On ten thousand dollars more he would be able to retire from this strenuous life.

# CHAPTER XXXIII

## THE SONG OF THE UNTAMED

Buck and his father were learning of a thousand crimes charged against Dan. Wherever a man riding a black horse committed an outrage it was laid to the account of this new and most terrible of long riders. Two cowpunchers were found dead on the plains. Their half-emptied revolvers lay close to their hands, and their horses were not far off. In ordinary times it would have been accepted that they had killed each other, for they were known enemies, but now men had room for one thought only. And why should not a man with the courage to take an outlaw from the center of Elkhead be charged with every crime on the range? Jim Silent had been a grim plague, but at least he was human. This devil defied death.

These were both sad and happy days for Kate. The chief cause of her sadness, strangely enough, was the rapidly returning strength of Dan. While he was helpless he belonged to her. When he was strong he belonged to his vengeance on Jim Silent; and when she heard Dan whistling softly his own wild, weird music, she knew its meaning as she would have known the wail of a hungry wolf on a winter night. It was the song of the untamed. She never spoke of her knowledge. She took the happiness of the moment to her heart and closed her eyes against tomorrow.

Then came an evening when she watched Dan play with Black Bart—a game of tag in which they darted about the room with a violence which threatened to wreck the furniture, but running with such soft footfalls that there was no sound except the rattle of Bart's claws against the floor and the rush of their breath. They came to an abrupt stop and Dan dropped into a chair while Black Bart sank upon his haunches and snapped at the hand which Dan flicked across his face with lightning movements. The master fell motionless and silent. His eyes forgot the wolf. Rising, they rested on Kate's face. They rose again and looked past her.

She understood and waited.

"Kate," he said at last, "I've got to start on the trail."

Her smile went out. She looked where she knew his eyes were staring, through the window and far out across the hills where the shadows deepened and dropped slanting and black across the hollows. Far away a coyote wailed. The wind which swept the hills seemed to her like a refrain of Dan's whistling—the song and the summons of the untamed.

"That trail will never bring you home," she said.

There was a long silence.

"You ain't cryin', honey?"

"I'm not crying, Dan."

"I got to go."

"Yes."

"Kate, you got a dyin' whisper in your voice."

"That will pass, dear."

"Why, honey, you *are* cryin'!"

He took her face between his hands, and stared into her misted eyes, but then his glance wandered past her, through the window, out to the shadowy hills.

"You won't leave me now?" she pleaded.

"I must!"

"Give me one hour more!"

"Look!" he said, and pointed.

She saw Black Bart reared up with his forepaws resting on the windowsill, while he looked into the thickening night with the eyes of the hunter which sees in the dark.

"The wolf knows, Kate," he said, "but I can't explain."

He kissed her forehead, but she strained close to him and raised her lips.

She cried, "My whole soul is on them."

"Not that!" he said huskily. "There's still blood on my lips an' I'm goin' out to get them clean."

He was gone through the door with the wolf racing before him.

She stumbled after him, her arms outspread, blind with tears; and then, seeing that he was gone indeed, she dropped into the chair, buried her face against the place where his head had rested, and wept. Far away the coyote wailed again, and this time nearer.

## CHAPTER XXXIV

## THE COWARD

Before the coyote cried again, three shadows glided into the night. The lighted window in the house was like a staring eye that searched after them, but Satan, with the wolf running before, vanished quickly among the shadows of the hills. They were glad. They were loosed in the void of the mountain-desert with no destiny save the will of the master. They seemed like one being rather than three. The wolf was the eyes, the horse the strong body to flee or pursue, and the man was the brain which directed, and the power which struck.

He had formulated no plan of action to free Buck and kill Silent. All he knew was that he must reach the long riders at once, and he would learn their whereabouts from Morris. He rode more slowly as he approached the hotel of the sheriff. Lights burned at the dining room windows. Probably the host still sat at table with his guests, but it was strange that they should linger over their meal so late. He had hoped that he would be able to come upon Morris by surprise. Now he must take him in the midst of many men. With Black Bart slinking at his heels he walked softly across the porch and tiptoed through the front room.

The door to the dining room was wide. Around the table sat a dozen men, with the sheriff at their head. The latter, somewhat red of face, as if from the effort of a long speech, was talking low and earnestly, sometimes brandishing his clenched fist with such violence that it made his flabby cheeks quiver.

"We'll get to the house right after dawn," he was saying, "because that's the time when most men are so thick-headed with sleep that— "

"Not Whistling Dan Barry," said one of the men, shaking his head. "He won't be thick-headed. Remember, I seen him work in Elkhead, when he slipped through the hands of a roomful of us."

A growl of agreement went around the table, and Black Bart in sympathy, echoed the noise softly.

"What's that?" called the sheriff, raising his head sharply.

Dan, with a quick gesture, made Black Bart slink a pace back.

"Nothin'," replied one of the men. "This business is gettin' on your nerves, sheriff. I don't blame you. It's gettin' on mine."

"I'm trustin' to you boys to stand back of me all through," said the sheriff with a sort of whine, "but I'm thinkin' that we won't have no trouble. When we see him we won't stop for no questions to be asked, but turn loose with our six-guns an' shoot him down like a dog. He's not human an' he don't deserve—oh, God!"

He started up from his chair, white faced, his hands high above his head, staring at the apparition of Whistling Dan, who stood with two revolvers covering the posse. Every man was on his feet instantly, with arms straining stiffly up. The muzzles of revolvers are like the eyes of some portraits. No matter from what angle you look at them, they seem directed straight at you. And every cowpuncher in the room was sure that he was the main object of Dan's aim.

"Morris!" said Dan.

"For God's sake, don't shoot!" screamed the sheriff. "I—"

"Git down on your knees! Watch him, Bart!"

As the sheriff sank obediently to his knees, the wolf slipped up to him with a stealthy stride and stood half crouched, his teeth bared, silent. No growl could have made Bart more terribly threatening. Dan turned completely away from Morris so that he could keep a more careful watch on the others.

"Call off your wolf!" moaned Morris, a sob of terror in his voice.

"I ought to let him set his teeth in you," said Dan, "but I'm goin' to let you off if you'll tell me what I want to know."

"Yes! Anything!"

"Where's Jim Silent?"

All eyes flashed towards Morris. The latter, as the significance of the question came home to him, went even a sicklier white, like the belly of a dead fish. His eyes moved swiftly about the circle of his posse. Their answering glares were sternly forbidding.

"Out with it!" commanded Dan.

The sheriff strove mightily to speak, but only a ghastly whisper came: "You got the wrong tip, Dan. I don't know nothin' about Silent. I'd have him in jail if I did!"

"Bart!" said Dan.

The wolf slunk closer to the kneeling man. His hot breath fanned the face of the sheriff and his lips grinned still farther back from the keen, white teeth.

"Help!" yelled Morris. "He's at the shanty up on Bald-eagle Creek."

A rumble, half cursing and half an inarticulate snarl of brute rage, rose from the cowpunchers.

"Bart," called Dan again, and leaped back from the door, raced out to Satan, and drove into the night at a dead gallop.

Half the posse rushed after him. A dozen shots were pumped after the disappearing shadowy figure. Two or three jumped into their saddles. The others called them back.

"Don't be an ass, Monte," said one. "You got a good hoss, but you ain't fool enough to think he c'n catch Satan?"

They trooped back to the dining room, and gathered in a silent circle around the sheriff, whose little fear-bright eyes went from face to face.

"Ah, this is the swine," said one, "that was guardin' our lives!"

"Fellers," pleaded the sheriff desperately, "I swear to you that I jest heard of where Silent was today. I was keepin' it dark until after we got Whistling Dan. Then I was goin' to lead you—"

The flat of a heavy hand struck with a resounding thwack across his lips. He reeled back against the wall, sputtering the blood from his split mouth.

"Pat," said Monte, "your hoss is done for. Will you stay here an' see that he don't get away? We'll do somethin' with him when we get back."

Pat caught the sheriff by his shirt collar and jerked him to a chair. The body of the fat man was trembling like shaken jelly. The posse turned away.

They could not overtake Whistling Dan on his black stallion, but they might arrive before Silent and his gang got under way. Their numbers were over small to attack the formidable long riders, but they wanted blood. Before Whistling Dan reached the valley of Bald-eagle Creek they were in the saddle and riding hotly in pursuit.

## CHAPTER XXXV

### CLOSE IN!

In that time-ruined shack towards which the posse and Dan Barry rode, the outlaws sat about on the floor eating their supper when Hal Purvis entered. He had missed the trail from the Salton place to the Bald-eagle half a dozen times that day, and that had not improved his bitter mood.

"You been gone long enough," growled Silent. "Sit down an' chow an' tell us what you know."

"I don't eat with no damned traitors," said Purvis savagely. "Stan' up an' tell us that you're a double-crossin' houn', Buck Daniels!"

"You better turn in an' sleep," said Buck calmly. "I've knowed men before that loses their reason for want of sleep!"

"Jim," said Purvis, turning sharply on the chief, "Barry is at Buck's house!"

"You lie!" said Buck.

"Do I lie?" said Purvis, grinding his teeth. "I seen Black Bart hangin' around your house."

Jim Silent reached out a heavy paw and dropped it on the shoulder of Buck. Their eyes met through a long moment, and then the glance of Buck wavered and fell.

"Buck," said Silent, "I like you. I don't want to believe what Purvis says. Give me your word of honor that Whistlin' Dan—"

"He's right, Jim," said Buck.

"An' he dies like a yaller cur!" broke in Purvis, snarling.

"No," said Silent, "when one of the boys goes back on the gang, they pay *me*, not the rest of you! Daniels, take your gun and git down to the other end of the room an' stand with your face to the wall. I'll stay at this end. Keep your arms folded. Haines, you stand over there an' count up to three. Then holler: 'Fire!' an' we'll turn an' start shootin'. The rest of you c'n be judge if that's fair."

"Too damned fair," said Kilduff. "I say: String him up an' drill the skunk full of holes."

Without a word Buck turned on his heel.

"One moment," said Haines.

"He ain't your meat, Lee," said Silent. "Jest keep your hand out of this."

"I only wish to ask him a question," said Haines. He turned to Buck: "Do you mean to say that after Barry's wolf cut up your arm, you've been giving Whistling Dan a shelter from the law—and from us?"

"I give him a place to stay because he was damned near death," said Buck. "An' there's one thing you'll answer for in hell, Haines, an' that's ridin' off an' leavin' the man that got you out of Elkhead. He was bleedin' to death."

"Shot?" said Haines, changing color.

Silent broke in: "Buck, go take your place and say your prayers."

"Stay where you are!" commanded Haines. "And the girl?"

"He was lyin' sick in bed, ravin' about 'Delilah' an' 'Kate.' So I come an' got the girl."

Haines dropped his head.

"An' when he was lyin' there," said Silent fiercely, "you could of made an' end of him without half liftin' your hand, an' you didn't."

"Silent," said Haines, "if you want to talk, speak to me."

"What in hell do you mean, Lee?"

"You can't get at Buck except through me."

"Because that devil Barry got a bullet for your sake are you goin' to—"

"I've lived a rotten life," said Haines.

"An' I suppose you think this is a pretty good way of dyin'?" sneered Silent.

"I have more cause to fight for Barry than Buck has," said Haines.

"Lee, we've been pals too long."

"Silent, I've hated you like a snake ever since I met you. But outlaws can't choose their company."

His tawny head rose. He stared haughtily around the circle of lowering faces.

"By God," said Silent, white with passion, "I'm beginnin' to think you do hate me! Git down there an' take your place. You're first an' Daniels comes next. Kilduff, you c'n count!"

He stalked to the end of the room. Haines lingered one moment.

"Buck," he said, "there's one chance in ten thousand that I'll make this draw the quickest of the two. If I don't, you may live through it. Tell Kate—"

"Haines, git to your mark, or I'll start shootin'!"

Haines turned and took his place. The others drew back along the walls of the room. Kilduff took the lamp from the table and held it high above his head. Even then the light was dim and uncertain and the draughts set the flame wavering so that the place was shaken with shadows. The moon sent a feeble shaft of light through the window.

"One!" said Kilduff.

The shoulders of Haines and Silent hunched slightly.

"Two!" said Kilduff.

"God," whispered someone.

"Three. Fire!"

They whirled, their guns exploding at almost the same instant, and Silent lunged for the floor, firing twice as he fell. Haines's second shot split the wall behind Silent. If the outlaw chief had remained standing the bullet would have passed through his head. But as Silent fired the third time the revolver dropped clattering from the hand of Haines. Buck caught him as he toppled inertly forward, coughing blood.

Silent was on his feet instantly.

"Stand back!" he roared to his men, who crowded about the fallen long rider. "Stand back in your places. I ain't finished. I'm jest started. Buck, take your place!"

"Boys!" pleaded Buck, "he's not dead, but he'll bleed to death unless—"

"Damn him, let him bleed. Stand up, Buck, or by God I'll shoot you while you kneel there!"

"*Shoot and be damned!*"

He tore off his shirt and ripped away a long strip for a bandage.

The revolver poised in Silent's hand.

"Buck, I'm warnin' you for the last time!"

"Fellers, it's murder an' damnation for all if you let Haines die this way!" cried Buck.

The shining barrel of the revolver dropped to a level.

"I've given you a man's chance," said Silent, "an' now you'll have the chance of—"

The door at the side of the room jerked open and a revolver cracked. The lamp shivered to a thousand pieces in the hands of Bill Kilduff. All the room was reduced to a place of formless shadow, dimly lighted by the shaft of moonlight. The voice of Jim Silent, strangely changed and sharpened from his usual bass roar, shrilled over the sudden tumult: "Each man for himself! *It's Whistling Dan!*"

Terry Jordan and Bill Kilduff rushed at the dim figure, crouched to the floor. Their guns spat fire, but they merely lighted the way to their own destruction. Twice Dan's revolver spoke, and they dropped, yelling. Pandemonium fell on the room.

The long riders raced here and there, the revolvers coughing fire. For an instant Hal Purvis stood framed against the pallid moonshine at the window. He stiffened and pointed an arm toward the door.

"The werewolf," he screamed.

As if in answer to the call, Black Bart raced across the room. Twice the revolver sounded from the hand of Purvis. Then a shadow leaped from the floor. There was a flash of white teeth, and Purvis lurched to one side and dropped, screaming terribly. The door banged. Suddenly there was silence. The clatter of a galloping horse outside drew swiftly away.

"Dan!"

"Here!"

"Thank God!"

"Buck, one got away! If it was Silent—here! Bring some matches."

Someone was dragging himself towards the door in a hopeless effort to escape. Several others groaned.

"You, there!" called Buck. "Stay where you are!"

The man who struggled towards the door flattened himself against the floor, moaning pitifully.

"Quick," said Dan, "light a match. Morris's posse is at my heels. No time. If Silent escaped—"

A match flared in the hands of Buck.

"Who's that? Haines!"

"Let him alone, Dan! I'll tell you why later. There's Jordan and Kilduff. That one by the door is Rhinehart."

They ran from one to the other, greeted by groans and deep curses.

"Who's that beneath the window?"

"Too small for Silent. It's Purvis, and he's dead!"

"Bart got him!"

"No! It was fear that killed him. Look at his face!"

"Bart, go out to Satan!"

The wolf trotted from the room.

"My God, Buck, I've done all this for nothin'! It was Silent that got away!"

"What's that?"

Over the groans of the wounded came the sound of running horses, not one, but many, then a call: "Close in! Close in!"

"The posse!" said Dan.

As he jerked open the door a bullet smashed the wood above his head.

Three horsemen were closing around Satan and Black Bart. He leaped back into the room.

"They've got Satan, Buck. We've got to try it on foot. Go through the window."

"They've got nothing on me. I'll stick with Haines."

Dan jumped through the window, and raced to the shelter of a big rock. He had hardly dropped behind it when four horsemen galloped around the corner of the house.

"Johnson and Sullivan," ordered the voice of Monte sharply, "watch the window. They're lying low inside, but we've got Barry's horse and wolf. Now we'll get him."

"Come out or we'll burn the house down!" thundered a voice from the other side.

"We surrender!" called Buck within.

A cheer came from the posse. Sullivan and Johnson ran for the window they had been told to guard. The door on the other side of the house slammed open.

"It's a slaughterhouse!" cried one of the posse.

Dan left the sheltering rock and raced around the house, keeping a safe distance, and dodging from rock to rock. He saw Satan and Black Bart guarded by two men with revolvers in their hands. He might have shot them down, but the distance was too great for accurate gunplay. He whistled shrilly. The two guards wheeled towards him, and as they did so, Black Bart, leaping, caught one by the shoulder, whirling him around and around with the force of the spring. The other fired at Satan, who raced off towards the sound of the whistle. It was an easy shot, but in the utter surprise of the instant the bullet went wide. Before he could fire again Satan was coming to a halt beside Dan.

"Help!" yelled the cattleman. "Whistling Dan!"

The other guard opened fire wildly. Three men ran from the house. All they saw was a black shadow which melted instantly into the night.

# CHAPTER XXXVI

## FEAR

Into the dark he rode. Somewhere in the mountains was Silent, and now alone. In Dan's mouth the old salt taste of his own blood was unforgotten.

It was a wild chase. He had only the faintest clues to guide him, yet he managed to keep close on the trail of the great outlaw. After several days he rode across a tall red-roan stallion, a mere wreck of a horse with lean sides and pendant head and glazed eye. It was a long moment before Dan recognized Silent's peerless mount, Red Pete. The outlaw had changed his exhausted horse for a common pony. The end of the long trail must be near.

The whole range followed that chase with breathless interest. It was like the race of Hector and Achilles around the walls of Troy. And when they met there would be a duel of giants. Twice Whistling Dan was sighted. Once Jim Silent fought a running duel with a posse fresh from Elkhead. The man hunters were alert, but it was their secret hope that the two famous outlaws would destroy each other, but how the wild chase would end no one could know. At last Buck Daniels rode to tell Kate Cumberland strange news.

When he stumbled into the ranch house, Kate and her father rose, white-faced. There was an expression of waiting terror in their eyes.

"Buck!" cried Joe.

"Hush! Dad," said Kate. "It hasn't come yet! Buck, what has happened?"

"The end of the world has come for Dan," he said. "That devil Silent—"

"Dan," cried old Joe, and rushed around the table to Buck.

"Silent has dared Dan to meet him at three o'clock tomorrow afternoon in Tully's saloon in Elkhead! He's held up four men in the last twenty-four hours and told them that he'll be at Tully's tomorrow and will expect Dan there!"

"It isn't possible!" cried Kate. "That means that Silent is giving himself up to the law!"

Buck laughed bitterly.

"The law will not put a hand on them if it thinks that they'll fight it out together," he said.

"There'll be a crowd in the saloon, but not a hand will stir to arrest Silent till after the fight."

"But Dan won't go to Tully's," broke in old Joe. "If Silent is crazy enough to do such a thing, Dan won't be."

"He will," said Kate. "I know!"

"You've got to stop him," urged Buck. "You've got to get to Elkhead and turn Dan back."

"Ay," said Joe, "for even if he kills Silent, the crowd will tackle him after the fight—a hundred against one."

She shook her head.

"You won't go?"

"Not a step."

"But Kate, don't you understand—?"

"I couldn't turn Dan back. There is his chance to meet Silent. Do you dream anyone could turn him back?"

The two men were mute.

"You're right," said Buck at last. "I hoped for a minute that you could do it, but now I remember the way he was in that dark shanty up the Bald-eagle Creek. You can't turn a wolf from a trail, and Whistling Dan has never forgotten the taste of his own blood."

"Kate!" called her father suddenly. "What's the matter, honey?"

With bowed head and a faltering step she was leaving the room. Buck caught old Joe by the arm and held him back as he would have followed.

"Let her be!" said Buck sharply. "Maybe she'll want to see you at three o'clock tomorrow afternoon, but until then she'll want to be alone. There'll be ghosts enough with her all the time. You c'n lay to that."

Joe Cumberland wiped his glistening forehead.

"There ain't nothin' we c'n do, Buck, but sit an' wait."

Buck drew a long breath.

"What devil gave Silent that idea?"

"*Fear!*"

"Jim Silent don't know what fear is!"

"Anyone who's seen the yaller burn in Dan's eyes knows what fear is."

Buck winced.

Cumberland went on: "Every night Silent has been seein' them eyes that glow yaller in the dark. They lie in wait for him in every shadow. Between dark and dawn he dies a hundred deaths. He can't stand it no more. He's goin' to die. Somethin' tells him that. But he wants to die where they's humans around him, and when he dies he wants to pull Dan down with him."

They sat staring at each other for a time.

"If he lives through that fight with Silent," said Buck sadly, "the crowd will jump in on him. Their numbers'll make 'em brave."

"An' then?"

"Then maybe he'd like a friend to fight by his side," said Buck simply. "So long, Joe!"

The old man wrung his hand and then followed him out to the hitching-rack where Buck's horse stood.

"Ain't Dan got no friends among the crowd?" asked Cumberland. "Don't they give him no thanks for catching the rest of Silent's gang?"

"They give him lots of credit," said Buck. "An' Haines has said a lot in favor of Dan, explainin' how the jail bustin' took place. Lee is sure provin' himself a white man. He's gettin' well of his wounds and it's said the Governor will pardon him. You see, Haines went bad because the law done him dirt a long time ago, and the Governor is takin' that into account."

"But they'd still want to kill Dan?"

"Half of the boys wouldn't," said Buck. "The other half is all wrought up over the killings that's been happenin' on the range in the last month. Dan is accused of about an even half of 'em, an' the friends of dead men don't waste no time listenin' to arguments. They say Dan's an outlawed man an' that they're goin' to treat him like one."

"Damn them!" groaned Cumberland. "Don't Morris's confession make no difference?"

"Morris was lynched before he had a chance to swear to what he said in Dan's favor. Kilduff an' Jordan an' Rhinehart might testify that Dan wasn't never bought over by Silent, but they know they're done for themselves, an' they won't try to help anybody else, particular the man that put 'em in the hands of the law. Kilduff has swore that Dan *was* bribed by Silent, that he went after Silent not for revenge, but to get some more money out of him, an' that the fight in the shanty up at Bald-eagle Creek was because Silent refused to give Dan any more money."

"Then there ain't no hope," muttered Cumberland. "But oh, lad, it breaks my heart to think of Kate! Dan c'n only die once, but every minute is a death to her!"


## CHAPTER XXXVII

## DEATH

Before noon of the next day Buck joined the crowd which had been growing for hours around Tully's saloon. Men gave way before him, whispering. He was a marked man—the friend of Whistling Dan Barry. Cowpunchers who had known him all his life now avoided his eyes, but caught him with side glances. He smiled grimly to himself, reading their minds. He was more determined than ever to stand or fall with Whistling Dan that day.

There was not an officer of the law in sight. If one were present it would be his manifest duty to apprehend the outlaws as soon as they appeared, and the plan was to allow them to fight out their quarrel and perhaps kill each other.

Arguments began to rise among separate groups, where the crimes attributed to Whistling Dan Barry were numbered and talked over. It surprised Buck to discover the number who believed the stories which he and Haines had told. They made a strong faction, though manifestly in the minority.

Hardly a man who did not, from time to time, nervously fumble the butt of his six-gun. As three o'clock drew on the talk grew less and less. It broke out now and again in little uneasy bursts. Someone would tell a joke. Half hysterical laughter would greet it, and die suddenly, as it began. These were all hard-faced men of the mountain-desert, warriors of the frontier. What unnerved them was the strangeness of the thing which was about to happen.

The big wooden clock on the side of the long barroom struck once for half-past two. All talk ceased.

Men seemed unwilling to meet each other's eyes. Some of them drummed lightly on the top of the bar and strove to whistle, but the only sound that came through their dried lips was a whispering rush of breath. A gray-haired cattle ranger commenced to hum a tune, very low, but distinct. Finally a man rose, strode across the room, shook the old fellow by the shoulder with brutal violence, and with a curse ordered him to stop his "damned death song!"

Everyone drew a long breath of relief. The minute hand crept on towards three o'clock. Now it was twenty minutes, now fifteen, now ten, now five; then a clatter of hoofs, a heavy step on the porch, and the giant form of Jim Silent blocked the door. His hands rested on the butts of his two guns. Buck guessed at the tremendous strength of that grip. The eyes of the outlaw darted about the room, and every glance dropped before his, with the exception of Buck's fascinated stare.

For he saw a brand on the face of the great long rider. It lay in no one thing. It was not the unusual hollowness of eyes and cheeks. It was not the feverish brightness of his glance. It was something which included all of these. It was the fear of death by night! His hands fell away from the guns. He crossed the room to the bar and nodded his head at the bartender.

"Drink!" he said, and his voice was only a whisper without body of sound.

The bartender, with pasty face, round and blank, did not move either his hand or his fascinated eyes. There was a twitch of the outlaw's hand and naked steel gleamed. Instantly revolvers showed in every hand. A youngster moaned. The sound seemed to break the charm.

Silent put back his great head and burst into a deep-throated laughter. The gun whirled in his hand and the butt crashed heavily on the bar.

"Drink, damn you!" he thundered. "Step up an' drink to the health of Jim Silent!"

The wavering line slowly approached the bar. Silent pulled out his other gun and shoved them both across the bar.

"Take 'em," he said. "I don't want 'em to get restless an' muss up this joint."

The bartender took them as if they were covered with some deadly poison, and the outlaw stood unarmed! It came suddenly to Buck what the whole manoeuvre meant. He gave away his guns in order to tempt someone to arrest him. Better the hand of the law than the yellow glare of those following eyes. Yet not a man moved to apprehend him. Unarmed he still seemed more dangerous than six common men.

The long rider jerked a whisky bottle upside down over a glass. Half the contents splashed across the bar. He turned and faced the crowd, his hand dripping with the spilled liquor.

"Whose liquorin'?" he bellowed.

Not a sound answered him.

"Damn your yaller souls! Then all by myself I'll drink to—"

He stopped short, his eyes wild, his head tilted back. One by one the cowpunchers gave back, foot by foot, softly, until they stood close to the opposite wall of the saloon. All the bar was left to Silent. The whisky glass slipped from his hand and crashed on the floor. In his face was the meaning of the sound he heard, and now it came to their own ears—a whistle thin with distance, but clear.

Only phrases at first, but now it rose more distinct, the song of the untamed; the terror and beauty of the mountain-desert; a plea and a threat.

The clock struck, sharp, hurried, brazen—one, two, three! Before the last quick, unmusical chime died out Black Bart stood in the entrance to the saloon. His eyes were upon Jim Silent, who stretched out his arms on either side and gripped the edge of the bar. Yet even when the wolf glided silently across the room and crouched before the bandit, at watch, his lips grinned back from the white teeth, the man had no eyes for him. Instead, his stare held steadily upon that open door and on his raised face there was still the terror of that whistling which swept closer and closer.

It ceased. A footfall crossed the porch. How different from the ponderous stride of Jim Silent! This was like the padding step of the panther. And Whistling Dan stood in the door. He did not fill it as the burly shoulders of Silent had done. He seemed almost as slender as a girl, and infinitely boyish in his grace—a strange figure, surely, to make all these hardened fighters of the mountain-desert crouch, and stiffen their fingers around the butts of their revolvers! His eyes were upon Silent, and how they lighted! His face changed as the face of the great god Pan must have altered when he blew into the instrument of reeds and made perfect music, the first in the world.

"Bart," said the gentle voice, "go out to Satan."

The wolf turned and slipped from the room. It was a little thing, but, to the men who saw it, it was terrible to watch an untamed beast obey the voice of a man.

Still with that light, panther-step he crossed the barroom, and now he was looking up into the face of the giant. The huge long rider loomed above Dan. That was not terror which set his face in written lines—it was horror, such as a man feels when he stands face to face with the unearthly in the middle of night. This was open daylight in a room thronged with men, yet in it nothing seemed to live save the smile of Whistling Dan. He drew out the two revolvers and slipped them onto the bar. They stood unarmed, yet they seemed no less dangerous.

Silent's arms crept closer to his sides. He seemed gathering himself by degrees. The confidence in his own great size showed in his face, and the blood-lust of battle in his eyes answered the yellow light in Dan's.

Dan spoke.

"Silent, once you put a stain of blood on me. I've never forgot the taste. It's goin' to be washed out today or else made redder. It was here that you put the stain."

He struck the long rider lightly across the mouth with the back of his hand, and Silent lunged with the snarl of a beast. His blow spent itself on thin air. He whirled and struck again. Only a low laughter answered him. He might as well have battered away at a shadow.

"Damnation!" he yelled, and leaped in with both arms outspread.

The impetus of his rush drove them both to the floor, where they rolled over and over, and before they stopped thin fingers were locked about the bull neck of the bandit, and two thumbs driven into the hollow of his throat. With a tremendous effort he heaved himself from the floor, his face convulsed.

He beat with both fists against the lowered head of Dan. He tore at those hands. They were locked as if with iron. Only the laughter, the low, continual laughter rewarded him.

He screamed, a thick, horrible sound. He flung himself to the floor again and rolled over and over, striving to crush the slender, remorseless body. Once more he was on his feet, running hither and thither, dragging Dan with him. His eyes swelled out; his face blackened. He beat against the walls. He snapped at the wrists of Dan like a beast, his lips flecked with a bloody froth.

That bulldog grip would not unlock. That animal, exultant laughter ran on in demoniac music. In his great agony the outlaw rolled his eyes in appeal to the crowd which surrounded the struggling two. Every man seemed about to spring forward, yet they could not move. Some had their fingers stiffly extended, as if in the act of gripping with hands too stiff to close.

Silent slipped to his knees. His head fell back, his discolored tongue protruding. Dan wrenched him back to his feet. One more convulsive effort from the giant, and then his eyes glazed, his body went limp. The remorseless hands unlocked. Silent fell in a shapeless heap to the floor.

Still no one moved. There was no sound except the deadly ticking of the clock. The men stared fascinated at that massive, lifeless figure on the floor. Even in death he was terrible. Then Dan's hand slid inside his shirt, fumbled a moment, and came forth again bearing a little gleaming circle of metal. He dropped it upon the body of Jim Silent, and turning, walked slowly from the room. Still no one moved to intercept him. Passing through the door he pushed within a few inches of two men. They made no effort to seize him, for their eyes were upon the body of the great lone rider.

The moment Dan was gone the hypnotic silence which held the crowd, broke suddenly. Someone stirred. Another cursed beneath his breath. Instantly all was clamor and a running hither and thither. Buck Daniels caught from the body of Jim Silent the small metal circle which Dan had dropped. He stood dumbfounded at the sight of it, and then raised his hand, and shouted in a voice which gathered the others swiftly around him. They cursed deeply with astonishment, for what they saw was the marshal's badge of Tex Calder. The number on it was known throughout the mountain-desert, and seeing it, the worst of Dan's enemies stammered, gaped, and could not speak. There were more impartial men who could. In five minutes the trial of Whistling Dan was under way. The jury was every cowpuncher present. The judge was public opinion. It was a gray-haired man who finally leaped upon the bar and summed up all opinion in a brief statement.

"Whatever Whistlin' Dan has done before," he said, "this day he's done a man-sized job in a man's way. Morris, before he died, said enough to clear up most of this lad's past, particular about the letter from Jim Silent that talked of a money bribe. Morris didn't have a chance to swear to what he said, but a dying man speaks truth. Lee Haines had cleared up most of the rest. We can't hold agin Dan what he done in breakin' jail with Haines. Dan Barry was a marshal. He captured Haines and then let the outlaw go. He had a right to do what he wanted as long as he finally got Haines back. And Haines has told us that when he was set free Barry said he would get him again. And Barry did get him again. Remember that, and he got all the rest of Silent's gang, and now there lies Jim Silent dead. They's two things to remember. The first is that Whistlin' Dan has rid away without any shootin' irons on his hip. That looks as if he's come to the end of his long trail. The second is that he was a bunkie of Tex Calder, an' a man Tex could trust for the avengin' of his death is good enough for me."

There was a pause after this speech, and during the quiet the cowpunchers were passing from hand to hand the marshal's badge which Calder, as he died, had given to Dan. The bright small shield was a more convincing proof than a hundred arguments. The bitterest of Dan's enemies realized that the crimes of which he was accused were supported by nothing stronger than blind rumor. The marshal's badge and the dead body of Jim Silent kept them mute. So an illegal judge and one hundred illegal jurymen found Whistling Dan "not guilty."

Buck Daniels took horse and galloped for the Cumberland house with the news of the verdict. He knew that Whistling Dan was there.

## CHAPTER XXXVIII

## THE WILD GEESE

So when the first chill days of the late autumn came the four were once more together, Dan, Kate, Black Bart, and Satan. Buck and old Joe Cumberland made the background of their happiness. It was the latter's request which kept the wedding a matter of the indefinite future. He would assign no reason for his wish, but Kate guessed it.

All was not well, she knew. Day after day, as the autumn advanced, Dan went out with the wolf and the wild black stallion and ranged the hills alone. She did not ask him where or why, for she understood that to be alone was as necessary to him as sleep is to others. Yet she could not explain it all and the cold fear grew in her. Sometimes she surprised a look of infinite pity in the eyes of Buck or her father. Sometimes she found them whispering and nodding together. At last on an evening when the three sat before the fire in solemn silence and Dan was away, they knew not where, among the hills, she could bear it no longer.

"Do you really think," she burst out, "that the old wildness is still in Dan?"

"Wild?" said her father gently. "Wild? I don't say he's still wild—but why is he so late tonight, Kate? The ground's all covered with snow. The wind's growin' sharper an' sharper. This is a time for all reasonable folk to stay home an' git comfortable beside the fire. But Dan ain't here. Where is he?"

"Hush!" said Buck, and raised a hand for silence.

Far away they heard the wail of a wolf crying to the moon. She rose and went out on the porch of the house. The others followed her. Outside they found nothing but the low moaning of the wind, and the snow, silver glimmering where the moonlight fell upon it. Then they heard the weird, inhuman whistling, and at last they saw Dan riding towards the house. A short distance away he stopped Satan. Black Bart dropped to his haunches and wailed again. Dan was staring upwards.

"Look!" said Kate, and pointed.

Across the white circle of the moon drove a flying wedge of wild geese. The wail of the wolf died out. A faint honking was blown to them by the wind, now a distant, jangling chorus, now a solitary sound repeated like a call.

Without a word the three returned to their seats close by the fire, and sat silent, staring. Presently the rattle of the wolf's claws came on the floor; then Dan entered with his soft step and stood behind Kate's chair. They were used to his silent comings and goings. Black Bart was slinking up and down the room with a restless step. His eyes glowed from the shadow, and as Joe looked up to the face of Dan he saw the same light repeated there, yellow and strange. Then, like the wolf, Dan turned and commenced that restless pacing up and down, up and down, a padding step like the fall of a panther's paw.

"The wild geese—" he said suddenly, and then stopped.

"They are flying south?" said Kate.

"South!" he repeated.

His eyes looked far away. The wolf slipped to his side and licked his hand.

"Kate, I'd like to follow the wild geese."

Old Joe shaded his eyes and the big hands of Buck were locked together.

"Are you unhappy, Dan?" she said.

"The snow is come," he muttered uneasily.

He began pacing again with that singular step.

"When I went out to Satan in the corral this evenin', I found him standin' lookin' south."

She rose and faced him with a little gesture of surrender.

"Then you must follow the wild geese, Dan!"

"You don't mind me goin', Kate?"

"No."

"But your eyes are shinin'!"

"It's only the reflection of the firelight."

Black Bart whined softly. Suddenly Dan straightened and threw up his arms, laughing low with exultation. Buck Daniels shuddered and dropped his head.

"I am far behind," said Dan, "but I'll go fast."

He caught her in his arms, kissed her eyes and lips, and then whirled and ran from the room with that noiseless, padding step.

"Kate!" groaned Buck Daniels, "you've let him go! We've all lost him for ever!"

A sob answered him.

"Go call him back," pleaded Joe. "He will stay for your sake."

She whispered: "I would rather call back the wild geese who flew across the moon. And they are only beautiful when they are wild!"

"But you've lost him, Kate, don't you understand?"

"The wild geese fly north again in spring," said Buck, "and he'll—"

"Hush!" she said. "Listen!"

Far off, above the rushing of the wind, they heard the weird whistling, a thrilling and unearthly music. It was sad with the beauty of the night. It was joyous with the exultation of the wind. It might have been the voice of some god who rode the northern storm south, south after the wild geese, south with the untamed.